THE BOYS OF BRIAR HALL

INTERNATIONAL BESTSELLING AUTHOR
ELENA LAWSON

ALSO BY ELENA LAWSON

The Painted Sinners Duet

White Rose Painted Red

Kings of Kilborn University

Soulless Saint

Ruthless Reign

Paranormal Romance Series

The Last Vocari

Arcane Arts Academy

The Wolves of Forest Grove

Queen's Consorts

CROOKED CROWS

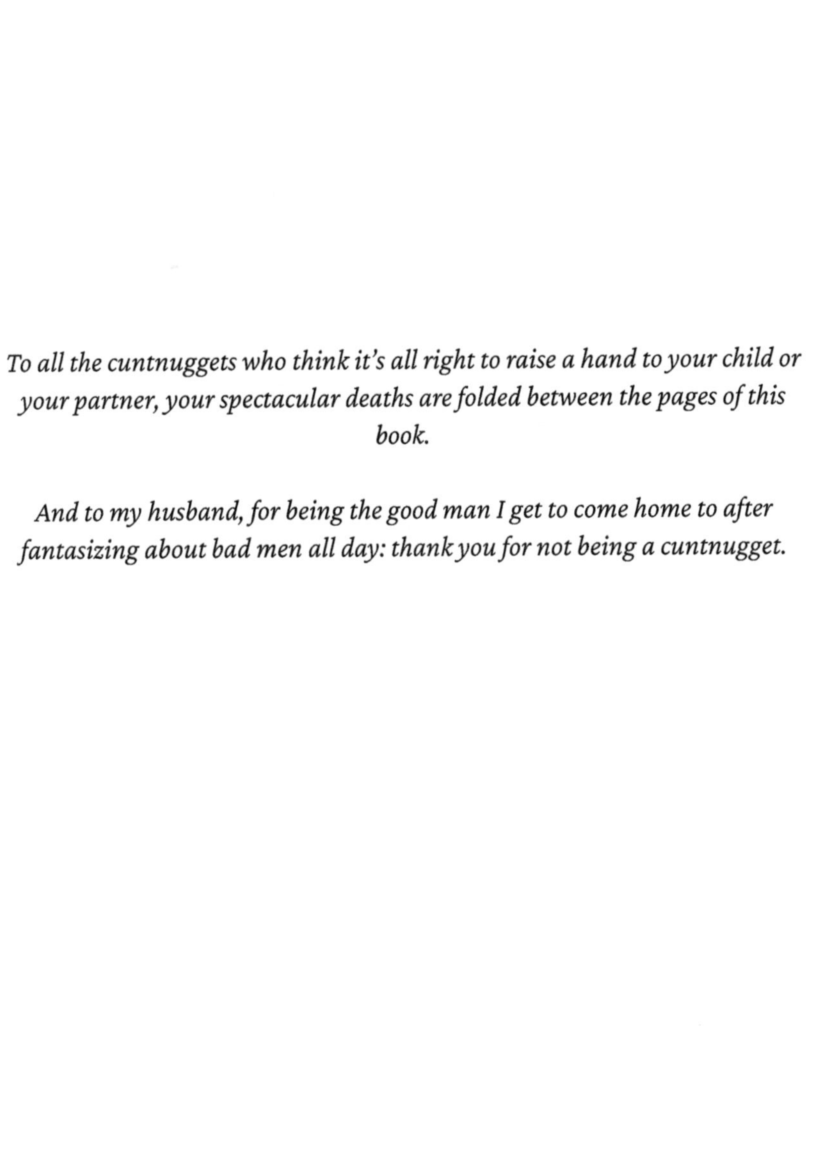

To all the cuntnuggets who think it's all right to raise a hand to your child or your partner, your spectacular deaths are folded between the pages of this book.

And to my husband, for being the good man I get to come home to after fantasizing about bad men all day: thank you for not being a cuntnugget.

1

CORVUS

Randy's body hadn't begun to smell yet, and judging by the still-tacky smears of blood around the carving on his chest, I'd say he'd only been dead an hour. Maybe less.

"You idiot," I seethed, glaring at his prone form as I drew my blade, giving a short, sharp whistle to alert the others that we may not be alone.

Rook and Grey's quiet footfalls sounded behind me as they jogged down the alley, slowing to a walk as they approached.

Rook cursed, rocking back on his heels when he saw the body half-laying, half-sitting against the side of a rusted green dumpster. He scrubbed a wide palm over his jaw. "The tip was legit."

No shit.

A chick from the after-hours stocking crew at the Valley-Mart was the one who tipped off the Saints about the body. Damn near the whole town knew better than to call the cops first, and the ones who didn't...they'd learn.

If there's blood in the streets, you don't want the useless rent-a-cops from Thorn Valley PD on the case. They don't care about you. They won't protect you. The Saints will.

I knelt to drag my red-stained fingertips over Randy's eyelids and bowed my head. Grey crouched next to me, reaching two digits to the hollow beneath Randy's chin, feeling for a pulse. As if someone this pale, this *still* could possibly be living.

His hand dropped not two seconds later, his head with it.

"I'll call it in," Grey said, dutifully drawing out his phone and rising from his crouch.

"Stay close," I growled when he moved to walk away.

"He was supposed to be made a full member at the next meeting," Rook mused aloud, biting on his lip ring. A habit he knew annoyed the absolute fuck out of me.

I stood, pushing off from my knees. "Not anymore." I held out a hand for the bag slung over Rook's shoulder. "Give me the tarp. Let's get this shit over with. I need a fucking shower."

Rook tossed me the bag, and I pulled out the folded blue square, wincing when the sound of it crinkling echoed back to us from the tall brick walls of the alley. The whole place smelled like trash, but there was an undercurrent of something out of place, too. Cologne. Or just some really terrible aftershave. Like a pinecone got ass fucked by a lime. My nose wrinkled at the reek of it.

"Keep an eye out."

Rook nodded, drawing his blade and hissing at Grey to get off the damned phone and help me.

"The carving," Grey stated as he ended the call, helping me lay out the tarp to roll the poor bastard's body onto it. "It was the Aces?"

The letter 'A' brutally carved into the pale flesh of Randy's chest would make anyone think so, but I wasn't convinced.

"We haven't had beef with the Iron Aces in months," I hissed. "There's no reason for this. Doesn't make sense."

"But the carving—"

"I know what it looks like, Winters."

At that, both of my brothers fell silent, and we wrapped Randy's body tightly in the tarp, binding him like a fucking sausage with half a roll of duct tape.

He was only twenty-four. Didn't have a family. No kids. Not even a girlfriend. Without any of those things, Randy would be given a whiskey-fueled farewell by the Thorn Valley Saints and then sent to a watery grave. It was the best many of us could hope for.

"Diesel's orders are to bring him to the Crow's Nest for now. Said he'd deal with it later," Grey told me as we finished, and I stuffed the rest of the duct tape back into the bag and tossed it to Rook.

When I didn't reply, still trying to work through the puzzle that was Randy's mangled corpse, Rook stepped to my side. "Want me to bring the Rover 'round?"

I nodded, jerking my chin for Grey to follow. "Go with him."

At least it was a cool night for early October in Northern Cali. Hopefully, his corpse wouldn't stink up the Rover too much before Diesel sent the cleaners to deal with it. Nothing worse than the smell of dead guy in the morning.

They turned to leave, but the roar of an engine coming to a stuttering, screeching stop at the mouth of the alley had me throwing an arm out to shield them, gun drawn, finger resting next to the trigger.

The sleek black sedan hadn't even come to a full stop before a body jumped out of the backseat.

I took aim.

Air rushed from my lungs in a heavy exhale. I relaxed as I took in long legs, a mane of dark brown hair, and an ass so fine it made my cock twitch beneath my jeans.

"Move the body," I hissed. Grey and Rook each took an end, pulling Randy with us into the shadows behind the trash bin and out of sight.

A driver exited the sedan as the girl pounded white-knuckled fists on its trunk. The bitch could hit. I'd be surprised if she hadn't left at least one dent in the thing.

"Miss," the driver pleaded. "Miss, the school is another mile *uphill.* Miss, please—"

"Open the fucking trunk," she snapped back at him, her voice carrying. It was laced with warning, and the pinhead driver must've sensed it because he lifted his hands in a placating gesture I knew well and retreated to the open driver's side door to pop the trunk.

"Ava Jade," came a woman's willowy voice from the darkened backseat as a window rolled lazily down. "You get back in the car this instant."

The girl, Ava Jade, I presumed, ignored the older woman's plea, hauling a massive suitcase and satchel from the trunk. When the damn thing fell over, it nearly took her with it, but she righted the suitcase, and herself, and took off in a huff, lugging all of her things up the road.

"Ava Jade!"

The girl paused, an audible growl tearing from her lips as she spun. A dark simpering fury in the set of her jaw. "I'd rather be at some bull-shit elitist academy than spend a single night at your fucking *museum*."

She didn't spare another second for the old woman. She turned on her heel and left, upper lip curled with distaste.

Both Grey and Rook craned their necks to get a better look, and I suppressed a groan.

"Is that Old-lady Humphrey?" Rook asked.

The bitch was rich; her dead husband came from old money. She lived in the big mansion over at Waverly Place all alone with, rumor had it, at least nine cats and a parrot that squawked all hours of the day and night.

"Looks like it," Grey replied, and I strained to hear the distant hum of more civilized conversation as the old bat instructed the driver to *leave the girl and take her home for Christ's sake.*

The car drove off after a minute, and we were left listening to the distant echo of the suitcase wheels bumping noisily over the pavement as the girl made her way down Main Street and up toward Briar Hall.

Both the guys darted forward after the red glow of the sedan's tail lights vanished, peering around the edge of the alley wall to get a better look at the chick.

"Should we..." Rook trailed off, a mischievous grin tipping up one corner of his lips, Randy forgotten for the moment.

"No."

"The fucker who killed Randy could still be around," Grey added. "We should at least warn her if not give her a ri—"

"I said *no*," I repeated, leveling the full weight of my glare on them both. Rook was quick to shrug it off, but Grey, he still didn't get it. He would though, even if I had to pound it into him.

I tucked my gun into the back of my waistband. "She isn't our fucking problem."

We weren't about to go out of our way for some spoiled rich brat who was going to be in the nurse's office all day tomorrow sobbing about all the blisters from her brand new heels. Not a fucking chance.

Grey stared after her a moment longer, and I didn't like the way his eyes followed her movements. Hell, even Rook still seemed bent out of shape that I wasn't going to let him loose on her. Turning his lip ring round and round with his teeth, his dark eyes gleamed with malice even though he was clearly trying to play it off like he didn't give a shit.

"There are finer asses than that in Thorn Valley," I said to Grey, attempting another tactic. "In fact, I'm pretty sure you left one in your bed an hour ago."

Grey tipped his head to one side, snorting a laugh.

We both knew I wasn't wrong about that last part, but fuck if I didn't know the first bit was total horseshit. I'd never seen a piece of ass that was worth wasting more than a night on. But *that ass*—that ass was trouble if I'd ever seen it.

It was in both of my brothers' curious stares as they took one last look at her before turning back to me for orders. I was going to have to do something about this *Ava Jade*. Fast.

"Get the Rover," I told them. "Looks like tomorrow we have a new student to welcome to Briar Hall."

2

AVA JADE

"*S*tupid *motherfucking bullshit wheels*," I cursed, kicking the suitcase back onto its front. The damned thing was overpacked, old as hell, and I lost one of the wheels about a quarter mile back. I tugged it along anyway, balancing it as it teetered precariously on the one wheel that was still working.

Everything I owned was in this bag. One way or another, I was going to get it up this hill.

As though in answer to my prayers, a break in the clouds allowed the moon to illuminate what was unmistakably a building taking shape amid the trees around the next bend.

A weathered brick exterior covered in young ivy came into view in bits and pieces. Darkened windows on the main floor were framed in black metal to match the large door set into the shadowy maw of a front stoop. Above the door in a bold pewter serif read *Briar Hall,* and below in shining silver cursive were the words *as the crow flies.*

What? No Latin inscription? How very modern.

I chuckled darkly to myself, wincing as the strain to my shoulders began to reach a breaking point. The damn suitcase chose *that* moment to catch a loose stone on the curving driveway and the case went down hard, nearly ripping my fucking arm from its socket.

I whirled around and kicked the thing as hard as I dared, cursing under my breath.

"What did that poor suitcase ever do to you?"

I had a blade out in half a second, letting the suitcase fall with a thud at my feet.

A girl emerged from the gloom beneath the front stoop, her shining brown eyes wide as she took in the slim blade gripped in my left hand.

"*Uh*, sweetie, I'm not here to hurt you. I'm just the welcoming committee."

That was when I noticed the haze of smoke in the air around her and how the heel of her knee-high black boot was stubbing out the remnants of a joint.

Not a heartbeat later the smell of pot-smoke wafted toward me on the cool breeze. I relaxed.

"Weapons aren't allowed on school property," she added, clearing her throat as I slipped the blade back into the garter belt beneath the hem of my skirt.

"I won't tell if you don't," I replied, inclining my head toward her foot and the stomped out joint hidden beneath it.

She laughed, bending to retrieve what was left of her midnight puff. I guessed that meant it was a deal. "I assume my aunt called ahead?"

The girl nodded, pushing long black hair back from her face. "Yup. Apparently, Mrs. June couldn't be bothered to welcome you herself since it's the middle of the night and all, so you get me."

"And you are?"

"Becca. Becca Hart. You'll be rooming with me."

She didn't sound too thrilled about that. Her smile tight.

"I was told I'd have my own room," I argued, a prickle of unease going through me at the idea of sharing with a total stranger.

If I'd learned anything, it was that people could not be trusted. And having a safe space to plop your ass down at the end of a hard day to sleep was paramount to survival.

A shudder ran through me, and it wasn't from the chill of the late hour. I shook off the imposing memories. This wasn't the time.

The girl, Becca, came down to the bottom of the stoop and reached out to help me lift my suitcase from the ground, showing off fingernails that were polished a perfect pearlescent black. Not a single chip.

Mine were a similar color, a deep plum, but shorter, chipped, and with all the color peeled off the right pinkie. She definitely noticed but said nothing.

"You do have your own. We share the floor as in: you have your own room, I have my own room, but we share the common living space. Most of the other students share at least four to an apartment. And on some floors, it's six. No one at Briar Hall has their own apartment except Bri. Well, and me, I guess, until *you* came."

"Shitty," I muttered as Becca helped me get the suitcase to the top step.

She made no comment to the contrary, but I felt her gaze roving over me as she shouldered the heavy metal door open and ushered me inside.

"The elevators are usually reserved for the Crows, but since they aren't here and it's the middle of the night, I think we're safe."

Becca walked across a wide marble foyer toward the single elevator against the far wall. To my left was a hallway twice as wide as the ones at my old school, a wooden sign on a wrought iron hook hanging from the ceiling farther down indicated the main office. Opposite that hallway on the other side of the foyer was a curved staircase leading up to where I imagined the classrooms to be.

The whole place smelled of oiled wood and old paper with an undertone of chemical cleaning product.

A loud *ding* in the dim foyer brought me back to reality, and I saw Becca striding into the elevator, throwing out an arm to keep the door open.

"Hurry up, would you? Before someone sees."

I did as she said, not because I was afraid of some mysterious *Crows* but because if there were any way I could avoid lugging this fucking thing up all those stairs, I was taking it.

Painfully aware of the trail of dirt and bits of gravel I was leaving in my wake on the waxed marble, I strode into the elevator and Becca released the doors.

"Who are the Crows?" I asked, my curiosity getting the better of me as Becca jabbed a button, careful to wipe it with her sleeve when she was finished.

Better to know in advance who to be on the lookout for.

I had to get through this last year of school, and then I would be home fucking free. Nothing was going to get in the way of that freedom. Not if I could help it.

Like Pops always said, *head down, eyes open, Ava Jade, that's how people like us make it in this world.* I'd never been very good at the *head down* part, but a girl could change.

Becca cut a sidelong stare my way, arching a brow. "You really aren't from around here, are you?"

"Is it that obvious?"

She bit her lower lip, thinking something through before she responded. "Tomorrow afternoon," she said finally as the doors opened again, letting us out in a long, dark hall.

"Tomorrow afternoon *what?*"

She shushed me, indicating the doors as we passed them, and I got the picture that these were the dormitories. The doors were too close together for them to be the larger rooms. At almost two in the morning, all of the students would be asleep.

Once we were clear of the corridor, Becca led me through a set of double doors and around a steep turn in the hallway. A sign in the same pewter serif as the front door of the building read, *East Wing.*

"At lunch," she continued as the door closed behind us. "I'll explain everything you need to know."

She took out a handful of keys from her pocket and separated two rings, handing me one. On it were two silver keys. Though I noticed there were not two, but three keys on hers. "We're just through here."

Becca unlocked the wooden door with the number 3 on it and pushed it open, flicking on a light switch as she stepped inside.

And holy motherfucking shitballs.

Equal parts stupefied, ecstatic, and disgusted, I strode past the wide foyer where a row of neat iron hooks held several jackets and hats and into a fully furnished living room. A black sectional U-shaped couch hugged a polished black square of a coffee table. On the gray stone wall across from it, a fire licked lazily at its chimney.

Behind the couch was a kitchen made up of a long bank of cabinets with a fridge at one end and a stove near the other.

Not like a cooktop or something. No, this was a monstrosity of polished chrome and black glass. With at least six burners. Matching cherry wood doors stood opposite one another to either side of the main living space. One sealed shut, the other slightly ajar.

"Holy shit."

I didn't realize I'd spoken aloud until Becca stepped up beside me, making me jolt. "Yeah. I like black. It just kinda matches everything."

When I didn't reply to her right away, she pursed her lips. "I mean, I can live with some color if you wanted to change anything—"

"It's fine," I hurried to say, picking my jaw up off the floor.

The living room and kitchen alone were damn near the size of mine and Dad's basement apartment back home. Definitely bigger than the trailer we lived in before that.

A painful jab in my chest made my lips tighten.

"I like black. But I thought we weren't allowed to change anything in the rooms anyway? My aunt drilled me on all the rules on the way here."

After she tried to convince me to stay with her and have Jarvis, or whatever the hell that dickwad driver's name was, drive me to school every day. Until I shut her the fuck up by literally jumping from the moving vehicle. No way in hell that was happening.

Becca shrugged. "My dad donated a new library to the school and has promised them a new gym, too."

She paused.

"*After* I graduate."

I cocked my head at her. Did she just say what I thought she'd just said? That her dad was literally blackmailing the school with fancy new shit so his daughter could do what she liked? Fucking rich people. But even I had to admit, that was pretty ballsy. He could just as easily have gotten her kicked out pulling shit like that.

"Sounds like an upstanding citizen of Thorn Valley."

She barked a laugh.

"As if. The formidable Mr. Hart doesn't live here. He just shipped *my* ass here so he wouldn't have to worry about me doing drugs or riding dick. Don't think he realized there are drugs and dick in every nook and cranny of this country, and I have my way with both no matter where I'm at."

She shrugged.

"I don't mind him feeling guilty though. His guilt got me this room. Oh, and my Audi. So I can '*drive home for the holidays.*' "

I narrowed my eyes at her, still a little taken aback at her drug and dick comment. I expected goody-two-shoes. I expected brown-nosers and posers and assholes. I didn't expect...

Whatever the hell Becca Hart was.

We might just get along after all.

"Fair enough," I nodded. "I'm assuming that's my room?"

I gestured to the door that was slightly ajar. Becca didn't strike me as an open-door sort of chick.

"That's the one," she trilled, capping off the sentence with a yawn as she dragged herself to the kitchen and rifled in one of the cupboards for a bag of peanut M&M's.

She stopped with a hand on her door handle. "Find me in the cafeteria at lunch," she added before leaving me alone in the living room. "I'm bagged, and you won't see me in the morning. I have somewhere I need to be."

"All right," I replied, hefting my suitcase over the hardwood, afraid to let the mangled wheels rub against the polished surface.

Huffing as I leaned my bag against the wall inside the room, I felt around on the cool bumpy surface for a light switch, cursing when I stubbed my toe on something.

I flipped it on, and the overhead light flashed to life, bright enough that I damn near turned it right back off. But in the end, curiosity won out.

The bed was the first thing to catch my eye. It was covered in a frilly purple monstrosity, with matching pillows. Who the fuck needed eight pillows anyway? I was lucky to have one at all half the time.

I cringed inwardly, making a mental note to get a new set the first chance I got. The rest of the space wasn't really that bad, though. The wall with the light switch was covered in a textured pearl wallpaper, and the deep purple color of the other walls looked pretty good with it.

The thing I'd stubbed my toe on had been a long dark wood desk with one of those fancy brass lamps on top of it. There was what looked like a walk-in closet to the left of the bed, and to the right, another door led to what I *prayed* was a bathroom.

Nearly tripping in my haste, I rushed to check it out, finding the light switch more easily this time. Fuck yes.

The room had its own en suite. Complete with a glass encased shower and removable shower head. Double sinks because...*rich people.* And a bright band of light embedded in the mirror. Stepping closer, I noticed there was a blurry bit and reached out to touch it.

The light brightened.

I touched it again, and the light changed from an orange hue to a blue one, making the dark pink circles beneath my dull eyes pop.

Jabbing the mirror again to darken my reflection, I tried to remember where I'd stuffed those big t-shirts in my suitcase. I could feel the tackiness of my own sweat drying against my skin beneath my clothes. A shower was absolutely mandatory before I crawled into bed and stuffed my blade beneath the pillow.

I noted the panel of shower buttons and my lips fell open.

It was official. Ava Jade was *not* in the Lennox ghetto anymore.

Sighing, I tore myself away from the awaiting spa experience and surveyed the room, checking the vents and every nook of the walk-in closet before I found what I was looking for. A loose board in the wood paneling beneath a shelf and hanging bar. I used a blade to carefully pry it free and peered into the dark hollow within.

It would have to do for now.

I upended the contents of my suitcase on the bed and pulled back the lining. The wrinkled Manila envelope filled with cash from my last job came free with a sharp tug, and I set it into my new hidey hole, notching the small panel back in place.

Chances were I wouldn't need it anymore. Not with a rent-free roof over my head and three square meals a day provided by my aunt's tuition payment, but if I couldn't do what she expected, I'd wind up right back where she found me on the streets of Lennox. Not fucking happening. I'd die before I went back to that shithole.

I set my blades right outside the door to the shower and stepped inside, hoping I wouldn't need a manual to work the thing. I jammed a few buttons, cursing when nothing happened.

"Come on," I groused, hitting the up arrow to increase the heat. "Let me simmer in my hell water you stupid fucking—"

I gasped as water sprayed from not one but five different places. Cool at first, but growing in temp until my skin flushed red. Just how I liked it.

3

AVA JADE

I rushed to the bathroom, the sound of sirens in the distance getting closer by the second. My pulse pounded in my ears, drowning out all other sound as I crashed through the door, hands scrambling to turn on the rusted faucets, smearing them with blood.

"Come on," I urged, as though by sheer force of will I could make the plumbing in our tiny trailer cooperate just this once. *"Come on!"*

My entire body trembled as the first flickers of red and blue lights swept into the trailer.

No.

If I could just get it off, they wouldn't know. I just had to get it off.

I scrubbed at my hands until they were raw, ripping the tips of my nails off when I couldn't get the blood out from beneath them and prodding them down the drain.

Fists pounded on the front door. If they hit it any harder it would collapse and they would come inside. They would find me. They would see what I'd done.

Hot tears pricked at my eyes as I shut off the faucet, ready to strip the crimson-soaked t-shirt off next, but not knowing where I could possibly hide it in the closet-sized bathroom.

The pounding began again, and I heard a muffled groan from next to the bathroom that could only be Mom waking up.

"Get fucked!" she slurred in a drugged stupor, groaning. Something shattered in the room as the mattress springs groaned beneath her. "Now look what you made me do!"

I turned off the taps and whirled, vision blurring at the edges enough that I had to slap myself back into the present. But something sticky and wet was left behind on my cheek, and I knew what would come next. I knew because it was what happened every time. A hopelessness filled my bones, weighing them down, and I sank heavily to my knees.

My hands were coated in his blood again, and I let them rest against my dirt-streaked jeans, giving in to the nightmare. I couldn't beat it; I'd tried so many times before. It didn't matter if I washed it away again, it would come back as if I never even fucking tried.

I clenched my shaking hands to fists and set my jaw, waiting for the officers to come and take me away like they always did. But I wasn't shaking because I felt guilty. My breaths weren't coming short and sharp because I regretted what I'd done.

No.

It'd been a rush unlike anything I'd ever felt before, and I wasn't sorry. As the darkness had finally taken over, pouring strength into my adrenaline-addled muscles and malice into my mind, I'd smiled. The bastard deserved it.

I'd do it again. *And again.*

I only feared what kind of monster that made me. I only feared a life in a cage.

I AWOKE WITH A STARTLED GASP, MY CHEST COVERED IN ICY SWEAT AS I HEAVED to get air into my lungs. No matter how deeply I breathed, it was like there would never be enough air to blow away the shadows clinging to my bones.

"Fuck," I muttered, throwing back the covers and rising on shaky legs to strip the bed, tossing the damp sheets and pillowcases into the wash basket. The more I moved, the more the fluttering beneath my ribcage came under control. But only once I pulled on a pair of joggers and a loose hoodie, sliding my sneakers onto my sleep-numbed feet and my earbuds into my ears did I truly feel a sense of calm.

I hesitated before grabbing my blade, hand trembling before I came to my senses and snatched it up, tucking it into my pocket and keeping my fist curled around it.

It didn't matter that it was barely dawn, or that it was cold as all hell as I crept through the room, down the still-vacant halls, and out into the early morning.

My breaths came easier as fresh air finally filled my lungs. I did a quick stretch before taking off toward the back of the old building, thumbing my phone until the haunting tones of Ruelle poured into my ears, singing to me of a game of survival.

A game I would win because I couldn't afford to lose.

I sang along, setting a brisk pace, relieved when I found a trailhead beyond the manicured field and gardens at the rear of Briar Hall. The trees welcomed me into their shaded embrace, and I breathed in the heady scent of petrichor, finding a sense of calm I hadn't had in days.

Had it really only been that?

Days?

Since Dad...

Since what happened.

I shook my head, savoring the burn starting up in my legs. The wind tugging at the ends of my loose ponytail.

What was done was done, and now, because of my father's incredible stupidity, I might just have a chance to do what he couldn't: escape the life I was born into.

Since Mom left a few years back, Aunt Humphrey was now the only person standing between me and the streets. After it happened, I thought I was fucked. Being eighteen meant that I was completely on my own. I'd have made do. Dropped out of my shitty high school and worked as many jobs as I needed to in order to keep a roof over my head.

Hell, I had already been paying most of the rent for Dad anyway. But then she showed up in her fancy town car with her ridiculous hat and an offer of a lifetime.

Aunt Humphrey and Dad didn't get along. I could see why, the woman was completely insufferable, and Dad was...well, *Dad*. About as much her opposite as opposites went.

She offered to take me off his hands when I was practically still in diapers so that he could spend the formula money on gambling. A proposition I bet my left kidney he considered well and good before turning down.

It almost felt like a betrayal taking her up on her offer now, knowing he'd refused her before.

It was too tempting to turn down, though. Only an idiot would.

She offered a comfortable allowance, to pay for my education, and buy me a small flat in the city, but it came with a caveat; I was to spend my final year of high school at Briar Hall, stay out of trouble, and get accepted into a good college by the end of the term.

If I could do that, she would set me up for a whole new life. The escape I'd always dreamed of back in Lennox was within my reach. All I needed to do was follow a few rules and be a good little Ava Jade, and I could have it.

I snorted through heavy breaths as I ran, giving my head a shake. As long as the privileged offspring of the wealthy and famous here at rich bitch academy stayed out of my way, it would be easy as pie. I could act the part of a nice girl and keep my head down for another nine-ish months, right?

Damn right.

A *crack* in the distance made me slow, tugging out an earbud to scan the trees, my free hand in my pocket, curled around the slender metal of my blade. I thought I saw a flicker of movement, but I couldn't be sure it wasn't just a trick of the slow-growing dawn light.

Shit. I needed to be getting back anyway. With one more good look, I decided there was nothing there and turned around. My skin prickled as phantom eyes followed me all the way back to the manicured lawn.

4

ROOK

"Are you sure you locked it?"

Mrs. June's voice came out in a rough pant as I shoved her over the edge of the pew, lifting her long skirt and nudging her legs apart with my knees.

"It's locked," I told her, though honestly, I couldn't remember if I had. Didn't really give a shit.

I ran a hand down the line of her thick ass, flicking her skin-tone panties aside to press two fingers against her opening. Her hands lifted to grip the back of the next pew as a stuttering moan left her lips.

She was already so wet for me. She always was.

"You like that, Care?"

"Call me Mrs. June," she cried as I shoved them inside of her, feeling her pussy clench around the digits.

I unbuckled my jeans and let them drop, exposing my hard on to the cool air in the chapel only for a second before I buried it into the heat of her cunt, not bothering to give her time to adjust. Groaning, I slapped her ass, leaving a bright cherry-red handprint behind.

"*Yes*," she cried out, and I reached forward, clamping a fist around the prim little bun of blonde hair at the nape of her neck.

"*Quiet*," I hissed. Not because I gave a flying fuck if anyone heard her, but because it ruined it for me when they spoke. She moaned as I eased out, driving back into her hard and fast, pulling so sharply on her hair that a whimper escaped her lips.

Her manicured nails dug into the old wood of the pew as I fucked her like a man starved. Until her little moans turned to startled cries, and she wriggled beneath me, trying to tug her hair free from my grasp.

"Rook!" she croaked between my thrusts, and I bent over her, wrapping my other hand around her dainty little neck as I drove into her from behind. I never really liked blondes, but Mrs. June had the body and the willingness to oblige my *tastes* to make up for that.

"Shut up, *Mrs. June.*"

My hips pounded against her ass, no doubt turning them as red as her pretty neck as I increased my speed, battering her against the pew until the thing started to come loose where it was bolted to the floor. Fucking her until all of my frustration was spent and the image of Randy's pale corpse faded from my mind.

The fucker who killed him was a dead man walking, he just didn't know it yet. I hoped Diesel would let me be the one to do it. It'd been a while. Too long.

I didn't let myself nut until Randy was fully purged from my skull. Not until the haunted memories seeing that carving in his chest brought back were gone, too.

"*Fuck,*" I roared, burying myself in Mrs. June until she found her release, her pussy clenching around my cock in a way that had me groan as I poured into her. Every meticulously crafted muscle in my body tense and writhing beneath my tatted flesh.

I released her throat, and she took a strained, gasping breath. Guess I was squeezing a bit too hard. I'd only meant to apply pressure to her carotid, but like Corvus always liked to remind me...I sometimes got carried away.

My phone went off in my pocket and I pulled out of Mrs. June, slipping my still-damp cock back into my jeans as I yanked them up.

Before I could get the phone out to check the message, Mrs. June whirled around. I saw the slap coming a mile away but didn't bother to stop her as the little slut's open palm cracked across my face.

Mmmm. My skin bristled, and I licked the dribble of blood from where the force of her strike tore at my lip ring, grinning at her.

"What's wrong, Caroline? I thought you liked it rough."

She moved to hit me again, defiance in her haughty stare and curled upper lip, but this time I stopped her. Snatching up her wrist, I yanked her in until she was close enough that her disgusting vanilla musk perfume filled my nose. Even in heels, she seemed so small, so insignificant as I stared down at her. "Hit me again and you will live to regret it."

Her bottom lip trembled for a moment before she got control of herself, snatching her wrist away to attempt to right the mess that was her hair and adjust her shirt to try to cover the marking my hand left behind on her throat.

"*Heathen,*" she snarled at me as she stuffed her feet back into her shoes and made her way toward the door. The door that was not locked after all as she opened it without the need to undo the deadbolt.

She growled her frustration, turning back to give me one last blistering glare before leaving.

"You know you love it. The rough fuck. The fear of getting caught. It's what you need to get off, *Mrs. June.*"

She took off into the north wing of Briar Hall, leaving me with only the sting of her slap and the scent of her sweet pussy lingering in the air. She'd be back.

I rolled my shoulders, pressing my thumb to my phone to unlock it.

GREY

New girl is in our homeroom. Hasn't shown her face yet though

I had absolutely no doubt Corvus made some midnight phone calls to make that happen. The guy never missed an opportunity to control a situation.

I stuffed my phone into my pocket and pushed my dark hair back, shooting a look at the statue staring down at me from the dais. "What?" I asked Jesus, shrugging as I reached into my other pocket for a cigarette. Lighting it up, I inhaled deeply, tipping my head to the side to work out the kinks in my neck. "We're just going to play with her."

And this time, I had a feeling I was going to enjoy the game.

5

AVA JADE

Late on the first day.

Joy.

Even though Becca warned me she wouldn't be there in the morning, I had to admit I was a little disappointed to find the flat empty when I returned from my run.

I wanted to ask her how to get to my homeroom and where I needed to go to wash my sheets. Tucked away in the pamphlet and massive rulebook my aunt gave me before carting me off here had been a map, but I couldn't find either in my things. I was pretty sure I left them in her town car after I hopped out in the middle of the street.

She hadn't called, and I wasn't going to be the one apologizing. She only said I needed to finish the year and be well behaved at Briar Hall. She said nothing about sitting there mutely while she badmouthed my father before he was even cold in his fucking grave.

"*Where is it?*" I muttered to myself, searching the entryway of the school for any sort of map. Of course, the office was completely vacant even though the bell had rung for first period five minutes ago.

"You look lost."

The voice was deep and gruff but playful. When I spun around in the corridor, I found him leaning against the wall in the mouth of the darkened corridor labeled *North Wing*.

I spluttered for a response, taking in what was surely *not* a high school boy but a combination of my best dream and worst nightmare all wrapped into one.

With lips clearly stolen from a Greek statue and a square jaw sharper than a razor's edge, his allure was undeniable. But painted over his knuckles and poking out from the top of his black shirt were tattoos. I was willing to bet that beneath the jacket concealing his arms, there was even more ink to be found. That, combined with the dark gleam in his eyes spelled trouble in big ass bold letters.

His teeth bit lightly at a lip ring at the edge of his mouth as he watched me curiously. Like one might watch an ant before busting out a magnifying glass to sear it into the pavement.

"Do you know where room 701 is?" I finally managed around the lump in my throat, lengthening my spine. It didn't matter that in my rush to shower and get to class I'd had to forego my usual five-minute makeup routine in favor of some hastily applied mascara. Or that all my clothes were wrinkled to shit from being stuffed haphazardly in my suitcase. At least I had my baggy black sweater to cover most of it up, though that wasn't exactly pretty either.

It didn't matter one little bit.

"701?" he repeated, making me wonder if he was daft. Someone as gorgeous as he was had to have some sort of flaw. As he slid his tatted fingers through his damp dark hair, I noticed the word inked into his knuckles was, in fact, *ROOK* and that his knuckles were bruised and cut. I also noticed how his left cheek was blooming with a patch of red that looked suspiciously like a handprint.

"That's what I said," I snapped and then remembered myself. *Play nice, Ava Jade.* "Could you tell me where it is?"

"I'll do you one better."

Without another word, he brushed past me, a nasty vanilla scent trailing along with him that made my nose wrinkle. I assumed he meant to show me instead.

I considered saying fuck it and finding the room myself, but in a building this massive, it could take me all day. So, instead, I caught up to the guy, brushing the stray hairs that'd snuck out of my messy bun back behind my ears.

"Won't you get in trouble for being late?"

If the rules were as archaic as the old building, I was willing to bet they beat you with rulers for a tardy.

He seemed amused by my question and his lips tipped up into a crooked grin. "Nah."

We fell back into silence and that suited me just fine. I wasn't about to make friends with a guy who looked like he might be here to stage an attack on the place. Though I did do a sweep over his hand and neck tatts again, checking for any discernible gang ink.

Finding none, I was satisfied for the moment.

We passed several classrooms where teachers prattled on to the whispered drone of student conversation until I noticed the pattern of the numbers.

"I think I can find it from here," I said, eager to leave the guy behind in the hallway. His nearness was setting my teeth on edge, and not least of all because he kept sneaking glances at me when he thought I wasn't looking.

I called back a hasty *thanks* before rushing forward to room 701 which should be...*ah*. Right there. I shoved my way inside, pulse thrumming in my ears. My sigh of relief turned to something entirely different as the teacher halted mid-lecture, his gaze piercing me in place.

My eyes skimmed over the class, searching for one specific face, but not finding it. No Becca. Great.

"I, *uh*, I'm Ava Jade, I just started—"

"You're late," came his sharp reply, and my first instinct was to snap right back at him with a comment about his Harry Potter wannabe glasses, but I smothered it with a forced nod.

"Sorry, sir, it won't happen again."

"See that it doesn't. Late students aren't welcome in my classroom, is that clear?"

"Yes, sir."

"Well don't just stand there, find a seat."

I bit the inside of my cheek and surveyed the rest of the class, face heating as I realized all eyes were on me. Eyes ringed in false lashes and faces framed in too-perfect hair. Clothes that looked like they were stolen right off the mannequins at Prada or Chanel.

The door bumped into my ass as it reopened at my back, sending me staggering forward toward the two empty seats in the room.

"Sorry," I muttered at whoever's way I was in, gaping when I saw it was the guy from the hall.

"Rook," the teacher said, removing his glasses to pinch the bridge of his nose with a sigh. "Glad you decided to grace us with your presence."

What?

Was he seriously not going to give the guy hell for being late after basically just verbally bitchslapping me for doing the same? Awesome, so the school was sexist as well. Why wasn't I surprised?

"Of course, Mr. Jameson." Rook tipped his head to the teacher, giving a little salute and absolutely no excuse as to why he was late.

He shouldered past me and took his seat, leaving me only one option: the desk and chair in the absolute center of the classroom.

Rook had taken the seat behind me and to the right, but he wasn't who I couldn't seem to peel my eyes away from.

Directly behind the empty seat was a guy who was staring at me like he was contemplating murder.

If it weren't for the scowl twisting his face, I might have said he was handsome. With a whisper of dark blond scruff on his jaw and menace in his bright baby blue eyes. The guy was big and thick through the shoulders, though not as big as his pal Rook, who was whispering something into his ear.

"Take your seat!"

I shot Mr. Jameson a glare before rushing to sit down. I didn't have to turn around to find out that the guy behind me was still staring. I could feel his eyes on the back of my head as if he were leaning into me, making the hairs on my arms and neck stand on end and my hand twitch toward the blade strapped to my ankle beneath my bootcut jeans.

Mr. Jameson launched back into a lecture on something I had absolutely no hope of absorbing, but at least I could try to take notes for later. I dug into the desk, ignoring the whispers and stares all around me, but my hands came up empty. I thought...

I thought the handbook said I would be provided with textbooks and study materials and supplies on my first day. Entirely unwilling to raise my hand in this den of vipers, I resigned myself to just sitting still, which was a feat of its own.

As Mr. Jameson lifted a piece of chalk to scrawl something in unintelligible handwriting on the blackboard, someone tapped my shoulder.

I glanced back, finding the guy who I'd briefly seen sitting to the other side of the psycho-looking one. He was holding out a few sheets of paper and a pen.

"The fuck you doing Grey?" the one in the middle hissed to the one holding out the shit for me, his voice dripping venom.

"*Umm*," I muttered, glancing back and forth between them. "I'm good. Thanks."

"Just take them," the one called Grey insisted, shoving them at me. He didn't look like he belonged with the other two. Where they were all dark and edgy, he was an All-American stud. With one of those short on the sides and long on top haircuts in a brassy gold too shiny to be dyed.

A winning smile split his face, and he wielded it like a weapon, slashing away any hope of my being able to deny him.

"Okay then." I cleared my throat as I spun around in my seat, paper and pen in hand. I caught the girl next to me glaring in my direction as I began to try and decipher what Mr. Whatshisface wrote on the board.

I gave her a *the-fuck-do-you-want* look, eyes bugging out of my skull in question until she finally looked away, her barbie pink upper lip curling in distaste. She had long blonde hair flowing in a perfect wave down her back with a solid gold pin keeping it tucked back behind her ear. Her outfit screamed money and her unblemished skin told me she hadn't had to work for a damned thing in her entire life.

There was no way those tits were real, either.

Fake bitch.

She gasped, and I realized I'd muttered the words aloud and clamped my jaw shut, redoubling my efforts to focus on the lesson and not on all the eyes watching the new girl.

Once they got their eyeful and made their judgment, they'd move along.

"Are you just going to let her talk to me like that?" The girl hissed in a low voice. Unable to curb my curiosity, I tilted my head to the side to see her baring her pearly whites at Grey.

His eyes lifted to the ceiling as he leaned back in his chair, looking bored as hell.

"Chill, Bri. You'll smudge your lipstick sneering like that," Rook crooned and an angry flush rose to her cheeks, mostly concealed by the thick layer of makeup she wore. She spun back around, her hands curling into claws atop her desk, practically shaking with rage.

Wow. Bitch really needed to get a grip. It wasn't like I'd called her a cunt or a whore, but judging by her reaction and the way she immediately looked to the nearest dick-bearing human for protection told me she was likely both of those things, too.

I studiously took notes for the next thirty minutes, droning out the whispered conversations around me and the way the asshat behind me kept 'accidentally' kicking my chair leg. Though, when the guy got up to use the bathroom I saw how gigantic he was so, maybe it *was* an accident after all.

Where Rook was all wide shoulders and dense muscle, this guy was tall as fuck. Like, he had to be close to clearing seven feet. Six-five at a minimum. For all I knew he probably couldn't help catching his size thirteens on my chair, but judging by the bitter look he gave me as he passed, he wouldn't have given a shit either way.

The blonde next to me, Bri, had her phone open beneath her desk and a coy smile tugged at the corners of her lips as she thumbed a message. Not more than a few seconds after she sent it, an audible buzzing sounded behind me, and she passed something back to Angry Face

My immediate suspicion was drugs, but then I had to remind myself where I was and amend my suspicions. Not drugs—*designer drugs*. There would be no tic-tacs or cloudy crystal here. It was likely all blow and bath salts at hoity toity prep.

And no search dogs, bag checks, or metal detectors to catch them.

At least I could keep my blade on me in class now. Having it close by almost always settled my nerves, even if in most circumstances I wouldn't need to use it.

Piggybacking on Dom's private self-defense lessons for the last two years back home made me just as lethal without it. Speaking of, I wondered how long it would take her to notice I was gone. It hadn't exactly been a priority to let anyone know I was leaving. Besides, she was sequestered up at her dad's place for the next two weeks while he defended some crime lord in court. Being a lawyer for one of the bigger gangs in California came with certain...risks.

He always made her stay with him in Madison Heights when he was going to trial. There was no telling what his clients might do if he lost on their behalf. Good thing he never did.

It was why he made her take the lessons in the first place. Why he didn't complain when I tagged along with her—since it seemed to be the only way his daughter would go herself.

"Hey," Bri whispered and it took me a full ten seconds to realize she was talking to me.

I squinted at her, checking to make sure the teacher was busy before replying. I didn't want to incur his wrath twice in the same morning. "What do you want?"

Her lips pressed together as she tapped a piece of paper in her glittery pink three-ring binder. Groaning inwardly, I leaned over to look at what she'd written and froze. Burning rage seared through my chest and steamed my cheeks, turning them no doubt a blistery red.

In a deep red ink were the words:

GO BACK TO YOUR TRAILER, LENNOX. YOU DON'T BELONG HERE.

Great, so everyone already knew exactly who I was then. I wondered if they paid off the office admin for the info or if they'd just handed it over with no questions asked. Neither would surprise me.

The darkness I always kept at bay slid up my throat like poison, making me have to choke it back.

I smiled sweetly and slid my middle finger over my lips, pretending to blend imaginary lip balm. *Fuck off,* I mouthed and earned myself a chuckle from Grey, who was at the perfect angle behind us to read my lips.

But Bri's grin only magnified at my slight, a deviant glimmer in her bright green eyes as she turned to the teacher, her expression morphing completely.

"Thief!" she shrieked, standing so sharply that her desk jostled, her perfect row of multicolored pens scattering to the floor. "Mr. Jameson, she stole my bracelet!"

I rolled my eyes. Yep. A cuntnugget for sure.

Mr. Jameson's beady eyes slid to me accusingly, his face in a disgusted pucker. "Now, now, class," he said firmly, making the chatter of the other students lower as he cut between the aisle of desks with his sights set on me.

I put my hands up, knowing the drill, even if Mr. Jameson wasn't an officer of the law. He might as well be here. Plus, if your hands are up, they're less likely to shoot.

Of course, you're still not totally safe even then. Getting one that'd had a bad day almost always ended in at least a few bruises from a baton or a getting tased for 'resisting' even if you were statue-still. At least, that's how it worked in Lennox.

"I didn't take anything," I said preemptively, cutting off the teacher before he could speak. "I don't know what she's talking about."

Mr. Jameson glared between Bri and me, his face growing redder by the second. "Miss Moore, is it possible you simply left your bracelet in your room?"

"No," she whined, pointing her finger in my direction. "Check her pockets."

Jesus fucking Christ.

Sighing, I turned out my right pocket and then my left, knowing the drill and just wanting this bullshittery over with. But something cool brushed my fingers a second before it toppled from the pocket of my baggy sweater. The dainty silver bracelet hit the polished floor with a little tinkle, and the rage I'd been working to squish back into the jar where it belonged began to overflow.

"I did *not* steal that," I said through gritted teeth as Bri crossed her arms over her chest, dignified in her accusation now that it was proven correct. I wasn't an idiot; I knew how this looked. And how weak my rebuttal sounded.

Mr. Jameson collected the bracelet and handed it back to Bri who looked far too pleased with herself for my liking. I wondered if she'd look so damned smug with two black eyes but managed to rein myself in, clasping my hands together beneath the table in a vice.

"Theft is not tolerated at Briar Hall."

Bri shared a conspiratorial look with the guy behind me, and it all made sense. The bitch had set me up. She'd passed the bracelet to the douche canoe behind me, and he'd slipped it into my pocket when she made me lean over to read her stupid note. I'd been played.

Wow. Touché, bitch. *Tou-fucking-ché.*

"Do you have anything to say for yourself?"

I glared up at the teacher, running my tongue over my teeth and half expecting to find fangs. When I didn't give Mr. Jameson the response he wanted, because I'd be damned if I was going to admit to something I didn't do, he shook his head.

"Gather your things and get out of my sight."

With pleasure. There was no sense arguing about it, not when the evidence was right there for everyone in the entire class to see.

"Detention," Mr. Jameson called back over his shoulder without turning to look at me as he made his way to the blackboard. "Every day this week after last period."

Bri grinned gleefully at me as I gathered up my notes, and I got an idea. It wasn't nearly as much as she deserved, but I remembered one of the cardinal rules of Briar Hall from the pamphlet my aunt gave me.

No cell phones in class.

I knocked my hip into Bri's desk as I bent to retrieve the pen I'd purposefully dropped, easily slipping my hand into the darkened mouth of her desk to grab her phone.

"Oh, so sorry about that," I said, my voice dripping sarcasm and growing loud enough that the teacher would be sure to hear me. "I didn't mean to make you drop your phone."

Her eyes went wide.

"Here." I dropped it onto her desk, and she went white as she scrambled to grab it, eyes shifting to Mr. Jameson who looked like he was ready to blow his top.

"Miss Moore, you should know better."

"Mr. Jameson, I didn't—"

"Detention," he shouted over her plea. "And I'll take that for the rest of the day."

I gave her a one-shoulder shrug as she fumed with a declaration of war clear in her haughty stare. I hadn't waved the white flag like she wanted, like she expected, and I got the feeling she didn't know how to handle someone who stood their ground.

On a whim, I tossed a wink at the asshat who'd colluded with her to set me up, letting him know that I knew exactly what he'd done. That I wouldn't forget it.

His stony blue eyes watched me, never wavering, as I left homeroom. It was me who had to break the connection, my throat going dry as I recognized something in his stare: a darkness that should've terrified me, but instead had me curious to see how deep it ran. My finger aching to press his buttons.

No.

I shook my head, clearing it of any lingering shadows. Freedom was within my reach. One school year away.

Another run before second period sounded like a good idea. If I stayed here, I couldn't guarantee I wouldn't wait around to give that blonde bitch a rude awakening after class.

At Lennox High, I was the girl everyone knew better than to cross. All it took was my curling a fist around the disappointingly small cock of the Lennox Lions' quarterback, and pressing one of my blades firmly against its base. I only drew the tiniest dribble of blood, but it did the trick.

If the jerkoff didn't already think I was insane for turning down his offer to fuck me in his truck, the blade helped finish the job.

By the next day I was branded a psycho and shunned by the rest of the school. Just how I liked it.

I half wondered if the same trick would work here before remembering the way the guy behind me had been staring. If I got his vibe right, the fucker would probably enjoy that. I sighed, tucking the idea away in a back pocket of my mind just in case I needed to use it.

6

AVA JADE

By the time lunch rolled around, my legs were stiff from my run and my brain was absolute mush from second period history.

Left with only my baser instincts, I followed the smell of roast chicken like a stray dog, practically panting as I found the entrance to the dining hall.

Dear sweet baby Jesus, I was *starving*. How long had it been since I'd eaten anything? A day at least. Probably more. My stomach burbled loudly as I made for the serving line, eyes saucer wide as I took in the heaps of steaming, glistening goodness along the self-serve counter.

Every kind of salad you could imagine. Not one but *three* different soups. Sandwiches with little toothpick flags sticking out of their tops. Steaming trays of lemon and herb chicken. Seared tofu. Artfully cut fruit that looked too pretty to actually eat. Sushi. There was fucking sushi.

"Drool much?" A girl sneered as I got into line behind her. She abandoned her tray, leaving the line presumably just to get away from me.

Her loss was my gain. She'd already filled one small plate with salad, and not knowing where she'd gotten the tray, I helped myself to hers, adding a bowl of creamy soup and three sandwiches to the pile. I promised myself I'd come back for some sushi after I was finished when I realized there wasn't room on the small black tray for anything else.

I spotted Becca as I turned and blew out a breath, glad to see a face that wasn't staring at me like I might be contagious. She flashed a smile my way, and I slid into the seat next to her, barely getting out a 'hey,' before stuffing the first sandwich in my mouth.

Becca picked at an orange on her plate and watched me with an amused look on her face.

"What?" I managed between mouthfuls.

"Just get out of prison?" she joked, eyeing my plate and mayo coated fingers.

I laughed around the bite in my mouth, swallowing it down with a grimace. "I might as well have."

I winced, realizing I'd said that out loud, but Becca didn't comment or question, just snagged a grape from the top of one of my salads and plopped it into her mouth.

The girl from this morning strode in a moment later with three other girls strutting behind her. They had to be related, I thought at first. All three were blondes, though after closer inspection it was easy to tell at least one of them wasn't a natural. Her brows were too dark and her roots were beginning to show. I assumed it was a prerequisite to join her clique and snorted, going back to my lunch.

"I heard about this morning," Becca said, drawing my attention back to her.

Why wasn't I surprised?

"People are saying Bri has it out for you."

I rolled my eyes.

"Yeah. She's sort of like the queen of Briar Hall. A legacy student. Her family has been going here for generations."

Woop-de-freakin'-do.

Becca licked her lips and scanned the students in the dining hall like she was considering how she might want to chop all their heads off.

"You look murdery," I commented, wiping my hands on a napkin before swapping out my sandwich for the soup.

Her expression softened, and she smirked, one corner of her deep crimson lacquered lips tipping up as her eyes leveled back on me. "A bad case of resting bitch face," she explained. "Inherited from my mom. I checked and there's no cure. I always look stabby. Probably why bitches like Bri generally steer clear of me."

"Teach me?"

She chuckled. "Maybe. If you're lucky."

I set the spoon down in favor of drinking the rest of the soup straight from the bowl, wondering if it was too soon to go back for seconds. So much fucking food must get wasted here. Enough to feed all the students from Lennox High who couldn't afford a proper lunch. It looked like most of them weren't even eating, going straight for the sparkling water and not much else.

"So, you were going to give me the low down," I said, sitting back in my chair to give my stomach a moment to adjust itself before I attempted to pile anything else into it. "Anyone besides Bri I need to be wary of?"

She jerked her head to the side, gesturing toward the door. The three guys from my homeroom were just entering the cafeteria. The one who'd colluded with Bri to accuse me of theft scanned the student body, making heads spin away from him as though they were afraid to be caught staring.

When his cold stare found me, I stared back, tipping my head to one side, raising a brow.

His jaw twitched as the blond one said something, and the trio went to sit at a table in the back corner of the cafeteria. I didn't miss how it was the one vantage point that would give them an unobstructed view of the entire room, *and* ensure no one could slip behind them undetected. It was where I would have sat. Where I *did* sit when I actually ate in the cafeteria at Lennox High.

"Yeah. Kind of figured. They were in my homeroom," I mused as the blond guy went to pile a plate sky high with food and carry it back to the table. Grey. I thought he was going to share it—the bitch boy going to get everyone's lunches—but he kept the tray to himself, immediately diving in. Demolishing the mountain of food like a starved beast.

The guy was thick with muscle, but if he ate like that all the time, you had to wonder where it all went.

"You shouldn't stare," Becca said. "They're the Crows."

I lifted a brow.

She leaned in, her brown eyes cutting to the table in the corner and back again as though she were afraid they might hear her from this far away. "They're Diesel St. Crow's adopted sons."

I knew that name. Where the hell did I know that name from?

"The Saints," Becca said when she saw I was having trouble catching on. "The Thorn Valley chapter. Diesel's one of the original three. This was ground zero for the gang. Now there are chapters all over Cali. One in

Phoenix, too, I think."

Heat licked up my back, and my appetite for food vanished, replaced with something more savage. Of fucking course they were part of a gang.

I thought I was escaping that bullshit when I agreed to leave Lennox and come here. I should've known better.

"They're members then?"

She nodded, absently picking at the orange on her plate. "What's his deal?" I asked. "The one who keeps staring."

"Corvus? He's kind of their leader, I guess. Hot as fuck, but still a psycho. Totally a Scorpio."

"A what?"

"Scorpio," she repeated, her cat eyes taking in the long line of him before flitting to the guy next to him. The scary sexy one with the dark hair and the lip ring. "And that's Rook. I have him pegged as Aries."

"What about the one eating like he's on his way to death row?" I asked, curious. I never paid much attention to horoscopes or whatever, but clearly Becca lived by them.

"I'm not sure. I go back and forth between Gemini and Taurus for him. He's a hard one to read."

"And me?"

She pursed her lips, considering as she eyed me up and down. "I haven't decided yet."

I opened my mouth to tell her, but she stopped me with a look. "No, don't tell me. I'll figure it out."

A knot began to form between her brows, and I sensed she had more to say, and it wasn't to do with which star sign I fell under.

"What?" I prodded.

She readjusted herself in her seat, her face pinching as she considered how to say something.

"Thorn Valley can either be the safest place you've ever lived—or the most dangerous."

"Depending on what?"

Her eyes flicked up to meet mine and then zeroed back in on the Crows. "Them."

"So, hypothetically, if I'd already maybe pissed one of them off—"

"*You did what?*"

"Well, I didn't exactly *do* anything. The guy looked like he wanted to erase me from the face of the earth the moment I walked into homeroom, and then he *helped Bri* set me up."

Her eyes widened. "Which one?"

"The tall one with the permanent scowl."

Her cheekbones flared. "Shit, girl. If Corvus James has it out for you, you should just leave."

I barked a laugh, but the sound died in my throat when her stony expression didn't crack.

"I mean it. It isn't worth staying."

My fingers automatically went to my lap, inching lower toward the blade hidden beneath the hem of my jeans. "I'm not going anywhere."

Her lips quirked up at one side. "Then you're an idiot."

I shrugged. "I've dealt with worse."

"Something tells me you aren't lying."

She inhaled deeply after a moment, biting on her lower lip. "Fine. If you're staying, then it's only fair I give you a proper welcome."

Becca eyed my clothes. "Friday, there's a party. Maybe you can make peace with the vultures...What size are you?"

I looked at her in question.

"We might have to go shopping first," she explained. "There's a place in town here that I love. I'll take you after school."

I cringed even thinking about buying something at a place where she shopped. Not because I wouldn't like it; the price tag and I might have some differences of opinion.

But if they didn't have alarm tags on them then...

"Shit. I can't," I huffed. "I have detention."

Her lips parted in surprise. Clearly the *whole* story hadn't circulated yet.

"On the first day? I mean, I'm impressed. Took me a full week to earn mine."

This girl just kept surprising me.

"Took the queen down with me, too. I have detention all week, but she has detention today, too."

Her eyes lit up.

"Brianna Moore has detention? That's new. She'll probably find a way out of it, though."

Becca glanced conspiratorially across the table. "Okay, so here's what you do. Ms. Wood runs detention, and she's an ornery fucker, but lucky for you I've learned how to tame that dragon. Listen closely and you'll have her eating out of the palm of your hand by the dinner bell..."

7

GREY

Three scraps of paper and a pen and suddenly I'm the fucking devil. Corvus got over it, but Bri...

My phone went nuclear at lunch. The instant we entered the cafeteria, she and her little posse turned up their noses and left. She barely waited two minutes to send the first in a slew of bullshit messages.

None of which I replied to.

She knew what we were. I made it clear to her from the start, and she agreed we wouldn't get serious. That didn't stop her from trying to lay claim to me in other ways, though. She'd already run one girl out of Briar Hall for daring to get too close to me. I didn't doubt that was precisely what she planned to do with this new one, too.

The mere thought of the new girl had my cock hardening beneath my jeans. She was not what I expected, and I'd gotten good at knowing what to expect. How to play those expectations to my advantage.

Ava Jade was frustratingly, and refreshingly, divergent from all my expectations. I didn't know what to make of her.

Callous. Vulgar. Sly as a fox.

And smarter than she looked.

We shared AP calculus third period, and she finished her work for the day *before me.* I thought she'd handed it in unfinished, or riddled with errors, but I saw the look on Mr. William's face when he marked her answers. Looking at her like she was some fascinating puzzle he'd like to unravel.

I couldn't blame him.

Hers was not a conventional sort of beauty. Not the type best suited to be wrapped up in silk or adorned with flowers and jewels.

Ava Jade's was a brutal beauty. Forged of sharp edges and heavy contrasts. Lips bowed and turned down at the corners. Eyes dark despite their arctic color, hooded and calculating.

Rook elbowed me hard in the ribs, and I cleared my throat, readjusting my cock as Diesel stood from his seat to go to the bar.

The warehouse was a temporary meeting place since the new headquarters weren't finished being built. We'd grown out of the old lodge but still laundered money through it—and about eighteen other properties from here to Stockton.

Thirty or more shot glasses were lined up in two neat rows along the bar, filled to their brims with whiskey. Enough for nearly everyone here to have two if Rook didn't drink his usual five first. Whispered conversations from the other members quieted as Diesel lifted one.

His cut-glass eyes skimmed the faces of the members. Pausing briefly at the low table where the other guys and I lounged near the open doors and the barbeques pouring burger scented smoke into the night outside.

"To Randy," Diesel said, suspending time for an instant before knocking back the whiskey and upturning the glass on the bar.

His eyes glimmered with malice as he licked the shine of the drink from his lips. "His death will be avenged."

A few shouts of assent rang through the gathering.

Diesel moved aside for the next member to pay his respects to a drumbeat of fists pounded on cheap tables until someone flicked the radio back on.

"What's up with you?" Corvus asked, his jaw working as he picked at the label on his beer, eyes boring a hole into me. Looking like he knew exactly what I'd been thinking about and didn't fucking approve.

"Bri," I lied. "She's still in a fit about homeroom."

Corvus rolled his eyes but visibly relaxed, smirking. I got the sense he was glad Bri decided she didn't like Ava. Less work for him if he wanted to get rid of her, which seemed like exactly what he wanted to do.

Stooping to helping *Bri*—a bitch he'd made no secret of disliking—set the girl up for theft? Since when did Corvus need help getting rid of a body? If he wanted her gone so damn bad, then why was she still here? I had a feeling there was more to it than I thought. He must've seen something in her, or knew something about her that we didn't. I wouldn't have been all that surprised if he'd already nicked her file from the office and used our contacts to dig into her past. He didn't like wild cards.

"What is it about the new chick that's got you all twisted?" I asked, regretting the question almost as soon as it left my lips. His cheekbones flared, and I was narrowly saved by Diesel coming to the table.

He slapped his hand down onto Corvus' shoulder and gave a squeeze. "I'm going to need you this weekend," our adoptive father said, slipping into the chair next to Corv, the mask he wore for the others slipping around the edges.

His exhaustion was apparent in the heaviness of his shoulders and the flare of red veins in his eyes.

Diesel rubbed the edge of his mouth, thinking, before wiping his palm down his short blond beard. Barely forty, but in this moment he could've passed for closer to fifty with all the hard lines creasing his forehead.

"Recon?" Corvus asked, running his tongue over his teeth as he turned his mind from the banality of Briar Hall back to business.

Diesel nodded.

"I don't think it was the Aces," Corvus said. "Doesn't sit right."

"We can't assume anything. Not until we have something concrete to base it on."

Corvus clearly disagreed, but said nothing else.

"Good?" Diesel asked, his gaze resting on each of us briefly before he stood again.

"Good," he said when none of us rebuked his order. We rarely did. "Now go pay your respects and get out of here. It's late. Grey, I'll get Cook to wrap you up a plate."

My stomach pinched at the mention of food even though I'd just eaten before we left home. "Thanks, Dies."

Corvus was the first to get up, abandoning his half-drank beer to head to the bar.

Rook stared on, his leg bouncing rapidly beneath the table as he twisted his lip ring around and around with his teeth between drags of his cigarette.

Corv was right. He had the itch. If we didn't get him some action soon, he'd go catatonic. "Hey, man," I said, nudging him. "Let's go get some whiskey, yeah?"

He rolled his shoulders and tipped back the rest of his beer before getting up, stomping out his smoke, and looking bored. A dangerous thing for Rook Clayton to be.

"Want to rally on the way home?" I offered and his lips twitched into a grin. We owned a good-sized patch of dirt just outside Thorn Valley with a few buildings on it. The Saints mostly used it for storing shit and taking apart stolen cars. We used it as a racecourse to destroy old junkers for kicks.

"No pussy shit," he said, framing it like a question even though he already knew what my answer would be.

"No pussy shit," I agreed. "We'll bust out that old Subaru SVX Corv found. I might even let you drive."

"You want to die?" Corvus said, reappearing like a fucking ghost out of thin air. "Because that's how you die. You want to rally at one in the morning, fine. But Grey drives."

"Suits me," Rook said as though he didn't care. We both knew he'd drown himself in whiskey before we left, anyway.

A familiar beat poured out from the speakers overhead and my throat went dry at the sound, all movement stilling as the first lyric dropped.

Corvus' face slackened as he registered what it was and calmly crossed the room to change the radio station.

Rook's black eyes scanned the room with unease before finding Corvus again, his analytic stare changing to a pained sort of pride.

I lowered my voice as Corv returned, still reeling but doing a good job of hiding it. "Man, was that just playing
on The Edge—"

"Shut the fuck up," he hissed. "Not here."

I snapped my mouth shut.

"You coming with?" Rook asked him, the moment erased as though it never happened.

"No," Corvus said in a shaky breath. "I'm heading to the gym."

"*Man,*" I started, but stopped myself when I saw the look he gave me.

Corvus barely slept, that was normal. He woke at the smallest sounds around the house and refused to wear earplugs or move out to the loft where it'd be quieter. But lately, it'd been worse. Like he wasn't bothering to try to sleep at all anymore.

For a guy who didn't let us have any secrets, he sure kept a lot of his own. He knew everything about Rook and me. Our pasts. The things we'd done, both before we wound up at Barrett's Home for Boys and during. I shuddered out of the memories trying to pull me under.

He never talked about his own past though. Not ever. I'd have been lying if I said I didn't wonder what kept him up most nights—what led him to Diesel and the Saints years before we were in the picture.

"Check in when you get back to the Crow's Nest," Corvus added as he stalked out the open door and into the night, not bothering to look back as he picked up his pace, starting a slow jog back toward town.

"Should've brought his Ducati if he was going to ditch," I mused aloud, my gut twisting as he vanished from view, swallowed up by the dark.

I shook my head. He'd be fine.

"I'd be shook, too," Rook said, clearing his throat. "Shit's on the radio now. There's no taking it back."

"Think Dies will recognize his voice?"

"Nah. I doubt it."

A muscle in his jaw twitched before his gaze trailed away from the cool night and back toward the bar. "Let's grab a drink and head out. I'm not in the mood for mourning."

"I'll let you have your fill first," I joked. "Let me know if there's any whiskey left when you're done."

He licked his lips and tossed me a wink before carving a path through the throng to the bar. I had to remind myself it wasn't drugs, that at least we'd gotten him off his weeklong coke benders. Booze and cigarettes we could deal with. When he was on blow, he was a fucking hurricane, and neither of us could do a damn thing to stop him.

Watching the other members, most almost twice his age, part like the fucking Red Sea made me smirk. People outside of the Saints always assumed Corvus was the psycho, but he was just the most lethal of us. Rook was the one they needed to be wary of. Where Corvus would plot your murder, taking into consideration every risk and possible outcome over a course of weeks before acting, Rook was liable to just snap at any moment.

And that moment was coming.

I'd have to call Julia tomorrow. See if she had anything new for us from the helpline.

My pocket buzzed, and I dug it out in a rush, thinking it must be Corv. That the Ace who carved that shit into Randy's chest was still around. But it was just Bri. *Again.*

Her message, the twentieth since lunchtime today, flashed over the screen.

BRIANNA

Meet you at your place around seven before school? I'll let you make it up to me...

My brows pinched, and I looked down at my traitorous cock. The thing wasn't even the least bit excited to get some action.

I readjusted myself.

Nothing.

Frowning, I thumbed out a quick reply. Annoyance washed through me, but I wasn't sure if it was directed at myself or her.

GREY

Busy.

BRIANNA

Are you serious?

Was I? I'd never turned her down before. The annoyance I'd felt before magnified as the new girl's face blew through my mind again. Bri didn't have any sort of claim on me. It was time I stopped letting her act like she did.

I started a reply that I would've regretted the next time my cock craved pussy but deleted it. The worst punishment for a girl like Bri would be not to answer her at all.

8

AVA JADE

Ms. Wood nodded as I left detention for the second time this week, her stubby fingers knuckle deep in the bag of Takis I brought her.

Becca was right. Ms. Wood was easily plied with a simple bribe of soda and snacks from the stash she kept in our shared apartment.

The only vending machine in the school was stocked with zero sugar protein bars, rice chips and some fruit things that looked like they belonged in the compost.

I didn't blame Ms. Wood for wanting a bit of junk food.

With her off-label clothes and unwaxed upper lip, she looked like she'd gotten the job at Briar Hall based more on her willingness to deal with the worst of the students than anything else. In fact, I think she might have worked at Lennox High for a while during my freshman year. As a janitor if I was remembering it right. I rarely forgot a face.

Becca was right about Bri, too. The bitch never showed yesterday. Looked like money and status really could buy you anything. Even a one-way ticket out of high school detention. I snorted to myself, hefting my books down the hall to the main atrium and the stairs leading up to the dorms.

Talk about a waste of power...

I fully expected another attack from her today in homeroom, but she didn't show up there either. Or anywhere else on campus for the rest of the day. Then again, neither did blondies 1, 2, or 3, so I had to assume they were all ditching together. Fixing their spray tans, I bet.

If I thought ahead, I might've been able to sabotage that...

Oh, well. There would always be next time. I'd have to learn where Bri liked to frequent just in case she was intent on continuing to try and make my life hell.

Two could play at that game.

I paused in the atrium, peering down the hall leading in the direction of the cafeteria. It was vacant save for the chatter of students eating dinner, just like it had been yesterday. And I had it on good authority—*thank you, Becca*—that the Crows didn't board here, which meant they'd already be gone for the day.

No one would know.

I backpedaled across the marble floor and used my elbow to jab the button on the elevator, bouncing on my heels as I waited for it to open. The thing was ancient, but at least it was better than lugging all these textbooks up three flights of stairs.

What kind of asshats *claimed* an elevator, anyway? Total bullshit if you asked me.

The doors pinged open, and I winced at the volume of the sound before stepping inside. Despite the masochistic part of me that almost *wanted* to get caught, I sighed in relief when the doors shut, boxing me in without being seen.

I made sure to jab the button for the main floor when I stepped back out on my floor, not wanting there to be any question as to whether it'd been used. And by whom.

No reason to poke the bears, especially when they hadn't taken a swipe at me today.

I'd almost been disappointed—the three of them seemed distracted as hell in homeroom. Barely paid me any attention except to stare. I could feel it, even if I didn't allow myself to turn around in my seat to check if my suspicions were on the money.

It would be better if they ignored me, but I got the feeling they were only biding their time for a better opportunity.

The sound of the shower and sweet smell of Becca's shampoo greeted me when I shoved through the door, making sure to lock it behind me. I sagged against the frame for a second, happy for a moment spent utterly alone.

Detention wasn't a group activity here. Not like it was at Lennox High, with a good mix of jocks and junkies. Loud jeering, tossed notes, and music playing so loudly through headphones that the cacophony of nine different songs echoed off the walls.

There were only two students with me in the borrowed science classroom used for detention at Briar Hall. So quiet, too. Like they were afraid to provoke Wood's wrath.

Worked in my favor, though. I couldn't imagine a more peaceful place to do all the work I was expected to catch up on. At this rate, I'd be ahead of the class by the end of the week.

Eager to set my books down, I kicked off my sneakers, stooping to draw the fifty I lifted from a buff dude that kept looking at my tits in math today. It was practically falling out of his back pocket anyway. At a place like this it was likely to be swept up and tossed out with the rest of the trash.

I'd make better use of it.

Hope the fucker enjoyed the show.

My phone chirped when I entered my room, and I tossed the pile of books onto the bed before flopping down next to them, snatching it from the nightstand.

Shit.

Twelve texts waited for me to read them, and if the cracked screen wasn't lying to me, three missed calls, too.

Dom.

I flicked through the messages, finding a slew from her. Asking me where I went. If I was coming back. If I was alive. And then, the last two, sent within the last fifteen minutes, assumedly after she decided to go looking for answers herself.

DOM

Holy shit, babe. I'm so sorry. Why didn't you tell me what happened?

I'm here if you need anything. Text me when you can.

My chest panged at the reminder, and I grimaced, closing her conversation without replying. Not ready to have that phone call just yet.

Here, people didn't know. They wouldn't treat me with pity or with any added scorn. I liked it better that way. I wasn't ready to think about it too hard. Not yet.

Dom would understand. We were friends, but not the kind who really knew each other's business. I didn't know how to be that kind of friend, so Dom had to settle for a halfway friendship. The kind where we shared self-defense training and sometimes some fast food afterward. Where she poured her heart out to me, and I listened.

Giving next to nothing in return.

I flicked through the other notifications, bristling as I came across one from my Aunt.

> **FEMALE HITLER**
>
> Detention on the first day, Ava Jade. Not off to a good start.
>
> **FEMALE HITLER**
>
> Answer your phone.

Not wanting to ruin my chances of a big payout from dear ol' Auntie Humphrey, I thumbed a quick reply.

> **AVA JADE**
>
> Won't happen again.

Big allowance. Big apartment in the city. Freedom. Big allowance. Big apartment in the city. Freedom.

I repeated the mantra in my head, trying to picture myself in that life. Just a girl in college, with aspirations of being a...whatever the fuck college girls wanted to be. With a cushy savings account, a nice boyfriend, and a local eatery on speed-dial for late night study sessions.

Yeah. Nope. Couldn't picture it. I'd spent too long in the dirt, up to my elbows in bills and my mom's vomit. At least Mom was someone else's problem now if she weren't dead.

I wouldn't be like her, not if I escaped this place. I could be the college girl I pictured. Carefree. On the road to a good paying nine-to-five, taking vacations twice a year. It's what I should want.

I mean, it's what I *do* want.

I groaned at the next message. Sent from Kit.

MY TICKET TO RIDE

> You missed the last session. Dom's worried about you. Want to come over for a bit?

My thighs squeezed at the offer. I'd been fucking Kit for almost as long as he'd been giving Dom and me self-defense lessons. She thought it was gross, since he was nearing thirty, but he was the only guy who'd ever been able to give me that big, glorious *O*. I wasn't about to give that up over something as trivial as an age gap.

Fuck. I could use the release right now, but he was an hour away and I had no way to get there. Maybe he could come...

No.

Sighing, I shut off my phone and rolled onto my back, setting it on my chest. It went off not two seconds after I shut my eyes, and I groaned inwardly, lifting it to my tired eyes.

I assumed it was another scolding message from my Aunt, or a worried one from Dom, but it wasn't either of them.

UNKNOWN

Hello, Ava Jade.

I clicked through to see the number, but didn't recognize it. A grand total of six people had my cell number. Six. And none of them would be giving it out in a hurry.

I considered how to reply. Obviously, the person had the right number...

Two sharp raps on my door had me bolting upright, a sizzle of heat racing up my spine.

"*Whoa,*" Becca said, holding up her hands as she appeared in the doorway. "I come in peace." She grinned, crossing her arms over her chest and leaning against the door frame as I relaxed.

Her hair was still dripping wet from the shower, but she had it pulled back in a long ponytail. Dressed like she was going out.

"How was Wood? She miss me?"

"Yeah, she made a point of mentioning that detention just isn't the same without you," I drawled.

She put her hand to her heart, sighing dramatically before bursting into a laugh. "Thought you'd be down at dinner. You eat yet?"

I shrugged. "Not hungry, I guess."

"You sick or something? Or just finally full? I never met anyone who eats like you, except maybe Grey."

I swallowed, a prickle of unease making goosebumps rise on my skin as my screen flashed to life again.

UNKNOWN

No run today?

"Did you give my number to anyone?" I asked, ignoring her other question. Other than my aunt, she was the only one in Thorn Valley that had it.

Her eyes narrowed, glancing between me and the phone clenched tightly in my palm. "No. Why?"

I shook my head, tossing the phone back onto the nightstand with a clatter. "It's nothing. Someone must've lifted it from the office."

Becca pursed her lips, but didn't disagree that it was a real possibility. Probably Bri. Trying to scare me away with ominous messages. How very boring.

"Well, *uh*, I have to go out for a bit. Help yourself to anything in the fridge if you're hungry. I had this eating *issue* a few years back. Now my dad has the fridge stocked with fresh groceries every week. It usually ends up in the trash so just help yourself."

I cocked my head at her, considering her thin frame in a different light.

"I don't have that problem anymore," she assured me, a muscle in her jaw ticking. Her body language shifted to discomfort. Shuffling on her feet. I looked away, clearing my throat.

"I didn't say anything."

"You didn't have to."

"You want company?" I offered as she pushed off the wall to leave, but her hesitation told me everything I needed to know.

"Actually, I forgot I have a history assignment I have to finish for tomorrow," I rushed to say, beating her to the punch. "I'll just go for a run if there's time after."

"You do that a lot. Run, I mean. Friendly tip? Stick to the main trail at the back of the field."

"Why?"

"There's an old service road that runs parallel to it. It goes up the cliffside to the Crow's Nest. You don't want to be anywhere near there."

"Crow's Nest?"

"It's where they live," she said offhandedly.

"There's a joint in the tin under the coffee table by the way," she offered with a wink. "History is better high."

I grinned, unable to disagree.

"Oh shit, I forgot. I got you something," she said, rushing out of my doorway and back across the apartment.

"You got me something?" I called after her, confused.

She reappeared a minute later with a crisp white shopping bag and tossed it to me. She had terrible aim, but I managed to catch it before it hit the floor by my feet.

"I guessed your size."

My stomach clenched.

"If you don't like it..." she started, trailing off. "I mean, I can always return it."

I peered inside, finding a swath of dark fabric. My fingers brushed the satiny dress and I grimaced, drawing it out of the fancy bag.

My first instinct was to bite her head off. I didn't need new clothes. Nothing was wrong with my clothes. I didn't need or want to look like the girls who went here.

"You don't like it," she said after a beat of tense silence, and I found her uneasily chewing her bottom lip.

I bit my tongue, seeing how clearly self-conscious she was about the whole thing. Maybe Becca was just as shit at having friends as I was.

Ease up, Ava Jade.

"It's actually amazing," I said.

And it was.

With a tight bodice and deep cut V in the front and a keyhole cutout in the back, it was a dream. The color was incredible, too. Black at first glance, but with a tint of dark navy and galaxy aqua when the light hit it just right.

The price tag almost gave me an aneurysm, though. It would eat up a quarter of the money I had stashed away if I were to have bought it myself. Plus, I didn't have the time or resources to case out a job in this town yet.

I hoped she didn't want me to pay her back.

"You shouldn't have bought me anything, though. I don't uh…"

"Have access to Old Lady Humphrey's bank accounts?" she finished for me.

I shook my head.

"I figured. I don't know much about her, but her tight purse strings are legendary in Thorn Valley. It's no biggie anyway, it went on Daddy's AMEX like everything else does."

Must be nice.

"Uh, well. Thanks."

"Welcome," she said, noticeably more chipper. "I thought you could wear it to the party tomorrow."

My mind immediately jumped to conclusions.

Wondering at her ulterior motives. She probably didn't want to be seen with me in my regular off-brand, thrift store clothes. Or maybe she was just wrapping me up as a gift to feed to the wolves to earn herself favor. Maybe…

Guilt gnawed at my stomach, and I shut down the part of my brain that always had to be suspicious of everything. Admitting there was a very good chance Becca just wanted to do something nice for her new roommate.

That thought was a harder one to swallow, and made my throat tight with emotion I didn't know what the fuck to do with.

"Yeah," I muttered. "Can't wait."

9

CORVUS

"This it?"

Grey pulled the car we borrowed from underground parking in town up to a neat white house with blue shutters, a doubtful frown turning down the edge of his mouth. "Thought that asshole lived down on Freemont, near the trailer park. That's where we picked him up the last time."

Rook chewed his lip ring in the backseat, already hedging to the door, his hands twitching.

"Yeah, I'm fucking sure," I growled, cutting Grey a look. "What? Shitty people can't live in nice houses?"

He inclined his head, knowing that all too well himself.

I inhaled deeply to calm down, knowing I was ornery as fuck. I'd have preferred to plan this little visit over at least a few days, if not a week, but we were running out of time.

Tomorrow was the monthly full moon party down at the docks and we needed to be there. The location, though it was perfect for parties, was right on the edge of our territory. The *one time* we didn't go, a group of junior Aces crashed and almost drowned a chick. We couldn't have that in our town.

If we didn't do this now—for Rook—then we'd have to leave him behind. I hated that idea almost as much as the idea of bringing him with us when he was like this.

"What are we waiting for? Let's fucking go," Rook gritted out, his tatted hand poised on the door handle in the backseat.

"Hold it. We need to scope it out. Julia said the kid usually leaves around this time to sleep out with a friend. We got to make sure he's gone."

A muscle in Grey's jaw twitched and Rook kicked the back of the seat, cursing.

I'd already gotten everything else into place, this was the one moving piece that I wasn't sure of, and it made my fucking skin itch.

"Stay here," I said, slipping out of the car and around the side of the house, skirting the hedges. It was a quiet rural street, and all the lights in the neighboring houses were out. Silent as the grave.

Except this house.

Around back there was a light on in the kitchen and the radio playing on low inside.

I crept to the sliding door and peered within, finding the whitewashed kitchen empty save for the row of empty brown bottles by the sink.

Soft footsteps drummed down the steps after two minutes of waiting and I lowered myself next to the door, crouching to be hidden by the deck's banister.

A boy, no more than eleven, rushed into the kitchen on quick, quiet feet, his runners in his hands. A fresh shiner bloated the flesh around his left eye and what looked like a fresh cigarette burn sat angry and red just below his jaw. I'd seen enough just like it on Rook, though his asshat of a step-uncle preferred cigars. His new tatts hid the scars well unless you knew where to look for them.

The boy's name was Thomas.

He'd called the number on our flier three times in the last six months after calling the cops did nothing to help him. Twice, we'd given his joke of a father very straight forward warnings about what would happen to him if he didn't stop. But apparently a broken arm and five cracked ribs weren't enough.

First warning, we scared them. Told them what would happen if they didn't comply.

Second warning got them at least five broken bones. A burned appendage. Maybe some missing fingernails.

Depended what kind of mood Rook was in.

But three strikes...

He's out.

The same rule didn't apply to child molesters though. They didn't get second chances.

Better no parents at all than ones like Thomas'.

We knew from the helpline that Thomas had an aunt he could live with, who'd been trying to get custody of him. But the ones who had no one else...we saw to it that they had the right connections in the system. That they weren't hurt anymore.

We weren't heroes.

We were just boogiemen who developed a taste for the flesh of villains. Someone had to sate that need. Who better than pieces of shit like Frank?

I vanished into the shadows beneath the deck as Thomas eased the patio door open and pushed through, his breaths coming quick. His shoulders up to his ears. Inside, a loud thud made him jump and gasp before he took off like a shot into the dark, sprinting through neighboring backyards until he disappeared over a low fence and was gone.

No better time than the present.

I walked back to the side of the house and nodded to my brothers in the old Camry before tugging the ski mask from my back pocket and pulling it over my face.

Rook's breath clouded in the cool night air as he came around the back of the house, his chest wide and heaving.

I nodded.

"We take him," I ordered before setting him loose. "I don't want to clean up a crime scene here."

"Fine."

"No blood."

"*Fine.*"

Rook went into the house first, and Grey and I followed, double checking the yards and area for anyone who might see.

All clear.

Even if the name *Saint* was enough to ensure we wouldn't be bothered, at least on our own turf, I liked the added layer of security. The residents of Thorn Valley may not go to the cops, but a few had tried blackmail in the past. Didn't work out for them the way they hoped, but I'd rather not deal with that shit.

"*No!*" came a shout inside the house, and my jaw locked tight as I followed Grey inside and shut the door behind us, flicking off the lights.

"*Rook,*" I hissed, following the sounds of struggle through the kitchen. "*Too fucking loud.*"

A second cry was abruptly cut off with an *oof* of breath, and I heard Rook breathing in through his nose like he was snorting a line. He liked the smell, he said. The smell of a man's fear.

I had to admit, it was a favorite of mine as well.

Almost as nice as the smell of a woman's.

Rook dragged the guy into the kitchen before Grey and I could get any deeper into the house, his bulging biceps cutting off poor Frank's air supply.

He struggled, his bloodshot brown eyes going wide as he took in the sight of Grey and me standing in his kitchen. Recognizing our masked faces from the last two times. Knowing what it meant that we'd returned.

The fucker doubled down his efforts to escape, tucking his chin to bite into Rook's arm like a feral dog. He got free, rushing forward like he actually thought he could get through us. Stumbling on his drunk ass feet.

Rook's blood spurted onto the tile floor, and he bared his teeth, rushing forward after Frank.

What a goddamn mess.

I shoved Frank back as he ducked in an attempt to slide through Grey and me and the fucker ping ponged off of Rook and then the kitchen fridge, making it pop open.

Rook got a hold on him again, but the damage was done.

Grey stared at the bare refrigerator, his eyes glinting venomously in the blue tinted light as he took in the empty shelves. Two slices of processed cheese and six beers.

Nothing else.

"Grey..."

His fists clenched.

Rook licked his lips.

"There he is," Rook whispered with excitement, his tongue sliding over his teeth as he took in Grey and held Frank steady for him.

My youngest brother shook as he turned his fury on Frank, and I stood watch as Rook shoved the asshole forward, giving Grey his turn.

The *crack* of his fist against the bastard's cheekbone was sweeter than any music I could create.

Grey hit him again *and again,* mute, his face a mask of stoic calm with only the barest glint of rage. He didn't stop until Frank was unconscious and lying in a puddle of his own blood on the floor.

"How hard is it to buy a loaf of fucking bread, you piece of shit," he seethed, getting one more good kick in before he began to settle, his shoulders dropping as the rage went out of him. He wiped the sweat from his upper lip, panting, and Rook stared down at Frank with glee.

There was a difference between inflicting pain for business—on orders from Diesel—and doing it for pleasure. This?

This was *all fucking pleasure.* For all of us.

"You finished?" I asked Grey with a raised brow. If he'd killed him, we'd need to find another asshole for Rook to play with. Luckily, he was just knocked out. Fucker would have one mean ass headache when he woke up. But not for long...

"Yeah," Grey said on a breath, slamming the empty

fridge closed and rolling his shoulders back, a calmness stealing over his features.

"Good. Go find the bleach. You're cleaning that shit."

10

AVA JADE

My breath fogged in the air as I jogged down the trail, one earbud in and the other tucked away in my pocket. The road ahead was gravel, narrow, winding up a fairly steep incline.

I told myself I just wanted to see which road Becca was talking about—to know where to *avoid* going but...

It was past midnight, and I couldn't sleep. I kept thinking about Dom, and Kit, and where the hell Becca kept going at all hours of the early morning and night. And, if I were being honest with myself, I couldn't stop thinking about *them*, either. This burning urge to know more ate at me.

Know your enemies.

I'd feel better if I knew what I was dealing with.

Where they lived. If I knew how far it was from the school.

It didn't take much to convince myself before I was stepping off the gravel road and into the shadows of the trees running alongside it, speeding back up to a run over the leafy ground.

A cool wind stole over the ridge, flash cooling the sweat slicking my arms and back, making the small hairs there stand on end.

I clenched my teeth, tapping my earbud to switch off the husky whisper of Primal Ethos singing to me of savages and saints. Just in case.

Statistics would warn against it, but night runs were my favorite. Especially in the hours just after midnight or just before dawn. When the whole world seemed to hold its breath, steeling itself against the coming of a new day. Only the night creatures chirped and chattered in the dark. Creating their own sort of music.

The house came into view about two miles up, where the road began to level out onto a flat, treed lot.

I squatted in the shadows, putting my hands to the damp earth as I squinted through the branches, keeping low as I moved closer.

I could see how the place got its name.

The Crow's Nest was a modern structure, tall and narrow, built of grey wood with big square windows and a sharply slanted roof. Orange tinted light shone out around the heavy black curtains on the middle floor, but every other light within was out.

There was a garage, built similarly, next to the odd house, and a smaller structure down to the right, almost hidden in the trees. A shed?

It wasn't built to match the others, it looked old. Ancient, really. And I wondered if it was the original structure here before they built the monstrosity of a house.

A camera hid in the alcove above the big black front door, facing downward. I checked for others before mentally giving myself a smack.

It was habit. Casing the place for weak points to exploit.

I mean, it looked like the sort of place where I'd find a metric boatload of cash. Probably weapons. Jewelry. Watches?

With only one camera, it was doable—

No, Ava Jade.

Jesus fuck.

What happened to not poking the bears?

Worst. Idea. Ever.

I sighed, deciding to leave well enough alone, placated knowing that they were at least eight miles from the school in total. Not far enough, but at least they didn't live on the grounds.

The sound of car tires chewing gravel made me duck lower in the shadows and I narrowed my vision. An old model light blue Camry sped into view, peeling into the lot in front of the house and coming to a jarring stop.

I should leave.

I should really *leave.*

I settled in, biting my lower lip as the engine went dead, and I held my breath to keep from making a sound.

A bulky shadow spilled out of the passenger door and pulled a black ski mask from his face. As he lifted his face skyward, taking a long breath, I saw that it was Corvus. Odd sounds filtered to me on the breeze. Whispers, and was that...

Was that whimpering?

"Get him. Let's get this over with," Corvus said as Grey and Rook popped out of the small car, both of them heading for the back of it.

Grey opened the trunk, and what was unmistakably a man with his hands bound clambered out and fell onto the driveway with a thud and a groan, breathing heavily.

Fuck.

With a reach like the strike of curved talons, Rook grabbed a fistful of the man's hair, wrenching his head back.

"N-no," the man choked. "He's lying. I-I didn't do anything. If you let me go, I'll...I'll pretend I never saw your faces. I won't say shit. I-I can pay you. I can—"

"Shut the fuck up," Corvus growled, slamming his door shut to join the others around the back of the Camry. "We warned you, asshole. And you didn't listen. This is on *you.*"

"Please..."

It was hard to tell this far away, but it looked like Rook was fucking grinning. And not just like a little grin, either. He was fucking *beaming* down at the guy. Like he wanted to lick the smears of dried blood off his face.

"Take him," Corvus nodded to Rook, and he licked his lips, hefting the guy to his feet by his hair alone. Like it was nothing.

The man spat at Corvus' feet as Rook began to drag him away.

Corvus just stared at him like he was the most insignificant thing on the planet. A speck of dust in the wind.

"Fuck you!" the man shouted at Corvus, spewing more saliva with his words as he turned his attention to the others. "Fuck *all* of you."

The smell of blood and urine reached me on the wind, and my nose wrinkled.

"Fucker pissed himself," Rook said, holding the guy out at arm's reach with a scowl as he roughly manhandled him across the lot, carving a path to the shed at the far right of the property.

Corvus followed and Grey rushed ahead to unlock it and flip a light on. From my angle, it was hard to see inside, and I leaned to get a better look, snapping a twig.

Corvus froze mid-stride, his back lifting.

I clenched my teeth, sinking as low as I could go without moving too much.

He turned, his face cast in moonlight looking so violent, all bones and shadows and contrast, that for a second, he looked like a skeleton come to life. Like a grim reaper searching for prey.

His hollow-eyed gaze swept over the lot and the trees before he continued, following his brothers into the small shed and shutting the door behind him.

It took about five seconds before the screaming started. Loud at first, and then muffled as though someone had stuck something in the man's mouth. They were torturing him.

My stomach lurched.

In Lennox, the Kings ruled the streets, but they didn't have the reach the Saints did. Or even the Aces. The Kings stayed in Lennox, keeping to their turf, never expanding.

I supposed I could see why.

If the junior members got their kicks torturing people, then how were the senior members?

Fucking gangs.

My upper lip twitched into a snarl.

Gangs stole my innocence. They ruined my mother. And now they'd taken my father, too.

Fuck the Crows.

They were just bad news wrapped up in pretty paper.

For a heartbeat, I considered setting the shed on fire with them inside of it. It'd be easy. Older cars were simple as fuck to hotwire. I'd just back it up to the door, blocking their escape, pop open the gas tank and drop in a match.

I'd probably be doing the world a favor.

But I was short exactly one match.

And the energy required to run for the rest of my life from one of the largest gangs in the western USA.

Tearing my gaze away, I stood and turned from the Crow's Nest, right at the exact second the shed door banged back open and Grey strolled out, shutting it firmly behind him and rubbing a palm over his jaw.

My heart vaulted into my throat.

He started toward the front door of the house, and I allowed myself a small breath, backing slowly away from the house, never letting my gaze falter from his back.

Grey stopped before he reached the door, tilting his head to one side.

No.

He whirled around, and it was too late to react.

Our eyes met.

I was fucking *gone.*

Without bothering to see if he was giving chase, I bolted through the trees, skidding down a slope and barely clawing back to my feet as I pressed forward, heedless of the trees jutting out of the earth like long fingers trying to grab me. To stop me from getting away.

I weaved through the forest, my focus dialing in like it always did when that blessed spike of adrenaline injected itself into my blood. My feet moved with more surety, keeping an unfathomably quick pace as I expertly avoided the worst of the branches, knowing exactly where to step on instinct.

As the drumbeat echo of my pulse quieted, my ears opening back up to the world around me, I heard him.

It was a second too late.

The inclined path worked in his favor as he tackled me from behind. My face and chest collided with the earth, skidding through sharp twigs and over gritty earth. The taste of blood and dirt coated my tongue as I worked to get him off, coughing, my hand reaching down to my ankle, to the blade strapped there.

His knee dug into my back, pressing me down as his hands wrapped like iron manacles around my forearms, effectively pinning me beneath him.

A little tremor of fear ricocheted up my spine when I couldn't wriggle free. When my mind immediately went back to another time. Another place.

Another man holding me down.

"Let me up you *motherfucker,*" I spat, just managing to eat more dirt.

"*Ava Jade?*"

The knee in my back let up just enough for me to get my feet under me, prying his metal grip from my forearms. I sent a backward kick into his face but missed, hitting him in the shoulder instead.

He groaned, reeling back enough for me to get to my feet, drawing my blade as I rose.

I held it out in front of me, blinking the grit from my eyes. It was a shame I only had one or I'd throw it. I hadn't practiced in over a week, but I rarely strayed from a bullseye.

Not worth the risk of losing it if you miss...

Grey panted in the dappled moonlight, taking me in with narrowed eyes as though he couldn't believe what he was seeing. He held his hands out, his eyes jerking to the glint of the silver blade, back to me, and behind him.

Like he was waiting for something. Or someone.

Backup.

Had he tripped some sort of alarm? Did he somehow have time to fire off a text in the split second before he gave chase? Did he shout? I couldn't remember.

But I liked my chances against one a hell of a lot more than my chances against three.

I darted forward, taking a stab at him when he twisted for another look behind him. He only *just* managed to knock my hand away, going for a grab of my wrist, but missing. I slipped free and danced back two steps, ready to try again, my body electric with energy.

"Shit," he cursed. "What the fuck are you doing?"

He tipped his head to one side as though seeing me in a new light.

"Who are you with?" he asked suddenly, his bright eyes darkening, hooded by drawn brows. "Who the fuck sent you?"

He stepped forward and I gave a warning swipe. "Don't think I won't carve up that pretty face," I warned. "Just turn your ass around and *leave.*"

"I can't do that."

A moment of brittle silence passed between us, and a scowl twisted his features. I hadn't noticed before, he usually wore long sleeves at school, but now, in nothing but a loose tank, I saw that he was covered in tattoos. Just like Rook. One entire arm. A half sleeve on the other. Except Rook's seemed to be done in shades of black and Grey's were all painted in vivid color.

"Who are you with?" he asked again, each word dripping venom as his fists clenched. "The Aces? Did they plant you—"

"I'm not with a gang, asshole," I spat, trying to judge whether or not I could get away if I tried a second time to run. I'd have to incapacitate him first. A good slice to the inner thigh would do it if I could get close enough. He might even survive if someone found him within a few minutes and got him to an emergency room.

But I didn't hear anyone else coming. Besides, then what would I do?

Run? Hide?

Grey's eyes carved a path up and down my body, taking in my jogging pants and cropped tank. My running shoes.

"Little late for a run, isn't it?"

"I couldn't sleep," I muttered, not sure why I was continuing a conversation with a guy who was clearly part of a murder-in-progress not even half a mile up the hill.

Grey lifted his shirt, turning to show that he was unarmed. He stooped to lift the edge of his jeans, too, showing his ankles, keeping a steady eye on me the whole time. He had more tattoos on his calves and the outline of something started on his ribs.

"I'm not armed," he said. "You say you're not with a gang? I'm going to need you to prove that if I'm going to let you go."

Let me go?

"Yeah, right," I said under my breath. As if he was just going to let me go after what I'd just witnessed.

He arched a brow. "You see something you shouldn't have?" he asked dubiously.

"I didn't see anybody."

Shit.

"I mean, I didn't see *anything*."

"Well that *nobody* earned what he's getting tonight...if it makes you feel any better."

"I don't give a fuck. Not my business."

That seemed to surprise him, and he pursed his lips, eyes flitting to the blade and back to me again. "I'll ask you again, new girl; Did you see something you shouldn't have?"

"Depends," I countered, challenging him. Praying that he wouldn't tell the others I was here. "Did *you*?"

He grinned. "Maybe. Maybe not. *Depends.*"

"On?"

"Whether or not you have gang ink."

I frowned.

"I'll need to check," he said, his teeth dragging over the corner of his lip as he looked over me again. "Or you could just take it all off for me."

"*Hell* no."

"Then I'm afraid I can't help you," he said with a shrug and lifted two fingers to his lips, ready to whistle.

"Wait!"

His lips split into a mischievous grin again and he crossed his arms. "Shall I check, then? Or would you rather give me a show?"

There was no way I was stripping down naked in the fucking trees. I wouldn't be able to keep a steadfast hold on my blade.

"You can check," I decided, inhaling deeply.

"You going to put that away?" he asked, nodding to the blade.

"Nope."

His jaw flexed, and he hesitated before stepping toward me. I liked the uncertainty in his expression. That he didn't know whether or not I'd cut him.

Hell, neither did I.

I stood very still as he closed the gap and slowly lifted the edge of my cropped shirt, exposing my black bra and breasts to the chilly air, making my nipples harden beneath the worn-out fabric.

He tugged at the waistband of my joggers, and it took everything inside of me not to use the opportunity to put him down like a dog. But if he was serious, if he was going to let me go when he found no gang ink, then I'd rather avoid a war.

I'd rather pretend this never happened and stay the absolute fuck away from the Crows and their murder nest.

I was an idiot for coming up here. A damned fool.

Grey circled me, tugging my joggers a bit to check my ass.

"Like what you see?" I gritted out when he seemed to be staring a little too long.

He grunted, letting the elastic waistband snap back against my hips before bending to check my ankles and calves. His hands sliding up my legs to push away the fabric made my breath catch, and I had to snap my mouth shut to keep from making a sound.

He moved to my back next, lifting the shirt out of the way to inspect my shoulder blades. Nudging my messy ponytail to one side to check my neck and behind my ears, his warm breath fanning over my neck, the twin sensations of danger and desire making me...

"You finished?" I snapped, pulling away and whirling on him. "Satisfied?"

"Not even remotely," he replied, his voice a low rumble as he took me in with new appreciation.

I *really* didn't like the way he was looking at me.

But my greedy vajay sure as fuck did.

Why? Why were the bad ones always so fucking hot?

His brothers are up there murdering *someone,* I reminded myself. Or at least they were torturing him. I should *not* be turned on right now.

Bad vajay.

"Who are you?" Grey asked in a distant voice, as though the question was more for himself than for me to answer. Good, because I wasn't about to tell him anything more about me.

"Can I go now?"

He ran a hand through his blond hair, considering something.

"One last thing."

"What?"

He didn't reply at first, but the bulge in his pants told me everything I needed to know. "I'm not fucking you," I bit out. "And I'm not sucking you off either, so forget it."

He barked a laugh that sent tremors racing up my spine, making my nostrils flare in worry that someone might've heard. How long did we even have before one of the others realized Grey was gone? Before they came looking?

I needed to get clear of here. *Fast.*

And hope to fucking god that he didn't tell them.

"You think I'm the kind of guy that needs to blackmail blowjobs, babe? No, when I fuck you, you're going to beg for it. You're going to scream my name until your throat is as raw as your pussy."

"You're a pig," I snarled, tough words coming from a girl who might be kind of, sort of, a little bit wet.

He smirked. "Just a kiss."

"You're kidding. A kiss? What are we, twelve?"

He shook his head. "A fair trade, I think. A kiss in exchange for *not* telling my brothers you were spying."

"I wasn't—"

"*Uh, uh,*" he warned. "Don't lie to me."

I pressed my lips into a tight line.

"What do you say? It'll be like this never happened. Like you were never here."

"Or I could just gut you and run."

"You could, but something tells me you won't."

"Won't your girlfriend be jealous?"

He snorted. "She isn't my girlfriend."

"But you knew exactly who I was talking about, didn't you?"

He licked his lips, ignoring me, even though I saw a knot form between his brows. He didn't like the idea of people thinking he belonged to her. I didn't think he liked the idea of people thinking he belonged to anyone.

"We doing this or are you gutting me? I haven't got all night."

My knuckles turned white as I lowered the blade. "This is fucking juvenile."

"Then it should be easy."

I stiffened as he came to me without warning, his hand coming up to grip the back of my neck as his mouth came down on mine. Heedless of the blade I was still holding at my side. Testing my will to use it against him. Daring me to.

Motherfucker.

His rough fingers pressed hard on either side of my neck, locking my lips to his, tipping my head up as he pushed inside with his tongue and stole all the breath from my lungs. Breathing me in like he could reach inside and snatch my soul clean off my bones.

He tasted like salt and caramel.

Felt like hot coals.

His hand skated down my side, gripping my hip to pull me hard against him. His hard cock pressed into me, and it was that touch that woke me to reality. Sending a burning fury licking down my spine to pool in my stomach like acid.

I shoved him back, breathless, lips swollen.

I didn't even realize I'd cut him until he inhaled violently through his teeth.

Grey gripped his biceps. Dark fluid dripped down to his forearm, rising to the surface even as he worked to stop the bleeding.

Oopsie.

It would need stitches, but he'd be fine. Not my fucking problem.

"We're square," I said, the words hollow as I strode past him.

He caught me by the arm, and I jerked to a stop, giving him a look that I hope conveyed how fucking glad I would be if he gave me another reason to cut him.

"Don't come back," he hissed. "Next time, I won't save your ass."

I tore my arm from his grip, a snort of derisive laughter steaming in the air between us. "Next time I won't hold back."

11

ROOK

Frank came apart beautifully.

His seams loosened bit by bit until his eyes grew wide and distant with hysteria. Until his sounds were nothing but whispers falling from quivering lips. Until his insides became his outsides.

With every piece of him that fell away, a piece of myself was returned. Until I was whole. And he lay broken at my feet.

His dirty soul in exchange for a moment of peace for mine.

Corvus coughed, and I remembered he was still there, standing at my back, like he always was.

I turned off the blow torch, stepping back to properly admire my masterpiece, tilting my head to get a better angle.

Bits of incinerated Frank floated in the sweltering heat of the old woodshed, sticking to my sweat slicked arms and bare chest. "I think it's my best work," I muttered with a smirk, looking to Corvus for confirmation.

He had his mouth covered with his ski mask, brows pinched from the smell. Corvus didn't like the smell of cooked asshole, but I'd grown accustomed to it.

Corv cleared his throat and dropped the mask. "You think the Met might be interested? We're low on cash. Could use the payout."

I snorted. "Dip him in epoxy and...*maybe.*"

Chapter 11

Corvus shook his head. "Nah, the fucker doesn't deserve to be admired."

"To the lake, then?"

"I was thinking the woodchipper, then bury the rest."

"Even better."

Corvus pushed out the door, and I hollered after him, not quite finished in here. "Can you pick me up another acetylene tank? I'm almost out."

I tossed the near empty one to the side and let myself fall onto the short stool in the corner of the shed, where I could watch the little Frank flakes dance in the moonlight on their way out into the dark. I fished out a cigarette and lit it lazily, twisted the pre-rolled mix between my blood and ash coated fingers before taking a drag.

Fuck.

I tipped my head back to rest against the rough wood wall and inhaled deeply through my nose, relishing the feel of *nothingness*. The stillness of my body. The quiet in my head.

Fucking *peace.*

Just like the first time.

Grey followed me that night, when I snuck out of Barrett's Home for Boys. I knew he was there, tailing me in the shadows, but I didn't tell him to go back. I think part of me wanted him to watch. So he'd be scared away. As he fucking should've been.

But he didn't come out. Not when I stole an empty jug from the back of a department store. Or when I siphoned gasoline out of a car.

Not even when I snuck into my aunt's house while she was out at Bingo, like she always was on Wednesday nights. Or when I doused my uncle's bedroom in gasoline and set it on fire.

Grey didn't come out until the windows were bright with orange flame and inside, we could hear my uncle screaming until he didn't scream anymore.

He sat with me, slung his arm over my shoulder, and didn't say a fucking word until the firetrucks and police and ambulances showed up. With all the chaos, they didn't even notice we were there, tucked away in the dark entry of the abandoned house across the street. It wasn't until they had the fire almost completely subdued that he stood up and extended his hand.

"Best barbecue I've ever been to," he said. "But I think we should get back before anyone notices we left."

That was when I knew: he was more than a kid I met at some lame excuse for a group home. He was my brother.

I could still taste the phantom flavor of gasoline on my tongue. Acrid and tangy. I licked my lips.

"Well, Frank," I said, stretching out my kinks as I stood again, snubbing out my cigarette on the top of his charred skull. "It's been a pleasure."

Grey cursed when I stepped into the doorway to leave and almost ran him over. He grimaced, and I wasn't sure whether it was me or Frank that offended him. Probably both. I was almost as covered in gore as our buddy inside.

It took me a second to register why he was standing awkwardly, his hand clutching his upper arm.

"The hell happened to you?" I asked, my veins flooding with heat. My hand jerking back in case I needed to draw my gun. I peered over his shoulder, looking. Listening.

Grey pushed past me, using one hand to dig around the various tools of my trade. "I thought I heard something," he said. "Ran into the trees to check it out and sliced myself good."

"On what?" I asked, scrutinizing the amount of blood soaking his arm. Still trying to squeeze past his fingers. "Are trees growing fucking razorblades?"

"Do you still have that stitch kit in here or not?" he hissed, shooting me a glare. I didn't miss how his eyes kept darting outside.

Either he was expecting company, or he didn't want Corvus to see this.

"*Rook?*" he pressed. "A little fucking help, bro?"

I gave my head a shake, deciding I didn't exactly care what happened, as long as the idiot didn't let it happen again. Hopefully, he learned his lesson.

I knocked a still smoking Frank from his chair and brushed off his ashes. "Sit down. I'll get the kit."

12

AVA JADE

"You think Bri will be there?" I asked Becca as we got in her Audi, the all-black interior swallowing us up before she started the ignition and the dash came to life, painting her in shades of blue.

Becca pulled out of the school lot, giving me a curious look. "Why? You miss her?"

Turned out she went on a shopping trip to LA. Or at least, that's what Becca thought. Bri went every year around this time for some big annual sale a designer put on in the fall. It would be just my luck if she got back in time for the party.

"So much it hurts," I replied, my voice dripping sarcasm.

It was a relief not having to deal with Bri the last few days, but I'd still had to weather the Crows this morning. I'd have been lying if I said I wasn't just a little bit on edge walking into homeroom, not knowing whether or not Grey would hold to his word to keep last night's unfortunate rendezvous between us.

It seemed he had, though. Corvus was his usual quiet, menacing self. Rook looked almost...*serene*. And Grey? Grey just kept on fucking staring at me. Not even bothering to try to hide it, either. Earned himself a solid jab to the ribs by Corvus at one point, too. Though I didn't know why.

Best not to question it.

Not to even think about it at all.

Banishing all thoughts of the Crows from my mind, I sank back in the seat, letting the supple leather conform to my curves. "Hey, nice car by the way."

"Thanks."

I took note of how the passenger side seat was slid all the way back and lowered, as though someone tall frequently sat in it. I wanted to ask, but it wasn't any of my business. I wondered if he was handsome. Older, I was betting. Maybe a teacher?

Becca had the air of someone much older than she was. I could totally see her banging a teacher. I just hoped it wasn't that Harry Potter wannabe from homeroom. *Ugh.* Or Mr. Williams from AP math. That guy gave me the creeps.

"What?" Becca asked after a few minutes of quiet driving. "Do I have something on my face?"

I laughed. "No. You're good."

"You clean up pretty nice, yourself," she said, giving me a smirk as she jabbed some buttons on the center console, connecting it to her phone, and Halsey came on. I should have known we'd have similar music tastes.

"It's amazing what a bit of mascara and a new dress can do, am I right?" she asked.

Well, she wasn't wrong. Even though I was loath to admit it.

The dress fit unlike any second hand one ever could. Hugging my body like it was made for me. The deep 'v' showed off just enough tit to be sexy, but not enough to be straight up slutty. The length was perfect, too, not so short that I would have to keep tugging it down, but not too long that it bordered on prudish.

The short heels Becca lent me to go with it, and the small miracle she worked on my unruly hair, really brought the whole thing together. I looked fucking *amazing* and I knew it. All thanks to Becca.

"So, anything I should know before we get there? It's at the docks, you said?"

Becca turned the music down a click as we veered off a main road and onto a side one without any streetlights. Though it was harder to see in the dark, she didn't slow. She clearly knew the road well, even though it wound and curved down the hillside.

"It's an old pier. Been abandoned for a few years now. It's basically just an old warehouse building on stilts over the lake."

"Sounds super safe."

"Not really," Becca said, checking her lipstick in the rearview, signaling to me that we were almost there. "But only one person ever actually drowned. Lots of close calls, though."

Noted.

"Just stay away from the balcony on the far side," she continued. "The boards are rotten. Bri got her heel stuck in one once, almost broke her ankle."

"I'd have paid good money to see that."

Becca lifted her shoulders and sighed like she got a case of the warm and fuzzies. "It was glorious."

I laughed, reaching to turn up the music as my current fave came on.

"You like Primal Ethos?" Becca asked as I hummed along. "Not many people have heard of them."

"I've been listening since his really old stuff."

"I heard he's on the radio now. Oh! And there's a show in Lodi next month. You *have* to come with me. It's going to be epic."

"I didn't think he was doing any more shows?"

She shrugged. "Guess he changed his mind. People are dying to figure out who he is. There's this whole online forum dedicated to sleuthing his true identity."

I wasn't surprised. I had to admit I didn't really care as long as he kept making music, but even *I* was a bit curious. When the video went up of his first live show, his face was done up in *killer* skeleton makeup, black hair slicked back. Eyes covered in whiteout contacts.

He was a mystery.

Honestly, I was no expert, but it seemed like nothing more than a great marketing ploy.

"No shit. Who do they think he is?"

She snorted. "*A prince.*"

"A prince?"

"Yeah, like of some European country. Hiding his identity and coming to Cali so he can do what he loves without the royal family breathing down his neck."

"I would've pegged him as an ex-con or something. I mean, have you paid attention to his lyrics?"

I turned up *Gravedigger* so the next lyric could play loud and clear, proving my point.

"Maybe he's just a twisted prince? Like that one from Game of Thrones, *oh fuck,* what was his name?"

"Joffrey?"

"Yeah! That fucker."

She had a point. "Maybe. Power does go to your head."

As we wound around another sharp curve in the road, the docks came into view and the thumping bass of music in the distance warred with Becca's playlist in the car. She turned it down as we drove down and into a parking lot running along the water's edge.

The pier was alive with a crush of people in the parking lot smoking and chatting. Others walked down the narrow planks out onto the water where the building perched on stilts loomed at the end.

It didn't look as beat up as I thought it would. But I should have expected that. If it was too atrocious the students from Briar Hall wouldn't dare go near it. As it was, the 'docks' seemed like they would be something of a novelty to them. Like rich folk who spent their weekdays in condos and their weekends 'roughing it' in cottages on the lake.

"Pretty cool, huh?" Becca said as she turned off the radio and parked.

I nodded. "Not bad."

The rough plank exterior of the building was done up in swirls of graffiti. I thought I caught the signature fleur-de-lis tag of the Saints amidst the blocky letters and vulgar art. Discernible from the religious symbol by the elongated bottom, formed to look like a blade. There was an *A,* too. The gang tag used by the Aces. Though it'd been badly covered over in artwork.

Clearly this was disputed turf. Noted.

The whole roof was strung with hundreds of little lights on strings —the only light illuminating the area for miles save for the moon and flashlight beams on camera phones.

The music grew louder as we stepped out, the sound of it echoing off the lake making the bass reverberate in my breastbone. I only recognized a few faces from the school, the rest looked a bit older. Anywhere from late teens to late twenties seemed to be in attendance.

Thorn Valley didn't seem a particularly large city though, and I was willing to bet there was very little *this* exciting happening here on any given Friday night.

Becca looped her arm through mine, taking my cell phone from my hand to pop it into her purse since I didn't own one of my own. "I don't see Bri's car," she said excitedly as we made our way to the dock leading out to the pier. "That's a good sign."

I hadn't seen the Crows yet either.

Could it be that I might actually have *fun* tonight? A smile pricked at my lips as we waded into the sea of bodies walking the plank.

The floor shook under our feet as we crossed into the large building and I instinctively put my arms out to stabilize myself.

Becca laughed at the expression on my face. "Trust me, it won't fall," she shouted over the music. "There'll be twice this many people here within the hour. Then the floor *really* shakes."

Jesus.

I let Becca drag me to an area to the right, weaving through dancing and chatting groups of people, many already piss drunk. The colorful strobing lights made their movements seem jerky and robotic with each flickering color change.

Despite the cool night air outside, it was fucking hot in here, and I was glad I'd accepted the dress from Becca instead of wearing the jeans and long sleeve I'd planned to.

She swiped a red cup off a stack from a table, and I snatched it from her, eyeing the punch bowl with horror. I could smell it from here. Artificial sweetener and way too much booze and likely a whole lot more than that.

It was wide open, ripe for drugging.

"You're not seriously going to drink that, are you?"

She cocked her head at me, smirking as she drew a mickey of gin out of her bag. "I'm not drinking at all," she said, pushing the gin and cup into my hand as she drew a joint out from between her tits. "And if I were, do you really think I'm stupid enough to drink *that*?"

No, I thought, a bit guiltily. I really didn't think she was that stupid. I gave her an apologetic grimace, and she bumped my shoulder with a smile, lighting up her joint to take a long drag.

"Don't worry about it. The punch is probably safe, anyway. This is Crow territory. No one would dare roofie the punch unless they wanted their eyeballs used as ice cubes in Rook's bourbon. But still," she shrugged. "Better safe than sorry."

I grimaced, able to vividly imagine Rook poking out eyeballs with a skewer after hearing the screams from their shed last night. *Ugh.*

Biting my lower lip, I considered the gin and cup before handing them back to her. If the Crows were here after all, then I should tread lightly.

"Maybe in a bit," I told her, stealing the joint for a quick puff instead. She shrugged and put it back in her purse, discarding the cup.

Me and alcohol had a rocky relationship at best.

Let's just say my particular flavor of darkness liked to bathe in whiskey. I'd once blacked out a whole evening only to find out the next day that I'd apparently ripped a chunk of Bethany Vargus' hair out and shaved off her brother Kenny's eyebrows after he passed out drunk. Their crime? Not caring that their family dog went missing during their party.

I was only fifteen.

And I really liked dogs. I also thought I was letting them off easy.

It happened again last year, but that time someone wound up being taken away by ambulance. No one knew who hurt the guy, but I did. Even if I couldn't remember. Those cuts could have only been inflicted by someone who knew their way around a blade. And mine were stained red when I woke up the next day.

Probably best not to see how gin affected me.

"Come on," Becca called over the music, taking back her joint. "Let's dance."

She skipped through the party goers, finding a place in the middle of the floor, already rolling her shoulders with the beat.

All around us, warm, half naked bodies ground against one another in time with the thud of the music. Lips met in sloppy kisses. Hips rolled and greedy fingers grasped and groped. These spoiled rich kids might've thought they were better than all the rest, but they were just as down and dirty as any you'd find in Lennox. Hell, maybe even more so.

I was pretty sure that girl over there was straight up getting finger fucked on the dance floor, but by the way her head was tipped back against the guy's shoulder in ecstasy, I didn't think she minded the audience. Probably enjoyed it.

A group of scantily dressed girls next to us shouted *cheers!* and tapped their little white pills together as though they were champagne flutes, before swallowing them down with shrieks of elation.

A guy with a black backpack counted cash one of the girls stuffed into his hand and nodded toward the back of the building.

That was when I saw them.

The Crows roosted atop a raised platform at the back of the warehouse-like structure. With the majority of the overhead lights pointed at the dance floor, they were mostly concealed by shadow, little flickers of their faces visible with the brightest of the colors.

Behind them stood a pair of double doors, their square windows showing low lighting within. A guy, barely visible on the other side, pressed down on a pretty blonde head and then tipped his back in ecstasy. Uncaring that everyone outside could clearly see his slack jawed expression as the chick sucked him off.

"They call it the Red Room," Becca explained, her voice rising over the din of music and conversation. "You know? Like Fifty Shades?"

So they had an orgy room...

Classy. I rolled my eyes before unintentionally letting my gaze fall back to them.

The Crows sat on a long black sectional, looking like kings overseeing their kingdom.

Rook, with his feet kicked up on a low table, took a swallow from a silver flask before passing it to Grey. I spotted a bit of white gauze poking out from beneath the sleeve of his t-shirt and felt all warm inside. Knowing that marking was mine, and that it would likely scar, forcing him to remember me every time he looked at it.

Corvus leaned forward over his knees, his eyes laser focused as they dragged over the bodies crowding the pier. Until they found me, and stopped.

"Show me what you got!" Becca shouted, spinning in a circle as she shook her hips to a top forty song, oblivious to the eyes watching us. Now three sets instead of just one.

A muscle in my temple jumped as I clenched my jaw, willing them to look away. Nothing to see here. Move. *The Fuck.* Along.

Instinctively, my gaze slid to Grey, and I found him smirking, leaning back to settle in, crossing his arms over his chest in a move that told me he wasn't planning on looking anywhere else anytime soon.

Fine. They wanted a show? I'd give them a show.

I came here to have a good time. Something I hadn't had in too long to remember. And they weren't going to ruin it for me.

I began to dance, feeling the music, letting it pull and twist and curl my body, closing my eyes to welcome it in and block them out.

"Damn, girl!" Becca said as she dropped the last of her joint on the wooden floor and stomped it out with the toe of her boot. "You can move!"

"Got my mom's stripper hips," I hollered back, regretting the admission as soon as it slipped out. I danced around Becca so my back was to the dais, and the Crows, but I could still feel them watching my every move.

Becca's eyes narrowed for an instant, lines of confusion between her brows before she seemed to decide

she didn't care, or that it wasn't her business.

I wondered what dive of a strip club my mom was undressing at these days. Or if, maybe, she was finally dead.

After what she did, she was lucky Dad didn't kill her. Hell, she was lucky *I* didn't. But that was before I became *this*.

This broken thing filled with hate, running on instinct and reflex like some kind of animal. Something less than human.

I didn't know what to do when she hurt me. Or how to react. I hadn't seen it coming. At least, not from her. She was always a druggie and a bad parent all around, but she hadn't ever done *that*. Not until she got the dirty drugs, cut with who the fuck knew what, and decided I was the devil incarnate.

Explaining the bruises to Dad the next day when he came back after losing all our money at the racetrack was the hardest conversation I'd ever had. For a second, I thought about lying. Covering for her. But...I just couldn't. I was done. Done covering for her. Done being the grown up at barely thirteen.

Dad made her leave that same day.

She never came back.

"Need a break?" Becca asked as I began to slow, sagging beneath the weight of the memory. Why did I have to bring her up?

I panted, my mouth parched from the heat and exertion. "I think I'll take that drink now."

She lifted a brow questioningly, but handed me the gin. I twisted the cap and drank straight from the bottle. Not too much, just enough to feel the burn of it slithering down my throat, pooling warmly in my belly. Fixing the ache there.

I recoiled from the taste, shaking my head to get rid of the lingering tang of juniper.

"Better?" she asked as I took one more swig for good measure and passed it back.

"Much."

The air was clogged with the smell of smoke, both tobacco and pot. Thick with a muggy dampness that clung to my skin.

"Hey," a deep voice rumbled into my ear and I spun, my pulse picking up speed, but it wasn't a Crow who'd slipped into our tight twosome. It was a guy I recognized from my second period math class. "It's Ava Jade, isn't it?"

"Josh?" I tried, though I was good with faces, I wasn't always as good with names.

His alcohol glazed eyes widened in appreciation at my memory before narrowing coyly, snaking down the line of my body. "Yeah," he said, moving his hips in time with the beat, inching closer. "Want to get some air? I could show you my truck."

Annoyance flared through me before I could fully

stifle it. "Well, *Josh*, I'm dancing with my friend. Or did you not notice?"

Becca laughed, putting her hands on my hips seductively from behind, beginning to pull me away. "Sorry, Josh, this little birdy is all mine."

"Catch you in class, then?" he called as Becca attempted to save me from being preyed upon. Little did she know it was a hell of a lot more likely she was saving *his* ass.

I almost slipped on a puddle of spilled beer trying to turn around amid a cluster of hot, dancing bodies. I caught myself on Becca with a yelp, who giggled as she spun me away from the mess to drier ground. And right into a bubblegum pink catastrophe.

"*Lennox?*" Bri sneered, her upper lip curled in disgust as she dissected my outfit with her eyes, casting an accusing stare in Becca's direction. Because clearly it couldn't have been me who put an outfit like this together. Ha! There was a difference between *having* style and *having the money* to fund that style.

"Barbie?" I countered, making my eyes wide with false surprise. "Thought you'd be taller."

Her glossed lips pressed together as her little group of minions stopped what they were doing to stand behind her, their stares just as skeptical as their master's when they recognized me.

"What? Never seen real tits before?" I asked the one on the right and her head snapped up, moving her line of sight where it ought to have been from the start. I mean, I was flattered but...

"You trailer trash *hoe,*" Bri said on a laugh, smug as fuck with her hands on her hips. And *god* that outfit was awful. So pink it hurt to look at. Paired with sky high stilettos that proved she hadn't learned from the first time she almost broke an ankle here.

I grimaced. Damn, the hem of her dress was about two inches from showing the entire party her lady bits.

She wanted to call *me* trash? While she was wearing that?

"Whatever you say, Malibu Barbie. If you'll excuse us—"

I moved to brush past her with Becca on my heels but she stepped once to her right, blocking our path and forcing me to stop or plow her over.

She was lucky I was trying so very hard to be good, even though I could already feel the rush of that unnamable *thing* inside of me rearing its ugly head. Uncoiling like a snake.

Rising like steam until my cheeks flushed red and my scalp dampened with sweat.

"I don't think so, Lennox—"

"It's *Ava Jade,*" I bit out, interrupting her.

"You don't need to be here, hon. Don't make this difficult. Just go back to where you came from, 'kay?

Nobody wants you."

I opened my mouth to form a reply, but Becca beat me to it.

"Oh, fuck off, Brianna. *I* happen to like Ava. She's much better company than you ever were."

"You little fucking bitch—"

Bri made a grab for Becca and that was it. When her manicured claws curled into Becca's hair, I saw *red*.

Letting go was always easy, even when I wished it weren't, but this time it was a motherfucking pleasure. I bristled with ecstasy in the split second before I launched my closed fist at her ugly ass face.

She released Becca the instant my knuckles cracked into her nose, a stunned look making her eyes round and distant as she staggered back, blinking to keep from passing out.

I didn't even realize I'd hit her again until I tasted blood on my tongue and realized I was splattered with it.

Someone screamed and hearing the sound of approach, I whirled, ready to take on whoever else wanted a fucking piece. I didn't even want to use my blades right now. I would if I had to, but the sting in my knuckles was *giving me life*.

The blonde who'd raced forward to try to attack me backed off when she saw the look on my face. Everyone backed off. Even Becca. The music continued to thud even with a floor devoid of dancers.

In the blink of an eye I'd transformed them from carefree partiers to stunned onlookers.

One of my best tricks.

Let them watch, my darkness whispered. I wasn't finished. Not quite yet.

I went back to Bri, who had fallen and was trying to get up on shaking legs, slipping on the smear of her blood. I gripped her by her hair like she'd gripped Becca's and ripped her head back.

She screeched, clawing at my hands, but I couldn't even feel it. The darkness was flowing freely now, blocking out the pain. Blocking out anything and everything I didn't care to feel. Anything I couldn't *use*.

"You'll pay for this, Lennox," she cried. "I'm going to fucking *end* you."

I put my mouth level with her ear, twisting her wrist back behind her when she made a swipe for my face. "1323 Rochester Lane. Big white house. Blue shutters," I whispered in her ear and reveled in the way her breath caught in her throat. The way her body stiffened.

It was easy to find her address, and one of the first things I did that very first day after the cow set her sights on me. A bit of social media sleuthing and reverse google image searching and *voila*. I had it. Just in case.

"Go ahead and come after me. See what happens."

I threw her head down and let her clamber to catch herself on the floor, inhaling deeply as the rush began to wear off, lingering only in my twitching fingers and the heat licking up my spine.

Three sets of eyes found mine when I lifted my gaze.

The Crows watched from their makeshift throne, expressions of shock and hostility reigniting my embers to flames. Did they want a turn?

"Come on," Becca said, and I flinched when she grabbed my bloodied hand. "We should get out of here, like *now*."

I let her pull me out, drunk off the rush, and grinning ear to ear.

13

CORVUS

The music pulsed as I leaned forward on the couch to watch as Ava Jade collided with Bri's backside, and the bitch turned feral. I had to admit, I was curious how she would react to the self-proclaimed queen of Briar Hall.

"Hey man," a kid no more than sixteen stepped up onto the dais, blocking my view. "You think I could talk to—"

"No," I growled. "Now get out of the fucking way."

"But Grey said that maybe—"

"*Move.*"

The kid opened his mouth a third time, but one look from me silenced him and he bolted for the exit.

Practically shaking.

"Dude, that was Jesse's kid. He wants in," Grey hollered. "He wants to take the trial."

I shook my head, searching for the new girl again in the crowd. "He isn't ready," I retorted. "The kid was about to shit himself."

I wasn't wrong. And Grey didn't argue. I wasn't about to stick my neck out for some pipsqueak with Diesel when I knew full well he wouldn't last a *second* in the trials. Besides, Dies didn't take on kids. You had to be a legal adult to be initiated into the ranks.

Bri sneered something at Ava Jade, and I took in how her body shifted, the minuscule movements seeming second nature, putting her in a fighting stance whether she was aware of it or not.

Her file had been missing from the office when I went to have a look through it the other night after Randy's send off, but that didn't stop me. It took me a couple of days, but I now knew all there was to know about Ava Jade Mason.

She lived in a trailer park with her dad before he was killed. His very brief police report alluded to gang involvement, but it didn't look like they were doing anything about it. I doubted they ever would.

Her mom was a mystery. It was noted in her files at Lennox High that she was no longer a point of contact, so I assumed she split.

Ava Jade wasn't pictured in any of the yearbooks aside from the obligatory class photo each year which led me to believe she was a loner.

A loner who seemed to know how to handle herself, and who carried a blade. I wondered if she knew how to use it. Why she felt the need to carry it in class?

Bri turned her venom on Becca, but it was Ava I couldn't peel my eyes away from. I'd already noticed her curves, despite the fact she liked to hide them beneath baggy sweaters and ripped jeans, but tonight...

Tonight she wasn't hiding. In that dress, with everything she had on display, she was fucking taunting giants. She knew it, too. I saw the way her face changed when she noticed us watching. Flustered at first, but then rife with defiance as she began to dance.

My brow furrowed as she stiffened now, her body going rigid as she watched over her new roommate. When Bri launched herself at Becca, Ava Jade was primed and ready.

When her fist flew, sending Bri staggering back, my cock throbbed in my jeans.

Grey moved to stand, but I signaled him to stay put. I wanted to see how this played out. She had an audience now, even Rook was sitting up and taking notice, a gleam of appreciation in his dark stare. His cigarette forgotten, left to burn out between his fingers.

There would be no taking this back. Ava Jade was royally *fucked*.

Bye-bye, little sparrow.

In a move not even I could've anticipated, she fucking

hit her *again.* As if once wasn't enough to seal her fate. You didn't mess up Gregory Moore's daughter's face and get away with it.

Bri's nose shattered under Ava Jade's fist on the second hit, spraying blood in an arc over her face. Somehow, the red warpaint suited her, and I ground my teeth to keep my body in check at her savage beauty.

"Jesus *fuck,*" Rook groaned, and I caught him pawing at the front of his jeans, practically salivating, his shoulders shaking with a shiver of rabid desire.

A hollow chasm gaped open in my stomach. That wasn't good.

Ava Jade wasn't what I thought, and I didn't know if I should be as turned on as Rook, or even more wary of her than I already was. I hadn't wanted something, *someone,* in a long time. Dolls broke too easily under pressure and the ones here were made of porcelain.

Ava Jade was made of something much stronger. Maybe not even a doll at all.

Would she break under my fingers? Would she shatter?

I'd been worried about what a girl like her could do to us, from that very first moment my brothers and I saw her. Their interest had me on guard, eager to get rid of her as soon as possible. My primal nature viewed her as a threat and my job had always been to eliminate those. To eliminate any possibility of distraction, but...

Bri fell to her knees, choking and spluttering. Ava Jade was on top of her in a second, ripping her head back to whisper something in her ear, and *the fear* on Bri's face. If that wasn't the most beautiful fucking thing I'd seen today...

What did she say to her?

For a second, I had to wonder if she'd use her blade. I knew she carried. I clocked it the very first day. Not because I saw it, or even its outline through her jeans. It was the way her fingers twitched low, toward her means of protection. The way her ankle hitched up when I stood to use the bathroom, just to get a better look at her. If she drew, I'd have no choice but to stop her.

My own hand inched to my gun, jaw tightening. Maybe we should stop this before it got any worse.

Bri's tear-stained gaze lifted to us, pleading without the need for words. Hurt and anger brightening her dull brown eyes.

A sneer curled my upper lip, and she let her head hang, defeated.

"Should we do something?" Grey asked, hollering over the music.

I shook my head. "I'll do it. You stay here, keep an eye."

Becca pulled Ava away, and the pair weaved their way out. I let out a breath as they shouldered past awed onlookers as Bri did her best to look *not* like the bag of shit she clearly was. Batting away helping hands left and right with a scowl.

"Corvus," Grey warned before I could leave. "Let me do it?"

I didn't like the look on his face. The way his eyes darted to her and away, or how his brows were drawn, jaw clamped tight. He was...*worried*...about what I was going to do. To *her*.

The beast inside me stiffened, making my blood sizzle in my veins, but I didn't let that show. Instead, I fixed Grey with an impassive stare.

Not for the first time, I questioned the truth of his excuse for vanishing last night. And for the too-perfect slice in his arm. He was keeping something from me. I had a feeling I knew exactly *who* it was.

"Nah," I replied easily, searching his eyes for any betrayal of emotion. "Why don't you shovel Bri off the floor? Looks like she might need a hand."

It was easy enough to find them. The partygoers scattered like roaches from an exterminator as I passed, letting me catch up to them without needing to hurry a single step.

When I stepped onto the dock, any lingering people outside fled too, except for the two girls who hadn't yet noticed I was trailing behind them.

Ava Jade tipped her head back and howled a laugh at the moon halfway down the dock while Becca continued trying to tug her along.

"Fuck," I heard her curse, her body shuddering on a long sigh. "That felt *good*."

Becca stopped short, yanked to a stop with Ava Jade. "Look, crazypants, that shit might fly in Lennox for keeping the wolves at bay, but it won't here. You just started a war."

Ava Jade leveled her stare on Becca and smirked, giving a one-shoulder shrug. "Worth it," she said, and Becca shared in her next laugh.

"We'll see how *worth it* you think it is on Monday. Come on, let's get back."

"Rebecca," I growled and her back stiffened. "A word with your new friend, if you don't mind."

Her throat bobbed as she glanced at Ava Jade, whose full attention was squarely on me. Where it should be.

"*Uh…*" Becca started, her discomfort evident in the tension between her eyes. In her stilted movements.

"No thanks," she answered, her icy stare narrowing to slits that would cut a lesser man down to the quick.

My lips twitched. "I wasn't asking."

"Corvus," Becca started, "Bri was—"

"I don't give two shits about Bri."

Ava Jade looped her arm back through Becca's, lifting her chin with a false smile. "We have somewhere to be."

I shook my head. "You're making a mistake."

"Am I?"

Becca tugged her close and whispered something in her ear, prompting her to roll her eyes before pulling her arm back from her friend.

"*Fine,*" she gritted out through clenched teeth. "But I'm not going anywhere with you while you're armed."

Smart girl.

I stared at her, trying to read the truth in her pinched expression, but for once, came up empty handed. She was a wild card, this Ava Jade. I didn't like that. Not one fucking bit.

"I'm not—"

"Don't fucking patronize me," she said, *interrupting me.* Heat licked up my neck, making my shoulders strain with the sudden urge to hit something. An urge I never let get the better of me, no matter how hard it tried to.

I closed the gap between us, sensing more than seeing the group gathering at the entrance to the pier at my back. She didn't balk at my approach, even though I stood almost a full head taller than her in heels, and she wasn't even that short to begin with. Maybe five-six.

I drew my gun from the back of my waistband and watched as her keen stare alighted on it, while her fingers jerked toward the hem of her dress.

Becca flinched when I passed the gun to her. "Go on," I told her. "Take it. If there's even a single scratch on it when you give it back…"

I left the punishment up to her imagination, keeping back a laugh as she grabbed it out of my grasp with two fingers, holding it as though it might explode if she weren't careful. "Safety's on, sweetheart," I told her. "Maybe best to keep it out of sight, yeah?"

She swallowed hard before carefully setting it into her purse and stepping out of my way. She mouthed *sorry* to Ava Jade, and I swept an arm out for her to take the lead.

"You first," she insisted, not budging an inch until I took the first step, guiding us down the dock and through the parked cars along the water's edge. She kept up, only a few steps behind me. I could feel her tension like a rubber band stretched as far as it could go, waiting for its opening to snap.

We rounded the last car and stepped off the gravel and onto the dirt where a sheer rock face jutted up out of the earth, curving like a hand cupped around the edge of the lake. You could climb it from just down the trail. Jump in from the forty-foot height if you were brave enough.

It wasn't exactly a thrill I was seeking tonight though as much as the silence and privacy the dark shadow of the cliffside would provide.

"Well, you got me out here, all alone. Congratulations. Now what the hell do you want?"

I cocked my head at her, not used to being spoken to that way by anyone, never mind a girl. I didn't know whether I wanted to sew her lips shut for the offense or lick away the blood still staining a corner of her frowning mouth.

"Do you have any idea what you just did in there?"

"Thought you didn't care?"

"I don't."

"You have a funny way of showing it."

"Where were you last night?" I asked, changing tactics. Needing to clear my head.

A flicker of recognition danced over her eyes before they settled back to a glare.

"What?"

"Don't patronize me," I said, using her own words against her, but she didn't squirm under the pressure of my accusation. "You wouldn't happen to know what happened to Grey, would you? Seems he had a run-in with a particularly feisty tree branch."

She crossed her arms, making her tits swell above the cut of her dress. They, too, were freckled with crimson, and I locked my jaw, grinding my teeth at the sight.

"I don't know what to tell you. Maybe he needs glasses if he's running into trees."

A laugh got stuck in my throat, held back by the dam of my lips.

"Bri's right, you know," I uttered, side stepping her, forcing her to mirror my movements to keep the distance she was so set on maintaining between us. "You don't belong at Briar Hall."

"I don't think you do either," she muttered, seeming to regret the words once they'd vacated her lips.

I lifted a brow, my body hardening as I began to cage her in, making her back up toward the rough rockface. Not knowing if I wanted to see how those lips tasted or toss her over the bank and into the lake. Would she cut me, too, if I tried?

I might like that.

I couldn't remember the last time I wasn't able to make a decision. The uncertainty was foreign. Yet another thing I was quickly growing to hate.

Once I had her boxed against the cliff side, I decided. I'd see exactly what I was dealing with here. Either she'd fight, or she'd crumple.

Which would it be?

Ava gauged my move a moment before I made it, her hand reaching for the blade she had concealed beneath the hem of her dress as I rushed in. My fist closed around her wrist, trapping it to her thigh while I blocked a hit from the other, pinning it to the stone at her back.

She panted through a snarling mouth, trying to get her hand free. I squeezed, forcing her to drop the blade with a little grunt. I kicked it away and it ricocheted off the rock before sailing like a glimmering arrow over the edge of the bank and into the lake.

If I thought she was pissed before, she was furious now. She tried harder to get free of my grip. Her relentless struggle made me have to use my hips to pin her. My thickening cock pressing against the cool bite of metal zipper.

"You're a monster," she spat, her harsh tone and curled upper lip disguising the truth her body couldn't hide from me. She was fighting the same indecision I was. Unsure if she wanted to fuck me or bite my head off.

She shivered as I leaned in, putting my mouth at her ear.

"You're damn right I am."

A bitter grin pulled at my lips. *Fuck.* I couldn't remember the last time I'd smiled.

"You should run, little sparrow. While you still can," I warned, unsure I'd even give her the chance to if she tried.

"And if I don't?"

"Then I'll swallow you whole."

Her resistance waned and for the briefest second, her blistering cold stare settled on my mouth—before she heaved her hips forward, knocking me off balance.

I staggered back a step, licking my lips at the ache in my hip bone.

"If I can't find it," she hissed. "You owe me a new blade."

She stalked past me like a panther, dark hair wild and blowing in a sudden gust of wind. She stopped for a second to tear the heels from her feet, tossing them to the side. Completely unbothered that her back was now to me. That if I wanted to, I could get my hands around that pretty neck and...

"Oh, and Corvus," she added as she unfurled back to her full height. "I'm not going anywhere."

She tossed me a wink over her shoulder before she dove, dress and all, into the lazy waves below, pushing herself deep into the black water to hunt for what she'd lost.

14

ROOK

I took another swallow of my whiskey, rolling my neck as the warm burn of it forced my muscles to relax even with the thud of the music rattling my bones. I was still a bit hard from the new girl's spectacle. She was fucking brilliant.

A goddess.

I'd admit it, I was intrigued by her coarse nature from the start, but now...

Fuck.

My cock twitched in my jeans, re-hardening at the mental image of her covered in blood. The pattern of it splattered over her sharp cheeks. How she didn't even fucking flinch as it sprayed over her. The way her eyes went hyper focused, and also blank as she hit Brianna for the second time. Like she didn't even realize she'd done it until it was too late for her to stop herself.

I shivered, my fist clenching and unclenching until I curled it around the arm of the weathered sofa to stop the habit, my teeth twisting my lip ring instead.

I wanted her.

My jaw twitched, resisting the admission.

Another swig of whiskey and the flask was empty. *Damn.*

Grey knocked his knuckles on my shin, and I followed his line of sight to the door, where Corvus was making his way back inside.

That was quick.

Corvus' brows were pulled tightly together, shadowing his deep-set eyes as he stormed through the crowd. He cast a curious stare at Brianna as her friends tried to help her clean the blood from her face near the punch bowl, before he jumped up onto the dais.

He gave Grey a look before running his tongue over his teeth, clearly still inside his own head. I knew that look. It was the one he got when he was trying to plan out a particularly difficult job. His mechanical mind going over every option. Every possibility. Finding ways to control the situation in our favor.

Exhausting.

I'd rather have one of them shoot me in the head than have my every move planned out to within an inch of error. That wasn't living. Where was the thrill in that? Where was the fire?

But Corvus needed that control. It was why Grey and I didn't often challenge the fucker. If he didn't have his control, he got so goddamned nasty that neither of us could stand to be around him.

So he made plans. And we mostly followed them. Sometimes ruined them. It was a tossup on any given day.

"You scare her away?" I called to him over the music, not really giving a shit if he had, but curious all the same. She'd only just sunk her fangs in, gotten my interest. I didn't really want her gone, I realized. She was too interesting.

A spec of vivid color on the otherwise dull canvas of my life.

"Not fucking likely," Grey replied, securing himself another scowl from Corv.

Corvus said something I didn't catch over the music, and I gestured that it was too loud. "Can't hear you, Brother," I hollered, lifting a hand to signal the pledge standing down at the end of the dais to get me more whiskey.

He rushed over, catching the flask when I tossed it to him. "Fill it," I ordered and he vanished, lost in the crowd on his way to the tiny, locked office where we kept some personals.

"She's going to be fucking trouble," Corvus said, and

I was left piecing together his grumbled words through the music.

A vein in his temple throbbed, and he tightened his jaw as he turned away from us, signaling the two chaps by the door to keep an eye out. They were seniors at Briar Hall. Two in a small group of five that wanted an in with Diesel.

They knew the best way to do that was through Corvus. They did what we wanted, when we wanted, on a fucking prayer that we'd give them the *in* they so desperately wanted.

One of them might even be worthy of the opportunity. The others were not.

Corvus jerked his head toward the Red Room for us to follow.

My buzz intensified as I stood from the sofa and I reveled in the staticky numbness, following my brothers through the double doors.

Red tinted light played over naked bodies as people fucked on every available surface. The sounds of their ecstasy and pain blotted out the music as the doors shut behind us, mingling with the wet slap of bodies on bodies and lips wrapped around cocks and

tongues toying with clits.

My feet unconsciously drew me toward the girl three guys had strapped to the spinning table. One of them pounded mercilessly between her legs while the other choked her with his cock at the opposite end. Her throat visibly swelling with each of his thrusts.

A third guy leaned over her tits, snorting a line of blow from the tops of each mound. I bristled, my eye twitching at the sight.

I was stopped short when Grey pulled at the back of my shirt. "Focus," he said.

"*Out,*" Corvus thundered, his hulking frame seeming to grow in the red lights like a shadow come to life.

I drew out a cigarette, lighting it and inhaling deeply as the fucking stopped all at once and heads swiveled to the door.

Fun ruined.

"I said get the fuck out!" Corvus bellowed and the nude statues frozen mid-fuck burst into action, gathering up clothes and shoes, rushing to remove strap-on dicks and unstrap people from the various devices stationed down the hall-like room.

I watched the cocaine slip from the woman's tits as she was unstrapped and ground my teeth as the phantom taste of it burned at the back of my throat. I finished my cigarette in the second inhale, dragging it all the way down to the butt before dropping it to stomp on its carcass. The need mellowed, at least for the moment.

The few red lights affixed to the low ceiling made the naked bodies look like cattle being prodded through a narrow corridor as we stepped out of the way for them to leave like they were told.

My fingers found a pretty throat, locking around it before the girl who'd been strapped to the table could escape. She gasped, her baby blue eyes going wide as she took me in, her body going rigid.

"Rook," Corvus warned as I leaned in, inhaling the sweet aroma of fear and arousal on her still mostly naked body. I bent, dragging my tongue over the remains of the blow on her tits with a groan.

"Wait outside," I told her, licking my lips. "This won't take long."

Someone needed to take care of the ache in my jeans.

She managed a nod and tried to swallow past the dam of my palm pressing against her windpipe. A taste of what she was in for. She gasped as I released her, and she scrambled out the door, uncaring that she dropped her panties.

The doors sealed out enough of the loud music and raucous shouts from the crowd outside that we could speak without shouting or being heard in here. I sighed, leaning against the black-painted wall to cross my arms.

"What's up, Brother?" I asked him, my attention briefly pulled out the window, checking to see if that little rat was back with my whiskey yet.

"That girl is going to be a problem," he repeated, huffing as he tipped his head up to the ceiling. The red lights deepened the shadows beneath his eyes, exposing the exhaustion he was trying hard to hide.

Even half drunk, it was easy to tell. He was my brother. I didn't have to cut him open to know what I'd find inside. We were made of the same stuff, just different flavors.

Grey's gaze roved over our brother, a knot forming between his brows. "Man, I think you just need to get some sleep. You know how you get when—"

"I don't need fucking sleep," he snapped, stepping up to Grey in a way that would've made him reel back a year ago. "*I'm fine.*"

Corvus began to pace, his eyes shifting over the floor at his feet like it might hold an answer he was looking for. "She's got to be part of a gang," he muttered. "Maybe the Aces? Kings maybe since she's from Lennox? Planted here to keep an eye on us? I've looked into her and there's no evidence to support the theory but she's...it would just make the most sense."

Not surprising that he'd already dug into her past. I should've guessed he would.

I considered what he was saying, casting her in a rival's role in my head, but the image wouldn't stick. It wasn't impossible for her to be a member of a gang. Rare for a woman, definitely, especially one so young, but not impossible.

Diesel's wife had been a full member of the Saints.

And apparently, she was the most brutal of them all.

Quietly deadly. A snake in the grass. How I wished I could've met her.

There was a woman in the Lodi chapter, too, but she was nearing thirty and had earned her *in* when she put herself between a bullet and Damien St. Vincent. One of the original three Saints.

"She isn't part of a gang," Grey said, making Corvus stop pacing to glare up at him.

"How would you know that?" he demanded.

Grey shrugged. "I just do."

He was growing some balls. *Fuck.* Didn't think he had it in him.

"And she won't be a problem," Grey continued. "Not if we can get her on our side."

"You're fucking serious?" Corvus scoffed, scrubbing a palm over his chin. When Grey didn't budge, staring down our brother with a *give-me-one-reason-why-not* look, Corvus ground his teeth. "Even if we wanted that, her dad was killed by the Kings. She's not interested in having anything to do with us. Or any other gang."

Hmmm.

Maybe Grey was onto something.

We didn't need to bring her in, and judging by the look on Corvus' face that wasn't an option, but maybe...

"Leverage then," I said, kicking off the wall to join Corvus and Grey at the middle of the floor. Thinking through the problem as best I could with my brain swimming in whiskey. If we could control her then whatever threat Corvus insisted she posed would be neutralized. We could go back to business as usual. And maybe get a little something extra in the deal.

"We don't need to bring her in, we just need some leverage."

Corvus' brows furrowed.

"Control," I added, speaking his language. "Give the dog a bone."

Grey's lips pressed into a tight line, but Corvus was intrigued.

"What the fuck are you saying Rook?"

"I'm saying we help her out. She just made a huge mistake with Brianna Moore. What if we cleaned it up for her? And in exchange, we get her docile obedience. You get to keep your reign of terror at Bitch Hall, and we get a new pet."

I let my proposition sink in, picturing Ava Jade's face contorted with pain and pleasure as I tore her sweet cunt to shreds, as I made her scream…

I swallowed, leveling my stare on Corvus. "I might even share her," I joked, smirking now. I liked this idea.

"If there's anything left when you're done with her," Grey muttered, seeming wholly uninterested in this plan. I thought he'd be all for it. He was clearly into her. He spent the entire hour of homeroom staring at her back like he could will her to want him as much as he so obviously craved her.

I may not have been as attentive as Corvus, but people were easy to read. And Grey had always been an open book.

Corvus brooded silently as he considered my idea, shifting from foot to foot.

They wouldn't blackmail her for sex, which really was a shame, but then again any of us could get that whenever and wherever we wanted. We hadn't had a drudge in a while, though, and I was willing to bet the idea of controlling the uncontrollable was *right* up my brother's alley.

"Awe come on, Brother," I pushed. "You can't tell me you aren't at all interested. I see the way you've been watching her. I bet you'd like to have her play fetch for you."

Corvus was more difficult to read than Grey, but his obsession was clear from the start, and it'd only gotten worse in the week that she'd been here.

His jaw tightened.

It seemed I'd misread him, too.

"Or maybe I've read you wrong," I baited him. "If you aren't interested at all then at least don't spoil the fun for the rest of us."

"She won't go for it," Grey warned, and I knew he was probably right. I had to admit, I'd be disappointed if she did.

I shrugged. "Didn't know we were planning on giving her a choice."

After another few seconds of thought, Corvus lifted his chin, fixing Grey with one of his rare expressions of support. "You good with this?" he asked. "Bri will shit a fucking brick."

I grinned darkly to myself, knowing damn well she would. But she wouldn't deny us if we told her not to breathe a word of what Ava did here tonight. If we told her to lie about what happened. Keep it hush. Grey would bear the burden of this call, though.

No more heiress pussy.

And he would be the one who had to deal with her hysterical ass when she realized that we'd chosen to protect this new girl over her. No matter the reason. Unlikely that he'd give her one anyway.

Grey nodded solemnly. "Bri was just a decent lay who happened to have connections we needed last summer. It should've ended a long time ago."

He wasn't fucking wrong there.

Corv and I had been telling him as much for *months*.

I bristled with anticipation, waiting for Corvus to give the word.

His gaze slid back to me, calculating, trying to read my intent.

I gave him nothing.

"We'll try it your way," he decided, and I let a fresh smile slither over my lips. It was the closest thing to an admission we would get from Corv that he wanted the girl, too. At his beck and call. Submitting to his every whim. That's how he liked them.

"Don't look so smug," he growled at me before turning to face Grey again. "Go find Bri before she calls the fucking cops."

15

AVA JADE

I read the message for what must've been the twentieth time since I woke up Saturday morning to see it staining my phone screen. And now, Monday morning, the feeling of dread still lingered.

Four years ago near the train tracks in Lennox, I went full dark.

It consumed me, and I let it.

Those repressed, terrifying, *powerful* feelings took the wheel...and I killed a man.

This wasn't Bri. It couldn't be.

She couldn't know that.

No one knew about that. No one was there.

It had to be a coincidence. I could remember walking along the tracks a handful of times back from downtown, anyone could've seen me. This didn't mean anything. Right?

But then who was it? Why the anonymity?

The number that sent this message late Friday night wasn't the same one that sent the others on Thursday, but the feel of them was the same. If they were sent by the same person, then why use two different numbers?

I could reply. Ask who it was. But my gut told me that would only be inviting even more messages from someone who was giving off major stalker vibes.

Ignore it and whoever it is will get bored and stop.

"Are you waiting for it to sprout legs and run away?" Becca asked, sweeping out of her bedroom fully dressed for the school day. The smell of her earthy body spray filling the room with her.

I blinked, glancing up from my phone and realizing how tightly I'd been holding it. Any tighter and I might've cracked the screen even more than it already was. "Oh," I swallowed. "No. It's just...I got this weird message on Friday."

She cocked her head at me, and I lost my nerve, not wanting to give whoever this creep was the attention he or she so clearly wanted. Not wanting to give Becca even the tiniest clue as to the potential meaning of the message still trespassing on my phone's drive. What would she think if she found out what I'd done?

"Never mind," I shook my head, stuffing my phone down deep into the pocket of my jeans.

Her eyes narrowed for an instant before she seemed to decide not to press. "So," she said, dropping onto the soft leather beside me on the couch with a snicker. "How excited are you for homeroom?"

I groaned, letting my head fall against the backrest with a roll of my eyes.

All weekend I'd been waiting for the *Bri* hammer to drop. Becca warned me that there would be retaliation, if not actual police involvement. Apparently Mr. Moore, the poor fucker who sired the queen bitch, didn't take kindly to people touching his precious girl. Being more of a strait-laced sort of fellow, his retribution would likely come in the form of a lawsuit or some other legal bullshittery that I did *not* want to deal with.

Frankly, I'd rather he send a hired gun. I had a much better idea what to expect and how to handle that than I did a lawyer.

If he dragged police and shit into this there would be no way to keep it from getting back to Aunt Humphrey. *Good-bye ticket to freedom.*

"That excited, hey?"

"Why hasn't she done anything yet?" I moaned.

Becca barked a laugh. "She must be cooking up something *really* special for you."

I'd spent the weekend catching up on assignments for the most part, but I also spent a solid three hours doing recon on Bri. I now knew where she went to get her nails and hair done. Where she liked to shop and grab coffee. What type of car she drove *and* her license plate number—what kind of dumbass doesn't at least blur that out for a social media photo?

I felt pretty confident that if she retaliated in any way not legally driven that I'd be ready to beat her right back, even if just the idea of wasting that kind of time on her was exhausting.

"Bri can be a cantankerous bitch, there's no doubt about that," Becca added as she got back up to pillage a handful of peanut M&M's from the kitchen counter for her breakfast. "But if I were you, I'd be more worried about the Crows."

The mere mention of them made me sneer. I hadn't been able to find the blade Corvus lost in the lake. I searched for a solid fifteen minutes in the chilly lake water, digging through seaweed and litter, but it was gone. I had three more from the set, but that wasn't the point. They were a gift from my dad. The last thing he ever bought me.

I now kept *two* on me at all times. If I'd learned anything from my run-ins with both Grey and Corvus last week, it was that one just wasn't enough. At least, not for them.

"That asshole owes me a blade," I grumbled, crossing my arms over my chest.

Becca snorted. "Yeah, good luck with that. I can't see Corvus James replacing your precious metals, babe."

Oh, he'd replace it. Even if it wouldn't be the same.

"Is that his last name?" I asked. "James? Why didn't Diesel give him his last name when he adopted him?"

Becca shrugged. "None of them are St. Crows. They all kept their last names. People say it's because Diesel only adopted them for his wife after she died. Because she always talked about wanting to give a few kids a better life."

"What do you think?"

"I don't think it's that. I've only seen him with them a couple times, but he definitely considers them his sons. I'm sure there's some other reason."

"Like?"

"Like maybe a *don't forget where you came from* kind of thing? Or maybe he wanted them to have a choice about joining the gang. If they took the St. Crow name, they'd have big ass red targets painted on their backs. Using their given surnames adds a layer of anonymity."

I lifted a brow. This girl was smarter than I gave her credit for. *Damn.*

Becca hopped up with a sigh. "I'm going to grab a water, want one?"

I shook my head, mulling over everything I knew thus far. At least one thing was for certain: Monday morning felt like a point of no return.

Bri told me she didn't want me here. Corvus told me I should run.

If I wasn't a stubborn ass with an ax to grind, I'd already be long gone. But their threats only made me dead set on staying. Nothing was going to ruin my chance at a ticket out of here. A ticket to a completely new life. One without gangs or worrying about casing the next job before I ran out of funds. Speaking of...

After a little jaunt into town with Becca to buy some new bedding and a couple incidentals, I was running dangerously low. I could ask Auntie dearest for an allowance, but honestly, I'd rather suck a goat.

I'd take the apartment in the city and college tuition when the time came, but for now, I'd do what I'd always done: take care of my damn self.

"Shit, we should head down," Becca said, rushing to toss her phone back into her bedroom. "The bell's going to ring any second."

Sighing, I saw that she was right. At least I'd get to see the look on both Bri and Corvus' faces when I deigned to show myself in homeroom this morning. It would be worth whatever came after.

I tossed my phone onto my bed and hurried to follow Becca out the door, making sure she locked it.

She split off from me as we reached the bottom of the stairs just in time for the bell. "See you at lunch!" she hollered, rushing to make it to her homeroom class before the tardy bell rang in three minutes.

I rushed across the atrium, knowing Mr. Harry Potter Glasses wouldn't let me in if I was even a second late. And I was *not* missing my chance to rub it in their faces that I wasn't going anywhere.

"Oh! Ava Jade, could you come here for a moment?"

My brows furrowed as I caught sight of a woman with a tight blonde bun sticking her head out of the office. She gestured for me to come to her, and I forced a face that wasn't the death glare I wanted to give her.

"Sure," I chimed as I hurried over, gauging how much time I had left to make it to class on time.

The woman held the door open, and I stepped into the quiet office, my nose wrinkling at a terrible vanilla musk scent that reminded me of something, but I couldn't place it.

A secretary typed away on a computer behind the main desk, and a few staff members chatted lazily in the corridor beyond that.

"I'm so sorry for your loss," she said, catching me off guard.

"What?"

"Your, *um*, your father, was it? He recently passed?"

My jaw clenched. "What is this about?"

"I'm so sorry, I'm the Vice-Principal, Mrs. June. It seems our secretary misplaced your file—"

"I told you, Caroline, I didn't misplace it. I wouldn't—" The secretary paused mid-typing to huff.

"Yes, yes." Mrs. June interrupted the secretary, waving off her words and earning herself an ugly face from the woman behind the desk. "Anyway, I seem to recall there being a request for you to see the counselor. I just wanted to let you know that she's been away on vacation this week but that she should be back by next week to see you, all right? If you need anything in the meantime, my door is open, just ask Janice here, and she can buzz you back."

Well, fuck me. I really hoped this wasn't some hidden stipulation of Aunt Humphry's because that was a *hell fucking no* from me, thank you very much.

"You must be mistaken," I said with my best apologetic smile. "I see a private counselor online."

The lie rolled off my tongue like butter and the VP lapped it up, looking relieved to be off the hook. "Oh, that's great. Well, if you find you need any more support, just let us know and we can try to set something up."

I nodded. "Sure thing. I should probably..."

"Oh, yes. Go on. Don't want to be late."

"Fucking counseling?" I muttered to myself as the door shut behind me, and I rushed down the vacant hallway, shaking my head.

The last time a school forced me to see a counselor I lasted a full five minutes before vowing to never subject myself to that again. I mean, Dom went to therapy and she said it helped her and that was great and all, but when people asked me prying questions, my first instincts were to either stab or run.

The counselor at Lennox high was lucky I'd decided on the latter.

The bell rang just as my hand closed around the handle of the door, and I stepped through before it finished ringing.

"Cutting it a bit close, Miss Mason?" the teacher drawled, peering at me from the corner of his eye while he sat atop his desk, hands folded over a knee.

"Sorry, sir," I bit out. "I was—"

"Don't care," he said with a strained smile, and I braced myself, my blood flooding with enough adrenaline to make me shiver as I turned my attention to the class, making my way slowly to my seat.

What was this?

I caught the briefest glimpse of Corvus' smirk before he dropped it in favor of his trademark scowl. He was fucking *pleased* to see me. The bastard. He knew I wouldn't run. His shoulders flexed beneath the leather of his jacket, making an audible creak.

Rook stared openly from beside his adoptive brother, leaning over his desk like he might launch an attack at any given second. His dark hair shadowing his even darker eyes. His knuckles popped as he cracked them into his palm one by one, the tattooed letters spelling his name moving like a wave.

Grey slouched back in his chair, running a thumb over his lower lip as his eyes scraped down the length of me inch by inch. He had his tattoos on display today in a short sleeve V-neck that showed off a lot of muscle I hadn't paid proper attention to before. Not to mention, the bandage still in place over the cut that was no doubt crusting over into a good scar by now.

Their interest wasn't missed, not by anyone in the class, but least of all by motherfucking Brianna Moore.

I took a good long look at her, *sitting at the other end of the classroom,* before I slid into the one vacant seat, directly in front of Corvus. Like he planned it that way. For all I knew, he did.

I smiled to myself as I set down my books and settled in to listen to the drone of the teacher prattle on about some shit that he prefaced by saying wouldn't be on a test—which basically meant I didn't care at all what he was saying. Good, because I was too busy replaying the epic visual of Bri in my head and biting my lip to keep from laughing.

No amount of makeup could hide the two black eyes, and *man* did she look absolutely ridiculous in that nose splint. I was surprised she came at all, though I had to assume it was to host her very own pity party.

But to sit all the way on the other side of the classroom? To not even give me a good *glare* when I came in?

Had I scared her that much?

Huh.

If a little threat was all it took, then I'd have done that to start with. Avoided this whole mess of bullshit drama.

"Find what you lost?" Corvus asked in a rumbling whisper behind me, and I wriggled in my seat, not liking what the sound of his voice was doing to me.

I really needed to get laid...

"You mean, what *you* lost, jackass?"

An intake of breath from someone nearby made me smile to myself.

"You owe me a new blade," I reminded him when he didn't reply, and got a pointed look from the teacher that I studiously ignored. I got what I came for, he could kick me out now for all I cared.

I missed the peace of detention with Ms. Wood.

Though, I really didn't relish the thought of having to explain myself to my aunt again. Yeah, *fuck that.*

"Is that so?" came Corvus' delayed reply, and I stiffened, feeling his fingers brush against my back and curl into my hair. For a heart stopping moment, I thought he might jerk my head back right there in the classroom, punish me for daring to speak like that to him. Right in front of everyone.

He might've even gotten away with it.

But he didn't, and I let out a breath as his fingers retreated, shivering. Telling myself I'd have had his hand nailed to the table with six inches of sharpened steel if he tried it.

"Yeah," I said, wetting my suddenly dry lips. "And it better be a nice one. The one you so rudely stripped me of was a gift."

He grunted as though amused, and I sensed more than heard him sitting back in his chair, leaving the conversation only half finished. If he thought I was kidding, though, he was dead wrong.

Not wanting to incur the wrath of the teacher and earn myself another week of detention, I decided *not* to poke the bears any more than I already had. At least for today. Surprisingly, they seemed keen to just lounge in their chairs and stare at the back of my head.

I had to admit, it had me feeling a little...*special?*

No, maybe that wasn't the right word.

Powerful.

Yeah, that was the one.

I'd hardly done anything to warrant it, but apparently speaking your mind and not letting bullies push you around was enough to make the notorious Crows sit up and take notice.

It'd be easier for me if they *didn't* take notice. I knew that, but taunting them was kind of...dare I admit it?...fun. I hadn't felt this alive since what happened to Dad. Maybe longer than that if I were being honest. Maybe all the way back to that night at the train tracks.

Run, the rational part of my brain demanded, at war with the dominant part that whispered to push them to their edges and see what they did when they fell.

Like a cat pawing a glass of water, nudging it to the edge of a countertop. Unable to help myself. Wanting to crouch down and peer over the edge to see the broken pieces after it fell. Tail flicking with satisfaction.

Stupid? Definitely.

Tempting as fuck? Hell yes.

I gathered my books and left before the teacher was through speaking at the end of class, not wanting to linger there with them barely a step behind me. Not trusting myself enough to not say anything more than I already had.

Be good, I reminded myself, mentally fighting those dominant urges.

Just one fucking school year of this bullshit and I would be free, but only if I followed Female Hitler's rules.

I got to the front atrium, almost to the stairs when I was jolted to a full and complete stop by his voice alone.

"Hey, Sparrow," he said, his voice booming in the cavernous atrium, drawing a lot more attention than just mine.

I gritted my teeth as I turned to find him standing in the elevator, Rook and Grey behind him. Students scurried past the gaping metal doors as he thrust an arm out to hold them open.

They cast me worried and curious stares as they went.

"Join us," Corvus said. Not a question. Not a command. But somehow both at the same time.

"I'm good," I replied, sending him a beaming smile I hoped screamed *fuck off* as loudly as I was screaming it in my own head. "But you boys have fun in your little box of privilege. Wouldn't want to spoil your VIP sausage fest with a street taco."

Corvus lifted a brow as a dark grin pulled at his mouth. "It was good enough for you on Friday," he said, and my lips parted but no sound came out as I choked on another sarcastic reply.

How had he found out? Who the fuck told him?

Reflexively, my gaze swept the atrium, hunting for the telltale red glow of surveillance camera lights. But I found none.

This was so fucking stupid.

Corvus stepped out of the elevator and Rook held the door as his brother crossed the floor to me. All six-foot five of him radiating the kind of smugness that only came from an overabundance of power.

The VP, Mrs. June, stepped out of the office for a moment but turned around the instant Corvus locked his eyes on her. He hadn't even needed to say a word and she was *gone.* Closing the door behind her and averting her stare.

Maybe I'd underestimated these three just a smidge.

"Get in the elevator, Ava Jade."

I clutched my books tighter to my chest, wondering how hard I'd need to swing them at his head to knock him off balance long enough to get away. If it would be worth the fallout afterward.

"Or what?"

Fuck!

I scolded myself as the air left my lungs, forced out by the pressure of his shoulder as he easily tossed me over it, scattering my books on the floor. *I could've stopped him,* I told myself, face heating.

"Put me *the fuck* down," I snarled, pounding on his back, helplessly unable to reach the two blades strapped to both of my ankles in this position.

"Stop squirming," he growled, locking me in place with his biceps and holding my legs down with his other arm. "Grab her books," he said, and footsteps sounded on the parquet floor. I got an upside-down view of Grey collecting my books from the floor before he followed Corvus back to the elevator.

He all but threw me down as the elevator door shut, leaving me to wobble unsteadily for a second before I was able to find my footing, my face burning from all the blood rushing to my head.

Corvus jammed the emergency stop button, and

I dove for my blades.

"*Whoa,*" Rook said from behind me, and I spun in the enclosed space, blade drawn. "No need for that. We just want to talk."

The bell rang, signaling that I was now late for class. *Great.*

I pressed my back to the elevator wall, holding my blade out in case any of them dared come closer. "Don't think I won't use it," I warned. "I can have the three of you on your asses and be halfway to Canada by morning."

Rook pointed at me, giving Corvus a *told you so* look that made me think I was missing out on some private joke between them.

"I know you could use it," Corvus replied, sliding his gaze stealthily to Grey and the arm I'd sliced open just a few days ago. "But I don't think you will."

Cocky fucker.

"What do you want?"

He lifted his brows as though affronted by my question. "It's not what we want, Sparrow. It's what we can give you."

My face must have pinched up because his smugness intensified.

"Brianna Moore," Grey explained. "You wonder why you weren't hauled off by police Friday night? Why she hasn't retaliated?"

I had to admit, I was wondering that, but the idea that they had anything to do with it just infuriated me even more.

"It's because we paid her a visit before she returned home to daddy dearest," Rook whispered huskily, his eyes gleaming with malice. "Saw to it that she wouldn't speak a word about her little *accident* at the docks."

"And why would you do that?"

It dawned on me as soon as the question left my lips: to bring me under their control.

They were offering me a life vest, a ticket out of the mess I made Friday night, but in exchange for what? I had to admit having queen bitch off my back permanently would make finishing out this year and getting my sweet, sweet freedom so much easier, but at what cost?

Corvus shrugged. "Call it a gesture of goodwill."

"Everything has a price."

He licked his lips. "Well, now that you mention it, there is one thing we all agreed would be a fair trade for our services."

"And what's that?" I spat.

Corvus' icy blue eyes flicked to both of his brothers before settling back on me with his reply. "Your obedience. You fall in line. Do as you're told. We say jump, you ask how high."

Unable to help myself, I barked a laugh, so caught off guard that my hold loosened on the blade for just a second. Hot tears stung my eyes and I flicked one away before it could fall, sniffling at the absurdity of it all. "Oh my god," I said once I settled down, seeing that none of them looked even the least bit joking. "You're serious? You want me to be your little bitch girl, is that it? At your beck and call?"

Corvus' brows drew together, his stare turning deadly instead of just spiteful, but he didn't deny that was exactly what they were after. They hated that they didn't control me. Couldn't fucking stand it.

"That's not exactly it," Rook deadpanned, and I turned my blade on him, but that only perked him up. "But I'll accept your *full* surrender if you're offering. I've never tried Lennox pussy."

He licked his lips, stepping forward until the tip of my blade was at his throat, just above the edge of a tattoo peeking out from beneath his black t-shirt. He pushed harder, until the freshly honed edge drew a droplet of crimson from his flesh.

My breath rushed out through parted lips, and my traitorous cunt throbbed beneath my jeans as Rook devoured me with a single look.

"We'll keep the bitch at bay," Corvus explained, placing his hand against the flat side of my blade to push it away from Rook's throat before he could impale himself on it. "But in exchange, you will belong to us. You will do as you're told."

"I'm not a fucking possession. You can't *own* me," I scoffed.

"I can, and I will. Whether you agree to it or not. This way's easier, Sparrow. Don't fight it."

He reached out a hand like he might try to smooth out the sour pucker tightening my lips, but I knocked it aside with a scowl.

"Hard pass," I hissed. "I can handle my own shit. I don't need your help."

His smug look faltered and pure satisfaction raced through my veins, bringing a smile to my lips.

"Fine," he seethed through a false smile. "Have it your way."

Corvus jammed the emergency stop button again and the elevator completed its trip to the second floor. The doors *pinged* open as he stepped out of my path, but he stopped me before I could leave. His hand curled around my upper arm.

I let him have his moment of control, even though if I'd wanted to, I could've sliced his fingers clean off his palm.

"Don't forget your books," he said, and Grey passed them to Corvus, who held them out to me, releasing my arm. "Last chance, pretty bird. All you have to say is yes and you can be living on easy streets for the rest of senior year…"

I snatched my books, burying my blade between the pages as a student ducked her head and scooted past the open elevator door. "I'd rather die."

Corvus nodded, pursing his lips as he pressed another button inside the elevator and the doors began to close before Grey slipped out.

"Walk you to class?" he offered with an entertained gleam in his eyes as the elevator whisked the other two away.

I groaned, frustrated heat licking up my back as I stormed away.

The sound of his muted laughter followed me to class.

16

GREY

Josh *fucking* Richardson.

You have got to be kidding me.

I knew something was up the minute he slid into the seat next to hers in math today. He always sat in the bottom left corner of the classroom. Where he could play games on his phone in the shadow of his desk without being noticed. Josh Richardson was the kind of guy that escaped notice most days anyway.

Flying below the radar of popularity even though his family was among the wealthier ones at Briar Hall. He treated school like a holding cell. Like it was just a thing he had to sit through to make it to whatever came next. I didn't think I'd ever seen him hand in an assignment, and yet he was still here. Still just below the top of the class. At Briar Hall, your money didn't just buy you nice clothes and a straight-toothed smile. It could also buy you halfway decent grades. I wondered if his parents would continue paying for A's when he went to college.

I didn't give a flying fuck about Josh *fucking* Richardson. Until today.

He leaned into Ava Jade's side, whispering something I couldn't hear from four desks back.

I should've sat next to her.

Why hadn't I sat next to her?

Oh, right, because I didn't want to push my luck and get fucking stabbed again. She'd do it. I had no doubt. But I also wanted to give her a little space. A little time to think over Corvus' offer without me right there, hovering. Show her that not all of us were as hard as Corvus or as bloodthirsty as Rook.

Being the nice guy got you absofuckinglutely *nowhere*. Corv was right about that. It turned out he was right about a lot of things.

When Ava Jade laughed at something Josh said, my jaw clenched tight. No matter how hard I tried to relax it, to not let this *thing* inside of me swell too big, it didn't work.

Was she trying to goad me? Was that it? Was she doing this on purpose?

She couldn't be serious, right? This had to be a joke.

This guy?

I caught the way her arctic eyes flitted over him. In an analytical way. Like she was taking a measure of him. Of his ability to please her. Like she might eat him alive if he couldn't perform. She twisted her ankles together beneath the table, and I wondered if she was imagining his cock inside of her. Pressing her thighs together against the ache forming between her legs.

My pencil snapped in my hand and a few eyes turned to me before they fled back to their work. But not her. Ava Jade didn't turn. She didn't look.

I dropped the pencil remnants to my desk and ran my teeth over my lower lip, leaning forward slightly. Trying to hear.

Was he handsome?

I critically evaluated the fucker from head to toe. He was tall. My height maybe. Not as tall as Corvus. A decent face, young and bright, like the darkness of life hadn't tainted him yet. Hadn't seeped into the hollows beneath his eyes or carved premature lines in his forehead.

His hair was dark, a chestnut brown that shone in the classroom lights like it was covered in a thin film of oil. I grimaced. Did she prefer men with darker hair, then? Men who looked like they would take you for a late breakfast at IHop after fucking you gently and texting another side bitch in the bathroom when you weren't looking?

Fucking *Christ*. I was jealous.

I was *jealous* of Josh *fucking* Richardson.

I couldn't remember ever being jealous with Brianna.

Not for even a fucking second. I wasn't even sure if that *was* the emotion I was feeling. Couldn't remember ever experiencing it before. But I knew one thing for sure, the idea of jumping to my feet and smashing Josh's smug ass face into his desk sounded really good right now. Magical, even.

I wondered if she'd smile at him then? When his nose was broken and his face covered in blood.

No. She might like that.

...fuck

This is madness.

The bell couldn't ring fast enough. I gathered up my unfinished work, stuffing it into the crook of my arm as Ava Jade put her hand on Josh's arm.

"Thanks," she said, and he grinned at her like a starved kitten who'd just been given a bowl of milk.

Thanks? Thanks for what?

He nodded vigorously. "No probs," he said, the epitome of douche.

As she went to hand her work in to Mr. Williams, I rushed Josh, not even fully aware of where I was going until my shoulder collided hard with his, almost knocking him on his ass.

"Sorry," he muttered, gripping his shoulder as he steadied himself on a desk. "Didn't mean to get in your way."

"Watch it," I sneered at him and caught Ava Jade smirking at me from the head of the class, where Mr. Williams was casually trying to get a peek down her shirt while she was distracted.

"Yeah, man, my bad," Josh mumbled, stooping to lift his scattered blank pages and binder from the floor.

I tore my gaze away from her and stalked from the class, my body flooding with unspent adrenaline, making my muscles shudder and twitch.

Maybe Corvus was right. That girl was trouble with a capital T. Bolded. Underlined.

But I didn't want her gone. I wanted her all to my fucking self.

I wanted all her smiles. Her laughter. I wanted her thighs to squeeze at the image of *me* inside of her.

They would, I decided, picking up speed as I thundered down the corridor and jabbed the elevator button.

Yes, I thought, the rage that'd been making my stomach clench loosening by the second now. *I will have her.*

I relaxed, rolling my taut shoulders back and cracking my neck. Grinning to myself in the solitude of four metal walls.

No girl had ever refused me, and I'd never backed down from a challenge. I wasn't going to force Ava Jade into Corvus' agreement. I would have her eating out of my palm without the need for forced coercion. It would just take some time, and time I had, since she'd made it very clear she wasn't going anywhere.

My phone buzzed in my pocket and I dug it out, seeing a message there from Corv.

CORVUS

Cafeteria.

I snorted. Knowing now that she had her talons in him just as deeply as she had them in me. We rarely ate in the cafeteria, preferring to take the Rover out to the Crow's Nest or get takeout instead. Since Ava Jade showed her pretty face on the streets of Thorn Valley, we'd only missed a single school-provided meal. Not the coincidence I originally thought it was.

I wasn't sure how to feel about that. Or the fact that Rook clearly wanted to take a literal bite out of her, too.

I didn't feel the same *thing* toward my brothers, as I did Josh, but Corvus... He'd always been possessive. If he decided she belonged to him, there would be no room for negotiation. Unless...unless...

Oh. *Oh.* This would be good.

I found my brothers in our usual spot, set near the back of the cafeteria, in the only spot that afforded us an unobstructed view of the entire room. I nodded to them before going for the food. I snatched a tray from between two queuing students and skipped ahead of the line to grab what I wanted, not really paying attention to the *what* as much as making sure I had enough to fill the unfillable void that was my stomach.

Rook tipped the contents of a flask into his glass of OJ, securing himself a scowl from Mrs. June, who seemed to be on cafeteria duty for the day. She didn't say anything, though, and she wouldn't. He'd been working her since our first day at BH. If Diesel St. Crow wasn't enough for the majority of the teachers and staff to turn a blind eye to us, Rook had the VP herself by her married little cunt.

A word from him could ruin her career and her marriage now. He had tapes of them. Several. They liked to fuck in the mornings in the rarely used chapel. He had one of Jesus' eyes carved out and replaced with a micro camera. It had to be some sort of blasphemy, but if there was a hell, we were all headed there anyway.

I fell into my seat opposite Corv and dug into my food, considering how best to broach the topic.

Rook rubbed a coin between his thumb and index finger, rolling it through his knuckles and flicking it to spin atop the round table. He was oddly pensive as he sipped his boozy afternoon drink.

I followed his line of sight to where she sat with Rebecca Hart. Honestly, she was about the only other girl at this school who wasn't a vapid, self-absorbed debutante. I'd be glad they were friends, if it weren't for the fact that Rebecca Hart would *definitely* be smart enough to warn Ava Jade away from us instead of goading her toward us, like the majority of the others bitches here would.

Ava Jade *inhaled* her lunch. Putting Becca's small bowl of low-sodium soup to shame with a tower of finger sandwiches and a bowl of fruit that I wonder if she knew was meant to be scooped from, not taken in its entirety to her table.

Was she left alone as a child?

Had she gone hungry?

Was she forced to fend for herself?

My stomach audibly rumbled, prodding me to pick up the next in a row of sandwiches on my own plate and take a large bite.

There was a time when a sandwich the size of the one in my hand right now would have looked like a feast to my 8-year-old eyes. When all there was were crumbs to be found beneath kitchen cabinets and mom had been gone for two weeks.

She came back sometimes. But the guilt of seeing me, rail-thin, gaunt, and starving always drove her away again.

I didn't only starve for food. I starved for her. For human connection. To not be left alone in the house out in the country with only my dead stepfather's library for company.

If a teacher from my school hadn't come by the house to check up on me after the phone was disconnected, I wouldn't be sitting here. I was almost gone. At the point of organ failure.

Literally starved to death.

My stomach turned now, remembering that pain. The *ache*. The eventual nothingness that followed.

Stop it.

I gave my head a shake, coming back to the present. Deciding there was no better way to do this than to just give it a shot. I set down the sub sandwich dripping tomato juice down my wrist and swallowed the tasteless lump in my throat before speaking.

"I have a proposition."

Rook's glass halted an inch from his lips. He raised a brow, setting the glass back down.

Corvus cocked his head at me, trying to read the words I hadn't yet spoken in my stare.

"A game," I explained. "Winner takes all.

Winner takes Ava Jade."

Rook perked up, leaning forward over the table with a gleam in his eyes. I had his attention.

"You want her," I said, telling Corvus what he wouldn't admit. "So does Rook."

I sat back, sighing. "So do I."

Corvus crossed his arms over his chest, his jaw working behind the wall of his lips. "What are you suggesting?"

"You were right," I admitted. "She was never going to go for our deal."

"Thought we weren't going to give her a choice?"

Corvus asked, eyeing Rook before turning his attention back to me.

"She'll fight us tooth and nail," I said, shaking my head. We didn't know her. Not really. But that much I thought we could all agree on.

No one denied it, so I went on. "What if we didn't use...the usual tactics? What if we tried to reel her in instead? The only way she's going to be controlled—unless you want to get rid of her..."

I let that thought hang in the air, banking on them not wanting to vote for that option. Their eyes widened before they settled back into mute scowls, trying to play it off like they didn't give a shit. Liars.

"...is if it's on her terms. Like, if she were with one of us. We make it a contest, first one to fuck her wins. First one to fuck her gets to keep her."

Rook liked this idea, I could tell by the way he twisted his lip ring with his teeth, his breathing heavy.

Corvus' face pinched. He stared at me like that, unmoving, for so long I almost began to squirm in my seat. But letting on that he was getting to me would only boost his already massive ego.

"You want to *date* the new girl?" he hissed, studying my face for a reaction.

My stomach twisted, but I kept my cool.

Did I?

Was that what I was suggesting here?

Shit.

"Never mind," I muttered, snatching up my water bottle for a long pull. This was a stupid fucking idea. What was I even hoping to accomplish? All I'd done was show my cards. Admitted I was a pussy. Right to their faces. Proved to them how weak they already thought I was.

Probably made Corvus even more certain that he needed to make her disappear. Proved to him that she was the threat he thought she was from the start. A thing that could come between us. Distract us. Infiltrate our ranks and destroy us from the inside out.

But I'd win, the thought whispered through my head. *And they know it.*

It was at that moment Josh Richardson entered the cafeteria, carving a path through the tables toward the one Ava Jade and Becca shared across the room.

"Get your head straight," Corvus uttered, stealing a thin chicken strip from my plate and tossing it into his mouth. I lifted a brow at him, not over what he said, but over the fact that he had just eaten a fucking strip of breaded, deep-fried chicken.

"What?" he grunted, but dropped it when Josh stopped at Ava Jade and Becca's table.

Josh flashed Ava Jade a smile, leaning down onto his elbow to put himself closer to her eye-level as they chatted. Becca glanced between them, her interest clearly piqued by the whole encounter. Ava Jade hadn't told her friend about her little conversation with Josh

Richardson in math class today. Was that because she didn't think it was important?

Because it didn't matter?

"The fuck is Richardson doing?" Corvus demanded, swiping the back of his hand over his grease-stained lips.

I wondered if it looked the same to my brothers as it did to me: like a fucking golden retriever propositioning a lioness.

Fucking *cringe*.

"He was all over her in math today," I told my brother. "I think they exchanged numbers."

Corv couldn't whip his head to me fast enough, his accusing stare fixed on me. "And you let that happen?"

My mouth popped open. "Should I not have?"

"We gave her an out this morning," he said. "Made a deal. She is *ours*."

"She didn't agree," Rook corrected him. "In fact, I'm pretty sure she said she'd rather die."

"And we're just going to let her get away with refusing us?" Corvus demanded, his slanted eyes cutting between Rook and me. "Have you gone soft there, Rookie?"

Rook frowned, back to looking like his usual bored self. Exhausted with Corvus' antics.

He wouldn't rise to the bait. He rarely did.

When I made no reply, Corvus fell back in his chair and pressed his lips into a tight line, his disappointment clear as he let his eyes track back to Ava Jade. She was still locked in conversation with the senior prick, smiling in a sultry way that told me she knew exactly what she was doing to him.

When Josh rose to say his goodbye's, he remained slightly hunched, angling his body away from Ava Jade. Hiding the chub in his pants.

Becca immediately descended upon Ava Jade, leaning far over the table with wide, glimmering eyes, demanding details.

Corvus' chair screeched against the linoleum floor as he shoved back and stood, following Josh Richardson from the cafeteria, without another word.

17

AVA JADE

I let the murdery lyrics of Primal Ethos' *Fuckface* drive me onward, using the unfiltered rage searing through my veins as fuel for the cruel pace I was forcing my body to endure. My sneakers pounded the blacktop and the chill of the evening licked at the warm sweat on my arms and chest. Stoking the fire inside.

Downtown Thorn Valley wasn't much to look at. Especially not at ten on a Monday night. All the shops running along either side of the historic city center were shuttered for the night. Their wide windows dark, *come back tomorrow* signs hanging in doorways. The only lights still on that I could see were from a small cafe at the end of the block, and the low lights from the Valley-Mart I'd already passed four blocks before.

The hill from town to Briar Hall was the only chunk of this route not alive with at least some public activity, and I was delaying the return trip.

Fucking asshole.

Whoever sent that text was ruining my only escape. I'd been running down the hill and through town since Saturday. Only using a short arm of the trail behind Briar Hall in emergencies of frustration to blow off some steam between classes before my lid could pop.

It wasn't that I was afraid, at least, not really. It just creeped me out.

Whoever was sending these messages was clearly watching me. They knew I liked to go for runs. They were at the docks during the party Friday night. For all I knew they'd *been* watching me all this time, though something told me that wasn't the case. That coming here somehow triggered this. This person was from Thorn Valley, but had seen me in Lennox years before. I was on their turf now.

Running alone in the dark through the trees, where no one except maybe the Crows might hear me scream just didn't have the appeal it did a few days ago. It irked me that someone could be out there, where I couldn't see them, fucking jerking off behind a tree or some shit.

Gross.

I vacillated between wanting to avoid it at all costs and going on a fucking hunting trip to find the bastard and carve his eyeballs out. I might still go on that hunting trip,

but maybe best to let everything else die down first.

I held no illusions that my refusal of Corvus' idiotic offer meant that my 'protection' from Brianna Moore and her wealthy father had been terminated. It was only a matter of time now before she launched her attack.

Corvus.

Fucking Corvus.

And the rest of them.

Smug bastards. As if they thought I would actually agree to...*to be their plaything.* To kneel like a peasant at their gilded feet and open wide for them to use my mouth like a fucking cum dumpster. I'm sure they would love that. They were probably getting off on just the *idea* of breaking me. Corvus for sure.

The worst part was that for the briefest second, I actually considered it.

My little *problem* with Brianna would evaporate. No legal problems. No cops. No retaliation. No more issues with teachers. No more detentions. Not while I was under their protection. Fuck, I'd even get laid.

I bet they were good, too. I bet...

Don't go there, Ava Jade. You are not for sale.

Besides, Josh would do.

He was tall, stalky. Big feet. Long thumbs. All the telltale signs that he should be at least somewhat well-endowed downstairs. Whether he knew how to use it or not was a mystery, but one I'd solve soon enough. He didn't strike me as the type of guy who dated, which suited me just fine. I wanted a fuck buddy.

Like Kit.

Speaking of, I really should message him back. And Dom, too. And okay, *fine,* Aunt Humphrey as well.

I slowed, hunching over with my palms braced on my knees to catch my breath for a minute, my throat burning. Sweat dripped down my temples and between my breasts. I could taste the salt of it on my lips.

I'd been out here too long. I needed to get back. Get some water. Some food. Sleep might also be a good idea. Hadn't had much of that in the last few days.

A long shadow stretched down the sidewalk from up ahead, bouncing lightly as the person approached. I moved to the side, resting my back against the shop next to the illuminated cafe so the late-night walker could pass.

But he stopped, instead. "Ava Jade Mason?" he asked, and a sliver of adrenaline spiked into my bloodstream, making me vividly aware of the stranger's nearness. Of his height and build. Of my hand's proximity to the blades at my ankles.

"Who's asking?" I panted, tipping my head up to get a look at his face while remaining hunched, overacting my tiredness to emphasize that I was weak. No threat to him. So that he wouldn't be expecting it when I proved to be the opposite. Keeping my hands on my knees because that's where they were closest to my blades.

The man wore a dark windbreaker over black slacks. His shoes were polished leather, scuffed lightly on the sides. His hair was cropped short. His face square, clean-shaven, light eyes searching.

He had a certain look to him that made warning bells ring loudly in my ears, but I couldn't place what it was about his demeanor that was throwing me off.

Was this my stalker?

No.

This guy didn't look like a stalker psycho, he looked...

The man reached into his windbreaker and I drew my blade, ready to disarm him, but he came out with something I hadn't been expecting instead, rushing back two steps with wide eyes as he took in my weapon. My fighting stance.

Oops.

He held his other hand up. The one not holding the police badge.

Slowly, I lowered my blade and tucked it back into the sheath at my ankle, covering it over with the edge of my sweats. "Sorry," I muttered, hands raised slightly to show that I was no danger to him while trying to assess whether or not he was carrying.

The officer narrowed his gaze on me before tucking the badge back into his windbreaker and clearing his throat. "Name's Vick," he said, still studying me warily.

"Was I running too fast or something," I sniped, panting lightly from the run and the burst of adrenaline still thrumming through my swollen muscles, making me feel lead-limbed and tired. I didn't want to deal with this right now. Whatever *this* was.

Officer Vick let out a breathy laugh at my smart-ass response. "Nah. Nothing like that. Could we talk? In private?"

He gestured to an alleyway carving a dark path down the side of the cafe and scanned the street up and down. What was he looking for?

"*Uh,*" I hesitated, feeling a creep of unease set in like phantom fingers tripping up my spine. "What for?"

If the cops in Thorn Valley were anything like the ones in Lennox, going down that alleyway with him could be just as dangerous as going down it with any random dude off the streets. Maybe more so.

"Just a talk."

The officer lifted his jacket, doing a slow spin, showing me that he was unarmed.

"Can I see that badge again?"

The man balked, but when I didn't move a muscle, he wrinkled his nose and retrieved the badge, holding it out to me again.

Victor Stoll. Thorn Valley PD.

Okay, looks legit. That doesn't mean he isn't here on an errand from Mr. Moore, though. A hired gun sent to intimidate the girl who dared raise a hand to his daughter.

I gave him another once over and decided I could take him if I had to. I didn't need to add a cop to my list of enemies in Thorn Valley unless I had no other choice.

"All right," I agreed, and followed him into the alley, going no further than just into its shadowed mouth.

When he saw that I would go no more he stopped, sighed, and leaned casually against the brick wall, kicking a bit of trash out of his way. He folded his arms and fixed me with an investigative stare.

I should have had him pegged as a cop from the moment I saw him. It was written all over him. The shoes. The haircut. His posture. The fucking navy windbreaker. Standard issue.

Christ, I needed to get out of my own goddamned head and pay closer attention.

"I hear you've made some *friends* at Briar Hall," he said, the words a verbal nudge. A prompt he wanted me to finish.

I didn't.

His jaw ticked. "All right. No beating around the bush." He lifted himself to his full height, all traces of *good cop* gone. This was business now. "It's been brought to my attention that you've drawn the interest of a particular three students. You might know them as the Crows: Corvus James, Rook Clayton, and Grey Winters."

This was *not* where I thought this was headed.

"I'll take your silence as a yes," he continued, not even bothering to give me more than a few seconds to formulate a response. "Now, I've done some digging. I know that your father, a Mr. John Mason, was recently killed in a gang-related incident."

My skin prickled with heat, fists curling.

"That's not how the cops in Lennox see it," I bit out.

He pursed his lips. "No. But you seem like a smart girl. I'm sure you know that these things aren't always dealt with as they should be."

He and I could agree there, but he wasn't painting himself in the best light. What made him any better than those useless badge-toting rednecks in Lennox?

"I want your help," he said, surprising me for the second time. "The Saints are squeaky clean. My department can't seem to make anything stick to those slippery bastards. And my boss...let's just say his allegiance is and always has been *questionable* at best."

That was a serious accusation. One he was making to an eighteen-year-old girl in a dark alleyway at nearly 11pm.

He wants my trust, I realized. He was trying to put himself on my level. Make it seem like we were in on some private secret.

I don't trust it.

"Why don't you just ask for a cut and turn the other cheek like all the other asshole cops do?"

A knot formed between his bushy brows.

"It's...personal," he offered, giving no more than that.

I nodded silently, imagining a million possible scenarios without his needing to utter a single word.

"Okay. So what do you want?"

"I think you'd like to see those boys and their entire empire fall just as much as I would."

The screams of the man in the shed returned to me in sharp clarity.

Corvus' rough fingers around my wrists.

Rook's malice.

Grey's attentive stare.

"I want your help," he repeated again. "I need an informant. One Diesel and his psycho sons won't see coming."

"I don't—"

"Wait," he interrupted, rushing forward a step like he might try to cover my mouth. Stuff my refusal back in. "Don't answer now. Think about it. If you've seen anything—if you *see* anything—just..."

He dug into the pocket of his slacks and opened his wallet, digging out a crinkled white business card. He thrust it out to me. "Just call me. The Crows don't mess around, Miss Mason. I can help you. We can help each other."

Victor Stoll left me standing there in the alley with his card in my hand as the only evidence that this encounter happened at all. Heels clacked on the sidewalk not far away, and I slipped the crumpled paper into my bra as a woman appeared in the entrance to the alley. A black apron covering her long-sleeve gray dress. A trash bag held at arm's length.

"Uh, you can't be back there, hon," she said, pointing up. "Read the sign."

18

CORVUS

"What do you think he wants?" Grey asked as we made our way into Sanctum.

"He has a job for us," I muttered, holding the heavy door open for my brothers, allowing classic rock music to spill out onto the midnight street. I didn't know for certain, but that was usually the reason Diesel asked to meet us here. He had something for us that he didn't want to take to the table. Something unofficial. Usually.

The bar at the edge of town was one owned by the Saints. Complete with an illegal boxing ring in the basement and a fully functional escort service running out of the two upper levels. Top tier. Two-dollar hookers weren't welcome in our city. Only the finest for Thorn Valley's privileged upper-class.

The boxing ring had been Rook's idea.

The escort service had been mine.

And with Grey helping run the books, the money was cleaner than it'd ever been.

Sanctum brought in a good chunk of the gang's income and helped tide us over when things got tight. Like they were right now.

Sasha winked at me from the bar as we entered, leaning over the ledge to show her new tits off to a drunk guy who looked like he was about halfway into a midlife crisis. He'd already removed his wedding band, the white slice of untanned flesh on his ring finger probably brighter than any silver or gold.

She could be his for the night if he could afford the ride.

"My sons," Diesel called to us from the back of the bar where he was setting up a shot at one of the pool tables. Playing himself and winning.

"Want some real competition, old man?" I asked him as we approached, shrugging off my jacket to toss it over a chair back. This late on a Monday night, there was little happening at Sanctum, and the echo of Diesel's 8-ball sinking shot rang through the mostly empty hall.

Diesel snubbed out his cigar and removed the ashtray from the table side, his silver rings glinting in the vintage table light above. "Always. Here, rack it up, and then we'll talk, yeah?"

He tossed me the rack, and I caught it, emptying the ball return to set up the game while Rook signaled Sasha for a drink, and Grey slumped into the nearest booth, frowning at his phone. Probably still dealing with an onslaught of messages from his former fuckbuddy. He still hadn't given Bri the green light to hit back at Ava Jade, even though I'd told him to the moment she refused us. He thought I didn't know, but it was obvious. Bri would've had Ava Jade carved like a Thanksgiving turkey by now if she thought she could get away with it. Or, she'd have at least tried to.

I'd let him think he was in control, at least for now, until the right moment.

Diesel polished off his beer and sighed. Not a great sign. He rarely drank. That, coupled with the deep lines in his forehead and the darkness beneath his eyes told me he was more stressed than he was letting on.

The more vocal members of the Saints were calling for blood after what happened with Randy. They wanted retaliation, and he promised it would come, but only once we had solid intel. The A carved in Randy's chest could just as easily have been an A for Arty. A member of the Kings who Diesel gunned down last year for stepping where he shouldn't. Or it could've been a member who acted alone.

There was that one time a year back when they tried to retake the docks. We lit them up like Christmas morning. Bells and all. Two Aces fell that day. It was only because their leader wasn't aware of the attack that the Aces still existed at all.

Or the whole thing could've been a set-up.

Dies wouldn't act until he knew what he was dealing with, no matter how vocal they got. But it was him who needed to deal with them all in the meantime.

"All right, son," Diesel said, giving a tight jerk of his head for me to have a seat before we started our game. "Let's talk."

I nodded and followed Dies to Grey's booth, nudging my brother to move further in so I could sit across from our leader. Grey obliged and Diesel slid in opposite me.

Rook joined a second later, whiskey in hand. Diesel clapped him on the back, giving his shoulder a tight squeeze. "You look good," he told Rook. "Up for a fight in a couple weeks? Some upcoming MMA aspirant wants to take a stab."

A sly grin played over Rook's lips.

"Has he ever done an underground cage match before?" I asked, needing more details before Rook could agree to it.

Diesel pursed his lips. He hadn't.

I shook my head. "Rook will kill him, Dies. Bad for business."

"I'll make sure he knows what he's signing up for," Diesel agreed. "We could use the cash."

That was the end of that then. Diesel had already decided. And Rook looked like a pig in shit. Swirling the golden liquid in his glass with a shiver of delight.

"Anyway, that's not what this is about."

"What's up Dies?" Grey asked, slipping away his phone to give our old man his full attention.

"I'm going to need you boys over the next couple of weeks. I know you have your own shit going on, but that's all going to have to be put on hold. I'll need your focus. All of it."

My skin bristled and without warning, a mental image of Ava Jade surfaced in my head. Put her on hold? I wasn't sure if I could do that. But for Diesel, if he needed it, I'd try.

"What do you need?"

"I've set up a gun deal with the Reapers MC. They have a shipment for us, coming in next week. We need some more firepower and I have a buyer for half the order down south."

Damn. I thought it was the last time *last time* we made a sale to the

Mexican cartel. I didn't like being involved with them. But neither did Diesel. He wouldn't be setting this up unless we really needed it.

"I need you boys to case the trade point and find out where they got the guns. The Reapers don't usually run guns. Drugs are their MO. I don't want fucking blowback after the deal is made. Make sure their source is legit and report back to me."

"You got it."

This was something I could do. Something I was good at. Planning. Recon.

The things Diesel used to do himself before I came along. His need for control *nearly* rivaled my own. Trust no one but family, that was his adage. And I had no doubt it was the only reason he was still alive at almost fifty.

"I don't want you missing too much school," he added before I could start asking more questions to flesh out the situation. My jaw clenched.

We all knew how Diesel felt about our education. It was a stipulation for us to join the ranks of the Saints. He didn't give two fucks about college but wanted us to do what he didn't in his teens and finish high school. Graduate. The whole idiotic shebang. He made a very generous contribution to Briar Hall to get us in. So generous in fact that they even took his suggestion of a motto change and ditching the antiquated uniforms.

They didn't know they were letting a pack of wolves in to have their way with the sheep. Or maybe they did but didn't care. The antiquated academy was on the verge of going under. It *ran* on hush money and bribes from wealthy parents now.

"We'll swap out," I offered. "Two of us on the job, one in class to pick up assignments. Good?"

"Good."

He leaned back, blowing out a breath. There was more.

We waited.

"That's not all," he admitted. "I've set a meet with the Aces."

"What?" I growled, fists clenching beneath the table. "When?"

"Two weeks. Right after the gun deal."

"Is that smart?" Rook asked and his trepidation lent weight to the question. If he of all people questioned the sanity of the decision, then I felt fucking justified in my rebuke.

Diesel's jaw set and he lifted his chin. The minuscule movement undetectable to most spelled the words *no fucking reproach allowed* clear as day to me. He'd already decided this. It was too late to change his mind.

"I want you three there. I can't trust the others to keep level heads. Randy was...he meant a lot to them. Like a surrogate son to some."

He didn't have to elaborate. Though we did larger jobs with the other members from time to time, we were a unit unto ourselves. Joined and yet somehow also separate from the rest. We didn't form attachments. Not beyond this.

Not beyond family.

"We need to know if they were involved... If that mark carved in Randy's chest was theirs, then they'll own it. Why else make it so obvious? And if it was them, we deserve to know why. If the bastard who did it acted alone or on behalf of Lenny Ace. We'll have to retaliate. I need to keep my men under control. This needs handling."

"Bloodshed?" Rook asked, his brows lowering, but not enough to shadow the gleam in his dark eyes. "Or a trade?"

"If the person acted alone, a trade. The killer's life for Randy's. If Lenny doesn't agree to that then, yes. There will be blood."

"And if it was them? If Lenny sanctioned the kill?" I asked.

His dark look said it all. If it was sanctioned by their leader then we wouldn't be the ones to initiate the bloodshed. They already had.

"Where is the meet point?"

I wanted to case that out, too. Make sure there was an escape route. No way for them to come at us with uneven numbers without us knowing well in advance.

Diesel signaled Sasha for another beer, also signaling that this conversation was coming to an end. "Haven't decided yet. We'll give it to them same day. Like usual."

No time for them to set anything up, but plenty of time for us. It would be up to them if they wanted to take the risk and honor the meet. If they didn't, it would mean they had something to hide and we'd find them and kill them anyway.

If it wasn't them, all they had to do was say so and Dies would walk away. He would find out the truth eventually, he always did. And if they were smart, they'd know that lying to Diesel St. Crow bought you nothing but a bullet with your name on it.

"Let me do it," I offered. "I'll find a good meet point. Somewhere in no man's land. I'll scope it. Rig it. Make sure there's an easy escape if needed."

"You've got enough to do over the next couple of weeks, son. I can handle it."

I nodded, a muscle ticking in my temple, making my eye twitch. I'd rather do it myself, but Dies was the one person I trusted implicitly. He'd get it done.

"Everyone good with this?" he asked as Sasha dropped him off a fresh beer and slid Rook a fresh whiskey.

"Can I get anything for anyone else?" she asked, and Grey shook his head. She didn't wait to hear from me before leaving with a little extra pop in her hips. She'd been trying to get Diesel between the sheets since she started here. She wouldn't have any luck.

"Alright." Diesel clapped his hands together, effectively ending the conversation. His cunning stare slid to the pool table and returned to me with a renewed spark of life. "Ready to get your ass kicked, son?"

The king of pool at Sanctum, Diesel hadn't ever been beaten. Not by anyone. But maybe tonight would finally be the night that the apprentice overtook the master.

I scoffed, flipping my internal switch. There were enough hours between now and dawn that I'd have plenty of time to start the recon Diesel asked for after we left.

Business later.

For now, I had a Saint to dethrone.

19

AVA JADE

asty.

I wiped drool from the corner of my mouth with a frown, my nose wrinkling at a cloying smell tainting the air of my bedroom. *Ugh.* What was that? I lifted an arm to make sure the gross limey odor wasn't coming from me.

"*Ew,*" I mumbled, rolling out of bed to wash the drool off my hand and rinse out my mouth. I never drooled. Couldn't sleep deep enough for that. At least, not usually. I swished the cool water from the tap in my mouth and spat, opting to just take a shower in case I did actually smell like a fucking stale ass gin mojito.

At least the deep sleep brought with it some clarity and as the scalding water prodded my dead muscles back to life, a plan formed.

To be fair, it started forming the minute the fucking Crows decided to try to cut me a very one-sided deal. The little visit from Officer Vick just cemented it.

The way they saw it, I had two options.

Option one: take the deal and become their little plaything. Kneel.

Option two: be forced to take the deal by whatever devious bullshittery they came up with to try to force me into it.

Officer Vick had provided me an option number three, but honestly? I didn't fucking like cops. Sixty percent were corrupt. At least thirty percent were power-tripping dickwads. The last ten percent were just fucking useless. Or stupid.

Biased? Maybe. But you haven't been a starving kid living in a trailer with a crackhead mother and a father with a gambling addiction. Or maybe you have. And then you know.

I was going for option number four. It was time to take these Crows down a peg. If I'd been smart, I'd have taken photos of the stolen car that night with the guy in the shed. I'd have filmed Rook dragging him to the shed. Captured his screams on camera.

Two could play the blackmail game. I'd been focusing my attention on the wrong threat. Bri was a blimp on the greater scale. The Crows were the real enemy. They were the ones who deserved my attention. I'd find out every little thing I could about them. Their dirty secrets. Their plans. And then I would use that knowledge to buy my freedom.

It would take time, and I'd have to do it right, but it could be done. I just had to make sure I didn't break along the way.

"You trying a new perfume?" Becca asked as I made my way into the living room, making a spectacle of plugging her nose. "Babe, that is so *not* your scent."

My shoulders slumped. "You smell it too?" I asked, relieved. I was starting to think I was going crazy when it didn't go away after the shower. It was somehow soaked into my blankets. In my pillows. Whatever I ate yesterday, I was never eating it again. *Barf.*

She poured herself a coffee from the elaborate chrome machine in the kitchen and pointed to a second cup. "Want one?"

I moaned, chasing the aroma of fresh coffee to the kitchen. "Careful," I warned. "I could get used to this."

She snorted, but set another cup under the weird coffee drippy thing and started frothing some milk. "Here," she said, nudging the already made cup with her elbow. "Take that one."

I took a sip, and it didn't even matter that it nearly scalded my tongue. It was fucking *divine*. Like, call me religious because I might have just been converted to a devoted member of the church of Becca Hart Lattes.

"*God.*" I groaned, clutching the mug under my nose to inhale. "I'm going to steal you away from whoever you go see in the mornings and make you my coffee bitch."

Becca barked a laugh but didn't reply, instead eyeing my outfit. The usual knock-off jeans, softened by too many owners, paired with a long sleeve black t-shirt today. "No run this morning?" she asked as she finished pouring off the frothed milk into the espresso basted cup.

I shook my head. "Nah, I had to wash that stink off. Two showers in one morning goes against years of two-minute shower conditioning. Just can't do it."

"Speaking of," Becca said, leaning against the counter to sip her latte. "Maybe close the oven after you're done baking. When I got home last night it was hot as balls in here."

I winced. I'd always been taught to leave it open, especially when it was chilly outside. It was a waste of heat to keep it closed. But I supposed that wasn't a worry here, where the air temp was controlled to within an inch of its life by the crazy touchscreen panel by the fireplace. I probably only managed to make the AC work harder. I snorted. "Sorry. Habits."

She smirked, getting that look she sometimes got that told me she didn't really understand but was trying to.

"No worries. You saved me a cookie, so I guess I'll let you off this once."

"So kind."

Becca swirled the coffee in her mug. She looked amazing in whatever the thing was she was wearing. A one-piece black romper with a long gold necklace and cage heels. But then, she always looked like a supermodel next to me. It was a wonder the Crows didn't take an interest in her instead. She wasn't like the other girls here, either.

Then again, maybe they had. What did I know?

"So," Becca started, a mischievous gleam in her brown eyes. "Has Josh texted you yet?"

I shook my head. "Nope."

She bit her lower lip. That wasn't what she wanted to ask. I could tell she was holding something else back.

"What?" I hedged. "Just spit it out. Is the guy a creep or something?"

Becca pursed her lips. "No, it's not Josh. It's just...people are saying they saw you in the elevator yesterday. With the Crows."

The flash of betrayal in her eyes cut me to the quick. "Oh."

"Oh?" she pressed.

"Look, I didn't say anything because I didn't want you to freak out."

Her brows lowered, worry creasing the spin between them.

"See?" I said. "You're already freaking out."

She smoothed out her expression and gingerly sipped her latte. "Well, what did they want? Someone said they saw Corvus *literally* fireman carry you into the elevator."

I gritted my teeth.

Becca set her mug down with a clatter and crossed her arms over her chest. "They're dangerous, babe."

"They wanted me," I admitted before she could say anything else. "They said they'd make what I did to Bri Friday night go away if I agreed to fucking bow down to their reign, be a good little girl and keep my pretty mouth shut unless they asked me to open it."

Becca's face screwed up into a scowl. "And you didn't take the deal, did you?"

"You think I should've?"

"*Hell yes*, you should've. I'd take *sit down and shut up* over possible jail time any day of the week and twice on Sundays. Never mind that your refusal means that you get to keep them as your enemies, too."

Heat licked up my neck, making my body shudder. "I'm not like that. I can't just..."

"Fuck. You're right." Becca huffed, pinching the bridge of her nose. "You're right. It's not my call to make. I just don't want to see you run out of here or worse, you know?"

I didn't know, but I was trying really hard to accept the fact that someone, a friend, did actually want me here. A smile beat back the frustrated heat still trying to find a toehold in my veins.

"I know. Don't worry, Becks. I'll handle it."

I always handle it.

"Taurus," she said suddenly, her eyes widening before a sour look took hold. "No, wait, that's not it, either."

"My birthday's in—"

"No," she interrupted, her mug clattering back down onto the counter as she reached over and slapped a palm over my lips before I could finish. "Don't tell me. I got this."

I laughed against her hand, and she pulled back, chewing her bottom lip as she considered me.

"Good luck with that," I muttered, finishing off my coffee. "While you stew over it, can I have another latte?"

I WENT INTO HOMEROOM EXPECTING TO HAVE TO DEAL WITH THE CROWS, knowing it was likely they would try to corner me after class was through again, but...that didn't happen.

As I walked in, a full two minutes before the second bell, I found only a lone Crow there waiting for me. Grey met my gaze as I entered the room, tipping his head in greeting.

"Morning, AJ," he whispered as I slid into my seat and I turned to give him a warning scowl before settling in for the day's lecture. He said nothing else to me through the entirety of first period.

And then the following day, it was only Rook. He didn't speak a word to me, though I could feel his hard gaze on the back of my neck. Could hear the *chink* of metal as he spun his lip ring with his teeth.

Thursday it was only Corvus, and I realized they were all switching out through the week. One in class, to collect assignments, maybe to keep an eye on me, and the other two off doing god knew what.

That was what I needed to figure out. I got the sense something big was going down. They would be here to terrorize me every chance they got if there wasn't something monumentally more pressing that needed to be handled.

I had to up my game.

Corvus all but ignored me Thursday. He seemed so distracted. His face a pinched mask of focus.

As if that weren't strange enough, I was still waiting for Bri to hit back. She hadn't made a single move even though I'd turned down the Crows.

And I hadn't received a single text from the unknown number in days. I wasn't foolish enough to think it was a coincidence that I stopped getting the creepy messages at the same time as the Crows being too busy to continue trying to make my life hell.

It would be too much a coincidence, right?

It had to be one of them.

By Friday, if I were being honest with myself, I was fucking bored as shit. Frustrated that I still didn't have anything worth mentioning on the Crows. I'd been returning to the Crow's Nest at night for days. Watching like a shadow from the darkness of the trees. But there was nothing happening.

No one there.

At least not between the hours of ten and two a.m.

My other endeavors were coming up empty, too. Usually, a bit of cash was all it took to get information, but not with these guys. I'd gotten nowhere trying to get their records from before their adoption to Diesel St. Crow.

All I knew was that Grey and Rook had been together in Barrett's Home for Boys when Diesel snatched them up as a pair.

I knew that Corvus James was adopted three years prior to that, at the age of nine.

But I had a few little gems of info now that I didn't before.

For instance, I now knew that Corvus was adopted from fucking *Lennox.*

That's right. *My* hometown.

I wasn't the only one from the wrong side of the tracks.

I also knew that Grey was short for Greyson. Greyson Winters.

And that Rook was a nickname. His real name was Sawyer. Sawyer Clayton.

I wondered why none of them took Diesel's surname when they were legally adopted. If that was their choice or Diesel's?

It wasn't enough though, none of it was really useful. None of it told me *who* they really were. What they'd done. What they'd been through. What made them tick.

I needed more. I needed something that I could use. Preferably before they were finished dealing with whatever it was they were dealing with and had the free time to harass me again.

After so many nights spent casing the Crow's Nest from a safe distance, I'd found a path. I had it all mapped out in my head. Exactly which direction I would need to approach from, where I would need to step, and pause, to be able to get inside without the camera seeing me. If I could get my hands on a decent bug, I could plant it. I doubted they were very careful with what they said while at home.

After all, no one was foolish enough to fuck with them in Thorn Valley.

I was so absorbed with my own thoughts, trying to figure out where would be my best bet to find what I was looking for in this foreign town *without* the Crows finding out, that I almost didn't see him.

"Josh?"

His back stiffened, hand stilling on the door handle to the office.

I only had about a minute before my last class for the day started. "Hey," I added when he didn't turn around straight away. I carved through the other students in the atrium rushing to class. "You haven't been in class."

He hadn't answered either of my texts this week, either, but I didn't really care about that.

My thirsty punani did, but she could deal.

"Where have you—"

He spun around and whatever I'd been about to say ghosted my lips.

The way he was looking at me, and also not looking at me, spoke volumes. So did the angry purple bruise swelling his left eye almost completely shut.

I could see the anger in the tension around his still usable eye. The embarrassment in the pink of his cheeks. The discomfort in the shifty way his gaze moved over the atrium. And I knew.

"What did they say to you?" I demanded, all desire to fuck this cowardly jackass gone in the blink of an eye.

Josh shook his head, his jaw tightening. "Look, I'm just here to grab my shit. I'm transferring to LA."

"*Josh*," I hissed, leveling the full weight of my stare on him. "What. Did. They. Say?"

He recoiled from me slightly, surprise flitting over his eyes as he took me in in this new light.

The bell rang, signaling that I was now late, but I didn't give a fuck. My muscles twitched, constricted beneath tight skin. So tight it made me itch. Made me sick.

"Fucking spit it out."

"It was Corvus, all right," he said, lowering his voice even though we were the only students still lingering in the atrium. "He...he warned me away from you. Told me I should leave."

"And you just packed up and went like a good little sheepy?"

His brows lowered, lips pressing tightly together.

"If you knew what was good for you, Ava Jade, you'd leave, too."

I laughed, shaking my head at the ludicrousness of this whole idiotic situation.

"What did he say, then, hmm? That I was his or some other bullshit?"

Without missing a beat, Josh replied. "Yes. And he didn't just warn me away. As of this morning, no guy in this entire school is allowed to go near you. They've...they've claimed you."

The way he said it, with pity, made my teeth grind. I got the sense they hadn't ever done anything like this before. Never claimed someone for themselves.

Fuck if I was going to let the bastard get away with it.

I wouldn't let them back me into a corner. Into a cage.

I said *no* to their deal, and I would stand my motherfucking ground.

A growl tore from my throat as I chucked my books to the floor and spun on my heel, storming toward the stairs, and leaving Josh in my dust. I shivered, my edges coming unglued, fingers of heat inching up the back of my neck.

My vision narrowed, tinted crimson.

My thoughts were a mess of disjointed things rattling in my head.

Those entitled motherfuckers.

Friday. Today was Friday.

Grey.

Grey was here.

Last period.

He would be in room 910. Biochem.

I was there so fast that I could barely recall from which direction I came, how I'd managed to climb two flights of stairs and jump down three different hallways. It felt like barely a second had passed since Josh poured gasoline on my fire.

The door flew open, battering loudly on the opposite wall as I stepped inside. Heads swiveled. Startled eyes took me in. But I was looking for a specific pair.

"*Excuse me*," the teacher all but shouted, rising from behind her desk with a pointed stare in my direction. I didn't even have to look at her to know that she was five foot nothing, rounded through her middle, and absolutely no threat whatsoever.

"You," I growled, latching onto Greyson Winters at the back of the classroom with my eyes alone. "We need to talk."

"I said, *excuse me*," the teacher repeated. "We're in the middle of—"

Grey lifted a hand, silencing the teacher with a lazy *shhhh*, without taking his eyes off me.

My heart beat in my temples, thudding so strongly that the room seemed to expand in shades of red with each pulse. I inhaled deeply through my nose, regaining control as the initial burst of adrenaline leveled out into a steady rush, sharpening my focus. Centering.

If I'd found Grey one minute earlier, I might've bit his head off.

"Excuse us, Mrs. Waters," Grey said as he rose from his desk, inclining his head to the ruffled teacher. He left his books and pencil behind as he waded through the whispering students toward the door.

"AJ," he said with a nod as he approached, the tiny tick of enjoyment squirming at the edge of his lips was enough to set my blood boiling anew. I snatched his arm and dragged him through the door, slamming it behind us.

I didn't stop there.

"Where are we going?"

I growled to myself, curses falling from my lips as I towed Grey along with me until I found what I was looking for. I shouldered the door to the ladies washroom open and shoved him through it.

"*Um*, hello?" a small voice called from one of the stalls inside.

"*Get out*." I snarled.

The girl was spurred into action, rushing from the stall with a furtive and fearful glance between Grey and me before she rushed out the door. I checked the other stalls, punching the doors open one by one until I was certain we were alone.

I locked the door and swallowed back the acid in my throat. Crossing my arms over my chest, I faced Grey, unable to trust I wouldn't just haul off and deck him right in his stupid mouth.

"I thought I made myself clear," I started, surprised at the level tone of my voice, now only edged with a sharp bite. "I am not something you fuckheads can own."

Realization registered on his face and his self-righteous smirk morphed into a taut line.

"Watch your mouth," he said, his upper lip curling. Though it wasn't hostility I found when I met his heavy gaze. It was something else entirely.

Grey's fists clenched and unclenched at his sides as he took me in, his broad chest heaving beneath the crisp white t-shirt he wore. His tatted biceps flexed, stretching the inked images.

"Or what?" I challenged. "Going to put me down like you did that guy last Thursday night? If you are, just get it over with. But I'm warning you now, I won't go down without a damn good fight."

A muscle jumped in his temple, and his fists uncurled. "There are a lot of things I want to do to you, Ava Jade," he said, his voice dropping an octave, the sound of it making me squirm. "Killing you isn't one of them."

My breath caught in my throat.

Grey stepped forward, closing the gap between us, and I felt my own wetness like warm silk in my panties.

I didn't move so much as an inch as he approached; to back away or go for a blade would be giving him too much credit. He wasn't armed, at least not with a gun. I'd given him a thorough once over when I spotted him at the back of the classroom. I'd cased each step as he approached. He wasn't packing. At least not anything but the hard angled shape in his back left pocket.

His cell phone.

His cell phone.

I suppressed a grin, biting my lower lip.

Grey stopped before me, standing nearly a full head taller. Inches of space between us. His dirty blond hair burned with strands of gold in the bright vanity lights over the bank of sinks at my back.

I jerked, twitching toward my blades as Grey took my jaw into his hand, his callused fingers rough against my skin. He studied my face as though he could read something hidden there. A secret code. A riddle to be solved.

"Who are you?" he asked on his next breath, his gaze narrowing as if he looked hard enough he might find the answer he was looking for. He'd asked me the same question that night in the woods. This time, I'd answer him.

"Someone you shouldn't fuck with." I'd meant it to sound threatening, but it came out differently. My breath stuttering.

"Is that so?"

I swung my arm up to knock his hand away, my anger flaring again at his arrogance, but he caught my wrist instead, holding it there with a cruel smirk.

"Fuck you," I spat, tugging the arm he had hostage, but his grip only tightened, drawing me into him. His scent engulfed me. So familiar. Like the forest just before dawn. When the air is thick with the smells of settling dew and damp earth. The stronger smell of engine oil was at war with it, giving the heady, soft aroma a bit of unusual bite.

A small sound escaped my lips, and my traitorous pussy throbbed beneath my jeans, aching at his nearness.

I could feel more than see his smile as he dropped his lips to my ear. "I dare you."

Motherfucker.

I shoved him back and his hand snapped off my wrist. He stumbled back a step, surprise in his wide stare.

Grey grinned, recovering quickly and coming at me with renewed spite pinching the skin between his brows. He shoved me back, and I let him, catching myself on the bank of sinks, lips parting.

I didn't even have time to catch my breath before he claimed my mouth, stealing whatever dregs of air remained in my lungs. His fingers twisted into my hair, securing me to him as he shoved me against the cool stainless steel. It bit into my lower back, and I clutched it until my fingers strained from the pressure, trying desperately to ward off the flutter taking over deep in my belly.

I don't want this.

Lie.

I don't want him.

Lie.

"Stop fucking fighting it," he demanded between kisses, pressing in between my hips, making me moan into his mouth as his erection nudged my belly.

Fuck it.

I released the countertop, letting him lift me with ease until I was seated atop it, able to wrap my legs around his middle. To yank his shirt off.

"*This means nothing,*" I panted as it fell to the floor, my voice a breathy growl.

"Absolutely nothing," he agreed with a smirk.

I stopped his advance with a palm pressed flat to his warm chest, making him look at me. Forcing him to understand. He was still my enemy. I was not going to hold back. As long as they fucked with me, I would fuck with them. Mercy wasn't something I was ever given. I wouldn't be offering it up. Not to them. Not to anyone.

Understanding made Grey still, made his smirk fade.

"Now fuck me," I demanded, loosening my grip on him with my thighs to allow him closer. Regret slammed into me even before he unbuttoned his jeans and let them fall, showing off one of the most beautiful cocks I'd ever seen.

No amount of premature remorse was going to stop me from having him.

Grey undid my jeans next, looping his fingers through the belt loops to wiggle them and my panties off. He paused at the sight of the scars marring six inches of flesh on each of my thighs, and I jerked him closer, forcing him to look at me. Not at them.

"What—"

"None of your fucking business," I hissed as I kicked my jeans the rest of the way off and spread myself to him.

But the sight of them had distracted him, and his thumb bumped over the perfect white raised lines, making me shudder.

He dropped to his knees, and I convulsed as his warm breath skated over my inner thigh. A gasp turning into a cry as his warm mouth pressed against my scars, kissing my inner thighs higher and higher until...

Fuck.

Yes.

His mouth closed over my clit, making my back arch violently. I thrust against his face as he began a slow, tortuous pace with his tongue. The fast-building orgasm was a testament to how badly I'd needed this fucking release.

Grey ate my pussy like a man starved. Like this was a heist he'd been planning forever, and I was the prize. I bucked and writhed against the counter, making Grey have to lock his hands around my thighs to hold me down.

"Just like that," I moaned, feeling the build deep within. "Fuck, don't stop."

He slowed just a fraction, and I about lost my shit, digging my fingers into his golden hair to make him keep going. He obliged, quickening the pace with his tongue and adding his fingers to the mix, pushing them inside of me at the perfect moment to increase the pleasure past the breaking point.

I clenched around his fingers, writhing against his mouth as I shattered, my head smashing back against the mirror so hard I heard the glass crack.

I hardly noticed as he slipped his fingers out and flipped me. My feet hit the floor and my belly met the hard countertop as he thrust into me from behind, making my thighs slap against the metal and a gasping moan press out through my lips.

He groaned, his length filling me exquisitely.

I gasped into the counter, face down as he splayed his hands over my back until they were curled around my hips. I braced, my breath hitching as he drove into me again, using his grip on my hips to push in deep and hard, grinding his hilt against me.

My hands grasped for something to hold on to, finding faucets. My back arched with his next thrust, and I found us in the broken mirror.

A hundred fractured pieces of pleasure and pain. Of reserved fury and sated desire.

Grey was a myriad of ink and flesh. Of control and chaos.

The build of another orgasm began again, and I bent to the sensations ricocheting through my body like fucking buck shot, crying out as he pumped his cock into me. He set a blistering pace I was sure would leave me fucking bruised, but I didn't care. All we had was this, here and now, and I was *starving* for it.

Grey grabbed my ass, squeezing hard as the fractured reflection of his face hardened in the mirror and his body began to tense.

"*Fuck,*" he cursed through gritted teeth.

I slipped my hand down between myself and the counter's edge, my fingers finding my slippery clit. They brushed against his length as he fucked me, and he shuddered at the dual sensation as I rubbed myself.

"*Christ,* AJ," he grunted, and I splintered, then broke, coming on his cock as he bent over my back, gasping. His hand slid over my mouth, muffling my scream as we came. His hot release filled me as his hips jerked their last.

I let the satiated delirium take me, but only for a few seconds. Only long enough for me to catch my breath, then I slid out from under him and stooped to snatch my jeans and panties from the floor. Easily plucking the cell phone from the back pocket of his jeans to tuck it into the lump of mine in my arms.

I strode to the door and unlocked it. "Thanks for the ride," I muttered, unable to meet his stare. Unwelcome guilt swirling in my stomach. "Now get the fuck out."

20

GREY

I could still taste Ava Jade on my lips when I left Briar Hall for the day, deciding to swing by Sanctum for a long workout before heading home.

We had a decent home gym at the Crow's Nest, but I didn't want to run on the treadmill or bench today. The heavy bag was what I was after, and I didn't stop until my knuckles bled.

I couldn't figure her out.

She wanted me, that much I was certain of, but she was so hot and cold. One second, she was fucking my mouth, grinding her round ass against my cock, crying out, fucking *screaming,* and the next...

I hit the bag again, gritting my teeth at the sting.

What did she want?

Where did she come from?

For the first time in forever, I had an itch I couldn't scratch. I wanted to know more about her. I needed to know what made her tick. In my head, I considered every place Corvus might've put the files he'd gotten on AJ. I couldn't ask him for them. Didn't want to see the smug look on his face when he passed them over.

If I wanted to read them, to know what he knew, then I'd have to find them myself.

Breathless, I stopped my assault of the heavy bag and rolled my aching shoulders back, walking off the frustration still clinging to my bones.

At least there was satisfaction in knowing that if the guys *had* gone for my little contest idea, I would've won.

My phone buzzed on the stool near the back of the private warm-up area in the basement of Sanctum. Sweat dripped down my temples as I shucked off my gloves and tossed them in the bin, snatching up my phone with a grimace.

I'd fucking dropped it in the girl's bathroom this afternoon. I hadn't even noticed for almost an hour after AJ kicked me out. At least when I went back to look for it, it was still there. Face down against the wall beneath the bank of sinks.

The screen was cracked now, a single long slice running from one corner to the other, making the message from Corv look like it'd been cut down the middle.

CORVUS

Where are you?

I thumbed a quick reply, sighing.

GREY

Sanctum. Heading home now.

CORVUS

Good. We have work to do.

I swiped his message away and tapped on Chrome, my thumb hesitating over the search bar. Habit.

My gut twisted as I pressed the search bar, and her name came up as a recent search. Siobhan Winters.

Fuck.

Changing my mind, I deleted the search history and dropped it back onto the stool.

I didn't care where she was. I didn't care if she was dead or alive. I didn't care why she never came back.

I wiped a palm over my face and shucked off my gym shorts in favor of the clothes I'd been wearing earlier, purging her from my thoughts.

I'd wait to shower until I got home. If I didn't leave now, I'd get another message from Corv in fifteen minutes asking why the fuck I wasn't back yet.

At least I knew that if some shit ever did go south, Corv would be the first one to figure out what went wrong and drag my ass out of trouble. We had about a thirty-minute window for answering our big bro before he came looking. And if you took more than thirty minutes to reply, you better hope your ass was dead because you'd never hear the end of it.

I may not have known what it was like most of my life to have family. To know that multiple people had my back no matter what. But at least I did now.

I took the back roads home, sticking to the routes I knew AJ sometimes liked to run, hoping to catch a glimpse of her. No luck.

One of Diesel's cars, the nondescript navy-blue Impala was parked up near the front door, and I drove around it, parking along the side of the Crow's Nest. They'd been doing some recon work, then. Otherwise Corv would've taken the Camaro.

The smell of roasting chicken greeted me when I entered, and I inhaled deeply, scenting lemon and garlic.

Corvus was cooking, that was a good sign. He hadn't cooked anything all week, forcing Rook and me to live off takeout and leftovers. If he was cooking, it meant they had a successful day.

Rook was just wandering to the kitchen from the living room as I entered, leaving the video game he'd been playing running on the load screen. It almost felt like a regular Friday as I snatched a bottle of water from the fridge and fell onto one of the stools at the kitchen counter.

"Hungry?" Corvus didn't bother turning as he stirred sauce in a small pan atop the stove, pausing every few seconds to toss a pan of green beans.

"Fucking starved. How'd it go?"

"Good," Corvus replied as Rook settled into the stool opposite me, pouring himself a fifth of whiskey from the bottle on the counter. He eyed me suspiciously as he swirled the liquid in the glass, his dark eyes narrowing.

"The MC's source is legit. We're good to go for the swap."

I snorted, impressed. That didn't take long. Now it would just be a matter of casing the meet point and then we'd be solid. More firepower.

A solid payday. At least things were starting to look up, with that one thing at least.

"Any word from Dies? How's the meet looking with the Aces?"

Corv gave a shrug. "He's deep in it right now. Not sure what's up. He'll let us know."

He played it off like it wasn't a big deal, but I could feel the tension radiating off him from here.

"Shit, I forgot the bread in the car," he said suddenly, flipping off the burners and tossing the dish towel on the counter as he stalked from the kitchen.

Rook leaned conspiratorially over the counter, and I lifted a brow at him. "What?"

He inhaled deeply and let out a sigh, his lips curving into a sultry grin. "What happened at school today? Anything exciting?"

I couldn't school my face fast enough, the memory of AJ's tight pussy wrapped around my cock came stampeding back to the forefront of my mind. I swallowed. "Not much."

"*Liar*," Rook said, calling me on my shit with a knowing look. "Leave you alone for one fucking day..." He shook his head, tossing back his whiskey. "How was she?"

Fucking Christ.

It was my turn to shake my head at him. No one gave the fucker enough credit. They saw him as the crazy one. All fists and fury, no brains. But my brother was the full package. He saw things other people didn't. Saw them easily. Without even trying to. He'd always been that way.

I licked my lips, leaning back in my chair with a slow shaking inhale, conveying to him without the need for words just how goddamned good it was. Lips twitching into a suggestive grin.

He blew a breath out, shoulders twitching as a shudder rolled down his spine.

Corvus returned a second later, and I winced, hoping Rook would keep this between us, at least for now.

He tossed me a wink and poured another whiskey, sipping it this time, a distant look in his eyes.

"So," I said, clearing my throat. "Work tonight; are we doing the job Julia texted about earlier?"

Julia sent a group text to the three of us like she always did. She got a call this morning at the helpline from a pair of little girls. We'd already visited their abusive father once. So this would be strike two for Billy Parker.

We had the address of a butcher shop he owned and intel that he often worked late Friday nights to prepare for the weekend rush. That he often worked *alone,* drinking in his locked up shop before driving home drunk to take out his rage on his five and nine year old daughters and their mother.

We knew Mrs. Parker tried to leave him once before, and that he almost killed her for it. She dropped her petition for sole custody less than twenty-four hours after she made it.

But...Diesel specifically said to hang up everything we were doing. He didn't know about our little humanitarian project, or at least, he pretended not to. Either way, he wouldn't like us going off to do our own thing with everything else going on right now.

It was why we all agreed to let AJ simmer on the backburner for the time being. Until we had more time to devote to her eventual surrender.

"Yeah," Rook answered before Corvus could. "It'll be quick."

There was no room for discussion, then.

Rook rarely took an assertive role, but when he did, it wasn't worth arguing. He'd go off and do it alone if we didn't follow him.

Corvus grunted his agreement, carving up and plating the chicken and beans, pouring the sauce over it.

He set our plates down on the kitchen island, drying his hands on the towel slung over his shoulder. "Eat," he ordered, turning his attention to me and wrinkling his nose.

I stiffened, thinking he could smell AJ on me as easily as Rook could, but then his gaze tracked to my sweat-greased hair. "And get washed up. We'll leave after dark."

21

AVA JADE

248 Fletcher Street, unit 4.

I double checked the slip of paper I'd written the address on so I wouldn't forget it. This was definitely the place. The small L-shaped shopping plaza near the northern ridge of Thorn Valley had already emptied for the night. Only a single car remained in the lot, an older model Ford truck with rust around the wheel wells and a cracked side-mirror.

The large square windows of the shops were all dark, caged over with metal to prevent break ins. Except for unit 4. The window of Parker and Sons Butcher Shop still glowed with a dim light from somewhere deeper inside the narrow space.

I really had no idea what I would find here, but this was the break I'd been waiting for.

After Grey left the ladies room, I locked the door behind him and *prayed* his phone wasn't solely fingerprint enabled or I would need a lot more time, and a computer, to bypass it.

I almost had a panic attack when it came up with the print scanner, but swiping across the screen brought up an alternative option. Not a code, but the option to draw a password shape.

I couldn't make out the finger smudges, so that was out. I had three tries before it locked me out and he'd know it was messed with. It'd been a hot minute since my pickpocketing days, but I still remembered the three most common shapes.

Grey didn't strike me as a basic bitch, so I threw out the first two options and went straight for the third. A simple enough swipe path, but not so common that just anyone would be able to get in. I got in on the first motherfucking try.

I wondered if Rook's or Corvus' phones would be equally simple to break into, but once I was inside of Grey's, I realized the reason it wasn't as protected as I assumed it would've been.

It wasn't a burner. Not exactly. But it was clear they did change phones semi-regularly. There were only three numbers stored in the device. Corvus. Rook. Diesel.

Every other call came in as an unknown number.

And aside from a few useless messages between Grey and Corvus (it was obvious he wiped the phone clean daily) there was absolutely nothing save for a single text message from an unknown number that was sent to all three of them.

UNKNOWN

Billy Parker. Strike Two. 2248 Fletcher Street, Unit 4. He works late. Doesn't get home until after midnight on Fridays. Accept?

The only reply was a single word from Rook in the group chat.

ROOK

Accept.

That was it.

I had a date and an address. A place where they were going to be tonight. I wasn't sure who Billy Parker was, but I was glad I wasn't him.

Strike two?

I had to assume it was something to do with a debt owed to the Saints. That they were going to collect or take payment in blood. If I could get something on camera, then maybe it would be enough to buy my freedom. Or at least, it would be a good start. I had no illusions that they wouldn't just as easily kill me if I tried to blackmail them, but if they took me down I'd make sure whatever footage I had of them went absolutely viral.

Dom once explained to me how to do that, because this one time the Kings did it to her dad. They blackmailed him with footage of Dom getting double teamed by two college guys at a frat party she'd snuck into. They told him *exactly* what they were going to do with the little movie they bought from the two dickwads at Theta Kappa Nu. Down to the minute details.

Dom never forgot because dear 'ol dad never let her live it down.

Her father saw to it that they got off on all charges like they asked, even though the mess they'd gotten themselves into should have wiped them off the face of the planet.

Fucking gangs.

I'd offered to castrate the little fucklets for their crimes, but Dom made me promise not to, something about not wanting me involved.

I crept around the back of the building, careful not to be seen. A single security camera watched over the parking lot from the southern corner of the plaza. Easy to stay out of view. Around back, in the wide alley between the plaza and a closed down pharmacy were the back entrances to each shop.

Big green dumpsters lined the alley opposite the back doors. There were no windows back here. None at all. No cameras, either. *Fuck.*

How the hell was I supposed to see what was going on inside without straight up peeping into the front window?

I settled next to one of the dumpsters, wrinkling my nose at the smell, but at least I was out of direct sight here, tucked away in the shadows.

The text message from the unknown number insinuated that Billy Parker would be here until midnight. It was just past eleven now. No sign of the Crows.

My phone buzzed in my pocket and I quickly drew it out and tapped the side button to silence the sound. The screen flashed with two messages.

BECCA

Hey, you asleep? Want to watch bad horror movies and get high?

KIT

Are you ever going to call me back?

Stage four clinger alert.

I swiped ignore on Kit's message for the moment, re-upping my promise to myself to get back to both him and Dom ASAP. Knowing that might not happen for a while. I really was complete and utter shit at being a friend.

AVA JADE

Out for a run, sorry. Raincheck?

I didn't wait for a reply, toggling my phone to silent and slipping it back in my pocket. I didn't run twelve fucking miles out to this sketchy ass plaza all the way on the other end of town for nothing. I was getting in there. One way or another.

Resolving to check the front again for a good vantage point, I stood only to drop back to a crouch as the door at the back of Parker and Sons burst open.

I tucked myself into the shadows, the cool nip of the metal trash bin biting even through my long sleeve black shirt and joggers.

"I can't tonight," a man said, speaking over a garbled voice on the other end of a call. He chucked a bottle into the bin I was hidden beside and it shattered. The smell of stale beer wafted to me on the cool breeze.

"All right, all right. Look man, borrow the truck, I'll leave the keys under the visor, but if you score, I want a cut."

A pause.

"Be back by midnight. You walking over?"

Another pause.

"All right. Yeah, yeah, I'm going."

Keys jangled, and Billy Parker cursed as he dropped his phone and fumbled to pick it up, angrily striding around the back of the other shops toward the parking lot at the front. The instant he was out of sight I sprinted across the alley to the door he exited and stepped through into the dimly lit shop.

The space was narrow. At the front, a long bank of refrigerated displays poured their blue-tinted light toward the front window. That must have been the ambient light I was seeing from outside. Nearer to the back, to the right of where I stood, was a large structure built into the wall. I crept to the front of it and found the door slightly ajar, leaking icy air out into the main shop.

A side of beef hung from a hook in the ceiling, all vivid red meat and yellowed fat and bone. Several stainless-steel shelves held long slices of aging beef along the back wall. More hooks dangled from the metal sliders in the ceiling, waiting to hold more mangled cow bits for Billy Parker to cut down to size.

Okay, think Ava...

Kicking myself into gear, I rushed for the front counter, digging in a low shelf between two display cases until I found what I was looking for. I began folding down a paper bag, my fingers working deftly until I was left with a good size chunk of paper. Peering over the display cases, I could see Billy Parker slamming his truck door shut to make his way back inside.

I let out a breath of relief when he veered left across the lot, going around the back of the plaza to the rear entrance.

Once he was out of sight, I hopped the counter and unlocked the front door, stuffing the wad of paper into the lock slot. There were no bells or anything else I'd have to worry about. If I needed to make a quick getaway, I should be able to slip out undetected through the front.

I padded to the right of the display case and sank into a crouch in the nook between the edge of the case and the wall just as the back door banged back open and Billy re-entered the shop. The exhaust fan from the display case pumped warm air around my ankles, but at least the soft noise of it would mute any sound from my shuffling feet as I maneuvered myself into place.

From where I crouched, facing the back of the shop, I could see the rear entrance door and the door to the massive walk-in cooler. If the Crows tried to come in through the front, I might be seen, but if they went around back I would be safely hidden from view by the metal cart piled with stickers and pre-cut butcher paper in front of me.

I was banking a lot on them taking the back entrance.

And this was only going to work if they attacked Billy Parker here in his shop. If they waited for him to leave to snatch him then this whole thing was just a total waste of my fucking time.

But it was the first bit of useful information I'd gotten. It would have been idiotic of me not to at least *try*. The Crows poked the wrong fucking bear and they would see what happened when the bear hit back no matter how long it took me.

A taste of their own medicine wouldn't kill them.

They tried to blackmail me first, after all.

The wait was longer than I hoped. Twice, Billy wandered too close to the front of the shop, taking breaks from sawing apart the massive cut of beef hanging in his cooler. Twice, I'd had to disappear into a tiny ball of black fabric and dark hair to avoid being seen. If he wasn't at least six beers deep, there was a good chance he'd have spotted me by now.

The guy liked to talk to himself, I'd learned. Though maybe *mutter* was a more accurate word since I couldn't really tell what he was saying beyond a word here and there. Something about *little bitches* and *that hoe.*

He was an asshole. It was easy to tell. Something in the drunken swagger. In the way he carried himself. In his snarling upper lip and the way he tossed back violent swigs of his beer, seeming to grow more enraged with each one he finished.

His buddy came and took the truck, honking twice before he pulled out of the lot.

Billy Parker had a lot to mutter about that guy. Apparently he was a no-good piece of shit, but Billy was really hoping he'd score for them both. I wasn't able to get the best look at his face, but Billy was a tall, lanky guy. With lean muscle and a pin-up girl neck tatt. His skinny legs swimming in the bootcut jeans he wore. He ditched his Mötley Crüe t-shirt sometime past eleven, working bare chested, a dusting of dark brown curling hairs on his chest making him seem somehow even more pale than he was.

I was about to call it and head home, drawn by the promise of a joint and bad horror movies, when I heard a car veer off the main road and into the lot. I wiggled in my little hidey nook to get a better look, finding a silver sedan slowly rolling through the parking lot. I ducked my head as it passed Parker and Sons, but I could still make out the shapes of three figures inside.

Where the hell were they getting all these different cars from?

I mean, I had my own ideas, but their supply of borrowed vehicles seemed to be endless.

The car vanished around the edge of the lot, and I closed my eyes, hearing the faint sound of an engine rumbling somewhere in the distance. I was willing to bet they'd parked out behind that closed down pharmacy. That was where I would've parked.

The idling stopped.

I held my breath.

The *bang* of the door being kicked into the opposite wall rattled the building and rang in my ears.

I sank impossibly lower, drawing out my phone as I waited for the perfect shot.

"*Oh, Billy boy!*" Rook rasped, and three reapers spilled into the shop.

Dressed all in black, they appeared to almost blend into the shadows. The stark white of their *Scream* masks with their hollow black eyes and overexaggerated smiles making their heads seem to float in midair.

Dammit.

Unless they said something to give themselves away or removed the masks, any footage would be pretty much useless.

I ground my teeth as I switched my camera screen to record and nestled it against the corner of the metal trolley to get a clear and unwavering picture.

A clatter from the meat cooler and rushing footsteps.

The tallest of them, Corvus, threw his foot into the cooler door before Billy could lock them out, not even flinching as it thudded against his boot. Between their dark bodies, I saw Billy Parker fly backward, knocking into the hanging meat before slipping to the floor with a shout.

"Billy, Billy, Billy," tutted Rook, stepping past Corvus and popping his knuckles.

Grey entered last, and I guess luck was at least a little on my side because no one moved to close the cooler door behind them, offering me a fairly clear view of what went on inside.

"We warned you, Billy," Corvus drawled, his voice a detached rumble.

Billy put up a good fight as Rook stooped down to grab him off the floor. He squirmed, alternating between grunts and curses, but one good fist to the face and the drunken butcher was too dazed to fight anymore.

"Hold that hook," Rook said, his masked face tipping up to the curved piece of shining metal in the track on the roof. Grey obliged, gripping the topmost part of it to steady it as Rook lifted Billy with ease.

My stomach turned as he slid Billy onto the hook, the metal biting through the skin of his back. Through his muscle.

Billy screamed, an awful drawn-out sound that ended in a sob only to start again. Scream after scream until his throat was raw and he choked up bile. Until his back was coated in red and it began to pool on the stained tiles below his hanging feet. Until he stopped trying to reach the hook with wildly flailing arms, realizing he couldn't dislodge it himself no matter how hard he tried.

"You about done?" Corvus asked

He kicked a milk crate under Billy, enabling him to stand on his tip toes to alleviate some of the pressure no doubt shifting the bones of his shoulder blade. *Ugh.*

"P-please," Billy pleaded, his arms hanging in defeat. "Don't kill me."

"We're not going to kill you, Billy," Grey said, crossing his arms over his chest, making his fitted long-sleeve black t-shirt bulge around his biceps. My mouth went a little dry, and I chastised my aching cunt for wanting another taste of his cock. Even now. Even while I watched them *torture* someone, she still thirsted for him.

I mean, I knew I was fucked up, but...that had to be some next level shit. Maybe Aunt Humphrey was right; I needed therapy. Copious amounts of it.

"We explained this to you last time," Corvus droned. "That was strike one. This? This is strike two. Your last warning."

Snot dripped down Billy Parker's face, mingling with the drool leaking from his gaping mouth. "I won't..." he said, the words choking off on a pained intake of breath. "I won't ever touch them again, I swear."

Silence in the meat cooler.

"*I swear,*" he repeated. "You've...you've made your point. Now please, *please* just let me down."

"Oh no," Rook said. "We're nowhere near finished."

If it were possible, Billy went even paler. His eyes, wide and round, terrified as he took in Rook.

"What was it you did to your little Ashley two nights ago?" Grey asked, his voice so cold, so different from the playful cocky tone I'd come to know as his. "Oh, right. You broke her arm."

"And to Stella?" Corvus asked. "Go ahead and tell me what you did to your five-year-old daughter."

Wait...*what?*

Billy began to sob quietly, hanging his head as my thoughts raced to catch up with exactly what I was witnessing here. This was clearly not what I thought it was. This wasn't gang business at all.

My chest burned, ignited by the accusations they were slinging at Billy. By his inability to deny them. If it were true, this coward of a man *broke his daughter's arm.* And apparently that wasn't all he did. Nor was it the first time.

My eyes burned and a muscle in my jaw twitched, remembering the time my mother hurt me. How it'd felt. The man at the train tracks. The feeling of helplessness after the initial shock subsided. Of being too small to do anything to stop it. Too weak.

"Say it!" Rook demanded, gripping him brutally by the arm and pulling downward, making the metal skewer in his back dig deeper. Billy whimpered, trying to pull away, and I hoped it fucking hurt.

"I..."

"Say it, motherfucker," Grey growled.

"I...I hit her."

"And then what?" Corvus prodded, his voice dangerously level.

"And then she fell," Billy croaked, his voice a hoarse mess of broken sounds. "She...she hit her head on the table and p-p-passed out."

"Go on, you piece of shit. *Then what?*"

"I..."

Rook gave Billy another sharp tug and his eyes bugged out of his skull as bloody foam gathered in the corners of his grimacing mouth.

"I locked her in her room," Billy blurted, the words overlapping so I wasn't even certain I heard him correctly. "For two d-d-days."

"Without any food," Grey finished for him in a snarl, his body going taut, his hands flexing at his sides.

Corvus stepped forward, but stopped, digging his hand into his back pocket as an audible buzzing broke the tepid silence.

"Hold that thought," he said, lifting the phone to his ear.

I held my breath as he left the meat cooler and walked toward the front of the shop, tugging off his mask. "Yeah," he said as he answered the call. "I'm a little busy at the—"

His words cut off as a garbled voice on the other end of the receiver interrupted him. I rushed to check the angle of the camera, to see if I caught him removing the mask, but he was just out of frame. I reached out to tilt the camera, but then he turned sharply toward me, pacing along the bank of refrigerated display cases. Fuck. I couldn't stick my hand out there without risking him seeing it. I'd have to pray he wandered back in view without that mask on.

"It's late, what are you doing calling me right...*shit*. All right. Yeah. Yeah, I have a sec. What is it?"

Corvus paced behind the counter, and I flattened myself against the side of the meat cooler, willing myself to be invisible.

"I told you, Max, I'm not interested. I can't be away that long."

The voice replied on the other end of the call, distinctly feminine despite the name, but I couldn't make out what they were saying.

"Well, I'm not most people, am I?" Corvus' voice was growing more irritated by the second, his steps quickening as he paced the short length of linoleum flooring behind the register.

"Merch? I don't fucking know. I'll have Grey make something."

Corvus stopped suddenly, and I dared a peek around the edge of the display case to find him pinching the bridge of his nose as he inhaled. "I might have something new. Do you think we could...yeah, all right. I'll try to make it. Thanks, Max."

He hung up, and I whipped my head back around and closed my eyes as he lifted his gaze, praying I was fast enough. That the shadows were thick enough to keep me concealed.

Shit.

Fuck.

Fuck. Fuck. Fuck.

He cleared his throat, and I almost cracked a tooth for how hard I was clenching my damned teeth.

"All right," he said, sighing, and his heavy footfalls retreated, heading back to the cooler. Mask back in place. "Where were we?"

I blew out a breath, tucking my blade slowly back into the strap at my ankle.

"I think we were just about to show Billy here what happens when he doesn't heed our warnings," Grey replied, and I heard a sharp intake of air and looked through the shelves of the trolly to find Rook *smelling* the guy. He shuddered.

"Please..." Billy pleaded again, his voice distant now, heavier.

Corvus slapped Billy hard enough to start to draw him out of his stupor. "Hey. Pay attention."

Rook licked his lips.

Corvus slapped him again, and Billy slowly came around, his watery eyes widening in surprise like he was waking from a dream to find a nightmare waiting for him in real life.

"Pieces of shit like you aren't welcome in our town," Corvus said. "We see *everything*."

Well, not everything, I preened internally. They didn't see me barely fifteen feet away from them. Watching. *Recording*.

Billy's lower lip trembled.

"This is strike two," Grey added. "I think you know what happens if you get to strike three."

They let the threat hang in the air for a moment before Grey backed away from Billy to lean against the right wall of the cooler where I couldn't see him. Corvus backed up, too, leaning casually against the doorframe with his arms crossed over his chest. Blocking most of my view of Billy.

"What happened to you?" Corvus asked Billy.

"...w-what?"

"I said *what happened to you?*"

"I...I had an accident. I fell onto a hook."

"That's right." Rook answered him, and I could hear his smile even if I couldn't see it behind his mask. "You also might've broken some bones. Maybe smashed your face into a table, too. Guess you should stop drinking at work."

"*Wait—*"

"Let's get this over with," Corvus said simply.

"No!" Billy screamed a second before a sickening *pop* and *crunch* tunneled into my ears. I knew what it was without having to see it. Rook had broken his arm, just like Billy had broken his daughter's. It's what I would've wanted to do, too.

An eye for an eye.

When the second break came and there was no end in sight, I carefully removed my phone from the shelf and stopped recording, gripping it tightly in my hand.

It would be almost useless. They were wearing masks. They didn't say each other's names. They would have been smart enough to take a vehicle not registered to them and even then, they would have carved a wide path outside of view of any surveillance cameras.

All I'd done here tonight was witness something I wished I fucking hadn't. I didn't want to feel this...connection.

And honestly? I wasn't sure what I'd do with the footage even if it had been usable. God*fucking*dammit.

I didn't flinch as Rook snapped more bones and Billy screamed and cried until Rook eventually knocked him unconscious. I listened, hating how much I wished I could hurt him, too. How the sounds of his agony had almost no effect on me.

A five and nine-year-old? They were too young. Too innocent to be subjected to that sort of abuse from someone who was supposed to love them.

I'd have just killed him, the thought came viciously to my mind and a sour taste coated my tongue, making me grimace and clench my fists.

People made mistakes. Hell, I'd made plenty, but I learned from them.

This fuckwad would continue to make mistakes. I could see it in his face. Hear it in his voice. Who was to say that he wouldn't kill one of his little girls the next time he was angry? Then it would be too late. Then *strike three* would only be vengeance instead of prevention.

I pressed my head between my knees as the Crows took a limp Billy down from the hook and left him on the floor in a pool of his own blood. My breaths came heavier. My pulse throbbed in my temples. Fingers twitching.

I worked hard to fight it, trying to stay calm. Stay quiet. Not let the darkness grab hold. Flashes of the man at the train tracks scorched into the back of my eyelids, and I forced my eyes open to erase them, sweat beading at my hairline.

A loud metallic *chink* rang out through the shop. Grey had snapped off the lever inside of the cooler and wiped it down for prints before tossing it to the floor. It scraped over the linoleum tiles and came to a clattering stop near my feet.

"What are you doing?" Corvus asked.

"Seeing how he likes being locked up," Grey replied stoically and closed the cooler door as he shouldered past Corvus.

"And if no one finds him?" Corvus asked, and I got the distinct sense that he was waiting to judge Grey's answer. That this was a test, and Corvus wanted to see if Grey would pass it.

"Then no one finds him," Grey replied and left, pushing through the back door of the shop to vanish into the night.

Corvus nodded quietly to himself. He passed.

"You hungry?" Rook asked. "I could really go for some McDicks right now."

"Seriously?"

Rook shrugged and Corvus snorted at him before the pair left to follow Grey out into the dark.

I couldn't be sure how long I stayed there, leaning against the metal, just breathing. Taking in everything I'd seen and heard.

A thousand questions swirled in the adrenal wasteland of my brain. What they were doing...did it make them any better than Billy?

They were murderers.

Fucking psychopaths.

None of them so much as balked as Rook broke Billy apart.

Neither did you, the darkest part of my mind whispered, and I swallowed hard, forcing my legs to push me back to standing. My back ached from crouching there for so long, and I took a minute to stretch it out.

A thud sounded, echoing in the butcher shop.

Then another.

"H-hello?" A weak voice called, muffled by thick steel and insulation. "Is anybody there?"

I judged whether I'd touched anything in the shop and did one last wipe of the front door to be safe. It was time to get the fuck out of here.

Another thud as Billy pounded a fist against the door. "Help!" he shouted. "Someone please!"

I groaned to myself, stopping near the door to the cooler. The handle was right there. I could just pop it open and vanish. I could free him.

But why in the absolute fuck would I do that?

Heat licked up my spine, and I took two steps toward the back door to leave before something made me stop. Invisible hands wrapped around my ankles like ghosts demanding proper justice.

I didn't even know what they looked like, his little girls, but I knew that they'd be better off without him. But was that enough?

What was I really considering here?

No one had seen me. I'd been careful. I'd triple check for prints.

What am I doing?

"P-please! I've been attacked! Please, someone open the door!"

"*Fuck,*" I gritted out through my teeth, the flood of new adrenaline vaulting up through me in an eruption of rage.

I stalked back to the walk-in cooler and wrenched the door open. Billy poured out, falling onto the floor with a wet *slap.*

He twisted, fear in his swelling eyes as he took me in. A relieved gush of air passed his lips, and I wrinkled my nose at the acrid smell of beer and blood mingling in the air.

"Thank you," he sobbed, reaching his bloodied hand, the one that wasn't broken, toward my shoes. I stepped back. "*Thank you.*"

I bent, the dull side of my blade sliding along my fingers as I drew it from the strap.

He lifted his head and his eyes met mine.

Something registered there after a second. The relief smoothing the lines of his weathered face vanished. He stopped breathing.

"Who—"

A hard and quick arc of my blade.

A clean slice.

I left him there to die, dancing away from the spray of crimson as it rushed to leave his severed carotid. I was gone before Billy Parker even finished choking on his own blood.

And I felt...*incredible.*

22

AVA JADE

I slept like a baby after butcher butchering night.

Well, for the four hours I managed to sleep before the sounds of Becca moving around in our shared dorm woke me.

It'd been an entire week since then and only a couple days ago the stiffness and aching in my legs from the twenty-four-mile return trip to and from Parker and Sons finally leveled out to the normal daily burn. Really, I should've added two more miles to make it a murder marathon.

I kind of missed the ache if I was being honest.

It kept my mind off other things. Things I *shouldn't* be thinking about.

Billy Parker's murder hit the news just this morning. They found his body two days ago and the fact his wife didn't report him missing and start an investigation sooner only served to cement I'd done the right thing. I didn't know what it meant that I slept better after killing a man. That I didn't lose my appetite. That I felt...*good*.

Not at all like the first time.

This time, I was certain there was nothing at Parker and Sons tying me to the murder. No prints, I'd wiped everything down that I touched. No camera footage, I was very careful to avoid the one camera in the plaza and honestly, I doubted it was even functional, judging by the antiquated look of it. There was nothing tying me to his death except for a very clean slit in a redneck bastard's throat.

And that could've been done by anybody. More likely the same people who caught his fishy ass on a hook to be flayed. Though, I was fairly certain they hadn't left any traces of themselves there, either.

I almost felt guilty when I finally secured the bug I'd been covertly trying to acquire on Monday night. And that same guilt ate at me when I planted it on Tuesday.

I *hated* that I felt guilty. I shouldn't. Not after the shit they'd pulled. Even if the self-proclaimed Queen of Briar Hall still hadn't attacked, I knew they weren't done toying with me. Once their meeting with the Aces and the other shit with the Mexicans was done, I'd be fair game again.

It was just like I'd planned. Easy in. Easy out. I didn't go inside the Crow's Nest to plant it. Not wanting to risk leaving so much as a stray hair behind to be found.

I'd had to settle for planting it just outside the kitchen window. It was strong enough to pick up conversations inside the house, albeit, not as clearly as I'd have liked. And the old wood siding gave me the perfect little knot to cram it into.

It wasn't top quality and the battery needed to be replaced every three days, but barring a trip back to Lennox to visit my usual contact, it was as good as I was going to get.

They had exactly three things planned that I was now aware of:

In three days, on the holiday Monday, they were meeting with the Aces whom Corvus didn't trust, but didn't think was at fault for the death of some guy named Randy.

In two days, Sunday, they would be making some kind of exchange with the Mexicans. I had to assume guns or drugs but couldn't be sure. They were all a little on edge about that one.

And tonight, in exactly three hours, at eleven, Rook would be up against some sorry sucker named Conor Jones in an illegal fight ring in the basement of a bar called Sanctum.

Two of those things, I was planning to attend as a ghost. The fight and the Aces meet.

The thing with the Mexicans was too far. I could jack a car, but from the sound of it, it was in the middle of nowhere, so they'd easily spot a tail. And the ride would be too long for me to be able to get away with climbing into their trunk. An option I was considering for the Aces meet to avoid the thirty-mile round trip run to what they liked to refer to as no man's land. Which was basically just a fancy way of saying Spirit Lake, the all but abandoned village just east of Thorn Valley. The only place within a hundred-mile radius *not* claimed by a gang.

Talk about a useful bug, am I right?

Though knowing all of this paled in comparison to the fact that I was pretty sure Corvus would shit an actual brick if he knew I'd one-upped him and was eavesdropping on *everything.* The thought alone brought me so much joy I'd been living on cloud nine all week.

I'd gotten even *more* ahead on all my projects, academic and extracurricular. Becca and I had a new routine of evening horror movie watching and popcorn when she or I weren't out—which I actually enjoyed. Way more than I thought I ever would.

She seemed sad lately, and I didn't feel bold enough to ask her about it, so I simmered in silence hoping that one day whoever made her upset would cross my path so I could cheerfully gut them.

But all good things had to come to an end.

I lowered myself behind the burgundy SUV across the street from Pop's Midnight Cafe where the owner, a balding man in his late forties, would soon be exiting with his weekly cash deposit to drop off at the bank on his way home. Like he had done the last two Friday's before this one.

It paid to pay attention. Literally.

If I wanted to get into Sanctum, I needed cash. If it was what I thought it was, it would be pay to play. All attendees would need to place a bet before entry. A hefty sum of which would be raked by the house.

If I showed up with my last three hundred bucks, I'd be laughed out. If I showed up with the 8-10k I thought might be in that faded gray cash bag, I'd have a better chance of being let in.

I needed to see what I was up against. Watching Rook fight might give me an advantage if we ever came to blows. More than that, I wanted to see the man himself. Diesel St. Crow. I wanted to take a measure of him. See if he was made of the same things as his sons.

At least, that's what I was telling myself. It definitely *wasn't* because

I wanted to see Rook beat Conor Jones to a bloody pulp. Not at all. And fucking *definitely* not because I haven't been able to stop thinking about all three of them since last Friday night.

Listening to the recordings on the bug only had me more confused. They talked about some show they had later this month, and I got the idea it was a concert. I *prayed* it wasn't the Primal Ethos one Becca was taking me to. That would be a surefire way to ruin my fun.

Oh, and Corvus cooks. Who would've thought? He also got up several times a night and wandered to within range of my bug by the kitchen for water and to grumble wordlessly to himself like a total lunatic.

I adjusted my wig, the short black bob had bangs and when it shifted, they tickled annoyingly at the skin just above my brows.

I groaned, hushing rapidly as the bells jingled and I peered around the edge of the SUV to see Mr. Jordan Hughes exiting with his big 'ol bag of cash. Right on schedule.

Fuck, he walked so slow it hurt to watch him. Made my skin itch.

Come on, fucker, hurry up. I don't have time for this.

Sanctum was across town and word on the street was that attendees were locked in when the show started. Unable to leave until it was over. Something about preventing a raid. If I didn't get there before eleven, I wasn't getting in at all.

I'd have to make this quick.

At this time of night, the streets were all but empty, but of course, because my luck was total shit, a patron exited the cafe right after my mark.

She went the opposite way, but would be quick to turn around if there were signs or sounds of struggle.

Awesome.

So, plan B it was.

Mr. Hughes whistled to himself as he unlocked his car and slipped into the drivers' seat. He didn't even balk as I opened the passenger door and slid into the passenger seat opposite him other than to give me a confused look.

"Uh, miss, I think you have the wrong ca—"

I jabbed my blade against the base of his ribs, and he flinched away, eyes wide, hands raised, faded gray cash bag dropped onto the center armrest.

"Don't scream," I warned before his mouth even opened. "All it would take is one thrust and this will pierce your lung. If it does, there's about a fifty-fifty chance you'll live long enough to get to a hospital."

His face paled and his Adam's apple bobbed in his throat, but his wild, jerky eyes were narrowing. Fixing on me.

My blood boiled, and I pressed harder with my blade, just enough to nick him. A small blood offering to keep my darkness at bay. "Don't fucking look at me," I hissed. "*Drive.*"

The prosthetic nose, double layer of lip plumper, and colored contacts would be enough to protect me, at least here in the dark of his SUV. The nose at least, would have to be removed before I entered Sanctum. I ran out of Dermabond and this bitch was held on with a bit of school glue and a prayer.

"Let's go, dickface," I urged when he hesitated.

Mr. Hughes fumbled to dig his keys out of his jacket pocket and took three tries to get them in the ignition. Already the high was wearing off. This man was pathetic. Not even a challenge.

I sighed inwardly as he roughly turned the SUV away from the curb, making me jerk in the passenger seat. Idiot.

"Turn left," I ordered as he came to the next street corner, and I got an idea. Maybe I didn't have to walk *all* the way back across town after all. There was a dead-end road I'd found on a run a few days back near Sanctum. Well, near enough that it wouldn't take me that long to get there. Far enough that if Mr. Hughes woke up before I was finished, the cops wouldn't find me anywhere in the immediate area.

"What do you want?" Mr. Hughes asked, his voice the tone of a man trying his best to be brave and failing miserably.

I shifted and paper crinkled at my side. I noted the edge of a crayon picture sticking out between the seat and center console. It was upside down, but a name was visible as we passed under the last of the street-lamps before I guided my mark down the dead-end road. Bethany.

I already knew enough about him to have dismissed him as any sort of threat, but judging by the drawing, the ratty old booster in the back-seat, and the wedding band on his ring finger, I doubly knew he wasn't going to fuck around.

Not if he was a good husband. Not if he was a good father.

Not if he wanted to go home to his family.

"Just keep driving," I replied, the leather glove on my left hand creaking as I gripped the blade tighter. How I'd missed them. They were faded black, well worn, and fitted to every curve and knuckle of my hands like a second skin. "We're almost there."

Mr. Hughes began to shake as we passed the *dead-end* sign and kept on going.

"Please," he said, the word a breathy plea. "I have a family. You...you don't have to do this."

I rolled my eyes. Fucking yawn.

"Park."

He did.

"Here's what's going to happen," I told him, slipping the faded gray bag onto my lap. "I'm going to take this, and you are going to forget that you saw me. You're going to say it was stolen out of your car. I'm sure your insurance will cover it."

He swallowed again, eyes shifting to the gray bag on my lap like he might make a play for it.

Try it, fucker.

Mr. Hughes didn't answer me, a knot forming between his brows.

"I'd hate for anything to happen to Bethany."

His head snapped up and a fire lit in his eyes. I'd struck a nerve. Good.

"I know where you work, Jordan Hughes. I know where you live. I know where you like to park and jerk off to amateur porn before going home to your wife. I know where darling Bethany goes to school."

His lips parted, a raw form of terror taking over his features. My thighs clenched, and I ground my teeth, a rush of power pulsing through my veins.

"Do we understand each other?" I asked after a second.

Hughes nodded and I flipped my blade away from his ribcage and lifted myself in the seat, using my full body weight to drive his face into the steering wheel. His sharp intake of breath was the only sound before a sharp blare of the horn. Then he was out. His body sagging against the wheel, arms hanging down.

The engine revved as his foot hammered down on the accelerator and I quickly shut off the engine and nudged his leg off the gas.

I slipped my blade away and unzipped the cash bag, flipping

through the stacks of cash. They were nearly organized in bundles of fives, tens, twenties, fifties, and hundreds.

The smaller bills would be coming back to Briar Hall with me. The larger ones would be my bet.

I judged the sizes of the stacks, quickly tumbling through the bills for a rough count. About seven grand in larger bills.

I fucking hoped that would be enough.

"Thanks."

I gave Mr. Hughes a gentle pat on his arm and slid the money into the inside pockets of my oversized jacket. It cost me thirty bucks at the small Thorn Valley thrift shop, but it held all the cash easily. I'd find a place to stuff it and two of my three blades once I got closer to Sanctum. They'd undoubtedly be doing pat downs before entry, and I didn't want to be caught with big ass wads of small bills and knives.

I opened the door and stepped out into comparably chilly air, breathing it in to erase the lingering tang of his fear and stress-sweat clogging my nostrils.

"Here," I offered, digging a few tens out of the stack and tossing them onto the booster in the backseat. "Buy your kid a better booster seat, asshole."

SANCTUM.

Not exactly a covert name for a pub owned by the Saints of Thorn Valley. But then again, I didn't think they really needed the anonymity. Hell, it seemed they strived for the opposite.

I was sure it helped officer Vick's pals know exactly who not to mess with. Where not to step foot.

It didn't look like all that much on the outside. A heritage building at the edge of the strip, taking up the full corner lot. Three levels. Well, if you knew about the basement, anyway.

On the top floor, cherry red curtains hung in the windows, backlit with diffused light. I'd heard talk that there was a brothel of sorts up there, but hadn't confirmed it just yet. Couldn't go asking too many questions of the locals, especially when they were so clearly as enamored with their *Saintly* St. Crow and his merry band of misfits as they were with themselves.

I bypassed the burgundy painted front entry of the pub and went around the side of the building to the nondescript black service door near the parking lot behind the bar.

I felt naked in the skin-tight black dress I wore after getting rid of my larger jacket and the rest of the cash. But the long sleeve little number was easy to move in, made the girls look killer, and hopefully, would help me blend in. I knocked. Waited.

The door opened three seconds later and the burly bouncer gave me a once over.

It was five to eleven now. I knew I wasn't too late, but by the look on his face, he was going to turn me away.

"I think you're in the wrong place, sweetheart."

He began to close the door.

I tugged the cash from my thrifted designer purse and thrust out a palm to stop him.

He eyed the cash. "Don't call me sweetheart," I deadpanned. "You want my money or not?"

"Fighter?" he asked, his shoulders tensing as he frowned at me.

"Rook," I replied. I didn't even have to know a goddamned thing about his opponent to know where my money would be safest. If I could double it. The More the better.

But it still physically wounded me as Mr. Bouncer ushered me into the narrow space at the top of a set of stairs going down and took the wad of cash from my hands to feed it into a counter.

When it was done eating my spoils, he stuffed it into an envelope and wrote the amount on the front. "Name," he barked gruffly.

"AJ," I replied on a whim, kicking myself when it was too late to take it back. I had a cycle of names I usually used. All variations of Evangeline. That name had *so many* short form variations. Eve, Eva, Evie, Vanna, Angie, Lina, Gilly, the list went on and on. Made it easier to remember and if I forgot I could just say Evangeline and they would connect the dots themselves. *Voila.*

But *AJ?* Fucking, really?

I groaned inwardly, telling myself that AJ could stand for any number of things while mentally kicking myself.

He added the name beneath the amount and sealed the envelope before prying open a metal drop shoot in the wall and chucking it in.

The *shhhhh* of the paper sliding down the metal shaft made a weight settle in my belly.

Bye-bye, my sweets, I'll be seeing you and your cousins very soon, I promised each bill.

The bouncer looked me up and down, judging my ability to hide a weapon somehow beneath the skin-tight dress I was wearing. The heels, the ones Becca lent me the night at the docks, were strappy and wouldn't conceal anything, either.

"Spread," the bouncer decided, and I heard a few cheers erupt from deep below. I could hear the faint thud of music, too, but it was all so muffled up here, they must have invested a small fortune in sound-proofing.

I lifted my arms and spread my legs as the guy completed a very thorough search. Above his head, I noted the blinking red light of a surveillance camera set into a nook on the ceiling. I wondered if they already knew I was here. I held no illusions that this disguise would fool the Crows, but if I managed to stay in the choked crowds of people I assumed would be surrounding the ring, I may skate by unnoticed.

"About finished?" I asked the burly fucker as his fingers trailed up my left thigh, hedging below the hem of my skirt. Another inch and he'd know exactly what I was hiding down there.

He frowned, but released me, snatching my small purse to look inside that, too. He grunted as he stepped out of my way and thrust the bag back at me.

I had a fake ID prepared, but it seemed my money was good enough to neglect the need for one even though I could smell the strong tang of mixed spirits and beer below.

"Good luck," he barked as I took the first step down into the bowels of Sanctum. I heard the deadbolt slide shut behind me and my heart skipped a beat, mouth going dry.

This was going to be one interesting night.

23

ROOK

"How is it?" Grey asked, finishing the wrap on my right hand. I flexed my fingers, making sure there was enough movement, but not so much that I'd easily break bones. I mean, I didn't mind a few breaks, but like Corvus and Grey liked to keep reminding me, if I broke the bones in my hands any more than I already had over the years I wouldn't be able to use them for shit when I got older.

Not to hold a gun.

Not to take a piss.

Not to jerk it when I woke from fever dreams of Ava Jade.

I hadn't dreamt a goddamned thing in years until now. I'd almost forgotten what it was like.

"Hey," Grey pressed. "You good?"

"Is he ready?" Corvus asked, storming back into our private area with a sour look on his face.

I lifted the dregs of my whiskey from the stool next to me and swallowed them down. Fight nights were the one time I let Corv regulate that shit. I'd had exactly four ounces of whiskey since we arrived an hour ago, and I wasn't allowed a drop more until *after* the fight. Something about not wanting to kill the other guy.

Personally? I thought it would make for an exceptional show.

"Yeah," Grey answered for me, and I knocked my glass back down onto the stool, glancing up through the dark hair covering my forehead to the clock.

Two minutes.

Heat swelled in my core, pouring steam into my muscles. I rolled my shoulders and twisted on my stool, stretching out my back muscles. I'd already gone through the rest of the stretching and pre-fight bullshit earlier, but my lower back was tight as fuck and I didn't want to risk it locking up in the ring.

"How's it looking?" I asked, shaking my head at Grey's offer of water.

"Better than we hoped. Conor Jones talked a big game. Won his last five consecutive fights. The bets are stacked against you, but not by much. A last-minute bet pushed it closer to even."

Which meant that when I won, the payout would be greater for our proxies, and therefore, *for us.*

"Just put on a good show," Grey said, clapping me on the shoulder and giving a squeeze as he fixed me with a pointed stare.

"Don't I always?"

He snorted. "And don't kill him."

"No promises," I muttered, getting to my feet as the crowd outside began to grow louder than the thudding music. After I killed that one guy back in April, they were hesitant to let me fight again at all.

If the roar of the crowd out there was an indication, I'd say it helped.

Deep down, people were more fucked up than they liked to believe. Even the investment bankers and the mortgage brokers and the lawyers. They came here tonight not just because there was a fight and they could make some coin. They came because those dark parts of themselves craved chaos. Blood. The possibility of death.

The only difference between them and us was that they wouldn't admit it. They choked it down and snuffed it out. Pretended it wasn't there. Trauma hadn't destroyed the barriers their darkness hid behind, but it'd shattered ours. Setting us free.

Corvus gripped the thick black curtain, and I grimaced.

This was the part I didn't care for. Growling quietly to myself, I waited, bouncing from foot to foot, letting that unnamable thing inside of me slither to the surface. The rawest, most primal parts of myself awakening as a spark of adrenaline ignited them.

I shook my head, opening my mouth to allow Grey to shove the guard in. He gave my cheek a hard slap, and I let it ricochet in warm waves through my body, stoking the fire.

Fuck yeah.

I grinned over the mouthguard as the music changed, shifting to the entry song Grey chose for me. The distant echo of cheers accompanied the synth sounds as *Fire* blared over the speakers, and I stepped out.

I kept my head down as I stalked toward the ring, bristling as shouts and jeers assaulted my ears. As unfamiliar hands attempted to clap on to my back and arms, reaching, keeping me hemmed in on both sides. Stopped only by the look on my face and the weak half fence holding them back. I envisioned cutting each hand clean off at the wrist as I passed, which made it all bearable.

This was part of the show.

A part I endured as a means to an end, but when a meaty hand slapped against my cheek, my lid popped and I whirled, striking him once in the jaw. He stumbled and fell, making the surrounding crowd have to catch him.

Silence fell for an instant before the cheers erupted anew, louder and more wild than before as the unconscious man was forgotten, left to fall unceremoniously to the floor.

"Back the fuck up from the fence," Corvus snarled as he and Grey moved to form a protective barrier on either side of me. "I said *move* assholes."

Funny how these pissants thought my brothers were protecting me from the crowd and not the other way around. A smirk curled my lips as I stepped up the three short stairs and bent to slip through the two red ropes.

The spotlights always took some getting used to. So fucking obnoxiously bright. I squinted into the crowd of shouting, animated faces. Finding Diesel at the edge of the room, just next to the bar, his arms crossed. He nodded to me, and I grinned maniacally.

His fingers slyly came up to tap his jaw. Three times.

He wanted me to go at least three rounds before putting Conor down.

I nodded back. I'd try, but Diesel knew just as well as my brothers that I couldn't always control what happened once that bell rang.

The music shifted and Conor Jones entered from the other curtained off section of the wide, black-painted space. He pounded his fists together and lifted his chin, slapping the hands of the crowd on his way down to the ring. A swagger in his step. A showman.

Unlike me, Jones' body was entirely devoid of ink. A blank canvas. Unblemished. He looked like a baby. If babies had eight packs and a sick fade. Something in his clean-shaven face only heightened the illusion. The guy could've been sixteen or twenty-six. It was anybody's guess. Corvus would know, but I didn't care to ask.

He'd be prettier covered in purple and red. When I was finished.

Jones stepped into the ring and raised his arms, shouting into the crowd as they cheered for him.

A chant of *Con-or Jones, Con-or Jones, Co-nor Jones* began, and I held in a snicker. He brought some fans. Cute. I wondered if he spotted them the minimum bet, too. I knew his type. I wouldn't doubt it if he had. He'd be expecting a cut of his winnings, which he clearly thought he had in the bag.

We squared off, and I hesitated before bumping fists, letting him question the look in my eyes. His cocky grin faltered, recognizing that I was a predator. Or maybe that he was the prey.

Pinky positioned himself between us, getting ready to signal the start of the fight. That was basically all we had a ref for down here. There weren't really rules in the basement of Sanctum.

I glanced up one last time, looking for Grey and Corv. I found them in my corner, waiting for the end of the first round. Kit and water already in hand.

My lips parted. Breath catching as a sharp set of brown eyes met mine from the edge of the room. I'd know those eyes anywhere, even if they were tinted with false color. They'd been haunting my dreams for days.

It didn't matter that she was wearing a short black wig and heavy-handed makeup, there was no mistaking her. She shuffled uncomfortably, turning slightly and breaking eye contact.

Yeah.

It was her.

I'd know that ass anywhere.

Ava Jade had come to Sanctum. Ava Jade was going to watch my fight. I didn't know why I was surprised. I had no reason to be. Of course she could get in. Of course she could get the money for the minimum bet. I didn't think there was much she *couldn't* do.

The animal within preened like a motherfucking peacock, and I licked my lips, my focus back on my target. Blood buzzing in my ears.

Oh, I was going to make this good.

"Fight!" Pinky roared, dropping his hand swiftly between us before rushing to back up out of the crossfire. It was time for the beast to play. I lunged.

24

AVA JADE

He saw me. I was sure of it.

Rook went at his opponent like a hurricane. A tatted hurricane with storm cloud eyes and a shock of black hair. And *fuck* if it wasn't the hottest thing I'd seen in my entire life.

His muscles rippled and flexed beneath the ink with each skillful blow. His focus was singular. Blind to the world around him as he danced and parried around Conor Jones, making him look a fool.

This man was born to fight.

Conor landed a blow to Rook's jaw, tearing his lip. Blood dribbled down his chin and splattered on the floor. He wasn't shocked though, I could tell he was grinning even with the mouth guard making it look more like a grimace. It was in his eyes. The high he was getting from not only inflicting pain, but receiving it as well.

I began a slow walk around the perimeter of Sanctum's underground club, getting different angles on the fight. I was certain of it on the next hit Conor landed; Rook had allowed it. It wasn't a lucky hit. Rook was letting the pasty-skinned fucker hit him *on purpose*. A slow grin spread over my lips, and I shook my head, unsure what to make of that.

I would have my work cut out for me with him. If Rook got close enough, I wouldn't be able to take him on my own. The admission stung. I ground my teeth, but it was the truth. It was why I'd come. I needed to know what I was up against.

Grey was a challenge, but I could take him if necessary.

Corvus... I had no fucking idea because I'd never seen him lift a finger. All he needed was his voice and the authority it commanded to get shit done. For all I knew, he could be a crap fighter. But I knew he packed heat, and I had no doubt about whether or not he knew how to use it. Learning to shoot would've been one of the first things Diesel St. Crow taught his adopted son.

Rook, though...seeing him now, he was not only dominating this fight, but also playing with his food like an animal toying with his kill before the final blow. I knew that if I had any chance with him, it would need to be at a distance.

I needed to brush up with my blades.

I'd practiced throwing all of *twice* since I arrived at Briar Hall. I'd need to keep that skill more honed than that if I stood a chance.

The first round came to an end and while Conor fell onto his stool and barely had the energy to lift his head to accept the straw his buddy offered him, Rook paced the ring. Only when Corvus climbed up and corralled him to his corner, did he go.

I paused my slow turn about the room and narrowed my eyes, watching Rook come back to himself. The faraway look in his eyes faded, and his heavy breaths subsided. He blinked, and it was like whatever possessed him in that ring was gone. He'd managed to beat back the beast within. Rook sagged a bit and pushed away the water, shouting something at Grey I couldn't hear over the crowd.

Grey's eyes narrowed, and his head turned on a swivel. Corvus' did, too.

Fuck.

I spun, finding a heavy dark curtain and slipping behind it. It was dark back here, but I could make out the shapes of heavy bags, weights, stools, and other equipment. Not a gym exactly, that would likely be under lock and key, but maybe a storage area.

I waited until the bell rang again and the second round started before I leaned against the wall to peer out the slit at the edge of the curtain. The burning desire to watch Rook too much to deny.

My lower lip stung as I bit down on it, getting momentarily

distracted by his ink. It covered him almost completely from his waist up. Two full sleeves stretching down to cover his hands. One of them stretched over to cover his right pec and creeped up the side of his neck. And his back…holy motherfucking shit. His back was fully covered in an angry crow captured mid-flight. Surrounded in expertly shaded clouds that appeared to be dripping blood instead of rain.

In the myriad of black lines and swirls and shapes, I could see stars, feathers, flowers, a portrait of a woman with long dark hair. And a roughly done tally grid running up the inside of his left forearm.

I could imagine what it was meant to keep track of.

He was a fucking masterpiece.

If he was a Saint, I might have to start praying.

No, Ava Jade.

Shit.

My stilted breath left my lips in a sigh, remembering why I was here. Why I needed to…

What did I need to do?

Blood burst from Conor's nose as Rook landed a vicious hit, his eyes slanted and wild as whatever *demon* inside of him took over once more.

I double checked to make sure no one could see me from my dark corner, hidden away behind the curtain, and licked my lips as an ache formed between my thighs. I twisted, leaning back against the cool wall to try to stifle the *need,* but it was too strong.

I hitched up my dress and braced my heel against the edge of a flat bench and tipped my head to the side to keep eyes on Rook through the slit at the edge of the curtain as he accepted a blow from his opponent and made a show of looking dazed when the sharpness in his stare told me he was anything but.

Moving my damp panties aside, I circled my slippery cunt, biting down hard as the sensation pulsed through my whole body, making my legs shake.

Holy shit.

Rook jabbed Conor in the ribs, and I *swear* I heard bone crack, even over the roar of the bloodthirsty crowd.

I moved my fingers faster, breaths coming hot and quick through my parted lips.

This is bad.

This is so fucking bad.

This is incredible.

Rook's dark eyes swung over the crowd between blows, catching on mine. A wicked curve drew up one corner of his bloodied lips and my lips parted in a silent surrender as my orgasm threatened to send me to my knees.

"Sparrow."

I froze, gasping as he pulled me from the wall. As my back met the solid warmth of his chest, his fingers curled around my throat, securing me to him. I blinked, my blade freed without thought from its sheath between my legs, the pointy end jabbing threateningly into his thigh.

"Let go," I gritted out, fury racing through me, tainting my still burning desire. Trying to figure out how he'd crept up on me from the shadows behind the curtain. Where and how he'd even gotten back there. "Let go or I'll cut your artery and leave you to bleed out back here on the fucking floor."

"If you were going to cut me, Sparrow, you'd have done it already."

My breath caught as he slid his other hand down my ribs, inching lower. I writhed against him, angry as fuck but also aching to finish what I'd started.

He guided my view back to the slit in the curtain with his thumb, squeezing my throat in a way that made me shiver. I caught sight of Rook striking like a cobra, his lithe body a weapon made of flesh.

"Watch." Corvus breathed against my neck. "Watch him all you like, but it's *me* you'll feel. It's *me* you'll come for."

His fingers grazed my inner thigh, and I squirmed, pressing more firmly on the blade, enough that I knew if I pushed any harder, it would slide right through his thick denim and into his flesh.

"Fuck you."

Corvus' fingers slid higher, brushing against my wet opening. His body shuddered against mine, and his breath came in a gush of heat against the back of my neck. "Go ahead, then," he said, his voice low and teasing. A rumble against my spine. "Tell me to stop."

I opened my mouth, but no words came out. The scent of him, like leather and lead was seeping into my nerve-endings, making them misfire. The truth I wouldn't dare utter hid within the confines of my lips. Unable to be spoken.

I don't want him to stop.

From my periphery, I watched as he lifted his damp middle digit to his mouth and slid it over his tongue, sucking off my sweetness.

"Mmmm."

An ache spread low through my belly, and I tried to look away from Corvus' finger in between his lips, away from Rook. Tried to force the insatiable need to dissipate, but Corvus only tightened his grip on my neck, prodding my line of sight back to his brother.

"Watch," he commanded, emboldened by the fact that I hadn't refused him. He had no idea that his force was only turning me on even more, or maybe he did know. Maybe this Crow knew exactly what he was doing.

When he slid that same middle finger and one more inside of my throbbing cunt, my back arched, and my mouth popped open on a moan. My grip on my blade faltering.

I wouldn't come, I decided as he began to pump his fingers into me, circling my wet clit with his thumb. I would *not* come for him.

"That's it," he cooed roughly against my cheek, and my head fell back as he did some fuckery with his fingers that was seriously going to make me fall apart.

No.

"Stop fighting it," he growled, speeding the movements of his fingers. "You *will* come for me, Sparrow."

"No," I managed through gritted teeth. "I won't."

Somehow, the round changed from second to third, and the sound of the bell ringing again sent Rook flying into action. Different this time. He wasn't holding back anymore. His movements were reflexive, not practiced. He was a beast caged in human flesh as he dragged Conor Jones around that ring, pummeling him like he was nothing more than a sack of meat and bones.

"Yes," he rasped. *"You will."*

"Fuck," I managed past the stopper in my throat, trying so hard not to let on what both of them were doing to me.

Rook landed the perfect blow to Conor's jaw, and his eyes went blank as he stumbled back, dazed and trying to regain his wits. Covered in blood from his temples down to his chest.

The chanting changed. They were no longer shouting for Conor, they shouted for Rook.

Rook, Rook, Rook.

"Finish him!" I heard Grey roar above the cacophony of voices.

Rook stepped up, and I cried out, my core tightening to beyond anything I could control. I squirmed in Corvus' grip, and he fought me the whole way, forcing me to come just like he promised he would.

No.

His merciless thrusts and rough circling of his thumb came impossibly faster, finger fucking me to within an inch of my life as Rook took the final swing.

I came hard on Corvus' fingers as Conor Jones hit the mat and Rook was declared the winner to a roaring crowd. My blade hit the cement floor with a clatter as I rode the wave of my orgasm, my knees weak and shaking.

He withdrew his fingers, and I spun away, but his fist around my throat remained, and he pushed me to the wall, his mouth finding mine in a cruel, bruising kiss. His hard length pressing against my belly.

The sound of my own moan broke me free of the trance he had me in, and I chalked it up to low O2 levels.

I thrust my arm up and knocked his away, freeing my throat while I used my other to grip him and pull, twisting us until *he* was the one backed up against the wall with my forearm across his throat. Shock registered in his cold eyes for an instant before his gaze leveled out into a wicked sort of triumph.

I pushed hard against his windpipe as I shoved myself away, making him cough to clear the ache from his throat.

He laughed ominously to himself as I collected my blade from the floor and pulled my dress down to cover the evidence of what he'd just done. What I'd just *allowed* him to do. My face turning a shade of red that I hoped the shadows concealed.

"Hope you got what you came for, Sparrow."

"Go fuck a goat, Corvus."

The bastard laughed some more as I pushed through the curtain and back out to the chaos of the main floor. I shoved my way through the throng of wealthy drunks to leave, feeling Rook's eyes on me all the way to the exit.

25

ROOK

I'm not sure what possessed me as I raced from the stage, heading straight for the cash room to smash my bloody fist on the door. Corvus was nowhere to be found, and Grey was right on my heels, barking at the crowd looking to congratulate me to step back.

I pounded harder, faster, until the lock disengaged and I shoved through, knocking the glasses off Jimmy's face. "Rook? The fuck you—"

"Who'd she bet on?" I asked, as if Jimmy would fucking know. "The girl. The girl with the short dark hair and tight black dress."

Jimmy's eyes crinkled with confusion as he righted his glasses.

"Move," I growled, shoving past him into the counting area, searching through the baskets of envelopes and cash on the table. Money spilled, and I could hear Grey shouting behind me, but I didn't give a flying fuck. If I didn't hurry, I wasn't going to catch her.

I needed to know.

If she got into Sanctum, it meant she'd placed a bet.

She must've...

I flicked back to an envelope I'd just passed, yanking it out of the *paid* basket. It said AJ on the front. Ava Jade. It had to be hers. She bet seven thousand...on *me*. I opened it, a slow smile turning up one corner of my mouth, straining the cut there.

Christ. My cock twitched in my pants, hardening as I choked on a laugh and shoved back through Jimmy, only pausing when Grey stood in the doorway to block my exit. A snarl tearing from my mouth.

"What the fuck is going on over here?" I heard Diesel roar, and I clenched my teeth, staring down Grey as Diesel tried to shove through the crowd toward the cash room.

"Move, Grey." I enunciated the words slowly as I leveled my stare on him. The blood dripping into my eyes stained my vision with a crimson tint, and my inner beast perked up like a bull.

Grey's nostrils flared, but he moved, knowing there would be no stopping me. "Brother," he said in a hard whisper as I passed, a warning in his voice to match the worried knot between his brows.

"I just want a minute," I cut back at him. "Stall them."

His jaw flexed as he looked away, and my neck heated, right eye twitching as I tore myself away from my brother and the cash room, launching myself up the stairs.

"Which way did she go?" I asked in a growl as I passed Diesel's newest recruit, the bouncer whose name I could never remember.

I shoved through the door and glanced back to see the big oaf pointing down the street to the right. "That way," he said. "Think she took a left on Churchill."

I nodded and began to run, my ankle protesting each step from a rough kick by my opponent. The cool air licked at the sweat and blood still clinging to my skin, making the cut on my lip and the gash above my right brow sting.

An odd scent, like rotting limes, permeated the air, and my nose wrinkled as I rushed past it onto Churchill, slowing to a quiet jog. The street was silent as the grave. A few small shops clustered near the main street gave way to a residential area of apartment buildings and a few older homes. Most lights were snuffed out for the night, save for a small handful of oven lights and late-night TV screens.

I stalked down the streets, the damp *slap* of my bare feet on the rough pavement the only sound aside from my breaths and the thudding of my black heart.

I could feel eyes on me, watching, and pursed my lips to contain a grin.

"Come out, come out, wherever you are," I called into the dark, licking the blood from my lip. "You forgot something."

Waving the envelope, I followed my gut, letting that *other* sense lead me toward the side of one of the more rundown apartments. I glanced down the narrow gap and caught a jerk of movement near the end.

Got you.

I sprinted down the side of the building, cut glass biting into my heel, making me snarl as I rounded the corner and stopped dead, my shoulders expanding and heaving with each slow pant.

Ava Jade waited there, a large black lump of fabric at her feet, her blade raised. Fire in her eyes. The delivery area was devoid of trucks tonight, leaving it wide open save for a bank of trash bins. Only one streetlamp illuminated the lot, and she stood just outside of it. Her blade glinted in the light. A threat that I'd take as a promise.

I licked my lips.

"Where are the others?" she demanded, her gaze jerking to the alley I'd just come from before checking her six.

"Not here," I shrugged, tapping the cash filled envelope on my palm. "Thought you might want this."

Her cheekbones flared, giving her away.

"How kind," she replied, her voice dripping sarcasm.

I stepped forward, and she stepped back.

I cocked my head, stepping in and to the left. She stepped back and to the right.

Smart.

She'd seen what I could do, and clearly she knew she wouldn't be a match. Judging by the way she was holding that blade, though, she knew how to throw it. I was willing to bet she was a crack shot, too.

"You don't seem very grateful."

"You don't seem like the considerate type," she lobbied back, still eyeing the alley and glancing down at her blade. Checking the reflection? I shivered.

"You don't know me."

"I don't want to."

"*Liar.*"

Her face heated, jaw tightening with anger. If it were possible, she looked even more beautiful when she was angry. Almost as good as she looked when she was covered in blood.

I dangled the envelope from my two fingers. "Come on," I challenged her. "Just come get it."

She scoffed, giving her head a slight shake, but I could see it, the instant she made the decision. Her eyes snapping to the envelope. She *did* want it. I could imagine what she might've done to get the money in the first place, and now she'd doubled it, betting on *me*.

It was a lot of cash to kiss goodbye.

"I won't bite," I told her, taking another step forward. She didn't retreat, her gaze jerking from my face to the cash and back again.

"*Liar*," she hissed, turning my own word against me.

I smiled, all teeth, giving her a glimpse of my monster.

Conor Jones balked when I let him see, but Ava Jade...her darkness smiled back.

I saw in her what I'd only seen in three other people in my entire life. It made me stop. Take stock. The intense need to know every dark corner of her mind took root in my mind, festering.

Without ceremony, Ava Jade lifted her shoulders and closed the gap between us in eleven long strides, stopping just out of my reach. Her dress was wrinkled, and her wig was slightly askew. She noticed me looking and tugged it off, tossing it on the asphalt as she shook her hair out of the spiral she had it contained in. It swirled around her shoulders in a wild mane of darkest auburn and something in my chest cracked.

Her lips popped open when she noticed the scar on my collarbone. Her eyes narrowed as she followed the line of it down, finding other scars to match it, and different sorts hidden within the ink. I didn't cover them because I was ashamed, I covered them to avoid this. The look of pity from others. The disgust.

I braced for it, but it didn't come. Her eyes jerked back up to meet mine and she betrayed no emotion at all except a sort of calm understanding that did things to me I wouldn't dare speak of.

Ava Jade made a valiant grab for the envelope, but I lifted it out of her reach, catching her wrist with my opposite hand. She had her blade to my throat faster than I could blink. I rolled my hips, soaking in my hunger for her.

"You saw my cards," I whispered, lowering my head so our faces were only inches apart. "It's only fair that I see yours."

Her eyes widened a second before I twisted away from her blade and pulled hard on her wrist, sending her stumbling to catch her footing.

I stuffed the envelope of cash in the front of my shorts, against my slowly building erection. Ava Jade whirled on me, her upper lip curling.

I beckoned her forward with a curl of my fingers.

She rolled my challenge around in her mouth before glancing down at her blade. She gripped it tightly and reeled her arm back for a sniper-like throw. I closed my eyes. Waiting for it to impale somewhere vital, but the *thunk* of it came and I felt nothing.

When I opened my eyes, her blade was embedded in the pock-marked wood of the streetlamp beam. She attacked while I was turned, and the breath whooshed from my lungs as I went down, my legs swept out from under me. My ribs and temple cracking against the pavement, a ringing forming in my ears.

Damn.

I was up and ready before she could launch her next assault, blocking a throat jab and a knee meant for the family jewels. Ducking from a punch that, if delivered in just the right place, might've been my end.

Fucking hell.

She roared her fury as she came at me again and again, and I blocked her, waiting for my opening. She went for a jab at my lower back, and I was too slow to block it. Pain exploded through my abdomen, making me clench my teeth.

When she went in for another hit, misjudging my level of pain, I narrowly dodged it, yanking her arm to get her off balance. She fell, and I was on top of her in a second, using the full force of my body weight to pin her to the pavement.

She struggled, cursing and writhing, trying uselessly to find any opening to get free, but my weight was greater than hers. Her legs were locked down. Her arms pinned. My cock against her belly.

She was trapped.

I saw the moment she realized it, too, her breaths coming faster. Panicked.

No.

Her face went white as a sheet, her body trembling, but it was her eyes that I couldn't stop staring into.

I knew that look.

Distant. An echo of past trauma lighting her up from within with blind terror.

Without thinking, I fell back, jostling to my feet in my rush to get off. The scent of pure fear putrefying in my lungs. The need to take it back wrestling with my still pounding need to dominate. To destroy.

"*Shit,*" Grey shouted as the sounds of two sets of footfalls reached me through the ringing still growing in volume in my ears. "What did you do?"

"Fuck," came Corvus' grunt, and I let him pull me back another step away from her.

Ava Jade slapped Grey's hand away as she got to her feet, unable to look at any of us. "Don't fucking touch me," she growled, shoving him hard in the chest. Making his eyes narrow.

She stormed away, snatching up the bundle of black fabric and retrieving her blade from the wooden post.

"Wait," I said before I could stop myself, reaching down the front of my shorts for her winnings, but by the time I looked up, she was already gone. The bramble at the edge of the lot shifting from her ghost.

I lurched forward but was stopped by a firm grip on my shoulder. Corvus. I bared my teeth, feeling too many things I didn't want to fucking feel.

"Leave it, man," he said. "Just leave it."

I shrugged him off and pegged the envelope to his chest, forcing him to take it.

"I need a fucking drink."

26

AVA JADE

I used the back door, like I always did, creeping into the silent lemon-scented halls of Briar Hall. Pro tip? No one ever checked to make sure that one was locked, and slipping a plug into the lock slot on my way out had always worked. Though I thought I could climb up to my window using the weathered brick facade and climbing vines if I ever needed to.

A violent buzzing almost had me tripping over my own feet, and I cursed in the dark as I rooted around in the lining of the oversized jacket for my cell, expecting a text from Becca.

Instead, the screen lit green with a text from another *problem* I didn't fucking need right now.

UNKNOWN

You should have killed the dark one while you had the chance, but now I see I'll have to do it for you.

Nobody touches what's mine.

Rage flared back to life in my veins like liquid fire and I saw red, my thumbs jabbing the keypad to the point of cracking glass.

I closed my eyes and took a deep breath in before flicking over the screen to get the unknown phone number, I committed it to memory before blocking it. Even if it wouldn't help, since whatever piece of shit this was liked to change phones every few days, at least it would shut him up for tonight. I had enough on my goddamned mind as it was.

Safe to say it wasn't Corvus, though, or any of the Crows as I'd once thought, unless this was an attempt at misdirection, which was also entirely plausible.

Groaning, I stuffed the phone back into my jacket and pushed the hair from my face, deciding to stuff away the added stress in a back corner of my mind. Ignore it. At least for now.

I could analyze later. I could find whoever it was and pour bleach in their eyeballs and chop off their thumbs *later*.

Removing my heels, I padded up the narrow back staircase the janitors used, avoiding the main floor and second floor cameras. I fumbled with the keys once at the door, my hands still infuriatingly unsteady after what happened.

I swallowed past the dry lump in my throat, cursing my weakness, as I finally sheathed the key in the lock and twisted. The door opened out of my hand before I could even push. The darkened shape of a disheveled Becca filled the entry.

"Hey," she said, bag of M&M's in hand. "Thought that was—"

She paused mid-sentence, backing up a step to flip on the hall light. I lifted an arm to shield my eyes, wincing.

"Girl, what the fuck happened?" she demanded, hustling me inside and shutting the door behind me.

I tossed my jacket and the small clutch swaddled within it to the floor and ran my palms over my face, sighing as I dragged my tired feet to the couch. Fear Street was paused with a still-image of a screaming female face filling the entirety of the sixty-inch screen.

Becca shut it off and my own reflection appeared in the black, not looking much better than the girl that'd been there before. She rooted around under the magazine covered coffee table until the rattle of her metal tin rang out around us.

"Here," she said, passing me a joint. "You look like you could use it."

I put it to my lips gratefully, leaning forward on the sofa as she flicked on her torch lighter. I inhaled deeply, my tensed muscles relaxing already as I blew out a cloud of pot smoke.

I passed her the joint and glanced up in search of smoke alarms.

"I disabled those months ago," she said without my need to ask. "I usually just smoke outside, but fuck it, they won't say shit to me anyway."

She took a long drag and went to pass it back, but I shook my head. The edge had been taken off, any more and I wouldn't be able to stay as sharp as I needed to be.

"So, you going to tell me what the hell happened, or...?"

I sighed heavily, letting my head fall back against the cushions.

"I mean, you don't have to, I just—"

"It's fine," I interrupted her. It might be nice to talk about it, and even though I'd only known Becca for a few weeks now, I really felt like I could trust her. But feeling like I could and *knowing* I could were two different things. There were some things she could know. Others, not so much. Not yet.

"I went to Sanctum tonight," I admitted, trying to suss out how much I wanted to share. "Rook was fighting there, in the basement."

"I've heard of that place," Becca mused. "I think my dad actually went there once for a match, before the Saints started buying up all the properties in Thorn Valley and pushed him out further South."

She snuffed out her joint and tucked her legs up under her on the sofa, getting comfortable. "If Rook was the one fighting, why do *you* look like shit?"

"Thanks," I scoffed, bringing two fingers up to pinch the bridge of my nose. There was a nasty headache forming behind my eyes, and it was just adding insult to injury. "I fought, too," I told her. "Afterward. With Rook. In the street."

"What?" she gushed, leaning in. When I chanced a look in her direction, her brown eyes were wide with worry. "Why? Oh my god, are they coming after you?"

Becca's gaze flicked fearfully to the door.

"No, I don't think so."

She cocked her head. "*Okay*, I don't think I'm following. What exactly is going on?"

I met her stare, curious if she would be able to see the truth in my eyes. The one I didn't want to admit. Not even to myself.

She gasped, her hand going to her mouth. "Shit," she said on a breath. "You want them, don't you? And they've made no secret about wanting to claim you."

I looked away, and she stiffened next to me.

Becca blew out a breath. I couldn't look at her as I worked my jaw, unable to confirm or deny her suspicions. I wanted to dick punch them as much as I wanted to fuck them, but that was just semantics.

"Fuck, babe. That's…"

"Insane?"

"*Hot.*"

I twisted back around, my face screwing up into a scowl. "*What?*"

She shrugged. "I don't know, I mean, they're dangerous. Fucking total psychos. Criminals. But…"

"But what?"

"But they are three of the most powerful men in this city. They are *definitely* the hottest guys in this school. Girl! You could have your own reverse harem! And I *know* you can handle them. I mean, I've had some pretty vivid dreams about *handling* them myself."

My stomach soured.

She laughed, oblivious to my green-eyed monster trying to lay claim to property that was definitely *not* hers.

She stopped laughing abruptly, her eyes gleaming. "Oh fuck! Bri would absolutely *shit* if you ever fucked Grey."

I winced.

"Oh my god *you fucked Grey?*"

"A little bit."

She shoved me, pulling a blanket into her lap to get comfortable. "Tell me *everything*."

So, I did. At least the parts I could. About my confusing split feelings and how I wasn't sure yet if I wanted to fuck them or bury them. How I might just do both. It didn't change anything though.

Tomorrow night when they went to meet with the Aces, I was going to be there. I *would* buy my freedom by whatever means necessary, whether or not I dreamed of Corvus's hands on my body tonight. Or Grey's cock thrusting into my pussy. Or Rook's dark eyes, his blood-stained face. The power behind his punch.

...the moment I thought he was going to kiss me when he lifted that envelope out of my reach. How my traitorous heart nearly stopped.

None of that mattered because they made their stance clear. To them, it was either me on my knees or hell on earth at Briar Hall. That shit wasn't going to fly. Not as long as I was still breathing.

It was time to trap some Crows.

27

CORVUS

The Rover chewed gravel as Grey pulled out of the driveway and bumped onto the road leading down past Briar Hall and into Thorn Valley. The tension in the front seat enough to form a physical weight on my chest. Meanwhile, Rook picked something out of his teeth with a switchblade in the back, lounging over the entire bank of seats like we were headed to a fucking picnic instead of a meet with our would-be enemies.

Sometimes I envied him. His ease in high-tension situations. He'd always been more at home in chaos than in calm. It was immobility, idleness, that was his kryptonite. My jaw flexed as I thumbed a quick message to Dies.

CORVUS

On our way.

DIESEL

ETA 12.

We'd hang back if we looked like we'd arrive before him, better to pull in all together. And since Diesel refused to ride with us, this was the best we had. Dies would park near the old warehouse, but not right at it. Just in case anyone fucked with the Rover. Having two getaway vehicles wasn't the worst idea, but I didn't like the idea of him riding alone.

I wished he'd at least brought Pinkie or Cash. Or, hell, both of them, but I could understand the reason he didn't, too. Diesel had control over his men, but vengeance could sometimes outweigh sense when push came to shove. I couldn't say I wouldn't go absolutely fucking feral if anything happened to my brothers or Diesel. Heads would roll. And I wouldn't be waiting to find out for certain who was at fault and who wasn't.

My back stiffened as the phantom scent of Ava Jade passed under my nose, my lips parting to taste it. I concealed a soft groan with a clearing of my throat as I shut my eyes, cock twitching in my jeans as last night's encounter replayed in my mind. Fuck, she'd smelled so good. Fresh and soft like spring moss and sandalwood, but also sharp, like some kind of strong herb. A poison that lingered in my memory longer than anything else.

Damn.

I shook my head, trying to dislodge the ghost of her from my thoughts. I needed to focus.

"Five minutes," Grey warned as we turned off Freemont Street and onto Clove Drive, leaving Thorn Valley.

I polished off the last of my coffee, setting the metal mug down with a thud back into the cupholder. *Still*, the scent of her lingered, distracting me. Like a stain left branded on the inside of my skull.

The feel of her tight little cunt squeezing my fingers, hungry for me even though she tried so hard to fight it.

The moment she lost that fight.

Her expression as she came, her muscled body hard and soft in all the right places.

I didn't sleep at all last night.

Not even for a fucking second.

I was afraid of what I'd see when I shut my eyes.

"*Fuck*," I muttered, inching my window down for some fresh air. Praying it would wash away the stain of her long enough for me to focus on *this*. On tonight.

"What's eating you?" Rook asked from the backseat.

A snarl curled my upper lip. What was eating me? Rook had been smug as fuck since we left the Crow's Nest, like he had a secret he was happy to keep all to himself. It made me wonder, not for the first time, what happened between him and Ava Jade in the street last night.

"We're here," Grey said.

I sat up straighter, squinting out into the gloom. The sleepy town was all but uninhabited these days, but here, just outside of it, it really was no man's land.

An old industrial area that housed only rickety old buildings and warehouses left to desiccate on a pockmarked gray paved road. Grey rolled to a slow crawl up the street. The area we wanted was at the very end. Another half a mile up the road into the dark.

"Where's Diesel?"

As if on cue, headlights bounded behind us, and I drew my weapon, finger on the safety. Rook did the same and Grey lifted his from the back of his pants to lie flat on his lap. We had a few higher-powered weapons already hidden strategically at the meet point. Just in case. But if their plan was to box us in on the road, this was all we had.

The uneven canter of my pulse steadied, settling into the focused rhythm of a hunter. My vision sharpened, and I blew out a slow breath, watching the approach of the car until I recognized the distinct shape of the headlights. Saw a flash of red paint.

"It's him," I said. "keep going."

"Anything on cams?" Grey asked, and Rook tapped on a small tablet screen in the back, bringing up the feed of the area. It showed a view of the rear yard of the largest warehouse, where the meeting would take place. Diesel had the camera well hidden, and it hadn't sent a notification of movement, so I had to assume the Aces hadn't arrived yet.

"No, nothing," Rook replied, and I heard the swish of liquid in metal as he took a nip from his flask.

"Hey," I warned. "Not too much."

"Fuck off, Corv. I'm fine."

Heat licked across my back, but I didn't push him. He'd been in a way since last night. I wasn't sure if he slept, either.

That girl was going to get us all killed.

Destroy us from the inside.

She was everything I worried she would be and then some. And yet,

I couldn't imagine letting her escape our reach. If she ran, I knew my beast would hunt her. Drag her back. Make her mine.

"Let me see," I growled, twisting an arm to the backseat for the tablet, scraping her from my bones.

He dropped it into my palm and leaned back, draping an arm over the seatbacks, letting his hand hang down into the trunk space.

The screen showed a wide-angled view of the lot behind the old warehouse at the very end of the road. Stacks of old tires lined the edge nearest the tree line, wrapping around the bulk of the yard. Stacked haphazardly, some piles having fallen over, leaving an obstacle course of tires strewn over the dirt and gravel.

An old bobcat and some other equipment withered in the yard. Broken and rusted. The bobcat closest to the southern side was where our extra firepower was hidden. It was where we'd approach the yard and make our stand and would provide the best cover and quickest escape should we need to use it. Meanwhile, the Aces would be mostly hedged in by the mountains of old tires on the other side.

They wouldn't like it, but if they had nothing to hide and wanted to clear their names from Diesel St. Crow's shit-list, then they wouldn't have a problem with it.

Dies veered off to park near the front of the warehouse while we went off road, bouncing over a cement piling and onto the overgrown grass between two warehouses, driving right to the yard at the back.

Grey spun the Rover around in a sharp U, letting the back end fishtail out so we were parked just ten or so meters from where the meet would take place, the Rover positioned for a fast and easy exit.

"Good here?" Grey asked to confirm, and I gave him a nod. He could've had a career as a professional driver if *the life* hadn't claimed him first. As it was, I wouldn't trust another soul in that seat. Not even myself.

"Shit." I hopped out of the Rover and gripped my gun with both hands, glaring as the unmistakable shape of Diesel rounded the edge of the warehouse, walking toward us alone. "What the fuck, Dies, you were supposed to wait for us to come get you."

"It's fine," he said with a wave of his hand, his face coming into view as he stepped from the shadows and into the moonlight. "They aren't here yet."

I grit my teeth but didn't argue. It was no use with him.

He stalked past me, running a hand over his beard, rings glinting in the light.

"You set up a spotlight?" I asked as he went to double-check the bobcat, showing us where the guns were hidden in the rusted metal bucket.

He nodded. "It's on a timer. Should be on any—"

The light clicked on, expanding to shed its glow over the yard.

"—second," Dies finished. "It's not as bright as I thought, *shit.*"

"It's fine," I assured him. We could do this just as well in the dark, but the light would keep anyone from trying to draw on us while concealed in the shadows. Plus, Diesel liked to look in the eyes of those he met with. He said the truth was always written there, no matter what words fell from their mouths.

Rook and Grey did a quick sweep of the neighboring warehouse yard, keeping tight, guns up and ready.

"Clear," Grey announced as they made their way back, Rook tossing something up and catching it in his palm. I thought it was a rock, but as they came back into the light, I cursed.

"Rook, we said no fucking grenades."

He wrinkled his brow at me like he had no idea what I was talking about.

"Don't look at me like that. We talked about this."

"It's just one," he argued, tossing it up again and catching it. The pull-pin rattling.

Diesel laughed, clapping Rook on the shoulder as he came to stand with us, and my jaw flexed, frustration rolling down my back. A crooked grin pulled at one corner of Rook's mouth, but it faded when he lifted his gaze back to me.

"Killjoy," he muttered and pocketed the grenade, lifting a cigarette to his lips.

Unbelievable.

The unmistakable sound of a vehicle's approach filtered into my ears, and I lifted a hand, signaling for silence as I listened.

"They're coming," I told them. "One car. A van maybe. A max of maybe eight Aces."

"Just like we thought," Diesel replied, drawing his weapon to click the safety off only to return it back to the sling across his chest beneath his leather jacket. "Get into position, boys."

We did the same, readying our weapons and getting into position near the old bobcat, but not directly behind it. Close enough that we could dive for the automatic rifles in a pinch.

Headlight passed by the gap between warehouses and the roll of tires stopped on the other side, out of sight.

I cursed Diesel's lack of foresight in not installing a cam on the road-side, too. I'd have liked even a thirty-second advantage of knowing how many there were before they made their way to the yard.

Diesel seemed to notice his mistake, too, a frown turning down the edge of his mouth for an instant before his all-business mask was tacked back into place. The unfeeling face of the founding Saint.

The crunch of boots over dry dirt sounded at the opposite end of the warehouse as the Aces made their way down the alley toward the yard.

Movement in my periphery drew my attention for a heartbeat and I stilled, my hand twitching toward my gun, my mind racing with possibilities of an ambush. My brows lowered as I registered what it was. A reflection in the crooked mirror on the rusted-out bobcat, reflecting the image of the Rover parked at our backs.

The breath was robbed from my lungs as the shadow of legs appeared beneath the chassis.

Shit.

The softest click of a door closing told me the fucker was *inside* the Rover. Maybe the whole time.

I hedged closer to Dies, ready to give him an elbow and a signal to the threat at our backs when she crept out from behind the sleek black SUV and darted for the tree

line.

No.

Fury and dread coiled in my chest, burning and sinking and heavy.

My little sparrow didn't make a sound as she flew to the trees, concealing herself in their darkness. My eyes jerked to the guys, to Dies, to the Aces piling into the yard across from us.

No one else noticed her.

There was jack shit I could do.

If she was discovered spying, she'd be killed. Or at the very least interrogated to within an inch of her life. My pulse throbbed in my temple and the muscles of my neck stiffened, burning.

Stupid fucking woman.

What the hell was she thinking?

I should have known. *Her smell.* Her scent had been all over the goddamned Rover, and I chalked it up to another sleepless night. Convinced myself she was driving me insane when all the while the little viper was hidden away in the trunk.

Stupid.

So *so* dangerously stupid.

Diesel elbowed me, and I blinked, refocusing my attention to where it should be. Squarely at the seven men standing opposite us in the yard.

"Welcome," Diesel said, lifting his arms, the warm welcome serving the dual purpose of showing them that he wasn't holding his weapon and telling them that he wouldn't use it so long as they didn't give him a reason to. "I think we all know why we're here, so let's get to it, shall we?"

28

AVA JADE

I forced the air to enter and exit my lungs in slow, quiet breaths, clinging to the base of an old redwood for cover as I watched the exchange unfold.

Four against seven.

I didn't like their odds, but Diesel St. Crow and his sons didn't seem bothered by them in the slightest. In fact, with the exclusion of Corvus who looked wound tighter than a top, they all looked calmer than they had right to be.

Rook especially. I eyed him suspiciously. The fucker had draped his arm over the seat and his fingers brushed into my hair. Like an idiot, I shied away, moving away from his touch. Unless he was more drunk than he was letting on, there was no way he hadn't figured out there was something back there that shouldn't have been. But if he'd known, then why not say something?

Why not call the whole thing off?

Turn around and take care of their unwanted passenger?

It didn't make any sense to me.

He didn't make any sense to me...and yet, he didn't have to. I felt like I knew him on a level where *sense* didn't have to play any part at all.

"Welcome," Diesel called into the chasm of devoid space between their two gangs. "I think we all know why we're here, so let's get to it, shall we?"

I dug out my phone and flicked to the video screen, tapping record.

I hadn't had a chance to spot the man himself last night at the fight and now, seeing him for the first time, I could see why he was their leader.

Formidable. Tall and thick through the shoulders with hooded eyes that cut like a shard of ice. A tapered beard and strong jaw. But it wasn't his looks alone that made him exude power. It was something in his stance. A relaxed power. A predator's grace. The unfeeling, unflinching mask of his expression gave not even an inkling of what he might be thinking beneath it.

If I was a weaker person, I'd cower at the mere sight of him. It was said many had, but he only served to pique my interest further, and I watched him closely, trying to figure him out.

A man across the yard stepped forward, putting himself a few paces ahead of the others. It was clear this was their leader, though he didn't have the same atmosphere about him as Diesel.

I'd done a bit of digging, well, as much as I could without drawing unwanted attention, to know that his name was Leonard Boniface. Aka Lenny Ace.

Shorter than I thought he would be. Younger, too. With coiffed brown hair and a clean-shaven, gaunt face. In a black t-shirt, bulky with what was unmistakably a bulletproof vest beneath, with two silver-handled pistols proudly strapped over his chest, lying flat against his ribcage.

He was the original Aces leader's nephew. Took up the position when his uncle died a couple years back under *suspicious* circumstances. As an outsider, it was easy to see how the death wasn't an accident. That it was very likely Lenny Ace himself that did it, but his gang brothers didn't seem to mind. They all stood in a neat row behind him, ready to give their lives for whatever their leader deemed a fair price.

"We heard about your man," Lenny replied. "Sorry for your loss."

Diesel cocked his head at Lenny, and a moment of silence stretched on between them. Long enough to make me squirm internally, my pulse picking up speed with anticipation.

"Appreciate it," Diesel replied finally. "Though I'll admit we were under the impression you might've had a hand in it."

A tick made Lenny's jaw jump. From my vantage point set a ways back from mid-field, I could see it easily, but I wondered if Diesel could. If his sons were paying close enough attention because that man was definitely *lying*.

He may not have pulled the trigger himself, but he knew something. I was certain of it.

I glanced to the Crows, finding Grey and Rook watching intently, studying Lenny and his entourage as closely as Diesel seemed to be. But Corvus...Corvus' eyes skimmed their faces. Unseeing. His brows were pinched tight and there was a distance in his eyes like he was a million miles from here. It wasn't what I expected from him and made my insides chill.

What was he doing?

Why wasn't he paying attention?

"Us?" Lenny asked, a brow lifting. "What made you—"

"The 'A' carved into Randy's chest. Your gang tag. The same one you paint over your territory."

Lenny's jaw ticked again.

This wasn't good.

"Now," Diesel continued, raising a hand in a calm gesture, not allowing Lenny to rebuke him. "I'm not saying it was by your command, but perhaps one of your men went a little rogue. It happens. You understand, Lenny, that blood must be paid for the life that was taken. Think carefully before you speak again."

The thinly veiled threat hung in the air like a promise and a thrill went through me, making me shiver despite the warm black pullover I wore.

The thrill quickly morphing to something else as I spotted one of the Aces slip a gun from the back of his jeans and press it to the side of his thigh. His black hair was slicked back, giving a fully unobstructed view of his face. The way his upper lip was twitching into a snarl.

He was at the very end, closest to me. The light from the battery-powered spotlight hung off the back of the rusted metal warehouse wall didn't quite reach him. The only one who might've been able to catch his movement, or the glint of his gun in the moonlight, was Corvus, and he was clearly distracted as fuck.

Look, I wanted to shout. *Pay attention, you fucking idiot.*

I had to reposition my phone, having lowered it while I, myself, was distracted by everything they seemed to be missing.

"I can assure you, Diesel," Lenny replied after a moment. "None of my men would have acted so recklessly. They wouldn't dare go against my orders."

Unlike yours... Lenny seemed to be implying and a small fissure formed in Diesel's perfectly crafted facade. That struck a nerve. So the king didn't have full control over all of his men, then. Though I doubted any gang leader did. It came with the territory, didn't it?

There was clearly a history between these two, one I wasn't privy to.

The man with the greasy black hair fixed his sights on Corvus and my lips parted in wordless alarm as his thumb pushed the safety off.

Oh god.

Why wasn't anyone noticing?

I raced to check all the other Aces, checking to see if they were readying weapons, too, but none seemed to be. Just this one. The one at the end looking like he had an ax to grind.

Fuck.

Fuck. Fuck. Fucking fuck.

"You wouldn't lie to me would you, Lenny?" Diesel asked, his tone one he might use on a child who'd misbehaved. Trying to tease out the truth with the promise of accepting it without punishment.

Something told me Diesel would, too. If Lenny admitted one of his men had acted without his permission, Diesel would have demanded that life in exchange for Randy's and no others.

A fair trade if you asked me.

People had to pay for their mistakes or else they'd just keep making them.

Blood for blood.

It was the one adage of theirs I could get behind.

But Lenny wasn't going to budge, I could tell by the way he was standing. Defensively. Chin raised.

It had to be this clown at the end, the one still looking at Corvus like he might want to carve out his eyes. Maybe?

Ugh.

If Corvus would just fucking *look* then…

The Ace's hand moved to rest beside the trigger and I could *feel* his readiness from here. Like a strain in the air I was breathing. Making it harder to inhale. Thicker.

He's going to shoot him.

"No," Lenny told Diesel. "I wouldn't lie to you."

"You know I don't like being lied to."

"And you know the Aces own their shit. I'm telling you we had nothing to do with it."

Diesel bristled. "Very well. If you had nothing to do with it, then might you know who *does*?"

Lenny opened his mouth to reply, but I wasn't paying attention to him anymore. My body flooded with heat, flushing my cheeks as a fresh wave of adrenaline pulsed through me, narrowing my focus.

Don't do it, I mouthed, eyes fixed on the guy with his sights set on Corvus. I slipped a blade from my ankle and held it loosely in my palm, turning to flatten my back against the rough bark of the tree, positioning myself. My phone was forgotten, slipped into my pocket with the video still recording.

I hesitated, my hand jerking with my own indecision.

If Corvus was killed, there was a good chance my problems would be over.

With Corvus killed, the remaining three Saints would stand even less of a chance against the seven Aces.

Once the first shot was fired, and the first man fell, I had no doubt it would be a bloodbath.

If I let that greasy motherfucker shoot him, I could be kissing my problems goodbye. I could delete the videos, slip out of here and go back to a boring life of books and a future of freedom.

I tested the weight of my blade, lifting it over my shoulder, pinching the edge of it, at war with myself. My pulse pounded in my temples until all I could hear was the rush of blood in my ears, making every other sound distant and garbled.

I couldn't hear what Diesel and Lenny were saying, not really. I couldn't even hear my own breathing, though I knew it would be shallow and slow, measured as I lifted from my knees, my sweater catching on the bark as I uncurled to my full height.

Sweat beaded at my brow.

All you have to do is let it happen, I told myself. *Just close your eyes and let nature take its course.*

My stomach turned, and I swallowed back acid, my teeth grinding.

The man with the black hair bared his teeth, and Grey noticed, squinting at him, but he couldn't see what was hidden at the guy's side. It was too late.

I saw the moment the Ace made his decision, jerking forward, his arm snapping up like a whip, his gun trained on Corvus.

My heart stopped.

I threw.

The bone-chilling *pop* of gunfire ricocheted through me, the sound coming only a split second before the Ace's shriek of agony. My blade speared through the meat of his palm. His gun thudded uselessly on the ground.

The shot went wide, and I sighed loudly, my breath leaving me in a painful gush when I found Corvus alive.

Guns raised all around.

Grey and Rook were fast enough to grab what looked like fully automatic rifles from the bucket of an old bobcat. Corvus and Diesel had their guns drawn, too. Safeties clicked off. Hammers were drawn back. Fingers rested on or next to triggers.

I waited for the bloodbath with bated breath, but it didn't come. The standoff held until Lenny broke it. They must've known that one more bullet would spell all of their deaths.

"Shut the fuck up, Carl!" he snarled, shouting at the hunched form of the black-haired man clutching his hand to his chest and whining obnoxiously loud. He was lucky I didn't aim for his thick skull. If I'd had the time to, I would've. As it was, the best option I could think of was to make him drop the gun or at least alter the trajectory of his shot.

Lenny side-stepped, keeping his sights trained on Diesel as he kicked Carl's gun far out of his reach. "Idiot," he hissed and then chanced a look into the trees. I ducked down, crouching in tight to the tree again, trying to shrink into the shadows, cursing myself for not beginning the quiet retreat straight away. For being too damn curious.

"What the fuck was that?" Lenny demanded. "Who do you have out there?"

Diesel's face betrayed nothing as his lightning-quick eyes flitted toward the trees and away again.

Corvus held his gun high, but his face visibly paled and his chest heaved.

Rook smirked, and my spine tingled when I realized he had a grenade clenched in his left hand while the rifle was butted to his shoulder and held with his right.

Grey was a study in mute power. His sights fixed on the injured Ace and nowhere else. Murder in his eyes.

"It's not ours," Diesel admitted, though I was willing to bet he hated owning to it. An honest man, I'd give him that. I wondered if he thought the next blade might be meant for him.

"Not yours?" Lenny hissed. "Then who the fuck—"

"Get out of here," Diesel barked right back. "We'll handle it."

I froze, drawing out another blade as I tried to soundlessly back away from the gun-toting gangsters in the yard before me.

Lenny squinted at Diesel, confused, but the Ace's leader backed up, gesturing to his men to get their fallen man and move out. I wouldn't question it either if someone gave me a get out of jail free card.

"Not him," Diesel said in a cold monotone, his gun still trained on Lenny's head as his eyes flicked to the injured Ace. "He tried to kill my son. The reason for which I'm sure you will fucking explain to me at a later date. But for now, I'll accept his life as payment for his *mistake*."

Lenny's Adam's apple bobbed.

"Boss?" Another Ace pressed, torn between helping his buddy Carl and leaving like he was told to.

I lost sight of them as I crept backward, remaining crouched as I began my slow retreat.

They are coming for you, my darkness whispered, unspooling to her full power in my gut. *Any minute now. If you don't get away, your heroic display there will have been for nothing. It'll be them or you. Blades versus bullets.*

Time to find out if all that running was worth it.

I may not be faster, but I would bet my left kidney I could run *longer.* Go farther.

Then what, idiot? That's your blade in that asshole's hand.

The Crows will recognize it. They'll know it was you, even if you do get away.

Stupid didn't even begin to cover what I'd just done.

"Leave him," I heard Lenny order, and a cry of protest came from Carl before a gunshot rang out in the night, marking the start of my sprint.

I jumped to my feet and ran like hell. Flying over dirt and rock and tree roots. Honing in on those other senses. The ones that only flourished under extreme pressure. Relying on reflex and the strength of my body alone.

The feel of the blade clenched in my fist gave me the extra dose of fortitude I needed to keep pushing when the sounds of them giving chase reached my ears.

My legs pushed me impossibly fast until I was soaring through the darkened trees like an arrow shot from a bow.

The dirt and tree roots gave way to rockier terrain and the ground underfoot turned upward, the earth and grass giving way to a rockface slick with moss. I had no idea where I was going or where this path would lead me, but I didn't like the look of the long incline ahead. The trees were more sparse here, and thinner. There would be nowhere to hide if...

A shot blasted apart a thin tree to my right, the splinters of it exploding into my path. If I hadn't been running with quick, jerky movement in a zigzag, it would've hit me, I had no doubt. My heart shriveled in my chest, imaging one of the Crows on the other end of the bullet.

Corvus shouted to stop, but another shot was fired, this one narrowly missing me. The bullet tucked itself into the stone at my right with a *crack!*

The inclining stone sloped down sharply to my left and when I thought I had enough cover, I dared the fall, jumping down to skid on my heels all the way back down to level ground. My ankle twinged with pain, but I didn't let it stop me, pushing forward.

With the tree cover, they wouldn't be able to see me from above, but more importantly, they wouldn't be able to get a clean shot on me. I growled inwardly as the pain in my ankle grew, forcing me to slow despite the adrenaline still pushing me onward.

I wouldn't be able to go much farther.

Fuck my life.

Rocks slid and tumbled as they made their way down the incline after me.

I would be shot like a fish in a barrel if I didn't hide or run, and since the latter seemed to be out for the moment, I crouched low and made for the deepened shadows of a fallen tree. It was held up by the rock face, and I folded myself into its dead, scratching branches, sandwiching myself in between stone and insect infected wood.

Cobwebs tickled my neck and face, but I didn't let myself think of all the things that might be crawling in between layers of my clothes right now. It wasn't important. Not even a little. I drew my last two blades, promising them I'd retrieve their brother from the dead guy in the yard if I made it out of this alive.

There were four Saints in these trees, and they all had guns.

If I had all four of my blades and the ability to throw them, I might've stood half a chance, but now, with only two, my only chance would be to stay hidden. To not be found.

I held my breath as their footfalls grew louder, until I could hear their heavy breaths.

Please, I sent a plea to whatever gods could hear me. *Please keep going.*

"Diesel," Corvus said, and I shuddered, closing my eyes against an assault of mixed emotions.

His father hushed him violently and all sound ceased. They were listening for me. I gave them nothing to hear.

"You hear that?" Diesel asked after a moment.

"I don't hear anything," Grey replied.

"Exactly," Diesel said in a husky whisper. "They stopped running. Whoever it is, they're hiding somewhere."

"Dies, come on," Corvus said, his voice taking on a tone I didn't recognize. What was up with him tonight? "They're gone. Let's just—"

"Spread out," Diesel barked, cutting Corvus off. "Rook and Grey, that way. Corv, you're with me. We'll find this son of a bitch."

They spread out, and I evened out my breathing, not moving a muscle as I caught sight of two silhouettes approaching. Grey and Rook.

Rook broke off from Grey and headed further away to the right, bent low with a mischievous grin on his face, his gun raised. This was all just a massive game of hide and seek to him. Unlike the others, he didn't seem bothered by the fact that the person they were hunting had blades, and maybe even a gun. Or maybe he'd already put it together.

The thought struck a nerve. Rook knew I was here.

What would he do if he found me?

But it wasn't him I had to worry about as he moved further and further away, it was Grey, who was carving a path almost straight for me.

"Clear!" Corvus shouted from somewhere far off in the distance.

"Clear!" came Diesel's brusque voice, closer than I'd have liked.

"Clear!" Rook.

Grey stooped low, tipping his head to the side as he examined the hollow between the tree and the stone. I held my blade high, but my hand trembled as he crept closer.

Don't make me kill you...

He darted forward, yanking a branch out of the way, handgun raised.

I could have thrown. I could have stopped him. I didn't.

I stood there in full view, blade at the ready if he looked like he might fire.

He didn't.

Grey's lips parted in silent horror as he took me in, his gun lowering.

"Grey!" Diesel snarled from somewhere far too close.

Grey blinked, stepping back and releasing the branch. His eyes didn't leave mine as he hollered back. "Clear!"

Then he was gone.

I sighed, my breath tripping from my lips, broken as I let the relief cascade over me. My breaths loud in my own ears, but they'd already moved on. I didn't think I could hear them anymore.

Never let your guard down, that was rule number one that Dad taught me when he took me on our first job. When he bought me my blades after a good win at the private casino. Rule number fucking one, and for just a second, I forgot.

I didn't even see him coming. His hand curled around my forearm and dragged me from my hiding place, tossing me to the ground as though I weighed no more than a sack of potatoes.

My shoulder and the side of my face knocked into the hard dirt, and I scrambled to get to my feet in the dark, shaken but regaining my balance quickly.

I lifted my blade, ready to throw it straight into the heart of Diesel St. Crow before he could lift his weapon to take aim.

"Sparrow, don't!"

Corvus' shout shattered my resolve, but I held there, blade at the edge of my fingers, ready to throw as I heard their footsteps running toward us. In a second, I'd be surrounded.

In a second, it would be too late to do anything.

I'd lost my chance.

Diesel's blisteringly cold stare bored into me like a spike of ice as he trained his gun on my face, but I showed him no fear. I always knew I'd meet my end by the bite of a bullet or the slice of a blade. I'd just hoped it would come later. Much later.

"You know this girl?"

29

GREY

AJ wouldn't allow us to disarm her, and Diesel didn't push for it, so we didn't either. She stood between Rook and Corvus, with me at her back, letting us corral her back the way we'd come. She limped slightly, but she was doing a good job of hiding it.

What the fuck was she doing here?

Did she have a death wish?

My pulse thrummed uncomfortably behind my ribcage, making my stomach twist. This wasn't good. Already, my mind raced with possibilities, options that might end with her somehow still alive. We had a shadow once. A guy who thought he'd strike it rich blackmailing the Saints. Diesel found him, too.

He never saw daylight again.

Our father might be called Saint, but he was merciless when it came to protecting his found family. His brothers and his sons.

That guy was a threat, and now AJ was, too.

"In the warehouse," Diesel snarled from up ahead as the yard came back into view through the trees. The spotlight dying with the battery so there was only a diffused glow over the tires and the dead guy lying among them.

"You're a fucking idiot," Corvus muttered, and I realized he was talking to AJ. I'd picked up on it earlier, how neither of my brothers seemed at all surprised to see her here. I had to wonder if they were in on it. Or had seen her somehow before I had.

"Yup," AJ replied, popping her lips on the 'p,' like she didn't care at all that she might be chum for the sharks before sunrise. "Saved your ass though. You're welcome, asshole."

Corvus visibly stiffened, but said nothing as Diesel slammed a palm against the door to the warehouse, shoving it open, the rusted hinges screeching in protest.

We escorted AJ through, and her shoulders tensed, immediately on edge, the blades in her hands twitching.

I left the door open, squinting into the dark to find Diesel hunting through the place, throwing random bits of scrap into a barrel. He dumped gasoline over the mess and flicked on his lighter, igniting a bit of stray paper before tossing it into the metal drum.

Fire roared as the pile of scrap wood ignited, illuminating enough of the space to see that the warehouse was devoid of anything more than some withering old wooden pallets and a sagging desk in the corner.

"Who are you?" he demanded, coming at AJ with a look in his eyes that made my guts twist.

When she didn't answer or so much as flinch when he stopped just short of her, he turned his fury on Corvus. "Well?" he pressed. "Who the fuck is she?"

"Ava Jade Mason," Corvus replied, and only then did AJ betray any discomfort. I wouldn't like Diesel St. Crow to know my name either if he wasn't my family. Especially not if he was looking at me the way he was looking at AJ right now.

"Who do you work for?" Diesel asked her, his nostrils flaring. "Who sent you?"

She locked her lips tight.

"*I asked you a question.*"

"She isn't with a gang," Rook replied with ease, leaning back on a stack of pallets like we were at a casual bonfire.

Diesel's steely gaze moved to Rook, studying his second eldest son before bringing his sights back to AJ. "Check her," he ordered.

I moved in to do it before Corvus could, unsure of why. "Lift your arms for me, AJ," I murmured, low enough that Diesel would have a hard time catching it over the roar, pop, and hiss of the flames in the metal drum.

My back warmed from the fire as AJ grudgingly lifted her arms, her knuckles white from her grip on her blades. I patted her down.

"Be thorough," Diesel commanded, and I re-doubled my efforts, careful to caress every inch of her body. The curve of her breasts. Between her legs.

"No wire," I announced, but as my fingers dipped into her pockets I found something else and winced. Her phone.

Diesel would've seen the shape of it sagging in the pocket of her baggy pullover, so I drew it out. "Phone," I announced.

"Check it."

I did, flipping the screen to her first. "Password?"

"Fingerprint," she replied without a lick of trepidation, but her face betrayed what her voice wouldn't as it paled when I pressed the digit to the fingerprint reader.

I flicked through the main screen as Diesel waited, his trigger finger twitching.

Bile rose up the back of my throat as I flipped through to videos and found not one, but two.

The dots connected in my mind, seeing Billy Parker trussed up like a pig in his cooler. We'd heard he was found dead, now we knew why.

She'd killed him.

But she'd also saved the video.

I wasn't sure what that meant.

And the other video was of tonight. I didn't watch more than a few seconds of either before deleting them, my mouth going dry.

"Well?" Diesel prodded.

"Nothing," I gritted out, giving AJ a loaded look as I handed her phone back to her. I didn't let go straight away when her fingers curled around it, making her have to tug it out of my grasp. If she survived tonight, she had some fucking explaining to do.

I wasn't even sure why I deleted the evidence of her crimes. Why the fuck was I trying to save someone who so clearly was trying to blackmail us?

Were you not blackmailing her first? The traitorous thought echoed back to me, bouncing off the recesses of my skull.

Something told me there was more to it than what it appeared to be.

"Then she's collateral," Diesel snarled, raising his gun.

I blocked his shot, lurching into the line of his bullet at the same time Corvus made a move to disarm him.

"*Don't*," Rook growled, and all eyes turned to him, no longer lounging easily against the pallets but standing like a hulking shadow, his arms tense at his sides, shoulders heaving. "No one touches her."

"Just what the fuck is going on here?" Diesel shouted, his carefully constructed mask crumbling as betrayal flashed across his eyes. It cut deep to see it, making me shudder, but I didn't budge. I wouldn't.

What the fuck was wrong with me?

"Dies," I managed, able to keep my voice level despite the chaos raging within. "A word?"

Corvus whirled on me, his brows drawn as if to ask what the fuck I was playing at.

If he wouldn't do it, then I would. AJ was worth at least *trying,* wasn't she?

Diesel glanced between the three of us, calculating. Studying.

His upper lip curled, and he dropped his gun, stepping back with a hiss. "Don't let her out of your sight," he spat at Corvus and Rook as he shouldered through them both and vanished back out into the night.

"What are you doing?" Corvus asked as I turned to follow him, giving AJ's arm a squeeze, an apology unspoken on my lips.

"What we should have done from the start."

"What?" Diesel snapped as I walked out of the warehouse, going to where he was pacing near the Rover. "You want to tell me what the hell is going on, Son, because I'm two seconds shy of—"

"We know her," I admitted. "She goes to Briar Hall."

Diesel's breathing evened out at the level tone of my voice, or maybe it was something in my face. But he softened, running a palm over his beard with a heavy sigh.

"I don't know why she followed us, but I do know that she's the only reason Corvus isn't the one lying dead in the yard."

Diesel stilled. He didn't like that.

"And we both know what would've happened if that motherfucker killed Corv."

It would have been anarchy. We'd have been lucky not to lose another. Or all of us...

"What are you saying, Son?" he asked, clearly exasperated as he shuffled, dropping his head to take a long slow breath. "You saying she's friendly? Hmm? Is that it? That she came here, what? As...as unsanctioned backup?"

I frowned, shook my head. I didn't know what I was saying exactly, but I needed to drive this point home. "She saved our asses, Dies."

"You saying you trust this girl? This *outsider*?"

I flexed my jaw. "Yes."

"And your brothers?"

"They trust her, too."

Not any further than they could throw her, but that wasn't the point right now. The point was saving her life like she'd just saved my brother's, and possibly all of ours.

"We owe her a debt of life," I pushed, speaking in terms he would understand. The unwritten code of the life.

Diesel's lips pressed into a taut line as he considered that. "She's a liability. She's seen what went down here tonight. The girl can't go free."

"No," I agreed. "But maybe there's another option."

"Speak it, then."

"We bring her in." I spoke the words quickly, my stomach dropping at the implication of them. It was what I'd been saying since the beginning, since I looked at her, *really* looked, and saw someone my soul recognized. That'd only happened three other times in my life. I had to trust it.

"Let her take the trial," I continued when Diesel looked at me like I might be losing my mind. "If she survives, she'll be in so deep that she'll never be able to use anything she's seen against us without burying herself, too. If she doesn't..."

I let that hang between us for a second, knowing he might like that option better.

"...then I guess you won't have anything to worry about."

"You're serious."

I nodded, and he turned pacing away only to return again, rolling my suggestion around behind the dam of his lips. Eyes unfocused.

"She's a girl," he argued.

"It's been done before. Mom was a Saint."

He bristled, and I realized belatedly it was the wrong thing to say. Comparing AJ to his dead wife.

I waited, unable to take it back now that it was said, but when the silence stretched too long and something inside me felt pulled so tight it was near snapping, I continued.

"You saw how good she is with a blade. She can fight. Sly as a fox, too. She could be useful."

He looked at me, his stare darting between my eyes as though he might find some truth there I was saying out loud.

"Do you have feelings for this girl?"

"No."

"Don't lie to me."

I clenched my teeth.

"I've never asked you for anything," I said, using the last tool in my arsenal. It was the truth. I'd always done what I was told. Everything I was trained to do. I was a good soldier. A good brother. A good son. I didn't push for anything, because in my limited experience, when you pushed, sometimes the person would never come back. But I was pushing now. I would push for her.

It was what was owed.

"I am asking for this. *For her.*"

The hurt in his stare almost broke me, but I hid the pain well. Stood taller instead.

"So be it," he said, his gaze turning dark as he stalked past me, unable to look me in the eyes anymore.

"She doesn't leave your sight. Not for a second. Not until the trial begins," he called back, and I stood there, mute and numb until I heard the sound of his engine roaring to life and his tires peeling away from the warehouse, carrying him home.

30

AVA JADE

After Grey returned, they escorted me to the Rover and closed me inside. I could hear snippets of their heated conversation through the bulletproof glass, but not enough to piece together what was going on.

Grey sat with me in the car while Corvus and Rook cleaned up Carl's body. The air permeated with anger and things unsaid.

It must've been hours before they finally returned from the dark of the trees, coated in dirt streaked sweat.

I thought of running again, but with my ankle still in bad shape, I knew I wouldn't get far. The only other option I saw was to slit Grey's throat and make a stealthy getaway instead of a rapid one while the others were busy disposing of the evidence of Diesel's kill, but...

I couldn't.

Just like I couldn't let that greaseball shoot Corvus.

I stewed in silence, angry at myself and trying to work through the puzzle of my thoughts, only bothering to speak once Rook slid into the seat beside me and Corvus hopped into the front seat.

"I'll fight back," I warned, crossing my arms over my chest as icy dread pooled in my stomach. I could take one of them. *Maybe,* I could take two. But all three? I could fight, but I knew what the outcome would be.

Rook lifted a brow at me, and Grey swiveled in the front seat, his face drawn. Corvus didn't bother to turn, sitting stoically in the passenger seat to stare out into the growing dawn.

"Just make it quick, would you?" I requested, sinking into the seat as Grey turned back to the front and started the engine, pulling slowly back onto the road.

They didn't speak to me the entire drive back to the Crow's Nest. Rook twisted his lip ring round and round with his teeth, his dark gaze slipping to me and away, only to return again a few moments later.

He kept his distance, lounging in the seat closest to the opposite window, knee bouncing behind Corvus' seat.

Somewhere around the halfway point, Grey turned on the radio, drowning out the tense silence with the early morning show from the local radio station.

The reality of my situation didn't seem to truly hit me

until we bumped off smooth pavement and onto gravel and the Crow's Nest came into view. But it wasn't what I couldn't stop staring at. The small shed at the edge of the property, half hidden by trees as the first rays of dawn lit the metal roof made my stomach plummet to my toes.

I was *this close.*

This close to freedom.

Why couldn't I have just bowed like a good girl and done what I was told.

Oh yeah, because I wasn't a good girl. I didn't bow. And I did whatever the fuck I wanted *whenever* the fuck I wanted.

The real question was, why couldn't I be someone else?

Someone else wouldn't be about to die in a tiny ass woodshed, their body parts hacked up and hid over three different states.

Fuck.

I gripped my knives, letting the darkness come, beckoning it.

I could kill them.

Maybe not before, but this was different. It was kill or be killed.

"We need to talk," Grey said as he shut off the engine, sighing.

Corvus muttered something I didn't catch to himself as he shoved out the passenger side door and slammed it, stalking into the house.

Rook whistled low, a smirk playing at the edge of his lips as he opened his door. "Want a whiskey?" he offered. "You're going to need it."

What?

"We aren't going to kill you, AJ," came Grey's exasperated voice from the front seat as he withdrew the keys and stepped out himself, shutting his door as he opened mine. I shied away, lifting a blade.

He looked between it and me, a tightness around his eyes. "And you aren't going to kill us, either," he challenged as I caught sight of Rook in my periphery, going into the house, too. "I think you made that pretty clear tonight."

"If you aren't going to kill me, then why the fuck am I here?"

He bent his head, pinching the bridge of his nose, making his dirty blond hair fall forward, shining with streaks of purest gold in the soft early morning light.

"Don't make this harder than it has to be. Either you come willingly on my word that you won't be harmed, or I call my brothers back out here and we drag you inside. Your choice."

I rolled my eyes and stepped out, forcing Grey to move out of my way or be hit. He shut the door behind me. "Good choice."

"The only reason I'm going in there is because Rook said there's whiskey, and I'm hungry enough to eat a whole fucking turkey," I grumbled, knowing how I must sound but unable to stop myself.

"If you say so."

"Fuck you."

His hand closed around my wrist, and I lashed out, slicing his forearm as he tossed me against the door of the Rover. Grey bared his teeth as he moved to box me in, the blade between us the only thing keeping him from closing the last few inches of the gap. Blood dripped in a slow stream from his arm, but he didn't seem to mind. Didn't even seem to feel it.

Fury burned in his eyes. A deep, pained thing that hurt to look at.

"Do you have any idea what I just risked to save you?" he demanded, his anger so hot that I could feel it soaking into my skin. Making the small hairs on the back of my neck raise. "What we'll *all* risk to keep you alive?"

"What are you talking about?"

"And after you were trying to...to what? Blackmail us?" he continued, drawing back with a dark laugh. "I saw the videos, AJ. I know what you did. What you were doing—"

"You gave me no fucking choice!" I shouted, my own fury rising to meet his, the icy dream in my belly turning quickly to acid.

"Yeah, you gave me no choice, either," he scoffed.

"Just remember that."

"What's going on out there?" Rook called lazily from the front door, sipping a short glass of amber liquid. "Come inside so we can all join the fun."

I growled in frustration, shouldering past Grey toward the front door. I snatched the whiskey right from Rook's hand and tossed it back in one long burning swallow before shoving the glass back at him and going inside.

They wanted to talk. *Fine. Let's talk.*

I knew the basic layout of the house since I'd been stalking it on and off for weeks, and I took an easy left from the hall in the entry, through to the kitchen, where there was a whiskey bottle open on the counter. I snatched it up and kept going, through the kitchen to the right into the living room.

Corvus was already there, sitting on the couch, the dirt streaks gone from his face and hands. His dirty jacket missing, leaving him in only a black shirt, dark wash jeans, and sock feet. It felt strange to see him so comfortable. I didn't think there was a place on earth where he wouldn't be ready for an attack at all times.

He lifted his head, and upon seeing me, threw the item he'd been twirling in his fingers at me. My lips parted in surprise as I caught it, the blade cutting into the pads of my thumb and forefinger. The blade that'd been embedded in Carl's meaty hand.

"You're welcome," he grunted, fixing me with a deadly stare.

I tucked it into my ankle sheath with its brother, keeping one at the ready in my palm just in case. "Yeah, well you still owe me one."

He shook his head.

Grey and Rook entered behind me. I fell into the only armchair in the room, forcing the others to all share the sofa on the other side of the long, narrow coffee table. It acted as a line in the sandy carpet, and I didn't intend to cross it again until it was time to leave.

I took a swig of the whiskey, then leaned forward to set it down on the table, noticing Rook eyeing the bottle.

He grabbed it, taking a pull straight from the bottleneck, too, and licked his lips.

Grey leaned forward between his two brothers, elbows on knees as he regarded me coldly.

"I've told them what I found on your phone," he began and already I was on edge, my fist tightening on the blade, regretting the whiskey already starting to nibble at my reflexes and senses.

"There are no secrets between us," he continued, though already I knew that was a lie. Maybe they didn't keep the important shit from each other, but I knew damn well that Corvus had no idea Grey and I fucked. I didn't think he'd like that after his possessive touch and words on fight night.

I waited for him to go on, and when he didn't, my irritability skyrocketed, fueled by whiskey and exhaustion. "How nice for you," I said with a false smile, my voice dripping sarcasm. "Do you also pick daisies on Saturdays and wish upon shooting stars?"

A tick in Grey's jaw was the only giveaway that my comment annoyed him, but I'd take it.

"This isn't a fucking joke," Corvus butt in, his eyes on fire. "Do you know what would've happened if Grey didn't stick his neck out for you?"

"Do *you* know what would've happened if I didn't throw that blade?" I countered, my voice rising in volume.

"Would you shut the fuck up for one second and listen?"

"*Corv*," Grey warned, and earned himself a snarl from his brother.

Corvus got to his feet and paced down to the edge of the coffee table. I thought he might leave, but he turned around, his jaw flexing, and sat back down.

I wasn't sure I'd ever seen him this worked up. I didn't think he *got* this worked up. It made me want to poke him some more, see how long it took before he snapped.

"What does he mean?" I asked Grey, instead, tabling the idea of provoking Corvus, at least for the moment. I didn't like the way they were looking at me. How they seemed to be hesitating to tell me something. "About you sticking your neck out for me?"

"Diesel wanted you dead, AJ," he said. "The instant you threw that blade, you became a liability. A threat."

"But I also saved his precious son," I pointed out. *"Who I wouldn't have needed to save if he was paying any attention at all."*

"Maybe I could've paid more attention if I didn't see your ass creeping out of the back of the Rover."

"Enough," Grey hissed, and Rook snorted, taking another swig of his drink, seeming to be having way too much fun just sitting there watching this conversation happen.

Corvus' nostrils flared, but he fell silent, content to sit there and glare at the carpet.

"AJ," Grey hedged, drawing my attention back to him. "I asked Diesel to bring you in."

"You did what?!"

"I asked him to let you take the trial."

I was on my feet, the burst of shock hauling me up like marionette strings, making me move. "He didn't agree to that."

Diesel St. Crow wouldn't agree to that, would he?

Grey's eyes slid from my face. "He did. I've never asked him for anything. Not ever. I asked him to spare you and let you take the trial. If you pass, you'll be in so deep there's nothing you could do to hurt him, or us, without also burying yourself."

I barked a laugh at the ludicrousness of what he was saying. This wasn't happening.

"And if I fail?" I asked, my tone light, joking. As if I were really going to take the trial to become a motherfucking Saint.

"You die," Corvus said, detached, his hard stare seeming to penetrate deep into my soul.

I flinched as though slapped. A trap door opened beneath my feet, and I was plummeting, searching for anything to hold on to. To pull myself out.

"I won't do it."

"Then you'll die, anyway," Rook interjected, finally speaking up, unlike the others, there was no apology in his eyes, no ire, either. Just amusement. Fucking bastard.

"Then I'll run."

"Diesel won't let you get away."

My heart beat out a discordant rhythm in my chest, fluttering like a caged bird. I worked to catch my breath, cursing myself for the hundredth time for not being able to be that *someone else*. A girl who could be controlled.

"Sparrow," Corvus urged and something in his stature changed. It made the lead in my bones turn to quicksand, melt into glass. Shatter. "You don't have a choice."

WICKED TRIALS

1

ROOK

Ava Jade stood there, a phantom in my room, dressed in light. Her lithe silhouette watched expectantly from the foot of my bed.

What was she doing in here? Grey had been changing the lock on the spare room door when I made my way past to my own bed.

She was asleep inside, face down on the pillow.

Out cold.

They were locking her in.

I didn't doubt she'd have no trouble getting free, but I didn't expect retribution so soon. No light leaked through the edges of my blackout curtains, which meant it'd barely been an hour or two since she passed out.

"Ava Jade?"

My voice sounded hollow. Dull, as though spoken through cloth.

Her lips tipped into a sharp, one-sided grin as she lifted a blade, the glint of the steel spearing into my eyes as it caught the light from the hallway behind her. She twirled it in her fingers.

My cock hardened.

"Come to exact your revenge?" I asked, slowly kicking off the thick blanket covering my naked body. I tucked my hands behind my head on the pillow to prop myself up. Getting a better view of her.

"Go ahead, Ghost," I baited her, adjusting my hips on the mattress to afford her an unobstructed view of my cock.

Her haughty gaze lowered, taking it in. Taking me in as though she were consuming every inch.

She threw the blade.

I closed my eyes.

It *thunked* into the wood of my headboard, and the sting of air on a fresh cut brought me roaring back to life. I lifted two fingers to my cheek, and they came away wet.

I groaned, biting my lip ring, the movement making the sting deepen.

"Come on then," I goaded her, happy to take the punishment for my brothers' actions if *she* was to be my executioner. "I'm ready."

Her eyes sparked as she vaulted over the footboard and was atop me in an instant, a new blade at my throat. I shivered, tipping my head back to afford her a better angle.

She leaned in, her warm breath brushing beneath my ear. "If I wanted to kill you, you'd already be dead."

"Then what do you want?"

Her fist closed around my cock, and I stiffened, my body reacting to her touch in a way it'd *never* reacted before.

My nerve endings blazed.

Hot.

So *fucking* hot. *Burning.*

But I'd burn to ash for her. She only had to light the match.

Ava Jade ran the blade at my throat down to my collarbone, skimming it over my chest and down my stomach, toward my rock-solid cock still clutched in her fist.

Her fingers, tight around my girth, slipped a little and the tiny amount of friction made me groan, my hips aching to thrust into her palm as the sharp edge of the blade skated around the base of my manhood.

Fucking hell.

"Tell me what *you* want..." she coaxed, her tone a wicked combination of desire and hatred.

My lips parted on a breathy sigh.

"Cut me. Burn me. Bleed me. I'm yours."

She shifted her weight, and I bucked as her mouth closed over the head of my cock, warm and wet and...

"Rook!"

Corvus' voice echoed down the hall, and I clenched my teeth, inhaling sharply as Ava Jade curled her tongue around the tip.

Not now, Corvus.

"Rook, get up."

I moved, plunging my hands into her hair to hold her there, my fingers twisting into the silky locks as my hips thrusted upward, fucking her mouth as she held her blade to my femoral artery, pressing firm enough to let me know who was really in charge here.

Something knocked into my chest, and I woke with a curse on my lips, scrambling to sit up, my head spinning, still drunk on the feel of her.

"*The fuck, Corv?*"

"Get out of bed," he ordered, ornery as ever with a sour sneer on his lips. Fuck, just because *he* couldn't sleep didn't mean he had to ruin it for the rest of us. I happened to have been having the best fucking dream I'd had in years.

The *only* dream I'd had in years. So rare and so real I thought...

"You have a test in Sociology today," Corv grumbled, tugging my bedroom door shut behind him as he left.

"We're leaving in ten," he called from outside.

I fell back onto my pillow, letting my hand fall to my sweat slicked chest.

I didn't dream.

Hadn't since I was a kid.

When sleep claimed me, it was a dark thing. A numb thing.

And when I woke, it was as though no time at all passed between night and morning. The only evidence it had was the light of the new day, my sore muscles, and morning wood.

I lifted the blanket to glare down at the swollen head of my cock, aching for a release. The visual of Ava Jade in my head, so crisp only a few seconds ago, was already beginning to fade. I clutched at it, willing it to stay with eyes squeezed tightly shut.

But it was fleeting, vanishing before I could trap it in my memory.

"Damn," I groaned, rolling to the side to snatch my phone from the nightstand. I winced as the screen flashed to life, blinding me for a second before my eyes could adjust.

I sent a text and forced myself out of bed.

ROOK

Chapel.

Her reply came as I finished tugging on my jeans and a pair of socks.

UNKNOWN NUMBER

Meet you there in fifteen.

I shook my head with a smirk, tucking my hard on into the waistband of my jeans with a grunt as I threw on a t-shirt and ran my hands through my hair to force it back into shape.

A shower might've been nice, but fuck it. Mrs. June wouldn't mind.

I paused in the hallway as I left my room, my eyes still burning from the light.

With two fingers, I tried the handle to the room where Grey laid Ava Jade to rest last night. It was locked tight. Listening, I could hear the faint sound of her even breathing inside.

Grey bounded up the stairs at the end of the hall, pausing when he saw me outside of her door.

I pointed toward the locked door, lifting a brow to ask the question without speaking.

He sighed, coming to snatch me from the hallway and drag me down the stairs with him.

I glanced back, my throat suddenly dry, before the door was out of view and we emerged into the kitchen.

"Let her sleep," Grey said. "I checked on her half an hour ago, and she didn't even stir. She's exhausted."

"We're leaving her here?"

"The door's locked," Corvus said, entering through the other side of the kitchen and prying the fridge door open to grab a Gatorade. "Grey'll come back and get her at lunch."

I laughed, shaking my head at him as I ran my thumb over my lower lip, smudging out a smirk.

"And if she wakes before then?" I asked.

Corvus whirled, pulling the bottle from his lips to swipe the back of his hand over the shine there. "Then she'll know her place."

I shook my head, biting my lip ring to keep from smiling. That would only make him even more grouchy than he already was, and I wasn't in the mood to poke the beast today. Maybe later.

"She won't wake up," Grey assured me. "She was dead to the world when I checked in. Twenty bucks says when I come back to get her at lunch she's still a corpse."

My lips pressed into a tight line.

"Your funeral," I muttered, brushing past Grey to grab myself a bottle of water from the still ajar fridge. "Are we leaving or what? I have someplace to be."

She rushed through the chapel doors like a thief in the night, spinning rapidly to ease the large wooden pane closed behind her, wincing as the lock caught with an audible *click.*

"Caroline," I greeted her, leaning against the back pew with a grin.

Her brows lowered as she turned and took me in, confused by the state of my clothes and something on my neck. Dirt, I assumed from the gritty feel of it. From digging the Ace's grave last night.

"Problem?" I asked her.

She hurriedly shook her head, wetting her lips as she walked over to me. Hips swaying, cheeks flaring pink beneath her makeup.

Mrs. June reached for me, going for a kiss, but my stomach twisted, and I stopped her, my fingers rough around her throat. I shook my head.

"No," I said on a breathy growl. "Kneel."

Her eyes lit with her smile as she dropped to her knees, thin fingers unbuttoning my jeans as she wetted her lips again.

I moved my hand to her head, messing up her prim little blonde bun as she freed my cock from my jeans. I tipped my head back as she took me into her mouth, waiting for the *need* to take me.

Her tongue lapped at my flaccid cock and she added a hand to pump its base when that didn't return it to the rock-hard state it'd been in earlier.

She did that thing I liked with my balls, and redoubled her efforts with her tongue, pumping double time with her fist now.

My patience waned, and I snatched up a fistful of her hair and thrust my cock deep into her mouth, making her choke on it.

She gagged and moaned, happy to open wide and let me do as I wanted.

Except...this wasn't it.

The image of Ava Jade passed through the fog of my thoughts like a ghost and I grimaced, sneering as Mrs. June struggled to breathe. Then a more vivid image. The image of her beneath me, pressed between my thighs and the pavement on fight night when I held her down. The look in her eyes.

The panic.

"*Fuck,*" I hissed, grinding my teeth as I pulled out of Caroline's popping lips.

She stared up at me, her eyes wet with tears from choking, her mascara smudged and running down her left cheek.

A week ago, I'd have fucked her throat raw.

A week ago, I'd have gotten hard at the mere sight of her teary eyes and smudged mascara.

A week ago, I wasn't being haunted by Ava Jade Mason.

"Wh-what is it?" Caroline asked, breathless. "Do you want my ass? You can—"

"Get out."

Her face broke. "What?"

"Get the fuck out."

She didn't move so I bent, batting her hand away from my still limp dick, snatching her by the throat in the process to force her to stand. She made a shrill little sound and pulled back, clawing at my hand and wrist as she tried to step away. "But—" she croaked, her words cutting off as I squeezed.

My monster reared its ugly head, solidifying my body, widening my stance. The *thump thump* of it echoed in the empty chasm of my chest.

"*Caroline,*" I warned, throwing her away, making her choke and cough from the pressure on her windpipe. She gasped, catching her breath as she spun unsteadily on her heels to leave. She didn't look back.

I wiped a palm over my jaw as the chapel door fell closed behind her.

I tugged my jeans up and forced the monster back into its cage with a nip of whiskey from the flask in my back pocket.

This was a fucking problem.

Whiskey might do the bare minimum to tame my beast.

I lit up a cigarette and inhaled deeply, blowing smoke toward the altar.

Cigarettes might help take the edge off.

But sex...

It was an equally important remedy to the growing dark within.

Damn.

I smirked at the ridiculousness of it. At the ridiculousness of *her* and what she was doing to us all.

Score one for the ghost.

Zero for the Crows.

2

AVA JADE

y mouth tasted of lead and whiskey.

That was the first thing I noticed when I opened my eyes Tuesday morning. The second was the locked door.

Really?

A locked door.

What did they think this was, amateur hour?

I rolled my eyes after trying the handle for a second time, my fingers sleep numbed and body heavy with the after effects of Rook's whiskey and lingering dread. I'd let Grey lead me to this spare room sometime in the early hours of the morning. I'd been in a daze, still reeling from everything that'd happened, and everything that *would* happen now that I'd been forcibly enrolled in the trials.

"*Hey,*" I hollered through the wooden pane, the sound hoarse, vocal cords demanding coffee before they'd function properly. I pounded a closed fist on the wood, shouting a second time. "Grey?"

I listened carefully, closing my eyes to await the sound of footsteps, but none came. The only sounds in the Crow's Nest were the ominous noises houses made when nobody was home. The whir and *shhh* of the air conditioning. The scratch of branches on window panes. The creak and groan of flexing floorboards.

Speaking of, there were no windows in this closet of a fucking room.

For all I knew it *was* a closet. One they'd converted to a ten by ten atrocity of a guest bedroom. With a lumpy single pushed against the wall and a wobbly nightstand and not much else. It was clean though, not a speck of dust in the air or coating any surface.

Honestly, it was more than I'd had in Lennox, but I'd gotten used to the grandeur of my shared suite with Becca back at Briar Hall. And that shower...

Mmmm, I could use one of those right about now. I could feel dirt under my fingernails. Forest debris in my hair. Stale sweat making my skin tacky.

"Either you open this door, or I'll open it my damn self," I tried one last time, tipping my head to the side for a stretch as I rolled my shoulders back and inhaled deeply to force my heavy limbs to wake.

"Fine," I growled. "Have it your way."

I had my blades on me still, but nothing small enough to try to pick the fucking thing, and it was an exterior lock. The kind with a key. Installed with the key side in. A new one by the look of it. I had to wonder if they'd somehow managed to install it while I was asleep. I couldn't remember noticing hardware that strong on the way in, and I would've noticed. At least, that's what I'm telling myself.

I was a real wreck last night. Apparently, I also hadn't noticed the lack of alternate exits in the room.

These Crows were going to be the death of me.

At least falling asleep in my clothes also meant passing the fuck out in my shoes. The runners wouldn't get the job done as well as if I'd worn my shit stomping boots, but they'd do.

I limbered up, stretching my quads and calves and rolling my ankles.

I just needed the right amount of pressure in the right place and...

My heel connected with the door, an inch too high, but still it rattled, the metal lock bits beginning to come apart. If this was an exterior door, I might've been fucked, but lucky me, it was the bustable interior wooden kind.

The second kick ricocheted up my leg and I grimaced, cursing each one of the vultures for each subsequent kick.

"Fuck."

"You."

"All."

The metal lock *pinged* as it hit the floor and the door fell open, busted up into a mess of chewed wood around the lock and hanging on now by only one hinge.

"Bastards," I heaved, catching my breath as I strolled out. I went to the window down the hall, clutching the sill to peer out onto the gravel drive. The Rover was nowhere in sight.

What day was it again?

Tuesday.

Right.

Still morning by the look of it. Had they really locked me in a room with no fucking bathroom and gone to class?

They told me they had to keep an eye on me. I remembered that part of the conversation. Something about Diesel making me their responsibility, and then there was the part about him not trusting me. And why should he? I wouldn't trust me, either.

I found my way back down to the living room, scanning the low coffee table and couch until I spotted my phone. I jammed the side button, but the screen stayed dark. Dead.

Figures.

Briefly, I thought about tearing a few gashes in the expensive looking sofa before deciding they weren't worth the trouble of honing my blades later. But I couldn't let them get away with locking me up, they had to know I was not some pet to be caged. No matter what they thought. No matter their orders.

It took me about ten minutes to find a Phillips head screwdriver tucked away in a small toolkit in the hall closet upstairs. It took me another fifteen to remove the door handles from every bedroom and bathroom door in the house and stuff them in a pillowcase to sling over my shoulder.

I couldn't help noticing the differences in their rooms, and my ability to tell whose was whose with barely a single glance.

That part surprised me, made something shimmy uncomfortably beneath my skin. I didn't want to know them, but there it was. Like it or not, they'd embedded themselves in my life. Made a home in my mind. Roosted in the cage of my bones.

Corvus': a neat, modern space with soft dark fabrics and espresso finished wood. Not a single item out of place. No personality, either. No posters on the walls. No books or CDs. Nothing that would tell me for certain it belonged to him other than its sterile, magazine page feel.

Grey's dead giveaway was his desk.

The rumpled bed could've been Rook's, but that desk, it was all Grey. A study lamp perched in one corner, school texts lined up neatly against the wall. Notepads galore, and...a drawing tablet. Unexpected, but also not surprising. I wondered if he were any good.

I couldn't see much of Rook's room. He had blackout curtains on the one window and barely a glint of natural light filtered into the space. The overhead light was burnt out, or perhaps purposefully removed from its socket in the ceiling. But I could smell him. Whiskey and tobacco and that musky man smell that did things to my insides. And I didn't need light to see what looked like empty cigarette packs, clothes, and bottles strewn over the floor and a fur blanket spilling off the side of a large bed. Fucking *fur*. Since this was Rook we were talking about, I had to wonder if it was real. Looked like it could've belonged to a black bear, maybe. Or a few black bears judging by the size.

Good luck sleeping in your dark cave without a door handle, asshole.

Good luck taking a shit, too.

I bounded down the stairs with my prizes, feeling lighter even with the five pounds of useless metal added to my frame. I strolled out the front door and spun, flipping the bird to the camera above the door before going around the Crow's Nest to the back. And then farther, through the sparse trees, up a small rock slope and to the edge of the cliffside to stare down to the rocky shore below.

Upending the pillowcase over the ledge, I watched with glee as the metal globes tumbled down like little bells, ringing against the rock until they finally laid to rest in the white-capped waves, burying themselves in the sand.

I sighed, looking toward the horizon as the sun peeked out from behind a hazy pink cloud, warming my cheeks. For a minute I could almost pretend my whole life didn't just go to shit in the last twenty-four hours.

But the minute passed, and my victorious smile waned.

Fuck.

I turned and started a slow jog down past the Crow's Nest and into the trees, making my way to Briar Hall. My legs protested nearly every step, but I made it, slipping in unnoticed through the back door and up to my room.

For a heart stopping moment, I wasn't sure I had the key, but remembered I'd tucked it safely into that tiny, mostly-useless pocket on the inside of my pants.

"Becks?" I called, squinting to see the clock in the kitchen. It was past eleven. Not quite lunch yet, so she was still in chem, and I was supposed to be in AP math. I couldn't wait for the inevitable text from Aunt Humphrey after she got yet another call from the office to report my absence. Fucking *joy*.

Coffee would have to wait. A shower was absolutely mandatory before anything else. My sweat was sweating, and I had a sneaking suspicion that the sour smell clogging my nostrils was my own.

I plugged in my phone on the way, promising myself I'd figure out my life just as soon as I was caffeinated and didn't smell like a dead mule.

3

CORVUS

"Which one is it?" Rook asked as we crested the top of the stairs, sending a trio of girls fleeing in the opposite direction, whispering as they went.

"That one," I growled, my back tensing with frustration as I jabbed a finger in the direction of her room. The silver number three marking the otherwise plain door.

Rook tried the handle. "Locked."

I banged on the wood twice, the thudding sound echoing back to us in the long hall of female dorms and apartments.

She didn't come.

I threw a fist through my hair, an audible growl vibrating in my throat. Christ, why couldn't she have stayed put? Grey was going to head over and let her out for lunch, escort her back to campus for the end of the day.

Fuck, it was his idea to leave her there in the first place, to *let her sleep*. I only agreed once he changed the door handle and locked her in, and only because I doubted she would wake any time soon.

She was dead to the world when I looked in on her. Sprawled facedown with one leg hanging off the mattress, like she just flopped and didn't bother moving to get comfortable.

I'd kill to be able to sleep like that. Just once.

"Grey," I gritted out, stepping back so he could slip ahead. He dropped to his knee and pulled out his wallet, drawing two pins from one of the card slots to pick the lock.

He cracked it in less than fifteen seconds, and we were in.

Her shared apartment sprawled before us. A wide space that would've been bright with all the natural light from the long windows across the floor, if not for all the black sucking the life out of it. Black couches. Black tables. Black cabinets in the kitchen. Even black throw rugs under our feet.

"AJ?" Grey called, but I was already moving. I could hear the shower running in the room to the right, and I headed for the door, shouldering through into her bedroom. Her smell permeated the air, like citrus fruits and salty caramel, making my jaw tighten.

I shoved through the bathroom door just in time to see her arm snake out of the shower and her wild eyes shining through wet dark hair as she threw a blade at me with a shriek.

I only just managed to dodge it, stepping to the left as it embedded in the door where my fucking head was a spit second earlier. A goddamned kill shot.

"Fuck, Sparrow!" I cursed, staring between her and the blade.

"Fuck me?" she howled, stepping out of the shower ass naked and dripping wet, making my fury heat into something more potent. "Fuck *you!*"

She angrily ripped a towel from the hook to cover herself, and I opened my mouth to say something, but she looked at me like she might kill me if I dared. She didn't know how much I'd have liked to see her try.

Rook appeared at my back with Grey only a step behind him.

"Great, now it's a fucking party," she hissed, tucking the corner of her towel down between her perky little tits.

"Can we rewind?" Rook asked, biting his lip ring as his heavy-lidded eyes narrowed on her body. "I think I missed the show."

Ava Jade rolled her eyes. "I should carve each of your stupid eyes out," she said, but I could tell she was quickly losing steam. Exhaustion dragged down the corners of her eyes, fucking with the usually bright and tawny color of her skin.

I couldn't help noticing the bruises.

And the scars…

Her short towel did almost nothing to hide them. Perfect little lines of white raised skin in neat rows on her upper thighs.

Self-inflicted.

My upper lip twitched up into a scowl, wanting a villain to blame. A face to smash. A life to end for her suffering.

I stopped myself. Cut off the thoughts with clenched teeth.

"I can't believe you locked me in that tiny ass room," she said, shoving a heavy mass of wet hair away from her face as she approached us. Seeming to be completely unbothered that I'd seen every inch of her naked body.

"*Uh*, move or I'll move you," she sneered at me, shouldering past us all and into her bedroom.

"I mean, what the fuck did you think I was going to do? Stay there like a good little bitch? Maybe chew your furniture a little if I got hungry? Piss on the floor? Wag my little tail when you got home?"

Rook snorted.

"I was going to come get you at lunch," Grey said in defense, and she whirled on him with a glare fit to smite him to ashes. I didn't know how I didn't see it in her from the start.

Her power.

It would have to be tamed if we were going to get her through this alive.

I pinched the bridge of my nose as Rook settled in to lean against the wall, loosely crossing his arms over his chest as she rummaged for clothes in the closet. He watched her like a starved lion before a feast. Transfixed. Like when he finally bent for the kill, he might not stop at blood and bone, but go for her heart, too. Her soul. I'd never seen that kind of obsession in him before, not even in his drug days, and it made my own blood chill to ice in my veins.

The edge of a dark duffle bag poked out from behind a stack of haphazardly folded jeans and I snatched it, shoving it at Grey. "Pack her a bag. We're taking her back to the Nest."

Her back stiffened, but she didn't turn as she strolled to the edge of her bed, dropping her towel to give us an unobstructed view of her ass.

Jesus fucking Christ.

"I had a really good shower think after my rude awakening this morning..."

My cock thickened as she bent to tug on a thong and then a pair of jeans, jumping on the spot to hitch them up over her peachy ass. The searing urge to string her up and fuck her until she screamed herself hoarse made my muscles bunch and my erection push insistently down into the leg of my jeans.

"I decided the whole thing is a hard pass. I'm not doing it."

"Doing what?" I asked through gritted teeth as she pulled a fitted tank over her head, going braless beneath the thin navy fabric.

"The trials," she retorted, shooting me a raised brow glare over her shoulder. "I'm not interested in being inducted into your fucking cult."

"Cult?" Rook asked, squinting then nodding as though he might agree with the assessment.

"Sect," she tried again, rolling the word around in her mouth. "Whatever the fuck you call a group of sinners dressed as Saints."

"It's too late for that, AJ," Grey said, perching on the edge of her desk. The growing light of the day deepened the shadows beneath his eyes. Our roles reversed for the moment. He didn't sleep last night either. I heard him pacing in his bedroom. Rifling through pages until long past dawn. "We've been over this."

Did she really think this was optional? The frustration heating my blood made me unsteady on my feet, and I had to grit my teeth to keep my frame from wavering. Last night wasn't the only one I hadn't slept through. It'd been days. My bones were heavy with fatigue, muscles strained from overuse without rest.

"It's already begun," I intoned, my voice flat. Dead. "Your first trial could be today. We won't be in on all of them. They can happen anytime. Any place."

"Yeah. Yeah. And anyone or anything is fair game. If I don't comply, I die. If I fail, I die. And if I somehow make it through the whole fucked up thing alive, I'll be in so deep that your dear ol' dad will own my ass for the rest of my life. *I remember.*"

"You should be grateful, Sparrow. If Grey hadn't done what he did, you'd be six feet under.."

"Ha!" She sneered, her face contorting with rage as she stepped up to me, jabbing two fingers into my chest, poking the beast within. "If *I* hadn't done what *I* did, it would be *your ass* buried six feet under."

A muscle in my jaw ticked, and she must've seen something in my stare because she backed off a step, dropping her arm with a grimace.

"There's no way out of this," Rook said, joining the conversation with a cavalier shrug.

Ava Jade clamped her mouth shut, and I knew she was already thinking of ways she might do just that. Though I doubted she was about to share any of them with the group.

"Aves?" Becca called from outside the room, the front door of the apartment sweeping closed behind her with a click. "You in here?"

Ava Jade tipped her head up to the ceiling with a sigh and closed her eyes before tossing her towel toward the bathroom floor and leaving the room.

"Babe, where *were* you? I texted, but you didn't..."

Rebecca Hart's words trailed off into shocked silence as we followed Ava Jade from her bedroom.

"Sorry, Becks," Ava Jade said, her frustration clearly evident in her voice. "I got *held up.*"

She sent a pointed glare in our direction as she pilfered through the coffee on the counter, trying to dump way too much espresso into the portafilter.

"Um," Rebecca said, swallowing as she glanced between us and her roommate, making her way carefully toward the kitchen. "Here," she offered, gingerly taking the portafilter out of Ava Jade's shaking hands. "Let me do it."

She stooped to whisper something to Ava Jade, who gave her head a miniscule shake.

"Apologies for the intrusion, *Becks*," I said. "We've just come to collect Ava Jade, and then we'll be on our way."

Her mouth opened in a little 'o' of surprise as the color leached from her face. She didn't respond to me, instead looking to her roommate for confirmation.

Ava Jade leaned heavily against the counter with a soft groan, watching the espresso drip steadily from the portafilter into a bowl-shaped mug.

"Grey," I growled, and he turned, heading back into her bedroom to begin packing the duffle still clenched in his fist.

"Aves?" Rebecca asked, her panicked whisper meant only for my Sparrow. "Are you really going with them?"

"*No,*" she replied, locking eyes with me across the room. "I'm not."

"Yes," I argued, taking another step toward the kitchen. "You are."

Becca turned off the steamer wand and slammed the metal jug of hot milk down atop the marbled counter top, making some slosh out the top as she spun to face us.

"Look, I don't know what the fuck you're doing here," she said, her dark eyes alight with fear and the misplaced desire to protect her friend. "But if Ava Jade says she isn't going with you, then she *isn't going with you.* You should leave."

I lifted a brow, trying to reconcile this Becca with the one I thought I had pegged as a docile non-threat.

When I glanced at Ava Jade, she was staring at me, doing an analysis of her own.

"It's okay, Becca," she decided, reaching out to squeeze her roommate's arm. To reassure her. "Corvus knows I'm not going with him. He's smart enough to know that no matter how many times he drags me back to the Crow's Nest that I'll just keep escaping. And that I might just decide to slit a few throats on my way out next time."

"*Mmmm,*" Rook moaned almost inaudibly.

Heat rushed across the back of my neck at her defiance, making my hands curl and stiffen, my jaw clench.

Touché, little Sparrow.

Becca nodded to her roommate, busying herself pouring the frothed milk into the cup with the espresso before handing it over to Ava Jade, who looked like she might come on the spot at the first sip. A curl of wicked jealousy wrapped its green fingers around my stomach.

She peered at me over the brim of her cup, waiting for me to play the next card.

"Aww, let her stay," Rook said, sauntering toward the kitchen. He cut in between Ava Jade and Becca, scooping a mug from the top of the espresso machine with his pinkie. He held the mug out to Becca with a grin, ignoring Ava Jade completely. "Can I get one of those, love?"

Flustered, Rebecca cleared her throat and took the proffered cup with a little nod, setting to work making another latte.

I sent Rook a pointed glare, telling him without the need for words that we'd talk about his idiocy later.

"*Fine*," I said just as Grey exited Sparrow's bedroom with a duffle full of clothes, my skin practically fucking *itching* with irritation. If she kept pushing me, I was going to blow.

How did she *do* that?

Nothing affected me like this.

I made sure of it.

Always calm.

Always level headed.

Except with her.

"She stays," I announced, turning my attention back to Sparrow, fixing her with a hard stare. "But one of us stays with you. One of us is with you at all times."

She paused, her latte frozen in mid-air with a grimace.

I drew my phone from my pocket and thumbed in her number, my angry strokes messing it up twice before I got it right. It was one of the first things I memorized from her file.

I sent her Rook, Grey, and myself as contacts via text. "I just sent you all of our numbers. If I text you, you reply. If I call, *you answer.*"

Her expression soured.

"And if I don't?"

My spine tingled.

"If you don't, I'll drag your ass back to the Nest and design you your very own fucking prison cell," I warned, the image of her locked behind iron bars, chained, and as naked as she'd been only minutes ago made my cock thicken once more.

"Don't think I won't do it," I added. "Nothing would make me happier."

4

AVA JADE

otal. Fucking. *Jackass.*

I grumbled wordlessly to myself through the last two classes of the day, barely able to focus on anything at all. At least fifty times the thought crossed my mind to just take off.

But even in the two classes I didn't share with any of the Crows, their authority was ever present.

I didn't doubt if I stepped one foot out the door of the classroom that somebody would be sending Corvus my movements. I'd already caught two seniors watching me. Guys who looked like they might be on their way to roles in the gang for themselves someday, if they made it through the trials.

If Diesel even deemed them worthy enough to take them.

I could get away though. I knew I could.

But did I want to?

Did I want to risk having to spend the rest of my life, or at the very least, the next several years running? Constantly checking the rearview? Only to possibly be dead before I could even hit legal drinking age?

Fuck. That.

They said there was no way out of this for me, but I knew of at least one. If I took them all down, then they couldn't own me. I could trade their secrets for my freedom. Ruin them from the inside.

I had one card left to play, and it was nestled safely behind a wooden board in a dark and cobweb infested nook in my closet. Officer Vick would be happy to help me if I decided to take him up on his offer.

My phone buzzed audibly in my pocket a few minutes before the end of the last class of the day, and I clenched my teeth, glancing up from my blank worksheets to the teacher.

Mr. William's gaze met mine for an instant before he looked away, ignoring the sound.

Huh.

I drew out my phone in full view, curious now.

A text flashed over the screen.

DICK FACE

Grey will be outside your class waiting for you.
Don't make this hard.

I rolled my eyes, not bothering to reply before slipping the phone back into my pocket.

Mr. William met my gaze again, his lips pursing before he went back to reading his book.

Not a coincidence then.

He really wasn't going to take my phone or even reprimand me.

Perks of forced proximity with the infamous Crows.

I'd take it.

I'd take it all.

I stuffed my blank pages in the textbook as the bell rang and made a beeline for the door, eager to get back to my room before Grey could escort me there. I didn't need to cement it in people's minds that they owned me. Corvus already did a good job of making them all think that without my help.

"AJ," Grey said as I breezed through the door, making me grind to a halt, a tremor of annoyance zipping down my arms, making my fists clench.

"Oh good," I said on a breath, not letting my frustration show. "You're here. Right on schedule. We're going for a run."

"What?"

"*A. Run,*" I enunciated, giving him a dubious look. "You know, like walking but faster."

"I'm starving. I thought maybe we could—"

"You thought wrong. We'll eat after. Hope you have some better shoes with you."

I glanced down at his brown leather boots, the tongue flapping out, laces loose. He'd never be able to keep up in those. Not that I cared. I needed to run. Now. Before I exploded with all this pent-up energy and rage. If Grey didn't want to be in the blast radius, then he'd better shut up and go along with it.

Grey opened his mouth to argue, but shut it again instead, pressing his lips together as he swept a sarcastic arm toward the hall. "Fine. Let's go for a run. Lead the way."

We didn't speak as I led him back to my shared apartment, changed and laced up my runners. Not even as we walked back down through the halls and out to the back gardens toward the trailhead at the back of campus, our shoes scuffing along tile and stone and eventually grass.

A little tremor of unease skated down my back, remembering the ominous messages from my would-be stalker still taking up space on my phone's hard drive. I hadn't run this path in weeks, but now, with Grey to accompany me, I supposed it was safer.

Perks.

I stuffed my earbuds in my ears just as he opened his mouth to say something. I pointed at them with a false apology curling my lips into a frown. "Sorry. Can't hear you," I told him as I hit play and broke into a jog, the crisp air in the shade of the matured trees already working small miracles on my nerves.

He kept pace easier than I thought he would in those boots. Laced up tight like he wore them now, I supposed they weren't completely useless.

I kept my eyes ahead after that, trying my best to ignore the fact that he was there as I let the exertion, the wind, and the smells of the forest swallow me up.

The sounds of Lola Blanc's Angry Too blared in my ears, distracting enough to keep my mind from wandering to bleaker territory again.

A smile curled my lips when I remembered that at any minute, Rook and Corvus could be noticing their missing door handles. I held onto that little joyous tidbit, letting it propel me onward. I thought for sure they'd have gotten a notification from the camera when I left earlier.

Actually, they might've. It was probably why they came looking for me, but they didn't know that the pillowcase slung over my shoulder contained nearly every door handle in their entire house.

"AJ," Grey said some time later, his voice barely audible above the song in my ears.

Maybe if I didn't answer him he would shut up and stop ruining this for me. He better not be tired already. I was nowhere near finished.

"*AJ!*"

Fuck.

Moment ruined.

I stopped, tearing an earbud from my ear, heaving as sweat trickled down my back. "*What?*"

"Look, can we just..." Grey trailed off, a bit breathless, his dark green t-shirt stained darker from sweat around the neckline. His face pinched.

"Who is that?" he asked, gesturing to the earbud pinched between my fingers and the sounds of Primal Ethos' *Anthem of the Broken* blaring through it.

I rolled my eyes. *Of course* he wouldn't know who Primal Ethos is. He probably only listened to top 40 songs and whatever was playing on Virgin radio like his vapid bitch of an ex-girlfriend or ex-fuckbuddy or whatever she was.

My stomach soured, and I cursed myself for the wave of jealousy that sank deep into the marrow of my bones.

"You wouldn't know it," I barked, sniffling as I caught my breath, bouncing on foot to foot so I wouldn't ruin my runner's high. "That would require you to have actual taste in music."

His eyes widened, lips parting on a reply that he didn't bother speaking.

"What do you want, Winters?" I asked after another beat of silence. "You're kind of ruining my high right now."

He jerked his head back toward the path. "Come on, we can talk and jog."

I growled, pissed that he fucked with my high, but was happy to start moving again at least. Grudgingly, I popped out my other earbud and tucked both of them into the pocket of my running shorts.

"I wanted to apologize," he said, head bent to the earth, his jaw taut.

This surprised me enough that my own jaw clenched in response. I didn't want to hear this. I didn't want an apology. I wanted my goddamned freedom back.

If I didn't hold onto my anger, I would have nothing left to shield me, and I was going to need one heck of a shield for what was to come.

"For what?" I demanded. "For taking my freedom? For trying to own me? For locking me in that—"

"For all of it," he interrupted, his brows drawing together as he looked up at me.

I looked away. "You're not sorry," I muttered. "Your 'apology' isn't for me. It's for you. To assuage your guilt. Own your shit, Grey."

"That's not—"

"It doesn't matter. What's done is done."

"AJ..."

"Just stop, okay?" I stopped dead on the trail, forcing him to stop with me. "I don't care if you're sorry. Sorry doesn't fucking help me."

A muscle in his temple twitched and the sky above us rumbled, accentuating my anger. Beneath the shade of the trees, I hadn't noticed how the sky had begun to darken. Storm clouds rolled overhead, casting Thorn Valley in a mottled darkness.

"Besides," I continued, sighing, my runner's high officially dead now. "I have a feeling it wasn't you who locked me in that fucking room."

He winced.

"Your brother has a control problem."

He pressed his lips together.

"Or more like an *asshole* problem," I muttered, more to myself than to Grey.

He brushed a hand through his damp blond hair. "You just don't know him like we do," he said, his voice softer now. "He comes across like a controlling asshole, and, well, he sort of is, I guess, but he's also fiercely protective of us. He's—"

"I don't care," I cut him off, spinning on my heel to start the slow walk back toward Briar Hall, smelling rain in the air.

"Wait," Grey started, snatching my wrist and pulling me to a stop. "Just give him a chance. Get to know him. I know he wants to get to know you."

I laughed, a loud, howling thing.

"The bastard lost my blade," I started, tugging my wrist away, but moving closer, letting him see the resolve in my eyes. "Which he still hasn't replaced, by the way. He tried to blackmail me. Tried to own me. And that's not even including the fact that he's unbearably controlling *and* a rude dickface. I don't give a fuck if he wants to know me. I don't want to know *him*."

It was a lie, I realized as the final words fell full of venom from my lips, and that only made me even more furious than I already was.

I threw my hands up, exasperated.

"It wasn't just him," Grey said quietly after a moment. "We...Rook and me, we did a lot of those things too."

He was right, of course. The blame wasn't all on Corvus, but for some reason he was the easiest one to hate, and I wasn't ready to let go of that.

I tipped my head back, breathing deeply to soothe the waking darkness within. "You know what, let's just get back."

My phone buzzed audibly in my pocket, and I clenched my teeth. "Speak of the devil," I snarled, anticipating another message from Corvus. Furious that I would have to be dealing with his bullshit text messages, and no doubt phone calls, for my foreseeable future.

But it wasn't him.

UNKNOWN

What a mess you've made, Ava Jade. I thought you were smarter than this.

My breath caught in my throat and immediately my head snapped up, scanning the forest on all sides, but there was nothing. Nothing save for overgrown weeds and trees.

My phone buzzed again in my hand.

UNKNOWN

First the blond one. I knew that was just a mistake. But then you let that asshole touch you behind the curtain, and you even looked like you enjoyed it. Disgusting. And now you're right where Diesel wants you and you have no one to blame but yourself.

"What is it?" Grey asked, moving closer.

I stepped back, turning away from him as another two messages popped up onto the screen.

UNKNOWN

You're just confused, I know, but that's no excuse.

UNKNOWN

Don't worry, my love, I'll help you...but if you let them touch you again, I'll have no choice but to punish you.

Got you, you fucking ASSHOLE.

It was him. It was him *all along*. Taunting me. Teasing me. Trying to scare me.

The bastard.

No one knew we were behind that curtain on fight night. *No one* would've been able to see us. The slit in the edge of the curtain was tiny. There was no way...

It was Corvus.

Had been from the start.

"I'm going to kill him," I deadpanned, taking off at a sprint into the trees, carving a path directly toward the Crow's Nest with Grey lagging behind, shouting for me to wait. To tell him what was going on.

Distantly, I heard a grunt as he fell. Good. Now there was no chance he would catch up.

The darkness I'd been working to suppress came rushing back, gushing up from deep within like a geyser.

From the start, I had a feeling it was him. I should have trusted my gut. Now there was no doubt.

It was funny how even though this wasn't the regular route I took to the Crow's Nest, I still knew exactly where I was going. Its location was anchored in my memory, a magnet to my compass. It drew me in as though I'd been going there my entire life.

My focus narrowed and the sound of Grey in the forest fell away, moving to nothing but a distant drone in my ears.

I couldn't believe Corvus' nerve.

This was a whole new low, even for Corvus. I understood icing me out. I could even understand trying to control me and attack me when he thought I was a threat. But this was just cruel. What was the purpose of it?

What was he trying to pull here? Did he want me to run? Was he trying to scare me away? So that Diesel would kill me? That way he wouldn't have to get his hands dirty himself.

That had to be it. I could see no other reason why he would do this. Unless he just got a kick out of making girls feel uncomfortable. Which, from what I knew of him, was entirely possible.

Either way, he wasn't going to get away with it. And if Rook and Grey were in on it with him they would go down, too. But something told me they weren't. This had Corvus written all over it. My chest began to ache around the same time the burn in my legs rose to an all-time high.

Until I was just an inferno of aching, burning fury.

The truth of it stung like a betrayal. But that was ridiculous, how could I feel betrayed if there was never trust to begin with?

I burst through the trees onto the gravel drive leading up to the Crow's Nest.

The front door stood ajar, and the Rover was parked in the driveway, the back hatch lifted to reveal several grocery bags and a flat of bottled water. It looked like they'd just returned home.

Corvus appeared in the doorway, exiting the house to retrieve the last of the groceries from the Rover.

I saw red.

My hands trembled as I stormed toward him.

"Motherfucker."

His distant gaze found me, brows drawing together. His lips parted, caught off guard to see me.

"Sparrow?"

I rushed him. Surprise registered in his icy blue eyes, one second too late.

I shoved him back, with my phone still clutched in my fist, the other slapping flat against his wide chest.

He stumbled back three steps, lip twisting into a sneer.

"What the fuck is your problem?" I demanded.

"AJ!" Grey shouted, breathless as he jogged up the drive.

I ignored him.

A shadow moved behind Corvus inside of the Nest, and Rook appeared in the hall, casually leaning against the wall as though there wasn't a seething dragon in his doorway.

"Suppose we have you to thank for our new open-door policy?" he asked with a crooked smile.

"What?" Corvus snapped at him, gaze jarring between Rook's unruffled posture and my flaring nostrils, his own frustration rising to meet mine.

Triumph at my success with my little doorknob trick would have to wait. I had more pressing matters to attend to.

"How long have you been stalking me, asshole?"

Corvus feigned confusion.

That's when it clicked.

A long fucking time.

The stalker saw me that night on the train tracks. The stalker knew my darkest, dirtiest secret.

Corvus knew what I did that night.

Shit.

No, no, no.

"I'll ask you again," Corvus said, inhaling deeply to rein in his control. "What in the actual fuck are you talking about?"

Cold dread filled my veins, dousing the fire that burned there only a moment before. I didn't realize I was still gripping my phone in my hand until Grey snatched it away.

"Don't!"

The fire roared back in an instant, and I launched myself at Grey to get it back.

"Hold her," Grey growled, and Corvus was able to get his arms around my middle, fastening me to him as though we were welded together with steel.

"*What the fuck,*" I gritted out, writhing. "Let go!"

"What are you doing?" Rook asked Grey so calmly that it just infuriated me even more.

"It was something on her phone," Grey mused. "She read something and then just took off like a bat out of hell."

"Shit," he cursed. "It's locked. What's your password?"

I continued struggling against Corvus' hold, but the way he had my arms tight against my sides, getting free was proving to be a chore and a fucking half. The muscles in my biceps and forearms flared from the effort while he grunted through my attempts at escape, his scent overwhelming my senses, playing tricks on my mind.

"Fuck you!" I spat at Grey. "I'm not telling you shit."

"*Sparrow...*" Corvus warned, his breath hot against my ear.

Fine. They wanted to play it like that? They could have it their way.

I stomped as hard as I could on Corvus' instep. When his hold loosened, I swung my leg forward and launched my heel back into his kneecap.

His hold on me broke enough for me to squirm free as he dropped to his good knee on the gravel drive.

He cursed loud and long, thick fingers reaching to try to grab me again, but it was too late. I was already on top of Grey, fighting to get my phone out of his grasp.

I didn't want to hurt him, well at least not that much, so I took him down gently. My version of gently.

My phone knocked from his hand as he fell. The wind gushed out through his lips from the impact with the gravel. I snatched my phone and stood, glaring at all of them. At Corvus on his knees. At Grey on his back. At Rook leaning against the door jamb with a prideful smirk on his mouth.

Smart fucker, not joining the fray. I wouldn't have gone easy on him, and I doubt he'd have gone easy on me, either. It would've been glorious.

A lot of that hot, angry wind in my sails died down as the realization of what Corvus knew truly sank in. I was still pissed, but also very wary of him telling the others... That was, if they didn't already know.

"AJ, can we stop for a second?" Grey asked, a note of impatience in his tone as he got to his feet and brushed the gravel dust off of his ass. "Could you just tell us what's going on?"

I pointed an accusing finger at Corvus, my chest heaving.

"Why don't you ask him?"

Grey's eyes slipped to his adoptive brother.

"Don't fucking look at me," he said, raising his arm in a shrug. "I have no idea. Maybe it's that time of the month."

Fucking prick.

I chuckled darkly to myself, the sound bordering on mania as the muscles in my jaw tightened again. I hadn't really realized how stressed and creeped out the messages had been making me with everything else that'd been happening, but now, at least, it was over.

With fingers rigor mortis stiff, I jabbed the phone screen until one of the newest messages from the unknown number appeared. The one detailing what Corvus and I did behind that curtain on fight night. I closed the small gap between us just as he finished getting to his feet, barely able to put any weight on his right leg.

I thrust the phone out, forcing him to look.

"So, you're telling me this *wasn't* you?"

Corvus' nostrils flared, his face growing red as he squinted to read the message on the screen. Leaning in, his sneer turned quickly to a frown.

"Sparrow, I didn't send that."

"Oh, and I suppose you didn't send any of the others, either?"

"Others? How many messages like this do you have?"

Concern pinched the skin between his eyes, and the muscles around his mouth. It certainly added to the effect of his claimed innocence. I had to say, I almost believed him.

"You're so full of shit."

"Ava Jade," Corvus pressed, straightening to his full height, and for some reason, the look on his face combined with the succinct way he spoke my name gave me pause. "I did *not* send that."

Rook, curious now, moved from his leaning stance against the door jamb to stand next to Corvus. "What is it?"

"But..." I trailed off, not breaking eye contact with Corvus even as my own began to burn from not blinking. There was no lie in his stare. He was either a *damn* good liar, or he wasn't lying to me at all. "It has to be you."

He shook his head once.

"Corv doesn't lie," Grey affirmed for his brother. "He owns his shit. If he does something, he does it with purpose. Without apology."

Corv gave Grey a grateful nod, and I could see it.

It made sense.

If it were him, he wouldn't have lied about it. He would have given me that infuriating smirk of his with a satisfied *gotcha* gleam in his bright eyes.

"Let me see the other messages," Corvus said, not a request, but a demand.

I faltered back a step, swallowing hard. "No," I muttered, blinking as I tucked my phone back away in my pocket. "No. It's nothing."

I cursed myself for not deleting all the other messages sooner. The one about what I'd done at the train tracks, especially. Now this stalker's words felt as though they were burning a hole in my pocket.

My relief at knowing this wasn't Corvus after all was overshadowed by a whole new brand of dread.

This person, whoever they were, had been watching me more closely than I'd thought. They were there, somehow, on fight night, and less than twenty-four hours ago, at that yard out behind the abandoned building.

The worst part was, I hadn't sensed it. If I had a tail, I should've noticed by now. *Why* hadn't I noticed?

Oh, yeah, probably because I've been fucking distracted by three *vultures* bent on making my life hell since the moment I got here.

Maybe Corvus wasn't Mr. *Unknown Number,* but it was his fucking fault regardless.

"It's *not* nothing, let me see," Corvus continued.

"AJ, just give him the phone."

"Just forget it," I snapped, promising myself I'd delete every single message from this asshole as soon as I got back to Briar Hall and had a moment alone.

"I told Becca about fight night. I forgot. It was probably her being stupid," I lied.

"What about fight night?" Rook asked, his teeth slipping across the silver loop of his lip ring.

Shit. Okay. *Just shut up, Ava Jade.*

By the way Corvus was eyeing Grey from his toes all the way up to his *blond* hair, I knew he was piecing that part of the message together right at this very moment.

This was *not* what I was after when I came here.

Steeling myself, I clenched my teeth and spun on my heel, snatching Grey's wrist as I went. "Come on, I'm hungry. Let's get out of here."

Grey shrugged at his brothers, and I caught Rook saluting him from the corner of my eye before we began the slow walk back down the hill.

"Want to tell me what that was about?" Grey hedged, a dark aura around him, shadowing his light.

Behind us, I heard Corvus ask what Rook was saying about an open-door policy and stiffened.

"Keep up," I told Grey, releasing him. I picked up my pace, pushing my aching legs into a quick jog to escape before the nuclear fallout hit.

5

GREY

When we got back to AJ's room at the academy, we ran into Becca on her way out.

I'd been about to ask her more about what happened back at the Nest, but the appearance of her friend silenced me for the moment. I may not have been as perceptive as the others, but I got the sense AJ wasn't telling us everything. She was downplaying the message, or *messages*, since she said there were others.

Guilt lingered long after the short-lived altercation with Corvus. I shouldn't have taken her phone, or told Corvus to hold her while I tried to read the messages.

But...

The distress, *the fury* in her eyes when she read whatever was on her phone was too much to ignore. I needed to know what it was. What could possibly drive her to that level of anger that quickly. I wanted to crush it. Shatter it. Burn it to ashes.

I wanted to ask her to tell me, now that the others weren't with us, what it was that she'd read. Of course, I could ask Corvus, but from the way he was looking at me before we left, I got the sense that I'd done something to piss him off.

He was already on edge. Best to leave him alone until he managed some shut eye. But they weren't letting this go, either. My phone buzzed nonstop the whole run back to the academy, and I knew it was them.

"Oh, hey girl!" Becca trilled uneasily, glancing between us as we nearly bumped into her leaving their shared apartment.

"Hey," AJ grumbled, pasting on the ghost of a smile for her friend.

"I was just on my way out," Becca continued, jabbing a thumb back toward the door. "But," she paused, eyes slipping toward me. "I can stay if you want me to."

AJ waved her off, kicking her shoes off to step farther into the living room. "Nah. I'm good. You go ahead."

"When will you be back?" I asked, earning myself a confused look from Becca and a pointed glare from AJ, who paused on the threshold to the kitchen.

AJ's nose wrinkled. "Leave her alone, Grey."

"I just want to know when to expect her back," I explained, not allowing AJ to overrule me on this. She didn't understand the stakes here. What exactly was going to be happening to her over the next sixty days. Her trials could happen anywhere, at any time. Someone entering the flat could just as easily be a member of the Saints, come to attack her in bed. Testing her ability to react in the heat of the moment.

If I heard an intruder in the night, I could at least give her a few seconds head start. Wake her up. Tell her to be ready for attack. And maybe not to kill whoever it was.

They were prepared for that, though. I'd have killed the one who surprise attacked me during my trials if he wasn't wearing a vest and tactical gear.

"Um," Becca replied, uncomfortable now. "I don't know—"

"You don't have to answer that," AJ told her friend.

"It's fine," Becca replied with a little wave of her hand.

"I don't know exactly when," she told me. "But it'll be late. Midnight, maybe. One, the latest."

I cocked my head at her. I hadn't expected that response. That was late. Really late. Where was she going?

Not my business.

"Thanks," I said with a tip of my head. "I have your number. I'll text you so you have mine. If you wouldn't mind texting before you get back, that would be great."

"You have my number?" she asked, surprise paling her salon-quality tan.

"Have a good night," I replied, my words punctuated by a loud groan from AJ in the kitchen, followed by muttered curses as she began messing with pots and pans in the cabinet.

"Uh, yeah," Becca replied, in a bit of a daze. "You, too."

She left without another word, and I leaned over to lock the door behind her, bending to unlace my boots.

A *snap* preceded a light sting on my forehead, and I jerked my head up, finding an elastic on the floor by my feet and AJ shooting mental daggers at me from the kitchen. "Don't harass my friend or the next thing I launch in your direction won't be as nice."

The cast iron pan clutched loosely in her hand accentuated her point. I sighed.

"It's for your own good," I tried, seeing that I was going to get nowhere with her tonight. Not while she was riled up and still on edge about whatever was happening on her phone.

"*It's for your own good,*" she mocked, turning on the gas burner and dropping the heavy pan onto it with a loud clamor. "If you're eating here, then you can at least help me cook. Get over here and peel the onions."

It was going to be a long night.

My hip bone and shoulder ached, pressed against her bedroom floor.

I shifted, trying to get comfortable with only one pillow to work with and no blanket.

I explained after dinner how I'd need to sleep in her room. Diesel's orders meant as little separation from her as possible. If I slept in the living room, she could easily slip out her bedroom window without me noticing. I checked it out earlier, it wouldn't be all that difficult to climb down.

As it was, with me on the floor between her bed and the window, escape using that route wouldn't be possible. She could sneak out the front door, but I was a light sleeper. Unless she was ninja quiet, I'd hear her.

Not like I was getting any sleep, anyway. Though, neither was she.

She tossed and turned in her bed two and a half feet up and five feet away from me. Restless. Sighing heavily every few minutes.

I had no doubt it was my doing. The fact that I was here, in her personal space. Corvus was the same way. The only time he ever slept was alone in his room with the door both locked and deadbolted. His phone right beside his head. The light from his studio closet left on in case he needed to see anything when he woke.

I wondered if she was thinking of earlier, when I made her sit in her bathroom with me while I showered off the sweat from our run. I thought she might turn away. Not look as I stripped down and stepped into the glass encased shower, but she didn't.

She folded her arms over her chest and stared openly, her expression betraying nothing as she watched me step inside and then wash myself meticulously from top to bottom.

It was almost impossible not to be turned on with her watching me like that, even if it was a cold kind of stare. A stare that said, *you don't affect me,* even though the slight squeeze of her thighs betrayed the feeling she concealed beneath her mask.

Ava Jade groaned slightly before sitting up in bed. I listened as she sighed again, checking my phone for the time.

It was just past eleven, and there were already several more messages waiting on there from the guys in the group chat.

CORVUS

Did she tell you anything more?

CORVUS

If she's not going to fess up, can we hack into her phone? We need to see what else she's hiding from us. Those messages seemed threatening. I think she's lying about it being Becca.

Angling my phone so she couldn't see, I typed out a quick reply, knowing neither of my brothers would sleep until I did. Ava Jade shut down my questions all night about the texts she claimed were from Becca, making me even more on edge. It took all the restraint I had to let it go, but only because I knew we'd find out whether she wanted to tell us or not.

Corvus' reply was immediate.

Ava Jade rose from her bed and padded to the door, stepping out into the living room, and even as tired as I was, I was grateful to have to get up off the solid floor.

Corv liked his bed hard, the mattress so over-firm it was uncomfortable even to sit on. But not me. I liked a good soft bed. Pillowtop. Plush. More like Rook's, though fur and Egyptian cotton weren't really my thing.

I'd take either over this, though. This floor was going to leave me with goddamned bruises.

I stretched out the kinks in my bones and went to the door, squinting out into the moonlit space. AJ was in the sunken area by the couches, searching beneath the coffee table for something. When she didn't find it, she huffed, moving onto the fireplace mantle and eventually the little cabinet beneath it. Getting more and more annoyed as she searched.

What was she looking for?

AJ paused as she pulled something forward from the back of the cabinet, tilting the box-like shape toward the light.

She pressed a button on it and it whirred to life as she leaned back, grabbing something from the top of the coffee table.

The television mounted above the slim fireplace flicked on, the blue light expanding until it coated the room with its eerie glow, making AJ reel back for a moment from its brightness.

It was clear what she was doing when she changed the input and drew what was unmistakably a controller from the back of the cabinet. She wiped the dust off the controller with her shirt and then toggled to the downloaded games as the console finished coming to life.

She chose a first-person shooter. A zombie game I hadn't heard of. There weren't a wide array of choices. She wasn't half bad, either. It took her a few rounds, a few virtual deaths, before she hit her stride, cutting down zombies and their offspring with ease, zooming through challenges and levels.

Her hair kept falling in her face as she played, and she roughly threw it back between zombie kills. The urge to hold it back for her, to pull it up into a ponytail out of her way gripped me, and I frowned.

It was an odd thought. What did I care if her hair was getting in her eyes?

Sitting how she was, cross legged on the floor, backlit in blue, she looked like my own personal poltergeist. Disturbing my routines, throwing my life into chaos.

And yet, just like before, I couldn't say I wanted her gone.

Or that I wished she never came here.

On the contrary, I wanted her more.

Even knowing what she was trying to do to us before the night at the warehouse didn't change anything. If I was in her shoes, I'd have done the same. Hell, I might've done worse.

The strap of her shirt slipped off her right shoulder, and she flicked her hair back again, sweeping it to the side, away from her slender neck. So fucking beautiful.

My cock thickened in my boxers, and I pawed it, trying to readjust.

I did say I wanted to talk to her, but maybe talking wasn't going to fix anything. Apologizing to her with words for earlier wouldn't mean shit. But maybe I could show her in other ways.

I was thinking with my cock again, a flaw Corvus constantly reminded me I needed to fix, but right now, I didn't give a flying fuck if this was a good idea. Or if she'd stab me for trying.

"I know you're there," she said quietly, her attention still focused wholly on the game. Her neck craned upward to see it. "I'm not going anywhere so you can just go back to sleep."

"I wasn't sleeping," I replied, my voice huskier than intended.

Her shoulders gave a slight shudder that I took to mean I was on the right track, my erection pressing harder against the front of my boxers now, but it wasn't me who'd be getting his rocks off.

Not yet, anyway, this was an apology after all.

I knelt behind her, and she faltered, getting attacked by a zombie, her health depleting a little before her virtual avatar managed to fend him off.

"What are you doing?" she asked, a note of impatience in her tone as she jammed the attack button on the controller, grunting as she took down another three of them on screen.

I leaned in, inhaling her scent, my nose brushing along the soft skin just below her right ear. "Apologizing," I replied.

AJ shied away as though I'd tickled her, and I wondered if she was ticklish. Something to explore another time. I slipped a hand around her middle, caressing her ribs before my fingers splayed over her belly.

She let me, at least at first.

The controller went lax in her hands, a horde of zombies taking advantage of her distraction, and she grabbed my hand, stopping its downward trajectory.

"Just let me touch you," I crooned, and her grip on me held for another few seconds until it relented.

"Why should I?"

"Call it an apology. You know, since *words won't help*. I thought this might."

She hesitated another second, the muscles in her arms swelling as she clutched the controller tight and then set it down.

"No," I blurted. "Keep playing."

"What?"

"Bet you can't keep focus," I taunted, making it a game. A challenge.

I got the feeling she didn't back down from those often.

I swore I could almost hear her smirking from my position behind her as she took the controller up again just in time for another zombie to attack. I placed my hand back on her stomach, and she let out a small gasp as I dipped it below the waistband of her little pajama shorts.

"Focus," I reminded her as my fingers brushed her clit, making her hips buck forward slightly, pressing her sweet cunt into my fingers, aching for more. I rested my chin on her shoulder, sitting with my legs pressed against her, wrapping her in my scent. Marking her as mine.

I shivered internally, her need making my own soar. My cock ached in my boxers, throbbing in time with my pulse as I began a slow circular motion with my fingers, light and teasing.

She made a small moaning sound, and I clenched my teeth to keep myself from jumping her right there on the floor. From tossing the controller out of her grasp and forcing her onto her back.

No. This was about her. Not me.

Not today.

I pushed through her slick folds, finding the heat of her center as I slid in first with one finger, then with two.

Her shots on screen went wide, and she stopped altogether as I added my thumb to the mix, rubbing her clit as I fucked her with my fingers.

"Uh, Uh," I warned with a tight smile on my lips, pressing them lightly against her neck. My cock ached inside the confines of my boxers. I slowed, almost stopping, and she continued playing. Redoubling her efforts to focus on the game. "You stop, I stop," I murmured in her ear, licking the fingers of my other hand before wrapping it around her to join the first below the waistband of her shorts.

I rubbed her clit mercilessly with one hand while I pumped my fingers in and out with the other, gaining speed. But it wasn't enough. I wanted more. I wanted her screaming.

I wanted her to shatter with my name on her lips.

AJ let out a small whine as I withdrew both my hands and moved to kneel. I grabbed her waist, lifting and moving her until she was seated on the edge of the coffee table.

My knees brushed the soft rug as I found my place in front of her and looped my fingers into the waistband of her shorts to tug them off. She obliged, wiggling her hips with a knot between her brows as she continued her game.

She opened her mouth to speak, but I hushed her. "This means nothing," I said for her, an echo of our last encounter in the bathroom. It was written all over her expression: how much she wanted this, *needed* the release, and how much she hated that she wanted it.

I hated wanting her, too. Or at least, I did.

Before.

Now?

I didn't think there was anything I could hate about her. Not even if I fucking tried.

I pried her legs apart and buried my face in her pussy before she could change her mind and push me away. Her sweet heat coated my tongue and *fuck* she tasted so. damn. good.

Her thighs squeezed, muscles clenching from the attack of my tongue, little gasping moans stuttering from her lips.

I was good at this, I knew. She got a taste in the bathroom, but today she would get the full experience.

With one hand clenching her hip to hold her in place, I slid the other between her legs, slipping it beneath my chin to join my tongue. I pushed inside, never ceasing the quick flicking motions with my tongue even as I began viciously finger fucking her.

AJ moved, squirming from the pleasure. You'd almost think she was trying to get away with how much she squirmed, but my bruising grip on her waist held her steady. Forced her to feel *everything*.

She stopped fighting a minute later, instead, grinding herself against me. AJ fucked my face like a woman starved, and I ate up every fucking second of it. Increasing the pace with my fingers to match her. We moved together, every thrust of her hips, every flick of my tongue, every stroke of my fingers, perfectly in sync until the controller clattered to the floor, and her fingers dove into my hair, gripping tighteningly, holding me there with a shout as she came on my lips.

I continued through her orgasm, forcing it to lengthen, making her shudder and twitch, trying to pull away, but I didn't let her. Not until the violent pull of her fingers in my hair began to soften and eventually to cease.

Only then did I stop, staring up at her with her wetness gleaming on my lips. She looked down at me with something I couldn't identify in her eyes. Heat, but not hatred. The knot never left the space between her brows, not even when she slumped back onto the coffee table, hands going to her chest as it heaved. Utterly spent.

I got uncomfortably to my feet with a grimace, my cock so disgustingly sensitized that even the brush of it against my boxers was like the phantom stroke of her fingers.

Her eyes were heavy-lidded, face flushed and slack.

She was so tired.

"Come on," I whispered, stooping to lift her from the table, slipping my forearms beneath her knees and around her shoulders.

She didn't protest as I carried her back to bed, setting her onto the soft mattress and drawing the blanket up to her chest.

"Sleep," I ordered, and her eyes shuttered despite her efforts to keep them trained on me.

She was uncomfortable, but maybe it wasn't because of me after all. Maybe it was because she knew as well as I did that someone could come in here for her first trial any minute. Or maybe it was something else I wasn't even aware of.

"I'll keep watch if you like," I added on a whim, and she looked at me strangely. Pained almost.

Her gaze flitted to the other side of the bed and for a heart-stopping moment I thought she might draw back the covers, invite me to sleep there with her on the bed. But then she turned away, drawing her knees to her chest without a word.

For a girl who always had something to say, her silence was disconcerting. I didn't know what it meant. While I cleaned up the evidence of what we'd done in the living room, I tried to analyze it, wishing I could be as perceptive as my brothers.

A key slipped into a lock as I shut off the TV and grabbed AJ's wet shorts from the floor. I froze, rushing to the edge of the fireplace as the intruder pushed inside.

I'd be damned if I was going to let him ruin her sleep. After how hard I worked to send her off.

I stepped into the wide entry, making my shoulders wide and thick as I lifted my head. "Not tonight, asshole. *Leave.*"

"*Um,*" squeaked a very female voice. "I just want to go to bed."

The small pod light in the entry flicked on, and I reeled back at its brightness, taking in all six feet of Rebecca Hart in a pair of strappy black heels, her hair in disarray.

Her wide eyes zeroed in on AJ's shorts in my hand, and the erection next to them.

My face heated as I covered it with the shorts, clearing my throat.

"Shit," I muttered, trying to keep my voice low so I wouldn't wake AJ. "Sorry, Becca."

"I texted," she said, defending herself. "Just like you asked."

Right. Except I left my phone in AJ's room.

"All good," I replied, already moving away. "My bad."

"Who…" Becca trailed off, her brows drawn. "Who did you think I was?"

Again, my bad. Obviously, AJ hadn't told her about the trials. She *should* tell her. Everyone was fair game after all, but it wasn't my place to do it for her.

"No one," I told her. "Don't worry about it."

I jabbed a thumb back in the direction of AJ's room. "I should probably…"

Becca's brown eyes flitted down to my erection and then away. "Yeah. You two have fun. 'Night."

AJ was going to kill me.

I paused after only a step, a prickle crawling over the back of my neck. "Actually," I said as I turned back to face her, keeping my voice as low as I could. "If I ask you something, could you keep it between us?"

Becca's gaze slid to her friend's bedroom door and back to me again, narrowing. Her jaw clamping tight.

"It's important," I urged.

Grudgingly, she pursed her lips. "Depends what it is."

I stifled the urge to shout, remembering AJ's twisted face in the woods.

"Did you text AJ earlier today? A little while after last period?"

She frowned. "Why?"

"Answer the question."

Her throat bobbed. "No," she finally said after a few beats of tense silence. "No, I didn't text her."

Fuck.

"Thanks. That's all I needed to know."

6

AVA JADE

Grey became my very own warden for the entire week. Nobody said it, but I suspected it was because Corvus was too angry to be around me for any length of time, and they didn't trust Rook not to eat me.

That was the vibe I got, easily surmised from the fact that Corvus hadn't spoken to me since Tuesday night over the phone, and when Rook offered to take over for Grey yesterday after class, Corvus and Grey replied a resounding *no* at the exact same time.

Rook shrugged it off with a roll of his eyes and a wink in my direction, but something told me it bothered him more than he was letting on.

"So, what now?" I asked after last period on Friday, barely looking up to check if Grey was waiting outside of class as I exited, heading for my room. His distinct footfalls padded along beside me. I'd grown accustomed to them over the last few days.

"Corv said we had...."

The hairs along the back of my neck pricked as the elevator down the hall pinged dully, the doors sliding open. Grey's sentence trailed off as his brothers exited, scattering the students that still lingered in the corridor.

"We have a pick up out of town," Corvus announced.

Grey stiffened. "*All* of us?" he asked. "What about her?"

He jabbed a thumb in my direction, and I tried not to let the heat of my anger rise. I hated when they talked about me like I wasn't even here. Like I was cargo. An obstacle. Like I didn't have a choice.

Corvus' cold blue eyes slid to me and then away. "She's with us. Diesel wants all three of us on the job."

"And he wants us to bring her?" Grey challenged, a doubtful note of sarcasm in his tone.

Corvus visibly tensed, annoyance in the knot between his brows. "He offered for us to drop her off at Sanctum with him," he all but growled, watching Grey carefully for his reaction.

"That's what I thought," he continued. "So, she's with us. When we're close, we'll blindfold her. And she can wait in the car."

"Could you all stop talking about me like I'm not right fucking here?"

"Problem, Sparrow?"

"Yeah, actually. I have plans tonight."

"Cancel them," Corvus bit out, a muscle flexing in his jaw. "And in the future you might want to check with me first before making *plans.*"

"Asshole."

Rook laughed, his teeth pulling lightly on his lip ring as he watched me. "Come on, Ghost," he said. "I'll buy you an ice cream."

Ghost?

Corvus turned to raise a brow at him but said nothing.

"Better be one hell of an ice cream," I sighed. "I'm missing movie night for this shit."

"Trust me," Rook replied, a gleam in his dark eyes. "It'll be worth it."

I drew out my phone and ignored the newest text from Aunt Humphrey while thumbing a quick text to Becca, telling her I was sorry but I didn't know when I'd be back.

I could put my foot down. Refuse to go. But I figured that was exactly what Corvus wanted. He'd fucking love that. An opportunity to flex his control muscles. To try to throw me over his shoulder again, kicking and screaming through the halls of the academy as he dragged me to their car.

I wouldn't give it to him.

Besides, this was exactly the sort of intel I'd need to be able to bring them down. And ice cream was just the cherry on top of the pie.

Corvus jammed the elevator button again and stepped in as the doors re-opened, Rook following, and Grey ushering me in behind them.

"Get those handles replaced?" I asked innocently, breaking the silence on the slow descent to the main floor, basking in my triumph for the first time. God, it felt good.

The air in the elevator seemed to heat in the split second before Corvus replied.

"No," he growled. "They were *imports.*"

"We have another two weeks of our new open-door policy before they'll arrive," Rook put in, looking nearly as smug as I felt, until his dark gaze fell back to Corvus and his smirk faded.

"Too bad," I sighed, turning back to face the doors, injecting some drama into the words.

The *ping* of the elevator rang like a dinner bell in the hot silence, and I was dragged backward as the door opened, the fist in the back of my shirt tossing me against the wall. The air knocked from my lungs as Corvus pressed me there, his forearm a bar against my throat. But I was ready for him this time, my blade pressed firmly against his side, just below the ribs, angled up.

Unbothered by the blade, he pressed against my throat, his blue eyes burning with the heat of a thousand suns. The red veins bright as fresh blood against the whites.

"You think this is fucking funny?" he demanded. "*Hmm?*"

"Actually, yeah," I spat back, my voice strained from his arm. "I do."

Corvus choked on a reply as Grey gripped him by the shoulder and hauled him back with a grunt.

"*Stop.*" Grey's voice resounded in the elevator.

"Just stop," he repeated as I gasped for a full breath, still keeping a wary eye on Corvus. Grey was giving his brother the same look, though his was tainted with worry and something else I couldn't name. I got the feeling Corvus didn't often show his anger in a physical way. He reserved that level of animosity just for me. "When was the last time you slept?"

"Don't fucking start," Corvus sneered. "You try sleeping with no goddamned door handle, see how you like it."

"Right, because *the floor* is so much more comfortable."

Corvus glanced between Grey and me, his right brow lowering in question. He hadn't expected that. Did he really think I was letting Grey cuddle up to me every night? Even after his *apology* Tuesday night, I wasn't about to go soft. It was a release I needed, and I could already feel that pressure building again, but it didn't change anything.

They were still my enemies.

"Want to trade?" Grey pressed, challenging his brother. "I'll take no door handle over rock solid floor any fucking day."

Rook raised his hand, a sly smirk tugging up one corner of his mouth. "I'll trade," he crooned, eyeing me up and down. The path of his eyes leaving a scorching heat everywhere it touched, making my insides squeeze. "Anytime."

Corvus scrubbed a shaky palm over his face as he sighed. "Fuck it," he said finally, dropping his head as he shook it, inhaling deeply. It was as though I wasn't even there anymore and I realized he'd just gone back to ignoring me. Pretending I wasn't there was easier than admitting I was getting to him. That I was *always* getting to him.

Under his skin.

Into his head.

I could see it.

And I fucking reveled in it.

"Let's go get this pick up handled. The sooner it's over the sooner she's out of my sight."

My chest squeezed, and I swallowed hard to squelch the unwelcome sensation, strutting from the elevator as though I didn't have a care in the world when the doors opened.

"Sounds peachy to me."

I thought I had some idea where we were headed, at least for the first hour of the drive. But now, closing in on two hours of driving, I needed to admit I had no fucking clue where we were going. The fact they hadn't even blindfolded me yet told me there was still a decent amount of ground to cover. So much for making it back in time for late night movies with Becca.

I grumbled wordlessly to myself, almost as loud as the growling in my belly, as I checked the map app on my phone again. Still heading south. We were basically in the middle of butt fuck nowhere. This county road seemed to lead to some tiny place called Eugine, but as far as I knew there was no Saint presence this far away from Thorn Valley. And I'd been doing my research, a lot of it.

Grey's gaze flicked to me in the rearview, his reflected eyes falling to the device in my hand before flitting away again. It wasn't the first time I'd caught him watching me, or rather, watching my phone, and my reaction to what I'm looking at on its screen.

He wasn't sold on the idea that my little outburst earlier in the week was nothing. I didn't think any of them were, but Grey seemed the most suspicious. The others, at least at the surface level, seemed keen to just let the whole thing drop.

I thought I'd better send a quick reply to Becca's earlier texts since they'd likely be taking my phone and putting it into airplane mode around the same time they blindfolded me.

BECCA

Hey girl, where are you?

BECCA

What time are you coming back later?

AVA JADE

Not sure and not sure. Sorry. I'll let you know when we're on our way, though.

Another text pinged through before I could repocket my phone.

BECCA

Are all the guys with you?

AVA JADE

Yeah. Why? Everything okay?

She took so long to reply this time that I almost called her, wondering why she'd want to know where they all were. If she was in some sort of trouble. Diesel-sized trouble. I wouldn't put it past him to use her against me in the trials, but if he did, it would be a massive mistake.

My finger hovered over the dial button when her reply came in.

BECCA

Everything's fine! Sorry, I just got a call from my beau. I'm off to see him. Don't wait up for me, k?

AVA JADE

Have fun!

Rook shifted, stretching his leg out further as he lounged in the back seat next to me. A frown turned down the edges of his mouth as he, too, stared at the device in my hands. I shut it off and cleared my throat, pocketing it with a sigh.

I'd deleted every trace of the so-called stalker from it, but I knew there were ways to recover those messages. Grey seemed like the type to know exactly how to do that, so I needed to make sure I didn't give him an opportunity to. I slept with it under my pillow all week, refusing to give him any opportunity to snatch it from my bedside table.

Other than that first night, I'd barely slept more than an hour at a time, every time he shifted against the hard floor, sighing, I woke, ready to smother him with a pillow in sleepless frustration. It was a wonder he still drew breath.

"How much longer?" I asked, speaking over the low hum of the radio for the first time.

"As long as it takes," Corvus grumbled in reply from the seat in front of me, his elbow resting on the window's ledge, his thick fingers propping up his heavy head at his temple.

I rolled my eyes and caught him giving me a spiteful look in the side view mirror. To which I flipped him the bird and he looked away, appearing bored, but the vein throbbing thickly in his neck told a different story.

"I'm fucking starved," Rook groused, sliding his tongue over his lower lip. "Let's stop for food, yeah?"

"No," Corvus deadpanned.

My stomach rumbled at the mention of food, and Rook shot me a smirk.

"Awe, come on, man. I promised the girl an ice cream."

He winked at me and *dammit* if my toes didn't curl.

"I don't care."

"It's five now," Grey put in. "By the time we get back, it'll be past eight. We should eat."

Rook reached a tatted hand around the headrest to squeeze his brother's shoulder with a triumphant grin. "Majority rules," he said, smug as fuck.

"Fine. But make it quick."

"There's a diner up ahead," Rook said, his teeth spinning the lip ring at the edge of his mouth. "Stop there."

Corvus made a disgruntled sound and sank lower in his seat, blood-shot blue eyes fixed on the horizon.

The diner came into view as we crested the top of a low hill. A short, squat building that looked like it hadn't been renovated whatsoever since the eighties. Only three cars were parked in the front lot and through the fogged glass windows, I could only see a handful of people seated at purple pleather coated booths.

I'd eaten at worse. Dad always joked I had an iron gut. Forged on trailer park water supply and fifty cent street hotdogs for dinner. I could eat whatever the hell I wanted here and be fine tomorrow, but these guys?

I doubted they could say the same.

"Pull around back," Rook directed as Grey slowed, the Rover's tires moving from uneven pavement to the dirt and gravel drive of the diner.

Grey cast Rook a look in the rearview, but did as his brother asked, driving us around to the back of the building to park beside a rusted old black van I assumed belonged to the owner or an employee.

"Who's going in?" Grey asked. "We should grab some shit to go. I want to be back before dark."

Rook nodded, his glimmering gaze hedging in my direction.

"We'll send her," he decided, still turning his lip ring.

"I'll take their fattest burger," he told me, licking his lips. "With fries and a shake. Chocolate."

"Oh, so now I'm your fucking butler, too?"

"She's not going in alone," Corvus huffed, as though he was explaining something for the tenth time to a bunch of dimwits. It wasn't lost on his brothers, either.

Grey's jaw tensed as he shut off the ignition. "Where the fuck is she going to go?" he asked, and it was odd seeing this side to him. Ever since that night out at the warehouse, something in Grey has shifted. Hardened. He wasn't who I originally thought he was.

Not their weakest link. Not by a longshot.

Though that's what he'd have you think.

Corvus lifted his head from resting on his knuckles to give Grey an appraising look.

"She's not to be out of our sight."

"There's nothing for miles," Rook chimed in. "She could run as far as she wanted in any direction and we'd find her in half a minute."

He wasn't wrong. The terrain here was desert-like. A flat expanse of hard packed, hot dirt with the odd shrub or stunted tree jutting up from the cracked earth. Nowhere to hide. Nowhere to run to.

Corv's jaw flexed, but he didn't reply.

Guess that meant I was playing servant.

Though the prospect of being alone without any of them to shadow me, for even five minutes, felt like anything but a punishment.

Grey removed his seatbelt with a sigh. "I'll go with her."

"You won't," Rook snapped, cutting his brother a meaningful look before his expression levelled back out. "She's got this. What'll it be, Brother? Clubhouse?"

Grey's brows lowered, his lips pressing together as he considered his brother.

Was I missing something?

"Yeah," Grey replied. "With fries and gravy."

"Corv?" Rook asked, expectant.

"Not hungry."

"He'll have whatever looks the least greasy."

"I said I'm not fucking hungry."

"Ignore him. He'll be less of a hangry grump once I've stuffed dinner down his throat."

I bit back a laugh as Corvus growled quietly to himself, his jaw grinding.

I slipped out the door, but Rook stopped me. His rough fingers slipping around my wrist, making me shudder internally. "Don't forget your ice cream, Ghost."

He slipped a small wad of bills into my hand and released me. "Oh, and I'll be needing you to leave your phone with me."

A bolt of ice struck low in my gut. "Why? I probably don't even have service here."

A lie. I did have service, and I fully intended to make a call while I was alone inside. I needed a better bug. The one I'd planted in the knotted wood beneath the kitchen window at the Nest was a fucking dud. It barely lasted more than twenty-four hours after the second charge. Useless. I needed the good shit. The kind Kit's contact could get for me. If I made it worth his while, I was willing to bet I could even get him to drive it out to me at Briar Hall.

Rook's devilish grin told me he knew exactly what I'd been plotting. Or at least, that I'd been plotting *something*.

He held his hand outstretched, the tough leather of his palm flat and expectant.

My jaw clenched as I slid the phone from my pocket and dropped it into his hand.

"Fine."

He closed his fingers around it and nodded. I reassured myself that there was nothing they could do with it here in the middle of nowhere, without a computer and the proper cords to bypass my password and hack into the device's backup drives.

My call to Kit would have to wait. At least for now.

I shut the door behind me, maybe a little too forcefully, as I could feel Corvus' eyes burning a hole into the back of my skull as I stalked around the building towards the front entrance. The smells of greasy bacon and home cooked chicken soup drew me in, and my stomach twinged in hollow discomfort.

I should've eaten more at lunch, but Becca had about a million questions and I wound up leaving with my plate still half full. A waste of perfectly good food. Enough to have fed Mom, Dad, and me once upon a time.

I wanted to tell her the truth of everything that was going on, but wasn't sure what exactly the rules were. Not that I was averse to breaking them...more like I just didn't want to deal with Corvus' bullshit if I did.

The bell atop the yellowed glass door jingled as I stepped into the diner, the humidity kicked up a notch from the dry heat outside. I inhaled deeply, reveling in the greasy scent. I wondered if I could eat a burger fast enough to keep my ice cream from melting.

Sounded like my kind of challenge.

I ignored dirty looks from an older couple seated in a booth to my right and approached the counter, sliding between two tall pleather coated bar stools to flag down the waitress at the other end.

She caught sight of me and gave an apologetic smile to the man she was working down at the end. He looked like he was about a minute away from asking her to marry him. And from the look on her face as she turned away from him, she knew it, too.

If he looked beyond the pound of makeup on her face and her big tits, he'd have noticed the slight swell of her belly beneath her apron. The way her pupils were more dilated than they had any right to be given the lighting.

She had a nice body, I'd give her that. But in less than, maybe about six months, she'd lose the belly and trade it for the babe growing inside. If she had her way, though, she'd be one baby daddy richer, too.

Poor bastard.

Men could be such idiots. Only seeing what we wanted them too. Not bothering to scratch any deeper than the surface. I wished the three bozos out back were as stupid as the man in the plaid shirt at the other end of the counter.

"Can I get you somethin', hon?" The waitress asked as she walked up, her shuffling steps giving away sore feet.

"Yeah. I need a few things to go."

"You need a menu?"

I shook my head as she dipping her fingers into the apron of her faded pink uniform and drew out a notepad and a pen. "Name?"

"Evangeline." The response came automatically, my nom de guerre rolling from my lips almost easier than my own. Another thing dad taught me. If they don't need to know your name, don't give it to them. Everybody could be a mark someday. Give nothing. Take it all.

"Pretty. What'll it be, then?"

"A clubhouse sandwich with fries and gravy."

She nodded.

"Two of whatever your best burgers are, with fries and one chocolate milkshake. A salad. Don't care what kind. And an ice cream, what flavors do you have?"

The bell jingled behind me, and I didn't have to turn to know it was Rook. His footfalls gave him away, and I cringed inwardly at how I'd somehow already memorized the sound of each of them. Their mannerisms. Fuck, they even breathed differently.

Like air wasn't a necessary thing for them. Like it was lucky to enter their lungs at all.

I rolled my eyes. They couldn't leave me alone for even five fucking minutes.

The waitress lifted her head from jotting down my order. "We have chocolate, strawberry, and va—"

Her words choked off, eyes widening at Rook just behind me with a gasp.

Yeah...he had that effect.

A startled cry from one of the patrons by the door sank into the pit of my stomach.

Maybe it wasn't Rook, maybe it was...

I carefully ran my fingers down the side of my leg, ready to make a grab for my blade.

Before I could whirl on him, he had me.

The barrel of a gun pressed to my temple. His gloved hand snaked around my waist, securing me to him, enveloping me in the scent of him.

Rook.

What the actual fuck?

"Everyone down on the ground, hands behind your head," he shouted. "Now!"

His warped image reflected back to me in the old mirror backing on the other side of the counter. Unmistakable eyes, even distorted, but the rest of his face was concealed beneath a black ski mask.

A muted shot hissed in my ear, and I snapped my head up to see he'd fired a round into the kitchen, a silencer on the barrel of his gun. It wasn't a kill shot, but a warning that had the knife brandishing cook with the Kurt Russell moustache dropping his knife and raising his hands in defeat.

"Any other heroes want to take their chances?" Rook hissed, and I could hear the smile in his words.

The gun pressed back to my temple, and I realized what was happening and had to keep the smile off my face, wear a stricken look of horror instead.

It was a con.

A motherfucking con.

Adrenaline flooded my veins, making my fingers twitch and my breaths come heavy. My face heated, and my vision swam. It probably only added to the effect of *armed robber takes hostage*.

"No," I cried. "No, please! *Please* don't kill me."

It was easy to summon the tears, they were always there, held back by the force of a strong dam I'd had in place since I was barely a teenager. They poured freely now, streaking down my face.

Rook stuffed a wad of white cloth into my hand, and I took it, hands shaking.

"Open it," he ordered me, and I clumsily found the opening to the pillow case.

He gave my waist a little squeeze that I felt all the way to my greedy little cunt.

Fuck.

"You," he hissed, momentarily training his weapon on the waitress lying on the ground muttering prayers to herself. "Get up."

She tripped as she stood, stumbling into the counter.

"Just do what he says, Cher," her plaid wearing hero called from where he lay face down on the dirty linoleum flooring next to his stool. "It's okay, doll. Everything's gonna be—"

"Oh, shut the fuck up," Rook groaned as Cher stood. "Fill it," he ordered her, the cold steel barrel back at my temple.

When she hesitated, he cocked it back and I felt the *click* all the way to the marrow of my bones. Like a current of electricity plugged straight into my flesh. I gripped the countertop, a hard breath gushed past my lips at the sensation of being *alive*.

Curiously, I peered toward the gun. Not many handguns needed manual cocking. I was no expert, preferring my blades, but Dad showed me a thing or two.

It was a Browning Hi Power. Semi-automatic. A sleek black number with a worn mahogany grip. He held it like an extension of his arm.

Why was that so damned *hot*?

Cher hurriedly emptied the register, pulling out wads of fives and tens and a few twenties. Nothing to get excited about, but right now, I didn't care, this was the most fun I'd had in *ages*.

I forced a whimper as she cautiously stretched her arms over the counter and dropped the bills into the pillowcase.

"You want the money out of the safe, too?" she asked, her voice a meek whine.

Was this bitch serious?

I hear the cook curse to himself in the kitchen and Cher realized her mistake, going whiter than the pillowcase between my fists.

"How very accommodating," Rook replied, tugging me closer to him, letting me feel the slight bulge of his erection against my lower back.

I pushed against it, biting my lip, making him grunt and pull back.

"Hey!" he shouted, spinning us both around to face the man who'd been in the booth by the door. The one with his cell phone in his hand. "*Uh, uh, uh,*" Rook cooed and roughly shoved me over to the man, forcing me to my knees at his side. He snatched a fistful of my hair, pulling until my scalp stung and I shivered.

"In the bag, *hero*," he said through gritted teeth, and I opened the bag for the man to drop his phone inside to join the cash. He wasn't giving me any dirty looks now, was he?

Dick.

"You too," Rook ordered his wife. "Your phone. In the bag. Everyone! Phones out, lay them beside you. *Now!*"

I feigned injury as Rook dragged me to my feet and forced me around the diner, collecting phones from the floor. "I'm sorry," I whimpered as I took each one, depositing them into the bag until we got back to the counter.

"Get his phone," Rook growled at Cher, gesturing to the cook in the kitchen with his gun while I took Cher's phone from the counter and dropped it in with the others.

"I don't have a phone," the cook lobbied through the pass-through window.

Cher's breath caught, giving away his lie.

Rook's rough fingers moved from my hair to my throat, the leather of his gloves flexing as he squeezed. I made a show of choking, letting my eyes bug out of my head.

"P-please," I begged.

"Do you want her blood on your hands?" Rook bellowed, his voice ringing out in the diner. "Hmm?"

"All right, *all right!*" the cook said, his hands raising palms out in a stop gesture.

I gasped for breath as Rook loosened his grip on my throat but kept his fingers there, brushing the sensitive skin on the side of my neck.

The cook reached very slowly into the front pocket of his stained apron and tossed the phone through the pass.

Cher grabbed it a second after it clattered to the floor and thrust it at me.

"Now, how's about we open that safe you mentioned, Cher?"

She sent an apologetic look to the red-faced cook before dropping to her knees and opening a small cabinet beneath the register. The telltale tinkling sound of a dial being turned gave me goosebumps.

Cher came up with an armful of cash. Stacks of bills elasticized together with little receipts at the tops of each one that denoted the amounts contained within each stack. My blood buzzed with a euphoria bordering on madness as she shakily stuffed them into the heavy bag clenched between my hands.

"Th-that's everything," Cher told Rook. "Now...now just let the girl go and—"

"An ice cream cone," interrupted Rook. "With all the flavors. Pile it high."

Her brows drew together.

"Did I fucking stutter?"

She jumped and sped into action, rushing down to the end of the counter to scoop ice cream onto a waffle cone.

Butterflies.

This psycho just gave me butterflies.

My thighs squeezed and he must've sensed where my mind went because he let his fingers slip lower, brushing down my collarbone, and lower some more until they caressed the tops of my breasts.

A soft moan escaped my lips just before Cher rushed back with a monster ice cream in her hand.

"Be a good girl and grab that for me, would you, love?"

I closed the sack of money and phones into one fist and took the ice cream with the other.

"Everybody stays down until that clock over there strikes six. If you get up, you die. If you call the police, *she* dies."

"The girl!" The cook called from the kitchen as Rook began dragging me backward to the door. "You said you'd let her go."

"Did I?" Rook asked. "*Hmm.* Don't think I did."

"Please!" I begged. "Please let me go!"

"If these good people here forget what they saw, you'll get your freedom."

"Please," I croaked, my plea meant for the patrons in the diner now as Rook hauled me out the door and around the side of the building.

Once we were out of sight of the windows, his arm around me dropped and I let out a small laugh, unable to hold it in for another second.

"That was the most—"

He ripped his mask off with one hand as he shoved me with the other, my back hitting the rough wall behind us. His lips parted as he stared openly at me, his dark eyes darting between my light ones. Trying to find something in their depths.

"Rook?"

I barely got his name out before he stole it from my lips with a brutal kiss that tore through every inch of my body like a shockwave. I gasped against his mouth as a sensation that bordered on pain twisted like a knife in my belly. The butterflies there turning to iron, their edges sharper than honed steel.

Rook's tongue slipped between my lips, and I let him take me. Lost in the feel of him as his hands gripped me roughly, fingers pushing into flesh like hot branding irons.

When his lips left mine, I blinked through a dizzy haze, unable to breathe.

His fingers gripped my chin, forcing my eyes to meet his. "You did good, Ghost."

"What?" I breathed, struggling to focus.

"You just passed your first trial."

7

CORVUS

"Is that...?" Grey trailed off as Rook emerged into the back lot of the diner, dragging Ava Jade along by her wrist. Both of them grinning like fools as ice cream dripped down Ava Jade's fingers, all the way down to her elbow, and a heavy sack swayed in Rook's fist.

They rushed for the Rover, faces flushed and eyes bright.

Fuck.

"Start the car!" Rook called before they were even inside, hurriedly tearing open the back door to help Ava Jade into the backseat before slipping in himself.

"I said *go,* man," he repeated, giving Grey's arm a shove. "Unless you want us all to be ID'd and arrested."

Sparrow laughed, leaning back in her seat with stars in her eyes as she caught her breath. I'd never seen her like that, and something within me pulled, straining against the confines I'd set for myself as a boy.

"What the fuck did you do?" I growled as Grey started the ignition.

"Forward, brother," Rook said when Grey tried to put the Rover in reverse.

"But—"

"Just do it, we don't need them seeing the Rover."

Grey muttered something to himself but did what Rook demanded, driving over the cement barrier and out onto the hard-packed dirt of the desert terrain. He'd find a way to avoid the road for as long as he could before slipping back onto it.

"What. Did. You. Do?" I asked again, whirling in my seat as the Rover bumped over uneven ground.

Rook leaned back and wrapped an arm around my Sparrow, smiling down at her in a way that made my teeth clench. She leaned into him, wiping away a tear from the force of her laughter. "Fuck," she said on a breath. "That was fun."

"Our little misfit here just passed her first trial," Rook said with a lopsided grin, and I frowned.

"What the fuck did you just say?"

"Diesel was busy," Rook explained with a shrug. "He said I should devise something for her first trial until he could get around to having something set up."

His words were like a punch to the gut.

Diesel had asked *Rook* for help with her trials, but he didn't even *tell* me. He always told me.

He never kept me in the dark.

He wouldn't—

He would, I realized, the knots in my stomach tightening for an entirely different reason now.

Damn.

Diesel asked Rook *specifically* to facilitate her first trial because he thought Rook would scare her off. He'd be the most likely to. And the least likely of the three of us to care what happened to her.

Except Diesel was wrong.

About Rook.

About Ava Jade.

He was wrong about a lot of things.

He didn't know that Billy the Butcher's blood was on her hands. Grey had filled us in on the footage he found on her phone. Footage he'd erased from the drive for good. She'd been there, watching us, and not only had she done nothing to try to stop us from giving Billy his warning, she'd decided that wasn't good enough.

She'd not only hidden quietly as we tortured him, but also finished him off after we left. Even *I* still didn't know what to make of that. My controlling nature told me she should be punished for her insubordination. We had a system. A way of doing things, and she was upsetting that. Fucking it up beyond repair.

And my inquisitiveness had me begging the question of whether it was the first time she'd killed. I didn't think it was. She wasn't haunted by it. I'd seen her the very next day, and she'd looked rested. Happy, even.

Like Rook after a kill. As though something inside of her had been sated.

She'd surprised us in every possible way. She *continued* to surprise us. She would continue to surprise Diesel, too, until she would win him over. I was sure of it. So long as she lived long enough.

"We should dump the phones," Sparrow said, licking around the base of the ice cream cone to clean up the drips of vanilla in a way that drove me absolutely mad.

I shook my head, the situation coming back into focus as Grey drove over a deep hole in the terrain and I bounced in my seat, hitting my head on the roof with a curse.

"Phones?"

"We took their phones," Sparrow explained. "We should dump them before we get too far away so they can't trace our route."

I narrowed my gaze on Rook, who shrugged.

"You held up the diner?" I asked redundantly. "With *her*?"

"You should've seen her, man." He bit his lip ring as he gazed down at her eating her ice cream, happier than a pig in shit. "She didn't know shit, but when I put the gun to her head, she played them all like fiddles. Could've had a career as an actress. I'd watch that movie on repeat."

She let out a little giggle, still high from the job, her pupils wide and dark.

"You put a fucking gun to her head?" Grey demanded, making Sparrow squint at the back of his head in the front seat while Rook began picking cell phones out of a bag of cash and tossing them out the rear window, unperturbed.

"She's still alive, isn't she?" Rook asked with a raised brow and Grey shook his head, his jaw flexing from what I could see of his side profile.

My face heated with rage, and I turned back around to face the moving landscape around us, trying to maintain a sense of calm. "It was stupid to organize it alone," I deadpanned. "You should've come to me. What if you missed something?"

"I didn't."

"What if—"

"I know how to run a fucking job, Corv. There's no CCTV out there. We parked around the back. No one saw the Rover. No one saw my face. My hands. No tatts. We took the phones. No prints. *It's fine.*"

"They saw *her*," I corrected him.

"They saw the face of a victim. A hostage."

"And when the hostage is never freed? When *the hostage* never goes to the police? When does your *hostage* start looking like an *accomplice?*"

And there it was. The hooked bait.

It was half the point of the trials, wasn't it? They saw her face. But as long as she did what she was told and didn't betray the Saints, we'd back her. She'd always have a solid alibi. She'd have access to the best lawyers money could buy. She'd stand before a judge who'd already been paid handsomely for the outcome of her trial.

So long as she was *one of us.*

Ava Jade put her face to the hot, dusted wind blowing in through her window and smiled, not giving two shits about the argument going on right next to her. I doubted she was even listening.

Rook, ignoring my comment, rifled through the bills in the bag before pulling out two large stacks and dropping them into Ava Jade's lap. She startled. Looking down at the cash and back up to Rook.

"Your cut," he explained, winking at her. "You earned it."

The way she smiled at him...

She'd never smiled at me like that. Never smiled at me *at all.*

"You still owe me," she replied, smug as she licked her ice cream. "I bet seven grand on you."

"A solid investment. Too bad you lost it on your second gamble, Ghost."

She pursed her lips, but even that couldn't hide the smile still trying to weasel its way onto her lips. I got the feeling I was missing some private joke between them and jealousy roiled in the pit of my stomach.

I turned around at the same time Rook reached forward and jammed the auxiliary button, connecting his phone to the car's speakers. The beginning notes of Queen's *We Are the Champions* played low before he reached forward again to crank it louder. I watched in the mirrors as he sang along, putting his arm back around Ava Jade. Rook rocked her side to side as the main chorus played, until she sang with him.

He gave Grey a shove in the front seat. Then kicked the back of the seat until Grey sang with them too, driving us off the uneven desert terrain and back onto a side road, leading to our next destination.

"Come on, Corv," Rook called over the music between verses. "*We are the champions—*"

"We are the champions," Sparrow and Grey echoed. The dark cloud that'd been hanging over Grey for days seemed to lift, his eyes brightening as he gave himself over to a second hand high.

So easy for him to forget his burdens. To shuck off the weight of his reality.

I wished it were even half as easy for me.

8

ROOK

The moon cast an eerie glow over the road as we veered off the highway and entered Thorn Valley at half past nine.

Ava Jade still munched on cold, stale fries from our fast food stop two hours before. She seemed determined to finish every last one even though she'd been full after just the enormous double decker burger she ordered.

She sighed as she ate the last one and set the paper container back into the bag at her feet, setting a hand on her stomach. She cooperated well with the pick up after our little stunt at the diner, seeming almost eager as I drew out the blindfold and wrapped it around her eyes, pulling it tight to her head.

I doubted it would do much to dull how lethal she was, but it did the job of hiding the location of the pick up and our arms dealer's faces from view.

My Ghost checked her phone again, flicking through notifications with a frown. I caught Rebecca Hart's name before she flicked that one away too with another heavy sigh.

Tricking her felt wrong.

My brothers didn't seem particularly at peace with it, either, but we all agreed it was necessary. After Grey told us Becca had nothing to do with the texts that had Ava Jade wound up tighter than a top, we agreed on the need to know who *did*.

It was always the plan to stop. Always the plan to have Ava Jade leave the Rover and leave her phone behind.

Grey was ready with his laptop—the software he'd need loaded up and primed for use—along with a micro-usb cord to connect it all together. It was all beneath the passenger seat.

It would take him some time to decrypt the deleted messages recovered from her phone's drive, but he had what he needed now so it was only a matter of time.

She didn't know it yet, but whoever was trying to fuck with her was a dead man walking. No one fucked with the Crows. *No one* fucked with our girl.

I winced as my lip ring tore through skin, the coppery tang of blood filling my mouth. I hadn't noticed I was biting on it.

"Think you can still get a movie in?" Grey broke the silence, turning down The Edge as he drove off the main road and up towards Briar Hall.

Ava Jade shrugged. "Maybe. But Becca went out since I wasn't coming, so..."

She shrugged again.

My phone buzzed in my pocket at the same time Grey's chimed and Corvus' chirped. It meant only one of two things and my blood sang in hopes of one over the other.

Please be Julia.

DIESEL

Corv, I need you. Grey, Alicia needs help with the month end shit from September. Go give her a hand before she has a fucking aneurism.

It was sent through our group chat, and I jammed the side button on my phone after reading it in disappointment. Would've been fun to take my Ghost to a strike two.

Ooooo, or a strike three.

I wondered if she would join me in the shed like Corvus. Watching over my shoulder as I worked.

I peered at her from the corner of my eye, trying to judge if she'd stay or if she'd run. If it would make her sick...or if she'd want to help.

The prospect of the latter made my cock harden in my jeans and I rolled my hips, savoring in the pleasure that image brought.

"Dies needs us," Corvus said from the front.

Grey shifted. "For what?"

"The books, for you," he replied. "That new one he hired is useless."

Grey didn't disagree. "What does he want you guys for?"

Corv shook his head. "Just me, and I'm not sure why."

Corvus thumbed out a message to Diesel and my phone buzzed again as it was received in the group chat.

Ava Jade, no longer staring out the window, sat up straighter in her seat.

"Should we bring her to Sanctum with us?" Grey asked and I snorted, rolling down the window to rest my arm on it, feeling the cool breeze on my neck as I dug deep into my pocket for the cigarettes there, lighting one up.

"He doesn't need me," I said, ashing my smoke out the window as they shared a look.

"I don't want her near Dies. Not right now," Corvus said to Grey. I might as well have not even bothered speaking. Not that I cared.

"Can't Rook come stay with me at Briar Hall tonight?" Ava Jade asked, and I tipped my head to one side, considering her in the moonlight. It was a simple enough question, but not one I'd ever expect her to ask.

She watched me string up Billy. Watched me beat him. Carve him up.

She was there the night outside the shed with Frank, too. Grey hadn't admitted it, but he didn't have to. Corvus and I both knew where he got that too-perfect cut on his arm. We knew who'd given it to him. Who was watching from the shadows as we unloaded poor Frank, stinking of piss and stale beer, and dragged him to my shed.

She knew what I was, and still she asked the question.

Her sea-glass eyes found mine in the dark, and in them, I saw a resolve few of the strongest men I knew possessed.

My Ghost wanted to know if she could handle me alone.

Maybe almost as much as I wanted to know it.

"Nah," I said, my lips turning up of their own accord. "Come back to the Nest with me. Have a drink. One of the others will drive you back to the Hall later."

"Why?"

"Do you have whiskey in your room?"

She shook her head.

"I do."

She pursed her lips as though to say *can't argue with that,* giving a small one shoulder shrug. "Okay, but I'm not sleeping in that closet of a room. Either you drive me back later or I'll walk back myself."

"It's settled then. I'll keep an eye on her. It'll be fun, won't it, Ghost?"

Grey's hand tensed on the wheel, and Corvus chewed on my words, his jaw grinding through the side view mirror as I finished my smoke.

Ava Jade gave a low chuckle, settling back into her seat as Grey drove us past the turn off to Briar Hall and around to the road running parallel to its grounds, around and up the mountainside.

The five-minute drive was tense, but when we got to the Nest, that tension broke as Ava Jade hopped out of the Rover. Like she was going to visit an old friend, not off to spend a few hours with a man who'd lost count of how many other men he'd killed.

This girl...

I shook my head as I stepped out of the Rover. The things I wanted to do to her. What would it take to make her scream? To make her beg?

Would she ever?

Or would she die silently? Resolute in her desire to not give in?

Mmmm...

Fuck.

"Rook," Grey called from his window, and I paused as Ava Jade went up to the front door.

"Yeah, Brother?"

He struggled with what to say, but I saw the truth of what he wished he could say written all over his face. *Don't hurt her.*

No. Worse than that.

If you hurt her, you'll be hurting me.

It stung.

Just as much as the watchful stare of Corvus from the opposite seat. A warning stare.

Where was the trust?

I'd admit I hadn't earned it, at least not in this respect, but still.

She was taking the trials. A Saint to be. A Crow in girl's clothing.

We didn't kill our own.

They should've known better.

They should've known *me* better.

I hurt women, sure, but only the ones who wanted to be hurt. They knew the risk. They *liked* the risk. Just because that one almost bled out last year didn't mean I would push it that far with Ava Jade. I wouldn't.

Would I?

I pasted on a smirk. "Don't worry, Brother," I crooned. "Her pretty face will be just as you left it when you get home."

...though I couldn't say the same for her pussy.

He nodded, his throat bobbing as he shifted gears into reverse and turned the Rover 'round. I watched the red taillights bob over the gravel drive for a moment before looking away.

Ava Jade waited in the doorway, her arms crossed over her chest. She lifted a brow. "What was that about?"

I stalked toward her, and she shifted to one side, letting me pass to unlock the front door. At least she'd left that handle and the one to the back door alone. I stepped inside, and she followed, kicking off her shoes and trailing me into the kitchen.

"I asked you a question," she pressed as I pulled two glasses down from a cupboard and poured two whiskeys, one shorter than the other. She took the fuller one before I could hand her the one with less and I smirked.

Too slow...

"My brothers worry too much."

"About you?"

"About other things."

"Should *I* be worried?" she asked, leaning against the counter by the stove to sip her whiskey, her lips tightening in a slight grimace at the taste, though it didn't stop her from taking another sip. A larger one.

I didn't answer her, downing my whiskey in one gulp to pour another.

She took my non-reply for what it was: the uncertain truth.

I couldn't tell her one way or the other if she should be worried. Tonight? No.

In the future? Possibly.

There were too many factors.

Too many nights I didn't remember, where I woke up covered in red.

But that was before I got clean. Now, I remembered my kills. Now, I have more control.

More than my brothers thought I had.

"They should trust you more," she said after a few minutes spent in easy silence, sipping whiskey. "You're family. Their brother. Family means trust. Or, at least it should."

Her face darkened and I felt something in me darken at the sight. Sea-glass eyes fell to the floor, shifting as her fingers clenched her glass a little tighter than they had a moment before that.

"Who hurt you?" I asked, the words evicted from the dark place inside. The decision to speak them wholly unconscious.

Ava Jade looked up, her lips parted, then closed. She cleared her throat. "No one."

She kicked at the floor and then grinned. "Do you want to fuck with them?"

"What? Who?"

Her eyes lit with mischief, and I licked my lips.

"The others. They don't trust you like they should. I say we fuck with them. Tit for tat."

She watched my tongue travel along my lower lip, her breathing growing heavier as she shifted her feet.

How could I say no to that? How could I ever say no to her?

I grinned.

"What did you have in mind?"

9

AVA JADE

I'd be sticky for days after this, but it was going to be worth it to see their faces.

"Hurry up," I urged Rook, they could be back any minute.

He ladled more of the red liquid from the metal mixing bowl onto my stomach, letting it drip and puddle on the kitchen floor.

"Does it look real?" I asked, trying to arrange my limbs in an unnatural way. The way I'd have fallen if I was a hundred and twenty pounds of *dead* Ava Jade.

"*Shit*," Rook hissed, stepping back to admire our handiwork. He bit his lip ring, sucking a noisy breath in through his teeth. This was turning him on, I could see it in his dark eyes.

It'd been easy to mix up a couple liters of fake blood. You only needed a few household ingredients. Hell, we had all those ingredients back at the trailer and that was saying something since our cupboards were chronically empty. But with corn syrup as the main ingredient, it was going to take some elbow grease and a full bottle's worth of shampoo to get it all out of my hair and off my skin.

Worth it.

Unless they killed Rook, but I was banking on that not happening. They'd probably say something like *I knew this would happen*, or *I told you so*, and then offer to help get rid of my body.

That's when I'd jump up and shout *surprise motherfuckers*, and hopefully scare the ever-loving shit out of them.

Solid plan.

Definitely a solid plan.

Rook sloshed more blood to the floor and nodded to himself. "You're a masterpiece," he said.

I smiled. "Hurry, let me see before they get back. Take a picture."

I put on my dead girl face and held my breath while Rook took out his phone and snapped a picture, kneeling in the fake blood afterward to let me see.

Damn.

"It looks so real," I said on a laugh. Getting my skin to look so pale hadn't been easy, but the darker reddish-purple circles around my eyes weren't faked. They were *au naturel,* courtesy of Diesel's watchdog order. Sleeping with another person in my room didn't bode well for comfort.

The blood though...it was looking super realistic. Pooled on my belly until it was dark, concealing the fact that there wasn't actually a wound there. Spilling over onto the floor, pooling around my 'corpse' until it soaked into the edges of my dark hair, fanned out over the floor.

One of my blades on the floor next to me, just out of reach of my bloodied fingertips.

So fucking dramatic.

Tires over gravel had Rook pocketing his phone. "That's them. They're back."

"Go!" I hissed. "Like we planned. You come in from the other room when they get to the kitchen."

Rook's lips pressed into a smile as he shook his head. "This is so fucking cruel."

"They deserve it," I whispered, hearing a car door open outside. "Now get the fuck out of here."

He lifted a hand to scratch the back of his neck, the first and only sign that he might've thought this wasn't as good of an idea as I did.

He'd see. It was a *great* idea.

I owed Corvus a mountain of vengeance after the way he'd been treating me. I was only just getting started.

I took a few slow, shallow breaths as the front door opened, willing my body into stillness. *I am dead.*

I am dead.

Dead girls don't breathe.

Dead girls don't move.

My body grew heavier, each limb forced into a state of relaxation. Limp. Numb. I got ready to only permit myself the shallowest, tiniest of breaths.

"I need a real bed," I heard Grey mutter from the doorway, continuing their muffled conversation from outside. "I have bruises on top of bruises from that floor."

"So buy a mattress."

A pause.

Clearly Grey hadn't considered that as an option.

Corvus sighed. "Fine. I'll stay at Briar Hall with her tonight. Tomorrow we'll go get a fucking cot or some shit. Sound good?"

"Yeah. Thanks, man."

"I still say it'd be easier to chain her up here."

Grey chuckled and a wicked sense of satisfaction raced through me.

My blood sang with anticipation, making it almost impossible to stay still as their footfalls echoed down the hall, coming closer.

Oh my god.

This was going to be fucking *priceless.*

They entered the kitchen.

Don't breathe.

"Good luck with tha—"

Grey's words abruptly cut off, along with the sound of their footsteps.

"*AJ...*" Grey's voice was no more than a whisper. A rough exhalation of air.

He flew into action a split second later. Uncoordinated footfalls pounding on the floor as he rushed to me.

"AJ!"

I could sense him at my side, my heart pounding so loudly in my ears it was a wonder he couldn't hear it as his hands hovered over me, brushing over the surface of my skin, my clothing, as though he were too afraid to touch me.

A playful whistled tune drifted into the room, along with the sound of crinkling plastic as Rook dragged a tarp into the kitchen as we planned.

But, unlike we planned, his whistled song paused. So did the sound of the tarp dragging over the tile floor. It took everything within me not to open my eyes and see what made him stop.

"Corvus..." Rook trailed off, his brother's name on his lips almost a question. Confusion evident in his tone.

"*What...*" Corvus snarled, trailing off as he struggled to inhale. "*What did you do?*"

"Come on, man, she was a liability and you know it."

"*What the fuck did you do!*"

Something crashed and there were five stomping steps that shook the ground as Corvus went after Rook.

Another crash, the sound of something raining down onto the plastic tarp.

"Stop!" Grey called, his voice sounding oddly broken, pitched all wrong. But he didn't go to help Rook or to stop Corvus; he stayed with me, his hands less fluttering now, but insistent as they struggled through the sticky blood to find the hollow under my chin, searching for a pulse as he twined the fingers of his other hand through mine, squeezing tight.

This...this wasn't funny anymore.

Rook coughed as a loud *thud* resounded in the kitchen. The cough turning into a laugh. The fucker knew this would happen. He was probably banking on it. I doubted he was even fighting back. Reveling in the pain like I once did.

Another thud, and I shuddered. This wasn't what I wanted.

"She was one of us!" Corvus roared, and I heard Rook struggle for breath.

Enough.

Grey found my pulse.

"She's still alive," he called, but Corvus was beyond hearing him.

I squinted an eye open, wincing at the sight of his face, drained of color, frantic. "Gotcha?" I said, biting my lip to draw attention away from the feeling squirming around in my gut.

He fell back, blinking like he was seeing me for the first time. The reality of the situation slowly registering as Corvus threw Rook against a wall at the other end of the kitchen.

"Christ," Grey said on a breath, scrambling to his feet, slipping on the blood. He caught himself on the kitchen island, getting his footing as he called to his brothers.

"Corv, stop!"

Corvus' hands were around Rook's throat. His back tight and biceps flexed to bursting.

Grey grabbed hold of him. "I said stop!"

But Corvus flung him off, blind to everything but his target.

Shit.

"It was a joke," I blurted, standing. "Corvus."

No response and Rook's face was turning a scary shade of red, though it didn't diminish the gleam in his eyes. Just like I thought, he wasn't even fighting back, not really. He held Corvus' arms, staring his brother square in the face. Daring him to finish what he started. His lip dribbled blood. A fresh shiner swelling on the edge of his left brow.

It hurt to watch.

I closed the gap, batting Grey's hands away when he tried to stop me from advancing. "*Corvus,*" I hissed.

I put my hand on his arm near the wrist, gripping him. Forcing him to *see* me.

He flinched, his burning stare finding me through his rage. His pinched face twitched, a knot breaking and reforming between his brows as his bright blue eyes flickered with recognition.

"Let him go."

His hands loosened, and Rook choked for air, bending over to hack until he could breathe again.

"You could've killed him," I said, the words venomous. Not how I intended them.

"Sparrow?"

His fingers brushed my cheek, and I pulled back, flushing hot.

"It was a joke," I repeated, angry, though I couldn't peg the reason why. "Just a stupid fucking joke."

I licked my fingers violently to prove the point. "See? Corn syrup."

His lips parted on a breath, a vein throbbing at his temple when he clenched his jaw again. "*A joke?*"

"Yeah."

"You think this was fucking *funny?*"

He shook his head before shoving past me, the smack of his firm body into my shoulder sending me back a step. I felt the hit all the way down to the pit of my stomach. It festered there, the ache spreading to my chest.

The front door slammed a second later. Then another door. The garage outside.

We all listened to the backdrop of Rook's strained breaths as an engine started. A motorcycle. And then he was gone. The whine of the engine and exhaust loud as he sped away from the Nest.

Rook found his way to the sink, hunched, running the water cold and cupping it into his mouth with his hand to spit reddish water down the drain. He swiped the back of his hand over his mouth when he finished, reaching for the whiskey on the counter to take a swig.

Grey's hands balled to clenched fists at his sides, his expression darkening by the second.

"Grey?" I hedged. "I didn't mean—"

"I need a minute," he interrupted, walking away before I could finish as he left too. Following Corvus' path out the door, to the Rover, and away down the road.

I pressed a hand to my stomach, hating the guilt that I felt lying heavily there. "That was way less funny than I thought it would be," I muttered.

Rook shrugged, setting the whiskey aside. "I thought it was pretty funny."

"You're an idiot."

"So I've been told."

He laughed and winced, coughing.

"You're hurt."

He licked the blood from his lip and looked away.

I went to him, lifting the edge of his shirt to see his chest. He lifted a brow, but didn't stop me as I ran my fingers over his tan, muscled abdomen. Over the tattoo on his hip and up higher, to the rapidly darkening bruise on his ribs. I pressed gently over each rib until he hissed at my touch at the fifth one up.

"It might be broken."

"Wouldn't be the first time."

I cocked my head at him. "Do you often try to kill each other?"

"Brothers. It's what we do. He wouldn't have killed me. He'd miss me too much."

"Sure as hell looked like he was doing his best to," I scoffed.

"You don't know him like we do."

A silence stretched between us as I continued to lightly trace the edge of the tattoo curving over his hip bone and disappearing into the low-riding waist of his dark denim jeans.

"What happened to you?" I asked, truly curious. Needing to know what forged him. If he was born or made.

I liked to think I was born good. Happy. Healthy. Without even a touch of madness.

I also hated to think that, because it would mean that the darkness took root later. After mom did what she did. After that man bled out near the train tracks in Lennox. It would mean that I *let it* take root.

Did Rook's darkness bury itself deep inside him after a trauma? Or was it there all along? Was mine?

Did our darkness lurk deep inside since we took our first breaths? Waiting for us to give into it...

"I'll show you mine if you show me yours," he said in a whisper.

I swallowed hard.

"The person who hurt you..." Rook trailed off, catching my hand as it traced a path across his lower abdomen, trapping it in his iron grip. Making me look at him. Making me remember the man by the train tracks. The weight of him pressed against my body, holding me down. The feel of him between my legs. Of his blood spraying over my face and bare chest. "What was their name?

I shook my head. "It doesn't matter."

"It does."

"It doesn't matter because he's dead."

He didn't seem surprised. A bit disappointed, maybe, like he was sad he wouldn't get the chance to play with whoever it was in his torture shed.

It really was a shame. I'd have liked to watch.

"You?" he asked simply, and ice bloomed behind my breast. A cold sweat slicked my chest and forehead. I'd never told anyone since the day it happened and that old fear came rushing back. The image of a cell, cold, with iron bars and a toilet in the corner flashed over my eyelids as I shuddered, closing my eyes.

But the man on the tracks wasn't the only man I'd killed now. There was Billy, too. You could even say I had a hand in the death of the Ace at the warehouse. And I didn't lose any sleep over them like I did that first kill.

I was smarter, more careful.

And they deserved it.

I nodded.

I placed the hand not clutched in Rook's tattooed fingers to his stomach again, slipping my hand along bumps of muscle to his back, finding the puckered ridge of a burn hidden beneath his ink. "And the one who did this?"

He didn't move as I fingered one scar, then another, staring at me like he was looking for something he couldn't easily find. "Barbequed."

A smile found its way to my lips, and his brows furrowed at my reaction.

"Good."

Rook jerked forward, taking me by the throat to pin me against the center island. The hard marble countertop slammed into the base of my spine, and I gasped, kicking up a heel to snatch a blade. He could've, but he didn't try to stop me as I drew it and pressed it between us, to the zipper of his jeans.

His hold on my throat didn't waver.

"Tell me to let go," he challenged, leaning in until his warm breath was a promise on my lips. His own upper lip raising in a silent snarl. He squeezed, and I moaned.

I fucking *moaned* as he leaned in ever closer, a knowing smirk on his lips.

"Go ahead and cut me, Ghost. Leave your mark. I will."

"You can try," I croaked before thrusting my arm upward, taking him by surprise. His hold on my throat was broken, and I ducked low, rolling out of his reach, my blade drawn as I fixed my stance, a thrill going through me.

He ran his tongue over his teeth like a wolf might right before a kill and my breathing hitched.

"Will you kill me?" I asked seriously, the ache between my thighs begging to be quelled in the way I thought only this Crow could quench it.

"Want to find out?"

My nostrils flared.

Did I?

I saw the madness in him almost from the start, but it was a familiar thing. An intelligent sort of insanity. Others didn't trust him. Thought he had no self-control. I was willing to bet it was the complete opposite. He had all the control in the world, he just decided to let it go sometimes.

Was I willing to stake my life on it?

Rook darted forward, and I parried to the right, going around the kitchen island to put it between us, stepping carefully to avoid the tacky smears of fake blood on the floor.

He watched me with the eyes of a predator, still, and calm. Waiting for his opening.

I shook my head, laughing to myself. At the idiocy of tempting the devil.

But that was exactly what I was going to do.

From the first moment I saw him, I wanted him. He was the forbidden fruit and I was fucking *starving*.

"Fuck it," I muttered, ditching my blade. Letting it join its cousin on the floor as I leapt over the kitchen island, tackling Rook until *he* smashed into the countertop. He took me like he was the one who was starving. Defiling my mouth with his wicked tongue.

A low sound in his throat made my knees quake as he took a fistful of my sticky hair and held me there, stealing all the air from my lungs. Bruising my lips with his kiss. His lip ring cutting into me until I tasted blood.

His hard cock pressed insistently against my belly, and I reached my fingers between us to stroke it through his jeans, making him groan. Little hard nubs ribbed his cock, and he shuddered as my fingers brushed over each one. His teeth found my lower lip to bite down hard, the pain adding to the eruption of sensations making my body shudder and shake.

I unbuttoned his jeans, rushing to lower the zipper. Wanting to see what I could feel through his jeans. To free it.

Rook's cock sprang free, nudging against my palm. Hot and thick and harder than steel. Lined with a row of frenum piercings running up the base like a ladder. I counted eleven. Eleven to form Jacob's Ladder. I'd always wanted to be fucked by a pierced cock, and I licked my lips at the sight of him. I jerked him hard, making him thrust forward at my pull.

He laughed, hot against my mouth. "You want to play rough, Ghost?"

His fist in my hair pulled down, forcing me to my knees. "We can play rough."

I knew what he meant to do. To force his way past my lips, but I was already two steps ahead of him, taking him deep into my mouth, making him curse.

I took him deeper still, wanting to feel him at the back of my throat. The laddered piercing ran over my tongue, pushing back until I choked. Rook stared down at me incredulously as I opened my mouth wide for him, holding him there until I could hardly breathe.

"*Fuck...*"

I wanted him. I wanted him so fucking badly it hurt.

I needed him to show me his darkness, because then maybe...

Maybe I could show him mine.

He pulled back after another second and I gasped for air.

"Fuck my mouth," I demanded. "Don't hold back."

Fear flickered over his features, gone so quickly I questioned whether I saw it at all as he slammed back into my mouth, using his fist in my hair to hold my lips around the base of his cock.

And then he did what I asked.

He fucked my tight little throat until it burned, until I was gasping and tears burned in my eyes. Until my panties were ruined from my own wetness. My cunt throbbing with a vicious ache, demanding to be touched.

I reached my hand down, fumbling to get my fingers below the waistband of my pants as Rook continued to pound into my mouth, low, rough grunts falling from his lips.

"No," he growled, popping out from between my lips, leaving me gasping. He had me by the throat again, and I was beyond fighting him, giving myself over to whatever he wanted. Happy to *not* be in control for once. Even if it meant my end.

My back found the countertop of the center island. The air knocked from my lungs as Rook dragged me to its edge, releasing my throat to tear my pants off.

They were still hanging uselessly from one leg when he pushed between them and slid two fingers against my wet heat, making me startle with a sudden cry at the violent sensation.

My back arched, and I pushed closer to him, aching for him to take me.

A tug on my ankle and I realized he'd taken my last blade from its sheath there. I bucked again as he laid the flat edge of it against my stomach, cold and hard.

I watched as he traced a line with it downward, turning it slowly to its freshly honed edge.

He watched me carefully while he moved the blade, biting his lip ring, breathing hard.

His cock was almost level with my opening, jutting out from him, throbbing in time with his heartbeat. The little silver balls catching the light. Menacing and glorious and *all fucking mine.*

"Do it," I told him. "Do it all."

He flicked the blade just below my hip bone, and I sucked in a breath as the fresh cut met the air. He bared his teeth, sucking in breath through them as his muscles bunched. Watching transfixed as the warmth spilled down my hip, rolling onto the counter.

It was shallow. I cut *myself* deeper than that.

"More," I hissed, the feeling of being *alive,* of *feeling* awakening something inside I thought long dead. "*More.*"

This time when he pressed the knife to my flesh on the opposite side of my hip, I pushed into the blade, my eyes rolling back at the sweet, *sweet* release of the pain.

Rook drew back and the blade slipped out, leaving a fresh trail of red over the counter. He blinked, snapping out of whatever held him hostage and threw the blade, embedding it in a cupboard. It was a good throw, and I squinted at him.

"You aren't the only one who knows how to use a blade, Ghost."

He grinned, rough fingers curving around my thighs, lips glistening as he watched the streams of crimson flow out of the wounds like ribbons wrapping around my hips and waist.

He pulled at the same time he thrusted, seating himself inside me to the hilt in one movement.

I lurched as he hit something deep inside me, whimpering as he settled himself there. There was no time to adjust to his size before he was edging out, his Jacob's Ladder rubbing in the most delicious way before he thrust again. Harder. His thighs slapped noisily against the counter. My body heaved against the cool marble.

I cried out, and he tipped his head back, his jaw taut as he released sounds of his own ecstasy.

"Fuck, you're so wet for me," he groaned as he thrust again, the pain pleasure mix of his fucking already sending me dangerously close to the edge.

"Rook!" I blurted on his next thrust, baring my teeth at his bruising force.

"Does it hurt?" he asked, never ceasing.

"Yes."

"Do you like it?"

He doubled his speed until I bounced on the countertop, his fingers digging deep into the meaty flesh of my thighs as he fucked me.

"*Yes*," I moaned, biting down on my lip to keep from screaming as my orgasm built.

He changed the angle, pitching himself forward, and I screamed at the loss of the build he'd been laying stroke by stroke. But then his fingers left my thigh to wrap around my throat and my eyes flew open to meet his.

When his other hand grabbed my aching clit, I arched again, unable to scream this time for the dam blocking my air supply. He pinched it hard, and I buckled, then he soothed the ache with gentler circular movements, never changing the pace of his cock between my legs.

"Holy fuck," I whimpered when his grip on my throat loosened just long enough for me to draw a breath.

He began to slow, and I growled. "If you stop, I'll kill you."

He smiled, bending to take a nipple into his mouth through my shirt, I clutched his head with a crow of surprise when he bit down, my fingers tangling in his hair, gripping so tightly I'd be shocked if I didn't rip a bunch out.

"*Oh god,*" I said on a breath, feeling my climax build.

Rook, sensing it, re-tightened his grip on my throat, rolling my nipple between his teeth, forcing me to jump from that ledge.

He grunted, pained and shuddering, coming to his own release, and it was that knowledge that broke me. I came hard on his cock, gripping him like he was the only life raft in a turbulent sea. Stars burst against the back of my eyelids as I struggled for breath.

He pumped his last with a feral sound stealing from his lips. When his hand around my throat opened, I cried out, shouting as the orgasm continued to tear through me, making my muscles tighten and spasm, legs shaking, cunt throbbing.

Rook remained there, seated inside me, lightly flicking my swollen clit to keep the orgasm rolling even when I tried to fight him off, tried to squirm away, unable to take any more.

His cock slid out, hands dragging down my body until he was upright again, breathing heavily.

The front door burst open, and I pulled my knees in, rolling from the countertop to snatch a blade from the floor as Grey raced into the kitchen, wild eyed.

I made my gaping mouth shut, staring like a kid caught with his hand in the cookie jar.

Rook leaned back against the counter by the sink, wholly unbothered. His cock still hard but softening slowly.

It took Grey a moment to realize there was no threat. The grip on the gun in his right hand loosened as he swallowed, replacing it into the back of his jeans.

"If you gotten back just a little sooner, you could've joined us," Rook said, bending to grab his pack of cigarettes from the floor, tugging one out to put it between his lips.

Grey frowned.

"You know how Corvus feels about smoking in the house," Grey said, his shoulders tensing as he waltzed through the kitchen past us to the stairs. "Go outside."

"Grey," I hedged and he paused on the landing, his knuckles going white from their grip on the banister.

"Stay here tonight," he said without turning. "If you don't want to sleep in the spare room, I'm sure *Rook* won't mind sharing his bed."

With that, he left us, ascending the stairs. His footfalls echoed in the silence, but there came no slammed door. Just the faint tap of wood on wood. Of a door closing without a handle to keep it properly shut.

I winced, dropping my head with a sigh.

"Want a dart?" Rook offered, and I turned to find him lighting the cigarette between his lips while holding another out to me.

I stole the one from his lips instead, inhaling the tarry smoke and exhaling it on a sigh. I wasn't a smoker, but there was something about a good smoke after a good fuck.

I took another drag before passing it back. "You held back," I accused him. I felt almost cheated. The truth was, I could tell he was holding back *a lot*. The fact that he *could* hold back boded well for my survival, but I'd told him not to. I wanted it all. Every dark, depraved part, but he'd denied me that. Why?

The smug look dropped from his face. "I…"

"You what?"

He jerked his head to the stairs. "Come on, Ghost. You need bandages—and a shower."

10

GREY

I couldn't believe the two of them. How either of them thought for a second that their little prank would be funny was beyond my fucking ability to understand. What I felt in that horrible moment when I saw her there on the floor, pale and bloodied and still...

It was unlike anything I'd ever felt before.

The *loss*.

The terror.

The fucking pain.

All felt through a sieve of numbness. Like I was in a nightmare. Like it wasn't real. Couldn't be real. Like I was beside myself, not really inside the cage of my bones anymore, but forced to bear witness as a phantom bystander. Able to feel all the pain, but unable to do anything to make it stop.

A prank.

A fucking prank.

More like a slap in the face, but maybe one I deserved for not trusting my brother. He'd crawled and clawed his way to the man he was now since Barrettes Home for Boys and since the years we don't talk about that came after.

My bicep ached and burned as I lifted the dumbbell for the last rep of the set, grimacing as I lowered it down to the ground for a moment before switching sides. Across the home gym we built into half the garage last year, Rook pummeled a heavy bag, dancing around it like there wasn't anyone or anything else in the room.

I gritted my teeth as I began reps on the left side, watching his lithe body strike blow after blow, ducking low, keeping his face protected.

Funnily enough, their *prank* wasn't what kept me up half the night.

I truly didn't know whether I wanted to punch him in the face or pat him on the back. I'd been vacillating between the two since I walked in on them last night in the kitchen.

As if my brother knew exactly where my head was, hadn't spoken to me at all since he came in to train twenty minutes ago. He just gave me a nod and went about his business. Patiently waiting for me to make up my mind between that punch or that pat. Happy to accept whatever I decided on.

She's good for him, the logical part of my mind argued. I'd already noticed some positive changes in him over the past few weeks. The itch he usually had by now wasn't nearly as prominent. He was drinking a bit less. He seemed *happy*. And not *I-just-killed-someone* happy, but actually happy. Rook never trained in the mornings, either. He reserved mornings for late wake-ups, spiked OJ, and the inevitable shouting from Corv for him to move his ass.

I wanted to be happy for him, but there was the other part of me—the one that whispered through clenched teeth *she's mine*.

I had her first, after all.

She liked me best, didn't she?

But didn't she also like Rook? And even on some level, Corvus, too?

We'd shared before. Once or twice. But those girls didn't matter. Not like AJ.

Inside the Nest, I heard heavy footsteps thudding down stairs and sighed, letting the dumbbell back down to the mat for a stretch and a break before my next set. Whatever he was coming to say, I didn't want a dumbbell in my hand when he said it. As it was right now, I was liable to throw it at him.

He came home in the early hours of the morning, not bothering to be quiet as he parked his Ducati and entered the house. He spent the hours leading to dawn pacing his room or rifling through the kitchen. I was having a hard enough time sleeping as it was *without* his noise keeping me up.

Corvus stepped through the open door to the garage, his back raised and jawline tense. "Why aren't you watching her?" he demanded of Rook, his bloodshot blue eyes laser focused on my brother.

Rook fell back a step, wiping the sweat from his upper lip before lowering his wrapped fists. He pointed two fingers at himself. "Me?"

Corvus' brows lowered, his cheekbones flaring.

"She's asleep," Rook defended. "Besides man, she ain't going anywhere."

"If she does, it's on *you* to explain that shit to Dies."

"Fine."

But Corvus wasn't finished, his shoulders shook so slightly that if you didn't know him well enough to know the signs of his anger, you'd never notice. And right now, Corvus was furious, and he had something else to say.

"Fine," he growled. "Maybe you want to explain to me why she's naked in your bed, then?"

...so I guessed we weren't going to be talking about their little prank last night then.

Rook raised a dark brow at him. "You're smart enough to figure that one out."

His nostrils flared for a moment before he turned his rage on me. "And you?" he pressed. "You've fucked her too, haven't you? And don't fucking lie to me."

I lengthened my spine, standing to place the dumbbell back onto the rack with a sigh.

"I did," I admitted, my tone filled with more animosity than I intended. I never lied to him. I never lied to either of them. Except for her. To protect her.

When I turned around, crossing my arms as I leaned against the half rack, he was still watching me. That animalistic gleam in his eyes told me he was on the very precipice of his control. I'd never seen him this bad this often. Maybe he was right. AJ was a threat. She might just be the death of us.

But oh what a sweet death it would be.

As I began to come up with ways I might restrain him if he actually went feral, something in his stare changed and the muscles near his cheekbones twitched as he began to calm and eventually to sag, sighing heavily.

He wiped a palm over his mouth, partially covering a shaky breath.

"I don't get it," he said finally, no longer looking at either of us, but searching the mats at his feet instead, like they might hold an answer he was seeking. "Why..." he started but stopped.

"Why not you?" Rook supplied, and I squinted at him, confused.

That wasn't what I thought Corvus was getting at, but I could see it now. The tightness between his eyes. The set of his shoulders. He was angry, yes, but he was fucking *jealous,* too.

When Corvus didn't reply, giving away the truth, Rook stopped the heavy bag from swinging gently back and forth and began unwrapping his hands, squatting to sit on a low weight-lifting bench. "Because you're a complete and utter dick."

I cleared my throat to cover a laugh. "He's right," I agreed. "And a controlling asshole to boot."

"When it comes to Ava Jade, at least," Rook added, and I snorted.

"Name someone he's *not* a controlling dickhead with?"

"Don't fucking push me right now," Corvus warned and, rolling his shoulders back. "I'm only like that with her because she—"

"She likes to push your buttons?" Rook interrupted with a mischievous smirk.

"Because she refuses to be controlled?" I added.

"Oh!" Rook blurted. "I know, because you want her all to yourself and you can't stand the thought of her wanting us more than she wants you. Is that it?"

I grimaced.

"Low blow, brother," I leaked out through another grimace.

Corvus' face reddened for a second before the blood drained back out.

"I already want to skin you alive for that fucking shit you pulled last night, Rook. *Don't. Push. Me.*"

He pinched the bridge of his nose. "It's not because of that," he said. "Not *just* that, anyway. It's..."

"Because you care about her?"

I could see it now and wasn't sure how I hadn't seen it clearly before. Corvus cared about Ava Jade. Similar to how he cared about us. It wasn't just control for the sake of control. He didn't give a flying fuck what happened to any other girl, or many of Diesel's men. He didn't try to control *them* because he didn't care about them.

He was a controlling prick with us because he cared. He demanded a reply when he texted because he cared. He wouldn't let Ava Jade out of our sight for the same reason. I doubted it had anything to do with Diesel's orders at all.

He just didn't understand her—the things she needed. What she would and wouldn't tolerate or understand. She didn't know him. How could she when he was always so busy erecting walls to cage himself in?

"Admitting it doesn't make you weak," I continued. "We all care about her."

Corvus opened his mouth with a rebuttal, but I shut him up with a glare. "Don't lie to me," I said, turning his own words against him. "Lie to yourself if you want, but don't lie to us."

"If you were right, which I'm not saying you are..." He trailed off, and I caught Rook rolling his eyes when Corv wasn't looking. "How would I...*you know*...make it up to her?"

"Stop being such a dick, for starters," Rook put in, going back to the heavy bag bare-fisted for another few hits.

"You could try giving her some trust. Some freedom."

His upper lip curled.

"Or...you could try flowers?"

He blinked at me like I just said the stupidest thing in the world. "All right, yeah, that won't work for AJ." I thought about it. "You owe her a blade, don't you?"

"I say get her a flamethrower," Rook grunted between hits.

"You're *not* getting a flamethrower," I told him.

"It's not for me, it's for her," he argued, pausing.

"Sure it is."

"You really think I can fix this?" Corvus asked, stopping my and Rook's little sidebar stone dead. "She hates me."

I shook my head. "Not as much as you think she does."

"She's one of us," Rook said to Corvus, his heaving breaths evening out as he sniffed and reached for his water bottle. He fixed Corvus with a hard stare as he took a swig and set the bottle back down, his stare never wavering. "You said so yourself last night. Remember?"

"I didn—"

"*You did,*" Rook barked. "She's a Crow and you know it. She belongs to *us*...and we belong to her. The sooner you both stop fighting it, the sooner we can all be exactly what we're meant to."

11

AVA JADE

My stomach rumbled as I rolled to the edge of Rook's bed and forced myself to sit up with a sigh. I glanced back at the disheveled fur covers and silky black sheets and pillows, but he wasn't there. My thighs clenched, cunt aching as I recalled vivid images of him between my thighs last night. Of his thick, warm cock in my mouth.

I traced the line of the small two inch cut running crossways below my hip bone, and shivered, all my little hairs standing on end.

I shifted against the soft sheets and searched the floor for my clothes, but couldn't find them even with the light from the hall filtering in through the half open door.

The smell of cooking bacon that woke me made my mouth water as I stole a swath of black fabric from the floor. It appeared to be a top sheet that I'm assuming a housekeeper put on his bed only for him to kick-off the first night it was there.

A house full of boys didn't stay this clean without a little help, though in all the times I'd spied on them here or listened in, I'd never heard or seen a cleaning person anywhere near the Nest.

I folded the sheet lengthwise and wrapped it around my back, crossing the ends in front to tie at the back of my neck. It was the ugliest toga you ever did see, but it was soft as fuck and would have to do for now. I'd go down naked to get the bacon if I had to, but the morning brought with it a chill and the makeshift dress did just enough to stave it off.

The Nest grew warmer the further outside of Rook's den I got, and I wondered if he kept it purposefully colder in there than the rest of the house. If he actually slept with those heavy furs covering him all night, he must've because there was no way I could sleep beneath them without sweating my ass off otherwise. And I had slept beneath them, like a fucking baby.

The best sleep I'd had in weeks.

I couldn't even remember the feel of him lying next to me, which made me question whether he even had slept next to me. Or if after I slipped into his bed, still damp from the shower, and he laid the heavy covers on me, he'd just left?

I followed my nose down the stairs, salivating as the smell of breakfast grew stronger with each step. I paused on the landing, finding Corvus swirling and tossing a pan of small-cut potatoes shimmering with oil.

He expertly switched between three different pans and checked the bacon in the oven, pulling it out to place it atop a cooling rack on the counter.

His back stiffened slightly before he turned, feeling my eyes on him maybe. His lips parted as they took in the swath of silky black fabric covering my naked body, before he turned back, the tension never leaving his shoulders.

"Morning," he said curtly.

"Uh...morning."

I went to the sink, searching through the cupboards for a cup to fill with water before planting myself at a stool at the kitchen island, the furthest one from Corvus.

"Hungry?"

"Starving."

I peered around the edge of the doorway leading to the living room, but couldn't see the others. Where did they go?

"*So,*" I said, playing with the condensation on my glass. "You're not still angry about last night, then?"

A derisive laugh told me everything I needed to know, but he replied anyway. "Oh, I'm angry, but I told Rook I'd skin him alive if he ever pulled something like that again."

I pursed my lips, noticing for the first time how *clean* the kitchen was. I'd passed the fuck out after my shower so who...

"Did you..." I trailed off. "Did you clean up the, *um,* the mess?"

"Fuck no. It was spotless by the time I got back."

Rook, then. I smirked. I owed him one for that.

"You don't give him enough credit, you know. He isn't the loose cannon you think he is."

"You don't know him that well."

"*...well enough,*" I muttered to myself, squirming in my seat right next to the spot on the kitchen island where we'd...

Best not to think about it or I'd sully his pretty sheets.

Corvus grunted, going back to focusing on the stove. He flipped the eggs before taking down two plates and beginning to fill them with crisp bacon, sautéed spinach, hash browns, and eggs. Maybe the others weren't here, then, or maybe it was presumptive of me to assume I was going to be offered a hot breakfast.

Once he'd finished arranging everything how he wanted it, he turned, pushing a plate down the length of the marble counter to me.

I must've had a look on my face because he frowned. "Thought you said you were hungry?"

"I am," I admitted, swallowing to clear my mouth of saliva.

"Eat," he ordered. "You've dropped at least five pounds in the last week. You need to keep your strength."

I ignored the way it sounded like a command because in truth, I planned to fucking annihilate everything on this plate and lick it clean. Even the spinach, and I didn't even like spinach. But he did something to it to make it smell like green gold.

The eggs were perfectly cooked. Buttery soft with slightly runny yolks. The toast was some freshly baked ancient grain blend that tasted like it came straight from 1892.

Unable to help myself, I moaned as I bit into a piece of bacon and caught Corvus watching me as he stood at the other end of the counter, eating his own breakfast slowly. The tiniest smirk tugged at the edge of his lips, and I schooled my face back to its usual hostile wariness, making myself slow down so my stomach wouldn't be aching when I was finished.

I couldn't remember the last time someone made me a meal. I must've been very young. A child.

"So, who's with me today?" I asked when I was nearing the end of my breakfast, resisting the tempting urge to run my fingers over the juices on my plate and lick them clean. I didn't want to give him any more satisfaction than I already had. That prank last night was far less than he deserved after all the shit he'd pulled over the past weeks.

"I have an essay to write and want to change my clothes. I need a run, too."

Corvus mulled over my request, chewing his food painfully slow as he considered.

I jumped as a man's garbled electronic voice screeched from the front entryway.

"*Door!*" It yelled. "*Door!*"

"Is that your fucking doorbell sound?" I asked, my heart pounding.

He was really smirking now, and trying to hide it.

"Rook chose it," he said by way of explanation before leaving the kitchen to answer it, wiping his hands on the tea towel slung over his shoulder.

I took the opportunity while he left the room to hop down and grab two more pieces of bacon from the tray on the counter, stuffing them quickly in my mouth before going to sit back down and chew furiously, eyes rolling at how good it tasted.

He must have done something to it to make it taste so good.

I overheard a muffled conversation at the door and let myself relax. I half expected it to be an intruder. Maybe my would-be stalker. Or a Saint come to give me another trial.

The door shut and Corvus came back into the kitchen just as I finished swallowing the wad of bacon in my mouth.

"What was that about?"

That's when I noticed the long, slim black box in his hand. I lifted a brow at it.

"It's, *uh*...It's for you actually."

What the fuck did he just say?

Corvus repositioned himself, leaning against the counter near his half-eaten meal and slid the box down the length of the marble countertop, making me have to stop it from careening off the edge.

The box knocked against my palm and something inside of it shifted. Something heavier than anything that size ought to be.

"I'm good," I replied tensely. "Whatever it is, I don't want it."

"You'll want this one. Besides. It's not a gift, so don't look so damn uncomfortable."

Was it that obvious?

"It's payment for what's owed."

I held the box between my fingertips, a muscle beneath my eye twitching.

"Go on," Corvus prodded. "Open it."

I sighed but did as he asked, lifting the top off the box...and gasped.

"You like it?"

It was a blade. Similar to mine, black with gleaming metal edges honed to perfection. Though that's where the similarities ended. A silver crow in flight emblazoned the tang, etched into the black coated metal so that it gleamed silver in the light. A tiny blue gemstone set into the place where it's eye ought to be.

I didn't have to ask to know it was a sapphire.

"I know it isn't the same, but..."

I lifted the blade out of the box, carefully running a finger along its edge. Turning it in my palm to feel the even weight distribution. Finding the crow's wings wrapped all the way around the tang to the other side.

It was beautiful craftsmanship.

But what did it mean?

An unnamed emotion roiled in my gut like a tightening fist. Was he trying to tell me I, too, was a Crow?

Or was this meant to assert that I belonged to them. A weapon to be honed in their image, to be wielded once Diesel owned me.

I clenched my teeth at the warring possibilities. Trying to pretend I hated both of those options, but the hopeful ache in my gut told me the truth my rational mind tried to deny.

I set the blade back into the box and glanced up, finding no evidence of either in Corvus' stony blue eyes.

"Do you like it?"

I swallowed hard before replying, to ensure my voice came out without any indication of what was going on within. "It'll do."

He nodded.

I cleared my throat. "So, about who's supposed to be watching me today—"

"Go whenever you like. I'll come get you later."

I cocked my head at him.

"I have some things to take care of here and Dies needs the others tonight. If you wouldn't mind." He gritted his teeth and I wondered how hard it was to *ask* me something rather than demand it, "could you stay here one more night? There's a loft above the garage you can use. It's furnished and has windows and doors that I promise won't be locked when you wake up. *Or* you can have any bed in the house you want. No one will be using them tonight."

This was...weird.

I opened my mouth to reply but shut it again. I wanted to argue for the sake of arguing. I liked the way his face soured when I told him no, but this was different.

He was giving me something. Trust. My freedom, even if it was for just a few hours. In return he asked for a small favor. In all honesty, I'd sleep just as shittily no matter where I laid my head tonight anyway.

"Fine," I replied. "Just tonight."

The ghost of a smile brushed over his lips before it was gone, and he nodded. "Good. I'll text you when I'm on my way."

"Okay," I said, jumping from the stool and remembering what I was wearing. I wouldn't be running anywhere in a fucking sheet.

"You wouldn't happen to know where my clothes are, would you."

He jerked his head toward the entryway. "They're washed and in the dryer. The laundry room is through the door at the end of the hall, but I guess you already knew that since you removed the handle."

I bit my tongue, rushing from the kitchen to go and get my fresh clothes before I said something that might ruin my chances at a few hours of freedom.

My spine went ramrod straight as I walked into the laundry room, finding my phone sitting atop the dryer. *Fuck.*

What was wrong with me?

A good prank and some good dick and I lost all fucking sense.

This was *not* me.

I'd told myself this once, and I'd keep saying it; these Crows were *literally* going to be the death of me one day. At least as long as they lived.

I snatched my phone and checked for any messages they might've somehow read. I had three missed messages, but I'd changed my settings so the lock screen wouldn't show message previews anymore, only the sender.

One message was from my Aunt Humphrey, another was from Kit. The last said only *unknown*.

I stiffened, leaning back against the wall as I unlocked it and thumbed over to read them.

I scrolled to the one I dreaded the most first, reading only the first line of text before I swiped to delete the message without reading the rest.

UNKNOWN

I warned you…

Whoever it was could *warn* me all they liked. Whenever they wanted to stop talking shit and *do* something, I'd be ready for them. Come at me, fucker. I dare you.

Next on the list of messages I least wanted to read. Dear ol' Aunt Humphrey.

AUNT HUMPHREY

If you don't return my calls, I'll have no choice but to revoke my offer. How you expect to finish the year with the grades necessary to get into a half decent college is beyond me. You have to actually attend class for—

I stopped reading. That was enough of that.

KIT

Dom's worried about you. If you aren't going to call me back, you should at least call her. I miss you.

I ignored Kit's message and thumbed over to my previous conversation with Dom, typing out a quick apology.

> Sorry girl. I'll try to call this week. Shit's been crazy. I'm fine so don't worry, k?

I was a terrible fucking friend.

I dressed quickly, rushing to my five seconds of freedom. I peered into the kitchen to tell Corvus I was leaving, but he wasn't there anymore when I walked past.

"Bye, dickface," I muttered quietly to myself as I tugged on my shoes and went to slip my newest blade into the sheath on my ankle, but thought better of it, deciding to keep it on me instead.

My skin prickled as I stepped outside into the growing warmth of the early afternoon, and I scanned the trees surrounding the Nest as I stretched for my run. Searching for anything out of place. Eyes that shouldn't be there.

There was someone watching me, that much was certain, but were they watching me right now? Were they out there at this very minute, waiting for an opportunity to pounce?

Did they see what Rook and I did last night? I glanced back, seeing through the window to the kitchen beyond it. A clear and unobstructed view of the kitchen island.

I shivered.

"*Fuck this,*" I hissed. If whoever it was wanted to attack me, let them. I had a new blade to break in, and I'd pledged to carve out their eyeballs. I couldn't do that if I was hiding inside, now could I?

No music for my run today. I needed all my senses keen and sharp. Just in case.

A small pang surprised me as the unconscious thought that I wished Grey was running with me crossed my mind.

I shook it away and started at a slow pace down the gravel drive, picking up speed as the gravity of the hill pulled me down its slope. Soon, the wind whipped through my hair, lifting sweat slicked strands and cooling the sweat beginning to coat my chest.

But still my runner's high didn't come and my mood soured, hating a nameless faceless person. Hating Mr. Unknown for ruining the *one* thing I had that was mine.

In the distance, the sounds of the forest, my favorite sounds, became ominous things.

The snap of a twig could just as easily be a rabbit as it could be Mr. Unknown.

The rustle of leaves: a bird or a man?

It wasn't fear, not exactly, it was the same self-preservation *readiness* that always took over when there was a threat. When my adrenaline knocked at the thresholds of my veins, waiting to be released.

Like the world had gone from low-fi to high-def in the blink of an eye. Vision sharper. My ears picking up even the tiniest sounds. I couldn't enjoy the pounding of my feet on the earth or the sensation of flying as I soared over miles of woods and road. Not with this itching feeling scratching at the back of my skull.

"Fucking damnit," I groaned to myself through pants, slowing to a jog as I veered off the road and into the trees toward the trailhead at the back of Briar Hall. If I stuck to the road, I'd have to go all the way around. This way I could cut through and save myself fifteen minutes. I'd have loved to have those fifteen minutes before, but now? What was the point?

I jumped over a low red-berry bush and onto the trail, seeing the lit opening in the trees ahead that would put me out at the back gardens of the Academy.

I saw him before he even moved. A dark shape lurking in the shade behind an old redwood. My feet dug into the ground as he rounded the tree, and I readied my new blade to throw, cursing myself for not arming myself with one of my own blades. My aim may not be perfect with this one yet. We hadn't been properly acquainted. I held it up all the same, the dirt underfoot bunching under the sides of my sneakers as I slid to a stop.

"*Whoa,*" a familiar voice spoke, raising his hands to carefully peel back the hood of his dark windbreaker jacket, revealing his face.

"Officer Vick?"

"Put the knife down, girl."

Hesitantly, I lowered it, but didn't put it away or move any closer.

"You shouldn't be here."

He snorted derisively. "Do you know how hard it's been to get to you? You've been with at least one of them every bloody hour of the day and night."

My face pinched. "What do you want?"

"What do *I* want? I thought we wanted the same thing...you haven't called."

"Because I didn't have enough to give you yet."

Officer Vick narrowed his eyes on me, stuffing his fists into his wind-breaker pockets. "It's true what I've heard then," he said, a look of disgust twisting his features. "You *are* taking the trials. They've turned you, haven't they?"

I frowned, a sneer curling my upper lip. "*Never.*"

He snorted and my face flushed hot, hands clenching.

"I didn't ask for this," I all but snapped. "It was the trials or death."

He cocked his head at me, interested now. "You saw something, didn't you? Something you shouldn't have. Tell me. Tell me and this can all be over."

My breath caught in my throat. The videos had been erased from my hard drive, but there was still a body. The body of a dead Ace in the ground out behind that old warehouse with one of Diesel's bullets in his skull. Would the body be enough?

"Would you need testimony?"

Officer Vick's hard look faltered, he hadn't expected that question. "Depends on what sort of evidence you've got."

"And if I didn't have any at all except my word and a body buried in the ground..."

He ground his teeth, considering the best way to reply, and I knew already what his answer would be. If the court was going to be able to do anything with the evidence, my testimony would be paramount. And a trial could take weeks. Months, even. And no amount of police protection would be able to stop Diesel St. Crow from slitting my throat before it ever went as far as a conviction.

My stomach soured. Would the guys be implicated in that or just Diesel? Could I keep them out of it?

Did I want to?

"Like I said," I continued before Officer Vick could say a word, wanting to cut this conversation short before I said something I couldn't fucking take back. "I don't have enough yet."

"When?"

"I don't fucking know.

He nodded. "The trials can be quite..."

"I know."

"If you help us, there's a possibility we'd be able to offer immunity for any crimes committed in the process of obtaining the information we need."

"Gee, thanks."

Vick ran a hand through his short hair, glancing between me and the end of the trail a good twenty feet behind him. My chest grew cold at the idea of someone seeing us here, like this. Officer Vick and I out in the open.

"We really need—"

I held up a hand to stop him from pleading his case any more than he already had. "I'm *working* on it," I gritted out. "But you can't approach me again. *Ever*. If someone saw..."

I shuddered.

"But—"

"I can't give you anything if I'm dead."

I fixed him with a hard stare before starting back at a slow jog. "*Move*," I growled and he stepped to the side as I pounded past him.

"We need you, Ava Jade," he called as I emerged from the path. "Don't disappoint me."

12

CORVUS

There were a few things I was good at that didn't involve violence. Cooking being one of them.

I spooned the honey Dijon white-wine sauce over the roasted chicken and potatoes, laying small sprigs of thyme on each. I wrung my hands in the tea towel, sighing as I hesitated to bring Ava Jade's plate in to her.

The television in the living room remained quiet as she flicked through the options on one of the streaming services Grey had hooked up to the TV. She'd been trying to decide for nearly twenty minutes already. At this rate, I wasn't sure if she would find anything at all.

I set down the tea towel on the counter and scooped up the plates, bringing them to the living room. Breaking my own rules. We never ate in the living room. Dinners, at least when I made them, were eaten together at the kitchen island.

It wasn't the only rule I was going to have to bend if I wanted Ava Jade to hold me in the same regard as she did my brothers. If I wanted her to stop hating me. *Did* I want her to stop hating me?

I shook my head, upper lip twitching at the idiocy of the internal question. *Of fucking course* I didn't want her to hate me. It was just easier that way...in the beginning.

"Hey," I said gruffly as I walked into the living room, the hot plates burning into my palms. "You hungry?"

She didn't turn from where she sat cross legged on the long couch to the right of the room, her side profile facing the television. Showing off the regal shape of her face. "I already ate dinner," she muttered, shifting on the cushion as she finally settled on something to watch. Cueing up a Marvel movie.

My grip on the plates tightened. "I didn't ask you that. I asked if you were hungry."

I couldn't help the tinge of acid in my voice and I cleared my throat to get rid of it, clamping down to get a hold on myself, purging myself of the angry thoughts vying for dominion in my mind.

She set the remote down on the table and peeked up at me, catching sight of the plates in my hands. Piled high with perfectly roasted chicken and potatoes and buttered carrots.

"Touché," she replied, the smallest smirk on her lips. "I'm always hungry."

"Just like Grey."

"Why is that?" she asked as I closed the distance between us and handed her a plate.

"You'll have to ask him. It's not my story to tell."

"What *is* your story then?" she pushed as I went to sit on the armchair across the coffee table from her. My back muscles tight and head heating as the hideous memories flooded my skull.

A small grumbling sound escaped my throat as I fought them back and my Sparrow frowned, dropping her head to her plate. "Sorry, not my business."

"No, it's not."

Fuck. There I went again, but I couldn't help it.

Appetite thoroughly ruined, I set my plate down on the coffee table and leaned back in the chair to watch the movie, attempting to clear the poison seeping in.

The *pop pop* of gunfire. The feel of their blood, hot at first, and then later, sticky and cold and stinking. The gore of it all. The numbness. The darkness. The whispers...

Not even Rook and Grey knew what led me to be brought in by the state, left with not a single blood relative to care for me. The only one who did was Diesel. I had a different name, then. Diesel wanted us to keep our surnames when he adopted us. Until we were adults, old enough to make the decision for ourselves. The St. Crow name was a dangerous one to call your own. He wanted us to be certain we wanted to wear it.

We all planned to take the name after graduation, becoming the Crows we've always been in practice on paper.

James wasn't my last name, though. It was my middle name. I'd never own to my true surname. Not ever. I couldn't *fucking* wait to change it. I begged Diesel when I was younger, but he told me it was important to remember where I came from. That I didn't have to use the name, but I had to bear it until I came of age.

I came of age last year and Grey suggested we all wait until graduation to make it official. What was another year after being forced to carry it for over ten?

I switched to watching my Sparrow when the movie did little to help distract me. Already over halfway through her meal, she closed her eyes briefly with every bite she took, unable to hide how much she enjoyed it.

Her cutting blue-gray eyes caught me staring and she pulled the fork from between her lips with a small blush. "Where did you learn to cook?"

"Diesel taught me some things," I replied, and she lowered her brows as though she hadn't been expecting that response.

"What? Does it surprise you that a gang leader would be a good cook?"

"Well, kind of, *yeah.*"

I bit out a short laugh. "Well, he only got me started. Showed me some of the recipes his wife used to make before she passed. The rest I taught myself. I like food that tastes good."

"What happened to her?"

I resisted the urge to bark at her. The second-hand pain of her loss I'd had to feel from my surrogate father since the day he adopted me swelling in my chest.

"She died," I said simply, realizing how my fingers were curling into the armrest of the chair. I loosened them and coughed to clear my throat, lifting my plate again to try to force myself to eat. If I wasn't going to fucking sleep, I knew I needed to at least eat well.

"I gathered that," Sparrow murmured, but she didn't press the question.

I only knew the gist of it anyway, heard from the other Saints, but never from Diesel himself. He'd been injured in a shootout, hospitalized, and on the brink of death.

His wife, strongest woman I'd ever heard of, led the attack on the offending gang. She'd planned it expertly. Not a single Saint lost their life that night, but there was a reason you never heard the name *Viper* anywhere in Cali after that. She wiped them from the face of the earth. Vengeance for her lover.

All the Vipers dead except for one.

The leader's son, hiding like a coward from the fight. It was his bullet that ended her once the fighting was through.

The Saints held him until Diesel was ready to deal with him himself. I shuddered to think what was done to him, but I know that if it were me, he'd have suffered for days before I allowed him to die. Weeks even.

I watched Ava Jade finish her meal and set the plate down, leaning back to drop a hand onto her belly. What would I do if someone took her from me?

She was *mine*.

Ours.

Grey needed to hurry up with decrypting those messages from her phone. Diesel needed him again tonight, to help with some tax shit that was past due. But Grey promised he'd be on it as soon as he was finished with that. Rook tagged along with him, happy to drink at Sanctum to allow me some time to try to repair what I had broken with Ava Jade.

She caught me watching her again and winced, shifting awkwardly. "Are you a good baker, too?" she asked, changing the subject.

"Why?"

She shrugged. "I like cake."

I snorted.

"I'm not bad," I told her. "It's Rook's birthday soon. He doesn't like to celebrate it, but I usually make a cake anyway. No candles or any of that shit. Just a big ass chocolate cake."

"Chocolate's my favorite, too."

"Of course it is."

She tipped her head to one side, considering me before going back to watching her movie.

I half expected her to have fled when I went to pick her up a couple hours ago, but there she was at the door, ready to go when I knocked. If not a little grumpy. Rook had been right after all. She wasn't going anywhere.

She knew what running would get her.

I finished firing off an email to Max on my phone, getting last minute details sorted before the upcoming show. Later tonight, I'd have to finish the new song I was working on if I planned to unveil it in Lodi. And I needed the others to help me once I was through. Rook was mad good at syncing everything together for me and Grey was the only one I trusted to make the lyrics really *hit*.

Though showing them the song would mean admitting to them what I'd only just managed to admit to myself...

"So," I asked after Ava Jade clicked through to start another movie once the credits rolled on the first one. "Did you decide where you want to sleep?"

She shrugged. "I'm good here. I probably won't sleep anyway."

I snorted. *You and me both.*

My phone buzzed in my hand, and I looked down to see a reply from Max and a text from Grey.

GREY

How goes it? You kill each other yet?

I covertly snapped a pic of her across the room, illuminated only by the bluish light flickering out from the TV in the dark room. I sent it.

CORVUS

Still alive.

GREY

Why are you sitting so far away? Go and sit
with her.

My teeth clenched.

I glanced at the two empty cushions next to Ava Jade and pressed my lips into a tight line. My attention snagged on the outlet by the wall at one end of the couch, and the charger cord sticking out of it.

My phone still had twenty percent battery but it could use a charge.

Clearing my throat, I rose, crossing the room to fall casually into the cushion at the far end of the couch, reaching for the cord to plug in my phone.

Sparrow raised a brow at me as I settled the phone onto the armrest and turned back to the TV.

"Needs a charge," I explained, leaning back to watch the next Marvel movie in the queue.

CORVUS

Anything from her phone yet?

GREY

I haven't had a chance. Diesel needs this done before the start of the business day tomorrow. I'm on it as soon as I'm done.

CORVUS

This needs to take priority. I'm about three seconds from tying her up and forcing her to tell me herself.

GREY

Because that will get you all the brownie points...

CORVUS

Fuck off. You know something isn't right about that shit. Becca said herself that she didn't send Ava Jade the messages. We made a deal. I play nice so long as you get us those messages so that we can see what the fuck is up for ourselves.

GREY

I know. Don't worry man, I'll get it done.

I clicked off the phone with a sigh and caught Ava Jade sneaking glances at me from the corner of her eye, curious about the rapid-fire text conversation I just had, but not curious enough to ask. Not enough to want to appear like she cared.

I wasn't sure how long we sat like that, quietly watching Marvel movies until my eyes burned like the fire of a thousand suns and the muscles around my right eye began to twitch. Until my Sparrow slumped over on the couch, curling herself up in a tight ball on the two cushions between me and the other end of the couch, doing her absolute best not to touch me.

It wasn't much longer until she fell asleep, though her face never completely softened. A tightness lingered around her eyes even though her breathing evened out and her mouth softened. Free of any of the sharp edges I was used to seeing.

Instinctively, I reached down to lightly brush a lock of hair from her cheek and she stirred, making a small sound of malcontent as she tried to stretch out her legs and was stopped by the arm of the sofa.

Without consciously thinking about it, I guided her to my lap, softly lifting her head as she did all the work of moving herself up with her feet braced and stretching against the armrest.

Her eyes fluttered open for a second and I held my breath, removing my hands from her shoulders, but she didn't fully wake, only enough to snuggle down, sighing as she fell back asleep.

Her hand brushed against my cock, and if she didn't stop nuzzling it, she was going to get a really rude awakening when it fully hardened. I gritted my teeth, multiplying math equations in my head until she settled and I could breathe again.

Extra carefully this time, I brushed her hair back, studying the curve of her face. She shivered at my touch. I tugged the throw blanket down from the top of the backrest and draped it over her, laying an arm over her shoulder to hold her there.

That tightness around her eyes loosened as she fell into a deeper state of sleep, her breaths coming slower. Her perfect lips parting just slightly. She really was the most beautiful girl I'd ever seen. I may not have thought so at first, but now...I couldn't imagine anyone I'd ever want more than I wanted her.

My chest tightened, and I ground my teeth against the ache. I already had too many people to keep alive, and I'd shatter if any of them were taken from me. I couldn't lose anyone else I cared about. I couldn't afford *to care* about anyone else.

I relaxed as the realization set in and a hopeless sort of wonder took hold.

It didn't matter.

It was too late.

She was already my Sparrow.

And I was already her Crow.

13

AVA JADE

I shifted in bed, my neck stiff and legs hopelessly tangled in blankets. No. Not bed.

The leather creaked audibly beneath me. The denim under my cheek shifted as I stiffened.

I closed my eyes tightly, heat crawling into my cheeks as I very carefully lifted my head, turning just enough to see if my suspicions were correct.

Blinking to clear the sleep from my eyes, I peered up at him, ready with a snide comment o pounce from my lips about how he was the absolute worst pillow in the world.

But...I barely recognized him.

I sat up straighter, pushing the dark hair from my face.

Corvus was asleep. His body slouched low on the sofa, and his head was tipped back against the headrest, turned slightly to one side. His dirty blond hair sat in a mussed halo on his head, tipped forward to shadow one eye. Without his trademark sneer, he looked so different. He still had wicked cheekbones and a jawline sharper than a razor's edge, but now it didn't look ominous or threatening.

He looked like a Saint.

Or maybe an angel. He was only missing the wings.

Get it together, Ava Jade, I scolded myself internally, giving my head a little shake. It didn't matter what the dick looked like when he was sleeping. All that mattered was how he acted when he was awake.

A new blade and a couple meals weren't enough to fix anything. Though, I had to admit, if he kept feeding me, I might have to forgive him eventually. I'd gone through much worse than Corvus James to get a half decent meal and his were *divine.*

Careful, AJ, my smarter self warned. *You're getting too close to them.*

And I was. My walls were crumbling with each passing day since the start. I couldn't afford to let that happen. I needed to keep them at a distance. If I let them in too close, I was terrified I'd only want more. That I wouldn't be able to push them back out again.

It would only lead to pain in the end. When push came to shove, I knew where their true allegiances were. And I knew where I stood.

Carefully, without shifting the couch, I untangled myself from the navy throw blanket trapped in my legs and climbed from the couch, stretching until my spine and neck cracked. I winced at the ache in my neck, wondering how in the hell I'd managed to crawl into his fucking lap in the night. I hadn't even meant to fall asleep. Didn't think I would even if I tried to.

But there we both were, sleeping. Him, right next to someone with enough blades to ensure maximum bleed out and me, on the lap of someone I vowed to loathe for all eternity.

Quite the fucking pair.

Yep, they would be the death of me for sure.

After one more stretch, I tiptoed from the living room, resolved to use the opportunity of being fully unsupervised in the Nest to have another good snoop around. If I'd been smart, I would've done it days ago when I broke out of the windowless closet room, but I'd had only vengeance on my mind that morning, and the haze of the whiskey from the night before.

Not a great combo for productivity.

The stairs creaked as I ascended and I paused, waiting to see if the noise woke Corvus, but after a few more seconds without the sound of him waking, I continued. I stuck to the outside bits of the stairs instead of the middle, spreading my weight to avoid any more unwanted noises.

I wasn't exactly sure what I was looking for, but I'd know when I found it. There had to be something here I could use as leverage. Or as proof of crimes that would see them all put behind bars. My stomach rebelled against the idea, and I pressed a palm to it, wincing.

May be wise to use the bathroom before Corvus woke up, too, since there was no door handle and I was pretty sure he'd stand in the open doorway while I peed out of spite. Ah well. Let him watch.

The first door belonged to Corvus' bedroom and it seemed as good a place as any to start. Perfect, actually. His offer for me to sleep in any room I liked had me thinking it was possible I wouldn't find a damn thing at all. If I was going to find something, I was willing to bet it'd be here, though. I would never have picked his room to sleep in, and he knew it.

I pushed the door open and stepped inside, finding it the exact same as the last time I'd seen it.

A bed, sleek with sheets and blankets pulled tight enough to bounce a coin off of, pushed against the far wall between two rectangular windows covered in modern blinds.

Against the wall to the right of me stood a tall mahogany dresser, it's top wiped clean of dust. The only thing marring its mirrored surface was a slender lamp that was really just a slim steel column with a light bar running up one side.

Aside from the night tables to either side of his bed, there was only a desk. Low and long, it dominated the space along the left wall. Three monitors perched on its surface along with some other equipment. A folding chair leaned against the desk, ready to be opened and used when needed. A temporary fix, I had to assume. It looked like our dining room chairs back in Lennox. The likes of Corvus James wouldn't be caught sitting on something so *cheap*. Not when the rest of his room screamed modern luxury.

I decided to start with the computer, walking over to tap on the keyboard, making it whir to life. I felt around under the monitors, searching for the volume buttons and finding them before the power on could make any sounds.

The password screen popped up and I cursed under my breath, but my attention snagged on several cords running along the floor below the desk. I cocked my head, following them to where they disappeared into the wall next to a closet door.

The fuck?

I took a breath. *Come on, baby. Give Mama something good.*

I opened the door with a flourish and stopped dead at what I found in the dark room beyond.

My fingers slipped along the wall inside, searching for a switch. I found a dimmer instead and pushed it up, slowly illuminating the closet.

No. Not the closet.

The entire six by eight space had been gutted. The walls covered in dark bumpy soundproofing the whole way around. The cords jutted from the wall, snaking up a metal pole to the boxy microphone resting at its apex.

A barking laugh fell from my lips before I could squash it.

I had no fucking idea what I was expecting, but this sure as hell wasn't it.

Did Corvus fancy himself a rock star?

Or...*oh my fuck*...did he rap?

Pretend to be the next Slim Shady. Corvus James, *please stand up.*

I giggled to myself, unconsciously stepping into the closet to touch the mic, stepping up to it like Corvus must.

I bit my lower lip, finger on the switch to turn it on, a dark chasm opening in my gut. My heart thudded in my ribcage, and I swallowed past the wave of emotion threatening to drag me under.

I couldn't remember the last time I sang.

No. That wasn't true. I could remember. There was only one person I ever sang in front of. My dad. The last time I sang was four days before he was murdered. He played his guitar, and I sang one of his favorite songs. When I was finished, he smiled at me and set the guitar aside.

That night, he did what he always did. He gave my chin a squeeze before getting ready to leave. He kicked on his work boots and pulled on his navy-blue plaid sweater. He pocketed the money meant to pay the rent and promised to be back soon. Further promising that *this time* he would win enough money to get us out of 'the hole.'

I didn't fight him on it. I knew from experience that it was no use and he would only go anyway. No matter what I said or did.

He said something different that night, though. He told me that if anything ever happened to him, that I should leave and never come back.

I didn't ask him why. I knew why. Even if he never told me himself.

You didn't teach your daughter how to throw knives and run jobs because you hang with the *right* sort of people. Good people. You taught your daughter those things and told her to run because you hang with the *wrong* sort of people.

I learned my lesson with mom. It was her debt that'd almost gotten me killed that night on the tracks. That's what that *filth* said.

Your junkie mom couldn't pay, so you'll *pay for her.*

I never did get the courage to ask her if she'd offered me up or if the slime ball of a man just decided to take what was owed in flesh instead of dollar bills.

She had her breakdown barely a week later and then she was gone. If I ever saw her again, I promised myself I would ask.

I hoped I never saw her again.

The mic felt cold against my fingers and when I slicked it on, the electronic hum of it filled the air, making the tiny hairs on my arms stand up.

Licking my lips, I shut the door, closing myself into the small sound-proof box and cleared my throat. I belted a few notes; they were rough. Like I said, it'd been a while, but I'd never sung into a microphone before, and I liked how it made my voice sound. I went louder, testing the quality of the soundproofing, then stopped and opened the door quietly to listen for Corvus.

Nothing.

Huh. Not bad.

When I closed the door the second time, that same overwhelming feeling of grief took root in my stomach again. I caressed the mic in my palm and closed my eyes, taking a deep breath, remembering sitting with Dad on the ratty old rust orange sofa in our living room.

Remembering how he'd fallen into the seat next to me and dragged his guitar across his lap.

"Sing me a song, my girl," he'd said, plucking a few strings to let me know which one he wanted.

I'd rolled my eyes like he was the most annoying human being to ever walk the earth, but that was the furthest thing from the truth. I loved to sing, and I loved when he asked me to sing for him. It was one of the few things we ever did together that didn't involve sharp objects or criminal activity.

In the moments where I sang and he played his beat-up guitar, we were a normal family. A dad and his daughter, doing dad and daughter things.

My eyes burned as I began to hum the first few notes of his favorite song, but I couldn't do it. I couldn't sing that, not without him there to hear me. I would never sing that song again. The ache behind my breastbone waned as a more familiar emotion grew to replace it.

How could he leave me like that?

After everything he taught me, it was *him* who didn't know better.

I didn't care what I promised him anymore. I left Lennox like he asked, but I would go back...at least for a single purpose: to find whoever killed him and make sure they knew the real meaning of pain before they died.

It didn't matter that there was no evidence. There was always something. Whispers. People who knew. It was the Kings, it had to be. I just needed to figure out which one.

The silent promise made breathing easier. Became a balm for my broken soul.

And then I knew what I wanted to sing.

Primal Ethos' Anthem of the Broken filtered past my lips, quiet at first, no more than a whisper. I felt the lyrics in my bones, filling in the cracks and fissures, mending me as I let the song carry me away from all the dark awful things swirling just out of reach in my mind.

There was only me and this song. This moment and the words.

Knowing that there was at least one other person in this world who knew what it felt like to have this hollow pit inside, so deep there was no hope of it ever being filled, made me feel like I wasn't alone.

Somewhere out there, someone understood.

Someone had felt the betrayal. The loss. The heartache. The confusion. The fucking *pain* I'd felt, and they made this song.

My voice began to crack as the final lyric leaked out, my throat burning at the release and the acknowledgement I hadn't allowed myself since the day it happened.

He was really gone.

He wasn't coming back this time.

The dam I'd been struggling to hold up all these past weeks crumpled in an instant, and I wasn't fast enough to hold my breath before the waves of my anger and grief crashed over my head. Filled my lungs until I choked. Until I was so full of it that it leaked out, dripping down my face, onto the floor as I crouched, clutching my skull between my stiff hands.

I'd never sing for Dad again.

He'd never stumble home drunk of the rush of a win and declare it Ava Jade Day at five in the morning and demand that I get dressed because we were going for ice cream.

Not ever again.

It could have been only minutes, but it felt like hours as I cried for the first time in...I couldn't even remember how long. By the time the tears slowed and then stopped, my eyes burned and my nose was so stuffed up that I probably wouldn't breathe right for days. But I felt somehow better, like a weight had lifted from my chest and getting back to my feet felt just a little bit easier than before.

I switched off the microphone and used the hem of my shirt to dry away the tears still wet on my cheeks, and stepped out of the closet.

Corvus sat barely six feet away, folding chair facing the closet door. His body bent, elbows on knees, fingers pressed together in front of his lips like a prayer. His eyes, shadowed by the sweep of hair hanging low on his brow, found me from their darkness. His jaw twitched, clenching as he stared.

My stomach twisted.

"How much did you hear?" I demanded, my voice still half broken from crying.

He dropped his hands and looked away. "Enough."

I swiveled my head, finding the computer screens along the desk all powered on, a little red microphone light in the software he had open blinking instead of solid now that the mic was shut off.

My hands clenched to fists.

"You're an incredible singer," he said, meeting my spiteful stare again. "Has anyone ever told you that?"

"And you're a hateful prick," I hissed, hating how my lungs were constricting in my chest. How my stomach plummeted to my toes. "Has anyone ever told you that?"

He didn't reply. Didn't even look angry at my barb.

"What do you even use that room for anyway, *hmmm?* Fancy yourself a fucking rock god or some shit? Or does the sound of your own voice turn you on so much that you have to record—"

"I turned it off," he interrupted, completely ignoring every word I said. "When you started…I turned it off. I didn't listen."

"Oh, so I should thank you then?"

"Sparrow—"

"I'm not your fucking Sparrow!" I yelled, my nostrils flaring as a wicked heat sizzled up my spine.

He heard me. He heard me *break*. No one had ever…

No one would ever again.

I moved to storm past him, and he snatched my wrist. Unable to stop myself, I reflexively struck. The flat of my palm cracking loudly against his cheek.

He didn't let go. Even when it started to bloom red.

"You don't have to hide your pain from me."

My eyes burned anew, and I couldn't take it. I couldn't take any of this.

I ripped my arm out of his grasp and ran for the door, taking the stairs two at a time until I somehow got outside and the fresh air filled my aching lungs. I forced the tears to obey, swallowed them back down until I felt only heat and fury.

"*Ava Jade*," Corvus called from inside the Nest, but I was already gone, running barefoot through the trees.

14

ROOK

I flipped a coin over my knuckles, sighing as Ava Jade and Becca chatted in the living room while music played in the background from a Bluetooth speaker. I leaned against the black marble countertop, sipping the bourbon spiked coffee Becca made for me, glancing at my phone every few seconds.

It was getting late, but neither of them seemed ready to call it a night, happy to chat the night away and pretend I wasn't here at all.

Ava Jade had hardly spoken to me since Corvus dropped me at her door hours ago. She'd opened it, taken one look at me, and walked away, leaving the door open for me.

I was guessing it didn't go well between her and Corv. Judging by the light bruise on his cheek, she'd actually hit him. And somehow, he hadn't retaliated. Corvus was a monument to self-control, but you didn't touch him. You touched him and you died.

He let her hit him, and he did absolutely nothing.

I didn't know what to make of that.

But whatever he did had nothing to do with me. We'd had fun the other night, hadn't we? I knew I did.

My jaw clenched as I remembered the strain of touching her. The tremble in my fingers I hoped she hadn't noticed.

The aching need to choke her a little longer, to cut a little deeper, to fuck her raw...

Being unable to do it.

The idea of scaring her away from me—

Of going too far and—

I tapped my phone impatiently for the third time in as many minutes, distracting myself as the screen illuminated to show no new messages or missed calls. Grey offered to come and stay with Ghost tonight, but we needed those messages cracked *yesterday*.

We all wanted to think we were overreacting, but I think each of us knew that wasn't the case. I had a bad feeling. A hollow, ugly pit that'd been yawning open ever since that day she accused Corvus.

Something was very wrong, and we needed to know what it was.

If someone was threatening her...

I clutched the coin in my hand, a tremor racing down my spine, making my back heat.

They wouldn't be a *someone* when I was through with them. They'd be a nothing. A pile of ash at my feet.

Becca and Ava Jade turned to me, and I realized I'd begun tapping my foot, and stopped, polishing off my coffee and bourbon instead before swiping the back of my palm over my lips and refilling my mug from the flask in my back pocket.

"There's cola in the fridge," Becca offered. "If you want to mix that."

I shook my head. "Too sweet."

"Suit yourself."

They went back to talking about some event they were going to soon. Becca was asking Ava Jade if they'd have to bring one of her *shadows* with them because they only had two tickets. My Ghost said *fuck no*, but she was wrong if she thought Corvus was going to let her go anywhere, least of all out of fucking town to Lodi, without one of us with her.

It was cute that she thought she could get away with it, really.

"You want to tell me what's going on?" Becca asked in a hushed tone I wasn't meant to hear, her dark brown eyes slipping in my direction before falling back on her friend as she leaned in. "They haven't left you alone for weeks."

Ava Jade shrank back from her friend, the discomfort evident in the tightness around her eyes as she struggled with what to say. "Are *you* going to tell me what's going on?" she asked, replying to her friend's question with one of her own meant to divert the conversation back to safer waters.

I knew the tactic. Grey was a fan of that one.

"You've been here a lot lately," Ava Jade prodded. "You've only gone out, what, once or twice in the last week to see your..." she shimmied her shoulders. "*Friend.*"

"He's just...been busy." Becca frowned, pushing her pin straight hair behind her ear. "Seriously though, Aves, why are they here? You know you can talk to me, right?" She lowered her voice, and I caught her brown eyes shifting to me in my periphery. "Maybe I can help you."

Shit. If she were dead set on staying here, Ghost really needed to come clean with her bestie. Before things got real fucking messy.

I busied myself on my phone, trying to give them a modicum of privacy to chat. Besides, I was wholly uninterested in anything Becca Hart naively thought she could do to help Ava Jade out of this inescapable situation or her sexual escapades with her booty call boyfriend for that matter.

Once upon a time I'd tried to get her into bed, but she didn't hold a candle to Ava Jade. No one did. She turned me down, anyway. Smart girl. The things I'd have done to that tight little body...

She never would have recovered.

I flicked over to the group chat with the guys and thumbed out a quick message.

ROOK

What the fuck is taking so long?

His reply came after a minute.

GREY

I have them.

My teeth locked.

GREY

On the phone with Corv. One sec.

The fuck?

ROOK

Three way me in.

My phone rang a second later and I picked it up, the mug in my hand clattering as I set it down harder than I meant to. I felt Ava Jade's and Becca's eyes follow me all the way into her bedroom.

"You there?" Grey asked.

"Yeah. Go."

I closed myself into the bathroom.

"It's worse than we thought."

"Fuck," Corvus hissed.

"Read them," I ordered. "Read them all."

Grey's voice wavered between a growl and a rasping whisper as he read out a slew of text messages from Ava Jade's stalker.

That was exactly what this motherfucker was.

With each message he read aloud to us, the tension on the line grew, coiling just as tightly as the knot of wrath forming in my gut. My skin prickled with the urge to *kill kill kill,* but I had no outlet here. Nothing to crush or break or burn or bury.

I gripped the ledge of the counter, bending my head as I breathed hard in through my nose.

"What is he talking about? The train tracks? What does that mean?" Corvus roared down the line.

I had an idea, but it was Ghost's story to tell. Her choice who she told it to.

"And *the dark one,*" Grey added. "That was sent on fight night. Whoever this is, they're talking about Rook."

"This ends now. Can we trace this guy?" Corvus asked.

I cared little about the threat to my life, but I knew my brothers wouldn't be taking it lightly.

What I was more concerned with was the threat to Ghost.

I'll have to punish you, this piece of shit said.

For being with us. For letting us touch her. Like she *belonged* to this...this coward who hid behind a set of electronic keys and the mask of being *unknown.*

"He sent most of them from different numbers. All burners. I can't get a trace on anything. That's why it took so long to get them decrypted in the first place."

"We need to talk to Ava Jade," I grunted down the line, that dark urge still souring in the pit of my stomach. Scratching at the back of my skull.

I twisted off the cap of my flask and drank deeply until the burn of the alcohol seared away some of the darkness, numbing the places where it used to be.

"We need to lure this bastard out," I added as I set the flask down.

A pause before either of my brothers replied. A muscle beneath my eye twitched.

"He's right," Grey said. "She should've told us. Especially after whoever this is threatened Rook."

I could almost hear Corvus nodding on his end of the phone as he came up with a plan. "Tomorrow," he said. "Take her to the chapel instead of homeroom. We'll meet you there."

I wasn't able to hold back a growl. I wanted this handled *now*. I wanted blood *now*.

"Be cool." Grey spoke calmly, letting out a shaky sigh. "This guy, whoever he is, is clearly a coward. He's just talking. Threatening her. Trying to scare her. He hasn't actually *done* anything."

"You think he's all talk?" Corvus asked.

"Maybe."

What did it fucking matter? My vision darkened.

I heaved, my breaths coming heavier, making my voice come out a husky rasp. "I don't give a fuck! No one threatens our girl."

"No one threatens our girl," Grey agreed.

Corvus grunted his assent. "Grey, how soon can you finish up with that shit Diesel sent you to handle?"

"A few hours maybe. What about you? Didn't he need you to settle a dispute upstairs at Sanctum?"

"That's where I am now."

"And?"

"It's going to be a minute. Some fucker stiffed one of our girls and made off with an iPad. I'm tracking it down now, and then Tiny and I have to go handle it."

"Rook, can you make it until morning without saying anything? If you confront her about it, she's going to lose her shit."

"What's the difference if she loses it here or in the chapel tomorrow?"

"Grey," Corvus supplied. "Grey is the difference."

It was clear it pained him to admit it, but he continued anyway. "She trusts him. You see how she is around him. Less on edge. Relaxed. He might be the only one of us that she won't stab first and ask questions later."

She would listen to me.

I didn't say it, because even though I thought it was true, I knew I wouldn't be able to speak calmly if she tried to deny the messages or continued trying to hide them or downplay them.

Grey could though.

"I can wait."

"Good," Corvus replied. "And Rook?"

"What?"

"I overheard Dies planning another trial for her earlier tonight when I was down at the pub."

"When?" Grey asked. "Which one?"

Corvus sighed. "Don't know. He stopped talking when he saw me. He seems determined to keep us out of it now that he has the time to administer the rest himself. Thought you should know in case it happens while you're with her."

"Don't kill anyone, man." Grey warned me. "It's not worth it."

"I know."

"Dies will shit a brick if you do, and she can handle herself."

"I said I *fucking know*."

"Sorry," Grey muttered.

"In the morning, then?" Corvus confirmed.

"Yeah," I said, and hung up, tossing my phone on the counter before I ran my palm down my face, trying to smooth away the angry lines I could still feel tight like pulled strings across my forehead and at the edges of my eyes.

Two soft knocks came at the door.

"Rook?" Ghost asked softly. "Everything okay?"

My chest ached.

Why did she think she had to endure this kind of shit alone when she had us? I wanted to throttle her and wrap her up in my arms at the same time. I could do neither.

Someone was threatening her, and she acted as though she wasn't bothered in the slightest when her reaction with Corvus proved that was anything but the truth. I pressed my palm to the door and sighed, the anger ebbing away almost as fast as it'd come. I winced at the loss of it, confused at how easily she could draw it out of me, like blood drawn from a wound.

What was this girl doing to me?

"Rook?" she hedged a second time, and I swallowed, pocketing my phone and the flask again before opening the door.

"What's up, Ghost?"

She studied my face, her cold gray-blue eyes darting back and forth between my dark ones. She'd find nothing there, though. I was a master at what Grey affectionately called *going dead eyed.*

Her brows pinched. "Who was that on the phone?"

"Corv and Grey," I replied. "Why?"

The knot between her brows smoothed out and she shrugged aloofly, like she didn't care. "No reason."

I cocked my head at her, my gaze snagging on the shape of her phone in her front pocket. Heat seared over my flesh, making it prickle as I wondered what other messages could be lingering there that she hadn't told us about. How much worse they could be than the ones we'd already read.

Tomorrow.

We're all going to sit and have a nice little chat about this fuckery tomorrow.

"I'm going to bed," she announced, grabbing a threadbare white t-shirt from the shelf of the closet outside the bathroom and tossing it on her bed before snatching up a throw blanket that was haphazardly draped over the top of her purple covers.

"Here," she said, pushing it into my hands.

"You going to make me sleep on the floor?"

"You can if you want to," she replied sweetly. "But I'm not going anywhere. Take the couch. You'll be more comfortable."

Her words didn't match the lack of sincerity in her tone. I saw this for what it really was. Her walls were finally starting to come down, and she didn't know how to handle it. So, like the Ava Jade we knew, she was going to fight it with everything she had.

It was a fight she'd lose.

"Did I do something?" I asked. "Because as far as I could tell, you thoroughly enjoyed yourself the other night."

"I don't sleep with other people."

"Good. Apparently, I don't, either."

Her nose wrinkled at that, confused at the dual meaning.

"No. I meant that I don't *sleep* with other people as in; I can't sleep when there's someone in bed next to me."

"You did just fine in my bed."

She opened her mouth to reply, shut it, and seethed. "That was different."

"Was it?" I challenged, brushing past as I left her bedroom. "Sleep well, Ghost. Maybe if you're lucky, I'll be the one haunting your dreams tonight."

A cute growl preceded the slam of her door behind me, and I laughed to myself, not bothering to try to hide the sound.

Becca stared at me from the kitchen, pausing after she finished filling herself a glass of water.

"What?" I asked.

"Nothing," she muttered, shaking her head as she walked to her own bedroom, but I caught her gaze fall to my cock beneath my jeans, and I knew why she was staring. Looking for the outline of my stainless-steel *accessories.*

Ava Jade told her. I wondered what she said. I glanced back at Ava Jade's door and smirked, mindlessly grabbing the pack of cigarettes from my back pocket.

"Could you, um, *not* smoke that in here?"

I blinked, coming back to myself before I could tug a smoke from the packet to find Becca hesitating in her doorway.

"I hate the smell."

"You smoke pot in here."

"That's different."

I raised my brows, and she dropped her gaze, clearing her throat as she closed herself into her bedroom. She wouldn't push the matter, but I would never hear the end of it from Ava Jade.

She said she wasn't going anywhere. Guess now was as good a time as any to test that. Corvus had left her to her own devices for hours yesterday, and she hadn't run, what was another hour? I could use the fresh air. It was late, but after hearing those messages, I wasn't fucking tired.

For once, I might get a taste of what it was like for Corvus. Exhausted but unable to shut my eyes.

I ditched the blanket on the couch and slipped a finger under the collar of my leather jacket hung on the back of a stool in the kitchen and shrugged it on. My teeth clenched as I wrapped my fist around the door handle, hesitating to leave.

Whoever was texting her had sent threats. Maybe Corvus was right and it was all talk, but what if it wasn't?

On a whim, I dipped my fingers into the pocket of Ava Jade's jacket on the hook by the door, digging for keys. I pushed past a thick piece of paper and heard them jingle. Drawing them out, I tossed them in the air and caught them, stepping out of the shared apartment and locking the door behind me.

I pocketed the keys and thumbed a quick message to Ava Jade.

ROOK

Going outside for a smoke. If you hear the door, it's just me coming back in. I locked it behind me.

She didn't reply, but the message showed as *read* after a second and that was good enough for me.

I hustled down the stairs and out the back door, stalking towards the basketball court protruding from the back of the academy. Automatic lights flicked on and I grimaced at their ridiculous brightness, lighting my smoke for a long drag as I leaned against the rough brick beneath the basketball net.

The academy grounds were quiet at night and everywhere outside of the ring of white security lights appeared so dark I couldn't see more than a few feet into it. Frowning, I moved away from the lights and settled myself just out of range from where they would detect me.

The dark swallowed me up again, and I waited for my eyes to adjust, the orange glow of the cherry on my cigarette now the only light as far as I could see toward the north lawn and gardens.

I scanned the trees, my fingers twitching toward the knife in my right boot. Corvus wouldn't let me bring a gun, and maybe that was for the best. Especially if Diesel chose tonight for her next trial.

Normally they were more spaced out, just long enough between them to make you start to get comfortable. Start to get complacent. But he was known for running a few back to back, just to mix things up.

My Ghost would pass the surprise attack with flying colors. Fuck, she almost had *me* that night out behind the apartment buildings. If she hadn't panicked, I had no doubt she'd have gotten free of my hold, too.

I rubbed out my smoke on the brick and walked back to the door, satisfied to have seen no threats lingering in the trees outside.

The keys jingled in my pocket and I plucked them back out as I neared the back door to the academy, but my arm jerked when I tried to open it.

I tried again, but it wouldn't budge. Locked.

Someone locked it.

ROOK

Did you fucking lock me out? Really?

No reply. No read receipt.

My stomach twisted.

Diesel.

It was fucking Diesel.

Or rather, whoever he sent after her. They knew I was a loose cannon at the best of times. They wouldn't want me interrupting her trial, and I gave them the perfect opportunity to lock my ass out.

I chuckled darkly to myself, heat making my leather jacket unbearable. I slung it off, discarding it onto the concrete as I rounded the building, picking up speed.

She can handle herself.

I believed it. Really, I did. But I didn't like being locked out. Chained up. Held back.

I wanted to see my Ghost go full poltergeist on their asses. I wanted to watch. I needed to be there *just in case.*

If she somehow failed the trial and was taken out, Corvus and Grey would blame me. Rightly fucking so.

It took me only a minute to find what I was looking for; the slim half-window at the base of the building on the west side, leading down into an old file storage room in the basement of the academy. A regular meeting place for Mrs. June and me before they cleared it out and added a space for the teachers' *quiet reflection.*

I bent and threw my elbow into the glass, sucking in a breath at the sting of air on a fresh cut. Licking my lips, I twisted, booting out the rest of the glass with the sole of my boot before pulling myself through.

I shouldered through the locked door to the filing room and stalked down the hall, taking the stairs up to the main floor three at a time.

"Hey!" Mick, the round-bellied security guard who was absolute shit at his job shouted as I rounded the corner into the main atrium, making for the stairs. I was surprised he'd even left his office, but by the disheveled look of him I'd woken his ass up from his one a.m. nap with the window breaking.

His flashlight beam caught on me, and I gave him a half a second of time. A single look that had him dropping the beam.

"Oh, fuck. Sorry, Mr. Clayton. I thought it was—"

I was gone before he could finish, up the curving staircase and down the hall, keys out, metal slipping into the lock, It was already open. *Fuck.*

I walked in and Becca appeared in her doorway, her eyes wide and wild and face pale in the moonlight as she took me in, confused. Her nightgown all twisted.

A loud *bang* echoed through the apartment and Becca cried out, her attention jerking to Ava Jade's closed door. Not a gunshot. Something hard knocking into an even harder surface.

I gritted my teeth and clenched my fists, the desire to go straight for that door and mow down whoever was behind it stronger than any urge that'd possessed me in a long ass time.

"*AJ,*" Becca breathed as the sounds of a struggle came louder through her friend's door. She made a break across the apartment and I headed her off, catching her around the waist. A bit surprised at her willingness to run into danger for her friend. I'd misjudged her.

"You can't help her," I muttered in Becca's ear, the smell of her essential oil perfume filling my nose.

She struggled to get free and shoved me, making me jerk a step back. "Don't you have a gun or something?" she blurted, and I sighed, my back muscles going taut as the sound of something else crashing in Ava Jade's room echoed all around us.

I snatched Becca's wrist and jerked her back when she made another go for Ava Jade's door.

"Go back to your room," I ordered her. "I'll handle it."

She frantically looked between me and Ava Jade's door, her eyes gleaming with frustrated, confused tears. It wasn't fair for Ghost not to tell her friend.

"She's taking the trials to become a Saint," I explained simply. "This is one of them. She's going to be fine."

Becca's brows drew together, but after a beat, her shoulders lowered slightly, and she closed her mouth on a heaving breath. "It doesn't sound like it."

Ava Jade cried out and a tremor of wrath flashed up my spine like lightning.

"Just go to your room," I growled at Becca before turning for Ghost's door, my vision darkening at the edges. Hot air pushed out from my lungs as I waited outside, listening carefully to the sounds within.

A male grunt.

A hard blow.

A cry of fury that could only be my Ghost's.

I was inside in an instant, dodging an elbow as Ava Jade tackled the tall masked man to her bed. They rolled off onto the floor, and she gasped for air as they struggled.

She has this.

He'll back off any second. Tell her she passed.

She managed to get on top of him, and I strode farther into the room, watching her as her fist connected with his jaw, knocking his head violently to the side.

Yes. Come on, Ghost.

I groaned at the violence of it. At the look on her face as she hit him again. A quiet determined fury edged in something sharper.

Wait...

She wasn't detached like she was that night with Bri at the Docks. She was on edge. Something about this attack spooked her.

I didn't like that.

Not one fucking bit.

Who was this guy? He was in a mask for the trial, but still, I should've recognized him. He was tall. Wide through the shoulders. Crowley? No, maybe Derrik?

My Ghost's eyes alighted on me for an instant and it was the opening the Saint needed to turn the tables. He flipped her onto her back, and I saw a flash of something silver in the moonlight.

Ava Jade shrieked, stopping whatever it was with a forearm, her teeth bared.

I couldn't help her.

It would render the trial void, or worse, result in an immediate fail.

She would either have to go through something like this again, or her trials would be at an end, and I shuddered to think what that could mean.

Shit.

"*No,*" she hissed, and then frantically, she shouted. "Rook!"

My beast responded. It didn't matter who he was anymore.

I didn't even register what I'd done until he was off her and I'd knocked whatever was in his hand onto the floor before throwing an elbow into his face. The window shattered and he sailed through it. Tossed out like trash to drop the two stories to the ground below Ava Jade's window.

The *thud* of his body against the earth was followed by silence only broken by the sound of Ava Jade's coughs and strained breathing.

I stomped to the wall and flicked on the light, finding her clutching her throat where a ring of quickly darkening bruises were rising to the surface of her skin. Heat seared along the back of my neck, and I bristled, nostrils flaring as I knelt and drew her against me. She fought my hold, her voice hoarse and cracking, making her cough as she tried to speak.

"*He...*" she managed hoarsely, getting her voice back. "*...in...*"

I rushed into her bathroom and filled a glass with water, hurrying back to kneel once more and put it to her lips.

She took it greedily, sitting up straighter and wincing as the cool water snaked down her throat. "He was trying to inject me," she said after another watery cough.

"What?"

Her mouth opened in surprise as she darted forward, almost knocking me over as she retrieved something from beneath her bed. She stared at it in her hand, barely breathing.

A slender plastic syringe with a short, needled tip was gripped there. A clear substance in the chamber.

I snatched it from her, turning it over in my fingers before looking her over for injection marks. "Did he get you?"

"No," she breathed. "No, I don't think so."

She coughed again, rubbing and massaging her windpipe.

"What the fuck was he going to inject me with? I didn't sign up to be fucking drugged."

I shook my head, my stomach turning. This wasn't right.

There was one trial that involved ingesting a substance, but not drugs. Never drugs. He wouldn't dare. Not after what I went through. What many Saints had gone through, the lives they'd come from and left before joining the gang.

I raced back to the window, leaning out, ready to climb down and demand answers from what was probably a corpse but...there was no one there. No body, living or dead. I jerked my head up, searching through the trees to the left and the edge of the parking lot and curving road leading to town to my right.

Nothing.

"Fuck," I hissed, pocketing the syringe in favor of my phone.

Corvus answered on the first ring.

"What is it?"

"We have a problem."

"Tell me."

"Get over here now. Bring Grey. Either Diesel's lost his damned mind or there's a bigger problem."

"Get out," I heard Corvus growl, and Tiny began to protest when I heard the Rover door shut and the engine rev.

"Be there in ten minutes," he snapped a second later, and the line went dead.

Ava Jade stood, her baggy white t-shirt torn to expose part of a breast. Stained red with blood dripping from a shallow cut in her forehead. "Do you want to tell me what the hell is going on?"

"Depends," I snapped, the fury still making my vision blur with patches of darkness not so easily released this time. "Do *you* have anything you want to tell me?"

A muscle in her jaw clenched.

I ran my hands through my hair and inhaled sharply, trying to get control. Bending forward, I planted my palms on my knees and leaned against the wall until my vision cleared.

"Rook?" Ava Jade hedged and I couldn't stand it anymore. I shoved the door to her room open, making it bounce loudly against the oppo- site wall as I stormed out.

What was Diesel thinking?

If this was Diesel...

And if it wasn't Diesel...

Someone was going to pay for this. We just needed to figure out who.

15

CORVUS

The tires skidded as I drove us into the parking lot, not fast enough to cut the wheel before making us knock into a low cement piling. Grey and I both jumped out, slamming the doors behind us. I could inspect the damage to the Rover later. I had a gut wrenching feeling whatever I was about to walk into would put that damage to shame.

Rook rarely sounded like he had on the phone exactly nine minutes ago.

I braced myself for whatever was bad enough to get him that worked up, the muscles in my arms flexing and unflexing with the clenching of my fists as we found our way into Briar Hall through the front door. I'd already called ahead and told security to have the door open.

"She's okay, right?" Grey asked in a solemn tone as we shoved through the front doors unimpeded and marched up the stairs.

"I don't know."

"Was it a trial?"

"I don't know."

"Well, did Rook say anything about—"

"*I don't fucking know anything,*" I growled at him, slicking my hair back as we neared her door.

I hadn't seen my Sparrow or heard from her since this morning. I didn't know how I'd handle it if she asked me to leave.

Watching her break this morning opened some long-forgotten wounds deep inside. I *felt* for the first time in a long time. I felt her pain as acutely as I once felt my own before I learned to block it out.

I'd never wanted so badly to be someone who had the ability to comfort someone else. And that song. *My* song.

I couldn't get the sound of her voice singing my words out of my head all fucking day. I got why Rook had taken to calling her Ghost. She was haunting me, too.

The door was open when we got to it, and we pushed our way inside with ease, my hand unconsciously going to the butt of the gun tucked neatly into the back of my jeans.

Rook sat, elbow on knees on the couch, his fingers steepled against his lips. Ava Jade and Becca sat on the couch opposite him, and it seemed we'd interrupted some hushed conversation between them. Becca was deathly pale. Her bloodshot eyes strained with the knots in her forehead.

I shouldn't have been surprised to see her there, and yet I was. Did this have something to do with her?

That's when I noticed the bruises. In a ring of purpling flesh around Ava Jade's throat. The crusted blood in her hairline and the shallow cut it'd come from. How pale she was, too.

"AJ," Grey said on a breath and her eyes snapped to mine for an instant before falling away as Grey approached her, going down on one knee before her on the couch to reach up and gently touch the bruising on her neck.

I wanted to break the hands of the person responsible. Saint or not.

"The attack trial?" Grey asked, and I cleared my throat, drawing his eye. I looked pointedly at Becca.

"She knows," Rook said, finally dropping his hands and sitting up straight. "We should have told her from the start."

My jaw ticked, but arguing wasn't going to help whatever the hell this situation was right now.

Rook pushed to his feet and gave Grey a nudge with his boot before shouldering past me towards Ava Jade's room. His face betrayed a storm cloud of dark emotion he was working hard to keep under control. "A word," he muttered as he passed, and I glanced between Ava Jade and him, jerking my head to tell Grey to follow.

Becca tucked herself into her friend's side, avoiding the blades strapped to Ava Jade's thigh and the one clutched in her hand. The one with the crow etched into the handle.

I made myself leave her there; it took everything I had not to demand answers right there and then. I wanted to shake Rook. To shake *her*. Make them tell me exactly what the fuck happened and why the fuck she thought it was okay to lie to us about her mystery texter for so damn long.

But that wouldn't win me any fucking points now, would it? And with the sound of her broken song still in my ears, I found I just couldn't do it.

Rook shut the door behind us and drew something out of his pocket. It took me a second to register what it was.

"What the fuck is that?" I asked, even though it was obvious. My skin prickled, burning up like my edges had been ignited and I was nothing but paper. "Is she on drugs?"

Rook's dark eyes met mine, and he shook his head once.

I noted the broken window behind him and frowned.

"She was attacked," he explained. "And whoever attacked her tried to inject her with it."

He was fucking playing with me. There was no way...

Grey snatched the syringe from Rook and pressed on the plunger enough to let a drop of the liquid slip out the top of the short needle head. He rubbed it between his fingers and sniffed.

A smell like limes tickled my nose. Familiarly mixed with the tarry scent of pine. I leaned in towards the substance coating Grey's fingertips, but it wasn't whatever the liquid in the syringe was. That was odorless, this was something else. So faint I could barely detect it, but it was there all the same. So familiar it grated on my nerves that I couldn't place where I'd smelled it before.

"Do you know what it is?" Rook asked.

Grey shook his head, but he already had his phone out. He dialed a number. Hung up and dialed again. On the third attempt, the line connected. "I need you to ID a substance for me."

A pause.

"Greyson Winters."

An exclamation on the other end.

"I need you to come and get it from Briar Hall. It'll be waiting for you with security. I need to know what it is within the hour."

Another pause.

"Tell no one of this. You are only to give the information to myself or my brothers. *No one else.*"

He ended the call and pocketed the phone.

I didn't know who it was, didn't care, my mind was still reeling. I stared openly at the syringe, my blood going cold. "Diesel wouldn't..."

"If not Diesel then I can think of only one other potential," Rook put in, his anger flaring across his cheekbones.

"Her stalker," Grey uttered, curling his fingers tight around the syringe.

"Tell us the rest," I demanded, and Rook explained the entire thing from front to back, humoring me each time I asked for clarity.

He'd left her alone, like a fucking idiot, but it was too late to fix that. And the lack of anything useful in his story drove me near to madness.

"You didn't know who he was?" I asked for the third time. "Are you sure?"

Rook pinched the bridge of his nose. "I told you, I couldn't tell. It was dark. He was masked. Could have been a Saint. Might not have been."

"It could've been a Saint and still you threw him through a window two stories above the ground?" Grey asked, raising a brow as though that was surprising.

"Could *you* have stood there and let someone strangle our girl?" he challenged Grey and that shut him up. He dropped his gaze, pensive as he considered the implications of his response.

I began to pace the narrow slice of carpet between her bedroom and the bathroom, thinking. Connecting. Formulating a way to move forward.

"Okay," I said after a minute. "Okay, so we can't ask Diesel if this was him because he'll know something is up, and I'm not sure we want him knowing if this is something *other* than a trial. At least for now. He doesn't need more reasons to want her gone."

"We can find out ourselves if a Saint has been injured," Rook suggested, and I'd been getting to that. "He'd been fucked up pretty good after that fall. Wouldn't be hard to pick him out."

I nodded.

"This couldn't have been Diesel," Grey said, repeating what we were all thinking, and I felt like an absolute piece of shit for even considering it.

But he'd made his obvious distaste for her clear. He didn't want her around us. He didn't trust her.

"How far would you go to protect your family if you thought there was a threat?" I asked, meeting each of their hard stares, nodding when neither replied.

"We can't rule him out, but I don't think this was him. If it were a trial, he'd be ringing your neck for interrupting it," I told Rook, and his upper lip curled.

"Not if he felt guilty for trying to alter the results with whatever's in that syringe."

"We need to explore the other option," Grey said, his eyes fixed on the door and the Sparrow beyond it.

He was right. This wasn't going to be pretty, but it needed to be handled. After tonight, there was no way she was being left alone again. Not even for a second. She needed to know why. She needed to know that we knew what she'd worked so hard to hide from us.

I followed Grey through the door and back out to the living room where Ava Jade was placing a warm mug of tea in her friend's hands. Leave it to her to comfort her friend after she was the one who was attacked.

"She doesn't need to be here for this," I said before I could soften my tone, indicating Becca. "Do you have somewhere you can go?"

Sparrow curled a hand around her friend's wrist to stop her from standing. "She stays. I don't want her going anywhere alone right now. Whoever that fucker was could still be outside somewhere."

Becca shuddered and remained sitting.

"Fine," I managed, resisting the urge to press my argument.

Grey walked into the living room, sitting on the edge of the coffee table facing Ava Jade so there was only an inch of space between their knees. He leaned over, and I could imagine the gentle expression he would wear as he told her.

"We know about your stalker," he said, his tone somehow managing to sound hard and gentle all at once. It brokered no room for argument. He was stating a fact, and giving her an opening to tell him the truth.

Her mouth pressed into a hard line. "I don't know what you're—"

"You should have killed the dark one while you had the chance, but now I see I'll have to do it for you. Nobody touches what's mine," Grey said, repeating the text message from where it's seared into his memory.

Her brows drew together and a flash of hot fury danced in her eyes.

"Don't worry, my love, I'll help you...but if you let them touch you again, I'll have no choice but to punish you."

"Stop," she growled in reply, and I saw how Becca was clutching her friend now, worry in the tight lines around her eyes.

"Aves?" Becca prodded. "Why didn't you tell me?"

"I was handling it," she all but hissed in reply, fixing her stare on Grey. "You went through my phone?"

He nodded slowly. "The, *uh*...the day at the diner. It was all planned. I had the laptop ready when you got out. Took a while to decrypt the files, though."

Her face reddened and she opened her mouth to speak, but I beat her to it.

"You should have told us," I said as gently as I could, given the situation. "Especially after whoever this clown is threatened Rook. Definitely after he threatened you."

Some of her anger seemed to burn off at that, and I placated myself in the knowledge that she clearly knew what I was saying was true, even if she didn't want to admit it to us or to herself.

I knew how hard it was to ask for help. To admit you might not be able to handle something alone. I'd chosen the harder path, but if I could go back and change that choice, things might've been different for me.

I might've been different.

"Has he sent anything else since the messages about fight night?"

Her ice-cold stare burrowed into me. "I didn't read it," she admitted. "He sent something, but I only read the first line. *I warned you...* then I deleted the message."

"Can you recover it," I asked Grey.

He nodded. "Yeah."

"Give him your phone."

Ava Jade balked at the command, and I gritted my teeth. I wanted to punish her for this. I wanted to bend her over my knee and bring my hand down on her bare ass until it was cherry red. I wanted to make her admit her mistake and apologize for putting herself and my brothers in danger.

But what I wanted didn't matter right now. What mattered was keeping us all safe, and the only way to do that was not to scare her into running or make her pull away from me even more.

"Please," I barely got the word out, and I sensed Rook stiffen beside me at the request, his eyes boring into the side of my face. "We need to know what it said."

"You think this was him, don't you?" she asked. "It couldn't possibly be your perfect gangster pops," she scoffed.

I shook my head. "We aren't ruling that out."

She was taken aback at that, and thought quietly to herself for a second before plucking her phone from her pocket and handing it to Grey.

"Do you have any idea who this person is?" Grey asked, catching her hand in his. He gave it a reassuring squeeze before she pulled away.

She shook her head.

"Someone from your past, maybe?" Grey asked. "A spurned lover?"

What?

I stared at the back of Grey's head, wondering what other messages he'd recovered along with the ones from the apparent stalker. Clearly more than we knew.

Ava Jade glared at him. "No. It's not Kit."

"Because you don't want it to be or—"

"It's just not him. Trust me."

He nodded. The conversation done for the moment and already I'd committed the name to memory, ready to scour every inch of Lennox for this guy.

"I'm going to take this downstairs," Grey said and held up the syringe as he stood, leaving the apartment to bring the syringe down to whoever was waiting on him.

Rook sauntered back into the living room and fell onto the sofa opposite the girls with a deep sigh. "Until we figure this out, you can't stay here," he told Ava Jade. "The window will take time to fix and the Nest is more secure."

"No. I already told you I'm not staying there. Besides, I won't leave Becca here alone. What if he comes back?"

Rook nodded. "Okay. Fine. She comes, too. You can both stay in the loft above the garage."

Surprise flashed in Sparrow's eyes, and I mirrored the sentiment. What the fuck was he thinking? But if it got Ava Jade to agree to stay with us, I'd deal with it.

"*Uh,* I'm good," Becca croaked, speaking up for the first time. "I really don't want—"

"At least until the window's fixed and you can have your dad install a security system," Ava Jade interrupted her, suddenly liking the idea if it meant she could ensure her friend's safety. Clearly that was more important to her than her pride. "Please? I can't leave you here."

Becca slumped. "Fine. Yeah, I guess that wouldn't be too bad."

Honestly, I expected her to put up more of a fight, or request to stay elsewhere. I was sure her millionaire daddy would happily put her up at The Vandermark just outside of town. I would have rather that, but if I wanted to stay on Ava Jade's good side, I could allow this. At least temporarily.

"Pack up," I said, planting my hands on the back of the couch either side of Rook's head. "This is your last night at Briar Hall for a while."

16

GREY

Diazepam.

Sally from the twenty-four-hour pharmacy in town took longer than I'd requested, but at least she managed to ID what was in the syringe. Enough Diazepam to sedate someone for hours. It would have taken effect within fifteen seconds.

Rook had been pummeling the heavy bag non-stop since I told him and Corvus on Monday night after moving the girls into the loft. Rook knew that drug better than most ever could. It was what they used on him at the psychiatric hospital in Stockton. The one Barrettes Home for Boys sent him to after they found one of the group leaders with a broomstick up his ass in the janitor's closet. The words *Rook was here* carved into the meaty flesh above his tailbone as he cried against a dirty rag in his mouth.

I never asked why he did it, and he never told me. It was just one of those things I knew was off limits for discussion, but my imagination came up with the worst things. Which was why after Diesel adopted us and made us what we were now, I paid a visit to that group leader. I didn't ask *him* what happened, either. I put two pieces of lead between his eyes and never said a word to a soul about it.

Helped me sleep better knowing that whatever he'd done to my brother, he would never be able to do again.

Rook was at the psych hospital for two months before they cleared him to return, and he was never quite the same after. The brooding, angry Rook I knew came back from that place aloof. Without a care in the world for anyone or anything except me. And that made him more dangerous than he'd ever been prior to that.

He only told me about his time there once, when he was blind drunk and all his words were slurring. For a month straight they injected him with Diazepam to put him down for not following orders like *take your pills,* or *paint a picture of a tree,* or *wait your turn.* They were happy to jab him with that needle at even the smallest infraction.

"Rook," I interrupted, stepping into the garage to a wave of warmth and the heady smell of sweat and aftershave. Heaving, he paused, blinking as his eyes focused on my face. He dropped his fists, shaking them out as he bounced from foot to foot.

He was getting super wound up. We were going to need to find the time to peel back his lid and let out some steam soon. Julia still had nothing for us, but I held onto the hope that she would soon.

We could always widen our net like Rook suggested several months back. Post the helpline fliers in the neighboring cities and towns, but then we might wind up with the opposite problem. Too much work to handle instead of not enough. If we left even one kid in a lethal situation...

If even *one* died because we didn't get to them in time after they called the hotline...

It would be one too many.

"Yeah?" Rook asked, swiping the moisture from his upper lip.

"It's almost time to go. You coming?" I asked, but it wasn't really a question. Diesel had sent us all the group message on Monday night after the girls got settled in.

DIESEL

Saturday night. Sanctum. Bring the girl.

Well, it was Saturday now and getting dark. Dies hadn't given a specific time, but nine was a safe bet and it was nearing eight thirty now.

Rook shucked off his gloves and methodically peeled some tape from his knuckles and fingers. "We still don't know what this is about?" he asked, his slitted gaze finding my face.

I shook my head. "No. We have to assume it's another trial."

"So soon?"

I shrugged. "It's not that soon if he had nothing to do with the attack last weekend."

Rook's lips pressed into a tight line.

We hadn't found a single thing to indicate the attack was at Diesel's request. None of the Saints were injured or unaccounted for. Diesel hadn't come to ring Rook's neck for interfering or given Ava Jade a fail.

There were no prints on the syringe.

None anywhere in Ava Jade's room.

Rook was still skeptical, but I believe this wasn't Diesel. This was her stalker. It had to be.

"Anything more on her phone, then?" Rook prodded, flexing his fingers before taking a long swallow from the glass of whiskey he had perched on top of a wooden stool by the wall.

"Nothing."

He slammed the glass back down and a muscle in my jaw ticked.

Ava Jade's stalker had been eerily silent since the attack last weekend. She hadn't received a single message. Either we scared him off or he was biding his time. Or, maybe he was just recovering from the two story fall out the window of her room.

There was no way he'd escaped unscathed from that drop. We'd checked the hospitals though. Every one within fifty miles. Of the few patients admitted with injuries that would've been consistent with the fall, none fit his description.

Tall. The same height as Rook—give or take an inch. Strong with a slender frame packed solid with wiry muscle. Neither Rook nor AJ thought he was very old. Maybe older than them, but not by much. Certainly less than thirty-five.

Only one man fit that description. And he'd met the cold barrel of Corvus' gun and wet himself two days ago when he was released from the hospital. It wasn't the guy. He was paid enough for a new pair of designer pants and sent on his way with a warning.

Rook licked his lips, and I could see the spark of madness in his eyes as they flashed in the overhead lights.

"We're going to find this fucker," I assured him. "We're going to find him and then you're going to take him apart piece by piece. I'll help you."

His gaze narrowed on me, a curious furrow in his brow. The unspoken question on his lips. *You will?*

I nodded.

Rook nodded back.

"I'm going up to get the girls. Corv is nearly ready."

As I said it, we both heard the front door close in the house beyond the door to the garage and the engine to the Rover start in the driveway. It was cold as fuck out there tonight, chances are he was just warming it up, but he wouldn't want to be kept waiting long.

Rook finished his drink and went in, headed for the shower.

I took the old entrance up to the loft. The one that required the use of the narrow staircase at the back corner of the garage.

Corvus had one of Diesel's contractors in on Monday while the rest of us were in classes. They finished the small renovation within six hours as requested and by the time we returned after last class, there was a new entrance to the loft, accessible through the other end of the upstairs bathroom.

Corv hadn't liked my loft idea, but instead of arguing about it, for once he just shut his mouth and found a quiet solution. One I was angry I hadn't thought of myself.

If he didn't have the new entrance made, they would've been sealed off from us. It would take too long for us to get to them in case of an emergency, and would leave them with only one route in and out— which was why Ava Jade was keen on the idea, too.

I rapped twice on the door and waited a beat before hearing Becca call for me to come in.

The loft opened up before me as I crested the last few steps past the threshold and into the little studio we never used.

Becca was perched on the edge of an oversized desk chair, pausing in painting her nails to inspect them for imperfections before sliding her hand beneath a UV light dome.

"What? Sometimes they need a fix between appointments," she explained. "And I haven't been able to get to the salon all week."

I wasn't going to ask, and I wasn't wondering, but I nodded all the same. "Where's AJ?"

She jerked her head toward the other end of the loft. "Shower."

I started into the loft but Becca's next question stopped me. "Got an ETA on those door handles yet? As much as I love showering with an open door in a house full of dudes...oh no, wait...I *don't* actually love that."

Fair enough. "Corv says they'll be here Monday."

"Thank fuck for that."

"Anything new we should be aware of?" I asked Becca, lowering my voice. "Messages, or..."

She looked at me like I'd sprouted another head. "Ask AJ," she said with a heavy sigh. "You really think she's still going to lie to you about it after that shit last weekend?"

The truth? I wasn't sure.

I wandered to the bathroom door, tapping on the wood pane lightly so it wouldn't open under my touch. "AJ? We have to get moving."

"What?"

The shower was off inside, but the exhaust fan likely made it difficult to hear.

"Time to go," I called louder, and she growled inside. The only response I was likely to get.

I sat heavily on the small chest snugged up to the end of the bed Ava Jade and Becca shared. The loft wasn't anything special, but it was enough for the two of them temporarily.

The bed was a queen, the mattress and bedding brand new. It had a small kitchenette in the farthest corner from the door and a sectional facing the wall in the opposite corner with a modest thirty-inch TV mounted on the wall. And the desk, of course, where Becca watched me warily as we waited for AJ.

The space was meant as a gift for Corvus. One Rook and I thought would help him get the peace and sleep he so desperately needed, but he never moved out here. Now that there was easier access to the rest of the Nest, I wondered if he would when the girls were gone.

I felt a pang in my chest, and I cleared my throat as Ava Jade exited the bathroom in ripped jeans and a tight-fitting, cropped tank top with no bra beneath. Her nipples like little Hershey's kisses beneath the dark fabric.

Her makeup was done, but her hair was still damp from the shower, falling down her shoulders and back in soft, wet waves.

"You got a blow dryer?" she asked.

I shook my head. "No. No time, either. I think Corv is already waiting in the car."

Right on cue, a long, blaring horn sounded outside.

"You going to be okay here alone, Becca?" I asked, and she opened her mouth to reply, but it was Ava Jade who spoke instead.

"You said it was safe," she spat back accusingly.

"It is."

"It better be. It's definitely safer than getting her any more involved in my shit than she already is. The last thing I want to do is parade her in front of Diesel."

I tipped my head to one side, pursing my lips. She had a point there.

"Besides she won't be here all alone anyway. You have plans tonight, don't you, Becks?"

Becca smiled at AJ meekly before shaking her head. "No. No, I'm just going to stay here."

AJ crossed the floor to her friend, lowering her voice as if I couldn't still hear her clear as day. "You haven't been out at all this week. Did something happen between you and your mystery guy?"

Becca shrugged, sighing again. "Fuck if I know. I think he's avoiding me. He does that sometimes," she shrugged. "Gives me time to catch up on some BioChem homework though, so whatever. I don't need him."

AJ squeezed her friend's shoulder. "You sure as shit don't, babe, but nobody ghosts my bestie and gets away with it. Want me to track him down? Drag him over here for a little chat?"

Becca barked a laugh that quickly died in her throat when she saw AJ's expression and realized her friend wasn't joking in the slightest.

"*Uh*," she said, laughing for a different reason now. "I'll let you know, 'kay?"

AJ nodded. "Hopefully we won't be long," she turned to me. "We won't be long, right?"

"Sorry. We haven't been briefed. No idea what's going on. Could be twenty minutes. Could be all night."

I hated admitting it but there it was, we were carting Ava Jade to Sanctum with absofuckinglutely no idea what was going to be waiting for us when we got there. It wasn't for a lack of trying to find out. We'd been snooping around Sanctum and the warehouse, and I'd even made an excuse to go and *pick something up* from Diesel's house just to have a little snoop there, too. Straight up asking him had gotten us nowhere, either. So, here we were.

"Is it another trial?" Becca asked, and AJ visibly tensed.

She'd had no choice but to come clean to her friend after the shit that went down at Briar Hall. It was about time, really. And as much as we didn't like it, it wouldn't have been fair to leave her in the dark, especially not if she was going to continue to stay here with AJ, which seemed like it might be the case.

AJ lifted her hard gaze to me, and I sighed.

"We don't know," she admitted, echoing my thoughts.

"You'll take care of her, right?" Becca asked me, fixing me with a venom laced stare that made me pause. I understood that she was pissed about what happened at BH, and that AJ was being swept up in all this, being out in danger, but there was more than worry there. There was hate.

And then it was gone, erased with Ava Jade's short laugh at her friend's demand.

"*Them* take care of *me*?" she said, grinning at her friend. "Don't worry, Becks. I don't need anyone to take care of me. I'll be back before you know it."

Becca's expression darkened, but she nodded. She really was in a foul mood. I hoped her boyfriend called her back soon. Otherwise, I was afraid her claws would only get longer. Her bite, harder.

"All right, then," AJ said, snatching a faded jean jacket from the back of the chair Becca was sitting on, sensing the tension in the air and wanting to leave before it got any thicker. "Don't wait up. Keep everything locked. You remember how to use that blade I left you?"

"Stick 'em with the pointy end," Becca replied, miming a stab gesture that needed a *lot* of work. AJ laughed at that.

"And the other part?"

"Stab first, ask questions after."

"You're going to be a pro in no time."

Becca waved us off after Corvus honked for the second time. "Go already before he blows a fucking fuse."

Ava Jade checked the door twice before we left to make sure it was locked and secure. She checked the garage door and the front door, too, wistfully tilting her head up to the small illuminated window set above the garage doors, worry creasing her forehead.

"She'll be okay. Corv installed all those new cameras. If you want, I'll put the app on your phone on the way there. That way you can check them whenever you want."

She smiled at me with her hand on the door handle to the back seat. The first smile I'd seen from her in a week. "Can you?"

"Yeah," I said and held the door as she slid into the seat next to Rook, who was staring out the window like the trees themselves might grow claws and fangs and come for his girl.

I cleared my throat, nudging the back of the passenger seat. "Corv, can you drive?"

"What the fuck for?" he growled.

"I'm going to put the app for the cameras on AJ's phone."

He grunted. "Give it here," he said, holding out his hand for AJ's phone without turning around. "I'll do it for her."

She hesitated, but reluctantly unlocked her phone and placed it into his hand, sitting up straighter in her seat to watch over his shoulder.

Either she had something to hide or she wanted to see if he would try snooping so that she could give him hell.

My skin bristled at the former option, wondering if there were any new messages between her and *Kit*.

I clenched my jaw as I circled the Rover and hopped into the driver's seat, pulling us out on the road.

"Nothing more from the stalker?" Corvus asked in a tone that I knew was trying hard to sound casual and not demanding but failed on all counts.

"Nope," AJ replied, popping the *p*.

Turned out the last message Ava Jade deleted before reading the whole thing was just that first line. Recovering it and decrypting it was a total waste of time.

But seeing the three words for myself was enough to make my blood boil anew.

I warned you...

He warned *her*? Ha! Motherfucker was a dead man walking.

We'd considered the option that he could have crawled off somewhere and died of his injuries, but somehow I doubted that. It would be a waste. There was a deep, dark part of me that wanted him to still be alive so I could have a hand in killing him myself.

"Grey," Corvus said, edging my name in a question, and I realized how tightly I was holding the steering wheel and forced my stiff fingers to relax. Made myself slow the speed of the Rover as we pulled into the back lot at Sanctum and Corvus handed AJ back her phone.

She was the first to hop out, appearing to not be at all worried about what might await her inside.

I sighed after her door closed and flinched when Corvus gripped my upper arm in an uncommonly gentle gesture. "You good, man?"

I swallowed and gave him a quick nod. "Yeah. I'm good, just..."

"I know," he replied before I could properly articulate what I wanted to say. "We got this. She's going to be fine."

The Rover rumbled to a standstill as I twisted back the key and stepped out into the crisp night air, inhaling deeply through my nostrils.

Food.

I needed something to eat. The banana I ate at breakfast and the pizza pocket I warmed up at lunch weren't even a fraction of my normal intake. No wonder I was so fucking irritable. No wonder my hands felt like they were trembling.

AJ flipped through the newly installed camera feeds through the app on her phone as we made our way inside, seemingly satisfied to find nothing but the shuddering shadows of trees moving in the wind and the quiet house on the screens.

"All clear?" I asked her with my best encouraging smile.

"Yep. Looks fine. She knows to call if she hears or sees anything. She'll be fine."

I wasn't sure if she was telling me that or herself, but either way, I agreed as we entered the main floor of Sanctum and the music from inside washed over us along with the smell of beer and whiskey.

I gave Sasha a nod as we entered and upon seeing us, she drew out Rook's favorite bourbon and poured him a glass without asking.

"Hey, sweets," she called, drawing the attention of the others. Sasha set the bourbon down on the bar for Rook and grimaced before taking it with a grateful nod. "Anybody else want anything?"

"No," Corv growled, his gaze tracking across the pub in search of Diesel.

"I'll take a water," AJ asked, and I caught her gaze dipping to Sasha's chest. It was hard not to, the way she wore her tits almost hanging out of her shirts. They were some nice tits, too. Fake, but sometimes those were even nicer than the real kind.

"Sure thing, hon," Sasha replied and filled a glass with ice and water, plunking in a slim black straw before handing it to AJ.

"You, Grey?"

"Nah, I'm good," I replied as I began looking for Diesel, too.

It was busy enough for a Saturday night and Sasha was quickly called away to help the other bartender fix drinks at the other end of the bar. Mostly Saints and their girlfriends or fuckbuddies graced the bar and tables. Pool balls knocked noisily into one another from the area at the back. A few locals drowned their sorrows in cheap beer at the bar and a handful of girls in too-short dresses eyed the leather-clad Saints not already spoken for from a booth near the door. Giggling as they adjusted their cleavage and hair.

I couldn't see Diesel anywhere.

Which meant he either wasn't here yet, or he was in the private room around the other side of the bar out of sight.

"Diesel here yet?" I went to ask one of the servers, a girl called Cat.

She shook her head. "Haven't seen him, but the others got here about an hour ago. Who's your friend?"

I glanced back at AJ. "That's our girl," I said before I could change my mind. "You get her anything she wants and if anyone so much as looks at her funny, I want to know about it."

Her lips twitched into an awkward tight-lipped smile as she replied. "Sure thing. I'll make sure everybody knows."

Rook growled behind me, and I turned to see him staring after a stumbling drunk asshole, leaving me to wonder if the guy'd accidentally bumped into him. He downed his bourbon and took off after the guy.

"Rook!" I called, but he was already gone, lost to the crowd.

"He muttered something about going to the bathroom," Corvus

said, giving me a strange look. Obviously he hadn't seen the look on Rook's face. Or maybe I was just overthinking it.

I grunted, giving a nod.

"I'll do a lap," Corvus offered, he and Ava Jade stepping up behind me. "Grab a table and wait."

"No, I'll go," I said, stopping him. "I need to stop by the kitchen and grab something to eat."

He looked like he might argue, but upon studying my face, stepped back to allow me to go. I must've looked as shit as I felt.

They found their way to an empty booth near the pool tables, Corvus slipping into the booth seat opposite Ava Jade.

"Hey, man!" Axel shouted over the music, clapping me on the back as I made my way through the crowd. His blue eyes hooded and glazed with intoxication. "Where's your pops at? I wanted to—"

"Don't know, Ax. He should be here soon," I interrupted, leaving no room for more conversation, but that didn't stop him.

"Hey! Hey, Grey, man I just wanted to let you know it's all set up like he asked. I didn't start drinking until it was done, you know. They're ready for him in the back."

What is? I wanted to ask the question but didn't. Then he'd know I had no fucking idea what he was talking about.

"Where?" I asked instead. "I need to check on them."

His face screwed up in confusion, and I worried I said the wrong thing but I stood my ground, waiting. "Well?" I pushed. "Where are they?"

"Kitchen," he said as another Saint began tugging on his arm for a reply to a question. "Bottom shelf of the cooler. I did it exactly how he asked, man. Just like always."

Like always?

Fuck.

"I'm sure you did, man. Thanks."

I left Axel to his friends and hurried through the back end of the bar, pushing into the kitchen. At this hour, it was closed and every stainless-steel surface gleamed. Satisfied it was empty, I crossed to the walk-in cooler and yanked it open, a blast of chilled air wafting into my face as I stepped inside.

Down low on the shelf to my left were two chalices made of heavy silver, the Saint emblem of a fleur-de-lis with a dagger protruding from the bottom embossed into the sides of each cup. Inside of each, a golden liquid reflected the horror on my face.

I swiped a palm over my face and began to pace the narrow slice of concrete floor, going over the limited options to prevent what was about to happen.

17

AVA JADE

"I told you," I groaned as Corvus pushed the pool cue into my hand. "I don't know how to play."

"It's easy," he told me, snatching a cue from the rack for himself. "It's all angles and calculating force. Grey tells me you're ahead of him in your math class. You'll pick it up quickly."

I fumed quietly by the edge of the pool table Corvus just cleared of players with a single look. My teeth ground together as he gathered up all the colored balls on the table and put them into a triangular frame, plucking some out to move them around to the right spots.

I hated that I could still barely look at him after the other morning. There were only a handful of people who'd ever seen me like that, well, maybe *handful* wasn't the right word. My dad was the only other person who'd ever seen me cry. And now there was Corvus.

It'd done something between us, and I wasn't sure I liked it. He was being *nice*. Cautious. Like he was afraid if he said the wrong thing, I'd shatter again. It was driving me fucking mental.

I cried. So fucking what. He needed to get over it. *I* needed to get over it.

If he kept treating me like I was made of porcelain, I would show him just how sharp my broken edges could be.

Grey appeared behind me at the pool table, lightly brushing my elbow with something cold and wet. I whirled on him with a snarl to find him holding out an iced drink with a slim black straw. It smelled like dark soda with a bite of...rum, maybe?

"Here," he said, pushing it toward me. "I got you a drink."

"No thanks, I'm good."

His face fell, lips parting as though I'd just refused a fucking proposal of marriage instead of a damned drink.

"*Jesus,*" I said on a laugh. "It's not like I kicked your dog. I just want to keep a clear head."

He cleared his throat. "Right. No worries. I'll just, *uh*, hold onto it in case you change your mind."

I lifted my brows. "*Okay*, then. You do that, Superman."

Grey's face pinched, his lips quirking up into the tiniest smirk before he stepped past me to go and sit in the booth next to the pool tables. Rook slid in a second after him, appearing out of nowhere. He leaned back in the booth, plucking a napkin from the silver dispenser on the table to wipe something that looked suspiciously like blood from his fingers.

"What?" Corvus asked and followed my line of sight to where Rook was now discarding the napkin atop the table and flagging Sasha for another drink.

"For fuck's sake," he cursed, and I followed him back to the booth in time to hear Grey hissing over the table at Rook.

"What the hell did you do?"

Rook gave a one shoulder shrug, his eyes looking lighter than they had in days. "He called her a whore," Rook said offhandedly, his wicked gaze flitting to me and away again.

Was he talking about me?

Corvus leaned over the table, his fingers splaying over the worn wood. "Who?"

"Some idiot."

"Rook?" Grey pushed. "Where is he?"

Rook sighed, graciously accepting a fresh bourbon from Sasha with a wink. "He's alive."

He didn't seem particularly thrilled about that. "He just won't be talking shit about our girl anymore. Or...talking much at all I'd imagine."

Oh my god. "You cut out his tongue."

It wasn't a question. I knew it, and he loved that I knew it, grinning at me wildly.

"Bingo."

That...that was kind of sweet. In a super fucked up, totally psycho kind of way. I bit my lip, hoping the sting of it would quell the rise of heat in my bloodstream.

"Fucking hell, Rook. You know the rules. No bloodshed at Sanctum. Diesel's going to shit," Corvus said, his face reddening.

"Relax, brother." Rook rolled his eyes. "I took him out back. I know the rules."

Grey relaxed some, nodding absently. "Fucker kind of deserved it," he muttered, making something flutter in my belly. Corvus didn't disagree, but he groaned, standing upright as he pinched the bridge of his nose.

"At least he didn't kill him," Grey told Corvus. "Progress."

Corvus shook his head, fixing his stare back on Rook, who was sipping his bourbon like he didn't have a care in all the world. "All right. Just...just fucking clean yourself up. There's blood on your jacket."

Corvus grabbed my elbow and steered me back to the pool table, away from the *situation* that was his brother.

"You want to break?" Corvus asked, indicating the neat triangle of colored balls on the table.

I knew enough about pool to know what he meant, but that was about it. Besides I was still reeling from Rook's blood display of affection. "*Uh*, I don't even know how to shoot."

"Come here," he offered. "I'll show you."

I snorted, imagining it. Imagining Corvus adjusting my hands on the cue. Him telling me to bend over and get a good line of sight down the cue to the ball while he positioned himself behind me. His warm body wrapped around mine. His warm breath on the side of my neck as he guided my cue into position with his hands on top of mine.

It was probably the fantasy of any girl in this room, and I'd have been lying if I said it wasn't tempting. But I didn't want to reenact cliched scenes from romantic comedies. Besides, I could figure it out my damn self. Just as soon as I shook off this feeling still heating my cheeks and making my knees weak.

"Well now," a rough voice called over the raucous laughter and music in the pub. "You boys didn't tell me she could play pool."

"Diesel," Corvus said, his jaw flexing as he stared somewhere over my right shoulder.

I turned, keeping any trace of discomfort from my expression. I'd show him no fear. Men like him could smell it in the air. They thrived on that smell. Bathed in it. I wouldn't give him the satisfaction.

"I can't," I said for myself. "Your son was just going to teach me."

I couldn't help rubbing it in just a little—that his sons chose *me*. Had chosen to let me live despite what Diesel might've preferred. That they liked me enough to teach me how to shoot pool. To cut out a man's tongue for calling me a whore.

It was stupid and maybe a little childish, but I didn't care. I didn't ask for any of this, and I wouldn't go down easy.

"Is that so?" Diesel's question was meant for Corvus, and I turned back to him expectantly.

"Yeah. Passing the time till you got here. Took you long enough."

"We got held up," Diesel replied, and I watched him shrug off a busted up old leather jacket and pass it to an enormous guy to his left. I recognized him as *Tiny*. The bouncer from the illegal boxing ring downstairs.

Tiny carefully draped his boss' leather jacket on the back of a tall chair, as though he were afraid too much force might tear it in two. He wasn't wrong. The thing looked to be holding on by threads and a prayer. Not the sort of thing I'd have expected the leader of one of the largest gangs in Cali to wear.

"If you don't mind, son. I'd love a go," Diesel said, crossing the floor to hold out a hand for Corvus' cue.

The level of sound in Sanctum had dropped exponentially since Diesel's arrival and as I spun in a slow circle, I noticed how many of the Saints who'd been drinking merrily five minutes ago were now watching. Rapt at the exchange between Diesel and his sons.

Between Diesel and their potential *female* new recruit.

Fuck.

Corvus reluctantly handed over the cue and Diesel flipped it over, holding it up to his eye to stare down the length of it.

Should I have done that?

"What do you say, princess?" he asked, his voice carrying in the pub as he set the cue down and fixed me with a ready stare. "Humor me with a game?"

"I told you, I don't know how to play. And don't call me princess."

He inclined his head, studying me from head to toe.

I took the opportunity to do the same. This was only the second time I'd seen Diesel St. Crow in the flesh and the first time, I'd been more than a little preoccupied.

The man was taller than I remembered. Handsome, for an older guy, with a trim, but muscled figure and bright eyes that I knew saw more than he let on. I normally didn't like beards, but somehow his suited him, long and tapered, mostly straight and groomed. I couldn't picture him without it. He had a relaxed sort of power. Like a lion at rest. He could spring up and strike whenever he wanted, but why would he when he had a pride at his back ready to do the work for him?

"Very well. Corvus? We're overdue for a game, I think. Why don't you take Ava Jade's cue? Or shall we just get started with the real reason we're all here?"

"Want to tell me what that is?"

Diesel smirked. "Why the rush?"

Corvus hesitated before coming to me. "Unless you'd rather just get this over with?" he muttered, holding a hand out for the cue.

I opened my mouth to reply *yes,* because *fucking duh,* I just wanted to go back to the house, but Corvus grabbed the cue before I could reply, taking my split second of silence as a non-answer. Or maybe he just wasn't ready for whatever *it* was to begin.

Grey beckoned me to the booth, and I went while Corvus bent over the raised edge of the pool table and broke the triangle of balls apart with a loud *clack.*

"How about that drink?" Grey asked, sliding the rum and Pepsi over to me.

Why was he so insistent on me having a drink? I wasn't a joy to be around sober, if I started drinking I was liable to knife someone.

"There's not much rum in it," he said. "It's just a single."

I met his gaze, finding a worried crease between his brows.

"I think you need it more than I do," I joked but took the proffered drink, swirling the straw before I removed it and downed the icy cold drink in two long swallows. The ice made my teeth sting.

Grey visibly relaxed, and I peered into the bottom of the glass. "If this was roofied or some shit, I'll kill you."

Rook smirked at that because *of course* Grey wouldn't roofie me, but with how bad he wanted me to drink the damn thing, it was a valid comment.

I noticed he hadn't bothered to clean the blood splatter from his jacket, wearing it as a badge of honor instead. The color suited him.

Corvus and Diesel's game was over in a matter of minutes, Diesel coming out the victor.

He went to his adopted son and gave his shoulder a squeeze. "You're distracted," I barely heard him tell Corvus. "Let's have another round later, yeah?"

"Yeah," Corvus muttered.

"Good." He clapped Corv on the back. "Let's get this over and done with. Grab the girl and meet us in the back room. Her second trial is tonight."

Corvus stiffened.

Diesel's eyes cut into me like shards of ice before they flicked away and he turned his attention to Tiny and another man behind him. Together, they vanished into the crowd.

"Any idea what it is?" I asked Corvus when he got close enough that I wouldn't have to raise my voice.

He shook his head. "A couple of ideas, but no."

I looked at the others. Rook and Grey sat stone faced and silent in the booth.

Great.

"The trials are always different for each person. There are a few that get repeated, sort of like tradition, but they're almost never given in the exact same way," Corvus explained.

He held out his hand for me and I stood up without his help, the little bit of rum I'd just slammed going to my head. I ignored his hand and he dropped it, seemingly unbothered. "If you need a minute," he offered but I was already shaking my head.

"No. I want to get back. Come on, let's just go do this."

Rook and Grey slid from the booth and fell in behind Corvus and me as we wove through the pub, making for a set of double doors around the quieter side of the bar in the back of the building. We stepped through them into a dark antechamber. Ahead were swinging doors with windows in their tops that showed a gleaming kitchen. To the right was a sign for bathrooms and to the left a long hallway that led to a single black painted door with a polished silver handle.

That was where we headed.

I steeled myself, cooing to my darkness as it began to swell, coming to life in my gut.

Corvus held the door open and Grey stepped ahead of me to go in first. Rook followed right behind me. The lighting inside the large room was dim, casting an eerie glow over the space.

To my left, a bank of expensive looking sectional couches held a few Saints, lounging quietly, drinks perched between their fingers. To my right sat a large rectangular table made of what looked like polished black glass at first. But as we neared, I saw it wasn't glass at all, but some kind of dyed epoxy, a golden fleur-de-lis turned dagger embedded down the middle.

Diesel St. Crow sat at the opposite end closest to the wall, and only one other chair waited at the other end of the table. It wasn't rocket science to figure out who it was meant for.

Without being told, I stalked past Grey and folded myself into the chair, sitting up straight as I pushed myself into the table ledge. With my lower body concealed, it was easy to stealth a blade from my thigh through the wide tear in the denim. Style and accessibility. These were my favorite jeans.

I laid the blade on my thigh and lifted my hands to the top of the table, feeling more confident knowing it was only inches away if I needed it.

Diesel's biting gaze watched me carefully, his line of sight flitting low before rising back to my face. Either he knew what I'd just done or he guessed. I didn't give a fuck either way. He didn't really expect me to go anywhere unarmed, did he?

I knew he was packing a piece. I'd seen it in the pub. And I also knew all of his sons were packing heat, too. What was a blade compared to guns? In the hands of someone less skilled, nothing. But in my hands...

Maybe one day Diesel would find out.

"Is this a staring contest?" I asked after another minute of terse silence. "Because if it is—"

Just then the door opened again and Tiny stepped through with two silver chalices on a serving tray. He went straight to Diesel and bent, whispering something in his ear before setting the tray down and leaving the room.

Corvus cursed and Rook let out a growl so low I wondered if I imagined it.

This wasn't good.

"May we have the room," Diesel said, his shining eyes flicking over the many faces eager to watch whatever the fuck was about to go down.

The Saints left one by one, and I turned my head to see Grey, Rook, and Corvus still standing just a few feet behind my chair.

"Do I need to repeat myself?"

Diesel's jaw flexed.

"You can wait outside," he offered them. "I'll let you know when you can come back in. I'd like a word with our new initiate in private."

"Is this really necessary?" Corvus asked, and Diesel narrowed his stare on him. "It's an antiquated tradition. We should—"

"This isn't up for discussion."

Slowly, I turned back to face Diesel, saying nothing.

A prickle of unease skated down my spine, making my stomach sour with dread, but I didn't show it. Not even as Diesel's sons dutifully left the room as they were asked.

Something I don't think they would have done if any of them truly believed he was the one responsible for the man who tried to inject me with fucking Diazepam.

That was enough to quell the rising dark within at least a little bit. Though we all knew Diesel wasn't interested in making me a Saint. That he didn't trust me and would do anything in his power to see to it that I failed. So, maybe the darkness could hang around just a little longer, in case I should need it.

"Ava Jade Mason," Diesel intoned, leaning back in his leather high back chair like a king on his throne. "Eighteen years old. Deceased father. Addict mother. Lived in Lennox your entire life until recently coming into the care of your aunt and moving here to Thorn Valley. Right so far?"

I didn't answer, but my fingers itched to reach for the blade in my lap.

"It was difficult to find very much information aside from that, however, given your street smarts and skill with a blade, I'd wager you had a *difficult* childhood. Is that right?"

"What does this have to do with anything?"

He shrugged. "I like to know what sort of snakes I'm inviting into my house."

"And?"

He tapped his fingers absently on the table. "And I like to know who my sons have invited into theirs."

"Well, now you know."

He pursed his lips. "Not nearly enough."

"If there's something you want to ask, just ask."

He cocked his head to one side, considering me in a new light. "I don't trust you, Ava Jade. I think you're a viper. All shining scales and alluring eyes. Lulling my boys into a sense of false security while you await your perfect moment to strike."

Officer Vick crossed my thoughts, but I pushed him away, afraid Diesel would be able to see the truth hiding just below flesh and bone.

"Then why agree to let me take the trials at all?" I asked instead.

He didn't like that question. It was clear in the way his expression soured. "My son asked me for this favor," he told me, surprising me with the truth. "Greyson has never asked me for anything. Not since the day I took him in. *Not a single thing.*"

His eyes found mine, holding me there with a warm intensity. "He asked me for *you.*"

"And you think he made a mistake?"

"I know he did. I just hope they all see that before it's too late. There are some lessons I can't teach them. Ones they'll have to learn themselves."

Something in my chest cracked at his admission and in the haunted look darkening his eyes.

He snapped out of it after a second, sitting up straighter in his chair to fold his hands atop the table.

"I want you to know, Ava Jade, if you betray my boys—if you harm them—I will hunt you to the ends of the earth. You may think you know the meaning of pain, but you're wrong. You will hurt and you will bleed. And when I'm finished with you...you will die."

I let that sink in, his promise etching into my bones.

It was violent and a clear threat and yet...

I respected him for it.

An ache formed behind my breastbone, and I swallowed back a burning in my throat. The memory of my own father dredged back up from the depths where I'd banished it. I had to admire Diesel for his willingness to do whatever it took to protect his sons.

I loved my Dad, but if I'd had a parent as viciously protective as Diesel, I might not have turned out the way I did.

"I understand," I replied with a nod.

"Good."

He rose from the table and lifted the two chalices from the tray at his side, carrying them both over to me.

He set them down in front of me on the table, one next to the other.

"Both have two ounces of good whiskey," he paused. "In one of them is a fast-acting poison."

My pulse quickened.

"You decide which one you want to drink. I will drink the other."

"You would poison yourself?" I asked dubiously, my mind racing.

He regarded me with cat-like eyes. "Yes. If you choose correctly. The poison is strong. The side-effects...unpleasant. But the likelihood of it being lethal is low."

Low, but not zero. Fucking awesome.

"What the fuck is this supposed to prove?" I asked, unable to help myself. "Blind obedience?"

"Sometimes obedience is necessary, even if it poses great risk to yourself. *If* you pass these trials, I need to know you'll do what is asked of you no matter if you don't agree. Even knowing it could cause you bodily harm. For the good of the many."

"And how is *this* for the good of the many? It's *poison.* This is some idiotic Princess Bride shit."

He smirked at that, but I wasn't joking.

"It's tradition," he added before indicating the chalices again. "Choose."

I narrowed my gaze on the chalices, grinding my teeth.

This is fucking stupid.

But...I realized a little belatedly, he'd just told me what this trial was meant to prove. If I didn't drink, I failed the trial. My refusal would prove my inability to follow an order.

If I didn't drink, *Diesel would win.*

Couldn't fucking have that now, could we?

I settled myself knowing that if Diesel killed me his sons would never forgive him. At least, Grey wouldn't. I didn't think Rook would be too happy, either. Corvus would probably get over it.

I could handle a little stomach cramping, right?

"Can I check them?" I asked and Diesel nodded.

I lifted each to my nose, smelling the bite of strong whiskey in each, but nothing else. I swirled them, angling the chalices to the light to check for swirls of a liquid that might have a different viscosity, or powder residue on the bottom. Both seemed clean.

Maybe there was no poison at all.

Maybe it was just a test of obedience and all I needed to do was drink to pass.

Too many maybes. Too little time.

I sighed, deciding on the chalice to my left, the one furthest from Diesel. I held it up, the cold silver damp with condensation. "To your health," I said with a wry smile, and he smiled back, all teeth as he lifted the other chalice and knocked it against mine.

I swallowed down the drink in two burning gulps and swiped the back of my hand over my lips, knocking the heavy metal chalice back onto the table.

"Boys," Diesel called loudly, giving me a knowing grin as he made his way back down the length of the table to his seat at the opposite end. With him gone from my side, I tucked my blade back into its sheath.

The guys came back in a second later, their faces shadowed as they took in the empty chalices in front of me.

A sharp pain lanced through my stomach, and I fought the urge to double over, clutching the underside of the table. *Fuck.*

"Go on, boys. Get her out of here. I don't want her making a mess on my floor."

18

ROOK

Ava Jade didn't make a mess anywhere as Diesel suggested she might. We brought her straight home, all of us tense with nerves as we waited for the inevitable pain.

But it never came. Nothing more than the knot between her brows to prove she was in any discomfort at all. I didn't know what the fuck to make of it.

I remembered the night after my poison trial and I wouldn't have wished it on anyone. Except maybe the motherfucker stalking her. The cramping had been bad, but it was nothing compared to the pounding headache that lasted days, or my stomach expelling every ounce of its contents and then some. And don't get me started on how badly I destroyed the bathroom.

I shuddered, hefting the massive water bottle onto my shoulder to trudge it up the stairs to the loft to replace the one Ava Jade and Becca had emptied.

I rapped twice on the door and Becca answered, stepping aside for me to enter. She'd hardly left the loft at all since they moved in, and I was curious if she was too afraid to. I wouldn't blame her. Fear was a powerful form of natural self-preservation, that's what Diesel was always trying to remind me, anyway.

"Ghost?" I asked as I placed the jug onto the cooler, popping the seal so the water could flow down into the chamber.

"Bathroom," she replied with a sigh, and my stomach tightened. Had it finally started? Ava Jade went straight up to the loft when we got back last night, and we hadn't heard from or seen her since. We all agreed to stay clear of the upstairs bathroom to give her some privacy while she was sick, but I never heard a peep.

Even with my bedroom the closest. There were no vomiting sounds. No pained cries. I would have brought her water. A cold towel.

"How long has she been in there?" I asked, staring at the closed door across the room.

Becca lifted one of her dark brows at my question, hesitating before her reply. "Um, why?" she asked, like it was the most ridiculous question and she couldn't for the life of her figure out why I'd want to know.

I considered that. "Is she not sick?"

"Sick?"

The door opened, and Ava Jade stepped back into the loft, fixing her hair with a pin. My cock jumped in my jeans at the sight of her, my mouth going dry.

She definitely wasn't sick.

Looking more like a wraith than a ghost in all black with a leather skirt and a tight black shirt with little cutouts running up both sides from her waist to her underarms, exposing more than a little side boob. Dark makeup on her eyelids with wicked slashes of black liner making them look winged.

"Rook?" she asked, and I realized I was still staring.

I gave her all black outfit one last go over before reining in my expression. "Whose funeral is it?" I asked, my lips pulling upward on one side.

"I haven't decided yet," she quipped, smiling back with a wink.

She really wasn't sick. Had Diesel not poisoned her? That didn't seem fucking likely. He always poisoned both chalices. He'd done that trial in some capacity or other on every member of the Saints. He was used to the poison, had built up a tolerance to it over the years that allowed him to get by without too much discomfort. Plus, there was the antidote always at the ready just in case he should need it.

The antidote...

My brain worked to solve the equation, trying to figure out how she got away unscathed.

Grey. That sneaky son of a bitch.

I should have seen it before. He went off to do a loop of the bar, said himself he was headed for the kitchens. The poison needed to be kept chilled. He'd have found it in the cooler. But how had he gotten his hands on the antidote so fast? It was a ballsy move, but I couldn't say I wouldn't have done it myself given the opportunity.

We'd have to tell Ava Jade eventually. Diesel would want to know she suffered. The only way that was going to work was if she were in on the lie. A problem for another time.

"Are you almost ready, Aves?" Becca asked, leaning over the desk to look into a small circular mirror as she applied dark cherry lipstick. "We should get going."

"Going?"

"We have a concert to go to tonight," she said offhandedly. "Thought I already told you guys'"

"You didn't."

"Oh. Too bad. If you're all busy tonight then it's no problem, Becca and I will be just fine without you."

Devious little fucker.

Why did her defiance just make me even harder?

I licked my lips, sucking in a breath as I bit my lip ring. Until I realized what today was and my amusement waned.

"I think not, Ghost," I replied without room for argument, not bothering to explain. She knew why we couldn't let her go anywhere alone. It was more than Diesel's orders now. There was someone out there who'd tried to put her down with a sedative. I could vividly imagine a thousand reasons why and none of them would *ever* happen if I had any say in it.

"Always such a buzzkill," Ava Jade muttered and I lifted my brows.

"No. That's Corvus. Not me."

She tipped her head this way and that, pursing her lips to show she agreed.

"What show are you going to?" I asked in an uninterested tone, leaning against the support beam at the center of the floor. "Anyone I'd know?"

"Doubt it," she replied with a haughty sort of disdain.

"Humor me."

She looked me up and down as she sat on the edge of the bed to tug on a pair of calf height boots, zipping them up tight. "Primal Ethos," she said finally, watching me for any trace of recognition.

"He's good," I said, eager to drag more detail from her lips. "Not amazing, but good."

An inside joke she wouldn't get, but inside, I was laughing.

Of course she would be a fan of Primal Ethos. I should've guessed it, but this? Her actually *going* to one of his shows? A bolt of wild anticipation tore up my spine.

"Ha!" she barked. "He's a fucking god and nothing less."

"*Amen*," Becca added, making a wicked sign of the cross as she shimmied her shoulders.

I couldn't keep the amusement from creeping onto my face this time, and my Ghost looked at me like I might have lost my final screw.

"What's so funny?" she demanded, and I cleared my throat, swallowing back my smile.

"Nothing at all."

She rolled her eyes, snatching up some cash and what looked like a fake ID from her nightstand. "Ready, Becks?"

"Yeah, just let me use the ladies room, first."

The door shut behind Becca, and Ava Jade adjusted her tits as she strode toward me. I let out a growl, loud enough for her to hear. She grinned at my reaction, leaning in close to my side to whisper in my ear. "So, will you be joining us?"

Her scent filled my nose, and I twisted a fist into her hair, knotting it in my fingers at the back of her skull to hold her there, inches from me.

Truth be told, I wanted to be there to see her face...but I had plans tonight. A little recon of my own. Off the books. All of us were carving out time to try to find the bastard who attacked Ava Jade, but so far we'd turned up nothing. I couldn't accept that. I needed his blood coating my hands. Splattering my face. I needed to hear his screams and watch the light leave his eyes so that I could sleep at night.

Tonight, I had one job. Find him. Or at the very least, find a fucking lead.

"Can't, I'm afraid," I murmured a breath away from her lips. "But I'm sure Grey would be happy to accompany you."

"Too busy for me?" she asked, her steely grey-blue eyes flitting to my lips and back up again.

I tipped my chin down, desire aching through me like a searing blade as I replied. "Never."

Her breath tripped from her lips in a quiet gasp as I tightened my fist in her hair, making her eyes squint with the bite of pain. She closed her eyes and moaned, but as the bathroom door opened, I released her, stepping away as though the moment between us never happened. She tripped forward a step, flushed and breathless, blinking at me standing three feet away like she couldn't fathom how I'd moved so fast.

"Aves?" Becca asked, staring at her friend's back. "You okay?"

She shook her head at me, the threat of returning my teasing ten-fold clear in her eyes.

"Fucking fabulous," she replied. "Let's go find Grey."

She sauntered past me behind Becca on their way out, and I smiled in her wake. I snatched her hand before she could vanish down the stairs into the garage, pulling her up short.

She glared at my hand holding her tight and lifted her chin with a question in her hard stare. But I didn't mean to stop her from going. "You're armed?"

She visibly relaxed and lifted the hem of her leather skirt, flashing me the twin blades strapped to either side of her thighs and a damn good view of her black panties. I clenched my jaw, nodding.

"Good."

I released her.

"Be careful."

"Ghosts can't die, Rook," she told me in a light tone. "We're already dead."

19

GREY

I fired the message off to Corvus. The seventh message I'd sent him in as many minutes.

"Could you move your seat up?" I snapped, shouting over Primal Ethos' Gravedigger and Becca singing along to it.

AJ whirled around in her seat, her eyes gleaming in the neon dashboard lights. "Nobody asked you to come," she reminded me. "And I'm not scrunching up my legs so you can stretch out back there. Turn sideways or something. And stop being so grouchy. You're killing my vibe."

"Awe come on, Grey," Becca added once Ava Jade was finished, turning down the music a few notches. "Are you worried we won't be able to scalp you a ticket? I'm sure we'll—"

"No," I interrupted her. "I'm not worried."

Becca recoiled as though slapped and turned the music back up, leaning over to whisper to AJ. "What crawled up his ass?"

"Not a clue."

"Oh, I love this one!" Becca shouted excitedly, turning the volume up to ear ringing levels now as we took the Lodi exit. "Come on, Aves. Sing with me!"

AJ smirked, dropping her head as Becca began to sing, but she didn't join in.

"Come on, babe," Becca continued to prod. "This is my favorite part!"

I went back to my phone, flicking through unsaved numbers until I found the one I hoped was Maxine's. Hers was a number I had yet to memorize.

GREY

Max. We have a problem. Have Corvus call me as soon as you get this.

Fuck. This was going to be nuclear if AJ recognized him. Or worse, if he saw AJ in the crowd and knew I'd done nothing to stop her from coming. If he thought rationally, which I doubted he would, he'd realize that nothing I could've said or done would've prevented her from going.

If I'd said no, she would have found another way. If I'd taken the fuse for the fuel pump out of the car, they'd have just hired a cab, or fucking fixed it for all I knew. If I tried to lock them in, AJ was liable to break down a wall to get free, and kill me on her way out.

Apparently, Becca and Ava Jade had been waiting and planning for this concert for weeks. Over a month. There was nothing that was going to stop them short of fatal injury, and I wasn't going to go that far. I *couldn't* go that far.

If we were lucky, the tactics we used to conceal his identity from the masses would also work on Ava Jade. But when had we ever been lucky? And when had AJ ever been fooled by anything we'd done or said?

It wasn't lost on me that if I hadn't slipped her the antidote to the poison that she would have been too ill to have gone. I guess this was karma coming back to bite me in the fucking ass.

Fuck. Fuck. Fuck.

On a last-ditch effort, I tried texting Rook.

GREY

Any brilliant ideas? I could use a hand.

The bastard had just walked right past me grinning when AJ announced where they were headed and said I had five minutes to get in the car or they'd leave without me.

His reply came a second later.

ROOK

Enjoy the show.

Fucker.

He was enjoying this.

Becca elbowed AJ in the front, and she began to sing the chorus of the next song with her friend, her voice rising in Becca's Audi like a rogue wave. It took me a minute to process it, how incredible she sounded. Her voice weaving almost expertly with his voice as it poured through the speakers. I wanted to tell Becca to stop singing, just so I could hear her better.

She must've sensed me watching her because after the chorus, she stopped singing abruptly and sank back into her seat while Becca squealed excitedly.

"Shit, girl!" Becca said, shoving AJ lightly. "You didn't tell me you could sing."

AJ shrugged it off, staring ahead into the dark, but the tiniest smile teased at the edge of her mouth. At odds with the sadness in her eyes that I could see through the side view mirror.

The concert venue came into view up ahead and swarms of concert-goers crowded in on both sides of the street, making their way to the main entrance from the parking lot we were turning into.

GREY

AJ is here. I'm sorry man, I couldn't stop her.

Concert nights were the *one time* Corvus set his phone aside to get his head in the game for the show. The only time he would ever ignore a call or a text. Max, his manager, usually held onto it for him until afterward, but even that bitch wasn't answering my goddamned messages.

It was just as likely that she'd read them, saw that the content might throw him off his game and decided not to tell him. He'd have her head for it, but at least the show wouldn't be ruined. Maxine was all about the money and when Corvus agreed to do another show, it was a guaranteed packed house. I wouldn't doubt it if the merch we'd ordered last minute was all gone before he even went on stage.

The mysterious Primal Ethos. The bone man, as some had taken to calling him. Everybody liked a good mystery. Maxine had been right about that, at least. Corvus' need for anonymity was part of the reason he'd grown in popularity so quickly. The ominous skull face paint added an edge of horror to the whole charade that matched his branding perfectly.

For a dead woman walking, even I had to admit Maxine was fucking fantastic at her job. It would be a shame to lose her. I might even miss her bossy tone and filterless attitude.

My phone buzzed as we stepped out of the car and I almost dropped it in my haste to tear it from my pocket.

UNKNOWN NUMBER

I don't know what's going on, but save it for post-show, alright? He's already stressed enough about the new song, he doesn't need whatever shit you're about to bring to the table, 'kay. Thx.

Max.

"Grey, come on! We have to find you a ticket before the show starts!" Becca beckoned, locking her Audi and waving a hand to me.

"Just one sec," I lobbied back, stepping further away from the car as I dialed Maxine.

Come on.

It rang, and rang, and *fucking rang.*

"Hey!"

"Maxine, oh thank fuc—"

"You've reached Max. I hate voicemails so this better be fucking important. If it is, make it quick, otherwise, email me at—"

I ended the call with a deep sigh and nearly cracked my phone from clenching through the frustration.

"Grey!" AJ shouted, and I spun to find them both waiting by the sidewalk expectantly.

You know what...*fuck it.*

I tried.

Corvus said himself that AJ was one of us. If he meant it, then there was no reason for him to want to rip my fucking head off. If he didn't...well, that would be his problem to deal with because I couldn't very well go and hunt him down backstage and leave Ava Jade's side. Not with the possibility of her stalker still being out there.

He could be here right now. From his text messages, it seemed like he was always lurking. *No*, I'd stay with her and deal with the consequences later.

"Coming," I hollered, jogging over to them as I pocketed my phone, reaching for the joint dangling from Becca's fingers at her side. I put it to my lips for a good long drag and exhaled deeply, coughing a bit as the smoke scraped up my lungs. It was good shit.

"*Greyson Winters*," Becca trilled, taking her joint back with a look of approval. "Welcome to the party, handsome. Let's go find you a ticket."

20

AVA JADE

Dare I say it?

As Becca dragged me through the paint chipped doors of the underground venue, jostled on both sides by other anxious fans, I had to admit it...I was having *fun*.

We weren't even in the main venue yet, and already I could feel it, a bubble of excitement in my chest ready to explode. As we were herded down the narrow corridor and out onto the floor, a smile pulled at my lips and lifted the edges of my eyes. Eyes that must've shone with the glow of the neon lights pulsing above in time to the music.

The band currently on stage was one I wasn't very familiar with but enjoyed listening to nonetheless. I let Becca pull me into the meat of it, brushing shoulders with her and Grey and about six other people as we danced.

Becca laughed as the song came to an end and those around us cheered, I tipped back my head to let loose a wolfish howl, raising my hands to clap with those around me.

I caught Grey staring and whatever bit of ice remained crusted around my heart began to thaw at the look on his face.

It was as though I could read his mind with that single glance. *I'm happy you're happy*, he seemed to say, but more than that. There was relief there, too. So deep that it hurt to look at. Had I been that withdrawn lately?

Thinking back to the night of the attack, I realized I had been. I'd hardly left the loft save for classes and the odd meal with the guys. And they'd left me to process everything on my own, only popping in every now and again to ask questions, showing that they were working to hunt down my stalker just as surely as I was.

They wouldn't like what I had planned to finally catch the motherfucker, but if everything worked out, whoever it was would be dead and then none of us would have to worry anymore.

If he wasn't dead already. My phone had been oddly devoid of threatening messages since last week, and I was starting to think the fall really had been too much for the bastard to recover from after all.

It would make things easier for me, that was for sure, but truth be told, I wanted to be the one to finish him off with my bare hands, and maybe a blade or two. It was a waste for a sadistic fuck like him to die without my being a part of it.

Too easy.

"Hey," Grey shouted as the band on stage announced that they would play one last song before welcoming Primal Ethos on stage. "Where did you go just now?"

"Hmm?"

"Come back," he urged me with an encouraging grin, slipping his hand into mine. But something pained flickered behind his amber eyes and I saw worry there that I hadn't noticed before. Something was going on, but whatever it was Grey seemed resolved not to let me carry any of the burden of it. Preferring to be a grouch the whole way here, at least until now.

"Stay in this moment, AJ. You deserve it."

Something fluttered in my chest, and I gave his hand a squeeze, nodding that I agreed even if a part of me thought I deserved all the misery the world could muster to give me. I'd ask him what was eating at him later. Help him if I could.

"Come on, Aves!" Becca screamed, twirling as the last song from the opening band started to play, holding her hands out to me as she came to a stop. "Dance with me, babe!"

How the hell could I say no to that face?

Grey stuck close by us as Becca and I danced and my eyes popped open when she stealthily drew a tiny bottle of Jack from between her breasts. I snatched it from her and looked around, making sure no one saw. "Are you trying to get us kicked out?"

She laughed. "Look around, babe! You see any security?"

I did as she asked and this deep into the heart of the floor, there was no security at all and in fact, I noticed several others drinking their contraband booze, and laughed.

"It's for you," she shouted, still swaying to the beat as the song began to slow to its end. "I have to drive."

I didn't comment on the fact that she seemed totally at peace with driving high, shaking my head at her instead as I held up the tiny bottle to Grey. "Want some?" I offered.

He gestured to me in reply. "All yours."

All righty then...why not?

I'd been handling my liquor pretty damn well these past few weeks and that was saying something since my life had been reduced to a pile of smoking ash.

"Bottoms up," Becca cheered as I downed the small bottle in one go and passed the empty to Grey when he reached for it. It seared a path all the way down to my belly, and a prickling warmth bloomed through the rest of my body, making me shiver.

But...

"Nasty," I said, shaking my head as my tongue recoiled from the flavor.

Becca laughed. "We'll try Crown next time. That's my favorite."

I had no idea what she was talking about, but I nodded, a heightened sense of ease taking root. "Whatever you say, boss."

The crowd broke into cheers, and we turned to give our attention back to the opening band, screaming and clapping with the others.

"That's it for us, Lodi!" the main singer called. "We had a blast tonight and we're fucking gutted to have to leave y'all, but it's time for the next act."

The decibel level as the crowd went wild reached an all-time high in anticipation of Primal Ethos.

I noticed how Grey had positioned himself behind Becca and me and was blocking several overly rowdy concert-goers from knocking into or jostling us. I smiled at him gratefully. Not that I couldn't have handled it, but it was nice to have him watching out for Becca, too.

"Let's welcome him back to the stage for the first time in over a year! Who are you here for, Lodi?"

"Primal Ethos!" the crowd responded, and slowly, a chant began to grow, echoing all over the tightly clustered space.

"*Bone Man, Bone Man, Bone Man!*"

Becca and I joined in while Grey remained silent at our backs, tense and so pensive I almost asked him what was wrong, but then the lights all went out, plunging the room into a darkness so deep that I couldn't even see Becca beside me more than her faint outline. I clutched her arm, reaching back to tangle my fingers with Grey's on instinct as the crowd hushed.

A black light flickered on the stage only a moment later, giving us a stilted, shuttering view of a bone-white skeleton face staring coolly out at nothing.

Becca squealed, her voice rising with the others as the black light flickered for the last time, now blooming to cast its eerie glow on the man standing center stage.

As the others around me screamed and shouted, welcoming Primal Ethos on stage, I could only stare, a deeply rooted emotion growing from deep within to claw up my throat, silencing me.

He truly was a real person. This man who sang of things few could ever really understand. Not in the way he did. Not in the way *I* did.

A beat started and the crowd began a new wave of cheers as the man with the skeleton face on stage lifted a microphone to his lips. He hummed the first notes with the beats, his smoke and honey voice reverberating in my chest just as surely as it was in his as he felt out the music, letting his body flow with it, too.

He looked like the devil incarnate. *The Bone Man*, they called him, and I could see how it fit. Dressed all in black with dark hair slicked back and white contacts covering his eyes, all that was clearly visible of him was his size, tall and muscled, but lithe. And his made-up face, done in a stark contrast of black and white that managed to look so real you almost had to wonder if it was.

The Bone Man's voice rose with the first lyrics of Anthem of the

Broken and my breath caught in my throat, stuck there, held back by a burning dam.

"We march up this mountainside alone.
Tired and broken, we push on.
One foot. Another. Do it all once more.
We crack and shatter while they rush past,
over jagged peaks with wings of steel...
...while ours are porcelain."

Becca's voice rose to meet The Bone Man's, lifting up and filling the space with hundreds of others all singing his anthem. But how many of them really understood his words? How many were crushed under the boots of the mighty? Forced into silence? How many could relate as he sang the verse about finding your hands red with blood and wondering what you'd done?

About not being sorry, but being afraid of finding yourself immobile, shut up behind bars, locked away with only the voice in your own head for company. About how insane that would make you. About how that purposeless life wouldn't just break your already crumbling wings, but shatter your soul, too.

As the song grew in strength building up to the chorus, I felt something in my soul lift.

"Find your broken crew,
'Cause they're the only ones who can save you."

My skin prickled as a new voice rose to join The Bone Man's on stage and the crowd absolutely rioted at the new addition. The female voice weaving with The Bone Man's on stage, mingling with his in a way that couldn't be described in mere words. I searched for the other singer, expecting a guest act to have joined him, but he sang alone, like he always did.

It shouldn't have taken me so long to realize why the voice woke something inside of me, but when I did, I almost hit the fucking floor.

How?

How had...

Tremors of fear and unease raced up and down my spine and a cold dread filled me all the way down to my toes.

"Oh my god, she's amazing!" Becca shouted, teary eyed and screaming as she swayed to the chorus. She hadn't noticed.

I turned to find Grey staring past me toward the stage, his lips parted and brows drawn.

Oh god.

I turned back and followed his gaze, pushing up on my toes to see.

Tall and lean, broad through the shoulders. You'd never know it if you hadn't spent weeks imagining what it might feel like to feel the crunch of his nasal bones under your fist.

No.

The chorus ended, segueing into the end of the song and the crowd roared. Not just for *him*, but for *her*.

For the new voice.

For *my fucking voice.*

My voice that Corvus not only heard in his little makeshift studio but *recorded*. That he'd edited and added to his song like it was his right to use whatever he fucking pleased. Because he *was* The Bone Man.

Primal Ethos.

That was Corvus *motherfucking* James on stage.

My stomach heaved, and I pushed free of the crowd, shouldering past Grey, tearing away from his reaching hands as I shoved through people all around me, itching to use my blade when a few resisted.

Finally, I found cleaner air and fell forward, catching myself on my knees to try to breathe as my head spun.

"AJ!" Grey shouted, and a second later I felt his hands on me, curling around my shoulders, helping me up. "AJ, what's wrong?"

I tugged away and whirled on him, a little off balance, my stomach still in knots, the threat of vomiting a real and present danger.

"What's wrong?" I echoed, glaring at him.

His expression darkened, confirming my worst nightmare.

"Jesus fucking Christ," I spat, lifting myself back to my full height to push my hair away from my face and find somewhere to sit down, not bothering to check if Grey was following me.

Corvus...fucking *Corvus* began another song. Another one of my favorites and my skin bristled, every tiny hair standing on end.

I fell into a seat in a vacant row at the far right of the floor, up one level.

"AJ, listen—"

"Nope."

"Just hear me out—"

"If you say another fucking word, I will cut you."

Mercifully, Grey fell silent, and I leaned over my knees, head clutched between sweaty palms.

My mind raced in a million different directions, trying to come to terms with this new information. It was clear that no one else knew. I doubted even their dear ol' dad did. I doubted he'd approve of the spotlight, or of his precious second in command doing anything that might take away from gang business.

Those weren't the important questions, though. The ones I really wondered about, I fought the hardest.

What did this mean?

I'd followed Primal Ethos for years. I'd loved his music for years.

Knowing that there was even a single other soul out there who understood me had gotten me through so much. His music had gotten me through so much.

Corvus' music.

Fuck.

I wanted to hate him, it was easier to hate him, but...

How could I when...

"I'm going to be sick."

Grey set a palm on my back, and I flinched, making him remove it immediately. "I'll go get you some water, okay, just...just don't move."

As if I even could right now.

"Becca, there you are. Can you sit with her for a sec," Grey said, and I wished I could disappear into myself as Becca rushed me, kneeling in front of me, right in the firing line if my stomach won the battle with my mind.

I swallowed my bile back as she set her hands on my knees. "Shit girl, you look like a ghost."

I almost laughed.

"Was it the Jack? We didn't really eat anything, maybe that was it. Do you feel sick?"

I shook my head and did my best to sit up, letting the chair back hold me up, but then he was in full view again. Up one level, I could see him clear across the concert venue, above the heads bobbing and swaying in an ocean of bodies on the floor.

I'd wondered before if The Bone Man had ever really experienced the things he sang about, but I didn't have to wonder anymore. Not while he sang about digging shallow graves. About the sound a bullet makes as it left the chamber of a gun. About how blood goes cold after a while, but still stains you forever, and no matter how many times you try to wash it off, it will linger, like an invisible tattoo only you can see.

Until you're just red. Nothing but red painted over shades of gray as you dig your graves.

"Incredible, right?" Becca shouted, and my heart squeezed painfully in my chest.

I couldn't reconcile them together. Corvus and The Bone Man.

I hated him for not telling me. For using my voice. For all the awful things he'd done and said. For every time he'd tried to control me.

But how could I hate him completely when now, through his music, I understood him?

His song, Protector, showed me why he had his need for control. How he couldn't survive without it.

And the others showed me...more than I wanted to know about him.

I sat there for so long, contemplative and numb that I didn't notice when Becca waded back into the crowd, leaving me alone, sitting there with Grey at his request so that at least she could enjoy the rest of the show.

I'd told her to go, or at least, I thought I did.

Somehow we'd been there for an hour or more because suddenly The Bone Man was announcing his final song of the night.

His voice, his non-singing voice, expanded into the cavernous underground space, and I'd have known it anywhere, even if he was adding an extra level of gruffness to it to try to mask it.

"I have one last song for you," he said and accepted a mic stand from a woman in black leather leggings when she walked it onto the stage and retreated with a quick red-lipped kiss blown into the crowd.

Corvus set his mic onto the stand and looked up into the black light. Something in his sharply defined skeleton face softening.

"You won't know it. It's something new I've been working on. It's... it's a little different from my usual, but I think you'll like it."

A few rogue shouts of *fuck yeah* and *whoop!* Went up.

He exhaled, the sound of it like a whispered prayer electrifying the air. He settled in as a beat a bit slower than his usual tempo began to filter through the speakers. All haunting piano keys stuck intermittently with the ominous sounds of breathing and an echoed beat. It made my skin bristle anew.

"This one's called *Sparrow.*"

I snapped my attention to Grey, spine going rigid.

He offered me a small impish grin, nodding slightly. *Just listen,* he mouthed, as if I could do anything else.

"She makes me mad
She makes me mean
She haunts my dreams
I call her Sparrow."

Something cracked in my chest, and I got up abruptly, letting my feet drag me forward.

"AJ!" Grey called, but I was already gone, vaulting over the railing and into the crowd, dipping and weaving and pushing toward the front.

That motherfucker.

How dare he.

After everything...

The crowd pushed back, not allowing me past as I continued to find a way forward, realizing belatedly that I should have just gone around. There would have only been a couple of security guards to deal with if I had, it would've been easier than slogging through this.

"Wicked as they come,
I'm coming undone.
Hate, fear, pain, love
Don't you know what you've done?
Sparrow."

A guy attempted to grab me when I carved a space out for myself against the front rail in front of the stage, but a single look from me had him moving *far* away.

What now? An angry voice asked in my head, and the whisper of my darkness coming alive in the pit of my stomach warmed the chilled blood in my veins. I wanted to jump this fucking railing, climb up on stage and get my fist super acquainted with his jaw, but, I also didn't want him to stop singing.

Caught between warring desires, I stood there, smushed against the rail, sandwiched on both sides by screaming girls whose worst day probably looked something like a busted heel and a declined credit card, unable to do a damn thing as he sang of his Sparrow.

Me.

In that voice.

The one I should have recognized the very first moment he spoke. And maybe I had, but I'd denied just like I was trying to convince myself still that it wasn't true. Except, there was a part of me, however small, that wanted it to be true now, too.

However impossible it seemed.

It also felt right, in a way that was so so fucking wrong.

Confusing didn't even begin to cover this.

Maybe it was my lack of enthusiasm. Or my lack of movement that set me apart from the others, but something drew his eye to mine, and I saw the moment he recognized me.

A muscle in my jaw ticked at the shock on his face, and my anger fizzled out when some emotion much stronger flashed in his white eyes.

He sang the last line, his eyes never leaving mine.

"She's the spark,

I'm drenched in gasoline

...I can't wait...

....I can't fucking wait to burn."

He stepped back from the mic, back from the black light to a raucous jeering of applause, until he vanished into the darkness backstage.

He wouldn't get away that easily.

Not a fucking chance.

I hopped the rail and kept low, racing across the base of the stage to the narrow corridor leading around to where I assumed the dressing rooms were.

"Hey!" A security guard bellowed somewhere behind me but I didn't stop, ducking below a velvet rope barrier.

Another guard ahead moved to mid-hallway, blocking my path.

"Now turn around, you don't want to get yourself arrest—"

I ran the last three steps, faking to the right so that I could clock him on his left temple, sending him down in a useless heap of overpaid muscle.

Nothing was going to stop me.

Corvus *motherfucking* James had some explaining to do.

414

21

CORVUS

My phone screen blared with missed texts and calls, dropped off in the private dressing room by Maxine sometime during the show. She was fucking lucky she wasn't here or I might have had to murder someone tonight.

I slammed the phone down, wincing when I heard the distinct sound of the screen cracking.

Wasn't this what I wanted?

I knew writing that song with the help of the guys and deciding to perform it would mean having to tell her the truth eventually. *Eventually* being the key fucking word. Not yet. Not right now.

I thought I had at least until it was recorded and released to make sure this was the right call. I had to know I could trust her first. This wasn't gang secrets. This was *my* secret. One my brothers helped me keep.

Would she help me keep it, or would she use it against me? I hated not knowing the answer.

A door down the hall outside opened, slamming into a wall.

"Corvus!" Ava Jade roared, her voice muffled through the heavy steel door of the room, almost drowned out by the still screaming fans out on the concert venue floor.

Another door opened. Another roar. "*Corvus!*"

Fuck.

I went to the door, with no other choice. If she kept calling my name, my very fucking *distinct* name, she was going to blow my damned cover. But when I got to my door, the handle was ripped from my fingers and the panel of steel flew open.

"*You!*" She seethed, breathing heavily. Her mascara smudged around her eyes. Her teeth bared.

So many roiling emotions in her eyes I couldn't peg down any particular one. It was like she was forcing herself to look at me against her own will. Making herself see me through the skeleton makeup still mostly intact on my face. Through the white contacts covering my ice blue eyes and the dark hair paint making my hair appear black.

My stomach clenched, fists balling as we stared at one another in a silent standoff for what could've only been a few seconds but felt like minutes. Or even hours.

I waited for the attack I knew was coming, resigning myself to stand there and take it, confident she wouldn't kill me. Maybe that confidence was misplaced, but the lyric rang true. If I would burn for anyone, it would be for her. I'd burn away just for her to be reborn from my ashes.

When she came for me, I stiffened, closing my eyes to accept my punishment for stealing her voice. For lying and hiding this part of myself from her. For everything.

But, when her claws dug into the skin at the nape of my neck, yanking me down to her, there was no killing blow. She crushed her mouth to mine in a feral kiss, sharp nails biting down into soft flesh so deeply that I felt blood welling from the half moon cuts she was digging into me. But I wasn't focused on that. If anything, that pain only added to the perfection of it.

Of her lips on mine.

A growl rose in my throat and she moaned in response, making something tug loose in my chest. The growl louder now as I gripped her around her waist, lifting her to my height. Her legs went around my hips, and she fisted her free hand in my hair, pulling and twisting sharply against my scalp.

When her tongue pushed between my lips, I couldn't inhale her fast enough.

I hadn't kissed a girl, or been kissed by a girl, in years.

Fucked, sure.

Sucked off, often.

But this was a line I didn't cross.

Hadn't wanted to.

Until now.

My tongue warred with hers and her next moan almost sent me over the edge of control. Her shirt tore open at the back, ripped apart by my hands. She gasped, and I swallowed the sound, devouring her, body and soul.

"You're a fucking asshole," she whispered harshly between kisses, redoubling her efforts to cut me with her claws.

I grunted, twisting my neck to push into the bite of them.

"Never claimed to be anything else," I muttered, and she kissed me again before I could finish, tilting her hips forward so that my rock-hard cock pressed against her heat. Too many layers of fabric between us.

"I hate you."

"I hate you right back."

But that wasn't true anymore, was it. I hated that I wanted her. I hated that I recognized in her someone who could not just withstand me, but fit into the mold with me to be reformed as something new. Improved.

Twice as lethal and twice as strong.

It'd been there from the start, her spark. I thought it would be the end of us, but I was wrong. She was the ember that would ignite us, spurring us into a forest fire that would eat all our enemies away, render them to ashes. We would burn together.

She was the catalyst we'd been waiting for.

My Sparrow reached down between us, pulling and tearing at my dark denim jeans, trying to get my cock free and failing miserably. Even just the brush of her fingers there made me convulse with *need*.

I thrust her against the wall, no, the mirror, and it cracked. The narrow shelf beneath was covered in pots of dark and light makeup and I bent, clutching her to me to swipe everything onto the floor before dropping her on the ledge of the high shelf, pulling her shirt the rest of the way off to reveal a threadbare bra beneath.

We'd have to fix that.

I curled my index finger beneath the connective bit of cloth between her tits and ripped hard, the whole thing coming free with barely any force.

Her nipples were so hard for me. Breasts swollen and perky and begging to be worshipped.

"You're going to pay for that," she hissed, clutching the ledge of the shelf to keep from being pulled off. My dark makeup smudged all over her cheeks and down the slope of her nose.

"That's the plan."

A tentative smirk played at the edge of her mouth, and I kissed it, breathing in her scent. So sweet but with a smooth edge like fresh tobacco smoke or musk. I couldn't get enough of that smell. It was why I kept one of her shirts in the top drawer of my dresser, the urge to steal it having come over me in a way that I'd never experienced before. I just knew that I wanted something of *hers*. To touch when I wanted. To breathe in when I wanted. A part of her that I could control.

I sighed as the drug of her settled into my veins, getting me high.

Nothing beat the real thing.

Her fingers were surer now when they reached for the front of my jeans, jerking me closer. The top button popping easily now. The zipper racing down.

Fuck.

I gripped her hand, stopping her, and her lips froze on mine before pulling away.

"There won't be any going back after this," I warned her, unable to look her in the eyes. It was the truth, and she deserved to be able to make this call.

If we crossed this line, she would belong to me, and I would *never* let her go.

I could feel the beast in me swelling, taking over. Promising a possession so fierce there was no way I'd ever temper it. No point in even fighting it. She would be mine.

Ours.

She reached forward and clutched my chin, dragging my gaze up to hers. My nostrils flared as I let her see the agony there. The pain I kept pushed down so deep that sometimes I could forget it was even there.

It was, though. Always had been. I didn't think there could ever be anyone I could share that with. Nor anyone else I could want to be responsible for aside from my chosen family.

But I would do it for her. If she would have me.

Please have me.

Her jaw clenched, and I braced for rejection, pulling my face from her hand, but she didn't let me go so easily.

"I don't make promises I can't keep," she said. "And a big part of me still wants to slit your throat..."

I snorted.

"But there's a bigger part that..." She trailed off, and the hope taking root in my chest hurt more than any pain ever could.

"I understand now," she said instead of finishing the thought, wading into safer territory. "I don't like it, and I haven't forgiven you."

Despite myself, I flinched, my teeth grinding.

"I want to, though."

"You do?"

"I think so."

I let out a shaky breath and put my forehead to hers, watching her eyelids flutter closed at the contact. "I can't promise to be better. I'm broken, Sparrow."

"So am I."

"No, you don't understand. I'll *always be broken.*"

There was only silence in reply, and I watched everything I wanted vanish against the backs of my eyelids, but then she spoke.

"If this is *broken,* then I don't want to be fixed."

She finished freeing my cock with a flick of her fingers, and I groaned as she took it into her hands, stroking the silky length of it gently at first, then she gripped it tight, and I grunted again, eyes flying open.

"Now, fuck me, *Bone Man,* or I'll go find someone who will."

My beast growled with possessiveness at her threat, but she didn't have to ask me twice. She'd made her decision. Now, she was mine.

I thrust into her palm, pushing my fingers into her hair to tug her head to the side, putting my teeth to her throat. I scraped them down the length of it to the nape of her neck and bit down, tasting her on my tongue, marking her for everyone to see. She shivered at the pain, and I pressed between her legs, knocking them aside to put my cock flush against her panties.

Her *wet* panties. She was drenched. Practically dripping for me, and I shuddered as her wetness soaked through, making the slip of my cock against them feel like a fucking dream.

"Panties," she panted, nails digging into my back, the word a plea.

I bit her again, resisting the urge to tie her up. Tie her down. Force her to her knees and tell her she was a good girl as I pushed my cock down her throat. Not yet. Not this time.

Not our first time.

"*Patience.*"

"Fuck that."

She reached between us and tore her own panties off, tightening her legs around my waist to impale herself on me. My glutes tightened, pushing me in deeper on instinct alone as Ava Jade held herself there, adjusting to me. And it *was* an adjustment. There was a reason the few girls I'd brought to bed in Thorn Valley liked to call me their Mount Everest. A summiting that could just as easily end in victory as it could in tears.

"*Jesus fuck,*" Sparrow said breathily against the skin below my ear, breathing heavily, and I smiled into her hair.

I started to move, aching to feel her clench around me as I withdrew and thrust back in, but she whimpered, clawing up my back.

"I can stop."

"Don't you fucking dare."

My smile widened.

The kind of smile only she knew how to drag out of me.

"As you wish," I teased and flattened a palm against her chest, forcing her to retract her claws and return to clutching the ledge of the shelf. I wanted to watch her.

My Sparrow squirmed as I grabbed her thighs, spreading her wider for me as I withdrew and thrust back in with a stuttered groan.

She tipped her head back, letting herself be consumed by the sensations, moaning in a way that was driving me slowly to madness.

She was so fucking tight.

"Just like that," she said in a breath as I picked up the pace, pumping into her hard enough to rock the whole shelf she was seated on. To make the cracks in the mirror behind her head spider out, erasing the reflected image of me from view.

"Is this what you want?" I asked, my upper lip curling as I fucked her harder.

"*Yes.*"

She tipped her hips up for me, allowing me even deeper. So deep she could barely catch her breath.

"That's a good girl," I cooed, releasing one thigh to grip the side of her face, forcing her to look at me. I wanted to see her ecstasy. Needed her to know that this meant the end of everything. And the beginning.

"*Fuck*, Corvus," she whimpered, unclenching one hand from the shelf's ledge to rub her greedy little clit, eyes boring into mine. The sight of her touching herself while I slammed into her almost sent me over the edge, and I had to shut my eyes, slow my breathing.

What was she doing to me?

I truly was coming undone. All my carefully erected walls coming down. The cement blocks of my control crumbling to fucking dust.

Dangerous.

Incredible.

Terrifying.

"Fuck, I'm going to come," she announced, and I bit down, my own orgasm shuddering down the length of my cock.

I dropped my head and pulled a pebbled nipple into my mouth, making her back arch as I bit down on it, forcing her to that summit before I hit it first.

She cried out as her orgasm took her, her convulsions milking my cock of everything it had to give. The sound of my own release mixing with hers.

A loud *chink* was the only warning that the shelf was going down, and I was almost too slow to catch her before she fell, rolling myself to take the brunt of the fall with my jeans tangled around my ankles so that she could land on my chest, my cock popping free of her cunt.

A little squeal left her lips as she landed hard on my chest, knocking the air from my lungs. Makeup pots and brushes jammed into my back, and I groaned, coughing to get a full breath.

She rolled off and our gazes met.

Then, she laughed.

A laugh that started deep in her belly and reverberated up through her throat, filling the whole room with its musical sound.

I laughed too, the sound foreign as it found its way past my lips. Deep and rich.

She kicked my leg as though it were my fault we broke the fucking shelf, and I kicked her right back, laughing harder.

She swiped a tear from her eye and sat up, looking around at the state of the room. At the state of us.

"We're a fucking mess," she said.

"You are," Grey announced, and as one, our heads swiveled to the door, finding Grey standing there leaning against the doorframe with Becca next to him, covering her mouth with both hands, eyes wide as she took in her friend.

"Sorry!" Becca chirped and turned around, striding away from the door. I guessed she was one more person to add to the list of those that now knew my best kept secret. That was a problem. I glared at Grey, deciding to deal with him later.

"I was wondering when you were going to show up," Ava Jade said to Grey. "Ten minutes earlier and you could have joined us."

22

AVA JADE

"Uh, Aves..." Becca trailed off, and I groaned sleepily, refusing to open my eyes even though light was searing the back of my eyelids. "Wake up, girl. I think someone left you a present."

That had my attention piqued, but still my stiff joins protested movement as I rolled over in the bed to find Becca standing by the door leading down to the garage. She held up a smooth black box with a piece of paper taped to the top of it. Scrawled across it in black sharpie was a single word: Sparrow.

I pulled my pillow back over my head, the whole thing coming back to me now.

The concert. *Backstage* at the concert.

Me gathering my things and telling Corvus that I needed time to process everything. That I wanted space.

So much for that. He was already bringing gifts to my fucking door. Prick.

My cunt throbbed at the memory of him inside me, and I clenched, feeling a pleasant ache still there from his size.

"You want me to open it?" Becca asked. "Or should we send it back?"

I moaned in response, disliking both options.

"I vote we open it, and since you're in no shape to be making any life decisions pre-caffeination, my vote counts for you too."

I pulled the pillow off. "No, wait—"

But she already had the top off the box and was staring excitedly down at whatever was inside. "Oh. My. God."

I sat up, the last remnants of sleep rolling off my shoulders like a bad vibe. "What is it?"

She tiptoed over to my bed like a crazy person and dropped the box in front of me. Black tissue paper spilled out, revealing something in a stunning magenta color. I used my pinkie to lift the dainty slip of lace fabric and my mouth fell open.

It was a thong. A lace thong.

"Look!" Becca trilled, clapping her hands before snatching something else from the box. "It's the matching set! Look at this thing!"

She held it up to her own boobs through her shirt as though checking to see if she might be able to borrow it.

I grabbed it from her and threw it and the thong panties back into the box, covering them back over with the tissue paper, my heart racing.

Becca calmed almost immediately, settling onto the bed with crossed legs. "I know we didn't talk about it last night, but I'm, like, hella curious what the fuck happened and—"

She caught my look and stopped babbling.

"Okay, so I *know* what happened. I just...I thought you didn't like him. I actually thought you hated him. Is it just because he turned out to be you know who? Because I *did not* fucking see that one coming. Corvus James: cold hearted prick, gang member, part-time psychopath, and *rock star?* You just can't make that shit up. Guess all the fan theories are wrong then."

She was wrong. So wrong, but I couldn't bring myself to correct her. I hadn't fucked Corvus because he was The Bone Man. I fucked Corvus because when I laid eyes on him in that dressing room...I saw him for who he really was. Not for the mask he wore.

I saw his soul. Bared. Naked.

And I wanted to claim it.

Becca laid her hand on mine, and I blinked back to myself, realizing I'd gone quiet. "Hey," she said. "You totally don't have to talk about it if you don't want to. I may kinda sorta be trying to live vicariously through you. I mean, since..."

She didn't finish the sentence, and again I was reminded that somewhere out there was an asshole who'd drawn her in and then ghosted her. If he didn't come back and apologize, I made no promises against finding his ass and forcing the apology out of him.

"It's fine," I told her with a forced smile. "I just don't really know how I feel about it yet. I do hate him. Or, I *did* hate him. I don't know. I'm just—"

"Confused?"

"Doesn't even begin to cover it."

She laughed. "Well, with a dick that big, I'd take my time considering my options."

I cocked my head at her, cheeks tinging red as something uncoiled in my belly.

He's not yours to get jealous over, Ava Jade. Cool it.

She held up her hands in a placating gesture. "No, I just mean it was a nice dick, that's all. I think I'm going plastic for a while. The real thing just isn't worth it sometimes."

"Ain't that the motherfucking truth."

My phone buzzed on the nightstand, and I grabbed it, catching Becca's barely concealed excitement at the sound.

"Is it him?" she asked, scorching closer.

I shook my head. "Just an email."

I almost set my phone back down before noticing who the email was from. *Vicky.* I didn't know a Vicky. I clicked on it.

To: Ava Jade Mason

From: Vicky Doyle

Subject: Swap Notes

Hey, Ava Jade, it's Vicky from English Lit. I was hoping we could swap notes for the upcoming project like we talked about. Can we meet? I was thinking maybe Sunday morning. I'm not going to be able to help you if you don't help me. Last chance. I'll send you the address later! Thanks.

My stomach dropped.

Vicky.

Officer Vick. He was trying to covertly set up a meeting without drawing suspicion.

Crafty fucker, and maybe a bit smarter than I gave him credit for. I had no idea how he got my email address. He was giving me exactly a week to make my decision.

An impossible decision, but one I think I'd already made.

"You good?" Becca asked. "Is it your hag of an Aunt again?"

I clicked off my phone and shook my head. "Nope, just a stupid scam email."

"Ugh, I hate those."

Becca jumped up from the bed to check her face in the small mirror on the desk, rubbing a mascara smudge from beneath her eye.

Her phone went off, and she lifted it eagerly, only to frown at whatever was on the screen.

"All good?" I asked.

"Yeah. Just my dad. Asking if I'm coming home for Thanksgiving."

"Will your mom be there?" I asked, realizing she only ever talked about her dad, never her mom. I assumed they were separated, but I honestly had no idea.

Becca stiffened, swallowing as she turned back to me, a sadness in her brown eyes. "No."

"Oh, you don't get along, or?"

"We did," she said with a somber smile. "Before she died."

My heart twisted.

"Guess we have that in common," she pointed out, and it was easy to tell she was trying to play it off like it was no big deal when it was. She immediately began picking at her fingernails, an act I'd come to realize was one of her stress responses.

"You have a dead dad. I have a dead mom. And our other parents are mostly MIA, other than when they want something."

I hadn't told her much about my mom. Only that I hadn't seen her in years, and only heard from her exactly once. A phone call from a payphone asking me to bail her out of jail.

"What happened?" I asked, getting a sinking feeling in my gut.

Becca clenched her hands together. "It was an accident. A bad one. The wrong place, wrong time kind."

Her lips pressed into a tight-lipped smile, and her gaze found mine before slipping away quickly. She sighed.

"I'm so sorry, babe. Do you want to talk about it?"

God, I was shit at this sort of thing. How were you supposed to comfort your friends if you couldn't slay their demons for them?

"It was a long time ago." She shrugged, and her eyes lit up, hands unclenching in her lap as she perked up.

"Hey! Do you know when Corvus' birthday is?" she asked after a second, turning a bit to lift a curious brow in my direction.

Um...talk about a one-eighty...

"Why?"

"I'm not sure if I pegged him right anymore, you know? I always thought he was a Scorpio, but now I'm thinking maybe Gemini?"

So, we were changing the subject then. Got it. I laughed for real this time. She really wouldn't give it up with this horoscope stuff.

"No, I don't know when it is. Rook's is next weekend though."

She gasped. "No way! I thought for sure he was Aries, but of course *he's* the Scorpio! Should've seen that one coming a mile away."

I hoped he liked his gift. It wasn't much, but I had a feeling it might mean something to him. Something more than chocolate cake or anything bought from Amazon. And I wouldn't make a big deal out of it since Corvus told me he didn't like to celebrate.

I shook my head at Becca.

"You figure me out yet?" I asked with a challenge in my tone, and she pursed her lips at me.

"You're a tough one. I think I've almost got you, though."

She wandered back to the bed. "You've got to help me figure out the other guys. They've legit never had a birthday party or anything in all the years I've been at Briar Hall with them. I'm starting to wonder if they were made instead of being born. Like crazy gangster robots."

We both burst out laughing, and it was hard not to picture it. Which only made it even more funny.

I sighed, swiping a tear from my eye as I calmed down. "Fuck, I think we need to get out more. We're laughing about fictional gangster robots."

Becca cut herself off mid-laugh and reached under our shared bed, drawing out two lumpy parcels with the Crow's Nest address on them.

"Say no more," she announced and ripped into the first one then the second.

She waited for my reaction, but I just stared, wondering what in the actual fuck I was looking at here.

"For the full moon party!" she said when I didn't get it. "It's a few days before Halloween so everybody's dressing up. I got us costumes!"

Truly, I'd been planning to find a way out of going to that, but I couldn't do that now, not with Becca looking so excited. Though, if the rumors were true, Bianca, *the bitch*, was talking shit around Briar Hall about 'taking me down.' So, the night might not be a total bust. Maybe I'd borrow the trimmers from under the sink, give her a new hairdo. The idea made me smile.

I lifted silky black fabric from one package, noticing the Prada label on the sheath-like dress, and what looked like horned headbands from the other.

"Do you get it?" she pressed, and I winced, staring between the two items with confusion.

"The Devil Wears Prada," she said, losing some of her steam. "You know, like the movie? Or the book, I mean, both were fucking phenomenal."

My lips pressed tight, and she gasped.

"You haven't seen it? Are you shitting me?"

"Sorry."

She shoved all the clothes and horns out of the way and took both my hands, hauling me up from the bed. "We're fixing that right now."

She pulled me through the bathroom, to the upstairs hallway of the main house. I pulled back, not wanting to face anyone just yet, but she only pulled harder. "It's just Grey, and he's working on something in his room, see?" She waved an arm to his open door. "No one else is here."

Grey lowered his headphones to his shoulders and spun in his office chair. "Hey, what's up? You need anything?"

"Just to borrow your TV," Becca said. "And to be left alone for a minimum of two hours."

Grey blinked, clearly as confused as I was but waved us on. "Our TV is your TV. Have at it."

"Come on, girl. Miranda Priestly is my fucking spirit animal, I can't wait for you to see this!"

"THE GUYS ARE ALREADY OUT BY THE CAR," BECCA SAID, PEERING OUT THE SMALL octagonal window at the front of the loft.

"They can wait another sec. My liner is almost out."

I shook the tube, forcing the last dregs of the black liquid eyeliner to saturate the brush tip. "Fucker," I cursed as a glob of black splattered on my black Prada dress that I was definitely going to pay Becca back for some day.

"Sorry," I muttered, trying to brush it off, but only managing to make a mess.

Becca laughed at my growly attitude, coming over to help. "You can't even see it. Here, give me that before you wind up looking like a raccoon."

I passed her the liner and reached for a makeup wipe, cleaning the black smudges from my fingers while she eyed up my eyes, getting a lay of the land. "Okay," she said, mostly to herself as she knelt and leaned in. "Close."

I closed my eyes, feeling the gentle press of her fingers at the edges of my eyes and then the cool swipe of liquid product over my lash line. She fixed the other side to match and then stepped back.

"Open."

She smiled. "There. Have a look. Maybe a bit bolder than your usual, but it's Halloween, so I think you can get away with it."

I checked my reflection, surprised at how the slight change in my liner could make my eyes look so much brighter than they usually did. And fuck if those wings weren't perfect. Combined with the dark lipstick, horns, and mega contouring, I really did look like a devil risen from the depths of hell. A sexy one.

"You're hired," I joked, trying to inject some real excitement into my tone.

She put her hands on my knees, and I found her staring curiously up at me. "You okay, babe?"

I nodded. "Yeah. Of course I am."

Becca's face fell a bit, but she recovered quickly, and I was reminded why I loved her too damn much. She didn't pry. Never pushed. But I knew she'd be there whenever I needed her to be. It made me feel guilty for never allowing Dom to get this close to me. Made me wonder if she and I could've had this. It didn't matter much now, though. After a quick chat this week, it was clear Dom had moved on with her life in Lennox, and I couldn't blame her.

You could only hold out for your *non*-friends for so long.

Kit was still trying though. He'd even gone so far as offering to come all the way here to visit since I'd told him I couldn't—*more like wouldn't* —come to Lennox.

"Well, you know I'm here if you need me," Becca said, standing with a sigh as she adjusted her boobs, making them appear even fuller over the top of the black bustier.

I smiled at that, a real smile, and stood with her, double checking everything of mine was in place, too. Deciding to whip my mopey ass into a better gear.

Just because all three guys were being moody bastards who'd barely left their bedrooms this week, didn't mean my fun had to be ruined.

It was obvious, wasn't it? The fucker who'd been texting me crawled off into a hole somewhere and died like the rodent he was. It was sad— not getting the chance to maim him myself, but I was over it. Why couldn't they get the fuck over it, too?

I followed Becca down the stairs and out to the front, where the guys waited by the Rover under the moonlight. Corvus, with his arms crossed leaning against the hood. Rook smoking a cigarette like it was his fucking job, and Grey texting something furiously on his phone.

My stomach twinged with discomfort as Grey, seeing me approach, quickly stuffed his phone back into his pocket, the muscles in his jaw clenching.

I couldn't help wondering who he was texting. If it was Bianca.

My fists clenched.

"Let me guess," Grey said, painting on a forced grin. "The Devil Wears Prada."

Becca put a hand to her chest and smiled widely at him. "A man after my own heart." She tossed a wink my way. "He's a keeper, Aves."

"Good flick," Grey added, gesturing to the bag Becca was carrying. "What the hell are you bringing in that?"

I thought she just had her larger black purse with her, but I realized now that it was more like a mini duffel bag.

"I had a feeling you three would be lame asses and not bother dressing up for your own Halloween party, so I got you these."

She dropped the duffel down onto the hood of the Rover, earning herself a little glare from Corvus as she unzipped the bag.

"One for you," she said, handing one to Grey.

"And you, Rook."

"And you, too, *Bone Man*."

"Becca," Corvus warned.

"I know, I know. Only in private, oh powerful prince of darkness."

"What the hell are these?" Rook asked, seemingly annoyed as he stomped out the remnants of his cigarette beneath his boot.

But it was obvious, wasn't it? The shape gave them away, even in the minimal light pouring onto the front drive.

"Crow masks," I said, not even realizing I'd said the words aloud.

"Come on," Becca urged them, planting her hands on her hips. "At least try them on. I had them custom made."

Corvus' nostrils flared, and Rook lifted a brow at her.

"She said try them on," I repeated, adding an edge of violence to my tone that was just enough to spur them to listen.

"Aren't they great?" Becca squealed as the guys finished tying them on with the oiled black laces.

They covered half their faces from forehead to just below the nose and were both a shining and matte black with an iridescent blue in some parts. The beaks extended out, but not so far out that they appeared bulky or looked foolish. They looked badass. Like, straight out of a horror movie.

"What do you say, boys?" I pressed. "Becca went out of her way to have these made for you..."

Grey cleared his throat. "Thanks, Becca. These are great." He elbowed Rook.

"Yeah. Whatever. They're cool."

"And you're already used to wearing a mask, so I'm going to assume this suits you just fine, Corv." Becca patted him on the chest. "Though I like you better in skeleton makeup."

He growled slightly, and I steered Becca toward the back seat. "Okay. That's enough. Let's go."

We barely got outside of the town limits before Becca pulled a joint from the smaller purse she had hidden in the duffel and lit it up, blowing the smoke out the rear window while she hummed along to Boy Epic pouring out of the speakers.

"Here," she said, passing it. "You need this more than I do. Loosen up a bit. Tonight's going to be fun, and it's my last night at the loft."

I took the joint with a sigh. "I really wish you'd reconsider staying a bit longer."

"Why? The window's fixed back at Briar Hall, and besides, you barely sleep at all with me there."

I opened my mouth to argue, but she held up a hand, and I took another drag instead.

"I'm not taking any offense," she said. "So I hope you won't either when I tell you that when you *are* actually sleeping, you're a terrible sleeping buddy."

"What?"

"Seriously, like, I'm pretty sure I have bruises from you kicking me."

I snorted. "Liar." I hardly moved in my sleep.

"Okay fine, I just miss my bed. Happy?"

I shook my head, and when I went to pass the joint back to Becca, Rook stole it from my fingers, lifting it to his lips instead.

"You mind?" he asked Becca, and her brows lifted.

"Not at all."

He smoked it down to the nub and tried passing it back, but Becca just gave him an unimpressed look. "You might as well finish it now."

I shivered as the cool night air pumped into the backseat from the open windows, and from the pot working its way into my muscles and making them tingle. It was stronger than her usual stuff, and I hummed contentedly to myself, leaning my head back against the seat as we veered off the main road and down towards the edge of Thorn Valley and the lake.

"Good shit," I muttered, letting the high sink deep into my bones.

"The best," she agreed. "I was saving it for—"

Her words cut off abruptly, and I was almost too slow to brace myself on the front seats as a black sedan peeled out in front of us, forcing Grey off the road.

Becca squealed while we swerved, the Rover's movements jerky and making my stomach fill with the bad kind of butterflies.

"*Fuck,*" I shouted as we skidded on the gravel at the road's edge, coming to a stop just a few feet from hitting the ditch.

I clutched my stomach, heart racing as car doors popped open all around and Becca screamed as black gloved hands dragged her from the Rover.

Her eyes went wide and wild as her body fell from the seat faster than I could snatch her back. My doped up fingers fumbled with my seatbelt as I shouted. "Becca! Someone get Becca!"

I got free and jumped from the car in time to hear a crude grunt. Headlights blinded me as I turned to find what made the sound, reaching for a blade.

"Aves!"

I spun, but it was too late. The blade was knocked from my hand and a black sack was pulled over my head, arms sharply hauled back and bound tight.

I kicked back, but my leg was only hooked by whoever had set upon us, sending me sprawling face first into the gravel. The earthy copper taste of my own blood filled my mouth, and I gagged as I swallowed it back, rolling to get back to my feet.

"Becca!"

Someone made a grab for my arm, and I bent my knees, throwing my whole body into the round house kick. I nailed whoever it was real fucking good, but without my arms for counter balance, I only ended up on the ground again, my shoulder aching from the fall.

"Sparrow, stop fighting," Corvus bellowed, and I hesitated as I rose back to my feet again, trying to see through the black hood over my head, but there was only light and shadows.

"What the fuck is going on?"

The hands came for me again, and I thrashed, but this time I didn't fight, choosing, maybe very stupidly, to trust Corvus.

"Awe, don't ruin the game, Son," Diesel's distinct voice rose right after a car door opened somewhere far off to my right.

"Just let her go!" Becca cried, and I could hear the struggle in her voice. Someone was holding her back. Was someone holding my guys back, too? Or were they watching this happen and doing nothing?

My chest ached for an instant before I realized what this was.

Another fucking trial.

Of course.

I forced my breathing to even out and straightened my back.

"It's okay, Becks."

"What's going on? What is this?" she demanded, and I wanted nothing more than for her to be *far* away from this place. Far from Diesel St. Crow and his men.

"Take her away," I said, in no direction in particular, the order meant for the guys. "Get her out of here."

"You heard the girl," Diesel said. "Get her little friend out of here."

"What are you doing?" Grey demanded, and I could see his expression in my mind's eye from his tone alone. The tension that would be between his brows. The sour curl of his upper lip.

A pause before Diesel answered. "I didn't want to ruin the surprise, but anticipation sometimes makes it even sweeter. We're having a hunt."

"A hunt?" Rook asked, his voice a lethal rasp.

"Yes. Like we did for Foley a few years back."

"Foley died in the hunt," Corvus deadpanned, and my mouth went dry.

"What?" Becca all but screamed, and I could hear the scratch of heels against the pavement as she struggled some more, making my heart twist in my chest.

A shuffle of feet and I saw what I thought was the shadow of Diesel move closer to his boys. Their three shadows were surrounded by many others standing in front of the headlights.

"Yes, well, Foley had questionable intentions, and in the end, he just wasn't good enough. He would've been a liability. A risk."

The way Diesel said *risk* told me exactly how he felt about them. Like father, like son. Corvus was just the same.

"We're taking her with us," Rook said, and I heard him step forward, saw the shadows close it, and then nothing. No movement.

"If you interfere, she fails," Diesel told his son. "You know the rules. I've already made one exception. I will not make another."

"You boys have a party to get to," the man holding me added, tightening his grip on my arm. "You'd best get going. You know how shit is with the Aces right now. If you want to keep your *Docks,* you have to be ready to defend them."

"Diesel," Corvus said, his father's name on his lips like a plea.

There came no reply for his son, but an order hissed from his lips. "Take her."

I didn't struggle as they led me away, already trying to come up with a solution on my own, but my thoughts were slow. Addled by the third of a joint I'd smoked in the fucking Rover.

"Wait!" Becca shouted as we passed her, and her hands grasped my arm, trying to keep me there while the men holding us fought to keep us apart.

I slowed my pulse and swallowed. "I'm going to be fine," I said, in a voice that sounded so certain I almost believed it myself. "Don't worry about me, 'kay? I'll see you later."

"Promise?"

"Promise."

Her nails scratched my arm as she was pulled away, and I heard her gasp as she was passed off.

"I've got you," Grey said. "It's okay. She's going to be okay."

"Are you sure?" she asked, the watery sound of her voice making my eyes burn.

"Positive," Corvus replied instead of Grey, making me feel stronger.

"But what if she isn't?"

I was shuffled from warm hands to cold ones and a trunk opened. I ground my teeth as they shoved my head down, folding me into the dark, cool space and closing me in. My phone was taken from my back pocket just before the trunk slammed shut.

Rook's reply was the last thing I heard before the engine started and the menace in his voice woke the dark parts of me back to life. Stoked my fire back to life, burning me back to a sense of sobriety.

"*She has to be.*"

23

GREY

The thumping bass vibrated through the rickety floor of the Docks, reverberating up through my feet. Setting my fucking teeth on edge. Becca sat with us on our makeshift stage, picking her fingernails at the far end of the worn leather sofa, her stare distant, thoughtful.

I snapped my fingers, and a pledge rushed over. I gestured to Becca. "Get her a drink."

"What should I get for her?"

"I don't know," I snapped, heat rising in my core. "Why don't you fucking ask *her*."

He nodded before running away to do just that, and I pressed my palms into my eyes, trying to grind out the ache forming behind them.

Rook threw his flask at the pledge now begging Becca to pick something to drink so that he could go and get it.

"Refill," Rook snapped while the pledge bent to retrieve his flask from the floor. "Now."

The guy scurried off, and I turned to where Corvus sat next to me, hunched over his knees, fingers steepled near his lips in complete stillness. Utter silence.

"We need to cut that one loose. He's useless."

Corvus grunted in response, and I got the feeling he hadn't even heard me.

"Corv, are you listening?"

"Hmm?"

My head pounded, making it almost impossible not to throttle him. How could he be so fucking calm right now? How was he not freaking out?

The Hunt was the worst ever idea for a trial Diesel had ever concocted. And he'd only come up with it because he decided he didn't want Foley to make it through the trials. And Foley, the twenty-five-year-old college drop-out, already knew far too much to be cut loose.

Diesel was right, of course, like he almost always was. It turned out he was being worked on by a cop. And Foley, being the weak link Diesel was beginning to think he was, was close to folding. Close to becoming an informant. Close to being formally inducted into our ranks, where he would've had access to even more sensitive information.

The Hunt was designed for a single purpose, to *kill* the hunted.

My stomach soured, and I got up, needing to move. To *do* something. But black spots crowded my vision and a wave of vertigo sent me back to the couch with a groan. "Fucking shit."

"The fuck is wrong with you?" Rook asked, raising his voice to be heard over the music and the chatter of the crowd before us.

I shook off the fleeting feeling. "Nothing."

But when I lifted my head to the strobing dance floor, the faces blurred in and out of focus, making my pounding headache that much worse.

Devil faces and witch faces and Barbie faces and every other Halloween costume that could be worn as a lingerie set with heels paraded past. They spun and jumped. Swayed and fell.

But none of them were AJ.

When the pledge came back, I snarled at him to get me some painkillers, hating my inability to control the rage I felt building inside.

Bianca's face filtered past with the others, trying desperately to catch my eye, her bunny ears bobbing as she sashayed past the raised stage, biting her lower lip.

I didn't know what part of *stop fucking texting me* she didn't understand, but obviously it wasn't sinking in.

She took a step toward the stage, and something in my face must've made her reconsider. Hurt gleamed in her eyes as she stepped backward instead, falling back into the crowd.

Good. I couldn't deal with her shit tonight. Not on top of everything else.

"The meet with the Aces coming up," Corvus said, his voice so low and deep it was almost impossible to distinguish it from the throaty bass. "I don't think it's a good idea. Something's up."

I couldn't keep the shock off my face. "How the actual fuck are you thinking about that right now?"

Rook stared off into the crowd, but by the tiny twist of his lips, I knew he was listening, too.

"Diesel wants us with him for the meet. I'm trying to come up with the best way to play it."

"*Right now?*"

I knew what he was doing, but I wasn't fucking having it. He was deflecting. Not thinking about the thing he couldn't control by thinking about something he could. A defense mechanism that wasn't going to save our girl.

He'd just fucked her, you'd think he could act like he cared whether she lived or died for five fucking seconds.

"I have an idea," Rook said, slipping from the arm of the couch to flop down onto the cushion next to Corvus. "Kill them all. Problem solved. Danger avoided. Risk factor? Reduced to a big fat fucking zero."

His dark eyes glimmered with drink and malice in the red-tinted lights. "We could start tonight."

Corvus finally broke his pose, fingers leaving his lips as he twisted to lay his eyes on Rook. "You can't just kill every person you have a problem with, Rook," he chastised our brother. "There are better ways of handling shit."

"*Smarter* ways," I added, not knowing why I was bothering to add anything to this pointless conversation right now.

Rook shrugged. "Not easier ones."

The pledge returned with some white pills and a bottle of water, and I swallowed them both down, guzzling the whole bottle before tossing it back at him. "Go."

Rook and Corvus regarded me with matching lifted brows, and I grimaced. "Fucking headache," I explained. "Lay off, okay."

I never took painkillers. *Never*. But if I didn't do something about the piercing, throbbing ache behind my eye sockets, I was going to snap.

A girl with light hair in an angel costume walked up onto the stage, swaying her hips as she approached Rook, bending to his eye level with her tits pushed out. I couldn't hear what she whispered to him, but I saw the way her gaze tracked to the Red Room door and back and how she bit her lower lip.

Rook gazed up at her with a haughty disdain, giving her a one-word reply.

When she redoubled her efforts, placing hands on his thighs, his entire body tensed, and he shoved her back, sending her sprawling to her ass with a yelp as his nostrils flared.

He snapped at her like a wild animal as she scrambled to her feet, sending her scampering off back into the crowd, red-faced and shaking.

His rejection only made *her* come rushing back to the forefront of my mind.

I pinched the bridge of my nose, pushing my thumb and index finger into the fleshy corners of my eyes. "She's going to be okay, right?" I asked, feeling something grow and clench behind my rib cage.

"I don't know," Corvus answered, and I let out a shuddering breath.

"Diesel wouldn't..." Rook trailed off, settling back onto the couch, but he couldn't finish the sentence and there was a reason why.

Diesel *would* if he knew something we didn't.

He *would* if he believed beyond a shadow of doubt that she would be our downfall.

"There's nothing we can do but wait," Corvus hissed.

"It's not good enough."

"You don't think I fucking know that?"

"Even if she lives, Diesel won't be finished with her," Rook mused, swirling his whiskey in the flask, staring down into the neck of it like the amber liquid inside might hold some secret to fixing this whole fucked up mess.

In a move so fast I hardly saw it coming, Corvus stood and flipped the low coffee table, throwing it into the unsuspecting crowd with a roar.

Becca squealed, and I heard the clack of her heels over the music as she backed away from the stage.

Corvus whirled on Rook. "What would you have me do?" he demanded of Rook, his eyes like burning embers. His teeth bared. "If we stop the trial, she fails, and she dies. If we save her, we've interfered, and she fails *and dies.*"

"We could leave," I said, not even realizing I'd spoken out loud until Corvus' searing gaze found mine, his nostrils flaring. "We could save her and then leave."

He paled, and I felt the blood draining from my own face, too, giving the migraine wreaking havoc in my skull a pulse.

"No," Corvus said after a minute, saying aloud what I wished wasn't true. "We can't."

"You said she was going to be fine," Becca said, and the three of us turned at once to see her standing behind the sofa, her arms tense with balled fists and trembling at her sides. "You knew she was going to die, and you just *let her go.* You fucking liars! You fucking pieces of shit!"

I stood, hopping the back of the couch to grab her. She just needed to understand, we didn't have a choice. But Becca snatched her arm away before I could grab her and spat at my feet.

"If she dies, I'm coming for you. I'm coming for all your useless asses."

She shouldered past me, the blow shaking me all the way to my core. She didn't have to worry about retribution. If Ava Jade died tonight, I was coming for my fucking self.

24

AVA JADE

The drive wasn't a long one. No more than five minutes and the car whose trunk I was currently folded into began to slow, and then stop.

Judging by the curvy path they took, and the steady inclination of the road, I guessed we were no more than a few miles from the Docks. Maybe three. Four at a maximum.

I didn't know if knowing where I was would help me, but I would take any information I could, tuck it away in the back of my mind in case I should need it.

Like the fact that there were at least five of them, but no more than seven. In two vehicles. One a sedan, whose trunk I was currently in, and the other, the dark SUV that drove us off the road.

I knew Diesel was here. And Tiny. The others I couldn't be sure of.

I also knew that I was fighting a high I wished to hell I hadn't decided to ride, and that in about three more seconds, I'd have the ties binding my wrists together at my back completely sawed off.

One, the sedan's ignition shuttered to a complete standstill.

Two, the doors clicked open.

Three, a key slipped into the lock on the trunk, and the latch popped.

The ties snapped apart, but I kept my arms behind me as the trunk opened, the almost total darkness brightening some under the dappled light of the full moon through the black bag.

Roughly, someone gripped my arm, and I clutched my wrist to keep my arms from popping apart as he hauled me from the trunk and threw me against the rear fender. I grunted as the blow to the back of my knees almost sent me to the ground, giving me the perfect opportunity to play it up the injury, and bend, groaning so I could slip two fingers beneath the back of my dress and snatch a blade from the garter on my thigh.

I wondered if I could kill them.

I mean, would that be breaking the rules?

The guys said to try not to, but if push came to shove? If they actively tried to kill me? If killing them was the only way to 'pass' the trial?

The other vehicle pulled up nearby and the headlights flashed over me before going out as the ignition shut off.

I sensed more than knew it when Diesel St. Crow stepped out of the other car, like a shift in the air. Similar to how it felt when one of his sons entered a room. As though they disturbed the fabric of the universe, taking up far too much space for beings their size.

I lifted my chin, waiting.

A second later the black bag was pulled from my head, and I blinked, disoriented and a bit nauseous from the bumpy ride in the trunk.

My lips parted, and a tremor of dread ran down my spine like an icy fingertip. Before me were six men, but I didn't recognize any one of them. It was too hard to tell in the masks.

A wolf. A bear. A stag. A panther. A snake. And a crow.

Their faces were fully covered by their animalistic masks, dark hollows where their eyes should have been. And in each of their hands, a crossbow.

Motherfucking crossbows.

I assessed my surroundings, finding myself ensconced in dappled darkness, surrounded entirely by trees. The road we'd driven in on was a dirt one. The air smelled of cooling earth and still warm wood with an undercurrent of something unpleasant, like sour mulch...or decomposing corpses.

"Untie her," someone said, but when the bear, Tiny, stepped

forward, I loosened my hands, showing him the empty one. No need to let them know I was armed yet.

"Hmm," someone grunted, a sound of surprised approval I thought might've come from Diesel.

"What is this?" I asked, folding the blade in my hand so it laid flat against my wrist, hidden from view, but easy to throw in a hurry if I needed to.

"Escape or stay alive until dawn and you will have passed the trial," the snake said in a voice I didn't recognize.

"That's it? There aren't any rules?"

The bear and the wolf shared a look, but no one replied, and I understood they didn't expect me to last very long.

"You have a one-minute head start," Diesel said, his voice ringing true even through the crow mask he wore. I hated that it looked similar to the ones Becca had custom made for the guys. "Don't waste it."

"Fifty-nine," the snake said excitedly, limbering up his legs for a chase. "Fifty-eight."

"Fifty-seven," the stag joined the countdown, adjusting his hold on his crossbow.

I sent one last look Diesel's way, letting him see that I would not go fucking quietly, before I bent, tearing the bottom of my dress away and kicking off my heels. And then I was running. Drawing on the part of myself that I would need to survive. My darkness bloomed to life, spurred to wake by the adrenaline pumping through my veins. Making my vision clearer. Senses sharper.

It was the darkness that whispered sweet nothings in my ear when a sharp rock cut deep into the fleshy underside of my left foot. And when a tree branch whipped across my face, leaving a potent sting in my right eye that forced it closed.

Speed was key here.

Escape was the goal. I had no doubt they would find me if I tried to hide.

But first I needed to outrun the distance their crossbow bolts could travel, and then I needed to find my way out of these woods, onto a road, to somewhere there were houses I could break into or cars I could hotwire.

If there were no rules that meant I could use any means to escape. I just needed to find those *means*, and right now it looked like all there was for miles as far as I could see were trees and darkness.

Twenty-two, twenty-one, twenty...

The countdown continued in my head, and I veered right on a whim. They would expect me to run straight forward, to put as much distance between me and them in sixty seconds as possible. They may not have expected a deviation.

Four, three, two...

The rest of the countdown finished out in my head, and a renewed burst of energy seared like white hot lightning down the length of my body, propelling me faster until I was sailing over the uneven earth, launching over fallen forest debris and dodging low hanging branches like it was my fucking job.

Just stay ahead of them. If they can't catch up to you, they can't shoot you.

It had to be a scare tactic. The guys had made it clear they cared what happened to me, which I was still processing, so the Saints wouldn't...they wouldn't actually shoot me, right? At least, not kill shots? Maybe that was why they were using crossbows. I liked my chances against a crossbow versus a gun a lot better.

An arrow *thunked* into the tree directly beside my head, and I hit the ground with a gasp, my eyes widening.

Wrong.

I was so wrong.

I was also up and running again, distantly hearing the brush of booted feet over the ground behind me. Someone shouting far off to my left. Someone else shouting back, also far in the distance.

Whoever was on my tail, though, they were closing in.

Was it wishful thinking to hope it was only one? That the others spread off into five other directions?

Gritting my teeth, I kept running, and the next low hanging branch I found, I grabbed hold of instead of sliding beneath, pulling myself up to the next branch and the next. Until I was at least fifteen feet from the ground and would be absolutely fucked if there were more than a few of them following me.

Or at a very good advantage if it were just one.

I held out my blade, peering down through the sparse leaves of the old oak tree, breathing quietly. I steadied myself with my free hand planted against the rough bark of the oak's trunk.

He came less than twenty seconds later, crossbow up and ready as he moved stealthily through the brush and bramble. The snake.

I leaned forward on my toes, trying to get a better angle as he approached and the branch I perched on creaked under my weight.

The snake jerked his head up, raised his crossbow, and fired. I dodged the bolt by a hair, falling, and threw, having to curve the blade to account for the lower branch.

I reached for a handhold, but my fingers clutched at nothing, just empty air as gravity worked against me, pulling me back down to earth. With a grunt, I hooked a leg out, catching myself on the branch below me to hang upside down. Brutally tearing something in my knee.

Dammit.

I drew the second blade as I flipped from the lower branch and prayed to land anywhere that wasn't on my face. It was a surprise to land on my feet, though the ache in my knee sent me bending to one side to account for it.

It surprised my attacker even more, though.

His eyes went saucer wide at the sight of me, more or less unharmed while he clasped his hands around the blade protruding from his gut. Hands slick with red.

His crossbow was discarded on the ground, two bolts scattered around it.

He went for the handle of the blade, but I lifted another and it flashed in the moonlight, drawing his attention. "As much as I'd love to have that back," I hissed, careful to keep my voice low. "If you take it out, you'll die, and I'm not entirely sure what that means for me."

I wasn't not sure what I expected, maybe for him to suck it up and take his defeat like a champ, bow out of this stupid *hunt* like the harmless reptile he was pretending to be, but that's not what he did. Not by a fucking long shot.

"She's over here!" he called, his voice carrying in the night, and my skin iced over with a new layer of cold sweat.

I reeled back and kicked him hard in the knee, satisfied to hear him cry out in pain as he slumped to the ground in my wake. I stomped on his crossbow too for good measure.

Run, bitch, I scolded myself. *You got this.*

But my knee was aching, and every step felt like another thread torn in whatever was holding the whole fucking hinge joint together. I pushed through the pain anyway, resolved to get the fuck out of here.

I stopped, only for an instant to hear sounds of pursuit, but I heard something else instead. Faint. Super distant, but it was there.

Music.

Dance music. A house party?

Or was it...

It could be...

I ran in that direction, trying to listen to the far-off sound of the bass to guide me.

It was almost impossible to hear it over the sound of my own breathing. And the thudding of my pulse pounding in my ears made it hard to distinguish one from the other.

Shit.

I rounded a boulder, crouched down behind it to listen again, holding my breath even though it made my chest burn. *There.*

More to the east.

I jumped back to my feet and was thrown forward, a whistle the only sound before I hit the ground, the air leaving my lungs in a pained gasp. Dirt and blood filled my mouth and the pain came all at once. An increasing pressure in my shoulder that was reaching a volcanic eruption size breaking point.

Still gasping for air, I twisted my head and came face to face with the arrowhead protruding from the fleshy bit of skin connecting my right shoulder to my torso. Blood dripped from the black metal tip and on a stomach twisting glance back, I saw the rest of it, sticking out the other side. Wood fletching and speckled feathers.

Holy shit.

They shot me.

Good thing I was a lefty.

The shooter's footsteps approached and even though it went against every instinct screaming in my nerve endings, I rolled to defend myself, snapping the wooden back of the arrow on the ground as I threw my blade, brokering no fucking mercy.

The wound in my shoulder protested in blazing agony and white spots flashed over my eyes as I pushed myself to my feet.

The blade embedded in the stag's eye, and he fell, thrashing wildly on the ground. The mask saved him from the extra inch of the blade that would've been his death. Too bad I'd have to waste another because he was making way too much fucking noise.

I went to draw my last blade, but my hand came up empty, and I cursed, searching the ground for it, but I saw no glint of steel on the dark mulchy ground.

"*Would you shut up,*" I hissed, reaching for the last resort. The blade Corvus had given me. The one I still wasn't entirely comfortable with. I guess now was as good a time as any to consecrate it unless I wanted to tear the blade from his eye and risk him screaming bloody murder before I could slit his throat.

A loud *knock* made me jump, and I spun to find the stag fucker knocked out by the boulder, his body limp and blood running down his mask. He'd thrashed so hard he knocked himself out. I resisted the manic urge to laugh, snorting instead, wondering offhandedly if my own blood loss was getting to me because that had to be the funniest shit I'd seen in a while.

Did that make me crazy?

Guess it didn't matter.

"Okay, then," I said, and before I could think too much about it, grabbed the metal arrowhead and forced it out of my shoulder with a grunt. Nausea rolled in my stomach, and I swallowed back bile, kneeling on the less sore knee to tear another strip from the hem of my tattered Prada dress.

Becca was going to kill me for ruining it.

I used the swath of overpriced fabric to tie tightly around the wound, winding it under my armpit and pulling it tight with my teeth. Not my best patch job, but it would have to do.

I hesitated before leaving the half dead stag, fingers itching to retrieve the blade sticking out of his eye. Odd, how I felt absolutely no remorse for permanently blinding him, but all the guilt in the world for leaving that blade where it was to hopefully prevent him from dying out here in the dark.

He looked young. Strong. What if he was like my guys?

He could have his reasons.

Just as I had mine.

Try not to kill them, Grey told me.

I made no promises, but this was me *trying* like he asked. Fucker better appreciate it because my shoulder hurt like a bitch, and my left hand was happy to dole out revenge.

With one last groan, I took off again, slower this time. Methodical. Focusing more on keeping quiet and hidden than covering ground. Since the latter didn't seem to be working out for me.

One blade left. I'd have to use it wisely with four more goons stalking the woods looking for me.

I followed the sound of the music upward, which seemed odd since I thought the road was the opposite way. Unless my sense of direction was just completely screwed at this point.

The trees ahead thinned out and more moonlight pushed between the trunks, making their shadows slant down over the ground like black bars in a ghostly cage.

I shivered, my mouth falling open as the view ahead opened up.

I knew exactly where I was.

Gripped with a sense of foreboding, I pushed my aching legs to move me the rest of the way up the slope to its ledge and stared out over the lake.

Moonlight kissed the rippling black water seventy feet below me, and to my right, maybe a mile as the crow flies, the Docks perched on wooden stilts over the lake. Pulsing with music and light and *life*.

So close.

So fucking far.

The sound of an arrow being notched into a bow had me dropping to the ground, crouching to find my attacker, crow handled blade lifted, pinched between my thumb and forefinger.

He stepped out of the shadows of the trees to my right, unfurling to his full height like he'd been there this whole time. Waiting. Like Diesel St. Crow knew it would come to this. Here. Right now.

"You aren't throwing," he crooned, inclining his masked head to the blade in my fingers.

"You aren't shooting," I countered, swallowing hard.

"Not yet."

Nothing in my periphery. No one else was here, but they would be soon. This cliff side ran the whole way around the lake, there was nowhere else for them to go.

Diesel, moving slowly, removed his mask from his face and discarded it on the ground, taking a deep breath as though it'd been suffocating him.

"Do you know how many bodies I've buried in these woods?" he asked, lifting the crossbow in a way that told me he knew very well how to use it. Maybe almost as well as I could use a blade.

I leveled out my breathing, deciding not to play his little game of intimidation. He was either going to shoot me or he wasn't, the rest didn't matter. I needed to keep my eye trained on his trigger finger. If it so much as flinched, I'd throw.

And wouldn't it be some kind of irony if Diesel St. Crow was killed by a blade his own son put in my hands?

"I've lost count," Diesel admitted after another moment, shifting to his left a bit, making me readjust my position to counter him.

He grinned at my movements, interest piqued.

"But there's one," he continued. "Buried right there."

His gaze indicated a spot only a few feet from where I stood. "His name was Foley, and he begged for a spot on my crew. I gave him a chance, and do you want to know how he repaid me?"

"Not really."

His lips twisted into a cruel smirk. "He was going to betray us. He was going to take down my son."

Something in my stomach fluttered, and I worked to clamp it down.

"Do you want to know how he died?"

"Let me guess. Crossbow?"

Diesel shook his head. "No. When I caught Foley in these woods, I fought him man to man. No weapons. Just fists. It was personal, you see. *No one* hurts my family."

A pang in my chest at his words made my brows draw together and my grip falter for a second before I was able to recover.

"I'm not what you think I am," I said in a low whisper, meeting his stony gaze, but the words sounded like a lie even to my own ears. And Officer Vick's face flashed in my mind's eye, making my throat tight.

When he didn't say anything, and I heard the muted sounds of movement approaching, I chanced looking away from Diesel and into the trees, trying to judge how much time I had left before I was fully surrounded.

I was fucked.

Was this his plan all along? Keep me pinned here until his minions could get to us? So that he could have one of *them* kill me. For him to be able to keep his hands clean of my death?

Idiot. I should have run.

I still could if...

"*Uh, uh, uh,*" Diesel chided, seeing what I had planned in the jerky movements of my gaze. "They'll be here any second. There's only one way off this rock that might end with your survival."

His cold stare tracked to the water below and back.

"Why not just shoot me?" I asked, my stomach already fluttering at the prospect of the long drop. There were rocks down there, too. Big ones. And smaller ones. It would be a small miracle not to hit any of them.

He hesitated, his hands tightening on the crossbow.

He couldn't, I realized. He wouldn't risk alienating his sons for good. He could let someone else do it, though. Or he could let me jump and hope the rocks below would do the job for him.

They might forgive him for that, in time.

"Make your choice, girl," Diesel snarled, his tension rising as the others closed in. "Do it now."

I inched closer to the ledge and a piece of stone chipped off under my foot, falling down to smash into another rock protruding from the waves below.

"And if I survive?" I asked, swallowing, my blood singing with what I was about to do.

Diesel tipped his head to one side, not understanding.

"If I survive, will you stop trying to kill me? Will you give me a real shot at passing these trials?"

He frowned, considering my requests, and maybe, my chances of survival.

"Perhaps."

Fuck.

It would have to be good enough. There was no time left.

"There!" someone shouted, and I sheathed the crow blade, backed up, took three running steps, and launched myself from the edge of the cliff.

The ground vanished and my body dropped like a stone, hurtling through chilled night air, my hair flung back from my face. I tried to right myself, knowing feet first was the only way that wouldn't result in injury, but at the last second, the wind shifted and I turned, flipping until I was face down, staring at rock and water and my impending death.

25

ROOK

During the last hunt trial, Foley was dead within thirty-five minutes.

I jammed the side button on my phone, displaying the time and a text message from one of my contacts in Lennox. A drug dealer who'd sold to me when all the ones in Thorn Valley were threatened away by my brothers.

DAN THE MAN

> Sorry man, no one with that description or injuries. I'll keep my ear to the ground though. Can I get you anything? I got some real good Columbian shit. Pure.

My mouth dried at the offer, and it took me a full minute before I forced myself to delete the message without replying. Keeping the knowledge in my back pocket for if Ava Jade...

No.

It was after midnight now. She'd been gone for over two hours.

It was either a very good sign, or a very bad one.

Happy fucking birthday to me. Putting her in the ground on the day I was born would just be the cherry on the bad memory pie. I already wanted to expunge this date from existence. Wipe it from the calendar completely and pretend it was never there. I didn't think it could get any worse.

As usual though, I was wrong.

Corvus had a drink in front of him, and though he hadn't touched it, it was the closest I'd seen him come to drinking in years.

Grey was a fucking wreck, getting up to pace every few minutes, only to sit back down. I knew the feeling. The sense of being absolutely useless dug deep into the marrow of my bones. Festered there.

Corvus had been right. There was nothing we could do but wait.

Ava Jade needed to prove herself, just like all the other Saints had to. Just like *we* had to. I could hardly blame Diesel for going harder on her given her history, but I would blame him if something happened to her. If she didn't come back...

I couldn't even imagine it.

Couldn't let myself go there, or else I'd lose control.

No one would be safe until I saw that she was with my own eyes.

Another drink. Another minute of blissful numbness.

Wait. And drink. And wait some more.

I hadn't worried about her at all in the previous trials, but this was something different. She was heavily outnumbered. Likely outgunned. I had every confidence in her, but with those odds?

I wasn't even sure any of us would come out the other side alive, and we had a fuck ton more experience than her, not to mention firepower where she only had blades.

The last of the whiskey in my flask flowed down my throat, and I lit up a cigarette, the last one in the pack, and sneered. "You going to drink that or just stare at it?"

Corvus' pale blue eyes slid to me with a murderous look before he lifted the short glass from the now-semi-busted coffee table and put it to his lips.

He paused, and I snorted, until I saw why he wasn't drinking it. Something drew his eye and I followed his line of sight, searching, the shriveled black thing in my chest squeezing ever tighter.

"Ghost?"

Ava Jade stood no more than fifteen feet away, and for a second, I thought I was hallucinating her. Thought she was a phantom come back from the dead to haunt me.

Pale. She was so pale. Her long dark hair dripping wet and hanging in her face. Mascara running to her chin. A bleeding wound in her shoulder. All her weight on her left leg. Her dress in sopping wet tatters.

It was the best costume here, but it wasn't a costume at all.

I saw it in her face just before it happened and rushed from my seat, off balance from too much drink, but not even that would stop me. I caught her as she collapsed, fingers curling over the back of her skull only a second before it would've connected with the wooden planks beneath our feet.

"Ghost!" I shouted, pushing wet strands of hair away from her face. "Hey. Hey, stay with me."

A hand came down on my shoulder, and I whirled, my upper lip curling at Corvus.

"It's me," he said, and Grey was there, too, looking white as a sheet.

Corvus tried to take her from me, but I held her tighter, my mind in a fog filled with flashing lights and Ghost, Ghost, Ghost.

"Okay," Grey shouted, pulling Corvus back from me so that he could step closer.

Around us, a crowd of onlookers was gathering, and I glared at them, my vision wavering so their costumed faces looked as though I was seeing them through a fun house mirror.

"We need to get her out of here," Grey was saying and I focused, blinking to clear the haze from my eyes. "Take her to the back room."

Out of here. Yes.

I lifted her to my chest, almost losing my footing until Corvus righted me. "Hurry. She's lost a lot of blood, Rook."

No. She was fine.

She would be fine.

Her wetness seeped into my clothes, drenching me in a brutal cold, nearly as cold as where my hands held her bare arms. She was too cold. She needed to be warmer.

Grey ran ahead of me, opening the door to the back room. He flipped a breaker and the music and lights behind us went dead as the heavy door shut. The partiers screamed and shouted their protest, but already their footfalls seemed to be retreating, leaving the Docks. Good.

Corvus knocked bottles and glasses from the top of the short black bar where we kept our stock, sending them shattering to the floor. The intoxicating smell of good bourbon and very good whiskey filling my lungs.

"Lay her down," Corvus ordered, and I grudgingly set her down on the damp bar.

"She's cold," I managed, coming back to myself, the influence of the whiskey still churning in my stomach, waning in the face of an injured Ghost.

Warm. She needed to be warm.

I threw off my leather jacket and laid it over her chest while Grey worked to untie the strip of black cloth around her shoulder. The knot came loose, revealing a water-puckered wound. Too messy to have been a bullet.

"Diesel," I growled, picturing the crossbow bolt that would've gone straight through her. In one side and out the other. Invading her flesh, corrupting her perfection.

I'd kill him.

I'd kill whoever shot her.

It didn't matter who it was.

"Rook," someone said, but their voice was so distant I couldn't be sure it wasn't just in my head.

"Rook!"

I found Corvus' blue eyes and flinched as he clutched my arms, shaking me. "Hey. Stay with us here, okay. She's okay. She's alive. She escaped."

"She passed the trial," Grey added, using his teeth to rip open a packet of gauze and jam it into the wound.

Ava Jade coughed, squirming as Grey packed her injury with the gauze, her storm-cloud eyes going wide. "*Fuck,*" she croaked, just barely holding onto consciousness.

Her fingers curled into my leather jacket over her stomach, pulling it tighter to her.

"Sparrow?" Corvus shouted, going around the other side of the bar to assess her. He lifted his phone flashlight high and pulled down her eyelids, checking dilation.

She weakly batted him away, her face screwing up in a sour frown. "S-stop," she stammered, her teeth beginning to chatter.

"What happened, AJ?" Grey asked, winding a clean bandage around her wound.

She blinked, her eyes coming more into focus, and focusing on me.

I went to her, and when she reached for my hand, I let her take it, holding her clammy fingers tight until some color returned to her cheeks.

"I j-jumped," she said, and Corvus and I shared a look.

"Hold on," Grey muttered, running to the couch at the other end of our small private bar area and the arsenal of guns locked up against the wall. He tore down the woven Saints banner hanging from the wall there and brought it back over, draping it over my jacket and her whole body. She shivered, giving him a grateful look.

"You jumped from where?" Corvus asked, his gaze lethally steady as he waited for her to reply.

"The c-c-cliffs. A mile from here."

"You swam a mile injured?" Grey asked, incredulous.

"A mile..." Corvus trailed off, the realization I'd just come to dawning on his face. Diesel had taken her to the same place he'd taken Foley. The Deadwood. Where we'd been burying traitors and enemies for years. Which meant...

"That's a seventy-five-foot drop. At least."

"What the hell were you thinking, Sparrow? You could have died."

Her eyes flashed with malice. "I would have died if I *didn't* j-jump."

Heat rushed up my spine and warmed my face. This had gone too far.

The trials were meant to be a challenge and more than a few had died before they could earn a space on our crew, but the trials were always fair. A challenge, made to push the one taking them to the limits of what they could survive, but *fair*. There had been five Saints with Diesel. Six in total, against one.

Even with the head start I was certain he'd have given her, where was the fairness in that?

"Who shot you?" The question passed my lips without conscious thought. "I want a name."

"*Rook*," Grey warned, and I gave a look that dared him to challenge me again.

Ghost smirked, a tiny laugh stopped by her closed mouth that turned into a cough. "The stag," she said and my brows furrowed in confusion. "But don't worry, I took one of his eyes."

It was my turn to smile now, and I gave her hands a squeeze. "Of course you did."

"D-did you guys really think I wasn't going to make it?" She coughed again, her whole body racking. "Glad to know you have s-so much faith in me."

Her gaze slid from us to survey the dimly lit room, a knot forming between her brows. "Where's Becca?

Grey dropped the empty packets he was holding and scratched an imaginary itch on the back of his head. "She *uh*...she got kinda pissed at us and took off."

Ava Jade sat bolt upright, the color draining from her face again. Her eyes went unfocused as the sudden movement made her dizzy. "Well go and *find her*," she scolded, back to her fiery self already.

Corv gave Grey a nod, and he leaned in to kiss Ava Jade on her head before leaving. "I'll be right back."

"You should lie back down," Corvus said, but Ava Jade just looked at him like he'd grown a second head.

"I'm good." She winced as she tried to move her injured arm and peered up at me through her lashes. "I'll take a drink, though."

I rounded the bar and pulled a bottle of water from the small fridge beneath, handing it to her.

"*Not* what I meant," she said with an eye roll, but took the bottle and drank half, shivering again. "I think I drank enough lake water to be hydrated for the next year."

Corvus' knuckles turned white where he gripped the counter, but he relaxed them when he caught me looking.

He was doing a shit job of pretending he didn't care.

Grey told me he and Ava Jade had finally fucked.

It wasn't exactly the kind of news I wanted after searching for endless hours and coming up empty handed in the search for Ava Jade's stalker, but that's life.

And Corvus deserved happiness just as much as any of us. More so than I did for sure.

Ava Jade passed me the other half of her water. "Drink," she demanded. "You look like shit and smell like a distillery."

"Shall I get you a mirror?" I joked, earning myself a glare, but I took the water, knowing a level head might prevent a few deaths tonight.

The door creaked open behind us, and Grey returned, a bit breathless. "The whole place is cleared out," he said. "I don't see Becca anywhere."

"What?" Ava Jade demanded, growling as she stepped down from the bar and almost fell flat on her face, grimacing as she gripped her right knee.

"You need to sit the fuck down," Corvus growled, hopping the bar to grab her from behind, picking her up off her feet despite her protests.

"Let go!"

"No. You calm the fuck down and *sit,* and then I'll let go."

Ava Jade, too tired to fight him, slumped, defeated in his arms as he carried her to the couch and tugged his phone from his back pocket. "Here," he said and handed it to Ava Jade. "Call her."

"Already tried that," Grey said, and Corvus sent him a scathing look.

Ava Jade dialed her friend, tensing with each ring that went unanswered. She didn't leave a voicemail, instead hanging up to switch to messenger. She thumbed out a text to her friend and then waited.

Corvus crouched to her eye-level. "We can—"

"*Shh.*"

"She probably just—"

"*Shh.*"

The phone pinged in Ava Jade's hand a second later, and she sighed as they read the message on the screen.

"She's okay," she said, typing out a less hurried message. "She's with her boyfriend."

"She has a boyfriend?" I found myself asking, doubtful. A fuck buddy maybe. Rebecca Hart didn't seem the type to be pinned down.

"Something like that," Ghost replied, finishing off the message. "He's been ignoring her for a while. I guess he finally came to his senses and realized what he had. Good thing too because I was about twenty-four hours from tracking him down and forcing an apology out of his sorry ass."

She sighed, handing the phone back to Corvus. I read Becca's reply over his shoulder before the screen went dark.

My jaw clenched, the lack of punctuation reminding me of the way someone else's messages often arrived on my phone.

Just a coincidence. It had to be.

I started for the door.

"Where are you going?" Ava Jade asked, stopping me.

"To have a chat with Diesel."

To my surprise neither of my brother's protested, but my Ghost did.

"Can we stay together?" she asked, and when I saw the uncertainty in her eyes, I couldn't say no.

"If that's what you want."

She seemed to think about that for a moment, then lifted her head and got shakily to her feet. "Take me home?"

26

AVA JADE

There was no way in hell I was taking the pain killers, too afraid they'd knock me out to the point of full unconsciousness. So, sleep was just not a thing likely to happen.

Sighing, I hauled my achy ass out of bed, gingerly touching the bandage on my shoulder. The sharp edges of the stitches Rook sewed into my skin poked me through the gauze, and I winced but continued to prod the area, testing my motor ability with the new injury. My knee was feeling all right after some ice and a borrowed knee brace from Grey. But the shoulder was going to take some more time.

I could lift it until it was level with my face but no higher. At least the arrow hadn't pierced anything too important. Or at least I hoped it hadn't, only time would tell since going to the hospital was out of the question.

I flicked on the light switch and limped quietly to the bathroom, trying not to make too much noise as I splashed cool water over my face and down my neck to staunch the feverish heat from getting any stronger. Honestly? I half expected to find Corvus in here.

Or Grey. Fuck, even Rook.

Each of them insisted I sleep with them or at least down on the couch where they could watch over me. I'd said fuck no on account of being absolutely exhausted and wanting to actually *sleep,* which I wouldn't be doing with an audience or a bed buddy. Turned out it didn't matter anyway. Sleep was a no go regardless of whether I was alone in my dark room or not.

I inched the door on the other end of the bathroom open and peered out into the dim hall, lit only by the pre-dawn filtering in through the window down at the other end.

Corvus' and Grey's doors were shut, but Rook's stood open, a draft whistling through to where I stood.

I bit my cheek, hurrying back into the loft to retrieve what I'd stolen from him a little while back. I wondered if he'd even noticed it was gone, but seeing as I found it tucked mostly behind an old photo on his dresser, I could see why he wouldn't.

Hell, it made me wonder if my brilliant idea for a gift was even a good one if he kept it hidden away. Maybe he didn't even like it.

Oh well. No going back now, and I had to return it to him eventually.

When I got back to his door, I pushed it open, poking my head inside. "Rook?" I whispered, squinting to see into the gloom as the smell that was uniquely *Rook* filled my lungs, making me smile.

"Out here," came his whispered reply, and I followed his voice to the open window next to his bed, the dark curtain billowing inward in the breeze.

The dark shape of him sat outside on the roof, a blanket loosely pulled around his shoulders.

"Couldn't sleep?" he asked as I crawled through the window to join him, the chill of the early morning air brushing over the bare skin on my arms and legs.

"No. You?"

He shook his head and lifted one side of the blanket, holding it open for me.

A muscle in my jaw ticked, but the hesitation only lasted a second before I curled up beside him, letting him drape the large furry blanket over my shoulders. His body heat enveloped me as I tugged the blanket around myself, huddling in closer to his side.

His fingers wrapped around the dip above my hip bone, tugging me against him with a small grunt. "You're freezing."

"It's cold out here."

"Nice though, isn't it?"

I couldn't disagree. It was nice. The fog that'd been clinging to my brain while lying in the stuffy loft had been blown away, replaced by a clarity only gained by inhaling clean, crisp air.

It seemed to have affected Rook in the same way. Though he was still tense, this was the calmest I'd seen him in days. Maybe even a week.

I wondered if the clean air was the only culprit or if something else had contributed.

We didn't speak for a while, content to sit there, staring at the slowly brightening sky in each other's warmth and company, but I'd come out here for a reason.

"So, um..."

"Hmm?" Rook said, coming out of whatever thought had taken him. He turned to me, his dark eyes searching my face.

"I'm not going to say it because Corvus sort of told me you don't like to celebrate."

His brows drew together.

Maybe this was a huge mistake.

"Everyone always forgot my birthday growing up. I mean, I didn't care that much because when they did remember all I got was a gas station muffin with a lit match as a candle but...I guess I just thought maybe—"

"What did you do, Ghost?"

I licked my suddenly very dry lips and reached into my Panama pants pocket, a slithering sensation of unease crawling through my gut.

"I found it in your room," I explained as I tugged his hand close to me beneath the blanket and peeled back his fingers. "It was broken, and I thought it might mean something to you so I...well I sort of gave it to this girl in my English Lit class whose dad owns a jewelry shop in town, and he fixed it."

I placed the necklace into his palm and felt him jerk at the feel of it, his expression darkening.

Shit.

He didn't speak for the longest moment, holding the necklace beneath the blanket while he stared off into the shadows of the trees across the drive.

"Fuck, I'm sorry," I spluttered, heat growing in my cheeks and the tops of my ears. "I don't even know what I was thinking. I should've just left it like Corvus said and—"

His wide hand closed over my mouth, muffling my next word. "Stop talking," he said, a strain in his voice as he slowly turned his attention back to me and dropped his side of the blanket to look down into his palm.

His warm hand came away from my face, and I stared down at the necklace, too. It looked so small in his large hand. So delicate.

The black diamond caught the pink light of the rising sun, and the brand-new clasp that the jeweler had to have custom made glinted like it was made of pure starlight on the thin white gold chain.

That, too, had been broken. Bent and twisted as though it'd been snatched off the neck of whoever had been wearing it.

I was dying to ask, but it was clear I'd already overstepped my bounds so I just waited instead, hoping he wouldn't be too pissed that I'd touched it.

"It was my mother's," he said finally, just when the silence was starting to get too heavy to withstand.

"What happened to her?" I asked before I could stop myself, then added quickly. "You don't have to answer that if you don't want to."

His lips quirked up slightly, making the tension behind my breast-bone ease enough to breathe.

"She died," he explained in a rough voice. "Childbirth."

My stomach twisted.

"She was going to be famous, you know? Julia Clayton. The rising star; that's what they called her."

"Is she the woman in the photograph?"

He nodded, and I remembered the black-haired beauty from the picture frame on his dresser. I'd honestly thought it was whatever had come stock with the frame. The woman in the photo too beautiful to not have been retouched and edited to within an inch of her life.

But it made sense, if Rook was her son. Beautiful, lethal, Rook.

"I'm sorry," I whispered. "Is that how you ended up at Barrettes Home for Boys?"

Something in his gaze shifted and his hand curled back around the necklace until his knuckles turned white.

"You've done some digging."

I shrugged. "And you haven't?"

"Me? No. But I can't say the same of my brothers."

I waited.

"Yes," he said on a breath. "But I didn't wind up there right away. I was put into the care of my aunt for years before that. She never missed an opportunity to remind me that I ruined her sister. That she died so a little shit like me could live. She didn't bat an eye when her boyfriend took out his very particular brand of violence on me. I think part of her wanted him to do it. To punish me for taking my mother from this world."

"He's the one who gave you these?" I gingerly brushed a finger over the scars on his arm, the ones hidden by all the ink covering his skin.

His upper lip curled and my inner fire burned hot, wanting retribution on his behalf. To scar the fucker in all the exact same places and in all the exact same ways as he'd scarred Rook before killing him slow.

"I thought I deserved it."

"It wasn't your fault she died."

"I know. I didn't back then, but I do now. I found this journal she wrote in just before my aunt finally had enough of my shit and sent me away to the group home. Everyone was telling her that having me would destroy her career. That she should abort me and never tell the father. She didn't ever tell him, because apparently he was a fucking monster, but wrote that she did want me. She wanted me more than she ever wanted anything else in her life."

"She sounds like an incredible woman."

He smiled a sad smile. "I like to imagine she was. I don't know what would've happened if I hadn't found that journal, but soon after I went to Barrettes home for Boys, I met Grey. And not long after that, I went back to my aunt's house on Sycamore Street and burned it down. With my uncle inside."

"Good."

His eyes met mine and something unspoken passed between us

before he shifted, turning slightly to face me. Rook lifted the necklace between us, his face growing hard. "Will you wear it?"

My stomach flipped and my lips popped open in surprise, but he said nothing else, only waited for my response as the first rays of morning sun broke over the horizon, painting him in brilliant gold.

Everyone thought he was the devil, but I could see it now. In just the right light, he wasn't a devil at all but an angel of justice. My dark prince.

Wordlessly, I turned, using my good arm to push all my hair out of the way, holding it up off my neck.

His hands brushed my collar, making me tremble as he draped the dainty chain around my throat, the black diamond weighing heavily in the dip of my clavicle.

Once he finished with the clasp, he brushed his thumb over the chain against the back of my neck, guiding me back to facing him.

His cheekbones flared as he took me in, in the dawn light, eyes passing between the necklace and my face. He smiled.

"It suits you."

I touched the stone with my fingertips, a sense of belonging taking me so strongly that it hurt. Mixing with a heavy guilt so crushing that it took all the breath from my body.

In less than twenty-four hours I was going to meet with Officer Vick. And thanks to Diesel's admissions in the Deadwood, I actually had something I could give him. If Diesel killed Foley with his bare hands and buried him at the edge of that cliff, his DNA would be all over the body. I could take him down. I could take them all down.

But when I looked into Rook's eyes...

His trusting, bleeding heart eyes.

How in the world could I ever betray him?

How could I ever betray *them*?

Was it worth my freedom?

Did I even want to be free anymore?

Rook lifted a hand to trace the line of my cheekbone, pushing my hair back behind my ear in a move so gentle it sent shivers all the way to my toes.

"What is it?"

I schooled my face, blinking away what was definitely not fucking tears.

"I don't deserve this."

Amusement crossed his eyes, making them slant playfully as he leaned in to whisper against my lips. "You belong to us, Ghost. And we belong to you."

27

CORVUS

The knock came at the door only a few hours after dawn. The distinct three rap cadence of it giving away who was on the other side, making my irritability skyrocket.

I set down the whisk and wiped flour coated fingers on my jeans. The sky might've been falling down around us, but I'd never skipped a birthday. Rook would have his cake, and he would fucking enjoy it. Ava Jade would enjoy it, too. She deserved it after that bullshit last night.

The door banged noisily into the wall when I ripped it open, finding Diesel standing a few feet away, peering up toward the octagonal window to the loft above the garage. Heat bloomed over the back of my neck, but I reined it in. I had no doubts that he knew she was staying here, but I didn't like the look on his face.

"What are you doing here?" I asked, unable to keep all the accusation out of my tone.

Diesel lowered his gaze to mine, hurt pinching at the bridge of his nose.

"I came to return the girl's things to her," he replied, handing me two clean blades and her cell phone.

"Where's the other one?" I asked, knowing she was missing all three of her blades. She was going to be pissed if another one was gone for good.

Diesel shrugged, indicating the blade in my left hand. "I pulled that one out of Galen's eye."

So it was Galen who shot her.

"And that one out of Dimitri's stomach."

"She said you didn't give her any ground rules," I reminded him, my teeth on edge.

"A mistake I won't make a second time. I underestimated her."

A flutter of pride had me lifting my chin. I'd underestimated her once or twice, myself. I wouldn't make that mistake again, either.

Diesel's gaze tracked back to the window above the garage and my jaw tightened. "She's sleeping," I told him. "And I won't wake her."

He lifted a hand to wave me off. "I didn't come to speak to her. I came to speak to you."

"About?"

He jerked his head toward the drive behind him, where his car was parked up next to the Rover. I set Ava Jade's things down inside and followed Diesel out, words I wanted to sling at him battering at the closed barrier of my lips.

When we were clear of the Nest, he stopped, leaning against the back of the Rover, and before he could speak, some of what I wanted to say came rushing out.

"What was that bullshit last night?"

Surprise lit up his eyes, followed by the lowering of his brows.

"Six?" I pressed when he didn't answer. "*Six* men with crossbows against just her."

I jabbed two fingers into the air, pointing to where she lay now, safe in our Nest. A part of me wished I could keep her there, bar her in and guarantee her safety forever.

"She survived, didn't she?"

My fists clenched.

"The trials are meant to be fair," I ground out. "To test loyalty and strength and wits. That was a fucking massacre that Ava Jade somehow managed to escape and you damn well know it."

Some of the rage Diesel kept tampered down tight came surging to the surface, and my own fury fought to be set free at the sight of it. If he could lose control, then so could I.

"So she didn't tell you I had the jump on her, then?" he asked, his voice like a whip, cracking against my defenses. "I could've killed her. It would've been a fair death. Just her and me at the edge of that cliff."

I heard what he was saying without the need for him to speak, piecing it together in my mind.

...he let her jump instead, leaving her death up to fate.

It didn't absolve him from this, but it softened some of the blow.

He left out the part that if they faced off on the edge of that cliff, Ava Jade could just as easily have ended him with a toss of her blade. And she didn't.

There was restraint on both sides.

"I didn't come here to argue about a trial I had every right to put her through as the leader of our crew," he hissed, running his teeth over his lower lips. "I came to warn you."

I started, my beast roaring *what now* in a way that made my rib cage rattle.

"About?"

His gaze dropped to the ground, where he dug the toe of his boot into the gravel and worked his jaw. "It's going to get ugly," he said after a minute. "I know you don't agree with me, Son, but it's my job as your father to look out for you."

My stomach twisted.

"You don't want to hear this, but I'm going to say it anyway," he continued, this time looking me dead in the eye. "She isn't who you think she is." How the fuck would he know who she is? He hadn't even tried to get to know her, and he would only know the same things I did from looking into her past There wasn't much to find. Unless he found something I hadn't? Or knew something I didn't? But if that were the case, why wasn't he sharing with the motherfucking class?

"Don't say anything." Diesel cut me off before I could say a word. "Just listen. She's fooling you. She's a liar and a con artist and you, my son, all of my sons, are her long game."

"You don't know what you're saying," I argued, my nostrils flaring as the fury worked its way to a head, filling mine with steam.

Ava Jade wouldn't...

My Sparrow *wouldn't.*

He was wrong about her. He would see that eventually, but I couldn't let him kill her in the process.

"I'm going to show you who she really is," he promised.

"How many more trials do you have planned right now?"

He was caught off guard by the question but answered honestly. "One, though there are several others I'd been consider—"

"No," I cut him off. "*One.* You can have your one, but no more. If she passes it, that's it. It's over. You accept her as a Saint and make her one of us."

His upper lip twitched, but I could tell he was considering my not-so-subtle request. He knew that shit in the Deadwood last night was pushing it to the limits of what would be considered a fair test of skill. By the look on his face, he was willing to negotiate if it meant peace between us. As a way of admitting his mistake *without* actually admitting it.

"And *when* she fails?"

A chill wormed its way into my belly, reaching icy fingers up to squeeze my lungs and crust over the thing beating behind my rib cage. "*If* she fails...if she truly is what you say she is, then we'll deal with her ourselves."

Diesel's expression evened out, and he sighed, placated by my response. He closed the gap between us to place a hand on my shoulder, squeezing in a way that told me he was sorry without the need for words. "All right, Son. All right. One trial and no more."

"When?" I asked as his hand slid from my shoulder. "She's injured. She needs time to heal."

Diesel nodded solemnly. "I make no promises."

28

AVA JADE

I checked my phone for the fifth time since I texted Becca two hours ago, finding only another passive aggressive text from Aunt Humphrey.

FEMALE HITLER

> I finally got to speak to several of your instructors this past week. It seems all your grades are well above average, however that doesn't excuse your lack of attendance.

Her way of apologizing?

Another message came through before I sent it back down.

FEMALE HITLER

> Also, dinner will be at 7 o'clock sharp at the manor for Thanksgiving. If you're bringing anyone along, please let me know in advance so I can make the appropriate arrangements.

Um, yeah...hard fucking pass.

"Anything yet?" I jumped out of my seat at the desk and winced as the torn ligament in my knee stretched too far.

"*Fucking shit fuck,*" I cursed, bending to rub the ache out of it.

472

"Sorry," Grey said, raising his hands in apology. "Didn't mean to scare you."

I sighed heavily, falling back into the chair at the desk and shoving my history notes out of the way so I could rest my arm there instead. "No. I haven't. She hasn't texted me back at all, and she won't answer my calls."

Grey's frown deepened. "Are you worried?"

I shrugged. "A bit? I don't know. She's always slow to text me back when she's with him, but not like this."

"Yeah, she doesn't usually spend the night," Grey mused aloud, and he was right. Becca always wandered back into the apartment at Briar Hall sometime in the early hours of the morning. She was never gone this long.

I shifted my notes around on the desk, stacking them into a neat pile atop my textbook, officially done with studying for the test this week. I doubted anything was sticking in my head right now anyway.

I'd overheard Diesel outside with Corvus this morning. I didn't catch everything, but I did catch something about things getting ugly and one trial. Hopefully, that meant there was only one left. I couldn't decide if that was a good thing or a bad thing, since Diesel St. Crow seemed set on me not surviving to the end.

"Hey," Grey hedged, coming into the loft. "If she isn't back for class tomorrow morning, then we'll go and look for her, 'kay?"

I wasn't sure how we'd find her since I had absolutely no fucking clue where she went when she drove off to meet her—

That was it! However she'd gone to meet her guy friend last night at the docks, it wasn't with her car. That was still parked in the school lot. I'd walked there with Rook earlier to check, and to stretch out the shit that was all twisted up in my knee.

"Do you think the GPS in her car has passive tracking? Like, to see previous routes?"

The corner of Grey's mouth lifted. "Yeah. I think it probably would. Just have to hack in, and lucky for you..." He rubbed his knuckles over his chest, smug as fuck. "You happen to be sharing a house with someone who knows how."

I smiled back. "Thanks, Grey."

His gaze softened and some of that smugness faded, transitioning to something harder to name. He cleared his throat. "Can I, *uh,* get you anything? How's the shoulder? We should probably redress it."

I shook my head. "Already done. And it's good."

I rolled it to show him, unable to conceal all the discomfort from my face, but somehow, mercifully, the arrow hadn't hit anything important. So, while it hurt like the devil's asshole, it would be just fine.

"Right. Good. That's good."

He was stalling, and for half a minute I considered asking him to stay. I'd been isolating myself from them since the Primal Ethos show, and I knew they were all uncertain about what the shift meant. Hell, so was I, but it didn't change things. Even if Rook and I had a moment last night. Even if a part of me wanted to rip every bit of Grey's dark track-suit to shreds and fuck him until I couldn't breathe. And even if I couldn't stop remembering the feeling of absolute freedom that'd come with letting myself *feel* something other than hate for Corvus.

A shred of doubt nagged at the back of my skull.

This wasn't what I came here for. I came here for a fresh start. A chance at a new life free of violence. Free of gangs and guns and *hate.*

Each day that image of what I wanted when I set foot in Thorn Valley has shifted. Every day spent with the Crows has been another bar welded onto a cage that I might never escape from if I'm not careful.

And that cage would trap me in the life I swore I was leaving behind when I took my Aunt up on her offer.

I didn't know what the fuck I wanted anymore, and that was a terrifying thought. But one I needed to figure out before it was too late.

"Thanks," I muttered, but still he hesitated. Wanting to say something more? Wanting to feel useful? It was hard to tell, but I knew they all partially blamed themselves for the Hunt. For letting it happen even though they didn't have a choice. Or, at least, that's what I was trying to believe.

"Maybe, if you don't mind, I'll take another piece of Rook's cake?" I said with a shrug, and his eyes lit up.

"Yeah," he said in a relieved sigh. "I can do that. Be right back. I'll make you some tea. I have this Rooibos blend that'll be really good with the cake. Might help you sleep, too."

He was gone before I could say anything. Like, what the actual fuck is Rooibos? I didn't peg him as an herbal tea kind of guy, and the new information made a small laugh escape my lips as I shook my head. I could use the sleep aid, though. It was already half past ten and I wasn't even remotely tired yet. Probably something to do with my three-hour morning power nap in Rook's bed. With Rook.

I hadn't planned to fall asleep there. I'd just wanted to sit with him a little longer after the blinding sun got to be too bright for our overtired eyes. Next thing I knew, I was drooling on his pillow, not for the first time.

I slumped in my chair, but sat bolt upright again as my phone buzzed violently with a new message. Becca's name flashed over the screen.

About fucking time.

Lifting my cell, I saw that it wasn't a message at all, but a video. I unlocked it and hit play and felt my whole fucking world crumble around me.

Becca screamed through the silvery tape covering her mouth, her black eye makeup running four inches down her face. Cords of metal chains hung in heavy circles around her slender neck, the skin beneath red from her struggling.

The clip was only four seconds long, and played again when it ended, starting a loop of horror.

I jumped to my feet, rushing to the bathroom to scream for the guys when another message came in, this time, a text. Making my racing pulse stop dead in my chest.

Becca: She's at the warehouse in no man's land. Come alone. Your trial begins now. You have thirty minutes. D.

What?

I replayed the horrific video of Becca, my hands shaking, stomach in knots.

There was a red glow over her right shoulder. I paused the video. It was blurry, but clear what it was. A timer. The red numbers 29:32 telling me the countdown had already started.

The chains around her neck...

He wouldn't.

But the guys' words echoed clearly in my mind, and I had to clutch the edge of the desk to keep myself from passing out at the wave of adrenaline going straight to my head.

Anyone or anything is fair game.

Come alone.

I couldn't even remember getting my blades strapped on, or putting on my shoes, but suddenly the keys to the Rover were in my hand and I was sneaking out the garage door, rolling beneath the seven-inch gap to keep from making too much noise. At least until it was too late for them to stop me.

"AJ," I heard Grey call out from upstairs in the loft just as I got to my feet.

Fuck.

The Rover chirped when I unlocked the door and got inside, and I saw Grey's face in the octagonal window as I started the ignition. His mouth opened wide as he shouted something I couldn't hear. Something not meant for my ears.

But I was already gone, peeling out of the gravel drive and bumping down the road, the Nest flickering to nothingness in the red glow of my tail lights in the rearview mirror.

Becca.

Of course Diesel would use the one friend I had here against me.

She was never going to want to see me again after this. She'd run for the fucking hills without looking back. Would she blame me? Hate me?

My stomach soured, and I groaned as the choppy pavement switched to clean smooth blacktop with a hard bump in the road.

If Diesel hurt her...

All bets were off.

I'd promised to *try* to not kill any Saints during the trials, but I'd have his fucking head if she died. And the heads of any others involved.

The minutes slashed away as I drove, barreling down side roads until I got to the edge of town, to the border of no man's land. They kept falling until ten were already gone. Then fifteen. Hedging on twenty even as I pushed the Rover to the breaking point of how fast she could go, nearly losing control more than once as the uneven pavement leading down to the old industrial area tried to slow me with potholes and scattered debris.

The tires screeched, and the throat clogging stench of burning rubber filled my nose as the Rover slid to a standstill, knocking against a cement barrier. The glass of the passenger window shattered, raining down over the seat and my lap as I shoved the door open and raced out into the night, making a beeline for the warehouse.

My peripheral sight expanded all around, tracking movement as I slipped a blade between my first two fingers, holding it loosely at my side.

I lowered myself to a crouch, skirting the edge of the warehouse, listening carefully as I neared the open bay doors at the front.

A soft whimper inside twisted my insides, and I grimaced, lifting the blade to throw as I stepped out of the shadows and into the gaping doorway of the abandoned warehouse, my mouth falling open.

Becca thrashed when she saw me, the tape covering her mouth muffling a fearful shout as her eyes widened.

A mechanical whir sounded from outside and a spotlight flared to life, blinding Becca, painting her in a halo of white.

She stood atop a rickety old pallet pack over twenty feet up at the other end of the warehouse. The metal chains around her neck were attached to a rusted metal pulley hanging from the rafters above. The other end of the chain reached down toward the ground where I assumed it was tied off, but I couldn't see where for all the walls and debris blocking my view across the space.

It didn't look the same as it had that night all those weeks ago.

There were stacks of tires and old pallets and crumbling partition walls like before, but they were moved. The low piles of dirt and loose stone on the cement floor in lines across the room gave it away.

It was a course, I realized.

Diesel had put together an obstacle course, and I needed to get through it to the other side in time to save Becca.

Shifting movement inside the maze gave away at least one Saint's position inside. Looking up, I saw Becca eagerly staring down into the maze and back at me, giving me his position somewhere close by on the left.

A chirp had me jerking my gaze upward, to the red numbers on the timer near Becca's head ticking down.

I had a little under ten minutes to get through it, but this time, I wasn't going to hold back.

A blinking red light drew my eye, and I found myself staring into the lens of a surveillance camera placed high in the far left corner of the warehouse.

Becca moaned and growled against the tape covering her mouth, and then sharply, she breathed in deep as the tape came loose, pried off with her tongue. One side fell from her lips, and she sobbed.

"It's okay, Becks," I told her. "I'm going to get you out of—"

"I'm sorry," she cried, the tears dropping from her cheeks catching the spotlight like falling stars. "I'm so, so sorry, Aves."

What?

What could she possibly have to be sorry for? This was my fault. If I hadn't made friends with her—if I hadn't brought her into this—she wouldn't be here right now.

She was here because I cared about her and Diesel wanted to use that against me. To see how far I was willing to go for someone whose life mattered to me.

He was about to fucking find out.

"Just hold on, Becks!" I called, keeping low as I darted forward, ready with a blade to throw at the Saint waiting just inside the row of tires to my left. A sharp snare snapped around my ankle, slicing into skin as the crude trap dragged me upward. My head smashing against the concrete as I was hoisted high into the air upside down. My fucked-up knee protesting the pull of the thin rope.

Dark spots crowded my vision, and I worked furiously to blink them away, my head throbbing.

I groaned, seeing the attacker coming just a second before it would've been too late. He charged forward from his hiding place, upside down, a knife raised high in his black gloved hand.

Blades against blades this time. Diesel was trying to be fair.

I threw my blade and it sank into his heart, sending him staggering back with a grunt.

Except, it didn't strike his heart at all.

The Saint lifted his head with a grin spreading wide over his lips, gripping the handle of my blade to tear it out of the bullet proof vest.

Motherfucker.

I reached for another, the move also saving me from my own blade as it was hurled back at me to *thunk* into a pallet wall six feet to my rear, deeper into the maze.

This time, my aim was lower, and the blade found a home in the meaty flesh of his inner thigh. I heaved my body upward, climbing the length of my leg to reach the blade at my ankle. Unsheathing it and cutting the trip wire holding me up in one fluid movement.

The air gushed from my lungs as I hit the cement floor, and I croaked even as I rolled, getting to my feet. I stormed forward, gasping as the Saint worked feverishly to staunch the flow of blood around the blade protruding from his thigh.

His eyes widened, flashing with terror in the ambient glow of the spotlight.

"Yield!" he hissed through clenched teeth, backing away from me. He released the pressure on the wound gushing his life's blood over the cement to tug another two knives from his belt and toss them to the floor. "*Yield*," he repeated as he knelt, lowering his head.

The muscles in my face twitched as I struggled to get air into my lungs, my left hand tightening around the handle of my blade as the darkness roared within, beckoning me.

Kill.

"Please," he muttered, and I growled as I rushed the last four steps to him, reeling back to kick him in the head, sending him off to dreamland. I grabbed his off-balance blades from the ground and threw them high, embedding them in some wood shelving twenty feet off the ground where no one would be able to use them. They would be no good to me. I wanted *my* blade back.

I tore it from the fucker's leg, unwilling to permanently part with another of my babies. He could bleed out for all I cared.

"*Yeah*," Becca said, but her voice boomed all around me, and I looked up to find her on her hanging block, head bowed as she sobbed. "*One of them is staying with her tonight at Briar Hall.*"

A recording. I searched and found the speakers placed high on other pallet racks around the warehouse.

"*Which one?*" A male voice asked, and a shiver rolled down my spine, making my toes curl.

"*Grey.*"

"*And the others?*"

"*I don't know.*"

"*Think you could find out for me, baby?*"

What...

What the fuck was this?

The tape skipped and a new recording played.

"They went out of town for something," Becca said in the recording, while my best friend sniffled across the warehouse, unable to look at me.

"For what?" the man asked.

"I don't know. She just said they would be back later."

"Do you know when?"

A pause.

"I could text her to find out."

My stomach soured, and I held back the violent urge to vomit, heat searing across my chest.

I remembered the timer, and I looked up to find I had less than six minutes now. I started forward again, pulling my other blade from the pallet board and tucking it away so I held just one in each hand.

Whatever Diesel thought she'd done, he was wrong.

He had to be wrong.

She was telling someone things about me and the guys, but so what? It probably wasn't what it sounded like. Or if it was, then she... she was being manipulated. Maybe even blackmailed. Maybe...

The recording started again, and I paused, my lungs wringing themselves of air in my chest.

"Listen, baby," the male voice said. *"You know they're monsters. Killers. They killed one of our men just last week. Diesel put a bullet between his eyes."*

My mouth fell open as it all began to fall into place in my mind, the jagged pieces fitting perfectly together where I wished they wouldn't.

Becca was dating an Ace. That was why she was so secretive about him. It wasn't because it was a teacher or an older guy or any of the taboo things I might've assumed. It was because he wasn't allowed in Thorn Valley. And if the guys had found out she was with someone from a rival gang, her life at Briar Hall would've been over.

The sound of something shifting on the recording alluded to movement I had to assume was Becca.

"If my crew takes Thorn Valley, it'll be safer, you'll see. And if the Saints were gone, your Dad could finally come back. If Diesel isn't here to keep

buying up all the vacant properties, he'd have no reason to keep buying further south."

"I just..." Becca trailed off. "I just don't see how feeding you information on my friend is going to help you do all that."

A condescending laugh from the Ace. *"Don't you see? She's one of them now. The Crows are Diesel's best weapons. Take them out and he's just an old man with a gun."*

No. No, Becca, why?

"*I don't—*"

"Listen to me!" the Ace thundered and something banged loudly, crumbling as Becca gasped on the tape, making my skin crawl.

"You're scaring me!"

Heavy breathing. *"I'm sorry. I'm sorry, baby. I don't want to scare you. I just need you to listen to me."*

"But they aren't like you think. They're good guys. Ava Jade is my friend."

"You're so naive. You have no idea what the world is really like. You know the Saints are the reason your mother died. What more incentive do you need?"

Another pause. So long I thought the tape had ended, but then Becca spoke again, a resolve in her tone that hadn't been there before.

"If I help you," the recording said, making my blood chill in my veins. *"Will you promise to leave Ava Jade out of it?"*

Becca cried harder, her sobs echoing around the warehouse, but this time, I couldn't bring myself to feel empathy for her pain.

"All right. Fine. Now, tell me about the trials. And I want to know where they are at all times. Can you do that for me?"

"I..."

"This is for us. *So we can be together. Isn't that what you want? Don't you trust me?"*

Oh god. The betrayal stung more than I could've thought possible and my eyes burned with hot, angry tears.

"Yes."

"I didn't do it!" Becca said through her sobs, shouting from the top of the pallet rack. "I couldn't. I saw how you were with them. How they were with you and I...I couldn't. *I hate the Saints.* I hate that if it weren't for them my mom would still be alive, but I wouldn't do that to you! You have to believe me!"

But he *ghosted* you, I thought to myself.

This Ace, whoever he was, he'd cut Becca off. Stopped texting her. Stopped seeing her.

If he hadn't ghosted her, would she have told him the things he wanted to know? Would Becca have caused the deaths of my Crows?

"When he texted me from that unknown number," she said between sobs. "I mean, when *Diesel* texted me pretending to be him wanting to meet up, I was going to end it for good, Aves."

I forced myself to look at her, my chest a hollowed-out shell filled with dark, but she brought the light.

There was no lie on her face. She'd fucked up. She'd made a mistake. She fell in with the wrong guy. Becca was smart, but even the smartest women could be fooled by the vilest of men.

A miasmal sense of foreboding wrenched the air as I wondered what exactly Diesel and the Saints would do with this new information. An Ace was trying to infiltrate Thorn Valley, gather privileged information, and take them all out. Diesel had been right not to trust the Aces. They were working against him in secret all this time. This was how gang wars started.

Wars that almost always resulted in innocent casualties. Likely what happened to Becca's mom.

And I remembered.

I remembered why *I hated the Saints.* Why I hated all gangs.

They'd taken Becca's mother.

They'd also taken my father.

Would I not have done the same thing if I were in her shoes? Did I not promise myself that I would return to Lennox and collect on the blood debt owed for my father's life?

And then it clicked.

This trial was never *if* I could save Becca.

It was whether I *would* save her.

Which meant I'd already failed.

The timer began to beep as the countdown rolled to 59 seconds and Becca started crying anew, her whole body shaking.

"*Oh god,*" she croaked through the tears.

"Call them out!" I shouted to her, racing around the pallets. "Becca!"

A gasp, and then she screamed, "On your right!" and I went skidding to my knees, throwing a blade for the Saint's neck. It sliced across the side of his neck as he dodged the throw, sending a spurt of blood cascading in an arc over the floor. He immediately went to his knees, choking as he tried to splutter a *yield* from his lips.

There was no time to disarm him or make sure he didn't get back up so I moved on, the crow handled blade and my blade at the ready in each hand.

I rounded a tower of tires and Becca screamed, "Watch out!"

I ducked just in time to miss an axe coming straight for my head, using the Saint's momentum against him to drive an elbow down into the back of his neck, hearing the satisfying *crack!* of bone as he went down. Went still.

"Hold on, Becks!" I called as she worked furiously to get her hands free from the binds keeping them tied behind her back.

The timer read twenty-seven seconds and my throat closed as I sprinted through the last of the maze, every muscle in my body burning. The wound in my shoulder and the tear in my knee begging me to stop, but I didn't dare.

I rounded the last wall of pallets and lifted my blade, not hesitating this time when Diesel came into my field of vision. He threw an ax, but I dodged it, rolling and up again before he could reach for an alternate weapon. I tossed a blade and it found a snug home in his Achilles, sending him to his knees with a look of utter shock on his face.

He reached behind himself for the gun my fingers were already on. I tugged it from the back of his jeans and aimed it at his head.

"She betrayed you!" he hissed just as the buzzer sounded and two men, no more than shadows outside of the spotlight's reach, pushed against the base of the pallet rack, trying to knock it from beneath Becca's feet.

She screamed, and I fired two shots at the shadows. I didn't think either hit, I was a shit shot, but the deafening sounds were enough to stop them.

"Touch that fucking rack again and I'll kill him," I hissed, aiming the gun lower, level with Diesel's head.

"Boss?" one of them called.

"It's all right, lads," Diesel called in reply, his voice strained as his blood pooled around his ankle on the cement floor.

I found where the chain was connected to a metal beam against the wall and edged toward it, keeping one eye and the gun on Diesel while I freed the chain.

"Becca," I called. "Can you climb down?"

"My hands!" she cried, a hitch in her voice.

"It's just zip ties," I said, assuming they used the same thing they used to bind my hands for the hunt trial. "Pull your wrists apart to put tension on them and then reach your arms back as far as you can."

"Okay."

"Okay now as hard and fast as you can, pull in toward your body and apart. It'll hurt, but it should break them apart."

She grunted. "It didn't work!"

"It's okay, babe. Try again. You got this."

Two more grunts, and I heard the satisfying *snap* of the plastic.

"I did it!"

"I knew you could. Now just climb down."

"You're making a mistake," Diesel said, seemingly unfazed by this entire ordeal. He just kneeled there, grim, and angry on the cement floor, eyeing me.

I gritted my teeth, so angry I wanted to beat him to death with his own fucking gun. "No." I seethed. "*You* made a mistake. She's an innocent girl whose mother you stole. She was played. Manipulated. And tonight she almost died because of you."

"She was feeding an Ace intel on my *sons*."

"So, what? You thought, hey, two birds one stone? Your men could've swarmed me all at once but they didn't. You *wanted* me to save her, so that I would fail the trial. So that you could turn around and kill us both."

He didn't deny it and that only made me even angrier.

But even I wasn't stupid enough to think that I could kill Diesel St. Crow and get away with it. If I shot him, his men would shoot me. They'd kill Becca, too. I needed to get us out of here. *Now.*

The pallet rack squeaked and trembled as Becca made her way slowly down, holding onto the rusted metal for dear life until she was back on solid ground. She sighed when her feet connected with the concrete, but when she saw the Saints on the other side of the rack, she squealed and raced to my side, putting herself behind me.

"I really wasn't going to tell him anything," Becca said to Diesel. "I swear I wasn't. I was just—"

"You don't have to explain yourself to him," I snapped, cutting off whatever Becca had been about to say next. "You owe him nothing."

She fell quiet, and I saw her chin quiver in my periphery as she held back the urge to cry. "I'm sorry," she whispered. "This is all my fault. I should've told you about him from the very start."

As if she was blaming herself right now. She and I were going to have a good long chat, just as soon as I got her out of here. "Come on, Becca. We're leaving."

I glanced toward the two goons still waiting in the shadows. "And if *anyone* tries to follow us, I *will* kill them."

We backed out through the rear exit, and I kept Becca tight to my side as we made our way to the front. To the Rover I hoped would still fucking start after what I'd put it through.

"Stay close to me," I reminded Becca, and she rushed to keep up as we stepped onto the road. Headlights flared on the road and the roar of an engine had me picking up the pace, grabbing Becca around the wrist with my blade hand.

She winced when I accidentally nicked her but she didn't pull away, letting me guide her to the Rover. "Get in!"

"AJ!"

I whirled, stopping with my hand on the door handle as the car skidded to a halt and the three of them jumped out.

"Sparrow, are you hurt?" Corvus demanded, rushing to close the gap between us while Rook fed a magazine into his gun and cocked it back, eyeing the warehouse like he dared someone to come out of it.

"We saw what happened," Grey rushed to say, his gaze sliding to where Becca was hesitating to get into the back seat of the Rover. His jaw clenched.

The surveillance camera. Diesel had sent them the live feed. And by the way they were looking at Becca...

I aimed the gun at Corvus, making him slow his forward trajectory. His brows drew together as he finally stopped.

"AJ, what are you doing?" Grey asked, stopping too, while Rook continued to watch my six, his gaze jerking warily between my gun and the warehouse at our backs.

"Get back in the car and go," I hissed.

"Sparrow..."

"No." I shook my head. "Tonight I'm not your fucking Sparrow, Corvus James. I'm the girl who almost watched her best friend *die*. Because of you. Because of all of you. Saints. *Ha!* Fucking sadists."

"We can work this out," Grey said, inching closer.

"*Don't.*"

I shot the ground barely a foot from Corvus' boot, but none of them even flinched. They all watched with unconcealed hurt and horror at what they were seeing, but I couldn't make myself stop.

They weren't saying Diesel was wrong. They weren't apologizing. They wanted to *work it out*. Work it out *how*?

I didn't want to find out.

"If you aren't going to leave, then get the fuck out of my way."

Corvus met my gaze and something inside me broke, twisting and shattering until drawing my next breath felt almost impossible.

"Ghost?" Rook asked, his gun lowering now, and I couldn't bear to look at him, because I'd already decided what I needed to do next. "This isn't right. Let me come with you."

The necklace still clasped around my throat weighed heavily against my breastbone, making it even harder to get air into my lungs. But as much as I knew I should, I couldn't bring myself to remove it. Not yet. "I can't do that, Rook."

"Just wait," Grey all but begged. "Let us talk to Diesel. Maybe...maybe this is all a misunderstanding. We can fix this."

My teeth ground together, bone creaking against bone. "*You can't.*"

It wasn't something that could be fixed. Not by anything they could say. Only by something I could *do*. Something that could ensure this never happened again. That no more mothers or fathers needed to die senseless deaths for the whims of a merciless kingpin. The Saints of Thorn Valley, The Iron Aces of Edgewood, or the Kings of Lennox...they were all the same.

I just needed reminding.

"Let her go," Corvus said, his tone the one I remembered from when we first met. Cold and detached. Emotionless.

"*Corv*," Grey tried to argue.

"Move," Corvus replied. "Let them go."

Becca hopped into the Rover, not needing any more incentive, and I got into the driver's seat, turning over the engine. It started on the second try, and the cement barrier scraped along its side as I put her in reverse and turned around just as Diesel exited the warehouse, the two goons helping him walk out. The other injured Saints limped and grimaced behind them. One fewer than there had been inside.

At least one dead, then.

I couldn't bring myself to care.

"Keep your head down," I growled to Becca and hit the gas, bearing us away from no man's land. Leaving the Crows and everything they were a part of behind before I could change my mind.

My throat burned as I drove, aching until I couldn't hold back the pain anymore and it overflowed, tracing warm paths down my cheeks. The gaping hollow spot in my chest where *they* used to be now scraped raw.

"Where are we going?" Becca asked quietly behind me, and I swallowed past the lump in my throat.

I pulled off to the side of the road, the Rover's tires bumping over uneven ground, and yanked my phone free of the side pocket of my pants. My hands shook as I found the email I was looking for.

To: Vicky Doyle

From: Ava Jade Mason

Subject: RE: Swap Notes

I have what you need. Give me a location. I'll be there.

"Aves?" Becca pressed, and I set down my phone, calculating the hours remaining until dawn.

"There's something I have to do."

TWISTED GAMES

PROLOGUE

UNKNOWN

The pain woke me.

Its angry claws dug into my chest and arms, dragging me up from the depths of a deep and dreamless unconsciousness.

A foul taste defiled my dry mouth and I resisted the swift and sudden urge to turn over and vomit onto the cement floor. But, unwilling to move just yet, I forced the rank taste of death down as I swallowed, trying to moisten my aching throat. Knowing there would be nothing to throw up even if I succumbed to the urge. My body felt frail, wisp-like as though hollowed out and stuffed with leaves.

My sight returned in increments, eyelids heavy and crusted so thickly my eyelashes plucked themselves free of my flesh as I worked to open them.

Breathing hurt.

My brain was on fire.

I couldn't feel my fingers.

But I was alive.

My neck strained as I turned stiffly on the sweat-soaked pillow beneath my head, trying to blink through the haze clouding my eyes.

The cold room wavered in and out of focus. I groaned, but that only made my ribs scream in protest of the vibration.

Fuck.

I couldn't be sure how much longer I lay there in a pool of my own sweat and blood and piss and stink, but long enough that the feeling returned to my fingers. Long enough that I could draw a fuller breath and the dim light no longer seared my eyes. Until I could move enough to reach over my battered body to the IV needle I'd haphazardly jabbed into my vein when the fever came on, bringing with it a delirium so complete that I saw four of my own arm as I fed the needle into my skin. I tugged it out with a grunt, and felt the warmth of fresh blood pool and spill down my forearm.

The IV bag hung shriveled where I'd fastened it to the wall above my cot with a blade stabbed directly into the wooden beam.

I had no doubt it was that bag of hydrative solution that prevented my death.

I'd misjudged the injuries.

The broken ribs were more a nuisance than anything, and gratefully none had punctured a lung. The fractured elbow would heal. The bleeding into the skin and soft tissues around my chest was ugly as shit but it would fade with time and proper circulation. It was the head trauma I'd misjudged. The internal bleeding had seemed slight. Manageable without emergency intervention.

But instead of better, it'd gotten so much worse.

It was a small miracle I was alive. That I still had the ability of rational thought.

Though I doubted the throbbing ache pressing on my skull like a drum would ease any time soon.

Hands shaking, I carefully eased myself upright, shutting my eyes against a wave of vertigo I was sure would take me to the floor. But my grip on the cot's edge saved me from the fall and I waited until it passed.

My cell phone peeked out from beneath the cot and bent to grab it, coughing when the movement sent a bolt of lancing pain through my side.

The screen flashed to life, blinding me, the battery icon in the top corner red and blinking.

This couldn't be right.

I'd been on this cot, unconscious for five days. Nearly a fucking week.

Slowly desiccating in this dungeon of my own making.

My upper lip curled into a snarl.

What had I missed in those days.

Where was she?

Was she still alive?

How many times had she allowed them to touch her?

My blood heated with a fury so swift and all consuming it made my vision blur and tint with crimson. Made my weak muscles shudder and ache. The Crows would be punished for touching what was mine. No amount of pain or weakness would stop me from meting it out.

It'd been too long.

A week since the fall from the window, and I could do nothing in this state. I had to wonder if I could even stand, much less follow her.

Ava Jade. What have you been up to?

The question ate at me, striking a new fire in my blood. Enough to propel me to standing.

My legs buckled, but I braced myself on the cool wall, damp with condensation.

It took minutes to cross the small room, but I got there, to the long desk and the sleeping monitors awaiting the stroke of my fingers to wake them.

I slipped into my chair, numb fingers turning each one on in turn before reaching below to the small fridge to grab a bottle of water.

The unwatched video and audio files were in the hundreds. I settled in to watch and listen to every last one, sipping the chilled water as they began to play, their sounds filling the space. Filling my mind. Sharpening my focus and my resolve.

It took hours, and with each recording, my muscles tensed. Until they burned. Until *I* burned.

My knees popped as I rose once more, going to the wall where I kept her.

Her face stared down at me with anger. With disdain. With resolve. With eyes sparking with life.

I pressed a palm to one of the photos I developed. The one of her asleep in her room at Briar Hall. So innocent. So peaceful. It was a face I doubted any other man had ever seen. I treasured it most of all.

I thought she would, but she didn't wake when I crept in. Not when I hid in the shadows at the edge of the room with her panties in one fist pressed to my face and my cock in the other. I liked that she smoked pot with Becca some nights before bed. Those were the nights she slept the soundest. Though I wouldn't tolerate such behavior once she was in my possession.

My eyes shut as I recalled that scent. The scent of her pussy. The taste, diluted by the soapy flavor of her laundry detergent.

Soon, there would be nothing to dilute that taste. Nothing to corrupt its singular essence.

When she was mine, and no one else's.

I traced the red line of string fastened between two pins on the wall, the one tracing upward, to the blueprints for Briar Hall, and across to the picture of Rebecca Hart. Her network of red lines flaring out like a spider's web over the top of the wall. To her father and his business dealings. Her mother's death certificate. Her connection to the Crows. She was always my mark. The girl Rook Clayton had taken a sexual interest in last year. The girl who had every reason to hate the Crows. The girl who, if I worked her just right, would prove a worthy asset and informant. I'd hoped, eventually, to turn her into a full blown spy. Convince her to bed them, gather better intel. For me. For *us*. For all the things she ever wanted but couldn't have.

Once, Becca's was the only female face on this wall.

And then everything changed...

I could hardly believe it when I saw Ava Jade all those weeks ago on the pre-dawn streets of Thorn Valley. There she was, muttering curses to herself as she hauled a swollen suitcase up the street. Though I didn't know her name then, only her face. Those fiery eyes. The whip of her sleek black hair.

I wasn't certain at first, but I followed her, unwilling to lose her again if fate had brought us back together.

I'd searched for her after that night in Lennox at the train tracks, but I never found her. I assumed she'd run after what she did.

The memory made my cock hard in my soiled jeans and I pawed at it, a shuddering breath passing my lips.

If I'd known how she would haunt my every sleeping and waking moment, I'd have taken her then, but I was younger. I hadn't come into myself. I didn't know what it was to own another person. To bend them to my will. To break them. To burn myself so irrevocably into their minds—to imprint myself so fully onto their souls—that they were no longer *them* anymore, but just extensions of *me*.

Mine.

And just like Ava Jade, there was no one to miss them when they never resurfaced again.

But I wouldn't bury her.

Her, I would keep. I would practice restraint *for her*.

She would see, I could be her everything and more.

How serendipitous, that if I hadn't taken her father's life, she never would have left Lennox. Never would have gone to Thorn Valley. I might never have found her.

Fate.

She just needed time and a strong hand to show her what she couldn't see for herself. That she was better off without her father. Better off without The Crows. Better off with me.

It would take time and patience to show her. To smother her fire and teach her obedience.

I would do it for her. I would do anything for her.

But first, there were three *problems* to deal with.

Well, more than three, but I would start with them just as I'd always planned to. *The Crows.*

It would be to both my personal benefit and my advancement in the gang to decimate them, and after all the recon I'd been doing I was finally ready.

I'd do it for Ava Jade.

But I was also going to do it for *me*.

We deserved Thorn Valley and all the territory between. It should've been ours from the start. If our leader had half a brain, it'd already be in our hands. But no one seemed to understand that a man's greatest weapon was his mind. Not his gun. Nor the number of bullets inside it.

His *mind* and what he could do with it. The things he could make happen simply with knowledge and know how.

I reached for the new papers resting in the print basket atop the desk and tucked a few into Ava Jade's file from Briar Hall to inspect with a closer eye when my head stopped throbbing. The others I placed on the board, tacking them on, running red thread between every other thing they could be connected to.

The connection formed immediately between two items and I grinned. *Gotcha.* Snatching a permanent marker, I wrote *does daddy know?* Beside the gps location I just pinned. A concert venue.

I grabbed a burner phone from the basket next to the printer and slid the cheap plastic backing off to shove in a prepaid SIM card, powering it on. A message waited for me there. One I hadn't expected.

UNKNOWN

This ends now. If you have even a shred of dignity, meet me in person. I want to see the face of the coward who tried to drug me.

I smiled.

Not yet, my love.

But soon. Sooner than you think. Once they're gone, and it's only you.

I quickly powered off the phone and pulled out the sim. I couldn't use it now. Too risky.

I'd have to get a message to the boss another way. Let him know I was alive. Still undercover.

And Becca. After what I saw and heard from my surveillance, she would no longer be of use to me. A shame. She'd proven great practice for the real thing. A testament to my ability to control my darkest urges. It wasn't without great difficulty at first, but once I began to look at it as the game it was, it became easier. Easier still when it was a game I kept winning.

I'd take this minor loss and learn from it. As I had every other loss before it.

The Crows wouldn't catch me off guard again.

I unpinned the single sheet of paper containing my false identity next to Becca's photo and tore it in two.

For Becca, I was Jericho.

But I had different names for others.

None of them my real name.

I couldn't stand the sound of it spoken aloud.

All I could hear was my mother's voice in that name. Her threats. Her dominance. Her manic commands to do it more, do it better, do it, *or else*.

My self reckoning happened the day I turned the tables. The moment I took the control from her hands and put into my own. Wrapping those hands around her pale throat. The transference of power flooded me like a drug. And I couldn't get enough.

I wouldn't ever get enough.

It was time for a new persona. A new face. A new way in.

And I had just the thing.

They wouldn't even see me coming.

1

GREY

The Rover's tail lights vanished from view, carrying Ava Jade and Becca away from Nomansland. Away from us.

Numbly, I watched them go, only half aware of Diesel exiting the warehouse behind us, grunting as the others helped him walk.

"Get in the fucking car," Rook growled, stalking back toward the stolen Civic still idling with three doors open wide to the night air. "We need to go after her."

"No," Corvus called, his voice a deadened monotone.

When Rook spun to glare at Corvus, nostrils flaring, I cringed at the mosaic of pain and fury in his black eyes. There wasn't much that affected him like that, mostly because he didn't give two shits about anything in this world except for us.

Us and *her*.

"*No?*" Rook demanded, his body heaving as heavy breaths flooded his lungs and a muscle twitched in his upper lip. "What do you mean 'no'?"

Corvus' hurt gaze dragged to me, but I wouldn't help him. I couldn't.

Didn't know what to do.

She left.

She *left*.

Becca betrayed her, betrayed *us*, and she saved her anyway. Saved her and left us behind.

"Boys," Diesel called, his voice tight.

Blinking, I looked away from Rook's seething anger and Corvus' cold eyes, finding my feet as I turned to face our father.

Neither Corvus nor I stopped Rook as he stormed back, his face pinched as he strode straight to Diesel, making our father stand straighter, shucking off the help of Pinkie and Axel helping him stand.

My stomach turned as Rook stopped no more than a few inches from Diesel, his entire body shuddering with barely controlled rage. "Why?" he hissed in Diesel's face.

"You know why, Son," Diesel replied calmly.

"Becca is a girl who made a foolish mistake," Rook snarled, his fists turning to claws at his sides. "She was manipulated. Played. She—"

"Is a girl who could've gotten you all killed," Diesel finished, snapping back at Rook.

My brother scoffed, bringing up a hand to rub over the stubble coating his jaw as he stepped back, purposefully putting distance between himself and Diesel, not trusting his control.

"Boss, here," Pinkie said, setting a chair in the middle of the abandoned road for Diesel to sit on, a first aid kit hanging from his pinkie. "Sit down, let's patch that up—"

"No," Diesel replied. "I'll do it. Leave the kit. Get the others to the Vet before they bleed out. We'll come back for Garrett's body."

Ice water filtered into my veins, and I closed my eyes against a wave of stomach-churning vertigo.

I knew Garrett. He was a good man. But I couldn't fault AJ for doing what she felt she needed to survive. This was as much Diesel's fault as it was hers.

"Boss..."

"*Go.* I need to talk to my sons."

Pinkie hesitated, eyeing us all in turn before doing as he was bid, piling the other injured Saints into a van before taking off.

Diesel kept a wary eye on a pacing Rook as he sank onto the chair and opened the first aid kit with sloppy fingers. He was pale, I realized.

Chapter 1

Far too pale. The hollows beneath his eyes darker than I'd ever seen them.

I wanted to be angry with him like Rook. I wanted to hate him. To run after Ava Jade and put my arms around her. Keep her safe. Take her far away from here.

But also...

This man was my father. The only father I'd ever known. A man who would do anything to protect his sons. *Anything.*

I could never run if it meant betraying him. If it meant betraying this family.

Teeth clenched, I went to him as the van sped past us, bumping from the gravel at the side of the road onto the pavement. I bent to my knee and took the kit from him, unzipping it the rest of the way to lay it out on the road next to us. I didn't ask what happened, only gripped the edge of his jeans and tore them all the way up to his knee, exposing a gnarly injury to his Achilles and a puddle of blood forming around the sole of his boot.

My hands stilled for a moment, and I grimaced. It was beyond my skill to mend. It would be a miracle if Ava Jade hadn't severed the tendon and nerve endings. I could patch it for now, stop the bleeding, but it needed seeing to by a professional if he expected to walk properly on it ever again.

I glanced up at him, conveying that I was out of my depth here. He nodded. "Do what you can."

"You should see a surgeon."

"This is more important."

I didn't argue, and the smell of tobacco drifted to me on the cool breeze as I did my best to sterilize and suture the wound, winding it tight with gauze and tape. It was a hack job if I'd ever done one, but it would do for now.

Rook hardly finished his first cigarette before stomping on its ashes and lighting another, gaze fixed to the pavement as he paced.

Diesel gave me a nod as I finished and put away the gauze, flipping the first aid kit closed as I pushed back to standing.

"This is fucked." Rook growled to himself, halting his pacing to stand near Corvus, who for once, seemed to have absolutely nothing to say. "You should've told us what was going on, Dies. We could've handled it."

"You might not like the way I decided to handle things," Diesel challenged him. "But I wasn't wrong about her. I'm *not* wrong about her."

His phone chimed in his pocket, and he drew it out, the edges of his mouth turning down as he read whatever message waited for him there.

"You *are*," Rook argued, and this time, I had to agree with him.

"He's right," I told Diesel, speaking for the first time since she left. My voice hoarse and raw. "What Becca did was stupid. She shouldn't have gotten herself mixed up with an Ace in the first place, but from the sounds of it, she was played *hard*. AJ is a lot of things, but she isn't stupid. She wouldn't let her friend die for making a mistake."

It took everything I had in me to hold Diesel's accusing stare. It was obvious he thought I—out of all of us—would agree with him. And I did, to a certain extent.

When I didn't buckle, Diesel sighed, leaning back heavily in the old wooden chair, looking for all the world like the king of anarchy he was, amid the scattered debris and abandoned buildings around us. "Perhaps I may have taken things a *little* too far, but I promise you boys, I am *not* wrong about the girl. And I can prove it."

He had our attention now. Even Corvus seemed to come back to himself, gaunt face lifting to peer over at Diesel. "What do you mean?"

"There's something I need you all to see, and once you see it, you can decide for yourselves what is to be done with your *Sparrow*."

Corvus winced.

"And if we decide she's worthy after seeing whatever it is you intend to show us?" I hedged, needing to be clear.

Diesel locked his cool blue eyes on me, analyzing the meaning behind my words before replying. *You won't,* his eyes said, but his mouth said something different. "Then I won't fight you. I will welcome her as a Saint."

Hope bloomed in my chest, but it couldn't grow past the iron cage of my ribs, making the doubt seep back into my bloodstream and coat my thoughts like poison.

There was another unknown variable in all this, and it hurt to even allow the thought to take root.

We might've already lost her anyway.

What if it were too late?

After this, would she even want anything to do with us? With the Saints?

Rook began pacing again, two steps to the right, turn, three steps left, and back again, a knot between his brows. "This isn't right. I don't fucking like it."

He stopped, his back to us as he stared down the road as though he could make her come back with the force of his will alone.

He whirled on Diesel. "What is it that you know?"

"I need you to think rationally, son. I understand your anger. It isn't entirely misplaced. But right now, I need you to trust me. There's someplace we need to be."

He looked between the three of us, holding each of our gazes before speaking again. "Are you with me?"

The dual meaning of the question wasn't lost on any of us and my teeth locked, making it impossible for me to answer him.

"Grey, help him up," Corvus decided for the three of us. "We'll take the Civic."

The stiffness in Diesel's shoulders abated, but the hardness creasing the skin around his mouth and eyes never ceased.

Corvus' reply told him all he needed to know. We would go with him, but that didn't mean we were *with him,* not when it came to Ava Jade. I wished I could reassure him. Wanted to. But it felt like a betrayal.

The same emotion was mirrored on both my brothers' faces.

If faced with a choice between Ava Jade and Diesel, we wouldn't choose.

We couldn't choose.

Would whatever Diesel intended to show us change our minds?

My stomach soured as my mind filled with a million possibilities—the ways in which she could be permanently expunged from my heart and mind. There weren't many, and I doubted any of them would ever fully do the job of erasing her from the empty places inside of me she'd filled but...

What if Diesel were right?

What if there were a way?

Could I bring myself to do what needed to be done?

Hollow, I pulled Diesel's arm over my shoulders and hauled him to his feet, taking the bulk of his weight. We followed Rook and Corvus to the Civic, each footfall feeling as though it was taking me one step closer to my destruction.

504

2

AVA JADE

"Are you sure he's coming?" I asked Becca for the second time, my fingers tightening on the wheel.

I squinted into the growing dawn light outside of her father's Thorn Valley office building, trying to find signs of life. We were sitting ducks here. It was possibly the *worst* fucking place Becca could have asked her father's driver to pick her up, but she'd hung up my cell before I could tell her to make alternate arrangements.

"I'm sure."

I vibrated in the seat, muttering to myself. "Come on. *Come on.*"

"Aves...can we please talk about—"

"*There!*" I interrupted her, jerking forward to point at the sleek black sedan pulling around the building. "Is that him? Do you know the plate number?"

I unsheathed a blade and sat up straighter, watching as the car inched closer.

"No, but..." Becca leaned forward from the back seat, her body fitting easily between the two front seats. "That's definitely him."

I relaxed, though not entirely. I could feel Becca's eyes on me, but I couldn't bring myself to look at her. Didn't want her to see how much her betrayal had shattered me.

"You need to go," I said, swallowing past the lump in my throat. "Do exactly as I said. Your driver has your passport, right?"

I caught her slow nod from the corner of my eye. She'd asked him to bring it during their call.

"Good. Then you go straight to the airport. Go to your dad's vacation home in Europe—"

"It's in Paris, you should come—"

"*Shhh*," I hushed her sharply, my body flushing with heat. "Don't say anything else. I don't want to know where it is."

"Do you really think they'll come after me?"

At the fear in her voice, I finally cracked, turning just enough to see the gleam of it in her brown eyes. "I don't know," I told her honestly.

She inhaled shakily and cleared her throat as the black sedan pulled up beside the Rover in the empty backlot of the building. "Are you going to be okay?" she asked in a watery voice.

"I don't know that either," I admitted. "But I'm done running. It's time for these *Saints* to pay for their sins."

Becca's grip on the seat tightened until her knuckles were white. "I can't talk you out of it?"

"No."

She hung her head. "For what it's worth...I really am sorry. I should've—"

"*Should've* doesn't help me, Becks," I snapped, completely unable to keep a leash on myself. She needed to leave now before *I* became the danger she needed to run from.

Hurt could turn to fury in the blink of an eye, and if I let myself go there...

"I need you to go. *Now*. Call me when you land, and again when you're settled in the house, but don't call from a landline. Get a burner at the airport."

"Okay."

I nodded, and she hesitated for only another few seconds before she pushed out the door and shut it behind her, climbing into the back of the sedan. I waited until it left the lot and then followed it, trailing it to the edge of town. Once it left the limits of Thorn Valley, I let the Rover's engine slow and pulled onto the shoulder, my throat burning until my vision blurred with tears.

I slammed my open palms on the steering wheel, and when the sting settled something inside of me, I did it again. And *again.*

Until the tears were gone and my palms were red and throbbing. Only then did I even bother trying to slow my breathing. Only then did I do a quick sweep of the Rover for any GPS trackers and then ease off the shoulder and back onto the highway, pulling a tire-squealing U-turn to head down the side-road a few miles back the way I'd come.

Toward the Docks. Where *Vick* would no doubt already be awaiting my arrival.

I couldn't let myself think about what I was going to do when I got there. Not about what I would say either. I'd lose my nerve.

I *couldn't* lose my nerve.

Fresh, morning mountain air blew into my face from the open window, and I closed my eyes, thinking how easy it might be to just let the wheel go. Let the Rover drift...

The tires jerked, bumping onto the shoulder, and my eyes flew open, hands working to pull me back onto the road, my pulse thudding in my ears.

Fuck.

I jammed the radio button, twisting the volume dial to crank it. Needing to distract myself.

The host of *The Edge* came on, and I almost changed the station to something that was actually playing music when his next words made me pause.

"If you were lucky enough to catch their show in Lodi, then you might already know what all the fuss is about. Not only did The Bone Man feature a whole new song, but also a whole new *voice*. The mystery surrounding the man himself has doubled as we all try to figure out who she is."

"That's right, Randy," the other host, a woman, added. "It's such a unique voice, but one that complemented Primal Ethos so perfectly. A tall order if you ask me."

Something in my chest tightened.

"And for him not to have even credited whoever it was..." Randy trailed off.

"Do you think we have another mystery singer?"

A laugh. "Definitely possible."

"All right folks, here it is from Primal Ethos, the live version of his brand new song, *Sparrow!*"

The opening notes of the song flowed into the Rover, and I was thrust back in time. To that night in Lodi, and as his voice came over the air, that thing that'd been tight in my chest only a moment ago shriveled to dust.

Corvus' brusque voice flowed through the speakers in surround sound, echoing inside of my skull. "This one's called Sparrow."

I jammed the off button before he could begin to sing, feeling sick and hot and freezing cold all at once.

He'd just stood there. Mute while Grey and Rook at least had the decency to speak. To try to work through what had happened, but Corvus became statuesque. A lump of useless muscle and flesh with a brooding aura. He just stood aside and told them to let me leave. I didn't know what to think about that. The unfeeling, unflinching monster in his stare had shaken me to my core.

But Rook...

He'd wanted to come with me.

The weight of the hard black stone against my clavicle felt almost too much to bear, but still I couldn't seem to make myself take it off. I would later. When I was alone. And I would find a way to get it back to him. I wanted Diesel to suffer. On some level, I wanted the Crows to as well, but I wouldn't become the Ghost Rook named me for before returning this last memento of his mother to him.

The Docks came into view as I rounded a corner in the bending road, and I flinched as warm orange-hued light blinded me. The sun cleared the horizon, and its reflection glimmered off the rippling waters of Spirit Lake, practically burning out my fucking retinas.

My mouth went dry as I pulled into the lot, searching for another vehicle. A police vehicle. But there was nothing. Not even the standard issue undercover sedan I'd thought he might arrive in. He was smarter than I gave him credit for then, not parking anywhere near here.

I cursed myself for not having that same foresight. This was Saint property, after all. I assured myself they wouldn't be coming anywhere near here with weeks still until the next full moon party, and put the Rover in park, sitting there while it idled for a minute, letting the calm lake and the warmth of the sun on my itchy, blood-spattered skin bring me a measure of peace.

For a second, I could almost pretend the last twenty-four hours hadn't happened at all. My best friend hadn't been plotting behind my back. Diesel hadn't tried to kill her *and me*. My guys...

No, not mine.

They were never mine.

Sighing, I stepped out of the Rover, realizing I was barefoot and trying to remember when I'd lost my shoes. Back in the warehouse, no doubt. The sharp gravel bit into the soft soles of my feet as I made my way to the dock, until it was replaced by the sharp prick of splinters instead.

I couldn't bring myself to care about either. At least the sting with each step reminded me that I was still alive. And living girls could have their vengeance before they became dead girls.

The weathered barn-like door creaked and groaned as I pushed it to one side, old green paint flaking off the wood. Inside it smelled of stale liquor and regret. Across the floor stood the low stage. Atop it, discolored leather sofas languished in the shadows. Desolate. Thrones without their kings.

I could picture them there so clearly. I had been standing just over there when I noticed them watching me that night. How their dark eyes had glittered with malice and a hunger so deep it roiled in the pit of my own stomach.

Forcing myself to look away, my jaw ticked as I turned my attention to the narrow doorway at the back of the warehouse. Standing ajar, it allowed the morning sunlight to filter into the space, along with a welcome breeze off the lake that carried with it scents much less assaulting than the ones currently cloying up my nose.

The shuffle of boots over wood outside and I knew that he was already here. Had likely been waiting a while. Why else venture out into the open unless it was to get away from this stink?

Just in case, I moved with quick, careful steps to the raised stage and snagged a broken bottle, careful not to let the glass ring against the wood. I couldn't bring myself to take the gun I'd stolen from one of Diesel's men back in Nomansland. If I were being honest, I hardly knew how to use one, anyway. I'd left it in the Rover, wiped clean of my prints.

It was a small miracle I hadn't accidentally shot Corvus when I was aiming for the pavement near his feet to show him I meant business.

My throat went dry, and I methodically tried to force a burning swallow, nearly coughing.

"Ava Jade?"

Officer Vick's distinct tone filtered into the warehouse, and I managed to somehow both relax and stiffen anew at the sound of it.

My fist clenched around the bottle neck as I made my way to the back exit and out onto the narrow deck surrounding the pier. I lifted my free hand to shield my eyes from the sun as it washed me in warm bright light. Officer Vick stood against the railing, next to a hold in the rotting decking that I had on good authority was made by Bitchface Brianna's fat ass feet.

It was easier to focus on that than look Vick in the eye.

"You won't be needing that," Vick said, his index finger indicating the broken bottle clenched in my fist.

My nostrils flared as I forced my clenched fist to relax, dropping the bottle near the door, close enough that it would still be within reach if I needed it.

"Glad you came," Vick continued unprompted, turning to rest his forearms on the edge of the railing overlooking the morning lake. A foolish move if you asked me. It looked about five seconds from giving under his weight.

If he fell and smashed his thick head on one of those rocks down below at least I wouldn't have to tell him jack squat. The thought burned through my mind, and I had a sudden intense urge to push him. To force those weather-weakened boards to crack under his weight and send him toppling over to the treacherous and rocky waters below.

As though he could feel my intent, Officer Vick shifted, turning back to face me while taking a step away from the railing.

"You look like shit."

I shook my head, remembering all at once *why* I was here.

The sting of their betrayal hit me all over again, just as crushing as it had been when it was fresh, barely five hours ago.

Had it really only been five hours?

It felt like more...

And less...

I grimaced, grinding my teeth as I lifted my chin to meet the officer's stare.

He lifted a brow, and for a beat, I had to wonder how truly terrible I must look. Barefoot. Clothing torn and bloodied. Hair a rat's nest sans rats on my head. Saying I looked *like shit* was probably a compliment.

"So," Vick began again. "What do you have for me?"

I opened my mouth to reply, but a stopper in my throat made it damn near impossible to speak. I swallowed hard, wondering where exactly I should start.

I had my phone tucked into my panties. Did Officer Vick and the other shitforbrains cops down at Thorn Valley PD have the tech to recover the videos Grey deleted off my phone?

They might.

Or would my intel be enough?

Diesel had been clear that the Deadwood was full of bodies. Several he'd put there himself. They were bound to contain some of his DNA. Or at least some slugs that might match his gun.

I could come clean about the diner incident. He'd promised me immunity. I could feel Rook's phantom hands on me, holding me tight. Holding me close. Pressing the barrel of a gun to my temple as I helped him rob the joint.

No.

I squeezed my eyes shut, a wave of dizzying vertigo making me thrust a hand out to the railing myself, to find my balance.

"Ava Jade?"

"Just...just give me a minute," I said, speaking for the first time, my voice a hoarse, cracking whisper.

I cleared my throat, blinking as a wave of nausea hit me so hard I had to fight not to double over and vomit on Vick's shoes.

"Take all the time you need," Vick crooned, and I flinched back as he moved close, a hand outstretched. I smacked it away, standing straight.

"Don't touch me."

He lifted his hands, eyes going round. "All right."

His close standard-issue sport's jacket reflected the light and I squinted to see him better. He looked a little rougher around the edges than I remembered in the daylight. Scruffier. More gaunt in the face. His hands thick and callused. Different than each time I'd seen him before. Once at night and once in the shadows of the trail just off campus at Briar Hall.

It somehow made him seem more human. Relatable. Like he was just a regular guy who might've seen some shit—been through some shit—himself. And I remembered he said the reason he wanted to bag the Saints so bad was personal. Did they take someone from him like they'd taken Becca's mom?

Like the Kings took my dad?

I sighed.

"You're doing the right thing," he said in a low voice. "The Crows and their father are monsters. Murderers."

My skin bristled.

"The world will be a better place without them."

"You're wrong."

The words were out of my mouth before I could trap them and shove them back down my aching throat.

I shook my head, my chest hot and swelling with each breath as they became heavier.

Officer Vick narrowed his eyes at me. "I am?" he challenged, a muscle in his jaw straining.

"The Crows are fucking idiots. Total assholes. And I can't say a single kind thing about their father except that he loves his sons more than anything in this world, but *no*. I don't think the world would be a better place without them."

I remembered the feel of my blade as it slit across the throat of Frank the butcher. The man who broke one daughter's arm and starved the other. *The Crows* found justice for the broken and oppressed people of Thorn Valley. Without them, those little girls would've continued to suffer. How many other pieces of trash had they cleaned from these streets?

How many lives had they saved?

Just as many as they'd taken?

More?

It didn't matter, I realized with a start.

I fell back a step.

I didn't have to do this.

They'd betrayed me. They didn't care for me the same way I had begun to care for them, but that didn't mean they deserved *this*. I could just leave. Disappear like I should've done from the start. Leave them to their nest of cruelty and vengeance. To their father.

I could still try to take Diesel down, but it would hurt them and I...

Despite everything, that was the last fucking thing I wanted to do.

Physically, I wanted to crush them. Drive over them with a fucking tank. But this?

I couldn't do this. It went against everything I stood for.

What I could do was cut a deal for my freedom with Diesel. He didn't want me anywhere near his sons; he'd made that clear as crystal. But he also couldn't risk losing his son's devotion by killing me without just cause or provocation. Hell, I'd bet the bastard would even pay me to leave, rendering Aunt Humphrey's inflated bank account completely useless to me.

I could even negotiate for Becca's life.

It would be a win-win-win.

Even if it felt more like losing everything right now.

"Do you really believe that?" Officer Vick asked, incredulous at my admission. "That the world wouldn't be better off without men like them in it?"

"Men like them..." I trailed off, sticking a hand down a tattered hole in my dress to retrieve my cell phone from where it was pressed hard into my hip bone. "Other gang members? Maybe."

Officer Vick eyed my phone, unable to hide his lusting after it. He was practically drooling, the dog.

He watched as I pried off the back, the metal warm to the touch from my body heat, and popped out the sim card.

"But other gang members *aren't* like them. No one is."

I snapped the sim. Vick's mouth opened in a silent, horrified gasp. I pressed the busted pieces into my fist with the phone and reeled my arm back.

Vick lurched forward, but he was too late. The phone whistled through the air, dropping, dropping, until it *plunked* into the soft waves of the lake and a weight the size of fucking Texas took its boot off my chest.

I sighed.

"I'm sorry," I told Vick as he clutched the railing, scanning the little white-capped waves for any sign of the device. "I can't help you. And Vick?"

I waited for him to look at me, the skin between his almost unibrow pinching.

"Don't ever contact me again. If you do, I'll tell the Crows all about you. Where you live."

His mouth pressed into a thin line.

"What kind of car you drive."

"How—"

I lifted my hand to stop him. I wasn't finished. Anyone with half a brain could use a name to search for an address. And anyone worth their salt could have a pleasant little run past said address to scope it out, thus finding a personal vehicle, plate number, and a hot-rod red tricycle in the driveway.

"Don't approach me again and you have nothing to worry about."

Vick took a moment to compose himself, his gaze drifting to the open doorway at my back like he couldn't wait to leave.

"I understand," he replied.

A loud clap echoed within the warehouse at my back, and I whirled, dropping to the ground to snatch up the bottle and roll back, putting distance between myself and the doorway and even more space between Vick and me.

The clap came again, louder this time, followed by another, and another as the shadowy form inside the warehouse came closer, their steps awkward and stilted, until eventually he stepped into the light.

Diesel St. Crow emerged from the bowels of the Docks, inhaling deeply through his nose as a breeze brushed over us from the lake. He continued his slow clapping as he turned to face me, seeming to be completely unperturbed by the police officer at his back.

The police officer who seemed wholly unsurprised to see Diesel there. No, not just unsurprised, but like he'd been expecting him. Like he knew him.

My mind reeled at the scene before me, trying to read between lines I'd somehow missed entirely.

"Thanks, Colin," Diesel said, jerking his head to Vick who gave a quiet nod before departing with one last glance in my direction, some-thing like a smirk playing on his lips.

He removed his jacket as he left, revealing arms covered from shoulder to wrist in tattoos. The sharpened fleur-de-lis sign of the Saints in solid black on the back of his left biceps.

What. The. Fuck.

I held Diesel's stony gaze, trying and failing to read what was going on in that twisted head of his. Noticed how fucking pale he was. No doubt thanks to my blade work.

Before I could form the beginning of a laundry list of every curse word in the dictionary and then some, the floorboards inside the ware-house creaked again and the Crows stepped out behind their father.

My pulse skittered before pushing back to a strong, steady rhythm as tangling tendrils of guilt, fear, and murderous intent wreaked havoc on my nervous system.

Diesel stopped clapping, but it was the Crows I couldn't take my eyes off no matter how much I wished I could. Jumping from the pier myself began to sound like a pretty damn good idea. I liked my chances.

My eyes darted to the lake, judging the distance.

"Don't," Corvus said.

My teeth clenched.

He had no right to look so damned betrayed. None of them did.

They started this shit. They roped me in. Pushed me into a corner. What did they expect?

But still, the hurt in their stares stabbed into me like knives, making it harder to breathe.

"I have to admit," Diesel said, a flicker of his concealed rage crossing his face. "This wasn't how I anticipated things going down."

"We had a deal," Rook growled, his hulking form vibrating beneath his leather jacket.

Diesel's upper lip curled into a snarl before he spoke again. "So we did."

The man hobbled forward, and I worked hard to stand my ground, bottle at the ready, checking him over for anything that looked even remotely like a concealed weapon.

He lifted a hand, his face back to an unreadable mask.

One I'd like to peel from his skull with the broken edge of the bottle in my hand for what he did.

"Welcome to the Saints, Ava Jade."

I looked at his outstretched hand. At his sons watching the exchange like they could force me to take it through sheer force of their will.

The bottle clattered to the decking at my feet, breaking.

I turned and walked away.

3

ROOK

There was no way in hell I was going to watch her walk away from us a second time. The pit in the bottom of my stomach clenched tight, walling in the darkness growing like an electromagnetic fog there. Like fucking poison.

"Rook?" Grey asked cautiously, sensing the presence of the monster within.

I turned to meet his stare and shook my head.

No.

I wasn't going to let her go. How could he? How could Corvus?

A muscle twitched above my lip, and I clenched my teeth, shouldering past Diesel.

"Son," he called after me, but I was done listening. My brothers liked to joke that whatever internal meter that read what was wrong and right in my head was broken, but they were wrong. Maybe it was their meters that were broken, because letting her leave felt like the most *wrong* thing on the fucking planet.

Sure, she was talking to a cop. Or at least, she'd thought she was, but she didn't tell him anything. And I knew that she never would've. No matter what. Didn't they know that, too?

Wasn't it us who backed her into the fucking corner?

This wasn't something she wanted to do. It was something she felt like she had to do. Probably because of what happened to her father.

It didn't mean I wasn't angry with her, of course I was, but I was willing to bet she was ten times more pissed at us.

I rounded the corner of the old pier warehouse and followed her. She was already a solid fifty paces ahead of me, but by the slight tensing of her shoulders, I knew she was fully aware someone was following her.

In fact, I was willing to bet she already pegged it was me.

Just like I could peg any singular sound at the Crow's Nest as either her or not her. The soft sure sound of her stealth silent footfalls. The way she opened cupboards, whip-quick like she expected to find a monster behind the panes of wood. Her soft sighing sounds in the shower, like she'd never had a proper one before in her life.

Ava Jade paused by where the Rover was parked looking out over the lake, but then continued, leaving it there. Her hands clenched at her sides as she started up the road, but she forced them to unclench, splaying her fingers wide. Forcing herself not to give in to what she was feeling inside.

I knew what that was like. Better than anyone.

"Ghost," I called to her, but she didn't stop, forcing me to hustle to catch up with her. She didn't bother acknowledging me when I slowed to walk alongside her, pushing my dark hair away from my face.

Her face, usually so composed, betrayed a raging hurricane of pent up emotions. Pinched, her eyes hard and jaw muscles working.

I opened my mouth to begin, but something made me pause.

She wasn't ready.

I swallowed deep and turned my attention back to the winding side road ahead, keeping pace with her. I didn't say anything, we just walked like that for a time. She didn't tell me to fuck off, and I was taking that as a good sign, it kept me going.

That and the intermittent glint of sunlight on the black diamond bobbing against her clavicle. She hadn't taken it off.

The dead thing in my chest squeezed, almost painful. The best kind of pain.

"I should've left Thorn Valley when I had the chance."

Her voice sent a shudder racing down my spine. So hopeless. I never wanted to hear it sound like that again. "You don't really believe that, do you?"

"Was it really all bullshit?" she asked in a low voice, ignoring my question, biting her lower lip as she stared at the ground disappearing beneath our feet. "Was any of it real?"

"Hey." I pulled her to a stop, and she let me, her cut glass eyes finding mine for only a fraction of a second before she looked away, disgust twisting her mouth. "I could ask you the same fucking thing. Talking to a cop...?"

"He wasn't even a fucking cop," she spat back.

"But you thought he was, didn't you?"

She growled, tugging away from me but staying stationary. She wanted to have this out just as badly as I did, even if she wouldn't admit it.

"I don't get it. I looked him up. Found his address. He's listed and everything. He's on the force—"

"All a trick," I interrupted her. "Dies has done this before. He went by Vick, right?"

Her lips pressed tight.

"It's how he's always smoked out rats. There *is* an Officer Vick who works for Thorn Valley PD. How else could the ruse hold up. All it would take is one call to the station or one online search to find out the name was bogus. The real Vick doesn't use social media. He's a total fucking recluse. Barely leaves his big house aside from taking his kid to the park down the street. No photos of him online."

"The perfect identity."

I nodded.

Her face darkened, and I could see how deeply this had all cut her. Ghost was someone who didn't trust easily. Fuck, probably didn't trust *ever*. But she'd trusted Becca and her friend had betrayed that trust. Lied to her. Plotted against her...whether she went through with it or not.

And Vick, he wasn't even a real cop. Damn, I applauded Dies for implanting him so quickly. I had to wonder whose eyes noticed we were getting close to Ava Jade and told him. One of the pledges trying to earn brownie points? The fucking night security guy, Mick? It could've been anyone.

But worst of all was the hurt we'd caused. I could see it in the way she wouldn't hold my stare.

In her own way, she *had* begun to trust us, and when we didn't come to her defense against our father. When we didn't defend Becca and reassure her. When we let her fucking go...

We never should have let her go.

"Did you know about Vick?"

"Hmm?"

"Did you know?" she pressed, and I came back to her from the dark place my mind had wandered.

"No."

She looked doubtful.

"We didn't know until about four hours ago when Diesel told us and led us here to listen in during your meeting."

She waited. Wanting more.

"He was hoping you were going to give us up."

"So that you would kill me yourselves?"

I didn't respond. I didn't want to say it, and frankly, I didn't need to. She already knew the answer. She didn't ask the most important question though...

Would we have done it?

I didn't want to answer that either.

"What's going to happen to Becca?" she asked instead of the questions we both knew the answers to, and at least this one, I could speak to.

I inclined my head. "Diesel won't hurt her."

"*Pfft.*" She shook her head.

"He won't, I'll make sure of it personally."

"But?" she pressed, not fully satisfied with my response, knowing there was a catch.

I wouldn't sugar coat it for her. "She'll need to answer some questions. As long as she cooperates, nothing will happen to her. She can stay here."

Though something told me Becca Hart was already long gone. Ava Jade would have seen to that.

She nodded, and even though I could see she didn't believe me, maybe didn't trust me, she wasn't going to push it. Cementing my suspicions about Becca already being gone. Maybe that was for the best.

"It wasn't all lies," I added after a minute, answering her question from before. "It was all real between us. But you already knew that. I get that it's easier to think we were all out to get you from the start."

That struck a nerve, she flinched, and my stomach soured in response.

Yes.

I knew what that was like, too.

Not being able to accept that there were people out there who cared about you. *Really cared.* Searching for hidden meaning in every word they spoke, in every gesture. Trying to untangle imaginary lies from truths. Looking for ulterior motives *always*.

"I know what you're thinking," I continued and this time she looked at me, searching my eyes to see if I was right. "You're going to leave."

The truth was clear in her eyes as she held me there, captive in her burning stare.

"You're going to disappear. Tell me I'm wrong."

She couldn't.

I let out a heavy breath. "Don't."

"Why shouldn't I?"

"Dies...he shouldn't have done what he did with Becca, but even you have to understand the reason wh—"

"I do!" she countered, her shoulders rising like a cat getting its back up. "I do fucking understand and that's the problem. I want to hate you. Them. *Him.*"

She paced back three steps before returning, her chest heaving. "But I can't. I can't, and it's fucking absurd."

I shrugged. "Then don't."

She laughed darkly, shaking her head at the ground.

"We need you, Ghost. I need you. Tell me you'll consider staying. Please."

Ava Jade stiffened, her head snapping up, the laugh dying in her throat.

I couldn't remember the last time I'd used that word. *Please.* It tasted bitter on my tongue, full of hope that only she could smash.

"I..." she started, but didn't finish, swallowing, her eyes glassy.

"Don't answer now, just think about it. And…and if you decide to go, I'll do everything in my power to make sure no one comes after you. But I'm telling you now—"

I stepped in close, sealing off the offensive gap between us to take her face into my hands. "If you leave, that's it. You can't come back. Not ever. I can't do this twice."

Her lower lip quivered, and on instinct, I pressed my mouth to hers, consuming her fear as if I could steal it from her and carry it as my own.

Her lips, soft and resistant at first, pressed harder against mine as she deepened the kiss, our tongues flicking out against each other. She tasted of salt and copper, and it made my body ignite with a need so strong my blood rushed in my ears, drained from my face to fill my cock as it thickened in my jeans.

She moaned against my mouth, and my fist found the hair at the back of her neck, twisting in and holding her hard against me as her fingers searched for something of mine to hold on to.

My Ghost ground her hips into me, and I shuddered at the contact, wanting this—her—right now, more than anything I'd ever wanted in my life. But she hadn't chosen us. Not yet.

I yanked her head back with my grip on her hair, breathing heavily as my cock throbbed in my jeans. "If you decide to stay, you know where to find us," I whispered against her mouth.

Before I could change my mind and strip her naked right there in the middle of the road, I released her and stepped back. Back again. Taking in the long shape of her body, every curve, every blemish on her skin, her face, the face of an avenging angel come to take my soul.

And then I turned and walked away, heading back in the direction I'd come, stuffing my fists deep into the pockets of my jeans.

4

AVA JADE

I could still feel the tingle of Rook's kiss on my lips as I entered Briar Hall, almost knocking into a student in my daze.

"Sorry," he muttered, pausing to stare before limping past me to go outside through the back door.

Judging by his small gasp, I had to assume I looked like death warmed over. Or worse. I definitely smelled worse. The trademark lemon pledge scent of these halls was almost completely covered over by it. *Ugh.*

A deep silence followed me as I made my way up the long staircase to the apartment and something about that seemed off.

Was it a school day? No.

Sunday.

It had to be Sunday.

That's why it was so quiet at this time of the morning.

Not like it mattered.

Numbly, I fumbled with the door to the apartment, shoving the key in the lock only to find that it was already open. I frowned, lifting my back straight as I twisted the handle and pushed the door in, ready for an attack.

The creak of someone shifting their weight in a chair forced me further inside, a lick of heat rolling up my spine. My adrenaline sparking but seemingly unable to ignite, its resources utterly fucking spent.

A man, unarmed, sat at the long stone counter on the living room side of the kitchen.

My heart jumped into my throat at the thought that this could be my stalker as he lifted his gaze to mine. Lack of energy be damned, if it were him…

"Who the fuck are you and what are you doing in here?" I sneered, picking out the knife block across the other end of the kitchen, judging my ability to get to it before he could stop me.

He was a big guy. Over two hundred pounds for sure, but much of that weight looked to be muscle. He'd be strong, but slow.

The big guy followed my jerking gaze to the knife block and back again, unbothered by my question. Unbothered that I was considering carving his eyeballs out with the paring knife. His bald head, partially covered in tattoos, gleamed as though freshly polished in the light and that's when the finer details started to take shape.

There was a heavy black canvas bag on the counter next to him. Beside it sat several small plastic cups that almost appeared to be the lids off plastic bottles. Filled with blue and black ink. A tattoo gun rested next to them, and a stack of paper towels and a small container of petroleum jelly waited next to it.

"Diesel sent me," he explained simply, indicating the stool next to him. "Depending if you want anything additional to the fleur-de-lis, this will only take about thirty minutes."

I blinked, the reality of exactly what was happening right now dawning on me like a smack upside the head. Unable to help it, I began to laugh.

"Fucking, really?"

He didn't look like he was joking. The man watched me with a wary disdain. Fuck, he almost looked bored. And my laughter didn't seem to throw him off in the slightest.

"Sit down," he said plainly, reaching for a pair of black plastic gloves in his bag to tug them over his large hands.

I shook my head, the laughter dying on my lips. "Get out."

He lifted a brow.

"I said get the fuck out. *Now.*"

I couldn't deal with this right now. When he didn't make a move to leave, an ache formed behind my eyes and I pinched the bridge of my nose to try to ward off the frustration headache from getting stronger.

"Look, girl, I'm here to do my job, not deal with a fucking tantr—"

"If you don't leave right now, I am going to slice off every one of your fingers and shove them up your ass."

He had the decency to look at least a little put off by the threat, but he didn't seem to think I would make good on it. Clearly, no one had told him about me. I was far from kidding.

He held my gaze for another moment before grimacing as he tossed his gear back into his bag, leaving the ink pots on the counter as he shouldered it and slid off the stool.

"I'm too old for this shit," he said under his breath as he strode past me, vanishing down the hall outside with loud, echoing steps.

I waited until I was sure he'd made it outside before closing the door and locking it, going to the window across the apartment to watch him shove his shit into a shiny black truck with *Forbidden Ink* decaled on the side in sharp lettering.

I surreptitiously checked the rest of the apartment bit by bit, pausing only when it came to Becca's bedroom door. I'd never been in her room. It'd always been firmly *her* space. I'd assumed she was just private about her things, or maybe left a bunch of vibrators lying around, but now I knew the truth.

She probably had things to hide.

Without overthinking it too much, I pushed open her door and stepped inside, quick to get eyes on every inch of the space in case there was anyone else waiting to jab me with fucking needles.

Seemed like everyone's fetish these days.

Satisfied that I was alone after a quick scope of the walk-in closet and the bathroom, I turned in a slow circle, taking in the space.

It smelled like her. Like jasmine and something a bit musky, like old wood.

Just like the rest of the apartment, her room was done up in varying shades of black. Polished black. Matte black. Faded black.

But with pops of indigo and violet, like the canvas artwork of a girl's face painted in shadows of lavender with her eyes crossed out in black, slashes of gray painted haphazardly over the entire piece.

A bit morbid, but it sort of suited her and something about it was very feminine and pretty despite the slashed out eyes.

My fingers trailed along the top of a sleek black dresser, falling down until they reached the top of the first drawer. I pulled it open an inch before shutting it again. Unable to bring myself to snoop through her things even after what she did.

Maybe later.

I needed a nap and goddamned shower before I even started to try to pick up all the pieces and try to figure out how they all fit back together after everything that'd happened.

But first, I had a promise to keep.

Briar Hall was eerily quiet as I found my way down to the main floor after removing my tattered dress in favor of sweats and a baggy t-shirt. The phone room, a relic of a time before cell phones, was nothing more than a narrow room with a bank of old black corded phones hanging on the wall, divided with thin panes of wood for privacy.

The whole space was covered in a fine layer of dust and instead of sitting on one of the moth-eaten chairs, I leaned against the wall as I lifted a receiver.

Shit.

They weren't working.

I tried the other six, sighing when the last one in the line at the very back of the room hummed with the electronic dial tone.

I'd memorized Becca's number weeks ago, and each digit beeped in my ear as I hit the cold metal buttons. She really should've gotten rid of her phone. I should've told her to get rid of it, but I was banking on her being out of reach across the country by now, or at least soon.

The line only rang once before it went straight to voicemail.

"This is Becca Hart, make it quick or text me like a normal person."

An almost smile pulled at the edge of my mouth.

"Hey, it's me. Just checking that you got there safe. Leave a message with the office when you get this, 'kay? I, *uh,* I lost my phone so don't bother texting. Hit me up on socials, but make sure all of your location sharing is turned off on your phone. Actually, maybe just get a new one. Toss that one before you get where you're going."

I paused, not sure what else to say.

"Be safe," I said finally before hanging up, dragging my dead ass to a shower and my bed.

5

GREY

I got up from my desk for the fifth time in as many minutes, running a palm over my face as I circled my room.

It had been almost twenty-four hours since Ava Jade walked away from us at the Docks and still it felt wrong being back here. Here without her.

Her, alone, wherever she was. With her stalker possibly still out there.

Maybe I shouldn't have cared, but I did. Even after everything. After she protected the friend that betrayed her and could've gotten us killed. Even after finding out that she was talking to a cop. Not just talking to him, but seriously considering ratting us out.

It didn't matter that Colin wasn't a real cop. She thought he was and that was enough.

It hurt.

It hurt more than I thought I *could* hurt anymore. This was why I didn't form attachments. The reason none of us did outside of the family.

You get attached, you get burned.

And I knew from firsthand experience that those scars never fully healed.

I shouldn't care. But I do.

I still wanted her, and even though there was a loud voice shouting in my head that she could no longer be trusted, there was another voice. One that whispered how badly we'd hurt her, too.

The voice insisted I consider what she had to go through in the last forty-eight hours and view the situation through that lens. Through her eyes.

If she could forgive us, could I forgive her?

It didn't help that I'd barely slept more than a few hours since we got home, if you could call passing out head down at my desk sleeping. My rest-deprived brain throbbed with too many unknowns. I pulled at my hair, and the pain grounded me.

Blond threads drifted down to the carpet when I let go, and I inhaled deeply as I watched them fall, remembering a time when I was so malnourished you could count each one of my ribs without even needing to remove my shirt.

How my hair had begun to fall out in clumps near the end, when I was close to death. Too stupid to leave the house and get help. Naively convinced that if I just kept waiting, my mom would come home.

I growled before sweeping the contents of my desk onto the floor, breathing hard.

A sharp pain bloomed on my arm as I pressed my palms to my eyes, trying to gain control. Liquid dripped down to my elbow and I found a thumbtack jutting out of my biceps, a little pinhead of green.

Rolling my eyes, I ripped it out and went to find a paper towel to clean the damn mess.

I sat on the floor when I was finished, the room reeking of stain remover. That was when I noticed the little flick of black nail polish on the side of the spray bottle and sagged.

I needed to talk to her.

But if I were being honest, I knew the real reason I was about to march my ass down to Briar Hall. Because I still felt a keen sense of responsibility for her safety. Or maybe that wasn't the right way to describe it. It wasn't responsibility. It was worry.

She was exhausted at the Docks. It was written all over her face. What if she went back to Briar Hall and took a nap. What if, tired as she was, she didn't hear it when someone broke in. Was too out of it to stop the stalker when he tried to inject her again.

What if...

Fuck it. I was going. Now.

I stood, and as I tossed the spray bottle and wad of paper towels onto my barren desk I noticed Corvus from my bedroom window overlooking the drive. He was wheeling his motorcycle out of the garage, looking down the road like it might grow teeth and bite him.

I leaned over my desk and hammered the side of my fist on the glass until he turned, looking up. I held up a hand, shouting at him to wait through the glass.

It took me all of two minutes to throw a clean shirt and deodorant on before I was outside.

"You going to see her?" I asked as I shut the door behind me.

His hands tightened on the handlebars as he threw a leg over the seat.

"Corv?" I pressed when he didn't answer.

"Where the fuck else would I be going?" he said, his voice the same flat monotone he'd been speaking in since last night. It reminded me of how he was when I'd first met him at eleven—before he trusted us and eventually accepted us as his brothers.

"You coming?" he added, and I swallowed hard, not giving him a reply as I got on the bike behind him and the engine rumbled to life beneath us.

I peered back at the Crow's Nest, searching Rook's black window for any sign of him, but I saw nothing. He was probably asleep. We'd picked him up along the road on the way back from the Docks, and he'd gotten in without a word. His expression dark.

Of course I wondered what she said to him. What he might've said to her...

But it wasn't the time to ask.

The gravel road turned to pavement as we sped toward Briar Hall, Corvus barely slowing at all until we were in the actual parking lot.

"What if she isn't here?" I asked as I stepped off.

"She will be," he replied, and it sounded more like he was trying to convince himself than me.

I followed him to the front door of the academy, the words *as the crow flies* mocking me as I passed beneath them.

Mick nodded as we passed through the atrium and took the stairs up to the third floor and down the hall.

"Rook?" I asked, surprised to see him sitting against the wall three feet from her door, his elbows on his knees, a lit cigarette hanging from his lips. Ashes all over the floor between his feet.

He cocked his head, glancing up at us.

"How long have you been here?" Corvus asked, tugging the dart from Rook's mouth to stamp it out beneath his boot, his nose wrinkling.

It smelled like dirty old ashtray in here.

I dug into the inside pocket of my jacket and passed him a stick of gum.

He grudgingly snatched it from my fingers and popped it into his mouth.

In less than an hour, all the students in the building would be waking up for classes. Some probably were already awake, terrified to leave their rooms to shower because of the Crow smoking in their hall, looking out of his damned mind.

"I left after I showered," he said, his voice rough.

But he'd showered only a few hours after we got back to the Nest yesterday. And we'd only made the one stop to drop Diesel off with the vet to have his injury looked after.

"Have you slept?" Corv demanded.

Rook shrugged. "Maybe. Might've dozed off."

He was here the whole time. Making sure she was safe through the night alone.

Guilt ate at me, and I dropped my head.

"Seen her?" I asked.

He shook his head, making a chunk of black hair fall into his eyes that he swept away with a shaky hand. "No, but she's in there. I heard her snore a bit earlier. Nothing since."

Relief exploded through me, so strong it made spots of light dance across my eyes.

I was starting to think Corvus had been right all along, this girl was going to be the end of us.

"I've been waiting until she woke up to knock," Rook added. "But I think she's still passed out."

I cocked my head at him. He was *waiting* for her to wake up? Rook?

The guy who did literally any fucking thing he wanted, whenever he wanted?

"How long has it been?" Corv asked.

"I don't know, but it's been quiet for at least sixteen hours."

"Then she can wake up now," Corvus decided for all of us, lifting a fist to the door. He pounded the wood and it rattled in the doorframe.

No sound came from inside as we waited and Corvus' lips pressed into a taut line as he knocked again. "Ava Jade," he called through the wood. "It's us."

When no sound came still, ice crept up my arms. What if...

"Grey, open it before I kick it down," Corvus growled, and I stepped forward, digging my pick kit from my wallet and kneeling down.

"Chill the fuck out," came AJ's tired voice from somewhere deep in the apartment, and I stopped, slipping the metal pieces back where they came from.

The ear-cringe sound of something heavy being dragged across the hardwood came before the sound of her bedroom door opening. She'd obviously pushed her desk in front of it while she slept. At least she wasn't too out of it to realize she might not be safe alone in the apartment.

Her stomping footfalls approached the door before they paused and I squinted through the wrong side of the peephole, catching a flicker of movement before she opened the door.

She stood there in an oversized gray t-shirt that looked distinctly like a man's, with nothing else but black panties poking out from beneath the hem. Her hair, usually pulled back into a messy bun or ponytail, was in messy waves of darkest brown. Like she'd showered and passed out before she had the chance to brush it.

The natural texture of it suited her. Gave her the lion's mane she deserved.

AJ took us all in in turn, saying nothing.

She pushed the door the rest of the way open and spun on her heel, heading to the kitchen. Letting us in.

It was a better start than I thought.

"Ava Jade," Corvus hedged as we closed the door behind us, wading into the apartment.

She held up a hand from where she stood in front of the espresso machine. "Shhh," she hissed. "No one speaks until I have a cup of coffee in my hand."

"We really should—"

She fingered a small paring knife from the block next to the espresso machine and tossed it. It landed three inches from my foot in the hardwood with a *thunk*.

"I throw the big one next," she warned, searching the back of the stainless steel beast for a switch.

Corvus walked into the kitchen, nudging her out of his way despite her glaring at him. "Let me do it," he grumbled, tugging four cups down from the warmer on top. "Move."

Her jaw tightened, but she didn't argue, crossing her arms to lean on the counter next to him as he filled ground beans and filled the thingy that let the creamy espresso drip out, frothing milk while it finished filling the bottoms of two mugs.

He passed one latte to AJ first, indicating Rook for the other, while he started the process over again, making two more for himself and for me.

I took the warm mug he offered, and no one said a damn word until he was finished cleaning up the machine and all its parts. Until Ava Jade had drunk at least half of her latte, trying to conceal how much she was enjoying each sip.

"Can we speak now?" he asked her, grabbing his latte and her elbow to tug her toward the living room.

She jerked away from his touch, making the latte almost slosh out of her mug, little lines of caramel liquid dripping down its side. "Look what you almost made me do," she sneered, flicking her tongue out to lick up the lost droplets before they could fall.

And fuck if that tiny thing didn't make me a bit hard in my jeans.

She continued into the sunken living room on her own. "Speaking of things you made me do..."

"Don't pretend for even a second that you talking to Colin was our fault," Corv argued.

AJ whirled on him, stopping him from following her with two fingers jabbed into his chest. He stiffened but remained in control. "It *was* your fault. All of you."

Rook and I shared a look.

You didn't touch Corvus James, not unless he wanted you to.

But this wasn't the first time, and I had a feeling it wouldn't be the last.

"She's not completely wrong," I said, earning myself a wicked stare from my brother. "And I think you know that."

"You know, it's funny," Ava Jade said, flopping onto the longer of the two black couches with a laugh that told me she definitely didn't think whatever she was about to say was funny. Not even a little bit. "For a split second I thought maybe you were here to apologize. But how could a *Saint* ever be wrong? Why would a *Saint* apologize for their sins?"

"It's why I came," I said. "Or at least, it's part of the reason."

She stared at me incredulously, her lips popping open in surprise. An emotion I couldn't name swimming in her eyes.

She watched me as I made my way to the couch opposite her, discarding my untouched latte on the coffee table between us. "Diesel went too far," I started, trying to remember everything I'd planned to say on the way over here if we found she hadn't skipped town.

"But he was trying to protect us."

Her lips twisted.

"And...a part of me gets that you probably felt backed into a corner. Colin is good. He probably pulled all the right strings."

"She almost fucking destroyed us," Corvus argued, standing a few feet behind AJ, halfway into the living room still.

"But she didn't," Rook said, sitting next to AJ, laying his arm over the back of the couch, not quite touching her but close enough that he could if he wanted to. "Did you, Ghost?"

She shivered, gray eyes snagging on the empty space between them before she pressed her hands together between her knees.

"I couldn't," she admitted. "It's not..." She trailed off, unable to find the right words.

"It's not what you do," I finished for her. "You aren't a rat. I know you. You don't trust law enforcement."

She didn't reply, and I knew I was right.

"It doesn't mean I'm not pissed," she clarified. "I'm still considering cutting all your balls off and keeping them in a little trophy jar on my nightstand."

This earned her a laugh from Rook as he lifted his ass from the couch seat and drew out a blade, flipping it over in his fingers so the handle was facing her. "Here you go, love. Carve away."

She eyed the blade, but didn't take it, rolling her eyes at him.

"I'd like to keep my balls, *Rook*," Corvus said, finally coming to sit with us, putting himself next to me on the couch. He was tight as a nun's asshole. Every muscle jacked, the vein in his neck popping as he leaned over his knees, steepling his fingers. Looking at the coffee table like he wanted to hack it to kindling.

"You didn't leave," I pointed out, trying to get us back on track. I needed to know what she was doing. I needed to prepare myself for the worst. "Does that mean you're staying?"

She bit her lip. "I don't know yet."

"Stay," Corvus said, breaking a momentary silence. The one word drawing all of our attention to him.

AJ's chin quivered, just once, before she got control of herself. I wondered if I was the only one who noticed just how much we'd hurt her. How much she was hurting.

"Why should I?"

"Because," Corvus breathed, some of the tension leaking from his shoulders. "I want you to."

"So do I," I agreed.

"You know what I want," Rook intoned, grazing the back of her neck with his knuckle, making her glare at him before inching farther from him on the couch.

She considered us all for a minute, pulling her hands from between her knees to clench them into little fists. "I don't have anywhere else to go," she said in a low voice, and the urge to go and pull her into my arms almost dragged me from my seat. But I didn't think she wanted that right now.

"You belong here," Corvus said. "With us."

Her eyes darted back and forth over the coffee table. "I'll stay," she decided. "But if Diesel pulls any more shit like he did the other night, I will kill him my fucking self. I don't care who he is to you."

Rook looked away. Corvus re-stiffened. But none of us challenged her. I didn't know what that meant.

"And I'm not coming back to the Nest. I need...I need some space."

Corvus looked like he was going to blow a fuse.

"Okay if one of us stays with you here, then?" I asked before Corvus could *demand* something instead. "Especially since you don't have a phone right now?"

She nodded slowly.

I didn't know what the next little while was going to look like for us, but one thing was startlingly clear. There was trust lost. On both sides. And I wasn't sure yet if we could get it back. But if there was anything in this world worth fighting for, it had to be her.

6

AVA JADE

Their phones blew up, and it was a welcome interruption after the conversation we'd just had. After I agreed to let one of them stay with me here, a terse quiet had fallen.

I hated it.

It felt unnatural.

Something between us all had been broken, and I didn't know if it could be fixed. Still wasn't sure I wanted it to be. But what I told them was true. I didn't have any place else to go. Lennox was the last place I wanted to go back to, but where else in this world was there a place for me?

With the so-called best friend who betrayed me?

With my female Hitler of an aunt?

This was the only place I'd felt like I'd fit in so long I had to wonder if I ever felt like I fit anywhere else before this.

"What is it?" I asked as they all read the messages on their phones, noticing how their faces had turned stony.

Rook dropped his phone into my lap and I glanced between it and him before picking it up to read the message on the screen.

DIESEL

We have a meet with the Aces tonight. Sending details and location later. Be ready for 10 pm.

DIESEL

Becca Hart got on a plane this morning to
Europe, but we need her back here. She's our
only source of intel on the piece of shit who was
trying to make a move on you. Make it happen.

"I'm coming with you tonight," I decided, rising from the couch to go and discard my mug in the kitchen sink. Feeling Grey's eyes on my ass as I walked.

"I don't think that's—"

"I wasn't asking. I'm a Saint now, remember?"

Grey nudged Corvus' arm, giving his head a little shake. Telling him not to push this right now. I was willing to bet he would try to convince me to stay behind later. He wouldn't have any luck.

I needed to speak to his father. I needed to make a couple of things clear if I was going to even *try* to stay in Thorn Valley.

Corvus' nostrils flared. "Fine," he growled. "Are you coming to class?"

I lifted my head to the clock on the kitchen wall and sighed, the word *fuck* silently forming on my lips. There was already lots of noise in the hallway outside. Classes would be starting in barely twenty minutes.

"We can pick up your assignments," Grey offered, and I looked at him curiously for the second time this morning.

He was giving me this weird vibe. Like he was stepping on eggshells. Tip-toeing around me. It wasn't like him.

The air was still charged with everything said and not said. It felt fragile, like even the smallest push would send everything we'd built tumbling down to ruble and ash. I wondered if he felt it, too. If he were afraid of what might happen if he pushed too hard.

"No, I'll go," I decided. "I don't need another absence right now."

Really, I didn't need to deal with more angry texts from my psycho aunt right now. No wonder my dad never talked about her. But more than that, I wanted the distraction.

"Rook?" Grey asked, and I watched the exchange between them, wondering why Grey was offering to pick up his assignments. Why he assumed Rook wasn't going to class.

His dark eyes betrayed nothing, but he gave Grey a tight nod, lifting his gaze to me. "Mind if I stay here?"

"*Uh...*sure. I guess."

He leaned back on the couch, lifting his legs to cover the area where I'd just been sitting, laying his head on the armrest. His forearm lifted to cover his eyes.

"I'll meet you guys down there," I told the other two, going to change.

"We'll wait," Corvus decided for them both. "Hurry up."

Don't stab him. Don't stab him.

I had a mind to make them wait as long as possible, but that would only see to it that I got locked out of homeroom for being late. Though, with my new status around here, maybe I could walk in whenever I wanted. Maybe I didn't have to ever be marked absent at all.

I'd have to see about that.

For today, though, I'd behave, if only because I wanted to save myself enough time to drop into the dining hall on the way to class and swipe a bagel.

Rook didn't so much as stir when we left the apartment, and I found myself shutting the door quietly behind me, twisting the knob to avoid the catching sound of the metal.

"He isn't a newborn," Grey commented, and heat bloomed over my chest, but I didn't give him the satisfaction of my attention or a reply.

Something told me he hadn't slept last night after we parted ways in the road. I felt maybe just a little responsible for that.

The few students remaining in the hallways parted, scurrying to get out of our way as we made our way to the elevator at the end of the hall, who jabbed the button, and stepped inside.

Funny how barely a month ago I had to sneak into the thing to use it. Now it was as much mine as it was theirs.

Perks: they were the silver lining holding everything together right now.

When the doors opened with a solemn chime, the three of us froze.

Heads turned, eyes latching on. Whispers dying on parted lips.

The main atrium was filled with students, but they weren't what we couldn't stop staring at.

Pasted to every available surface in the entire space were photographs. On the banister. On the walls. Scattered over the floor.

I wasn't sure what I was seeing at first, until I knelt to lift one to inspect it more closely.

They were photographs of Rook...

And...

"Is that the vice principal?" I asked, turning the photo of their entangled naked bodies in what appeared to be the unused academy chapel. In this shot, Rook had his fist around Mrs. June's throat while he drove into her from behind, her face the picture of bliss. Her tits spilling out of her blouse over the back of a pew.

I scanned the others on the floor close to us, finding at least ten other pornographic images. I couldn't help but notice the different bits of clothing they wore. The different lighting. Proving that this wasn't a one-time thing but a *very* regular occurrence.

Corvus lifted his phone to his ear and growled down the line. "Get down here. Now."

We stepped out of the elevator, and it closed behind us.

Numbly, I lifted another two photographs to look at them more closely, hating how my stomach was twisting into knots.

"What the fuck are you staring at?" Corvus demanded, eyeing the gape mouthed students still hovering all around the atrium. He reached behind him, lifting the edge of his jacket, where the distinct shape of a gun was pressed between his jeans and his lower back.

I dropped the photos, grabbing his hand before he could draw it.

"Get the fuck out of here," I yelled, and the ones who hadn't already fled, raced to follow their wiser peers, dispersing within seconds.

Behind us, the elevator chimed again and Rook appeared, leaning lazily against the door with dark circles beneath his eyes.

Corvus bent and scooped a handful of photographs from the floor, shoving them into his stomach, putting him off balance as he grabbed them.

"The fuck, man?" he groaned, lifting them.

His surprise quickly turned to an approving smirk, his brows lifting. "Damn. Some of these are really good. I told you that camera was a good investment."

"Did you do this?" Corvus hissed, pushing Rook into the elevator to give them some privacy as the bravest of the students still lingered in the archways leading out the classrooms.

"Why the fuck would I?" Rook shoved Corvus back, tossing the photos unceremoniously on the floor. "She was useful in my back pocket. She won't be now."

"It was a power play, then?" I found myself asking aloud, needing to know.

Rook tipped his head slightly to one side as he considered me. "You worried, Ghost?"

My blood pulsed with electricity at his words, and I was wholly unable to stop myself as I reentered the elevator with them, shouldering Corvus out of my way. Making the doors chime loudly as they were kept from closing again.

"If it was a power play, then I'm impressed."

He frowned.

"But if you ever touch her again I'll have to kill her. And cut your balls off."

That frown vanished, his eyes sparking with amusement.

I could hardly believe I'd said it, but I realized I meant every word. He was mine and no one else's.

He licked his lips. "Understood."

"Good."

A bang outside the elevator made the three of us exit to where Grey still stood, watching the scene playing by the office.

The principal, a man I'd only ever seen once besides now, tried to maintain order among his staff as Mrs. June was escorted out of the office between two police officers.

She caught sight of Rook and paused, her chin beginning to quiver.

Rook pressed two fingers to his lips in a silent salute to her, not a care in the world. Mrs. June spat onto the floor in his general direction, her face going red despite the thick coating of makeup covering it. "Fuck you," she shouted. "You sick bastard!"

"You loved it," Rook called after her as the officers moved in to restrain her, dragging her from the building now as she struggled, cursing and kicking all the way.

Another officer exited the office, leaving the principal's side with his sights set on Rook. And wouldn't you fucking know it, his name badge read *Vick.*

I snorted.

He looked nothing like his phony counterpart. Round through the middle with a saucer sized bald spot on his crown that he was trying to cover with a midlife crisis toupee that looked more like roadkill.

"Sawyer Clayton," the officer said, and I sensed more than saw Rook stiffen beside me. "We have a few questions if you wouldn't mind coming down to the—"

"I would mind," he hissed. "And it's *Rook.*"

"Mr. Clayton—"

But Rook was already gone, vanishing down the north hall, likely headed straight for the exit.

Officer Vick cleared the gap between us with uneasy steps, fumbling to get a card from his pocket.

He held it out to me instead of the two guys at both of my sides.

It wasn't so long ago another Officer Vick was handing me a card. I wasn't going to fuck this up twice.

"Would you give me a call when he's ready to talk?"

I took the card he offered with a smile and tore it into four equal pieces, letting them fall to the floor to join the photographs when I was finished.

"If that's all?" I prodded when he just stared, his face going a little green around the edges.

He left without another word and a rush of pure ecstasy rushed through me, making me almost cringe at its intensity. Man, if you could bottle up that feeling and sell it...

The PA system crackled to life as the principal made an announcement to the academy from the front office.

"Good morning students, please be advised that all classes for the day have been canceled. Any due assignments are to be submitted through the online portal unless otherwise instructed by your professor. The computer lab, cafeteria, and library will remain open for your use. Thank you."

"Well, *shit.*"

Corvus and Grey were staring at me, I realized. Looking more than slightly impressed by my little spectacle with the real Vick.

I gave myself a spiritual pat on the back and shrugged. "What? I wasn't about to fuck that up twice."

Grey smirked, clearing his throat as he went back to studying the picture in his hand. The obvious question in his eyes likely the same one we were all thinking.

"These are definitely from Rook's hidden camera," Grey mused. "But if he didn't do this, then who did?"

7

CORVUS

The road to the old outpost north of Thorn Valley could be a bitch in bad weather, and right now? Right now it was absolutely *pissing* down.

I cursed Diesel for picking it as the meeting point tonight, not just for the crap location, down thirty miles of gravel road, but because there wasn't a secondary way out.

It was a dead-end at the outpost. Nowhere to go but back the way we came.

A great tactic if you didn't think you'd need to make a hasty getaway, but tonight, all bets were off. If Lenny Ace admitted the little bitch who'd been grooming Becca was doing so at his command, Diesel would put two pieces of lead between his eyes.

It would either be them leaving here tonight, or us.

Maybe Diesel was counting on that.

But if Lenny Ace had half a fucking brain, he wouldn't even come here tonight unless it was because he thought we could part ways without bloodshed. He had to know if it came to blood, they wouldn't stand a chance. Their larger numbers be damned.

No one fucked with the Saints and lived. Not after Mom died. And especially not when the supposed target this go 'round was Diesel St. Crow's sons.

The wipers slashed across the windshield, and I squinted to see through them, getting tense on Grey's behalf even though he looked calm as ever as he maneuvered us toward the meet point. Deftly avoiding potholes and sections of washed out road as the rain beat out a pelting rhythm on the roof of the Rover.

"Does anyone have a phone I can use?" Ava Jade asked from the backseat.

"What for?"

Behind me, the whiskey in Rook's flask sloshed for the eighth time since we'd left Briar Hall, signaling another swig. He didn't bother answering Ava Jade, and I had a feeling he was still on the edge from earlier.

No one called Rook Clayton by his given name.

No one except his bastard uncle and the people at the sanitorium where they'd stuck him when they couldn't handle him at the group home.

There was a reason he couldn't stand the sound of it.

Much like certain words and symbols triggered memories from my past, and an empty refrigerator triggered Grey, it was Rook's own name that triggered him.

"I don't have a phone," Ava Jade reminded me. "I just want to check socials and my email."

"Becca?" I asked, not really expecting a response. I'd tried to talk to her about it earlier, but she'd shut me down. Diesel was right though, we needed the intel only Becca could give us. Like what the guy looked like, and whether he had any discernible tattoos. And everything he'd ever said to her.

"You can use mine," Grey offered, but I was already lifting my ass from the seat to pull mine from my back pocket.

I slipped it to her between the seats, taking in her narrowed eyes.

She didn't think it would be me who offered.

Why not?

It wasn't like there was anything to find.

"Two, Seven, Four, One," I told her as she took it. "That's the code. Don't forget to sign out and wipe the history."

"No shit."

I watched her in the rearview as her thumbs tapped over the screen, the blue light deepening the shadows of her sharply angled features.

Ava Jade Mason.

My Sparrow.

My undoing.

I couldn't believe what went on with her and Diesel's cop bait, and the only thing that kept me half-sane was thinking that she never would've gone through with it. That she knew she wouldn't from the very fucking start, but needed to feel in control.

Like me.

Having that option in her back pocket and knowing that she *could* use it if she wanted to was what she needed to get through the rest of it all.

She chose us, I reminded myself, the sick feeling turning my stomach again.

I cracked the window, making Rook snort behind me, annoyed when some rain flung back at him without warning. But he didn't tell me to roll it up.

Good, because I needed it.

It helped to distract myself with other thoughts. Like whether or not I should install some form of tracking device on the new cell phone I ordered for her late last night.

If I could get away with it, I probably wouldn't have given it a second thought, but I knew she would strip the thing and search it inside and out. That was, if she even agreed to take it from me in the first place. It was a healthy step up from the usual burners. The newest model, actually.

Better even than my own phone.

At least now her stalker would have no access whatsoever to her number.

My teeth clamped tight at the reminder, and I breathed deeply through my nose of the rain-scented air to regain the calm I needed to get through this fucking meeting.

With any luck, the motherfucker who'd tried to inject her was already dead, but something told me it wasn't that simple. Especially after what happened at Briar Hall this morning.

It could've been the Aces, sure. But that didn't sit right.

Ava Jade slipped the phone back to me over the seat, our fingers brushing before she pulled back from the contact.

"Anything interesting?" I prodded.

"Wouldn't you like to know."

"*Sparrow...*"

She sighed, exasperated as she leaned back in her seat, swiping Rook's flask away for a little swig. He didn't seem bothered, but took it back from her as soon as she was finished. "Nothing from creepy stalker fucker if that's what you're wondering. He was a text guy though, remember?"

"*Was,*" I emphasized. "Not sure he's going to like not being able to communicate with you anymore."

"If he's even alive," Grey grumbled from the driver's seat.

"Good," Ava Jade said. "Either way I won't have to deal with being skeeved out every fucking time my phone chimes."

"This is it," Grey said as he pulled us around the last bend in the road to the sleepy little building nestled in the woods. It was a ranger's cabin once, before they built a more modern one thirty miles south.

No one used this one now except hikers looking for a night's refuge or someplace warm and dry to escape a storm. The shit brown siding was riddled with graffiti, but no gang tags. None that mattered anyway. This was just as neutral as Nomansland and a meeting place we'd used on other occasions several times over the last two years.

Diesel was already there, sitting in a plateless black truck idling in the wide drive. It looked like Tiny was beside him in the passenger seat, though it was hard to tell in the rain, and as Grey pulled us around to the other side, we saw the nondescript dark green van next to him.

No doubt filled with at least five more Saints if not more than that.

This location made me uneasy. Unlike usual, we didn't get the details ahead of time. Didn't have a say. We got jack shit from Diesel, actually, besides the time and location at the last minute.

He didn't want help setting it up, and he didn't even reply to my text cautioning him against meeting right now. This soon after finding out about the snake.

We'd be showing them our cards instead of trying to use what we knew to figure out what cards they were trying to play. Not to mention we had a dead Saint to bury, and I had it on good authority from Pinkie that Dies was told he should stay off his feet for at least ten days to let the knife wound to his Achilles heal.

I knew he wasn't thrilled with what happened back at the Docks, but I had to wonder how long he intended to punish us.

I bent my head, grimacing as an ache formed in my skull.

"I still can't believe you insisted on coming tonight," I found myself saying out loud.

Diesel wasn't going to like this, but he hadn't said *not* to bring her. What he did say was to watch her. How else were we supposed to do that if he asked us all to come out here?

"This is what you wanted," Ava Jade said plainly. "Remember?"

Grey flinched at that, but none of us contradicted her. Whether it was Grey who did the asking or not for her to take the trials, it was a fact that every single one of us wanted that same thing. It was better than the alternative.

"Get out," I told her. "I have something for you in the back."

I stepped out into the rain, bristling as the chilled droplets snaked through my hair, dripping down the back of my neck, bringing my focus back.

Her door opened, and she rushed to the trunk, squinting through the rain, her arms wrapped around herself as the rain soaked through her black long sleeve shirt.

I took out the vest I'd purchased for her more than a week ago, though it only just arrived this morning. It was the closest one to her size I could find. The adjustable straps should ensure it was a snug fit.

"Put this on."

She looked between me and the bulletproof vest. She hadn't been expecting this.

Her hesitation was making me grind my teeth again. They'd be worn down to stumps in no time if she kept being so damned stubborn about every little thing.

I lifted the edge of my grey t-shirt, showing her mine beneath it. Everyone here would be wearing one tonight. Except for Rook, who never wore one no matter how much we tried to push him into it. He had the bullet holes to prove it, but not even those could persuade him. He wore each one like a trophy. A time where death could've come for him but didn't.

"Just put it on, Sparrow."

She relented, stripping off her shirt without another word to lay it in the trunk, her skin reflecting the moonlight, bathed in rainwater. The tops of her breasts prickled with gooseflesh.

I adjusted my stance to block her from the view of the van as she turned around to slide her arms through. I helped her get it on and adjusted and then tugged her damp shirt back on over top of it.

Though nearly everyone here would be wearing one, it was bad form to show it. This was a courtesy meeting after all. Wearing a bullet-proof vest meant you expected blood. And if you expected blood, you would often find it.

"It's still visible," she said, trying to adjust her shirt so it would cover the top part of the vest covering her perfect tits, but it was no use. I slipped off my leather jacket and flicked off the rain before settling it around her shoulders.

"Zip it up. No one will know."

She touched the collar delicately for a second, like she wasn't quite sure what to do, and the urge to push her up against the Rover and punish her for everything she'd put us through almost took me. But then she zipped it up like I told her to do and gave me a taut nod. She looked amazing in it.

"Good girl."

She bit her lip.

Jesus fuck.

The rain started to let up, and I heard the truck door open, instinctively stepping forward to put myself in front of Ava Jade. She made a sound of annoyance at my tiny shove but didn't fight me.

No. She just stepped back around me to put herself directly at my side as Diesel appeared outside the truck, shrugging his worn jacket to pop the collar as a defense against what remained of the rain.

Grey and Rook got out of the Rover, coming to stand with us.

Diesel didn't seem the least bit surprised to see Ava Jade there as he pulled a long stick from the truck seat and set it on the ground.

A cane.

I felt Ava Jade stiffen beside me as Diesel approached us, using the sleek black cane to hold the majority of his weight.

He stopped a few feet away.

"What's the—" I started, but he interrupted me.

"You're here," he said, sniffing, his icy gaze fixed on my Sparrow. "Good."

Good?

What?

"After you threatened Rick, I wasn't sure you were with us."

She'd done what? Rick was our tattoo guy, owned a local shop in town. Had Dies already sent him to her? And she'd clearly refused the ink. It wasn't negotiable.

Ava Jade jutted out her chin, offering no explanation.

"You must've been very tired," Diesel said, looking at her as though she were a wounded little girl in need of coddling. I wanted to tell him if he looked at her like that for even another second, she was going to attempt to gouge his eyeballs out but that would only make matters worse.

Instead, I covertly wound my fingers around her wrist, feeling her tendons taut as a whip with her hand balled into a fist.

"Not tired enough not to make good on what I promised him."

Diesel's jaw ticked. "You need to be inked next time, or you won't be welcome."

I squeezed her wrist tighter. *Calm down.*

"Anyway," Diesel said, inhaling deeply, the moment past. Time for a subject change. He jerked his head at Pinkie, who stepped forward to hand Ava Jade a white cloth.

More like dumped it into her hands.

The clatter of metal told us what was inside.

She unwrapped her blades, the ones she'd lost back at the warehouse. "Thought you'd be wanting those back."

Her fingers curled protectively around them. She offered Diesel nothing, just a strained nod by way of thanks even though they appeared to have been cleaned and sharpened by our blade guy.

I doubted the gesture would have the effect he hoped for with Ava Jade, though. I doubted she liked other people touching her blades, never mind honing them for her.

The others from the van exited now, forming a semi-circle of six behind Diesel and Tiny.

I didn't like the way they were looking at Ava Jade. Like she was an outsider. Like they wanted to...

If Garrett hadn't been a newer implant into the gang, Ava Jade would've been in for a lot more than some hateful stares for killing him.

It's a truth universally known among us that people died during the trials, but usually it was the ones taking the trials, not the ones administering them. It wasn't the first time it'd happened, but it definitely wasn't common.

There was a reason we'd told Ava Jade to try not to kill anyone.

It would take her twice as long to earn their trust—their respect—now, if she ever got it. There was also the matter of her having a different set of *parts* to consider. There were only two female gang members I'd ever heard of besides Ava Jade and it'd taken them years to earn their places.

"What's the plan?" I asked when the silence stretched on.

Diesel tipped his head to the cabin. "You four inside. Pinkie and Tiny, you're with me inside, too. Axel, I want you in the driver's seat of the van, don't budge. Derrik, Crowley, Shane, and Lee, you're in the woods. Watch their entry, warn us if they're packing more than they should be. If Lenny Ace leaves the cabin before me, light him the fuck up."

So it was like that.

Ava Jade snatched her wrist back from me while everyone's attention was elsewhere, sending me a scathing glare.

"Everyone got it?"

A chorus of *yeah boss,* and *let's get it done* rising up all around as the rain finally let up.

Four of our men dispersed into the tree line, vanishing into the shadows, careful of where they stepped to leave no boot prints in the muddy roadway. Axel went back to the van, seeming unhappy with his assignment, but they all respected Diesel. Each one knew that if they followed his orders as he spoke them with no room for interpretation, their chances of surviving until another sunrise were a lot fucking better than if they didn't.

The graves of the outliers proved that, without the need for Dies to throw his weight around.

"Arm up if you aren't already," he told us, and Ava Jade made a show of slipping her blades into the empty places on her ankle sheath and into the new knife slot at the top of her bulletproof vest beneath her shirt.

Diesel watched with a raised brow, and I knew what he was thinking, but he wouldn't say it. She needed a gun. He was only half right about that.

"Let's head inside. They'll be here soon."

We fell into step behind Dies and Tiny, but there was something else bothering me about this whole thing. Probably because he didn't bother to give details about anything to do with tonight's meet even though he knew how it would drive me to the brink of fucking insanity to not know.

"What exactly do you expect to get out of tonight?" I asked, making Diesel pause briefly at the bottom of the short staircase leading up to the front door of the old cabin.

He turned, just enough for me to see the twisted side profile of his face.

"The truth. Either they give it to me, or they live *and die* with the consequences of that choice."

8

AVA JADE

Headlights poured across the weatherworn floor of the cabin as the Aces approached the meet point.

Three cars, I counted as their headlights passed over the front window one by one. Heavy vehicles. Trucks and vans like the ones Dies and the others drove in on by the sounds of their tires as they hit deep potholes and drove over sections of puddled road.

Diesel rolled his shoulders back and lengthened his spine, hiding a wince as he passed the cane to Tiny.

"Boss, you heard what the vet said—"

"Get rid of it."

Without another word of protest, the Saint took two steps to his right and chucked the cane out the shattered back window of the cabin.

Diesel adjusted his footing before taking two steps forward and then three steps back. Testing his ability to appear uninjured.

He did a damn good job of it, but I knew it wouldn't be without a monstrous amount of effort that his face stayed placid as a lake. I'd done a damn good job of fucking up his Achilles, and if he kept walking on it, it wouldn't ever heal properly. I was no doctor, but I was pretty sure he'd wind up with a limp for the rest of his life doing that.

Though, I understood his need to appear strong. Especially now.

I caught his gaze flick to me as he returned back to his place,

553

standing elbow to elbow with the rest of us to the far right side of the cabin. This side had the only window other than the one next to the front door and therefore the only side with an alternate means of escape.

Though the other side was more heavily strewn with old discarded furniture that could prove useful as cover if it came to a gunfight.

With Rook and Grey beside me, I felt an odd sense of responsibility for them. Like, if something happened to them it would be at least partially my fault as the person who was at their side. Meant to have their back. Meant to cover them from fire.

From their tension and the way they both inched ever so slightly nearer to my sides as the sounds of heavy thudding footfalls ascended the stairs outside, I knew they felt similarly.

I counted the footsteps.

Eight of them coming inside. Another five? Maybe six waiting outside by the idling vehicles.

We were six in here.

Eleven in total.

Decent odds for normal people.

Fucking amazing odds for us. I knew I could take at least four before they saw me coming. And my guys? They could easily handle the rest, Diesel or no Diesel.

My own certainty surprised me, but I felt it like a truth carved into my bones, and lifted my chin as the Aces entered.

I clocked weapons as they came in. Finding the tactical edges of bulletproof vests poking out from under collars and sleeves. They were ready for this to go south, too.

Nothing bigger than a handgun, though, unless someone had a particularly deep anal cavity.

I searched the faces of the Aces here tonight, trying to decide which one could've been Becca's beau. The man who'd manipulated and conned her. The one who was after my Crows.

Their eyes betrayed nothing.

The man from that night in the yard of the warehouse emerged from the group, putting himself at a slight lead from the others at his back. Diesel did the same.

I recognized him easily enough. He had a distinct look about him. A thin, angular face with coiffed hair that made him appear taller than he was. And suddenly I was back there, knelt down in the shadows of the trees, watching as Lenny Ace and Diesel St. Crow spoke. As the Ace on the end of the row eyed Corvus, his trigger finger twitching.

It was that one thing that sealed my fate. If that other Ace hadn't tried to kill Corvus... If I hadn't saved his life.

I might not be here right now.

"Lenny," Diesel said.

"Diesel. To what do I owe the pleasure?"

Lenny sounded bored. Almost annoyed. It was clear from his tone he wasn't happy to be here. That it was a major inconvenience.

Not the sort of tone Diesel St. Crow would take kindly to.

"Have you nothing for me, then?" Diesel pressed, his hard stare unwavering on Lenny Ace.

Lenny had the decency to look confused at the question. "Should I?"

Diesel bristled, and I thought he was going to end this meeting right here and now in a hail of gunfire, but then the atmosphere around him shifted. The switch reminded me of something—someone—else, and I glanced at Corvus, finding the same practiced restraint in his features and stature.

"You have nothing to prove your man's death is on us," Lenny continued when Diesel didn't give him the courtesy of a reply.

"And you have nothing to prove it wasn't," Diesel continued, and it took me a moment to realize they were continuing the conversation from all that time ago at the warehouse. About the guy The Crows found dead in Thorn Valley...with an A carved into his chest?

I didn't know the particulars. Only what I picked up on from my bug and what I'd heard since.

"It was probably Devon," someone else behind Lenny piped up. "He was always a loose cannon."

Lenny turned his head slowly, and the look in his eyes promised a slow death to the man who spoke if he said another word.

He shut up.

"Convenient then, since he's buried on the spot where he tried to shoot Corvus and can't defend himself," I couldn't help saying.

Lenny's blue-eyed gaze found me for the first time since they entered, analyzing me from the top down.

"Who the fuck is this?"

"That's not your concern," Diesel replied. "And I didn't ask you here tonight to talk about Randy, though I still think there's something to be spoken to about his death."

"Then what *did* you ask me here for?"

The Aces tensed behind their leader, anticipating a fight.

I could feel it, too. Like electricity in the air that I could taste if I just flicked my tongue out to touch it. My blood hummed with it. With the possibility that tonight, I might kill a man. And fuck if I wasn't looking forward to it. That inner darkness thirsting for violence.

Rook made a low sound in his throat next to me, and I inched my hand to move to the side, brushing my knuckles with his, feeling a static shock. His dark eyes gleamed in the low light, and I knew he was feeling it, too.

"One of your men is out to get my boys."

A dark laugh rattled out of Lenny's chest as he shook his head, dropping it to pinch the bridge of his nose like something Diesel said was funny.

I didn't find it fucking funny.

My fingers flinched, pulling away from Rook's to hover at my side, ready to spring for a blade.

"You're paranoid, old man," Lenny said, sighing. "No one is messing with you. No one is after your sons. At least, not *my* crew. I'd start looking to your enemies, there is where you'll find—"

"Maybe you didn't hear me," Diesel interrupted Lenny. "*One of your men is out to get my fucking sons.* It wasn't a question. It isn't a suspicion. It's a fact."

Lenny's lips pressed tight. "If you truly believed that, we wouldn't be talking right now."

"The only reason we are is because I'm giving you the benefit of the doubt, Lenny. I'm not making your insides your outsides right now because I recognize it might be one of your men acting independently and not on your command."

"Diesel—"

"I'm not finished. Either you have something to do with it and you have a death wish, or one of your men, someone you trust, is working an angle without your knowledge."

Lenny's face was growing redder by the second. Unlike Diesel, he was wholly unable to keep his emotions from playing on his face. And right now, he was angry. Feeling disrespected. I had an urge to push him a little more to see how he might react.

I opened my mouth to do just that, but Grey stepped on my foot. The slight shake of his head the only hint he knew what I'd been about to do.

"You're wrong, Dies," Lenny said.

"I'm not. I have the proof I need; what I don't have is a name."

"I can't give you what I don't have."

"You have ten days to give me that name," Diesel continued, ignoring Lenny completely. "Give him up and declare peace or you renounce your territory claim and *leave*."

"Excuse me?" Lenny scoffed. "We've held that territory since my grandfather—"

"I don't care if you've held it since the dawn of time. You give him up, or you better get as far away from northern Cali as you can go."

Lenny stepped forward, cinching the gap between himself and Diesel. To Diesel's credit, he didn't so much as balk at the advance. Actually, he smiled.

It was worse than when he was expressionless. Much worse.

"And if we don't?" Lenny asked, a muscle in his upper lip twitching as he snarled.

"Then you have chosen the path of violence, and we will not hold back."

Diesel lifted his hand in a circular motion, and Grey tugged me to follow him from the cabin.

My head pounded with the throb of unspent adrenaline in my veins as we exited back out into the damp night. I stayed by the door until Rook was outside. Diesel and Corvus were the last ones to leave, and I didn't fall back into step until Corvus tugged me to him, making me follow beside him instead of behind.

I didn't trust them.

There was a vibe there. I couldn't explain it, but I knew there was something more to this feud than what it appeared on the surface. If I was right, it wasn't going to take much more for the tenuous truce to snap.

Before there was all out war on the streets.

A sharp whistle and Diesel's other men exited the tree line, surprising the small gathering of Aces waiting by the idling vehicles on the left side of the parking lot.

They strode past them like wraiths and the Aces watched as they hopped into the van with Axel, silent.

"Get back to Sanctum. I want you combing over those tapes for *anything* we can use," Diesel told Pinkie. "Go with the others."

Pinkie nodded before going to the van.

"I want the rest of you ready. Wait for my orders at Sanctum."

"Where you going, boss?" one of them asked as Corvus continued to drag me slowly to the Rover.

Diesel's eyes found mine, and I stopped short, dragging Corvus to a stop with me.

"I'm following my sons back to the Nest," Diesel told him. "I need to have a little chat with our newest member."

The van door slammed and the engine turned.

Diesel held my stare for another moment before his eyes flicked to Corvus and then to Rook and Grey. "You make no stops. We don't need to give them any advantage or opportunity. Got it?"

"Yeah," Corvus replied gruffly. "I got it."

There were no surprises on the route home, though I half expected an ambush, and by midnight, we were pulling up alongside the Nest with Diesel's headlights bouncing behind us.

"He's going to want the intel only Becca can give us," Grey said solemnly as he shut off the engine. "He'll want you to get it."

"I know."

Grey twisted in his seat to see me in the back, trying to gauge something from my stare. Perhaps whether or not I would comply. I wasn't yet sure if I would either, so it was anyone's guess.

Depended on how Diesel did the asking and whether or not he would agree to certain...*stipulations.*

I knew from the email Becca sent six hours ago that she landed, was safe, and had gotten rid of her phone like I told her to. It put me at least moderately at ease to know she was so far away. Out of his reach. Well, maybe not entirely, I didn't know how large his web of contacts expanded, but I was counting on it not being large enough to reach her there. At least not this quickly.

Diesel's headlights behind us blinked off, and we all stepped out of the Rover, meeting him outside.

"Here," Grey said, going to Diesel's side to try to take his arm, take some of the weight off his injured ankle. "Come on, I think we might have something you can use for a—"

"I'm good." Diesel waved him off, walking alone unassisted instead, though he was no longer trying to hide his limp. "It's splinted."

"You still shouldn't be walking on it," Corvus said, agreeing with Grey, but Diesel ignored both of them as he passed, making for the front door.

"You want to help? Stop yapping and let me in so I can sit down."

Corvus opened the door for Diesel, and we all followed him through the dark house to the living room, flicking light switches as we went. All of us on edge as the rooms each lit up in turn, as though there might be monsters waiting in the shadows. Because...there might be. Not the kind with big scary teeth and claws, but the kind with guns, or in my case, syringes full of fucking sedatives.

I only allowed myself to partially relax once we were all seated in the living room. I thought about trying to get out of joining this little chat, but knew Diesel would only insist if I tried.

Awkward didn't even begin to describe the atmosphere in the living room in the minute between sitting down and when someone decided to break the silence.

"Want a whiskey?" Grey offered Diesel, pushing the low coffee table nearer to him so that he could lift his leg to rest on its edge.

"No."

"Fuck yes."

Diesel and Rook said at the same time.

Grey's face screwed up into a sneer at his brother. "Dude. Get it yourself."

Rook huffed as he pushed off from the sofa next to me and went to the kitchen, the sound of rattling glass and tinkling ice the only thing to be heard until he returned.

"No need for small talk then," Diesel said, his eyes roving over each of his boys with a flicker of disappointment before they settled on me. "We need intel only Rebecca Hart can give us. I know she skipped town. I have a rough idea where she is and the area gets narrowed down by the hour. I have no interest in sending my people in to get her, but I need her back here. Now."

I rolled around his words in my mouth, contemplating spitting each one back in his face.

"I won't tell her to come back here, if that's what you're asking. Not without guarantees."

Diesel sat back on his cushion, extending his arms wide over the back of the couch so his reach nearly touched Corvus and Grey spread out far at his sides near the edges of the sofa. "What kind of guarantees?"

"Her safety, for one."

"Is that all?"

"No."

He waited.

"You want to speak to her at all? You have questions for her? They go through me. You've traumatized her enough."

A muscle in his temple bulged.

"And I can ask said questions on your behalf while she's away. There's no need for her to come back here."

Not until I'm certain I can trust you, I wanted to add, but didn't. We both knew that was unlikely to happen. Ever.

"And if I need her to ID a face?"

"I'll send her a pic."

Fucking obviously.

"When the heat's died down and whoever this fucker is, is six feet under *then* I'll tell Becca it's safe to come back to Thorn Valley. She shouldn't be here right now. The man who was using her for intel knows just as well as we do that she is the only person who can ID him. Who has information that could lead to us finding him."

I let him fill in the blanks. If Becca came back here, it wasn't just Diesel she had to be afraid of but also *him.*

"I won't bring her back here to die. You can't ask me to do that. No matter the reason why."

He held my stare for a long moment. "You care for this girl? Even after what she did to you? Could've done to them?"

He indicated his sons.

"I didn't say I forgave her," I corrected him. "But there's a difference between making a mistake and a calculated move."

He nodded quietly to himself, and I knew he had to see some reason in what I'd said. What good would Becca be to him if the man who was grooming her got to her before we did? Before she could ID him?

"All right."

"All right?"

"We do it your way. She have good security where she is?"

A vivid image of the man whose voice played over the tapes in the warehouse attacking Becca in her European flat flashed in my mind. "I'll make sure she does."

Another nod. "I want an established line of contact between you and her by tomorrow, and I'll have a list of questions by morning."

Had we just come to an agreement without blood spilling?

Damn.

I'd be more surprised if it weren't for knowing the ultimate—and mutual—goal here was the assured safety of his sons. It was the one thing I thought that could force us to work together.

"Want me to drive you back?" Grey asked, pushing up from his knees. "We can get rid of the truck for you."

Grey's face had remained impassive all night, and I got the distinct feeling that a war was waging beneath his carefully painted mask. He wasn't just walking on eggshells with me. He was doing the same with his adoptive father.

It made my heart hurt to watch him.

"We aren't finished," Diesel said, staring at Grey until he sat back down. "There's something else, and I wanted to bring it to you three before I put it to a vote with the others."

Three.

So, not me then.

Noted.

This had Rook sitting up, his whiskey dangling from his fingers between his legs, forgotten for the moment. "Total annihilation?"

Diesel faced him with the smallest of smirks at the edge of his mouth. "No, Son, not yet."

Rook grunted and sat back again. His excitement gone.

"I want to ally with the Kings."

"What?" Corvus roared, his head whipping around to face his father. "Why the fuck would we do that? We've never allied with anyone and there's a fucking reason for that."

"We trust our own," Rook added. "No one else."

"That's what you taught us," Grey echoed their opinion.

Diesel's light eyes found mine for an instant, and I wondered if he waited for my opinion. I couldn't give it.

The Kings.

They were the reigning gang on the streets of Lennox, my hometown.

I suspected they were also to blame for the death of my father. He was borrowing money from someone. He'd told me as much in so many words. I knew he was in over his head. I just wished I'd acted sooner.

I wished I tried harder to break him of the habit that killed him.

Wishing never got me anywhere.

They continued to argue, and I felt the tension in my shoulders wind until it was close to snapping, every muscle across my back burning like I was standing on a pyre instead of sitting in a living room discussing a treaty with the enemy.

Huh.

Keep your enemies close...

If the Kings allied with the Saints then I might get the chance to find out what happened to my father. Who killed him. And return the favor.

I'd always known that vengeance would be mine someday, but this? This could be the opportunity I needed to follow through.

My stomach fluttered at the thought of King's blood all over my hands.

"He's right," I interrupted something Grey was saying. "If the Saints don't ally with the Kings then the Aces might."

It was what Diesel was trying to tell them if what I heard in pieces while plotting my own revenge was any indication. But I needed to put it to them plainer.

This needed to happen.

"If the Aces and Kings join together it'll be a lot worse for us. A much, *much* bigger mess to clean up if things go south, and I think we all know that's exactly where this is headed. There will be more loss of life. It's the logical move."

I focused my attention squarely on Diesel now. "You should do it. Now. Before the Aces do."

He considered me as though seeing me in a new light. Maybe one he didn't particularly loathe. I had to wonder why he didn't shut me up. He clearly had no desire to hear my take.

He's learning, I thought. Watching and learning. Seeing how my addition to this threesome would affect his future with his sons. How he could use it to his advantage. Weighing the risk versus the potential rewards.

This man was far more cunning than I gave him credit for. He knew when to speak. When to throw his weight. And when to be quiet; a thing most men in positions of power never quite learned.

Diesel looked around the room at his sons. "Boys?"

"I don't like it," Rook said, sneering as he finished his whiskey. It wasn't a clear cut opposition.

"Neither do I," Corvus agreed, but he, too, was already nodding, his sights on me. "But they have a point."

"Grey?" Diesel pushed. "I need the green light on this from all three of you before I'll move on it."

Grey's brows knotted.

"We form the alliance," Grey said, casting the deciding vote. "But as a means to prevent them from joining with the Aces. I don't want to work with them. Not unless we have to."

That would make my plans more difficult, but I'd still take the win.

"Agreed," Diesel said, and winced as he brought his leg down from the table. The bandage poking out from beneath the hem of his jeans was soaked through with crimson.

I guess we really weren't going to talk about *that.* Or the million other things still left unsaid between us over the past weeks. It was probably for the best. If we started talking, I wasn't sure I'd be able to keep talking from becoming *stabbing.*

He hopped to his feet, and Grey got up to follow him.

"Stay," he told Grey, and his son obediently sat back down.

Diesel paused in the doorway to the kitchen. "Oh. There was just one last thing."

There was more?

"That business at Briar Hall this morning? What was that about?"

Of course he would know about that, though it didn't keep me from wondering exactly *how* he knew.

"Just some cunt fucking around. Probably a prank. Doesn't seem like the Ace's style."

Diesel shook his head. "No. Not their usual MO, but my guys are looking into it anyway."

"I got this," Corvus said, his shoulders flexing.

"Do you?" Diesel asked him. "Remember who runs those halls, son. Things like that can't go unpunished. Clean it up."

Corv nodded, and Diesel's gaze strayed to me. To the blade I was unconsciously twirling between my fingers as I thought of brutal ways to use it against our mutual enemies and some of my own.

"And for the love of god, someone teach her how to use a fucking gun."

Diesel left, but it did little to fix the knots in my stomach or the ones still burning across my back.

I stood.

"Where are you going?" Corvus demanded.

"Back to Briar Hall."

"For what? It'll be dawn in a couple hours. Not like you're going to sleep."

He wasn't wrong.

"I have an idea," Rook said, licking his lips as he rose from the couch, trying to dump the last few drops of his whiskey down his throat.

Corvus blanched, and I got the sense that when Rook had an *idea* it didn't always end well.

"Let's blow off some steam, yeah?"

He brushed past my shoulder on his way to the kitchen, his warmth and scent flooding all my senses.

"You coming?" he called from the front door, and the rest of us shared a look before following him from the Nest.

Anything was better than staring at the ceiling for the next four hours, right?

9

ROOK

"*Fuuuuckk*," Ava Jade screamed with a smile as Grey cranked the wheel, whipping the old Volvo around a stack of tires in the middle of the massive field. Making her press hard into my side in the backseat, sucked close from the g-force as we spun out.

Grey didn't let the car stop for even a second, turning the wheel hard and gunning it until we fishtailed out of the spin and were barreling over the dry dirt and patchy grass again.

"Why didn't you take me here before?" Ghost called over the roar of the engine and the music blasting from the speakers, completely at ease without a seatbelt in the middle of the backseat as Grey drove us at double the legal limit over uneven terrain. She held herself from being sucked back with hands gripping the edges of the front seat, legs spread wide like she was riding a bull instead of a backseat.

I licked my lips. "Crank it!" I ordered Grey, and he cut the wheel, throwing Ava Jade back into my lap before she could adjust her hold. I caught her before she could smash her head into the window, running a possessive hand down her side to grip the inside of her thigh.

She looked up at me in the dark, eyes gleaming with danger, and smiled.

I knew this was a good idea. We hadn't been up here to rally the cars in ages. Not since the night we found Randy's body.

"Shit, Grey," Corvus hissed from the front seat, and I realized he wasn't as lucky as Ava Jade, his head having knocked into the window.

He rolled it down, letting a blast of cool wind into the car as Grey kept going, taking hard turns and speeding so fast it made Ava Jade squeal.

I didn't think I'd ever seen her so alive. So blissfully empty of all her darkness if only for just a moment.

She pushed away from me and tipped her head back, howling like a wolf, her back arched to the wind, arms spread wide, eyes shut. Either she trusted Grey's control of the vehicle implicitly or she didn't care if we crashed.

I knew I didn't.

Sometimes I craved it.

Imagining the press of cold steel as it fed through my flesh, twisted with my bones. If it weren't for my brothers in the car, I just might give in to that tiny voice whispering *what if you just let go of the wheel.* I supposed it was a good thing they didn't let me drive.

"What is that?" Ava Jade shouted, leaning over the center console to point out the windshield, far into the distance at the jump we built last summer. The old property Diesel bought three years back was nearly a hundred acres of empty fields with nothing in any direction for miles. We'd been making it into our playground every chance we got. And that jump was one of three that were complete. The others, not so much.

It was the smallest of the three, but still a rush at fifteen feet.

Grey jerked his gaze to Corvus, and my eldest brother nodded, giving him permission. A small grin pinning up one edge of his mouth.

"You should hold on to something, Sparrow."

She braced herself on the seats again, widening her legs as she planted her feet firm against the floor.

Grey switched gears and pushed the Volvo to its max, the night time landscape rushing by in a blur of dark shapes. I let the pull of danger wake and tame the black thing rumbling deep within. Tipping my head back as the cold wind stroked it. As the g-force made it quiver.

My hand found the inside of Ava Jade's thigh and skated higher.

Her eyes found mine as Grey sped us to the ramp, shifting gears every second. She held my gaze there as I pressed my hand flat against her cunt through her jeans, feeling her warmth.

She shuddered as my fingers began to rub and the ramp came into full view in the dim headlights out the front windshield.

"Hold on!" Grey shouted, and I took it literally, squeezing her juicy little cunt hard so she tried to squeeze her thighs closed, her lips popping open in surprise as the Volvo hit the base of the ramp, thrusting us into the air.

For one blissful, weightless second, we floated, the dark becoming an ocean, the wind its waves.

Ava Jade's hair lifted from her shoulders as the car dropped, and there was that one second of complete silence before the front tires hit the ground. The Volvo jerked and Ava Jade was violently tossed to one side of the car, her cunt slipping free of my grasp as she barreled into the opposite door *hard* and came up laughing like a maniac as the tires spat dirt until we were at a stop.

I could see her pulse thudding in her neck, quick and steady. Not frantic.

Just like mine.

She caught me staring and licked her lips, her gaze alighting on the hand that'd been firmly attached to her just a second ago.

I grinned at her wickedly.

"We have to do that again," she said, breathless, shouting over the spluttering radio.

She perked up, spinning away from me to push out of the Volvo. She opened the driver's side door next. "Get out," she told Grey. "I want to drive."

Hairline cracks formed in Grey's confident smile.

"Fuck no," Corvus said, turning down the music. "Get back in."

She planted her hands on her hips and continued to stare at Grey. I kicked his seat. "You heard the woman, get the fuck out and let her drive."

I dug my whiskey bottle from the bottom of Corvus' seat, happy to find it still intact, and took a pull, relishing the burn.

"Not tonight," Corvus said, giving me a pointed look through the cracked side mirror, but Grey was already getting out of the car, spreading his arms wide with a flourish.

"Your chariot?"

"Why, thank you," she replied, slipping into the seat, her hands caressing the wheel. I could see the goosebumps on her arms from here. Each peachy blonde hair raised like she was brimming with electricity —energy that needed an outlet. Right now, this was it.

"Come on, Corv," she said, nudging him with her elbow. "I think you kind of owe me. Live a little with us, please?"

He inhaled, face pinching. "Fine. No hero shit, though. I mean it. Leave that to the professionals."

Grey smirked at the insinuation as he slid into the back with me. He seemed out of place in the seat, and I could honestly say I couldn't remember a time I'd ever seen him not up front.

He seemed just as weirded out by it as me, looking around and trying to find a place to put his feet comfortably.

"Put your fucking seatbelts on."

I rolled my eyes at Corvus, shaking my head at Grey as he and Corvus buckled themselves in.

"Where's the faith?" Ava Jade asked, rolling her eyes when Corvus reached across her body to yank down her seatbelt, notching it in despite her protest.

"You can drive stick, right?" Grey asked as Ava Jade adjusted her seat.

She shrugged. "Guess we'll find out."

"Are you fucking ser—"

Whatever Corvus had been about to say was cut short as Ghost gunned the engine, the tires spinning on the spot for a second before she threw it into second gear and tore off downfield with a holler, turning the music back up between shifting gears.

The Volvo bumped over the uneven terrain as she leaned forward in her seat, squinting out the windshield to see as the night sky began to brighten, bruised by the purples and pinks of a new day.

The engine groaned as she pushed it to its limits, axels near snapping as she cut hard corners and nearly hit the fucking shed where the other old beaters and some guns and ammunition were stored.

Corv gripped the holy shit handle like his life depended on. Grey's face turned ashen after barely five minutes.

I elbowed him. "Corv is the one with control issues. Relax. Enjoy the motherfuckin' ride, Brother."

He swallowed, taking the bottle of whiskey when I offered it for a quick swig. He shook his head, grimacing, but it did the trick to help ease the tension through his shoulders, and I polished off the last of it before chucking the bottle through the window as far as she would go.

The car dragged to a stop as Ghost finished a round of doughnuts that left a massive circular tread in the field. But the look in her eyes told me she was far from finished.

Her breath caught.

"What?" Corvus growled. "What the fuck are you looking at?"

He tried to follow her line of sight through the dim, but couldn't find whatever it was.

I didn't have to see it to know.

It was ramp numero three.

The largest of the set we completed last summer.

One Grey had only jumped with me once and we'd busted the whole chassis of the car we used.

It was at that moment that the song on the radio switched to a new, familiar beat. The opening line of Primal Ethos' *On The Edge* the spark she needed to light her fire.

She cranked it as high as it would go and threw the Volvo into gear, speeding over the earth like a bullet.

"*AJ, no,*" Grey yelled. "It's too high!"

"Sparrow, *stop.*"

But she was beyond hearing us and inside my heart beat to a mantra of *yes, yes, yes.*

"Punch it!" I called as she neared the base of the ramp. This one jumped over a pond, and if she didn't hit it hard enough, we'd never clear it.

She did as I bid her.

Corvus grabbed the brake.

Fuck.

It broke off in his hand, and he chucked it from the window, cursing.

"Ava Jade!"

The ramp was only milliseconds away now.

I shut my eyes.

Blinding yellow light shocked the backs of my eyelids and Ava Jade screamed, blinded by the dawn.

I acted without thinking as the car's perfect trajectory wobbled. We weren't going to hit it right. She couldn't see.

I was through the seats in a second, curling a fist around the wheel to jerk it to the right as the tires hit the base of the ramp.

The world tipped up, and my head cracked against something hard as the Volvo rolled, my stomach in my throat as the metal contracted all around us and dirt and broken glass pattered against my face and neck, burying themselves in my skin.

The rolling stopped. Or my head stopped spinning. The Volvo balanced precariously on two wheels at the end of its spin before falling back to all four, the cloying smell of engine smoke and dry dirt filling my nose.

Someone coughed, and I reached for Grey, jerking his arm.

He tapped my hand as he continued to cough, letting me know he was all right as *On The Edge* continued to play intermittently on the busted radio.

The light made it hard to see through the dust cloud as Ava Jade grunted, disentangling her leg from where it was trapped beneath the wheel well with Corvus' help to lift the gnarled metal.

My stomach clenched, but then she was free and Corvus was inspecting her leg, the only injury he sported a shallow cut in his temple leaking crimson down into his eye.

That's when she started laughing.

A dull chuckle at first, morphing quickly into a full belly laugh, her eyes leaking as she clutched her stomach. Tears clearing tracks through the dirt coating her face.

I couldn't help laughing too, a lightness taking shape in my chest so wide and all-consuming that it blotted out the dark.

Grey chuckled too, slapping me on the leg as he shook his head, incredulous that we were somehow still alive.

Corvus' door opened with a creaking groan as he stepped outside, kicking it shut behind him. The dawn light covering him in its vivid orange hue as he stalked away.

"Corvus!" Ava Jade called after him between fits of laughter. "Where the fuck are you going?"

He didn't answer her, just kept walking, shoving his hands into his pockets, his back up. And I knew he needed to leave. It wasn't a matter of choice. He was going to lose himself if he stayed, and Corvus James never lost himself. Never lost his control.

Too bad.

It would set him free.

10

AVA JADE

"What crawled up his ass?" I asked as we continued to laugh, my legs pulled up to avoid the smashed footwell, twisted in my seat to see the guys.

I was met with the steady eyes of Grey, staring at me with a hot intensity that curled my toes as his laughter faded. His Adam's apple bobbed, lips parting to let out a shaky breath.

Lips that looked pillow soft in the dawning light.

He bit his lower one and something tightened in my belly, the adrenaline still pumping blood through my veins making my fingers twitch.

A slight curl at the corner of his mouth sent me over the edge with a wild lust that swallowed me whole.

I was through the seats, a fist in the short hair at the nape of his neck to crush his mouth to mine. An animal sound ricocheted through my chest as his hands came up to hold me there, tight on either side of my jaw.

"*Mmmm,*" Rook groaned somewhere to my right, and I reached a blind hand out for him, finding a fistful of shirt to grab hold of. I yanked him close, tearing myself from Grey to find Rook's lips.

He tasted strongly of whiskey, and it sent a spike of surprise sparking in my eyes like starbursts. His tongue flicked into my mouth, and I moaned, but a strong hand gripped my neck, hauling me back. Hot and urgent. Until I was kissing Grey again, their intermingled scents driving me to a hazy delirium.

A sound of surprise squeaked up my throat as Rook grabbed hold of my legs, hard fingers working the button and zipper of my jeans.

I moaned loudly into Grey's mouth as Rook violently undressed me and Grey ravished my mouth with his tongue. My breasts with his greedy hands. Their touches almost frantic in their intensity.

Like they were afraid at any moment I would stop them.

I should.

I really should.

But right now? I'd rather die than have them stop for even a fucking second.

I was high off the moment. Wanting to keep living fast, ready to die hard if that's what this demanded of me.

"Fuck," I croaked as Grey's mouth trailed kisses down my cheek to my neck, suckling lightly on the tender flesh there. Marking me.

Rook grunted as he struggled with my pants, finally kicking the warped door open to get out and rip them from my legs. Yanking me down to lay me across the seat in the process. Bits of chunky glass and dirt biting into my skin.

My panties went next, the distinct sound of steel cutting through cotton making me shiver as he sliced them from me.

I tried to heave myself up to see what Rook was doing, but Grey kept me locked to him, jerking my chin until our mouths met again in an upside down kiss.

My back arched, breath hitching as Rook buried his face in my pussy.

I whimpered into Grey's mouth, and he ripped the top of my shirt, exposing my breasts to the cool morning air, making my nipples pebble.

He groaned into my mouth as he twisted one, rolling the sensitive top between his rough fingers until I was convulsing against the seat at all the sensations rebounding through my body.

Rook feasted on my greedy cunt like a man starved until I wrapped my legs tight around his shoulders, crying out when Grey finally released my mouth to lean over and suck one of my nipples into his warm mouth.

This was...

Fuck, this was the most incredible...

A blade dragged up my inner thigh. I would know the feeling anywhere.

I pressed into it, hungry for more.

"*Fuck, Rook,*" I choked out, squirming so much now in the seat that he had to move his free arm over my waist like a bar, holding me down.

Cold metal brushed my opening beneath where his tongue was setting a quick, flicking pace.

I pushed against it, the cold making me suck a breath in through my teeth as I felt the blunt edge of the tang thrust slowly inside of me.

Holy. Fucking. Shit.

"You like that?" Rook asked, sounding almost incredulous as he pushed the blade further inside of me. I found a fistful of his dark hair and dragged his mouth back to my pussy.

"Yes," I said. "Don't fucking stop."

He didn't.

My nipple popped out of Grey's mouth, and I reached my other hand above me, feeling down the length of his torso until I found what I was looking for. The solid bulge beneath his jeans. The perfect cock I knew was bound beneath it and begging to be set free.

I tried to undo the button, but the angle made it almost impossible. I whimpered, shuddering as Rook fucked me with the handle of the blade.

"Take these off," I demanded breathily, tugging on Grey's jeans. "*Now.*"

I didn't have to tell him twice. He got his door to open and stepped out to remove them, coming back with his cock fisted in his hand.

I opened wide, salivating at the sight of it, looping my fingers around his thigh to force him to move faster. He knelt on the edge of the seat and fed his thick cock into my mouth. I stretched my neck, taking it in, using my grip on his thigh to bring him closer.

The salty taste of him slid down my throat and I moaned against his cock as he withdrew it, letting me circle the tip with my tongue.

"I want you to fuck my mouth," I told him, breathless, readjusting myself on the seat so my head was flat and he stood behind me. I wanted him to fuck my mouth while Rook fucked my pussy with his knife.

I didn't think I'd ever wanted anything as much as I wanted this.

"Do as the woman says," Rook growled from between my legs and Grey obliged, pushed past my lips to slide his cock over my tongue, all the way to the back of my throat.

I relaxed my gag reflex as he grunted, fucking my tight little throat until I could hardly breathe. It only turned me on more.

An orgasm began to build, coming on faster than a jet, with just as much power.

My pussy clenched around the hilt of the blade.

Grey, sensing my closeness, reached down and rubbed my nipples with wetted fingers until I came. The orgasm ripping through me like a thousand tiny explosions. Like a car crash I wanted to relive over and over again. The bruises and bumps and scrapes forgotten in favor of the *release*.

If I believed in souls, I'd say mine just left my fucking body.

I screamed around Grey's cock as the orgasm came to a head, my vision blurring, fingernails biting into flesh.

It continued for what felt like minutes, and just when I thought it was finally going to release me, the blade and Rook's tongue vanished from between my legs and I gasped as he lifted my ass end high, plowing into my pussy with his pierced cock.

Grey's cock was knocked from my mouth, and I dragged in a breath.

"Don't lose it," Rook told me, breathless, the gleam of my wetness still on his lips as his dark eyes watched me. "I want another one."

He thrust into me, holding my legs locked around his neck, making Grey have to climb into the backseat to reach my mouth. I took him back in as he braced himself on the seats, nudging the back of my throat again.

"Come on, Ghost," Rook demanded, and as if on cue, I began to spiral into another orgasm. The feel of his Jacob's ladder rubbing over my sweet spots driving me fucking insane.

"Choke her," Rook roared, and Grey gave me a chance to catch my breath before his fingers curled around my throat, tightening the channel his cock ruthlessly fucked.

My fingers clutched the worn seat beneath me until it tore, the lack of air priming my body as one orgasm began to roll into the next.

Teeth bit into my calf, and I cried out as they broke the skin, the pain mixed with the pleasure bringing me a release so absolute it made tears sting in my eyes. Grey cried out as his warm heat spilled down my throat, and Rook stiffened between my legs, giving himself over to his own release, filling me.

I swallowed, utterly spent with the orange glow of sunrise staining the backs of my eyelids. The only sound besides our heavy breaths and the chirp of the sparrows in the trees.

The hum of the tattoo gun filled the apartment as I leaned over the back of one of the kitchen stools. I wasn't sure what I expected for a pain level, but this definitely wasn't it. It was kind of nice, actually.

I didn't know what that said about me, but the heavy handed path of the needle working its way down my spine felt almost therapeutic. Fuck, it would've been if it weren't for *what* Tattoo Guy was inking into the flesh between my shoulder blades.

"You sure this is all you want?" Tattoo Guy grunted as he completed the tattoo and set down the gun on the counter. "Dies pays well in case his men want additional ink to compliment the tag. Pinkie got his in the eye of a tiger, and you might've noticed all The Crow's tags are woven through with their other ink."

My face screwed up at that as I pulled my tank top back down to cover the fresh ink.

"Hey, hold up. I need to bandage it."

Groaning, I lifted my shirt back up as Rook wandered from my bedroom, a towel hanging low on his hips. His body glistening with fresh droplets from the shower, flushed red.

My jaw tightened. If Tattoo Guy could've waited just another twenty fucking minutes to show up at my door, I could've joined him.

Judging by his cheeky smirk, he knew what I was thinking.

Rook tugged my shirt the rest of the way out of Tattoo Guy's way as he cleaned the tattoo, wiping it down before applying a thin clear bandage to it, pressing it down tight, making the fresh needle wounds sting.

"That's it?" Rook asked, echoing Tattoo Guy's question.

I shrugged his hand from my back. "I didn't exactly have time to think about it."

He frowned, and Tattoo Guy finally finished with my bandage, starting to pack up.

"If you want anything added, just give me a call. I'll make time." He flipped a card from his wallet, pressing it flat to the countertop. "Rook," he added, nodding in his direction. "We still on for next month."

"Pending my demise," Rook replied with a wink, making my stomach clench.

"Any idea what you'll have yet or are you going to make me draw it up same day again?"

Rook shrugged, pursing his lips. "You'll know when I do."

"So yes then."

"See you, Rick."

Tattoo Guy shook his head, slinging his back over his shoulder as he left.

Rook didn't speak again until the door shut behind him. He put a hand on my shoulder and squeezed, his name flexing over his knuckles. "You good?"

"Feels like a betrayal," I found myself saying, the honesty almost too heavy.

"Because of what happened to your dad?"

I nodded. It wasn't the only reason, but it was the biggest one. The fact my mom got the drugs that drove her half mad from the Kings didn't help. They were also the reason she became an addict. And the reason the collector came knocking for money she didn't have. Why he decided to take what was owed from my flesh instead of her empty purse. Why he gave me no choice but to end him. Awakening my darkness and changing me forever.

Rook nodded solemnly to himself, brooding.

"It's fine," I muttered. "It needed to be done. Now Diesel will stop bitching at me. Worth it for that alone."

My attempt to lighten the mood seemed to work only halfway, but I'd take it.

Rook had spent the last two nights with me at Briar Hall, in my bed, and somehow I'd managed to keep my hands to myself after the slight setback at the rally field.

It wasn't without herculean effort though, and seeing him now, naked save for the towel and dripping wet...

I want to lick him.

My skin bristled at the traitorous thought and I cleared my throat as I went through the motions of making two shitty lattes, my skill at frothing the milk seeming to only get worse day by day.

I'd made it clear to Grey and Rook after the fiasco in the smashed car that what happened between us didn't mean I'd forgiven them or that I trusted them. They didn't say it, but I could see in their eyes that it didn't mean I'd gained their trust back yet, either.

And Corvus...

Well, Corvus barely said two words to me since rally night. He showed up for classes and threw himself into finding out more about whoever set up the art display in the school atrium last week, doing everything he could to ignore me.

I knew he was pissed because someone could've been hurt in the crash, or, you know, if I'd actually managed to take the thirty foot jump, but we were all still alive, weren't we?

In hindsight, *maybe* I was being reckless, but fuck if it wasn't fun. We'd needed that.

I slid one of the latte's to him on the counter. "You should go get dressed or we'll be late."

"Does it matter?"

My brows drew. Did it?

"Corv has already spoken to administration."

"What do you mean?" I asked.

"You're exempt."

"From?"

He grinned mischievously behind his mug as he took a sip. "From everything. Being marked late. Absent. Using your phone during class, if you still had one. And a myriad of other fun things."

"Like not getting expelled for fucking the vice principal?"

He lifted his mug in a salute. "Exactly."

"Well, if it's all the same to you, I'm hungry as fuck and have absolutely no desire to cook."

"Cafeteria?"

"Please."

He strode back to the bedroom to get dressed, standing in such a way that he damn well knew I could see him as he let his towel fall to the floor and pulled on his jeans.

His back tatts extended down to cover part of his magnificent glutes and the urge came again. To taste him. To bite him like he bit me on rally night. The twin crescents of his teeth marks in my calf were crusted over now, but I fully planned to scrub the scabs off in the shower later, ensuring the markings would scar.

"You talk to Becca any more this morning?"

"With what?" I asked. "I don't have a phone, remember?"

"As if you couldn't break into mine."

I pursed my lips, nodding.

"No. I haven't. Not since our calls Tuesday and yesterday."

I'd done as Diesel had asked and set up a call with Becca. Her on a payphone and me on Grey's burner cell. We now had a good idea of what the creep looked like. Brown hair long enough on top to show it was wavy. Blue eyes. A pale complexion. Slim, but muscular. About six feet tall. She had no photos of him since he wouldn't let her take any, smart fucker, but the description was good. So was the other intel.

Diesel already knew where they were meeting since he'd bugged the place. It was a little bunkhouse on the edge of Thorn Valley that Ace had been renting in cash for several months. But Becca's intel also told us that he sometimes asked her to meet him in other places. Or rather, to pick him up in other places. Which explained why the passenger seat of her car was always set for someone much taller than I was.

Specifically, from a Quickie Mart just inside Ace territory.

It cemented the theory that he was an Ace, but on the next call, when I'd asked Becca Diesel's new question about his gang ink, she'd said he didn't have any. No ink at all.

She'd been fucking this guy for months, so I wanted to believe she had an intimate knowledge of every inch of his flesh, but... that may not have been the case.

The guys I slept with before the Crows never saw my scars and there were six inches of them cuffing both my upper thighs. They didn't see them because I didn't want them to see them. If I could hide that, this guy could hide a little 'A.'

"Is it getting any easier?"

"What?"

"Talking to her."

My chest tightened. "Not really."

I got off the phone as fast as I could each time we spoke even though Becca was brimming with questions of her own. Was I okay? Was I in any trouble because of her? Did I need her to come back?

The questions were only put on hold for the apologies.

I knew she meant them, but I wasn't ready yet. Trust was a fragile thing, a *new* thing for me. I didn't know how she could earn it back or else I'd tell her.

"You guys'll work it out," Rook assured me, sounding so sure.

"How do you know that?"

"You think the guys and I haven't gone through shit? Man, I could tell you stories... This one time Grey—"

"Grey what?"

"Nah. It was a long time ago. We were younger. Still learning how to trust each other. It wasn't always easy, you know. It won't be for you and Becks, either, but she's your sister. Maybe not by blood, but by choice. You don't throw that shit away for one mistake."

I must've pulled a face because he snorted, coming over to tug the empty mug from my fingers. "Come on, Ghost. Let's eat."

11

CORVUS

I checked my phone again for a reply from Rook as I waited in the atrium, but none came, and I scrubbed a hand over my face, feeling the prickle of day-old stubble. I needed a shave, and probably a fucking shower, but after we discovered the security guard, Mick, was missing, I needed to figure out why.

All security footage of Monday morning last week had been scrubbed from the drives. It went black around three in the morning and then flicked back to life around seven, when the first of the students began to wander downstairs to find the pornographic photos.

It drove me to madness thinking there was someone else in the academy, just a couple floors below where Ava Jade slept. She'd been alone. It didn't matter if it was an Ace or her stalker. In either case, the person had wanted to hurt us, and I couldn't think of anything that would hurt us more than something happening to that girl.

Groaning, I texted Rook again.

CORVUS

> Where are you guys? The bell rang five minutes ago.

I punched the elevator button and waited, giving in to the urge to go up there and see for myself, even though I knew damn well what I could be walking into. Imagining their bodies tangled together, flushed and violent, made me almost crack a tooth.

I knew when Grey wandered home several hours after I left the rally field exactly what happened when I left. He had that *rocks off* glow. The one he rarely got from fucking Brianna, but I knew the face. Nail marks all over his neck and shoulders told me the rest.

I didn't ask because I knew it would only stoke the internal flames to know whether or not they had her at the same time. Without me.

It had become something of an unwritten rule from the start with Ava Jade; that she wasn't interested in choosing. That she would take her pleasure from each of us as she wanted, without asking permission. Without guilt.

The guys and I had shared before. A handful of times. But those women never mattered to us. Not like her. And my inner beast roared that she belonged to me even though the still rational part of my brain was almost *glad* she'd found a home in my brothers' hearts, too.

It was the only way she could be one of us.

It couldn't work any other way.

I jerked back as the doors to the elevators opened and Ava Jade and Rook stepped out.

"Hey, Bro," Rook said nonchalantly, his hair damp from a shower. Ava Jade's was dry and styled in a high ponytail with little pieces left out to frame her face. Either she blow dried it or they didn't share a shower.

I stuffed the need to know down deep, burying it.

It didn't matter.

"Lose your phone?" I found myself growling back at him.

He tapped his pocket. "Nope."

"I texted you."

"I saw. We were on our way down. I knew you'd be waiting here."

"Where's Grey?" Ava Jade asked, peering around the atrium for any sign of him.

Grey entered through the front door five minutes later than he said he'd be and came over to us, a curious knot in his brows. "Thought you'd be in class, didn't the bell—?"

"I was waiting for them," I interrupted him, indicating Rook and Ava Jade. "You get those books handled?"

Grey nodded. "Yeah. All taken care of. I have more news, too."

Chapter 11

"What?" Sparrow asked.

"The alliance with the Kings is official. Dies made the move last night."

I didn't miss how Ava Jade's fists clenched at her sides, at odds with the next words to leave her lips. "That's good, right?"

Grey's lips pressed together. There was something more.

"Apparently they weren't satisfied with an alliance in name only. Victor asked Dies for our crews to meet in good faith." He paused. "So, Dies has welcomed them to join us for the next fight night."

"*Fuck.*"

"It's not like we didn't think this might happen."

"I didn't know you were fighting again," Ava Jade said to Rook. "When?"

She didn't seem the slightest bit surprised or perturbed at the new turn of events.

Rook shrugged at her. "I fight when Dies tells me to."

"He hasn't found an opponent for you yet," Grey explained to Rook. "No one wants to take their shot since how badly you beat Conor Jones last month."

"Pussies."

Sparrow laughed at that.

Now was as good a time as any.

I tugged the slim box free of my back pocket and passed it to her.

Her laughter ceased as she took it, taken aback by the brand emblem on the cover.

"What's this?"

"Your new phone," I told her. "It was supposed to get here days ago, but it was late."

When she opened the box to see the slim silver cell inside and said nothing, I continued. "You haven't bought yourself a new one, and we need to be able to get ahold of you. I, *uh*, I hope you don't mind. If you don't like it, I can order something different."

Jesus Christ, I sounded pathetic. I could feel my brothers watching me.

"Well?" I gritted out, trying to force a reply from her.

Despite my change in tone, she smiled up at me, shaking her head and the heat that'd been crawling up my neck died out.

"Thanks, Corv," she said, taking the phone out to hand the box back, powering it on. "Guess this means you're done being mad at me?"

"Depends. Are you done trying to get us all killed?"

"For now."

A smile stained my lips to match hers, and I wasn't sure where to put my hands. What was this girl doing to me?

"*Ava Jade Mason,*" a woman's voice shrieked as the door to the main office burst open. Standing there in the doorway with a hat twice the size of Texas wrapped in a dead thing instead of a bow, was Ava Jade's aunt. The Humphrey widow who lived across town in the big secluded mansion all alone.

Fuck if she wasn't a terrifying creature. With a botched face lift and droopy lips painted a dark red. A cashmere coat draping all the way to the floor, baggy on her five foot nothing frame.

I could smell the mothballs from here.

"*Fuck my life,*" Ava Jade breathed, sighing heavily as the woman waddled over to us.

"You guys should scram," she muttered to us.

"No way in hell I'm missing this," Rook replied, standing up straighter as though he were a fine upstanding citizen of Thorn Valley and not a fucking shark in human skin.

In the black sweater he wore, with his tatted hands behind his back, he could almost pull it off, too.

Grey and I followed suit.

I inclined my head to the woman as she approached. "Madam Humphrey," I said graciously, stepping between her and Ava Jade. "It's a pleasure to meet you. I'm Corvus James."

She balked at my extended hand, taking in my too perfect smile and towering height.

"Oh!" she exclaimed. "Who?"

"Corvus," I repeated, taking her frail hand in mine to shake it, hearing Ava Jade grumble something unintelligible at my back. She should've been thanking me. Thanking all of us. There were non-violent ways of getting what we wanted, and though they were less fun, we used them often.

Grey cranked up the charm to eleven and took my place in front of the woman. "And I'm Grey Winters. Your niece and I share AP calculus. I was the top of the class before she dethroned me."

Humphrey blinked rapidly, taking us in like her puny little brain couldn't compute what was happening. She was trying hard to maintain her frustration, but it was waning fast.

Rook put the last nail in that coffin.

He swept forward, taking her veiny hand up to his lips for a kiss. "Rook," he said simply. "A pleasure."

"What are you doing here, Aunt Humphrey?" Ava Jade asked, shoving Rook out of the way with a little more force than she needed to, giving him a pointed look.

"I...well I was..."

Well shit, we broke her.

Her face reddened, and she cleared her throat. "I came to see you."

"Why?"

"What do you mean, *why*?" Humphrey demanded, coming back to herself. "You've been ignoring all my calls. My text messages. I thought you'd left."

"I lost my phone."

Humphrey's gaze alighted on the brand new cell phone in Ava Jade's hand. "Just like your father, always telling lies."

Ava Jade trembled with rage at her aunt's comment, and I winced, anticipating a number of things that could leave her mouth now.

"It's a new phone," she said through gritted teeth. "And I'd *appreciate* it if you didn't talk about Dad like that."

She waved away Ava Jade's words like they were coils of a particularly odorous smoke wafting near her face. "Yes, well, it's true, but never mind that. You never replied about Thanksgiving."

Ava Jade cocked her head, staring with open incredulity at her aunt. "You're not serious."

"Why shouldn't I be? We're the only family we have now, dear. I should like for you to join me at the house for dinner."

It didn't sound like a request, and I wondered why Ava Jade put up with the old cow. Was it truly just because she paid her tuition here at the academy? Fuck, I'd pay it myself to get the hag off her back.

"I don't do Thanksgiving," she replied in a careful monotone. "Haven't since I was, like, four."

"That's just sad, Ava Jade. Your parents should've—"

The woman cut herself short, clearly not completely immune to my Sparrow's murderous stares.

Humphrey turned her attention to me. "Well, just ask your friends. You boys must have Thanksgiving plans? Would you rather sit alone at the school?"

"Actually," Grey interjected. "We don't. Our father lost his wife the day before Thanksgiving, so we don't celebrate it."

Humphrey's hand went to her chest, fingers clutching the pearl necklace around her throat. "Oh, how very unfortunate. Should you like to, you'd be welcome to attend Thanksgiving dinner at my home with Ava Jade. Everyone should have somewhere to go for Thanksgiving."

Ava Jade's eyes went wide at the offer, her mouth dropping open. "They wouldn't—"

"We'd love to join you, madame," Rook said, making me choke. I had to cover the sound with a cough and a smile. "What a gracious offer."

"It's settled then. I'll send you the details, Ava Jade, dear. Mind your phone. I don't want to have to come all the way across town again."

Ava Jade seemed temporarily mute, glaring at Rook so vehemently that I was surprised she didn't reduce him to ash with the look alone.

"It's a new phone," I reminded her aunt, making her pause before departing. "But I'll be sure to have Ava Jade text you so you have the new number."

Her mouth opened into a tiny 'o.' She didn't like the insinuation that she'd wrongly accused Ava Jade of lying. But she only nodded. "Thank you, dear."

"You're welcome."

"Now get to class, the lot of you. I don't want my niece getting you into trouble for being late."

Ava Jade stared after her aunt red-faced, her little fists tight balls at her sides until the front door closed behind the old woman.

"You're not coming to Thanksgiving." She seethed at all of us.

Rook put a hand to his chest, a fake look of hurt crossing his face. "But, Ava Jade," he said in a terrible Madame Humphrey impression. "We were invited."

"I'm going to murder all of you."

12

AVA JADE

My skin itched. I had to wonder if just being near my aunt had caused some sort of allergic reaction. She reeked of mothballs and that awful old lady perfume she always wore to try to cover it up. My eyes felt puffy from it. Definitely allergic to her.

"Why do you put up with her?" Grey asked, following behind me to grab a tray and fill it up with what remained of the breakfast buffet and the start of lunch items being brought out in the cafeteria.

Ahead of me in line, Brianna picked at a bowl of grapes, sneaking glances at me from the cover of her lashes. I wanted to stuff her face into the potato soup, but that would only render it inedible, and it was my favorite.

"AJ?" Grey hedged when I didn't reply right away, drawing my attention back to him.

"Because her aunt is paying for her tuition here," Corvus replied for me, and I rolled my eyes at him. Not even a little bit surprised that he would know that. He'd done his homework. I'd done mine too. At least as much of it as I could. His history had been the most unattainable of the three. With almost no information whatsoever anywhere in the state or the neighboring ones.

"Is that it?" Grey asked, confused. "You're a Saint now, AJ. If you want to go to school here, we'll cover it."

I didn't know how to explain it to them: the deal I had with my aunt. Maybe the whole thing was a moot point now.

My aunt promised me tuition to a good college or university plus my own apartment in the city and a monthly stipend. I could have all of it if I graduated Briar Hall with good grades and got accepted into college. It was her guilt-wrapped gift to me for not being around when my dad was still alive.

But what did any of that matter now?

I'm a Saint.

No matter how many times I repeated that to myself, it didn't ever sound any more true. But it was a fact. And I couldn't see Diesel St. Crow being chill with me going away to college and renting an apartment in the city. What good was my aunt's money now?

I couldn't explain it to them because it didn't make sense why I was still dealing with her bullshit other than the one thing she said that struck a nerve; we're the only family we have now.

It was true.

Mom was gone, and I hoped she never came back. Dad was gone now, too. Mom's family was never around and Dad's sister, Viola Humphrey, was the only living relative he had left.

The only one *I* had left now that he was gone.

They didn't get along, but he mentioned her sometimes. How he worried about his older sister alone in her big house after her wealthy husband passed away.

How he wished he could've seen eye to eye with her so that I could have grown up with a rich aunt to spoil me.

It felt like spitting in his face to say to her what I really wanted to: to fuck off and never contact me again.

She's right, Dad would tell me. *I was a shitty dad. A liar. Always gambling our money away.*

My dad was a lot of things, but he knew exactly who he was and what he was doing to us. He was just powerless to stop himself. Like my darkness, something greedy and morally gray writhed within him that he couldn't purge.

I knew I wouldn't be able to purge mine, so how could I be angry that he couldn't do the same?

"You going to ladle that?" Grey asked, and I blinked, realizing I was standing with the soup ladle poised over my bowl. Empty.

I shook my head.

"Sorry," Grey muttered as I went back to filling a bowl of soup. "You don't have to explain yourself to me. Family's...a tough subject. I get it."

Something told me he really did get it, and I was glad at least one of us did.

We went to join Rook and Corvus at the table, one of only three still occupied by students this late in the morning.

I knew Brianna transferred out of homeroom sometime last week, the fucking coward, so I wasn't totally surprised to see she'd opted for an open period instead of enrolling in a new class this late in the term. But the others, her little posse, seemed to have joined her, and I knew for a fact they were still in homeroom with us.

The other table was just two guys studying. More students with an open first period.

Fuck, if I had an open first period, I'd be spending it sleeping.

I slid into a seat at the table beside Rook, and Grey slid in next to me. Corvus drank a smoothie, scowling at his phone. Rook drank a glass of orange juice that suspiciously didn't look or smell to be spiked. Surprising.

Grey started with his glass of water as I munched on a stick of celery and set about getting my new phone operational. I added all the necessary apps, checking for any Corvus may have added before giving it to me, and signed into my email and all socials. I needed to keep that shit open in case Becca needed me.

I checked the phone's system settings to get the number and pushed through an email to Becca containing it. Telling her to only text from a burner, and change burners every few days. Better safe than sorry.

Corv set his phone down with a clatter on the table.

"Max again?" Grey asked him.

"Yeah."

"She still pissed you canceled those shows?"

"She's threatening to fire me as a client."

Grey laughed. "Yeah, right."

"She won't. You're her number one, Bro," Rook agreed.

Corvus' brows drew together. He looked so tired, I realized. The hollows beneath his eyes dark and purple hued. When was the last time he'd slept?

"Why did you cancel the shows?" I asked. "You only had two others lined up this season, and they weren't far. All in NorCal, right?"

He shook his head. "Too much heat right now. I need to be here."

Not for the first time, I wondered how he'd managed to juggle his gang life and a secret music career. But the answer was staring me right in the face the entire time. He *wasn't* juggling it. Either one suffered or the other did. Right now, his alter ego of *The Bone Man* needed to take a back seat so Corvus James could do what his father expected of him. What his makeshift family needed.

Was it what he wanted?

His steely gaze flicked up to meet mine, lips tight as he considered saying something else.

I lifted a brow. "What?"

"I might've promised Max you'd work on a new track with me, and we could unveil it at the next show after Christmas."

"*You did what?*"

Corvus lifted his hands in a placating gesture. "Before you say no—"

"Yes."

"What?"

"I'll do it. But I want fifty percent of all royalties earned on it *plus* a cut of the ticket sales from the Lodi show. Only fair since you recorded me without my knowledge and used said recording on stage."

He stared at me dumbfounded.

"What? A girl's gotta earn a living and... I didn't sound half bad."

"*Ha!*" Grey balked. "You were incredible, AJ. There's a reason every music blogger on the West coast is trying to figure out who you are."

I flushed and tried to hide it by taking a bite of bacon. "I want vocal training too, though."

"Done." Corvus grunted. "I'll train you myself. Best I can do. We can't take you to a professional vocal coach. It'll draw too much attention."

"What do you think my name should be? I'm thinking something epic like..."

"Sparrow," Corvus interrupted before I could finish my train of thought. "Obviously."

"Bone Man and *Sparrow*?" I groaned. "That's lame."

"How about *Ghost*?" Rook interjected, sipping his OJ.

"The Bone Man and The Ghost." I rolled the titles around in my mouth. "Has a better ring to it, don't you think? More...ominous?"

"So you think Rook's nickname is better than mine?" Corvus asked, a slight curl at the edge of his lips. He was playing.

I didn't know if I wanted to join the game just yet, though.

"Maybe," I acquiesced, putting an end to the conversation for now as I got ready to dig into the food that was going cold on my tray.

Grey's tray rivaled my own in terms of how full it was, and he smirked at me as he set into eating a massive pile of scrambled eggs, eyeing my tray right back.

"There's no way you're going to finish all that," he said between mouthfuls, indicating my mountain of food.

"Wanna bet?"

"Fifty."

"Make it a hundred," I replied cheerfully, ditching the spoon for my soul to lift the bowl to my lips instead.

"You're on.

Rook snatched the bowl before it reached my lips and hot soup sloshed over my hands and the rest of the food on my plate.

"The fuck, Rook?" I hissed, shaking soup off my hands.

He held the bowl to his nose, smelling it.

"If you wanted some you could've just got your own."

He didn't reply, and something in his dark eyes made my frustration wane. He dipped his index finger into the soup and put it in his mouth, tasting it.

A growl ripped from his lips.

"What is it?" Corvus demanded.

"It's been tainted," Rook spat back. "Drugged."

Um...what?

"Are you sure?" Grey asked.

Corvus' hand curled around his smoothie cup until his knuckles turned white. "What's in it?"

"I can't tell, but it's something. Pills. Crushed up. I know that smell. I know the taste."

The sanatorium...

What the fuck had those people done to him there?

Without another word, Grey shoved his tray away and lifted the dripping bowl of soup from the table as he stood, walking away.

"Grey, where are you..." Corvus started, but trailed off, and I spun on the bench seat to see that he was carrying the soup to Brianna's table.

My food-deprived brain caught up to where his had already gone, and I remembered Brianna ahead of me in line. How she kept peering back at me. The fucking cunt.

I followed Grey, the others rising from the table with me as I stood, my vision tinted with crimson.

I thought I'd made myself fucking crystal clear. I warned her.

Grey dropped the bowl in front of Brianna and what remained of it slashed over her shirt, splattering the two other girls crowded in at her sides, making them squeal.

"What the fuck did you put in this?"

Brianna went a shade of sickly white, but kept her expression impressively neutral.

"I don't know what you're talking about, Grey," Brianna said, her brown eyes following me as I approached with a raised chin. "But you just ruined a three hundred dollar shirt and—"

Brianna gasped as I grabbed hold of her blonde ponytail, dragging her from her seat. She screamed, manicured nails scratching at my arm as I hauled her from the cafeteria. Not even feeling the shallow cuts she was digging into my forearm.

She tripped, screeching like a banshee all the way to the kitchen.

My spine tingled as I entered, a rush of power going straight to my head.

"Get out," I barked at the cooking staff, and they hesitated before seeing my entourage follow inside behind me and scattered like rats.

"*Stupid bitch,*" Brianna was shrieking between some very unattractive sounds as I hauled her size-two ass to the row of gas burners and switched the closest one on.

I put her face to it. So close the peach fuzz on her cheeks would be singed off. "What did you put in the soup?" I demanded.

She screamed.

"What did you put in it?" I repeated, my darkness surging in full now. Demanding blood. Demanding pain. My arm holding her to the burner shook with it.

Soon, I wouldn't be in control anymore. Any second now.

I pushed her closer still, and she let out a cry. Her hair came loose from the ponytail, and I curled a fist into it, the long strands almost in the fire now.

"Laxatives," she managed and I brought her back an inch. "They were just laxatives! I was trying to make you shit yourself. Fuck!"

My face screwed up.

Laxatives?

That was the best she could do?

Christ.

So pathetic.

"P-Please, I won't ever—"

The smell of burnt hair reached me and I recoiled from it, releasing her a second too late as her head burst into orange flame. Her hairspray drawing the fire to her like spilled gasoline.

She howled like a dying cat as she stood there, rooted to the spot in shock as the flames engulfed her head in a golden crown. Not the kind she wanted, but the kind she deserved.

"B!" someone cried, and I saw blondie numero uno rushing past the guys and into the kitchen, the other one hot on her tail. Blondie numero dos fumbled to get the extinguisher loose from the wall as the other one slapped uselessly at her friend's fiery hair.

Brianna continued to blare like an air raid siren until she passed out, slumping to the floor. Blondie doused her with the fire extinguisher, covering her in plumes of white until she came to again, coughing and rubbing at the chalky residue on her face. Struggling to sit up.

I pushed the blonde on the floor away to kneel next to Brianna, grabbing her by the shirt to haul her to her ass. Her hair was gone, all except for a few tufts of blonde still clinging to her scalp. Mild red burns crisscrossed over her flesh, but they would heal. Probably wouldn't even scar. Too bad.

Brianna clutched my hands holding her shirt, blinking past tears to stare into my eyes. *Fear.* She reeked of it. She was so terrified I was sure she'd piss herself. I'd be impressed if she didn't.

"P-please," she started, her lips quivering, but I didn't want to hear another word out of her mouth. She needed to shut up before my darkness clawed its way up my throat and ate her for fucking breakfast.

"If you ever come after me again, I'll end you, bitch."

She began to shake.

"Nod that you understand."

She nodded.

I released her shirt, throwing her to her friends. "Get her out of my sight."

They dragged her pathetic ass from the cafeteria and my darkness snarled, rebelling at my mercy. But she wasn't worth it. Fucking laxatives? What a joke.

I closed my eyes, cracked my neck, and rolled my shoulders back, inviting a foul smelling breath into my lungs.

When I opened my eyes again it was to see the guys standing near the entrance to the kitchen.

Corvus stared openly, analyzing my loss of control.

Grey's mouth was gaping.

Rook had his ringed fingers clasped to his mouth, dark eyes glittering. He looked like a deranged kid with fifty bucks in a candy store.

"Dibs," he said, biting on his lip ring as he strolled forward, tugging the plain silver ring from his pinkie finger.

"*Rook*," I warned as he bent to one knee.

"Marry me?"

I shook my head, ignoring the way my belly flipped.

"You're an idiot," I said, but I plucked the ring from his fingertips as I walked past him, slipping it onto my index finger since it was the only one it'd fit. "But thanks for the ring."

I got three steps past them before my phone chimed, making my darkness make a resurgence to the surface. It could only be Becca. I'd just emailed her. She must've replied to...

"Fuck," I said on an exhale, my insides twisting as I stared at the blemish on my very new phone.

An email gleamed on the screen in vivid color.

. . .

To: Ava Jade Mason

From: gh380xc@gmail.com

Subject: Miss me?

Why'd you let them put her out? You should've let her burn, my love. She deserved it.

P.S. I see you haven't been listening. Perhaps you thought my warnings were only idle threats. That was your mistake. Now you've forced me to do what you should've from the start. Say your goodbyes, Ava Jade.

Ice skated down my spine.

A hand on my shoulder had me tensing up, dropping low, widening my stance, on the offensive.

"Whoa, AJ, it's me," Grey said, his eyes searching my face. Falling to the phone clenched tight in my hand. "Is it him?"

Slowly, I scanned the kitchen, finding what I was looking for. The blinking red light of a security camera in the corner across the room. I'd thrown a blade before I was even consciously aware I'd drawn one. It embedded in the glass lens of the camera and sparks dripped down to the tile floor as a little puff of smoke curled up from the ruin.

"He has access to the cameras," I spat, my skin crawling so badly I wanted to soak in boiling water.

Grey took the phone from my hand, and I didn't stop him as Corvus and Rook rushed to crowd him, reading the email with murderous stares.

"He's alive," Rook growled while Corvus stormed out of the kitchen with his face set in a myriad of hard lines, pale, with a vein pulsing in his neck.

"Grey," Corvus hollered back over his shoulder. "*With me. Now.*"

"Stay with her," Grey told Rook before handing my phone back and rushing to follow Corvus. Likely to interrogate the office staff and fingerprint the security office.

"Come here, Ghost," Rook said, but I didn't want his comfort.

"He needs to fucking die," I gritted out past clenched teeth. I wanted to stay angry at the Crows, but I wouldn't just sit here and let this piece of shit threaten them. They were *mine* to be angry at. And I protected what belonged to me.

Rook nodded solemnly, his dark eyes looking almost black now. He curled a hand over my shoulder, and the small contact made me flinch and sag, needing more. No matter how much I didn't want to admit it.

I let him pull me close, closing my eyes against the hollow of his throat as he trapped me in his arms. "I know," he told me, squeezing tight. His scent filled my nose, setting my soul alight and soothing it all at once. I couldn't get enough of it. "He will. I promise you that."

13

GREY

"Again," Corvus ordered, kicking Ava Jade's feet wider apart. "Stop overthinking it."

AJ grumbled something unintelligible through her teeth as she stared down the short length of the barrel, aiming at the glass bottles downfield. She fired, and the M9 kicked back into her palm.

"Fuck," she hissed when the shot went wide again, missing all six glass bottles entirely.

I whistled low, drawing her eye. "I have to say, AJ, I thought you'd be better at this."

It was meant to be teasing. To bring a smile to her lips, but it only deepened the grooves between her pinched brows. She'd looked like that since yesterday's email. Up all through the night pacing, opening the fridge just to close it again, standing by the window like at any moment her stalker might appear outside of it and she could end him.

At four in the morning when she gave up and showered for the day, I joined her. Truth be told, I thought she might ask me to get out, but she turned as I stepped in with her, sighing under the stream of insanely hot water.

"I'm not in the mood," she'd said, exhausted, but that wasn't why I joined her. AJ let me wash her hair and scrub wide soapy circles over her back. By the time she got out, she couldn't fall into bed fast enough.

We'd only managed two hours of sleep, but it was more than I thought either of us would have after Corvus and I found *nothing.*

Nothing in the security office at Briar Hall.

The email traced back to an IP location in Lodi. It took a lot of ultimately useless sleuthing to find the exact pin. An alley where a piece of crap old laptop was stuffed in a dumpster, wiped clean of prints.

We had jack shit.

And it was taking its toll on all of us.

Rook chain-smoked as he leaned against a tree several feet away, his gaze unfocused as he watched Ava Jade try to hit a bottle and miss for at least the tenth time since we started.

She dropped her arm, rolling her shoulder, which was no doubt starting to get sore at this point. "This is useless. I'm just as lethal with my blades as you are with a gun. I don't see the point to—"

"Diesel said—"

"*Diesel said,*" AJ mocked Corvus before he could finish. "I could've killed Diesel five times over by now with my blades, but I didn't."

Corvus pinched the bridge of his nose, inhaling long and slow. If we weren't sleeping much, I knew that he wasn't sleeping *at all.* From experience, we all knew that could only go on so long before he got so grouchy none of us would be able to stand to be around him. Or worse, it could get as bad as it used to when Rook and I were first adopted.

When his insomnia was so relentless he'd start hearing voices. Seeing things that weren't there. His mind playing tricks on him.

If I thought I could get away with it, I'd drug his ass asleep, but I knew neither of my brothers would be chill with that as a tactic here.

"Sparrow," Corvus warned.

She huffed.

"I have a thought," I said, squinting into the distance to see the old barn and shed where we kept the rally cars and our backup arsenal. "We still have that sniper out here?"

Corvus looked up, considering where I was going with the question.

"Maybe this," I said, plucking the handgun from her grasp. "Is not her thing. Maybe we try something else. If she shows promise with a sniper, we work on that and then circle back to close range arms later."

Corvus bit the inside of his cheek. "Okay. Yeah. We'll try it."

AJ perked up at the mention of *sniper,* her eyes alight. "Are any of you any good with one?"

Rook dropped a cigarette to stomp out on the patchy grass with its friends. "Grey isn't bad," he said, speaking for me. "But Axel is our sharpshooter."

AJ lifted a brow at me. "He's right. I'm competent, but none of us are much good with one. I feel like you would be though. A lot of the same principles apply as with blade throwing. Distance perception. Wind speed and direction. Timing."

She pursed her lips, unsure, but clearly excited to give it a shot.

"Then Rook should be decent at it," she said. "I've seen him with a blade, too. He's good."

I nodded, but she was forgetting one thing.

"I don't have the patience," Rook admitted. "Who wants to sit on some perch half a fucking mile away from the all the fun, waiting for the perfect shot."

"Not you?" AJ asked, her tone dripping sarcasm.

"No, Ghost. Not me."

"If we climb up onto the roof of the shed, we should be able to get a good line of sight down the field," I said, pointing toward the barn and the smashed up Volvo we'd parked up beside it. "I'll grab a can of paint. We can put a few targets on the high jump."

"You don't need us then?" Corvus said, a tick in his upper lip as he read something on his phone.

I frowned.

He indicated the phone in his hand. "Dies. Wants two of us to deal with another client upstairs at Sanctum. He and the others are busy keeping tabs on the Aces."

"It's three in the afternoon," AJ protested.

"What?" I asked. "Is three too early to get laid? I didn't know a good fuck had time constraints."

She rolled her eyes.

"Yeah, we're good," I told Corv, gaze tracking to Rook, who looked torn between staying and going. Not wanting to leave AJ's side and needing to vent some of his pent up rage before he exploded. "Go," I added, jerking my head for Rook to follow Corv. "We'll be here when you get back."

He nodded, rolling his shoulders back with a sneer as he left.

"*So,*" AJ singsonged, the happiest I'd seen her since yesterday morning. "Show me the big gun?"

I laughed. "Let's paint the targets first, and *then* I'll show you the big gun."

She made a little growly sound that went straight to my cock, biting her lower lip as she brushed past me, heading for the shed. I grabbed my sketchpad from the stump next to me and followed her, tucking the graphite pencil behind my ear.

I'd promised Max I'd come up with a few new merch designs by next week and with everything going on, I hadn't had the time to even start.

"Just like I showed you," I whispered, lying next to AJ on the uneven roof of the shed, binoculars pressed to my eyes, watching the three ringed target dripping red a quarter mile downfield. "Don't hold your breath. Breathe evenly. Fire on the exhale. Slow."

She hesitated another moment before firing, and I had the satisfaction of watching the bullet *crack* into the wood of the jump just a few inches outside the widest ring.

AJ grinned, readying another shot, licking her lips.

I said nothing, smirking at her focus face as she leveled her left eye with the sight. It was the best focus face.

She readjusted her position, just slightly, pinkie up to feel the breeze, and fired again.

I was almost too slow to press the binoculars to my eyes, catching only the little burst of wood where her bullet buried itself into the red line of the second inner ring.

"*Damn,*" I said on a breath, pulling the binoculars down, twisting to face her. "Was that really only your second shot?"

She peered at me over the barrel, a Cheshire smile on her mouth.

I reached over and shoved the gun, messing up her aim.

"Hey!"

"I have to know if it's beginner's luck. Start again."

She groaned wordlessly to herself, but did as I said, finding the correct position all over again, feeling out the wind.

This time her bullet sank into the target just an inch outside of where my bullet went in when I was showing her how to shoot, grazing the inner ring of the target.

I set the binoculars down. "Well. I think we found your weapon, AJ."

"Secondary," she whispered, correcting me as she patted the blades on her belt. "It's okay, babies, I would never replace you."

I snorted as she lined up for another shot.

"Keep practicing," I encouraged her, getting off my belly to sit against the short wall behind us where the barn attached to the shed. I checked my phone again, waiting for word from the guys. It would be getting dark soon and they still weren't back.

Sighing, I lifted a knee, snatching up my sketchpad to try to get some other work done while I could.

She fired, and I watched her readjusting again. The long weapon at home butted against her shoulder. Fuck, she was more than I ever dreamed a woman could be. She was how I imagined Diesel's wife to have been before she was taken from him.

Before I knew it, I was drawing AJ instead of sketching new merch designs. It happened more often than not.

When she was finally ready for a break more than thirty minutes later, having put a good dent in Diesel's good quality lead, I was finished.

She fell against the wall next to me, rubbing out a kink in her neck, but she froze when she saw what was lying in my lap, her lips parting.

"Is that me?"

She leaned over me to get a better look.

It wasn't anything special. Just a series of dark and light lines, but they were unmistakably *her* lines. The cruel curve of her mouth. The angle of her face. Her delicate ears. Long fingers curled around the trigger of the sniper rifle.

"It's amazing."

I tore it off the pad and handed it to her. "Keep it."

She took it, staring at her likeness like she couldn't believe it was her.

"Wait, is that me, too?" she asked, tapping the pad in my lap with a black fingernail.

I barked a laugh, seeing what ripping the page off had revealed.

Another drawing of her. This one of her ass.

Specifically, her bare ass, peachy and lifted as she bent over a bank of sinks in the girls washroom at Briar Hall. The mirror over the mountainous peaks of her ass and dripping cunt broken to reflect back a busted up image of me.

She snatched the pad from my hands before I could stop her, flipping quickly through the pages.

There was no point in stopping her.

Besides, maybe she should know. How irrevocably she was burnt into my thoughts.

She flipped past images of herself. Her side profile. Her hands. Her breasts dripping with water in the shower. The arch of her back, artfully covered in a wave of dark hair.

She flipped to the last page and icy dread threaded through my veins at the image on the page. An old drawing. Of another woman.

Older. With short waxen hair and a small face. Her eyes scratched out with heavy black strokes. I could never get my mother's eyes right. Couldn't remember what they looked like. Probably because she never looked at me. Not even when I was right in front of her.

My stomach soured.

I took the sketchpad back from AJ and flipped all the leaves back over until it was closed.

"Who is she?" AJ asked.

"My mom."

She squinted at me. "How long since she..." she trailed off. "I mean, how old were you when..."

"She isn't dead," I found myself saying, muscles in my arms and across my upper back tensing. "At least, I don't think she is."

AJ squinted at the rough wood roof beneath us, trying to understand. I wondered if she could and a sudden burning urge to come clean seared through me.

"I look her up sometimes," I admitted. "Type her name into search engines or social media. Just to see..."

She cocked her head, a sadness in her eyes that made my chest ache, and I wasn't sure if I wanted to say any more. If I wanted her to know.

"She starved you," she said, not a question.

"Left me," I corrected her. "Alone in my dead stepdad's house. For weeks at a time."

"So you were taken away from her, then? That's how you ended up at Barrett's Home for Boys with Rook?"

I wasn't surprised she knew about that. I'd have been lying if I said I hadn't scoured Corvus' room for her files last month, trying to understand her. Who she was.

"Yeah. My teacher found me. I was almost dead. She never came back."

"That's why you look for her," AJ mused. "Because you want to see if she's still out there, living her life, free of you. If she forgot about you."

I cleared my throat, shifting uncomfortably. "It's pathetic. I know."

She grabbed my arm, making me look at her as she shook her head. "No," she said. "No, it's not. It's okay to wonder. To care. You can hate her and still care to know. I'd want to know why, too. Why she couldn't take care of you."

That was part of it. The itching need to know *how* she could do it. But there was another reason I couldn't help myself from typing her name into the search bar. The other part of me, the darker part, wanted her to suffer. Wanted to see what she would look like with her bones showing through her skin. With her eyes jaundiced and teeth falling from her mouth.

I was afraid of what I would do to her if I did find her. As if the precious few good memories of her somehow made all the fucking brutal ones tolerable.

"This doesn't make you weak," AJ continued. "You hear me?"

I smirked. "Yeah, AJ. I hear you."

I lifted a hand to cup the side of her face, her cheek cold against my palm. She pushed into my touch, offering me a small sad smile before she pulled away.

"So, you draw me. Like, a lot. When did that start?"

She rolled her shoulders, the heavy vibe tumbling off. Forgotten.

"Since the first time I saw you."

Her cheeks pinkened before she scraped to her feet. "The guys should be here soon, and it's getting late. I'm going to go pack this shit away."

"I'll be right behind you."

I breathed in the sunset, closing my eyes to feel the last of its dying rays warm my face and tint the back of my eyelids brilliant orange.

My phone buzzed in my pocket, and I tugged it loose. It was about time Corv answered me. For a guy who always expected an immediate response from us, he sure didn't seem to feel like he needed to abide by the same.

My thoughts cleared at the sight of the message waiting for me when I unlocked my phone. It wasn't from Corv. Or Dies or Rook. Not even Julia, though it boasted her trademark *Unknown* tag.

How the fuck...?

I swallowed, my teeth clenching as I reread the message, my stomach twisting.

UNKNOWN

Hello, Grey. How far would you go to protect your brothers?

Another message came through before the first had a chance to settle in my mind.

UNKNOWN

Let's find out, shall we?

14

AVA JADE

The ten day deadline Diesel gave the Aces was dwindling fast. They now had three. It was Monday, which meant by Thursday, fight night, their time would be up.

Each morning that came and went felt like another nail in their coffins. If Lenny Ace really had nothing to do with the douche canoe who'd conned Becca to get closer to The Crows, then why not just turn the bastard over?

He didn't have that big of a crew, it wouldn't be hard to narrow down the suspects. Find the culprit. Or fuck, choose one to use as a scapegoat to get out of the mess. Though, I was sure Diesel would see through a scheme like that.

"What are you thinking about?" Corvus asked, falling into step next to me as I made my way down to the cafeteria for lunch.

"What?"

"You had a face."

I shrugged. "The Aces. Their time is almost up."

His face darkened, gaze lifting away from me as we continued to walk. "You worried?"

I thought about it. Worried wasn't the right word. I didn't want anything to happen to them. To me. There was a modicum of discomfort simply because I couldn't predict the future—see what was going to happen. But that discomfort was entirely overshadowed by the clawing need to put bodies into shallow graves.

Erase the threat before it could erase us.

I wanted to *act* before we were acted upon.

The waiting was killing me.

Corvus let out a little snort, shaking his head. "You're fucking excited, aren't you?"

I licked my lips. It wasn't quite the right word, either. "Impatient," I said, correcting him. "If something's going to go down, I just wish it would happen already. I don't like waiting. Not knowing—"

"When?" Corvus supplemented for me. "Not knowing what they are going to do and when and how they intend to do it."

I nodded and Corvus scrubbed a palm over his mouth, sighing.

"It's fucking exhausting being prepared for every scenario."

"That why you're not sleeping again?"

His expression soured, and he didn't reply.

"If you need me to, I can—"

"I'm good," he rushed to say, his back up, brows down. "Don't worry about it."

I pressed my lips together, muttering, "If you say so," as we walked through the doors to the cafeteria to find the others.

A little sizzle of anticipation went through me at the memory of Brianna with her golden hair up in flames. The phantom smell of burnt hair still lingered in the air.

The guys had assured me nothing would come of what I'd done, and it turned out they were right. I didn't hear a single word from the office about it. Nothing from Brianna's father. Not his lawyers. The cops. No one.

If I wasn't careful, it would go straight to my motherfucking head— this new position I'd fallen into. One with the kind of power I'd only ever dared to dream I could have.

I paused before following Corvus to the serving line, shocked still by the girl sitting three tables away. Alone.

A girl in an oversized sweater and sheer black tights, with beat up leather boots on her feet and a shaved head.

Brianna must've felt my eyes on her because she turned her head just enough to catch sight of me in her periphery, and stiffened. Her makeup was darker than usual. Heavy coal lined her eyes, winged out at the edges. Damn good falsies fringed her brown eyes, and somehow, even with the slightly reddened patches of healing skin showing through her buzzcut, she rocked the look.

Her upper lip curled as she turned back to her mostly empty tray, tapping something violently on her phone until I could hear the music blaring through her Bluetooth earbuds from here.

Brianna's friends were sitting across the cafeteria, I noticed, with another girl I sometimes saw with them. It seemed that girl was the new queen. And Brianna Moore was the newest outcast.

A dark laugh escaped my mouth. "Welcome to the club, bitch," I muttered to myself, snatching up a tray to catch up to Corvus at the end of the serving line. Barely paying any attention to what I was putting on my tray. I'd have Rook give it all a good sniff before I ate any of it, though I didn't expect a repeat offense from the *former* queen of Briar Hall.

On a whim, I filled a bowl of the potato soup, slipping it onto Brianna's table as I passed. "You should try it," I told her. "It's not half bad when it's laxative free."

Rook smirked at me as I slid into the table, but I couldn't smile back, sensing something that was majorly off.

I couldn't place it for a minute, but a glance at Grey made it pretty obvious. He sat across from me next to Rook, his tray stacked high with completely untouched food.

"Grey?" I asked, and he blinked, taken aback as though he hadn't even noticed us sitting down.

"Everything good?"

"What? Oh. Yeah. Just..." he pushed his tray away, grimacing. "Stomach's bugging me."

"Never stopped you before," Rook said, leaning forward to rest his forearms on the table, getting a better look at his brother. "What's up, Bro?"

"I said I have a fucking stomachache, Rook. Leave it."

Rook lifted his hands in truce, reaching into his jacket for a quick nip of whatever was in his flask this morning.

Grey's gaze tracked above our heads, to the big round clock on the wall, and his jaw clenched.

A girly shriek rose above the din of lunchtime conversation, forcing all other sound to hush. I spun, ready to launch off the bench. Rook and Corv were primed, too, but Grey...

He didn't seem surprised.

I searched the crowd, finding the girl standing at the edge of the room like she'd just jumped from her seat. She pointed animatedly at our table. "Oh my god. Oh my god!" she squealed, practically fucking vibrating.

"It's him! You guys, it's him!"

The girl next to her got up, snatching the phone from the vibrating chick's hand to look at what set her off. She gasped, her hand flying to her mouth, eyes flitting between us and the phone.

No. Between *Corvus* and the phone.

The girl pointed straight at Corvus, her face tainted with a scarlet flush. "It's Primal Ethos! Corvus James is The Bone Man!"

Somehow, I found Corvus' hand on the bench next to me. His cold as stone under my touch. If he got any paler, he'd turn into the skeleton he'd worked so hard to hide from the world.

"Corv," I hedged, my pulse racing as the cafeteria exploded in a raucous outcry of sound. Students rushed to see what the girls were talking about. Phones chimed under tapping fingers, searching. Eyes watching, wide and incredulous. All of them on Corvus.

On The Bone Man.

Fuck.

"Oh my god, can I, like, have your autograph," a brunette asked, hurrying over with a sharpie while she pulled down the neck of her shirt to expose the tops of her round breasts. An eager gleam in her eyes that had my darkness roaring to the surface.

I was on my feet in a second, shoving her until her fat ass hit the tile. "Get the fuck back," I hissed.

Corvus rose behind me, the entire bench scraping over the floor as he pushed free of the table, the screeching sound sending the cafeteria back into a buzzing silence.

"*Wait,*" the girl on the floor whined, but Corvus was already gone. Storming from the cafeteria in a wake of a hundred whispering voices.

15

CORVUS

"Okay, so I know this isn't exactly what you wanted, but—"

"How the fuck did this get out, Max?" I growled down the line, pacing the floor of my bedroom, trying not to lose my fucking mind. My thoughts already racing through every possibility. Everything that would be completely *fucked* now that this was out. Whether there was a way to claw it back. Make it go away before it was too late.

"We're looking into it, but it looks like it was leaked by a blogger."

"Someone we know?"

"No. It's a ghost account. No posts before this one. Are you near a computer?"

I went to my desk and punched the power button on my monitor, but couldn't bring myself to sit. "Yeah."

"'Kay, the first post was made as a comment on that forum, oh shit, what's it called, *um...*"

"*Maxine.*"

"Oh right, the 'music is my medicine' one. You know where they have all those fan theories about your identity and—"

"Yeah. I'm there," I said, the website coming up on the monitor. "Where is it?"

"It should be at the top of the forum page. It has about twenty-thousand comments on it now."

The post at the top of the forum was titled *Who is the Bone Man?*

It was made by a user months ago and had a shit-ton of people following it, but I was looking for *one* particular user. The one who somehow figured out who I was. If I could find them, trace them, then I could have them take this shit back.

Maybe Grey could...

"Do you see it?" Max asked on the other end of the line as my fingers hovered over the mouse, re-reading the user name who'd posted not one but five comments on the post. Images. Facial mapping comparisons. Street cam footage of me getting off my bike and entering backstage at the Lodi show. And a signed NDA. The one I made Maxine sign when she expressed interest in managing me.

It was irrefutable.

"You see the blogger tag?"

I did, but I was still trying to process it. Knowing what it meant, but not wanting it to be true.

CrowKiller321.

The final comment uploaded at 11:25am this morning was signed off with a simple moniker. *Anonymous.*

The monitor cord ripped from the wall with a *snap*, sparks flying from the outlet as I chucked it against the wall. The sharp edge of it embedding in the drywall so it stayed there, half in the wall and half out of it like a demented form of artwork.

It brought me no fucking relief as I fought to level out my breathing, my skin cold and coated in an icy sweat.

Somewhere in the room, Maxine was calling to me, her voice broken by dead sound. I fell into the chair at my desk and lifted my phone from the floor, seeing a new call coming in on the screen. The one I'd been dreading since this afternoon.

Diesel.

"Corvus?" Maxine shouted. "Are you there, is everything—"

I ended the call with Max and answered the one from my father, inhaling shakily through my nose.

"Yeah?"

A heavy silence filled the other end of the call before Diesel finally replied. "It seems you've been keeping secrets from me, Son."

He let the statement hang between us for a moment, maybe

expecting me to fill the void for him, but I couldn't. I didn't have time to plan a response. Better not to speak at all.

"I'll be expecting you at the house in the next thirty minutes."

The line went dead.

I bent over my knees, pushing tense fingers through my hair to grip it tightly at my scalp. Downstairs the front door opened, and I heard Ava Jade and the guys rush inside, locked in heated conversation.

"Corvus," Sparrow crowed up the stairs. "Are you up there?"

Fuck.

I'd been so careful with this secret.

More than any other.

There were no leaks. None save Ava Jade and Becca fucking Hart.

Then again, the fucker had sealed documents from Maxine's office. Maybe it was her who'd sold me out. Though that didn't seem likely either since the mystery of The Bone Man was half the fucking allure. No mystery, no cold hard cash in her wallet. Or mine. Not anymore.

My door swept open, and Ava Jade stood there, framed on both sides by my brothers.

"We can fix this," Ava Jade said, the promise gleaming like hard stone in her eyes. "We just have to—"

"It's too late," I replied, detached from the words. "Diesel knows. It's over."

My Sparrow shook her head, gaze snagging on the monitor still protruding from my wall. "It doesn't have to be. Why shouldn't you be able to have both? It's fucking stupid. Being The Bone Man never stopped you from fulfilling your duties to your family before, why should it now?"

"Dies won't see it that way." Grey grimaced, his face pale and ashen like it was his secret that'd been put on stage for the whole world to see. It was a mite too close to looking like pity for my fucking taste.

I got to my feet and snatched my leather jacket from the floor. "Dies is expecting me. I have to go."

Ava Jade stepped out of my doorway for me to pass, reaching out to me before thinking better of it to claw her hand back to her side. Smart girl.

"Grey," I said, pausing in the hall. "The fucker who leaked the intel —I think it's the same bastard who's been messing with Ava Jade. I doubt you'll be able to trace him since we haven't had a break with anything leading up to now, but it's worth a shot. Max has the details you'll need to try the trace."

He nodded solemnly.

"Are you sure it's him?" Sparrow asked, horror plain on her paling face. "It could be—"

"I'm not sure," I told her, mostly because I didn't want her to blame herself for this. I didn't know why, but I *was* sure. I knew it was him. Either it was that fucker or it was the Ace Becca had been dating. He might've gleaned enough information from her to piece it together before Becca broke things off.

"Regardless," I added. "We need to find out who it is. Either it's a nobody who got lucky with a guess, or it's someone with a vendetta that needs to be crushed to fucking dust."

"I'm on it," Grey promised, turning to stalk toward his bedroom.

"Wait," Ava Jade called after me. "Maybe I could come with you? I could help Diesel understand—"

"You being there won't help, Sparrow. If anything, it'll just make it worse."

I couldn't bear to see how that comment hit, grinding my teeth as I stormed down the stairs. It was the truth. And sometimes, the truth wasn't kind.

The blacktop vanished beneath the tires of my Ducati as I sped across town, ignoring every road sign and light along the way. I tried to come up with a way to explain this shit to my father without breaking the fragile bond still healing from the cracks formed over the past weeks during Ava Jade's trials.

I'd own my shit. I always did. But a part of me wanted to chew his fucking head off. Tell him that I didn't have a choice but to lie about it. He never would have supported it, and I wouldn't have had the outlet I needed to keep myself his perfect soldier all this time.

My engine barked as I revved around the corner leading to his street, slowing to a static purr.

Diesel's car sat parked up in the drive of the house where I lived with him up until two years ago.

A modest charcoal gray house with a double car garage. Two-stories. A rose garden Dies' wife started before we came into the picture bloomed with crimson flowers beneath the tall windows next to the door. Pristine. He would settle for no less.

I bowed my head, stepping off the bike. My thirty minutes were nearly up.

I pushed into the house, the overwhelming scent of my prepubescent years filling my lungs. Cigar smoke, hot cast iron, and coffee. All of it cut with the smell that was uniquely Diesel's. It clung to the place.

I remembered when I first entered this house, an angry, scared boy with no place left in the world to go. It smelled like a mother then. The lingering scent of Dies' late wife had brought me comfort those first few weeks, before it inevitably began to fade. It reminded me of my own mother.

"In here," came Diesel's deep baritone from the living room down the hall to the right. I kicked off my shoes before going in, trying to cling to a singular racing thought so I could figure out how I wanted to handle this. But the truth of it was, I had no fucking idea what was about to come out of my mouth.

Diesel lifted his head from the laptop screen he was scowling at on the coffee table. His elbows on his knees, hands clasped tight.

He turned the screen to face me without a word.

On it was a webpage that read in massive white font on a black background *The Bone Man*. Below was the comparative images of mine and my alter-ego's faces, showing all the marker matches that confirmed our identities were one and the same. How this fucker had access to that sort of software was beyond me. But it wasn't the worst of the evidence. The signed NDA was what really made it undeniable. I was just glad I always signed as *Corvus James*, excluding my true surname.

A prickle of unease festered in my gut as I racked my brain trying to remember if that name was anywhere on that document. I remembered Maxine saying it wouldn't be binding without my full name, but had I used it? Had I given her...

"Is this accurate?" Diesel asked, and I pulled myself back to the here and now, forcing myself to stand straighter. "Your face is all over the internet, son. They were talking about you on The Edge this morning."

Fuck.

Of course he found out through the fucking radio. He always had that station playing.

"It's true," I confirmed, and Diesel's eyes glimmered with malice as he stared at me from his seat on the couch, jerking his gaze away as he stood, showing me his back. Just long enough for him to get control back.

He popped his knuckles, lifting his head to stare out the window, past the roses, onto the quiet street outside. "You kept this from me..."

"I did."

"For how long?"

"I signed with my manager a little over two years ago," I found myself saying. There was no point in lying about any of it. Not anymore. "But I've been uploading my music anonymously to different sites for longer."

He took a shaky breath.

"You've always been so good at keeping your secrets, Son," Dies trailed off. "You thought you were keeping your little humanitarian project from me too, but I've had Julia on my payroll longer than you have."

My teeth clenched.

"You knew? This whole time?"

"Of course I fucking knew. This is *my* city. I know everything that happens here."

...but I never had a show in Thorn Valley. And that was *very* purposeful. Which was why he never figured it out.

He turned back to face me, hard lines in his forehead. "But *this*? How could you keep this from me?"

A muscle in my jaw popped as I held back a thousand words I wouldn't be able to take back if I spoke them aloud.

"You must know," Diesel continued. "How *stupid* this is."

Heat flooded my chest.

"This gives our enemies a time and place where you're going to be. Show dates and times. Locations."

"Which was *why* I hid my identity."

"Oh? So it wasn't just to keep it from me, then?"

Breathe.

"For all you know, Son, it *was* our enemies who outed you."

"There's nothing I can do about it now. It's over."

Without the mystery of The Bone Man, the allure was gone. Max would probably fire me by the end of the week. He had nothing to worry about.

"Is it?" Diesel pressed. "Or is this what you want? Are you leaving? Do you want out? Is that what this is?"

"What?" I cocked my head at him. "What the fuck are you talking about?"

"Are you leaving the Saints? To become this... this *Bone Man?* Do your brothers know?"

He could see the answer on my face.

"So you've all been lying to me, then." He ran his tongue along his teeth, baring them in a small growl.

"I'm not leaving," I said, realizing what it was I needed to say. The only thing he wanted to hear. "It was an outlet. One I needed. But my loyalty, my *family* is here."

Diesel shook his head, clearing the distance between us with a stiff hand raised like he wished he could rip me apart with his bare hands. I didn't budge, and he stopped mere inches from my face.

"Family doesn't lie to one another," he spat. "I taught you better."

His words stung, and I recoiled from the truth in them. Guilt over the selfish need for him to accept this part of me made the anger fizzle out, sending the beast back to its cage. Leaving me hollow.

"There's only three more days until time's up for our enemies in Edgewood," he said. "I expect this mess to be cleaned up by then."

I nodded, turning to leave.

"And Corvus?"

I waited.

"Don't ever lie to me again."

16

AVA JADE

The thrum of bass and loud conversation filtered through the heavy black steel door leading to the underbelly of Sanctum. Corvus thudded his closed fist on the door twice before Pinkie opened it for us, stepping aside to allow us through.

"Good luck tonight, Rook," he said as we entered.

"As if he'll need it," I replied sweetly, throwing Rook a wink behind me.

I already figured as much, but it seemed the rules about being armed in Sanctum did *not* apply to Saints. We went down to the private fight club without so much as a second glance, never mind a pat down the likes of which I had endured last time.

Though if you had half a brain cell, you could see that we were all armed to the teeth. Tonight was *the* night. In a precious few hours, the deadline Diesel gave the Aces would be up, and as far as we were aware, there had been no word from them. The guys had contacts on Ace turf, though, and word was the streets of Edgewood were getting hella tense these past few days.

Arms passing hands.

Meetings held in private locations not usually used by the gang.

Security around Lenny Ace's place tripled in the last forty-eight hours.

They weren't running. They were getting ready to weather the storm.

Unless a miracle happened and they realized how very outmatched they were, there would be blood before the end of the night was through.

"Hey," Corvus said, his fingers touching my wrist to prod me to stop once we reached the bottom of the stairs. He jerked his head for the others to go ahead, holding only me back with him in the shadows.

"What's up?" I asked, trying not to let the tension I was feeling creep into my voice.

I was worried about him. About what happened on Monday. I could only imagine how it went with Diesel. He'd been ignoring all of Maxine's attempts to get ahold of him. Refusing to so much as look at any of the online commentary. He wouldn't talk to any of us about it. Or anyone else, either.

If anyone so much as looked at him funny at Briar Hall, he would growl in their direction like a poked bear, and they'd scatter. It didn't stop the fangirls from attaching notes to the windshield of the Rover or in his desk at homeroom.

Most were smart enough not to include their names. The ones who weren't... well two had already completely unenrolled from Briar Hall after barely five words from my mouth.

"Corv?" I hedged when he didn't continue straight away. I knew he was worried about me, too, but for an entirely different reason.

His jaw flexed. "Look, I know you think it was the Kings who took out your dad—"

"I won't kill anyone," I said before he could finish. "Not tonight, anyway."

"Sparrow..." he warned.

"You can't ask me not to nail the motherfucker to the wall and rip out his intestines if I find him. Tell me you wouldn't do the same if it had been Dies who was taken out?"

It was still a sore spot, I could tell. But regardless of what happened between them, I could tell that Corvus would still raise the entire city of Edgewood to ash if an Ace took Diesel down.

He made a low sound of agreement in his throat, and I nodded. "Look, I know Diesel needs this alliance right now, but there will come a time when he no longer does. And when that time comes, I want to have a name. I want to be ready."

He nodded quietly to himself.

"I'll help you," he said, surprising me. "When the time comes. But we keep this between us. I'm sure Grey and Rook know exactly what you're doing too, but the others don't need to know."

"What? You think I don't know how to not draw attention?"

That brought a small smirk to his mouth. "You? Draw attention? Never."

I punched his arm. "Jackass."

"Wait, Sparrow. One more thing."

I rolled my eyes. "Come on, Corv, I want to get a look at the other fighter."

He held my gaze for a few seconds before asking me for the one thing I couldn't give him. "I don't want you talking to Diesel."

"About?" I asked innocently.

"You know exactly what about."

I shrugged, adopting an innocent expression, batting my lashes. "Sorry, no idea what you're talking about, Bones."

"*Ava Jade,*" Corvus called after me, but I was already gone, weaving through the crowd toward the bar, where I knew Rook would be having one of the three ounces of whiskey he was 'allowed' before a fight.

I kept a vigilant eye on every face in attendance, easily discerning the Saints from the Kings, and the bloodthirsty rich citizens of NorCal from the gang members.

Soft hands, clean fingernails, unlined faces—definitely the bankers, lawyers, and corrupt high ranking officers.

Unarmed with callused hands and taut jaws—the Kings.

Armed, ready, and wary—our people.

I saw the guy whose eye I took during the hunt trial sneering at me from across the room. I gave him an apologetic shrug, and he looked away as I caught up with Grey and Rook.

"So," I said, glancing around to the other side of the ring and the drawn curtain set into the wall beyond it. "Where's the other guy?"

I had to shout to be heard over the din of conversation and music, the smell of whiskey rolling off Rook much stronger than three ounces worth. I didn't worry about *him* fighting wasted, but I did worry about the survival of the other guy.

"Not here yet," he muttered.

I took the shot glass poised between his fingers and slung it back, grimacing as it burned a path down to my stomach.

Rook lifted a brow at me. "Sorry, I needed that."

He turned to the little bar window cut out, tapping the shot glass on the polished cement bar top to signal he wanted another.

"How much have you had?"

He lifted his replacement to his mouth, but paused to shoot me a dark glare. "Not nearly enough," he said before slamming it back and I made myself shut up about it.

The guys hadn't had a call from Julia in weeks, and I was beginning to see just how much Rook needed them to stay sane. His darkness was so close to the surface that in the right light I could almost see it. Surrounding him like an inky aura with claws and teeth. Demanding to be sated.

This fight wasn't a good idea tonight, but there was nothing I could do to stop it now. Rook would never back down, and I'd never expect him to.

The Kings might've been in for more of a show than they bargained for...

I stepped past Rook to slap my palm on the bar, getting the bartender's attention. He was a slender guy with a shock of green hair in a black Sanctum t-shirt. I didn't think I'd seen him here the last time. It had been one of the girls from upstairs bartending if I remembered correctly. His nametag read *Johnny*.

"A water," I told him. "And a Guinness."

"Who's the Guinness for?" Grey asked as the bartender turned to get my order ready.

"Me."

He looked at me askance, with a knot between his brows.

I took the frothy black gold from the bartender and pushed the water into Rook's hand. "We were broke a lot," I found myself telling him. "But Dad always kept a few Guinness stashed away from Mom in the kitchen. It's filling and the taste isn't half bad. It grew on me."

Grey frowned, his brows drawing to cloak his eyes in shadow.

I hadn't meant to trigger him.

I took a long swallow and passed it to him. "Want some?" I asked with the closest thing to a smile I could muster, trying to erase the sour mood I'd just brought on.

For as often as we didn't have food, unlike Grey, I didn't starve. Not much, anyway, and not often. We lived close enough to several stores with poor security, which meant that if it got bad enough, I could pretty easily lift a few Twinkies from the low shelves to keep us fed for a day or two.

I'd had options.

By the sound of it, Grey hadn't.

Grey took the proffered beer and sipped it, still brooding. And shockingly, Rook was also sipping his water, even though the look on his face told me he thought it tasted more like donkey piss.

I laughed quietly to myself, still gauging our surroundings as Corvus finally made his way over to us, his cold stare passing over the faces in the private club.

"He's in the back," Grey told him. "On the phone. Sounds like there might be a problem with Rook's opponent."

Corvus nodded.

It would be the first time he'd seen Dies since Monday. The guys had been sent on a few errands and were still getting updates on shit with the Aces and what our game plan was, but as far as I knew they hadn't spoken.

Grey passed me back my Guinness, and I wrapped both hands around it, gulping down another few mouthfuls to quell the hunger pangs in my stomach. Rook had been with me at Briar Hall earlier, and we wound up doing some 'light' sparring in the living room to get ready for tonight. Once we were both sweaty, eating was the furthest thing from our minds.

Besides, we had a huge fucking mess to clean up by the time we were done. It was a good thing Becca wasn't around because I was sure she'd have something to say about the cracked TV screen and the half of the sofa that was now concave, the legs busted off.

I couldn't even remember how it happened or whose fault it was.

"Whoa," Grey warned, taking the Guinness back before I could finish it. "Slow down, babe."

I licked my lips, knowing he was right. Tonight wasn't the night to get tipsy. I didn't think we had anything to worry about on our turf, but Diesel could give the order to attack the Aces any time after the deadline was up. And right now, I didn't think he had a proclivity for patience.

My gaze hooked on a man hovering near the entrance, watching us.

I squinted at him, giving him an annoyed sneer until he looked away, crossing his arms over his chest.

The guys chatted about the fight, but I couldn't seem to focus on the conversation anymore. Something about the guy was bugging me.

He was pale. Tall. Broad through the shoulders but lean, with brown hair and narrowed blue eyes.

"AJ?" I heard Grey say, realizing it wasn't the first time.

"Hmm?"

"I was asking if you'd—"

"Who is that?" I asked, inclining my head to the guy across the room. Something about him seemed so familiar, but I just couldn't place it.

"One of the Kings," Corvus answered, and I should've known he'd do his homework on them, especially since making the alliance. "Don't have a name for him, though. I only managed to get intel on the major players. He's likely low on the food chain."

"Does something about him..."

"Seem familiar?" Grey finished for me, and I sensed him growing nearer to my side, trying to covertly get a better look at the guy.

And then it hit me.

"He fits the description," I said in a low voice.

"What description?"

"Becca's. He's about six feet. Brown hair, long on top. Pale. I don't see any ink."

"Becca's guy was an Ace," Rook said, bored.

I shook my head. He was right. I was probably just seeing things that weren't there. But I had a right to be on edge.

I shivered. "Whatever, the guy gives me the creeps."

"Me too."

I spun at the unfamiliar voice, finding a guy standing a couple feet away from us, a pint of golden beer in his right hand. The jeweled crown tattoo around the base of his index finger giving away his status as a

King. He looked... familiar, but then again he also looked like half the male students at Briar Hall. Great cheekbones, even better skin. With sandy blond hair cut short, a chin dimple, and a classic Cali tan.

But overshadowing it all was the weathered veneer of a man who'd already seen some shit in his short life.

Truly though, if it weren't for the roughness of his hands, the wicked gleam to his eyes, and the style of his clothes, the guy could've passed for the son of one of the bluebloods in attendance here tonight, too.

But he *wasn't* that. He was a King.

"WHAT?" I COCKED MY HEAD AT HIM.

"He's creepy as fuck," the guy repeated.

"Isn't he one of yours?" I asked, a rhetorical question, really.

The guy nodded. "Yup."

He turned, feeling the unanswered query still lingering between us.

His brown eyes roved the length of me before continuing. He leaned in closer, conspiratorially, making Rook growl low from behind him. Guy had balls, I'd give him that.

"His name's Aries," the King whispered to me, the smell of his grapefruit and sandalwood cologne strong in my nose. "He's always been kind of a loner. But he's lethal when Maverick needs him to be. He's the one we use when there's a message that needs sending if you catch my meaning. He's also our one man *cleanup* crew."

My stomach churned.

The guy they sent in when they needed to send a message...

Could that fuck be the one who took out my dad?

Unconsciously, my hands balled at my sides. I only realized when Rook dropped a heavy palm on my shoulder, shocking me back to the present. He dragged me back a step, pulling the King's attention.

"And you are?" Rook asked, his smile all teeth.

The guy stretched out a hand to Rook, inclining his head respectfully. Clearly he already knew who they were. "Drake."

Rook's upper lip twitched, but he took Drake's hand.

"And you must be Rook Clayton."

Drake nodded to Corvus and Grey. "Greyson Winters. And Corvus James. Your reps precede you."

"Afraid yours doesn't," Corvus said gruffly, staring openly at the guy.

Drake frowned, but there was still a smile lingering at the edge of his mouth. He wasn't offended, or at least he was doing his best to appear like he wasn't. "Well, shit, man. Way to call me out. We can't all be the sons of a veritable street god."

"Touché," Grey put in, throwing a covert elbow into Corvus' ribs. Reminding him that we were trying to make friends here, not enemies.

The guy snorted a laugh.

Corvus gave the guy a nod. "Enjoy the fight, man," he said before stalking away, likely gone to scope out the competition for Rook.

"What crawled up his ass," Drake whispered playfully, tossing me a wink before he turned to the bar for another drink.

Rook eyed him as he turned away, and I gave him a hard look. *Play nice,* I mouthed to him. The guy had paid me barely an ounce of attention. I pitied the fool who one day tried to actually pick me up in front of them. That guy barely flirted and Rook looked close to smash mode. Grey too, actually.

"What are you smiling at?" Grey asked me, confused.

I shook my head, clearing my throat. "Nothing."

He narrowed his eyes on me, as if he just looked hard enough he could see straight through skin, muscle, and bone to see exactly what I was thinking.

I heard Diesel over the music and peered to my left from the corner of my eye, finding him walking toward the high top table where he usually sat during the fights. Either the injury to his ankle was healing really well or he'd just gotten hella fucking good at hiding it. I detected almost no limp whatsoever.

He stopped, turning to bark something at Pinkie, who was following him. Pinkie nodded before taking off in the other direction, leaving Diesel to sit alone, adjusting his battered leather jacket with a sneer on his lips.

Now was my chance.

I rolled my shoulders back, wishing Grey had let me finish my beer.

"I'll be right back," I told them, not waiting for the protests I knew would surely follow before picking my way through the crowd.

Diesel's gaze snagged on me as I approached, watching with a wary distaste as I dragged the tall stool opposite him out from beneath the table and plunked my ass atop it.

"Ava Jade," he said, cold blue eyes burning into me. "To what do I owe the pleasure?"

I leaned over the table so he would hear me without the need to raise my voice. It was one thing saying what I was about to say to him, it would be another thing if he thought people could overhear us.

"You're being a dick," I told him, careful to keep my voice even, watching his face for changes in his expression.

He managed to keep a level of neutrality, but the slight downturn of his lips gave him away, even concealed by his beard as they were.

"I think I misheard you," he said.

I shook my head slowly. "You didn't."

"If you think—"

"Hear me out, and then I'll fuck off."

A vein throbbed in Diesel's neck, but he said nothing else. Probably just wanted to get rid of me as quickly as possible. I was banking on that.

"I don't know what you said to him on Monday—"

"That's between me and my son."

I waited, not letting his defense wake the dark within. This needed to be said. And it needed to be said in a way that he might actually listen.

"I know it is," I replied coolly. "Which is why I don't know what you said. What I do know is that he's been a shell of himself since then."

That seemed to strike a nerve. Good. Maybe I was on the right track, then.

"He won't return any of his manager's calls. He's completely given up on an entire part of himself. An entire chunk of his soul."

"That's fucking dramatic." Diesel scoffed.

"You don't get it, but that isn't a good enough reason for you to take it from him."

"He *lied* to me. I'm not having this conversation."

He jerked his head toward a Saint nearby. Axel, I thought his name was. *Get her out of my sight* written in his stare.

I lifted my leg, letting my black skirt fall up my thigh to reveal the blades strapped there. I held Axel's gaze, daring him to interrupt.

He glanced between Diesel and me, hesitating.

"Let me finish," I told Diesel. "And you'll never hear another word about it from me."

His jaw tightened, but Diesel gave Axel a little nod, rolling his eyes.

"Corvus lied to you because he knew you wouldn't understand. He knew you wouldn't condone him spending his time doing something that could take him away from all of this, regardless of how important it is to him."

"What's your point?"

I swallowed down the frustrated rage trying to claw to the surface, clutching the bottom of the table to keep from flying over it at him. For a guy who clearly cared so much about his sons, he was being so fucking dense about this.

"My point is that he's been The Bone Man for *years*."

I let that sink in.

"And has he ever once shirked his duties to his family? To the Saints?"

He didn't like being reasoned with.

"He'll resent you for this," I continued. "Whether he understands your reasoning or not. His music is a part of him."

There was so much of him, of his soul, his heart, in every word he sang. It would be a fucking crime to stop him from creating.

"You wouldn't chop off his arm, would you?"

"You don't understand our ways."

"I don't?" It was my turn to scoff.

Diesel's attention wandered, catching on something to our left, and I followed his line of sight to where Corvus was standing with the guys again near the bar. Grey pointed at us, and Corvus lifted his head, going white at the sight of me sitting across from his father.

"He asked me not to do this," I added. "But I care about him. I care that he's hurting."

Diesel looked doubtfully at me but said nothing.

This was the part my body physically fought against me saying, but Corvus and the shit with Primal Ethos was only part of the problem.

There was a rift between this father and his sons. And a large part of it was my fault.

A bigger part of his was his own damned fault, but regardless of who was to blame, I wouldn't take sons away from a father who would do literally anything in this world to keep them safe.

If only I'd been so lucky.

"All I'm asking is for you to consider what forcing him to stop might do *to him*. He *can* have both."

"If that's all—"

"I also know that *I* have been the cause of a lot of tension between you and them."

He lifted a brow.

"Even though the vast majority of that shit is your own fucking fault," I added, completely unable to help myself, then I sighed. "I don't want to carve a rift between you."

"Oh?"

"Which is why, I'm..."

He tipped his head slightly to one side, light eyes glinting with triumph.

"You know what, I'm not going to fucking say it," I decided. "I'm not sorry. I know you don't trust me. You don't like me. And frankly, I don't give a shit. I don't need you to like me. But I *will* try harder to not want to slit your throat... for them."

A slow smile spread on his mouth. "All right."

"All right?"

A Saint approached the table, clearly drunk, with two shots held between his fingers. He set them on the table in front of Diesel, sloshing half their contents over the wooden top. "Hey, Dies," he said. "Happy Birthday man! Have a shot with me."

"It's not my birthday," he told the Saint. "Not for a while yet."

"Oh shit man, I thought it was today. Gives me time to get you something; though, eh?"

Diesel shook his head, getting annoyed. "Crowley," he said, eyes indicating me across the table. "I'm in the middle of a chat with our newest member. Do you mind?"

"Oh fuck, yeah man. Sorry."

The Saint left both shots untouched on the table and left, giving me a wicked side eye as he went.

"Where were we?" Diesel said, pushing the shots away. But before I could open my mouth to say anything else, we were interrupted a second time.

Pinkie returned, leaning down to whisper something in Diesel's ear. His jaw tightened, and he cursed between clenched teeth.

My pulse raced in my chest, adrenaline spiking in my blood as my hand unconsciously went to my thigh, assessing the immediate area for threats.

"Relax," Diesel told me, sensing where my mind had gone. Then his stare deepened, considering me in a new light.

"You still have a line on Alpha?" Diesel asked Pinkie without taking his eyes off me.

"Yeah. You have someone for her?"

He nodded toward me. "We promised our new comrades a show. Make the call."

Pinkie turned, vanishing back the way he came, cell phone to his ear.

"Am I missing something?" I asked, skin still tingling as the burst of adrenaline began to fade.

"It seems the fighter we lined up for Rook soiled his big boy pants and took the first bus out of town."

I lifted my brows, scowling.

What a pussy.

Diesel nodded, agreeing to my unvoiced sentiment.

"But our new friends," he said, sweeping an arm over the gathering of Kings, Saints, lawyers and bankers. "Still expect a show."

"So you're replacing the fighter?"

"*Fighters*," he corrected me, and the smile crawling across his mouth made my insides shudder.

"Looks like you have a chance to prove that you meant what you said," he continued, running his tongue over his teeth. "You are now tonight's fighter, Ava Jade. I suggest you go get ready."

17

ROOK

Fucking coward.

It wasn't the first time some big talker failed to live up to the noise, backing down at the last second because of some bullshit excuse.

I finished my whiskey and hollered around the curtain for another, tapping my empty glass on the cement wall as I swiped the back of my hand over my mouth.

Lighting my last cigarette, I went back to the benches in the private room, inhaling deeply until my lungs were filled with the sweet tarry taste of tobacco.

Grey held up his phone, showing Ava Jade a video of Alpha; the female fighter Diesel had wanted to acquire for a fight here since we started the events.

"See how she uses her legs," Grey was saying, pointing to the screen, and Ava Jade nodded. "She weakens your stability like that so when she strikes up top you go down harder. She's good on the mat, too. Don't let her bring you down. If she does, you won't be able to get out of it."

Her cheekbones flared. She disagreed.

I couldn't say whether she was right or wrong about her ability to take Alpha. I'd only seen her fight once, but she was a lethal combination of speed and size. The other girl, even one in the same weight class as her, didn't stand a chance.

And Ava Jade was at least a full weight class down. Possibly two weight classes. But then again, she'd almost had *me* that night out behind the apartment buildings. She hadn't needed her blades then, just the incentive of getting her winnings from betting on me in the fight and the rush of a challenge.

As twitchy as I was that I wouldn't be smashing heads tonight after all, at least I got to watch this fight. It was the best alternative, and maybe I'd get a second hand release from watching her take Alpha down.

It wouldn't lift the heavy burden pressing down on my soul, but it might soothe it. For another day. Another hour. Another minute at least.

If Julia didn't call soon...

I finished off my cigarette and stomped it out beneath my boot.

"How are you on the ground?" Grey asked my Ghost, and her lips pressed together tight.

He took her silence and expression to mean something they didn't. It wasn't that she wasn't good on the ground, it was that if she got stuck in a hold, unable to move with someone on top of her, she panicked. It was that panic that would be her undoing someday.

It was a scar that we needed to help her heal. It could save her life.

"Focus on what you're good at," I found myself saying.

Her gaze flicked up to meet mine, burning eyes boring into me. "Too bad I can't use my blades," she said with a smirk that didn't reach her eyes.

"You don't need them," Corvus said, entering through the curtain with my fresh whiskey in his hand. He passed it to me, going to kneel in front of Ava Jade with thin strips of torn cloth to wrap her knuckles. "She might have more skill than you, but it's at a professional level. She won't fight dirty, and she won't be expecting you to."

"She also won't expect you to be able to take a hit as well as you can," Grey added. "You need to outlast her and wait for your opening."

"She's weak in the knees," I put in. "During the fight I saw last year in Lodi, she took a hit to her inner right knee, not even a hard one, and it almost put her flat on her ass."

Ghost nodded, taking it all in.

The noise and light from the main floor pushed into the private space as Diesel and Pinkie entered, throwing the curtain back shut behind them. "Alpha's here," he announced. "Fight's in fifteen. Is she prepped?"

"Almost," Corvus growled.

"Put this on," Pinkie said, and I noticed the tiny ass top and shorts in his mammoth fingers. He tossed it to Ava Jade, and she caught it in the fist Corvus wasn't currently wrapping.

Corvus snatched them from her fingers before she could get a good look at them. He pushed to his feet, holding them out to Diesel with murder in his eyes. A smile found my lips.

"The fuck is this, Dies?" he asked, holding the tiny shorts and sports bra between his fingers like they personally offended him. He shoved them back at Pinkie. "She isn't wearing that."

Ava Jade didn't hide her amusement at the exchange, calmly offering her hand to Grey for him to finish the job Corvus started.

"She is," Diesel said. "She can't fight in a skirt and a baggy band tee, son."

"That's fucking lingerie," he argued, jabbing two fingers to the outfit lying on Pinkie's palm.

"It's sport shorts and a sports bra," Diesel corrected him.

"Her tits and ass will be all over the place in that. She *isn't* wearing it."

Diesel took the outfit from Pinkie and strolled over to Ava Jade, holding out the bits of dark cloth for her. "Ava Jade," he said, making a spectacle of asking her permission. "Would you mind wearing this for your fight. Not only will you be able to move more easily, but its effect on many of the dimwitted rich in attendance will make for a better monetary gain."

She looked between Corvus' quickly reddening face and our father's, taking the skimpy outfit with a tip of her head. "If it'll help," she said, sharing a meaningful look with Diesel that I wanted to deconstruct. If my brain wasn't swimming in whiskey, I'd have been doing just that.

One thing was clear though, she was behaving. Doing as she was told. She agreed to this fight at the very last minute. Agreed to fight someone well above her weight class. Agreed to wear *that*.

And I got the sense she wasn't doing it for herself.

Corvus wiped a palm over his mouth, physically holding back whatever else he wanted to say.

Ava Jade sent him a wink. "Let them look," she said. "That's all they'll ever do."

"If any of them touch you, I'll fucking kill them."

Diesel raised a brow at his eldest son, but Corvus' hard gaze never left Ava Jade.

She smiled sweetly at him. "I would expect nothing less, Bones."

In a move not even I could've predicted, Corvus sidestepped closer to me and took the whiskey from my hand, draining it in one long swallow, a sneering grimace on his lips as he stared down Diesel.

"The match is five, five-minute rounds," Diesel told Ava Jade. "It's best if you can last at least until the third."

"So you're betting against me?" she asked him.

He didn't reply.

It was the wrong move. Even more so to let on that he had. It would only push Ava Jade that much harder to win. And win she would. Not without injury. But I felt bad for Alpha, she wouldn't have a soul left once my Ghost sucked it clean from her bones.

"Winner will be determined by submission or knock out."

She nodded her understanding.

"Or by climbing to the top of the cage."

The room went collectively still.

"You're dropping the cage?" I asked, something churning beneath my ribcage. "I thought we weren't doing that anymore since—"

"Since you killed your opponent?" he finished for me. "I don't think there's any risk of that happening tonight, and it adds something extra to the excitement."

"You okay with this?" I asked my Ghost. If she wasn't, Diesel wouldn't be dropping the cage. Period.

She shrugged. "At least she won't be able to get away."

She flexed her fingers, feeling out the wraps as she stood, holding my stare with a wicked gleam in her eyes. My cock thickened in my jeans as I realized what I was seeing in her stare. She was excited.

No. Not just excited.

She hungered for this.

Lusted after it.

An opportunity for her to quell the same darkness that lingered deep inside of her. A darkness that no doubt was on the verge of chaos with all the shit she'd had to go through, and continued having to go through, since she first arrived in Thorn Valley.

She wouldn't be getting what we knew she wanted out of tonight—to find the King who took out her father and start planning how she would take him apart—but this was a good consolation prize.

Corvus pushed my empty glass back at me before turning to Diesel. "I don't think the cage is—"

"She's got this," I interrupted, biting my lip ring as I looked over Ava Jade, seeing the readiness in every one of her muscles.

I nodded to Diesel. "We're good here."

"We'll give you some privacy to change," Diesel offered, pausing before he and Pinkie left. "And Ava Jade?"

"Yeah?"

"Thanks for filling in. The income from this match will be much needed in the weeks to come."

For the war to come, he might as well have said. I expected we'd be meeting as soon as this match was through to go over the plan.

Ava Jade inclined her head, and he was gone, back out through the curtain with Pinkie on his heels.

"This is bullshit," Corvus groaned, turning to pace a short stretch of concrete floor. "She hasn't had enough time to train. Even after all that shit, he clearly *still* wants her dead."

I stopped him, slapping a hand down on his shoulder, gripping tight. His nostrils flared. "She has this. She wouldn't have agreed to it if she didn't."

"She didn't know who she was up against."

"Doesn't matter, Brother. You can't beat a ghost."

The sound of Ava Jade's knife belt clattering against the bench drew our attention back to her. She removed her t-shirt and bra without a second's hesitation, wiggling her hips as she worked to get the skirt over her round ass to let it slip down her thighs to the ground.

The mark of my teeth in her flesh from rally night made my hard on jump in my jeans, and I pawed it, the phantom taste of her on my tongue.

Her nipples pebbled in the cool air under Sanctum, and here, under the lights, it was easier to see the evidence of all the shit she'd endured during the trials. Her body was riddled with bruises in all stages of healing. Some a purple so deep they bordered on black. Others so pale yellow they were hard to discern from her unmarked flesh. And cuts.

The ones in her hips, nearly healed now, put there by me, didn't bother me. The other did.

More than I ever thought I could be bothered by seeing a wound.

She was mine to mark. To mark in the ways she *wanted me* to mark her. In the ways the dark, deprived part of her craved.

No one else was allowed to mark her.

The darkness I'd been working to drown in whiskey and tobacco came back with a violent resurgence, making a heat lick up my back like flames.

Ava Jade pulled on the black shorts and the sports bra before pulling her hair back to twist it into a tight donut shape on the top of her head, securing it with an elastic.

She squatted, rolling her shoulders back and then jumping to get limbered up, her tits bouncing. No fucks given that we were all drooling in her direction with unconcealed chubs.

She widened her stance, striking an invisible opponent, light on her feet.

This was going to be good.

She'd already gone through some drills with Grey and a full body stretch. She was as ready as she was going to be.

Outside, the volume of the crowd turned up, and the sound of a mic turning on marked the start of the event.

"Shit, did someone pick me an entrance song?" she asked.

Corvus and Grey shared a look.

"Don't worry, Ghost. I got you."

Pinkie cleared his throat into the mic before starting the opening of the show, using his best Rogan copycat voice.

Ava Jade jumped on the spot, loosening up, and as the opening tone of Primal Ethos' Gravedigger came over the speaker and Pinkie shouted her name, I yanked her in for a viscous kiss, biting her bottom lip *hard*. She grunted into my mouth before pulling away, licking the small droplet of blood there with a malicious gleam in her eyes and a smile making the tiny cut open more.

"We're right behind you," Grey assured her, and she stepped out of the curtain, and all proof of her excitement or nerves gone in the blink of an eye. She stalked through the crowd, dead-eyed and with her chin raised. I wished I could've seen her face.

Not a single man in attendance dared reach out to touch her. Instead, they backed away as she walked, parting like the red sea. Going silent as the song I chose grew to a loud crescendo of violence all around us. Promising blood. Promising violence. Promising the show of their fucking lives.

Ava Jade. My ghost. Tonight's *gravedigger*.

Distantly, I could hear Corvus cursing at my back. Could see the distaste on Diesel's expression as he watched from his high top table near to the bar. Didn't give two flying fucks about either. It was the perfect song for her entry. And now that everyone knew it was Corvus, why hide it?

He needed to own that shit.

Take control of it before it suffocated him.

Ava Jade stepped through the ropes, the long line of her body bending in the most delicious way until she stood next to Pinkie, waiting, entirely immobile even though I could sense the latent power pulsing beneath her flesh and muscle.

"And in the opposite corner," Pinkie hollered. "*Andrea 'Alpha' Stone!*"

Gravedigger faded into another song, one I didn't recognize, but had to admit was pretty badass.

She swaggered out from the opposite curtain, and I watched her approach as I took the petroleum from Grey. I was always the one on the other side of these ropes. I wanted to be the face she saw when she got through her first round. Her second. Her third.

I would take care of her.

Alpha stepped up through the ropes, unfurling to her full height, and a sour taste filled my mouth. It'd been a minute since I'd seen her in the flesh, and she'd clearly gone up a weight class since then. Standing at about six-two with a frame damn near as wide as Grey's, she looked like a monster beside my Ghost. Her thighs roughly the size of Ava Jade's waist. Her blonde hair pulled back into a low bun at the nape of her neck.

Her lips twisted. Every muscle flexed.

"This is so fucking lopsided," Corvus growled, throwing a clawed hand through his mussed hair.

"She can handle it," I reminded him. "And Diesel knows it. It's why he set it up."

"He bet *against* her," Grey reminded me.

"Did he?" I challenged him, slipping a curious eye his way. "Or did it only make it seem that way to light a fire under her ass? Because he knows exactly what she's capable of."

Grey's brows drew, considering that.

I didn't even realize I'd be considering it until the words left my mouth, but there it was. And I'd be fucking shocked if it weren't the truth. She'd bested everything Diesel had thrown at her. If he thought she'd be taken down by this bitch, he wasn't the wise man I always thought him to be.

"...winner by submission or knockout," Pinkie was saying as the lights in the underbelly of Sanctum went low, all save for the ones above the ring. "Fighters, *ready!*"

My stomach fluttered, and I clenched my teeth against the sensation as it went straight to my cock.

Pinkie stepped back as Alpha's entrance song quieted and the metallic groan of the cage overhead sounded. Pinkie exited the ring as the cage clanked down, locking Ava Jade in with Alpha.

I gripped the cold metal, pushing up on a crate to make sure I didn't miss a thing.

"Ghost," I called through the bars, and she turned, her face so hard it could've been cut from marble. I pointed at her opponent with two fingers, never losing my hold on her attention. "End that bitch."

She nodded once and rolled her shoulders back, widening her stance as Pinkie lifted the shining metal whistle to his lips.

The sound of it rang through the room, sending Alpha into an immediate feral attack. I grinned, watching Ava Jade deftly avoid the advance, landing a solid jab to Alpha's ribs, and she rolled out of the way and sprang back to her feet, ready.

Alpha bared her teeth, the knot between her brows telling me she'd misjudged her opponent. It wouldn't be the last time.

Ava Jade blocked Alpha's next blow with her forearm, but failed to see the nasty kick coming, the blow to my Ghost's shin nearly sending her down.

The crowd roared at the hit, cheering for Alpha, and I wanted to eat each and every one of them for breakfast.

I settled for snatching up the nearest Armani shirt, yanking the fucker to me to knock my skull into his, rendering him a mess of unmoving muscle and flesh on the soiled cement floor. I spat on him, feeling Grey's arms tug me back a step to stop the kick I'd been about to throw into his abdomen.

Grey pushed me back to the metal bars, back to the fight, and I growled as I watched Alpha land another kick to Ava Jade's thigh, bringing a bright red tint to the surface of her skin.

If it weren't for the fact she took it with a smile, I'd have been tempted to rip through these bars and snap Alpha's neck.

Fuck, I wanted to.

Watching her wasn't helping.

It was making my *need* that much worse. My violent soul longed to go to war with hers. To be at her side. Fight as one.

Watching was a form of torture, but when Ava Jade landed the next beautiful hit, forcing Alpha to stagger back two steps, her hand reflexively going to her mangled jaw, I almost came.

"Yeah!" I screamed through the bars. "Take that bitch, Ghost!"

My hand found my cock through my jeans, and I pushed against it, trying to fix its position with a snarl on my lips.

Pinkie blew the whistle for the end of the match, just before Ava Jade was about to strike.

"No!" I growled at Pinkie, slamming my palms against the bars.

"*Rook*," Corvus growled beside my ear, but I was already climbing up, pushing and unlocking the cage door to step through, hollering back over my shoulder. "Get me a fucking whiskey."

Ava Jade came to the corner and Grey stepped through behind me, setting the stool down for my Ghost, but she didn't want to sit. She paced back and forth in the corner like a caged tigress, only stopping when I forced her, shoving her against the bars. I scooped the petroleum onto the back of my hand and held her against the bars as I swiped my fingers into it to run it over her forehead and cheeks. Over the cut on her brow to stop it leaking into her eyes.

"She hits like a fucking truck," Ava Jade said between panting breaths.

"Then you hit her harder."

She opened her mouth to allow the straw through as Grey pushed it in. She pulled greedily at the water, and I knocked the straw from her lips.

"Not too much," I cautioned. "You'll cramp."

Her jaw clenched, but she nodded, breaking free of my hold to storm back to center ring as the next round was announced.

"Rook, come on, man," Grey was saying, but his words were swallowed up in the roar of the crowd as Pinkie lifted the whistle to his lips and Ava Jade squared off against her opponent.

I let Grey pull me back through the cage door and slam it behind us, the whistle sounding for the second round. I jumped down from the ledge, fingers latched through the metal bars as they circled one another.

Fuck, she moved like liquid, dancing around Alpha as though there weren't bruises the size of bread loaves blooming on her legs. There was no denying it. My Ghost was bred for this. She was made from different stuff. Maybe the same stuff I was made from.

Something rougher, harder, *darker* than regular people.

Ava Jade feigned to the left, psyching out Alpha to land an insane hit to her right temple, jumping to throw her entire body weight into the throw.

Blood spattered over the floor at their feet as Alpha tried to regain her balance, but Ava Jade wasn't having it. My Ghost closed the gap between them, sweeping her legs out to knock Alpha to the ground. The big bitch went down hard, but she got hold of Ava Jade's ankle, twisting it to take my Ghost down with her.

"Get off the floor!" Grey was shouting.

"*Fuck,*" I heard Corvus curse behind me.

My teeth locked in my jaw, watching as Alpha dragged Ava Jade close, grabbing hold of her when she sat up to try to get free. The next bit happened so fast I couldn't be sure how they got there, but Alpha's arm snaked around Ava Jade's neck, her arm trapped beneath one of Alpha's knees, the other punching uselessly at Alpha's shoulder.

Ghost's face started to turn red, her light eyes bulging as Alpha choked off her air supply with a vicious sneer on her lips.

Corvus shouted uselessly, threatening murder if Pinkie didn't blow the fucking whistle, but I locked my eyes on Ava Jade, and when she found my gaze, I lent her the strength she needed. My head tipped in a small nod.

You know how to get out of this, I told her. *Stay calm.*

Her body sagged on cue, and Alpha immediately let her go, standing with a triumphant gleam in her eyes, but before Pinkie could blow the whistle, Ava Jade flipped, sending a kick upward into the bottom of Alpha's chin, coughing as she finally allowed herself to breathe.

Teeth rattled to the mat, and blood smeared over Alpha's mouth as she fell back, choking on it, spluttering as she blinked to get back full consciousness.

"*One*," the crowd started to shout.

"*Two.*"

If Alpha didn't get up, it was over. Ava Jade got unsteadily to her feet, spitting onto the mat between heaving breaths, her entire body gleaming in the lights as she gathered what remained of her strength and staggered toward Alpha."

"*Three.*"

"*Four.*"

Alpha groaned, flipping uneasily onto her stomach, using her arms to push herself up.

The crowd called her name. Chanting.

I'd rip out all their voice boxes if they didn't stop, the only reason I didn't—couldn't—was because I didn't want to miss a second of what would happen next.

I licked my lips, teeth dragging over my lip ring.

"Finish it," I whispered.

Alpha lifted her face, and Ava Jade took two running steps and plowed her knee into Alpha's cheek, sending her back down.

"*Stay the fuck down,*" she screamed at Alpha, every muscle in her back puffed up, her hands claws at her sides. This was her restraint. She didn't want to stop.

She needed Alpha to stop so that she could stop herself.

But Alpha rolled back to her knees again as the crowd started a thirty second countdown for the round to end.

Alpha pushed to her feet and began climbing the fucking cage, trying to get away. It was the coward's way out; if she made it to the top, the match would be over. Forfeited. Unless Alpha was trying to get higher to put power behind a hit.

Ava Jade bent her head and cursed, her upper lip curling as she went after Alpha before she could get high enough up to do anything useful.

"Get that cunt down!" I shouted, my pulse pounding in my ears.

She grabbed Alpha's bun and ripped her from the bars, making her fall with a resounding *thud* to the mat and roll over, coughing at the air that was knocked from her lungs.

Ava Jade was on her in a second.

"Ten, nine, eight," the crowd chanted, while others moaned and griped, calling for Alpha to get up. But she wouldn't be getting up. Not any time soon.

Ava Jade straddled the bitch, laying hit after hit *after hit* to her face.

"Seven, six, five, four," they chanted.

"She's killing her!" someone screamed.

And they weren't wrong.

"Three, two—"

Pinkie blew the whistle, and I launched through the cage door, racing to Ava Jade, hauling her off Alpha before she could finish the job she started. She fought against my hold, spinning to land a brutal blow to my jaw that I felt all the way down to my cock.

"It's me. It's me!"

She blinked, thrusting away from me, her breathing erratic and eyes full of dark stars.

She bent over her knees, almost gagging from the exertion, her head tipping slightly to one side to see the evidence of what she'd done. Alpha, lying bloody and broken, but still alive, in a puddle of her own blood.

Two of our men rushed in to tend to Alpha, fixing her with a neck brace, pouring cold water over her bruises and cuts before pressing bags of ice there instead. One shone a flashlight into her eyes.

Pinkie entered the ring, snatching up Ava Jade's arm to drag her nearer to the fallen Alpha. Alpha, who was trying to say something to the Saints helping her, and a moment later was helped to stand, her gaze distant, the whites of her left eye filled with blood.

"And the winner by knockout is...AVA JADE MASON!"

Pinkie lifted her arm, and she lifted her chin in turn, looking out over the faces in the club.

Alpha stumbled closer to my Ghost, and I stepped up, ready to cut her down if she tried anything, but she extended a shaky hand to Ava Jade.

She took it, swallowing past a lump in her throat.

"You're a fucking animal," Alpha slurred.

"It was a good match," Ava Jade replied, her gaze catching on someone behind me. I spun to find Diesel just outside the cage, clapping for her. His grin wide.

18

GREY

I pressed the ice pack to AJ's thigh, and she sucked a breath in through her teeth, snatching my forearm to squeeze tightly.

"Shit, does it hurt that bad?" I asked, pulling back, but she pressed the ice harder into her skin, her hot hand pushing down on the top of mine.

"Just fucking cold," she said, the words whistled through clenched teeth.

I knelt, holding the ice there for her, trying to get a better look at her face.

Alpha got a few good shots in, but she looked like she'd get away without too much facial damage. The blow to her brow made it swell to cave-man proportions, but she was holding a smaller ice pack there, and I was sure the swelling would go down before the night was through. At least her eyes weren't swollen shut.

The purple tint blooming on her jaw would hurt for a while, though. As though she knew what I was thinking, she opened her mouth to move her jaw in a slow circle, feeling out the injury.

"Anything that needs medical—"

She shook her head before I could finish.

"I'm fine, Grey. I've had worse."

I didn't doubt it, but I hated to imagine it. I hated seeing her hurt like this and the *idea* that she had ever been hurt *worse* than this made my stomach turn. Made my thoughts tint red as though my brain was soaking in poison.

Rook wasn't the only one who'd wanted to hop those fucking bars and rip Alpha's head off. I'd have done it happily if I didn't think it would piss Ava Jade off to the point where *she* wanted to rip my head off. If any of us had interrupted the match she would have taken it to mean that we thought she couldn't handle it.

She wouldn't have liked that.

I mean, fuck, she'd given Rook a damn good clock to the jaw for trying to haul her off Alpha, but I had a feeling that was done more blindly than anything.

The curtain flapped behind us, and Corvus and Rook stepped back into the private area. The party still raged outside on the main floor, the Kings mingling with the Saints just like Diesel wanted. The lawyers and bankers spending more money on drinks and games of cards at the tables in the other room.

Diesel hadn't opened that room in a while. We must have really needed the extra coin right now. Nothing worse than dealing with drunk gambling addicts who've just lost all their fucking money. *Not worth the trouble,* he used to say. Apparently, he'd changed his mind.

"How is she?" Corvus asked me.

"I'm fine," AJ answered before I could, and my stomach twisted. As much as I tried to forget it, I couldn't help the guilt still gnawing at me.

It was my fault Corvus' cover was blown.

But I couldn't do what that fucker wanted. I wouldn't trade AJ's life for my brother's secret and he *knew* it. He just wanted to fucking toy with me. I'd tried every night for days to trace those messages, but I was still coming up empty handed. The only thing that kept me going was the knowledge that all it would take was one slip and I would have his dead ass in the palm of my hand.

There was no reason to tell the guys about the text messages if I didn't have anything useful to offer. They were nothing but this guy trying to tear us apart from the inside.

Rook would have done the same.

Corvus would've done the same.

No matter how many times I told myself, it didn't ease the hollowness picking away at my insides.

"Here," Rook said, flopping down beside AJ on the bench with a glass of whiskey. "Have some, it'll take the edge off."

She eyed the whiskey like she might turn it down, but when Rook pushed it at her a second time, she took it, knocking it back in one swallow then grimacing and shaking her head.

Rook rubbed circles on her back. "There you go, Ghost. Better?"

She nodded.

He was going to turn her into a fucking alcoholic. We were going to need to talk about that.

Corvus scrutinized Ava Jade from where he stood, his light eyes roving over every mark, every scratch, every bruise, and getting darker with each one he found. "Dies wants to talk to us about—"

"Boys," Diesel said at that moment as he stepped through the curtain, counting through a massive stack of bills, pausing to lick his fingertips as he speedily walked his fingers through them, double checking his winnings.

"You bet on me," Ava Jade said, not a question, but it was clear she was surprised.

"You really think I'd bet against one of my own?"

AJ flinched at that but said nothing, her cut-glass eyes falling to cut the cement floor instead of our father.

Diesel pocketed the bills, and I moved the ice pack to Ava Jade's other thigh.

"Don't tell me you boys didn't bet on your girl?"

"'Course we did," Corvus said, patting his breast pocket. A tiny smirk tugged at the edge of AJ's mouth.

Diesel nodded and drew out his phone, the skin between his brows creasing. He turned the phone to us, displaying the time. "Time's officially up for the Aces," he said, digging in his front jacket pocket for a cigar. He patted his jeans pockets, frowning.

"Dies," Rook said and flipped him a lighter.

Dies caught it, a little off balance from his injury, and lit the cigar, blowing a cloud of sweet smelling gray smoke into the room.

"What's the plan?" Corvus asked.

"We'll meet at the warehouse to go over the plan. I'm going to need some time to round up the others and our new *friends*. You boys go ahead and open 'er up, but watch your asses. I'll be sending Axel, Pinkie, and Crowley right after you in case you run into trouble."

We all nodded and Diesel set his sights on Ava Jade. "Good fight," he said. "Wish it could've gone to a third round, but... I'm impressed."

She squinted at him, maybe trying to judge if he were fucking with her. He wasn't, but she needed to figure that out for herself. Our father gave credit where it was due. *Usually.*

Diesel's gaze snagged on Corvus before he spun to leave. He lifted a hand in the air making a circular motion. "Get a move on, boys, I want the Aces *folded* by this time tomorrow."

Ava Jade sighed.

"We can take you back to the nest on the way," I offered. "You should rest."

Her face scrunched up at that and she looked at me like I had shit on my fucking face. "Fuck no. Your pops would *love* that."

"It doesn't matter what he thinks," Corvus said, and I wished he would take his own advice.

But despite our protests AJ was still shaking her head. *"I'm fine,"* she all but growled. "I'm coming with you."

She pushed my hands away and dropped the ice pack from her head to the bench, pushing to her feet to grab the clothes she came in, pulling them on right over top of her sweat-dampened shorts and sports bra. Her fingers fumbled to buckle on her knife belt and attach it to the garter on her thigh.

I put a hand atop hers, and though she stared daggers at me, she let me finish buckling it up for her, shivering when I brushed my finger-tips up her thigh. I grinned at her, and she looked knowingly down at me.

"You are a fucking queen, you know that, right?" I found myself saying, wrapping my hands around her waist as I stood.

"About time you noticed," she said, her voice laced with heavy sarcasm.

I pushed her hair away from her face and bent my head down to kiss the top of hers, smelling her cheap shampoo. I'd come to love that smell.

Corvus cleared his throat, and I pulled away.

"We should get moving," Corv said. "We're the only ones with the code to get in, and if Pinkie and the others get there before us they're going to be pissed it isn't open yet."

Ava Jade nodded, doing her best to hide a slight limp as she walked up to Corvus and he fell into step beside her, an arm reflexively going up behind her, palm hovering protectively over her lower back without actually touching her.

"There you are," the guy from earlier, Drake, said, lifting his glass to Ava Jade. "Nicely done up there."

She tipped her head in thanks. I didn't like the way she smiled at him.

"Back up, man," I barked. "We have places to be."

Drake lifted his hands, backing up a step. "Sorry, man. Just wanted to congratulate the winner. Glad I put my money on you, Ava Jade."

Over his shoulder, I noticed the other guy, the one Ava Jade said gave her the creeps. The fucker who matched the description Becca gave of her booty-call boyfriend. He, too, seemed to have bet on Ava Jade and was lifting a stack of bills from an envelope with a wicked grin on his mouth.

His head jerked up, sensing my eyes on him, and he stuffed the money back in the envelope, flashing me a set of perfect teeth before turning away to head in the direction of the bar.

I boxed Ava Jade in on her other side and Rook trailed behind us, growling at anyone else who looked like they might interrupt our procession out of the club.

AJ's knuckles turned white as she gripped the railing, hauling herself up the stairs and out of the noise and heat of the club. When the door opened, she couldn't get through it fast enough, tipping her head up to breathe in deeply through her nose, staring up at the waning moon.

My ears rang in the sudden quiet, and I flipped up the collar of my jacket at the chill in the air. "You guys want to wait here? I'll bring the Rover around."

I didn't want her to have to walk all the way around the lot if she didn't have to.

Rook lit up a cigarette, nodding.

"Stop," Ava Jade said and something in her tone made my skin prickle.

She stared up at the building across the street, tipping her head to one side. I followed her line of sight and cursed.

"Get the fuck down!" Corvus roared, slamming his body into Ava Jade's, sending her down to the pavement just as the echo of the shot broke the sound barrier and the round embedded itself in the wall behind them.

My gun was out in an instant and Rook roared as a gang of men rounded the building and rushed us.

He sped straight ahead, zigzagging as the ten men fired at him, taking a bullet to his leg before he drew his own guns, firing wildly.

"Get her out of here!" I shouted at Corv who was hauling AJ to her feet.

I aimed and fired, hitting an Ace square in the chest before he could get another shot on Rook. The fucker crumpled to the pavement as Rook danced through the rest of them, a beast set loose on a herd of sheep.

"Fuck that," Ava Jade said, gasping as Rook was hit again. Corvus didn't try to stop her as she sprinted forward, following her instead, already firing.

The glint of the sniper's rifle above reflected in the moonlight, and I took off after them, making an uneven path.

"Don't stay still," I hissed at them as the first of the Aces turned their attention away from my brother and toward us. Big fucking mistake.

Rook grabbed the Ace by the head and twisted, the *crack* of snapping bone resounding in the street.

Headlights flashed over us before jarring to a stop, turning around to flee the scene.

The Ace directly in front of me lifted his gun to aim at my face, and I sped the final step, knocking it from his hand. But before I could fire a shot of my own, the whisper of steel cutting through wind filtered into my ears.

He went down with a silver pommel embedded in his neck.

Ava Jade's hard eyes found mine, and I nodded. "Keep moving!"

She nodded back, going to Rook as three more Aces began to surround him. She pressed her back to his and threw another knife. The gurgling cry of a dying Ace echoed through the night, telling me her aim was true.

Rook dropped his mag and refilled it, hooking an arm around AJ's waist to bring her to the ground as someone shot at her. As they both rose, blades and bullets flew. I rushed up and kicked one Ace in the back of his knee, sending him to the ground before pumping two bullets into his skull.

The screech of tires cut through the sounds of fighting and gunfire and my pulse picked up, doubling its tempo as I whirled to see the white van. To see its door opening and the men pouring out. Armed with a lot more than fucking handguns. An icy cold slunk down my spine.

Fuck.

The Aces never planned to go quietly. And they never planned to try to weather the storm. They were out for blood. Live or die. I should've fucking known. *We* should've known. Lenny Ace was nothing like his uncle was. He had no honor.

"Three o'clock!" I shouted, already firing, rolling to dodge a few stray shots.

"The alley!" Corvus bellowed. "Rook! Sparrow! *Move!*"

Rook finished off the last Ace in front of him and grabbed Ava Jade, dragging her to the alley. She fought against his hold, fingers reaching to jerk one of her blades out of the body of a man at their feet. The only blade she had. The rest, she'd already thrown.

No. Bad idea. The alley would provide cover from the sniper, but it would be like shooting fish in a barrel. Heat seared into my side, and I hissed, shouting as the realization that I'd been shot made the pain intensify.

"Grey!" Corvus was yelling, and I sensed Rook and Ava Jade had stopped.

A hail of gunfire sounded before I could move, and my eyes widened as I realized I was directly in its path, distracted.

A body knocked into mine and the *pop! pop!* of Corvus' shots rang in my ears as he laid down cover fire, hauling me away. Grunting as a bullet grazed past his face, brilliant red streaming down to his chin.

The others had to be on their way out.

There was no way they couldn't hear this. Right?

Even underground, with music pumping, Diesel would hear the pop of gunfire in the street outside, wouldn't he?

And the camera, it would've picked up something. But was someone manning the cams right now?

God fucking damnit.

Corvus shoved me into the alley with Rook and AJ, and I stumbled back, hand clutching the gushing wound to my side.

"Fuck, Grey!" AJ was shouting, rushing to me, tearing my jacket back to see the blood seeping through my fingers.

"He's hit!"

"We all are," Corvus growled, hesitating in the mouth of the alley. His gaze flicked to Rook behind me, fixing him with a dark stare. "Get them out of here," he muttered before turning back and running from the alley, drawing gunfire and the pounding of heavy booted feet after him.

"Corvus!" Ava Jade hollered, still clutching me. "He's going to get himself killed."

Her voice wobbled, and I didn't dare look, couldn't bear to see the pain I knew I would find in her eyes because she was right. And Corvus knew it.

"Fuck that," Rook said, switching out his mag to the last one he had on him.

I did the same, extricating myself from Ava Jade, removing my hand from the seeping wound to my side. Getting up.

It didn't seem to have hit anything important, and judging by the wetness leaking down my right ass cheek, the bullet had gone through and through. Blood loss would be my only issue. I'd survived worse.

"Stay here," I tried, grabbing AJ by her wrist, knowing it was useless. "Find someplace to hide and call Diesel."

She squinted at me, shaking her head once, slowly.

"Fuck, AJ."

"*Move.*" Rook pushed between us, jogging out the mouth of the alley as the booted footsteps approached. It was too late now.

"You need to get a gun," I told her, my voice hard. I lifted her hand to my mouth and kissed it, feeling the tacky wetness of blood smearing over my mouth.

She nodded, glancing down at her last blade clutched tightly in her fist. "We need to go."

Outside, Rook roared as he engaged the half of them that didn't take off after Corvus.

My brother needed me.

I let AJ's hand go and swallowed, holding my breath against the pain as I raced from the alley.

I barely managed to dodge the hard side of a pistol as an Ace whipped it at my face, coming around the corner faster than a Mack truck. I fell to my ass to avoid the hit, and AJ sank her blade into the fucker's jugular, not stopping at a single stab, but going at it three, four, *five* times before she was satisfied, reaching down to help haul me back to my feet just in time for me to shoot the next one and for her to throw her blade into the chest of the last one coming for us.

I nodded to her, and she nodded back, but something over my shoulder caught her attention, and her face went whiter than the ghost Rook named her for.

My guts twisted.

Corvus coughed, a sound of gruff pain, and I turned to find him ten feet from the entrance to the club, surrounded in Aces as they took turns stomping on him. Their heavy booted feet kicked and pushed down, making him jerk and cough, blood coating his lips.

I shot wildly, rushing past Rook, who'd disarmed the three remaining Aces near the alley and was going at them with vicious fists.

I felt AJ on my heels, but we weren't going to make it there in time.

An Ace, one I recognized from the meet at the warehouse drew his gun and aimed it low, directly at my brother's head.

I fired, but the gun clicked uselessly against my hand, out of bullets. I tossed it, and a fear unlike anything I'd ever felt before gripped my heart in a vise. *No. No, no, no.*

The door to the underbelly of Sanctum opened and a body stumbled through, grinning, his easy expression morphing the instant he saw the scene before him. Drake lifted his gun from the back of his waistband and fired.

The head of the man who'd been about to shoot my brother kicked back, and he crumpled to the ground. Ava Jade launched herself onto the back of the Ace next to him, and he cried out as she sank her teeth into his neck.

I nicked the gun from the one next to him and took aim, firing one shot after another, my bullets blasting from the barrel in perfect time with Drake's as the Aces in the circle around my brother went down one by one, taken by surprise.

Drake refilled his mag just as the door behind him smashed against the cement wall outside and Diesel came swiftly out, the others on his heels.

He wasted no time raising his gun, firing two rounds to finish off the two still doing a death dance with Rook.

I heard his outcry of rage at his prey having been taken from him, but he'd get over it.

"Sniper!" I warned. "Twelve o'clock"

Axel darted ahead to check it out, but it seemed the sniper had fled. There was no glint of metal barrel on the roof opposite us anymore.

"*What the fuck is going on out here?*" Diesel demanded, his face a mosaic of rage as he came to us, stooping to help a coughing Corvus from the asphalt.

"Fan out," he bellowed to the Saints at his back. "Clean this mess up. Bring me any still breathing."

"Son," he said, giving Corvus a slight shake. He gripped Corvus by the face, forcing his eldest son to look at him. "Look at me."

Corvus' blinked, coming back to himself with a grimace. He jerked out of Diesel's hard grip to spit blood onto the ground.

"Hey," Diesel said, slapping his cheek. "Look at me."

Diesel checked his eyes before judging the rest of him. "Are you hit?"

He lifted the hem of Corvus' t-shirt, checking for injury, his gaze snagging on me. On the dark red staining the front of my jeans. "Christ, Grey," he cursed, releasing Corvus to push my jacket out of the way and assess my wound.

"The fuck did you do that for?" Rook growled as he stalked closer. "I had it."

But when he saw Dies' face and Corvus' distant gaze and beaten body, he stopped talking, his gaze fixing on Ava Jade instead, assessing her.

"Good, Bro?" Rook asked, slapping Corvus on the back, making him cough again.

"Yeah," Corvus said, his voice garbled as he tugged away from Ava Jade's helping hands, standing on his own. "Good."

"Get me a fucking kit," Diesel hissed at no one in particular, pushing hard against the wound to my side, making air rush in through my clenched teeth.

"Fuck."

"Rook, get over here," Diesel demanded, and Rook came around. "Hold this."

Rook knelt in front of me and pushed the wadded up fabric against my wound as Diesel accepted a first aid kit from Pinkie and used his teeth to tear open a plastic bag. I bit down as he knocked Rook's hand out of the way and began packing the wound with clotting powder. Once he was finished, he looked up at me. "Good?"

I nodded. "Good."

Rook stood, and Diesel cursed. "*Rook.*" He seethed, limping to grip the back of Rook's jacket and tear it clean from his back. Two bullet wounds, one to his thigh and another to the dangerous area between his neck and shoulder seeped steadily. "Were you just not going to fucking say anything?"

"I'm good."

"Like fuck," Diesel said, muttering curses to himself as he grabbed more clotting powder, stuffing it into Rook's wounds angrily.

"And you?" he asked, turning to Ava Jade with another bag of powder clutched between his fingers. "Are you hit?"

Ava Jade shook her head.

"I could use some of that," came a voice from behind us. Drake struggled over, clutching his biceps, his gun dangling uselessly from his fingers. "If you don't mind."

Diesel tossed him the baggy, and he caught it, dropping to a knee to pack his own wound.

I went to him, wincing as I reached out a hand to help him up when he was finished. He stood, tossing his light hair away from his eyes. I shook his hand. "Thank you," I said earnestly, catching sight of another shadow behind Drake. Someone peeking out from behind the building on the next street up. Not fighting, just watching. Something about his posture, his shape, and height seemed familiar, but I couldn't place it.

"Axel," I shouted, since he was the nearest. I pointed and the shadow vanished. "*There,* one of those fuckers is hiding 'round the building."

Drake took his hand from mine and air expelled in a gush from his lips as Ava Jade pulled him into a hard hug.

His hands hovered over her back awkwardly, like he wasn't sure whether he should hug her back. Right now, I wouldn't kill him for it. We owed him.

But before he could decide, AJ pulled away. "Thank you," she said on a breath. "We owe you."

Drake shook his head, a sad smile on his lips. "Nah," he said. "You're good, angel."

AJ sighed, reaching out to twine her fingers with mine, unbothered that both of our hands were covered in blood.

"Got one," someone shouted, leading an only mildly injured Ace out from the alley by his hair. Likely the sniper, trying to escape unnoticed.

Diesel took the motherfucker from Axel and threw him to the asphalt just as the rest of the people from inside of Sanctum's underground began to pour out. The Kings looked on the carnage with a sort of awed surprise. The lawyers and bankers turned varying shades of green and red and white, but none could bring themselves to look away or leave.

This was what they came here for, after all. They wanted to see blood. Now, they could see what real death looked like. It wasn't pretty. There wasn't just blood staining these streets. Most men pissed themselves when they died and the smell of urine was just as strong in the air as the scents of blood and lead.

"Where's Lenny?" Diesel asked, cocking his engraved Desert Eagle to press against the Ace's temple.

The skinny fucker cringed away, but managed to keep from soiling himself.

"My father asked you a question," Corvus growled, accepting a bottle of water from Pinkie to sip.

"Not here," the guy said. "He only sent us. Said that it would be easy. That you'd all be here and we should pick you off as you exited."

"*Coward.*"

"Where is Lenny now?" Diesel asked. "Where is the rest of your crew?"

The Ace lifted his hands higher, his fingers shaking like leaves in the wind. "I-I don't know. I s-s-swear, man. They s-sent us and said they'd be right behind us."

"You wouldn't lie to me..." Diesel trailed off.

"N-no. No, man, *p-please*. I have family. I have a brother and—"

Diesel clocked him on the back of the head, just enough to stun him. "Shut the fuck up."

The guy began to cry, and Diesel dragged him to his feet, hauling him by the back of his shirt toward Corvus. *"Apologize,"* Diesel demanded, and I recognized the manic gleam in his eyes. Diesel St. Crow rarely lost his control, but he liked to toe the line, and right now, he was fucking dancing on it.

"You fucking heard me, asshole!" Diesel shouted, shaking the Ace.

"S-sorry," he choked out.

"Sorry, *what?*" Diesel prodded, and Corvus lifted his chin, waiting.

The Ace lifted his head to look Corvus in the eyes. "I-I'm sorry we tried to k-kill you."

Diesel dragged him two feet to his left, placing him in front of me. *"Apologize."*

My nose wrinkled at the smell of fresh urine, and I stepped back a step to avoid the growing puddle beneath the Ace's feet.

"I-I'm so sorry," the Ace said to me, his snot running down to his chin.

Diesel shoved the Ace away, making him fall to his knees in his own urine in front of Ava Jade and Rook.

"You aren't finished," Diesel roared, bending to grab a fistful of his hair to stop his whimpering, forcing him to look up at Rook and Ava Jade. Rook grinned down at him. AJ looked like she might carve his face into a jack-o-lantern and put it on her front porch.

"I'm sorry," he cried. "I'm so, so, so sorry. Please. *Please.*"

Diesel let him go, and he slumped forward, fists against the pavement, shaking.

"Satisfied?" Diesel asked Corvus.

Corvus' upper lip curled. "No."

"Grey?" Diesel asked.

"Not in the slightest."

"And you?" he asked Ava Jade.

She shook her head mutely.

"Rook? You satisfied?"

"Not yet," Rook said with a wicked gleam in his eyes.

Diesel's cheekbones flared, he nodded once, lifted his gun again and emptied the clip into the Ace's skull to a riot of screams from the fine citizens of Thorn Valley watching at his back.

19

AVA JADE

"Why are we even doing this? It's fucking ridiculous," I said, kicking Corvus' shoes out of his reach to keep him from putting them on.

He glared at me from the one eye he could see out of, the other one was completely swollen shut, and snatched his shoes from the floor.

"Because we said we would," he groaned, falling heavily onto the small stool in the hallway of The Nest, and I could tell it pained him to reach down to pull the shoes onto his feet. The five stitches in his cheek strained as he grimaced. He had two cracked ribs and some internal bleeding, but even battered as he was, I knew he wouldn't accept my help no matter how many times I offered.

And I *had* offered. Many times. After I'd laid into his dumb ass for trying to sacrifice himself Thursday night. What the actual fuck was that? I didn't know how I felt about it other than angry as fuck.

No one had ever put my life above theirs.

"Besides," Rook said, coming through the hall to kick his feet into his boots like the bullet hole in his leg didn't bother him at all. "Corvus won't be cooking jack shit with his gimp ass, and I'm hungry."

"Dick," Corvus hissed and Rook made a face at him, stepping out of the way for Grey to come through to get his shoes on as well.

"Dies doesn't want us here, anyway," he added. "It's too secluded. He knows where we're going and said it's a good idea."

I really wasn't going to get out of this, was I?

Fuck.

"We should be scouring every inch of Edgewood for those fuckers before they have a chance to regroup," I argued. "Just because the Aces *seem* to have gone to ground doesn't mean they aren't just biding their time. What if they make a move on Diesel? Is *he* all alone at his place?"

Corvus lifted a brow at me. "You think he's an idiot?" he asked. "Of course not. They're all at Sanctum with their families. Dies is keeping them all under lock and key until Lenny Ace is a fucking corpse."

I frowned.

I hadn't known that, but they still didn't share everything with me. I didn't think they kept it from me on purpose, they just didn't think I needed to know.

And maybe I didn't.

I wasn't sure I liked the difference in how I was feeling about Diesel St. Crow. The way he'd gone straight to his sons, tended to their wounds. The vicious way he'd forced that Ace to apologize before pumping lead into his skull. And now he was keeping not only his men, but all of their families safe at Sanctum?

He also had that street cleaned up within hours of the battle, the only trace of evidence that it happened at all: the bits of blood lingering between cracks in the pavement. I didn't have to wonder why the cops never showed up. Before we'd all gone back inside to sew up our wounds, Diesel had passed all his winnings from the match to Pinkie.

"Go pay our friends in blue," he'd said, expression tight from the loss of winnings.

"I don't want to go," I tried instead, switching tactics, rolling my shoulder, feigning injury from the sniper rifle practice session this morning. I forced an overdone wince. "I changed my mind."

"Too bad," Corvus said gruffly as he pushed to his feet. "Get your ass in the car."

I crossed my arms over my chest, and Corvus' brows drew as he caught sight of the blade strapped to my ankle. "How armed do you have to be to have dinner with your aunt, Sparrow?"

My jaw clenched. "As armed as I need to be to go into battle with a rival gang."

He caught my meaning. The fact that I had every one of my blades back where they belonged and at the ready had nothing to do with my aunt and everything to do with the fact that there could be an ambush of Aces waiting for us anywhere.

Though I doubted they would strike while it was still daylight.

"They're gone," Grey said, speaking aloud what all of us were thinking. "We exterminated over half their crew. They're hiding, licking their wounds somewhere. They won't be back for a while, if they ever come back."

Corvus nodded his agreement. "All our sources say there's been no gang presence in Edgewood since Thursday night. Lenny's Hail Mary failed. He won't risk his own ass to try some shit like that again."

"Maybe not," I acceded. "But they could just as easily ally with another gang as we did."

"Who would ally with them now?" Rook asked, making no effort to disguise how idiotic he thought my statement was.

I rolled my eyes at him.

"You know what, never mind. Just tell me you're all armed."

Rook opened his jacket, showing the sleek mahogany grip of his gun hooking from the top of his jeans. Grey lifted the back of his jacket, showing me his piece and the hem of his jeans, flashing me a row of mags strapped there.

I looked to Corvus.

He sighed. "Don't worry, Sparrow. I'm armed."

"Fine," I said in a huff. "Then let's go sit around a table and say what we're grateful for. Sounds like fun."

Grey chuckled, and I sent him a deadpan stare, telling him without the need for words just how *not* funny I thought this was.

It'd only been two days since fight night. Our bruises were at their darkest. Our cuts were puckered black scabs. The hollows beneath our eyes were deep and the most vivid shade of purple they could be.

We were liable to give my aunt a goddamned heart attack just showing our faces at the door.

"We were in a car accident," I decided. "No one was hurt beyond cuts and bruises, which is why we didn't go to the ER."

"Don't fucking smirk at me," I told Rook. "You're going to regret going to this dinner by the time the night is through. I promise you that."

My aunt's disgusting mansion loomed around a bend in the freshly cobblestoned road ahead, seen through the heavy iron bars of her front gates.

Grey drove us up to the intercom panel and reached out to jab the button. It crackled before a male voice came through. "Can I help you?"

"Yeah," Grey said, leaning down so the tiny camera could see his face. He flashed a smile. "Could you please let Mrs. Humphrey know that her niece has arrived for dinner."

A pause.

"Y-yes. Certainly. Please do come in."

The groan of a mechanical pulley system swelled in the tepid silence. The nearest neighbor was over a mile away and here, on the grounds of the Humphrey Estate, only birdsong and the distant sounds of the water fountains in the garden could be heard.

The amount of privilege and excess behind these gates was enough to make me want to vomit.

Grey drove us through, steering the Rover up the drive to the front door.

"It's not too late to turn back," I blurted, putting my hand over Rook's in the backseat to stop him from opening his door.

His face lit up. "Honestly, the fact that you don't want us to go inside so badly just makes me want to go in even more, Ghost."

I growled, letting him go as I pushed out my own door, hating how Corvus almost lost his footing as he stepped out. He gave me a cautionary look as he shut his door, trying to gauge if I'd seen. If I would tell the others he wasn't ready to be walking around yet.

My nostrils flared, but instead of calling him out, I looped my arm through his. "You're an idiot," I muttered, trying to covertly take some of his weight as we ascended the wide ivory staircase to the massive wooden front door.

Corvus scoffed in reply but didn't pull away.

The door opened before Rook could even curl his pinkie finger around the knocker, my aunt standing there in her grand foyer, cheeks pink from too much rouge.

"There's my niece," she trailed off, her wide, welcoming arms dropping as she got a better look at us. Red painted nails flying to her chest to ward off the start of the heart attack I'd warned my Crows about.

"Oh dear," she said. "What happened?"

"Car accident," I supplied, seeing a playful gleam in Rook's eyes I didn't like. "It looks worse than it is."

"You should've called," my aunt said, tutting as she ushered us through the door. "Come in, *come in*. Let's get you in out of this heat." She snapped her fingers and the butler, who's name I'd forgotten, rushed in. "Jackson, will you get ice waters for everyone?"

"Right away, ma'am," Jackson said, bowing, his dark hair not moving at all through the movement, held hard to his head like a helmet with too much gel.

"Could I get something stronger?" Rook asked, making the butler pause. Clutching his shoulder as though it was causing him a great amount of pain. "The damned doctor wouldn't give me anything for the pain. It's almost unbearable."

The butler, Jackson, looked to my aunt for guidance and she looked at Rook, assessing his suddenly drawn face. She gave Jackson a nod. "All right, dear," she said to Rook, going over to pat him on his opposite shoulder. "Would you like some Vicodin?"

Rook perked up.

"No," Corvus said for him. "Just a drink to take the edge off will be great, ma'am."

My aunt gave Corvus a tight smile. "All right, well, I suppose there's no sense in pretending eighteen-year-olds don't drink these days." She turned, hollering down the hall after Jackson. "Bring up a bottle of my late husband's best, Jackson. And a few extra glasses."

His muted voice called back that he'd heard, and Rook fought to hide a smile.

When I caught his eye, I shook my head at him, and he winked.

"Smells delicious," Grey offered, indicating the aroma filling the room. Far off, I could hear the clatter of cookware from the staff kitchen and wondered how many staff she'd hired just to make a fucking dinner for five.

The fact that Dad and I were living in a run-down trailer for most of my life, with barely enough hot water to shower, while his sister had been living *like this* just a couple towns over made me feel so ill I had to swallow back the taste of bile in my throat. Had to remind myself that it was my dad's *choice* to distance himself from his sister.

To not take her strings-attached handouts.

He was prideful and stubborn, but I didn't fault him for denying her. Wouldn't I have done the same thing on principle alone?

Besides, it wasn't even her money. It was her dead husband's.

My dad's favorite theory was that she'd poisoned him to an early grave, but I couldn't see it. The woman standing before us in a long silvery sheath of a dress with outdated blingy combs tucked in her ratty gray-brown hair wasn't capable of murder. Not even a coward's murder.

She didn't even look like she could tie her own damned shoes. If anything, I pitied her. Alone out here surrounded by stuffed dead things and priceless art and a butler who pretty obviously loathed her.

"The staff has been cooking all day," my aunt said, looking over our outfits now that she'd gotten used to the sight of our bruises. She smiled at each of my guys in turn, over-appreciative gaze finding tailored pants and brand name suit jackets left to hang open over crisp shirts. I had to admit they cleaned up *good*.

But they all grimed up good, so I wasn't surprised. I liked them just as well covered in blood and leather as I did in the clean cut styles they wore now. Maybe more so.

Definitely more so.

My aunt's smile turned into a frown as her milky eyes tracked over my attire, finding me in a thrifted skirt, black converse, and a tank top covered over in a soft black cardigan. That one wasn't thrifted, it was *lifted* from the racks at Nordstrom and felt like real cashmere. It was the nicest thing I owned, but she sneered at it as if I was wearing the skin of a dead goat.

"Ava Jade, dear, would you be more comfortable in a dress? I took the liberty of purchasing a few. They're upstairs in the spare bedroom if you'd like to—"

"I'm good."

"AJ, don't be rude," Grey said, and I slowly craned my neck, leveling the full weight of my fury on him, but it only served to make him even more triumphant. The fucker. "She'd love to change."

"No, I wouldn't."

Grey pouted, and I rolled my eyes.

Now was not the time for playing. We shouldn't even *be here.* Goddammit.

"Come on, Ghost," Rook said. "I'll help you into your dress."

He extended a hand to me, and my aunt gasped. It was her dismay that ultimately made me take his hand, slapping my fingers down onto his palm.

"H-how...how kind of your friend," My aunt stumbled over her words just as Jackson re-entered the grand foyer with a tray containing a crystal decanter of amber liquid and five partially filled glasses.

Rook stopped before the bottom stair and reached over, snatching two glasses with his index and middle finger. "Cheers," he said, winking at Jackson, who blanched.

Despite myself, my anger was fading fast, and I felt a traitorous grin worming onto my lips.

At least if the Aces somehow tracked us here, we'd have a veritable fortress to protect us. I knew for a fact my aunt had invested in a crazy system that locked down the entire place with metal shutters.

Silver lining.

I let Rook lead me the rest of the way upstairs while my aunt led Grey and Corvus through the dining room, not making them remove their shoes, which I remembered had been a *strict* rule for me during the one night I lasted in this fucking place.

"Thought it was Thanksgiving, not Easter," Rook said, squinting at a small collection of Fabergé eggs.

"Those aren't Easter eggs," I said, tugging him away from them before he could grab the closest one. "They're Fabergé eggs. Her husband gave her one every year they were married."

"Why?"

"Why do rich people do anything that they do?"

He frowned, shrugging.

"They're worth something like ten grand a piece, for the smaller ones."

"Those fucking eggs?"

I nodded.

"Fucking rich people."

"Fucking rich people," I echoed, indicating the door down the hall.

He pushed through, and the wafting odor of fresh potpourri made both of us recoil.

"Ugh."

Rook quickly grabbed the bowl of it from the low table just inside the door, dropping the amber liquid in its place. He crossed the room, opened the window, and tossed it outside.

I suppressed a giggle, seeing his eyes watering at the smell.

"I'm going to be honest, Ghost, I was planning to rip your clothes off the second we got into this room but..." He made a face, shutting the window again.

"What? My dark prince can't handle a bit of shitty potpourri? Who would've known that was your Kryptonite."

He narrowed his dark eyes on me, closing the gap between us in two long strides. He reached forward and grabbed my shirt, dragging me to him before tearing it into two pieces, the torn shreds catching on my arms as he ripped it off. My cunt throbbed, panties dampening at the heat in his stare.

"That was my nicest sweater."

"Not anymore."

"Oh!" Jackson exclaimed, appearing and then disappearing from the entrance to the room. He hovered just out of view, and I sagged, taking up one of the cups from the side table as the butler mumbled his apologies.

"I'm sorry, miss. Your aunt asked me to come and get you. She has a surprise for you and asked that you meet her and your friends in the sitting room. Again, so sorry, miss."

Rook loomed over me, licking his lips as he reached past me for the other glass, clinking it against mine. "You heard the man, get dressed, Ghost. Your aunt has a *surprise* for you."

I frowned, balking at his six foot frame, aching to have his tatted hands on my body. "Are you serious?"

His dark gaze flicked down to my pebbled nipples, and he let out a small growl before stepping away. "Deadly. Can't keep the woman waiting, Ghost. I can rip off your dress, too. Later."

I rolled my eyes but went to the closet, my greedy little cunt still pulsating beneath my skirt. Injured or not, I'd make him pay for this later.

"You've got to be shitting me," I groaned, looking at the three dress options hanging inside the mothball scented walk-in. Each one worse than the one next to it.

Dear god.

"Come on, Ghost," Rook was saying, a teasing tone coaxing me the rest of the way down the hall toward the low sound of conversation in the sitting room. "Let's go show your aunt how sexy you look."

"Rook, I look like a fucking peacock."

He pouted. "But such a cute little peacock."

I punched him in the arm, the one near his gun-wound, and he moaned at the pain, making me groan in response.

Whoever made this atrocity of a dress really had some fucking balls. I damn near came down in my bra and half torn shirt to keep from wearing any of the options my aunt had chosen. But Rook somehow managed to reverse psychology me into the least atrocious of the options. A fitted peacock green and purple bodice sloped down to a full skirt that ended just below my knees with little strings hanging from the hem that obnoxiously tickled my legs.

And clearly Aunt Humphrey hadn't thought to find shoes to match this fucking hideous dressed, so it looked all the worse from being worn with the black converse shoes I came in with.

Fuck it.

I stomped through to the sitting room, eyes turned up to a spot on the wall over all of their heads. "Go ahead, get it out of your system," I announced, waiting for the inevitable laughter, but it didn't come.

Aside from a rough cough from Corvus and a red-face from Grey, neither spoke.

"Oh, it looks darling!" my aunt said. "Wish I'd have thought to get the matching shoes. How marvelous. It'll be perfect for the surprise."

I pinched my brow, going to the tray of expensive bourbon to pour myself another glass and sink onto the low tufted sofa between Corvus and Grey, while Rook planted himself next to the alcohol.

"Is dinner ready?" I asked, drinking greedily from my glass. She didn't know me very well, but she knew I didn't like surprises.

"Patience." She tutted, looking into the bottom of her empty glass.

Rook, noticing, quickly snatched up the decanter and crossed the Persian carpet to her side, taking the glass from her fingers. "Allow me," he said, his voice smooth as silk.

"Oh!"

Rook filled the glass.

"Oh my, stop dear, that's far too much."

Rook gave her a devilish grin, and she fucking blushed at him. "Too much?" he shook his head. "You look like a woman who can handle her liquor, am I right?"

Her eyes widened, and Rook clinked the empty decanter against her nearly full glass.

"Garcon!" he called in no direction in particular. "We need a refill."

"Rook," Corvus warned, but Rook only flashed a set of straight white teeth at his brother and settled back down onto the sofa with his glass, lifting a leg to rest his ankle on his knee, so at ease I was actually sort of jealous of him.

Jackson entered from the foyer a moment later, hands clasped behind his back.

"Refill," Rook repeated, looking at the butler like he was daft, stretching out his neck like he could see if the butler was hiding the liquor behind his back.

"Right away, sir," Jackson replied, turning his attention to my aunt. "She's here, ma'am. Shall I send her in?"

My aunt got unsteadily to her feet, setting her over-filled bourbon down on the table to straighten her dress. Clearly she did *not* know how to handle her liquor.

"Yes, yes. I'll see her through."

"Who else did you invite?" I asked, something uncomfortable tightening in my belly.

She barely spared me a second glance as she followed Jackson from the room. "You'll see, Ava Jade. It's a surprise."

Heat flooded through my stomach, flashing over my chest until it was damp. Until the heat turned cold.

My stomach turned.

"We shouldn't have come," I said, barely recognizing the sound of my own voice because I was hearing *her* voice down the hall. Muted and distant and barely there, but even after all these years, I would know it anywhere.

"Sparrow?" Corvus asked, sitting up now. "What is it?"

My mouth went dry.

Aunt Humphrey came back through the entry to the sitting room, a wide smile beaming on her ashen face.

My mother followed behind her.

20

ROOK

Ava Jade launched to her feet, her breaths long and heavy as she watched the woman follow her aunt into the living room.

I didn't like the look on my Ghost's face. She didn't like this.

She was... she was fucking panicking.

"Who the fuck are you?" I asked, putting myself between the woman and my Ghost.

"Oh!" Ava Jade's aunt exclaimed, her hand flying to her mouth, but I couldn't be bothered to play nice anymore, not until I knew exactly *what* had just walked into the room.

"Sparrow, who is this?" Corvus asked, a vein in his temple throbbing as he made himself stand, too. Grey watched the woman, and I got the sense he already knew who she was. His expression was dark, and I didn't like it. My fingers twitched toward my gun, and maybe I shouldn't have had that last bourbon because it roiled in my stomach now like a poison.

"Her mother," Grey said for Ava Jade. "Right?" he asked her.

The woman clasped her hands in front of her, lowering her head.

And I could see it now.

Even though this woman looked like she'd been fed through a fucking wood planer, there were similarities. The long, dark hair, hers shot through with silver, coarse. The light colored eyes, her mother's bloodshot and surrounded in hollow flesh. The frame... it was hard to tell beneath the clothes hanging from her body, but it looked like Ava Jade's mother might've once had curves much like her daughter's. But drugs had eaten the meat right off her bones.

I knew the look of her better than anyone else could. She was strung out. Probably just coming down from a weeklong bender. Her shoulders were hunched. Her fingertips shaking. A slight twitch to her right shoulder.

She was trying to hide it, but even the expert makeup she'd hastily applied to her face couldn't hide the truth.

This woman was an addict, and my Ghost did *not* seem happy to see her.

It was enough for me.

"What are you doing here?" Ava Jade asked, her voice abrasive as she stared at her mother.

"I... I heard you were staying with—"

"*Oh,*" Ava Jade interrupted, smacking an open palm to her forehead like she was the idiot here. "I get it," she said with a poisonous smile. "*You heard* that dear ol' Aunt Humphrey took me in after Dad was *murdered* and you thought *wow, what a great opportunity to wring some cash out of the old hag.* How far off am I?"

"Ava Jade!" her aunt exclaimed, turning to the woman. "I'm so sorry, Valerie. I don't know what's gotten into her."

"Violet, would you give me a moment alone with my daughter?"

Ghost's aunt hesitated but left like she was asked.

Valerie turned her attention to the three of us, but none of us budged. At least the bitch was smart enough to know not to even bother asking. We weren't leaving.

"What is it this year, Ma?" Ava Jade demanded, taking two purposeful steps forward, making her mother cringe. "Blow? Smack? Fucking meth? How long since your last fix?"

Valerie lifted her chin, staring her daughter in the eyes, chin quivering. "I'm clean, baby," she said, and Ava Jade looked like she was going to vomit. "I came tonight because your aunt invited me. I wanted to see you. I wanted to... to apologize for—"

"Oh, Jesus fucking Christ," Ava Jade said, throwing up her hands. "We're out of here."

"*Please*," Valerie pleaded, and when she made to step closer to Ava Jade, I intercepted her, holding out a palm to stop her. I shook my head. *No.*

That was far enough.

Valerie looked between me and Ava Jade, clearly distraught, but not for the reasons she wanted Ava Jade to think she was.

"It's part of my recovery, baby. I need to apologize for the things the drugs made me do. I should've never…"

She stopped, unable to continue, and I felt my darkness rising like smoke through my veins.

What the fuck did this bitch do to my Ghost?

I shoved her back a step, and she put a fearful hand to the place where I'd touched her, cowering back.

"It's fine, Rook," Ava Jade said in a deadpan voice. "She can't ever hurt me again. If she tries, I'll fucking end her."

Valerie's throat bobbed.

"I really am clean, Ava Jade. I'm… I'm so sorry. I didn't mean to ruin your Thanksgiving."

Enough.

Before Valerie could turn away like the kicked dog she was pretending to be, I lifted the purse from her shoulder and upturned it on the carpet, shaking out all its contents.

Valerie shrieked.

I kicked around the lipstick tubes, dollar bills, and *panties* that were now dotting the Persian carpet, but didn't find what I was looking for.

I stuffed my hand into the purse, checking the other pockets and the zippered closure, but they were all empty. I thrust the purse back at Valerie, finding Ava Jade staring at me. "It's clean," I announced with a shrug. My Ghost didn't seem upset though, a deep understanding was all I saw in her eyes.

She knew I suspected her mother wasn't clean, and she trusted me. But the purse devoid of drugs or any drug paraphernalia begged to differ.

"You want to go, AJ?" Grey asked, settling a gentle hand on Ava Jade's back as her mother dropped to her knees to collect her things back into her purse.

Humphrey returned, glowering at the scene.

"How dare you, Ava Jade, that is *your mother*. She's been in rehab for *months*. I thought you'd be glad to see her."

Humphrey helped the woman to her feet, whispering reassurances in her ear.

Ava Jade seethed quietly, watching her aunt and mother with a mix of dark and painful things glittering in her eyes.

"I don't believe that for one second," Ava Jade said. "She's here to fleece you, Aunt Humphrey. Go ahead and call the rehab center she *claims* to have attended. I doubt they've ever heard of her."

That struck a nerve with Valerie.

She pulled away from Ava Jade's aunt and spat onto the carpet, her expression quickly changing from practiced weakness to the sort of deranged mania that only an addict could bring to the surface. "You always were a little bitch!"

"Valerie!" Humphrey exclaimed.

"Oh, don't act so surprised," Ava Jade slung at her aunt. "You *know* what she did to me and you still let her come here? You're just as bad as she is."

"I can't stand for this," Humphrey said, lengthening her spine, lifting her chin. "I must ask you *all* to leave. I never should have taken you in, you vile, *vile* girl. I should've known you'd turn out just as rotten as your father."

Ghost's eyes flashed with malice.

"When those men came here looking for money, I thought it was an opportunity to save you, but I can see now you don't want to be saved."

"What?" Ava Jade hissed, and I could see her pulse racing in her veins from here, could almost hear it. Taste it. Like when she was fighting in the ring, my Ghost *radiated* violence. My darkness was ready to go to war with hers.

"*What?*" Ava Jade repeated, showing her teeth. "What men?"

"Those awful gangsters. They said they'd kill him if I didn't pay what he owed but I don't negotiate with *criminals*." She folded her arms over her chest.

Ava Jade snapped.

She took out a blade and closed the gap between herself and her aunt in a flash, not even I was fast enough to stop her. Though, I didn't want to.

I watched, enraptured as Ava Jade held a blade to her aunt's hanging throat. "You fucking monster. You could've saved him!" her voice broke.

Grey and Corvus stood next to me now, watching as our queen exacted the justice she deserved. She didn't need our help here, as much as I would've *loved* to have a piece of it.

Valerie finished with her purse, dragging her skinny ass from the floor to leave. She was muttering something to herself, her words all jumbled together, spoken with too much saliva in her mouth.

"Never should have listened to that guy. Stupid motherfucker. Why did I listen to him?"

I reached to grab her, wanting to know what the fuck she was talking about. *Who* she was talking about. She stabbed something into my forearm and I hissed, drawing back, giving the cunt the perfect opportunity to grab my Ghost by the hair. Prying her from her aunt with a screech.

Ava Jade grunted as she jerked free, spinning on her heel like a dancer, her blade held out in a dangerous arc. Her mother managed to save herself from a certain death, falling backward just in time. The blade skated across her mother's throat, just enough to kiss the flesh there, to make bright red bloom over the pale skin. Not enough to kill her.

But there was still time.

"Oh my god," Ava Jade breathed, and I found her staring at me, all the frenzied rage in her eyes gone, replaced with a horror I didn't understand.

Until I felt it. The rush of euphoria taking over so swiftly I couldn't feel my legs under me. Couldn't feel my face. But I could see the needle now, stuck in my arm, the plunger pushed all the way down. I shut my eyes, grinning as the heroin shot through my blood, erasing all the dark.

"Rook!"

21

AVA JADE

I unlocked the door, and we pushed through into my apartment at Briar Hall. I held it open, ushering the guys in. Rook was held up with his arms between the shoulders of the others, looking not the least bit bothered about a damn thing.

"Do we need naloxone?" I asked, unsure what to do, my heart thundering in my chest as they laid Rook down on the couch and his head lolled to one side, a loose smile attempting to twitch up at the edges of his mouth. "I-I think they have some down in the nurse's office."

Grey knelt next to Rook, checking his pulse, his temp, and lifting his eyelids to check pupil dilation and light response. "He's going to be fine. *Fuck.* Why didn't we see this coming?"

He stood, swiping a palm over his face.

It was bad enough having to see my mother's face after all this time —bad enough to find out that my aunt could've prevented my father's death, but this?

This was a whole other level of bullshit to deal with.

Those cunts were just lucky my priority was Rook after we saw the syringe in his arm or I would've shoved their heads up each other's asses. I still might.

As it was, I hoped the nasty cut I'd sliced into my mother's neck got infected and she died of sepsis. I wasn't sure what kind of monster that made me, and I didn't care. I *knew* she hadn't changed, but for a second, *just a second*, she almost had me.

If it weren't for the suspicion in Rook's eyes, I might've bought it.

And now look at him.

I felt sick.

"This is bad," Corvus said, perching on the edge of the coffee table facing Rook. "He's been clean for almost two years."

I knew only a little of Rook's past, and I wasn't surprised he'd found solace in drugs. I didn't judge him for it even though I could've, but that was probably because he'd done the work. He'd gotten clean. He didn't let the drugs consume him, turn him into something else. But heroin?

"He was addicted to smack?" I asked, confused.

Corvus shook his head. "Blow. Doesn't matter though, this high could destroy all his work."

"We can't let that happen," Grey gritted out, starting to pace the floor. I hated how his pain was pinching his face.

"We won't," I assured Grey. "We'll lock him up if we have to."

Corvus' head snapped up. "We tried that once," he said. "Not a good fucking idea."

"*Urghhh*," I growled, wanting to rip the hair out of my head. "I just want to go back there and... and..."

"They aren't worth it," Corvus said. "But if you want them dead, just say the word, and we'll make it happen. You don't have to be the one to do it."

The monotone way he made the offer made me pause. He wasn't joking in the slightest. The promise was there in his eyes, clear as a brand new day. He'd wipe them from the face of this earth. All I needed to do was say the word.

"Don't decide now," he added. "Think about it. If you'd rather do it yourself then fine."

There was no third option. Corvus wasn't going to let what my mother did to his brother go unpunished, but I knew he wouldn't kill her unless I gave him the green light. He'd hurt her, though, I could see it in the beast pacing behind his icy blue eyes. It wasn't like she didn't deserve it, but...

"I think I have a better idea," I found myself saying, but right now, revenge wasn't the priority. They'd get what was coming to them. *Both of them.*

Corvus nodded without asking anything else as Rook began to gag.

Grey rushed to the kitchen, ransacking through the cupboards. He came rushing back with a silver handled pot and held it next to the couch as he guided Rook over it, holding him up by the shoulder as he vomited into the pot.

My throat burned.

I didn't like this.

Rook was supposed to be invincible.

And I realized in that moment that I'd been counting on him as the one person who wouldn't leave me. By choice or otherwise. Because I'd believed him to be something he wasn't. Immortal. Immune to the things that could send mere mortals to their knees.

But no one was immortal. Not even Rook.

I wished I could unsee all of it.

He vomited again, and I felt bile rise in my own throat.

A key turned in the lock to the front door, and I was so out of it that I didn't even reach for a blade as it swung open.

Corvus did, though, he launched over the couch, stepping in front of me, his gun raised.

Becca screamed, dropping into a crouch to cover her head with her arms.

Becca.

Corvus lowered his gun, all his air rushing from his lungs in a hard pant. "Fuck, Becca."

"Becca?" Grey asked.

I struggled to believe what I was seeing, blinking and swallowing past the bile to see her more clearly. She shakily pushed back to her feet, a small carry-on suitcase resting on the tile behind her. Dressed in leather leggings and a flowy printed top, she looked amazing. A heavy contrast to the peacock I was still wearing. The mixed emotions tangling behind my breastbone were almost too much for me to handle right now.

I didn't want to see her.

I was so fucking glad to see her.

"Becks?"

She was still struggling to catch her breath. "Hey, babe," she said, her voice pitched high, looking tentatively deeper into the apartment. She swallowed. "Bad time?"

Unable to stop myself, I pushed past Corvus and went to her, wrapping my arms around her, holding my breath to stop the sudden *ridiculous* urge to cry. "Shit, girl," she muttered, put off balance in her heels before she wrapped her arms around me too, hugging me tightly. "Are you okay?"

She rubbed my back. "Honestly, I expected you to kick my ass out," she muttered into my hair, her voice watery.

Maybe I should've, but it was too late now. She couldn't go anywhere unless it was on another airplane with a Saint escort.

"What's going on, babe? And what are you wearing, it's tragic as fuck."

Behind us, Rook vomited again, and she stiffened, pulling back, taking her essential oil perfume scent with her. Fuck, I'd missed that smell.

"Um, who's sick?" she asked.

"Rook," Corvus replied, stepping past us to drag Becca's suitcase into the apartment and shut the door behind her, locking it. She eyed his tailored blazer jacket with a raised brow, but made no comment.

"You're a fucking idiot," I told her, wiping the back of my nose over the sleeve of the dress.

She recoiled as though stung but then nodded, a tight smile on her lips. "Think we kind of already established that, but I did say I was sorry, like, a million times."

I shook my head. "No. I mean, you're an idiot for coming back here, Becks. Your guy is still on the loose somewhere, and you're the only person who can ID him."

"Yeah and apparently an all-out gang war happening on the streets of Thorn Valley," she added for me, indicating the bruise and cut on my face. I frowned at her.

She shrugged. "Daddy said not to come home because it wasn't safe. He said there was a whole ass gang fight in the streets and a bunch of people died and you weren't answering texts, so..."

"So, he said not to come back because there's a literal *war* going on so you... what? Hopped the first flight home?"

She rolled her eyes. "Look. This mess is as much my fault as it is anyone else's. If I can help or at least just be here for you, then that's what I'm going to do. You're my best girl, Aves. I couldn't stay there, knowing you were here dealing with all this shit alone."

I snorted. "Well, not alone."

She eyed Corvus. "Not the same," she said, and she was right. It wasn't the same.

They meant something different to me than Becca did, and I didn't realize how much I needed her here.

Had no idea that despite trying to hold onto my anger, I'd already forgiven her.

The bitch. I fucking loved her.

Rook had been right about that, too.

"You're still an idiot," I told her. "Now I'm stuck babysitting your ass."

Becca winced, but I just shook my head at her. "It's okay. I'm glad you're here."

"Glad someone is," she muttered, her gaze jerking from me to Corvus and back again before she cleared her throat and sighed. "Good. Now, what can I do to help?"

Becca took the handle of her suitcase and rolled it further into the apartment, her nose turning up at the smell of vomit on the air. "God, what did he eat?"

Corvus' haughty stare followed her, his jaw muscles flaring as he clenched his teeth. I grabbed the arm of his jacket and pulled it hard. "You don't have to forgive her, but don't be a dick," I whispered.

He pursed his lips but nodded.

Becca gasped, and the suitcase dropped to the hardwood as she caught sight of Rook for the first time. "Holy fuck," she said. "What happened to him?"

"He's been drugged," I said, going around to the other side of the couch as Grey helped ease Rook back down onto the cushions.

"Can you grab me a cloth?" he asked, but before I could go for one, Becca was already rushing through to the kitchen, running a kitchen towel under the hot water. She came with it and knelt next to Grey and Rook, lifting the cloth to wipe away the bits of vomit stuck to his chin.

Grey watched her with narrowed eyes for a moment before holding out his hand for the towel. "I got this," he said, and she dipped her head, getting uncertainly to her feet to pass it to him so he could finish the job she'd started.

She swallowed hard, tapping her wrists against her thighs. "So, uh, I'm just going to address the big fat fucking elephant in the room and say—"

"Becks, you don't have to do this now."

"I do. Just let me say it."

I shut up, wrapping my arms around myself at a sudden chill in the room.

"I fucked up. Really bad. But I think you should know the reason why I thought I was doing the right thing. I mean, at first. And really only for a minute."

"You were manipulated," I corrected her. *"Used.* It's—"

"No. It wasn't just that. I *wanted* to hurt them. If it weren't for the Saints, my mom might still be here. I blamed them even though she brought it on herself. She was only caught in the crossfire because she was cheating on my dad with a Saint."

"What?" Corvus demanded. Clearly, he hadn't known this and there was very little Corvus James didn't know.

Becca nodded. "My mom never took my dad's name. Her last name was Matthews. Eden Matthews. She was with Damien St. Vincent *before* he left to go start his gang chapter somewhere else. Her death was probably why he left."

Recognition flashed in Corvus' eyes, and I wondered what he knew about her. About what happened.

"I didn't find out about the affair until a few years back. It just made me hate the gang even more," Becca added, tucking a loose strand of her long straight hair back behind her ear.

I hadn't known this, and a part of me ached for her, but another part of me wondered why she'd omitted this part. Though, I hadn't exactly given her a chance to explain herself since all that shit went down.

Her brown eyes found mine, the apology clear there. "It wasn't just *him* influencing me. I was angry, and I wanted someone to hurt for making me have to grow up without her. I was wrong. I didn't know you guys, but when I *did* get to know you I knew I couldn't go through with what he wanted me to do. Especially not after—when I knew it would hurt Ava Jade."

"If you're asking for us to forgive you..." Grey said, his tone harsh as he trailed off.

"I'm not," Becca said. "But I wanted you to know why I agreed to help him. And ultimately, why I didn't go through with it all. You can forgive me or damn me, but either way, if my girl will have me, I'm not going anywhere."

I offered her a sad smile, and she returned it.

"I'm sorry about your mother," Corvus said. "If it helps you to know it, Damien St. Vincent loved her. He was broken after she passed. And you're right, it was the reason he left. Because he couldn't stand living on these streets anymore, knowing that he would never see her on them again. At least, that's what Diesel told us. It's a common story. The women we love are taken from us. It's dangerous business, falling in love with a Saint."

A knot formed between Becca's brows, and I could tell she was trying to rectify what Corvus had told her with the narrative she'd constructed in her own mind. She'd placed Damien St. Vincent in the villain's role in her head, with a wicked devil tongue that seduced her mother ultimately to her death.

She shook her head, clearing it. "Well, that's why I'm here. I'm not going to let the same thing happen to Ava Jade. Not if there's anything I can do to stop it."

Corvus nodded darkly. "And you would give your own life to save hers?"

It was a loaded fucking question.

"Corv," I said, giving him a *what the fuck* look, but he didn't retract his question, still waiting for Becca to reply.

Becca's lips pulled down at the edges, but when she answered it was with a conviction I hadn't seen in her up until now. "Yes. I would. She's my family, and I owe her my life."

Her words hit me like a fist to the chest, and a breath caught in my throat.

"You're forgiven," Corvus said. "But if you betray her again, I'll gut you myself."

She swallowed. "Um. Okay?"

"Grey?" Corvus hedged, waiting for his brother to weigh in.

Grey's gaze landed on me briefly before he spoke. "You're good," he told Becca without looking at her.

She smiled, relieved and pressed her hands together as though giving thanks to god above. "Fuck. That's so good to hear. I half thought you guys would be the ones to kill me if I came back so…"

She wipes the back of her palm across her forehead, laughing awkwardly. "Dodged a bullet here. Literally."

The room fell silent, and I went to kneel next to Grey, brushing stray black strands of hair away from Rook's face. Becca grabbed her suitcase, muttering something about going for a shower to give us some privacy.

"He'll really be okay?" I asked again, the ashen tone of Rook's skin making me think otherwise.

Grey took my hand, squeezing it. "Yeah. We'll take shifts keeping an eye on him, but he'll be just fine. We're all going to be."

I wish I believed him, but I couldn't shake the feeling that things were only going to get worse.

22

CORVUS

Sparrow slept curled in a ball at the end of the couch where Rook was still passed out, their feet tangled together. I'd managed to convince her to go take a shower and change, but she'd refused food and sleep until exhaustion finally took her a few hours ago.

Grey was dozing in her bed and had been since he declared Rook completely out of the woods. Lucky bastard.

It'd been days since I'd slept more than a few minutes, maybe an hour, at a time. With the Ace's deadline crawling nearer and Ava Jade's stalker back on the scene, sleep wasn't a priority.

And now...

Now that the Aces had made their move and vanished. Now that the stalker seemed to have gone eerily silent. Every minute was important. Every second. I could sense the tension stretching around all of us, flexing, tightening.

Something was coming, and I needed to be ready when it did.

I sighed heavily, my stomach aching with a hollow hunger, throat dry.

My tired bones creaked as I stood, head spinning as I made my way to the kitchen on quiet, shuffling feet, holding the counter to steady myself as I searched for a glass.

I drained two glasses of water before going to the fridge, seeing two of it for a second before I was able to realign myself with a sharp bite to the inside of my cheek. There.

There, that was better.

I grabbed some kind of premade salad and lifted some dressing from the door, rifling through the cupboard for some sort of protein. I found a bag of slivered almonds and dumped it on top of the salad with a bit of dressing, leaning heavily against the counter to eat.

Sparrow lifted her head sleepily from the couch and then snapped her head in my direction, wincing as the whiplash from the quick movement seared down her neck. She rubbed out the ache, groaning softly.

I lifted my fork in a silent *good morning*. "Sorry. Needed some food."

She pushed her sleep-mussed hair from her face and swiped a palm over the corner of her mouth, sitting up to check on Rook. She leaned over him, gently pressing the back of her hand to his forehead.

"He's really warm," she whispered.

I nodded.

"The fever is low. He's out of the woods, Sparrow. Don't worry."

She peeled the throw blanket from her shoulders and got to her feet, her spine popping as she stretched. "Did you sleep?" she asked when she was finished, her body sagging as she padded into the kitchen, going for the espresso machine.

When I didn't answer she stopped, peering over at me with a harsh gleam in her eyes. "Corvus, when was the last time you slept?"

I shrugged. "I got a few hours the other night."

She narrowed her eyes at me, setting down the portafilter. "You're lying."

My jaw tightened.

Fuck.

It had always been my tell, and if I wasn't so damned tired, I'd have been able to keep from doing it.

"You *are* lying. Jesus, you look like garbage."

I lifted a brow, shoveling another bite of salad into my mouth. "Thanks, Sparrow. Really laying on the compliments this morning."

She rolled her eyes.

"Grey's been in there for hours, go and wake him up and sleep in my bed for a while. Unless Diesel needs us for something, we don't have anything we need to do today."

I kept eating without replying.

"Corvus," she pressed. "Did you hear me?"

I swallowed. "Yeah, I heard you, Sparrow, but there's no fucking way I could sleep in someone else's bed. I can barely sleep in my own."

She mulled that over. "Then we can all go back to the Nest. You need to sleep."

I set the salad back down on the counter, my stomach souring. The idea of shutting my eyes for even a minute was repulsive. It didn't matter that I could feel the exhaustion like heavy lead in my veins. It didn't matter that behind my ribcage, my heart felt like it was slogging through mud one minute and fluttering like a caged bird the next. And the voices...

I knew they weren't real.

Just audio hallucinations. Like before. Distant whispers like radio static that would only become clearer the longer I deprived myself of rest.

I knew now not to fear them. I knew they didn't mean I was crazy. Just tired.

But sleep wouldn't come. Not now. Not with all this shit going on. There was no point in trying.

"You aren't even listening to me, are you?" Sparrow asked, her gaze darkening. "I'm warning you, Bones. I haven't had my coffee yet. Don't fuck with me."

I pinched the bridge of my nose, a frustrated heat rolling off my back, but I couldn't even fully feel that. My body not wanting to cooperate with connecting the proper neural pathways. "Look, Ava Jade, there's no way I'm going to sleep right now so—"

"What if I sleep with you?"

"What?"

She shrugged, dipping her head to hide the slight flush in her cheeks. "Neither of us thought we were going to sleep that night I stayed at the Crow's Nest with you. You fell asleep sitting up, and I wound up passed out in your fucking lap," she laughed uneasily. "So, maybe we can recreate whatever weird shit happened to make us both able to sleep like babies."

"So you can drool on me again?"

Her face scrunched up, and I felt a smile on my lips, tugging at the stitches in my cheek.

"If that's what it takes," she said, recovering with a grimace. "It's, what..." she looked at the clock on the stove next to me. "Just past seven. So, I only slept for about three hours. I could use a power nap."

She came over to me, leaning on the counter to look up at me through her lashes. "You'd be doing me a favor, really."

"You're relentless."

"It's why you love me."

Something in my core tightened at her words, and I had to bite down on my own tongue to keep from saying *yes*.

She might've been joking, but looking down at her now, her face soft from sleep, eyes slitted, hair an absolute fucking mess, I knew it was far from a joke.

I loved her.

She cocked her head to the side, considering me. "What? Why are you looking at me like that?"

I wrapped an arm around her waist and drew her into my chest, laying a rough kiss to the top of her head. Maybe it was the exhaustion talking, but right then I'd probably do anything she asked me to. It was terrifying.

I surrendered to no one.

...apparently no one but her now.

I let out a shaky breath. "If Diesel doesn't need us, then fine, Sparrow, I'll take a power nap with you. I'll try to."

"Would you be opposed to sleeping pills?" she whispered into my chest. "Because I'm pretty sure Becca has—"

"No pills."

She hesitated. "Okay."

Becca's door creaked open across the room and my Sparrow pulled away from me to see her friend exit her room, already dressed and ready for the day. I kept from smirking at her outfit. Fitted Lycra pants, combat boots that looked like they were from a designer label, a loose fitted tank top and ball cap that she'd pulled her long brown hair through in a tight ponytail. Not her usual attire. It looked like something Ava Jade would wear if she knew she might run into trouble.

"You make coffee yet?" Becca asked Ava Jade.

She shook her head.

"Good," Becca said. "That's my job."

She hesitated before entering the kitchen, craning her neck to see Rook in the living room. "He's still out?"

"Yeah," I told her. "But he's all right."

The crease in her forehead made it seem as though she had been legitimately worried about him and maybe she was. I'd detected no lie in anything she'd told us last night. And anyone willing to lay down their life for my Sparrow was okay in my book. But I'd also meant what I said. If she did *anything* to betray Ava Jade again—if she hurt my brothers—I would end her.

"And Grey?"

"Asleep," Ava Jade replied. Jerking a thumb to her bedroom.

"Not anymore," Grey said, wandering from the room in nothing but his boxers, stretching his arms high over his head, the veins in his biceps and waist jutting from his skin like snakes.

Speaking of...

"Come on, man," I hissed at the same time Becca cleared her throat.

Grey's hard-on was squashed between his stomach and the waistband of his boxers, a good two inches of its head poking out for everyone to see.

He looked down, bored. "It's a dick. Are you offended by dicks now? You'll be disappointed to know that you have one, too, Bro."

Ava Jade chucked a tea towel at him. "Go put some pants on," she said, her gaze sliding to Becca, a tick in her jaw.

She was jealous.

It was a good look on her.

"There's fucking vomit on them," Grey complained, covering his cock with the towel.

"Oh!" Becca exclaimed. "I bought these really nice Puma sweats for... well, it doesn't matter who they were for. I bet they'll fit you. One sec."

The reminder of Becca's mystery Ace boyfriend soured the mood in the room, and I had to wonder not for the first time whether we'd already killed the fucker.

I was willing to bet Becca was wondering that, too. Holding on to the hope that he was dead, which would mean she was in considerably less danger.

I doubted she was so lucky. I'd seen not a single Ace who truly matched the description she'd made. Though Ava Jade was right, that one King definitely *did* match.

My tired mind tried to work through the puzzle of it all, wondering whether or not Diesel had recorded anything of their conversations where Becca's boyfriend actually *said* he was an Ace. Though even if he had, what was this guy's word worth?

"Here," Becca said, returning from her room to toss Grey the sweatpants, and whatever I'd just been thinking about was knocked from my skull, and I couldn't claw it back.

Yet another symptom of insomnia. The inability to hold on to slippery thoughts. To make connections. To see things coming before they did and stop them.

My Sparrow was right. I needed to sleep. If I didn't, I'd start missing shit that was right in front of me.

Grey pulled on the sweats, and Becca was right, they fit him like a glove. He didn't seem to like that fact, but it was better than wearing around Rook's vomit until we could get back to the Nest.

Right on cue, Rook stirred, a low groan falling from his lips as he rolled lazily from his back to his side, arm flopping from the side of the couch.

Ava Jade abandoned her attempt to make coffee and rushed to the living room, grabbing the glass of water from the coffee table.

"Hey," she said, sitting uneasily on the edge of the couch, hand hovering over his shoulder like she was afraid to touch him.

Oddly, I didn't feel jealous as Rook settled his hand on her thigh and squeezed weakly, or when she helped him up and pushed the hair back from his face to pass him the water. I felt... glad.

So fucking glad that she was there for him just as much as we were. That she could give him things that Grey and I never could.

Rook sipped the water, grimacing, probably wishing it was whiskey.

His slitted eyes glanced around the room at the rest of us, and a frown curled the edges of his lips downward. "All right," he hissed. "Show's over. What the shit happened?"

"You don't remember?"

"I remember your mom being a cunt and then... just nothing."

"That was pretty much it."

Ava Jade dropped her head, unable to look him in the eyes. Maybe it was good if he didn't remember everything. If I were being honest, there was a small part of me that was afraid for Rook to wake up. It could've gone either way, with him pissed at Ava Jade and out for her mother's blood, or like this... his usual aloof self, not giving two fucks either way.

His hands shook as he drank more water, and he was pale and sweaty as fuck. He needed a shower and to be watched like a hawk at all times over the next couple weeks. He'd be twitchy.

To my knowledge he'd never touched heroin before, but I could vividly remember him coming down off a cocaine high.

Shit wasn't fucking pretty.

People died.

We just tried to make sure the *right* people died. It was all we could do.

If Rook couldn't have his next drug fix, he needed blood on his hands.

Grey rounded the sofa into the living room, sinking onto the coffee table to wait until Rook looked up at him.

Once he did, Grey studied his stare, nodding silently to himself as though he got all the answers he needed just from looking into the black depths of his brother's stare. "All right," he said.

"Satisfied?" Rook prodded.

"For now," Grey replied. "But you fucking tell me if I need to be more worried."

Rook gave a single terse nod.

"Hey," Grey barked. "I want to hear you say it."

"All right. *Fuck.* I'll tell you."

"Good."

Becca came into the kitchen, picking up where Ava Jade left off, making coffees for everyone.

"I'm not a very good cook," she said as she frothed milk. "But I can do pancakes if you guys want something to eat. Or we can order in."

Ava Jade shook her head. "Actually, if it's cool with everyone, we need to head back to the Nest once Rook's good to move."

The man himself flinched at her words, and she noticed, wincing with second-hand shame.

"What for?" Grey asked and my jaw clenched.

"Your idiot brother hasn't slept in days. Probably longer. I'm going to put him down for a nap."

Rook laughed at that, and even Grey smirked. Traitors.

I shook my head at her. "You're dangerously close to making me change my mind about the whole fucking thing," I warned.

But she only shook her head. "Nope. You're going to nap even if I have to knock your ass out to make it happen."

I bit my cheek to keep from grinning.

"Bet you fifty he doesn't sleep more than an hour," Rook said.

"Make it a hundred and I say he doesn't sleep at all," Grey countered, his eyes flicking to Ava Jade. "Not even if *you* ask him nicely, AJ."

Her cut-glass eyes narrowed on Grey and Rook. "You're on, motherfuckers."

23

AVA JADE

Shit. I fell asleep too fast.

I knew it the moment I opened my eyes, hearing the faint sounds of a deep rumbling voice coming from the closed closet door across the room.

Groaning, my arm stretched to the opposite side of the bed, feeling cool empty space where Corvus should've been.

Fuck.

I was going to be out a hundred and fifty bucks.

My eyelids peeled back, adjusting to the glow of late evening light.

Evening?

I quickly rolled to the other side of Corvus' bed, his engine oil and spice scent filling my nose as my legs slipped over his tightly tucked sheets to snatch my phone from the nightstand.

I flinched at the brightness of the screen, seeing that it was past eight in the evening before peering back to the closet door. He wouldn't have stayed in here for eight hours, would he? We got here around eleven, and I was probably passed out by twelve.

My muscles ached, protesting the movement as I swung my legs from the warmth of the covers and off the side of the bed, touching my toes to the carpet. I leaned forward, pressing my palm into the hollows of my eyes.

I couldn't remember the last time I'd slept this long.

The three hours I'd gotten last night plus however many I'd had now equaled a greater amount than I'd probably had since I was a fucking toddler.

And I'd done the sleeping next to another human being. Twice.

What was happening to me?

Inside the closet, something crashed and the door pushed open, an angry Corvus quietly stepping through to avoid waking me. Behind him, his mic was knocked against the wall, hanging from the stand awkwardly like he'd tossed it away.

He stopped in his tracks, seeing me sitting up in bed. "Fuck," he grunted, throwing a fist through his hair. "I didn't wake you up."

I shook my head. "You didn't. But you should've. Why'd you let me sleep so long?"

He gave a one shoulder shrug, and I noticed he was already dressed again, the boxers and t-shirt he'd slept in now joined by a pair of faded black denim jeans. "You needed it."

I pinched the bridge of my nose. "That wasn't the point. The point was—"

"Sparrow, I just woke up."

"What?"

"About an hour ago."

I couldn't contain my triumph as a relieved grin spread over my face. "Really?"

He nodded, seeming just as shocked himself. "Yeah, really."

"I knew it," I muttered to myself. "Those fuckers better pay up."

Despite having just slept for what I had to guess was a pretty good amount of time, Corvus still managed to look exhausted as he crossed the carpet and sank onto the edge of the bed with a deep sigh.

I crawled back across the tangle of blankets to sit next to him, indicating the tossed mic in the closet. "What went on in there?"

His jaw clenched. "I had an idea for something new and I thought..."

"What?" I asked when he didn't finish. "You thought what?"

He fell back onto the bed to stare at the ceiling. "There's no point," he said numbly. "Primal Ethos is dead. Besides, the gang needs me right now. I shouldn't be wasting time—"

"Shut the fuck up. Don't be stupid. Primal Ethos isn't dead, not unless *you* let it die."

His expression darkened, his gaze never leaving the ceiling. "You don't get it, Sparrow. It's over. The Bone Man—the *mystery* of him—that was the allure. Without it, I'm just another jackass with a microphone."

I couldn't help it, I laughed, and his forehead creased, betraying a rage he usually kept tampered down.

"I'm sorry but that's fucking bullshit. Have you looked online *at all* since you were outed?"

He didn't answer. It was answer enough. He hadn't.

I shook my head. "You should. If anything, they're even more mad for you now than they were before."

I wasn't going to let him do this. He was too talented to throw this all away. With or without Diesel's permission, he needed it. Pushing to my feet, I grabbed both his hands, dragging him up from the bed. "Come on, show me what you were working on."

"We need to check in with Diesel."

"He can wait another hour."

"Sparrow—"

"Just do this for me, okay? Show me what you're working on. Maybe I can help. And then as soon as we're done, I promise you we will go and check in with the others."

His resistance weakened as I hauled his ass to his feet and toward the closet, dragging him into the small enclosed space with me. I dropped his hands and lifted the mic back into position, fiddling with it until it sat properly in the stand.

"Okay. Now show me."

"It's just rough shit. It isn't even finished yet. It's... it's missing something, but I can't fucking figure it out."

I bit my lip to keep from smiling. Was Corvus James *nervous* to show me something? It wasn't a look I'd seen on him before. It was... kind of cute.

I reached past him and shut the door behind us, feeling a tingle go up my spine at the feeling of being in a confined space, of him being so close I could feel the press of him like a physical touch even though we were nearly a foot apart.

"I'm waiting," I prompted him, looking up at him coyly from

beneath my lashes. Fuck. Had he always been this tall? In the tight space, he seemed to tower over me, and from the way he was looking at me, I could tell his mind had gone to a similar place as mine.

I swallowed. Cleared my throat.

Corvus smirked before lifting his phone from his back pocket to tap the screen, bringing up what appeared to be some rough lyrics in a notepad app.

"Since you're here, mind giving me some rhythm?"

"Hmm?"

He hit a section of not padded wall with the side of his closed fist to create a simple beat, showing me what he meant.

I stepped closer, copying the beat until I had it right and he could lower his fist.

Surprising me, he reached up and caught the string dangling from the light above us and tugged it, plunging us into darkness. The rhythm of my fist on the wall faltered and my pulse picked up, but I recovered quickly, my belly tightening as Corvus began to hum into the dark. A deep sound that I felt all the way to my toes as he moved through the opening of the song.

He began to sing, filling the small space with his voice so fully that he could have been singing inside of my head. His rough voice ricocheting through my body as he sang of being stronger.

About how he thought he'd made himself into something that couldn't be affected. Couldn't be broken. Couldn't be hurt. How he never saw me coming.

The lyrics hit me hard. I could've written them myself, and when he began the chorus again, my voice rose to meet his, feeling the truth of the song flow through me like I was nothing but a vessel.

Our voices trailed off as one, and I was left momentarily breathless, body aching. Pulse throbbing with a need so pure it could've brought me to my knees.

"*Sparrow,*" Corvus whispered, and I felt him grow nearer in the pitch darkness. His knuckles brushed down the back of my arm, making me shiver and a little gasp escape my lips. "I think you were the thing that was missing."

Rough fingertips found my temple and skated down the line of my jaw until they rested against my lips, making them part.

"You were always the thing that was missing."

He pressed this thumb into my mouth, a slight groan on his lips as he slid it against my tongue, pushing to the back of my throat until I moaned.

"Tell me you want me," he said, so close I could feel his breath fanning over my lips as he withdrew his thumb, wetting my lips with it.

He moved fast, gripping the back of my neck to haul me closer, until I could feel the brush of his lips against mine when he spoke again. *"Tell me."*

"I want you," I muttered breathily, my panties already soaked, thighs squeezing at the hot ache between them.

"Good girl."

A ripple of unexpected gratification raced through me, making me shiver.

His lips pressed to mine, hot and full as they pried mine apart to allow his tongue entry. My back slammed against the padded wall, wrists held against the wall to either side of my head. I moaned into his mouth as he pressed into me, letting me feel the hard length of him against my belly.

I struggled against his hold, needing to be closer. Needing to take off the layers of clothing separating us, but he held me there, hands tightening around my wrists.

"Now, Sparrow," he chastised. "Did I tell you that you could move?"

My mouth parted, but no words came out. I'd never given over control like this before, but something about letting myself go, about handing that control over to him and not having the burden of it on my shoulders turned me on so much it fucking hurt.

I wanted him to make me his. I *wanted* to relinquish myself to him. And it scared the shit out of me.

"You will not move," he said, and a stuttering breath left my lips as he released my wrists, and I kept them there, high above my head as he traced a light line down them with his fingertips. Down past my shoulders, over my breasts, down my waist to the elastic band of my panties.

He hooked his fingers into them and pulled them down painfully slow. I tried to wiggle my hips to help him along, but he placed a warm palm flat against my lower belly and pushed, holding me still as he used his other hand to finish removing them.

"C-Corvus," I said, my voice breaking on his name as my arms started to lower of their own accord. I needed to touch him. Needed to feel him inside me.

Warm breath fanned over my greedy little cunt, and I bucked against his hand, my own hands delving into his hair to find something to hold on to.

He grabbed my wrists and spun me, pressing my chest to the wall as the sound of leather rushing through denim echoed in the darkness and his belt was wrapped tightly around my wrists, binding them together at my back before he flipped me back around.

Corvus kicked my legs apart, and I groaned as he laid a kiss to the sensitive skin of my inner groin.

"Stay still, Sparrow," he told me, and I cried out as he closed his mouth over my wet heat, tasting me, his tongue flicking over my swollen clit.

He groaned. "You taste so fucking good."

I whimpered, my body near to convulsing as he added a finger to the repetitive movements of his tongue, pressing it slowly into me.

"That's it," he cooed between teasing licks. "Sing for me, Sparrow."

He plunged another finger inside of me and increased the speed of his tongue, making me cry out at the intensity of the sensations, wrists trying to break free from their binds as I ground against his mouth.

"*Oh fuck*," I said on a breath, my orgasm building to the breaking point.

He feasted on my cunt, hands gripping hard at my waist to keep me pinned there, unable to move as the orgasm rushed through me, making stars burst against the back of my eyelids in the dark.

I tried to pull away, the orgasm almost too much to take, but he held me through it, forcing me to feel every last spark of it until the flames subsided.

"Holy fuck," I said, letting my head fall back against the padding to catch my breath. Was it bad that I wanted more? One of the best orgasms I'd ever had and I was already primed to beg on my knees for round two.

"You want more?"

I nodded, still struggling to catch my breath.

"I need to hear you say it, Sparrow."

"Yes."

Corvus pulled me down until my knees hit the carpet and I sensed him rise above me. Heard the shuffle of his clothes as he removed his jeans.

The light flicked on and I blinked at its brightness, staring up at Corvus as he finished removing his shirt, his chest covered in a tattoo I'd never seen before. Actually, I didn't think I'd ever seen Corvus without his shirt on. The name Emmanuelle was written over his chest in black script, surrounded with a myriad of imagery.

A crowned heart.

A massive crow.

A sparrow.

Roses and thorns.

I followed the lines of ink all the way down to the massive cock hiding beneath thin black boxers.

My mouth watered.

"I want to see you," Corvus said, his left hand sinking into my hair as he thumbed the waistband of his boxers and tugged them off, letting them fall to the ground at his feet. His massive cock sprang free and I remembered the feeling of it inside of me that night in Lodi. The fullness of it seated all the way to its hilt, hitting something so deep it bordered on pain.

How I'd been so angry and so turned on and so confused.

I wasn't confused anymore.

Corvus' grip on the back of my head tightened as he guided me forward. "Open," he ordered me, and I did as I was told, opening wide for him as he pushed between my lips. The salty taste of him coated my tongue, and I moaned around his girth as he shuddered, fingers knotting into my hair.

"*Fuck,* Sparrow."

I let my tongue slip over the underside of his cock, my arms straining at the binding holding my wrists together. I wanted to touch him. To feel the silky slip of his base against my palm.

Corvus picked up his pace, pressing in deeper, until I could feel him at the back of my throat. I could feel my own wetness smearing over my thighs as he pumped into my mouth and I pushed forward to meet him, trying to show him that I could take it. I could take it all. He didn't have to hold back.

I wanted him to choke me with it.

I wanted him to leave me gasping.

Sensing what I wanted, he lifted me until I was plastered against the wall, the back of my head cushioned by the padding as he fucked my tight little throat, hot hands clasped to either side of my face as he panted.

"Damn," he cursed, slipping out from between my lips as I gasped for air.

I was going to ask him why he stopped. I could feel that he was close, but before I could get enough air into my lungs to speak, I was jerked back to my feet and Corvus had me with my chest against the wall again. The belt slipped from my wrists at the same time as he lifted my hips and thrust into me.

I moaned at the fullness, adjusting to his size as my fingernails dug into the padding on the wall.

"God, Sparrow, you're so fucking wet for me."

He reached a hand around to my front, and I felt my shirt tear from my back as he ripped it clean off my skin, fingers finding a nipple to squeeze.

I jerked at the pain, arching my back. "*Yes.*"

Corvus squeezed the other nipple, harder than the first, as he eased out and slammed back into me.

I fought to stay on my toes as he fucked me from behind, his height making for a challenge.

"Come for me, Sparrow," he said, breathless as he continued a quick pace, and I felt a tightening at his command, the beginning of another orgasm spurred on by his command.

His hand slid down the slippery skin between my breasts until it found my clit. He rubbed it viciously as he fucked me, grunting into my ear as he held off his own release.

"Choke me." The words fell from my lips unbidden, and he did as he was told, wrapping his free hand around my throat from behind, cutting off my air supply at the perfect moment.

I came hard on his cock, writhing against him, grinding into his hilt as the orgasm spiraled through me.

"Fuck!" he hollered as he came with me, rough, wet fingers wrapping around my middle as he thrust his last, pressing me into the wall.

I gasped as he released my throat, both of us sinking to the floor, knocking the microphone against the wall. He hauled me to his chest as he sat awkwardly against the wall in the tiny studio, and I crashed against him, listening to the quick steady beating of his heart until our breaths began to even out.

"Do we have to leave this room?" Corvus asked after a few minutes, and I knew what he really meant because I could stay here forever, too.

24

AVA JADE

After all the shit that had happened in the last four days, going to class felt like the biggest waste of time, which was why when Becca and the guys banged on my bedroom door at Briar Hall exactly thirty minutes ago to wake my and Rook's asses up, I'd almost bitten off all their heads.

"Are you sure there's been nothing from Diesel? Nothing at all?" I asked Corvus for the third time since I'd peeled my eyes open.

Fuck, you'd think after all the sleep he and I had yesterday I'd be raring to go, but somehow, just after two in the morning, I'd sunk into a deep and dreamless sleep next to Rook as he finished sweating out the toxic substance still lingering in his bloodstream.

We hurried down the stairs to the front atrium with only minutes to spare until the bell, Becca breaking off from the rest of us with a blown kiss to rush off to her homeroom class.

"Nothing," Corvus confirmed. "The Aces are underground, Sparrow. They won't be poking their heads out anytime soon, not after losing that many men. They're *dead*, and if they know what's good for them, they'll stay that way."

I frowned. They weren't all dead.

Diesel had sent pictures of the deceased to Corvus late last night for Becca to flick through. He wanted to be certain her man was dead. But he wasn't among their corpses. All the morbid slideshow had accomplished was to make Becca barf up the meager dinner she'd managed to choke down an hour earlier.

I rolled my shoulders back, trying to let the lingering feeling that we should be doing *something* roll off my back, but it wouldn't leave. Something wasn't right. I could fucking feel it.

"Excuse me," called a man's voice from the front office, and as one, the four of us turned to find the principal sticking his long neck from the door, indicating toward me. His balding flaxen hair clung to the sides of his head like a bird's nest befitting of his long thin nose. "Miss Mason, may I have a word please."

I sighed heavily, turning to retrace my steps to the office as the bell sounded through the halls. At least with my new status as a Saint I wouldn't be marked tardy.

Unsurprising to me, but very surprising to the principal, the guys followed behind me, flanking me on either side.

"Problem?" Corvus asked before I could speak for myself.

The principal blinked, pushing the door the rest of the way open to stand in its mouth uncomfortably. "*Uh*, well, I believe it's a conversation better had in private."

I didn't budge.

"Whatever it is, you can say it in front of all of us," Grey said.

I nodded my agreement, just wanting whatever this was over with so I could nap behind my textbook in homeroom.

The principal's Adam's apple bobbed and he patted the front of his pressed slacks. "All right then, if you're sure." He cleared his throat, jerky eyes meeting mine. "It seems your aunt has unauthorized all future tuition payments."

He left the sentence open, hanging with something like a question, waiting for me to fill in the blanks he didn't have answers for, like who would be taking up those payments going forward for the next term.

I couldn't say I was surprised. I figured after the other night, the bitch and I were finally through with each other, which was good because I didn't con or steal from my family. And the things I intended to do to that woman would go a step above either of those.

"I fail to see the problem," Rook said, slinking between me and Grey to put himself nearer to the principal, his dark gaze fixed to the small man's face. "Perhaps you can enlighten me?"

The principal recoiled from Rook's nearness, glancing between Rook and me like I might do something to help. To stop any attack. I wouldn't.

"Oh, well, you see..."

"Yes?" Rook prodded, his body tightening, coiling like a snake.

The principal fell back a step. "I just wanted to congratulate Miss Mason," he blurted. "I wanted to, *um*, personally let her know, *uh*, that she's qualified for our scholarship program... and that her final semester of the year will be fully covered, including boarding fees."

The principal let out a small gasp as Rook slapped a hand down on his shoulder, giving it a squeeze. "Well, isn't that nice," Rook said, giving the man a little shake as he turned to face the rest of us. "Isn't that nice?"

"Very," I agreed. "Thank you. I'm glad I qualified."

In all reality, if I'd applied, I probably would've qualified for the program. If such a program existed. Though I supposed it did now.

"Yes, yes," the principal said, dropping his shoulder to get away from Rook and back into the office. "Just wanted to let you know. You'll get an official letter emailed to your academy address later this week."

He couldn't get away fast enough and as the office door closed, the four of us burst out laughing, rushing away from the office and down the hall to homeroom.

"*Fuck,*" I said, shaking my head. "You guys didn't have to do that. I could've just paid for it."

How expensive could it possibly be? I had about five grand sitting in my secret cubby upstairs in my room.

Grey raised a brow at me. "You have thirty-five grand?"

"*What?*"

"The price of privilege," Corvus said with a twist to his lips and then, "Don't worry, Sparrow, we didn't pay either. Diesel's *contribution* to the school wasn't a monetary one. He offered *not* to expose their century of corruption, racial and sexual preferences—"

"Don't forget that one priest they had before the church shut down," Grey added.

Corvus nodded. "Yeah, and *that*. Anyway, we had acceptance letters the next day and the school's motto was changed by the end of the following week. There are things in this world worth a lot more than money, Sparrow. Never forget it."

"*Shit.*"

"Shit, indeed."

I had to admit, it felt oddly liberating to be free of my aunt's promises. To break away from the future I *should've* wanted for the one I actually did want. The one where I belonged.

Homeroom went by in a half-dozed blur, and math was more of the same. I couldn't bring myself to focus on any of the problems we were solving in class, but it didn't matter. Thanks to *past* Ava Jade, I was still pretty far ahead of the class. That was going to change fast though if I couldn't get my ass in gear and focus.

My mind kept wandering though.

And not just to the Aces.

To the faceless enemy targeting not just me, but me and my guys now.

I had a feeling he was the one to blame for outing Rook's *thing* with the vice principal.

He'd admitted to watching us through the academy's security system the day I'd burned all the hair from Brianna Moore's pretty little head.

He had to be CrowKiller321. The fucker who'd exposed Corvus' identity as The Bone Man. Grey hadn't managed to reverse trace his IP. No surprise there. This guy, whoever he was, was fucking *good*.

And I knew he was far from finished.

Who would he target next?

What was he hoping to accomplish, playing these twisted games with us?

The itch to *do* something was so strong I found myself leaving AP Math with a whispered excuse of using the bathroom to Grey, needing to move. To think.

Halfway there, I pulled my phone out, bringing up the email from the stalker that day in the academy kitchens. My thumb hovered over the reply button, pulse picking up speed as my vision began to tint crimson.

I clenched my teeth, stopping near a long window in the hall of the upper floor, bouncing on the balls of my feet.

It was me he wanted.

What if I made him an offer he couldn't refuse? Would he leave the others alone?

I didn't know every skeleton in their closets, but I knew there were plenty to be dug up if you knew where to look. How deeply could he bury them if I didn't do something to stop him?

There was apparently nothing to be done about the Aces until they resurfaced, but *this*...this I might be able to put a stop to. I just needed a few minutes with this fucker and a freshly sharpened blade.

Swallowing, I clicked *reply*.

To: gh380xc@gmail.com
    From: Ava Jade Mason
    Subject: RE: Miss me?

Why don't you come out of the shadows and play? Or are you too much of a coward? It's me you want. Come and get me, motherfucker.

I hit send before I could change my mind, reassured by the heaviness of the four sharpened pieces of steel strapped to my limbs. By the fact that I knew any of the guys would have sent the same message if our roles were reversed. They couldn't be angry with me for this. Especially not if it got me the result I wanted.

This fucker's head on a spike proudly displayed at the entrance to the Crow's Nest as a warning to any others who might try to raise a weapon against my guys.

Feeling much better, I pushed into the bathroom, going to splash some water over my fury flushed neck and cheeks.

I pocketed my phone, on edge as the sound of shuffling feet beneath a stall alerted me to someone else in the bathroom.

The room fell silent.

My brows drew. "Hello?"

I bent to peer beneath the stalls, finding the small floor spaces all empty. But I'd definitely heard someone.

The fury came rushing back at the realization that the stalker would still want to keep tabs on us here even though Grey now had complete control over every form of surveillance on the property and was certain there was no outside access anymore. What if he were *here*? Watching in the flesh.

My upper lip curled back as I reached for a blade and kicked the first stall door open.

A girlish squeal from the stall next door made me hesitate, but only for a second before I kicked that one open, too.

The girl cowered in a ball, hugging her knees to her chest atop the toilet seat, her long brown hair hanging like a curtain to cover most of her face. Though it didn't cover enough to hide the fact that she'd been crying. By the look of it, she'd been crying in here for a while. Her eyes were puffy and red, mascara streaked down to her chin.

I thought I recognized her as a freshman who usually sat near the front of the cafeteria. Usually alone, or as a fifth wheel to another group of kids who mostly ignored her. I couldn't remember her name, though.

She stared at me like I was the grim fucking reaper come to inhale her soul. Jesus.

My stomach tightened, and I backed up a step, the fire in my veins spluttering. "Um..."

Fuck. I wasn't good at this.

"Are... are you okay?"

The girl burst into sobs at my question, pressing her face into her knees.

Oh god.

I stepped into the stall, awkwardly patting the girl's shoulder. "There, there."

That's what you were supposed to say, right?

"I'll, uh, I'll go get the nurse, okay?"

Her hand shot out, grabbing me by the wrist to stop me. "No!"

Something about the fear in her voice stopped me, and the hairs on the back of my neck pricked.

"Why not?"

"*Please*," she sobbed, wiping snot across the back of her hand. "Please just f-f-forget you saw me."

My phone chimed in my pocket, but I barely heard it over the rush of blood in my ears. Something bad happened to this girl.

This girl who looked like she couldn't be more than fifteen. This girl, who, under the running makeup and red eyes, looked sweet and innocent despite attending school at a place like this.

"What happened to you?" I found myself asking, sinking down to her eye level.

She spied the knife in my hand and gasped, prompting me to put it away. I lifted my empty hands to show her I meant no harm. "I'm not going to hurt you."

Her tears slowed as she considered me, clearly scared, but there was something else there too. A thing I recognized. A spiteful sort of anger, hidden beneath layers of pain.

"But that's what you do, isn't it?"

I cocked my head at her, not understanding.

She swallowed, her hair falling forward to shadow her eyes. "You hurt people. You and those other guys. The Crows. I've heard about you."

"Then you know that this town belongs to *them*. And that they take care of the people in it."

A twitch in her upper lip told me I might be on the right track. "Tell me what happened. Maybe I can help."

Fuck, how much I'd *love* to pummel one of the cocky, baby-faced jocks into the ground right about now. I shuddered just to think of the release. Maybe I'd even let Rook help me.

I couldn't get justice for me and the guys. Not yet. But maybe I could get some for this girl.

Her lips parted, but no words came out.

"It's okay," I assured her. "If you want, I won't even tell them it was you who told me."

She frowned, looking at me suspiciously. I could tell she was wondering how I knew it was a *someone* and not a *something* she was crying about.

"I can't," she decided.

"Then whatever happened will probably happen again."

Her lower lip quivered.

"His life would be ruined."

So it was a *him*. We were getting somewhere.

"Did he hurt you?"

She looked away.

Motherfucker.

I could feel my cheeks flushing with a renewed heat, and I struggled to keep my voice even. "If someone hurt you, you can't let them get away with it."

Her hands clenched to fists against her thighs. "You won't tell him it was me who told you?"

I shook my head, a sick feeling in my stomach at the look she was giving me.

A minute ago, I was sure what this was, but now I didn't think I was prepared for what she was about to tell me.

"I already called the hotline," she said. "You know that one for reporting crimes anonymously, but nothing happened. No one even called me back."

What?

I needed to get her back on track. I could examine that little tidbit later.

"Tell me what happened."

She squirmed against the toilet seat, her brown eyes looking everywhere but at me. "He offered me a better grade. It was just supposed to be that one time," she finally said and the force with which my rage intensified was like a bomb detonating in my stomach. I'd be shocked if there wasn't smoke coming out of my ears.

I managed to maintain a calm front, but my next words came out strained. "Go on."

The girl, whose name I learned was Layla, told me as much as she could before her face turned green and she couldn't talk anymore. Until she was shoving me out of the way so she could crawl down off the toilet, lift the lid, and vomit into the porcelain bowl.

I felt like joining her by the time she was finished.

She sat back heavily against the toilet, breathless from being sick as I rose to my feet, every inch of my skin vibrating.

"I'm going to take care of this," I told her. "You don't have to worry about Mr. Williams anymore."

"What are you going to do?" she hollered after me as I left the bathroom, but I didn't reply. She didn't want to know.

25

GREY

Mr. Williams barely looked up as I rose from my desk, leaving my shit as I exited the classroom ten minutes before the bell. AJ wasn't answering me, and she'd been gone too long.

I thumbed a quick message to the guys on my way down the hall.

GREY

Something's up.

Chances were I was being paranoid and she was just too fucking antsy to be stuck sitting in class, but if that were the case she would've answered my texts by now. I pocketed my phone and reached my hand back behind me, ready to draw the gun there if I needed to.

Heavy, thudding footfalls sounded around the corner ahead and I clenched my jaw, fingering the outline of my gun through my shirt, working the thin fabric up and out of the way.

"AJ?" I hissed, sweat slicking my chest.

Five more steps and there she was.

Ava Jade didn't stop as she rounded the corner, staring straight ahead, her hands in fists at her sides. Her face red. Her body rigid. Murder in her eyes.

I scanned her for injury, but she seemed unharmed.

"AJ," I repeated, stepping in her path.

"Move."

"Hey," I said, a lick of anger racing up my spine as I gripped her arm, hauling her to a stop. "What the fuck is going on?"

She spun, slamming her palm against my forearm to break my grip on her. Pain radiated up my arm, and it was my face that brought her back to me, if only for a second. She blinked, realizing what she'd done and stopped, inhaling deeply through her nose.

"Where were you?"

Footsteps ascended the stairs at the end of the hall and she stiffened, watching like a hawk until Corvus and Rook crested the top of the staircase, their faces hard as they zeroed in on us.

"What happened?" Corvus demanded, hurrying down the hall, his sights fixed on Ava Jade.

Rook drew his gun, stepping past us to peer around to the next hallway. "Clear," he muttered, replacing his gun in the back of his waistband, a knot forming between his brows as his gaze landed back on Ava Jade.

She was practically shaking with rage, her jaw locked.

"Ghost?"

Her light eyes tracked a path to Rook and the glass in them shattered, her shoulders shuddering as they fought to fall. "He's a fucking monster," she said, her hand unconsciously going to her stomach.

"Who?" Rook demanded, his gaze darkening. "Name him."

"Williams."

I cocked my head at her. "*Mr.* Williams?"

She nodded.

I racked my brain, remembering every time I caught him staring at her in class, but I'd just been with him during AP Math while she was in the bathroom. He couldn't have done anything.

"Did he fucking touch you?"

Her eyes found mine, confused. "You think he'd still be breathing if he had?"

No. I didn't. But then what the fuck was she talking about.

"Sparrow, start talking. What happened?"

She rolled her shoulders back, taking another shaking breath before she began.

AJ explained about the girl she ran into in the bathroom. She told us how the girl had given Williams head once for a better grade. And later, how he'd used a video he'd taken of her giving him head as blackmail to get her to do other things, threatening to post it on the internet and ruin her life.

"He took her somewhere. To a place that she said had a video camera set-up with a bed and nothing else. She didn't know where it was because he would blindfold her to take her there. He..."

She choked before continuing. "*Fuck*," she said, lifting her hand to bite her knuckles to stop whatever she was going to say next. "He's a fucking pedo. What were your rules about that?"

This question she posed to Corvus. "Hmm?" she prodded. "They don't get strikes. They go straight to the grave, right?"

A muscle in Corvus' jaw ticked. Rook was already glaring down the hall like he could will Williams to leave the classroom right this minute so he could shoot him in the kneecaps.

Corvus' brow pinched. "Not without proof."

"What that girl said isn't good enough?"

He shook his head. "No. If we relied on the word of fourteen-year-old freshmen there would be a lot more unmarked graves in Thorn Valley... filled with some very undeserving corpses."

Ava Jade's eye twitched.

"But," Corvus continued. "We will look into this."

"Fine," Ava Jade said. "We look into it *now*. Right fucking now."

Rook was already nodding. "Grey, get the address. The fucker will be busy with classes for the next few hours. We'll scout his place while he's busy here. If he was taking videos, we'll find them."

"And if he was?" Ava Jade prompted.

"Strike three," Rook confirmed, his nostrils flaring.

AJ nodded gravely. "I want to help."

Rook's lips parted, the creases in his forehead smoothing as he searched her eyes, then nodded.

I set to work logging into the staff side of the academy's online portal from my phone.

"Should we bring Becca? I don't want to leave her here."

"I'll call Tiny. He'll come and stay with her until we come back. Good?"

"Yeah. I'll text her to let her know."

"She's not going to like that," Rook said.

"She'd like coming with us a lot less."

AJ had a point. Becca was stronger than I'd ever given her credit for, but normal people had limits, and what we would do if we found out the girl was telling the truth would go far beyond Becca's. Besides, Tiny was basically a giant cuddly bear with a gun. He'd probably braid her hair and order her a fucking chocolate cake.

"Got the address," I announced.

"Let's go."

Behind us, the bell rang as we made our way down to the Rover, alert for any signs of attack.

Diesel would kill us if he knew we were going on a little side-quest for our humanitarian project right now, but Ava Jade wasn't wrong. If Williams was what that girl claimed, he had no place in Thorn Valley. Letting him get away with doing what he was accused of even one more time would be one time too many.

Plus, if he'd done it once, we knew from experience it was very fucking likely he'd done it before. Layla might not be the only one.

Williams' place was a pedo's wet dream.

Secluded at the outer edge of the city, surrounded by trees with no neighbors for miles.

Of course, that alone didn't mean he was guilty, but I couldn't help noticing it as we stepped out of the Rover and onto his freshly paved driveway. AJ shared a look with Rook and I knew she was thinking the same thing I was.

Ava Jade stormed ahead of us, rushing his front door. She kicked it in with one long heavy stroke of her leg.

Now was not the time to be getting turned on, but...

I cleared my throat, jerking my head after her. "Let's go."

We followed her inside, down a narrow hall that broke off into three directions. Up the stairs. Into a living room to the left, and a kitchen to the right.

Rook stormed up the stairs, where it looked like Ava Jade had gone if the boot prints on the off white carpet were any indication. Corvus went through to the kitchen, and I went the opposite way into his living room. My nose wrinkled at the smell of the place. It reminded me of the group home. Musty with an undercurrent of microwaveable food.

I tossed the couch cushions first, then moved on to the coffee table, tugging out both drawers to tip their contents onto the carpet. Nothing.

The bookshelves.

I tipped the spines, flicking each one out of its place until they were all in a pile on the floor at my feet.

A corner of white paper stuck out from one and I bent, lifting the heavy tome, a copy of a book called I'm Not Sam. I lifted the paper from the pages, but found it blank. Though, beneath were words that jumped out at me. I grimaced, reading a small part of the page the makeshift bookmark had been stuck in.

Was his taste in fiction enough to condemn him? I was starting to think it might be when I heard AJ call from upstairs. "Get up here," she shouted, and I let the book fall closed, dropping it to the pile at my feet with the others.

Corvus and I met in the hall, and I followed him up the stairs. "Anything?" I asked Corvus.

He shook his head. "You?"

"Super fucked up book. Not enough to be sure."

A door was open at the end of the hall when we got to the top of the stairs, bluish light bleeding onto the carpet.

The sound of a girl crying filtered past my ears and my stomach tightened as we went into the room, finding AJ sitting at a small desk in a small room, Rook hunched over her, his face a twisted mask. The heavy blackout curtains were drawn so tightly over the window that the entire room was black save for the light of the monitor screen.

AJ suddenly pushed away from the desk, knocking Rook back in her haste. "I can't watch anymore," she growled, shoving past me as she left the room, thudding back down the stairs.

I went to Rook, still staring at the screen like he couldn't peel his eyes from it even if he wanted to, the murderous intent in his stare deepening.

I didn't need to see it, didn't want to, but I needed to know what we were dealing with.

On the screen a video played. Recorded on a shitty camcorder in what looked like a dingy basement type of space. Mr. Williams wore a mask while he fed his cock to a little boy, but there was no mistaking it was him.

Behind the still-playing video was a wide finder screen with hundreds of tiny little video files. Each one labeled not with names but with ages and sexes.

I didn't want to believe the smallest number was accurate.

"Turn it off," Corvus roared.

Rook clicked over to another video instead, his body rolling with rage.

Corvus shoved Rook back and grabbed the entire monitor from the top of the desk and smashed it on the floor, stomping on it for good measure, his breaths sawing in and out through his teeth.

"In our fucking town," he hissed. "Right under our fucking noses."

Guilt pooled in my stomach like acid, and I swallowed back the taste of bile rising in my throat. I'd always known Williams was a bit of a creep, but this? I'd been in his class for months now, and I hadn't seen this. I should've.

Corvus' turned his fury on me. "Want to tell me how this fucking slipped your notice, Grey?"

A muscle in my jaw ticked. I shook my head. I had no excuse to give.

"He was clearly good at hiding it," Rook said numbly, his stare still fixed to the busted monitor. "His kind often are."

Not for the first time, I felt a deep peace at knowing I'd killed the man from Barrett's Home for Boys. I still didn't know exactly what he'd done to deserve the broomstick Rook shoved up his ass, but seeing him now, I thought I might have a better idea.

I wished I didn't.

"Come on," Corvus said, calmer now, putting a hand on Rook's shoulder. "We have some justice to dispense."

"Wait…" Rook trailed off, his eyes slanting as he considered some-thing for a second and then walked out the door to the room without another word. I followed him down the stairs, hearing what he'd heard. Noises from below.

We followed the sound to where the dining room table had been shoved to one side of the room, the oval shaped rug beneath thrown back to reveal an open hatch and dark stairs leading down.

The smell from below made me hold my breath as he descended into the darkness after AJ.

A lightbulb swung at the end of a long orange cord fixed to the ceiling. Casting a wavering light over AJ as she stared over a short double bed, the gray sheets stained with something darker. A rat skittered past our feet, its hind leg caught in a trap that it dragged along with it.

The culprit to the noise we'd heard from above.

"*Ugh,*" I cringed, stepping back. I fucking hated rats.

"Move the Rover," she said, the *zip* of a blade whizzing through the air preceding the sound of the rat's final squeal. "We do this here."

"I need my kit," Rook said.

"I'll take you," I told him.

"I'll wait here with AJ for him to get home," Corvus said. "Take the main roads. In and out. If you aren't back here in twenty minutes—"

"We will be," Rook promised Corv, and I believed him. There wasn't a single thing on this earth that would stop him from returning to this dank basement to dole out justice for the children who would be forever scarred by what had been done to them.

26

ROOK

"Grab the lighter fluid from under the sink, would you?" I asked, remembering we were out of gasoline as I made my way to the shed, skin itching. The pain in my abdomen, a symptom of the withdrawal, stronger now than it had been this morning. I grimaced through the pain, a muscle in my right arm spasming as the reaching hands of my darkness raked at the back of my skull, demanding to be fed.

Tonight, it would dine on the dirty soul of a pedophile.

But... it whispered. Dan the Man was only a phone call away. I could fix it. I could almost feel the chemical burn of cocaine on the back of my throat. Could almost fucking taste it.

I could skin Ghost's mother alive for doing this to me, but that wasn't a call I could make. My girl had promised me vengeance once our lives in Thorn Valley returned to a semblance of normal, and that was good enough for me. For now.

I unlocked the shed and stepped inside, the lingering scent of bonfire filling my nose. I breathed it in deeply, clutching the edge of my work table and shutting my eyes to get a hold on myself. I dug in my back pocket, drawing out a cigarette with shaking fingers to put it to my lips.

The flame danced on the top of my Zippo, an inch from the end of my cigarette as I froze in place, staring down at the surface of the table in front of me.

There, atop a torn slip of paper was a small black bag. Round and bulging. Knotted at the top.

The words were an afterthought, and I had to force my eyes to leave the familiar baggy to read them.

You're welcome.

That was it.

No.

Fuck.

I blinked hard, hoping that when I opened my eyes again, it wouldn't be there.

But it was.

"Rook," Grey called from outside and in a knee-jerk reaction I snatched the eight-ball of coke from the table and shoved it deep into my pocket, flicking the paper away.

"Hey, you good? We need to get back," Grey said, appearing in the door. "Got the lighter fluid."

I grabbed my busted up red toolbox and lifted my blowtorch from its nook with a pinkie. "Yeah. I'm good."

We got back to his house before he returned home, parking the Rover in the trees a little farther down the road.

The afternoon sun, so warm and so fucking bright, was at odds with the dark rising within, making me froth at the mouth as I waited, crouched low behind a boulder near the end of his driveway. The black ball in my pocket feeling like it might burn a hole straight through.

My knuckles rubbed over its outline through my jeans, and I gritted my teeth.

I heard the car coming and nodded at Grey through the living room window, tensing the thin length of rope between my fists. It was going to be hard not to end him right away, but filth like Mr. Williams deserved to suffer first.

The rope bit into my fingers as I stretched it to its limits, a shudder rolling down my spine as the images from his computer screen replayed behind my shut eyelids. I'd only had the pleasure of slaughtering one other monster like him.

The one I really wanted dead, the counselor from Barrett's Home for Boys, bit a bullet before I could get to him. Though I had a feeling I knew who'd done the job for me, and I was glad it was one of us. At least I had the satisfaction of knowing that he would have seen Grey's face and known the reason he was there. *Who* he was getting justice for.

Didn't change the fact that I wished I'd done it myself, felt robbed of the chance to get my revenge, but now. Here. Tonight. I would get my revenge for others who never could. Never *would*. Not in the way that they should.

My teeth clenched, baring in a snarl as tires turned from the choppy road to the smooth pavement of the drive, slowing.

A car door opened, and I rose from behind the boulder in one swift movement, grinning as I stalked around the back of his car on silent feet, my shadow lying over him as I approached.

He started, seeing it a second too late. I wrapped the cord around his throat twice, pulling it tight until my biceps strained. Williams choked and spluttered, clawing at the thin cord around his throat as I sent him to his knees, not letting up until his clawing hands turned to useless deflated lumps of flesh and began to sag.

I squeezed one last time before shoving him forward onto his face, releasing the cord. I kicked him hard in the side, and he replied with a coughing breath, going back to a limp stillness as he passed out. Couldn't have him suffocating before we'd had our fun, now could we?

Another car was coming, and I cursed, bending to lift the dead weight of his body onto my shoulder, the bullet-wound in my leg protesting the extra weight. I groaned, carrying him around the other side of his car until the other vehicle passed by.

I pushed a hip into his car door to close it before hauling him inside, through the house to the kitchen, where I dropped him down the hatch and watched as black-painted fingernails grabbed him by his ankles and dragged him into the dark.

I bit my lip ring, fingers fumbling for a cigarette before I changed my mind, climbing down into the hole, closing the hatch behind me.

Grey helped my Ghost lift Williams' limp body onto the bed.

I dropped my toolbox to the cement floor and crouched, digging into it for the zip ties. I grabbed a handful and tossed them onto the bed. "Tie him down."

Ghost didn't waste any time, grabbing a couple strips of plastic before tugging Williams' arm high above his head, securing it to the dated metal headboard while Grey did the same on his opposite side, securing his wrists and ankles in place until he was stretched into a long X on the dirty mattress.

Corvus watched from the edge of the room, arms crossed over his chest as he oversaw our progress, like he always did.

Once Ava Jade was finished, she drew out her blade and carved a long slit into his arm with a flick of her wrist, making him rouse. Crimson spilled over the sheets as the math teacher found his voice, letting out a low, pitiful sound, little gasping cries as he tugged on his extremities, only a little at first, then thrashing, moving the whole bed as he flung his body back and forth, tearing the skin of his wrists in the process.

Ghost's upper lip curled back, and she lifted her blade again.

"Patience," I said, and her manic gaze found mine in the dim space, her knife-hand stilling.

"We don't want it to be over too quickly."

A muscle in her jaw ticked, but she nodded. She understood.

My darkness fluttered.

"*Wh-whats going on here,*" Williams shouted, his voice breaking, pitched all wrong. It was the best sort of music. "Hey! Miss Mason, just what is it that you think you're doing?" he continued, staring up at Ava Jade with a crease in his brow before his eyes finally found me and he stilled.

I inhaled long and slow, taking in his fear.

He reeked of it.

I licked my lips.

"N-no," he uttered through quivering lips before those lips pulled back over his yellowing teeth. "I'll press charges," he threatened, and I grinned in response.

"I will!" he promised. "You won't get away with this."

"And you think we're going to let you get away with what you've done?" Ava Jade asked, her voice strangely calm, but with a note of mania that only I could recognize. She was only speaking calmly because she'd already decided exactly what she wanted to do to him and knew nothing would stop her from doing it.

Williams had the decency to shut his mouth at that, pressing his teeth together as he began tugging anew at his binds. He didn't deny it.

It was as much of an admission of guilt as we would get, not that we needed one after the evidence we found.

"You'll pay for this," he said.

Ava Jade only shook her head. "No," she said. "But you will."

She lifted her head, eyes landing on Grey, then Corvus, then me. A slow smile pulled at one corner of her sharp mouth. "Are you thinking what I'm thinking?"

"Take his fingers first?" Grey asked, eyeing his filthy hands where they flexed and squeezed, tried to get free.

Ghost shook her head.

"His cock?" Corvus put in, readjusting his stance against the wall to get a better view.

She shook her head again and I saw in her a version of myself when her eyes flashed with malice in the light.

"Fuck him in the ass with one of your blades?" I asked.

Her grin widened. I hit it right on the money.

Not a bad idea.

"Help!" Williams screamed, his voice frantic now. "Help! Someone, please!"

Ava Jade leaned over him. "Hold him," she told Grey, and to my surprise, Grey knelt on the edge of the mattress and held Williams' face steady as Ava Jade got hold of his tongue and sheared it from his mouth.

Blood spurted upward, spraying over Grey and my Ghost, coloring them with the most beautiful shade of red.

They fell back as Williams gurgled, craning his neck to keep from choking on his own blood as Ava Jade held his tongue up to the light, examining it before tossing it over her shoulder with a look of disgust.

If I'd ever had even a shadow of doubt about where she belonged, it was gone now.

Grey was right. She was our fucking queen, and I'd go to war for her no matter the cost or consequence. She was one of us.

As my gaze fell back to Williams, I was... almost jealous.

It was my turn to have some fun.

"I like your idea," I told Ava Jade, tapping the pads of my first two fingers to my chin as I rounded to her side of the bed, looking down at our soon to be masterpiece. "But the guys are right. We should take his fingers first. Then his junk. I'll cauterize the wounds, of course, so he doesn't bleed out..."

"And then I can fuck him with my blades?"

"We'll save that for the finale."

Too bad Williams was almost fully gone by the time I even got to use my torch, but still, it was a balm to my soul to watch his skin turn red, then black, then flake off to float beneath the light all around us like gray snow.

I coughed beneath the shirt I'd tied around my face, Williams' ashes tickling my throat.

My Ghost's hand pushed down into mine, our fingers twining as she drew nearer into my side, unbothered that my naked torso was covered in sweat, blood, and smears of ash.

Grey and Corvus stepped out, leaving the hatch open behind them to give some airflow as we finished up here. The plan was to set fire to the whole joint before we left, ensuring that everything here was turned to ash with Mr. Williams. His victims didn't need to relive the things he'd done to them if any of those videos should come to light. Their peers wouldn't ever look at them the same way.

They would be questioned. Their parents would want to know why they never said anything. No one could possibly understand.

It was better this way. Justice had been served and he couldn't hurt anyone ever again.

"It's kind of beautiful, isn't it?" Ghost said, indicating the still smoking remains on the concrete floor at our feet. Williams' charred shape was curled in on itself, in the fetal position, hands over his head, the white of his bones showing through the burnt remnants of his skin.

I'd thought Frank had been my best work, but Williams took the cake. I squeezed Ghost's hand in mine, lifting it to my lips. I pressed a kiss on the back of her palm. "It is."

She shivered at the touch of my lips, and I tipped my head to one side, peering down at her. Her lips parted at something she found in my stare.

"You're not the monster people think you are," she said, and the black thing in my chest tightened.

Her face pinched. She moved to stand in front of me, lifting a hand to brush the pad of her thumb over the top of my cheekbone. It came away stained black and red with blood and ash. Her breathing deepened.

I mirrored her movements, brushing my knuckle down her cheek, streaking a path through Williams' debris.

"I am," I assured her.

Her chin tipped up, defiant. "Then I guess I am too."

My brows lowered.

She pressed a hand to my stomach, dragging her nails low until they met the top of my jeans. Her eyes never left mine as she undid the button there, making me groan and my already thick cock turn to iron against the press of her hands.

I dropped my forehead to hers, a tremor rolling up my spine as she took my length into her hand, stroking it from tip to base.

"Fuck," I cursed into her hair.

Here? We were going to do this *here*? Now?

This was an entirely new level I didn't even know existed.

My fingers twisted into her hair, jerking her head to look up at me.

Some unspoken thing passed between us. A connection forged in blood and blades and fire. It was a joining of souls. Mine twisting with hers, hers with mine, creating something gnarled and twisted. Stronger. New.

"Fuck me, Rook," she pleaded on a breath, and I could see it in her eyes, she felt it, too. Her thighs pressing together, a pained expression crossing her sharp features. *"Please, Rook.* I need you."

I wouldn't make her ask me twice, but I wasn't about to take her on the defiler's bed or on his dirty corpse.

I lifted her onto me, and she gasped when I forced my tongue into her mouth, carrying her to the wall until her back was pressed into its rough, uneven surface, pinned there by my hips.

My cock pushed hard into her heat through her clothes, and she moaned as I moved against her. It didn't take long for me to feel her wetness seeping through and I inhaled her next moan as I stepped back, letting her fall back to her feet as I grabbed the waist of her jeans and pulled.

The button popped free and she had them halfway down her legs in the blink of an eye, clawing me back to her, her nails biting down into my chest and shoulder until I felt the well of blood. The caressing trails of it as it flowed down my warm flesh.

She had my cock in her hand again, and I groaned, convulsing as she pumped it, backing up against the wall again, guiding my hand back to her waist.

I did as she wanted, lifting her off her feet as she spread her legs wide for me, using a tight fist around my base to guide me inside.

My head pushed against her opening, and I sucked a breath in through my teeth as she thrust her hips forward, impaling herself on me with a cry, her hips rocking in ecstasy as she arched her back and let her head hang.

I cupped her perfect ass, holding her up as she moved against me, little panting gasps driving me to the brink of an entirely different kind of insanity.

Her tight cunt squeezed me gloriously as I began to move too, slamming into her hips with the taste of Williams' ashes still on my tongue. My lips curled back over my teeth, and I growled against the side of her neck, making her shake in my arms.

Pain exploded across my left shoulder, and I jerked as the sensation awoke something that had long been sleeping deep inside, adding to the intensity of my pleasure.

The glint of my Ghost's blade caught the light, and I smiled. "Do it again."

She stabbed the sharp tip of it into the thick meat of my shoulder muscle, pushing it in slow as I fucked her.

"Harder," she urged me.

I leveled my dark gaze on her, aching to taste her lips again. To feel their softness under the hard bite of my teeth.

"*Harder*," I urged her, the challenge clear.

She pushed hard, and I did the same, her body bucking between me and the wall until I felt her beginning to come undone. Her dripping cunt erratically tightening, *tightening, tightening* around my girth until my balls tightened and the fire of my orgasm shredded up my spine.

Reflexively, I lowered my head, biting into her shoulder, marking her in the same place she'd marked me. She gasped, releasing the blade in my shoulder to allow it to clatter to the floor as she coiled around me like a snake, coming on my cock just as my own climax hit like a fucking Mack truck, erasing all thought. Leaving us a tangle of trembling limbs against the wall, the heat of Williams' still smoldering corpse making it even harder to breathe.

27

AVA JADE

Mr. Williams' body still had yet to be found in the ash and rubble of his house at the edge of the city, though officials had been searching since the flames and embers died out early this morning. Soon, they'd find him. But for now, Thorn Valley seemed to collectively be holding its breath, waiting for good news.

All except for Layla Hopkins, who we found in the cafeteria at breakfast, staring up at the news channel on the widescreen television, her food untouched. Subtitles flashed across the bottom of the screen, telling the general public that so far, there was no evidence of arson or any form of foul play. For now, at least, they were treating this as an accident and the authorities suspected the fire came from a burner that was left on in the kitchen.

Which was exactly the story Corvus had fed to the fire chief along with a wad of bills and a cliff-notes version of what we'd found in his house in case the chief decided the bribe wasn't worth the man's life.

So far, everything was going to plan, and I couldn't help a smug smirk as I slid into the serving line, piling a plate high with scrambled eggs and bacon while the guys wandered to our table. I gave Grey a strange look, but he didn't see, his stare fixed to the screen over Layla's head.

Apparently, I was the only one eating this morning.

I mean, the sooty, acrid smell of Williams still clogging my nose would probably taint it all with a funny taste, but with enough hot sauce...

Yeah, it'd be fine.

The metal spoon clattered against my tray as I scooped some fruit into a bowl and set it on my tray. Layla twisted in her seat, doing a double take when she saw me. Her first reaction was fear, but I held her there, captive in my stare for a moment, waiting for it to sink in.

I nodded, and she slumped at my wordless admission, a breath puffing from her lips, eyes watering. There it was. The relief.

It solidified that we'd done the right thing.

Layla Hopkins should fear me, but she should fear for the real monsters more.

Better the evil you know than the evil you don't.

"Hey, Angel."

My fingers tightened on the tray, and I turned, finding a very familiar six foot tall frame also piling a tray high with breakfast.

"Drake?"

He peered up at me from the corner of his eye. "Yes?"

I looked to the guys, who were all staring at Drake's back with varying looks of unease.

Drake nudged me out of his way, reaching past my arm to grab some fruit for himself as though this was entirely natural.

"Um, what are you doing here?"

Behind him, I thought I saw another King entering the cafeteria, a girl from my English lit class on his arm, blushing as she bit her lower lip.

Drake tossed his light hair back from his face and lifted a strip of fatty bacon to his mouth, tearing off half the strip with his teeth. "Part of the deal with Dies," he said once he'd swallowed. "Apparently," he pointed to the ketchup behind me, "do you mind?"

I moved out of the way for him to grab it. He loaded it onto the mountain of eggs on his plate.

"Apparently, *what?*"

"*Apparently,*" Drake repeated, plopping the ketchup back down. "The Aces have resurfaced further south. They may or may not have cut a deal with the, *uh,* Skeletons?"

"Skeletons?"

"No, fuck, that's not it. *The Dead Men*. That's them."

I lifted a brow. I hadn't heard of them.

"You wouldn't know them," Drake said, reading my mind. "They're little league. Barely a blimp on the map, but together with what remains of the Aces..."

"Why weren't we briefed on this?" I found myself asking, as though Drake would know.

He started toward the table, *our table,* pausing to look back over his shoulder at me. "You coming?"

Drake slid in easily across from Corvus, setting his tray down with another piece of bacon hanging from his mouth. He caught Corvus staring and lifted the lip of his plate, tipping it in his direction. "Want some?"

Corvus' phone rang, and he lifted it to his ear. "Yeah?"

He listened for a minute to whoever was on the other end, eyeing Drake as I slid in next to him and he made some space for me.

"What's our move?" Corvus asked over the receiver, and I assumed it was Diesel calling to explain just what the fuck was happening.

"Got it," Corvus said and hung up, setting his phone down on the table.

"Pops?" Drake asked between mouthfuls of egg.

Rook tapped a coin on the table, sitting up straighter to peer over at Corvus. "Want to fill us in?"

"We got word that the Aces were cutting a deal with the Dead Men," Drake said before Corvus could.

"And apparently Diesel thought it might be a good idea to increase gang presence at Briar Hall in case they try anything," Corvus added.

"Surprise," Drake said sarcastically, an easy smile gracing his full lips. "We're homeroom buddies now."

Rook's dark gaze zeroed in on the other Kings entering the cafeteria. I spied the creepy looking fucker from fight night, the one that matched Becca's description, and wished she was down here eating with us so I could point him out. He hovered near the rear exit to the cafeteria, sipping something from a paper cup.

There looked to be a total of five new students at Briar Hall. Two of whom looked far too old to be here.

Drake, though, even with the evidence of a hard life carved into the weathered lines of his face, somehow managed to give off the aura of someone young and full of life. He fit in. The others really didn't.

Grey's foot slid into mine under the table, *hard,* and when I looked up, I found him watching me.

Watching me watch Drake.

Had I been staring that long?

I cleared my throat, my appetite suddenly gone. "I think I'm going to take this up to Becca. See if she's up to eating anything."

"Becca?" Drake asked, lifting a brow.

"My roommate," I explained. "She wasn't feeling well this morning. She's still in bed."

"Ah," he said, stabbing another forkful of eggs. "Want me to go with you?"

"We're good here," Grey said. "Why don't you go and sit with your guys, yeah? We'll let you know if we need you."

I pressed my lips together, holding back a grin.

Drake, unperturbed, stood, scooping up his tray. "Whatever you say, man." He flashed me another quick grin. "Later, Angel."

"I don't like him," Grey muttered, his hand curling into a fist on the table.

"If he looks anywhere below your neckline again, I'll have to carve out his eyes," Corvus added, the new skin forming over the puckered scar on his cheek, catching the fluorescent lighting. We'd taken the stitches out last night and it was looking a lot better.

"He saved your life," I reminded him.

He shrugged. "Doesn't matter."

Rook sat back in his chair, letting his coin roll over his tatted fingers as he watched Drake walk away. "I kind of like him," he said, making Corvus and Grey balk.

"Don't you, Ghost?" he asked me with a knowing gleam in his eyes.

I lifted my tray from the table, heat rushing up my neck. "I'm going to see Becks," I said, dodging the question. "I'll be back by the bell."

I heard Grey hiss something nasty at Rook that I didn't catch and listened to the throaty sound of Rook's laugh as I left the cafeteria, feeling the itch for a good long run.

"Oh my god, did you get this?" A girl by the elevator asked the guy standing next to her, and I hesitated when the doors pinged opened. "Check your school emails. There's no way this is real, right?"

"I got it, too! They don't mean Corvus like *the* Corvus, right?" the guy asked, and I dropped my tray, breakfast forgotten.

The girl looked up at the clattering sound of the tray hitting the tile and startled when she saw me coming, cringing back into the wall, sinking low into a ball, her phone outstretched to me.

"Hey, whoa," the guy next to her said, lifting his hands, getting in my way.

I decked him in the jaw, sucking in a breath at the sting in my still-bruised knuckles as he careened to the right, tripping to keep his footing.

"What the fuck," he groaned, his mouth sounding like it was full of marbles.

I took the phone from the girl's hand and lifted it to my face, scrolling back up to the top of the email on the screen.

"What is this shit?" I asked, nudging her with the toe of my boot.

"I don't know!" she wailed. "I swear, it just came to my phone."

The email was a photocopy of an old newspaper. Almost twelve years old.

The headline jumped out on the screen in bold text.

CULT KILLINGS: FIVE DEAD IN BRUTAL SLAUGHTER

What the fuck was this?

All around me, students paused on their way to breakfast and classes, their devices pinging as the email was circulated.

I scrolled lower on the screen, my pulse racing as the gruesome image of a crime scene devoid of bodies but not of blood screamed at me in black and white. It was a child's bedroom. Complete with train-patterned sheets, tiny toy cars, and a starscape nightlight. The entire thing was coated in blood. It puddled on the mattress, soaked into the carpet. Splashed over the wallpaper. A tiny dark handprint was left on the floor near the base of the bed. A child's handprint.

My stomach turned.

I scrolled lower, reading the first few lines before I had to force myself to stop.

It was a brutal scene in east Lennox this morning when the bodies of married couple Francine and Douglas Adler were found in their home along with Douglas' brother, Chris Adler, and their eight month old son, Emmanuelle. They are survived by their eldest son, who was admitted to Lennox General this morning with only minor injuries. Authorities suspect the killings were part of a cult ritual due to the nature of the deaths and the—

I couldn't bring myself to read any more.

Bile rose up the back of my throat.

Emmanuelle.

The tattoo on Corvus' chest.

Everyone in the state knew about the cult murders. The Adler family was only the first to go. After them, the Finches and the Hayes were found dead in their homes in similar ways. It was later learned that they were all in the cult together. That Douglas Adler was their leader.

I glanced back down at the text in my hand, seeing where the photocopy of the newspaper had been altered. A piece of paper cut into a thin rectangle covered a line of text that seemed to be saying how the surviving boy's identity would be kept confidential. On it were the words: CORVUS JAMES ADLER.

Fingers shaking, I tapped on the sender's email at the top of the screen.

CrowKiller321@gmail.com

My heart lurched in my chest, heat sizzling down my spine.

I chucked the phone at the wall, and it smashed into tiny bits, raining down onto the tile to the backdrop of gasps from the students in the atrium.

I stalked to the nearest student and knocked the phone from their hand. "Don't fucking read that." I seethed, staring at all the other students as they stared back at me.

In the cafeteria, a chair scraped back from a table, and I heard Grey shout.

"You fucking heard her," someone yelled and I turned to find Brianna *fucking* Moore on the bottom of the stairs. "*Put your goddamn phones down.*"

She knocked two phones from the hands of the students nearest to her.

From the corner of my eye, I saw movement and a face flashed clear in the daylight before it vanished around the corner of the west hall.

A face I recognized.

I drew a blade, and the students around me all screamed like little bitches, falling back, their phones suddenly forgotten in the face of something far more interesting: a girl on the edge of her fucking rope.

"Hey!" I bellowed after the King, giving chase as I sped through the atrium and down the hall, catching the flip of his jacket as he pushed through the exit doors at the end and went outside.

"AJ!" I heard Grey shout somewhere behind me, but I wasn't stopping.

It was him.

That creepy fucker from fight night. I was sure of it. Why lurk around the corner watching like that if he had nothing to do with it.

Why *run?*

Guilty.

Guilty.

Guilty.

"It's him!" I called back over my shoulder before I shoved through the heavy metal doors, bursting into the humid morning, squinting as the sun stabbed into my eyes.

I raced forward, lifting a hand to shield my eyes as I scanned the front lot for him, seeing nothing.

"Hey!" I screamed, rushing ahead to vault over the low hedges in front of the parking lot. "Come out, you fucking coward!"

I dropped to my knees and bent low, peering under the vehicles in the parking lot, searching for feet, for movement, for anything.

"AJ," Grey shouted from behind me as I rose back to my feet, storming around an SUV to peer into the bed of a truck.

Grey caught up to me, his gun at the end of his extended hands, aimed low as he looked over all the cars. "Where is he?"

I growled my frustration, my skin tingling with rage. "I fucking lost him."

I kicked the nearest tire, kicked it again. *Again.*

"*Fuck!*"

"Hey," Grey said, brushing a soothing hand down my back, but I didn't want to be soothed right now. I wanted fucking blood. I shrugged him off, putting my hands to my hips as I paced the narrow space between two cars, my chest and back slick with cold sweat, my head spinning from the aftereffects of too much adrenaline and not enough fuel in the fucking tank.

"We'll find him, AJ," Grey promised as I hunched over, hands braced on knees to pinch my eyes closed, trying to clear the spots from my vision. "But right now we need to get to the Nest."

"What?" I asked, and the reality of what'd happened before I saw the King fleeing the scene of his crime hit me. "Corvus."

Grey nodded gravely. "He took off."

My heart squeezed. "Alone?"

His jaw locked. "Rook went after him, but Corvus is faster than any of us. He looked like he was heading for the Nest though, so…"

I took one last long look over the cars in the parking lot, praying for even the slightest indication that the fucker was still here, but I really had lost him. He was gone.

But I knew who it was, and I would get answers from him. That was if Maverick still wanted to keep his fucking alliance with the Saints. I wanted him on a fucking platter, and I would have him one way or another.

Drake came rushing from the front entrance a second later, just the person I wanted to see.

"What just happened back there?" he asked, jabbing a thumb back toward Briar Hall. "Your guy just lost his fucking shit. Something about an email?"

"It was your man," I said, looking at Drake in a new light now, knowing we couldn't afford to waste much time here. I didn't like the idea of Corvus alone in the woods, even if it was only a few miles between here and the Nest. It could be exactly what the fucker expected. He could be waiting.

Drake's brows lowered over his eyes. "What are you talking about?"

I cleared the few steps between us and pointed my blade at him, bringing it to within an inch of his chest. To his credit, he didn't budge at my advance, only stiffened. "That creepy fuck from fight night. The one you said was your one-man clean-up crew."

"Aries?"

"I saw him lurking in the atrium when that mass email was sent out to the entire school. And when I pursued him, he fucking *ran*."

This seemed to surprise Drake, but not as much as it should've.

"Maybe he was just running because you were chasing him, Angel," he said with a shrug, but the tension in his jaw said it all. He didn't trust Aries, either. "I mean, he saw you fight. I'd run, too."

I shook my head. "I'll be having a little chat with Diesel about this," I warned. "If you and your leader want to keep this alliance, I want Aries served to me on a silver fucking platter. You hear me?"

Drake recoiled from the sting of my words but nodded. "It's probably just a misunderstanding."

"We'll be the judge of that," Grey said.

Drake nodded. "Understood."

I let my gaze rest heavy on Drake's for another moment before inclining my head to the Rover parked a few rows down. "Let's go, Grey."

28

CORVUS

A soft knock came at the door to my bedroom. I knew it was her. Something in the tentative double rap of her knuckles gave her away, and I shrunk into myself, resisting the urge to throw something at the door. Shout at her to fuck off and *leave*.

It was exactly what I'd been doing for the last two days, but even I knew I couldn't stay in here much longer. It wasn't that I wanted to hide from my past. It was the fact that I'd worked so fucking hard my entire life to push back those memories. To pretend what happened never happened.

To rid myself of the nightmares that left me in a tangle of sweaty sheets with bile climbing the back of my throat.

"Corvus," Ava Jade whispered through the door. "You can tell me to fuck off if you want, but at least take some food and water. Please?"

I sighed heavily, lifting from my core to throw my legs off the edge of the bed and hang my head. "Come in."

I'd eaten since Tuesday morning. Not much, but enough to keep me sustained. I'd crept downstairs during the early hours of the morning while everyone else in the Nest slept.

The only person I'd spoken to since I'd come home and thrown my door closed had been Diesel. He was the only one who already knew the truth of my heritage. The place and the *people* I'd come from. I didn't know who told him about the email, but it didn't matter. He'd called me right after putting in a vicious call to the principal, threatening to raze the academy to the earth if they didn't get to the bottom of who had sent the unsanctioned newsletter to the entire student body.

The conversation between my adoptive father and me wasn't a long one, and I'd said little more than yes or no to all the questions he had. A firm *no* to his offer to come by the Nest. Another *no* to his asking whether I knew why the guys and I seemed to be the ones under attack from the Aces.

We couldn't hide the truth from him for much longer, because the truth was whether we had proof or not, I knew it in my bones that this was Ava Jade's stalker. The Aces weren't even capable of these types of attacks. Weren't smart enough.

Whoever this was, they knew just where to stab us. How hard to twist the knife.

Diesel sent Pinkie and Axel since I'd declined his offer to put us up at Sanctum. Extra muscle packed with a small arsenal to back us up in case of an attack.

But it never came.

Tuesday blurred into Wednesday, and suddenly the sun was dawning on Thursday. Time seemed to have no bearing as I sat here, reliving the worst day of my fucking life.

Ava Jade knocked again.

I cleared my throat. "I said come in," I called again, trying not to let my frustration creep into my voice.

She pushed into the room, a bowl clutched in one hand and a water bottle under her arm. Steam coiled off the mountain of breakfast hash in the bowl, and my stomach rumbled.

She offered a sheepish smile and came in, tip toeing across the carpet as though she was walking a tightrope.

"I'm not going to bite you," I growled, accepting the bowl from her, suddenly aware of how terrible I smelled. I needed a fucking shower. Though if she cared, she didn't show it, settling anxiously into a seat on the bed beside me, her palms pressing into her thighs.

"Could've fooled me," she said with a half-hearted laugh, and I flinched at the reminder of all the angry things I'd shouted through that door over the past two days.

"I..."

"You don't have to apologize."

"So, want to tell me what I've missed?"

She bit her lip. "Not much. We've confirmed the Aces have allied with the Dead Men and are on the move. Looks like further south, but Diesel has people keeping tabs on them for now. We're planning an attack for the end of the week."

"Friday?"

Shit, was that tomorrow already?

She shook her head. "No. The guys are throwing Diesel a birthday party tomorrow at his place and then we have the full moon party later in the night. We'll hash out the plan at Dies' place and roll out early Sunday morning for the attack."

I grunted my understanding, able to tell she wanted to ask me about *it*. She wanted to divert the conversation back to what she'd seen in that email blast, but I wasn't ready just yet.

"So soon?"

"My idea," she admitted. "We weren't ready last time. We need to strike first this time. Strike hard. Put an end to it all."

She wasn't wrong.

"Where's Becca?"

She jerked her head to the door. "In the loft. Still sleeping, I think."

"Is that everything?"

Now I was just stalling, and I could tell she knew it, but she played along anyway.

"Almost," she said. "We think we might know who the stalker is."

I jerked, twisting my hips to face her. "*What?* Why the fuck didn't you tell me?"

She lifted a brow at me like I was the one being fucking daft. "Pretty sure you threatened to kill anyone who so much as came within two feet of your door."

"Who is it?"

"We aren't a hundred percent sure, but we think it's Aries. That King that was at fight night. You know the one. He was—"

"Yeah, the creepy fucker who was watching you. I remember. Why him?"

"He was watching in the atrium when that email went through. I caught him creeping around the hall, and when I went to confront him, he ran."

"What do you mean, he ran?"

"I mean *he ran*," she said again, exasperated. "And I fucking lost him and now none of the other Kings have seen him since that morning. He hasn't checked in with Maverick. Nothing. No word. No trace on his cell. He's just gone."

"He matched Becca's description of her ex fuckbuddy, too, right?"

"Yeah."

"Did she see him?"

She shook her head. "She was sick, remember? Grey showed her a still image from the security footage from that morning, but there was nothing that caught his face. She said he had the same hair and stature but that was it."

"So..." My throbbing brain struggled to piece together all the new information. "We think Becca's guy might also be your stalker? They might be the same person?"

She lifted one shoulder. "Maybe."

"And that guy may not have ever been an Ace at all, but a King the whole time?"

Seemed a bit fucking far-fetched, but I'd considered all the logical options and none of them were fitting.

She let out a long gush of air. "I don't know, Corvus. We're still trying to figure it all out."

"But if it's a King, then..."

"The alliance might be a set up," she finished for me.

"We have to tell Diesel."

She sagged at my words, and I knew she was thinking it was just one more reason for Diesel to hate her. If we told him she had a stalker that was targeting *us,* he wouldn't like it. But she was one of us now. And we protected our own. She would see.

This was the closest we'd come to any sort of lead on this guy, and I cursed my dumb ass for not being the one to figure it all out. Instead, I'd been locked up in here like some kind of depressed hermit, leaving all the work to them.

She held out the bottle of water to me, and I swallowed, accepting it from her. I set the bowl down on the nightstand, and she frowned at me.

"I'll eat it," I promised. "But I need to do this first."

"Do what?"

"Did you read it?"

She blinked, her face flushing pink as she realized what I was talking about, adjusting to the abrupt change in topic. Before I could leave this room and get back to business, this needed taking care of.

"Only the first couple sentences," she admitted. "Once I knew what it was, I stopped."

I believed her, but I was almost disappointed. It would make hearing everything I was about to say that much harder. It would make telling her that much harder.

"And Rook? Grey?"

She shook her head. "None of us read it," she told me. "We wouldn't invade your privacy like that."

I nodded to myself.

"Can you get the guys?"

Her nose wrinkled, but she nodded and left.

I drank half the bottle of water while I waited for them all to come back, my stomach both growling and turning at the idea of eating the small breakfast someone had prepared for me.

I would eat it though. It was the least I could do considering I hadn't slept in well over seventy-two hours. Again.

"Hey, man," Grey said, a muscle in his jaw jumping as he hovered in the doorway.

I waved him in.

"You good?"

A shaky laugh passed my lips.

"The truth? Not really, man. But what the fuck is new, right?"

His lips pressed in a tight line as he dragged the folding chair from my desk to a spot near the bed, unfolded it and sat down.

Rook and Ava Jade came in a second later. My Sparrow to the bed next to me, her back taut as she sat down. Rook bit his lip ring, crossing his arms over his chest as he toed the door closed behind him and leaned against it.

He nodded.

I nodded back, then blew out a breath, trying to get control of the ache forming behind my eyes. "I only want to tell you once," I said to them all. "And then I never want to hear about it again."

"You don't have to," my Sparrow was quick to say. "It's really not our fucking business."

I looked up, holding her stare, a fist clamping around my lungs at the depth of emotion in her eyes.

"I do, and it is. I know all about you," I told her. "I know where you come from. I know every black mark on your record. I know about your dad. Your mom."

She recoiled.

"I know about the older guy you were fucking well before it was legal for him to touch you. Kit, was it? Your friend's self-defense instructor?"

She pursed her lips. "Well someone did their homework," she muttered to herself, clearly trying not to be angry with me.

"I did," I admitted. "And that isn't even half of it."

She blanched, and I turned my attention toward Rook and Grey. "And you've both always been open with me about where you came from. What made you. I owe it to you."

Grey shook his head. "That's not how we see it."

"I know."

"You don't know everything," Rook put in, but he was wrong. I *did*. I wished I didn't. But I'd done my fucking homework on them, too.

I knew all about the fucker at Barrett's Home for Boys who liked to defile his charges. I knew all about his time at the Sanitorium. The drugs they fed him. How long they kept him in that padded room. And how often they tied him down.

I knew.

They deserved to know about me, too.

"My last name is Adler," I started, hating how that single word tasted on my tongue. Souring my stomach. "My father was Douglas Adler, the cult leader responsible for the deaths of a combined twelve people. It would've been a lot more if the cops hadn't figured out what was going on and stopped the three other families involved from *ascending* too."

"How old were you?" Sparrow asked, folding her hands tightly between her knees.

"Seven."

I didn't look up. Couldn't handle seeing her face.

"I didn't know much about what my family was caught up in. Only that people came to the house a few times a week and they would all go downstairs, to the basement, and... breathe."

"Breathe?" Grey asked.

"Yeah. Like, weird, fast breathing. Loud. Rhythmic. And then my dad would talk for a while and they would hum. Always the same tune."

The tune that had stuck with me, playing in my unconscious mind at all hours of the day and night, keeping me from sleep for the first month after they died. It had taken me years to finally rid myself of it.

"When my father decided it was time for us to *ascend*, my mother had doubts."

"She tried to stop it?" Rook asked, his expression darkening, hand closing to fists where they were crossed over his chest. I knew he was picturing ripping my father's throat out with his bare hands. I pictured the same thing for years.

"She told me to hide. Tucked me under my bed behind some bins and said not to make a sound."

Ava Jade's chin quivered, and I swallowed past the burn in my throat, needing to continue before I changed my fucking mind. "She said she was going to get my little brother next, but that was when my father came into the room. He told her Emmanuelle had already ascended and was waiting for them on the other side. I didn't know what that meant at the time."

I settled the tremor in my core and sat up straighter, disconnecting myself from the story. A tactic I was cautioned against when the therapist at the hospital told me I may be developing a dissociative disorder.

"She was hysterical," I went on. "But my father calmed her down, promising her it wouldn't hurt and that it would be over soon. He asked her to go and get me, but she told him that she'd already sent me away. Told me to run and to keep running and not stop until I got to town."

"He was angry, but said that I would find my own way to my ascension. That they needed to be strong so that the others would follow their lead into eternal life or some other fucking shit. The memory is all fucked up, but I do remember what happened next very vividly."

"My uncle came in, and my mom lost it. She was screaming and fighting them. I remember... I remember trying to plug my ears to keep from hearing it. I... I remember the smell of my own fucking piss in my nose. Most of all, I remember feeling completely helpless while they held her still. While she choked. Then it was Uncle's turn to choke and then my fathers. Through the small passages between the bins, I could see contorted, blurry images of them. Pale. Still. And the red. So much red. Soaking the beige carpet. Streaking their soft white skin."

"I don't know how long I stayed there. A long time, I think. But at some point I crawled out. Past their bodies. I remember thinking that they said Emmanuelle had ascended and I didn't know what that meant but I thought I needed to check on them because my parents weren't going to. They were never going to again."

"I found him in his crib."

Ava Jade choked on a sob, pushing the back of her hand to her mouth to try to keep it in. I tried not to feel it; what I felt when I looked down on my tiny little brother still, bloodless, and lifeless in his crib, surrounded in a puddle of dark crimson. A hollowness to complete that I didn't think anything would ever fill it again.

But then something did.

Anger.

A toxic rage so complete and so out of control that the state almost sent me away to juvie at eight years old. But Diesel found me. He recognized my anger. Taught me how to use it. To wield it when I needed to, and control it when I didn't. He was the one who helped me see that the anger was directed at myself, not anyone else.

I was angry because I'd sat there, hiding my face in the carpet, plugging my ears. Crying into my pajamas. Pissing on myself.

I was angry because I did nothing to stop it. Because I wasn't paying close enough attention. Because I didn't see it coming.

Diesel told me if I wanted, I never had to feel that way again, and I never had. Until recently. When Sparrow flew into my world and turned it upside down, a fucking faceless wolf on her heels.

"It wasn't your fault," Sparrow said. "You know that, right? You know you couldn't have done anything to stop them? You were just a kid."

"I know."

"That's some twisted shit, man," Rook said. "Even by my standards."

I laughed hollowly.

"Doesn't change how we see you," Grey interjected. "Not at all. You could've told us."

I pinched the bridge of my nose, sniffing, using the pads of my thumb and forefinger to clear the beginning of tears from my ducts before they could show on the rims of my eyes. "Yeah. I know. I just—"

"Wasn't ready?" Ava Jade supplemented, sighing, and I got the sense she understood more than she was letting on. I wondered if she'd ever share with us her own defining moment. The thing that twisted her beyond repair. Turned her into something powerful. A force of nature.

"I guess."

Her bright eyes cut away from me, finding a spot on the carpet. "Are you going to be okay? I mean. Do you want to stay home again today?"

I shook my head. "Nah. I don't give a fuck what any of them think."

"If anyone so much as looks at you funny, I'll cut them," Rook promised.

"Samesies," Ava Jade echoed, putting on a smile for my benefit. "You should eat. And maybe shower."

"That bad?" I asked, pinching the front of my shirt to sniff down the collar. Recoiling.

"Kinda," she replied with a wince, her hand finding my thigh to give it a tight squeeze before she considered her own state of affairs, lifting her fingers to the messy bun deflated against the top of her head. "Want company? My hair's fucking tragic."

"On that note," Grey said, pushing off from his chair. "I'm going to go check in with Dies about their missing King and then get back to trying to trace that email."

"You could come, too," Ava Jade offered, and Grey hesitated before his jaw flexed.

I tried not to get my back up at the idea of Ava Jade naked between us, water cascading down her breasts, filtering down her legs. His hands on her wet skin. The idea made my stomach tighten, but it was less repulsive than it had been a few days ago.

"Shower's too small," I said.

Grey and I shared a look before he winked at Ava Jade. "Next time, AJ."

29

GREY

"What is that?" I asked Ava Jade, gesturing to the brown box in her hands as we made our way out of the Nest.

She shrugged. "A gift."

"You bought Diesel a gift?" Corvus asked, incredulous.

I nodded to Pinkie and Axel as they pulled out of the driveway first, letting them know we were right behind them.

AJ pursed her lips. "It's his birthday, isn't it? Did you not get him anything?"

"What did you get him?" Corvus asked her, answering her question with one of his own, making her roll her eyes as she opened the door for Becca to slide into the backseat first. Her friend scooched all the way to one side, letting AJ sit in the middle between her and Rook.

"It's really nice," Becca said. "I think he's going to like it."

"So you told her what it was but you won't tell us?" I asked, pulling the driver's side door shut at the same time as Rook and Corvus closed theirs, sealing us all inside the Rover.

"It's not that big a deal. If you think I shouldn't give it to him, then I'll just leave it in the car."

She was getting frustrated now. We'd made her uncomfortable. Corvus and I shared a look in the front.

Rook patted the box on her lap with a smirk in the rearview. "Whatever it is, I'm sure he'll love it, Ghost. We'd have gotten him something, but he has a strict no gifts policy for his own birthday."

She lifted a brow in the rearview. "You could have told me that."

Rook lifted a shoulder. "Didn't think you'd be rushing out shopping."

"I didn't," she argued. "I ordered it online." A huff. "Fuck, I knew it was stupid. I'll just leave it in the car. Maybe one of you will like it."

"Sparrow, chill. Give him the gift. It might help soften the blow of... you know."

I pivoted in my seat, watching her face darken as I looked out the back windshield, reversing out of the spot to drive us down the choppy gravel road. It was decided that tonight we'd tell Diesel about AJ's stalker. How we suspected it was him who was to blame for the personal attacks against us and not the Aces.

Diesel was already made aware that we thought Becca's boyfriend, the one who'd been acquiring dangerous intel about us, might be a King. He was working that shit out with the King leader, Maverick, who'd promised to turn Aries over as soon as he was found.

Either the man was a damn good fucking liar or Diesel was losing his touch because he believed they had no ill-intent toward us. And my father could sniff out a lie from a mile off.

But as good as he was, he didn't know that AJ had a stalker. That we thought Aries and said stalker may be one and the same person.

Tonight, he'd find out.

I doubted AJ's gift would soften his reaction, but it couldn't hurt.

Becca squirmed in her seat, staring anxiously from the window. I tried not to be suspicious of her every action, word spoken, or tick of her face, but it was harder than I'd thought it would be.

I'd been on the voting side to drop her off at the Vandermark hotel on the way to Dies', but she'd been insistent on coming to look out for AJ. Not just in the den of papa wolf, but later, at the Docks for the full moon party.

I didn't know what she expected to be able to do if shit went south in any capacity, but AJ seemed content to have her with us at least for now. Tomorrow morning when we set off on the attack to obliviate the Aces and Dead Men, Becca would be deposited at the penthouse suite of the Vandermark hotel with hired security since we'd need all hands on deck for the fight.

At least she wasn't foolish enough to think she could handle coming with us for that.

"He's totally going to love it," I heard Becca whisper to her friend before inching her window down to light a little pinner of a joint, blowing the smoke out into the slowly darkening evening.

"Want some?" she offered to AJ, who shook her head, but Rook reached over and took it from Becca's fingers.

"Thanks, love," he said, rolling his own window the whole way down, leaning his head back against the seat in the path of the wind as he inhaled deeply. Something was up with him lately. I couldn't place what it was, but he was quieter than usual.

More reserved.

Less on edge.

I knew it was likely to do with the fact that he'd killed a healthy fucking number of people over the past couple weeks, including the things he did to Williams, but I couldn't help feeling like there was something more to it than all that.

Even after a strike three, he was never this reserved.

He adjusted himself in his seat, pushing his hand into the pocket of his jeans and keeping it there as he took another toke of the joint.

"Hey," Becca complained, reaching across AJ to steal it back from him before he could finish it. "God, ever heard of puff puff pass?"

Rook didn't answer, staring out his open window as we turned onto Diesel's road, the house ahead of us flanked by a line of Saint vehicles. A few of them loitering out by the rose bushes, smoking.

The space next to Diesel's car in the driveway was reserved for us, and I pulled into it. "In and out," I reminded the others. People were going to start showing up at the Docks in the next hour or so with or without us and with shit the way it was in Thorn Valley, we couldn't leave that turf unprotected.

We got out of the car to the sound of Primal Ethos playing on the radio and Diesel smashing his fist on the front window from inside, giving a stern look at the lads smoking near his roses. They fell back to the driveway, nodding at us in turn as we made our way inside.

Anthem of the Broken played low on Dies' sound system from the living room, and it didn't escape Corvus' notice, a vein in his temple throbbing as he worked his jaw. No doubt overthinking what it might mean. Likely it was just The Edge, but if Diesel was as pissed at Corvus about his musical career as he originally seemed to be, he would've changed the station by now.

"Is that Primal Ethos?" AJ mouthed to me behind Corvus' back, pointing through the wall to the living room on the other side, the box still under her arm.

It was a rhetorical question, but I gave her a nod anyway.

"What the fuck?" she mouthed.

I shrugged, noticing her wince as she shifted the box to her other side, rolling out her shoulder. She was getting scary good with that sniper rifle, but it came at a cost. I'd seen her shoulder when she stepped out of the shower last night, purple and blue in the shape of a rifle butt marring eight inches of milky skin in the groove between her shoulder and chest.

Even butting it properly, like I knew she was, it was still leaving marks. We'd need to give it a rest for a while.

"You good, AJ?"

She stopped rolling it and smiled. "Yeah. Why?"

"Nothing."

I pushed past Corv to enter the living room, knowing she didn't need the coddling, even if some foreign instinct inside me wanted to coddle her to fucking death sometimes.

"Hey," I said, finding Dies with a cigar pinched between his first two fingers, standing in the middle of the living room as he told the mustard gas story to a few Kings seated on his low sofa. He looked up as I entered and stopped right before the climax of the story to the shock of his audience.

"Ah," he said, eyes bright with drink. "There's my sons."

He ushered me into the living room, pulling me into his side to sling an arm over my shoulder. "You know these three, don't you?" he asked, pointing the gray ash end of his cigar at the three Kings on his sofa. The middle one was Drake, the other two were Lucas and Avery. They were the ones Dies had agreed to implant into Briar Hall to beef up gang presence there.

Drake lifted his beer in salute as he stood to go and get a refill, while the other two said a lame hello, clearly wanting Dies to get back to his story.

"Happy birthday," I told Dies, who blew off the sentiment.

"Don't remind me."

"What are you now, old man?" Rook said, slinking into the space to toss an arm around Dies' other shoulder. Fifty seven? Fifty eight?"

Diesel balked at him, releasing me to put an offended hand to his chest. It was good to see him in good spirits. Between his birthday and Christmas, they were the only two days of the year we were guaranteed to see him smile.

"Fifty," Diesel corrected Rook.

"Keep telling yourself that," Corvus said, entering with Ava Jade and Rebecca Hart on his heels. "You've turned fifty the last five years and counting."

Diesel leaned in close to Rook's side, whispering in his ear. "That was meant to be our little secret."

Rook laughed darkly, shaking his head.

It was a running joke among the gang. The oldest Saint members had been bringing balloons and cakes emblazoned with the number 50 for years with no signs of stopping the tradition. If Diesel survived to sixty, I had no doubt he'd turn fifty again that day, too.

"And look who decided to join us," Diesel said, craftily changing the subject as his sights narrowed on Becca. "Come here, darlin'."

Becca looked to AJ for guidance, paling, but AJ nodded her forward, a warning in her eyes meant for my father.

Becca came into the living room, swallowing as she took my father's outstretched hand, and he turned it, lifting it to his lips. "Bygones?" he asked her, holding her gaze with his trademark stare. The one that could hold you captive for hours if he wanted it to.

She choked on her reply, clearing her throat before she echoed his sentiment. "Bygones," she agreed.

Diesel grinned. "Good." He tugged her hand, spinning her away toward the couch. "Have a seat, love. The King who was sitting there seems to have grown bored of my story, but I think you'll like it just as much."

AJ stood on her tiptoes, peering around into the kitchen, where a group of Saints chatted, beers in hand, weapons at the ready. No one would be getting drunk tonight, but the potential threat wouldn't stop them from enjoying themselves. It was the one time a year Dies would have a drink with them, continuing the tradition his wife started of inviting the whole gang over for a birthday potluck each year.

"Is that Drake?"

"Yeah."

"I wanted to talk to him."

He looked like he was going out the back. "He's probably gone for a piss. Wait till he gets back."

She snuck a look at me, reading my suggestion for what it really was. A plea for her not to go off alone with him.

He was a handsome guy. I hated to fucking admit it, but it was true. And Rook was right. AJ did seem... interested.

I didn't know whether I wanted to slit his throat or roast him over a fire. I might wind up having to do both. It didn't matter if she'd already told me she intended to ask him about her father's death. That conversation could easily go sideways.

Ava Jade chuckled to herself, walking to the couch. She jerked her head at the King next to Becca. "Move," she said, and he ambled to his feet, giving up his seat for her.

She made no secret of being uncomfortable with the fact that Dies and Maverick seemed content to believe she'd just scared that creepy fucker, Aries, off. I mean, *okay,* she was scary, but only if you've done something to piss her off.

Or, maybe she was scary all the time. Judging by the way the other Kings looked at her, I was starting to think we'd just become immune to her.

She set the box down on her lap just as Diesel was about to start into the story anew.

"What's that?" he asked instead, taking a drag of his cigar.

AJ clenched her teeth. "I wasn't told about the no gifts rule."

"No shit?"

"Nope," AJ confirmed, her lips popping on the 'p.'

Diesel glared down at the box like it personally offended him, but Rook jabbed him with an elbow, and he cleared his throat. "Well let's open it then, shall we?"

AJ set it on the small ottoman in front of her and kicked it closer to him, nearly making the box topple to the carpet. Her forefinger spun the dented silver ring on her thumb, the one Rook gave her. It'd become something of a nervous habit over the past few weeks. Not for the first time, I told myself I'd get her one, too.

Something with a stone the color of her eyes. That actually fit her.

She should have one from each of us.

Diesel bent to ditch his cigar in an ashtray on the coffee table he'd pushed against the entertainment unit and lifted the box. He was still a bit unsteady on his leg, but was doing a good job of concealing it.

It pained me to know that he would likely use a cane in private for the rest of his life. It was a hard lesson learned for everyone, but sometimes lessons needed to leave scars to remind us not to repeat old mistakes.

Diesel pulled out a switchblade and carved through the tape on top of the box before re-pocketing it. He pulled out the item inside, letting the cardboard fall to the floor at his feet.

The conversation around us died the instant he held the leather jacket up to the light, his expression hardening.

Fuck.

Rook cursed under his breath and Corvus silently pinched the bridge of his nose.

"*What?*" AJ asked, glaring around at all the Saints watching Diesel carefully for a reaction.

We should've fucking told her.

I didn't think she'd get him a goddamned gift, though.

Why would she need to know that the beat up leather jacket Diesel wore was the last gift he ever received from his late wife?

No matter that it was falling apart. That he'd paid seamstress after seamstress to repair it despite them telling him it was a lost cause or the fact that he wouldn't agree to replace the lining or any part of it no matter the extent of the damage.

To AJ's credit, it was a nice fucking jacket. She'd likely paid at least a grand for it. And it looked to be Diesel's exact size. Thicker through the shoulders with additional leather and hand-stitched elbow patches. A muted matte black that seemed to absorb all light with a gunmetal silver zipper wider than my thumb, the pull tab custom fashioned into the Saint symbol.

Diesel lowered the jacket, laying it over the ottoman in front of him with a carefully crafted blank expression. "Was there something wrong with my jacket?" he asked AJ.

"*Dies,*" I tried. "She didn't know."

He held a hand up to silence me. "Answer the question."

Getting angry now with all the eyes on her, AJ lifted her chin, and I winced inwardly. "Not if you like the hobo-chic look."

Diesel turned his ire on me. "I think it's time for you boys to go," he said, and his stare brokered no argument. "Your Docks need manning."

He whistled sharply. "Axel, Crowley, Derrik. You're with them. Pack up. Get out."

AJ, skin bristling, stood from the couch, eyeing the jacket like she might take it back but ultimately thinking better of it. She hauled Becca to her feet with her. I guessed we weren't going to be having that chat with Diesel about AJ's stalker problem tonight after all.

"Come on, Becks," AJ said, her face red as she pulled Becca from the room.

Corvus whispered something to Dies, and our father clenched his jaw, but made no reply as Corvus stepped away, dropping his head instead.

"Later, Dies," I said halfheartedly, and he gave me a nod, clapping Rook on his back as we all left, some of the fire gone out of him at whatever Corvus had said.

"What did you say to him?" I asked as we moved to follow the girls back out onto the street. We'd barely lasted fifteen minutes in there. To be fair, it was ten minutes longer than I thought we'd last with AJ and Becca in tow.

"I told him that Jacqueline would've liked Ava Jade, and he knows it… and that he really needs a new fucking jacket."

I snorted. My brother wasn't wrong.

From what we knew, Ava Jade was just a younger version of Diesel's previous wife. Strong, with a spine sturdier than a roman column and sass for fucking days.

"What the shit was that all about?" AJ demanded, tearing open the door of the Rover a millisecond after I unlocked it.

"That shitty jacket he wears," Rook said, sliding in beside her. "It was the last thing his wife ever bought him."

"And no one fucking told me?"

"We didn't exactly expect you to get him a gift," I replied, reaffirming what we were all thinking.

"It's his *birthday*. That's what you do."

"Even for people who once tried to have you killed?" Rook asked, cocking his head as I started the ignition.

"If they also happen to be the father of the three guys you're fucking, then yeah. Even then."

She grumbled wordlessly to herself while Becca pressed her lips together to keep from laughing, a blush on her cheeks.

"Oh, Ghost," Rook joked, tugging her in against his side despite her protests. "You're nicer than I thought you were."

"Don't make me fucking stab you, Rook. Let me go."

She extricated herself from him, her glare sharper than her words.

He lifted a hand in mock surrender, digging into his right pocket for his blade to hold it out to her. "Don't make promises you aren't going to keep."

She rolled her eyes at him and sank back into her seat, simmering in her frustration with arms crossed over her chest.

"I bet you he wears the jacket by Christmas," I said, turning on the radio as I pulled out onto the road, waiting for Axel and the others to pull up behind us before leaving.

"Or he'll use it for kindling in tonight's bonfire," Rook said, and I sent him a look in the rearview.

What the fuck, man?

He shrugged. "What? It's the truth."

30

AVA JADE

Becca bumped my shoulder as we pulled into a parking spot at the Docks, over-eager party-goers already flooding the entire area.

"Come on, girl," she said. "Let's go get you a drink."

I grumbled wordlessly in reply, sighing as I followed her from the Rover, the guys exiting along with us. The music rose into the night, echoing across Spirit Lake and back to us as scantily clad bodies sauntered up the long dock to the twinkle-light covered pier. Inside the wide opening, people were already dancing. White and purple light twisted and flickered over the floor in time with the beat.

This was positively the *last* fucking place I wanted to be right now, though I understood the need to be here. Beneath the layers of graffiti painted all over the once green warehouse, you could still see the sharp spike at the top of a spade shape. The strong triangular form of a red 'A' since covered over with a glowy looking Saint tag.

If the Saints didn't hold the location, the Aces could make a play for it, though I doubted they were strong enough to do that now. I also fucking doubted something as idiotic as a pier mattered to them. Though the guys had told me when the Aces controlled the Docks the place was a fucking shit show. Young girls getting roofied. Dirty drugs causing overdoses. Less than willing participants guided, stumbling, to the Red Room.

That wasn't how they ran this place, and it showed. Teens and younger adults alike congregated here, wary of my Crows, but respectful of their authority. They knew exactly what would happen if they broke one of the rules. If they stepped a toe out of line. So they didn't. Mostly.

Apparently, Rook once tossed a guy over the railing out back for trying to sell blow laced with dirty fentanyl. The guy lived but barely.

As we made our way up the dock, Corvus accepted a small bag from a skinny twenty-something with messy black hair and dipped his pinkie finger in. It came out white, and he touched it to his tongue, tasting the cocaine. He nodded, indicating the larger bag the smaller one had come from, checking its contents. He lifted out a Ziplock with about thirty single pills in smaller baggies inside. "We don't allow these here," he told the guy, tucking the bag into the inside pocket of his jacket. "You can collect them at the end of the night."

"But—"

"Problem?" Rook hissed at the guy, and he shook his head, pulling the drawstring on his drug bag tight.

"No. Not at all. Thanks, man."

No one sold drugs here that didn't first pass through inspection from the Crows. And not without them getting their cut at the end of the night.

The dealer scampered off after the crowd, slyly making inquiries as he passed through couples and groups of friends bound to split by the time the night was through.

I sighed, hearing heavy booted footsteps behind me and turning to see Axel, Crowley, and Derrik coming up the dock behind us, each carrying a heavy duffle. One of which I recognized. I lifted a brow at the badly concealed heavy artillery. "Really?" I asked Axel, indicating the sniper rifle. "Is that necessary?"

The guys and I were already armed with our regular load-outs, theirs buffed only with additional magazines. The gear the other Saints were carrying seemed hella fucking overkill to me.

Though no one else seemed to notice or care.

Axel fell into step beside me. "Orders," he said with a shrug. "Grey knows how to use it."

I smirked. Grey wasn't the only one who knew how to use it

anymore, but Axel didn't need to know that. There was a quiet sort of satisfaction in keeping that fact to myself.

"So," Axel said, dragging out the 'o,' his gaze sweeping up to Becca walking a few paces ahead next to Grey, the pair of them chatting while they walked. "Your friend, is she—"

"Touch her, and I'll cut your balls off."

Axel coughed, his eyes going wide as he stared down at his feet instead of at her ass. "Cool. Noted."

Even if he wasn't a healthy ten years older than her, I didn't want Becca getting any more ingrained in this life with these people than she already had to be. With any luck, we'd get the Ace problem *and* my stalker dilemma resolved in the next few days and she could go back to her normal life without having to look over her shoulder, worried someone might want her dead.

Something inside of me crumpled at the realization that the only way she'd ever be truly free—really out of danger—would be for me to put distance between us, too. I was a Saint now. Like it or not and regardless of the tentative truce between Diesel and me, I doubted he was going to let me go.

Truthfully, I didn't think I wanted to be let go. Not if it meant being separated from my Crows.

"Well, I'm going to go stuff this shit in the back office," Axel said awkwardly, hefting the sniper bag higher on his shoulder as he took off into the pier, the other Saints following closely behind him.

"What'd you say to him?" Rook asked, rushing to catch up, tossing his finished cigarette into a sand pail by the entrance as we stepped inside.

I pursed my lips. "Not much. Just that I'd cut his balls off if he touched Becca."

Rook tipped his head to one side. "Can't blame the guy for trying," Rook said with a mischievous grin, his gaze tracking to Becca, who was drawing a little mickey of Crown Royal whiskey from her black purse, her hair falling over her face like a shimmering curtain.

No. I really couldn't.

Becca was hot as fuck.

If I swung that way...

"*Ava Jade,*" Rook said, and I hadn't heard him say my real name in so long that I startled at the sound of it leaving his lips, my stomach flipping. "Do I need to be worried?"

He glanced between Becca and me, speaking just loud enough for me to hear him over the music.

I snorted, shaking my head as I swatted him. "No. But just because I don't order from that menu doesn't mean I can't appreciate the options."

"Hey," I grabbed his chin hard, tugging his gaze back to me. "*I* can read the menu. Not you."

His lips split wide, teeth grazing over the ridge of his lip ring as he looked down on me.

"Aves!" Becca shouted, and instinctively, I bent at the knees, hand reaching for a blade.

"What are you doing?" she asked, holding out the small bottle of whiskey to me with a raised brow.

Fuck. I needed to relax. Just a little.

I shook my head, accepting the bottle to take a small sip, just enough to wet my tongue and feel a burn down the back of my throat. Tonight wasn't the night to lose control, no matter how much I'd have liked to. I still couldn't fucking believe Diesel's nerve.

That jacket was nine hundred bones. The most I'd ever spent on an article of clothing, like, ever. The only reason I'd spent the money was because it was gang income. Money I'd earned from the diner hold-up and my winnings from fight night. With the Crows covering literally all of my other living expenses and now with a free ride at Briar Hall, what the fuck else was I going to spend it on?

A girlish voice whispered beneath the hard shell formed in my mind... *shoes. Bras.* Those pretty lacy panties I'd seen in Becca's laundry. I wondered how much a pair of those cost.

I handed the whiskey back to Becca and shivered as Grey ran a fingertip down the back of my arm, slipping his hand into mine, our fingers twining. He grinned at me before leaning over to say something in Rook's ear that I didn't catch. Rook grinned eagerly, his black eyes flashing on me.

"Come on," Corvus shouted, leading the way to the raised stage at the back of the space, his body a long, rigid line.

I grabbed Becca and towed her along with us as we weaved through the crowd, Rook pushing ahead to catch up to Corvus.

Around us, I saw how everyone stared.

At all of us, but mostly at Corvus.

It was easy to tell if they were staring because they knew him as The Bone Man, their eyes bright and expressions filled with a devout sort of admiration. Or... if they were staring because they now knew him as the sole survivor of the Lennox Cult Murders.

Some of those looked on with pity, others with disdain. I released Becca, flashing my blade at the latter with a warning in my stare that had them turning their heads real fucking fast.

Corvus stepped up onto the stage, looking down on Rook with his brows lowered like he didn't particularly like something he'd just said. Axel and the others returned from their office drop off, settling onto the sofa atop the dais.

"Hey," Grey said, leaning forward to talk to Becca on my other side. "You good chilling here with Axel and the others for a minute?"

Her face screwed up, and she cocked her head at him. "I mean, I guess so, why, what's—"

"We need to talk to AJ real quick. Won't be too long."

Becca's lips popped open in a little 'o' and clearly she was catching on to something I wasn't. "Ah," she said after a second. "*Talk.* I got you."

She brushed against my shoulder. "Have a wonderful conversation," she said in my ear, giving me a knowing look as she sauntered up the two steps onto the dais and plopped herself down on the sofa between Axel and Crowley. Axel's eyes flicked up to meet mine for a second before he shifted a few inches away from Becca.

"So, what exactly do we need to talk about?" I asked Grey, catching sight of Corvus and Rook over his shoulder a few feet away at the edge of the raised stage, arguing about something.

"You'll see."

"What's going on?"

"Trust," he said simply, lifting our joined hands to press a warm kiss to the back of my palm. The sly gleam in his eyes gave me goosebumps, and I thought maybe I knew what they wanted to *talk* about.

Grey grinned, tugging me toward the door to the Red Room.

I bit my lip as I craned my neck to see Rook and Corvus still arguing.

Something in my belly tightened as Rook threw his hands up, his lips easily readable as he shouted at Corvus. "Fine. Your loss, man."

Grey opened the door to the Red Room and dragged me through as Rook left Corvus standing at the edge of the stage, his hands in fists at his sides.

The red light flicked on, and a gush of warmth rushed over my skin as we entered the room, the smell of lavender scented cleaning products and some kind of diffused oil thick in my nose.

I blinked to adjust to the light, skin tingling as Grey released my hand to remove his jacket.

My throat went dry, at odds with my greedy cunt as my gaze swept the room, finding it devoid of partygoers, but filled with a hundred other things that made adrenaline spike in my blood.

Leather straps affixed to the walls. A large silver hook where at least five different types of whips hung like a horse's mane from the low ceiling. A suspicious chest with a padlock on the side. A sex swing. A shining silver pole. Low, inviting black couches strewn with cock shaped pillows. Mirrors reflecting reversed images of us from the ceiling.

And the piece de resistance, a round table at the heart of the space with spokes jutting out from its cushioned leather edges, an assortment of leather straps and buckles flayed open, waiting for someone to latch on to.

Behind us, the door opened, washing louder music into the room for an instant as a couple tried to push through the door, giggling, already drunk.

Rook slapped a palm against this side of the door, stopping them from coming all the way in. "Room's closed."

They fell back, the guy putting his lady friend in front of him like a shield as they backed away. A little laugh escaped my lips as Rook shoved the door shut, tipping his head to one side to give me one of his rare wide smiles.

"So, Ghost... shall we put you to the test?"

"Depends..." I trailed off, trying not to let it show how badly I wanted to rip all their clothes off. After the bullshittery of earlier tonight and the bullshittery of our lives in general lately, I could think of no better release than this, but something was missing.

"Is Corvus coming?"

Rook's grin faltered. "No, Ghost."

"But he knows I've been with both of you, too," I reasoned, not understanding his reluctance to join us. I didn't realize how badly I'd been craving that.

Being with Grey and Rook together had been the most incredible sexual experience I'd ever dared to imagine, but having all three of them at once...?

Fuck. If it didn't kill me, it would only make me stronger, right?

"Knowing it is one thing," Grey said, kicking off his shoes, his gaze still heavy on my body. "Watching is another."

"Our brother has never been much good at sharing," Rook added. "At least, not with the things that matter."

I nodded, trying not to sound disappointed as a Primal Ethos song began to play outside, the lyrics of it filtering through into the room, muffled by the door. The throb of the beat expanding and contracting around us echoed in my chest.

It was almost like he was here with us, and I let a small, coy smile find my mouth.

Rook was right, it was Corvus' loss. It didn't need to ruin it for the rest of us.

As though he sensed the change in the atmosphere at my conscious decision to enjoy myself no matter what, Rook cleared the gap between us. I braced myself, a small moan coming from my lips. A jolt of pure, unfiltered lust struck me like lightning as his strong fingers carved a path up the back of my neck, twisting into my hair to tug my head back, his lips crushing to mine.

Behind me, Grey pressed a hot kiss to the base of my neck, his fingers finding the zipper at the top of the slinky black dress I was wearing. It raced down the length of my spine, hands running over my ribs as he pushed it wide open, fingertips tracing the solid lines of my Saint tattoo before coaxing the sleeves from my shoulders and down my arms.

Rook's lips left mine, his mouth finding my throat, teeth grazing the sensitive skin along my collarbone. I shuddered between them, my gaze finding the door behind Rook. "What..." I said on a gasping breath. "What if someone comes in?"

"Let them," Rook said.

"Fuck that," Grey said, his warmth leaving my back as we went to lock it, but just before his fingers could catch on the lock, the door opened and Corvus' six foot frame pushed through, shutting the door behind him.

Rook released my hair, and I let my head roll, feeling the brush of warm air on my chest and back as my dress hung awkwardly from my frame. Half on and half off.

Corvus' jaw tightened, his light eyes blackening.

"Stay," I said before I could stop myself. "Please."

He growled low, twisting his head down and away from me.

I brushed past Rook, and he let me go.

I gave Corvus no choice but to look at me as I planted myself in front of him, reaching past his wide frame to lock the door.

"Stay," I said again, slowly peeling my dress from my arms, pushing it past my hips to let it pool in a black puddle around my heels.

His hungry eyes roved over the blades strapped to my body and the lingerie he bought me after the Lodi show. The night he first had me and ruined my bra and panties.

I put a hand to his chest and felt him shudder beneath my fingers. "I'm yours," I promised him, letting that sink in but not without a caveat he had to understand because I would *never* choose between them. I couldn't.

And I didn't fucking care what that made me. What that made us.

I wouldn't have it any other way.

"*All of yours.*" I twisted to face Grey and Rook, both of them breathing heavily, waiting in the wings for the go ahead. "And *you are mine.*"

"Sparrow…"

"You don't have to stay," I told him. "But I want this."

He lifted his chin. "Then you'll have it."

I couldn't help smiling, my thighs squeezing as a violent need coiled up through my belly, making me clench my teeth. Making my toes curl.

Corvus' eyes lifted to something behind me before returning to my face. "Do you trust us?"

I turned to see what he was looking at, my throat bobbing at the sight of the table—the straps that would hold me down.

"That's a loaded question," I whispered, so low I didn't think he would've heard me, but he jerked my back against his chest, erasing the space between us as he lowered his mouth to my ear.

"Give me my answer, Sparrow."

I swallowed. "*Yes.*"

His hand snaked down between my breasts, lower to flatten against my stomach, fingers tickling at the edge of my panties.

Rook and Grey watched as Corvus slipped his hand beneath my panties, brushing over my soaked opening.

He groaned into my ear, nuzzling at my neck, making me shut my eyes against the riot of sensations coursing through my body.

Then he released me just as suddenly, pushing me forward. I thought I'd fall, but Rook was there, and he took me from his brother eagerly, dipping his head closer to mine, his fingers pressing hard into my waist. "You don't have to do this," he said, and somehow, coming from him, those six words made me *melt.*

I remembered the look in his eyes out behind the apartment buildings. When we'd fought and he'd held me down. His weight pressing heavily into my body, making it impossible for me to move. For me to get free.

I'd panicked, and he'd seen it for what it was. My trauma making a resurgence, wrapping it's spindly fingers around my throat. Suffocating me.

I shook my head, pushing his black hair from his eyes. "I want to."

Besides, these were straps, not vicious hands. And these were my Crows, not a dealer come to collect his due.

"Tie her down," Corvus said, and a flutter of anticipation beat against my ribcage.

Grey took my hand on the one side, and Rook snatched my other, both of them leading me to the table like a pair of magicians might lead their lady to a vanishing cabinet.

But I intended to be *very* present.

They helped me step up onto the table, my heels making it difficult.

I reached down to take them off, but Grey settled a hand over mine, stopping me, a wicked gleam in his eyes. "Leave them on," he said.

"Lie back, Ghost."

My heart thudded against my ribcage, echoing in my ears over the muffled roar of the music outside.

I sank to my backside and let Grey tug my legs off the edge of the table as I lay back, my head resting on the pillowed edge, nearly hanging off.

Rook stuffed a hand beneath my back and undid my bra with a flick of his wrist, tugging at the delicate material until it came all the way off, my breasts laying heavily against my chest, nipples pebbling from the slightest brush of the fabric.

"Mmmm." Rook groaned, bending over the table to grab my left breast and guide it into his mouth. I tried to reach for his hair, my hips bucking, but my arms were ripped away, pressed down against the cushioned edge of the table as Corvus buckled them in starfish wide.

I bucked against Rook's mouth, resisting the urge to pull my arms from Corvus' grip. This was what he wanted. What he needed.

My full surrender.

If he would give me what I craved, I would at least try to give him what he craved, too.

I opened my eyes, seeing my reflection in the mirror above. My torso covered over with Rook as he lavished my breasts, his mouth on one, his hand roughly pawing the other. And Grey at my hips, adjusting me so that my ass was on the cushion, legs hanging all the way off the table, before he fixed the wide leather strap over my lower waist, securing me in place.

And Corvus, studiously tightening the straps at my wrists. I could see the tension in his shoulders even from the birds-eye-view angle as he tried *not* to watch what Rook was doing.

I moaned louder as Rook bit down on my right tit, my head tipping back at the pain.

I reached uselessly outward, trying to find something, someone to hold on to. I wanted to touch them. Taste them.

Why were they making me wait?

"Patience, Sparrow," Corvus said, his voice a gravelly rumble from his chest.

Rook fingered a blade from where it was strapped to my thigh and twirled it in his fingers, making my breaths come uneven and my throat bob in anticipation.

I followed the glint of it in the red light as he lowered it to the hollow below my rib cage and carved a path downward, hard enough to let me know he meant business, but not hard enough to draw blood. Not yet.

I peeled my shoulder blades from the table, trying to watch, but a strong hand on my shoulder jerked me back down, finding the underside of my chin to hook my gaze backward. "Eyes on me, Sparrow," he said, holding me hostage with his icy stare as Rook sliced my panties off, exposing me to the air.

"*Fuck,*" Grey groaned and I felt fingers on my thighs, but had no idea whose they were. "She's so wet for us."

"Are you ready to come, Sparrow?"

A hot breath gushed from my lungs, laced with a need so strong it made black spots dance at the edges of my vision. "Yes."

Corvus broke eye-contact to give a tight-jawed nod to his brothers.

My eyes rolled back as mouths closed over the sensitive parts of me. A hot tongue circled my swollen clit. Teeth grazed over my nipples. Hands grasped and groped. And all the while, Corvus watched me, his own breathing growing heavier to match mine as he fed off my bliss.

I licked my lips, eyeing the upside down swollen bulge just inches from my face. "Fuck my mouth," I asked him, squirming as fingers joined the tongue lapping at my clit, adding the perfect amount of pressure to the mix. I strained, holding back a cry as a tiny cut opened up on the outside of my thigh, the sting of it meeting the humid air making my head spin.

"What do you say?" Corvus asked, his hair falling forward as he stared down at me, cocking his head to one side, eyes filled with fire.

"*Please,*" I begged, fighting against the straps holding my arms down.

He bent forward, his palm on the base of my chin moving lower to hold me lightly by the throat as he kissed me. I moaned into his mouth as his brothers continued their slow torture of my body.

When his lips left mine, his cock replaced them. Corvus moved to brace the back of my neck, tugging me as close to the edge as he could, giving me the angle I needed to take him in. The wide, salty girth of him slid down my tongue, pressing deeply at the back of my throat, holding there until I choked before pulling back to repeat the motion.

My eyes watered, the beginning of my orgasm built as Rook cut me again, and whoever was between my legs, *Grey* I suspected, increased his tempo. My body trembled against the table, and I could hardly catch my breath as Corvus began to fuck my mouth in earnest. I opened up my throat for him, taking breath when I could to keep the blackness at the edges of my vision from seeping any further in.

I cried out on his cock as my climax spun up from within unlike anything I'd experienced before. It crashed over me like a wave, centered around my breasts before ripping down the length of my torso to set fire to my core, making my clit pulse beneath Grey's mouth.

Had I just...had a nipplegasm?

"Fuck," I choked out as Corvus slid his cock from my throat, and I strained, catching my breath, squirming against the binds holding me down as Grey and Rook coaxed the orgasm to its fullest, making me scream. Colorful stars burst behind my eyelids until my entire body tightened so completely that I was on the brink of cramping.

Corvus grabbed my throat anew, pulling my heavy gaze back to him as my climax crested and began to fade, leaving me sated but still craving *more*. I would never get my fill of these men.

Not ever.

"Tell me what you want, Sparrow," he said, his teeth bared, cock just out of reach of my lips, glistening with a bead of pre-cum on its perfect head.

"You," I told him, jerking from his grasp to look at the others. Grey between my legs, his lips wet, and Rook hovering over my body like a wraith, his black eyes savage in the red light. "I want all of you."

I didn't care if that made me the biggest slut on the planet. I wanted to feel all of them inside of me.

"Spin it," Corvus said, and confusedly, I craned my neck up to see him, but then he was whisked away.

No, *I* was whisked away, my stomach flattening against my spine as the table spun viciously and I was left with Grey at my head and Corvus at my hips.

"Careful what you wish for, Ghost," Rook taunted, biting his lip ring, distracting me so that when Corvus thrust into my dripping cunt with one strong stroke of his hips, I didn't see it coming. My stomach lurched to my throat at the fullness of him seated inside of me, and my head tipped back. My cry of pain and pleasure stolen from my lips by Grey's kiss.

Corvus fucked me hard and fast, grunting into his thrusts as Grey stroked my breasts, his tongue meeting mine. When he pulled away, leaving me gasping, I found Rook touching himself beside the table, his dark stare tracking Corvus' movements. Looking equal parts like he wanted to skin Corvus alive and join him.

"Spin," Rook demanded, his upper lip curling as he was brought to the edge of his need. He gripped the nearest spoke to him and jerked it, giving Corvus no choice but to pull out of me as I was spun toward Rook.

Rook slapped my cunt before moving in between my legs, making me buck against the strap tight around my waist with a gasp rushing down my throat. He took me swiftly, lifting a knee to brace himself on the edge of the table to deepen the angle of his thrusts.

He slapped against my thighs until I felt them begin to bruise, felt my next orgasm building like a wave, rolling, growing, cresting.

He flicked my clit, bringing me to my edge with an animal grunt on his lips.

"Spin," Grey said, his tone dripping danger.

But Rook didn't let me go, holding tight to the spokes on the outside of his knees as he fucked me through my orgasm.

"I said *spin*," Grey hissed, and the table shuddered beneath me as the sound of snapping wood assaulted my ears.

I craned my neck back to see a busted wooden spoke in Grey's lifted hand. He'd ripped it clean off the table.

Rook gave in to his brother, spinning the table hard, making Grey have to catch me by the knee before I could soar past him. He leaned over me, his normally playful, kind eyes, heated to cracking. He bent his head, pressing a kiss to my stomach. Then lower.

"Untie my hand," I said, my voice more a moan than words as I tipped my head to the left, finding Corvus' bright eyes roaming the surface of my naked flesh. Looking everywhere but at Grey and what he'd begun to do between my legs, dipping his fingers into my wet cunt before gently prodding them against my ass.

I shuddered as he pushed inside with his thumb, slowly stretching me for him.

Corvus untied my left hand, and I stretched the extra few inches over the edge of the table to grab his cock in my hand, still slippery from my wetness. I stroked his length, watching his face closely until I had the pressure just right.

Grey removed his thumb and lifted my legs, pushing them together before tucking them over his right shoulder. He pressed his cock into my cunt for a second before moving it lower, pushing it into my ass.

I tipped my head up, finding Rook stroking his cock.

I licked my lips, and he took the cue, moving in closer, grabbing my jaw with his rough fingers to jerk my chin up, forcing my mouth open to push his cock inside.

Grey eased all the way into my ass, and I moaned around Rook's cock in my mouth, impressed with my ability to keep up a continuous stroking of Corvus' cock with my left hand.

"Holy fuck," Grey croaked. "You're so fucking tight, AJ."

I moaned in response, opening up my throat for Rook as he lengthened his strokes, fucking my mouth with a sort of slow gentleness I didn't know he possessed. His rough fingers holding my face steady so at odds with the torturous pace he was forcing himself to maintain, grimacing with each easy thrust into my mouth.

Grey gripped me by the hips, quickening his pace until he was pummeling my ass with his cock, hitting something deep inside that made fire race up my back and tingles fall down my legs.

Another climax began to build, my already battered nervous system shooting sparks into my blood at the oncoming storm, but I was powerless to do anything to stop it. To lessen the force of impact as Grey slipped a hand between my legs and added the pad of his thumb to the mix, rubbing my clit as he fucked my ass.

"I'm coming," I said around Rook's cock, and it triggered something in them all.

Rook wrapped a tight fist around my throat, blocking my airway, fucking my mouth faster. Corvus moved his hips in time with the strokes of my hands, shuddering, bending over the table, wide palms splayed over its surface next to me. His face pinched and breaking.

"AJ," Grey said, breathless. "Come on, baby. Come for me."

My body responded, as though on his command alone, I came again, this time, the black spots dancing around the edges of my eyes crowded in, and I sagged, my muscles spasming and screaming as the orgasm tore through me, making my legs go numb.

Grey grunted as he came, his hands gripping tight to my thighs like life rafts at the same time Rook released my throat, coating my tongue with the salt of his release.

"*Fuck,* Sparrow," Corvus growled, curling in against the table as his heat spilled down my knuckles, dripping onto the table.

"Untie me," I croaked as Grey slid out of my ass, lowering my legs.

"You good, Ghost?" Rook asked, his chest heaving as he caught his breath, his cock still steel stiff, jutting out from the top of his jeans.

I swallowed past the dryness in my throat, wincing at the ache.

"Get her a drink," Grey said, and I heard movement, and then Corvus was there, lifting my head from the table to feed me a sip of water from a freshly cracked bottle. It sloshed over my cheeks and down my neck as I drank greedily, but I didn't care.

"Better?"

"Yeah," I sighed.

I felt Grey's hands flying over my waist, undoing the wide strap there while Corvus and Rook worked the ones at my wrists.

I pulled my legs and arms in to my chest, luxuriating in the feel of my muscles recoiling back to where they belonged. As the creeping fingers of oblivion retracted their claws and I regained full consciousness.

"Are you hurt?" Corvus asked, peeling my knees back to get a better look at me.

I grabbed his wrist, and when he moved back, I went with him, letting myself be drawn from the edge of the table, unsteady on my heels for a second before my head stopped spinning. He held me there until I was good.

"That was..."

"Insane?" Corvus supplied.

"Incredible," I corrected him, sex drunk and grinning from ear to ear.

Rook slipped me a soft towel and I took it, cleaning the evidence of them from my body as I swayed toward the sofa.

"What is that?" Grey asked, and we turned in time to see him zipping up his jeans again, his head cocked to one side, listening.

Immediately, I was on edge, my fingers tripping down my calf for the blade at my ankle, still shaky.

But then I heard it, too.

Vibrating.

Corvus cursed, grabbing his jeans from the floor to retrieve his phone, but it'd already stopped ringing.

"Dies," he said, flicking over his phone screen.

The vibrating started again, and I looked down to find my phone screen lit up where it had fallen to the floor sometime since we'd entered this room.

I bent and picked it up, putting it to my ear while I jammed a finger in the other to hear over the subdued noise coming from outside the Red Room.

"Hello?"

"Jesus fucking Christ, does *no one* answer their goddamned phone anymore?"

"Diesel?'

"Shut up and listen. They're coming. You need to—"

"*What?*"

"Sparrow, what is it?"

"The Aces and the Dead Men, they're coming right fucking now," Diesel shouted down the line. "Do you hear me? Get ready. Our man just spotted them turning down the Dock road. We're still twenty-minutes out and they're right on fucking top of you."

31

AVA JADE

I tossed my cell to Corvus with Diesel still screaming down the line, rushing to kick off my heels and pull my bra and black dress back on over my naked body.

"We've got company," I said to Grey and Rook just as a loud bang resounded in the Red Room. I jumped, drawing a blade as the bang came a second time, louder. Someone was battering themselves against the door, trying to get in.

Becca was out there.

Grey drew his gun, lifting it to take aim at the door as it burst wide open and Axel came flying through.

"*Fuck, Axe,*" Grey said on a breath. "I almost fucking shot you."

"They're coming," Axel said, practically frothing at the mouth, his own gun held tightly in his right hand, aimed low to the ground. "We need to get these kids out of here."

"It's too late," I told Axel, shaking my head. "If they're already on the dock road they're going to be here any minute."

"Get as many of them as you can into this room," Corvus ordered. "Move the rest out back along the dock. We'll keep them as far away from the line of fire as possible."

Axel hesitated.

"Fucking *now,* Axel."

"Becca," I said, panicked, racing after Axel through the door. "Where the fuck is—"

"Aves!"

My breath caught when I saw her, standing with her arms tight around herself by the couch. "Becca!"

I went to her, flipping my blade into my palm to take her by the shoulders without cutting her. Her eyes were wild with fear. "It's okay," I told her. "You're going to be okay. Come with me."

"Sparrow," I heard Corvus shout behind me just as the music was cut and a loud gunshot rang through the room, soliciting screams from the crowd. I shoved Becca behind me and lifted my blade, but it was only Axel getting everyone's attention.

"*Everyone shut the fuck up,*" Axel bellowed, surprising me with the level of volume he was able to put out from his smaller frame.

The crowd quieted and Corvus took over, storming to the edge of the stage. "Listen up," he hollered. "There are some really bad fucking people on their way here right now. Hey! Hey you, *stop.* Don't try to leave, there's no time. These people don't have qualms about laying out a few innocent people to get what they want."

Somewhere to my right, several girls began to cry.

"*Calmly,*" Corvus said, injecting the single word with enough venom to put even the strongest man into a state of paralysis. "I need everyone to make their way to the Red Room. Hey! Did I say to fucking move yet?"

Those who'd already begun to push forward stopped, whispers and cries rising from the throng.

"You will *not* all fit. Once the room is full, lock the door. The rest of you make your way out onto the back deck. Spread yourselves out, but stay behind the wall of the warehouse. Keep low."

"Aves," Becca said, her eyes glinting in the still-blinking and sweeping lights carving paths over the floor.

I squeezed her hand in mine, trying to keep her calm.

"Okay now move," Corvus said and as one the crowd rushed the stage, pushed through and around us to get to the Red Room. Some people already running for the docks out the back door.

I pulled Becca through the oncoming stampede, barely able to hear her over the panicked voices clogging my ears when she asked me where I was taking her.

I could sense more than see or hear the guys hot on my tail as I weaved a path toward the back office. Unable to wait for a key, I kicked the door in when I got there and dragged Becca through.

When I let her hand go she shakily came around the bar, reaching for the shot glass and bottle of whiskey that had been left there. She poured herself an ounce and knocked it back, breathing out through her mouth.

I unzipped the closest duffel to me and dug inside, past an AR and a shotgun to find what I was looking for.

I tucked one Glock into a strappy holster and threw it over my chest, carrying its twin to Becca.

She looked between me and the gun in my outstretched hand like I'd lost my damn mind.

"Don't worry," I told her as the guys entered behind us and I heard the flinch-inducing sounds of guns being prepped for killing. "You probably won't have to use it but there's no fucking way I'm leaving you unarmed."

"*Oh god,*" she said, her chest heaving, tits swelling over the shelf of her corset top as she accepted the gun into her hand.

"This is the safety," I showed her. "You don't have to cock it. This is safety on. This is to turn it off. Got it?"

She blinked, clearly overwhelmed. She wasn't hearing me. She was going to fucking die.

Without thinking, I slapped her across the face and she cried out. All sound behind me ceased for a second before resuming.

Becca blinked, her shoulders settling, eyes clearing. "Fuck," she said. "I needed that."

"Safety," I repeated, and she swallowed, flicking it on and off with her thumb, a red handprint coming through on her cheek.

"Got it."

"You shoot anything that comes through that door."

"But what if—"

"We'll announce ourselves first if it's us," I assured her. "You can't afford to hesitate, Becks. Do you understand?"

"I think I'm going to be sick."

She bent, lifting a small black trash can to her face, the gun still tight in her manicured fingers pressed against the side of it as she hurled and then set the can down to run the back of her hand over her mouth.

"Do you think he's going to be here," she asked.

I knew who she meant, and a sharp cold bit into my bones. If the guy who'd been after my Crows was here…

"If he is, I'm going to kill him," I promised her. "He won't get to you."

She nodded. "Okay," she said, repeating the word again and again, nodding as she backed up to the wall, stopping only when it blocked her from going any further.

I pointed a finger to the corner. "Stay over there, by the couch. From there you should be able to see someone coming in before they see you—"

"Ghost," Rook growled behind me. "We have to move."

"Remember," I told Becca as she shakily moved to tuck herself by the couch in the corner of the room.

"Shoot first, ask questions later," Becca finished for me.

"You got this."

Grey held out two extra magazines to me, and I fed them into their places in the holster strapped over my chest as he snapped the buckle at my back, locking the whole mechanism in place. I was absolute shit with a handgun, but I only had so many blades.

"I see headlights!" We heard Axel outside the office.

"How long?" I asked, the question obvious. The only one that mattered. How fucking long did we have to hold out until Diesel and the others got here?

Corvus' eyes darkened, and he tossed me my phone back. I tucked it deep into the left cup of my bra. "About sixteen minutes."

It was going to feel like a goddamned decade.

I let my darkness rise within, felt it fill my chest with toxic air, breathe extra strength into my muscles as it danced with the adrenaline pumping through my veins.

I tipped my head to one side, cracking my neck as I double checked the mag in the Glock and slid it back into the chamber, pulling the slide back.

A delicious shiver rolled down my spine, and for one blissful second, I felt fucking bulletproof.

"Let's go fuck up some Aces," I said and Rook smiled wildly, his tongue trapped between his teeth as he sucked a breath in, his savage excitement ramping up my own.

"We hold out," Corvus said, his tone stern. "No hero shit. We hold the fucking fort until Diesel gets here. No one's dying tonight. Not on our fucking side."

Grey nodded his agreement, but Rook and I shared a look. A dangerous understanding passing between us.

If I had my way, there wouldn't be a single enemy soul remaining on this earth come dawn.

We moved, and I ignored the little choking sob of Becca behind me, needing to focus to get through this. To keep her and every other innocent person here tonight safe.

The silence in the booze scented room was so complete you could hear a pin drop as we moved through it toward the front bay door. Light flashed over the front of the building, blinding me for an instant as I dropped low, moving to stand in against the inside wall, peering out down the docks.

My pulse thudded violently in my chest at what I saw.

Car after car after car came screeching into the lot, stopping to let the Aces and Dead Men come pouring out.

We'd been so certain they wouldn't try an attack here, but now, looking at them, it made sense. They knew the Crows held this territory and partied here for every full moon. If they took us out before Diesel could get here, then they could hold the Docks, and all the hostages trapped within it.

And Diesel, having more honor in his pinkie finger than Lenny Ace did, would give him what he wanted to stop a slaughter.

It was the perfect plan.

I vowed in that moment to *never* underestimate my enemy's ability to be even more ruthless than I was.

"There are too many," Derrik shouted, light on the balls of his feet across from us against the other side of the bay door opening like he might flee. "We'll never hold them off."

He wasn't wrong.

We were almost too late to move out of the way as an automatic weapon pumped lead into the bay door from way down at the other end of the long pier. Some of the bullets pushed through the worn wood, leaving smoking holes for the moonlight to filter through.

"Anyone hit?" Axel asked.

No one answered.

But they would be soon.

This building wasn't going to hold up to that much gunfire and they were already slowly making their way up the dock toward us.

Rook took a running step and launched himself across the bay door opening, opening fire as he went, tucking in his chest to roll the last few feet to the other side, bullets missing him by a hair.

I peered through a bullet hole and saw that he'd gotten two of the bastards, but there were already six more there to replace them.

"*Watch out,*" Grey bellowed, knocking me to the floor, the air stolen from my lungs as another line of gunfire punched holes in a long line down the side of the wall right where my fucking head had been.

I crawled closer to the opening and made a snap decision.

They weren't going to stop coming.

Even as slowly and carefully as they made their advance down the dock, they'd be on top of us in the next two minutes, the group quickly growing as more vehicles arrived, Dead Men and Aces walking shoulder to shoulder, heel to toe.

We needed to stop their advance.

There wasn't time or the equipment required to blow the dock, but there might have been something else I could do.

I tore myself from Grey's grasp, my dress tearing as I ran like a shot back the way we'd come.

"Sparrow!" I heard Corvus call after me, but I wasn't stopping.

This had to work.

A gunshot sent me dropping to my knees as I slingshotted myself through the office door.

"*Jesus.*"

"Oh my god, Aves! *You said!* You said you would announce yourself."

Her hand shook on the gun. "It's okay. You did good."

I grabbed the sniper bag from the floor next to the bar and took off. "Just keep doing what you're doing!"

She shouted a stream of curses after me, but I was past hearing her, rushing to the back of the building.

"AJ, what are you doing!" Grey shouted, but no one followed me as I shoved through the back door to the shouts of the teenagers huddled against the wall.

"Hold still," I told the tallest looking one, stepping up onto their back to get a handhold on the old rusted ladder that was busted off at the bottom. I hauled myself up, my shoulders screaming their protest until I got a foothold and cleared the top of the ladder, throwing my legs over onto the roof.

I kept low as I raced over the debris, avoiding the soft looking spots where water was puddled, algae foaming around the edges.

My fingers fumbled with the zipper only for a second before I got it down, pulled out the sniper and yanked the tripod free, feeding bullets into the slot like Grey taught me.

I cocked it back to the sound of a cry below, my heart in my throat. It wasn't one of them. It wasn't one of them.

They're fine.

I lifted the barrel over the wide edge of the roof, butting the rifle to my shoulder, staring down the scope, adjusting it.

There was a flurry of movement as the enemy reached the entrance to the Docks and I heard Rook's throaty bellow as he went ape on the ones who'd managed to get inside.

I was too late to stop them, but I wouldn't be too late to slow the flow.

I breathed in, settled on a moving target, breathed out, and fired.

He jerked back, falling in a heap.

Heads snapped up.

I took aim. Fired again.

Again.

Two more shots.

Reload.

It wasn't enough.

They were still coming. Pouring over the docks like ants.

Fuck. Fuck. Fuck.

I reloaded, lifted back onto the ledge.

Found a face I recognized.

I twisted the dial on top of the gun, turning on the red dot sight. It pierced Lenny Ace square in the chest.

I saw the instant he noticed, his body going deathly still as he stared down at it, hands raising.

He shouted something, but I couldn't hear him from here.

Sweat dripped down my forehead, and I squinted, trying to keep it from getting in my eye, keeping steady.

Like dominos, the Dead Men and Aces stopped their advance. Guns were lowered.

"Stop!" I heard Lenny this time as he shouted, still raising his hands ever higher as three more gunshots inside the warehouse below me signaled the deaths of three more of his men.

My finger brushed the trigger, the darkness within beckoning, whispering violence in my ears. Kill him.

Kill him.

All shooting ceased, and I breathed slow out a small opening in my lips, my arm starting to shake from holding the heavy weapon steady.

If I killed him, one of two things would happen.

Either they would all disperse, or I would have created a martyr. Given the Dead Men's leader a chance to double the size of his gang by taking in Lenny's as his own.

There was the other option, of course. I could hold until Diesel got here. Clean up this mess for good.

My phone vibrated forcefully against my left tit, and I jerked, almost losing my aim, but able to right it again.

Carefully, I held the sniper in place with one hand while I fingered out my phone with the other, tapping blindly at the screen until the call was answered and on speaker phone.

"Sparrow?"

"I'm a little busy at the moment, Bones. Call me back later?"

"Don't shoot."

I ground my teeth.

This fucker tried to kill my guys.

He'd gotten each of them shot on fight night.

Those wounds had yet to heal.

He didn't deserve to live.

"Sparrow?"

"He needs to die."

"Can you hold?"

Fire flooded my belly. "Yeah," I gritted out. "I can hold."

But Lenny Ace, waiting for the others to do all the work for him at the far end of the long dock, stepped backward. One small step.

I dropped the barrel of the sniper half an inch and shot the pavement at his feet before immediately lifting it back to his chest. He started, lifting the leg nearest the smoking ground like a fucking flamingo before setting it back down.

His mouth moved, and I strained to hear what he was shouting.

"What the fuck is he saying?"

"He wants to leave."

"Fuck that."

"*Sparrow,*" Corvus warned. "If you kill him, the rest of them are going to rush the pier. The Dead Men didn't join with the Aces to lay down arms and give up whatever they were offered. If Lenny's dead, they'll try to take it and more. They won't ever get another opportunity like this. I need you to *hold.*"

I growled my frustration, stroking the trigger, a shiver rolling down my back.

Just a little more pressure and we could kiss this bastard goodbye for good.

Was Corvus right?

Hold, the rational part of my brain argued, buffing my biceps and shoulder, lending them more strength to keep holding the long weapon in place.

But the darkness was still whispering, and I wanted to feed it the blood it craved.

"Five minutes," Corvus' promised. "They should be here in five minutes, Sparrow. Hold."

The wind quieted enough that the next time Lenny Ace's vile mouth opened I could hear him. "We're going to leave," he shouted, his voice echoing across the lake.

Fucking coward.

"No one else needs to die tonight," he continued, his voice cracking, arms beginning to lower. "I'm going to back up now."

"The fuck you are!" I roared, uncaring if he could hear me or not.

Lenny took a step back.

"*Corvus,*" I hissed.

"Don't, Sparrow. It'll be a bloodbath. We can end this another time. On our terms."

I clamped my mouth shut, breathing in and out rapidly through my nose as I watched Lenny slip back a step. Then another.

Someone opened the side door of a van a few paces away from him and climbed inside, beckoning for him to follow.

NO.

We were *not* going to let them get away.

"Diesel and the others can stop them on their way out," Corvus promised, but if Dies was still five minutes away, they could take the dirt road leading around the Deadwood. They could get to the highway before he could intercept them. *They could get away.*

I watched Lenny through the scope as he dragged his foot another step back, but it wasn't his movement that made me do it. It was the look in his eyes as he tipped his head up, the moonlight catching on a wicked gleam there. Carving a little gray shadow where the edge of his lips were creased in a vile smirk.

No.

I don't fucking think so.

My arm tightened on the rifle, I breathed in. Breathed out.

And shot Lenny Ace through the heart.

32

CORVUS

T he *crack* of the rifle shot rebounded from the cliffs cuffing the edges of Spirit Lake. Time stopped. For one blissful second I enjoyed the fact that Lenny Ace was dead. Then that second ended and all fucking hell broke loose.

"Damnit," I growled through my teeth, dropping my cell phone to the wooden floorboards in exchange for my second weapon, lifting both guns to fire two shots at once, sending two Aces to their graves as the wave of them resurfaced, stampeding down the docks towards us now, the vibrations of their pounding footfalls ricocheting up my legs.

"Get ready," I yelled to the others, rolling out of the path of a bullet to put myself deeper into the warehouse, waiting for them to come rushing through so I could pick them off one by one. The opening was wide, but not wide enough for more than five to get through at once.

If we did this just right, none would make it further than a few feet inside.

A female grunt came from outside and someone shrieked on the docks.

"Ghost," Rook roared, rushing out into the opening, out into the night onto the docks to meet our enemies, foiling my plan completely.

"Fucking hell," I ran after him, my stomach vaulting into my throat at the deafening staccato of gunfire swelling in the atmosphere.

My Sparrow had jumped down, and I watched her swipe her blade over a throat, her other hand tossing a blade in the air to catch it with the business end pointed the opposite direction as she stabbed another attacker in the thigh, swinging her body low to avoid his flying fist before she danced around his back and stabbed him in the side of his neck.

A barrel raised in my direction, and I ducked low, sweeping feet out from under a body, pumping a well-placed piece of lead between his eyes.

They were still coming, and I saw the shine of a longer weapon, sharp angled and whistled hard and sharp, letting the others know we were about to be playing an entirely different sort of game.

"*Get inside,*" I bellowed. "Keep them back!"

I took out two more before I needed to change a mag and a Dead Man got the jump on me, butting the hard metal handle of his weapon into the side of my temple, making flares of light pop into my vision as I careened to one side.

I shook my head, trying to clear my eyes, alert and ready for another attack, but when I opened my eyes again, it was to look down the barrel of a gun.

My lips parted.

He fired.

Click.

He was out of bullets, the idiot. I disarmed him, throwing my entire body into the hit as I pistol whipped his ass unconscious.

Grey, Rook, and Ava Jade were almost all the way into the warehouse, and I grimaced, looking down the dock to the storm blowing our way. All the Aces and Dead Men who'd been hanging out by the vehicles, waiting, were coming this way now, too. A guy I recognized to be the leader of the Dead Men was at their helm. He roared, lifting an AK high over his head.

Shit.

I took a second to turn my attention beyond them, to the road curving up and away into the trees. There was still no sign of Diesel. Not even the faintest glow of headlights or even the rumble of engines approaching.

This wasn't good.

"Corvus!" Ava Jade shouted, and I turned, heat rushing through me as I raced back into the warehouse, quick, jerking movement making something in my belly pinch uncomfortably.

A warm wetness was seeping into my jeans, sticking against my thigh.

I pressed the side of my weapon and my knuckles to my stomach, my hand coming away vivid red in the flashing lights inside the pier.

I grimaced, baring my teeth as I growled through the pain, searching for Ava Jade in the fray as our people fought to keep any more of the enemy from entering the building.

I caught a flash of dark hair and went for it, keeping a wary eye trained on the door, picking off Aces and Dead Men at will as I made my way over to her.

She ducked to avoid a blow and came up like a fucking springboard, her eyes going wide at something over my head. The *zip* of her blade arcing just next to my head filled my right ear before someone behind me fell with a watery croak.

My Sparrow drew her Glock and fired toward the bay door, backing up over the pile of dead strewn over the wooden planks at our feet.

We were fending them off as well as we could.

Then Crowley went down, his brains exploding out the back of his head as he fell.

Derrik was next.

What had she done?

My chest squeezed painfully at the sound of Rook screaming through his own pain as he was hit, not for the first time.

I ran out of bullets. Out of magazines.

AJ's gun kicked back in her hand. Her too.

Fear flashed over her eyes as she searched the ground for something, *anything* to use.

This was it.

Lenny Ace was dead.

But my Sparrow had condemned us to die with him.

"Look!" Grey cried, pointing down the docks, to the headlights bouncing against the shoreline. The sound of squealing tires reached my ears, and I dropped to the ground, pinching a shotgun from a Dead Man's dead fingers, cocking it back and firing.

He was here.

We could survive this.

I rushed to stand closer to my brothers, closer to my Sparrow.

Grey whooped, firing the last few shots in this clip. "Fuck yeah, motherfuck—"

His head whipped back, his body crumpling to the wooden floor.

"*Grey!*"

He didn't move. I fired again. "Grey, get up!"

The shotgun kicked back into my shoulder, sending a violent wave of pain all the way down to the bullet wound still steadily seeping my life's blood down the front of my jeans.

"*Brother!*" Rook roared.

Guns fired further afield and our enemies turned their attention to the Saints and Kings now boxing them in from the other end of the dock, trapping them in the middle.

I dropped the shotgun, reaching for a discarded pistol, raising it as I backward walked my way toward where Grey had fallen.

Please, no.

Ava Jade screamed, and I chanced taking my eyes off the Aces and Dead Men now engaged in a firefight with the entirety of my father's force.

Rook's face was bent over Grey's, blowing into his mouth before he started compressions.

...compressions...?

My brain struggled to make sense of what it was seeing.

Couldn't unseen the garish wound where his right eye used to be.

...used to be...?

My body sagged, knees making impact with the wood, my heart beating out of rhythm.

"*Please,*" Sparrow was saying, her entire body shaking like a leaf in a hurricane as she hovered over Rook and Grey amid the carnage. "No, please! No. *No.*"

Numbly, I lifted my head, trying to see through the burning saltwater coating my eyes.

I let this happen.

My fault.

My fault.

Something inside of me snapped.

"*Why?*"

Sparrow turned her horrified gaze to me, her lower lip quivering as tears streaked twin paths through the blood and dirt on her face.

"Why couldn't you fucking listen to me?"

She crumpled. Something in her eyes cracking. Breaking. *Shattering.*

Ava Jade was shaking her head, muttering something I couldn't hear to herself over and over again as Rook continued his assault of Grey's chest.

His still body lurched from the movements and bile rose up the back of my throat at the *snap* of his rib bones.

"Fuck you!" Rook was screaming at Grey's lifeless face. "Wake. The. Fuck. Up."

He stopped pumping Grey's chest and slapped him instead, first with one palm and then the other, leaving red on both his cheeks. "*You don't get to fucking die. Not tonight.*"

He slapped him again and I couldn't watch anymore. "Rook, stop," I said, my voice laced with warning.

But then a choking cough spluttered from Grey's lips and Rook hefted him onto his side as Grey choked up blood, spattering the floor with it as he racked his lungs, his one eye opening wide, bloodshot, and strained from the pain.

I didn't know how I got there, but there I was, rolling him back to his back, prying his one eye open, checking his pupil dilation. Jabbing two fingers below his chin to take his pulse, the feel of it hard and strong against the pads of my fingers better than anything I'd ever felt in my whole miserable fucking existence.

I fell back onto my ass, a broken breath falling from my lips, my head spinning.

He was okay. He was going to live.

Ava Jade crawled to his side, reaching for him, and I saw red.

I checked her advance, cutting her off from getting any closer as he came slowly back to full consciousness. "Don't fucking touch him."

She recoiled from my words, falling backward onto her elbows, her eyes filled with hurt.

Rook was asking Grey if he could count the number of fingers he was holding up. Behind Ava Jade, I saw the stern face of my father leaving a trail of corpses in his wake as he burrowed a path through flesh and bone to get to us.

Ava Jade got shakily to her feet, dropping the useless gun still in her hand to the ground. "I'm s-sorry," she said, her watery stare fixed on Grey, who had lifted a hand as though he might be trying to touch her.

"He'll be okay, right?" Rook asked me, still crouched beside Grey's head, his bloody fingers brushing debris from the garish wound to his brother's eye. "He's going to live?"

Diesel brushed past Ava Jade, assessing the situation, rushing to Grey.

"Hey, where the fuck does she think she's going?" Rook said, and when I looked back up, Ava Jade was already halfway down the dock, jumping over corpses, ignoring the Saints calling out to her as she passed them. Running away.

"Ghost!" Rook called out to her, his voice hoarse. He tried to stand, but his leg was fucked, and he fell back to one knee, baring his teeth before trying again. "Ghost!"

I bowed my head. *Fuck.*

"What the fuck did you say to her?" Rook demanded, taking a shaky step forward, his left boot glinting crimson.

What had I said to her?

I could barely remember.

My heart faltered a beat, vision darkening. Beneath my knees, the docks were slick with a puddle of my blood.

I needed to go after her.

She couldn't be out there alone.

"I didn't mean..." I trailed off, my tongue heavy in my mouth, muscles unlocking from bone until I could hardly hold myself up.

"*Shit*," I heard someone curse and then hands were holding me up. "Diesel!"

I let my head fall back and looked up into mismatched eyes. Something about that seemed weird, but I couldn't seem to hold onto the thought as Drake called for Diesel a second time. "He's been shot," Drake said. "I think he's hemorrhaging."

Diesel pushed something against my lower stomach, and I shuddered, grimacing at the pain.

"We need to get him to the vet," Diesel announced, and he and Axel shuffled Drake out of the way as they lifted me from the floor despite my grousing.

"Wait," I said through gritted teeth, reaching out to grab Drake, haul him close.

He looked down at me, confused, edgy.

"Find her."

His gaze narrowed on me. "Who?"

"She took off," Rook supplied for me as Diesel set me on a plank of wood, my makeshift stretcher.

"Find her," I implored Drake. "Bring her... bring her..."

I could feel myself fading and fought it with everything I had.

"Don't worry," Drake said, peeling my rigid fingers from his forearm. "I'll find her."

33

AVA JADE

I had to shoot him.

I *had* to.

He was going to get away.

A chill rushed up my arms, and I shivered, trying to ignore the throb in the side of my thigh where a bullet had gone through and through. It wasn't so bad. I could keep walking.

Didn't matter.

So what if I collapsed?

So what if I fucking died right here in the road?

I'd almost killed them.

If Diesel had been even another minute later, I would've.

But he needed to die.

No.

I could've held. I could've let him go.

No.

I beat my fists against the sides of my head, growling my frustration, bending to a crouch.

Corvus was right. This was all my fault. Axel was still alive, but I'd seen the others among the dead. Crowley and Derrik. They wouldn't be going home to their families. Grey would never see right again. Rook was shot at least twice, if not more, his older bullet-wounds still healing. Corvus had been shot in the stomach, and even if he seemed all right, the recovery from that would be brutal.

My Crows.

I'd always thought *they* would be the death of me. Maybe it was me who was always destined to be the death of them.

The tears came hot and fast, welling from a spring deep down inside that I thought had rusted over a long time ago.

I beat my fist against my skull again, relishing in the pain.

I deserved it.

I deserved every bad thing that ever happened to me. That ever would happen.

My fingernails bit into my scalp as I rocked there at the side of the road in the dark, stuck between wanting to run and keep running and never come back...

...and turning my ass around and marching back there, to the place where I belonged.

I choked on a painful sob, swiping the backs of my palms over my eyes as I pushed myself back to standing, wincing at the wound in my leg. It could just fucking get in line with all the other aches and pains on the surface that did nothing to distract me from the deeper ache.

The one quivering in my chest like a dying thing.

Grey was going to live.

He would live and Corvus would live and Rook would live.

Diesel was alive.

The Aces and the Dead Men were dead.

I inhaled deeply, taking in the scent of the dry dirt along with the earthy tang of dried blood coating the inside of my nose. The crispness of mountain trees.

My stomach dropped at the realization that I would need to go back. I had to face them.

And fuck...*Becca.*

I'd completely forgotten about Becca.

She was probably catatonic right about now.

The twin beams of headlights swept up the road from behind me, and I turned, instinctively reaching for a blade that I didn't have. I didn't have any of my blades left. They were all sunk into the corpses of our enemies now. At least one of them permanently lost to the sea with an Ace I'd sent right over the edge of the dock.

My hands glared red in the headlights as I backed up further onto the side of the road, bending to conceal myself in the bushes. I squeezed my fists, blood making them stick like that, crimson stuffed into every crevice, dried onto the backs of my knuckles.

A van barreled past, Diesel at the wheel. Another van followed.

I stepped out of the shadows.

"Wait!"

A Jeep blared it's horn at me and a familiar voice called out the open window, mostly lost to the wind. "Angel!"

"Drake?"

He pulled up alongside me, leaning over to shove the passenger door open. "Get in. Corvus needs a surgeon. We're headed to the vet."

I hesitated, my mind reeling, feeling sick all over again at my mistake. *My mistake.* I pressed a hand to my stomach. "Is he…"

"Come on, Angel, get in. We'll meet them there."

I climbed into the Jeep, sitting up high to see if I could still see the van ahead of us around the next bend as Drake tore off down the road after them, his blond hair catching with strands of silver in the moonlight.

Drake cursed as he reached over my chest and grabbed the seatbelt, pulling it across my body to belt me in.

"This is all my fault," the words fell from my lips, the truth of them forming a hard ball in my throat.

Drake nodded, shifting gears, the back tires spinning against the dirt road as he pushed the vehicle to its limits.

Fuck. He could at least lie to me. I opened my mouth on a sharp remark, but stopped.

Drake's hands tightened on the wheel, an unnamable thing charging the air around him.

Something changed, like the plates of the earth beneath our feet were shifting all out of place, and I was losing my balance.

"Can I tell you a secret?" Drake said, his cheekbones flaring. His eyes seemed brighter, I thought, something in my stomach turning.

No. Just one eye.

He'd had brown eyes, though. I was sure of it. But right now, one was blue.

My pulse picked up.

There were brown roots peeking through the strands of his blond hair.

My breath caught in my throat, my hand inching slowly toward the buckle holding me in, readying myself to strike.

Could I survive a crash at this speed?

"*Drake?*"

He turned to face me, his expression unreadable, the carefree mask of Drake gone.

"I hope he dies."

A stinging pain bit into my thigh, heat spreading like wildfire up and down my leg.

The Jeep kicked out to the left as Drake wheeled right, putting us onto the dirt road leading through the Deadwood and away from the convoy of Saints.

I fumbled with the seatbelt, my fingers numb and sloppy, the back of my palm hitting something in my leg.

A knife.

No.

Something much worse.

My thoughts turned sluggish. Blood rushed in my ears, deafening.

In my leg was the plunger end of a syringe. I blinked, and a riot of colors were thrown over the back of my eyelids, blinding me. An odd smell stuck in my nose. Like limes and rotting flowers. I sagged against the seat, gravity churning my belly until I couldn't hold my head up any longer.

The syringe was yanked from my leg.

My eyes crossed, and I drowned in an all-encompassing dark.

WARPED MINDS

1

CORVUS

Grey stirred atop the thin cot, his face pinching as he woke.

His skin puckered where the surgical tape held the clean bandage against the garish wound where his right eye used to be.

Rook jerked his chin up, discarding the blade he'd been using to carve twelve more kill lines into the flesh of his right forearm. We left our silent vigil by the front window of Sanctum now allowing cold dawn light to filter through the tinted glass.

"He's waking up," Rook rumbled, lurching in Grey's direction, his leg fucked from not one but two bullet-wounds, one that would've shattered his knee-cap if it had hit just a few inches higher.

Grey coughed and Rook bent to slide a hand beneath his shoulders, helping him sit up. I moved for the glass of water set on the floor beside the cot and passed it over, concealing a wince at the sharp pain in my abdomen. "Drink," I ordered, not caring that the noise was waking the other injured Saints laid up on cots throughout the entire floor of the bar.

The smell of lead and injury was so strong it managed to overpower the usual reek of stale liquor permeating these walls.

Grey choked down some of the water, his one eye focusing slowly on us as he pushed through the haze of drugs our vet had to use to keep his ass down.

I pressed a hand to the bandage on my lower stomach, feeling the ridge of wiry stitches through the gauze as I rose back to my full height. I couldn't remember the vet digging out the bullet, but I could feel the phantom memory of his sharp tools where they'd scraped and nudged and pulled between major organs. Sewing back together bits of my insides and my outsides.

"Where is she?" Grey croaked and my jaw tightened, teeth clicking from the pressure.

Rook's fingers curled over Grey's shoulder, squeezing, but our youngest brother's eye remained trained squarely on me. As if he somehow knew her leaving was my fault regardless of the fact he was unconscious, near fucking death, when I'd said what I said to her.

"She took off. Isn't answering any of our calls," I said in a low voice, struggling to keep it steady. "I sent Drake to look for her hours ago. He texted just before dawn to say he couldn't find her."

Grey nodded solemnly, his eye narrowing as he considered that.

"She blamed herself for this," he said, lifting a hand to gently brush the bandage with a grimace.

"She had help," Rook hissed, his dark gaze sliding to me before returning to Grey.

Anger flared Grey's nostrils and tightened the lines around his mouth as he shook his head slow. "She'll come back. She won't leave us," he said with conviction. "She can't."

Rook nodded his agreement. "Yeah, man. She'll be back when she's ready."

Grey's shoulders sagged and for the first time he allowed himself to see the quiet chaos surrounding us all. "How many did we lose?"

"Eight," Rook replied.

"*Fuck.*"

"Injured?"

"What you see here. Vet says everyone'll make it, but Vance won't walk again."

I turned to the window, staring out into the early morning as though I could will Ava Jade to appear through the thin fog still clinging to the street.

She would be back.

She had to come back.

My throat burned, and I swallowed hard to snuff the aching, licking my dry lips and tasting blood. No way of telling if it belonged to myself or someone else.

Since we got back, none of us left this space save for Diesel and a small group of uninjured Saints and Kings. They went to see to the clean-up, make sure no one escaped alive.

"Hey," Becca said weakly, her voice thin and groggy as she padded barefoot through the cots of sleeping gangsters from the back room where we'd put her. She winced when she saw Grey but quickly covered it up with a small smile. "You're awake," she said. "Does that mean…"

"He's going to be fine," Rook confirmed gruffly, the words carrying with them a finality, as though Grey's survival was entirely up to him and he'd already made the call. Daring the reaper to *try* to come and claim a soul that was ours.

Grey's lips turned up at one corner. He cocked his head at Becca as she tucked a long strand of dark hair behind her ear. "Does it look that bad?" he asked.

She started, shaking her head vehemently. "What? No. No, it's, *um…*"

"It looks badass," Rook filled in, giving Becca a glare that could've damn near reduced her to ash.

"Yeah," Becca agreed, swallowing. "I just—it just looks like it hurts, that's all."

"It does," Grey confirmed, clearing his throat. "Feels like I got kicked in the head by a horse."

My guts twisted.

"And then a zombie with dull fingernails dug out my eye."

Rook's upper lips twitched. "Thanks for that visual, man," Rook deadpanned, going dead-eyed to cover up how bothered he was by his brother's pain. He patted Grey on the thigh. "I'll go get you some more morphine, you big baby."

Becca wrapped her arms around herself, tiptoeing toward where I stood back at the front window. She looked out into the morning, at the streets slowly waking for another gorgeous day in Thorn Valley. None of them aware that only miles away, just out of earshot, a battle left at least forty men dead by the shores of Spirit Lake.

"She still hasn't come back," Becca said.

It wasn't a question, so I didn't answer.

She shivered, her fingers tightening on her shoulders.

It was hot as fucking balls in here, so I knew it wasn't from the cold.

"Have you tried calling?" she asked.

I lifted a brow at her, and she deflated. "Sorry, stupid question. Of course you have."

"I take it you've tried too?"

She nodded and my stomach twisted.

Ava Jade would ignore us if she was upset, me especially, but Becca? If she wasn't answering calls or texts from her best friend either, that meant she was more hurt than I realized.

That or she'd lost her damn phone.

Or something far *far* worse.

I wished I'd had Grey install the tracking app on her new phone, but I was trying to let go of my need to control her. Giving her, her freedom. Look what fucking good it did me.

My fists clenched and not for the first time this morning, the urge to hit something until my knuckles cracked and bled raced up my arms like lightning, heat pulsing through my core. I shut my eyes against the sensations, a ragged breath slinking past my lips.

A hand gingerly touched my shoulder, and I flinched, gripping the window ledge to keep from throwing my girl's best friend across the damn room.

"She's fine," Becca said, though her tone lacked conviction. "She's always fine, no matter what happens. I'm pretty convinced that girl can't die."

....die?

Why the fuck did she have to say that?

I scrubbed a palm over the sharp stubble on my jaw, pulling away from Becca's touch.

The back door of Sanctum opened, and I had my gun out and aimed, Becca swept behind me, in the span of a single second.

"What took you so long?" I heard Rook say quietly, and my pulse steadied as Diesel strode into the main bar with a few men on his heels.

I tucked my gun back into the waistband of my jeans, avoiding the injury still singing agony through my core.

Our father took in the injured around him, the storm of his face not calming until he found Grey.

"I'm good," Grey confirmed and Diesel's Adam's apple bobbed as he cleared the space between them, sinking to one knee to check the wound and Grey's state himself. He nodded once he was satisfied, and some of the ice in his eyes melted away, leaving a glint on the surface before he blinked, sniffing hard and the tears were gone.

"You scared me, Son."

Grey smirked. "About time. I've been trying for years."

Diesel shook his head, rising back to his feet. "Smart-ass."

He lifted something from his back pocket and turned, throwing the slim phone in my direction. I caught it, my lips parting in surprise and dread.

"Found it on the roof at the Docks," Diesel explained as I pressed the side button, lighting up the screen to a barrage of missed call and text notifications. The battery almost dead. "Someone was trying to call it off the hook. Thought Grey could check it, make sure it's not one of theirs, or—"

"It's not," I interrupted him. "It's Ava Jade's."

I walked it to Grey, and he took it eagerly.

"It's locked. Can you get into it?"

Rook returned with a single tiny pill, but Grey didn't take it, staring at the lock screen like he could figure out her passcode just by staring at it.

"Do you need a laptop?"

He shook his head, thumb hesitating over the screen before he tapped five times and then sighed in relief.

"How did you know her passcode?"

"Saw her enter the first two numbers once. Wasn't hard to figure out the rest."

I resisted trying to pry the phone out of his hands as he scrolled through all our missed calls and texts.

"What do you mean?" Becca asked, confused.

"The numbers were two and seven. C. R. It wasn't hard to figure out the rest. It's a thumbprint entry, but her backup passcode spelled *Crows*."

His words were a sucker punch to the gut.

I didn't know how, but I was going to make this up to her. I'd fucking beg for forgiveness on my knees. I'd grovel at her feet for as long as it took.

She shouldn't have fired that shot, but I shouldn't have put the blame for Grey, for everything, on her shoulders.

And then there was the other possibility.

That I was wrong.

If Ava Jade hadn't taken the shot, it was possible Lenny Ace could've come back even stronger, with a better plan, and killed us all.

We lost good men, but *we* were still here.

Diesel was still here.

Maybe it was the right call. The call I was too hesitant to make.

"*Damn*," Grey cursed, his thumbs lifting from the screen as he paused his scrolling, staring down at something with his lips in a hard line.

"What is it?" Rook asked, but I was already pulling the phone from Grey's stiff grip.

It wasn't a text he was looking at but an email.

To: GH380XC@GMAIL.COM
     From: Ava Jade Mason
     Subject: RE: Miss me?

WHY DON'T YOU COME OUT OF THE SHADOWS AND PLAY? OR ARE YOU TOO MUCH of a coward? It's me you want. Come and get me, motherfucker.

"WHEN DID SHE SEND THAT?" ROOK ASKED, TRYING TO SCROLL BACK UP ON THE phone over my shoulder.

We both looked at the time stamp. It was sent days ago, and she'd received no reply.

"She was fucking taunting him," Grey said.

"Who?" Diesel asked, a knot forming between his brows.

"Let me see," Becca demanded, rushing over to stand on tiptoe to see the screen.

"Are we really surprised?" Rook asked gruffly as Becca let out a little gasp after reading the message.

"No," Becca replied to the rhetorical question. "But... you don't think she would go after him, do you?"

Heat surged through my chest, making my breaths come heavier.

I knew she *would*. But did she? After everything that happened, was that where her head would be right now?

"I don't think she can," Grey answered Becca. "I've exhausted every resource we have looking for this fucker. As smart as Ava Jade is, she couldn't find him alone."

"That's the fucking problem," I growled, struggling to regulate my breathing at the idea of this piece of shit's hands touching what was ours. "She's *alone*. And that's exactly what he wants."

"What the fuck are you talking about? *Who* are you talking about?" Diesel asked, reminding me he was still standing there, the other Saints who'd been with him scattered around the bar, checking on their injured brothers.

I met my father's cold eyes, lifting my chin. "We meant to tell you," I said, unable to sound even the tiniest bit apologetic. I had bigger fucking problems. "We were going to last night before—"

"Before you lost your shit on Ghost over a fucking jacket," Rook supplied, reaching over the empty bar to scoop a bottle of Jack from the other side and take a swig straight from its mouth.

Diesel pinched the bridge of his nose. "Mind explaining *now*?"

"AJ has a stalker," Grey started, and when Diesel shifted his hard stare to my brother, he lost his nerve, sagging at the raw emotion in Grey's eye. The fear. The pain.

He wore his worry plain on his face, not bothering to try to conceal it.

Diesel dragged a stool from the bar and set it down near Grey's cot, falling onto it, leaning his elbows over his knees. "Go on."

Grey told Diesel almost everything, not glazing over the gritty details. There wasn't any point. Once he caught wind of it, Diesel would find out all of those details for himself one way or another. And he needed to know. This person, whoever it was, had threatened not only Ava Jade, but us too.

If it were reversed, I'd want to know.

"You should've come to me sooner," Diesel said when Grey was finished, his icy blue eyes pacing the floor.

"You weren't—"

"You should've fucking told me," he cut me off, his tone sharp as he pushed to his feet. "Where is she now?"

My brows furrowed.

"Ava Jade," he clarified. "Where is she?"

"We don't know," Rook said, leaving the bottle on the bar. "This idiot told her all that shit down at the Docks was her fault."

I flinched, but I would own that.

"She took off," Grey added.

Diesel nodded. "I saw her storm down the dock. I remember."

"We should look for her," Becca said, piping up for the first time in thirty minutes.

Diesel's gaze slid to her like he was only just remembering she was there. "There's no reason to believe that this... *this filth* has her. She was upset. She left. She doesn't know you're here to come looking."

"She'd figure it out," Grey argued.

Rook shook his head. "She won't be ready to come looking. Not yet."

"Becca's right," I said, two words I never thought I'd utter. "We should look for her. I don't care if she's ready or not. She shouldn't be out there alone."

"Give her the day," Diesel suggested. "If she isn't here by nightfall, we'll find her. Send out teams of three to every place you think she might've gone."

I cocked my head at him. *We?* He was going to use our men to aid in the search for her?

"She's one of us," Diesel said plainly, looking at me as though I should've understood that. "And she's important to the three most important people to me. That makes her problems *my* problems. But I got to say, boys, the timing of this shit..."

He trailed off, not needing to finish the thought.

We all hoped the war with the Aces and Dead Men was at an end after the slaughter at the Docks, but we needed to be cautious. We needed to rebuild. Strengthen our ranks. With the Kings here to help bolster us, we were all right. We wouldn't be perceived as weak or vulnerable to attack any who wanted a piece of our territory.

But did that alliance still hold now that the threat was dealt with?

"Tonight, then," Rook said with a note of finality in his tone.

Diesel shook his head. "You three aren't going anywhere. The vet said Grey shouldn't be moving around for a couple days at least. You either, Rook. In fact, I recall him saying not to put any pressure whatsoever on that leg."

Diesel eyed Rook's torn off jeans and the bandages cuffing his thigh and calf. Blood was already showing through the starchy white gauze even though I'd changed the dressings for him twice. Unless I tied him down, he wouldn't stay sitting.

"And you," Diesel added, gaze sliding my way. "You're lucky the internal bleeding didn't put your ass in a casket. You need fluids and rest."

"Then we'll rest," I said through gritted teeth. "...until the sun goes down."

He threw his hands up, scoffing as he rolled his eyes. "Have kids she said," he muttered to himself. "It'll be fucking fun, she said."

Grey snorted, and I couldn't help the tiniest smirk at the reminder of the reason Diesel St. Crow took in three strays and made them family. His wife, who couldn't have children, but always wanted them. The woman who resolved to adopt... just before her life was ended.

"All right. Rest then," Diesel said after a moment. "We'll be back in a few hours. Got some things to check up on and Maverick wants to have a meet."

"You need us there for that?" Rook asked.

"It'll happen at Sanctum. I'll be back before he gets here."

"Wait," I said before Dies could take off again, remembering the other thing we'd wanted to talk to Dies about during his party. "Aries."

He quirked a brow.

"Maverick's man," I explained. "His clean-up guy. Ava Jade thought he might be the guy. Her stalker. He took off a couple days ago, after the newsletter was sent to the entire school about my... origin. We haven't seen him since."

Diesel's mouth pressed into a thin line as he thought through the new problem. Asking a gang leader to hand over one of his own men wasn't going to be pleasant, but Maverick could either give him over or let us hunt him down. If he was smart, he'd prefer the former.

"I'll bring it up at the meet," Diesel said finally. "You think it's him?"

I rolled the question around in my mouth.

"No," Rook answered for me. "The guy's a creep, but not a monster." He sneered. "Too weak. Besides, he's probably a hundred pounds soaking wet."

"AJ said—" Grey started, but Rook cut him off.

"Which is why we'll look into it. You actually telling me you think that little shit is the guy?"

Grey didn't have anything to say to that, falling silent.

"We just want to ask him a few questions," I supplied.

"A few questions?" Diesel scoffed, knowing exactly what that meant. He shook his head. "I'll speak to Maverick."

He whistled low and lifted his hand, making a circular motion with his ring and index fingers. The others who'd been with him gathered back to his side, following him from the bar. The conversation finished for the moment.

"Where the fuck do you think you're going?" Rook asked as I lifted my jacket from the back of a chair with my pinkie and slid it on, ignoring the pain of the movement.

"I can't just sit here."

"Where are you going?" he repeated.

"To check on Julia." I didn't have a specific place in mind, but the words rolled off my tongue anyway. It was as good a place as any. She wasn't answering our requests for updates on our humanitarian projects the last couple weeks or so. And hadn't Sparrow said something about that girl in Williams' class trying to call the hotline but not getting through?

Yes. I would check on Julia.

It was as good a thing to do as any if I was meant to fucking wait another two hours to hunt my Sparrow.

By the time I got back, no force on this earth, not even Diesel St. Crow, was going to stop me from finding her. I prayed she'd be back before I was. I didn't want to, but I would drag her back if that was what it took. Kicking and fucking screaming.

"Fuck. Wait," Rook huffed, a snarl on his lips as he put weight on his fucked up leg. "I'll come with you."

His leg buckled when he moved forward, and he caught himself on a table, cursing.

"No you won't. I don't need your gimp ass slowing me down."

"Fuck you."

"Besides, you and Grey need to be here with the others. Just in case."

"That's what the sentries are for," Grey argued, swinging his legs from the cot.

He wasn't wrong. Diesel left a team of men guarding Sanctum. There were five around the building and two on the roof. No one would even get close.

"You need to lie down," I reminded Grey. "And, Rook, you're already bleeding through your fucking bandages."

"You aren't going out there alone, man," Grey argued.

"I'll go with him."

At once, our heads turned on a swivel to where Becca was still standing quietly by a high-top table. She flushed, swallowing hard as she tried to appear confident, nearly succeeding.

I... didn't know what to say.

Fuck no seemed a good option, but I knew Sparrow wouldn't like that. "You should stay here," I said instead. "Where you'll be safe."

"Fuck that. I can't sit here anymore, either. Let me help. I'm a shitty shot, but I know how a gun works. I'll cover you."

I ran my tongue over my teeth, holding back another response I knew my Sparrow wouldn't like. "Rebecca..."

"Look, either you let me help you or I'm just going to go and start looking for her."

"No, you're not," Rook warned. "Not alone."

"If anything happened to you, AJ'd have our balls," Grey added.

She strengthened her resolve, lifting through her hips to stand taller, looking more like someone who could be Ava Jade's equal than I ever gave her credit for. "Then you're taking me with you."

2

AVA JADE

The sharp sound of a breath in my ear woke me, my limbs jerking against a hard wall. An even harder floor.

Streaky light slashed across my eyes, and I grunted, squeezing them shut only to force them open again, panic swelling in my chest as the feeling returned to my bones.

I pushed my back flush against the wall I'd been dumped against, blinking rapidly to force my eyes to see. The persistent rush of adrenaline in my bloodstream helped burn off whatever shit still clogged my veins, making everything feel sluggish. Forced. Harder than it should've been.

Pain ricocheted through my thigh when I tried to claw my way up the wall to standing, making me sink back down to land hard on my ass, a dizziness making my breaths come heavier.

"*Fuck*," I slurred, my surroundings dipping and spinning in a wild dance around me as they tried to come into focus.

Black spots bloomed in front of me like shadows come to life, and I weakly threw an arm out, trying to shove them back.

I coughed, the weak, wet sound of it rattling my lungs.

A room. I was in a room.

No. A box.

The thing in my chest squeezed at the sight of the gray walls. Four. In a square. No windows. A solid ceiling. A cold cement floor.

A door.

I pushed through the pain in my thigh, dragging my body in a sad attempt at a crawl, cursing the whole way as I tried to kick off the last of the drugs still in my system like a heavy blanket keeping me down.

I slapped a palm against the cool metal of the door, my forehead connecting next as I craned my neck to look up at the smooth surface. Entirely smooth.

No door handle.

No window.

I let my hand fall down the thin seam of the door.

No hinges.

No big deal.

There was always a way out.

Always.

My body seemed to disagree with me, my chest rising and falling faster, fingers vibrating with a tremor that coursed all the way up both arms.

Drake.

My slow mind slogged to catch up, piecing together everything that led me to this fucking box.

I remembered him. Drake. The wind tugging at his hair as we sped through the Deadwood. The malice in his eyes when he plunged a syringe into my leg. When he told me he hoped Corvus died.

Bones...

Oh god.

Grey.

The searing memory of him lying amid the carnage at the Docks, Rook bent over him, screaming. Screaming so fucking loud as he pressed his palms against Grey's chest over and over.

He'd woken, but that didn't mean he was okay.

And Corvus. I'd seen Diesel speed past like a bat out of fucking hell. And Drake said...

I couldn't believe anything Drake said.

Corvus was probably fine.

He would be fine.

He had to be.

None of them could die because of me.

Why hadn't I just listened?

Stupid. *So fucking stupid.*

My fault. *My fault.*

I clenched my teeth so hard I heard them click in protest, my fist shaking as I beat it against the door, heat rising in my face.

"Open this fucking door," I shouted, my voice hoarse and breaking. "You fucking coward!"

I listened for a reply, my heart a jackhammer against my ribcage. The darkness within pooled, sparking with rage.

I beat the door again, the hit reverberating down my arm. "*Hey!*"

Again. "*Hey!*"

Drake was a dead man. If that was even his name.

He could keep this door locked all he wanted. They would come for me.

They would come for me, right?

My stomach turned and a stinging ravaged my throat, bringing hot tears to my eyes.

Would they?

After what I'd done?

The darkness drained away, taking with it the last dregs of adrenaline still pulsing through me.

I wouldn't come for me.

The truth settled in my stomach like lead. "I'm on my own."

My eyes traveled the four walls, no more than seven feet in length each. The gray color wasn't painted. Not cement, I realized, squinting through the remaining haze still making the edges of my vision foggy.

I winced, pulling myself to the side to push my hand against the nearest wall. The spongy surface cushioned my fingers.

A padded cell?

No.

This wasn't padding. Not the kind you'd find in an insane asylum. I'd seen foam like this before. On the walls of the closet in Corvus' bedroom. In the little recording studio he'd built there. Soundproofing.

Wherever I was, Drake worried someone might hear me.

I dug my fingernails into the foam, the *shush* sound of it splitting as I peeled it from the wall making me shiver.

"Hey!" I shouted again, coughing.

I didn't stop there, making myself move, I frantically began tearing all the foam from the walls, ripping it off in great swaths and little chunks where it was glued down more heavily. I screamed as I worked. As the foam piled on the floor at my feet and I had to kick through it, rushing to do the next wall, and the next, ignoring the way my body protested the movements.

Ignoring the screaming pain in my thigh until I couldn't anymore, growling as I collapsed to my knees, a sharp cry on my lips as the impact tore something.

I pressed a hand to my leg and it came away red.

For the first time, I noticed the way my pants were hanging off my one leg. Torn from my ankle all the way up past my knee. The once white bandage wrapped tightly around my thigh was now stained every shade of red with blood. It was too much for the bandage to contain anymore and ran in wispy streaks down my leg.

I felt around my thigh, pressing gingerly on the exit wound around the other side.

Through and through.

Right.

I remembered.

But I didn't remember how this bandage got here.

Or the wiry ridge of stitches I could feel poking through the soiled gauze.

What else hadn't I felt?

I swallowed back bile, grimacing.

Somewhere outside the door, the loud clamor of another slamming shut echoed into the room.

Shit!

I got back to my feet, holding back a sound of pain as I spun through the foam, looking for something. Anything to use aside from the spongy material that would do *nothing* to help me unless I wanted to start a fucking pillow fight with a sadistic fuck like Drake.

My necklace. My hands flew to my chest, to the black diamond resting there. No. The dainty chain wouldn't be strong enough.

My gaze caught on the hem of my black dress, and I remembered the laces running up the back.

Heavy footsteps rang in my ears from somewhere far off, getting nearer.

I let my ass fall onto the pillow of foam and wasted no time twisting my arms behind me to the point of pulling them from their sockets, tugging the laces free. My fingers plucked and pulled until I had the full length of thin cord between my hands. I grinned, scrambling backward to the wall where the door was until I was close enough to use it to aid me in standing.

The bones of my back pressed flat against the tacky wall just next to the door, and I held my breath, winding the lace around each fist, pulling the length between them taut, praying it was strong enough. I shook my head, practically foaming at the mouth as the darkness woke once more, pushing back at the drugs trying to drag me down.

I won't kill him, I decided. That would be too easy.

Just choke him out, the darkness whispered. *So we can play with him later.*

Yes.

I smiled despite the whisper of my sanity begging to be heard as we threw it in a closet and locked the fucking door.

The steady rhythm of his strides in the hall meant he hadn't heard me screaming. Didn't know I was awake. That I was ready for him.

If I didn't take him down now, I doubted he would give me the opportunity of taking another stab at him. Not if he was as smart as he seemed to be.

It was a wonder he even left me with the laces in my dress. Either he needed to take off quickly, or he didn't expect me to wake up before he returned. Either way, his mistake.

His fucking funeral.

I stretched the cord between my fists, closing my eyes as his footfalls approached the door. Swallowed and breathed deep through my nose to calm my galloping heart.

An electronic chirp. A click.

The door swept open and he stepped in, his back going rigid at the foamy carnage coating the floor. His momentary shock was enough to take him by surprise.

I cried out as I launched at him, the pain in my leg forgotten as I wrapped them around his middle the same time I pulled the cord tight around his neck, dragging my fists back and down as though if I just pulled hard enough I could take his head clean off his shoulders.

He choked, clawing at his neck, his hard body flexing with bone and muscle as he fought to shake me off. The acrid scent of rotting limes filling my nose, making me gag.

I twisted my fists behind his neck, feeling the cord cut into my flesh.

"Come on," I hissed in his ear. *"Go to sleep, motherfucker."*

My stomach lurched as he pushed us backward until my back connected with the wall, a sliver where there was still enough foam to cushion the blow, but still the air left my lungs in a gush and I fought to maintain my hold on the cord, stars in my eyes.

He spluttered, almost no sound escaping his lips as he hunched, pressing his neck harder into the cord before he slammed me back again.

My sight darkened as the back of my skull connected with the sticky cement wall and my fists loosened, fingers slipping as I was thrown, my body flipping over Drake's to bounce hard on the foamy floor.

Somewhere, he was coughing. I could feel him, his nearness as I fought with everything I had to come out of the semi-unconscious state, trying to see through the black. To feel through the numbness.

No.

No.

I reached out blindly, wavering as I found my feet, claws slashing, ready to tear his face clean from his skull.

"Come at me," I screeched, the pitch of my own voice painful in my ears.

He did, the blackness abating just enough for me to dodge his attack and land a violent hit to the back of his neck, sending him careening forward to catch himself on the wall.

I slid my right leg behind me, lowering my body in a fighting stance as he turned back to me. I launched into a full attack before he could make his first move, but he deftly deflected my advance and suddenly there were two of him. The twin Drakes moving together and apart and together again.

"Stop," he growled hoarsely, and his voice in my ears only spurred the darkness into a feral frenzy.

I attacked again, and he knocked me away.

"You've lost too much blood, Angel," he continued, shoving me hard enough to send me to the floor on my next advance. I pushed myself up on my arms and the traitorous things shook beneath me, my palms slipping on something wet and thick beneath the foam.

Blood. It was blood. My blood.

I glanced down, finding my leg entirely red with it. A puddle of crimson forming in the foam around my knee.

Shit.

It didn't matter.

I roared as I went for his ankle in the tight space, pulling it in a sharp motion to make him fall. His back connected with the ground for barely a second before he was pulling his ankle away, pulling me through the foam, flipping me onto my back, my wrists pinned as I stared half consciously into his brown eyes.

"Stop fighting," he roared.

"*Never,*" I growled, spitting into his face.

He released my wrist, and I struck his nose, crunching it under my palm, but not before I felt the familiar sting of a needle sliding out of my neck.

NO.

A scalding tear rolled from the edge of my eye and down into my hairline as I felt the warm gush of whatever he injected me with sliding down my collarbone and into my chest. Filling me with a numbness so complete I thought it might paralyze my lungs. That I may not be able to breathe.

Was I breathing?

My vision doubled again, and I fought to hold onto consciousness.

"I miscalculated the dose last time." Drake's voice spoke to me as though from another dimension, coming across muffled as though spoken through cotton.

"That won't happen again," he promised as my heavy eyelids blinked up at the ceiling and my mouth fell slack.

My leg was moved and distantly, from the feel of pressure alone, I discerned that he was removing my panties.

Tugging at my dress.

"Clothes are a privilege, Angel."

"I'll kill you," I tried to tell him, but the words came out a garbled, wet moan.

"Hush. You need rest."

He slipped the black diamond necklace from my neck.

"Mother... fucker..."

My eyes crossed and the last strings tethering my mind to my body snapped, leaving me to fall back into the dark.

3

GREY

I needed to see it for myself.

I eased the bathroom door shut behind me, flipping the lock. With a bar full of Saints, it should have been assured that I'd be interrupted, but not today.

Not when the majority could barely roll themselves off the cots and pool tables where they were laid up to heal, most passed out from all the pain killers in their system.

Not me.

I'd gummed the little morphine pill Rook all but forced into my mouth and spit it out when he wasn't looking. I wasn't going back to sleep until Ava Jade was back. Until I knew she was safe.

A shaky breath filled my lungs as I turned, carrying the fresh bandages and clean cloth to the bank of stainless steel sinks. I took the time to wipe down the scratched surface before setting down the sterile materials and pressing my palms down against the cool metal.

I looked up, feeling a chill roll down my spine at the reflection staring back at me in the mirror.

It was unmistakably me, which was a sort of relief I supposed. But *fuck* did I ever look like shit.

The bandage taped over my eye was a gruesome shade of yellowish pink, soiled, bits of gray dust and debris discoloring the edges of the clear surgical tape holding it in place. My face was gaunt. Paler than I'd ever seen it. With dark purplish skin beneath the one eye I still had and the veins in my temple a striking blue against the thin skin covering them.

I'd managed to change out of my blood-covered clothes into gym shorts and a baggy t-shirt, one of the few extra sets of workout attire I kept here in the basement, but even the clean clothes couldn't cover up how absolutely *not clean* I was. There was still blood in the shallow wrinkles slashing across my neck. In my dirty blonde hair sticking out at every angle.

I needed a fucking shower, but that would have to wait. We'd planned to use one of the working girls' rooms upstairs to clean ourselves up after the meet. But without knowing exactly when Dies and Maverick would be showing up, we'd kept holding out.

I wanted to be there. Put the pressure on Mav if he even thought for a second about denying our request to hand over that little shit, Aries.

Rook was right, I didn't really think it was him, either. But then why run?

Why was he even there to fucking begin with? He was the clean-up crew, not a frontman. If he wasn't the guy, maybe he knew something that could help us at the very least. Something he wasn't keen to share.

I coughed to clear my throat, giving my head a slight shake to bring myself back to the reason I came in here. I was procrastinating, and it wasn't going to fucking help anything.

I licked my dry lips and gave my hands one final scrub under the hot water, drying them as well as I could before I set to work.

The bandages were practically fucking glued in place, and I cursed as I eased the edges of the surgical tape off my skin, leaving red marks behind.

"Grey," Rook's voice came through the door, followed by a soft double tap. "You good?"

"Fine."

"Sure you don't want help, Bro? You shouldn't be standing yet."

"Look who's fucking talking. How's the peg leg?"

No reply, but I could imagine his face on the other side of the locked door.

"I'm good, Rook," I cemented. "I need to do this myself."

I heard the faint sound of his hobbled footsteps retreating and finished lifting the last bit of tape from my skin, jostling the bandage enough to cause a sharp pain to shoot all the way back through my skull, setting off a persistent throbbing ache once it subsided.

I gritted my teeth, rethinking the fucking morphine for half a second before I forced myself to pull the bandage the rest of the way off, not stopping once I began to pull despite the agony making my fingers shake.

"Fuck," I gritted out, tossing the bandage into the sink and squeezing my one eye shut. The muscles around the missing one tried to flex as well, only serving to worsen the aching.

I slammed a fist against the countertop, the pain in my hand helping to dull the sharpness of the pain in my ocular cavity.

From the look of the bandage in the sink, it wasn't going to be fucking pretty, but I made myself look again.

I blew out a breath, finding something other than what I imagined.

Not a garish crater-like wound that was caving in half my skull.

Stitches ran down the middle of my upper-eyelid, sewing it back together. The skin of my eyelids and around my eye screamed in shades of purple, red, and yellow. Swollen and brutal.

The thin wet red slash between my eyelids where my eye used to be looked like something out of a horror movie. Just really good special effects.

An all red contact lens.

But I knew the truth. I knew there was no eye there, and what I was seeing was the backside of an ocular cavity injured by the force of a bullet.

It had to be a ricochet. That was the only way the bullet wouldn't have continued to travel, past my ocular cavity and deeper into my most vital organ.

The guys were right. I was lucky.

My chest squeezed at the thought of Ava Jade ever seeing this.

Not only would she always blame herself for it, but...

I was fucking hideous.

Maybe when the swelling went down... when it began to heal.

I laughed darkly. No. Not even then.

I'd wear a patch for the rest of my life. I'd make sure she never saw it.

All that would be left would be to learn a really good fucking pirate voice and buy a parrot that could ride shotty on my shoulder and the look would be complete.

I choked on the next laugh, swallowing past the bile rising in my throat.

Vance would never walk again, I reminded myself.

This was nothing.

But I'm already the weakest of us, my mind whispered. *Now Rook and Corv will only have to pick up even more slack for my sorry ass.*

Would I still be able to shoot with one eye?

Drive?

Would I have to relearn everything?

Before I could fall too deeply into a bullshit well of self-pity, I picked up the clean cloth and let the water from the tap run piping hot before soaking it under the stream.

I cleaned the wound, scrubbing off bits of dried blood and some other substance I'd rather not know well enough to name. Once the clean bandage was in place, I felt better, even if the soreness around the wound had only tripled as I cleaned it.

I took the antibiotics the vet gave me, scooping water from the tap to help ease them down my dry throat.

A fist pounded once on the door to the bathroom, and I jerked, hissing, "*What?*"

"Dies just pulled up," Rook said through the door. "You done? Mav should be here any minute for the meet."

"Yeah."

I dumped all my shit in the garbage and swiped the back of my hand over my wet lips before striding out, Rook watching me with a hawk's eye as I passed him, moving back to the front of Sanctum.

"How bad was it?" he asked as the sound of our father and the other Saints entering from the back door through the kitchen floated to us in the main bar.

I shrugged a shoulder. "It's fine."

"That's a bullshit answer."

I clenched my teeth. "It's not as bad as I thought it would be."

It was the truth but that didn't negate the fact I was missing an entire fucking eyeball. That I'd never get it back.

"Good."

From the way he was looking at me, I could tell. "You've already seen it, haven't you?"

"Course I have. Corv was passed out while the vet worked on you, but I watched the whole thing. He said you may be able to be fitted with a glass eye if it heals right."

So I could actually look like Frankenstein's monster.

Diesel pushed in through the door to the kitchen with a few Saints on his tail, scanning the bar until he found us.

"Mav's on his way," he said, striding over, trying to covertly get a look at us.

He dragged a stool from the bar and shoved Rook into it, dragging out another and patting the seat. "Lift your leg."

"*Dies*," Rook groaned.

"Lift your goddamned leg, or I'll do it for you."

Rook's face soured as he lifted his leg, but he barely got it more than a couple feet off the ground before it dropped and he cursed, his body jerking forward.

Diesel grabbed the underside of Rook's calf, below the bandage there and lifted it into place on the stool, his hand coming away red.

He glared at Rook, not needing to say a damn word, Rook knew he was being stupid. Now, whether or not he cared was another thing.

"Have either of you slept?"

I looked away.

Rook jerked his chin to Pinkie. "Grab me the Jack, would you?"

"No," Dies hissed, making Pinkie stop in his tracks. "You'll bleed out if your blood thins anymore."

Rook's upper lip twitched, but he didn't argue.

"No Ava Jade yet?" Dies questioned, his gaze tracking around the quiet pub.

The wrinkles in his forehead deepened. "Where the fuck is Corvus?"

I pressed my lips shut.

If Corv hadn't threatened the sentries Dies had placed at all the exits, they would've notified him Corvus left hours ago.

I assumed Corv planned to be back before Diesel was.

He texted an hour ago to say he wouldn't make it.

He was only digging his own grave.

"Goddammit," Diesel said between clenched teeth. "When did he leave?"

"Ten minutes after you did," Rook admitted, knowing Diesel would find out anyway. Besides, I got the feeling Rook was done covering for our big brother. His slight with Ava Jade wouldn't soon be forgiven. By either of us.

And if she didn't come back...

"Where did he go?" Diesel demanded.

"To check on a friend," I supplied. "We haven't heard from her in a while."

"Becca went with him," Rook added. "His *backup*."

Diesel tipped his head back, exasperated as he dragged a palm down his chin.

"The boy is fucking lucky we already swept the entire city. What was he thinking? With his injuries? Taking off into the streets still sour with the smell of spilled blood..."

It was a rhetorical question, and he lifted a hand to silence Pinkie when he tried to say something, lifting his cell phone from his pocket to dial Corvus.

I winced for my brother as the quiet sound of the line ringing filled my ears.

After a moment, the impersonal automated voicemail message from the service provider sounded, rattling off the phone number with a request to leave a message at the tone.

Diesel growled as he hung up, his thumbs flying over the screen as he typed what I knew would be a vicious text message. For a guy who expected us to reply to him immediately, he really did have a double standard with that shit.

Dies stuffed the phone back into his pocket and sighed, resetting himself as he stood at his full height. Out of the skin of an angry parent and back where he fit best, into the battle-hardened flesh of a gang leader.

"Let's do this downstairs," he decided. "We don't need Mav seeing this mess."

He indicated the broken men around us, not needing to point out the obvious. That the majority of the injured were Saints. Not Kings.

They didn't quite outnumber us now, but it was close.

Too close for Diesel's comfort.

Rook lifted his leg off the stool.

"Not you," Dies hissed at him. "You park your ass there and keep that shit elevated."

"You know he's just going to follow us," I protested.

Diesel glared at Rook, and my brother gave him a plaintive shrug.

"Not if I make you stay," he challenged, jerking his chin at Pinkie, who stepped forward.

Rook lifted his gun from his waistband and set it on the stool where his leg was only a second ago, between him and Pinkie.

"Try me, big guy."

Pinkie looked back at Dies. "Boss?"

Diesel's eyes glinted with malice as he sucked a breath in through his teeth. "So fucking stubborn," he said. "You remind me of her."

Rook smirked, replacing the gun back into his waistband, hobbling on his one leg. "It's why you adopted my ass, remember?"

"Help him down the stairs," Dies ordered Pinkie. "And see that he sits his ass down and elevates that leg."

"You got it, boss."

Rook allowed Pinkie to help him through the bar to the back stairs, and I followed behind them.

"You don't have to be such a fucking cunt all the time," Pinkie grunted without any real animosity, taking the brunt of Rook's weight.

Rook laughed hollowly. "You know I wouldn't really hurt my Pinkie Pie," Rook crooned, and Pinkie shoved him into the wall, making him groan.

"*Oops,*" Pinkie muttered, only drawing another laugh from Rook as they made their way at a snail's pace down the stairs to the underbelly of Sanctum.

4

CORVUS

Becca's arms squeezed tight around my waist as I drove us to Julia's. I removed a hand from the handlebars to lift her arms higher, away from the bullet wound.

"Sorry!" I heard her muffled voice through the glass fronted helmet on her head and the wind rushing over us, followed by a squeal as I took the next turn too sharply for her liking.

I'd wanted to be back for the meet with Maverick, but it didn't look like that was going to happen anymore.

We had to stop for food. If seeing Becca's pale complexion in the sunlight wasn't enough, the fact that she could barely stand on her own two feet cemented it. She needed food and water or she was going to pass the fuck out.

And I supposed I needed to eat, too.

We couldn't go get breakfast with blood and gore all over us, which meant we needed to shower.

Standing in Ava Jade's shower at Briar Hall, the safest place we could think to go, was harder than I'd thought it'd be.

Her room smelled of her, even after all the time she'd spent with us at the Crow's Nest. Her cheap shampoo, near empty conditioner, and bar soap scattered on the shower floor were so *her*.

And all right, if I was being honest, the only reason I thought to put

815

off checking on Julia and risk being late to the meet was because there was a chance she might've been here.

Alone. Waiting for us to come and find her.

Walking in to absolute silence was like being shot all over again.

Where are you, Sparrow?

My Ducati's engine revved as I pulled us up alongside Julia's place, and Becca couldn't climb off fast enough.

"I'm sorry," she repeated as she pulled the oversized helmet off, letting her still damp dark hair fall down her back. "I didn't mean to hurt—"

"You're good," I interrupted her, trying and failing not to be agitated with her presence.

Ava Jade would be glad I'd taken her with me. That I'd fed her and saw that she got herself cleaned up.

It was one small step toward my redemption.

One of many.

My phone vibrated in my pocket and I took it out, jaw clenching at the screen. The missed call from Dies and the text message.

DIESEL

Get your ass back here. Now.

I tucked the phone back in my pocket without replying. "Come on," I told Becca. "Let's get this over with."

"Um, do I, like, need a weapon... or...?"

I stopped, turning back to face her, quirking a brow.

"Okay. Gotcha. I'll just follow."

My nostrils flared.

I bent to pull the blade I kept at my ankle out of its sheath and handed it to her.

"I didn't know blades were your thing," she said, taking it carefully at first, like it might bite her, before she got the tang properly placed and held it with confidence.

"They're not," I replied. "You know how to use that?"

"Stick 'em with the pointy end," she said, a small smile on her lips.

If there was trouble up there, we were dead.

"Yeah. You do that."

Her smile faltered, and she fell into step behind me.

"Keep that thing pointed down if you aren't using it."

"Oh. Right. So, um, who lives here exactly?"

We walked up the drive to the small two story house set apart from the others farther up the street. Julia rented the upstairs apartment, despite our offer to put her up somewhere far nicer. She insisted she loved the view of the dense redwoods in the backyard and didn't need any more space.

Before I could take the first step, the *bang* of a screen door around the house stopped me, startling Becca into a little chirp of surprise.

My gun was out in an instant, but when the small stout woman who lived downstairs came stomping around the edge of the house in a huff, I hurriedly put it behind my back.

"*Oh,*" she exclaimed, seeing me and Becca on the stairs. "I thought you were Julia," she said, her face pinching, looking irritated and disappointed all at once.

"Have you seen her recently?" I asked.

The woman gave me another look, scrutinizing more closely. She was suspicious.

I put on my smooth voice and forced a worried expression of my own. "I'm her cousin. The family's been trying to reach her, but she hasn't been taking anyone's calls. We're starting to worry."

The woman's gaze slid to Becca.

"We were hoping to check on her," Becca lied smoothly. "You know, make sure she's okay."

This time, the woman's flustered demeanor melted, and she nodded sadly at Becca. "I'm sorry, dear, but I haven't seen her in weeks. She's past due with her rent and there's an awful stink coming from up there. I think she might've gone someplace and forgot to take out her trash."

"You haven't seen her in weeks?" I repeated. "And you didn't think to call the police?"

The woman looked taken aback at the question. "Well, no. Julia keeps to herself. She's gone out of town for a couple weeks before without telling me. And you know her, with that landline ringing all hours of the day and night. I don't think she had a cell phone."

She did.

But clearly she never thought to share the number with her landlady.

My stomach turned with unease.

"Would you happen to have a key?" Becca asked the woman, moving toward her. "Maybe we could find some clue to where she's gone."

The woman frowned. "I... well, yes. I do keep a spare, but I couldn't possibly—"

"Please," Becca pleaded. "We'll be in and out."

Becca paused.

"And maybe we could arrange for the payment of the rent she owed you in the meantime?"

This seemed to spark something in the woman's eyes, and her pursed lips slackened.

"It's twelve hundred," she said. "And I'll take next month's too in case she doesn't show."

Becca turned to look at me for confirmation.

Greedy old cunt.

I nodded.

"We can do that," Becca said.

The woman made a show of thinking it through before vanishing to find the key. She was back in less than five minutes, holding the key just out of Becca's reach.

I strode up to them, reaching into the inside pocket of my leather jacket for the short stack of bills there.

I counted out twelve hundred, packing the other four or five hundred back into the pocket.

"That's only one month," the woman protested.

"And you'll get the other month's rent when it's due," I told her. "And only if our being here today stays between us."

Her lips parted, perhaps finally recognizing me for who I was.

Maybe not my face or my name, but I needed neither to pull weight in Thorn Valley. My face screamed Saint, and if she knew what was good for her, she wouldn't refuse me.

She was lucky I played along at all instead of turning over her entire house to find the key myself.

"A-all right. That seems fair."

She backed away. "I'll just be inside if there's anything else you need. Just... just slip the key back through the mail slot when you're finished, will you?"

She didn't wait for a reply before taking off back the way she'd come.

"See," Becca said, lifting the key to dangle it in my direction. "I can be useful."

She dropped the key into my hand and took the blade back out from where she'd hidden it in her tits. How she'd managed to not slice one off was beyond me.

"Let's go, Hart. I'm already late getting back."

She hurried to keep up as I took the stairs two at a time, the feeling of unease only growing in the pit of my stomach the nearer we got to Julia's door.

Something was definitely wrong.

Julia knew the risks when she agreed to take this job.

Even with her identity concealed from the kids who called in for help, there was a possibility someone could figure out who she was. All it would take was one guilty child admitting who they called for help. One angry parent with a cop friend to trace the call back to her.

These were violent, sadistic pieces of abusive trash.

But having been abused herself as a teen, Julia knew the risks and didn't give two fucks about them. The way she saw it, if she could even help one of them out of a bad situation, it was worth it.

The smell hit us before I could finish feeding the key into the slot and I cursed, my nose wrinkling as I flicked the safety off my gun and pushed inside.

"Don't touch anything," I growled to Becca behind me.

"Oh god," she croaked, her voice nasally. No doubt plugging her nose. "What is that?"

I would know that smell anywhere. Flashes of time-tainted memory of my parents dead on the floor, their blood soaking into the carpets assaulted my mind.

I pushed through them, lifting the neckline of my t-shirt to cover my mouth and nose with my gun hand extended.

My eyes watered from the force of the odor, and I kicked past mail piled on the floor in front of her door and into the dusty apartment.

"*Christ, Julia,*" I hissed, knowing what I would find as I cautiously stepped through the kitchen, noting the upturned retro chair and the molding coffee in the antique mug on the table.

Everything in here was so outdated. Julia wasn't fucking around when she said she didn't need much. Everything in the whole place appeared to be thrifted if not dived for out of dumpsters. What the fuck did she do with all the money we paid her?

"Corvus," Becca said in a quiet voice behind me. "I-I don't think I can go in there."

"You wanted to come with me," I reminded her in a hushed tone. "Get over here. Stay close or I won't be able to protect you."

Her light feet rushed over, sticking to my ass like she was told.

"What *is* that?" she whined, choking on the smell no doubt coating her throat like it was coating mine.

There was only one thing it could be.

I peered through to the left and right, toward the open living room and bedroom, but nothing seemed amiss in either. Just more old furniture. Several stacks of yellowing paperbacks towering around her bed and filling the side tables.

In front of us were two doors. One no doubt led to a bathroom, but the other... the other would be her office. It was a stipulation of the job offer. She needed to have a separate office. One that could be locked. With a safe to keep her notes in and the ability to connect a landline phone.

I opened the door on the left.

Bathroom. Untouched.

Becca moved closer to my side. I couldn't hear her breathing anymore as I opened the other door, twisting the knob with two fingers before shoving it the rest of the way open.

I already knew what I'd find, but that didn't make it any easier to swallow.

"Fuck," I cursed, giving the room a quick once over before lowering my gun.

Behind me, Becca vomited on the floor, gripping on to my arm to keep herself from falling over.

I waited until she was finished and returned to standing.

The reek of her corpse was nearly enough to make me follow Becca's lead, but I'd smelled worse. Seen worse.

Though that didn't mean the gruesome picture of violence in front of us didn't unsettle the absolute fuck out of me.

Julia sat in the wooden chair in front of her wooden desk by the curtained window. Her head bent over a desk covered in scattered blank note paper. Motionless.

Her skin was tinted in shades of red and green, slipping in places where it should've been sedentary. But it wasn't the disgust of her corpse itself that made my stomach squeeze. It was the objects sticking out of her flesh. Hanging out now that time had worn her body down.

The sharp ends of pencils and pens and little silver bits I thought might've been paper clips.

A line of what looked like staples ran down the back of one of her arms.

But the piece de resistance, the cause of her death, appeared to be the cord from the ancient landline phone wrapped threefold around her thin neck, the skin bloated now around the tight beige coiled line.

"Oh my god, I just dumped my DNA all over this crime scene," Becca said, still trying to catch her breath from retching so hard.

"Don't worry about it," I told her, moving deeper into the small office space. "I'll be sending a clean up crew to take care of this. Cops won't touch it."

I noticed the safe to the side of the desk, open, papers spilling out. All Julia's notes on the kids who called. Meticulously taken by hand in black ink, areas highlighted, circled and underlined.

I nudged the safe closed with my foot and found blood on the dial.

Whoever did this forced her to open it.

I leaned over Julia, pressing my shirt harder into my mouth and nose to find the cord of the landline phone had been ripped from the wall.

Her cell phone was left on the desk. I tapped the screen, but it was dead. I picked it up and slipped it into my jacket's inner pocket, hoping there was something, anything on it that might lead us to the person responsible for this.

Maybe she'd started to type out a message to one of us. Or left a voice memo. Recorded the attack. *Something.*

Julia was smart, but was she that smart? Was she able to act that fast or had whoever did this snuck up on her?

My hand hovered over Julia's shoulder. I couldn't bring myself to touch her.

I let the hollow sadness of her loss fill me, but only for a second. She deserved for someone to grieve for her. She was only twenty-six and she had no family left that cared for her.

"I'm sorry," I whispered to her. "I'll find the person who did this and I'll make them pay."

I clenched my hand into a fist and lowered it.

"Make yourself useful," I told Becca. "Grab all those notes from the safe. Whoever did this will have taken the notes she had on them to avoid being caught."

"What?"

I forgot Becca didn't know about our humanitarian project.

There was a lot she didn't know.

Even more she shouldn't.

If she knew what was good for her, she would get the fuck out of dodge the instant Ava Jade came back. Maybe her friend could convince her to.

When I didn't answer her, she bent to her knees and began scraping the papers together, keeping as much of a distance from Julia's corpse as she could.

Once she had them all in a neat stack, she rose to her feet shakily and tucked them under her arm.

I checked the rest of the room for any other evidence, but my gaze kept falling back on Julia.

Something about her death, the nature of it, didn't sit right with me.

The assholes we visited vengeance on in Thorn Valley didn't seem capable of it.

They were drunks. Assholes. And one in maybe every fifty was truly unhinged, but all of those were dead.

Whoever did this appeared to be playing with her. Fuck, they turned her into a human fucking pin cushion. Sickly, it reminded me of something Rook could've done, though he never would've served this level of pain on an innocent person.

On a monster, sure.

But not to a girl like Julia.

Not on purpose.

And this was *very* fucking purposeful.

There was something here, and I was missing it.

"Corv," Becca said, gagging again. "Can we go?"

"What's that?"

"What's what?"

My brows furrowed at the rough scrape in the dark wood desk beneath a sheet of the note paper next to Julia's head.

I pushed the sheet of paper out of the way and found the carved line in the wood had a curve to it.

Quickly, I began to tear the sheets of paper from the surface of the desk, revealing jagged lettering carved into its surface.

"Sorry, Julia," I uttered, lifting her heavy head off the desk to hang back in her chair. A smear of her putrefied remains clung to the pages, gluing them to the surface of the desk, and I had to scrape them free, swallowing the taste of bile as it rose up the back of my throat.

I swiped what remained from the desk with my forearm and stood back to read the message left for me.

No, not for me.

For *us*.

No more carrion for the Crows

Below the hastily scratched in text were smaller letters. A signature.

I roared, rage singing in my veins, exploding in my eyes, tinting my vision red as I flipped the desk and spun, storming out of the office and through the kitchen, back to the front door. To the air I needed to get a hold on myself.

My fingers curled around the wooden banister, flexing the old wood to the point of snapping as I pushed the rage down. Swallowed it back.

Controlled it.

Control it.

"C-Corvus?" Becca hedged, hovering in the apartment. "What did it say?"

I whirled on her, taking the papers from under her arm, making her yelp as I threw them back into the apartment. "We don't need those," I seethed. "I know who did this."

5

ROOK

Maverick and a small group of his men entered the underground fight club, chins raised like the Kings they thought they were. Mav went straight for Dies, his hand extended, a carefully placed grin on his lips.

"A righteous win, St. Crow," Mav said. "My boys and I just finished sweeping the area west of Spirit Lake. None escaped."

Dies nodded, continuing the pre-meeting conversation with Maverick. Going over which areas specifically Mav and his men covered as well as several other things that needed to be seen to.

I spied Drake beside his leader and caught his eye.

He lifted his chin in greeting, excusing himself from Mav's side to come over to the edge of the room near the bar where Grey and I sat at one of the high top tables. The three chairs already occupied by both of us and my bum fucking leg.

I wouldn't be moving it for Drake's ass, either.

"Hey," he said, waving the bartender Dies called on short notice behind the bar for a beer. "Heard anything from your girl, yet?"

He pushed his sandy blond hair away from his forehead, leaning over the table to look between us.

"Nothing," Grey said, his tone clipped.

Drake shook his head. "I don't get it. I searched the entire Deadwood for her. She couldn't have gotten that far on foot."

"Wouldn't surprise me if she jacked one of the Kings' cars or bikes," I put in, also waving to the bartender for a whiskey.

Her jaw clenched and she stilled, brown eyes jerking between my father across the room and me.

"I'm only supposed to give you water," she said tensely after a second.

I ran my tongue over my teeth, sending Dies a glare.

Did he *want* me to take the painkillers?

Because taking away the only thing dulling the aching in my leg would've made most people turn to the drugs as the only other viable option for fucking pain management. As it was, antibiotics were all I was allowed, though I doubted those would work if I drank too much, either.

"Make you a deal sweetheart," I told her with a wicked smirk. "You give me two fingers of whiskey, neat, and I'll drink all the water you put on this table."

She grimaced, hesitating before pulling down that good Canadian rye whiskey I liked from the top shelf and pouring it into a short glass.

"Atta girl."

"Thanks," Drake muttered after the bartender dropped the drinks off at the table, including two brimming glasses of water next to my whiskey.

"If you haven't heard from her at all by now..." He trailed off, pursing his lips.

"*What?*" Grey growled.

"Well, I mean, she's probably gone for good then, yeah? Maybe this life wasn't for her after all—"

Grey tensed, but it was me who acted, dragging Drake across the table by his jacket, making the zipper done all the way up to his throat come partially undone.

"*You don't know what you're fucking talking about,*" I seethed, seeing something in his blue eyes tighten, the fear I was used to seeing reflected back at me absent.

He gripped the hand knotted in his jacket and pried it off, keeping eye contact. "I'm not your enemy, man," he said. "I didn't mean anything by it. Just... if she still isn't back, then where is she?"

Neither of us could answer that and instead of savoring my whiskey like I planned to, I downed it in one, baring my teeth at the glorious burn chasing the darkness back down my throat.

Behind Drake, Mav and Dies seemed to have begun the formal meeting, sitting opposite one another in the long table Dies had brought down and placed just next to the fighting ring. Pinkie sat next to Dies where Corvus would've been sitting if he'd made it back in time and three other seats sat empty on the right of the table.

Mav's men sat next to him, one empty seat near the edge of the table remained, and I assumed it was meant for Drake. I hadn't realized he was part of Mav's main men.

"Here," Drake offered, jerking his head. "Let me help you."

I snarled angrily, hating that I needed to be helped to my fucking seat like some goddamned senior citizen.

"I'm good," I retorted, nostrils flaring as I eased my leg down from the chair and went to take a step and nearly fell on my face as all the blood drained from my upper body to congregate in my leg, filling it so it felt near bursting.

"*Fucking hell*," I ground out, clutching the table.

"Come on, big guy," I barely heard Drake say as he dragged one of my arms over his shoulder and Grey took my other arm, leading us all to the table for the meet.

They deposited me in my chair next to Pinkie, and I sniffed, catching the scent of Pinkie's rum and Coke on the table in front of him.

I slid it over to myself, giving him a warning look when he opened his mouth to protest. He rolled his eyes, staying silent like a good Pinkie Pie.

"We all know why this meet was called," Mav began, and I studied him over the rim of my drink as I sipped away.

He was a big guy. At least two-twenty, most of it muscle, with tattoos up the right side of his neck and a teardrop tat beneath his right eye that looked pretty sick in combination with the word *SUBMIT* scribbled above his brow.

But I'd pegged him as a weak ally from the first moment I'd seen him.

His men were a different story—some of them were true warriors, but this guy? He looked the part but that was where it ended. Underneath that jerky gaze and all those pounds of muscle was a man who had no fucking idea what he was doing.

He lacked the confidence a man in his position should have. Lacked the sort of vicious bearing he needed to properly lead a gang of his size.

It was a wonder he'd managed for as many years as he had.

"We do," Diesel agreed. "But I'll hear your concerns properly voiced all the same."

Mav nodded, his gaze slipping to his men down the table beside him. "I need to know what this win means for our alliance."

I tuned them out, playing with the condensation on my glass, the alcohol working against me now. My vision blurred, and I shook my head sharply, regaining focus.

Unlike my brothers, I hadn't had the luxury of passing out from my wounds, and I couldn't fucking sleep until my Ghost was back where she belonged.

"Can I get some fucking food," I piped up, shouting across the space to the bartender, interrupting the pointless talks going on at the table.

Diesel eyed me, and I lifted a brow. "What?"

They went on with their conversation, and I sat back in my chair, ignoring Grey's quiet pleas to get my attention with his elbow jamming into my ribs.

"I'm fine," I hissed at him, finishing the cocktail only to get a bit more sugar into my bloodstream.

"We'd like to offer for the alliance to continue," Diesel said. "We have the arms connections you need and you have the clientele we need to get rid of the last of our smack. Besides, not having to circumvent Lennox to get to our arms dealers would save us a fuckload of time and resources."

Mav nodded as Diesel spoke, and I ripped the corn nuts from the bartender's hands as she brought them to the table, tearing into the packaging to dump the contents into my mouth.

"We accept," Mav said, like we all knew he would. He'd be an idiot to turn down Diesel's offer. And Dies would be the even bigger fool not to have offered for the alliance to continue in the face of our current losses.

"This isn't a permanent situation," Diesel added. "We'll continue the alliance on a trial basis. Temporary. For now."

It was the *for now* that gave Mav the hope he needed to conclude this meeting with any measure of triumph. A permanent alliance with the Saints would cement him and his gang among the top predators of this great nation. It wouldn't be given or won so easily.

Mav nodded again, slowly, to show he understood.

I nudged Dies, and his jaw ticked.

"There's one more thing, a condition of this alliance's continuance."

"A condition?" Mav repeated, his brows pulling together, gaze slipping down the table again, making me wonder if he was the one calling the shots here or if they formed more of a council between the four of them seated at the table.

I put a cigarette to my lips, cursing as I flicked my zippo and nothing but sparks came out.

"Your man, *Aries*."

Surprise registered in Mav's eyes, but he didn't reply.

"We have reason to believe he may have less than honorable intent toward one of my Saints."

I flicked again, a tremor of annoyance scraping up the back of my skull.

"How so?"

Diesel set his jaw again. He didn't have to explain himself to Mav, and it seemed, in this case, he wouldn't. It was a power move. He wanted to see if Mav would fight him on it or if he would bend, giving Diesel what he wanted without him having to work for it.

"What do you want with him?" Maverick asked after an uncomfortable silence.

A lighter slid noisily across the table between us and I glanced up to see Drake had tossed me his. I gave him a nod, abandoning mine as I lifted his to light my smoke, finding a set of initials engraved in the worn silver surface.

I inhaled greedily, shoving the lighter back across to him, catching a mean side eye from Diesel that asked me without the need for words if I was fucking finished.

I nodded.

"I want you to call him in," Diesel continued his conversation with

Mav. "Me and my boys would like to have a little… *conversation*… with him."

"What sort of conversation?"

"The kind where I will determine whether a man like him has a place allied to my crew."

"And if he doesn't?"

The silence carried with it the threat no one needed spoken.

If Aries turned out to be the monster my Ghost thought him to be, there was nowhere on this earth he would be safe from us.

Fuck, I would be just as likely to chase his ass to hell and torment him for the rest of his miserable fucking afterlife too.

Maverick glanced at his men at the table once again before nodding to Diesel. "I'd gladly give him up to you for your questioning," Maverick said, sighing even though his body only grew more tense. "But we haven't seen Aries in a few days. We thought he might've been spooked knowing it was going to come to a firefight with the Aces. I told my men it would be all hands on deck for the fight. Even his sorry ass. The kid's better with corpses than he is with the living."

Diesel visibly tensed. He wasn't all right with this answer.

"I don't give a fuck where he is. He's your man, and I want him. Find him and bring him here, or I'll be forced to reconsider our position."

Mav bit the inside of his cheek.

If he wanted to keep his fucking head, he should be saying *yes fucking sir*, right now.

"I think I can find him, Mav," Drake said from down the table. "I know where he likes to hang out. Let me take a couple guys. We should be able to get a hold of him pretty quick."

Mav nodded, visibly relieved. "Will that satisfy?" he asked Diesel.

"For now," Diesel deadpanned, and I stubbed out my cigarette, glad to be done with this bullshit.

The thunder of steps rushing down the stairs from the street entrance interrupted the tepid silence and as one, Saint and King alike stood, guns out.

All except for my ass.

It was Corv.

Obviously.

But that didn't mean I didn't also hear the urgency in his hurried steps. Or that it didn't coil something tightly in my gut, souring the meager snack I'd just managed to choke down.

My fist clenched beneath the table as he burst into the room, the door banging like a gunshot against the opposite wall as he stormed through. His eyes laser focused as they found Diesel. Us next to him.

"A *word*," Corvus snarled, his face a battlefield of barely contained rage. I'd never seen him this wound up. He didn't let anyone see him like this. Control was his mountain, and he never gave up the climb.

"Thought you were too busy to join us, Son," Diesel said smoothly, thumbing the safety back on his gun before tucking it away. The Kings opposite us sat, all except Drake, who looked like he was ready to go to war if only Corvus would give the order.

Maybe we'd keep him once this alliance came to its inevitable end.

"*Diesel*," Corvus all but yelled, his teeth bared.

"Excuse me for just a moment, would you, gentlemen?" Diesel said, giving Corvus a warning look as he caught my ass when I tried to stand and dragged my arm over his shoulder.

Corvus stalked through the club to a barrage of whispers from our guests, not stopping until we were all through to the back room where our guys counted the cash from fight nights.

Grey closed the door behind us all once we were inside.

"Interrupting a sanctioned meeting, Corv—" Dies began but Corvus laid a glare on him so heavy it made our adopted father stop whatever he was about to say.

"What happened?" he demanded instead. "Are you hurt? Where's the girl?"

Corvus paced the small space, throwing a fist through his hair. His face all sharp angles. "She's fine," he said. "She's upstairs."

"Then what the fuck—" I started but Corvus continued, talking over me.

"We found Julia," he said, a hollow laugh on his lips. "Dead. Dead for fucking weeks."

"She answered the phones, right? She had to know there would be risks with that job."

The dark parts of me flickered within, aching for retribution for the taking of a life that was *ours* to protect.

"How?" I demanded.

"She died badly."

Then so would the person who did it.

But that didn't explain why Corv was so riled up. He didn't give a fuck about anyone outside this room save for Ava Jade. Not really. Not in any way that would get him this fired up.

"That's not the worst part, is it?" Grey asked, catching on only a second after I did.

Corv stopped pacing, his head bent as he shook it, still trying to regain control. "It was him," he said, his voice so low I wondered if I heard him right.

"What?" Diesel pressed. "Who?"

"He left his fucking signature," Corv replied. "*No more carrion for the Crows,*" he added with another dark laugh. Signed *Crow Killer.*"

Fire. Liquid fire raced through my veins, and I ached to spread it. Spread it so vastly that everything would burn. Every tree. Every car. Every motherfucking building. Leaving him no place to hide from me.

"Wait, this was the stalker?" Diesel asked, his gaze jerking back and forth, not really seeing anything as he thought it through.

I stood, unable to sit anymore as the animal inside awoke, on the prowl.

"Rook, sit the fuck down," Diesel said, reaching for me, but I smacked his hand away.

"*Don't,*" I warned at the same time Corvus growled, "*Leave him.*"

"*AJ,*" Grey's soft whisper somehow managed to cut through all the shouting and my eldest brother and I froze in place.

I met Grey's eye, and it was like all the breath was snatched from my lungs.

My Ghost.

What if...

"We need to find her," Grey said in a rush. "We need to find her *now.*"

"Hold up, now," Diesel started. "This doesn't mean anything. You said yourself this happened weeks ago."

"I don't give a fuck what I said," Corvus replied. "Grey is right. We can't wait any more. *Fuck!* We shouldn't have waited at all."

Diesel thought through the problem, his one worry showing

through the careful mask he always wore. "All right. We bring this to the table. Get the guys on it. All of them. Yeah?"

I didn't like the idea of bringing the Kings into this, but it made sense to get as much help as we could. The more people looking, the faster we would be likely to find her.

Even if the dark beast within whispered that we didn't need any help. That we would be the one to find her. To eviscerate this filth so slowly that he would be pushed to madness before he would finally die.

"Yeah," Grey agreed.

"Yeah," Corvus put in.

Diesel waited for my word. I gave him a nod.

"I'll go with Drake," Grey offered. "He was going to put together a small team to try to find Aries. That's who AJ thought it was. It's as good a place as any to start looking."

"Fine," Corv said. "Then Rook and I will lead two other teams."

"Rook can't lead anyone right now," Diesel said. "I can—"

"The fuck I can't," I barked. "Corv will lead a team to search all the locations she could be. I'll lead a patrol team. You drive, I'll ride shotty. I want at least five cars on the streets until she's found. We'll connect with the radios. Divide into wards for patrol."

Diesel's mouth tightened, but he nodded. "All right. That'll work." He sighed. "So much for fucking resting, huh boys?"

"Rest is for the weak," Grey said.

"I'll rest when I'm dead," I added.

Corvus chewed his bottom lip, lifting his icy eyes to ours. "I'll rest when our girl is home and not a fucking second sooner."

We all moved to leave, the pain in my leg seeming to have leveled out to a static hum of discomfort after the crescendo of pain earlier. Good. I'd need to be able to walk. To run.

To fucking *chase* if I needed to.

"Ugh, fuck, wait," Corv said, making us pause. "What about Rebecca?"

"What about her?" I asked.

"The fuck do we do with her if everyone's out looking for Sparrow?"

She'd want to come, but judging by the look on Diesel's face he wasn't keen to involve her any more than we already had. We didn't need to tango with Mr. Hart if anything happened to his precious daughter.

Although... I'd never sampled the fear of a blue blood.

"She can stay here for now if she wishes," Diesel said finally. "But our protection ends there. She doesn't need it anymore. The Aces are dead and with them her boyfriend. If she's ready, send her home."

"Who's going to tell her?" Corvus asked, at his limit for patience.

Grey sighed behind me. "I'll do it."

I slapped a hand on his shoulder. He really was the best of us. In more ways than one.

6

AVA JADE

I ran through the dappled moonlight, my bare feet flying over uneven terrain. A laugh grew in my chest, and I couldn't fully contain it as it slipped past my lips. I'd missed this.

The sensation of flying as the still-warm Cali night air coursed over my body, twisting and braiding my long hair into a tangle. The exertion. The burn in my legs. So potent. So fucking perfect.

Another laugh escaped.

Shit.

They'd hear me.

My pursuers were close behind me, but they'd never catch me, not unless I wanted them to. And honestly? I did want them to. But I had to at least make them work for it, right?

I stopped dead, craning my neck to listen. I could hear them, but barely. They were still *way* the fuck back there. Damn tortoises.

"You want me?" I shouted, breathless, my hand curling into fists as more laughter ached for freedom from my lungs. "Come and get me, fuckers!"

A grunt somewhere far off, close to the Nest we'd all started this race from. Corvus. He was catching up.

A wicked idea curved my lips into a twisted smile, and I started running again, tugging my tank top off to discard it on the forest floor behind me.

My bra went next and I sucked in a breath at the sensation of the warm air rushing over my nipples, turning them to hard pebbles as my breasts bounced almost painfully.

I slowed to a hop to get my shorts off, tossing those behind me, too, leaving a trail for them to find.

My panties were already wet with anticipation as I pulled them off, running ass naked through the dark trees between the Nest and Briar Hall.

"*Sparrow,*" Corvus growled in the distance, angry as he found my clothes. I roared with laughter, pushing my legs harder. I didn't think I'd ever run faster, with nothing between me and the air. Nothing between me and the sky. If I just spread my arms and closed my eyes, I was willing to bet good money I could straight up fucking fly.

I closed my eyes, relishing the feeling.

When I opened them again, I recognized the small space coming up through the trees. I'd run through it tens of times since Grey and I shared our first kiss here. It was perfect.

I peered over my shoulder and slowed, waiting for them to catch me.

The anticipation sent little shivers rushing all over the surface of my skin, made the space between my legs hot, pulsing with an electric need that sent currents racing up through my belly.

The crash of footfalls got louder in my ears and my breathing picked up to an uneven, heavy pace, my eyes narrowing to slits.

Corvus' dark shadow wove through the trees, bursting into the space where I stood, naked in the moonlight.

He skidded to a stop, his light blue eyes catching in the silver light like reflective glass as he stared at me. Hungry like an animal who'd just sighted its prey.

The others were right behind him; Grey and Rook appeared through the dense foliage at the same time, rushing up to stand to either side of Corvus. Rook's lips parted as he caught his breath, his dark eyes devouring every inch of my body.

Grey licked his lips, his shoulders rising and falling, hands in hard fists at his sides.

"Well…" I beckoned, pulling my lower lip in between my teeth. "What are you waiting for?"

A vicious growl left Rook's lips as he stalked forward, not stopping until all the space between us had been annihilated. He twisted his fist into my hair, jerking my chin up until my lips had nowhere else they could go but to meet his in a feral kiss.

My heart twisted in my chest, and I let out a little moan of surprise, jerking as a hand that was not Rook's ran down the length of my spine, making my back arch.

Feather-light kisses trailed over the ridge of my shoulders from behind, turning harder, more insistent, until they weren't kisses at all, but bites. Hard bites that would leave marks for days to come.

I moaned, and Rook bit my lower lip, adding to the pleasure pain mix only to lick the pain away a moment later, diving into my mouth with his wicked tongue as though he could inhale my soul.

Hands wrapped around my ribs, reaching between Rook and me to find my breasts. They squeezed, rolling my nipples between the pads of thumb and index finger.

"*More*," I managed between fevered kisses.

I wanted them to use me until I was so spent they had to carry my ass back to the nest.

"*More*," I demanded a second time, pulling roughly away from Rook to look him in the eyes. He needed to know I meant business.

"Tell me what you want, Ghost," he said, lips swollen from our kiss, eyes so black I could fall into them and never come out again. "And it's yours."

"You," I said on a breath, grabbing Grey's hand on my breast. "And you," I told him, spinning until I found Corvus standing just a few feet away, his hand pawing at the erection begging for release from his jeans. "And you."

"That's a lot of cock, AJ. Sure you can handle it?" Grey crooned against the base of my neck, making me shudder.

I nodded. I never backed down from a challenge.

I yelped as Corvus lifted me high, tossing me over his shoulder. The yelp turning to a laugh as he spanked my ass. "Not hard enough?" he asked.

He spanked me again, and I jerked against his shoulder, the breath rushing out of me.

"That's a good girl."

My head spun as he threw me forward, catching me before I could fly into the dirt. I noticed the fallen tree he'd brought me to. No doubt to fuck me on, but I wanted to taste him first.

I immediately fell to my knees, unbuckling his jeans, letting that magnificent cock free. I took him into my mouth, the warm salty taste of him sliding over my tongue.

He groaned, his palm pressing on the back of my skull. "That's it," he said. "Open that throat for me."

I did as I was told and he pushed in deeper, his tight ass muscles flexing against my hands as he filled my throat, holding himself there until I choked on him. Choosing his cock over air.

Corvus barely waited for me to catch my breath before driving into my mouth again, fucking my tight little throat until it was raw.

Out of the corner of my eye, I found Grey striding over, his shorts discarded somewhere, his cock in his hand. Stroking himself.

The sight made my pussy quake, and I moaned on Corvus' cock, making him curse.

I reached for Grey, wanting to touch him. He obliged, pressing his cock into my hand. I pumped him, rubbing my thumb over that sensitive spot just below the tip on his underside. He shook in my hand, tipping his head back to close his eyes.

Corvus' cock popped free of my lips, and he dragged me to Grey. "Open," he said and I did, letting Corvus push my mouth onto Grey's cock.

I found Corvus' massive length again, stroking him while I let Grey have his turn in my mouth. But there was someone missing.

Rook lifted my ass, forcing me to balance on my knees as he reached between my legs, finding my wetness.

The first stroke raced through me like fire and I bucked, whimpering.

The flick of a blade opening made me sharply aware of everything around me, something in my chest tightening in a way that only Rook could untie.

Rook pressed his palm flat against the base of my spine, trying to keep my lower body still. He removed his fingers from their teasing stroked between my legs only long enough to flick open a small cut on my hip.

I sucked in a breath, only managing to inhale Grey's cock even further at the sting.

"More," I tried to say around Grey's cock, never relenting my pumping of Corvus' with my right hand.

Little flicks of the knife opened shallow wounds curving around the bone of my hip. I didn't realize what he was doing until he was nearly finished.

Grey pulled out of my mouth, and I took the opportunity to crane my neck backward, finding Rook admiring his handiwork. The name *Rook* bled against my moonlit skin, and I hoped he'd cut deep enough for it to scar because it was the most beautiful tattoo I could even imagine having.

"It's perfect," I said, voice hoarse.

"Enough of this," Corvus growled, snapping at Grey as he indicated the fallen tree. "Sit."

Grey's brows furrowed, but he did as he was told, sitting on the rough bark.

"Ready, Sparrow?"

I nodded, letting Corvus lift me from my knees, Rook following suit.

The sound of tearing fabric rushed in my ears, and I clenched my teeth as a strip of Rook's black t-shirt pressed against the fresh cuts in my hip, and he fastened it tightly into place to stop the bleeding.

"You said you wanted all of us," Rook whispered against my neck, biting the skin beneath my ear.

"You say that like it's a threat..." I trailed off, letting them see that it was the exact opposite.

"Step back, Sparrow."

I did, feeling Grey's hands wrap around my middle, drawing me onto him from behind. "Give me your ass, AJ."

The tiny hairs on my arms rose as I held myself up, letting him slowly work himself into my ass until I was grimacing at the initial pain and how it evened out to a glorious sort of fullness that I knew would only grow.

I used Grey's thighs to prop myself up, opening my legs for one of the others to enter me from the front.

Fear skated down my spine, but nowhere near as great as the dizzying drug of ecstasy pulsing in my blood, making my vision blur at the edges.

I tipped my head back as Grey adjusted himself inside me, getting even deeper. Strong arms wrapped around mine, pulling them back, securing them. Grey trapped me against his body, and I laid my head against his shoulder.

My greedy cunt throbbed, waiting for Corvus.

"What are you waiting for?" I all but growled, unable to handle another second of the anticipation.

Why was he making me wait?

I squinted into the dark to find him and something in my belly tightened, setting me on edge.

He... was fully dressed again.

So was Rook.

The pressure of Grey's cock thrust deep in my ass vanished, and I felt the textured fabric of denim against my bare ass. But still, he held me against him, not allowing me to move.

Corvus' eyes seemed to glow in the dark as he watched me, not with a hungry passion, but with something far more sinister.

What...

Somewhere, the sound of something dripping reached my ears and each little slap of water sent my heart into a faster rhythm.

Something wasn't right.

"Grey?"

I struggled to pull my arms free.

"Grey, let me go."

My pulse pounded in my ears.

"Rook?"

"Corvus?"

I glanced between them, between their shadows.

They were the monsters in the dark again, but this time I didn't want them to chase me. Had no desire for them to catch me.

"Step into the light," I shouted at them, needing to see their faces. Needing to make sure it was them.

That it wasn't…

Corvus moved first, taking two strong steps into the light.

I frowned, trying to make sense of the pained expression on his face. At the rage in his eyes, barely contained.

"What happe—"

I gasped, seeing the blooming rose of fresh blood turning his gray shirt a wet red just above his waistline. Blood poured from the wound, darkening the denim of his jeans, draining all the color from his face.

"C-Corvus?"

His upper lip curled into a sneer, and when he tried to take another step forward, he nearly collapsed, catching himself on the thick branch of a tree to hold himself up.

No.

Rook emerged from the dark and into the moonlight like the ghost he named me for, his face pale. But on his second step, he fell to one knee, a sort of anger I'd never seen from him before shaping his face into someone I couldn't recognize. He held my gaze, radiating hate as I began to notice the wounds in his leg. The gaping bullet holes, leaking blood so black it couldn't have been human.

"He'll never walk right again," Corvus rasped, looking so faint it made my heart nearly stop.

Something warm dripped on my shoulder, and I jerked my head away from Grey, twisting my neck until I could see him. See the garish wound where his eye used to be. The blood dripping down his perfect face, carving lines of darkest crimson against the pale skin of his cheek.

I screamed, the adrenaline in my veins giving me the feral strength I needed to pull out of his grasp. "No!"

I fell onto my front in the dirt, my chin and breasts scraping against the rough ground.

"No, no, no," I muttered, scrambling to get to my feet.

"Yes, *Sparrow*," Corvus hissed, his nickname for me a poisonous threat on his lips as he shoved me back down until I tasted dirt.

"Your fault," Grey added, and a booted foot collided with my rib cage, stealing all the breath from my lungs.

"Your fault!" Another kick and I coughed, seeing stars.

"*Your fault.*"

A great stabbing pain in my back made me scream, and the rush of blood leaking from the wound made me lightheaded.

I tried to stand, but something solid as a rock collided with my jaw, sending me back down, making my vision go dark. Making sound come to me slower. Muffled.

A gun cocked.

Through double vision, I watched him lift the gun. Watched The Bone Man's jaw clench until he looked like the skeleton I first fell in love with. Before I knew who he was.

"I won't let you hurt us anymore," he promised me, and I closed my eyes when he pressed the barrel of the gun to my forehead.

"It's okay," I told him. "Do it. I'm ready."

My darkness swirled, but I pushed her down.

Hush.

It's us or them.

"Goodbye, Sparrow."

"I'm sorry."

A loud *bang!* rang in my ears, and I tried to make sense of my surroundings.

Not a dark forest.

Bright. So fucking bright.

Heaven?

I groaned, rolling over to vomit onto the cold cement floor, my head spinning as my lungs struggled to fill enough to eradicate the fog shrouding my thoughts.

My eyes adjusted to the light, and I stared at my naked tits, my lips parting as I struggled to make sense of them. Make sense of anything.

My skin tingled everywhere it touched the floor, and everywhere it didn't. My throat burned with bile, but I managed to keep the next bout of nausea from turning up anything more I didn't have to give to the floor.

The hollowness in my stomach felt like an expanding universe. A black hole that would consume me if I didn't try to fill it.

Not heaven.

Hell.

I was in hell.

I scraped myself to a seated position against the wall, swiping the back of my hand over my lips only for my arm to fall back heavily to my lap. The drugs in my system not allowing me more than the tiniest of movements without a massive amount of effort.

Blinking, I noticed the bandage wrapped around my leg and willed myself to feel the pain of the wound there, but there was nothing.

Numb.

I was numb and utterly naked save for that bandage.

My eyes burned and my lips tightened, but I would *not* fucking cry. The bastard that stuck me in this cell didn't deserve to see that.

Vivid imagery from what my mind cooked up in my sleep assaulted me. How good it felt to have them. To touch them. To be touched by them.

How those touches soured. Turned violent. How it hurt.

How badly it fucking *hurt*.

I rolled my head to the left, finding the door to my cell.

It looked different, and I felt my brows try to furrow. Twitch instead.

It looked different because it was different. Drake had replaced the old door with a new one. One with a small plate glass window in the top so he could look in. And a slot near the bottom.

Things rested against the spotless cement floor there. A saturated paper bowl filled with something gray that I thought was porridge. Wedges of peeled orange on another paper plate, partially dried up from sitting too long. A paper cup.

My stomach ached at the sight, and I squeezed my eyes tight, ignoring the pain.

I couldn't eat that.

Who fucking knew what he put in it.

But...

Much longer without any food or water and I'd be useless no matter what.

And eventually... eventually I wouldn't be here at all.

I dragged myself over to the food, lifting a piece of orange to my nose, trying to smell the presence of drugs like Rook could.

I smelled only the pithy scent of orange peel and the juice waiting beneath. The porridge would be easy to spike. So would the small cup of water. But the oranges?

It was the best bet.

That's what I kept telling myself as I stuffed each sliver into my mouth, one after another, until they were all gone and I was licking the remnants of their juice from my fingertips.

I became aware of the drip dripping sound somewhere outside the cell again, and heat spread across my back, fizzling out under the pressure of the drugs in my system before annoyance could turn to rage.

I threw the bowl of porridge at the door. The congealed mixture ran down the stainless steel in clumps. "*Shut up,*" I hollered, pressing my palms to my ears, the back of my head against the floor. My skin tightened with gooseflesh against the cold concrete and I tried harder than I ever tried anything not to think about the fact that I've been naked in this room for fuck knew how long.

Not just naked, but passed out. Drugged.

Everything looked the same, but that didn't mean he didn't touch me.

My stomach rebelled against the orange slices, and I swallowed hard to keep them down.

I gasped, removing my hands from my ears at the sound of something else. Something new.

The dripping was still there, but.

"Hello?" I called tentatively, dragging my half numb ass closer to the door. "Is someone out there?"

I pressed my ear to a spot not coated in porridge, waiting.

Nothing.

I banged the side of my fist against the door. "Hey!"

A whisper, too close, filled my ears. Indeterminate. A string of word-like sounds that my sluggish mind couldn't make sense of.

"No."

I shook my head, pulling my knees to my chest to hug them close, pressing my head between them. There wasn't anyone outside.

It's just the drugs, I told myself when another indistinct whisper filled my ears despite them being firmly cut off by my knees. *Not real.*

I was *not* going crazy.

I wasn't.

7

GREY

Becca sat rigidly in a stool at the bar upstairs, staring at something on her phone that made tension radiate up her arms. She sighed, all but tossing her phone face down on the bar in favor of the glass of clear liquid I didn't think was water.

"Hey."

She jumped as I dragged out the stool next to her.

"I-I swear I'm going to pay for this," she stammered, indicating the vodka. "I just lost my wallet somewhere at the Docks and—"

"Becca, I don't give a fuck about the vodka, drink as much as you want."

Her cheekbones flared, but she nodded. "I just wanted the one. To take the edge off, you know?"

"Corv said it was bad."

"She was... until the Docks, I'd never seen a dead person you know. Well, not unless you count my mom, but they had her all made-up and pumped full of whatever the fuck they put in dead people to make them look alive at a wake. Julia was way worse than the Aces at the Docks. She died badly."

She was rambling, and she realized it before I could say anything, sighing before she sipped the vodka, her hands trembling slightly.

844

"What were you looking at just now?" I asked her. "Before I came up here."

Becca shook her head, snorting derisively. "Nothing from Ava Jade if that's what you're thinking."

It was hard to keep the disappointment off my face, but it was clear whatever it was upset her. If AJ were here, she'd ask her friend what was wrong. I didn't have a lot of time, but after all the shit Becca had had to endure over the past few months, deserved or not, I owed her at least a few minutes of my time.

"What was it?"

She bit the inside of her cheek, flipping her phone over to flick open the screen and slide it over to me.

On the screen was an open email. An acceptance letter to CalArts. No, it was a scholarship. As if Becca Hart needed scholarship money.

I'd all but forgotten her love of art. She was leagues better than me and my notebook scratchings. Her talent was probably what had gotten her in.

"Congrats."

"A couple months ago, I would have been over the fucking moon if I saw this. Now, I just... I don't *feel* anything." She sipped her vodka. "Doesn't matter anyway. I'm going to tell them to give the scholarship to someone else. My dad would never let me go. He expects me to follow in his footsteps. Already has an in for me at fucking MIT."

"But that isn't you."

"Tell him that."

She finished her drink and set the glass down, fixing me with a hard stare. "So?"

I lifted a brow.

"You didn't come up here to talk to me about potential colleges. What's up? Corvus didn't speak to me at all on the way back here, but I could tell something was up."

I reached over the bar to grab a glass and fill it with OJ from the hose, needing some sugar in my system before I crashed.

"We're going to look for AJ."

She sagged in relief. "Thank fuck. When do we go?"

I fixed her with a look.

"When you say *we?*"

I licked my dry lips. "I mean the Saints."

"I can help. You *know* I can."

I nodded, mostly to myself, because she probably could. She'd just seen a mangled body and was still here. Waiting to be helpful. Becca was more than I ever gave her credit for, and I was starting to see what AJ probably saw in her friend. Someone much stronger than met the eye.

"This is Saint business," I started, trying to hold a gentle tone. The one I used when I needed to do the sweet talking Corvus and Rook weren't always capable of. "And since your Ace is dead now, you no longer need our protection."

She stiffened at that. "How do you know?"

"They're all dead, Becca. We triple checked. And we don't think any got away."

She shook her head, swallowing before she spoke again, pushing the curtain of long straight hair back behind her ear. "I looked at every face, Grey."

"What?"

"When one of the Saints led me out of the Docks. I *made myself* look at every face. Every bloody, awful dead face. I didn't see him. What if he's still out there?"

She pressed her hands between her knees, shoulders drawing in until she looked very small.

"It's not possible."

"Isn't it?" she all but snapped. "He wasn't there."

I had to admit, it was odd, and kudos to her for being able to look at so much death and still be sitting here mostly stable. But her guy had to be dead. We left none alive, and Mav said himself they'd checked for any who might've escaped.

"All right," I said decisively. "Then I'll send you back to Briar Hall with a guard."

"I want to help."

"You will be helping. If you're at Briar Hall, we won't have to do rounds checking the academy. That way if AJ shows up you can call us."

She looked like she wanted to argue some more but also knew I wasn't wrong. And she wasn't going to get what she wanted this time no matter how hard she pushed.

"I guess."

Something scratched at the back of my mind, and I struggled to grasp it, remembering what Becca did to get herself tangled up in all of this to begin with.

Her boyfriend.

Her Ace boyfriend who she swears wasn't among the dead at the Docks.

One of them is staying with her *tonight at Briar Hall,* Becca said in Diesel's recordings.

I could text her *to find out.*

My mind raced, trying to recall the exact words.

I just don't see how feeding you information on my friend *is going to help you do all that.*

"Becca?"

"Yeah?"

"Your Ace boyfriend—"

"He's *not* my boyfriend."

"You said you had no pictures of him."

A knot formed between her brows. "I already told you that, he wouldn't let me take any. I gave Diesel his description and everything else I knew."

I waved off her concern, ignoring the defensive tone.

"Did he ask about Ava Jade a lot?"

Her jaw clenched. "He asked about all of you."

"Yes, but did he ask about *her* specifically?"

"*Ow.*"

I released her wrist, not even realizing I'd grabbed it or how my knuckles were white against her perfectly tanned skin. "Sorry," I muttered. "Becca, I need you to answer the question."

Becca rubbed her wrist, thinking. "I mean, yeah, but that was because she was a direct line to you three."

"Was it?" I asked, the question more for myself than her.

She opened her mouth to say something, but I stopped her with a look. "You're absolutely sure you didn't see him among the fallen at the Docks?"

She nodded slowly, going pale. "You don't actually think that Jericho and Ava Jade's stalker are..."

"I don't know," I admitted. "But it fucking tracks, doesn't it?"

I bit my lip, trying to connect the dots even though the pain in my fractured skull was reaching a breaking point. It was usually the others who figured out shit like this. The chances that *I* realized something this monumental before either of them were slim to none.

It could've been nothing.

It could be everything.

To find this guy and crush him once and for all.

"You don't have any pictures," I repeated.

"I already told you—"

"I wasn't finished. You don't have any pictures, but you're an artist. Can you draw him? Paint him?"

Her expression soured, but I could tell she would do it. No matter how much it would repulse her. "I can."

My fingernails dug into my palm. Why hadn't we thought to ask her to do that before?

Oh yeah, because before he was only a threat to *her*. Now, maybe, he was a threat to our girl, too. To us.

The door at the front of Sanctum opened, and I fixed Becca with a hard stare. "Keep this between us," I said before Corvus, Diesel, and Pinkie could reach us at the bar.

"But…"

I shook my head *no* to drive my point home, and Becca shut her mouth.

There was a damn good chance this would lead absolutely nowhere. That I was more than just wrong, wasting brain power on something so completely useless when I needed to be focusing on more important things. I didn't need to distract the others too if this was a dead end. Right now we needed to find Ava Jade. Once she was back here safe, we'd have a meet about it.

"We need to get moving," Corvus announced before they reached us. "We'll have one of the patrol's take Becca back to Briar Hall."

Another Saint ran into the bar, bringing a wrapped cloth to Corvus. "Only found three," the guy said, and I couldn't be bothered to recall his name right now, my head still spinning with possibility.

"There should be four," Corvus growled, unwrapping AJ's blades, still stained with blood.

The crow handled one, and two from her father rested in Corv's hand.

"That's all we found," the Saint shrugged, leaving the way he came in.

"She's going to be pissed," Becca said, leaning over the bar to put her used glass in the bar sink.

"We'll replace it."

Corvus' pocket vibrated, and he cursed, stuffing his oversized hand into it to wrench his phone free.

He clicked the side button and slipped it back in without answering.

"Who's that?" I asked, not able to interpret the look on his face.

"Max."

"You've been ignoring her calls for ages."

"Think there's more important shit to worry about right now, don't you?"

"Max," Diesel said. "That's your manager, right?"

Corvus didn't answer.

"Don't waste your talent, Son. Call her back."

I didn't have time to consider the fact that our father just basically gave his blessing before Corvus was snapping at him. "Not. The. Time."

Diesel lifted his hands in a placating gesture.

Becca hopped down off the stool, a little unsteady.

"I'm sending a guard with Becca," I announced, sliding off my stool as well. Corvus was already on his way back to the front of the bar but paused to peer over his shoulder at me with a questioning stare.

"We can't spare anyone," Corvus answered before Diesel could. "She doesn't need a guard. Her shit stain of a boyfriend is dead."

"I'll go with her."

As one, we turned to find Axel getting up from a cot, gritting his teeth as he did.

He managed to escape with moderate injuries even though he was there with us from the start, when our odds were a million to fucking one.

His shoulder was all kinds of fucked up, and the gunshot wound had nicked an artery, making him loose a fuck ton of blood, but he'd be okay *with rest.*

"You need fluids."

No sooner had Diesel said it than Axel removed the IV needle from the back of his hand and tossed it aside.

I shared a look with Axel, realizing he'd heard at least some of what Becca and I had been talking about from where his cot near the bar.

He may have been injured, but he was also probably the one who would take watching over her seriously. And the only one who Diesel and Corvus would consider sparing.

"Let me go, Dies. I'm not going to be useful anywhere else."

"You could've taken the fucking IV bag with you, genius," Diesel said, pinching the bridge of his nose.

I nodded to Axel and he nodded back. "I'll keep an eye on her," he promised.

"Thanks, Axe."

I turned to Becca, listening to the front door bang closed behind Corvus, who'd clearly grown tired of waiting. "And you, *uh*... you'll work on that thing for me. Tonight?"

Her brown eyes met mine. "I will."

8

AVA JADE

S omething shifted beside me, and I let out a weak noise, my eyelids trying and failing to flutter open.

"I was wondering what you'd choose."

His voice sent my mind rocketing to an alertness my drug-addled body couldn't keep up with. I tried harder to force my eyes open, seeing a blurry form next to me, sitting against the wall with an elbow resting on one knee. Looking for all the world like nothing was wrong.

My chest squeezed.

I squinted, the fuzzy outline of my dark prince coming in and out of focus. I could smell him. I reached a hand in his direction, but couldn't move it more than a few inches as the drugs wore off achingly slow.

"I half expected you to starve yourself, but I figured if you'd pick something, it would be the oranges. Probably seemed the safest. Which is why they had the most Haldol in them."

Of course he would know that. But why was he so far away? Why weren't we leaving?

"Rook," I tried to call to him, but my voice was nothing more than a muted rasp.

"Shh," he said, his hands wrapping around my arms to drag me closer, to lay my head in his lap. "I've got you now, Angel."

Angel?

He stroked my ratty hair, not with his fingers, but with a brush, taming the knots back to some semblance of smoothness.

His hand lay on my shoulder. My naked shoulder.

"Rook," I tried again, my body beginning to shake all on its own. Convulsing from trying and failing to fight the drugs in my system. Was this what he felt like in that place? The sanatorium where they kept him in line with so many different drugs he was only a shell of himself. Until Grey got him out. Or was it Diesel who'd done that?

"Rook," I tried a third time and this time his name came out a bit more clearly and the brush stroking through my hair paused.

"What did you say?"

The sharp edge to his voice threw me, and I realized the smell in my nose wasn't Rook at all. It was citrusy, concealed with some sort of musk cologne.

I'd smelled something like it before.

"Rook?"

This time, his name was a question I was afraid to know the answer to.

"No."

My stomach turned.

"Fucking... kill... you... motherfuck—"

"Save your energy, Angel."

I tried to heave my body away from him but only managed to put myself face down on the cement, arms flopping uselessly, unable to hold myself up.

Everything tingled as though a thousand insects crawled over the surface of my skin.

"I think it's time for another dose," he said easily, and I rolled my head to the side to see him opening a long stainless steel case, saw the syringe inside.

"No," I managed around the lump in my throat, struggling to pull myself away with fingernails digging into the concrete.

"Then behave yourself."

I stopped struggling.

He dropped the syringe back into the case and set it next to him. I looked away from it quickly, not wanting him to catch me staring. If I could just keep him talking. Get my strength back. Then maybe I could give him a taste of his own medicine.

I opened my mouth to ask him something. Anything. But my tongue still felt fat in my mouth, uncooperative.

Drake lifted a brow at my sad attempt, blowing out a breath as he messed with his hair. I had no sense of time in here. No idea how long I'd been stuck in this cell. But he looked worn as fuck.

With dark circles under his bloodshot eyes—so maybe it was night then.

I noticed the color of his eyes, remembering how one was blue and the other brown that night at the Docks. How the roots of his hair had appeared darker than the ends. How, if this man wore a good pair of contact lenses and dyed his hair, he could be someone else entirely.

He seemed content to just sit there and watch me lie, naked and pathetic against the cold floor, but I needed to know if the theory trying to stick in my slippery thoughts was right.

"Jericho," I managed, butchering the name, but I knew he understood me.

His face lit up with a wide smile, showing two rows of perfectly straight white teeth.

"I knew you'd be the first one to figure it out."

So, this was the *Ace* Becca was 'dating.'

My stomach flipped, and I groaned, trying to hold in whatever was still in there when I remembered how I'd felt about *Drake* not that fucking long ago.

Whatever I thought... whatever I felt...

It was long gone.

"Drake?" I asked. The feeling was returning to my tongue, but I slurred the word anyway. He needed to think I still couldn't move. Couldn't speak properly.

I never pretended to be a great actress, even during the height of mine and Dad's con days, but I needed this to be an Oscar-worthy performance for it to work.

He narrowed his eyes at me in reply. Of course that wasn't his name, either.

"Who?" I asked.

"Shhh," he hushed softly, smirking. "There will be time for all that later."

Pain sliced through my lower stomach, and I tried to pull my knees in.

"Bathroom?" Drake asked, and I realized that was exactly what the pain was.

No sooner did I realize it than my bladder completely lost control and warmth ran down my thighs, pooling around my middle.

"Oops, too late."

"Fuck... you."

His eyes roved over my naked body with a promise and I swallowed back bile.

"You know who I was with today?" he asked, changing the subject, seeming to be completely unfazed by the fact I'd just pissed myself and the stink of it was quickly filling the room despite the small drain in the middle of the floor slowly sucking it all away.

"Grey."

My heart shuddered to a stop, fire stirring from the dormant coals in my belly.

"We spent hours together. Searching for Aries."

I watched his face, looking for any sign of something more he might not have been saying, but the smug look was still in place as he returned the favor, searching my stare for information of his own.

"We didn't find him, of course. And we won't. I paid him to disappear. All part of the plan."

Something in my eyes must've flagged my worry because he crooked his head to the left. "Don't worry, Angel. Grey's fine. I *did* spend the evening dreaming up some very creative ways of killing him, but there were others with us and it's not time yet. Besides, he's the one I hate the least. And now, *pfffft,* I mean, he's not exactly a threat with just one eye. It's pathetic really. He could barely walk a straight line."

Grief and anger warred in my chest, flushing my cheeks with fresh blood, making my fingers curl in like talons.

At least he's alive, I reminded myself.

You can't believe a word he says, the darkness reminded me.

"Plan?"

"But I *will* kill him," Drake continued, ignoring me, his gaze unfocusing as he imagined it. I took the opportunity to wiggle my fingers and toes, see how far up my limbs the feeling went. "When the time is right. Once things have calmed down and the Kings have Diesel's trust, that's when we'll make our move. Take the territory that *I* should've inherited."

His gaze refocused on me, and I let my body sink heavily into the floor. "That's when the real work will begin for you, Angel. To remake you. But you'll have to wait your turn. I can only orchestrate so many masterpieces at a time."

I snorted. "Fuck, you're pathetic."

His brows drew together, and in his eyes, I saw a lick of something I hadn't noticed there before. Or maybe just hadn't been paying close enough attention to. There was a darkness there. A sickness. Like mine but also not. His sent a tremor of revulsion rolling down my spine.

"Don't resist this, Angel," he said, the hard edge to his stare never waning. "You will be mine or you will be no one's."

"Yep," I said, coughing against the cement. "Pathetic."

His lips pressed into a thin line.

"I can't... belong to a corpse," I said with a smile, forcing the words out sluggishly, making them sound weak. "And that's all you'll... be... soon. My guys will... come for me."

That struck a nerve. The sickness flashed in his gaze and goose flesh rose on his arms.

"Not *yours*," he corrected me, his gaze lifting to someplace above me as he considered something. The air in the room felt heavier as I readied myself to strike.

"Yes *mine*. And me... theirs. I'll never belong... to you."

"Hmmm," he said, rubbing his forefinger over his chin. "You have a point. They don't appear to want to give up looking for you, and I hadn't expected that. I thought once you were gone..."

I didn't hear the rest of what he said, the rush of blood in my ears as my body sang back to life blocked out all other sound.

They're looking for me.

They didn't abandon me. They didn't wish me dead. *They were looking for me.*

My eyes burned as precious H2O leaked down my face and my rib cage squeezed me tight. The tiny cell expanded around me, filled with possibility. My fists clenched and a reawakened resolve to get the fuck out of this hole filled me.

A shaky breath passed my quivering lips before I clenched my teeth.

"Oh well, it doesn't matter. They'll give up eventually."

They wouldn't.

Drake lifted the metal tin from the ground and removed the syringe.

I forced my body to stay very, *very* still. Dead girl still.

A slow, steady breath passed between my lips, and as he rolled off his backside to his knees, arm outstretched, I came back to life.

I pushed myself up from the ground and grabbed his wrist, pulling hard to bring him off balance.

He jerked forward, and my grip slackened as dark spots crowded my vision, trying to keep me down. I dodged a strike from him on a fluke and staggered back, almost slipping on the wet floor.

"So fucking crafty," he growled through gritted teeth as he lunged at me, lifting his right hand high.

I let the backhand connect with my face to focus all my energy on ripping the syringe from his other hand. I grunted when his knuckles knocked across my cheekbone and the piercing tip of the needle went straight through my hand.

I blinked rapidly, seeing the pointy end through the backside of my palm, a perfect teardrop of bad medicine hanging there, about to fall.

My mouth opened.

Drake paused.

Before I could think, I closed my hand around the syringe, the needle through my hand feeling so disgustingly foreign as my muscles and tendons worked around it.

I screeched as I ripped it away from him, my fingers slipping on the plunger, accidentally spewing all the sedative over my bare chest.

Fuck.

My heart lurched in my chest, feeling like it might give out at any second. The lingering sedative and adrenaline in my veins did *not* want to play nice together.

I shook my head fiercely, the useless syringe in my hand forgotten as I attacked, throwing myself at Drake with claws and venom. Ready to use teeth if I needed to.

I landed a hit to his jaw, and he grunted, deftly avoiding my next blow and delivering one of his own.

The fist in my stomach pushed all the air from my lungs, and I couldn't get air back into them fast enough, choking as stars danced with the dark spots in my eyes. As the taste of blood coated the back of my tongue.

His elbow jabbed hard into my kidneys, and I went down hard, gasping against the concrete.

"Someone needs to be taught a lesson."

A booted foot connected with my middle, and I hunched in, coughing as a cramping pain spread and vomit joined the blood in my mouth. He kicked me again, lower, below where my arms protected the soft flesh of my belly. The sharp pain in my cervix erased all other pain, and I bit my teeth together against a scream he didn't deserve.

"Had enough?"

"That all you got?"

He kicked me again and again. Until I couldn't breathe. Until it felt like my insides were liquified. But the pain reminded me I was still alive. And as long as I was, I could kill him.

Blood splattered from my mouth onto the cement on his next kick, and he stopped. I rolled onto my back, barely conscious, a hand over my broken, beaten, bleeding body.

I coughed, finding his face through the heavy curtain of unconsciousness snaking its way over my eyes.

Drake's body heaved with each breath he took, the bite of insanity in his eyes clear even in my state. But the lines in his forehead told me he didn't mean to take it this far. That poisonous stare roamed my body, angry, as though I'd done this to myself.

I smiled up at him, but my face twitched, not cooperating with my command. "Didn't think—"

My words were choked off when a sharp, stabbing pain stabbed into my belly and I groaned, a blanket of white searing through my eyes.

I thought he'd stabbed me, but when I blinked through the brightness, I found him still standing there, staring down at me with something like worry.

He knelt, reaching a hand toward my middle.

I knocked it away with a snarl. "Don't fucking touch me."

"I'm sorry, Angel—"

"I'm not your *fucking* Angel." I spat at his feet. "I'm a Crow. Always have been. Always will be. I belong to *them*."

He stared into my eyes, reading the truth there before rising steadily to his feet. "Not as long as they're still alive."

Cold fear and white hot rage curled opposing fists in my chest.

"I see that now." He threw a hand through his hair, nodding to himself. "Fine. They'll die first. It'll make taking back what rightfully belongs to me that much easier, anyway."

"They'll eat you alive."

Drake grinned at me. "No, Angel. I don't think they will. They won't even see me coming."

I clawed back to my stomach, trying and failing to drag myself to him. To stop him, cursing at the spoiled floor.

"Don't touch them!"

Drake stepped out the door, leaving it ajar.

I clambered to my feet, off balance, my belly aching with a persistent throb, the flesh there already turning fifty shades of blue.

My hand closed on the threshold, and I stepped out into the hall for half a second before he was there again, snatching my wrist, peeling my hand from the doorframe.

I threw a weak fist into his chin, but he ignored it, sticking a fresh syringe deep into the side of my neck.

"If it makes you feel any better," Drake said in a smooth voice, catching my body against his when my knees buckled. "There's one other problem I have to take care of first. Your *scavengers* have at least one more night to live."

I moaned, sickness roiling in my stomach as my face fell against his chest. He ran a knuckle down my cheek, and I felt the press of his mouth against my temple before the sedative stole my sight, his next words a garbled mess of sound in my ears. "Hush, now, Angel. It'll be over soon."

9

BECCA

I couldn't seem to get his hair right. The way it sometimes fell over to the side of his forehead, casting a shadow over his brown eyes. I dipped the thin brush back into one of the brown colors I'd made especially for this purpose, and painted in the lowlights.

A sour taste in the back of my throat made me reach for the gin and lemonade on my bedside table, taking a long swallow. Cringing.

The ice melted hours ago, and it was piss warm. I knocked it back onto the table, trying to swallow away the taste.

A soft double rap on my closed door sent a shiver rolling up my spine. "Axel?"

I winced at the panic in my tone.

"Just checking. Thought I heard something."

"I'm good," I replied, the tension across my back starting to relax again.

"You should try to get some sleep."

"On my way," I lied, tapping my phone screen.

It was almost three in the morning and there was still no way I'd be able to sleep. At least not until this was finished.

"All right," Axel said through the door. "I'm here if you need me. I'll do your check-ins for the rest of the night."

I rolled my eyes, but shouted a polite *thanks* back to him before I heard him retreat back to his place on the couch and the TV turned back on to a low drone.

Grey asked me to check in every hour on the hour. He said it was to make sure I was good, but I knew it was mostly because they wanted updates on Ava Jade. If she was here. To confirm she wasn't.

I bit the inside of my cheek, sighing at the watercolor pad in my lap and the face staring up at me from it.

Jericho.

It was him all right, even though it wasn't quite finished. What I'd managed to remember surprised me. The exact cut of his jaw. The way his eyes slanted down at the edges, just slightly. The tiny scar at the side of his straight nose. The way his brows arched, in a way that most girls would kill for.

And his lips. Full. Soft.

I shut my eyes against a wave of nausea, evicting the line of thought from my mind, convinced I was the most naive bitch on the fucking planet.

He used me.

Betrayed me.

Manipulated me.

Jericho almost talked me into hurting the Crows. Into hurting Ava Jade. And I almost let him. For what?

My mom was a big girl. She knew what she was getting herself into when she let herself get mixed up with Damien St. Vincent. She knew what could happen and she did it anyway. It didn't make me hate the guy or the criminal organization he stood for any less, but I could see now what I couldn't before—my mother wasn't blameless. She chose to be involved with him, even knowing it could mean my losing her. Growing up without her.

Love did fucked up things to people.

I didn't even *love* Jericho and look how messed up that shit got.

Fuck love. And fuck monogamy. Fuck the whole damn institution of it all. I'd marry when I was forty and found the perfect dick, with a padded bank account to go with it and not a second sooner.

I thought Jericho loved me, or at least that he was headed in that direction. But you didn't play with people you loved like dolls, only to toss them in the trash once they'd served their purpose.

If what Grey was thinking was true, then Jericho really hadn't felt anything at all for me. I was a tool. Something to be used to get closer to his true mark. My best friend.

My fist clenched around the thin brush in my hand, and I felt it snap in my palm, that acid-eaten pit of guilt in my stomach growing even more.

"Fuck."

The alarm on my phone went off, but I ignored the reminder to send a text check-in to Grey. Let Axel do it.

I tossed the broken paint brush to the trash bin in the corner of my room, missing it by a foot.

I snorted at myself. At how useless I was in this whole mess. I would've sent my ass home too. What good was I? I couldn't shoot a gun. Couldn't throw a knife. I couldn't even hold my breakfast down. Grey didn't need to know it, but I'd vomited twice on my way out of the Docks, escorted by Diesel's men back to Sanctum.

But I needed to know. I needed to see Jericho's face. I didn't think there was any way I'd ever feel safe again. Knowing he was dead would be the only way.

He is *dead.*

He had to be.

Then why are you painting him?

I lifted my phone, thumbing back to messenger to send off another message to Ava Jade. We knew the guys had her phone, but she could still check messenger without it.

REBECCA HART

You've made your point, babe. PLEASE come back now? They sent Axel McFuckMeEyes here to keep an eye on me. Save me?

REBECCA HART

I'm worried about you. So are your guys.

REBECCA HART

Love you, bitch.

I scrolled back up through the fifteen other unanswered messages I'd sent. Re-reading each one only compounded the cold dread in my blood until I needed to pull the covers around myself to stave off the chill.

When she got back, I'd help her disappear if she wanted to. We could both vanish. Get as far away from Thorn Valley as we could. A large cash advance from Daddy's credit card to get us started and then we'd figure it out from there.

Fuck college. If Daddy couldn't find me, then he couldn't make me go to MIT. It would hurt to let the CalArts scholarship go to someone else, but...

I could get a job.

I almost laughed at the image of me in some fast food uniform, apron stained with grease. Ava Jade wielding a stainless steel spatula like a weapon of mass destruction. Slaying burgers all day.

We could do it.

If she wanted.

I flicked a fresh brush over Jericho's lash line, pretending I was painting literally anyone else as I filled in his short lashes.

A door opened outside my room, and my heart lifted, paint brush stilling in my hand as I listened keenly.

I'd already run out there four times thinking I might've heard Ava Jade come in only to be disappointed. I wasn't going out there again. Not to have Axel fuss over me and ask me ten *more* times if I wanted to talk.

The low rumble of two male voices came muffled through my door and I sagged, discarding the paint brush on my duvet to push my hair away from my face with a huff.

I stared down at the painting, deciding it was as good as it was going to get. I snatched it up, accidentally tossing the covers over the still wet paints. Shit.

A loud thud outside made me jump, my pulse skittering.

I rushed to the door, but my hand paused on the handle, listening to what was unmistakably the sounds of a struggle on the other side. An icy cold stole over my chest, and I held my breath.

Another crash.

Axel cursing.

I couldn't move.

Couldn't think.

Shit. Fuck.

No.

No. No. *No.*

"Becca, get out of here!" came Axel's roaring command from the other side of the door, and I broke free of the ice coating my skin. My hand shook where it held the painting.

I dashed for my bed and the phone I'd left there, but the unmistakable sound of a silenced gunshot whispered in my ears and I stopped.

The painting.

What if...

Oh god.

I looked around, the panic a raging storm in my chest. A drumbeat echo in my skull.

I raced back across the room, my stare fixed on the massive self-portrait hanging on my wall. My shaking fingers lifted the base of the canvas and I shoved the sheet of paper with Jericho's face on it into the hollow behind the painting, running back to my bed.

Phone.

I threw the duvet cover back, rustling in the heavy fabric to find it, a scream rising in my chest.

Where the fuck was my...

The door to my room opened, and I froze, my legs heavier than lead as I looked up. Fingers of dread crawled up the back of my neck as I recognized the man beneath the mask. Behind the contact lenses. Under the dye coating each strand of his hair. I'd know that smirk anywhere.

"Miss me, darlin'?"

10

CORVUS

"The fuck you think you're doing?" I asked Rook as he pushed the passenger side door of the Rover open.

He hobbled out into the parking lot at Briar Hall, stretching out his lower back with a groan.

"I can't sit anymore, man."

"Too fucking bad, park your ass on the hood until I get back."

"Nah. I'm with you."

I shook my head, pushing down the swell of heat in my chest. It's been there ever since we found Julia's body, just below the surface, aching for release. Everything I'd worked almost my whole damn life to swallow—to control—was teetering on the edge of release. And no one wanted to see that shit.

A long breath and I sent my gaze skyward to the slowly brightening sky. The navy blanket of night already turning the purple of a fresh bruise. In an hour it would shift to shades of rust and roses.

Another night without Ava Jade.

She wasn't in any place I thought to look for her, and I'd considered every fucking possibility.

Diesel continued the patrol, rotating out the most tired Saints for fresher stock, but they'd searched every nook and cranny of Thorn

Valley and had even sent a contingent of Kings to Lennox to check there, too. It was where she'd grown up. Maybe she'd wanted to go home.

They didn't turn anything up, but as soon as we were done here, that was where Rook and I were headed. I wanted to walk the train tracks. Check the trailer she grew up in. Her school. Find her old friend Dom. And that instructor she had a thing with. Kit?

If she went to him...

I'd fucking kill him.

"In and out," I told Rook, jerking my chin to the back entrance of Briar Hall.

He slammed the door to the Rover.

"Hey. Use the crutches."

Rook's back tensed, but a second later he reached into the open window and dragged the crutches out, a dark shadow over his eyes as he struggled to get them into place.

I worked to keep my pace slow so Rook could keep up, even though it felt like wading through fucking water. I just wanted to get this over with.

Grey said Becca and Axel missed the last text check-in and neither was answering their phone. It meant one of two things. Either they both fell asleep, which I was banking on, or they were fucking. I wouldn't put either past Axel. And I had it on good authority Becca had a thing for dangerous men. And apparently, also for older guys if what people said about her and the substitute English teacher last year was true.

We took the elevator up to the third floor.

A text came in from Grey along the way, and I growled as I took it out. He was probably texting to say they finally checked-in and this whole goddamned side trip was a total waste of our fucking time.

Why he was even so insistent on sending Axel with her was beyond me. There was no danger, not for Becca, not anymore.

GREY

You there yet? Still haven't heard anything.

CORVUS

Just got here? Find anything on the cams?

GREY

Nothing.

"Fuck."

"What?" Rook asked as the elevator doors slid open on the third floor.

I pocketed my phone. "Grey. He still hasn't found anything."

What good was having access to all the local security cameras and the ability to hack traffic cams if it gave us absolutely nothing?

Sparrow, where are you?

My stomach twisted as we made our way down the quiet corridor. So quiet I had to wonder what fucking day it was. A weekday? Weekend? I'd lost track.

Either way, the dead silence only broken by the sound of our footfalls and Rook's crutches clicking against the marble tile was enough to set my teeth on edge.

Something wasn't right.

I lifted a hand to signal Rook to slow down, stay quiet.

I turned back to see him ditching his crutches against the wall in favor of his gun and a nasty limp. I drew mine, too, flicking the safety off.

Rook nodded to the door at the end of the hall.

Fire raced over the back of my neck when I saw what he was looking at. It was open. Just slightly. The low lighting from inside stained a slice of the floor with its hazy orange glow.

I quietly fingered my phone back out of my pocket, moving steadily, stealthily forward.

Rook knocked into my elbow as he passed me, rushing toward the door.

"*We need to call for backup*," I hissed, making a grab for him, but he was already gone, all attempts to remain silent abandoned as he shoved into the room.

I followed right on his tail, sweeping the hall, the living room, the kitchen.

"*Axel*," Rook roared, running to the kitchen, almost slipping on the trail of blood mopped over the floor from the living room to the coffee bar. "Watch my six."

I swept the rest of the living room and kitchen, kicking Ava Jade's door in to sweep the inside of her room and bathroom before returning to the kitchen where Rook was hunched over Axel's still form.

He lightly ran his thumb and index finger over Axel's eyelids, shutting them. Blood puddled around Axel's head. He was shot in the temple. The bruising around his jaw and over his knuckles told me he didn't go down without a fight.

"Fucker didn't deserve this," Rook said on a sigh, pushing back to standing.

My gaze fixed on the door across the living room and the blood in my veins went cold.

Rook looked there, too.

"Rebecca?" I called, raising my gun back to eye level.

My phone started to ring in my pocket, but I ignored it as Rook and I pushed forward, stepping over Axel, around the kitchen island, until we were standing at her door.

I met Rook's stare. He nodded.

Ready.

I kicked the door down and we ran in, guns raised.

"*Becca*," Rook called out, putting his gun away to rush to her ..

What the fuck happened?

Why?

Who?

I watched Rook ball up a wad of what looked like satin pajamas and push them against Rebecca's chest, his hands immediately soaked red.

Her skin glowed pale white in the lamplight. If you didn't know she usually had a perfect golden tan, you could almost believe she was asleep. With her eyelids fluttered gently closed. Her lips parted just slightly. Arms splayed above her head.

I failed her.

Rook slapped Rebecca's cheek, leaving a red stain behind on her skin. "Hey!" he shouted at her placid face. "Becca, *wake up*."

"She's gone, Rook."

"No she's not."

He slapped her again, pressing so hard against the bullet wound in her chest that I'd be shocked if he wasn't cracking ribs.

"Why are you just standing there?" Rook growled at me. "Help me."

I couldn't look at her anymore, my rage-stained thoughts making ration an elusive thing I couldn't quite grasp.

Come on, Corv. Make sense of this.

Rebecca should've been safe. Her boyfriend was dead with all the other Aces.

Who else would want her gone?

Diesel?

No.

He wouldn't make the same mistake twice. He wouldn't hurt someone Ava Jade cared about. Not anymore. Not now that she was one of us.

Then who?

Why?

My phone rang again, jostling my line of thought.

It cracked against the opposite wall of Rebecca's room, shattering onto the ground after I threw it. I didn't remember deciding to throw it.

"Corvus!"

Whoever did this had to have wanted her dead badly. No. *Needed* her dead.

Why?

Why?

"Corvus!"

"What?" I bellowed, my nostril flaring as I lost my train of thought again, ripples of vicious rage rolling up my arms.

"Call an ambulance, man. The fuck you doing?"

I blinked, my red-stained gaze refocusing on Rook. On Becca. He tipped her chin back and blew into her lungs. Rebecca's fingers twitched.

Jesus fucking Christ.

She's still alive.

"Corv!"

I raced to the busted up remnants of my phone, kicking them aside with a curse.

"Back pocket," Rook shouted between rounds of blowing air into the half dead girl at his knees.

I found his phone, but my fingers paused on the dialpad.

Ambulance?

I couldn't call an ambulance. Protocol was always the vet.

Hospital records were too difficult to scrub and surgeons too wealthy to afford to pay off.

"*Now,* Corv." Rook commanded, his black eyes fixing on mine with the promise of violence. "There's no time. She won't make it to the vet."

No. She wouldn't.

And we couldn't let her die.

"I need you to hold this."

I bent, ignoring the stab of pain in my abdomen as I took over holding the wad of soiled satin to Rebecca's chest while he focused on getting air to her brain.

"Hold on," I told Rebecca, as if by commanding her alone, I could will her not to die. Not to leave the friend who still needed her. "You don't get to die. Not today."

I dialed, lifting the receiver to my ear, ready to threaten the worst kinds of violence if the ambulance didn't arrive in the next two fucking minutes.

11

ROOK

"We'll meet you at the hospital," Corvus told the paramedic as they loaded Rebecca into the back of the ambulance, like it was a threat instead of a promise.

"If she dies, so do you."

The paramedic paled, giving us one terse nod as he climbed into the back with Rebecca, closing the doors behind him. Lights flashing and sirens blaring, they sped down the road into Thorn Valley, leaving a plume of sand in their wake.

I turned and decked Corvus in the jaw, catching him off guard. He stumbled back a step, hand going to his chin with murder in his eyes.

"Rook, what the fuck?"

"That's for being a fucking idiot," I spat at him, practically preening at the sting in my knuckles, salivating with the urge to hit him again.

"What—"

"*She was alive,*" I shouted in his face. "And you just stood there like a lump of dead flesh."

"I—"

"Save it, man. What is going on with you? I've never seen you so fucking out of it. Where's my brother? Hmm? Because we need his ass here right now, not this motherfucker who stands there like a mute statue instead of doing literally any*fucking*thing useful."

His mouth pressed into a thin line, a knot forming between his brows. I could see it. That thing inside of him that he liked to keep locked up. There it was, right fucking there, tormenting him, begging him to be let free. But he clenched his fists against it. Swallowed it down. Snuffed it out.

I shoved him in the chest. "Come on," I egged him on. "Let it out, Bro. If you don't, your brain's going to be drowning in it, and we need you right now. We need this."

I jabbed the side of his temple twice with my fingertips, making him recoil, his upper lip curl.

"We need to call this in," he said through gritted teeth. "Don't push me, Rook."

I laughed, but the sound of it was violent even to my own ears. I'd never been so fucking tired and so wholly unable to sleep in my entire miserable life. *Wired* didn't even begin to cover this feeling and the fact that the *thing* squatting in my chest was hungry again wasn't fucking helping.

My hands ached for violence. To do *something*. Anything that might bring me closer to my Ghost. Bring my Ghost back to me.

I was ready to go door to door with an AK and blow the heads off anyone who didn't have her face. I'd find her eventually. And when I did, we'd sharpen our blades together and gut the filth that hurt Becca.

A shuddering breath escaped my lips at the beautiful, bloodstained imagery playing like poetry across the backs of my eyelids.

"Fine," I said, the reel of promised revenge with my Ghost like ASMR to my fractured soul. I shakily brought a cigarette to my lips and lit it up, inhaling deeply. "Call it in. While you do that, I'm going to go back in and make sure we didn't miss anything."

I blew the smoke in his direction, watching the flashing lights in the distance vanish.

He should've been the one to do the looking, but he wouldn't find a damned thing, not with his brain soaking in unspent testosterone-fueled rage.

"You call," he argued. "You're already bleeding through your fucking bandages again. Stay here."

The laugh I was planning to have at his attempt to subdue me died before it could reach my lips.

"What time is it?"

His brows drew down. "Why?"

"Who do you think that is?"

I pointed the red cherry at the tip of my cigarette to the headlights flashing like strobe lights through the trees as the sun finally broke over the horizon.

I glanced back up at Briar Hall behind me, finding more than a few curious faces in the windows, watching from the semi-security of their bedrooms.

The last fucking thing I wanted to deal with right now was the principal. Though the mouse of a man would probably take one look at our blood-coated hands and turn his fat ass right around and go back home where he was safe.

"That's not the principal's car," Corv said, echoing my thoughts as the older model Volvo rounded the bend onto the front drive of the academy, pulling up in front of the entrance.

"Not the cops, either."

Corv made it clear to the operator that we only required an ambulance and not to send anyone else. Name dropping Diesel made arguing a moot point.

We watched as a man stepped out of the driver's side, unfurling to his full height, closing the door behind him.

I reached around my back and slid my tacky fingers around the smooth grip of my Browning Hi Power, flicking my cigarette away after one final drag.

The other door opened and a girl stepped out. Her height and the shape of her frame made all the weight fall from my shoulders, before the shadow over her head fell away. It wasn't my Ghost.

This girl had short dark hair and a small oval shaped face.

The two of them argued in hushed tones in front of the Academy before the girl finally shut her door too and they ascended the stairs to the front door.

"Who are they?"

Corvus shook his head. He wasn't sure either. "We're about to find out."

I followed him across the lot, listening intently to the electronic voice coming through the speaker at the entrance.

"I'm sorry, but we don't allow visitors outside of regular school hours, you'll have to come back another time."

"Well, when's that?" the girl asked in a whiny voice.

"Eight forty-five," the new security guard replied.

"Look, we just want to check on a friend. Her name is Ava Jade Mason."

The girl leaned down to shout into the mic while the other guy hovered behind her, hands shoved deep into the pockets of his jeans.

"She hasn't been answering any of our calls or texts and we're really worried that something might've happened to—"

"Who the fuck are you?" Corvus asked, and the girl gasped, pivoting to face us with surprise in her eyes.

"And how do you know Ava Jade?" I added, analyzing the pair of them.

The new security guard's voice came back over the speaker with a sigh. "Look, I've told you already..."

I stalked through the newcomers, forcing them to separate, and jammed the intercom button. "Stop talking," I spoke into the mic. "Go back to your Diet Pepsi and Takis like a good mall cop. Oh, and be a peach and turn the fucking cameras off, yeah?"

"Right away, Mr. Clayton."

I waited until the red light blinking on the overhead camera went dark before turning my attention back to the girl.

"I believe we asked you some questions."

Her throat bobbed.

The fear hitching her shoulders high, leaking into the azure blue of her eyes, made a smile pull at my lips.

"Look, I don't know who you are but this isn't your business," the guy said, glancing between Corvus and me with something in his stare that whispered to me not to trust him.

I didn't like the way he was looking at us. Like he was gauging our height. Our builds. The distance between us and him.

He widened his stance.

A fighter, then.

"Wait. I know you," Corvus said suddenly, ignoring the guy's misinformed statement. "You're Kit. Kitrick Dagwood. From Lennox."

He fixed his cold blue's on the girl next. "Which would make you Dominique."

Kit.

Kit?

I racked my brain, dredging up information from the bits and pieces I picked up on my own from my brother's more intensive PI work. The exhaustion clinging to my skull like lead weights made it difficult, but not impossible.

This was the self-defense instructor she'd been fucking. And the friend who all but abandoned her when she moved here.

I analyzed them in a new light.

Kit stood a little shy of six feet from the ground. With reddish brown scruff on his jaw that grew up into darker hair cropped short. Shit brown eyes. A decent jaw. If you liked the ass chin thing.

Not her type.

And fucking old.

Not that I was one to judge, but this guy had to be thirty five. And not a threat. It was clear Corv was thinking this pissant might be Ava Jade's stalker, but no. This guy couldn't be him.

"And you are?" Kit replied to Corvus, his Adam's apple bobbing.

"Your worst fucking nightmare."

"Look, man, I didn't come here for trouble. I came here to check on a friend."

"A friend?" I echoed. "Don't you mean fuckbuddy?"

Even saying the words made a twist of jealousy twinge in my stomach. Not my thing. Never was. But Ghost was *mine.* Ours. The fact that this pansy ass motherfucker came here meant on some delusional level he thought he still had a claim on her. He needed to understand that he didn't. And never would again.

"That's not your business."

Dead wrong.

"You should leave," I said, the one and only warning I would give. Only spoken at all out of respect for my Ghost and the fact that she may not like to return home to find her old friends dead.

Corvus squared off against Kit, who raised his hands in a placating gesture my end-of-his-rope brother wouldn't be placated by.

A shiver of anticipation rolled down my spine at the look in his ice cold eyes. The dead look. The one that spoke of murder. A smile pulled at my lips.

"Look, I get it. You're the new flavor of the week, right?"

Corvus didn't give him a reply, his eyes tracking Kit's every movement.

"You don't want to do this, man," he told Corvus, letting out an exasperated sigh, like he was dealing with a fired up toddler rather than one of the most deadly men in the state. "How old are you? Eighteen? Twenty? You've got too much to live for. Let it go, man. I'll crush you."

A hysterical laugh rose from my throat unbidden, and I hunched over at the force of it, sides aching as tears welled in my eyes.

"What's so fucking funny?" Kit asked, looking offended.

Dom grabbed Kit's shoulder, trying to pull him back toward the car. "Come on, Kit. Let's just go."

"No," he said, rolling his shoulders back, shucking Dom off. "I want to know what's so fucking funny?"

I swiped a tear away from my eye with my knuckle and leaned back against the wall, tugging out a cigarette to put it to my lips. "You should listen to your friend," I said through the last of the dark laughter still shuddering in my lungs. "Get the fuck out of here."

Kit looked between Corvus and me. "You know what, fine. I don't have time for this shit."

He shook his head, jabbing two fingers in Corvus' direction. "When you see Ava Jade, tell her I'll be waiting when she's ready to come back to a real man."

Ope.

Corvus rushed him. The self-defense instructor managed to dodge the first swing of his fist, but wasn't fast enough to evade everything else.

My brother kicked his legs out from under him and he went down hard, eyes wide and empty from the knock to the back of his head.

Corvus crouched over him, not wasting a second before snatching up a fistful of t-shirt to drag him up only to knock him back down with a beautiful throw of his fist.

Kit's head jerked back, blood spurting from his mouth.

I took a drag of my cigarette.

Corvus hit him again.

Dominique screamed.

Again.

My cock hardened.

Again.

Kit's eyes rolled back.

"Stop it!" Dominique screamed. "*You're killing him!*"

Blood sprayed over my brother's blackout face. The beast inside on full display.

I shook my head, in awe of him. Aching to join him. But he needed this. This one was his and only his.

Dominique raced in, throwing a roundhouse kick to Corvus' head. He was knocked to the side for an instant, but it didn't stop him from getting right back on that motherfucking horse, pummeling him into the flagstone. Painting the entryway red.

Dominique tried again, jumping on his back only to be thrown off, her eyes wet with tears as she coughed, inhaling dirt.

"Please!" she shrieked, and I realized the plea was for me. "Make him stop."

I took another drag and butted out the cigarette beneath my boot. "Sorry, love. This one's between my brother and that sorry bastard there."

Corvus hit Kit once more before dropping his limp body to the ground to lift his chest to the sky, tipping his head back in a feral roar. Breath so hot I could see the faint cloud of it in the night air.

He looked down at his handiwork, upper lip curling, hard breaths expanding his entire torso as he rose back to his full height, fist still clenched like he wasn't sure if he was done.

I put my hands together in a slow clap, drawing his attention. "Damn, Bro. Didn't know you had it in you."

A muscle in his jaw ticked, and he stepped out of the way as Dom rushed in, falling to her knees at Kit's side, trying feverishly to wake him.

Kit groaned and I frowned, a little disappointed to find he wasn't dead after all.

"Want me to..." I indicated Kit.

"Do what you want," he said in a distant growl, turning on his heel to leave without so much as another word. I watched his back retreat, not to the Rover in the parking lot, but around to the back of Briar Hall, no doubt to the trailhead that would take him back to the nest.

"Come on," Dominique was saying, still crying, and it was hard to believe Ava Jade took self-defense lessons with this girl. This girl whose clothes oozed money and whose demeanor couldn't be any more divergent from hers. Not to mention the divide in their skill level and ability.

Some people had a natural talent, a predilection for violence. Neither of these sad motherfuckers did.

"Get up!" she was shouting. "*Come on.*"

I considered the knife in my boot for a minute before deciding they weren't worth my trouble. Or the time. Time that we didn't have.

The door creaked open as I stepped into the academy, the sound of fleeing footsteps all around as I strode toward the elevator, cursing the limp I couldn't seem to contain.

By the time I got to the second floor, all the students who'd been lingering in the atrium, watching in the stairwells, from their windows, had fallen silent. Aware of the monster stalking the halls.

The drag of dissipating adrenaline from watching my brother finally come undone was almost too fucking much for my exhausted system to take.

But I knew how to fix it.

How to stay awake.

To keep looking.

My Ghost wasn't safe. I knew that for certain now. We thought Becca was and look what fucking happened to her.

She'd be back by now.

If she were able.

Cold dread and white hot rage simmered and spiked in my blood, sputtering before either could be the fuel I needed to keep going.

I lost count of how many hours it'd been since I slept. But if this was how Corvus felt most days, I didn't know how he handled it without a little something to pick his dead ass up off the floor.

The bathroom door banged loudly against the opposite wall as I shoved my way inside, flicking on the light switch.

My phone pinged, and I plucked it out only to shove it back in my pocket, fingering past the cool metal to the bit of plastic tucked away beside it.

Grey could wait for an update. Just a few minutes.

I set the small bag filled with white powder on the stainless steel counter, my mouth going dry.

How could I know it hadn't been tainted?

Nah.

This fucker wanted us to destroy ourselves.

No carrion for the Crows.

He took away our outlet.

Outing Corvus took away his mask. Put him under more scrutiny.

And this...

This was the fucker trying to get me to sabotage myself. I didn't know what he knew exactly, but blow wouldn't render me useless. And it wouldn't turn me against my brothers. What it *would* do was keep me awake for as long as I needed to be awake to find her.

It would make me a fucking wrecking ball of a human being, bulldozing everything and anything that stood in my way of getting to her.

I needed it.

Just for now.

I could stop.

I'd stopped before.

Before I could change my mind, I tore the baggy open, spilling the contents over the counter. I dipped my pinkie in the mound of powder and rubbed it onto my gums, tasting the familiar flavor.

Woody. It was pure. Had to be.

I waited a minute to be sure, feeling the small hairs on the back of my neck lift with the slow tickle of a high.

I fingered a card from my wallet, dividing the rest into two thick lines. Rolled up a bill.

My phone rang, and I set it on the counter, watching Grey's number flash insistently on the screen.

"Sorry, Bro."

I tapped *ignore* and put the rolled bill to my nose.

12

AVA JADE

I f I could, I would've chewed my own fucking arm off by now. But with the thick leather strap tight as a noose around my neck, that proved impossible.

The equally tight straps around my wrists afforded just enough wiggle room for me to annihilate the skin there trying to get them free.

Drip. Drip. Drip.

"Fuck!" I screamed into the room, the frustration and anger so intense it might take on a life form all its own and burst out of my skin.

Drip. Drip. Drip.

"I swear to fucking god..." I growled into the pitch darkness, promising a thousand things worse than murder to the nothingness.

My wrists were coated in wetness I knew was my blood, and a thin material hung off my slowly withering frame. An oversized t-shirt? I couldn't be sure. But I knew who it belonged to. The smell of his stench, piney with that sour tang of lime was embedded deeply into the fabric, unable to be washed out.

I'd have questioned why he put a fucking shirt on me and no pants but that became obvious upon waking, when hot urine burned its way out despite my trying to hold it in.

This fucking chair or whatever it was had a hole in the seat, big enough to let my mess pass through, drained away to a metallic sounding bucket beneath.

The worst part wasn't that I couldn't see. And it wasn't that I was strapped down. The worst part was that I felt... clean.

Smelled clean.

Like cheap strawberry shampoo and Ivory soap. I tried not to let my mind run away with all the possibilities of what else he could have done to me while I was out. The space between my legs didn't feel any different. It didn't feel sore or violated. So unless this guy had a micro dick, there was a pretty good chance he hadn't touched me. At least not yet.

I squinted into the dark, not for the first time since I woke up, but still I couldn't see anything. I had no idea if this was even the same room or a different room entirely. All I knew was that dick face had clearly grown tired of my antics and decided to strap me down. Honestly? It was probably the smartest move on his part.

But it didn't bode fucking well for me. I growled through a pained moan trying to claw its way up my throat when I tugged at my restraints again. It was no use. Even if I broke both my thumbs, I wouldn't be able to slide my hands free. No, if I could do literally anything to break them, I would've already tried that.

Drip. Drip. Drip.

If I had to listen to that *fucking* dripping for another second I was going to go mad.

Scratch that. I was already going mad. Unless there were other people in this room, hidden under the cover of darkness, whispering faintly.

I highly doubted that.

Which left one of two possibilities, either I was finally going insane —something I always thought was likely to happen someday—*or* the drugs asshat kept pumping me with had fully fucked up all brain function.

Insane people don't know they're insane, I told myself. Right? Wasn't that what people said?

I mean, just because people said it didn't really mean it was true.

But it was something to...

My rambling line of thought cut off at the sound of someone coming. Of *him* coming.

I wished I could spit fucking acid. That would be a handy talent to have right now.

A handle turned, and I braced myself against the wooden chair. Light burst into the room and with the flick of a switch, another light, brighter than the fucking sun blazed down on me, making me recoil, bending my head to protect my burning eyes from the sting.

I blinked, trying to see through the white, my eyes screaming as they adjusted.

The out of focus shape of Drake moved toward me. His fingertips brushed the broken skin on my right wrist, and I jerked, tearing more skin to try to get away from him. He tsked me, snatching my forearm above where the strap wrapped my wrist to hold my arm steady.

He bent to get a closer look at the wound.

My stomach turned at the sight, and I swallowed back bile.

It was way worse than I thought it was. Way fucking worse. I was no stranger to the sight of gore, but something about *my own* gore always sort of grossed me out.

A little blood was nothing. A gunshot wound? Sure. A nice clean slice? Fuck, I enjoyed those.

But this? This mangled mess of bloodied, raw flesh, torn down to white bone on the ball of my wrist?

"I can fix this," Drake said, finally releasing me. "Tighten the straps. Make sure you can't move at all."

So this would be how it continued between us. Moves and counter-moves. I used my clothing against him so he took it away. I proved to him that even half numb and semi-conscious, I would fight him, so he strapped me down.

Now, he would make it so I couldn't even move.

What next?

"Just kill me."

He frowned, lifting to his full height.

"I'm not going to be the *thing* you want me to be. I'd rather die. So go ahead. Get it over with. I'll come back and haunt your ass."

...and watch my men get sweet, sweet retribution for my death.

"No, Angel. Everyone can be broken. *Everyone*. You just have to know which buttons to push."

He leaned in close.

"And I think I might have found some of yours."

I spat in his face and his jaw ticked, but he didn't move, remaining hunched, staring into my eyes. Would've been so much fucking better if it was acid.

Maybe that was how I'd kill him. Slowly disintegrate him in a giant vat of acid. The mental image made a bubble of manic joy rise in my chest and my lips twitched.

"For instance," Drake continued. "I've just taken care of the first problem standing in my way."

My smirk faded, and I threw myself against the straps holding me down. "What the fuck did you do?"

It was his turn to grin.

My guys. *My guys.*

No. He couldn't. They'd eat him alive.

He shook his head as though reading my mind. "Those vultures you call Crows are still alive. For now. But Becca met the reaper just a few hours ago."

But... Becca...

Met the...

"You're lying."

"Thought you might say that."

Drake pulled two cell phones out of his back pocket, replacing the black one in favor of the sleek silver iPhone. He thumbed the screen for a second and flipped it to face me.

"See?" he said, and I couldn't tear my gaze away.

I'd never get the image out of my mind.

Of Becca lying on her bedroom floor, her body at an odd, uncomfortable angle. Blood coating her torso. Her eyes shut.

"Oh, shit, wait a sec," Drake said, pushing his light hair away from his forehead. "I didn't press play."

I couldn't help the immediate burn of tears in my throat, or the way my chin began to quiver as Drake turned the phone back to me and I watched Becca's bedroom door open.

Saw her face turn ashen with fear as she realized who'd just come in, frozen in her pajamas.

"Hey darlin'. Miss me?"

"Wait, Jericho, please... don't..."

Bang!

"See," Drake said, giving the phone a little shake. "I made it nice and quick. I did that for you. Now, I can't say I'll do the same for the Crows, but they have it coming."

I couldn't feel my face.

Couldn't feel a damn thing.

I was looking at him through red-tinted vision, with a bottomless well of guilt in my stomach threatening to swallow me whole.

"Don't give him the satisfaction."

I gasped at the very real sound of Grey's soft voice in my ear.

"Stay calm." Corvus' voice joined Grey's, and I closed my eyes, forcing tears to roll down my cheeks, no longer caring if I was crazy. If it meant I got to hear their voices, even for a second, it was well worth it.

Becca.

Dead. Because of me.

I should've stayed away from her.

Idiot. Such a fucking idiot.

I choked back another sob and then thrashed against the restraints when Drake ran a knuckle up the trail of moisture on my cheek. Pressed the knuckle into his mouth to suck off my grief at the loss of possibly the only real friend I'd ever had.

"The whole thing gave me an idea," Drake was saying, and I had no idea when he started talking again, but I only heard him distantly as he backed away. The sound of the gunshot that took out my best friend replayed in a morbid beat through my skull in time with my pulse.

"See?"

I dragged my burning gaze up and saw what was behind him. A standing desk with two monitors on it, side by side. He clicked a button on the mouse and the screens came to life. Showing several different surveillance camera feeds from some locations I didn't recognize... and some I did and wished I didn't.

My bedroom at Briar Hall.

Becca's.

The Nest.

Sanctum.

How long had he been watching us? What had he seen? And where the fuck were these cameras?

This was not the same room I was in before, I realized numbly.

It had cement walls and a cement floor like the other one did, but this one also had this desk. Outlets on the wall. A heavy but not impenetrable door in place of the solid slab of stainless steel that'd been in the other room. How big was this place?

"Pretty cool, right?" Drake was saying, continuing to speak like I actually fucking cared what he had to say. Like I wasn't imagining a thousand ways to kill him to try to keep the tears at bay.

"This way you can watch."

"Watch?" I found myself asking, my voice sounding unfamiliar to my own ears. Deadened. Exactly the sort of voice he wanted to hear.

I cleared my throat, lifting my chin. Refusing to give him anything.

Drake nodded, white teeth flashing. "So you can watch them all die."

13

GREY

"We're falling apart," I sighed into the sterile hospital room, scrubbing my palms over my face as I watched Becca's for any signs of life.

She looked so fragile lying there, with the tube down her throat and the IV in her arm and the monitoring devices stickered all over her body. She wasn't out of the woods yet. They put her in the coma to give her body a better chance at healing, but they still weren't sure if they'd be able to wake her up after. That would be up to her.

"Corvus lost it," I continued as though she could hear me. "He *never* loses it."

I lifted the Styrofoam cup of cold coffee to my lips and took a long swallow, not knowing how much longer I could stay awake.

"And Rook..."

A dark chuckle.

I set the coffee down on the linoleum tile and steepled my fingers, putting them to my lips. "I don't know, but there's something wrong there too. He didn't sound himself on the phone... we're breaking without her."

The back of her hand felt like ice under my fingertips.

"We need you to wake up, Becca. you might be the only one who can tell us who this motherfucker is."

I grit my teeth against the selfish request. Here I was urging her to wake up so that she could help me save her friend; meanwhile, somewhere inside of that beautiful broken body she was fighting to survive herself.

If only she'd finished the drawing we might've been able to avenge her, and maybe AJ, too.

"I'm so sorry this happened to you."

The sound of a man shouting down the hall touched my ears and I sat up straighter, craning my neck to see if I could get a look at him through the window by the door.

I leaned down, feeling the outline of the gun holstered at my ankle, waiting to see if the heavy thudding footfalls of the man were headed in our direction.

I saw his face in the window only a second before the door was wrenched open, and Mr. Hart entered the room with a nurse close on his heels.

"What is this?" he roared at the nurse, not even noticing me sitting silently in the darkened corner beside Becca's bed.

"You call this a private room?" he spat. "Do you have any idea who I am?"

"Yes, sir, of course. I'm going to put her on the waitlist for one of the larger rooms right now."

"And get the goddamn doctor in here right now, I want to know exactly what happened to my daughter."

The nurse raced back down the hall, and Mr. Hart inhaled shakily, putting his hand to his mouth as he took in Rebecca lying prone on the hospital bed. He noticed me a moment later and removed the hand that was covering his mouth, his big money mask back in place.

"Who the hell are you and what are you doing in my daughter's room?"

I met his hard stare with an even harder one of my own, remembering what Becca told me about her father forcing her to go to MIT instead of the school she really wanted to go to. I didn't think that was the only thing he'd ever forced her into.

"A friend."

Mr. Hart's cold brown eyes tracked from my head down to my feet and back up again, clearly deciding I was not friend material for his precious daughter only a second before recognition sparked.

"I know you. You're one of Diesel St. Crow's sons, aren't you?"

"Grey," I supplied.

His eyes widened.

"*You,*" he sneered. "This is all your fault, isn't it?"

He cleared the space between us, his chest puffing up beneath his tailored suit. I stood, but made no move to attack or defend. This dog was all bark and no bite.

I wouldn't lie to him, but I also wasn't going to give him the satisfaction of a reply.

"What?" he hissed. "It wasn't enough to take my wife from me? *Hmm?* You had to take my...*my daughter* too." his voice cracked.

"I'm sorry for the loss of your wife, sir," I said, monotone. "But it wasn't the Saints who took her life, and I think you know that."

"No?" he pressed, the cracks in his voice filled with acid now. "I'm not talking about her death, boy. Your kind took her from me *long* before she died, and I'll be damned if I allow you to drag my daughter down with her."

It was time for me to leave. I turned to Becca and bent, taking her delicate hand in mine despite her father's protests behind me. I gave it a small squeeze. "You can do this," I whispered. "We need you."

"Get away from my daughter this instant."

I felt something on her palm and pulled back, flipping it carefully to see the smears of dirtied paint drying in the cracks there. I peeled her fingers back and found paint under her nails, too.

Smiling, I brought her hand to my lips before laying it back down on the bed.

I shouldered past her father and out into the hall, already typing out a message to the group chat, ignoring her father's shouts to not bother coming back.

I jabbed the elevator button.

GREY

Meet me at Briar Hall. Becca might've left us a gift.

The doors dinged open.

"Greyson?"

"Uncle Damien?"

I stared at the man who was unmistakably Damien St. Vincent standing alone in the elevator with a knot in his brows. I hadn't seen him in a few years but he looked the exact same. With a salt and pepper shadow of scruff along his jaw and jet black hair that only deepened the contrast of his slate gray eyes.

Anyone else would've taken one look at him and run, seeing him for the predator he is. Much like Diesel, Damien commanded an air of respect and violence. But for me, he offered a small smile. And even though his attention clearly tracked to the bandage over my eye, he didn't stare.

"How you been, kid? I have to say, you've looked better."

He stepped out of the elevator and drew me into a quick embrace, slapping a palm on my back. "Hope you got the fucker that did that to your face."

"We did. What are you doing here?"

"Happy to see you, too."

Damien peered down the corridor, toward the room I'd only just left and it was all the answer I needed, but he gave me his own version anyway.

"The hospital informed me when she was brought in."

I frowned. "Rebecca?"

"She's Eden Matthews' daughter."

The woman he loved more than anything in this world before this world took her from him.

Damien nodded, something souring in his expression as he settled a cold stare on me, maybe reading the guilt I was sure was on full display there. "Did you have something to do with this, son?"

"Not exactly."

"Care to elaborate?"

"There's someplace I have to be," I said, knowing I'd be here all fucking night if Damien wanted the full explanation of why Rebecca Hart wound up in the ER at four in the morning and was now fighting for her life in a coma. "Are you staying in town?"

He didn't seem at all placated by my response, but nodded. "For the night at least."

"Good. Go talk to Dies. He'll fill you in."

"This have to do with the Aces?"

I remembered Diesel had Uncle Damien on standby in case we needed him when things were getting bad, but mostly, our gangs ran independent of one another. And Uncle Damien had his own territory to look after. A much larger area than we had.

"They've been taken care of," I said, jabbing the elevator button again. The doors opened, and I stepped past my uncle and into the box. "Talk to Dies. We'll come by and help explain if there's time."

Damien's eyes flashed a warning in the fluorescent lighting overhead.

"Oh and you might not want to visit just yet," I said as the doors began to shut. "Her father's in there with her."

His jaw ticked, and the doors sealed, carrying me down to what I hoped was the key we'd been looking for. The one that might open the door to take us back to our girl.

Rook shifted foot to foot at the front entryway, seemingly uncaring that one boot was tapping away at a dried pile of blood. Apparently *Kit* had come to 'check on' AJ, and he must've said or done something to make Corvus snap.

Not an easy feat, but with the way he'd been at the edge of his rope lately I wasn't as surprised as I should've been. We knew only from stories how he'd been when Diesel first took him in, it seemed now we'd get to see the monster for ourselves.

Speaking of the devil, the engine of Corvus' Ducati snarled as he revved around the corner and pulled into the lot.

"What's this shit about?" Corvus growled, stepping off his bike helmetless, with heat still lingering in his gaze.

He turned his attention to Rook. "Have you been here this whole time?"

Rook lifted a hand to shield his eyes from the morning sun as he squinted at Corvus. "Would you have rather I took the Rover, Bro?"

Corvus bristled at the reply, but I ignored them both, stalking past Rook to the front doors of the academy. "Let's go. You two can bicker later."

Corvus lengthened his strides to keep up, the three of us walking through the atrium, scattering students milling around between classes in our wake.

"Mind explaining why we're back here. I was on my way to Lennox when I got your text."

Rook punched the elevator button and then leaned against the wall, waiting, rolling a coin over his knuckles. "What do you mean she might've left a gift?"

I sighed. "I think Jericho is AJ's stalker."

No point in dragging it out.

"Jericho's dead."

"Is he? Becca said she made herself look at every face on her way out of the Docks. He wasn't there."

Rook shrugged, but I could already see his mind working behind the blasé gesture. "Then he died in the attack on Sanctum."

"I don't think so."

Corvus pinched the bridge of his nose, upper lip curling. "I'll ask you again, Brother, what the fuck is this about?"

"It was something he said in the recordings," I explained, ignoring my brother's misplaced hostility as we rode the elevator up to the third floor. "It made me think we weren't his only target. Think about it. He was asking about AJ. Wanting Becca to find out where she was."

"To get to us," Corvus said, but the conviction in his voice was gone. Even he was starting to see it.

"Maybe. Maybe not. Becca didn't have any pictures of Jericho, but she's an artist. A fucking good one. I asked her if she could draw him for us."

Rook glared after me when I walked out of the elevator. I could feel his wrathful gaze boring holes into my back. "You didn't think you should mention this sooner? Give her a protection detail?"

"I did."

"Axel was fucked," Rook argued. "He wouldn't have been able to stand up to a strong wind, never mind this sadistic motherfucker."

"I didn't know if I was right," I admitted, keeping my eyes trained ahead. "I still might not be."

Corvus dragged me back with a rough grip on my shoulder. "You should've fucking told us."

This time, I did meet his stare. "I know."

Rook knocked Corv's hand from my shoulder, giving him a warning glance before turning his black eyes back to me. "You fucking tell us if you think you know something. I don't give a shit how stupid you think it is. Hear me?"

"Yeah, Bro. I hear you."

"So." Corvus sighed. "You think she managed to draw him before he got to her?"

I shook my head. "Not draw. Paint. But no, I didn't think she had. Not until I went to check on her at the hospital and found dried paint on her palm."

I could see the same hope I felt mirrored in their tired expressions.

Rook all but ran past me, clearing the distance to AJ and Becca's room, not wasting another second.

We followed him into the apartment, through the living room and across to Becca's room. He shoved the door in and set to work.

"Paint," he called after tearing back the comforters on her bed. Smudges of varying colors stained her light duvet. Dirty paintbrushes scattered to the floor.

I lifted a pad of watercolor paper from the floor, fingering a torn bit at the top. "A sheet's missing."

"Fuck!" Corvus kicked the side of her espresso finished dresser, denting in the wood. "He took it."

I shook my head. No.

My blood cooled in my veins, dread hollowing my gut. "No. No, we don't know that. Keep looking."

Rook snatched the pad of paper from my grasp, the hope in his eyes replaced by deep shadows.

I stole it back. "Keep. Looking."

His dead eyes told me he'd already lost hope, but he gave me a terse nod anyway. Rook didn't care about much, but the things he did, he cared about fiercely. With no reserve. Giving up was never an option when it came to us, and it wouldn't be with our girl, either.

Rook began going through her nightstand drawers while I rifled through lacy panties and bras in her dresser. I didn't think Corvus would help at first, but as we worked, tearing through every inch of the bedroom, he became too uneasy to stand still and stomped into the bathroom to check there.

Rook paused when he pulled out the bottom drawer on the right hand side of Becca's bed and I rushed over, my heart jump started back to life. "What is it? Did you find—"

My words died on my lips at the absolute fucking *arsenal* of sex toys in the drawer. Every shape and size of vibrator and dildo. Anal beads. Butt plugs. Some weird device shaped like a rose. A whip. Fucking *rope*. And at least five different kinds of lube. All organized and lined up in categories and size order.

"*Damn*," Rook said on a breath. "That's quite the collection. He fingered a ball gag from the pile, and I swatted it out of his hand.

"*Dude*," I chastised, slamming the drawer shut. "Keep looking."

He shook his head, brows lifting as he set back to work, moving on to the desk against the wall.

I turned from where I stood, surveying the room. The dresser, bed, and nightstands we'd already checked. Where else could she have hidden it?

Please. *Please tell me you hid it.*

I'd tear the entire fucking room apart before I gave up on this.

I texted Diesel again, just in case she's shown up at Sanctum, even knowing damn well he'd have called one of us on the spot.

My gaze tracked over the floor, the window hung with heavy draping curtains next to her bed. The large self-portrait on the wall. The bookshelf.

The portrait...

It wasn't hung perfectly straight. Even though most other things in the room were lined up in neat rows. Precisely placed.

A smudge of brownish paint marred the otherwise flawless deep purple wall just next to it.

Emotion, raw and hot rose in my chest, and I covered a shaky exhale with my palm. "Holy fucking shit."

I was right.

I was right.

A tremor of harrowing worry ricocheted up my spine at what that meant. At the realization that Ava Jade was definitely *not* safe.

"What is it, man?" Rook asked, coming to stand next to me, his black eyes tracing the painting.

"The fuck are you two looking at?" Corvus demanded, standing in the doorframe of the bathroom.

Without a word, I walked forward and lifted the painting off the wall, flipping it around. There, jammed haphazardly into the back of the canvas framing was a lone piece of watercolor paper.

I slipped it from the frame, my stomach in my throat. Corvus and Rook crowded beside me as I flipped it over.

"Is that..." Corvus trailed off, his voice dripping malice.

"It is."

Rook tore the page from my hand to bring it closer to his twisted face, his dead-eyed composure slipping before it fled entirely. He threw the page away and stormed for the door. "He's *mine.*"

14

CORVUS

"*Rook, wait,*" I shouted, chasing him through the hall to the stairs. I only managed to catch up at all because his leg was slowing his ass down.

"*I said wait,*" I tried again, my growl echoing in the stairwell, making him whip around to face me, white knuckle grip on the railing, face a mosaic of unleashed fury. The mirror image of what I felt inside but was fighting past because we couldn't waste this. We had the advantage here. The upper hand.

And we couldn't let it all go to shit because we wanted this fucker's head on a platter.

"What?" he barked. "What the fuck are we *waiting* for?"

Grey caught up, letting the door bang closed behind him, sealing us into the stairwell alone.

"Stop and think for a fucking second," I implored him, noticing his rapid breathing. The way his whole body moved with the simple act of taking in air. I couldn't remember the last time I'd seen him like this. So wound up he could explode at any second. It was shocking he'd stopped at all. That he was listening.

His black eyes searched the dead air in front of his face as he tried to figure out what I was getting at, clearly getting more and more frustrated by the second.

Grey padded down the few steps from the landing to us, stopping in front of Rook. "AJ still isn't back. If my theory is right and I think it is then..."

"He might have her," Rook finished for him, his eyes wild now, but focused.

"And if we rush in guns blazing..."

"So, what then?"

I licked my lips, my body alive with a savage flutter behind my rib cage. The crush of anxiety I hadn't felt since I was a fucking teenager rearing its ugly head. Everything depended on us doing this *right*.

"We don't let on we know anything," I started. "First, we need to find out where he is."

Rook lifted his phone to his ear and I grabbed his jacket sleeve, jerking him toward me. "Who the fuck you calling?"

"Diesel."

I released him. "Tell him not to let on a goddamned thing."

He nodded, and Diesel picked up on the other end. "Dies, you alone?"

Rook shuffled down a few steps, turning around to speak to Diesel in hushed tones.

Grey ran a shaky hand through his hair. "What are you thinking? Tail him?"

"If Drake is who we think he is, it won't be easy. He's a smart motherfucker but that means we'll just have to be smarter. He probably has all his bases covered. He'll notice a tail straight off. We'll have to be more creative."

"So, we're just supposed to pretend we don't know? Be in the same room as this fucker? Breathe the same air?"

"Unless there's some way we can get our hands on him without setting a war in motion with the Kings."

"Fuck the Kings," Rook injected, coming back up to where we stood near the window, looking out over the rapidly darkening parking lot. "How do we know they aren't in on this shit? He's one of theirs."

"And if going to war is what it takes to get her back, then so fucking be it," Grey added.

The uncomfortable flutter behind my rib cage died, swallowed by the familiar heat of the animal within coming back to life. They were right. It didn't matter what it took.

"Where is he?"

Rook's lips twisted into a wicked grin. "At Sanctum. Diesel's going to try to keep him there."

Fuck. I gritted my teeth, shaking my head. "If Drake gets the feeling something's off, he'll bolt."

"Diesel won't let him."

A new worry took root. "Why's Drake there?"

"It was another meet with Mav and his main crew. About what happened with Becca. He's putting the pressure on Mav to bring Aries in."

But we knew now it wasn't Aries. Never was. He was always a distraction. Something to keep us busy while the real threat worked alongside us. Right under our noses. This whole fucking time.

"Who's with him?"

Rook lifted a shoulder in a half shrug, his expression filled with questioning annoyance, bouncing on the balls of his feet. Overeager for action. "I don't know, man. I heard Pinkie in the background. The others are still on patrol for Ghost."

The lines of exasperation in his forehead softened as he realized what I'd already figured out. Diesel was in a closed space with the enemy. Diesel and Pinkie and maybe one more Saint if he was lucky. Meanwhile Mav was there with Drake and the rest of their inner circle.

"We don't know for sure if the Kings even know about Drake. The alliance could still be legit. There's no reason to think..." Grey trailed off. The placation was more for himself than for us. He could be right, but I doubted it.

"We need to move."

Grey pushed the Rover to its limits as we sped across town to Sanctum, still better with one eye than any driver I knew with two.

"Slow down a bit," I warned as we turned onto High Street, nearing Sanctum. We didn't need to come peeling into the lot and set anyone on edge. We were going to walk in there, take Drake, and tell Mav that if he didn't cooperate, it would be his head.

The Kings might've outnumbered us now, but not by much. Not by enough.

Was I thinking straight?

I shook my head, blinking away the exhaustion clinging to my eyelids, trying to drag them down like lead weights. Sleep wasn't a luxury any of us could afford these days. If I didn't get my Sparrow back, I doubted I'd ever sleep again.

But if I did get her back...

I'd do whatever she wanted. *Be* whatever she wanted. I'd share her with my brothers. Let go of my control.

Falling for someone was never in the cards for me, but I didn't just fall for Ava Jade. I'd crashed and burned, and I'd keep burning for as long as she wanted to hold me in her fire. Love was something meant for story books and fairy tales. A lie people whispered to each other in the dark to justify and rationalize their most carnal desires. To control. To protect. To dominate. To fuck. To *own*.

I didn't love Ava Jade. What I felt for her went far beyond such a simple emotion. It was a nameless thing that kept me going, breathing life into my battered bones and weary mind. She was the spark.

Grey ground his jaw as he forced the Rover to a crawl and Sanctum came into view.

Rook's fingers dug into the front seats from where he sat in the middle behind us, ready to launch at a second's notice.

"Remember," I said, working to keep my voice at an even timbre so as not to set him off. "We can't kill him. Not yet. We need him alive."

"Fine."

"Rook."

"I said *fine.*"

Grey cranked the wheel to pull in next to one of Dies' cars out the front of Sanctum at the same time as a loud *bang*! rang through the evening air, forcing him to hit the brakes.

The front door of Sanctum crashed open and a storm of gray smoke chased Drake from the building.

Diesel.

Rook darted from the backseat, leaving the door open behind him.

I opened my door, the instinct to *chase* searing through my blood, but Grey shoved the Rover into reverse, jostling me back into the cab.

"He's going to get away," Grey shouted, throwing the Rover back into drive.

Drake straddled a motorcycle parked down the street from Sanctum, but Rook was almost there, his wraith-like shadow on top of him.

Diesel poured out of Sanctum with Pinkie and Mav right behind him, coughing.

My relief at finding him alive fled as the roar of the motorcycle's engine filled the night, droning out the sound of their coughing. Even the sound of our own engine, revving to give chase.

"How did he know we were coming?"

I barely registered what Grey had asked as he cranked the wheel, jarring to a stop only long enough for a cursing, out of breath Rook to clamber back into the back seat as we sped off after the single tail light curving up the blacktop ahead.

"Keep them here," I hollered out the window to Diesel, gaze cutting to a genuinely stunned-looking Maverick. "And call back the others."

Diesel nodded through another hard cough from the smoke bomb and whipped my head around, taking out my gun and checking the clip before pushing myself half out the passenger side window, into the whipping wind.

"We're going to lose him!" Rook roared and Grey punched it, propelling us like a speeding bullet down the road after Drake.

"Watch out!" I called and Grey barely managed to skate around a merging SUV, nearly jostling me out the fucking window.

Ahead, Drake's taillight grew smaller. Further.

No.

"Grey!"

I fought the wind, firing, but the shot went wide and still his fucking taillight grew smaller until it vanished around a corner.

"Hold on!"

I threw myself back into the seat before he pulled the e-brake, skidding us to the side before speeding off again, down the narrow alley between two buildings.

The side mirrors sparked, scraping against weathered brick as the Rover ran over empty bottles and cardboard boxes, smashing trash cans out of the way.

The instant we were clear of the alley, both Rook and I leaned out our windows, searching.

"There!"

The motorcycle dipped to the left off the end of Main Street, merging onto the southbound highway. Grey followed, swerving around two cars in the slow lane to slide all the way to the fast lane, pushing the Rover to its limits. Honking sounded all around, but he ignored everything except the Rover and the road and the bob and weave of Drake's tail lights ahead.

The unparalleled focus in his eye told me he wouldn't be letting Drake go. Not while this car was still moving and he was still behind the wheel.

"Get around this van," I shouted over the roar of the wind rushing into the cabin, pushing back out the window, taking aim.

The business end of my Colt traced the erratic driving pattern of Drake ahead between two other cars.

Fuck. If I fired I'd risk hitting one of them instead of my intended target.

Rook's gun discharged two shots, ringing in my ears. One hit the rear tire of the hatchback to the right, sending it swerving off the highway, spinning into the ditch, toppling onto its side. The other missed Drake, but the gunfire was enough to scare the other car off the road, leaving him with no cover for at least another couple of miles.

I clenched my teeth, ignoring the smoking wreckage behind us to focus my attention ahead.

I fired. Once. Twice. Drake jerked, the motorcycle swerving madly before he managed to right it.

Rook fired, but his shot went wide, pinging off the metal center meridian in a shower of sparks.

"Keep it fucking steady," Rook bellowed, and Grey, heedless of the lines on the highway, drove straight up the middle, laying on the horn to keep the cars attempting to merge onto the highway from getting in our way.

"Now," he shouted. "Do it."

Rook fired again and this time he would've had the fucker had he not swerved out of the way at the last second, using a break in the meridian to put himself on the other side of the highway, driving against oncoming traffic.

He bent low over the bike, flattening himself with his elbows wide as he steered through the speeding, honking vehicles.

"He's going to get away," Rook hissed, watching like a fucking bobble-head, trying to keep his sights set on Drake as Grey continued driving.

"No he's not."

"Shit!"

Two cars on the northbound highway crashed trying to avoid hitting Drake, a third flipped over the median into our path.

My head knocked against the window frame, neck screaming with whiplash as Grey avoided the collision, the smell of metal and gasoline heavy in my nose. The glow of fire in the rearview.

Cars piled up on the opposite highway, busting through the meridian, clogging the air with a thick, dense smoke.

"Do you see him?" I asked Rook, trying and failing to locate him in the wreckage or the now tens or maybe hundreds of cars slowing to a red-brake-light stop.

We did *not* just fucking lose him.

No.

I slammed my palm on the dash, my breath hot and heavy, coming out through bared teeth.

Rook grabbed my shoulder. "There!"

I followed his line of sight and found a single tail light as it curved, getting off the highway.

"Grey—"

"I saw."

He took the next exit, jamming the Rover into a lower gear as we whipped around the curve and took the first left.

With bated breath, we drove in tense silence, the whistle of the wind the only sound above the distant roar of fire and sirens as we took the exit road toward Edgewood.

We barreled down the road, passing every vehicle in our way, scouring the shoulder, the trees, the roads forking off in both directions.

The Rover rolled to a stop when the road finally reached a two way split, holding up traffic as it caught up behind us. Left would take us back to Thorn Valley. Right to Lennox.

There were no red tail lights in either direction.

Grey punched the steering wheel hard before grabbing it to anchor him through a feral war cry. "Fuck, fuck, *fuck.*"

The car behind him honked, long and loud and his eyes glittered with rage before he threw it into reverse, demolishing the front end of the car behind us before throwing it into park. His hands gripped the wheel as he fought to tame his breathing, leaning his forehead against the worn leather.

There was nothing Rook or I could say now that wouldn't make him feel even more like a failure than he clearly already did.

"You did what you could," I said, my voice terse and emotionally detached even to my own ears.

We fucking lost him.

And now he knew that we knew who he was.

I dragged a sweaty palm over the scruff growing on my jaw.

"Just fucking say it," Grey demanded, his voice hollow. "I never would've lost him before. The one fucking thing I'm good at and I—"

"*Don't,*" Rook sat back in his seat, laying his Browning in his lap to press his palms into his eye sockets. "How the fuck would you've caught a motorcycle driving on the other side of a fucking meridian in opposing traffic. Who the fuck are you, Houdini?"

Grey didn't reply, and the man in the car behind us opened his door, phone to his ear. Blood running in a straight line down the middle of his forehead.

Rook opened his door, flashing his gun at the guy. "Back in your car, asshole."

"We need to get back," I found myself saying. "Maverick needs to answer for this motherfucker. He knows something. He has to."

Yes. A new idea. A new angle. Something. I needed something to go on. Anything that could lead us to *her.*

Grey turned left, taking us back to Thorn Valley.

My phone vibrated and I took it out, knowing better than to hope it would be anything good.

And as usual, I was right. My stomach soured at the message lighting up the screen.

Sensing my tension, Rook leaned forward, trying to peer over my shoulder to read the text, but I thumbed the side button and the screen went black, reflecting my own carefully constructed mask back to me. "Who was it?"

"Diesel," I lied.

15

ROOK

"What are we doing here, Diesel?" Maverick's misplaced sense of superiority tainted his voice as it floated up to us from the underbelly of Sanctum.

"We're waiting for my sons."

"There are places we need to—"

"You'll wait."

Diesel's attention turned toward us as we came down the stairs and I shoved past Corvus to make a beeline for Maverick.

"You didn't catch him?" Diesel asked Grey and Corvus, stepping out of my way as I squared up in front of King's so-called 'leader,' seeing him in a new light.

Watching him cower.

"Tell me about Drake."

His lips flexed into a tight line, but his stare couldn't hold mine for more than a second before he turned his attention to Diesel. "What is this, St. Crow? I already told you I don't know why the boy ran."

"Like how you know nothing about where Aries went?" I pressed, thumbing my blade from my hip to flip it between my fingers, rolling it over my rings.

"Diesel?" he urged.

"You will answer my son's question, Maverick."

"Sit." I pushed the tip of my blade into Maverick's chest, guiding him to the seat behind his ass until he fell into it.

I perched on the edge of the meeting table, lifting my foot to rest on the chair next to him, never looking away. Watching the sweat bead at his hairline.

"I've already told your father, boy. I have no idea what Drake was playing at. One second he was sitting here at the table with us for the meet. The next thing I know he jumps out of his seat and throws a damned smoke grenade and a flash bang under the table and he's gone."

I looked to Diesel for confirmation. He nodded gravely.

"What was he doing before that?"

Mavericks thick brows bunched together.

"He was on his phone," Diesel answered for him. "Must've seen something that spooked him off."

Corvus and I shared a look.

We already knew Drake had eyes on us at Briar Hall. In the halls. The cafeteria. The fucking kitchens. Why not in Ava Jade's and Becca's room? We could've missed it. We weren't watching close enough. We should've been checking.

Should've.

Should've.

I would never *should've* again.

On that note.

I licked my lips, eyeing Maverick's men behind him. As per Diesel's rules, none of them were allowed in Sanctum armed, but judging by their shifty looks and hand placements, they weren't following the rules. And Diesel, dear daddy Diesel wasn't as on top of it as he should've been.

"That motherfucker nearly *killed* our friend," I seethed, remembering the feel of Becca's near dead body under mine as I fought to save her. She didn't deserve that. "And he might have my fucking reason for living in his filthy hands. *You know something.* Tell me."

The truth of it hit me like a Mack truck to the chest. *She* was my reason to keep going. For years I'd been just getting by. Keeping the ugliest parts of myself choked off, sated. I'd stopped giving a fuck whether I survived our next job. Our next run in with a rival gang.

Ghost was my reason to want to be more cautious. If only to keep from missing a single moment with her. My brothers filled the void. They were close to being enough, but she was *more.*

She was everything.

Maverick's upper lip curled. "I don't know a damned thing."

I punched him in the face, sucking in a breath at the sting.

His men rushed forward but Grey, Corvus, Diesel, and Pinkie raised their weapons in warning.

I watched the light come back into Maverick's eyes as they focused on me.

On me licking his blood off my rings and spitting it onto the floor.

"Try again."

"Rook," Diesel said, calm. The eye of the storm raging all around him.

Maverick's chair scraped back as he stood, twisting out from under my shadow. "I'm warning you, St. Crow," he said, unsteady as he swiped the back of his hand over the blood dripping from the fresh cut on his lower lip. "This is not how we handle business."

Diesel nodded, and I snarled at him. "He's *lying.*"

"And if he is, then he knows what will happen."

"This is bullshit."

I lifted my blade to Mav's throat and within half a second there was a barrel pressed to my temple by one of his men.

"I think you should go, Maverick," Diesel said.

He swallowed against my blade. "And our alliance?"

"Give me Drake and I'll reconsider severing ties."

Mav's lips parted in surprise. He hadn't been expecting this. Hadn't been expecting Diesel to support his sons over this absolute forgery of a fucking alliance.

"I told you, I don't know what he's up to."

"Then you have nothing to worry about."

"Dies?" I pressed, drawing a drop of blood from Mav's neck.

My father turned his attention to the man with the gun pressed to my temple. "You have exactly one second to remove that gun from my son's head or I'll blow yours off."

"One—"

The barrel dropped, and I pushed off of Maverick, away from the Kings reduced to fucking jokers in a court of bloody nightmares.

"Leave."

"Think about this, St. Crow—"

Diesel fired a round into the ceiling, sending them scattering like roaches. "*Leave.*"

Diesel remained like that, with his arm raised, the tail of smoke from the shot he fired still rising from the weapon gripped tight in his hand, until they were all gone.

"Now," he said, holstering the gun. "Someone want to tell me what the *fuck* is going on?"

"I still say you shouldn't have let him go."

I paced the short span of floor as Grey finished explaining about the painting of Drake and what it meant.

Diesel gave me an exasperated glance before responding to something Grey was saying. "So, you're telling me the Hart kid's gang boyfriend—"

"Becca," Grey corrected him.

Diesel sighed. "*Becca's* gang boyfriend who was an Ace actually wasn't an Ace at all but a King?" A pause. "A King who is also Ava Jade's stalker?"

Grey pinched the bridge of his nose. "Basically, yes."

"Well, that shit doesn't make sense."

As little sense as it made when we came to similar conclusions about Aries. But with Aries, it didn't fit. His little pansy ass couldn't have been Ava Jade's stalker. This guy, though? He could be.

I saw his darkness. A different flavor from mine but it was there all along. I thought it meant he could run with us, a new wolf to join our murder of crows. My Ghost saw it too. It beckoned her. Reeled her in only to trap her.

Bristling on the inside, I shivered on the outside, feeling the drag of coming down from my high like fingernails pulling at the back of my skull.

Corvus stopped stewing, giving the inside of his cheek a break from his incessant chewing. "It only doesn't because we don't have all the information. But it fits. It's him. It has to be."

About time he fucking said something. My older brother had been a goddamned mute since we left the crossroads in Edgewood. I read between his lines now though, catching onto what he wasn't saying.

If it wasn't Drake, then that would mean we had exactly zilch to go on in helping us find my Ghost. But I was with him on this. It did fit.

And without Grey putting the pieces together we wouldn't have this lead at all.

I flipped open my phone, scrolling to my old Lennox contact to fire him off another text.

ROOK

What the fuck is taking so long? I need my shit.

"I don't like this," Diesel was saying. "Rook's right."

I scoffed.

"Maverick was lying. That much was obvious, but we don't know what he was lying about. He might not have a clue what Drake is up to, if that's even his name."

"Doubtful," Corvus muttered, gazing distantly toward the exit before checking something on his phone.

Diesel rubbed a knuckle over his chin, thinking. "Either way, it might come to a fight with the Kings and we're weak. We lost a lot of men at the Docks and nearly half our fucking force are either down or at least badly injured."

"Bring in the newer recruits," Grey suggested.

"They aren't ready. Haven't even taken the trials."

"Make *this* their trial. It's better than being outmanned practically two to one."

Diesel didn't like that idea, but it was clear he was considering it.

"All right, we bring them into the fold, separate out the wheat from the chaff when this is through and run them through the trials. But we're outgunned, too, and low on munitions. We'd need more weapons and can't risk traveling through King territory to get what we need right now. And if we go the other route, to the dealers south of the border, it'll cost twice as much and we can't afford it."

"I might be able to fix that problem," I offered, remembering a certain someone's very expensive *very fancy* Easter eggs. Someone who deserved to have her mansion broken into, her precious gifts stolen. "You still have those art dealing contacts in the black market?"

Diesel crooked a brow. "Yeah, why?"

"I'll get us the cash. Set up a meet with the Mexicans for a few days from now. We'll get the weapons and munitions just in case."

Diesel looked like he might argue or ask questions, but instead he just set his jaw, and sighed, deciding he didn't really want to know.

"Boss?" Pinkie's voice drifted into the chilly room from the office by the exit where he was diligently watching the cameras. "St. Vincent's here. And the boys are back from their patrol."

Diesel gave Pinkie a nod and the big guy went back to watching the screens.

"I'll brief the others on what went down here. We'll have to drop it down to a single patrol on the streets for your girl. I can't risk spreading us thin right now."

"She isn't on the streets." I wished it wasn't true, but I knew in my gut it was. He had her.

He'd had her this whole time. The things he could've done to her in the days, nearly a week now, that she'd been gone.

The darkness within stirred, both fed by the remnants of the white powder still keeping me going and dulled by the aftereffects of it slowly leaving my system.

I needed more.

Now.

I lit a fresh cigarette with shaky fingers I willed to still themselves, checking my phone again for a reply. Ready to get moving again. We'd done enough standing around.

"We need to keep looking for her—for *him*," Grey told Diesel, mirroring my thoughts. Our father closed the short gap to where Grey was seated and placed a reassuring hand on his shoulder.

"I know, Son."

Grey stood.

"Check in every few hours."

"We will," Grey promised as our uncle hollered a hello from the stairs, trotting down to meet us. His nose turned up at what he found, brows furrowing.

"Hey, little brother," he said in greeting to Diesel. "Why do I feel like I just missed the show?"

Diesel shook his head, making for the bar. "Drink, Damien?"

"You know what I like."

Diesel lifted his chin in a silent goodbye as we left, finding a new day staining the sky purple, a slice of glowing orange blooming on the horizon.

"I'm going to see what I can dig up on Drake," Grey announced. "And try to access any cctv footage on the road where we lost him."

"Good call," Corvus said, making for Diesel's car.

"Where are you going?"

"I'm going back to where we lost him, try the road to Lennox," my brother announced. "You go back to the nest with Grey. I'll meet you there in a bit."

"We shouldn't split up," Grey argued.

Corvus paused with his hand on the handle of Diesel's car, his back stiffening. "What good am I sitting my ass at home?"

"Corv—"

"Let him go," I interrupted. "We'll meet you at home, Bro."

Grey shrugged off my grip on his arm, twisting away from Corvus as he slid into the driver's seat of Dies' Camaro. He always left the keys in it. No one was stupid enough to touch Diesel St. Crow's car in this city. No one except his son.

Grey stalked around the building to the Rover, a black cloud following him.

"Hey," I called after him, not even bothering to try to keep up as I lit another cigarette, coughing on the acrid taste of cocaine dripping down the back of my throat. "You still have that shit on all our phones, right? The tracking shit?"

He stopped, spinning on his heel, his brows drawn in question. "Yeah, why?"

"Corvus isn't going to the crossroads. He's lying."

"What?"

"Something's up and we're going to find out what."

16

GREY

"This is a waste of time," I grunted, shoving my phone into Rook's hands as I settled into the driver's seat. "We need to be trying to track this motherfucker."

"We might not have to," Rook answered, closing the passenger side door, his hand shaky as he swiped his way into my phone and I started the engine.

I frowned. "What do you mean?"

"Think about it. We know Ghost's stalker wants us out of the picture. If I was him, I'd want to get each of us alone. And he has the perfect bait to make that happen."

"Corvus wouldn't be so stupid."

Rook lifted a brow at me, challenging me to reconsider my response. "If this bastard threatened Ava Jade, you're telling me you wouldn't do whatever the fuck he said, *including* lying to us or going off on your own?"

My chest burned. I'd already done exactly that.

"Exactly," Rook sighed. "Now how the hell do I work this tracking app?"

I snatched the phone back, flicking to the app and keying in all the credentials to activate it before passing it back.

Rook zoomed into the map, finding the little blue dot that showed Corvus' location. He grinned.

"He's not going to the crossroads. He took a left on Compton."

What? "What's out that way?"

Rook shrugged, letting out a shuddering sigh. "Not much. A couple hotels. Restaurants."

He looked rough, I realized. Way rougher than I'd seen him look in a long time. Losing AJ, not sleeping, and all this shit with the Kings seemed to be getting to him. It was about time something did, but I hated seeing him like this. I selfishly wished he'd go back to being his aloof self, without a care, with all of the confidence that no one stood a chance against us. That we would get her back. Easy as fucking cake.

This Rook was a harder pill to swallow, and his anxiety only fed my own.

"Hey, you good, Brother?"

Rook narrowed his black eyes on me quickly before flitting them away, letting them go dead. "Just drive, Grey. We need to catch up with Corv."

Rook directed me through the streets of Thorn Valley as we slowly tailed Corvus across the city.

If this was a waste of time...

I inhaled deeply through my nose to settle the quake in my stomach. Unwound the taut muscle wrapping my arms like cords about to snap.

I had him. *I had him,* and I fucking lost him.

Anything that happened to AJ from here on out happened purely because of my inability to do the one fucking thing I did best.

"You're going to break it off if you don't let up," Rook said, smoking a cigarette out the window, gesturing with the burning red tip toward my grip on the steering wheel.

I didn't even bother trying to relax, gritting my teeth behind the wall of my lips, willing him to shut up so I could try to calm down.

This wasn't me. I was the group mediator. The make-everyone-happy brother. The calm one. The *nice* one.

The things I wanted to do to Drake were as far from nice as you could get.

"I want to rip his arms off," I gritted out.

"Mmm," Rook agreed, puffing out a cloud of noxious smoke, heavy-lidded gaze still focused on the phone, completely unfazed by what I'd just said. And why would he be? I was letting myself feel everything now and only now. With one of the only people on this planet who would understand.

Something beneath my breastbone trembled and heat scattered down my arms like sheet lightning.

"I want to castrate him and scalp him and roast his ass over a bonfire, and when I'm fucking finished, I want to serve his smoking head to her on a platter."

The volume of my voice increased of its own accord until I was shouting. The pressure behind my eye and the space where my other eye used to be making them feel on the verge of popping.

This finally got Rook's attention. He ashed his cigarette before snubbing out the still-burning cherry between his fingers.

"Welcome to the next level, Bro. Now use that shit. We're going to need that fire to find her and finish this motherfucker."

My pulse slowed back to a manageable tempo, warm cheeks cooling as my breaths evened out. "Is this what it's like for you all the time?"

All the rage? The vicious desire to smash everything within reaching distance just to let out enough of the fury to properly function. It'd been building since I woke up and AJ wasn't there. It'd gotten worse after finding out about Becca. But now?

Now it was almost unbearable in its intensity.

Rook's deep timbre filled the cabin with his reply. "Worse."

I sagged, trying to pull my focus back to the task. We were pulling onto the strip of hotels near the northern edge of the city. "Where is he?"

Rook pointed a ringed finger up the street. "Up ahead. Another few blocks, I think. I don't see the Camaro. He must've parked it in one of the underground lots."

"He's stopped?"

"Yeah. Looks like it."

I pulled into a parking spot on the side of the road, not wanting to get too close in case Corvus spotted us, but also sort of wishing he would just so I could throttle him for going off on his own, in the *complete opposite* direction from where he said he was going.

If either of us pulled this, he'd shit a brick and then use said brick to bash our heads in.

We stepped out into the growing dawn, the smell of the city in the early morning filling my nose.

Rook stepped up onto the sidewalk on his toes to get a look down the street before checking his phone again. "I don't see him, but if this is right, he's at the Vandermark."

The Vandermark?

I tipped my head up to see the length of the narrow gothic revival building currently dressed up in gaudy Christmas decor to match the banners strung on the lampposts lining the street leading up to it.

"Shit, there it is, right out front," Rook said, and I followed his eye to the Camaro sandwiched between two larger vehicles in a parking space close to the entrance. Corvus not inside it.

Why would he be going there? It didn't make sense as a meeting spot. Not if Drake's intent was to take Corvus out. There weren't enough fast ways to escape the tall building. Unless...

"The underground parking garage."

Rook nodded. "Let's move."

17

AVA JADE

Drake made it impossible for me to move and absolutely every*fucking*thing itched. That alone would've been enough to drive a woman insane, but with the drugs still lingering in my system, and that *incessant* dripping... safe to say I was absolutely mad. Delirious. Starting to question reality.

So when he came barging in, sweeping right into the room to head straight for the desk of monitors, I thought maybe he wasn't really there at all.

I mean, fuck, I thought I'd seen my dad chilling over there in the corner, humming his favorite tune to the sound of a guitar strumming in my brain just an hour ago. Or maybe it was a day ago. Who fucking knew.

Either way, my dad was definitely dead, and I was definitely crazy.

Which was why I started to laugh when Drake manically smashed the spacebar on the keyboard, muttering to himself as the computers woke from their slumber.

He whirled, sneering at me, a smear of blood on his jaw.

I immediately stopped laughing.

Whose blood was that?

Whose *fucking* blood was that?

914

He realized where my eyes had strayed and looked down with a grimace, peeling off his leather jacket with a hiss.

He smelled like smoke and gasoline.

My heart thundered in my chest and I spoke through my teeth, trying to find the darkness inside that seemed to have abandoned me to my crazy sometime between being stripped of my clothes and dignity and being strapped into this godforsaken chair. "What did you do?"

He bared his teeth as he tore the sleeve from his black t-shirt, revealing a bullet wound in his shoulder, bloody and gruesome and enough to tickle my insides with fucking joy.

They got him. If only they'd hit a little lower. More to the right.

Drake grabbed the first aid kit he'd used to wrap up my wrists and tore a pair of long metal tweezers out of a plastic sleeve with his teeth.

He let out a mean cry, gripping the underside of the desk with one hand while he dug the pointed tips of the tweezers deep into the wound, coming out with a bullet a few seconds later. He dropped it to the floor and it clattered as it rolled toward the door.

"*Fuck,*" he barked, closing his eyes tight for a second before continuing to sanitize and wrap the injury.

"What happened?" I pressed again, swallowing past the thick cloth Drake had used to bind my head and neck even tighter to the chair, squirming the tiniest bit that I was able. My lower abdomen ached with even the slightest contraction of my muscles and my face pinched.

"I'm fucking talking to you, dickface," I shouted hoarsely, coughing against the restraint of the cloth. When he didn't answer, the laughter came again, and with little control over what fell from my mouth, words tumbled out as though from a drunk Ava Jade. But these words I didn't care to stuff back inside.

"They figured it out, didn't they?"

I laughed some more.

"They kicked your ass! Look at you? Pathetic."

He turned on me, his fist closing around my throat, making me bite my tongue, my mouth welling with the coppery tang of blood.

I stared straight into his eyes, daring him to finish what he started, shoving down the knee jerk reaction to panic when my vision began to darken around the edges. I wouldn't give him the satisfaction.

Kill me then, I dared him with my stare alone. I wouldn't give him my soul, become the hollow shell he wanted to fill with his own desires, so he might as well take my life. Get it over with.

"Fucking *bitch*."

Red veins flared in his eyes, and he squeezed harder, shaking with the effort. My lungs burned. If he squeezed any harder, I was sure my neck would snap.

Just before the lights went out, his hands moved and a gush of cool, sharp air filled my lungs, making me choke and splutter. Reality came back in patchy images spotted with dark circles as I breathed through the razor blades in my throat.

"You think so highly of them..." he said, his voice distant as I ebbed somewhere just outside of full consciousness. "You think they're invincible, *hmm?*"

I tried to spit out the blood in my mouth between coughing fits, but only managed to get it all over the oversized t-shirt still covering my body.

"I'm going to show you just how mortal they are, Angel. And once they're gone, you'll see it was always *me*. I'll make you see."

"Come on AJ," Grey's voice soothed me and a morbid grin graced my blood-coated lips. "Snap out of it, baby. I need you to focus. Watch what he's doing on those screens."

I opened my eyes wide to correct the lingering double-vision while also trying to swallow.

"That's it," Corvus crooned. "Good girl."

The phantom touch of rough fingers brushed over the no doubt purpling skin on my neck, making me shudder. "Just picture him flayed and cockless," Rook whispered in my ear, and I leaned into his touch, but it wasn't there anymore.

And neither was he.

They were gone.

They were never here.

"...think they ruined my plans..." Drake was saying to himself, and I turned my attention back to him, squinting to try to see what he was doing on the monitors like Grey told me.

Like *I* told me, I corrected myself.

Not real.

Not real. Get it together Ava Jade.

"*Ha!* They might've made it more difficult but this changes nothing."

A phone rang somewhere, the echo of the factory setting ringtone bouncing all around the small room. Drake opened a drawer and pulled out an ancient flip phone, answering it.

"Go."

A pause.

"*Fuck.*"

He brought the phone away from his ear and squeezed it between his hands, closing his eyes, a muscle flexing hard in his jaw as he contained himself before putting it back to his ear. "Shut the fuck up, Maverick. No. Don't do anything. You fucking sit there and you wait for my instructions. Head for the warehouse. There's something I need to take care of, and then I'll meet you there."

Drake hung up before Maverick could've possibly given him a response, muttering to himself some more. And I thought *I* was crazy.

"What was that you were saying about them not ruining your plans?"

He stiffened but didn't come at me this time.

Honestly? A little disappointing.

I watched Drake open up a program with what looked like about a hundred different tiny video cameras on it. He clicked on several of them and they flew over to the next monitor, opening live camera feeds in small boxes. A door. A cityscape I recognized to be Thorn Valley. Where was this?

What was this?

"In about ten minutes, there'll be one less of them for me to worry about. One less of them in the way of me claiming what rightfully belongs to me. Thorn Valley should be *mine* by right."

Drake moved away from the monitors, giving me a clear and unobstructed view of the almost motionless footage. The only reason I knew it was live was because there were clouds moving in the sky.

He came around the chair, putting himself behind me. He bent his head to my eye level, pressing his cheek to mine, making my stomach turn as he pointed directly toward the image of the city skyline. "You see that, Angel? We're about to find out if Crows can fly."

18

CORVUS

Barely three seconds after I entered the lobby of the Vandermark, my phone rang with an unknown caller.

"Where are you?" I growled down the line, making the early morning hotel guests give me a wider berth as I turned in a slow circle, searching for his rat face among the ridiculously opulent Christmas decor. A rendition of Jingle Bells played over the sound system, a stark contrast to the black aura surrounding me.

"Go to the elevator."

"Fuck that. Where. Are. You?"

"Excuse me, sir, can I help—"

I spun on my heel, glaring down at the bellhop twiddling his thumbs nervously until he fell silent and stepped away. "Apologies, Mr. James. I didn't recognize you."

Eye twitching, I went to the bank of elevators. "Up or down?"

"Up," Drake replied. "All the way up."

"*Corvus—*"

The sharp strike of flesh on flesh contact followed by a hiss cut off the sound of her voice.

"*Sparrow,*" I roared into the receiver; my pulse picked up. There was no mistaking her voice, even hoarse and pitched high as it was. This monster had my Sparrow. It wasn't just a possibility anymore. It was a stark reality.

My phone screen cracked in my ear from my grip on it. "If you touch her—"

"You'll what? Up, Corvus. All the way to the top."

I stabbed the button, my chest tight. "Let me talk to her."

"No."

I stepped into the elevator, hitting the button for the top floor, a miasmal feeling tapping at my bones. Telling me to turn around.

"Don't!" Came my Sparrow's desperate plea in the background of the call, and I crouched to the floor, dizzy, every muscle screaming with useless adrenaline. I couldn't breathe.

Could do nothing to help her.

"Quiet," Drake hissed, and I heard her muffled shouts as he shoved something into her mouth.

The line buzzed faintly with dead air for a moment as the elevator carried me up and up, and I schooled my breathing, knowing I would never get the frantic sound of her voice out of my head. *Never.* No matter how hard I tried.

The gravity of it settled in my stomach like acid coated lead. The others didn't say it, but I knew they were thinking it. It was *me.* I was the reason she took off that night at the Docks.

I sent Drake after her.

Me.

"I'm going to kill you," I promised him, my voice unrecognizable.

The elevator doors opened at the top floor, outside of a single door to the penthouse suite. Drake didn't reply.

A muscle under my eye twitched as I rose back to my full height. "I don't have a key."

"Oh, you aren't going in there. Take a left. Go to the stairs, Corvus. All the way up."

Down the hall, an exit sign pointed to the door. Next to it a roof access sign hung on the wall.

I didn't budge. "What is this? What do you want from me?"

"Isn't it obvious?"

I gritted my teeth.

Drake laughed hollowly down the line. "I want you to die."

I shook my head, pushing the button for the elevator again. I wasn't playing this game. No fucking way. "You can suck my left nut, asshole."

The frenzied strain in his voice was clear in his reply. "Go to the stairs... or I'll kill her."

Bile coated the back of my throat.

He was bluffing.

All this just so he could have her. He wouldn't kill her.

"You won't."

A grunt on the other end.

A pained cough.

I set my jaw.

"Go ahead, Angel," Drake prompted. "Scream for your Crow."

Another grunt.

"Stop."

The tiniest whimper that told me just how hard she was working to keep herself silent despite the pain clearly being inflicted upon her.

"I said *stop*."

He'd made his point. He may not kill her, but he wasn't above hurting her to get what he wanted.

"Left. Take the stairs like a good little vulture."

The door crashed against the wall behind me as I whipped it open and took the stairs one at a time. Each step a march in the black parade that could only lead to one possible ending.

My phone vibrated in my hand, and I chanced moving it a few inches from my ear to see Grey trying to call.

I shut my eyes tightly, jaw clicking as I ignored it and the door to the roof came into view.

It went off again. Twice.

I checked again, reading three text messages on the screen.

ROOK

Where the fuck are you?

GREY

We're here. We found Dies' car in the parking garage. What the hell are you doing at the Vandermark?

My stomach twisted knowing they were somewhere in the building.

Looking for me. The fucking tracking app. I forgot to disable it. Or maybe subconsciously I'd wanted them to find me. To stop me.

I pushed against the door, but it wouldn't budge. "It's locked."

The door clicked. The lock disengaging.

For one beautiful second I actually thought he was really on the other side. That *she* was too. And I could finish this.

I raised my weapon and kicked the door open, ready to fire, and was left staring into the blinding amber light of a new dawn. Seeing the heart of Thorn Valley a few miles to the west of where I was standing. And nothing else.

Gravel crunched underfoot as I swept the roof but found nothing. No one.

I put the phone back to my ear, not bothering to speak.

"You look terrible."

My brows drew, and I looked more closely at my surroundings, finding the small black eyes of cameras placed in several places around the roof.

"I'm sure you aren't looking too hot yourself after taking that shot to the shoulder."

"Just a graze, nothing to worry about, but thanks for your concern."

"Enough. I'm done talking. Get to the fucking point."

"You see that ledge in front of you, the one facing the front of the building? Walk to it."

"And then what?"

"Jump."

"*Don't you fucking dare,*" my Sparrow growled, and I could hear the struggle in her voice. The strength shining through the hoarseness and the fear.

"How do I even know she's really there?" I ground out. "That that isn't someone else or a fucking recording?"

I knew in my gut it wasn't, but I was stalling. And I needed to be absolutely certain. I needed to see her. I needed Grey and Rook to find me. To stop me...

"You don't."

"Then you won't get what you want. I won't jump."

I hung up, my stomach plummeting.

He won't kill her.

He won't kill her.

It was less than a minute before my phone rang again. A different sort of ringing, and when I turned my phone to my face, I saw an incoming request for a video call.

My thumb shook over the answer button before I finally pressed it, my lungs refusing to take in air.

There she was.

My throat burned.

My Sparrow caged. Her wings clipped.

Tied to a massive wooden chair with thick leather straps, the chair bolted to the floor. Lengths of dirtied white cloth tied around her neck, her wrists, her forearms, her shins. Binding her so completely that I doubted she could move more than half an inch.

Fury and fear danced in her eyes, the dark hollows beneath them making the sharp sea glass color of them cut me to the bone. A red knuckle pattern marred her pale cheek. Blood stained the oversized white t-shirt covering her otherwise naked body. Her legs trembled against their binds.

Her chin quivered around the mound of gauze gagging her and she shut her eyes, trying to hide herself from me. To hide the reality of where she'd been. What she'd been through.

She didn't want me to see.

"There," Drake said and the image shook as he settled his phone somewhere so he could enter the shot. He strode toward her in the small room.

Cement walls. A drain in the floor. I couldn't see the roof.

It looked like a cell.

I took a screenshot. Then another as he ran a finger over her collarbone and bile rose up the back of my throat.

Her eyes shot open at his touch, and heat flooded my veins.

"*Oh,*" Drake said, a smile widening on his lips as he crooned in Ava Jade's ear. "He doesn't like that, does he? That's right. He's the jealous one. Can't stand to have anyone else look at or touch what he mistakenly thinks is his."

He snatched her chin, his tongue flicking out from between his lips like a snake to lick her from jaw to earlobe. Her muffled attempts to shout at him only made it ten times worse as her body convulsed in disgust.

"You know, you were right," he said, releasing her chin, his eyes on me while he reached lower, fingers dipping below the neckline of the t-shirt. "I won't kill her. And it seems hurting her isn't motivating enough, but…"

Her jaw clenched when he found her breast and the thin t-shirt material shifted as he squeezed it, hard.

My breaths came hot and ragged. The ground beneath my feet seemed to shake. But I couldn't look away, forcing myself to watch what I allowed to happen.

"But there are other things I can do," Drake continued, flicking his hair back from his face as he withdrew his hand only to snatch the collar of the shirt and tear it clean down the middle, exposing her naked body to the camera.

Fuck.

Fuck.

Her lower abdomen was a map of purple, black, yellow, and blue. Swollen.

I shut my eyes against a wave of vertigo.

"I was going to wait until she begged me for it, but maybe I'll sample her now."

"Don't touch her."

"Unless…" Drake looked at me expectantly.

My eyes tracked to the edge of the roof and back. No.

I needed to end this bastard, and I couldn't do that from six feet underground.

"Then just remember," Drake said, his smug expression souring with impatience. "This is on *you*. Not me."

He bit his lower lip, his dirty hands finding her breasts again, twisting her nipples until her eyes watered.

"Tell him how good it feels, Angel," Drake crooned, removing her gag as he twisted her left nipple again and she bit back a cry.

"*Fuck you,*" she hissed through gritted teeth, her eyes lifting to the phone. To me. "I don't care what he does to me. Hang up. Just hang up the phone. *Corvus.*"

Drake rounded the chair, kneeling in front of her, between her splayed legs, leaning to one side so I would have a better view while he pushed a hand up her thigh.

My knees hit hard gravel.

My Sparrow's gaze lifted to the ceiling, trying not to watch what he was doing between her legs, every tendon and vein in her neck taut and swollen. "Just don't look," she urged me, the fire in her voice almost enough to cover the edge of panic.

"Stop."

He did as I asked but didn't remove his filthy hands from my woman. "Jump now and I promise you I will not touch her again until she asks. And she *will* ask."

"How can I trust that?"

"You can't," Drake said with a smile. "But you can watch me fuck her if you prefer."

I met her eyes in the camera, lifting a trembling finger to the screen as if I could touch her through it.

The texts from my brothers were non-stop now, flashing over the top of the video, frantic.

They couldn't find me, I realized. If they did, Drake would only force them over the edge, too. And they'd go...

My mind was already made up.

Ava Jade gasped as Drake drove two fingers into her pussy, her jaw clenched so tight I could see every edge of the angled bone.

"*Stop.* I'll do it."

"No!"

He withdrew.

My Sparrow continued in an onslaught of threats and curses, all of them aimed at me. I deserved it. I deserved it all.

What better way to prove how sorry I was for everything? That I loved her?

I would rather die than watch him touch her for another second. I would rather spend eternity in the fiery pits of hell than see the strain in her eyes. Hear the fear she worked so hard to hide in her voice.

I should've died twelve years ago. In that bedroom with my fucked up family.

I should've died a hundred times since.

Numb, I lifted the phone to my face, hating that I'd never see hers again, but my brothers would.

"Rook and Grey will find you," I promised her, speaking over her broken, shouting voice.

I looked at Drake now, who pushed himself to his feet, the triumph in his eyes making my chest burn with rage. "I'll see you in hell."

"Looking forward to it."

My Sparrow sobbed, her curses and shouts weaker as she lobbied them through the dam blocking her voice. "I hate you!" she screamed at me. "Don't do this!"

But I was already walking to the edge, stepping up to the plate. Batting my last fucking round.

She'd be fine without me. They would all be.

Rook and Grey had a bond far stronger than I shared with either of them. *And who's fault is that?* My subconscious hissed.

My own.

I didn't let people get close. Wouldn't let them in. Let them see what hid beneath the layers I sealed myself inside.

And now I never would.

"I'm sorry, Sparrow. For everything."

I dropped my phone onto the gravel and turned away from the view of the city I'd come to call home, shutting my eyes. Spreading my wings wide. My heels shuffled beyond the ledge, hanging over empty air.

...and I fell.

19

ROOK

We rushed off the elevator from the parking garage, shoes screeching on the freshly polished marble of the lobby, searching for him.

I cursed as I brought my phone back down from my ear. Voicemail. Again.

"Check the app again," I snarled at Grey, making for the front desk, shoving a suit out of the way to get to the front of the line.

"It still says he's here. He should be right fucking *here*."

"Excuse me, sir, I believe that man there was ahead of you," the maître-d chirped at my advance, backing away from the counter, his button up suddenly too tight around his fat neck.

"Tall fucker," I said. "About yay high. Dirty blond hair. Scary looking face. Probably wearing a leather jacket. You seen him?"

His double chin bobbed as he tried and failed to utter a stuttering reply. "I-I-I'm not—"

"He took the elevator," a bellhop replied from further down behind the long desk. "Maybe five minutes ago."

"Which floor?"

The little pipsqueak's lips closed.

I snapped my fingers at him. "Hey! Which fucking floor?"

"I-I don't know."

I twisted to find Grey jumping the desk despite the maître-d's protests, shoving him out of the way of the computer. "Your security system. How do I get in?"

The fat oaf, flushed scarlet, waved frantically as he backed away from Grey. "Someone call security!"

I launched over the counter and took him by his too-tight collar, pulling him in until his face was inches from mine. "Your security footage. Now."

He let out a shrill squeal, and I saw the exact moment he realized *what* had a hold of him. Not a Saint. Not a Crow. But a fucking psycho who wouldn't hesitate to rip out his jugular if he didn't give exactly what was asked.

"I-it's there," he pointed weakly toward a room near the back of the large lobby, where a security guard argued with a petite woman I guessed was the manager trying to get him to do his job. Which he was clearly refusing to do. Smart fucker.

"Grey," I jerked my head to the security closet and released the cowering maître-d. "Call me when you find him."

I headed for the elevators, taking out my gun to a cacophony of gasps and squeals from the few people still lingering around the edges of the lobby. I pushed the barrel against the button to go up and slung off my jacket, discarding it on the lobby floor, my muscles rippling with unspent energy, burning off the last traces of the blow still clinging to my nerve endings.

I cracked my neck, stepping into the elevator car as Grey rushed across the lobby, shouting at the security guard to bring up the footage from the last ten minutes. All of it.

The doors shut, and I pressed for the first floor, twitching at the cringy Christmas music filling the pine scented box.

"Corvus!" I bellowed down the corridor as soon as the doors opened, stopping to listen. A woman exited her room in a bathrobe but at the sight of me, hurried back in and closed the door, latching it.

"Corvus!" I tried again, jamming the button for the elevator doors to close, punching the button for the second floor.

I fired off another useless text on the way, pulling the emergency stop when the elevator opened again to keep it from being called by anyone else.

"Corvus!"

My neck pricked with dread at the silence that answered. A disquieting sense of anticipation coated my chest in an icy sweat that had nothing to do with coming down.

Where are you, Brother?

I checked almost every floor, that feeling of something coming getting bigger in my chest until I couldn't take it anymore, clapping the hard side of my gun against my temple to get myself together before pressing the button for the top floor.

I checked the clip. The chamber. Sniffing as I wrapped my fist around the grip and the door opened.

My phone went off and I cursed, too on edge in the quiet.

"He got off at the top floor," Grey said. "But the angle is shit from the elevator camera. I can't see which way he went."

"I got him," I said before hanging up. There was only one door.

The penthouse suite.

I raised my gun just as the sound of shattering glass exploded through the door, pushing me to charge. My shoulder popped and bright stars filled the edges of my vision as I rammed straight through, leaving the thing hanging from its hinge as I caught myself.

And found...Gregory Hart standing in front of a broken flat screen TV, a half empty bottle of whiskey in his fist as he looked drunkenly down at his handiwork and then over to me.

"What are *you* doing here?" he slurred at me. "Come to take me down too? Go ahead. You've already taken everything else!"

I scanned the room for Corvus, trying to figure out what I missed.

"Where's my brother?"

His face scrunched, and he just managed to catch himself before he tripped over the broken flat screen on the floor. "Who?"

I shook my head. He wasn't here.

Then where...

The dawning light reflecting off the buildings in the distance out the panoramic windows gave me my answer.

When I turned away to rush out the door, the shadow of something blocking the sunrise darted down the wall.

No.

The unmistakable crunch of metal was followed by the blare of a car alarm and a woman screaming far below.

20

AVA JADE

The image of him falling backward from the roof played over and over against my closed eyelids despite the tears trying desperately to wash it away.

He's gone.

He just... fell.

I screamed my pain, thrashing uselessly against all the bindings keeping me caged tight. I screamed until my throat was raw. Until the pit in my stomach turned into a chasm, draining away all the good things until there was nothing but this.

Nothing but bad, bad, *bad.*

There would never be anything good again.

Through the tears, I found him watching me, his head cocked to one side as he relished in the sight of me broken. This time, I couldn't bring myself to care if this was exactly what he wanted.

I didn't care about anything at all.

I wanted to expunge the last three minutes of existence. Go back to hallucinating peacefully in the dark room.

Hallucinating.

That was it. Wasn't it?

It didn't happen.

It didn't happen.

"Oh but it did, Angel," Drake said, coming to sooth me with a palm against my cheek, and I realized I was chanting the words like a mantra aloud. I tried to bite him, but he pulled away too quickly, leaving my teeth to click against nothing.

"I'll leave you to process this... loss. I have some *things* to take care of. More Crows to turn to roadkill."

This made my breath catch, and my skin burned everywhere. I pushed and pulled against the chair, shouting obscenities at him as he backed out the door, letting it fall closed behind him.

As one door closed another door opened, and I jerked my gaze back up, blinking through tear-stained vision as Grey crashed out the door to the roof, rushing over uneven gravel to the edge of the building.

"Grey!" I shouted uselessly, knowing he couldn't hear me. I could only see him through the live camera feeds Drake left open on the screen. "Don't look!"

He tripped against the ledge, throwing his upper body over to look down, and froze.

I couldn't breathe, but the pain in my chest was beyond measure as I watched him take in Corvus far below. Grey staggered back from the edge, his eyes blinking, face white.

His head shook. His palms went to his knees as he bent his head, unsteady, lips moving wordlessly.

"I'm sorry," I croaked to the screen. "I'm so, so sorry."

He rose up suddenly and kicked the gravel, arching his back, his mouth open in a scream I couldn't hear but that still shattered my heart all the same.

Grey's lower lip trembled as he fell to his knees, eyes shut, face tipped up to the cloudless sky. Hands limp in his lap.

His grief filled me, doubling my own, pushing me to the edge of what I could take. A heart couldn't handle this kind of pain. Surely, *surely* any minute now it would just stop.

I hoped it would.

Grey's attention jerked to his left, back toward the edge of the roof, and I blinked through my tears as his hard gaze focused on something I couldn't see from the angle of the camera.

He scrambled to the edge, kicking up gravel in his wake. When he stood, it was with Corvus' cell phone in his hand. He tapped the screen furiously, dragging the back of his hand hard across his eyes as he searched for anything that he could use.

His fingers stopped moving and his upper lip curled at something he found before he lifted his head and spun in a slow circle. He stopped when he found what he was looking for, eyes locking with mine through the camera he was now stalking toward like a lion let loose from his cage.

Grey stopped just short of the lens, his rage and pain showing through in the tremble of every muscle in his sculpted face.

I couldn't hear him, but it was easy enough to read his lips when he roared into the camera.

I'm coming for you.

I won't stop until she's safe. I won't stop until you're a puddle of blood at my feet. You hear me, motherfucker?

You fucking hear me!

Grey lifted his head suddenly, his eyes searching all around as though he'd heard something.

My pulse spiked as a fresh wave of fear arced through my body, thudding in my ears.

He took off like a shot, darting for the door leading back into the hotel.

"No, wait, *Grey!*" My voice broke on his name. Whatever it was... wherever he was going... it was probably a trap.

Probably going to get him killed.

Get Rook killed.

Oh god, where was Rook?

This wasn't going to end, was it?

Unless...

Unless I put an end to this madness.

I stopped fighting against the agonizing images filling my skull like the strongest sort of poison, screaming as flashes of Corvus flicked past my closed eyelids. Him boxing me in against the cliff side at the Docks. Wanting him. Hating that I wanted him. The moment I realized he was the Bone Man. The moment I decided he was *mine*.

And the moment I saw the decision to jump flash in his cut glass eyes.

His body falling, arms spread in an attempt to take flight doomed only to fail.

Grey's grief at the loss of his brother. His body arching in pain as he roared his fury to a god who wasn't listening.

The darkness that'd been slowly sinking lower, beneath the crust at the floor of my being, started to break free. Something shifted, cracked, and it leaked out, twisting pain into white fire. Grief into the fuel I needed to keep that fire burning hot. Wild.

The smooth metal object in my hand almost slipped out, but I clenched my fist around it, setting my jaw.

The memory of Drake's fingers on my chest, between my legs, beaten back by the darkness whispering that we had something. If he hadn't come so close. Been so distracted. We wouldn't have been able to dip our two fingers into the outside pocket of his jacket. We wouldn't have been able to lift out the item there and stuff it between our palm and the wooden arm of the chair.

The lighter, well worn, with initials engraved in its reflective surface was the first spark of hope I'd had since I'd woken up in this horror show of a place. And I wasn't about to let it go to waste.

21

GREY

I drained the last of the coffee in the paper cup and tossed it to the floor to join the others discarded there, tapping through different security feeds to find the one I wanted.

There was exactly one gas station near the area of the Docks. The road leading up from the lake forked in two directions. One leading toward Thorn Valley and one leading through Edgewood and further south, to Lennox. The gas station squatted in between the prongs of that fork. Anyone traveling by car *had* to take one of those roads to leave the area.

And since Corvus sent Drake after AJ, it was safe to assume he took her that night. Which was why she never came back. Not because she didn't want anything to do with us anymore. Not because what Corvus said had hurt her so deeply it was enough to keep her from us all.

Because he took her.

The image of her, tied to a wooden chair in what looked like a fucking dungeon on Corvus' phone was seared into my retinas and would probably live there for as long as it took to get her back. Maybe longer. Maybe forever.

I'd hoped his phone would be able to give me something my brother couldn't anymore, but I'd already tried to work with the calls and phone numbers Drake used to call Corvus as a means of tracking him, but like I already figured, it was a complete waste of time. He'd covered his tracks too well, but I had one ace in the hole. Well, Diesel's Ace, actually. Someone in the bureau owed him a favor. He'd been saving that favor for years. Today, I asked him to use it, and he agreed.

There was no telling if the agent would do it, or if it would help, but it was worth trying. The last cell tower Drake's burner phone pinged off of to make a call would narrow down the area. And if it didn't, then I was fucking *praying* something in this footage would.

I lifted my gaze to Becca lying in her hospital bed, a machine assisting her to breathe with a tube jammed down her throat.

Or if you'd just do me a solid and wake up…

If she did, there might be something she could tell us. All I needed was a single thread to follow. To unravel it all. And I could find her. I could make this right before we lost anyone else.

I wouldn't lose anyone else.

I grimaced as a sharp pain stabbed into my chest and I hunched over the laptop propped on my lap, swallowing past the burn in my throat.

Everything hurt. My head throbbed in time with my pulse, each labored beating a hammer against my skull, but I wouldn't give in to the need to rest.

I'd rest when I was dead.

Or when *he* was.

My hand vibrated over the mousepad as I toggled over to another folder the owner of the gas station sent over at my 'request,' and I clenched my fist to stop it.

I wanted to be *out there*. Tearing down every building in search of her. Like Corvus would be. But I was better at this. *This* was where my talents were best put to use. Sitting here in this fucking chair, on this fucking laptop, batting my head against a proverbial wall.

"Just give me *something*," I growled at the screen, resisting the urge to throw the damned thing across the room.

A soft double rap at the door preceded my uncle's entry into the room. He took one look at me and all the paper cups littering the floor around me and set his jaw. "Nephew," he said, stepping in quietly, shutting the door behind him.

I nodded before going back to the video files filling my screen with small dark checkered images. I clicked on the first one, playing it with fast forward enabled to get through them quicker.

It would help if I knew what the bastard was driving.

Damien St. Vincent lifted the clipboard from the end of Becca's bed, flipping a page.

"No change," I said, saving him the trouble.

"But everything's stable," he argued. "She should've woken up by now."

He shoved the clipboard back into the slip and put his palm to his mouth, inhaling deeply.

He was right. She should've, and it wasn't a good sign that she hadn't. The longer she stayed in this coma, the less likely she was to wake up at all. But I wasn't about to tell him that. We'd suffered enough loss this week.

"How are you holding up?" my uncle asked, and I tensed, the knee-jerk reaction to tear a strip off him and shove him out the door making my eye twitch.

Or maybe that was just the abundance of terrible hospital coffee in my veins.

"How the fuck do you think?"

"It seems my brother wasn't entirely honest about the situation here. He said it was handled."

I laughed darkly. "Diesel doesn't ask for help."

I didn't need to tell him that. He knew it just as well or better than I did. Diesel handled his own shit. There were three chapters of this gang. His, Uncle Damien's and Uncle Ransom's, and they all operated fully independent of one another. None of them had ever asked him for aid, and he wasn't going to be the first to break that unspoken rule of doing business.

"No. He doesn't. But I wish he would've."

He paused, moving to perch on the edge of Becca's bed in front of me. His ringed fingers clasped in front of him but that was as far as I would look. I couldn't meet his stare. Not right now. I needed to fucking focus.

I clicked to the next video.

"This business with the Kings. Be honest with me. Are they a threat?"

"You need to talk to Dies."

"I'm talking to you."

I clenched my teeth. "We don't know," I answered honestly, doing what my father wouldn't if only to keep anyone else from a senseless death.

My gut twisted. "We have reason to believe they may come after us."

"How undermanned are you right now?"

"More than we should be."

He pushed up from his knees and stood. "That's settled then. You did the right thing, son. This conversation will stay between us. You have my word."

I tapped the spacebar, pausing a video just as a dark colored jeep came driving up to the fork in the road. I squinted, zooming into the still frame to see a shock of blond hair catching the moonlight. I checked the timestamp. It fit.

But the footage was grainy as fuck.

Whatever ancient system this gas station was using needed upgrading fifteen goddamned years ago.

Damien asked something, but I was beyond hearing him, clicking through the footage frame by frame as the topless jeep took the turn, not toward Thorn Valley, but toward Edgewood and Lennox.

It's him.

Holy fucking shit, it was him.

The frozen frame of his face in side profile was unmistakable. But then where was AJ?

I played the footage back a second time. A third.

On the fourth, as the Jeep bumped over a pothole in the road, I caught a glimpse of exposed skin.

I took a screengrab and moved it over to the software I'd purchased last year for cleaning up footage this shitty. I zoomed. Enhanced. Waited for the pixilation to even out.

And there she was.

Slumped over in his lap, her hair fanned over most of her face. That and the dark dress she wore concealed her almost entirely from the view of the camera.

"AJ..." I breathed, my heart pounding as my mind raced to work through what I could do with this.

This was the thread.

Now all I needed was to follow it and unravel everything. If this footage existed, there would be more. I just needed to follow the road. Every business nowadays had video surveillance for liability purposes. I just needed to go bang on every door from this point south. Follow his path south.

It would take time I didn't have, but it was something. Finally fucking *something*.

"Grey," Damien pressed, and I knew it wasn't the first time he'd tried to get my attention. "What did you find?"

I turned the screen to face him. "It's her."

His brows drew down as he analyzed the image. "Do you have a frame with the plate number?"

I'd already taken a screenshot of it. I brought it up and showed him. Damien nodded and pulled out his cell phone, typing something. "I'll see if my contacts can find the owner."

"It won't be the guy," I said. "He's too smart for that."

"Even the smartest of them make mistakes, son. That guy there," he pointed to the still-open image of Drake in the driver's seat. "He saw an opportunity, and he acted. I doubt there was a lot of time for being choosy about transportation."

I nodded, still thinking it would be a dead end but grateful to my uncle nonetheless.

An alarm blared into the hospital room, jarring us into motion. My uncle and I shared a look, both of us twisting toward the door, where loud, thudding footfalls echoed in the hall.

I drew my gun.

My uncle followed my lead.

A voice on the sound system called for security to room 308.

The door smashed open and Rook's pale face stuck into the room, breathing hard, his eyes wide black discs. "He's out of surgery."

22

CORVUS

My head pounded like a fucking jackhammer, making my vision waver and double, smeared with a hazy blur, smudged with bright spots. The lights burned. My body ached like it'd been crushed by a fucking steamroller.

Sour bile coated the back of my throat and I coughed, choking on it as I heaved my battered body up, half rolling off the bed to land on my hands and knees. I vomited onto the tile, the sharp twinge of broken bones along my rib cage protesting the squeeze.

Voices shouted all around me.

Cold fingers wrapped around my biceps and I flung them away, getting unsteadily to my feet.

"Where is she?" I roared, my voice a slurred, raw sound I didn't recognize.

A sting in the back of my hand had me tearing an IV needle free from my skin, untethering me. I crashed into a large square object that chirped at my attack. The machine whirred as I used it to get my balance.

"Doctor!" someone shouted.

A siren alarm sounded all around me, making me cringe as it bored into my ear canals, making the pain in my head double.

"Sir," someone was saying. "Mr. James, I need you to—"

I lashed out in the direction of the speaker, my arm connecting, sending the person to the floor.

"Where is she?"

I pressed my palm flat against my ears, hunching as a wave of intense vertigo made the floor beneath my feet shift. "*Where is she?*"

"*Move,*" a voice I recognized growled.

"Get away from him," another added, and I blinked, trying to get my eyes to cooperate as I lifted my head, stumbling into the wall, the heat in my chest suffocating under the pressure of whatever was wrong with me. Making my heart race and blood vessels constrict until I my ass connected with the floor and an icy sweat slicked over my chest.

"*Where...*"

"Someone turn off that fucking alarm," Grey hissed, and I struggled to lift my chin as the rough touch of my brother gripped me by the shoulders.

"Corv. *Corv.* You with us?"

"He can't be moving right now," a foreign voice joined theirs. "He needs to be lying down. He needs monitoring. We need to—"

"Shut the fuck up," Rook seethed at whoever was speaking. "We'll handle it, just give us some fucking space."

There came no more argument as the cool tile beneath me slowly brought me back from the edge of darkness, and I was able to focus on their faces.

Rook and Grey came into focus, kneeling on the floor of a mostly-destroyed hospital room. My upper lip twitched as the pain in my head and side grew sharper, whatever they'd given me to dull it wearing off faster than it should've been with all the adrenaline pumping in my blood.

"Where is she?"

Rook's jaw clenched.

I wanted to punch it.

They were supposed to find her. They were supposed to save her.

My mind chugged to catch up to the present moment, the rooftop coming back in broken pieces. They were supposed to find her because...

I remembered his hands on her body. Her struggle in that chair.

"Breathe, Bro," Rook pushed. "You need to keep your BP level. You're lucky to still be alive."

The sharp edge to his tone gave away what he wasn't saying. He wanted to shove me off that roof all over again for being so stupid. But he wouldn't have done it any differently, would he?

Now, with my thoughts disjointed and loose in my skull, it all seemed so fucking pointless. Why *had* I jumped?

What good would it have done if I died?

Would it have even stopped him?

I dropped my gaze.

"We need to find her."

I tried to get to my feet.

"Whoa," Grey chided, pushing down on my shoulders until I grunted, dogged by his resistance. "No, you don't."

"We need to *find her.*"

"You aren't doing shit," Rook said in a dead monotone. "Look at yourself, man."

This time when I looked up, I caught a glimpse of my reflection in the upturned metal tray leaning against the base of the hospital bed. Warped and blurry, I cringed at my own reflection, lifting an unsteady hand to my shaved head, finding a wide bandage at the top rear of my skull.

"You had a subdural hematoma," Grey was saying, adding something around burr holes and acute fractures that I didn't understand.

"*English*, Grey."

"Your brain was bleeding," Rook explained. "They needed to drill holes into that thick head to relieve the pressure. And you busted some ribs."

"Is that all?"

Rook barked a laugh. "If the roof of Dies' Camaro hadn't broken the worst of your fall, it would've been a lot worse."

Fuck.

"Don't worry, we convinced him to kill you *after* you finished healing."

"Where is he?"

"On his way," Rook answered. "Now come on, we need to put you back in bed."

I pulled against their attempt to help lift me. "No. We need to find her."

...before he...

I closed my eyes against another wave of nausea.

Grey let go of my arm. "I have a lead."

"What?" Rook and I said at the same time.

"I found footage of Drake taking AJ after the Docks. They went south. I'm going to follow their trail using every surveillance backup I can get my hands on."

I tucked a knee, curling to stand on my own. "What are we waiting for?"

A curse slipped past my lips as the pain in my ribs intensified and wetness spread over my lower stomach, dripping red on the floor.

"Nurse," Rook called, his voice back to the dead tone I knew meant nothing good. "Knock his ass out before he bleeds to death."

I twisted to glare at him.

He glared right back.

The nurse came forward with a syringe and I gave her a withering stare that made her hesitate.

Rook stood, snatching the syringe from her.

"Don't make me use it."

"You wouldn't."

He flipped the syringe around in his fingers, a sly smirk twisting one corner of his lips.

"Want to find out?"

"We're going to find her," Grey interrupted, his arm hooking under mine to grip me around the back, pushing my lame ass up to my feet. "But if we let you die trying to be the hero, she'll just kill the rest of us when we do."

I woke from a forced sleep sometime later, and if it weren't for

Diesel sitting there beside the hospital bed with a shotgun across his lap and thunder in his eyes, I might've tried to escape.

"Don't even think about it."

"I wasn't thinking of shit."

"Sure, you weren't."

He sighed, resting a hand on the barrel of the gun, lifting his eyes to meet mine. A rare glimpse of his true emotion showed through the veil of iron he wore, and I recoiled from it, guilt curling its ugly fist in my chest.

"Where are the guys?"

A muscle in his jaw ticked. "Gone after your girl."

I shot up in bed and nearly passed out from the sudden movement, falling back onto my elbows. "They found her?"

Diesel shook his head at me. "Not yet. But I got some info from that agent who owed me a favor, and Grey's been gathering security footage from every gas station, convenience store, and doorbell cam from the Docks, through Edgewood, all the way to Lennox since last night.

"And?"

"And they've traced his path from the Docks to a service road just outside Lennox before they lost him."

My chest ached with hope. "They're there now?"

Dies twisted his wrist to check the time. "Should be any time now. They're going to drive the area where the footage Grey found ended while keeping within the radius of the last cell tower his burner phone pinged off of."

He must've seen the desperation in my eyes because he lifted a hand to settle me. "It's a wide area, Corvus. At least thirty-square miles."

The hope cracked but didn't shatter. This was what we'd been looking for. Rook and Grey—they could work with this. And I had no doubt that they'd comb every square inch of those thirty-square miles within the next twenty-four hours.

They'd find her.

They *had* to find her.

Because I could barely sit up straight.

"It's your own idiotic fault, you know," Diesel said. "That you're stuck in here while they're out there doing what actually matters."

"Don't."

"Don't *what*, Son?" Diesel snapped. "Don't be upset that my son threw himself off the roof of a fucking building? Hmm?"

I pinched my eyes closed, remembering what it had felt like to give in. To fall.

The most terrifying thing about it was that it wasn't scary at all. It felt like the sweetest sort of release.

It didn't matter that I hadn't slept more than a few minutes at a time in weeks and wasn't thinking straight. It didn't matter that I'd almost killed a guy for making a backhanded comment about my girl in a blacked-out rage. That I'd been slowly, steadily losing this controlled version of myself since the first time I woke up to realize she wasn't there.

It didn't matter that now, in the light of day, lying useless in this fucking bed that I could see how completely pointless my death would've been. I *still* couldn't bring myself to fully regret it.

I'd do it again to save her.

And again.

And again.

If my death meant she suffered for even a minute less than she had to. I'd give her the knife and beg her to end me.

Diesel leaned forward over the shotgun in his lap, his expression hard. Lips in a taut line. "You've really got nothing to say?"

"You don't know what he was doing to her, Dad."

His lips parted at something he saw in my eyes.

"He had her tied. Practically naked. He was..."

A knot formed between his brows.

"...touching her. He threatened to..."

I couldn't even say it without the rage threatening to boil over inside. My head spun, the testosterone and adrenaline at war with the pain killers keeping me floating on a cloud where they couldn't quite reach.

"I couldn't watch him do it," I said after a moment of tense silence between us.

Diesel hesitated before responding, pressing the tips of his fingers together to steeple them in front of his mouth, thinking. "We're going to find this guy, and when we do, the things I did to the man who took my Jacqueline from me will pale in comparison to what he will suffer."

The promise of violence shining in his eyes made me shiver with relief.

"But you have to promise me, Son. No matter what this mother-fucker does, you will *not* throw your life away. You have far too much to live for."

I looked away. "I won't."

23

AVA JADE

Think, bitch.

Think.

I stared at the lighter through watery vision, as though it might whisper to me the secret to my escape. And my revenge.

Without the ability to move, it was useless.

I growled my frustration at it, pushing the darkness to new heights within. Little good it did me now. My skin prickled with it, my chest expanding wide with heavy breath. That nameless power I drew from in critical moments like this one was wasted on me.

What good was it if I *couldn't. Fucking. Move.*

I bared my teeth, carefully maneuvering the lighter between my fingers so I wouldn't drop it, flicking the flint wheel until spark and flame erupted from the metal. The heat of it singed my finger hairs, scorching my skin.

Shit.

I flicked the top closed and the flame snuffed out, the slight burn on my finger smarting with a dull pain.

"Yes," Rook crooned. "That's it."

I tipped the top back on the lighter again and struck a new flame, watching it dance above the wick.

My gaze strayed to the wooden arm of the chair that I was still tied to. It was solid. Ancient. Probably fucking half petrified. But it was *wood*.

The lighter stilled as the shake in my fingers steadied and whatever had been knotting in my chest unfurled. My lips parted, realizing there was one way I could still get out of here.

I couldn't twist my wrist enough to burn off the leather restraint. Or even catch the cloth gauze around the wounds there aflame. I could only touch this flame directly to the wood.

And if it caught, the fire would spread up the arm of the chair, burning everything in its path. The leather restraints. The tied cloth. *Me.*

All I needed was that one arm free and I could untie the rest of me.

...but it was going to hurt.

"Only for a second, AJ," Grey's smooth voice reassured me. "You got this."

"Whatever it takes," Corvus purred in my ear, the vibrations of his rich timbre shaking loose another tear from my eyes. I sniffed, clutching the lighter tighter.

"Burn it all," Rook urged, and when I opened my eyes, he was there.

His hand guided mine, pushing the flame ever closer to the wooden edge of the arm of the chair.

The tattoo over his knuckles...

The rings on his fingers...

He was so real.

So close.

I'd do anything he said if he'd just promise to stay.

I shut my eyes, trying to feel him, leaning into the madness. Willing this beautiful hallucination to carry me through as I pushed the flame to the wood and grit my teeth.

I bit back feral screams as I peeled my burned flesh from the flame-licked wood, the burning leather strap around my wrist stretching like pulled taffy until it finally released its hold on me.

The heat made rational thought the hardest thing I'd ever had to do. So hot. Too hot. Sweat coated my face, my chest. Ran down my arms. Doing absolutely nothing to douse the flames getting steadily larger as they ate the wood from under my arm.

I shook, my eyes rolling back at the ceaseless *burn*. If there was a hell, this was what it would feel like.

Darkness threatened at the edges of my vision, but I breathed through it, unable to look at the pink, red, white, and black menagerie of pain that was my left hand and forearm.

I choked on stomach acid as the fire worked its brutal magic, scorching the sensitive underside of my forearm for another few seconds before the cloth tie burned enough for me to pull through that too. I lifted my wrist to my mouth with a sob, biting down on the still burning gauze wrapped around my wrist to tear it off, screaming through my teeth as the cinders also left little burns on my lips. I spat the gauze out and cursed when it landed on my thighs.

I shuffled enough to let it fall between them, down to the piss pot below.

My arm shook violently as I pulled as far away from the fire as I could, taking my first full breath in what felt like a century, my entire body convulsing as the burning sensation rang through my entire being. Shot bright spots against the backs of my eyelids.

The wood cracked and sizzled.

Bright orange light had me snapping my eyes wide. The fire roared in my ears as the flames spread, licking higher, catching on the back part of the chair.

"Fuck," I managed through the dam in my throat, wincing as I shakily reached for the strap around my forehead. My fingers sloppily tried to work the buckle, putting my elbow back into the fire.

I jerked away reflexively, my stomach dropping.

"We don't give up," Corvus reminded me, and I held onto his voice, willing it to be louder than the wind of the fire rushing past my ears. Singeing my hair. "We *never* give up."

I thrust my elbow back into the fire, latching onto the buckle with renewed purpose, my fingers stinging and numb all at once.

The buckle came loose, and I let my head fall forward, choking on the cloth still tied around my neck. I worked on that next, coughing as the smoke wafted into my face, filling my lungs and already aching throat with its scratching claws.

As soon as my head fell free, I curled my body away from the flames, racing against the growing fire to untie the cloth and buckled straps on my right arm.

This wasn't the clean, sharp, pain of a perfect cut. It wasn't the press of fingers into flesh, caught up in a moment of bruising passion.

This pain didn't call to the broken parts of me, giving me release. It fucking *burned.*

It doesn't hurt, I growled in my mind. *It doesn't hurt. It doesn't hurt. It doesn't hurt.*

Another arm freed and I threw myself forward, using both tingling hands now to untie the rest of my binds, the fire licking at my back. Any second now and the baggy t-shirt was going to catch.

"Come on. *Come on.*"

One leg out and the shirt caught, the breath of the fire blowing hot air up my back.

I shifted my hips away, crying out at the pain in my belly as I threw myself to the floor with one ankle still strapped in, rocking back and forth over the cold cement floor until the fire went out.

The acrid smell of burned hair assaulted my nose and I choked on it as I fumbled with the last strap, kicking the chair when I was finally, fucking blissfully free.

Palm pressed into cement, I willed my body to ignore the burns, the aches, the exhaustion and *get up.*

The chair was almost entirely engulfed in flame now and black smoke stained the ceiling, billowing out toward the close walls, rushing downward.

"*Stay low,* Sparrow."

I made for the door, pausing when my hand wrapped around the handle.

The cameras.

"We need to know what he knows. What he's seen," my mind spoke with the voice of Grey, and I hunched, covering my nose and mouth in the crook of my elbow as I made for the screens, tapping the spacebar to open them up.

The monitors came to life, reflecting with flickering orange light from the fire burning behind me, warming my back through the remaining tatters of the t-shirt hanging from my frame.

My hands hovered over the keyboard.

"The folder with the video feeds," Grey reminded me. "Go to it."

I did, clicking through video feed after video feed, finding a feed of

Sanctum and then another. One that looked to be positioned across the street. Another that rested behind the bar in the underground fight club.

There were three in and around the Crow's nest.

Two in mine and Becca's shared apartment at Briar Hall. One in the living room. The other in my fucking bedroom. The angle was awkward and I struggled to figure out where it could be coming from.

There seemed to be countless others. One in front of Diesel's house. Another near the Docks.

These had to be top grade gear. Otherwise there was no way we wouldn't have noticed them. Was there?

I couldn't count the number of times I'd swept the apartment at Briar Hall, that the guys had swept the Nest, after my stalker had pushed his way into our lives.

Unless these were newer?

I tapped a saved video, my eyes burning from the smoke, throat burning, and watched Drake slither up to my bed at Briar Hall, hunching over my sleeping form in the dark.

My stomach turned, watching him reach down between his legs, his jerky movements giving away what he was doing under the cover of darkness. His body shuddered, and I watched, gagging, as he carefully touched his fingers to my lips, rubbing his seed there. Claiming me.

I exited the feeds, committing their locations to memory so we could take care of each and every single one of them when I got away from here, but a folder labeled simply 'Angels' on the desktop caught my attention.

I clicked it, knowing I was running out of time as the smoke thickened and the reflection of the fire on the monitor's surface brightened at my back.

Photos filled the screen, little snapshots of dead girls.

Each one more gruesome than the last.

All of them strangled to death.

The bruising on their necks clear in each overexposed frame.

They were his trophies, I realized, and the floor shifted beneath me when I realized something else. A similar quality between them all. Long, dark hair. Light colored eyes. Full lips. A familiar curve to their facial structure.

They all looked... like me.

I squinted through the burn in my eyes, coughing uncontrollably as I scanned the room quickly for something I could use, finding the long tweezers Drake had used to dig the bullet out of his arm. I grabbed them and a swath of fresh gauze in my fist and ran to the door, heaving it open to stumble out into the hall. The fresh gust of air drawing the fire to new heights, filling the corridor with smoke.

My watery eyes searched the long hall, finding more than a few doors lining the walls in either direction. Many not unlike the one I just exited. But there were more still that were the other kind. The kind like the one in the first room I wound up in.

Solid steel, with small openable slots near the bottom to push through food.

I paused only long enough to wrap the gauze around my burned arm, but finally allowing myself to look at it, I found I couldn't.

The skin from my wrist up the underside of my forearm was just... gone. Open and raw, a mosaic of colors that didn't belong. Black and pink and red and seeping yellow.

Not a fucking chance I was touching that.

I dry heaved, but managed to choke down the urge to vomit, looking away.

A blinking red light down the hall drew my eye and I stared into the lens of a camera there, knowing somewhere, on the other end of it, Drake was alerted to my escape. That he was probably watching me right now.

How long would it take him to get back from wherever he went? Could he remotely engage some kind of lock? Shit.

It didn't matter, I wasn't going to be here when he got back. No fucking way. I'd let the whole place burn and walk through the ashes to get free if I had to, mortality be damned. I'd become something *else*, something *more* to make sure this bastard got what he deserved in the end.

The sound of glass shattering from the heat in the room I left spurred me into action, and I spared only one glance back at the tongues of flame licking from beneath the door before smiling wide for the camera and taking off down the hall. My legs protested the sudden movement, but I pushed them to *work*.

We were built for this.

We were made *to run*.

And this time, he wouldn't catch me.

The door at the end of the hall was locked, but beyond it, through a small rectangular window, I could see a set of dirty stairs leading up. Out.

I leaned back and threw the force of my body into the door, but it didn't budge, and the aches in my body intensified to the point of nearly losing consciousness. The tweezers clattered to the floor, and I rushed to pick them back up, my panic-addled mind assessing the lock.

Old school. A key lock with a wide chamber.

I bent the tweezers back over my knee, prying them back and forth until they snapped into two pieces, each with a sharp, pointed end, and bent to my knees.

Picking locks was never my forte. It was Dad's specialty. Today, it was going to have to be mine.

The hallway began to fill with smoke as I worked. Great black clouds of it rolled over the ceiling, spreading fast in my direction. The fire spreading beyond the door to the cell he'd kept me in.

I hoped it consumed everything. Every nook and cranny of this accursed place needed to burn.

The lock clicked in protest at my advances, and I coughed raggedly, my lungs aching at the smoke working its way ever lower.

I closed my eyes, pressing my cheek against the still-cool metal of the door to steady myself, letting every sense other than touch fall away. Willing my trembling hands to still as they worked.

The lock made a loud *clack,* and I held the broken bits of metal tweezer in place, reaching for the handle, praying.

It opened, and if it weren't for the need for clean air battering at my rib cage I'd have paused to give Drake the finger through the camera.

I tripped up the steps, letting the heavy door fall closed behind me, one of the two long, sharp bits of metal still in my hand, wielded like a hunter's knife as I clutched the railing, hauling myself all the way up.

The darkness in the tight space was lined with a slice of light carving the stairs in two. Ahead, slanted wood doors lay nose to nose, and sun pushed through between them.

The sun.

I smiled to myself, burning tears from the smoke still tracking down my cheeks.

Unthinking I tried to lift the wood door with my left arm and screamed at the contact with the wounds there.

"Fuck!"

I pushed through with my right, bare feet leaving hard cement in favor of soft earth. Thick brush stood in my way on the other side, and I needed to claw through to get free, biting my lower lip to keep from screaming as it scratched along my wounds.

I fell to my knees in the dirt, twisting to look back at the hole in the ground I'd just crawled out of. You'd never know it was there unless you were looking for it. The worn wood of the cellar doors blended seamlessly with the rest of the overgrowth and the ruddy color of the forest floor all around.

Spinning in a small, slow circle, I took in my surroundings, finding nothing but trees as far as I could see in any direction. I could hear nothing but the chirp of birdsong. The hum of insects.

I found my footing, wincing as the burns along my arm protested the sudden temperature change. The warmth of the daytime sun clung to the forest, even here in the shade, and I sucked air in through my teeth as its humid heat washed over my chilled skin.

If this door was the only way in, then there had to be some sign of which way would lead me out. A road. A path. A tiny ass foot trail. There had to be something.

There!

But as I found my footing again, I realized the one weaving trail of hard packed earth leading away to the right would be the way Drake would likely use to come back, which he was surely already on his way to doing.

I couldn't go that way.

The sun pierced through the leafy canopy above, but I couldn't use it to place myself. I'd been underground too long. Had no sense of direction. No landmarks to orient myself. I had no fucking clue which way would carry back to them.

If I went the wrong way, I could wander for days and find nothing. There were more than a few places in northern Cali where even the most knowledgeable hikers could get lost. This could be a fucking nature reserve. Like in that true-crime horror movie Becca and I watched a few weeks ago. That monster had hidden his victims in a hole in the ground a lot like the one I just crawled out of too.

Maybe Drake was taking notes from Netflix hits.

I stepped in what I thought was a northern direction but hesitated, not wanting to be food for local wildlife, not after finally getting free.

I can wait here, my darkness reasoned. Let him think I'd escaped. Come rushing back. Right into a trap of my own.

I laughed at the absurdity of it, looking at the measly bit of semi-sharp metal in my hand and literally nothing else. I could hardly stand.

Revenge would have to wait.

Besides. Rook and Grey deserved their pound of flesh, too. I wouldn't take that from them.

"This way," I decided, pressing deeper into the trees when I heard the familiar blare of a train's horn, coming from somewhere far off through the denser wood to my left. I stopped to listen more intently, needing to be sure I hadn't imagined the sound.

The horn sounded a second time. Then a third. Then stopped.

I smiled.

If there was a train, then there were tracks. And tracks always led to civilization. I just had to find them.

My feet stung after miles of heading in what I fucking prayed was the right direction. As much as I wanted to, I couldn't mark my progression through the forest to avoid going in circles. If I did, Drake would be able to follow my path. And I was working *hard* to keep that concealed. Doubling back to take a new route every mile or so. Walking through streams when I could. On top of logs.

I was painfully aware of how slow I was going. Entirely unable to run or even walk at a decent pace. Every step felt like wading through water. Or mud.

I stopped being hungry long before my escape and I knew that wasn't good. I could go at least three weeks without food and stay alive, but not without sacrificing energy and strength. The mushrooms and berries of the forest were tempting, but I wouldn't go down like the dude from Into the Wild. Nope.

That wasn't the way to go.

So I settled for sips of stream water, hoping I didn't get sick from it, shivering at the glacial temperature made colder by the rapidly declining temp as day twisted into night.

My eyes fought to close, legs twin pillars of pure *strain*.

Nearly falling, I caught myself on the trunk of a tree, the jarring blow of the rough bark enough to rattle my consciousness back to the present. Away from the jaws of exhaustion.

If only the damned train would go by again, I could orient myself. See if I was going the right way, still. It felt like the right way, but everything looked the same.

A dark shape crouched far ahead, quivering between two thick-trucked redwoods and I froze, half tucked behind the tree I'd run into. My breath fogged in the air, obstructing my view, and I clamped my lips shut.

Gooseflesh rose on my arms.

Oh shit.

I patted the tatters of the t-shirt hanging from my body, searching uselessly for the long bit of metal tweezer no longer in my hand. I scanned the dark forest floor, but no metal glinted in the moonlight.

When I looked up again, the large shape stared back at me with reflective eyes.

I turned to run, my foot catching hard on a tree root that sent me whipping to the ground. My temple connected with hard stone, and I blinked slow, a ringing in my ears as the moon darkened... darkened... until there was nothing.

I came to with a pounding in my head, itchy dried blood tight over my forehead and down my cheek. A weak groan left my lips when I pushed myself to sitting, many fingers and toes numb from the chill in the evening air.

Evening? How long had I been out?

Orange light stained the ground. My straining eyes struggled to make sense of my surroundings, blinking through a gnawing sensation of danger biting at the back of my thoughts.

I pushed up from the cold earth, teeth chattering as I found my footing again.

Dried blood flaked away from my skin as I felt the new injury just above my temple, prodding the area to assess the damage. My pinched eyes flew open at the memory of what sent me tripping in the dark.

I whirled around, a shaky laugh falling from my lips at the moss covered boulder squatting fifteen yards away between two tall redwoods. I shook my head, wincing when that shook loose another shooting pain through my temple.

Now which fucking way was it?

"Guys," I asked, holding my breath as I awaited a reply from the madness in the voices of my guys. "I could use a little help."

In answer to my call, a train's horn sounded, loud enough to vibrate in my rib cage.

I darted through the trees, rushing toward the sound despite the protest of my body. Without caring about covering my tracks. I wasn't going to lose it this time. No fucking way.

"Come on, bitch," I urged myself, Ignoring the burn in my limbs. The pounding in my head. The desperate, *desperate* need for rest. The darkness consumed it all, spreading fresh adrenaline like a salve over my entire being.

I pushed my legs harder. Faster. Letting the sensation of flight as I soared over the earth, catapulting over fallen logs and darting around trees to provide me with the only fuel I needed to keep going.

Flashing images of my guys stood in the forest all around me, watching as I soared past them. Vanishing as soon as I turned my head.

Not real.

They're not real.

The echo of the horn faded, leaving me in the wide wild wood alone.

"No!"

I kept on in the same direction, not altering my path. So focused on keeping my body moving, I didn't notice the steep drop in the terrain or the break in the trees before it was too late. I sailed over the edge and slid on my knees over a bed of sharp gravel, my body flung against a hard iron bar.

Pain exploded in my rib cage and I curled in on myself, feeling the vibrations of the hit deep, deep down.

No. Not the vibrations of the blow to my ribs.

I gripped the iron track I'd landed on, feeling the rattle of the oncoming train a second before the horn blared again. The great metal beast charged from around a bend in the track, coming at me head on.

"Fuck!"

I ducked and rolled out of the way, scrambling backward over the gravel just as the train sped past, making my hair lash against my cheeks.

I tipped my head back, laughing up at the sky. The next curse out of my lips a much softer one. I fucking did it. And what was more. I knew these tracks. The train passed and I stepped into its wake, staring after it until its tail vanished around the next bend.

These tracks carved a path through Lennox. I caught movement from the corner of my eye and I fell back, whirling to see my father, pale and ghastly, crouched between the tracks.

I squeezed my eyes shut. Opened them again.

He was gone.

Jesus Christ.

I was losing it.

I shook my head, trying to get my rational brain working again. If I followed the tracks, they'd lead me to the trailer park on the outside of town where I'd lived with both my parents before Mom took off and Dad bit it.

And if I followed them a little farther, they'd take me past the spot where I'd taken my first life.

The night that set this whole goddamned mess in motion.

But I wasn't going to be taking a trip down memory lane today. Fuck no. The past was finished and I had too much to live for—too much to do—in the present.

I stepped off the tracks to the west, climbing the short bank back up into the woods on the other side, picking my way toward the road I knew wasn't more than five more miles away.

24

ROOK

I peeled the wrapping from a fresh pack of cigarettes, putting one to my lips as Grey turned onto a dark backroad we'd already driven down three times since this afternoon. Just like every other road within the thirty-mile radius Diesel marked on the map for us before we left.

"She has to be here," Grey muttered to himself. We'd already searched every nook and cranny of Lennox, tempting fate by crossing into King territory even though Diesel expressly told us to keep a low profile.

We were relying on the older model two-seater Jag with the super tinted windows—Pinkie's prized possession—to keep us concealed and so far, it'd been working.

There was only one instance where I might've been seen, during a quick in and out at the local pub under the guise of taking a piss.

Kind of disappointing that they hadn't noticed us yet. I hungered for pain. Thirsted for blood. I wanted them to find us, maybe then I wouldn't need the poison burning a hole in my pocket to keep me going. I could inhale their souls instead.

"Unless you want to start knocking down doors, Bro, this is what we've got to work with."

He didn't answer, and I knew he was thinking that knocking down some doors might not be a half bad idea.

"Where was that service road again? We should go back and check out that way. Maybe there's a dirt road we missed? A trail?"

"We already looked."

"Well, let's look *again*."

I held the dart between my lips as I opened the map app again on my phone, zooming into our location, scrolling to the left to find the service road again. "Take the next right and then it's a left about a half mile down."

My heart beat out an uneven rhythm in my chest, and I coughed to cover a violent shudder, grinding my teeth as I set my phone down in favor of tapping the armrest. Mouth dryer than if it had been scoured out with a fresh kitchen sponge.

I couldn't wait anymore.

"Pull over, man. I gotta take a piss."

"Again?"

I fixed him with a look, gesturing to the bottle of bourbon by my feet and the water in the cup holder he'd been making me drink alongside it.

He rolled his eyes before pulling the Jag onto the shoulder. I stepped out into the moonlight, stalking a little ways into the tree line, limping, making a show of stretching out my legs while the Jag idled at my back.

A quick glance over my shoulder showed Grey's face illuminated on the light from his phone screen. Checking the map again no doubt. We'd planned to do one more round of driving through this area before starting on foot into the forest around the place where Grey's found footage cut off.

I wasn't looking forward to that, but I had something that would help get me through.

I took the silver ball of foil (name) gave me at the Pub and opened it, careful not to drop any of the powder contained inside.

"Let's go!" Grey shouted out the window, honking, nearly making me drop it.

"Jesus Christ, I'm coming!"

I bent low, pretending to fix my boot lace as I fingered the blade from the sheath at my ankle, lifted a small mountain of white from the foil with the tip and snorted it from the sharp metal.

My eyes rolled back as the chemical burn shot through me, making my muscles ripple with it. The pull of exhaustion fleeing like a distant memory.

"Dude, are you taking a shit right now? Really?"

"Fuck, Grey!"

I heard the window roll up, and I wrapped the foil back over the blow, twisting it tight before sheathing the blade back where it belonged.

Rising to my feet, I luxuriated in the feel of a fresh white wave crashing through my system.

I stopped, squinting into the dark.

A light shone dimly through the trees ahead to the left. Headlights, I realized. Far away. On the road that intersected this one a half a mile up.

The car wasn't driving, though. The headlights were sedentary. Whoever it was, they were pulled over. On a random backroad. In the middle of butt fuck nowhere. At almost eleven at night.

A horn blasted, long and loud.

I raced back to the Jag, ripping the door open to throw myself inside.

"Did you hear—"

"*Drive*," I roared, dread singing in my veins, vivid images of my Ghost, pale and unmoving on the side of the road strobing in my mind.

I braced myself on the dash, my heart a jackhammer in my chest as Grey peeled away from the shoulder back onto the road.

My skin tightened, flexing, constricting me like a cage.

"What is it?" Grey shouted over the roar of the engine. "What did you see?"

"Go!" I hissed, urging him to speed up, my breaths coming ragged.

He took the turn at nearly eighty miles an hour and the Jag fishtailed out on the road, facing the minivan pulled over on the shoulder a hundred yards down.

The driver's side door hung open to the night air, and in the cabin light I could see the woman making wild gestures with her arms, lifting them high. Trying and failing to fend off the person attempting to steal her wheels.

A glint of steel in the moonlight.

A flash of dark hair whipping in the wind.

I was already opening the passenger side door before Grey could slow the Jag.

"Rook," he hissed, his fist twisting in the back of my jacket to stop me as the tires screeched, slowing the Jag and her face turned toward us, sea glass eyes violently unhinged.

Ghost.

I lost my footing, thrown to my damn face on the uneven pavement on the side of the road as I stepped out of the still rolling car.

She threw the woman from the drivers' seat onto the ground and stepped into the minivan.

"No!"

The Jag purred as Grey floored it, cutting her off, the front of the van crushing against the side of the Jag.

"Ghost!"

She fell from the driver's side door, coughing, struggling to get back to her feet. To run.

I chased after her, willing her to see me, hearing the Jag door open.

My Ghost limped as she ran, barefoot, wearing nothing but a bit of torn, dirty fabric on her naked body.

"Ghost!"

This time she jerked to a standstill, her shoulders heaving as she hunched her body, curling in on herself, her palms pressing tight to her ears. "No, no, no," she muttered.

"AJ!"

Grey blew past me, catching up to her.

"Not now," she was screaming, pounding on her head.

She lashed out as Grey neared, a skinny bit of sharp metal in her fist. She slashed at him violently.

"AJ. AJ, it's me. *It's me.*"

I panted, throwing an arm out to stop Grey from advancing on her.

"Ghost," I said, calmer now despite the buzzing in my veins.

I knew that look.

The sheen in her too-wide eyes. The pupils dilated to extremes.

When I got my hands on the filth that drugged her, I was going to rip him apart.

"This is real," I told her, shocked at the sting in my eyes. The ache in my gut that demanded I go to her. Touch her. Hold her. To make sure *I* wasn't the one hallucinating. "We're here."

I felt the moment Grey caught on to what was happening, his body stiffening against my still-extended arm.

"We aren't a hallucination."

Her fist clenched around the bit of metal held out in our direction, face breaking as her gaze darted between us.

Behind her, the woman from the van ran down the road, shouting for help, but I could barely hear her over the thump of my own heartbeat. Didn't give a fuck about anything or anyone else in this moment except *her*.

Ghost's grip on the bit of sharp metal faltered. "But..."

Her lower lip trembled, her watery gaze searching the air behind us as though there was something missing.

"If you're real, then..."

Her face broke and a heavy sob racked her body. She dropped her makeshift weapon, and I rushed her, pulling her into my chest, holding her tighter than I'd ever held anything in my miserable life. She shattered against me, her entire body shaking, making my darkness whisper sweet nothings in my ear about all the things we'd do to make sure this *never* happened again.

I pressed my lips to the top of her head, cradling her skull to keep her tight against me, tucked into the crook of my neck. Her scent, tainted by smoke and earth filled me. The feel of her, cold and small, made my primal instinct recoil when Grey tried to move closer, snatching her away from him. Keeping her close.

"I'm sorry," she croaked between sobs. "I'm sorry. I'm sorry. I'm sorry."

The black thing in my chest splintered.

This time when Grey came close, I let him touch her, but I didn't let go. I wasn't sure if I could. Not yet.

He brushed the hair away from her cheeks. "Hey," he crooned in that way only Grey could. "Hey, it's okay. It's okay, you're safe. We've got you. We've got you."

She pulled away from his touch, shaking her head against me. "No," she sniffed. "It's not okay. It's never going to be okay again."

"*Shhh*," I whispered against the top of her head. "It will," I promised her.

"I'm sorry," she said again. "It's all my fault."

Grey took her chin, forcing her to look at him from the cocoon of my embrace. "Hey," he said, sharp. "None of this is your fault, you hear me?"

"It's ours," I growled, feeling the guilt of it like water in my lungs, suffocating. "We should've never let him get his hands on you. We should've found you faster. *We should've saved you.*"

"But you *did* save me. You were all there with me. Helping me escape."

Grey frowned, his brows drawing down in confusion. "AJ, you aren't making sense. You saved yourself."

She shook her head again. "Not fast enough. Becca... *and Corvus,*" her voice broke on his name. "I wasn't fast enough to save them."

Shit.

I released my hold on her to hold her at arm's length, needing her to see the truth in my eyes.

Her body shook with another sob, and I thumbed a tear away from her eye. "Corvus is alive, Ghost."

She stilled, the fevered hope in her eyes spurring a fresh wave of tears.

"So is Becca," Grey added, and her lips parted in mute shock.

"Corv was hurt bad from the fall," Grey explained. "He's in the hospital, but they're hopeful he'll make a full recovery. And Becca... she's..."

"She's going to be fine," I lied, unable to tarnish the emotion I could see in her eyes.

She swallowed, her fingernails digging into my forearms where they held her, like she couldn't let go of me yet, either. "Take me to them?"

"*Shit, AJ,*" Grey rasped, and I realized how he was looking at her. *What* he was looking at.

My pulse quickened to new, impossible heights at the shade of the skin showing through a tear in the shirt she wore.

I clutched a strip of it and ripped it off, revealing her naked body and a sweep of bruises all across her lower abdomen. She tried to cover the injury with an arm burned from wrist to elbow, a raw mess of deformed skin colored in shades I recognized from my own victims. The kind of burns that usually preceded a long suffering death.

But on her. *On my Ghost,* it wasn't art.

I bent, my vision darkening at the edges as the shadow inside swelled, aching for vengeance, making me shudder.

"We need to get you to a hospital," Grey was saying, but it was like he was speaking underwater, growing more and more distant. "Come on, baby."

"Rook?"

I heard her call, tried to latch on to it, let it drag me to the surface, but there was a stronger call from the deep.

My vision tinted red as I rose up, watching Grey with Ava Jade cradled in his arms as he carried her back to the minivan, opening the side door to help her into the seat.

Her eyes locked with mine, disarming me like a pin put back in a grenade. The *need* there so clear that it rattled me back to myself, shaking liquid from the corners of my eyes.

I had no memory of movement, but suddenly I was there, stopping Grey from closing the door, slipping into the backseat with her, gently lifting her body so that she could lie across my lap. Her hands wrapped around my thigh, holding tight.

Grey shut the door behind us, jumping into the front seat.

I brushed the sweat-dampened hair away from her overheated forehead, hating how pale she looked. How frail he'd made her.

She shivered at my touch. "Promise me..." she said, her voice a low growl in the dark, beckoning to the most savage parts of me.

Grey pushed the Jag off the road with the minivan, grinding gears, alternating between drive and reverse, cursing under his breath until the dark backroad was clear and we were moving again.

"Anything."

"Promise me he'll suffer."

My vision darkened as I threaded my fingers through hers, gripping tight.

"No one will ever suffer more."

What the fuck was taking so long?

I tapped my foot on the tile, flexing my jaw, leaning over my knees with my hands clasped together.

"Shouldn't she be out by now?" Grey echoed my worry, pacing the hallway outside the door to the x-ray room at the hospital. The one fucking place the docs vetoed us from entering while they took comprehensive scans of her stomach and pelvic region, checking for anything worse than what we could see on the surface of her skin.

It was the last item in an hours-long endeavor to have every inch of her checked. Which she only agreed to *after* seeing Corvus and Becca for herself. Pinkie and a few of the other guys in the hall guarding both rooms regarded her with obvious shock, making way for her to pass with nods of respect. There had been no change in Becca's status, and Corvus was doing well, resting with a knot in his brows even in sleep.

I was going to wake him, but Ghost said not to, leaning over to kiss his forehead and brush her fingertips over the shaved hair around the new scars on his skull before taking a seat next to him.

The only reason she left to have herself checked out at all was because Grey made Pinkie promise that he'd call us the second Corvus woke up.

They attended to her burns first. My Ghost refused the offer of pain medication before they set to cleaning the burns, removing the dead skin and applying grafts. She bore it with a sort of numb resignation, the only indication it hurt at all the occasional twitch of her nose.

Grey and I each held a hand as a nurse performed a rape kit on her after she admitted she didn't know whether he'd violated her since she'd been unconscious most of the fucking time. She wouldn't look at us before or after the nurse finished, jotting notes down on a clipboard and promising the doctor would share them with her once the rest of her examinations were complete.

We waited as they inserted an IV needle into her arm to get her fluids she desperately needed. And while they drew blood afterward.

Always at her side.

Until now.

It didn't matter that we had the entire hospital filled with Saints now. Or that the staff were aware of a potential threat with all members of security holding a picture of Drake's face in their phones. Right now, this door separating us from her was the most repulsive object I'd ever seen, and if she didn't exit it in the next three seconds, I was going to break it the fuck down.

Grey's phone rang, and he lifted it to his ear, never ceasing his pacing footsteps in front of the door.

"What?" he answered.

"Who is it?"

"Dies," Grey replied, listening to something our father was saying on the other end. "He just got back."

I nodded.

"I can't right now."

I stood, feeling heavy and cold. My body aching for more of the white powder burning a hole in my pocket.

I didn't realize I'd stuffed my hand in, feeling the spiky edges of the foil until Grey snapped something at Diesel on the phone and I tore my hand free, swallowing the taste of acid on my tongue.

I lit a cigarette, putting it to my lips as I strode closer to the door, trying to listen to what was happening inside. The ceaseless Christmas music blaring through the halls wasn't fucking helping my nerves, either.

"You can't smoke in here, Rook," Grey said, covering the receiver with his palm. "It's a fucking hospital."

I lifted a brow at him, ashing on the floor. "Watch me."

Thanks to a generous donation from Diesel of the rest of our working capital as well as a blackmail threat to some jackass on the hospital board, we owned this place. At least for the next forty-eight hours.

Nothing would be reported to the useless sacks of shit at Thorn Valley PD, and I doubted a bit of laced tobacco smoke was going to change that.

He rolled his eyes, saying nothing as he went back to his conversation with Dies. "Come up here, then. I'm not leaving—"

"Go," I told Grey, knowing our father would want a full account of everything straight from the horse's mouth. He'd want to know where we found her. *How* we found her. And anything else she told us. Which at this point was almost nothing.

She'd been painfully silent since we found her, but I knew that would change. She just needed a fucking minute to catch her breath. I'd wait. And Diesel would fucking wait, too.

"What?" Grey snapped, his gaze straying to the closed door. "I'm not—"

"I've got her," I told him, taking another drag. "I'll bring her back down to Corv's room as soon as she's done."

His expression tightened, but he nodded, speaking more roughly as he replied to our father. "I'll be down in a sec."

He spared one more longing look at the door before turning on his heel to leave, storming down the hall to the elevator.

I inhaled deeply through my nose and stubbed out my cigarette beneath my boot, my hand absently going back to the tiny bulge in my pocket before I curled it into a fist and knocked hard on the door.

"Almost done in there?"

No answer. I tried the handle. Locked.

"Just a second," came a muffled reply from the nurse. I couldn't hear my Ghost.

I banged again. Harder.

"Open up!"

No answer.

My stomach dropped.

Three... two...

I stepped back, reaching for my gun to blow the entire handle off just as the door swung open and the nurse gasped at the sight of me, shuffling backward into the room.

I pushed past her to find my Ghost wincing as she sat up on the table, her legs dangling over the edge.

She smirked at me knowingly, the first sign of life I'd seen from her since we found her. "Can't go without me for more than five minutes?"

I narrowed my gaze on her. "Not if I can fucking help it."

She laughed, flinching as she got to her feet, walking around the wheelchair next to the bed.

"She should really be using that until the doctor goes over these x-rays," the nurse pressed, indicating the wheelchair.

I lifted a brow at my Ghost.

She stared at me deadpan.

"Nah," I said, reaching for her. "I got her."

"Mr. Clayton, you can barely walk yourself. In fact, you should be using a wheelchair, too. Crutches at least."

Ballsy, this one.

"She's right," my Ghost said, looking up at me with worry creasing her brow. "Your leg."

It was my turn to smirk. "I'll use the crutches if you sit your ass in that wheelchair."

Her lips pursed.

"That's what I thought."

25

AVA JADE

The broken pair of us used one another to stay standing as we walked back down the long hall toward the elevators. I choked on a breath, seeing my father standing behind the nurse in the box as the doors closed.

Not fucking real.

I squeezed Rook's arm, feeling how solid he was. *This* was real. I tried to make my tired mind remember the difference.

"Where did Grey go?" I asked.

Rook licked his lips, running his teeth over the piercing at the edge of his mouth. "Gone to tell Diesel what's up. We're headed down there now."

His hand trembled where I held it in the crook of my elbow. I squeezed it, but the tremble didn't quit. "Are you okay?"

A dark laugh passed his lips. "Am *I* okay?"

"That's what I asked."

He went from licking dry lips to biting them, his dark eyes downcast. A knot between his brows. He looked so pale, I realized. The hollows below his eyes were beyond normal Corvus levels and that was saying something.

Tonight, *he* looked like the Ghost. Not me. I wondered how long it'd been since he slept. If it was me, I wouldn't have wanted to sleep until I knew he was safe.

Scratch that, *I wouldn't sleep.*

At all.

I pulled him to a stop, making him turn his attention to me. Rook looked down at me with a question in his eyes. Deep brown overtaken with iris' blacker than I'd ever seen them.

My hand found his chest beneath the leather jacket he wore, and I pressed into him, needing him to feel me. To know that I was here and safe. That he could relax the tension I could sense all over his body. Pulling his shoulders tight. Flexing in his legs and up and down his tatted arms. He was wound tighter than a fucking top.

"I'm here, now," I muttered. "You can breathe."

Humoring me, he took a long, slow breath, but it came out shaky, and when he bent his head to mine, pressing our foreheads together, I felt the cadence of his heart beating against my palm.

A thundering gallop in his chest.

I gasped, pulling him closer, putting my ear to his chest, listening to make sure I wasn't mistaken. The insane speed of his pulse *thump-thumped* against my cheek like a cheetah at full sprint.

When I pulled away, I could see it written all over his face. The guilt and shame. The pain. *The fear.*

"What did you do?"

He looked away, his jaw grinding.

He wasn't going to get off that fucking easy. I snatched his hand and dragged him the few yards down the hall to a door labeled 'Supply Closet,' opening it and shoving him inside. I closed the door behind us.

"Where is it?"

He didn't even bother trying to deny it, instead his gaze tracked to his left pocket, and I dug into it, coming up with a small ball of foil.

Hot tears burned in my eyes as I clenched it in my fist. "*Why?*"

"I needed it—"

"That's bullshit."

He bristled, still unwilling to look me in the eyes.

"Where did you get it?"

My tired mind was already trying to work through the logistics of how to proceed from here. What I needed to do. Slit his dealer's throat was number one on the list, followed closely by chaining his rogue ass to something immovable until all of it left his system.

He backed away a step in the tight space, leaning against a shelf full of mop heads and jugs of bleach. The whole room stank of it.

"I asked you a fucking question," I snapped, closing the gap he tried to put between us, needing him to see how serious I was.

I may not have been there, but I knew what he went through from the stories the guys told me and all the things they didn't say about those dark years but communicated about with their solemn silence and looks.

It was bad. And it had been even worse trying to get him clean.

"That," he said, nodding at my closed fist and the drugs I held. "From a guy in Lennox. But the first eight ball came from—"

He cut himself off, clenching his teeth.

"From who?"

"Take a guess."

My lips popped open.

"He left it for me in the shed at the Nest. A gift."

"And your first thought was *hey, I'll just put this right up my nose?*" I was screaming now, but I couldn't help it. My skin was buzzing, *burning* with rage.

I shoved him hard in the chest. "What if it'd been laced? What if he was trying to kill you and you just—"

"I didn't do it when I fucking found it," Rook interrupted, hurt in his coked out eyes. "I had it for weeks before I did it. It was only when—"

"When what?"

"Fuck, Ghost, let me finish!"

I stifled the very real urge to punch him in the dick and walk out the door.

He sighed. "When you didn't come back. That's when I did it. When I realized that something was wrong and *you needed me*. You needed us."

His words dulled some of the anger and fear dancing behind my ribcage, but I'd heard excuses from my mom a thousand times before. Addicts would say anything to rationalize their actions. The reasons why they 'needed' to use.

I *tried*. I tried not to let those past experiences taint what was happening right here and right now, but the fear-fueled rage inside was already building.

"I couldn't let myself sleep," he added when I said nothing. "I needed to stay alert. I needed—"

I shook my head and he stopped talking.

The rage that'd been building didn't crescendo, instead it shattered, my chest aching. Because it wasn't rage at all. It was sadness. Fear. Guilt.

"You can't do this to yourself," I whispered. "I won't let you."

I opened my fist, looking down at the repulsive shining ball in the center of my palm, looking up at him.

Before I could drop it to the floor and stomp on it, Rook plucked it from my palm and did just that, grinding it under the toe of his black boot. "I don't need it anymore," he said quietly.

He reached into his jacket and grabbed the pack of cigarettes there, offering them to me along with a small metal flask he pulled from his back pocket.

"I don't need any of it. Take it. I just..."

His Adam's apple bobbed.

"I just need you, Ghost. I can't do this without you."

I swallowed past the lump in my throat, my eyes burning. "Do what?"

He gestured vaguely all around us. "Any of it. It's like I've been living in the dark, buried six fucking feet underground since you..."

He dropped his arms, defeated. "It's like I can finally breathe. Finally feel the sun. I couldn't go back. I *can't* go back. Not now that I know what this feels like. So take it. Take it all. I'll be whatever you want me to be."

I shakily took the pack of cigarettes from him, fingering one out to put it to my lips, looking up at him expectantly, a ball of emotion tight in my chest.

His lips twitched at the corner, and he held back a laugh as he took the lighter from his pocket and leaned in, lighting the tip as I inhaled long and deep.

I blew the smoke over our heads, my whole body sighing at the release from the tobacco.

"I don't want you to change for me, Rook." I tried to sound strong even though I felt far from it right now, with his words ringing in my ears, whispering that I was loved deeply. More than I ever thought I deserved. "Don't brighten your darkness or blunt your edges *for anyone*. You're perfect the way you are."

I pointed to him with the ash end of the cigarette, waiting for his eyes to align with mine, for him to see the darkness there, before I spoke. "But if you *ever* touch that shit again, I will fucking destroy you."

He grinned. "*Mmmm*," he purred, and a gear shifted between us. "Is that a promise?"

"I'm not fucking around."

He bit his lip ring, crowding me in against the closed door until I could feel his heat against my chest, his breath against my cheek. I took another drag of the cigarette, outwardly ignoring his antics even though inside, I was aching with a need for him so strong I thought it might tear me apart.

"Swear to me," I said, back arching of its own accord as his teeth scraped along the sensitive skin below my ear.

"Hmm?"

"If you get an urge that you don't think you can suppress on your own..."

He gripped my left hip, pressing his semi into my belly as he continued a torturous trek of teeth and tongue down my throat to my collarbone.

My toes curled.

"...that you'll tell me. So I can help you."

He pulled back, and I saw the war he hid from everyone raging inside. The one I was willing to bet he waged on himself every day, hiding behind an aloof exterior but always fighting the darkness, and the need to dull it by any means necessary.

The battle he was no longer hiding from *me*.

"I swear."

I dropped the cigarette, and he crushed the remnants of it on the cement floor, dropping the flask to the ground with a clatter as his strong fingers curled around the back of my neck, pulling my lips to his.

He kissed me like a man who'd just received a pardon from death row. Like it was the first time and the last time he'd ever be able to hold me.

I moaned against his lips as he took me, his tongue finding mine as he inhaled me deep, his fist twisting in my hair. I clutched his jacket like it was the only thing anchoring me to this moment.

My body ached inside and out with my need for him. When he pressed between my legs, I cried out, and he stilled, backing off, his lips leaving mine.

His eyes found mine in the dark before slipping low, to the bruises across my abdomen now hidden by the baggy hospital gown whispering against my pebbled nipples.

I could sense his hesitation, only making me grip him tighter. "No," I all but snapped. "I need you. *Right now.*"

I'd never needed anything more.

His grip on my hip loosened, and I swear to Christ I almost hit him, but he didn't let go, just relaxed his grip. His fist in my hair uncurled to trace a gentle path down the side of my neck to my collarbone. I shivered and his teeth flashed in the dim light.

"Then you'll have me."

Confused, I cocked my head, a question on my parted lips as he easily untied the string holding my hospital gown to my body and it slipped to the floor.

A muscle in his jaw ticked as his black eyes roved my body, finding evidence of my need for him and more injuries than I knew he could handle seeing.

He bristled, falling back a step, but I caught him before he could go any further, pulling his hand back to my body. I placed it over my heart, needing him to feel it.

"I'm alive," I said on a breath. "Let me *live.*"

The muscle around his right eye twitched as he closed them, tension clear in his jaw as he lifted his hand to cup my face, brushing his thumb over my jaw.

Rook pressed his lips to mine again, the kiss so slow and deliberate, so gentle that it broke me all over again.

His thumb drew a straight line down my body as he continued to kiss me slow, making my thoughts scatter. My fingers itched to grip him tight, to fist in his black hair, but I held still, letting myself indulge in the moment, knowing this show of restraint and tenderness wouldn't—*couldn't*—last.

"I told you…" I said, my breaths hiccupping as his tracing fingers found my inner thigh, turning their trajectory upward. "I don't want you to change for me. I want *you.*"

…and you're not gentle.

"This is me, Ghost," he purred against my throat, the rumble of his voice vibrating down the length of my body. "This is me taking care of you. Let me."

"But…"

"Shhh. The things I'm going to fucking do to you once you're healed can wait. Right now, *this*…"

His fingers found my wet pussy, and I gasped, fingers digging into the door at my back.

"…is what you need."

"*Roo—*"

He swallowed my cry with his mouth, pushing his fingers into me. I fought against the urge to clench my thighs, forcing them wider for him.

"That's it, Ghost."

Rook fucked me with his fingers, slow, adding a third until he had me stretched wide and dripping for him.

I buried my face in his chest, clenching my teeth, coming completely undone for him. He sucked a nipple into his mouth and I almost screamed at the dual sensation, my stomach flipping, pussy clenching tight around his fingers.

"More," I whimpered, holding his head there with a tight fist in his hair.

He ran his teeth over my nipple and I bucked against him.

"*More.*"

He bit down on my breast and I sucked in a breath at the sting, grinding against his hand between my legs.

My nipple popped from his mouth and he switched to the other one while he rolled the one still wet from his tongue between the callus pads of his fingers. Tugging and pinching until I thought I might come from that touch alone.

I jerked and clenched everywhere he touched me, my skin on fire. Alive with the feel of him. His scent in my lungs. His warmth, like a furnace. His *everything.*

"*Fuck*," I croaked, my orgasm building as he quickened the pace with his fingers, rubbing my clit viciously with his thumb.

I could feel his smile against my breast as he sucked my nipple into his mouth again, rolling his tongue over it, drawing me to the edge.

I bucked against him as my orgasm tore through me, evicting a loud cry from my lips. The strength of it tore through my body, and I recoiled from it, the sensation almost too much to bear.

But Rook wasn't having it. He kept my legs open with a knee to my thigh and pressed his free palm flat against my chest, shoving me back, holding me still against the door as he continued to fuck me with his fingers. Wringing every ounce of the earth shattering orgasm from my body, ignoring my claws in his forearm or the way my legs shook.

He didn't stop until I was shuttering against the restraint of him, seeing stars, my throat dry from panting. Knees weak.

When I was able to focus on his face again, the stars receding, I saw a glint of wicked triumph in his black stare. I also saw the hard ridge of his cock pressing against his jeans and my core tightened.

I looked up at him hungrily and he slowly slipped his fingers from my pussy, bringing the glistening digits to his mouth. He sucked his pinkie clean, licking his lips when he was finished, making my breaths come heavy against his palm.

When my gaze found his cock again, he growled, pushing me beyond all limits of my control. I knocked his arm away and fumbled with the buckle of his leather belt, unable to wrench it free because of the infuriating shake in my fingers.

"Ghost—"

I dropped to my knees and drew the blade from the sheath at his ankle, feeling the sense of pure *power* with it in my hand. I stood, slicing through the leather with ease.

"Ghost, you're hurt—"

I changed tactics, flipping the blade through my fingers, bringing it to his throat. "So are you," I hissed, my thighs squeezing as he closed his eyes, chin tipping up to allow me better access to his carotid artery with a rumble of desire in his chest.

With my other hand, I pushed below the waistband of his jeans, wrapping his thick, silky cock with my fingers, making him jerk upright, standing at attention with a broken laugh on his lips. The piercings down his shaft bumped over my fingers, the feel of them making me soaking wet.

"Tell me you don't want this," I challenged him and he brought his chin down, staring into my soul.

"Never."

I threw the blade and the lightbulb over our heads shattered as I shoved Rook back, out of the scattering glass and into the shelves at his back. Several broke, knocking mop heads and piles of cloth to the floor as I clawed his jeans from his body. He lifted me when I was finished, spinning us until my back was pressed against the shelves in the dark. His breath against my lips.

"Tell me if it hurts," he whispered, and I didn't know if it was because he wanted it to or because he didn't. Both options left me wanting more. He pushed his cock against my opening, rubbing it over my clit before slipping it inside.

I bit the inside of my cheek, tipping my head back as he eased himself inside, each piercing on his Jacob's ladder gliding in.

He curled a hand around my hip, fingers digging into my lower back. The ache in my belly was nothing compared to the immense pleasure of having him inside of me. Filling me.

"Ghost?" he asked, stopping.

I wrapped my legs around his waist, bracing myself on one of the shelves at my back, urging him closer. "I want every fucking inch," I demanded. "I want it all."

He sheathed himself inside me, groaning as he settled in to the hilt, his grip on my waist tightening.

I panted as I adjusted to his size, starting to move against him, needing to feel him move inside me.

Rook eased out, his piercings rubbing me just right, adding an edge to the pleasure that I could say with conviction I would *never* tire of.

His hand came around the back of my neck, holding me there, our eyes locked as he fucked me. No. As he made love to me, showing a restraint so beautiful it made me want to cry. As much as I craved all things distinctly *Rook*. His rough touch. The sharp bite of blades on skin. This hurt just as much, but in a different way.

I could feel myself unraveling as he thrust into me, pausing to roll his hips, grinding into my clit, making me tremble in his grip.

He looked down between us, at the joining of our bodies, his eyes heavy lidded. His grip on me changing, tightening as he struggled to contain his baser instincts.

"Fuck, Ghost, you feel so good."

He let out a little growl and the sounds of his pleasure started the quickening sensation low in my belly, making me move with him, pushing him faster, harder.

"Oh god, Rook," I moaned, licking my lips as my back slammed into the shelving behind me again and again.

"Fuck," Rook hissed, lifting me away from the shelves, wrapping my legs around his hips, holding me up with hands locked under my ass as he guided me up and down on his cock, our bodies rubbing together just fucking right.

I grinded against him, using my thighs to hold myself up as I rode him standing.

"That's it, Ghost, take it. Take it all."

His breathy exhalation against my ear send shivers down my spine, igniting the fuse, and I came so hard I had to stuff my face into his shoulder to muffle the sound of my screams. Rook grunted as he poured into me, his hold on my hips turning violent as he thrust his last with my name a whispered promise on his lips.

26

CORVUS

I came around with a weight on my chest and a thudding in my skull. My jaw tightened at the persistent and fucking obnoxious ache that didn't seem to want to quit. My body sank deeply into the thin hospital mattress, left arm numb.

Despite my distaste for the aftereffects, I clicked the switch in my hand with prickling fingers, giving myself another small dose of morphine.

A sigh left my lips and the weight on my chest shifted, sending a stream of fresh blood into the dead arm. Dark hair brushed against my chin and I blinked, forcing my burning eyes to open, my lips parting.

Her body curled against mine on the small bed, a leg tossed over my thigh. Her arm across my chest. Head in the crook of my arm. My chest tightened, a different sort of ache twisting deep there, making my throat burn.

I discarded the morphine switch and wrapped my arms around her, feeling her sleeping body adjust to my movement, nuzzling in deeper. I suppressed a hard sob, not wanting to wake her.

Not wanting to wake *me*, in case this was a dream.

Jesus *fuck*, it better not be a dream.

I bent my head to hers, pressing my lips to the top of her head, breathing her in. Her sharp spring herb and sandalwood scent was almost entirely overpowered by hospital soap and something sour, but it was there. I couldn't dream that up.

This was real.

They found her.

They brought her back like they promised. And they did it entirely without my help.

I peered through blurred vision over my Sparrow's head, catching Grey's eye where he sat in the corner of the room. He nodded slow, but I could see the strain still in his face. In his clenched fists on the armrests of the chair. It wasn't over. They brought her home, but Drake was still out there.

The Kings were still on our doorstep and there was no telling if they'd walk away or use a battering ram to try to knock down our defenses and take everything we had left.

I let out a shaky breath and nodded back.

My Sparrow let out a little whine of discomfort, shifting, pulling her arm in close. The arm covered in a thick coating of bandages and gauze from her wrist up to her elbow. Angry red skin poked out from the top edge of the bandage that'd slipped since it'd been applied and my stomach twisted.

Rook crashed through the door, making Ava Jade spring up like a fucking jack in the box with a gasp on her lips. I sent him a scathing glare as he righted himself, a drink tray filled with iced coffee in one hand and a greasy paper bag in the other.

"Sorry," he grunted, pacing to the window to throw back the curtains to a bright and blazing afternoon.

"What the fuck, Rook?" Grey shielded his eyes, and I averted mine, the pain in my head that'd only just started to numb from the morphine returning in full force.

"*Rook,*" I growled, and the blinds closed again.

"What? It's dark as fuck in here."

"Rook, what are you doing?" Grey demanded.

I could hear Rook's indecisive footfalls thudding and squeaking across the linoleum.

"I figured you'd all be sick of the hospital slop by now. I got takeout."

When I managed to see through the brightness, Rook and Grey's argument fell to the periphery as my eyes locked with hers. She looked down at me over her shoulder, with shattered ice in her blue-gray eyes, her jaw working.

"Hey, Sparrow."

She shoved me, hard in the chest, making me cough. My ribs creaked, screaming in protest. "You *idiot*."

"Uh, AJ," Grey said uselessly. "He's got a few cracked ribs."

She shoved me again, and I sucked in a breath, letting her get it out. "I—"

Shove.

"Fucking—"

Shove.

"*Know.*"

When I was finished coughing, I swallowed hard, grimacing at the coppery taste in the back of my throat. Sort of wishing I hadn't tossed away that morphine drip cord. "You... finished?" I wheezed.

"I haven't even started."

I braced myself for her next attack, ready and willing to accept any and all forms of punishment, but she pressed her lips to mine instead.

I grunted in surprise against her mouth, but that only made her kiss me harder, her lips almost to the point of bruising before she finally pulled back.

There was fire in her eyes when I opened mine to find her inches from my face. "I hate you for this."

"You should've hated me already, Sparrow."

Her brows drew down, confused.

"I should never have said those things to you at the Docks. I didn't know what I was—" I cut myself off, heat rising up my neck. "No, that's bullshit. I knew exactly what I was doing. Because it's the same bullshit I've always done. It wasn't fair to lay the blame for Grey... for all of that shit on your shoulders."

She rocked back to sitting, her face paling. "If I hadn't taken that shot at Lenny Ace then maybe—"

"*I* sent Drake after you," I blurted before I could change my mind, hammering the final nail into my coffin. "I fucking fell for his shit. I didn't see him for what he really was. After you took off, I asked him to find you and..."

The bed dipped, and I found Grey sitting on the bottom right corner with Rook at his back. "We don't have to do this now, man."

"I do," I corrected him. "She needs to know. She has to know that I'm the one that did this to her."

Sparrow frowned, a muscle flexing in her jaw. But she wasn't looking at me anymore. Wouldn't meet my stare.

Good. It was what I deserved. And more.

She didn't have to forgive me. Not now. But I would earn her forgiveness. No matter how long it took to do it. For whatever fucked up reason the devil wasn't ready to claim my soul and I wasn't about to waste this second chance at life with anyone else but her.

"You can hate me for as long as you want, Sparrow, but I'm not going anywhere. You're it for me. And I'm going to make you believe it."

She'd have to kill me to get rid of me.

"Did you lock me in a cell, Corvus?" she asked so quietly I wasn't sure I heard her right. "Did you drug me? Tie me up? Make me watch a man I love fall to his fucking death?"

"I—"

"You didn't do this to me. You fucked up. Royally. So did I. If I was able to control myself—"

"We might all be dead right now if you'd let Lenny Ace walk off that pier, AJ. No one knows what could've happened. We only know what *did* happen. And what happened was we annihilated the Aces before they could take us out. And all of us are still standing."

Grey's gaze found me lying in the bed and guiltily darted in Rook's direction. He shifted foot to foot, holding most of his weight on the rail of the hospital bed.

"Well, mostly," he amended.

"We had casualties," Sparrow continued to argue, and the way she said *we* made me sag with relief even if that *we* didn't include me. She still counted herself a Saint and that was a fucking win to me.

Rook shook his head. "There are always casualties. That's the cost of doing business."

Ava Jade's cheeks tinted pink, and I could tell there was more she wanted to say but wasn't sure how. She hadn't expected us to forgive her almost as much as I thought she'd never forgive me.

She was making it clear as fucking crystal that she was angry, but *anger* I could work with. I couldn't work with indifference.

"Grey's right," she said, leaning over to snag one of the iced coffees from the tray balanced on my shins. "It's done now. There's no point in dwelling on it."

Her hospital gown fluttered open in the back, revealing a slice of peachy ass and the little hollows at the top of her hip bones.

Not even near-constant pain and morphine could dull the start of a raging boner as it began to take shape beneath the thin hospital sheet. I lifted a knee, groaning at the movement to cover it up, nearly spilling the rest of the coffee.

Rook was fast enough to save it, a curse on his lips. "Corv," he growled. "That's it. No coffee for you."

He took the iced americano that was clearly meant for me and removed the lid, tossing it into the trash to drink straight from the plastic cup.

His nose wrinkled. "How can you drink this shit, man?"

"What? Not a fan of my quad shot americano, black, no sugar?"

He thrust it in my direction with a scowl, and I struggled to sit up and take it, thrown onto my back again when my Sparrow shoved me down, climbing from my side to stand on the floor beside the bed and hit the button to lift the top end. The motor whirred as my back rest rose, pressing me up to a sitting position.

"I'm not a fucking invalid."

She fixed me with a look that brokered no argument.

"...but I'll be one for you."

She rolled her eyes, taking the americano from Rook to hand to me, but she pulled it out of my reach before I could take it. "Wait a second. Are you even allowed to have coffee right now?"

The door opened behind her, and she turned, the ice in the coffee rattling as she jumped.

My doctor poked his head into the room, his gaze settling on Ava Jade instead of me.

"Ah, there you are," he said, entering the room, leaving the door open behind him. "Thought I might find you in—"

"Is he allowed coffee?" she interrupted.

The doc lifted a brow, glancing between my hard ass stare and the cup in Ava Jade's hand.

"Uh, well, no. Probably not the best idea unless it's decaf. It's a natural blood thinner and…"

He trailed off halfway through his explanation since Ava Jade was done listening and had already crossed the room and entered the small private bathroom with the cup. The toilet flushed, and she came back empty handed.

She lifted her brows in challenge at my glare. "Doc's orders," she said with a wide grin and settled into the chair in the corner of the room where Grey had been. She fingered the greasy paper bag from the floor and settled it into her lap, digging into the food. Clearly pleased with herself.

"Do you need the room?" Grey asked the doctor, glancing between him and me. "More tests, or?"

"No, I'm not here for Mr. James at all, actually. I was looking for Miss Mason. I've gone over all of your test results and was wondering if I might have a word in private?"

Sparrow looked up like a deer caught in the headlights, with her mouth stuffed full of french fries and another fistful at the ready, ketchup packet hovering over the greasy bundle.

"Huh?"

The doctor tapped the clipboard in his hand. "A word?"

She swallowed a massive lump of fries and cleared her throat. "Uh, yeah. Sure."

She dropped the fries back into the bag and wiped her palms on her hospital gown, swiping the back of her hand over her ketchup stained lips.

She stood.

"No," Rook said, the dead calm in his tone worse than if he'd shouted. He turned his head on a swivel toward Ava Jade and pointed at the chair behind her. "Sit down."

Surprising the hell out of me, she did as she was told, her eyes widening at Rook's sudden need to take charge. "I think we'd all like to hear whatever you have written down on that clipboard, Doc."

The doc fumbled with the clipboard before uncomfortably loosening the neck of his button up shirt, his gaze furtively darting between

Rook and Ava Jade. "Well there's patient confidentiality to be considered here, Mr. Clayton. I have protocols—"

"Fuck your protocols."

"AJ?" Grey asked, speaking up.

She didn't look at him when she replied, and I realized she hadn't looked at him at all, or really even spoken to him since I woke up.

"Is this okay with you?" he asked, and I watched his fist curl into my blanket behind his back with a knot in my gut.

Sparrow sighed. "Yeah," she said, though she didn't sound sure. "It's fine."

The doc closed the door behind him and flipped a page on the clipboard. "Well, we'll start with the x-rays. You've sustained a stable pelvic fracture, but judging by the fact you're walking, I assume, without much discomfort, we're happy to keep an eye on it for now so long as you don't do any strenuous activity or running for a while."

By the slight pursing of her lips I knew she'd already broken that rule, and for the first time since I woke up my critical mind kicked into a higher gear, demanding to know every detail of how my brother's saved her.

Finding that out would be first order of business after the doc finished giving us a list of Sparrows injuries... and everything we would do to Drake before we killed him.

"The second and third degree burns you sustained on your left forearm appear to have only damaged minimal nerve endings, but that coupled with the slight loss of muscle will make recovery a bit of a challenge. I'd expect full use of the arm and all numbness in the area, as well as any restricted movement in your hand and fingers from the nerve damage, to be gone within a couple weeks at most."

My inner beast skulked within, and I could see its siblings in my brothers' eyes, thirsty for blood.

"Scarring?" Grey asked.

The doc's downcast gaze scraped the floor as he nodded. "Yes. Even with the skin grafts we applied, I expect there will be lasting scarring."

"Is that all?" Sparrow asked, her breathing low and shallow.

"Well, there's just one more thing, but I'm not sure if it would be better discussed in private."

Rook let out a low growl and the Doc licked his suddenly very dry lips, flipping another page on his clipboard. It was then that I realized what other sorts of tests they would've run.

My Sparrow had been drugged, and that *bastard* had touched her. What if, after I jumped, he hadn't stopped. What if…

"The results of the rape kit performed by Nurse Fellows were difficult to determine, but she remains confident that you were not violated by the assailant."

The room seemed to sigh as one, but it didn't change anything. I was still going to feed the fucker his own dick.

"There's something else," Rook pressed, his face hard and pale in the light. Too pale. A sheen of sweat slicked over his brow, and I recognized the tremble in his hand, but I couldn't focus on any of that right now because Rook was right. There was something else. And it was clear the doc was hesitating to say it.

The doctor abandoned his clipboard, letting it drop down to his side as he fixed our girl with a sympathetic stare. "There is."

He swallowed.

"Due to the trauma you sustained to your lower abdomen, it appears as though your ability to conceive may be significantly reduced, if not altogether eliminated. I'm so sorry."

I didn't hear him offering for her to come to him with any questions, and I didn't hear him leave. Not really. It was like hearing something in another world, because in this one, my Sparrow stared dead-eyed after the doc, her lips parted as she processed how what Drake had done to her would impact not just the here and now, but the rest of her fucking life.

Rook crossed the room, kneeling in front of her, his hands on her thighs.

"What do you need, Ghost?"

The strain in his voice promised to make Drake his most macabre piece of artwork yet, but at least he said something. At least he could go to her. Speak to her.

I couldn't choke out a sound through the dam in my throat, cutting off my air supply. Making my face hot and full.

Grey watched Rook comfort our girl for another moment before turning his attention back to me with torment clouding his eye. I could see the same helpless torture he suffered reflected back.

Chapter 26

There wasn't anything we could do. Nothing except kill the bastard who took this from her.

"He dies," I promised Grey in a low voice. "*Slow.*"

27

AVA JADE

We left Grey alone at the makeshift command center he'd set up in Becca's hospital room, closing the door behind us. I'd wanted to check on her again, whisper to her that she was stronger than whatever was keeping her down. She was stronger than she ever gave herself credit for.

I needed her to wake up.

I needed *her*.

And selfishly, I wanted to rid myself of the added guilt on my conscience. If she woke up, I could let at least a small part of that crushing weight roll from my shoulders before I bought her a one-way ticket as far away from Thorn Valley as she could possibly get.

But I didn't get to whisper sweet nothings in her ear today. It was clear my and Rook's presence was distracting Grey from his work. His steady key-clacking on the keyboard balanced across his lap stuttered, the tension in his jaw spreading down to his neck and shoulders.

He wouldn't say it, but I knew he wanted us to leave.

Wanted *me* to leave.

I couldn't blame him.

Greyson Winters, known for being the hottest guy at Briar Hall. A heartless playboy with golden hair and a winning smile who could snap his fingers and have any girl naked and dripping for him.

But he wasn't that anymore. I'd disfigured him and even if I thought the black eyepatch he wore made him look somehow better than he did before, he clearly didn't think so.

I hadn't seen him smile once since I got back, and aside from the short embrace he gave me on that backroad outside of Lennox, he hadn't touched me, either.

I'd apologized a thousand times on that road. And a thousand more times between there and the hospital, but it was like he couldn't hear me.

"What is it, Ghost?" Rook asked, his fingers twining with mine as we made our way back toward Corvus' room. "Nervous about the meet?"

I snorted, shaking my head, happy for the excuse as to why I was so clearly sulking. "Which one?"

Grey would be meeting us in Corvus' room in an hour. It was finally time for me to go over, *in detail*, everything Drake did to me as well as anything I could remember about the underground shelter he'd kept me in. They'd waited patiently for almost two whole days, but both them and Diesel were getting restless.

Right after I went over the nauseating details with them, Grey and Rook and I would be going to meet with Diesel at Sanctum where we hoped to figure out some form of attack plan from my intel.

Except... I didn't have much.

Nothing that I thought would help. But a fuck ton that I knew would only hurt my guys to hear. I was already pulling apart all the details in my mind, trying to figure out what might be helpful and therefore worth mentioning and which parts I could omit for their own sanity.

"I know what you're doing," Rook muttered. "But you can't protect us from it. We need to know, Ghost. There might be something we can use that you don't think is important."

I bit the inside of my cheek.

"Besides," he continued without missing a beat. "I need to continue developing the plans for his... execution. If your intel isn't good for helping us find the bastard, then at least it'll help with that."

"You have plans?"

He lifted his brows, as surprised as I was. "Shocking, right? I don't do plans, but this piece of shit has me making sketches and a detailed schedule of events for his disassembly."

My lips twitched into a half smile that he returned, giving my hand a squeeze. "It's going to be fine."

"How do you know?"

"Because we've all faced wicked trials and twisted games, Ghost. We've survived the ugly and made a home in the darkness. We can handle your truth, because you handled ours."

His words spoke to the deformed parts of me, making me think their sharp edges could be forged into something new and beautiful.

"Okay."

I spotted the nurse from my testing and cleared my throat, untangling my fingers from Rook's. "Go ahead," I said, indicating Corvus' room down the hall. "I'll catch up. I wanted to ask the nurse something."

The shadows over his eyes darkened, but I gave him my best *everything's fine* smile. "I'll literally be twenty feet from you. Just go."

He rubbed his thumb over his lip ring as he considered the nurse in a way that had me fearing for her immediate safety. "You do you, Ghost. I know you don't need a babysitter."

His expression was at odds with his easy tone, but he walked away, adjusting his jacket across his shoulders as he did. I noticed his limp was getting better and sighed after him.

I swallowed, turning to lean on the high desk of the nurse's station. "Excuse me," I called over it, watching several nurses' heads turn in my direction. No doubt they'd all been told to give me everything and anything I needed. Just as the hospital security seemed to also be watching my every move, judging every other person in my immediate vicinity for threats.

Rook may have *said* he knew I didn't need a babysitter, but it seemed to me someone thought I did.

...or they're just trying to protect you, my rational mind tried to remind me. *Because they love you.*

It's not as impossible as you think.

"Nurse Fellows," I amended. "Can I ask you something?"

The other nurses went back to their quiet chatter, going over files and keying information into the computers while Nurse Fellows abandoned the file she was going over and plastered on a polite smile.

"Is everything all right?" she asked, and by the empathy clear on her face, I knew she'd been briefed on all my test results. She knew I wouldn't ever have kids.

I pushed the thought from my mind, hating how my mood instantly soured. I'd been trying hard not to think about it, but there it was. The one thing that might make my guys reconsider wanting me as their one and only.

It didn't matter that procreating was the absolute *furthest* thing from my mind... If I couldn't give them that, then would they want to find it somewhere else?

I swallowed, my grip on the counter tightening. "I'm fine," I blurted. "Well, maybe not fine, but, I..."

I trailed off, gaze lifting to the others within earshot.

"Would you prefer to speak privately?"

She waved a hand to a small exam room down the hall, and I nodded gratefully.

"Just let me grab your file."

I waited while she dug it out of a locked cabinet and led the way to the exam room, shutting us inside.

"Have a seat."

I shook my head, shying away from the exam table. "No, it's not—I mean, I'm fine. Physically."

"Oh."

I realized I was about to worry a hole through the hem of my shirt and made myself stop, stuffing my hands into my pockets instead.

"Are you having negative thoughts, or—"

"No, it's not that. It's..."

Jesus fuck, just spit it out.

"Can sedatives cause hallucinations?"

Her face pinched in confused worry. "Perhaps some very specific types, and only in large doses, though it's not common."

I nodded, more to myself than to her, ready to admit to myself what I feared since the first time I heard the whispers in my head. *I'm crazy.*

The hallucinations seemed to be petering off since the guys found me, but maybe that was just because I was under less stress. Maybe all the drugs Drake pumped into my system unlocked something that'd just been waiting to be set free and there was nothing I could do to lock it back up.

I'd always felt like there was something separate to myself deep down. The darkness. A mirror self. A broken part of me that hungered for violence, thrived off bloodshed, lusted for pain.

Hearing voices shouldn't have been a stretch.

"So then I'm fucking crazy."

As if on cue, Grey's voice whispered from beside me, as if he was standing right there. "All the best people are."

My heart began to pound in my chest. A bubble of manic laughter only to be choked off in my throat. This wasn't a laughing matter.

I was broken in more ways than one now. Not just physically, but mentally, too.

How could they want me now?

"Ava Jade, are you suffering from hallucinations?"

I blinked, peering from the corner of my eye to see if this hallucination was auditory only or if I was going to be graced with another full blown spectral vision of one of my guys.

The area to my right was empty, and I sighed. I hadn't seen them like that, as a hallucination, since the forest.

That was something at least.

"Hmmm?"

I couldn't remember what she'd just asked me for all the thoughts racing in my head.

"Are the hallucinations visual?"

I moistened my dry lips. "Not always. Mostly, it's just hearing things."

She nodded, flipping a couple pages in the file. "The doctor should have spoken to you about the possible side-effects."

"Side-effects?"

"Of the Haldol in your system. Ah, here it is." She passed me a sheet of paper covered in a graph with numbers and short name code I didn't understand.

"What am I looking at?"

"You see this, here," she pointed to a particularly high spike on the chart. "That's the level of Haldol that was in your system when you arrived at the hospital. And this here, that's the amount of Klonopin. That's ketamine. Not to mention a veritable cocktail of other narcotics of the legal and illegal variety."

"What does this mean?"

She took the sheet of paper back, tucking it in the file. From the lack of judgment in her eyes, I knew that despite Diesel's deal with the guy on the hospital board to keep things hush, at least this nurse and the doctor were made aware of where I'd been. They would have had to have been to know what to look for.

Heat flushed my cheeks, but Nurse Fellows didn't have pity in her pale green eyes, only a deep understanding that made me wonder what drove her to a profession as a nurse.

"It means that if you *weren't* hallucinating, I'd be more concerned."

I sagged against the exam table.

"Doctor Henry really should've gone over this with you, but it must've been missed given the rest of your exams."

"No shit."

She closed the file and came to lean casually on the edge of the exam table next to me. "You should also be aware that you could have some withdrawal symptoms given the amount of drugs that were in your system. From my understanding it was several weeks of usage?"

I nodded, still trying to reconcile everything she was saying.

"So symptoms such as headaches…"

Check.

"Nausea…"

Check.

"And anxiety…"

Check.

"Are all completely normal and to be expected for the next week or so."

"And the hallucinations?"

"Those should taper off naturally. I'd expect them to be gone entirely in the next few days."

"And if they're not?"

She gave me an understanding smile. "They will be. You're not crazy, Ava Jade. At least, not the kind of crazy that needs to be locked up in a psych ward."

I snorted. "You sure about that?"

She pursed her lips, shrugging, her gaze lifting to the small window in the door, and Rook's black eyes staring back at her through it. She shuddered, rising to unlock the door.

"Yeah, I take it back. You are crazy."

Nurse Fellows opened the door and dipped her head as she squeaked out an *excuse me* and slipped past Rook into the hall, making her escape.

"Get what you needed?"

I pushed myself back to standing. "Yep."

"Mind if I ask what that was?"

I winked at him as I exited the exam room, purposefully brushing against him as I passed. "Wouldn't you like to know," I teased, in higher spirits than I'd been in days.

So, maybe I was crazy, but at least it was the fun kind.

28

AVA JADE

"It's been five days." Corvus was snarling at the doctor when Rook and I entered his hospital room to find him struggling to untie the knotted hospital gown. "I'm done lying in that fucking bed."

"If you could just allow a few more tests to ensure—"

"No."

"Mr. James, it's important for you to keep your blood pressure down. If you could just sit—"

"I said *no.*"

"Corvus *motherfucking* James," I hissed from the doorway just as he managed to get his fingers on the strings at his back and untie them. His hospital gown dropped to the floor, showing all six feet five inches of glory that was his body. Even with the bruising over most of his left side and the bandages on his bald head, he was every inch the rock-god I knew.

Right down to the flaccid, but still insanely impressive length of his cock brushing against his thigh.

"Sparrow?"

"Sit the fuck down," I ordered him, but he stood his ground, somehow managing to look intimidating despite the fact that he was just as naked as the day he was born.

His hands curled in like talons at his sides. "I can't sit there anymore."

"Too fucking bad."

Rook cleared his throat, and I didn't have to turn around to see the smirk I knew I'd find on his lips. No one talked to Corvus James like this. No one except me could get away with it.

There was a thrilling sort of power in that. And call it a high from just finding out that I was not, in fact, totally insane, but I was feeling pretty damn good.

"Tell her what you told me," Corvus implored the doctor, whose expression clearly said he'd already given up on trying to make this stubborn bastard do anything he didn't want to.

He ran his hand through his sandy hair and sighed. "I said that he was progressing well."

"And?" Corvus urged, a vein in his neck bugging out as he crossed the floor on remarkably steady feet and grabbed a pair of folded jeans from the windowsill. The fact that the curtains were wide open seemed not to concern him as he bent to pull them on, covering himself.

"And that the scans we did this morning gave me cause to believe there won't be any lasting brain damage."

Corvus padded barefoot to the private bathroom, making us all wait while he took a piss before he returned to the room.

The doc leaned in to whisper in my ear. "To be cautious, I'd like to keep him for another day or two under observation."

"Then he'll stay."

"The fuck I will," Corvus growled, plopping his ass down in the chair in the corner to lace up his boots.

I vibrated with rage. "You're the idiot who threw yourself off a building," I spat. "The least you can do—"

"*Ava Jade*," he snapped back, inhaling deeply to check himself with palms rubbing down his face. "Rook told me you refused the wheel chair."

"That's different."

"It's not. I've stayed in that bed like my father wanted. Like you *all* wanted for five days. I have a massive fucking headache and my whole body hurts, but the doc says I'll be fine as long as I take it easy. Isn't that right?"

The stare he fixed the doc with would've reduced a lesser man to a stuttering fool in a puddle of his own piss. The doc lifted his chin. "I did."

Corvus jerked his chin in Rook's direction. "You got a problem with this?"

I spun to give Rook a warning stare to which he raised his hands and stepped farther away from me. "Fuck no. I'm not getting in the middle of this shit."

"What are you doing out of bed," Grey asked, stepping into the room behind me, forcing me to get out of the way for him to come in.

"*Thank you,*" I said. "That's what I'm trying to figure out."

Corvus tipped his head back, letting out an exasperated groan. "Look, Sparrow, I'll do whatever you want, okay? Anything except get back into that fucking sickbed, you get me?"

My nostrils flared. "Do the tests then."

"What?"

"Can you schedule all the remaining tests you wanted to do for this afternoon? We have to leave here by six."

The doc raised his brows. "That's a bit short notice, I'd have to move a lot of things around and I'm not sure—"

"Move them," I told him, leaning into that Saint power. "Corvus will submit himself to every test you want to run, and then he'll come home with us, but you will send a nurse to check on him every morning until you're certain he's in the clear."

Corvus pinched the bridge of his nose, clearly put off by my non-negotiable suggestions, but he'd finally shut his stubborn mouth so that was a win.

The doc's bedside manner mask slipped as he nodded, revealing just how pissed he was at this entire arrangement, and being the one on the hook for Corvus' recovery. I hated to think what Diesel St. Crow would do to him if Corvus didn't completely pull through from his injuries. It wouldn't be pretty.

"Thank you," I called after him earnestly as he left the room.

Corvus stood, going to fetch the shirt that went with the jeans Diesel left for him and pull it on. "Pretty fucking happy with yourself, aren't you?" he asked without looking in my direction at all.

"How does it feel to give up some of that control, Bones?"

At his nickname, he jerked his eyes up, and I watched something inside of him tighten with hope.

"Like I just swallowed a bitter pill."

"Get used to it, you'll be swallowing a lot more of them before we finish this."

I wouldn't make him suffer too much. I played a crucial part in our monumental fuck up, but there was one thing he was right about, and it was that I wouldn't stand for *any man* speaking to me the way he did that night on the Docks. I deserved to be reprimanded but not like that. Not from *him*. Not to mention that the jackass tried to kill himself to stop me being raped, as if one was worth the other.

As if stopping my pain and torment was somehow worth his entire fucking life.

That was what I was mostly angry about, despite how it also broke my heart in the most brutal, beautiful way.

Okay... *and* it was kind of amazing to watch him grovel.

Ava Jade, bringing big bad men to their knees since 2022.

"Speaking of bitter pills," Grey said, crossing the room to sit in the chair Corvus had vacated, opening a laptop. "Are we ready to get started? I've hit a wall with what I could find based on the information AJ gave us already. I need more to go on."

He spoke so matter-of-factly, I knew I couldn't be the only one to pick up on it. There was no emotion there. He'd cut himself off from me, and I didn't know how to stitch us back together.

My heart hurt, watching him *not* look at me as he adjusted himself in the chair, likely opening up a notepad on the screen to take any notes that might help him later on.

My guys watched me and with the searchlights of their stares blazing into me, I felt like I had an audience of thousands instead of just three.

"Take your time," Corvus said, all the stubbornness he'd been holding onto gone now with something more important for him to focus on. I could tell, even more than the others, that he'd been starving for this moment. His analytical mind hungry for information it could store and use to our advantage.

No time like the present to disappoint him.

I imagined myself as an omniscient presence in the room, watching myself speak instead of doing the speaking myself. It was easier to get through it that way, telling it like a scary story rather than as something real and tangible. A thing I'd experienced.

If I let the disgust—the absolute rage—show on my face while I told them how he'd kicked me while I was down and unable to move, touched me while I was tied down, and every other sick thing he'd done to me, it would only hurt them too. Exacerbate their rage.

And right now, I needed them thinking clearly.

We all needed to be thinking clearly if we were going to beat him.

I didn't like how quiet it'd been since I escaped. Quiet wasn't good. It meant Drake was planning something and we needed to stop whatever the fuck that was before he could follow through.

When I finished, none of them spoke. The room had a dark aura hanging over it, the sort of shadows not even the deep orange glow of the sunset through the curtains could cut.

"You set yourself on fire to escape?" Rook asked, his dark eyes stroking the length of the bandage on my arm with something close to reverence even though his face was a shade of pale green I'd never seen before.

I nodded. "It was the only way."

Grey squinted at me in disbelief. "And then you ran over twenty miles through the forest to the road?"

"About that. I don't really know exactly how far it was. That was what it felt like. It could've been less. I passed out somewhere in the middle."

"And then you two just happened to find her on the road?" Corvus asked the guys, and I didn't miss how they were focusing their inquiries on my escape rather than my capture. It took me a couple days to be ready to recap it. It would take them longer.

Rook nodded. "She was trying to hijack a minivan."

"How else was I supposed to get back to Thorn Valley? Walk?"

Rook shook his head, his attempt at a smile dying before it could be born. "No one's judging, Ghost."

"What do you think he meant about Thorn Valley rightfully belonging to him?" Corvus asked, changing the subject.

"I don't know, but I fucking knew Mav was just a front man. Guy has no balls." Rook sniffed, rubbing his nose between his thumb and finger. No doubt it was still bothering him.

At least my intel gave him something else to think about. I didn't realize I even had so many little useful tidbits until I started going through it all step by stomach-churning step.

Grey cocked his head to the side. "Does this mean we were right about the Kings gunning for us from the start?"

Rook sighed. "Diesel is going to shit a brick."

A tap on the door interrupted their questions and I didn't think I'd ever been so happy to see a man in uniform. "Mr. James," the doc said, coming in without an invitation. "We're ready for your final tests."

"You heard the man. Get your ass out of here."

His lips pressed into a taut line as he stood, coming to stand in front of me where I sat on the side of his hospital bed. He stared at me for a moment, with an emotion I couldn't name raging behind his eyes. Then he brushed the hair back from my chest, his fingers running along the skin behind my ear as he leaned in and pressed a chaste kiss to my forehead. "I swear to you," he whispered in my ear. "You will never have to endure anything like that again. Not while I'm still breathing."

His hand fell away, and he walked past me to the door. "Don't leave for Sanctum without me."

"AJ, if I bring up a map of the area around where we found you, do you think you could pinpoint the location of the underground shelter? Or at least the direction?"

Grey turned the laptop screen around on his lap, and I frowned at the crisscrossed lines of the map there. "I-I don't know."

"Try?"

I sighed, but got to my feet, crossing the room to kneel in front of him, squinting at the screen. "Well, there's the tracks I crossed."

I pointed to them, tracing the line in a northeasterly direction. "I crossed about here, so maybe somewhere in that direction."

Grey leaned over the screen, watching my finger trace a path further into the national park. He nodded. "Okay, that's good. I can work with that."

He turned the laptop back around, and when I didn't move from my spot in front of him, he lifted a brow at me.

"Thanks."

The word was a dismissal, and I felt it like a slap to the face.

"Come on, Ghost," Rook called for me, his hand extended in my direction. "I don't know about you, but I need a fucking drink before we head over to Sanctum. Want to go see what these docs keep hidden in their office drawers?"

"Only if we can go torment the emergency patients after."

"It's a date."

Something about leaving the hospital and driving the familiar streets to Sanctum felt surreal. And I realized that for all my stubbornness and shit talking in that fucking hole in the ground, I wasn't sure I'd ever be here again.

I rested my head on Rook's shoulder in the backseat as he smoked a cigarette out the window of the Rover, absently stroking his tatted fingers through my hair. I knew this wasn't going to last. The second we left this car and went into Sanctum, the little bubble that'd been forming around us in the hospital would burst.

If the Kings were out for Saint blood, it meant there was another war on the horizon. And the puppet master of the whole damned thing was still out there. He could be waiting around any corner. Hiding in the shadows. Waiting for the perfect opportunity to strike.

His number one target aside from me? My guys.

Even though my blood buzzed with the need for vengeance and a thirst for the blood of a dragon, I couldn't take it if anything else happened to them. Not because of me.

"You ready for this, Sparrow?" Corvus asked, catching my eye in the rearview from the passenger seat. "We can postpone."

"No we can't."

He worked his jaw, but nodded in reply, knowing I was right. Diesel had already begun putting precautions in place in case of an attack by the Kings. He'd also set up a meet with the Mexicans to get some more firepower. It was all hands on deck, now. The Saints were outmanned. But they weren't outwomaned, and maybe that would be the difference that saved us all.

It was me Drake wanted after all. And since we'd already discerned he was the true head of that Kingsnake, I'd just have to cut his off to end it all before it could begin.

Before any more of us could die.

I didn't know the other Saints very well, but I'd come to respect the hell out of most of them. Oddly enough, it was Axel's death that hit me the hardest out of those who lost their lives in this bullshit. Even though he liked to watch Becca with fuck me eyes, I knew he was harmless, and would never touch her if she didn't want that.

He was a good man.

So were some of the others who fell at the Docks.

All because I couldn't help pulling that trigger.

I let out a shaky breath as the three story building came into view at the end of the downtown strip. Would they want me crucified?

Were my chances of ever truly being accepted into their ranks dashed now forever?

I shook my head, sighing at myself, finding Rook staring down at me curiously, with a dopey smile trying to curl up the edge of his mouth.

"I'll cut anyone who looks at you sideways, Ghost. Promise."

"How do you always do that?"

"Do what?"

"Read my mind."

He shrugged, and I sat up in the middle seat, clutching the leather beneath me.

"Because it's the same as mine."

I snorted as we pulled into the parking lot out front. I hadn't seen Diesel yet, either. He'd been through the hospital a couple times since the guys found me, checking on Corvus, bringing some supplies to the Saints he'd positioned there as sentries. But our paths hadn't crossed yet, and I didn't know if that was coincidence or by design.

I wasn't avoiding him. Not really. Okay, maybe a little.

It was me who got his men killed. Who almost got his first son killed.

I was sure I wasn't wrong thinking it was more by design than anything else. He probably didn't want to see me any more than I wanted to see him.

I followed Rook from the Rover, chewing my lips as I tipped my head up, taking in the bar.

The shining tips of sniper barrels glinted in what remained of the sunlight filtering between the buildings, placed evenly in three of the six upstairs windows with another on the roof.

Turning, I found a further two in the building across the street. Diesel wasn't taking any chances, it seemed, and I hoped they were all at least a decent shot.

Instinctively, I headed for the door around the back of the building that would lead downstairs to the underbelly of Sanctum, but Grey whistled to get my attention, indicating the front door with the inclination of his head.

I fell in line behind and between my guys, who crowded me in as we entered the main bar. A sign in the window said 'Closed for Renovations' but the guys had told me Diesel had no choice but to set up all the injured Saints here. Better to keep everyone together, close, in case of an attack. And it seemed, even now that nearly everyone was back on their feet, he was still using the bar as a makeshift safe house and Saint headquarters.

The warehouse where they usually met was too in the open for comfort given all the recent threats.

Rock classics hummed at a low volume in the background as Saints chatted, sipping beer at the bar and racking up at one of the pool tables in the back.

Heads turned as we entered and some guy in the back lifted his pint, letting out a loud *woop!* Others followed his example until Sanctum echoed with the raucous cheers of everyone in the bar.

I dipped my head, shrinking behind Corvus for him to enjoy his welcome home with a ball in my throat at the warmth in the room.

"What are you doing, AJ?" Grey asked, gently tugging my elbow, guiding me back out into the open, where I realized they weren't looking at Corvus as they clapped and jeered, sloshing beer over the floor as they raised their cups. They were looking at... me.

"Welcome back, Ava Jade," Pinkie hollered, his throaty bellow reverberating in my chest from where he stood in the middle of the room.

I couldn't move.

Couldn't breathe.

"*A-va Jade*," Vance called from his wheelchair, turning my name into a chant that others soon joined.

"*A-va Jade, A-va Jade, A-va Jade.*"

My gaze caught on a familiar pair of steel blue eyes watching me from the bar, but I'd never seen them like they were now. Crinkled at the edges, pulled taut from how he was smiling around the cigar clenched in his teeth. Diesel stood from the stool, clapping with the others in time with the chant.

My stomach twisted. My throat burned. My hand went absently to my throat, fingers grasping at empty skin where a black stone used to rest.

I whirled on my guys, who'd joined the chant with the others. So much pride in their eyes.

"What is this?"

"This is for you, Ghost," Rook answered, his black eyes glittering in the light. "Welcome home."

A hand grasped my shoulder, and when I turned it was to find Diesel standing behind me... wearing the leather jacket I bought for him.

"The boys filled me in on what you went through escaping that bastard," he said, shouting to be heard over the chant. "Hope you don't mind, but I shared some of it with the others. You got guts, kid." He leaned in close. Squeezing my shoulder. "More than most of my crew."

I didn't know what to say, but I was hella fucking shocked when he pulled me in for a hug. My chest squeezed, making me clench my teeth to fight back the tears at the complete sense of belonging. The paternal sort of affection I thought I'd never feel again.

Diesel released me, and I quickly sniffed, covertly wiping my sleeve over my eyes as he spun back to face the crew of Saints in the bar. "All right, all right," he hollered. "Calm the fuck down."

The chanting slowly petered out, most of them going back to what they were doing, but Pinkie and a few others waded through the crowd towards us to greet me personally.

"Damn, kid," Pinkie said. "I already knew you were a badass, but..." he trailed off, shaking his head. "I don't think there's another girl on this planet better suited for our Crows. Isn't that right, boys?"

Despite myself, I blushed. Something about everyone here knowing I was intimately with not one, but *all three* of these guys made me just a smidge uncomfortable. But Pinkie wasn't judging, and the others next to him had only respect in their eyes.

"You know it, Pinkie—"

"Boy, if you call me Pinkie Pie one more time, I swear to god—"

I laughed, the ball in my throat shrinking until I could breathe again.

"Oh, you think that shit's funny, do you?" Pinkie challenged, fixing me with a mock glare.

I swiped a tear from my eye. "Fucking hilarious," I corrected him. "I wish I'd thought of that."

"Come on, you four," Diesel said, interrupting before a red-faced Pinkie could take a swing at any of us. "Let's talk, shall we? We'll bring the others into the room once we've reached a decision. Pinkie, with me."

"Yeah, boss."

We followed Diesel and Pinkie through Sanctum toward the back room, the one where I'd taken the poison trial. Fuck, it felt like ages ago now.

The door swung closed behind us, muffling the loud conversation and music outside to a dull hum.

"First thing's first," Diesel said, passing Corvus something.

Whatever it was clinked familiarly as Corvus unwrapped it, coming to where I hovered at the edge of the long table.

The others sat down as he laid the cloth wrapped bundle on the table in front of me. "You might be needing these."

He threw back the last bit of cloth to reveal my blades.

No, not just my blades. There were others, too.

The blue-eyed crow-handled blade Corvus gave me seemed to have spawned two more. One with a golden eye, and another with an onyx one. That crow had flames etched on wings. I loved them beyond words.

They made the fact that there were only two of my own blades remaining an easier pill to swallow.

"Here," Corvus said, seeming to pull a fistful of black straps and holsters from out of nowhere. "There's two for your belt. Two for your thighs. One for your ankle and a dual chest strap. I wasn't sure what you'd prefer."

"You should grovel more often," I muttered for his ears only as I took the bits of leather and Velcro from him.

He snorted, saying nothing as I set to adjusting the straps, fixing the new holsters over my chest in a cross, where I put two of the three crow-handled blades, adding the other one to my inner thigh and the two others to my ankle and belt.

I sighed happily, the remaining tension I'd been holding on to sloughing off like dead skin.

"Just like that," Rook said, snapping his fingers. "And my Ghost's back."

I smirked at him, sliding into the seat next to Corvus at the table.

"What do we have on this guy?" Diesel asked, not wasting any time, his stony gaze drifting over the four of us seated at the table with him and Pinkie before landing squarely on me. "The guys filled me in on some, but is there anything else?"

"We figured out a general area where the bunker could be in the national park, but we won't be able to narrow it down until we can get some guys out there to search the area."

Diesel nodded. "All right, but even if we find the bunker, your girl set it on fire, yeah? Likely there won't be much evidence left there to use to our advantage."

"But it's possible," I said before Diesel could continue. "Were there any fires in the area that emergency crews responded to?"

I posed the question to Grey, who shook his head. "Already checked. He must've gotten it under control before it could get out of hand."

"*Fuck*," I cursed under my breath, trying to think of another angle and coming up empty handed.

"All right, let's forget the bunker for the minute," Diesel suggested, leaning over the table. "This guy. Drake, Jericho, whatever his fuckin' name is. If we can figure out who he is, we might be able to trace him. So what do we know? Let's go over it."

Corvus sat back in his chair, sighing, clearly frustrated to be going back over intel we already had. "We know he's the true leader of the Kings."

"And we know he thinks Thorn Valley should be his by right," Grey added while Rook dragged a glass ashtray from the middle of the table over to where he sat and lit a cigarette.

"He was prying Becca for information on us and Ava Jade."

Diesel nodded, trying to find connections from all the puzzle pieces.

Rook ashed his cigarette. "He was working Becca before Ghost even got here, though."

"Wait. In those texts he said he wasn't sure if it was you when he first saw you on the streets of Thorn Valley. The texts started, what, like a few days after you arrived?"

"Yeah. Something like that."

"But you didn't go anywhere near town during that first week, did you? You ran the trail off campus, through the woods."

I shrugged. "Yeah, but I did have my aunt's driver drop me downtown the night I arrived. Well, I practically jumped out of the moving car. I couldn't stand another second with that bitch."

The guys shared a look, and something uncomfortable slithered in my belly. "What?" I asked when none of them said a word.

"We saw you that night, too," Corvus answered for them all. "Dragging your suitcase all the way up to Briar Hall."

My lips parted, confused. "I'm not following."

"That was the night we found Randy dead in the alley," Rook explained. "With an A carved into his chest. We had to drag Randy's body out of sight when Humphrey's fancy car squealed to a stop right outside the mouth of the alleyway."

Diesel held a hand up, a red tint to his cheeks. "Hold on a fucking second," he hissed. "You're saying this fucker was in Thorn Valley the night Randy was killed? In practically the same goddamned place?"

"Holy shit..." Grey breathed. "You don't think he...?"

Diesel was already nodding. "I do."

He stood suddenly, his chair scraping across the floor, his palms slapping against the table's edge before going to his head, pushing his hair away from his face. "Jesus Christ. Lenny wasn't lying when he said his men had nothing to do with Randy."

He hit the table again, and it rattled all the way down to where I sat. "Fuck!"

I was still putting it all together in my head. The guys being there from the very first moment I arrived in this place. Randy. The war with the Aces. The alliance with the Kings.

Oh my god.

"It was him this whole time."

"What?" Diesel asked, and when I looked up, all eyes were on me.

"It's obvious, isn't it?"

Or maybe it wasn't. If it weren't for the sick churn in my belly, I might've felt proud to have caught on before *the* Diesel St. Crow.

"He's been working you this whole time," I began, my heart thudding loudly in my chest. "He said it himself, he thinks Thorn Valley should be *his*. If he killed Randy, it was to push you into starting a war with the Aces. Which is exactly what you did. He wanted to hit you hard. Weaken your defenses. And *he did*. They weakened enough that you considered an alliance with the Kings."

"Which was also exactly what he wanted," Corvus picked up where I left off, his voice dripping with malice. "To get close to you, so that when the time came he could finish off the rest of us."

"He'd have no competition for hundreds of miles in any direction," Rook said, a dark laugh on his lips like he half respected the guy. I had to admit, it was a damn good plan. "He had you do all the heavy lifting. Taking out the Aces. The Dead Men. Leaving only us, weakened. For the first time since you and the other Saints created this empire, we're weak enough that someone *could* have the upper hand."

Diesel staggered back a step, his Adam's apple bobbing. He slunk back into his seat, still pushed back from the table, and bent, rubbing his palms over his face. "Who *is* this guy?"

The question was meant rhetorically, but I realized I might have one last clue that could help.

"He had this lighter," I said, and Diesel lifted his chin. "The one I used to set the chair on fire. It had initials in it."

Rook flipped his own zippo lighter between his fingers, his brows drawn down. "I remember," he said before I could finish. "He let me use it once. The initials were—"

"L.R.B."

Recognition flickered in Diesel's eyes. His body stilled, going practically rigid.

"Boss?" Pinkie pressed, worry in the creases on his forehead. "You don't think it's actually…"

Diesel stood, holding himself up with palms pressed flat against the table. He let out a shuddering sigh. "I think that's *exactly* who this is. *God dammit,* why didn't I see this sooner?"

"Who?" Corvus demanded, his hand curling into a fist on top of the table. "Who is it?"

When Diesel lifted his gaze to us, I felt the guilt in his cold eyes like it was my own. Saw the rage behind it. "My son."

29

CORVUS

"*Your son?*" I repeated, the throb in my skull pulsing double time now, seeing my adopted father through a red tint, my vision going hazy around the edges. "What the fuck do you mean, *your son?*"

"Carson."

"Carson? That's it. Care to fucking elaborate?"

The dark circles around my father's eyes deepened, making him appear as though all the energy had been sucked clean from his soul from uttering the name alone.

"That's not right," my Sparrow argued, shaking her head, staring at Diesel with narrowed eyes. "The initials were L.R.B. No 'C.' Besides, you would've recognized your own son."

I caught the way Diesel's jaw flexed, and no one failed to notice his lack of reply.

"Dies?" Rook asked, his tone even. The vocal equivalent of going dead-eyed. Hiding his feelings from the rest of us.

Diesel inhaled deeply, holding a long meaningful look with Pinkie. The big guy was a shade of green.

"That's because they aren't Carson's initials," Diesel finally replied, going for the decanter of good scotch by the far wall to pour himself a few fingers of amber liquid. He drained them and poured two more, bringing the bottle to the table with him. It thudded against the table as he folded himself back into the chair. "They're his mothers."

Rook curled his fingers, indicating the scotch and Diesel slid it all the way down the table, into Rook's waiting palm.

"Pinkie, you mind? Leg's bugging me."

Pinkie rose to get Rook a class. "Sure it is. Lazy ass."

"Diesel, I need you to start fucking talking here." The words rushed from my mouth, chased out by the slow-building feelings of absolute betrayal in my gut.

Diesel had a son? One that shared his blood?

How did I not know this?

Why hadn't he told anyone?

"L.R.B," he said on a breath. "Lilliana Rose Bates. The lighter belonged to his mother. The first woman I ever loved. His name is Carson Gregory Bates. Born March 31st, '96."

Rook filled himself a glass of scotch before sliding the decanter back down the table to Diesel, who'd already drained his second glass. I stopped it before it could reach him. "Keep talking."

Dies licked his lips, abandoning the glass to steeple his fingers in front of his lips. "I haven't seen him since he was twelve. He didn't look anything like he does now."

I could tell there was more he was holding back, trying to decide what to say first.

"I wasn't around," he admitted. "When I got Lilliana pregnant, I was... I was with Jacqueline."

"Are you serious?" Grey asked, disgust tainting his tone, offended on behalf of a woman he never had the chance to meet. But meet her or not, we knew her from the countless stories Diesel and the guys told about her. Their memories bringing her to life in our minds just as though we *had* known her ourselves.

Diesel was her everything. And we thought she was his, too.

"Not my finest fucking moment," he sighed. "Lily had this way about her. She could get you to do pretty much anything. Manipulative. You know the type. Anyway, Jacqueline and I had just gotten hitched and we were trying to have a kid. Well, Lily got it in her head to try to trap me before that could happen and split Jacqueline and I for good. She seduced me into her bed—"

"No. You don't get to put it like that," Sparrow corrected him.

I nodded, glaring at our father. "You fucked another woman. That was *your choice*. Own it."

His upper lip twitched but he gave a tight nod. "Yes. It was. She'd poked holes in the rubber and within weeks she was at my doorstep, waving a positive test in my face. She thought I'd leave Jacqueline on the spot. Do the right thing."

"You obviously didn't," Ava Jade put in, tapping the table, clearly more than a little put off by Diesel's past. But I had a feeling the worst was yet to come.

"Yes," he answered plainly. "I did do what was right. I stayed with the woman I vowed to spend the rest of my life with, and I offered Lilliana more than she deserved. I bought her a little place in Lennox. I sent monthly payments. More than enough to cover anything she needed."

Rook sipped his scotch before running the pad of his middle finger over the rim, not looking at Diesel. "And the kid?"

"Jacqueline and I just found out the week before that she couldn't have kids. I couldn't..." He choked on his next words. "I couldn't do that to her. Make her see the one thing she wanted most in this world and could never have. I never admitted the affair to her for fear she'd figure it out herself. The house and the money, they were contingent on Lilliana never telling a soul who fathered her son."

"Where is she now?" I heard myself asking.

"Dead," Pinkie answered before my father could. "For years now."

Diesel rubbed a palm over his beard. "Murdered, by her son...when he was twelve."

"He fucking strangled her to death," Pinkie added, his face twisting. "In her own bed."

My Sparrow let out a little gasp, and I remembered her telling us about all the photos she'd found on Drake's, no, *Carson's*, computer. Of women who'd been strangled. How they'd all sort of looked like her. I had to wonder if my Sparrow looked a little like Lilliana Rose Bates. His first kill. And whether that was why he'd been drawn to her.

Sour bile coated my throat, making my mouth fill with warm saliva. I choked it down. "That's when you saw him last," I said, not really a question, but I was damn sure expecting an explanation. "That's what you said."

"I went to see him in juvie. Offered to pay for him to get help. He didn't even know who I was."

"She hadn't told him?"

"No."

"I'm guessing he didn't take your offer?" Ava Jade asked and I could see the gears turning behind her sharp eyes, putting it all together.

Diesel's rings caught the light as he spun them round and round on his fingers. "No. But he found out soon enough who I was. He wanted in. To be a Saint. As if I could have someone like him anywhere near my Jacqueline. He started writing me letters after that. Pinkie?"

"Yeah, boss," Pinkie said, leaving the room.

"You kept them?" Grey asked, and it was hard to miss the hurt in his voice. I knew, for him more than the rest of us, our makeshift family was everything. Finding out Diesel had another son, a biological son, wouldn't sit right with him. Neither would the fact that Diesel left that son, just like his mother had left him.

"I did. They're in the office. The letters got more and more insistent, borderline psychotic. Before they stopped altogether about five years ago. The last one I got from him was the day he was released from Folsom State after a long lull between letters. In it he said he understood why I couldn't have him in my crew. That he would work on himself. Become *better*. Worthy of the Saint title. And then he would come see me. I never heard from him again."

Pinkie returned with the letters, dropping them on the table in front of me. Each yellowed envelope was stamped with the Folsom State Prison seal. Printed with its address, Carson's name almost illegibly printed in the blank space provided.

I lifted the one on the top before letting it fall back to the table. "I don't give a fuck about some letters he sent you years ago. You should've told us."

"I didn't think he would—"

"He was a threat," Rook interjected, slamming his now empty glass onto the table. "Not just to you. But to us. And now to Ava Jade, too."

"All because you abandoned him," Grey growled.

"He was a fucked up kid who wouldn't accept my offer to get him help, what was I supposed to do? He *killed* his mother."

"Did you ever ask him why?" Ava Jade asked our father with murder in her eyes. The still-beating thing in my chest ached at the pain in her eyes, realizing what made her ask the question. The things her own mother did to her. Except that was before my Sparrow found her wings. While she was still earthbound, trapped in the skin of her weaker self.

Diesel narrowed his steely eyes on Ava Jade. "The kid killed his mother," he tried to remind her.

"And now that same kid has also had a hand in killing off half your fucking men," she spat back. "He murdered at least twelve other women. For fuck sake's, he had Corvus *kill himself*. He almost…"

She trailed off, her face turning a shade of pale green.

"And you think I could've stopped any of that?"

"Maybe," Grey spoke up. "If you were there."

Rook tapped his glass on the table, and I shoved the scotch back at him. He poured. "Even if you couldn't have changed how he turned out, at least you might've been there." He took a sip before reaching over the table to offer the rest to Ava Jade. She shook her head, and he drained it himself instead.

"For what?" Diesel demanded.

"To put a piece of fucking lead between his eyes before he could hurt anyone else."

Diesel jerked back at Rook's words, and I knew my father well enough to see that he was coming to realize we were right. But they were all forgetting one thing.

"It doesn't matter now. What's done is done. Diesel might've had a hand in creating this monster, but now it's all of us that have to deal with him. Grey?"

My brother was already nodding, lifting his phone from his pocket. With this new intel, there had to be more we could find on this guy. Hopefully, it would lead us straight to him. "I'm on it. We need to get back to the Nest. I need my fucking computer."

We all stood, ready to leave. To get to work.

"I'm going to make this right, boys," Diesel promised, making us all hesitate before leaving. His guilty eyes found mine, holding fast. "I'm sorry."

I knew he meant it, but an apology wasn't going to fix this.
Blood and lead would.

30

GREY

One by one, our surveillance cameras went online. Two for every one of Drake's we removed based on Ava Jade's direction. It was a condition of being able to return to the nest. Not only would we bring half our remaining force with us, but also surround the place in tiny glass eyes where we couldn't watch.

That and trigger alert systems all along the road leading up to the Crow's Nest. Along with a handful speckled through the forest just in case the surveillance cameras became compromised.

The three land mines lovingly laid to rest six inches beneath the dirt by Rook around the house felt a touch overboard, but I wasn't about to argue. Not when it came to her safety.

If it was up to me, I'd have put her on the first flight to our cousin gang in Arizona under an alias. Have Uncle Ransom bury her so deep there that no one could find her. Not even us. Until this was over.

But I knew there was absolutely nothing I could say that would coerce her into leaving. She may have been finished with me, but she wouldn't leave my brothers. And as long as she stayed, there was a chance I could win her back. Missing eye and all.

I tabbed through each camera, flipping from a view of the woods to one of the road. The parking lot. Behind the Nest, toward the thinning wood that led to the cliff side. I watched the Saints Diesel sent with us skirting the buried mines on their way back inside. It was about to get real fucking cozy in here with all of them crammed in with us.

AJ gave up the loft Becca and she shared for a few of the more injured ones to sleep in proper beds. The rest would camp out in the living room or the garage.

Once I was satisfied that every cam was up and running, I grabbed the radio walkie from the desk. "All good up here," I told Pinkie. "Let Dies know we're set and then settle in, yeah? It's late."

"Roger."

I let the walkie clatter back onto the desk, rubbing my burning eye. Strange, even though the other one wasn't there, it somehow burned with exhaustion, and I pressed against the black eyepatch covering the place it used to be all the same.

"Grey?" AJ's voice came muffled through my bedroom door.

I pushed my hair back, sliding out from the desk to smooth the front of my shirt. "Come in."

AJ hesitantly opened the door, a mug of something steaming in her grip. "I, *uh,* thought you might like some tea. Figured you'd be up for a while, so it's that green blend you have in the cupboard, with a bit of honey."

She cringed when our eyes met and something in me deflated and I felt my shoulders slump with it.

"You don't like honey in your tea, do you?" she asked, staring down at the mug like she might shatter it against the nearest solid surface. "That's okay. I can make you one without. I'll drink this one. Be right back."

"Don't," I blurted before I could stop myself, my mouth going dry. "I like honey."

"Oh."

"Yeah, I was just—just surprised to see you is all. I figured you'd be with one of the others. Getting things ready for Sunday."

There was still the issue of a lack of funds to purchase our new firearms and ammunition from down south. Which we would desperately need if we were going to stand a chance against the Kings who outmanned almost two to one.

Surprisingly, it was Rook who came up with the solution for that problem. With Diesel's contacts in the black market, all we needed to do was pay a little unsolicited visit to Viola Humphrey.

*Un*surprisingly, AJ didn't so much as balk at the idea of breaking into her aunt's mansion at the edge of Thorn Valley. In fact, she was ready to lead the charge, almost giddily eager for the heist. She'd said each one of those Fabergé eggs were worth tens of thousands of dollars. Those combined with anything else we could find would fetch more than enough for all the munitions we needed.

And the old bag fucking deserved it.

She nodded. "I was. But they can handle getting the rest of it together without me. I thought maybe I might be able to help up here."

AJ padded across the carpet, settling the mug down carefully away from the monitors, but within my reach. She hunched down, squinting at the three screens now showing a myriad of surveillance angles.

She visibly recoiled, and I frowned.

"What is it?"

She shook her head, clearly trying to play it cool even though I could tell something had really bothered her. "It's just... Drake, I mean *Carson*... he had a set up almost exactly like this. Cameras and all."

The comparison made the muscles across my back flex and strain, but I knew she didn't mean anything by it. I just hated to have anything at all in common with the fucker. But if he had even half of the shit I had here set up, then he knew what he was doing.

"Sorry, *uh,* can you switch them to night vision? Might be hard to see much with these."

She pointed to the ones around the side of the house and the others in the forest.

I tapped a few keys and changed the upper right camera to night vision, showing Rook's kill shed and the rear ends of a few parked cars in vivid green light.

"*Awesome.*"

"Yeah?"

"Fuck yeah. I don't know why, but anything night vision just gives me such a lady boner. So cool."

I found myself smiling. "Yeah. Same."

Shit.

"I mean, not about the lady boner, but... you know what I'm saying."

She laughed nervously, pushing off her knees to return to standing, taking in my room as though it was the first time she was seeing it when we both knew that wasn't true. She wandered to the shelving across the room, fingering the neat rows of manga before she stopped. I didn't have to look to know she'd found one of my many hiding places.

Behind the manga, in a nook of carved out drywall, rested an old six shooter, loaded and ready to be fired if needed.

If she continued toward the closet, she'd find a go bag filled with money, a change of clothes, a fresh passport, a flare, and enough water and protein bars to last me several days. But she didn't continue to the closet to find my hiding spot, she turned suddenly, sharply, clapping her hands together. "So, is there anything?"

I cocked my head at her, not understanding.

"Anything I can help with," she amended, putting all her weight on foot before switching to the other one.

She was... nervous.

It became so utterly, painstakingly obvious, that my lips parted in surprise. I wasn't sure I'd ever seen her like this. Vulnerable. Almost afraid.

Of what?

"Not really," I found myself saying. "I have it all covered."

"Oh."

She bit her lip, her sea glass eyes darting to the door.

"But you can stay if you want."

She visibly relaxed, her body heaving a sigh as a small smile pulled the edge of her mouth. "Only if I won't be distracting."

But she was already settling herself on my bed.

I laughed quietly to myself, tossing her the stack of letters Carson sent to Diesel. "Might as well make yourself useful. Want to sort those by date and then we can go through them? Make sure there's nothing we can use."

AJ snatched them up hungrily, seemingly eager to be helpful. She tucked her legs beneath her, chewing her bottom lip as she focused all her energy on the letters, quickly pulling them from the envelopes and beginning to sort them.

It was harder than it should've been to pull my eye from her and return to the screens in front of me, but I found her reflection in the monitor on the left. Despite her wish that I wouldn't be distracted, I knew that wasn't a possibility. Not with her on my bed. No more than a few feet away.

I cleared my throat, dogging the erection begging for attention in my jeans with the firm press of my palm.

It took me twice as long as it should've to find anything on Carson Bates. There were the things I expected. His mother's obituary. Some other easily accessible documents. But nothing useful. No property in his name. No corporations. No medical records. The guy was basically a fucking ghost. Which I guessed I should've expected. But it frustrated the absolute fuck out of me all the same.

There was still no fucking sign of him or the Kings and with each day that passed, I knew we were edging closer to him making a move.

"You know, I don't really agree with Dies peacing out on his kid, but I think he did the right thing not bringing him in."

"What?"

I pushed away from the desk, wheeling my office chair around to face her.

She waved the letter she was holding in her hand. "Kid was fucked up. Right from the start. Some evil is made, but I think this monster was born rotten. He goes into *detail* in this one about how much he hates cats. Like, how he used to trap the ones in his neighborhood and beat and skin—"

I held a hand up to stop her there. I could watch a man be brutalized beyond recognition, but animals? Not a fucking chance. Something about their absolute naivety. Their innocence. Didn't sit right with me.

"Sorry," she said in a hush, setting the letter down. "I said I didn't want to distract you and that's exactly what I'm doing."

"You don't have to do that."

"Do what?"

"Make yourself so uncomfortable. You don't need to be in here at all if you don't want to. You don't owe me anything."

Someone had to say something. I needed it out in the open. So we could deal with it. So I could see if there was any chance for us or if I needed to lock myself away from her forever. Resigned to being happy for my brothers, but not enjoying her attention myself.

"Wait... *what?*"

The confusion on her face gave me pause. Her lips twisted.

Then she was shoving all the letters aside. "Come here. I think we need to get something straight."

I dragged my ass from the chair, not daring to hope as I slid onto the bed across from her. When I caught her looking at my eyepatch, I dropped my head, making my hair fall forward to cover it from her view. My jaw clicking.

She darted forward and grabbed my chin, dragging my gaze back to hers before letting go. "Don't do that. You don't have to hide it from me, Grey. I should be made to look at it. If it wasn't for me, you'd still be whole."

I snorted. "What?"

"I don't know what you're thinking in that big beautiful head of yours, but I'm only uncomfortable because you've carved a fucking line between us deeper than Mariana's Trench."

What?

"And I get it," she continued. "I really, really do. It's my fault and you're angry with me for it. You could've died and you were this golden boy. Fucking perfect down to every last hair and now—"

"I look like a fucking cyclops?"

Her face screwed up and for a second I thought she might hit me. My brain was still playing catch up, trying to figure out what was happening right now, but I couldn't seem to shut myself up and listen, speaking over her instead.

"...and every time you look at me you're disgusted and probably filled with guilt even though *it wasn't your fault at all.* So instead you do your best not to look at me at all. Tell me if I'm warm?"

A deep sadness filled her eyes. "I do feel guilty," she admitted. "But Grey, you're still you. You could be missing *both* eyes and both your fucking arms and I'd still love you."

It became clear all at once. Like swiping a hand over a fogged mirror to see the truth reflected back at you in all its startling *realness.*

I was sitting there thinking Ava Jade was disgusted by the sight of me. Wouldn't ever be able to look at me the same way because of my deformation and the fact that she thought she was the cause of it.

Meanwhile, she was over there, on the other side of the trench between us, thinking I was blaming her. Hating her.

I dropped my head, shaking it, a smile pulling at my lips. A soft laugh on my lips. My fists twisting in the sheets. I hadn't lost her at all.

She wasn't leaving me.

AJ was going to stay.

She would always stay.

My heart squeezed. "Well, I'm not planning on losing another eye," I choked out. "Or either of my arms. So, we have that going for us—"

She tackled me, knocking me onto my back as she pressed her knees to either side of my hips, lying over me until I could feel her hard pebbled nipples brushing my chest. Smell her hair as it tickled along my jaw.

"Greyson Winters," she said, holding back a smile of her own. "You are a monument to idiots everywhere."

"Takes one to know one, babe." I winked.

She let out a breathy moan as her mouth landed on mine with crushing force, stealing the breath from my lungs. I couldn't get my hands on her fast enough, running fingers up her sides, grabbing, pulling, digging in so deep that she wouldn't ever be able to disentangle herself from me again.

She moaned against my mouth, but the sound was spiked with pain, and I immediately loosened my grip, breaking the feral kiss. "Wait. Wait, wait, wait. I don't want to hurt you. You're still healing."

AJ grinned wickedly in response, gripping the collar of my shirt in her fist. I barely felt the pull on the back of my neck before she tore it all the way down to the hem, exposing my chest and abs to her.

She hungrily followed the line of my body all the way down to where my waist vanished into my jeans in a tight V. I adjusted my position, flexing the muscle there for her, making her jaw clench with need.

I meant what I said. I didn't want to hurt her, but I sure as fuck wasn't about to deny her, either.

She reached down, easily unfastening my belt before pulling it through all the loops and discarding it on my bedroom floor. My buttons were next and my throat went almost painfully dry as my breaths deepened. My cock, rock hard, twitched at the slightest brush of her hand as she worked to pull my jeans off, letting it spring free.

I lifted my hips to help her, seeing how much she wanted this written all over her face. Maybe almost as much as I did.

AJ stood back a second, her wicked stare fixed on my erection as she licked her lips. "Did I ever tell you that you have the most beautiful cock I've ever seen?"

A smirk twitched on my lips. I wouldn't tell her she wouldn't be the first person to tell me that. Instead I tucked my hands behind my head and cocked my head at her. "Is that so?"

"*Mhmm.*"

She crawled back onto the bed. "I don't think there's a single flaw."

Her gaze flicked up to my face, tracing every ridge. Every hollow. "In fact, I don't see a single flaw *anywhere*."

"Neither do I."

She bit her lower lip, making my body burn with a need for her so strong I worried she might go up in flames if she came too close.

But my girl didn't fear fire.

31

CORVUS

She had to be hungry by now.

The last time we ate was back in the hospital this afternoon. I was sure there was something I could scrape together with whatever was in the freezer and cupboards... since everything in the fridge had long since rotted.

Sparrow said I should grovel more often. She was going to get that wish. I'd make her see it. Stuff it down her tight little throat until she couldn't take it anymore. Until she begged me to stop. She would. Because she and I both knew that she *liked* it when I took control.

...most of the time.

I didn't bother knocking, but maybe I should've.

Ava Jade and Grey pulled apart as I entered.

Grey lay naked on his bed, his proud cock at attention, wet and glistening with my Sparrow's saliva. Her lips were swollen from all the work she was doing, on her knees, praying to the church of Greyson Winters like the devout Saint she was.

"Damn," I coughed, waiting, giving myself a minute to choose my next words more carefully since the first one came out all on its own. My Sparrow told me she wouldn't choose, and I knew she meant it, but there would always be a part of me, some leftover vestige of the possessive caveman I knew still clung to some part of my brain I couldn't fix.

Chapter 31

"Glad to see you've made up."

Grey lifted a brow, unfazed by my entry, while Sparrow glared at me with something halfway between hatred and hunger glittering in her watery eyes.

My fist curled, and I turned to leave them to their makeup fuck, half wondering if I'd get such a gift. It was the season of miracles after all. Might be time to make my Christmas wish.

"Wait," Sparrow called hoarsely. "Stay."

She didn't have to ask me twice. I slammed the door, coming for her like a bull let loose at the gate.

"No," she hissed, stopping me in my tracks with a hard look. "Watch."

"What?"

She indicated the computer chair to their right and kicked its base so it rolled over the floor to the corner of the room. Where she would have a perfect line of sight to me. And I her.

And Grey.

Fucking.

"Is this my punishment, Sparrow?"

She shrugged, leaning over Grey's cock to lick the bead of precum there, making him shiver.

"You're wicked," Grey said, his voice heavy with desire as he tipped his head back. "Let him join, AJ. I don't mind."

"I do." She jerked her chin to the chair. "Besides, you heard the doctor. No elevated heart rates allowed."

"He said no coffee," I argued.

Another shrug. "Same thing."

Fine. If this was what she wanted. I'd watch.

I stalked to the chair, sinking into it, gripping my thighs to hold myself there when it was almost impossible not to strip her naked, tie her up with her own clothing, and stuff my rapidly growing cock down her little throat for daring to try to control *me*.

As if she could sense where my mind went, she opened her mouth wide, taking Grey all the way in to his hilt. His hand found the back of her neck, hips tilting up to push his cock in even further, until she couldn't breathe.

Only then did she pull back, her hands digging into Grey's thighs, urging him to fuck her mouth. He did. Thrusting up into her mouth until his eyes rolled back and the veins in the arm that held her in place jutted out from his skin like snakes.

When he let her come up for air, it was me she looked at, a wicked curve to her mouth. "Enjoying the show?" she teased.

Challenge accepted.

I unzipped my jeans, pulling out my cock as evidence of just how much I apparently did, surprising the both of us.

I'd long since gotten used to the idea of sharing her with my brothers, and almost losing her cemented the entire beautifully twisted arrangement for me. If she would have me, I would have her in whatever way she would have me in return.

At least, that's what I'd thought at first, but now, watching them together, I knew it was more.

I wanted her for me.

But I wanted her for them, too.

Her lips parted, the bottom one swollen and damp, making me even harder as she damn near drooled over the length of iron dick I now stroked.

Ruffled at my reaction, her cocky grin faltered.

Grey took the opportunity with her distracted to catch her under the arms, lifting her swiftly, making her yelp as he flipped her onto her back and hovered between her legs. "Eyes on me, baby," he purred, a finger under her chin.

She smiled up at him, and for a moment I was entirely forgotten as she tugged his lips to hers, arching her back to help him remove her pants.

Grey didn't waste any time, tossing her jeans and panties like fucking party favors around the room. He pressed his fingers to her opening, and I watched her squirm at the touch of his fingers, her chest heaving. Nipples hard against the thin gray t-shirt she wore.

Fuck.

I reached for the lotion at the edge of his desk and pumped cool ropes of it all over my cock, sliding my hand over the slippery skin, adjusting my pressure.

Grey leaned down to taste her, and I groaned, licking my lips as if I could taste her sweet pussy on my own lips. My Sparrow's breaths quickened as he drove her to the brink of climax, her breasts heaving with each breath as she fought to muffle her cries with one fist between her teeth and the other twisted in the blanket.

I jerked off to her pleasure, gripping the armrest of the chair with my free hand.

I could see the moment she was going to come, her body fucking rigid as a corpse. Practically levitating, her back arched, lifting from the bed until she couldn't take it anymore, thighs crushing against either side of Grey's head.

Her moan was loud enough to wake the whole fucking house, but I didn't think she cared. I knew I didn't. Let them hear what we were doing to her. How she moaned and cried out *for us*.

Let them hear that she belonged to *us*.

Grey licked his shining lips as she released him, her whole body shaking from the aftershocks of her orgasm. But before she could fully recover, he flipped her onto her belly, lifting beneath her hips gently to avoid the bruising still hidden by her shirt there.

She lifted for him, shuffling to the edge of the bed like a lion stalking its prey in reverse. Her sharp gaze found mine as Grey fumbled with something behind her, getting himself into position.

My phone buzzed in my pocket, and I whipped it out, a bolt of panic racing through me, but it was only Max. *Again.* As if I could even fucking consider the tour or record deal she was trying to cram down my throat.

I silenced the call and tossed my phone onto Grey's desk.

"Now just relax for me, AJ," my brother warned her, and I lifted from my hips, never stopping the stroking of my hand, to watch as he slowly fed a massive plug into her ass. She closed her eyes against the sensation, a mix of pain and pleasure twisting her beautiful face.

She settled once it was all the way in, biting her lip.

"There you go," Grey whispered, curling a hand around her hip as he positioned himself at her opening. He looked at me with a teasing smirk as he slid into her, sucking a breath in through his teeth.

Sparrow gasped as Grey thrust himself into her balls fucking deep, settling himself there with a groan, his mouth slack.

"Fuck, AJ, you're so wet for me."

She pushed back against him, bending her chest to the bed, preening like a cat. "*Mmm*," she purred, and he began to move, pressing a palm flat against her lower back as he thrust up and into her sweet pussy, making stuttering moans fall from her pillow-soft lips.

I increased the pressure with my hand, focusing on the tip until my breaths came out stuttered too as I pictured myself deep inside of her. Feeding every inch of my massive cock into her pussy until she almost couldn't take it. She'd had little trouble after my show in Lodi, but I knew it wasn't without some discomfort. There wasn't a pussy on this planet that could take this dick easy.

Grey increased his speed and there were stars in her eyes as she lifted them to the ceiling, snaking a hand down between her legs to rub her greedy clit with a groan.

My brother bared his teeth, his knuckles white as he switched to holding her for dear life by the hips, close to his own climax.

"Fuck..." my Sparrow cried. "Grey!"

"That's right, baby," he said between pants, fucking her harder. "I told you... I'd have you... screaming my name."

She buried her face in the blankets, her shoulders flexing with lean muscle as she spiraled closed to orgasm.

"*Come on, Sparrow,*" I found myself saying on a breath, making her crane her neck to find my face through the haze of her ecstasy. "Come on his cock."

Her upper lip curled and her lethal gaze narrowed, but she did as she was told, winning the battle, but losing the war as she screamed my brother's name, shoving all three of us over that edge.

"*I want it,*" she cried, her voice strained as she tried to speak through her orgasm as Grey pumped his last, teeth bared as she buried his cock in her cunt.

She opened her mouth and I stood, brought to my climax the instant the head of my cock slid onto her warm tongue. She sucked greedily on me, making me catch a fistful of hair just to keep myself standing, shuddering against her perfect mouth.

32

AVA JADE

My mouth watered at the plate of food Corvus slid across the center island to me.

It was the third dinner he'd prepared for us all since we came back to the Nest. Three days and we still had *nothing*. I was getting restless, and I could tell everyone else was, too. Grey set to shoveling the brown butter potatoes and rare steak into his mouth, but I could tell he wasn't really tasting it. He had that faraway look in his eyes. The one he'd worn since the morning we woke up after he fucked me until I couldn't see straight.

He'd gone straight back to work, wrapped in a blanket instead of bothering to get dressed. And even now, as he ate, he was still fucking working. His scholarly mind trying to find an angle he hadn't already thought of.

Rook stood, elbows leaned on the center island as he pushed his steak and potatoes around on his plate with a scowl on his lips.

"Eat," Corvus ordered, glaring at both Rook and me as he slid into the last stool, dropping his own plate in front of him. "I didn't spend an hour mothering those potatoes for them to get fucking cold."

I sighed, popping one into my mouth. It was incredible, but so was everything he'd ever cooked for us. I couldn't bring myself to give a compliment tonight, though. We still had another day before our planned heist of female Hitler's fancy eggs and pearls. Grey needed a specific type of decoder to get past her home security system, which should be arriving tomorrow morning.

And then we'd have to wait a day or two while Diesel secured a black market buyer.

The day after that was the planned meet with the Mexicans, when we'd need to have the cash in hand no matter what happened any of the days before.

Once we had those weapons and ammunition, there was still the teeny tiny problem of not knowing where the fuck Carson was. Or the rest of the Kings for that matter.

While we sat here, eating a gourmet meal surrounded by grouchy sleep-deprived Saints, they could be planning their next move.

At least Corvus was looking and feeling better. And I had to admit the time spent at rest made all the difference for me, even if it wasn't what I wished I was doing. The burns along my forearm were still gnarly as fuck, but they'd stopped seeping, and in another few days I figured I could remove the bandages for good. The bruises along my stomach had turned a sickly shade of yellow, and would fade completely soon... even if the internal trauma couldn't be so easily healed.

But the main thing was the complete and utter *lack* of voices in my head. Aside from some very vivid dreams and night sweats, turned out that nurse was right. I wasn't crazy. At least, I wasn't *hearing voices crazy*. I was definitely the other kind.

"Try the horseradish sauce," Corvus urged, pointing the sharp end of his steak knife toward my plate and the white sauce spilling over the sliced strips of steak.

I let my fork clatter to the plate and sat up, leaning to my right to take Rook's half-drunk glass of the good bourbon he'd been slowly working his way through this week.

"I can get you your own," he offered, and I lifted a brow at the hostility in his tone.

"I don't want my own," I parried, tossing the rest of it back with a shiver as the burn flushed down my throat to my belly.

He gave me a look before going to get himself a brand new glass from the cupboard.

"Someone's grouchy," I muttered to myself, setting the empty glass down.

"How's the search coming?" Corvus asked Grey, and I caught the way he flinched at the question. It was all anyone wanted to know. The Saints asked him every time he left his room to take a piss. Diesel asked him every time he called. He didn't need the pressure from us, too.

"Would you leave him alone?" I snapped. "He's doing everything he can."

Grey stood suddenly, the legs of his stool scraping over the tile as he wiped his mouth with his napkin and tossed it over his half eaten dinner. "I don't need you to baby me, AJ. I'm going back to work."

My nostrils flared as I leveled a murderous stare on Corvus. "And what have you done, hmm? Aren't you supposed to be the one that thinks of everything?"

His brows lowered over his eyes, making the bright blue darken to a stormy navy under their shadows. The threat of thunder in the hard set of his shoulders and bulging biceps. "You think I haven't been doing everything I can to find this fucker, too? What is it you think I'm doing in my room all hours of the day and night because it sure as fuck isn't napping. I've exhausted all my resources. It's like the guy doesn't fucking exist."

"Well, he does, and he's still out there." I pointed toward the window, to the long road curving away into the trees down to Briar Hall.

The reminder that not only was I likely going to be a dead girl within the week, but I'd also be a dead *high school dropout*, just made me even angrier.

Going back to class was completely out of the question. There were too many opportunities for Carson to get to us there, not to mention the possibility of innocent teens being put in the line of fire. But whether the reasoning was sound or not didn't fucking matter to me. I'd worked *hard* to get to where I was with my grades, and it was all for nothing. Christmas break would be starting in two weeks and then it would be an entirely new semester with new classes. No way to make up for lost time or projects from the previous semester.

But who fucking cared, right?

Not like you needed a high school education to handle a weapon.

Dad would be so proud.

"You don't think I know that?" Corvus growled. "You don't think it makes me sick knowing he's out there, walking free, *breathing*, after what he put you through? *Hmm?*"

"Then why are you in here 'mothering your potatoes?' "

The darkness ebbed and flowed, fully set free to swell and crash against my walls inside. A part of me knew I wasn't being fair, but I couldn't seem to help it. Couldn't seem to stop.

Couldn't fucking sit here anymore.

Corvus snatched his dinner from the counter and pitched it into the sink, shattering the plate before he stalked from the room.

Rook slid onto the stool next to me as though nothing had happened at all, sipping his fresh glass of bourbon.

"Damn Ghost..."

He grabbed the bottle to top off my glass. "You really know how to clear a room."

He knocked his glass into mine in a mock cheers before draining the rest of his drink and lighting a cigarette.

"Corvus will kill you."

Rook smirked around the cigarette at the edge of his mouth. "Nah. He'll stay in there the rest of the night now."

He took a drag and ashed onto his plate. "No one gets to him like you do."

Rook took my untouched glass of bourbon and put it to his lips.

I bristled. "Thought we weren't sharing," I said bitterly.

He bit his lip ring, sliding the glass back my way. When I reached for it, he settled his hand over mine, and I noticed the fresh ink on his middle finger. A little ghost with black oval eyes. My rage slipped away, replaced by a fierce tightening in my chest that almost had me choking.

"We're all a little on edge right now, Ghost. For what it's worth, sorry I snapped at you."

I lifted his hand, studying the new ink. He grinned. "You like it?"

I shifted my gaze to the hand wrapped around the bottle of bourbon, and the name ROOK displayed over his knuckles, and I understood the significance. He fought for himself with that hand, but now I'd always be right here, on his left. The other thing he would go to his grave fighting for.

I opened my mouth to tell him how perfect it was when a horn blared long and loud out the window.

Saints rushed in from the living room, their weapons drawn.

Voices crackled over the radio.

"Incoming!"

The horn honked insistently now, over and over again as the sound drew nearer. Rook slid from his stool with a spark of life in his eyes I hadn't seen in days as he drew his gun. I loosed two blades from their holsters, making a beeline for the side door with Rook on my heels.

"Hold your fire!" Corvus bellowed over the radio, but I didn't hear the rest of what he said as Rook and I left the Saints behind, rounding the house, positioning ourselves behind a parked car, backs against the cool metal.

"Ready?" Rook asked.

"Ready."

We jumped out from behind the car just as the dark green truck appeared down the road. I reeled my arm back to throw, but Rook caught my wrist, stopping me.

"What are you—"

"It's my uncle," he hissed, releasing me as he stepped out into the road, waving his arms at the truck. "Damien!" he hollered.

"Rook, get out of the way!"

My heart lurched, legs poised to tackle him out of the truck's path and take the hit myself, but the tires screeched as Damien St. Vincent ground the truck to a stop, cranking the wheel sideways to spew gravel in our direction as it came to a jarring, shuddering stop. I sheathed my blades.

"What the fuck, Uncle D?" Grey slammed the front door behind him and Corvus as they stalked into the driveway and Damien St. Vincent shoved out of the truck.

"Get in,'" he said, his face flushed. "I just got off the phone with the hospital. She's awake."

The words were a punch to the gut, and my hand flew to my chest as tears sprang to my eyes.

She's awake?

A sob grew in my chest, and it let free as someone's arm came around my waist, breaking me out of my frozen state.

The driver's side door shut and Damien revved the engine as we raced to the back of the truck, launching ourselves into the cargo bed.

"We're right behind you!" one of the Saints, Mickey, shouted, tossing a set of keys to someone. The engines of all the cars in the driveway turned over as one as Damien chewed gravel, whipping the truck around to go back the way he'd come.

Someone squeezed my hand, and I glanced up to find Grey there, giving me a comforting nod as tears raced down my cheeks and the ball in my chest grew. I sniffed, squeezing his hand back, reaching for Corvus.

I squeezed his knee, and he gave me the same reassuring look. "Be ready," he said over the rush of the wind. "They could be waiting for us."

The hope and joy that'd been churning in my gut turned back to heavy lead, and I drew my blades again, ready for anything. I fucking dared him to try something now. There was nothing on this mortal coil strong enough to stop me from getting to that hospital. *Nothing.*

The guys and I led the charge into the hospital with Damien St. Vincent and the other Saints flanking us, ready for anything.

I'd been courteous enough to sheath my blades, and the guys had holstered their weapons, but it was clear to anyone with two eyes and a brain that we were all armed to the teeth. Whether long t-shirts or jackets concealed the majority of our weapons or not.

"Is she in the same room?" I asked Damien, gaze fixed on the hallway ahead, and the stairs that would lead up to the next floor where I would take an immediate left and find her room.

"As far as I know," he replied gruffly, starting to flag behind.

This made Grey pause, his sneakers squeaking on the tile floor. "You're not coming?"

"Why would I? She doesn't know me. Just... just let me know she's all right, would you, lad?"

"Yeah," Grey replied before I heard the rush of his footfalls hurrying to catch up to the rest of us as we blew into the stairwell. I had no patience to stand in the hall and wait for an elevator.

"There's no chance this is a trap, right?" Corvus asked, taking the stairs two at a time in stride with me.

His words sent a spike of ice stabbing into my chest. If this was some sort of trick... if Carson had used my best friend against me *again*...

"It's not," Rook answered before I could, putting my apprehension to rest. "Damien would've sorted that out quick."

His reassurance didn't rid me of the disquieting thoughts altogether, though. Thorn Valley had seemed eerily quiet on the way over here. And with still nothing from Carson or the Kings, I couldn't help feeling that something big was coming. There was no way they were just going to crawl into a hole and disappear for good.

Carson would come for me. I knew he would. It was only a matter of time.

I bulldozed through the door to the second floor with a hard lump in my throat, seeing a willowy silhouette sitting up in bed through the curtain to her hospital room.

Nurses whispered outside her door, shaking their heads. "Such a shame," one was saying. "Mr. Hart only just left to sign that merger. If he'd stayed another half day he would've been here when she woke up."

"He's assured us he's on the next flight back."

"Doesn't change the fact that she had to wake up alone. Poor thing doesn't have any other family—"

"Yes she does," I argued, shoving between the two nurses and into the room.

"Becks?"

My friend was shakily bringing a plastic cup to her lips, but stopped dead when we entered, her unfocused eyes squinting at me like she didn't recognize me.

My heart stopped.

"Rebecca?"

"Who..."

Her voice was a hoarse whisper.

She set the cup down, swallowing hard as her brown eyes flicked to the guys behind me, clearly struggling.

No.

"Becks, it's me."

I went to her side, sitting on the edge of her bed. I reached for her, but she shied away, her face paling. Fuck, she looked so frail. With her big brown eyes wide and fearful. Her body shrunken and weakened from being stuck in this bed. A weight settled in my stomach, yanking tears from my eyes.

"Sparrow..." Corvus hedged. "Memory loss is common in coma cases, maybe you should give her some—"

"It's me," I implored her, ignoring Corvus as I saw a flicker of recognition in her eyes, making my pulse pound. "There you are. It's me, babe. It's Ava Jade."

She dropped her head, shaking it, her eyes closed tight. Grimacing.

I gripped her cold hand tight between mine and this time when she lifted her head, her lips parted. "Aves?"

"Oh my god," I choked out, pulling her into a solid embrace. "*Becks,* you're okay."

Her arms came slowly around me, squeezing as well as she could. I felt her back heave as her tears stained the collar of my shirt, leaking over my collarbone.

"Holy shit," she cried, clutching me almost as tightly as I was clutching her now.

"Let's give them a minute," Rook said somewhere behind me, and I heard the door to the hospital room click shut.

I sniffed, pulling away from her shaking embrace to hold her at arm's length. "You scared the shit out of me."

"Me?" She sniffed. "You're the one that was just... gone. But, you're back. Where did you go? How could you just... just leave us like that."

She wiped the back of her palm over her nose, falling against the inclined back of her raised hospital bed as if she couldn't stay sitting up anymore on her own. I realized there was so much she didn't know.

Sensing where my mind had gone, she took my hand in hers. "Babe? You were just staying away because you were angry, right?"

I wished I could lie to her, but I'd decided a long time ago that I needed to stop doing that. This bitch was my ride or die and just woken up from a coma or not, she deserved the truth.

"No, Becks, I wasn't. But we don't have to talk about this now. The important thing is that you're awake. You're all right. I'm... *fuck,* I'm so sorry this happened, Becks."

She shook her head. "Did he...?"

I clamped my mouth shut.

Her nails dug into my palm. "Tell me everything. I want to know. I *need* to know. Is he dead at least? Did we get him? Did my painting help?"

"It did," I assured her, remembering the guys telling me how smart she was to hide the painting before Carson could get to her. I didn't care what anyone said about her, she was a badass bitch. "It helped so much more than you realize."

Because of that painting, Diesel dissolved the alliance with the Kings before they could act. She might've single handedly saved at least thirty lives.

"But he isn't dead, is he?"

Her hand went absently to her chest, to where a bandage covered the bullet wound an inch away from her heart. I could sense her fear in the way her body went rigid, her hand trembling in mine, but I could also see the fire in her eyes. The absolute feral rage simmering below the surface.

"No. He isn't. We can't find him."

"Did he hurt you, Aves?"

My non-response was response enough.

"Oh, fuck, babe. I'm so sorry. You don't have to tell me if you don't want to."

She leaned forward to hug me again, and I let her hold my broken pieces together for me, just for a minute, wondering how I'd ever gotten by without her.

"We're going to find him," she promised with a harsh whisper in my ear. "And he's going to pay. For all of it."

I nodded against her shoulder. I couldn't tell her right now, but once she was on her feet she needed to understand that there wasn't a *we* when it came to dealing with Carson Bates. I'd get my pint of blood of out of him on her behalf, but she wouldn't be anywhere near this place when that happened.

Someone tapped at the door, and Becks and I pulled apart as the guys came back in. "Hey, Becca," Grey said with a winning smile. "How you feeling?"

She tucked a length of rich brown hair behind her ear and tried to return his smile. "I'm awake," she replied. "So that's a start."

Becca's gaze flicked to Rook and filled with an anguished sort of warmth. "Thank you. The nurses said that you saved my life."

I frowned, turning to face my dark prince. He winked at my bestie. "Anytime, love."

I mouthed a *thank you* of my own to him, wondering why the fuck no one thought I should know that little tidbit. But of course he saved her. I doubted there was a reaper strong enough to take a soul Rook Clayton refused to give up. I was just glad he'd decided hers was worth holding on to.

"What the fuck happened to you?" Becca asked Corvus, her face screwing up at his new buzz cut.

Corv scratched the still healing puncture wounds on the back of his head. A habit I was trying to break him of. "I fell off a building."

"Fell?" I pressed.

He cleared his throat, waving a hand toward Becca. "You look good." Corvus coughed, not so sneakily changing the subject.

Becca gave a short laugh. "Right. And you're a good liar."

"I'll get you your things from Briar Hall," I offered. "Just text me the list and I'll bring it for you."

She shook her head. "They didn't have my phone."

I looked askance at my guys, but they shook their heads. Clearly Carson had taken it.

"Take mine," Corvus offered, shuffling over to slip his phone onto her lap. "Code's 26637. All of our numbers are already programmed in."

I smiled gratefully at him.

"I know it's not the time," Grey hedged, licking dry lips as he rested his hands on the rail at the end of her bed. "But we've hit a wall trying to find Carson and—"

"Carson?"

"Jericho," I explained. "His real name's Carson. He's Diesel's biological son."

She jerked back as though slapped, trying to process. "What? Wait. Slow down. Diesel has another son?"

I could tell we were going to need to fill her in on all the dirty little details. If we did, then maybe she would remember something that would link us to Carson. Or lead us to the Kings. I'd take any scrap of helpful evidence at this point.

"If you're sure you want to do this now—"

"I am. I want to know what happened while I was out."

I nodded. "Corv, can you ask one of the guys out in the hall to wrangle some peanut M&M's and a cherry cola for Becks? We're going to be here a while."

33

ROOK

The completely destroyed rose garden out front of Diesel's house told us three things.

1. That they were still out there. Waiting.
2. That Carson was furious.
3. And that he wasn't through with us.

The bastard couldn't help himself, he had to take the one thing our father had left of his wife. He knew where to hit him to inflict the most damage outside of killing us, and he didn't waste his chance. With all of us busy between Sanctum, the hospital, and the Crow's Nest, Diesel's place had been left almost entirely open to attack. All he'd had to do was cut the power to the street and there was no evidence of his presence. No video footage. Nothing.

It was an act carried out in spite. He wanted to scare us, but all he'd managed to do was piss us off even more.

Ghost nudged me in the backseat of the Rover, the moonlight shining on her face revealing a soft, sympathetic smile.

It'd been like pulling teeth dragging her away from her friend in the hospital to come with us for the heist. She'd only come at all because we left

1040

half the Saints that'd been with us there to guard her friend. Despite her father's loud ass protests when he finally arrived a few hours ago. They'd made themselves scarce, but they were under strict orders from my Ghost herself not to leave the second floor and cover all points of entry at all times.

It didn't surprise me that they'd taken her orders without question. My Ghost was born to lead.

"How's Diesel?" she asked, breaking the tepid silence in the Rover. She'd been in the shower when we got the call, and I was glad she didn't have to hear his explosion when Corv put the call on speakerphone. Distraught wasn't the right word. He was rattled. Broken. Breathing fucking fire.

"Not good, Sparrow," Corvus answered honestly from the front seat, his head propped up by his fist against the window. "Not good at all. It was all he had left of her. I've never heard him so..." He trailed off, his voice shaky.

"Is there anything we can do?" she asked, leaning forward in her seat. "There has to be something salvageable. Maybe we can replant it and—"

"It's done, AJ," Grey interjected, flicking his hard stare to her in the rearview. "Dies said there was nothing that could be saved."

I shifted in my seat, fucking hating how some ruined flowers planted for a woman I'd never even met could make me absolutely feral, ravenous for blood. Or maybe it was just the fact that I hadn't had anyone to punish for their sins in far too long. I told myself I was just saving it all up for one person who would be punished far beyond anything I'd ever accomplished before.

His anguish would be music to my fucking ears. I couldn't wait to smell his fear. Watch him bleed. Hear him fucking beg. I sucked in a breath and the air rattled in the empty vestiges of my chest.

I needed a fucking cigarette.

When I took out the pack, Ghost stole one from the stack, putting it between her lips.

Not more than a second after she had it there Corvus was reaching back between the seats to snatch it out of her mouth. He rolled down the window and chucked it out. "You're not starting that shit. It's bad enough he still smokes."

"Aren't you supposed to be groveling?" she asked, a dangerous lilt to her tone.

"I draw the line at letting you give yourself fucking cancer."

"Oh, but for Rook, it's totally fine?"

I smirked as I lit my cigarette, rolling down my window to blow smoke out into the night.

"You try making Rook do something he doesn't want to do," Corvus said lazily, going back to leaning against the window. "Call me when you succeed."

Ava Jade rolled her tongue over her teeth, sitting back in her seat to cross her arms. I knew if she didn't agree with him, she would've just taken another. But there was nothing like my tobacco mix to take the edge off a hard fucking day.

I took a long pull, holding the smoke in my mouth, and leaned over to her, kissing away the scowl on her lips. I blew the smoke into her mouth and she inhaled, her body pressing up against mine.

She blew it out with a haughty look in Corvus' direction, but my brother just rolled his eyes in the side view mirror before giving me a pointed, warning stare I knew to take seriously.

He'd let me poison myself all I wanted, but he *would* have my ass if I let her get addicted to this shit.

I rubbed out the smoke between my fingers and dropped the dead butt into the pack with the others. "So these eggs," I started casually, trying to forget about ruined roses and just enjoy the night. We hadn't had to pull off a heist in a while, and even though this shit was about as low key as it got, it was still making me hard thinking I'd get to do it with my Ghost at my side. "Do we know where all of them are?"

Ghost nodded. "I clocked each one the first night I spent there. There's four upstairs in the hallways and my aunt's bedroom. Another five on the main floor. One in the foyer. One in the dining room. One in the living room. Another in the drawing room, and one in the sitting room."

"What's the fucking difference?" Grey asked. "Between a living room and a sitting room and a—what was it?—*drawing* room? Isn't that all the same shit?"

"Rich people shit," Ghost said with a shrug. "Don't even bother trying to understand it."

Up ahead, the rich bitch's estate sprawled in rolling hills of gated off green, the mansion itself still hidden in the hills.

"Switch," Grey announced, pulling off to the side of the road so he and Corvus could swap seats. The convoy behind us slowed, pulled off as well. It was less than the contingent of Saints that Diesel wanted with us, but I had to agree with my Ghost. Becca needed just as much protection as we did. Maybe more.

Thanks to her we now knew of the existence of a 'factory.' Carson mentioned it to Becca a few times, and she'd figured it was just a story he concocted. Another lie. But there was detail there. He said he'd needed to meet his leader there not once, but three times during the time they were "dating," probably to get out of spending any more time with her than he needed to. There must be at least a hundred factories in between here and Lodi, but Grey was already looking into every single one. Open and operating. Shut down. It didn't matter.

If it was a place where shit was made, he was finding the name on the lease, looking for any cracks in the facade.

With any luck, by the time we secured our new firepower, we'd have them by the balls.

Grey opened his laptop in the passenger seat, tapping keys as Corvus pulled away from the road. "I just need to get within range. Pull up another mile, but stay out of sight of the cameras at the main gate."

Corvus grunted in reply as Grey rolled down his window and held a black box with an antenna outside, his hair blowing in the wind. There was silence for a minute before Grey said, "I've got it. Pull over."

He continued to hold the device with one hand and tapped away at the keys on his laptop with the other. My Ghost peered curiously over the seat, watching with squinty eyes. "How did you learn how to do this?" she asked.

Grey took a second to respond. "Trial and error. One of us needed to know how to hack and these two were both way too impatient to learn."

"Hey, man, I tried," I argued weakly.

"Yeah, two broken laptops later..."

"I said I *tried*. Didn't say I succeeded."

"What about you?" Ghost asked Corvus.

"No broken laptops. My talents were better put to use elsewhere."

"Like singing to yourself in your closet?" Grey asked with a playful lilt, tapping the final key with a loud stab that I knew meant he had cracked the coding.

"Fuck you." Corvus elbowed him.

I laughed, but Ghost was frowning. "Have you called Max back yet?" she asked seriously as Grey announced he was in.

Corv scratched the scars forming at the back of his skull. "No, but I will. When this is over."

"Okay that should be enough footage to loop," Grey said, mostly to himself as he did whatever magic he did to make it look to Old Lady Humphrey's cameras as though we were never here.

"Take us to the gate, Corv."

The other Saints pulled ahead to the service road down the way as we turned up the short stretch to the main gate. They'd wait there, tucked away in case we needed backup, until it was time to make our getaway.

Grey stepped out of the Rover and attached a small screened device to a port on the back of the big silver box with the number keys. It took him less than twenty seconds before an electronic horn sounded and the gates slowly swung inward.

Pleased with himself, he slipped back into the passenger seat. "Now it's just the home security and we're good."

"Like your new toy?" Ghost asked him as my brother practically stroked his new brick-like device like it was a newborn babe.

"I've always wanted one of these," he muttered.

She gave him a playful shove. "You're such a nerd."

He laughed and Corvus killed the headlights as we crept up to the imposing mansion.

"It's so dark," she said, her brows furrowing.

Corvus pulled down the narrow road that led to the caretaker's shed and the vegetable gardens on the east lawn, parking between the hedges.

"You think something's up?" I asked Ghost.

She lifted a shoulder. "Don't know. It's just, even in the middle of the night, there were always a few lights on. You know, the staff getting things ready for the next day. Cleaning and all that. My aunt hated them puttering around her during the day so she had them all work at night."

"She's a real piece of work," Grey sighed, gathering his new device into a black bag as he stepped out into the night air. Ghost and I followed, going around to the trunk to collect the duffles filled with packing foam to protect the eggs once we had them.

Ghost pulled on a pair of tight fitting leather gloves and flexed her fingers.

"Masks?" she asked the others as they came around to the back.

"Grey shook his head. "Won't need them. I'm going to shut down the whole system while we're in."

"Won't that set off some warning bells?"

"Not until your aunt realizes her shit's gone. They'll check the footage from the security cams and find a gap in the feeds."

"I wish I had one of you back in Lennox," Ghost mused. "Would have made a lot of our jobs go *a lot* smoother."

She'd mentioned before how she and her Dad used to run jobs together. Conning unsuspecting shop owners and the wealthy elite. But the reminder made me thirsty for something other than blood. I bit my lip ring, watching her double check the placement of all her blades before nodding confidently at me, scrunching her eyes at the look I was giving her. "You ready, Rook?"

"*So* ready."

This was going to be fun.

"Let's move," Corvus commanded, hunching low as we circled the hedges, stealthily moving over the lawn in the moonlight to the side entrance. The one the staff used to bring groceries into the house. Ava Jade keyed the code into the small pad above the door handle from memory, but it chirped at her when she was finished. The light turning red.

"Shit."

She tried again. Red light.

"Stop," Grey said before she could enter it a third time. "You'll have Thorn Valley PD crawling all over this place if you get it wrong three times."

"I'm not getting it wrong," she growled in a whisper. "That was the code."

"Then the old bag is smarter than we gave her credit for," Grey whispered, shuffling in front of Ava Jade to access the code panel. "She must've changed it after the shit show that was Thanksgiving."

He used a flat bit of steel to carefully pry the box back, revealing a shining green panel with connected wires. He dug in his bag, connecting his device with some copper clips. "Just give me a sec."

"Come on, come on," Ghost repeated restlessly, bouncing from foot to foot. We had five minutes to get inside before the motion detection on the camera above our heads sent an alert to the alarm company.

"Got it," Grey announced, detaching the device to reveal a green light.

"Move in," Corvus urged. "We have to get to the coms room."

We spilled into the mansion, greeted with the stagnant scent of musty old furniture made worse by the cover of expensive potpourri.

"Through here," Ghost whispered, leading the way even though we'd gone over the location three times already. I followed her lead through the kitchens and dining room, across the marble floor in the foyer and to the little closet sized room around the dark side of the curving staircase.

Grey got to work right away, accessing the system with ease. He erased the couple minutes of footage that showed us coming up the side lawn and got ready to make it all go black.

"Can't you loop this footage too?" Ghost asked, but Grey shook his head. "It's an old system. Making it go dark is the best I can do."

"Hold on," I barked, grabbing my brother's wrist before he could shut it all down. "Look."

I pointed at the old bubbled screens and the fuzzy images they displayed of the mansion in darkness. There were angles of almost every room in the whole place. And there wasn't a soul to be found in any of them.

"You don't think she left town?" Ghost asked, leaning in to get a better view.

"After what happened?" Grey asked. "I wouldn't be surprised if she left the state."

"Shut it down," Ghost told Grey, sliding from the room like a wraith in the dark on silent feet. "Rook, let's sweep the place. The staff quarters are down the hall, all the way to the end on the right. I'm going to check my aunt's room. They were the only ones without feeds."

I guessed the old bitch drew the line at her staff watching her sleep.

I nodded, drawing my gun more out of habit than necessity as I tiptoed down the hall. There was no reason to be silent, though. Ghost came back down the stairs to the foyer at the same time Corv and Grey left the security room and I came back from the staff quarters.

"Empty."

"*Empty,*" Ghost echoed with a laugh.

"Well this just got a whole lot easier."

"You mean more boring?" I corrected Corv.

He rolled his eyes.

A cunning smirk spread on my Ghost's lips. "It doesn't have to be."

She had me at the smirk.

I tailed her to the living room with the others following close behind me.

"What are you doing?" Corvus asked as she crossed the Persian carpet to fiddle with the modern sound system that looked painfully out of place among the cloth bound books and antique wood of the bookshelves. She plugged an auxiliary cable into her phone and flicked the dial, cranking the volume as one of my brother's songs came on, blasting over the surround sound.

Hide and Seek.

I felt my lips pull into a venomous grin, watching her move on her toes, a sparkle in her eyes.

"AJ, what—"

Ghost slipped off her shoes and my jaw flexed, legs burning with something other than the pain they'd been made to feel the last few weeks. They burned with the need to *chase.*

Her shirt went next and she threw it in my direction. I caught it with one hand and put it to my nose, inhaling deeply.

She bounced on the balls of her feet, her tits heaving in the lacy bra she wore as she looked around her, and I could tell she was thinking of all the places she could hide.

"I'm betting you'll never find me," she shouted over the blasting music. Over Corvus' haunting voice warning of the things he would do once he found his prey.

"Hide and seek, Sparrow? Really?"

I slung off the duffle bags and jacket, tossing it over the back of the couch, never taking my eyes off her. "You don't have to play, Bro," I growled. "I'll gladly have her all to myself."

"Fuck that." Grey was already setting his bag down and Corvus cursed, rolling his shoulders back.

"You have until the song ends, Ghost. Then you're mine."

She took off like a shot, and I put her shirt back to my face, breathing deeply of her before discarding it on the couch with my jacket. Instinctively, I bent at my knees, ready to give chase. I listened hard through the music, trying to hear her on the stairs. Or above on the second floor. But she was too good for that.

I smiled to myself, my fingers twitching as the song came close to its end.

The others weren't here anymore.

There was only me and *her*.

The predator.

And the prey.

The final note chimed and another song began, setting me free like the shot of a gun at a fucking horse race. I darted from the living room, catching the edge of the wall to slingshot around to the adjacent hall, my chest growing with each breath as I charged to the kitchens.

I heard my brothers on the stairs, but they weren't my prey. And they wouldn't find her.

I would.

"Oh, Ghost," I singsonged over *Gravedigger* playing muffled through the walls. "Come out, come out, wherever you are…"

The patter of little feet rained across the floor above my head, and I licked my lips, taking off at a sprint.

She had no idea what sort of monster she'd just unleashed.

34

AVA JADE

I tucked myself into the tight cupboard at the base of an old converted hutch in the grand bathroom upstairs, kicking towels aside to fit. My heart raced in the dark with the words of Primal Ethos' *Gravedigger* whispering of violence in my ears.

I regretted my choice of hiding place as soon as I closed the door, but it was too late. I could hear footfalls I recognized as distinctively Rook's thundering up the steps.

My breaths came heavy and ragged, and I closed my mouth, forcing the air to enter and exit silently through my nose. The others had gone down the other end of the hall, but Rook sounded like he was headed right for me. Like he knew exactly where I was.

I clasped my palms over my mouth, a thrill going through me as his dark shadow crossed the threshold of the bathroom, passing it by.

Even if I wanted him to find me, a part of me—the part that willingly decided I was the prey—instinctively wanted to run. Knowing this predator wasn't just a threat. He was apex. And if he found me, I didn't think even he would be able to control what he would do.

I'd seen a glimpse of it that night after he fought Conor Jones in the ring at Sanctum and he came after me in the streets afterwards. The thrill in his black eyes. The way he stalked around me, turning us in circles. A dance of villains and thieves.

Of primal desire and the need to *dominate*.

I pushed further back into the cupboard as the song switched, changing to the quicker tempo at the opening of *Run, Bitch, Run*.

Fitting.

A cold sweat coated my chest and slicked over my forehead as I heard Rook crashing through the rooms down the hall, growing closer by the second.

As though on cue, my ass knocked something solid hidden at the back of the cupboard. Something glass. A bottle. It tapped against the wood. Such a quiet sound, but I could feel the change in the air.

Like it was thicker to breathe.

"Shit," I cursed with a manic laugh, kicking out of the cupboard to scramble over the slippery tile, sloppily as I unfurled, finding my feet. I raced from the bathroom, conditioned air rushing over my bare stomach, whipping my hair back from my face.

At the end of the hall, Grey and Corvus tripped over each other exiting a bedroom. Behind me, I could feel Rook's presence like a heavy shadow.

"Got you," he snarled, far too close, and I gripped the banister, launching myself over it, my stomach soaring as I tumbled through the air, landing on the balls of my feet in the foyer, rolling to lessen the impact. The roll turning right back into a full sprint.

The floor beneath my feet trembled as Rook jumped down behind me with a loud grunt.

Oh god.

Oh fuck.

I crossed the living room in a split second, rushing through the dining room as *Run, Bitch, Run* hit its first base drop. I could hear him behind me. In the living room. He'd be on top of me in seconds. The others not far behind.

Glass shattered in the living room, and I sucked in a breath, spying the dark space beneath an oversized ottoman in the sitting room. I slid across the hardwood floor, disappearing into that darkness an instant before Rook crashed into the room.

A clatter sounded above me. The bottle I'd knocked against the back of the cupboard in the bathroom must've fallen.

"She's back upstairs," Grey shouted, and I was sure if they came any closer, they'd be able to hear my heart thudding as loudly as I could hear it in my own ears.

Two sets of racing footfalls departed, but there was still one set lingering. Even with the slightly heavier right foot from his injuries. I know the sound of him anywhere. Rook knew I didn't go back upstairs.

Run, Bitch, Run slowed, coming to an end, giving me the opportunity to hear him take a long breath in through his nose. Was he... trying to scent me?

Wetness slicked my thighs beneath my leather skirt and I bit down hard on my lip, wanting to run but also aching to be found. I pressed my thighs together as the next song started, gasping as the leather hugging my thighs creaked.

Fuck.

Strong hands gripped my ankles, and I let out a squeal that was stolen away by the raucous beat of the next song as Rook dragged me out from beneath the ottoman.

I twisted out of his grip, clawing the carpet to escape, but he had me again a second later, his hard body crushing mine into submission, face down on the floor. "Where do you think you're going, Ghost? You're mine now."

A feral sound escaped my lips as I reflexively struggled to find a way out, my heart racing like a trapped animal. His knee slipped from my spine, and I took the opportunity to flip onto my back, launching a bare foot into his chest. An *oof* left his mouth as he fell back, and I scrambled to my feet, hurtling over the couch.

He was up in an instant, and I stood there like a deer mesmerized by bright headlights as I watched his shoulders expand. Rook gauged the distance to me. The height of the couch between us. He stepped to his left, and I jerked to the right, the bulky couch the only thing stopping him from getting to me.

"Ghost..." he warned, his tone dripping delicious venom.

I licked my lips, trying to taste it, and then bolted.

The thud of the couch being tossed from his path made shivers of fear and anticipation electrify every step. I didn't even get back to the main living room before making the critical mistake of turning to see how far behind he was. My foot caught on the arched leg of a side-table in the entry, and I went crashing back to the floor.

I flipped to my back right as he descended on me. I raised an arm to strike, but he already had my wrists and pinned them high above my head, making me struggle and writhe beneath him.

"*Mine.*" His guttural declaration vibrated through his chest.

I cried out as he bent over my chest, biting the mound of my right tit, nearly breaking skin, making me see stars.

I got an arm free and raked my claws over his neck but that only excited him more. He fought to regain control, twisting my arm, my body, until I was facedown and entirely unable to move. I felt the press of cold steel against the base of my spine and shivered. But it was the press of his warm, hard cock through his jeans against my ass cheek that had me panting for him. Salivating.

Wanting.

Needing.

Begging.

"*Please.*"

He flipped up the hem of my skirt and sliced the thin string of my thong in one quick movement, exposing me to him. He pawed my left cheek before squeezing it so hard a yelp tore from my throat. His hand came down on the same spot an instant later, making goosebumps race along my body.

I arched, trying to move, that instinct to run still persistent in my blood, but he leaned over my body, and I felt the sharp edge of a blade under my chin, making my pulse skip a beat. "You aren't going anywhere, Ghost," his warm breath fanned over my cheek. "I *won*. Now I get to claim my prize."

"You found her," Grey's excited voice came from somewhere to my right and Rook's answering snarl made his steps falter, shuffle back a foot.

The sting of the blade nicking my skin made me suck in a breath as a droplet of warmth slid down my throat, finding a home between my breasts. I closed my eyes against the wave of endorphins, bristling beneath my dark prince.

"I found her," Rook roared and the possession in his voice made my toes curl. "I get to claim her first."

"Fair is fair," Grey replied cautiously, and the remaining struggle leached from my coiled muscles.

Rook scraped the blade down my throat just as *Anthem of the Broken* began to play, raising gooseflesh in its wake. "Now be a good Ghost and don't fucking move."

He released my arm, and I let it drop to the floor, wincing as the overextended muscle returned to its natural state.

My breasts pressed against the floor with each rise of my chest. The blade withdrew from my throat and without warning, Rook impaled me with his cock, tearing a scream from my throat as my fingernails dug for purchase on the hardwood. "That's right, Ghost, scream for your Rook."

I didn't catch my breath before he was rearing back to slam into my dripping cunt again, hitting something so deep I was sure the echo of him inside me would repeat forever.

Rook set a brutal, bruising pace, fucking me so hard I knew I'd feel him there for days after. But the pain shifted swiftly to a pleasure so intense I howled, his animalistic sounds, my moans, and the slapping of our bodies creating a song all our own.

I sucked in a breath, my chest lifting from the floor when he snatched my hair, pulling hard, making me have no choice but to hold myself up on my hands, pressing back into my knees as he drove into me with a feral possession, claiming me like he promised he would.

He came hard, the blade forgotten, dropped to the floor. His rough fingers grasped my hips tight as he arched his back and poured into me with a ragged cry. The sound of his climax brought on my own and I ground my cunt against his base, trembling against the floor, my core tightening around him, squeezing out every last drop.

Rook eased out and I fell onto my side, still riding the wave of my orgasm, drawing my knees in with a soft moan. He smiled devilishly at me, bending to press a kiss to my ankle. "So, hide and seek?" he asked, breathless, his pupils slowly returning to normal.

"My new favorite game," I admitted with a dopey smile, craning my neck to find Grey and Corvus hovering in the entry, their eyes burning with lust.

"It's not over yet," Corvus said dangerously, making my pussy tighten again.

He crossed the room, mindful of Rook as he wrenched me to my feet, and shoved me back onto the couch. Mine and Rook's combined release smeared over the luxurious fabric, and I opened my legs, helping it along. A wicked thought forming in my mind. I wanted to trash this place. I wanted to fuck on every surface.

"Want me to hold her down for you, Bro?" Rook asked, running his tongue over his teeth. "She's a slippery minx."

Corv jerked his chin in reply, and Rook lurched forward, grabbing me from behind, pulling me against his solid chest on the couch, wrapping his ankles around mine to keep my legs flayed. Arms locked between our bodies behind me.

Bones went to his knees in front of us, catching a decorative pillow Grey tossed his way. He ran the tasseled end of it over my slit, cleaning me. I gasped, throwing my head back into Rook's shoulder when he removed the pillow and dove for my pussy with his mouth, his tongue thrashing wildly against my clit as he ate me like a man starved. I struggled against Rook, the sensation almost too much after the initial attack, but he held me there, arms locking around me like iron bars.

"You're going to come for me, Sparrow," Corvus said between assaults. "Whether you like it or not."

He didn't have to fucking tell me twice. It was a useless fight and one I was already losing, the beginning of my climax spiraling through me like a tornado, sucking me up just as hard as Corvus was sucking my clit.

I screamed again as I came on his tongue, trying uselessly to get my legs free from Rook's hold, but they were both determined to make me ride out every stomach churning drop, until my body sagged, trembling against Rook. All the fight gone out of me.

"Give her to Grey," I distantly heard Corvus saying. Almost completely out of it as my body was moved, passed from hands to hands. Body to body.

An erection pressed into my lower back, and I moaned as the scent of Grey filled my nose, petrichor and heady engine oil. I lifted an arm lazily to reach for him behind me, my finger tangling in his hair. His lips found mine, and I moaned against his tongue as it lashed into my mouth, taking me.

"You ready for us, baby?"

Us?

Grey lay down on the couch, pulling me with him, our lips disconnecting as my head lolled back against his chest.

I did as I was asked and Corvus pulled my legs together, wrapping his hand around my crossed ankles to hold them high. "Think you can take two at once, Sparrow?"

Danger flashed in Corvus' eyes as he ran his pinkie finger through my wet slit, lower, to my other point of entry. I clenched my teeth as he prodded the opening with his pinkie finger, prepping me slow. Rook leaned over the back of the couch, flipping his hair back before lighting a cigarette, settling in for the show.

The burn as Corvus added a second finger made me groan, but I didn't want him to stop. I'd been craving this for longer than I could remember, and I wasn't going to let a little fucking discomfort stop me from having it.

"That's it, Sparrow," Corvus purred, releasing my legs and withdrawing his fingers. He settled them on either side of me.

"Lift your hips for me, AJ."

I did as I was asked and Grey guided the head of his cock into my ass, making me grit my teeth. It was nothing like the plug from the other night. As Grey fed every perfect inch of himself into me, I knocked my head back against his hard chest, only letting out the air in my lungs once he was fully settled there and had a second to adjust. He'd taken my ass once before, on the spinning table at the Docks, but it felt like the first time all over again.

When I opened my eyes again it was to the sight of Corvus taking his massive erection out of his pants. Letting them fall to the floor as he kneeled on the couch between both Grey's and my legs.

OH FUCK.

I suddenly wasn't so sure I could handle this. I mean, I was the one who declared I wanted all three of them, but seriously, how could they both fit?

Corvus flattened a warm palm on my belly as Grey began to rock, moving his cock in and out of my ass in controlled increments. It felt... good.

Really good.

Corvus pressed the tip of his cock into my opening and the stretch—the dual sensation—was almost too much. I struggled to catch my breath, aching for a pillow to scream into as he pushed in an inch further. Another inch.

"Oh fuck," I cursed, trying to lift up on my elbows, crooking a leg to try to shove him back. "Wait. It's too much. I don't think I can—"

"You're going to take every fucking inch of this cock, Sparrow."

I let out a yelp as he jerked my leg out of his way, holding it at arms-length as he eased even further inside, both of them filling me to fucking bursting.

"Look at that pussy stretch," Rook crooned, and I found his black eyes above me, smoke drifting around his sharp cheekbones. "Damn, Ghost."

Corvus locked into me, thrusting the rest of the way in, making my eyes roll back and a broken moan escape my lips.

I leaned up, needing to see for myself. Not quite believing I had them both inside me. At least not until Corvus started to move, his cruel strokes making my ass rock back and forth over Grey's cock. The twin pleasure coursing through had me clutching at anything, everything, to hold myself together because surely I was going to tear apart.

Rook snaked an arm down to me, and I clutched it, holding myself halfway up so I could grind on them both. My nails bit so deep into Rook's forearm that tiny tracks of blood raced to his elbow, making his eyes flash with lust.

"That's it, Sparrow. There's my good girl."

I cried out as an orgasm with the intensity of a fucking plane crash began spiraling down through me. Different, but good. The pulse of it tightened around Grey's cock in my ass and stole all the breath from my lungs.

"Fuck, AJ," Grey hissed in my ear. "I felt that."

"Another," Corvus demanded. "Rook, hold her leg."

Rook dragged my leg up the side of the couch, pinning it there with his free hand, allowing Corvus a better angle. His cigarette hung from his lips as he watched with rapt attention, his eyes fixed on mine as I rode out the last wave of the anal orgasm with a shuddering moan.

Corvus pounded into my pussy, the new angle hitting something even deeper inside.

He added his fingers, and I was a fucking goner.

"Fuck...yes..." I managed to get out between panting breaths, my legs starting to shake as another orgasm built, this one surging up through my core, making my back arch. "Bones!"

He slapped my clit hard, and I gasped. "Now, Sparrow! Come for us."

I screamed as my cunt clenched around his mammoth length, and he came with me, letting out a cry in time with the crescendo of Fuckface. Grey's hands on my hips squeezed, and I felt the moment he fully lost it, jerking against my back as they both poured into me and I split into a thousand pieces, my vision darkening for an instant before I came back, every muscle protesting the aftershocks of the orgasm still quaking deep within.

I shivered, letting my hand slip from Rook's arm as Corvus pressed a hot kiss to my inner thigh and took his time pulling out. Once he was, my legs fell closed and Grey lifted me easily, his cock leaving my ass.

He turned me until we were both on our sides on the couch, his body conforming to the shape of mine from behind as he pressed a kiss into my hair. My arm was at an odd angle, but I was too spent to bother trying to move and fix it.

Hearing someone coming, I slitted my eyes open to find Corvus coming back into the living room with something in his hand. I hadn't realized he'd left.

He knelt at the end of the couch, readjusting my hips gently to allow him access. He cleaned me with a warm cloth, making me sigh for an entirely new reason. He tossed the soiled cloth onto the back of an antique wingback chair in the corner and for some reason I found that so fucking funny.

"We should get those eggs," I murmured sleepily.

"In a minute," Grey whispered into my hair. "Rest, baby."

I snuggled into his embrace, worrying that if I closed my eyes I might actually fall asleep right here, naked on my aunt's couch.

My eyelids fluttered.

"What was that?" Rook asked, and something about his tone had me snapping my eyes back open, my exhausted body coming back to life.

"What?"

I followed his eyes to the window, peering out into the night through the gauzy curtains.

"There. Look out over the hill."

The glow of light over the hill could only be one thing. Headlights.

"They're supposed to wait on the service road," I growled, angrily forcing myself to my feet, searching for my shirt. My ruined panties could stay.

"They are," Grey replied, rushing to climb from the couch and get dressed too. He waved his phone at me. "They wouldn't move in. Not without saying something first."

"You don't think...?"

"Fuck," I hissed. "Cut the music!"

Rook ripped my phone from the auxiliary cord, plunging all of us into a ringing silence and tossed it to me. I caught it with ease, tugging my shirt over my head. "Fuck, the eggs! Move! I'll take the ones upstairs. You three split up down here. Remember where they are?"

"Yeah."

"Yah."

"Got it."

"Meet back at the Rover," Corvus added as I pulled my shoes back on and darted for one of the duffles, disappearing into the hall, spurred by the headlights now flashing across the windows in full streams of luminescent white.

I took the stairs two at a time despite the aching between my legs, muttering curses to myself the whole damn way. Couldn't a bitch get a nap after taking two dicks? Was that really asking too much?

I started at the end of the east hall, carefully scooping the eggs from the hall to place them into the foam.

The front door opened and I dropped to my knees, drawing a knife, but my aunt's haughty tone echoed up from the foyer, and I sheathed it again, knowing no matter how this went down, I wouldn't need it.

Want it, maybe. But that was a whole other gray area. I didn't want to murder a sad old lady. Bitch or not. But I also wouldn't spare her if she got in my way. Not after what she did.

Blood or not.

"Such a shame," she was saying. Her voice making me gag. Fuck, she really was repulsive. How I'd managed to spend more than a day with her or agree to her stupid arrangement was beyond me now. Past Ava Jade needed a slap. Preferably another spanking. From Rook.

"It really has gone downhill since the last time we visited, don't you think?"

"Yes, Madame Humphrey," her stuffy butler replied as I crept down the hall, closer to where I could hear coats being removed and luggage rolling over the parquet floors.

"And to think they actually expected me to take a junior suite. *Junior*, can you believe it?"

"No, madame."

I stayed low as I raced on tiptoe across the stairway, catching Corvus' severe face down the hall. He waved violently for me to get out from where he hid in the shadows, but I shook my head. I wasn't leaving yet. The real cheese was in my aunt's room. The most expensive of the eggs. Not to mention all her precious pearls and diamonds.

I wasn't about to leave any of it behind. That would just be wasteful, and I did not waste.

Out of sight of the foyer, I inched her doorknob to the right, twisting it until the latch released and I could sweep into her room without a sound, pulling the door back shut behind me.

It took me less than two minutes to add the egg to the others in the duffel and find her jewelry, grabbing it by the fistful to stuff into the duffel. I snatched the last of the pearls just when a shrill scream filled the mansion.

"My eggs!"

Oh no.

I bit my lip, tossing in the pearls and zipping the duffel, turning in a circle to find a better exit strategy. The balcony.

It was a second floor room.

Okay. No problem.

I rushed to the double doors, fumbling with the lock before managing to throw them open.

I could hear them coming up the stairs now.

A delicious thrill went through me, sharpening my focus, making a laugh bubble up my throat. I stopped it before it could escape, allowing myself a wide grin instead.

Down below, I caught movement in the bushes.

"Grey?" I hissed, and he spilled out onto the lawn, looking up at me with a furrowed brow.

"AJ?"

I tossed the duffel down. "Catch."

Grey cursed, racing forward to catch the delicate eggs before they could smash on the lawn. Vaguely, I heard him calling up to me, warning me against the drop most likely but it was already too late. I climbed over the railing and used what remained of my strength to lower myself as far as I could go before dropping the rest of the way to the ground.

A ripple of pain raced up through my heels, but I grimaced through it.

"The balcony!" Humphrey cried above, and I threw my head back and howled, grabbing Grey's hand to haul him away with me into the dark.

35

GREY

I went over everything I had to present at the meeting that would start in the next fifteen minutes, bringing the image up on the tablet screen before shutting it down to wait for the rest of the crew and Diesel to arrive.

This was it. The piece we'd been searching for. With a little luck, we'd have the Kings by the balls.

I pressed my palms together, resting on the bar upstairs at Sanctum, pressing my fingers to my lips. There was going to be blood. A lot of it. The fun of the last few nights was at an end. Now, it was time for war.

"Holy shit." Rook said beside me, choking on his whiskey as he squinted at something on his phone.

"What?" AJ asked, leaning over from his other side to see what he was looking at.

It spoke to the level of stress we'd been under lately that my stomach instantly soured before my brother could even respond.

"Humphrey," he said, pushing the phone toward AJ. "The bitch bit it."

AJ's eyes widened as she snatched the phone from him, scrolling through something on the screen there.

"She what?" Corvus asked from behind the bar, guzzling a bottle of water.

AJ let out a long breath and let the phone fall back onto the bar, looking at Corvus. "She's dead."

"What? How?" I demanded, a spike in my gut. Had Carson gotten to her? Was he there when we were there? Was he that close to getting his hands on AJ again?

"We killed her," AJ added.

"What do you mean, we killed her?"

"Heart attack," Rook answered. "She was pronounced DOA at the hospital a few hours after we made away with our fancy eggs."

I looked past him to AJ. "Are you okay?"

She bit her lip. "Fine. Is that bad? I feel... nothing."

"She was a bitch." Rook shrugged, finishing his drink. "She wasn't your family, Ghost, just blood. There's a difference. You don't have to feel a damn thing for that woman."

AJ nodded to herself, subconsciously agreeing. "I'd be lying if I said I hadn't considered doing her in myself after finding out she could've saved my dad."

"There you go," Rook said, reaching over to give her shoulder a squeeze. "This was you don't have to get your hand dirty. Did you finish the article?"

"No, why?"

"Her staff dumped her at the hospital and none of them could be reached for comments."

"They all took off?" I asked, incredulous.

Corvus' lips twisted into a wicked smirk that looked foreign on his usually severe face. "With all the good silver and artwork, I suspect." He laughed.

"So you can stop worrying about our DNA being all over the place. No one's going to be reporting any stolen goods any time soon, Ghost."

"That's some fucking luck," she snorted.

This girl, she still didn't get it. She wasn't running with the likes of a wannabe gangsters. The Saints were all but untouchable. Diesel had seen to making it that way. This was the weakest we'd been in the history of the gang since the very beginning when the three original Saints split ways. "We would've blocked the investigation before it could be elevated to the feds anyway, AJ. Not to mention the fact you're her straight A's niece and we spent Thanksgiving there. It would stand to reason our prints would be all over the place."

"And the *other* evidence?"

"We had a party while your aunt was out of town. Like teenagers do."

She shook her head, but there was a smile on her lips, and I realized I would do *anything* to keep it there.

"And fuck if it wasn't the best party I've ever been to," she played along, her thighs pressed together on the stool. I knew she was remembering it. It'd been almost thirty-six hours since the heist turned fuckfest, but it was still the number one thing on my mind. I'd had a rock solid hard-on off and on since I woke up the next morning.

A sharp whistle behind us had us all swiveling our seats.

Dies held the back door open across the mostly empty bar, his icy stare fixed on me. "Let's see what you got, Grey."

Hello to you, too, Pops.

He'd been easily irritable since what happened to the garden. It had been a shrine to his wife, and he'd tended it meticulously for as long as I could remember. I imagined it was like losing a part of her all over again.

"We'll be right down."

AJ slid off her stool, the pink flesh of her forearm looking better today than it did yesterday. Rook was walking with barely any trouble, and Corv's nurse finally stopped coming around. They were all mostly whole again. And I was starting to think a missing eye wouldn't be the thing that stopped me, after all. Target practice over the last few days had proved it. With some minor adjustments, I was just as good as I'd always been.

"What are you looking at?" AJ asked curiously, her brow lifting.

"You."

She gave me a cheeky look, coming to loop her arm through mine. "Come on, Superman. Let's go start a war."

The underbelly of Sanctum was packed with faces, new and old. In the corner, a few seniors I recognized from Briar Hall stood with their arms crossed. They were the ones the guys and I identified as potentially strong enough to join our ranks. They stood tall, trying to appear unintimidated by the battle-hardened criminals surrounding them.

Then there were the other potential candidates. The ones brought in by the others. They consisted of cousins and friends. Brothers and sons. All men who wanted an in with the Saints, and now they'd get their chance to prove themselves worthy.

This feud with the Kings, and the eventual bloodbath it would come to, would be their only trial. Honestly, I counted them lucky. The trials could be far, *far* worse.

"Where's Uncle Damien?" Corv asked, scanning the room. "Thought he'd come for the meet."

My good mood turned rancid in an instant. "Dies said he left town after Becca woke up. Guess he got what he came for."

"What's with the hostility? You know he's got his own fucking chapter to run down south. He couldn't hang around here forever."

I shook my head. "Yeah. Right. Just on edge."

My disappointment rolled off my back. If Diesel was too fucking stubborn to ask for help, then why should I have expected Uncle Damien to force it on him?

This—what we learned today—was a win. And I wasn't going to let anything ruin it. I'd worked too fucking hard.

Rook snapped at the guys from Briar Hall as we passed and when they jerked back from his shining teeth, he blew them a kiss, settling between two other new faces by the bar to ask Pinkie for another drink. The newbies gave him a wide berth, casting furtive glances his way as they cautiously sipped their beers.

I leaned into the side of the nearest one. "Just don't make any sudden movements," I warned with mock seriousness, and his Adam's apple bobbed. When Rook turned, drink in hand, he couldn't get out of the way fast enough, sloshing beer onto the floor.

"Hey," Rook growled, glaring at the poor guy. "Clean that shit up. This isn't your mama's house."

Diesel clapped his hands together at the head of the long table, getting everyone's attention. "All right, listen up, if you're a new implant, get the fuck out. The rest of you gather 'round. Grey has something to show us."

The new recruits filtered out as me and the others made our way to the table. I applauded Diesel's caution, but the new recruits were hardcore vetted by both Pinkie and myself. They had no connection to Mav, the Kings, or Carson fucking Bates. And when it came to blood, they'd be with us anyway. Pumping up our numbers. Giving us a better chance.

Human fucking meat shields with something to prove.

I waited until the last of them were gone before starting.

"This has got to be it."

I leaned over the table in Sanctum's underbelly, pushing the tablet into the middle so everyone crowded around could see it, too. The aerial view of the factory was pixelated. A snapshot courtesy of google maps. If it had been on a major road, we'd have better images, but the old metal manufacturing plant was set away from the hustle of Lennox, hovering far onto its outskirts, backing onto the national park.

"I almost passed over it at first, until I remembered Mav's real name isn't Maverick. Took a lot of fucking elbow grease, but I found out his real name is Clancy, and then I went over every factory *again*." I jabbed the screen with the pad of my index finger. "The lease on this factory is in the name Clancy Moore."

Diesel nodded at the grainy image. "You did good, Son."

"We still need to scope it out. I've looked everywhere but wasn't able to find any building plans or schematics for this place. We need to know all the entry and exit points. If there are cameras. Safeguards. We can't rush in blind."

"I'll do it," AJ offered. "I'm small, and I'm fast. I'll be in and out before they know I'm there."

"Fuck no." It was Diesel who said it, but it was the echo of what the others and I were thinking. "Sorry, Ava Jade, but last time my boys lost you they almost lost themselves, too. I'll send Mickey."

AJ's expression soured, but for once she didn't argue.

Mickey gave a terse nod from across the table, his already hollow cheeks sucking in as he worked his jaw. "I've got it, boss."

"Go prepare what you need. You leave after nightfall. I want that intel by morning."

"If you go through the national park to come up on it from the rear, watch for surveillance in the trees," I called after him, making him stop. "And if you see any trails or *anything* that looks like the entrance to a bunker, take note of the coordinates."

Mickey gave another nod and left.

"Have you secured the buyer for the Fabergé eggs and jewelry?" Corvus asked.

"It's done. We have the cash. The meet with the Mexicans is tomorrow and we'll have everything we need."

"You want us there for that?" Rook asked eagerly, but I could tell from Dies' expression that he was about to decline.

"No. I need you here to keep a lid on things. This is our second rendezvous with Los Diablos. We've been a good earner for their illegal sales. Despite what we thought at the start, I don't believe them to be a threat. In fact, they're shaping up to be a regular supplier. They're cheaper than our contacts to the east, and they've been in the business since before I was fucking born."

"Could be a mistake," Corvus put in, but Diesel was already decided.

"It's a risk we'll need to take."

I turned the aerial image of the factory around to face me, looking for weak points to exploit in the grainy image. "If this is it, what's the play?"

"We attack," AJ answered from my left, drawing the attention of everyone in the room. "We can't wait for them to hit us first. We don't have the numbers. We hit *them* first. Hit them hard. Leave no survivors."

"*Fuck*," I heard Rook groan under his breath, turned on by our girl's penchant for violence. I had to admit, it turned me on when she took control like that, too.

"She's right," Diesel announced and a few whispers went up through the crew.

"They might have the numbers, but we have this." He thumped a closed fist over his chest.

"And this." He jabbed two fingers into his temple.

"If we plan this just right, we can wipe them from the board with one stroke. Finish it for good." He pushed himself to his full height. "Get ready, crew. We'll be feasting on King flesh by the weekend."

36

AVA JADE

Mickey's sketches of the factory were fucking atrocious, but they would have to do. He confirmed it. The Kings were there. Holed up inside. He heard arguing inside and there had been at least fifteen cars parked along an old dirt service road leading up to the place.

There hadn't been a Jeep, but that didn't mean Carson wasn't there. He had to be there. We had eyes on the only exit road branching off from the service road now, and only one car had left while two others returned since Mickey got back.

They were definitely camping out there and the only exterior precautions they were taking were a few trip wires and from what Mickey could tell, only one security cam facing the road.

The plan was simple, and we went over it for the fifth time since its inception.

"Pinkie, you're coming in from the northwest with Greg. Mickey with Ryan from the southeast side."

"And we're hitting it direct from the southwest face," Grey finished for Diesel.

"Right. Each of you chucks your grenades into the windows, here, here, and here on my mark."

"That will filter them out through the front exit here where the rest of our force will be waiting," I added, practically knowing the whole damn spiel word for word now. "Now can we go?"

"There's one last thing."

We waited, chomping at the bit to go outside with the others packing the vans full of everything we needed.

"Ava Jade, I'm going to need you to stay back with the other snipers."

"What?" I demanded, my voice dripping venom.

"Look," Diesel said, raising his hands in a placating gesture. "Before you go biting my head off, hear me out."

I looked to my guys for help, but it didn't look like I was going to get any.

"I'd bet my left nut that you're a better shot than any of the others on your worst day. You're a natural. I need that kind of skill at my back. I need someone up in the nest who isn't going to take my head off trying to take out the enemy beside me."

"And you trust that I won't?"

"Well, if you keep looking at me like that, I might reconsider."

"I don't want to be way up on the hill, Dies. I need to be down there. With them," I gestured to Rook, Grey, and Corvus. I shoved Rook next to me. "Say something."

"It would be more fun if she was with us."

Diesel pinched the bridge of his nose. "Rook, that is such a shit argument I don't even know where to start."

"Corv? Grey?" I tried, but Corv was chewing his lips and Grey was toeing the carpet. "Seriously?"

Corv scratched the back of his head, where sandy blond hair had begun to grow back, covering the scars a little better. I'd give him new ones if he didn't pipe up. "Sparrow, it's not a bad idea. You are a crack shot. Just yesterday you hit a rolling barrel at two hundred fifty yards and still managed to hit within the second ring of the bullseye. You're the best we have. Even better than Grey."

"Especially now," Grey muttered, and I knew he was thinking about how his ability with the sniper had taken a hit with the loss of his eye. He had to handle the weapon on the opposite side, needing to learn it all over again.

"Not what I meant," Corv said to Grey before turning back to me.

"Think about it for a sec. If you're up there, you can eliminate any threats that come at us before we can ever see them coming."

"And if it gets too messy and you can't get a clean shot on any of them, then you're not so far away that you can't run into the action," Rook added with a wink. "I'll save you a few."

"I don't like the thought of her being alone up there, though," Grey said on a breath.

"She won't be," Diesel argued. "There will be two other snipers with her."

I groaned inwardly, breathing deep to suppress the wrath building in the shape of my darkness as I thought it through.

Fuck.

I'd hit Lenny Ace straight through the heart at two hundred yards despite the wind rolling in off the lake. It really was a beautiful shot. And honestly? I'd bet Diesel's left nut and his right, that I could do it again if I needed to. Being able to watch over my guys while they were down there wasn't a half bad idea, either.

"You have the comms, still?" I asked Grey, and he grinned up at me, digging in his black pack for them.

"Thought you said they'd be too distracting."

Grey scattered the little ear pieces on Diesel's kitchen table, and I lifted one up, inspecting it. "I did. But if I'm going to be watching from above, then it might be helpful to warn you if trouble's coming your way."

"You'll do it, then?" Diesel asked, trying to confirm as the screen door banged closed and Pinkie appeared in the hall.

"We're all packed up, boss."

"Yeah, I'll do it. But if it looks too hairy down there I'm leaving that fucking thing on the hill and I'm coming down."

Diesel offered me a rare grin. "Deal. If the other's come down with you just ditch all the ammo first, yeah? Don't need our enemies using our own hardware against us." Diesel's brows drew, his gaze flicking back to Pinkie. "What is it, Pinkie? Why are you hovering?"

"The vet's shitting a brick, Dies. You sure we need him with us?"

A muscle in Dies' jaw twitched. "I'll handle it. Go make sure the snipers packed Big Red. Ava Jade's going to be up in the hills with them."

"Nice," Pinkie said. "I'll go check."

Diesel followed him out the front door while I turned the ear piece this way and that between my fingers. "How's the range on these?"

"More than good enough."

"Is he always such a buzzkill?"

"Might as well be his middle name," Rook said with a rough laugh. "Where do you think Corv gets it from?"

Grey scooped up all the comms gear and deposited it back into his bag.

"Come on, let's go gear up," I said, my fingers itching for my blades as we left the house. One way or another, each one would kiss the skin of our enemies tonight. And one way or another, Carson Bates would be ours before the night was through.

"Should we do it now?" Grey asked as we stepped out into the night to a swarm of Saints double checking their weapons. Strapping on vests and other gear.

"Do what now?" I asked.

Rook caught my elbow, dragging me to the open back of a nondescript black van. "Diesel got a wide selection, but if there isn't one here that suits you, you can borrow one of ours for now."

"What are you talking about?"

Corvus stepped ahead of Rook, flipping back a swath of grey fabric laid in the bed of the van to reveal an arsenal of handguns.

Grey wrapped his hands around my shoulders from behind, looking over my shoulder at all the weapons. "Call it an early Christmas present."

A thrill went through me and I found myself grinning. "I get to pick one? Whichever one I want?"

"Yep," Grey said in my ear. "Personally, I'd recommend the Smith & Wesson or the Colt 1911." He indicated two near identical guns save for the difference in grip. One had a reddish colored diamond pattern grip that looked to be made of horn while the other was a lighter oak-looking wood.

"You know I'm a sucker for a Browning," Rook added, lifting a gun from the cloth that looked similar to his own, save for the darker grip. He disassembled it in a matter of seconds, checking the parts before clicking it all back together and handing it to me. "Looks solid."

"She can't go wrong with the Beretta or the Colt," Corvus spoke up, passing me another in my other hand. This one was a simple black number, sleek and smaller than the Browning. I tested the weight of each in my hands, truly feeling like a kid on Christmas fucking morning.

I set both down, deliberating, my eyes raking over the options until one caught my attention. The black cherry grip with a carved out starburst design was so unique by comparison, and I lifted it, feeling its weight. A winged pewter medallion in the middle of the grip reminded me of my Crows. It felt like the right size.

"Your girl has expensive taste," Diesel said, coming up behind us. "Not going to lie, I was kind of hoping she wouldn't choose the Wilson Combat. It's a beauty."

"Yeah?" I asked, holding it at arm's length to look down the sight, ensuring I wasn't pointing it at anyone. It was heavy enough that I knew the mag was loaded, but the safety was still on.

"Yeah," Diesel echoed. "It's a solid choice—basically what would be born if the Colt and the Browning had a baby. Here."

He reached around me to grab two extra mags. "They're a fifteen round capacity."

I took them from him, hating how this man could make me furious one minute and then *like this* the next. "Thanks for doing this, Dies. I appreciate it."

He nodded. "Of course. 'Bout time you had your own weapon *aside* from your blades. Here, I grabbed a couple holster options for you. Thigh, ankle, or chest?"

Considering I already had my blades across my chest and strapped to both ankles as well as my belt and one thigh, there was really only one free space. "Thigh," I said, but Corvus took the strap from Diesel before I could reach out and grab it, kneeling at my feet.

"Spread your legs for me, Sparrow."

Yes, sir.

He set to fastening the straps in place, anchoring them to my belt, attaching the gun holster, positioning it just right. "Gun."

I handed it to him, and he slipped it into place. "How does that feel? Good?"

I swallowed hard, tongue-tied, making Diesel clear his throat and excuse himself. "Yeah," I answered finally. "That feels perfect."

He gave my thigh a squeeze before rising back to his feet. "It suits you."

I ran my hand over the grip. "Yeah. He's a beaut."

"He?"

"Oh yeah, definitely a *he*. Jealous?"

"If you keep stroking it like that, I might be."

I laughed, realizing there were several other Saints looking my way. Some appraised my new weapon with admiration, but most wore grave expressions. Especially the newest recruits.

"This is going to work, right?" I asked my guys, keeping my voice down.

Rook nodded. "Yeah, Ghost. It'll work."

There was no other option.

A tingle of apprehension raced down my spine watching the vet breathe into a paper bag near the front door as Diesel patted his shoulder. For a guy who treated some of the most gnarly wounds I'd ever seen, he was far less butch than I thought he'd be. I still hadn't met him officially, but it was clear to anyone watching that this guy was *not* here of his own volition.

In his late thirties, he was built slim, with a whip of red hair that touched the tops of his ears and an overly pointed chin. He looked so out of place among all the beef and brawn surrounding us. But he wasn't wrong to be afraid.

The Kings still outnumbered us two to one, and if they got so much as a whiff of our advance, there was a good chance most of the men here wouldn't be coming home to their families.

But that was why we went over the plan a million fucking times.

Because it *had* to work.

"Don't worry about the vet," Grey said, reading me wrong. I wasn't worried about him. I fucking pitied him his complete and utter lack of balls. "He'll be hanging at the back of the advance. Dies only wants him with us to treat the wounded on site. We lost too many men at the Docks that he could've saved if we got them to him faster."

"I know," I replied. "He won't be armed, right?"

Rook shook his head. "*Pffft*, as if."

That was good at least. A gun in those shaky hands was sure to cause a fucking catastrophe.

"We ready to roll out?" Corvus called to Diesel, adjusting the straps on his vest before visually checking mine. I gave him a pointed look.

"Five minutes," Diesel shouted, and everyone on the lawn and driveway spread the word.

My blood buzzed with adrenaline and I blinked slow, shivering as a pool of it enveloped me in its warm embrace, making me tip my head back.

"Cool it, Ghost," Rook said, hauling me back against him so I could feel the start of his erection through his jeans. "Or I'll have no choice but to take you right here on this lawn in front of the whole crew."

Was it bad that I was thinking about letting him do just that.

The others nearby looked at us like we were crazy, and they weren't wrong. Where their faces were long and drawn or tight with worry, my dark prince and I smiled, thriving on the promise of violence.

The sound of a horn broke us apart, and I was about to cuss out whoever'd done it. They were going to wake the whole damn neighborhood with that noise and the last thing we needed was curious neighbors coming out onto their lawns.

But it wasn't one of ours. Headlights flashed bright across the lawn as a truck I recognized pulled right up onto the grass in front of us, followed by three other cars that parked down the street.

A few Saints drew their weapons, but Grey lifted a hand. "Lower your weapons."

Damien St. Vincent opened the door of his truck, standing on the kick bar to look out over the assembly, a bright smile spreading wide on his face as he found Diesel by the door. "Glad we caught you, Brother!"

"Damien?" What the fuck are you doing here?"

"A little birdy told me you might be able to use a hand."

He whistled, and those in the cars down the street exited, coming to join us on the lawn.

"No fucking way," Grey said excitedly, speed walking across the grass to where two guys approached with a group of others behind them. He embraced the first one and got tackled to the ground in a bear hug before the other one hauled him back up and into a back thumping embrace of his own.

"Who are they?"

Rook ran a thumb over his lip. "Well, shit. Now it's a fucking party."

The two guys waved at Corv and Rook, coming over. The one on the left had a smile that practically glowed in the dark, while the other, though he looked happy to see my guys, had an aura of danger around him like a black cloud I doubted ever saw sunlight.

"Hardin, Kaleb, how's it going, you fucking beautiful bastards?" Rook said, answering my question for me, slapping smiley guy's hand before tugging him in for a hug and fist bumping the other one.

"Shit, Corv, the buzzcut does *not* suit you man. You got to grow that shit out," the smiling one said, jerking Corvus in for a hug while rubbing the top of his head like a lucky charm.

"You always knew how to give a guy a compliment, Kaleb. Harind," Corv shook the other one's hand. "What are you guys doing here?"

"Shit, wait. We need to make the proper introductions," Rook said, completely interrupting Hardin's reply, earning himself a glare in the process. He put a palm to my lower back and shoved me forward. "*This is Ava Jade.*"

Hardin's bright eyes ran the length of me before giving a nod. "Nice to put a face to the name."

"No shit?" Kaleb said excitedly, snatching my hand to shake it roughly in his. I lifted a brow at him and yelped as he jerked me forward, using his firm grip on my hand to spin me in a circle before letting me go and giving me a good appraisal himself. "Damn. They don't make 'em like that in SoCal."

I snorted, changing my mind about stabbing him for the unsolicited dance. "So, who exactly are you guys?"

Kaleb put a hand to his chest, looking at my guys with wounded puppy eyes. "They didn't tell you about us. Now, I'm just hurt."

"Hardin St. Vincent," the brooding one said, extending a hand, which I took. "And this jackass is my brother, Kaleb."

"St. Vincent?"

"They're Uncle Damien's sons," Grey explained.

"You're here for the fireworks, then?" Rook asked, his black eyes alight with enthusiasm in a way that told me I could trust these two.

"Seems that way," Hardin answered. "D said you could use the help."

Kaleb shoved Corv. "Couldn't miss the chance to come up and see your ugly mugs."

I caught sight of Damien and Diesel speaking in hushed tones near Damien's truck, and looking around at all the now-hopeful faces of our crew, I truly hoped Diesel didn't turn down his brother's offer. I scrutinized Damien St. Vincent in a new light. I would've never pegged him as the fatherly type, but then again, I would've never guessed Diesel to be a father, either.

His sons didn't look much like him aside from Hardin's dark hair and wide-shouldered build. And maybe Kaleb's face shape, with the sharp edged brows and even sharper jawline.

They were pretty, but not pretty enough to go saying *my guys* had ugly mugs. Joke or not.

Damien wrapped an arm around Diesel, drawing him over to where we stood on the lawn while they continued their conversation.

"You know I can handle my own shit, Damien," Diesel was saying, and I wanted to fucking hit him.

"I know," Damien said. "But you don't have to. Besides, I'm looking forward to fighting alongside my brother. It'll be like old times."

Diesel's hard exterior seemed to crack at that, his lips pulling into a half grin.

The rest of Damien's men came forward, saying their hellos to my guys and Diesel, who graciously welcomed each one.

"This is all I could spare," Damien said, indicating the additional twelve men on top of himself and his sons.

"It's more than enough, Brother."

Damien let out a loud whoop, slapping Diesel on the back before tearing his jacket off to reveal a menagerie of polished steel strapped over his chest and around his waist. He stuffed his tatted hand into his pocket, and when he withdrew it, gleaming brass knuckles glinted in the moonlight as he raised his fist. "Move out! *Let's go kill us some motherfucking Kings.*"

37

AVA JADE

We moved on foot, under the cover of darkness, the only sound the *shhh* of branches brushing thick canvas and the crunch of boots over dry dirt. My guys flanked me as we made our way, them with their guns out and aimed low, me with two of my blades in hand.

As much as I was tempted to use my new gun, I wasn't acquainted with it well enough to choose it as my first line of defense. He'd get his turn if I lost my blades in battle, though.

I adjusted the sniper bag on my back, feeling the burn in the muscle across my shoulders from carrying it the four miles from where we parked back at a trailhead near the Lennox exit.

Grey wandered closer to my side. "Want me to take it?" he asked in a whisper, but I shook my head.

"We're almost there."

I could feel it. Mickey said it was about five miles in, and my body knew the distance from running my whole life. As if on cue, I squinted into the dark, seeing how the terrain changed, sloping upward. That was the hill. And somewhere below it, nestled in a small valley clear of trees would be the factory.

"Hey, Sniper," a guy called Donny whispered, jerking his chin up and to the right. "This is us."

Another guy with a sniper bag made his way over while the rest of

1076

them continued their careful pace through the trees. Diesel stopped at the head of them and the rest paused with him. He stared right at me, giving me a meaningful nod. *Watch over my sons,* he said without the need to speak at all.

I nodded back, and he twirled a finger in the air before butting his AK to his shoulder, continuing into the dark.

"Fuck, I change my mind," Corvus said, his jaw clenching tight. His eyes looking brighter than ever with the black war paint slashed over his sharp features. "Maybe you should come with us."

"You're the one who convinced me to do this," I argued, my whisper cracking like a whip. "I already agreed."

He cursed, his gaze fixing on Donny and the other guy whose name I could never remember behind us. "You watch her fucking back," he told them.

"We will."

"Bones, I'm going to be fine. We all are. And who do you really think will be watching whose back up there?" I challenged, leaning into the darkness, letting it bring me the confidence I needed to do what we were about to do. I was fucking *fast*. If anyone came up behind us, I'd be the one laying them out with my blade before either of these fuckers could even draw their weapons.

Corvus put his forehead to mine. "See you when it's over, Sparrow."

I nodded against his forehead, and he pulled back.

"Comms check," Grey said, tapping his ear piece. "Come in."

His voice echoed in my ear, and I nodded, tapping my ear piece. "I hear you."

Rook and Corvus nodded, signaling that they could hear me in their ear pieces, too.

"Let's move," Donny said. "We need to be in position before it begins."

Grey surprised me with a rough kiss before Rook stole me away with a first grip on my pussy through my tactical pants. I opened my mouth in surprise, and he used the opportunity to dive into my mouth with his tongue. I moaned into his mouth, and he bit my lip, drawing blood.

He released my wet cunt, and I blinked up at him, having to shake myself to get my focus back.

"Catch you on the flip side, Ghost."

"Be careful down there."

They turned away from me, falling into step with Hardin and Kaleb, the five of them moving like shadows through the trees. I watched until I couldn't pick them out from the others anymore, and Donny nudged my forearm. "Come on, there's nothing you can do for them from down here. Let's climb."

I sighed, sheathing my blades as we hiked the steep slope all the way to its summit, having to resort to digging my fingernails into the hard dirt and rock to get up the last fifteen feet to the mostly flat top. Jagged rock made finding good spots to set up a challenge and peering down over the lip of stone, I knew trying to jump down and run into the action would be more of a challenge than I originally thought.

I would be more likely to roll down the steep face than run.

The other two snipers and I got into position, and I knew it wasn't a mistake that they placed themselves to either side of me, Corvus' orders to watch my back likely still ringing in their ears.

I looked down through the trees as I set up Big Red just like Grey taught me, able to see the outline of the factory in the ambient moonlight. Cloud cover was pretty heavy tonight, which provided an added layer of cover we were all grateful for, but would also make everyone's jobs harder. Including mine.

Once Big Red was in position, I hunkered down in the dirt, lying out against the cold earth.

"In position," Donny said, his radio crackling.

A jolt of electrifying panic shot through me, and I rushed to look through the scope, making sure I had the angle I wanted. My breaths fogged in the air, stomach packing the dirt with each deep inhale.

My finger trembled as I rested it next to the trigger and I willed myself to calm down, blowing out a slow breath, tapping into that hyper focus still hovering just out of reach.

The factory loomed a couple hundred yards down the bank, settled on the flattest stretch of earth, surrounded on its left and back sides by trees set twenty paces back from the brick exterior. To the right, a long dirt drive was choked up with tens of vehicles. In front, where my sights were trained, a flat expanse of crumbling pavement stood between the large entry doors of the factory building and the tree line.

I looked all around, trying to find Diesel or my guys or anyone in the trees, but they were doing their jobs well. I couldn't find a single one for almost a full minute until I spotted Mickey getting into position, creeping forward through the trees to on the (direction) side. Which meant my guys were somewhere out there, behind the building, readying their grenades.

I swung my barrel to the right, trying to find the other team, instead I found a King. He reached into the open driver's side window of a car and pulled out a pack of cigarettes. He plucked one out and put it to his lips. Ten feet away, a Saint crept up on him from behind, using the parked cars as cover.

The air froze in my lungs as I watched, praying that they could take him out quietly. Quickly. Before someone noticed. I had a clean shot, but the echo would be worse than whatever sound the guy might make as he died.

The Saint rushed forward all at once, gripping the King around his face with a palm over his mouth. My eyes gaped wide as his neck snapped and the Saint set him down easy. I realized it wasn't just any Saint. It was Hardin. I watched him drag the body out of sight before darting through the maze of parked cars to the back of the building.

Damn. He was good.

"Get ready." Diesel's voice came over the radio, and I turned my sights back to the front doors, peering over the edge of the hill to find a line of Saints crouched like boulders along the tree line, waiting. Ready.

Goosebumps rose on my arms and that next level focus snapped into place as I watched Mickey race forward from the left and the other team rush up from the right, dipping between cars to get to the side of the factory wall.

My body tensed.

The *bang bang bang* of the grenades went off like dominos, echoing through the night. Vibrating in the air. Screams followed and orange light exploded out the sides of the factory, smoke rising up to the sky.

The front doors burst open, and just like Diesel said they would, the Kings rushed out, coughing and spluttering. Some injured, others with their weapons raised, ready for the fight they seemed to at least have some inkling was coming.

They were all armed to the teeth, but as Diesel and Damien led the charge from the trees, they were caught entirely by surprise. Gunfire sounded like firecrackers in the dark, and I watched as one King fell, then another. Waiting for my guys to join the fray. Looking for one specific face amid the absolute massacre.

Everyone was on strict orders not to kill Carson if they could help it. We wanted to take him alive. But I wouldn't complain much if he had a few non-lethal holes in him when they handed him over.

Donny fired next to me, and a King with a grenade in his hand went down before he could throw it, blowing himself and the guy next to him into pieces. My guys came through the smoke, charging forward like gods of war personified. Rook slit the nearest King's throat with a swipe of his arm and roared in the spray of blood as Corvus pumped two bullets into two more Kings and Grey narrowly dodged an attack by the third, getting his arm around the guy's head. He pulled up sharply, and the body attached to it slumped. He discarded the King, kicking him out of the way as they continued the charge.

Fuck, they were beautiful.

Shit!

Diesel fired the last round in his mag and it dropped to the pavement. He bent to reload and a King behind him lifted his weapon, aiming it at the back of Diesel's head.

I fired, and the King's head exploded, raining brain matter over Diesel's back. He gave a two finger salute our way before taking out another King in his path with his brother now tight at his side, watching his back.

I swiveled back to the guys, but they were doing just fine, dispatching justice like the cruel Saints they were.

Three more Kings exited the building and I recognized Maverick among them. I set my sights on him, but his sights were firmly trained on my guys. I watched him point their direction and the goons to either side of him raised their weapons. I fired, and took out the one on Mav's right, jerking back the lever to push another round into the chamber, but it made a metallic *chckk* in my ear and wouldn't pull back the full way. I tried again.

"Jammed."

Keeping an eye trained down the scope, I tapped my earpiece. "The door!"

Corv spun, firing, laying out the goon to Mav's left.

Maverick raised his weapon and a fucking fresh army of Kings emerged from the smoke behind him. Way more than there should've been. Double the force we knew about. I worked mercilessly to unjam my gun, shouting at the other snipers. "The door. Shoot them down!"

My heart pounded in my skull as sloppy fingers worked to pry back the lever. Donny shot. One round. Then another.

"Where the fuck are they all coming from!" The other sniper to my left cried, reloading.

"I don't know!"

The lever popped back, and I cried out in relief, dislodging the bullet. I reloaded and pried it back again, a cold shiver rushing down my back as I settled back into position, took aim, and fired at the first King I saw.

I chewed through all the rounds in a matter of what felt like seconds before I needed to reload again.

"There are too many."

"Sparrow, there are too many," Corvus' gruff voice echoed my own words in my skull through the earpiece, making all my muscles seize and burn. "Hold them back!"

"Donny, why aren't you firing?" I screamed.

"I'm out! I'm out!" he shouted back. "No more ammo. Fuck this, I'm going down."

Before I could say a word to stop him, Donny was over the ledge and rolling over sharp rocks and loose dirt, all the way down to the bottom of the hill.

I finished reloading and started firing again, doing my best to hold them back.

Fearful faces lifted in our general direction as their brothers fell at their feet, .50 Cal rounds in the center of their mass.

"Sniper!" I heard someone shout far below, and the Kings crowding outside the entry scattered, some returning back into the building, others into the trees. Others right into the waiting lines of fire of Saint guns.

I picked off two who tried to escape to their cars before I was out of ammo again and reached for more only to find my canvas empty.

"Shit! I'm out!"

I looked down my sights again, trying to find my guys. To know which direction to head once I launched myself off this hill. I found Diesel and his men fighting the bulk of Carson's force to the left, but where...

I found them.

Grey, Corvus, and Rook formed a tight circle, nearly back to back as they fought hand to hand against five Kings. Guns and shell casings littered the ground at their feet. Clearly everyone was out of fucking bullets.

Okay.

The other snipers and I managed to put a good dent in the extra men and from what I could see, despite their inflated numbers, we still had the upper hand. Though I cringed as I found several familiar faces among the dead.

I tapped my earpiece. "I'm coming down."

But just before I moved my eye from the scope, I caught sight of a familiar head of dyed blonde hair, and I gripped the rifle tight, following him as he skirted the left side of the factory.

"It's Carson!" I shouted, holding down the button in my earpiece. "Northeast corner of the factory, coming to the front!"

"Shoot!" I yelled at the other sniper. "There! The northeast corner of the factory! Take out his legs!"

He angled the shot and fired, missing Carson by a fucking hair.

"Again!"

"I need to reload."

"Fuck!"

"Don't," came Grey's voice, out of breath and muffled by the sounds of battle around him through the earpiece.

I found them again through my scope, and watched Rook dispatch his enemy and the one about to get a hit on Grey, bathed in blood. He put his hand to his ear. *"Where?"* he snarled.

I turned back to set my sights on Carson, just catching him as he doubled back and took off into the tree line to the northeast. "In the trees! Fucker's running!"

But he wasn't going to get away. Not this time. I stood, pushing sweat and hair away from my face as I assessed the drop one last time.

"Wait," the other sniper called after me. "They'll fucking kill me if I let you—"

I jumped, managing to land on my feet. My heels dug into the loose dirt and stones, sliding down the slippery slope.

"Sparrow, stay fucking put!"

I cried out as a rock jabbed into the soft part of my foot through my boot and fell onto my side, rolling, rocks and debris scraping along my arms and across my cheeks. My body was tossed from a sharp ledge at the bottom of the slope, and I landed hard on my stomach, crouching, tasting dirt on my tongue. I lifted my hand to my ear to tell them to meet me at the northeast corner, but my earpiece wasn't there.

It'd come out in the fall.

I reached for my phone in my back pocket. My fingers grasped at nothing but thick material and gritty dirt. I felt around me in case either landed nearby but came up empty handed.

"God*fucking*damnit!," I coughed, pushing to my feet, the volume of the battle happening no less than forty feet in front of me so loud now it was near deafening. My ears rang with it and my vision blurred as the earth heaved beneath my feet as I got my balance and the dizziness dissipated enough to move.

I drew two blades, ignoring how my left hand was slick with blood from where my still-fragile skin tore open in the fall, and took off after Carson. I couldn't waste any time. We couldn't let him get away this time. One way or another, this ended tonight.

I wouldn't wake up to another message from him on my phone. I wouldn't sleep with one eye open, worrying what he might have planned for my Crows. I *couldn't* do it.

Narrowly missing running straight into a tree, the last of the dizziness burned off as my muscles pumped fire through my veins.

They know where I'm going, I told myself. I'd said northeast corner, right?

They'd be right behind me.

Fuck, maybe they were already ahead of me. Maybe they had him.

That thought made my chest vibrate with the feline purr of my darkness.

Running steps off to my right had me tucking behind a tree before I could round to the northeastern side of the building and follow Carson's trail.

Damn.

I peered around the tree and looked down the barrel of a gun twenty paces away. It fired, and I just whipped my head back as tree bark exploded over my face. I bent low, rolling out from the cover of the tree, bullets puncturing the dirt in my wake. I threw.

His scream was abruptly cut off by a gurgle.

I leapt to my feet and ran, bending to tear my bloodied blade from his jugular to keep going. I'd never catch up with Carson if I didn't *push*.

The *crack* of another shot glanced off a tree as I ran passed it, but I kept on, altering my running steps into a messy zigzag with no pattern as bark snapped and scattered over my path with each missed shot.

Once I had a good idea where the fucker was, I mentally kissed the blade in my right and turned to throw it, knowing I didn't have time to retrieve it. It embedded in the burly chest of a King I didn't recognize, but I didn't wait to make sure he was down before I whipped my head back around.

I'd be too far from his line of sight soon, anyway.

I took a sharp left, going deeper into the national park where I saw Carson enter the tree line.

He could be so far ahead by now that I'd never catch up.

No, the darkness whispered. *We'll catch him.*

Yes.

I will.

I was born to run.

I took the other crow-handled blade from my chest, the one strapped over my heart. The one with the onyx eye and pushed myself even harder, feeling more than knowing that he was there. Somewhere ahead. Just out of reach.

The clouds overhead shifted, uncovering the moon long enough for its light to spill over the forest floor in dappled patches. A trail. There was a trail back here. A narrow channel of red dirt that carved through the forest in an almost straight line.

A large shape far to my right had me pausing, panting, lifting a blade to throw, but the clouds shifted again and my heart sputtered.

The large boulder squatted amid its wooden cousins, and it wasn't the first time it'd tricked me into thinking it was something other than a harmless chunk of rock.

And suddenly, I knew where I was going.

Where he was taking me.

I raced for the rock, grimacing as I scratched a giant X into its face, blunting the edge.

Please find me.

I set my sights on the trail, finding fresh tracks in the dirt.

Got you.

I caught my breath before pushing myself onward, following Carson's trail, marking several more trees with vicious slashes of my blades. Breadcrumbs for the Crows.

Until suddenly, there it was.

I skidded to a stop, falling onto my side in the dirt before managing to scrape back to my feet, huffs of moisture clouding in front of my face even though I was *far* from feeling cold. I was far from feeling *anything* except this burning desire to hunt. To kill.

The cellar door hung open in the middle of the small clearing, welcoming me into its dark depths with open arms. Smears of soot coated the wooden panels and filled the cracks and grooves in the cement steps.

My throat ached with dryness as I panted quietly, seemingly unable to make my feet move any closer to the door. The fire leaching from my arms, making my fingers stiff from an all-consuming cold.

I peered over my shoulder as if I could will my Crows into appearing, soaring through the trees to my side. The only sound was the whisper of the wind . the redwoods, and I gulped, knowing that the longer I gave Carson to prepare for attack down there, the worse my chances would be.

My grip tightened on my blades, and I pushed through the ice, letting my darkness melt it all away. One step. Another.

I dipped a toe into the inky dark on the other side of the cellar doors and then kept going, letting it swallow me whole. I felt along the wall as I went, remembering the exact reverse of this moment. When I'd climbed, burned and broken up these same steps and found my freedom.

Found my way *home*.

I'd find my way home again. But this time, I wouldn't go empty handed.

Careful not to make a sound, I descended to the very bottom of the stairs and reached for the door handle, seeing a trace of light through the soot covered window down the long corridor. The acrid smell of burned things stung in my nose, making it wrinkle.

I lifted a blade to eye level and released the handle, deciding to slip through the slim crack in the door instead of opening it wider, not trusting the hinges.

My tits pressed into the doorframe, and I sucked my ass in tight, just fitting.

I buried myself in the shadows of the corner next to the door, peering up where there was a camera. It was still there, but it was covered in gray ash like much of the floor, and the red light was dead.

Hopefully that meant it was, too.

No risk, no reward.

I crept along the wall, wiping the back of my hand over my eyes to get rid of the ash clinging to my lashes.

The light was coming from the very end of the hall, where a steel door hung open.

I wasn't falling for another fucking trick.

I took my time, inspecting every room on my way down the corridor. Some of the doors were still shut tight, locked, dark around their edges. But others... they were filled with evidence of his abuse. Chains bolted to the floors and walls. Crimson stains on concrete floors. Fingernails embedded in concrete walls.

My stomach turned at those, and I moved slower, checking each space as thoroughly as I could. Giving my guys more time to find me.

A sinking dread grew in my belly the longer it took them.

They should've found me by now.

What if me and the other snipers didn't take out enough of the Kings to even the odds. What if...

I couldn't bring myself to think it.

They'll come.

"Fuck!" Carson bellowed at the end of the hall, and I covered my mouth with a palm to stifle the sound of my sharp intake of breath when an entire computer tower and monitor crashed across the opening to the room, cords snagging, keyboard keys clicking over the concrete.

"Fuck, fuck, fuck!"

Now or fucking never.

I ran on my toes, hopeful that the sounds of him trashing the room would conceal my advance.

I pressed my back flat against the wall outside the door, lifting a blade as something else crashed against the door and spilled into the corridor. A basket full of fucking burner phones. My skin itched with savage desire and it took everything in me not to rush in knives *hot.*

Maybe I should.

I clenched my teeth, sinking down to a crouch, remembering in vivid imagery the feeling of being powerless. Trapped in a cocoon of my own flesh as the drug he dosed me with took away all my fight. I couldn't go through that again.

Angling the blade in my right hand, I pushed it closer to the door, trying to see his reflection in its freshly polished silver surface. I couldn't see him. What I did see was a cot pushed against a cement wall. And another wall covered entirely in maps and images and notes and newspaper articles and a lot more I couldn't decipher from the reflection alone. All of it centered on *us.* Me. The Crows. Diesel and the Saints. Rebecca. All interconnected with lengths of red string.

It was a serial killer wall. Fitting, since that was exactly what this filth was.

I twisted my blade just slightly and found a pair of blue eyes staring back at me. Carson cocked his head and I jerked my blade back, rounding the corner.

He dove and I threw, catching him in the thigh.

I threw my other blade, but he jerked a chair in front of himself and it embedded in the worn seat.

I bent to draw another from my ankle, unwilling to get closer to him, when he fired.

The shot grazed my forehead and knocked me back onto my tailbone. Blood gushed down into my eye, blinding me, but I couldn't feel it. I kicked off the wall, curling up behind a desk, narrowly avoiding his next shot.

"You bitch!"

I squeezed my blood-coated eye closed and spied his back around the edge of the desk. I hurtled my other blade from lying on my side, and it *thunked* into the meat of his side, burrowing deep.

He cried out, and three more shots fired in the room, finding homes in the concrete as he jumped to his feet and wildly fired after me as I sprinted back out into the corridor. My eye burned, and I hissed, gasping as I slipped on a phone, landing face first on the floor.

A heavy weight pressed into my back, and I screamed as his fist twisted into my hair, rearing my head back to smash my face back down into the concrete floor, dazing me.

I coughed, choking on the coppery tang of blood in my mouth, fighting through the pain and the black spots in my vision. Wondering if I could reach his gun where he'd dropped it a few feet away.

He reared my head back again, and I used the angle to my advantage, grabbing my last blade from its holster instead and sheering it through my hair like butter.

My head came free, and I used all my upper body strength, pushing up from the ground to knock him off me, coming at him with a feral cry, blade raised, short tendrils of dark hair stroking my cheeks.

Carson fell onto his back, catching my wrist before I could sink the blade into his chest. The tip of the blade pressed through his lips parted in fear, but it was met with a tough resistance I noticed the ridges of the vest beneath his clothes. *Damn.* This wasn't going to be easy. I bared my teeth, shouting my wrath into his face as I pressed down down *down* with everything I had.

"*You're no Angel,*" he spat in my face, the veins in his neck bulging like slithering eels.

"No," I agreed. "*I'm your worst fucking nightmare.*"

With another feral cry, I locked the muscle in my back and shoved down, sinking the blade past the vest, seeing the moment it broke contact with skin from the widening of his eyes. He choked, his eyes rolling back, hands leaving my wrist to claw at his chest, gasping.

My darkness preened within and together, we shoved off him, reaching for the Wilson Combat strapped to my thigh to knock him the fuck out and drag him back to Rook's murder shed. But the fucker was faking the punctured lung and he was *fast*. Faster than me.

My gun came free of the holster at the same time he pushed his against my breastbone, grabbing me by my vest to haul me close.

I gasped as Carson pumped two rounds through the Kevlar, one chasing the other, helping push it through the woven fabric to meet its mark. The shock waves rolled through me and I felt hot wetness seep down my stomach. My Wilson slipped from my grasp, my world tipped up, and I fell hard into whatever waited on the other side.

38

CORVUS

I pressed my bloody fingertip to the boulder, coming away with rock dust from where my Sparrow had carved an X in its face. "This way!"

My gaze dragged to a bush, where fresh blood-splatter painted the leaves crimson. I heard my brothers crashing through the forest toward me and hollered. "Bring the vet! She's hurt."

Not knowing how badly was making it harder to breathe as I picked my way around the boulder, finding a trail concealed in the darkness. I dropped to one knee, feeling out the tracks.

Rook came up behind me. "Grey's gone to bring the vet, which way?"

"She was fucking chasing him down," I gritted out through clenched teeth, sizing the two distinctly different prints in the dirt.

"It's okay, Bro. We're right behind her."

...except we weren't.

There had been so many of them. So many more than we'd planned for. How they'd managed to conceal such high number for so long was beyond me, but I was willing to bet it was something to do with the bastard my Sparrow hunted. It took us forever to cross that stretch of pavement and get to the trees. We'd had to fight the whole way. Steamrolling Kings, cutting through muscle and bone.

I checked the gun I stole off a King a ways back. There was at least half a mag left. It would have to do. The sounds of the ongoing battle raged behind us, but Diesel and the others had it. There weren't many left out front, and I suspected even fewer still lingering inside the building. I'd pointed to the tree line and shouted *Carson* when he'd shouted over the gunfire to demand to know where the fuck we were going.

With any luck, he and the others wouldn't be far behind, and no matter what happened when we found Carson Bates, he wouldn't be leaving this forest in one piece. He'd either be dead, or preferably, a prisoner.

Rook and I raced down the trail, each of us pointing out the trees where our girl marked her path, telling us we were on the right track.

The unmistakable echo of a gunshot shook the forest and both of us cursed, breaking out into full sprints.

Rook growled next to me, keeping pace despite his leg.

Three more gunshots rang out, nearer than before, and I knew what we were about to find before we crashed through the trees. The cellar doors hung open, and Rook and I skidded to slow down as we soared over the edge and onto the staircase headed down.

Two more shots fired off in rapid succession and my blood sizzled, something in my chest snapping as we blew through a metal door into a long corridor... and watched Ava Jade's body slump to the ground.

"Sparrow!"

Carson pushed himself up, gun raised.

I fired first, and red exploded where the gun had been. The shot knocking it from his hand and taking two fingers.

"Ghost!" Rook was already halfway to her, but I couldn't seem to keep my burning eyes from Carson. He bared his teeth, hissing as he dragged his legs from beneath Ava Jade's limp ones, reaching for his weapon with his other hand.

Rook reached my Sparrow, and it was the panic in his voice that finally broke me. "*Ghost, wake up!*"

I charged forward, crushing Carson's reaching hand under my boot until he screamed. I kicked him onto his back and emptied the entire clip into his chest, his body jerking and convulsing with each heavy hitting blow.

It took longer to register than it should've that the trigger was clicking uselessly. There were no more bullets to be used. I couldn't see Carson through the haze of tears as I tossed the gun aside and turned to face my blackest moment.

Rook pressed his hands over Sparrow's chest, but it was no use, blood welled between his fingers, streaming down. Her pale face rolled to one side, eyes lidded at half-mast. Lips rapidly turning blue.

I looked away, my stomach turning.

No.

No.

She didn't get to die.

I wouldn't let her.

"Move," I growled, shoving Rook back. I unzipped her vest and yanked it open, exposing the wound to her chest. It was on the left side. Maybe a little too far to the left to have hit her heart?

Please.

Please.

"Put pressure on it," I ordered and Rook tore his shirt clean off his chest, balled it and pushed it against the wound. I wasn't going to sit here and do nothing like I did last time. If it weren't for Rook, Becca would've died. But he saved her.

I could save my Sparrow.

We could.

Rook put his ear over her mouth as I positioned myself, starting compressions, crushing Rook's fingers in the process.

"She isn't breathing!" he screamed, and I could see he was losing it. Becca was one thing, but this was our girl.

He pressed two fingers to her throat and let out a relieved cry. "I think I feel a pulse!"

Then there was a chance. As long as we were here to fight for her.

"Don't let up on that shirt."

I lost count of my compressions and cursed, bending down to pinch her nose, tipping up her chin so I could blow into her mouth. Wishing I could push my own life down her throat.

Take it, I wanted to scream. *I don't want it without you.*

"Come on," I urged, re-starting compressions to the point where I was sure I was breaking fucking bones. *"Come on, Sparrow!"*

Heavy swift footsteps descended the stairs, and I heard Grey call, "Here! Down here!"

But his tone changed entirely a moment later. "AJ?"

His footfalls slowed in the corridor, and he vomited, the sound far-off, background noise for the incessant beating of my heart in my ears.

"Where's the fucking vet?" Rook demanded in a lethal hiss.

As if on cue, the vet tripped down the last three steps and Rook grabbed Grey, dragging him down to the floor to place his hand on top of the cloth. "Keep pressure."

Grey choked over our girl, his knuckles white as he pressed hard into her wound, tears spilling onto her chest as I continued compressions.

"*Move your fucking ass,*" Rook shouted and somewhere behind me the vet yelped, and I heard the scrape of something being dragged over the concrete before the thin man was unceremoniously deposited at my side. "Help them!"

"K-k-keep compressions," the vet said, fumbling with the Velcro on his field medical kit.

"The fuck do you think I'm doing?"

"The wound. L-l-let me see it."

Grey pulled the fabric back and on my next compression, a fresh well of blood gushed out, and I pulled my hands back.

"We need to stop the bleeding," the vet said, sounding more sure of himself. He pulled out a green packet and tore the top off with his teeth. The quick clot gauze toppled onto her chest and he grabbed it with shaky fingers. "Remove the shirt."

Grey grabbed it through the hole and tore it wide, giving the vet the clearance he needed to start packing the gauze into her. He stuffed it into her bullet wound like he was pushing magicians ribbon into a fucking hat.

She should've woken up.

There was no way you didn't wake up when someone was packing foreign objects into your ..

No way.

Rook paced behind me, cursing, hitting the side of his Browning against his temple as he muttered to himself, a low whine in his throat.

"Rook? Rook!" Grey was calling to him, trying to get his attention.

The vet put his fingers to her throat and cursed.

"What?"

"We're losing her. She's lost too much blood."

"Well, do something!"

He peeled her eyelid back and tugged on her blue lip. "She's not getting enough oxygen."

Heat sizzled up through the balls of my feet as I pushed to standing, reaching over the vet to snatch Rook's Browning from his hands and put it to the vet's temple.

"*Save her.*"

He stilled.

"Darryl, so help me god, if you don't start doing something useful, I will blow your goddamned head off."

The vet dug in his kit, coming up with a portable defibrillator and an ambu bag. They rattled against the concrete in his rush to get it all apart, wiping down her chest to place the pads where they needed to be. He shoved the bag at Grey. "Put that over her mouth, start slow compressions on the bag. Even if I can re-start her heart, she needs air."

My vision blurred, doubling, and I had to bend over my knees to keep from passing out.

Re-start her heart. Did I hear that right?

No.

"Stand clear."

Grey removed his hands from the bag, and the vet initiated the shock. Her torso lurched. He felt for a pulse and cursed.

I put the gun back to the vet's head. "*Again.*"

39

ROOK

The vet shocked her again.

"It's running out of juice!" he cried as Corvus shoved the barrel of the gun harder against the back of his head.

"Again!"

"Clear!"

Ghost's body jerked against the stained concrete for the third time. The vet put his fingers under her chin and stared wild-eyed up at Corvus. "*She's gone*, there's nothing else—"

He pistol whipped Darryl, making his eyes go unfocused as he keeled over, but Corvus wasn't about to let him go. He jerked him back upright. "You're done when I fucking say you're done!"

Grey muttered pleas over her body, begging her to come back while the vet set up for another shock with blood gushing from his nose.

I felt rooted to the spot. Like I was watching from some omniscient point of view as I lost the best part of myself.

My Ghost...

Gone.

I'd been fighting the depressive feelings of my withdrawal for days now, and I was getting through it because *of her*. But now?

Now I let them crash into me, break me apart from the inside. My eyes burned so hot it took me a minute to remember that this was what it felt like to cry. My chest caved in on itself and I sank to my knees under the weight of the stones I'd built up around my heart suffocating me. My heart bleated out an uneven rhythm and I bent, putting a hand to the cold concrete as my head spun from the lack of air.

But, I didn't want to breathe.

Not when she'd never share the same air.

I choked out a hard sob that felt like throwing up part of my soul, the heave of my body knocking loose the grenade from my torn pocket. It rolled over the floor, coming to a stop directly beneath my face.

It was the solution.

I let out a broken breath and reached for it, its ribbed surface fitting into my hand as if it was made just for me. Like she was.

...was.

"*Again!*" Corvus screamed, his voice breaking.

I lifted my head to say my goodbye. "I'm sorry, Ghost. I told you... I can't do it without you anymore."

"Rook!"

I looked to my younger brother, all the blood drained from his face as his sights fixed what was in my hand. "Rook, don't!"

I stood, shaking my head. "It was always going to end like this for me, Brother. I should've died a long time ago."

Corvus realized what was happening and dropped my gun. "Keep trying!" he shouted at the vet, lifting his hands to me as he advanced on me. "Rook, put it down, man. Don't *fucking* do this right now."

"Tell me you don't want to join me, Brother."

His lips parted, and I saw the truth in his eyes. He was willing to die for her once. What happened when your reason for living was no longer living herself?

I used his moment of inner reflection against him, taking the opportunity to pull the pin before I could lose my nerve.

"No!"

It dangled on my index finger, and I lifted the grenade high in my right hand, holding the lever down as I raced back down the corridor to the entrance twenty meters away. I was going down, but I would make damn sure I didn't take them with me. Their lives. Their choice.

"Tell Diesel this is what I wanted. No mourning. No fucking funeral. Bury me with her."

I let go of the lever and closed my eyes.

"Fucking Christ!"

The grenade was wrenched from my fist and Diesel slammed into my back, knocking me to the ground. He landed on top of me, his body forming around mine as the grenade exploded somewhere outside the cellar, deafening in its volume, shaking the fucking walls.

Concrete dust rained down around us, and I shoved Diesel off me, gripping him by his shirt. "Why the fuck did you do that?"

"Rook—"

"I wanted to end it!"

"Rook—"

"*You don't get to take that from me.*"

"*Rook,*" Diesel screamed, spittle flying into my face as he backhanded me, making the taste of copper explode on my tongue. "Look!"

A wet cough burrowed into my ears, and I couldn't move fast enough, shoving Diesel away, racing back down the hall.

My Ghost blinked up at the ceiling through blood and tears, choking, her lips blue.

I fell at her side, taking her cold hand into mine. "Ghost! Ghost, look at me!"

Her unfocused eyes searched, but couldn't see to latch onto anything.

"She's suffocating," Grey cried out, putting the ambu bag back over her mouth, squeezing it to try to get her air.

Her eyes started to roll back.

"Hey," I growled at the vet. "What do we do?"

He dumped his bag onto the floor, searching for something he clearly wasn't fucking finding. "I-I don't have what I need. It must've fallen out."

"*What?*"

"Her lung is full of blood. We need to drain it."

"*Get out of the way,*" I growled, kicking Darryl to the side as I took his place. "It's okay, Ghost. I'm going to make it okay."

I drew my blade and grabbed a length of tubing connected to a blood pressure cuff, slicing off a length of it before leaning over her. He didn't restart her heart only for us to lose her twice.

"Rook, what are you doing?" Corvus hissed.

"Saving her."

I felt along her slippery ribs, still so bony from malnourishment. We'd fix that. We'd fix everything.

"Hold on, Ghost."

I found what I prayed was a good spot and made a hundred promises to the almighty if he'd just let her stay as I stabbed my girl in the chest, deep. Deep enough that I knew I'd hit lung.

Thanks to my time spent taking apart men piece by piece, I had a good fucking idea of how far I needed to go.

She let out a pained gurgle, her eyes finding mine finally as her body writhed away from the pain.

"Hold her still!"

Blood spilled over her side as Corvus held her arms, and I fed the tube into the new wound I'd created, keeping my eyes on her. *Stay with us, Ghost.*

Blood funneled out of the tube, her filled lung draining onto the floor, puddling around my knees.

"Come on," Grey begged, moving to pull her head up into his lap, getting it higher from her heart level. *Breathe, baby.*

She jerked her head to the side and coughed, blood splattering the floor.

"That's it, Ghost, get it out."

"Slow, small breaths," the vet said somewhere to my side, sliding a stethoscope over her chest, his eyes on his watch. It was hard not to want to rip his arms off, but I needed to hold this tube in place as the blood continued to leave her lung.

The vet removed the stethoscope. "We need to get her to urgent care before she crashes again. She needs blood."

"Take mine."

"Are you the same blood type?"

"How the fuck should I know?"

"Do you know *her* blood type?"

My nostrils flared.

"If I give her the wrong blood, it could be fatal."

So we needed to move her and fast. She hacked again, and some of the color returned to her lips as air was greedily sucked down her throat. I leaned down to push her short hair away from her face, bringing her eyes back to me. "I need you to keep fighting, Ghost. A little longer."

"*Keep... fighting...*" she repeated in a wet voice, her chin dipping with a tiny nod.

"That's my girl."

Ghost's hand found mine again, and she squeezed weakly, letting me know she wasn't giving up.

A groan permeated the air to our left and my hackles instantly rose. Carson's booted foot moved as he woke.

Corvus was on him in an instant, wailing on his face until it was bloody.

"*We need him alive,*" I roared.

"The others are bringing a stretcher," Diesel said, kneeling next to me, putting a hand on my shoulder, his expression grim. I shrunk into myself at his touch.

My father's gaze strayed to where Corvus was getting off Carson, staring down at him with a hatred so fierce I worried my brother may never regain his perfect control again. How could he?

Carson gurgled, his nose smashed and cheekbone already swelling to double its size. The bullets riddled in his vest probably cracked some bone beneath, but his injuries were nothing compared to what we'd do to him when our girl was ready.

It was her hand that would end him, but only after we got our pound of flesh.

"*Father...*" Carson slurred, trying to curl onto his side, his red eyes pleading.

Diesel's jaw tightened as he stood to look down at his son with disgust twisting his features. "He's yours to do with whatever you will," he said. "That filth is no son of mine."

"You hear that, Ghost? He's all ours."

The fire returned to her eyes, and I knew that no matter what, she was going to be there when we took him apart. Not even death himself could stop her.

40

GREY

TEN DAYS LATER

"Are you just going to keep pretending like it never happened?"

Rook stiffened on his way back from his morning shower, the muscle in his back going rigid as he turned and shook the water droplets from his hair, tossing it out of his face. "What's with the ambush?"

"You tried to kill yourself, Rook."

"Today, Bro? Really? It's fucking Christmas."

I set my jaw, not budging from his door.

"Fine." He sighed, brushing past me into his dark bedroom, tossing the towel on the bed to throw on a pair of jeans. He zipped them over his junk commando and perched on the end of his bed. "Well, come in."

I stepped into the room and shut the door behind me, flicking on the rarely used overhead light. He shied away from the assaulting brightness, his upper lip curling. "Ghost will be awake soon, I wanted to be there when—"

"This will only take a minute. I'm not going to ruin her Christmas morning."

"You're just going to ruin mine, then?"

"You got something to tell me?"

I cocked my head at him, waiting for him to fill in the blank so I didn't have to. I didn't make accusations like this one lightly, but I knew my brother well enough to know when he was on drugs. I should've seen it sooner, but that night in that fucking bunker cemented it.

Rook was a lot of things, but he wasn't suicidal. *Unless* he was coming down. Then we had to stop him from offing himself in a blaze of glory almost weekly. It was the ugly, bitter truth we never spoke of. Other people saw the violence and the bloodshed. They saw the *crazy* when he was high, but they didn't see him come down.

No, those precious fucking moments were reserved only for us. And we'd kept them only to *us* for his sake. But I wasn't going through that shit again. If he was using, he was going to get clean *now,* and I didn't care how much he fucking screamed for a fix this time.

How had we missed this?

I felt like a failure for letting it get this far.

I surveyed his eyes under the light, my hands itching to tear apart his entire room drawer by drawer, floorboard by floorboard. I'd find it. It was only a matter of time.

"*Rook,*" I pushed when he didn't answer.

"You seem to have it all figured out, Brother. You don't need me to tell you."

My cheekbones flared, but I reined it in. It wouldn't help to get angry, it would only make him combative and we'd get nowhere. "You admit it, then? You're using?"

He leaned over his spread knees, pressing his face into his palms. "I was," he muttered.

"Was?"

"Yeah. When Ghost was gone."

"And what, you just stopped?"

He lifted his chin, narrowing his black eyes on me. "She knew," he said. "She knew right off. That first night at the hospital she cornered me about it in a fucking janitors closet. The look in her eyes... *fuck...* I never wanted to see that shit again. I crushed what I had left under my boot and rode out the withdrawals. Didn't you wonder why she was in my room all those nights after the hospital?"

My face screwed up. I *had* wondered, but I thought that was just where she wanted to be. That she'd chosen Rook those nights, and I'd been doing my fucking best not to be jealous about it. Not to mention the fact that at the time I figured she'd never want to share my bed again, anyway.

"We weren't having a goddamned picnic," he admitted. "She took care of me. Made sure I was okay. I asked her to wait for me to tell you guys myself once we'd gotten through all the shit with the Kings. There was enough to worry about."

I studied him carefully once more, and found pupils dilated normally under the light. Color in his face. That lazy grace about him where he'd be on edge and constantly moving if he were high.

"You're really clean?"

"Yes."

I nodded to myself, letting that settle.

"Does Corv know?" Rook asked.

"He'd have skinned you alive already if he did, but I think he suspects. Not much gets past him."

"Spit it out," Rook said when I didn't continue, knowing there was more I was hesitating to say.

"Look, I know it wasn't really you..." I started, knowing I needed to get this out before I could go wake up my girl and enjoy the moment we'd all been waiting for. "But fuck you for thinking if she was gone that you wouldn't have anything else to live for. That's horseshit and you know it, and I fucking hate you for it, drugs or no drugs."

"I deserve that."

I crossed the floor to him and jerked him onto his feet and into a hug. Hating that I almost lost two of the most important people in my life because of that motherfucker. "You're lucky you're clean or you'd be spending Christmas locked up tighter than Carson."

Rook barked a laugh in my ear, slapping me on the back. No one would *ever* be locked up tighter than Carson.

"Are you going to tell her?" I asked as I pulled away, watching his eyes for the truth of his answer, but they'd already gone dead.

When AJ woke up after surgery with all of us surrounding her, all she wanted to know was where Carson was and if the Kings were all dead. There wasn't a whole lot of opportunity for Rook to slip into casual conversation that he almost fucking offed himself in a manic depressive fit at seeing her dead on the floor.

"I should," he replied, dropping his gaze. "I don't want any secrets between us."

I squeezed his shoulder. "It's your call, man. I think she'd understand."

"Yeah, after she ate me for breakfast."

I laughed. "Well don't worry about it today. It's Christmas."

"Speaking of..." Rook said with a wry smile, going to gather her things from the top of his dresser. "We told her we'd be there when she wakes up."

"Then let's go."

I checked the surveillance app on my phone for the fifth time this morning as we made our way through to the loft.

On the live feed, I watched Carson shouting manically at whoever was currently stationed to watch him. There would be at least three Saints there, surrounding the cage in the underbelly of Sanctum. Having to listen to him squawk and scream for hours at a time without reprieve. Whatever switch he'd managed to keep off in his brain all this time had been flipped and the true Carson Bates was out to play in all his pathetic glory.

This feed was the only reason any of us could stand having her be alone without one of us there with her. Though she rarely was. One of us crawled into her bed in the loft with her almost every night. Taking turns. Last night Corv stayed with her so he'd already be there at her side.

It was harder than any of us wanted to admit not to take a little detour into town and carve off pieces of him to bring back and lay at AJ's feet. But he was *hers* to do with what she deemed fit. She would get the first taste of blood, and the last. Once she was ready. And today, with the all-clear from the doc for her to move around more than the twelve hundred square feet of the Nest allowed, it was time.

Her drains came out a few days ago and with the breathing exercises, her lung was expanding as it should be. The bullet wound was healing nicely. The scar almost a perfect match to the one Carson put in her best friend.

Marking them as sisters. Twins.

"Shit, did you do the decorations?" I whisper hissed before we reached the loft. I'd completely fucking forgotten. We were supposed to set them up after her sleep meds kicked in.

"Took care of it early this morning. Couldn't sleep," Rook whispered back. "You should see Corv when he sleeps with her, I've never seen the guy so relaxed. Had his fucking mouth open and everything."

"No shit?"

Rook nodded, waving an arm for me to hurry up and fuck if I wasn't excited. I couldn't remember the last time I'd looked forward to a Christmas this much. Diesel did his best for us, but we were already mostly grown when he adopted us and the season seemed to always remind him of Jacqueline We'd do a big turkey dinner and he'd hand us a stack of bills and a beer and say not to spend it all in one place.

This one was going to be different.

The tiny box in my pocket felt like it was going to burn right through and my mouth went dry again, worrying about whether or not she would like it.

Rook flipped on a switch when we entered the loft on quiet feet and hundred tiny lights flickered on, illuminating the space in white and red light. They draped across the ceiling, wrapped around the columns, draped over the headboard. Fanned across one entire wall.

Corvus startled awake, reaching for the gun under his pillow before he saw us standing there amid the pinkish glow. He rubbed his eyes, looking around himself like he'd just woken up in fucking candyland.

He might as well have. "What the fuck did you do?" he hissed quietly, trying not to wake her, rubbing his eyes.

"You like? I think it's got *pizzazz*, don't you?"

AJ stirred, letting out a small groan as she turned from her back onto her side, pulling her knees in close as she squeezed her eyes tighter. "No," she moaned, her voice still raspy, but nothing could ruin the perfection of slightly grouchy, sleepy AJ. She held up a hand. "Five more minutes."

"It's Christmas," Rook argued, going to kneel at her bedside, trying to pull the covers down from her face.

She dropped three fingers. "Two minutes then."

"Come on, Ghost, open your eyes."

"You better have coffee."

I winced. We forgot that part. Probably my fault.

"On it," Rook said, jumping to his feet, giving me a look that fully confirmed it was in fact my fault before racing through the Nest to get our girl her cuppa.

Corvus cleared his throat, still eyeing the lights like he might try to shoot out each one individually as he pushed up to lean against the headboard. "How the hell did he manage to do this while we were sleeping?"

The question was clearly rhetorical, but AJ answered it anyway. "Admit it, you're a big softy for your Sparrow."

She poked him in the ribs and he growled, shooting her a glare.

I folded myself on the edge of the bed, and she reached for me blindly, the mound of covers sighing as her hand found mine. I gave her a squeeze and felt something lurch in my chest.

This felt so right. Her here. All of us together.

I ran my fingers over her knuckles, and she peered at me from beneath her covers, her brows lowered in concern. "Hey, Superman, you okay?"

"Just... happy."

She grinned at that, blinking her big beautiful eyes open a little wider, letting the covers drop a little lower. She opened her mouth to say something, but the lights caught her attention, and she squinted, sitting up straighter to get a proper look around the room. "Did you do all this while I slept?"

"Rook did."

She smirked at that and I knew she was imagining big scary dangerous Rook hanging a thousand Christmas lights because I was too and it was fucking hilarious.

AJ chuckled, and I joined her. "Did you sleep okay? How are you feeling."

"Better. I feel good. Doesn't hurt as much to breathe anymore, either."

Corvus and I shared a look, and she wrinkled her nose. "What?"

She didn't know it yet but that was the right answer.

Rook returned with her coffee and she gave him a warm smile. "You didn't have to do all this."

He passed her the mug and bent to kiss the top of her head. "Sure, I did. Like it?"

"It's... a little harsh, but I love it."

"Present time?" Rook asked, eagerly rubbing his hands together.

"I thought we said no presents?"

"They're small ones," I reassured her, but it didn't erase the knot between her brows. She didn't need to give us anything, anyway. Having her here, alive, was the best gift we would ever be given.

"Me first." Rook bent to one knee next to her, fishing the items from his pocket.

AJ squealed as soon as she saw the ring and black diamond necklace, taking them from his hands with tears in her eyes. "I thought they were gone for good."

She went to push her hair back but found only empty air behind her shoulders, laughing dryly. Becca had fixed the chop she'd made to her hair in the bunker, turned it into a sharp angled bob that only further accentuated her high cheekbones and severe features. She passed Corvus the necklace behind her. "Help me?"

"Dies and the others found them when they went back to get rid of all Carson's shit," Rook said, his dark eyes following the path of the finger now carrying his ring.

The slight downturning of her lips was the only indication that the reminder got to her before she fixed a smile in place of the frown. It was crazy to think that if we hadn't chosen to attack right away like AJ suggested, we'd all be dead right now.

Carson had everything in place to annihilate us all without even lifting a gun, and it was all set to deploy less than twenty-four hours from when we attacked. We were right. He'd been busy.

We were just faster.

"Me next," I said, lifting the tiny box from my pocket, turning it in my fingers before I set it on the plush covers in front of her.

She glanced between it and me curiously. I found the antique leather ring box online and thought it suited her, but it was the ring inside I hoped she'd like.

AJ popped the little pin and cracked the box open. I held my breath.

Her eyes lit up. "Grey, it's gorgeous. I love it."

She couldn't tear it from the box fast enough, hesitating before she slid it onto a finger. The white gold ring had been crafted into a crow in flight, a diamond in place of its eye. "This isn't...?"

An unsure laugh passed my lips. "No, not exactly but—"

Corvus plopped his ring box down in front of her, flipping back the lid to reveal the princess cut diamond with two emerald stones on either side that he picked out. "We all wanted to be represented."

She gasped before pressing her lips together, the slight quiver in her chin giving her away. "This is too much," she told Corvus, indicating his ring. That diamond is like a whole carat."

"I called Max back yesterday. Agreed to the spring shows and took the record deal." He poked her ribs. "So let me spoil you."

At this, she perked up, whirling to tackle him in a tight embrace. She cried out at the contact with her injury, pulling back, but only enough to dull the pain. She clung to him, not letting him put any extra space between them. "I'm so happy for you."

"For us," he corrected her gruffly. "You said you'd go on tour with me, remember?"

"How could I forget?"

She put the two new rings on her fingers, holding her hands out to admire them. "A few more of these and Diesel and I will match."

I snorted. "Don't tell him that."

She sniffed, elbowing Corvus. "Well, there is one more gift that needs to be given."

Corv reached into the nightstand on his side of the bed, coming out with a clean black box, which he held out to me.

"What's this?"

"It was all Sparrow's idea, we just helped pay for it."

AJ paled, looking edgy in her seat. "You don't have to wear it. I just thought, *we* thought that you might want one and—"

I opened the lid and she fell quiet as I stared down at the glass eye swathed in dark navy silk. It looked so real that for a second I could've almost believed it was the one I was missing. Carved out, preserved, lovingly tucked in this box.

"Took a lot of back and forth to get the coloring just right and the sizing the vet gave us might've been off, so if it is we can get you a new one and—"

"AJ..."

"Yes?"

I couldn't seem to draw up the words to express how much this meant to me, my lungs burning, throat scratched raw. "It's..."

"Do you hate it?"

"What? No!"

I managed to pull myself together, clearing my throat as I slid the lid back on the box. "It's perfect. I'm going to try it out after we get back."

"Back?" Her head tilted to one side. "Where are we going? I thought Dies was coming here for dinner."

I could tell she had an inkling of where we were going with this, the hunger for it clear in her eyes. In the way her hands twisted in the covers, ready to use up all the rage she'd been patiently waiting to set free. It was a condition of our forgiveness for almost getting herself killed that she allow herself time to heal before we took Carson apart piece by bloody piece.

"We're not going to dinner, Ghost."

"It's time," Corvus confirmed. "The doc gave the all-clear last night."

"Merry fucking Christmas, babe."

41

AVA JADE

I tipped my head back, inhaling deeply as Carson's blood dripped down my neck. Sanctum smelled of whiskey and copper, and I filled my lungs with it, shivering even though it was far from cold.

We'd never get his blood out of the mat under our feet in the fighting ring. The whole thing would need to be replaced. The once gray-white color of it entirely stained with varying shades of crimson.

The splatter patterns from seven days ago when we started were the deepest color. A near black. While the freshest smears were still a raw red that looked almost pinkish by comparison. It was our canvas, and we'd painted it well.

I gripped the blade in my hand, flipping it edge over edge as I caught my breath and licked my lips.

At my feet, Carson let out a weak, wet moan from a toothless, tongueless mouth. He was fading fast.

Rook was right when he said we'd be here until New Year's Eve. I lifted my gaze to the clock on the wall across the space, finding it was already past nine in the evening and I promised Grey we'd watch the fireworks together. The four of us.

"Are you ready, Ghost?" Rook asked from behind me, and I instinctively leaned into him, resting my back against his solid chest, breathing him in as my panting subsided.

"Ghost?" he pressed when I didn't reply, my nickname a rumble against my back. He dipped his head, nudging my neck with his nose, making me sigh.

Fuck, I was so tired.

We'd been sleeping upstairs, in one of the back rooms of the bar each night since we'd been here. Showering on the third floor. Surviving on pub fare, water, and whiskey. It would be nice to be finished, but something inside of me still thirsted for vengeance. I didn't know if I *could* be finished. Not yet.

The things this piece of shit put us through.

What he almost took from us.

From me.

I didn't think I'd ever be finished. There was no ending fitting enough, *brutal enough*, for him.

Rook wrapped a hand around my middle, kissing the nape of my neck.

I closed my eyes, my core tightening.

They hadn't touched me, not like this, since I woke up in the hospital. A sweet kiss here and there. A warm body next to mine while I slept. But no more. At first, I thought they were afraid to break me while I was still healing. And this week? This week we spent every waking hour down here until we were all too tired to do anything but sit in a hot shower and fall into bed.

Carson let out another weak sound, ruining the moment. I drew my hand back to throw my blade and shut him up, but Rook caught my wrist. "Wait," he said, his chin jerking to our prey.

He kissed me again, and something in Carson's dying eyes betrayed discomfort. Anger.

The fucker still thought he had some claim on me? Even after everything I'd done to him. He'd never touch me, or anyone else again, and not just because he'd never leave this basement.

He didn't have fingers anymore.

And suddenly, I knew how I wanted to end it.

There was one more form of torture we hadn't explored.

Rook loosened his grip on my wrist, and I let my hand drop, spinning to face the others. Corvus and Grey lounged on the old black sofa we'd dragged down here a few days ago. Grey wiping down his hands and wrists, all the way up to his elbows.

He'd surprised me the most out of the three. I expected the ruthless thirst for blood from Rook, and even on some level, from Corvus. But Grey took his pound of flesh, too. This morning, with a sort of quiet resignation, he skinned Carson's back like a hunter might work to remove the pelt from a stag. In trained, precise movements as Carson screamed hoarsely.

When he was finished, he'd discarded the pieces and stood back to let someone else have a turn. Entirely unfazed.

"I'm ready," I finally told Rook, knowing this needed to end. We'd already taken everything from him that could be taken without killing him. Corvus, his balls and fingers. Rook, his cock, both nipples, and each one of his toes.

We'd taken our time, keeping him with us by cauterizing each wound with Rook's blowtorch. Sticking him with IV needles to replenish him with a steady supply of liquids.

But it was time.

"How do you want to do it?"

Grey finished washing up and pushed his blond hair away from his face with a sigh. "Together."

This had Corvus looking up from his phone, and Grey fixing me with a piercing stare.

"I want you to take me while he watches," I announced, discarding my blade on the floor. "All of you."

I wanted the last thing he saw to be his *Angel* getting absolutely destroyed by three Saints. Three *Crows*. I wanted him to watch as they made me come. As I enjoyed every touch. Every stroke. As I cried out *for them*. As they erased everywhere *he* touched me, replacing every last memory of him with more of *them*. Until he was expunged from my skin. My bones. My soul.

And then when we were finished, I would end him for good.

"You're still healing," Corvus said, but I could already see the hunger in his watchful stare as it traversed my loose, blood-spattered Primal Ethos t-shirt and tight yoga pants.

"So are you."

So were we all. But it'd been over two weeks since the bunker. I wouldn't be running a marathon anytime soon thanks to this fucker. I kicked Carson hard in the stomach, and he choked, the misshapen mitts of his hands pulling in close to shield himself from another attack. My shoulders rolled back as anger sizzled down my spine at the reminder of yet another thing he took from me, whether permanently or not.

No running for me, but I'd be damned if I was going to give up fucking, too.

Grey rose from the couch, removing his shirt in one swift movement, discarding it on the floor. His toned abs rippled all the way down to his low hanging jeans and the 'V' of his Adonis belt.

He undid his belt and slid it through the loops, coming to stand in front of me, never taking his eyes off me. "Take your clothes off, AJ."

My Superman.

I heard Corvus' rough curse as he, too, gave in, standing up from the couch, discarding his phone behind him on the seat. Rook was already helping me with my shirt as Grey lifted his arms high, feeding his belt through the grates of the metal cage overhead. Carson had stopped trying to run—stopped being *able* to run—days ago, but we still lowered it over the ring every morning when we came in to start the workday.

Once he had it so both ends hung down on either side of a bar, he lifted his chin. "Can you reach?"

I lifted my arms as Rook unlatched my bra, and I felt my breasts drop free of the soft material. I wrapped my hands around both sides of the belt, able to loop the leather around my palms but only if I rose up on my tip toes.

Grey nodded. "Good."

Corvus placed himself between me and Carson, lying half conscious on his side on the mat, his nostrils flaring. "I don't want him looking at you."

I released the belt, falling back to my feet to finish removing my bra, standing before him topless, my nipples already so hard they hurt. "This is *my* body, Bones. *My* choice. I want him to see. I want him to watch you take everything from me that he wanted for himself. And then I want to kill him."

His brows lowered as he rolled a reply around in his mouth before finally nodding, his veins popping. "You don't have to join us," I offered. "You don't have to be here."

Hurt crossed his eyes and I grabbed his hand, holding it tight in mine. "But I want you to be."

Corvus let out a shaky breath. "So do I, Sparrow. There's no place else I'd rather be."

I found Rook watching me, pawing his erection, and I smirked. "Sit him up. In the chair. I don't want him to be able to look away."

Rook righted the chair and reached down, hauling Carson up by the crook of his elbow like he weighed nothing. He shoved him into the wooden chair, strapping his head back. It wasn't the same chair he used to restrain me, that one was gone for good, but it was a damn close copy, and we'd used it quite a bit in the time we'd spent down here.

Carson's face pinched, the skin between his brows bunching as he tried to speak. I thought he was asking me to kill him. It was either that or he really wanted a cami. Hard to tell with the missing tongue and burned out throat.

Not for the first time, I felt a rush of skin tingling satisfaction at the sight of him broken. I promised him I would end him, and I'd made *damn good* on that promise. He thought he could fuck with our lives, hurt us, twist us against one another. Now look at him...

"You're going to watch," I told him, slowly removing my yoga pants. "Close your eyes and I'll have your eyelids."

"*Sffuck ouu,*" he hissed, trying to pry his head away from the restraints, but it was no use.

"*You* won't," Rook chided, his dark eyes sliding to me with a gleam of lust in their boundless depths. "But I sure as fuck will."

My core tightened as he slung off his jacket, chucking it toward the couch.

"*AJ,*" Grey whispered, the only warning before he took me by the neck, spinning me back around to face him, his plush lips colliding with mine, drawing a low moan from someplace deep. He pulled me close with a hand on my lower back, pressing me flat against him. His tongue slipped into my mouth, tasting me before he ran his teeth along my lower lip, sucking it into his mouth. He palmed my right breast, and I cried out into his mouth as he twisted the nipple.

"*Fuck, Grey,*" I panted, and he swallowed the words with another kiss. I could feel him hard against my belly through his boxers and eagerly reached between us to feel him. He groaned as I stroked him through the thin fabric, still claiming my mouth.

Carson let loose another slew of unintelligible curses and meaningless threats, only making me want *more*. He thought he could own me? That I could be twisted into some hollow version of myself that would do only as she was told?

No.

I felt Corvus crowd in behind me, his warmth radiating over my back. He swept my hair to one side and I gasped into Grey's mouth as he bit down on my neck, smoothing out the pain with the press of his lips.

I dipped my hand beneath Grey's boxers, but it wasn't enough. I wanted more of him. Of them. I'd been hungry for this for far too long.

"On your knees, Sparrow."

He pressed on my shoulders, guiding me down. I took Grey's boxers with me, letting his proud length spring free. My mouth watered at the sight of it.

"Open," Corvus said, and my belly flipped as he fisted his hand into my hair, taking control. I opened my mouth and Corvus guided it onto Grey's cock.

I flicked my tongue against his tip, tasting the perfect bead of precum there before I let Corvus push me further, forcing me to take the entire length of him.

Grey groaned deliciously, flexing his thighs as he pressed into my throat, feeling it yawn open for him. I choked and Corvus let up only enough for me to catch a small breath before guiding me back, using my face to fuck Grey's cock.

"*Holy shit*," Rook rasped, and I heard the jangle of metal before his jeans hit the floor and Grey slid from between my lips. Corvus lifted me, guiding me more to my left. I opened for Rook, feeling his Jacob's ladder rub over my tongue as he pressed into my mouth.

I felt his tremble as Corvus forced me to take Rook all the way to his base, until I couldn't breathe. Until my head started to spin. Only then did he pull back, letting me fill my lungs. A curse fell from my lips and Rook knelt, rubbing his thumb over my bottom lip, looking at me, at my mouth, in wonder.

I sucked his thumb into my mouth, and his lips parted, eyes heavy-lidded, drunk off the high of this moment. He licked his own lips in response before spreading them into a devilish smirk. "My turn."

A yelp escaped my lips as he hooked his fingers beneath my chin, dragging me up by my jaw as Corvus roughly grasped both my hands, raising them until my fingers brushed the leather hanging over my head. "Hold on, Sparrow."

I curled my hands around the edges of the belt, uncaring that the buckle was biting into my pinkie finger because Rook was between my legs, wrenching them apart.

Another breathy cry left my lips as he dove into my pussy without restraint, sucking greedily at my folds, his warm tongue sliding across my wet slit until I was bucking against his mouth, my hands slipping. Thighs pressing against his head, unable to hold them wide for him as a riot of sensation swirled down through my core.

"Grey, hold her other leg."

Strong hands came around my ankles, dragging my legs wide, prying my thighs from Rook's head. I fought against their hold, but rough hands slid up my calves, up my thighs, holding me in place, kneading the skin there. It was all I could do to hold onto the belt as Rook savagely attacked my pussy while Grey and Corvus held me open to their brother's whims.

"Fuck!" I howled as Rook bit my clit, the pain ricocheting through my body, shoving my head back from the force. He pulled me into his mouth once more, sucking away the pain before poking his tongue into the heat of my core as he pressed his upper lip to my clit, managing to hit all my marks with nothing but his wicked mouth.

The muscles in my legs contracted as I edged toward orgasm, my biceps burning from holding myself up as I began to rock against Rook's mouth, riding the wave.

"That's it, Sparrow," Corvus hissed, his lips pressing a fiery path of hard kisses up my calf as his fingers trailed higher up the back of my thigh. He grabbed a fistful of my ass at the same time Grey sucked one of my nipples into his mouth and I came on Rook's tongue, thrashing as my climax rolled through me. Rook lapped me up until I could barely stand it anymore, letting my head fall forward to watch him as his mouth came away from my cunt, lips glistening with my release.

I let go of the belt above me, and if it weren't for Grey and Corvus on either side of me, I'd have folded like a cheap tent on wobbly posts. Rook licked his lips before running the back of his hand over his mouth.

"Tell us how you want us, baby," Grey said, breathless with desire as he ran a knuckle down my spine.

I swallowed, ignoring the twinge in my ribs as I fought to catch my breath. "Like last time," I panted, remembering the feeling of being full to bursting with them. How I didn't think I could handle it. How I was so fucking glad I did once we were through.

Except, I was missing one vital part of our foursome. This time, I wanted them all.

"Except I want all of you."

Grey's brows furrowed. Rook's lifted with a keen interest. Corvus looked like he was trying to figure out where all the puzzle pieces would fit. I honestly didn't fucking care, as long as they did.

"Sparrow, I don't think you can stretch that wide."

"Try me."

"Hold up," Grey said, going back to the couch to gather the throw blanket haphazardly tossed over the back. He spread it neatly on the floor within Carson's line of sight. His eyes were rolling back, I noticed. The three shallow stabs I'd given him to his stomach must've been deeper than I thought. There was too much blood on the floor. We would lose him soon if we didn't cauterize them. But there was no sense in it now. Not while we were so close to his end.

I reeled my arm back and slapped him hard across the face, bringing him back around. "We're not finished yet."

He groaned, his eyes struggling to focus on me. I slapped him again and they focused. "There you are."

Carson reached a mitt toward me but I batted him away. "Try to touch me again and I'll take the whole fucking arm," I hissed before leaving him to continue enjoying the show.

Grey finished straightening out the blanket.

"Lie down," Corvus said, and I started to kneel, but he stopped me with a hand on my elbow. "Not you."

Grey watched Carson as he lay down on the blanket, his erection hard and pulsing an inch away from his belly,

Corvus used his grip on my elbow to jerk me nearer, scooping me up by the waist. He carried me over to Grey. "Bend your knees, Sparrow."

I did and he adjusted his grip, lowering me onto Grey, who gripped the base of his cock tight, holding it perfectly upright. My knees touched the blanket on either side of Grey's hips as his tip breached my opening, making me contract around him with a groan.

Grey's hands came to my hips as Corvus passed me over, finishing his brother's job guiding me lower on his cock until I was settled all the way down to his base. I shuddered at the fullness of him inside me, leaning forward to rock a little, making his hands on my hips grip tighter.

"You feel so good," I whisper moaned, leaning further down to press my lips to his as he rolled his hips against me, hitting all the right notes.

"You're so wet for us," he whispered between kisses, reaching down between us to rub slow circles into my clit, making me arch back into a seat, giving him more space, feeling him hit something even deeper inside me.

Rook caught my head as I tipped it back in ecstasy, shoving his tongue into my mouth, making me gasp in surprise as he inhaled me.

The rough pads of his fingers brushed my ribcage before sliding lower, taking over for Grey's hands. Rook moved my hips against his brother, pushing and pulling me as his brother teased another orgasm from my clit and Rook swallowed the sounds of my release as stars burst over my eyelids, my legs shaking against the blanket.

Grey's solid warm body pressed tight against my thighs.

"Grey, your legs. Make room," Corvus said, and I felt Grey spread his legs wider, making me shift forward as Rook positioned himself between Grey's legs.

"Ready to stretch for us, Sparrow?"

I nodded, still coming down from my climax with broken breaths. Corvus came to stand at Grey's head, his blue eyes boring into mine. "Lean forward, Sparrow."

I did, and he eased me down with a burning palm pressed against my bare back until I was almost flush with Grey. My Superman nuzzled into my neck, nipping my ear as he tangled his fingers in my short hair.

"In her pussy," Corvus said, and I startled, confused who he was talking to or what was happening until I felt the press of Rook's pierced tip push hard at my already filled opening.

"*Oh fuck*," I hissed out, hands reaching desperately for something to hold onto.

Rook wrapped one hand around my hip and pushed in a little more, his cock sliding against Grey's as it made its way inside of me. Fire seared through my pussy as it clenched around them both.

"*Fuuuuck, Ghost*," he managed to gasp out, and I dared a look behind me, watching him watch me stretch with a sort of dazed incredulity.

Grey groaned under me, tipping his head back to hiss as Rook settled inside, and I choked at the fullness, arching.

"*Fuck*," Grey cursed in my ear.

"Is it okay?" I asked him, the words a breathy exhale.

I pulled back enough to see his face and watch his eye close. "*Better*."

Corvus kneeled next to Grey's head, throwing his jeans open, taking his mammoth cock out. "I need it nice and wet, Sparrow."

I lifted slightly as Rook and Grey both fucked my pussy, one easing in while the other pulled back, stretching me to my limits. I opened for my Bones, and he lovingly caressed my cheek before catching me under the chin to pull my mouth onto him.

His salty taste slid over my tongue, and I moaned around him filling my mouth, making him let out a snarl, his grip on my face tightening.

"Rock between us," he said, his voice strained, and I began to move my body, rolling my hips over the two cocks deep in my pussy, rocking back onto them: forward to take Corvus deeper into my throat, and back again. Loving how they were all a part of this. All of them using me, filling me, claiming me.

Corvus pushed his fat tip to the back of my throat, and his hand slid to wrap around my neck as he thrusted into my mouth, fucking my throat. Rook slapped my ass, and the sting raced through me, making me cry out around Corvus' cock. He pulled out.

"Ready for the third?"

I moaned in reply, no longer caring what they did to me as long as they didn't fucking stop.

"I'm going to take your ass, Sparrow," Corvus warned in a rasp. "It's going to hurt."

"I don't care," I found myself saying, even though my stomach fluttered with nerves as Corvus slid a hand down my spine to my ass, priming me while he continued to stroke himself with his other hand.

I rocked against his fingers and their cocks, planting kisses over Grey's collarbone. He rested his forehead against the top of my head as he continued fucking me with his brother, grunting with each thrust like he was already so close to coming undone.

One of his hands left my hip to palm my breast instead, rubbing and teasing, tugging at the nipple, making me moan even more loudly than before.

Corvus added another finger in my ass, and I sucked in a breath as it settled there, opening me up wider. Then he withdrew.

My eyes flew open, wanting him to keep going, but when I saw him move... felt his warmth as he crouched over my bent back.

"Lean back, Rook."

I felt the angle of Rook's pierced cock in me shift as he did what his brother bid, making room for Corvus to hover above me. I bared my teeth as Corvus fed the thick tip of himself into my ass, the pressure of adding the third cock threatening to split me apart.

Grey reached a hand over his head to find mine, twining his fingers with mine against the blanket covered floor, giving me something to hold on to. His eye fixed on me, pouty lips parted as he watched me take his brother's cock in my ass.

"You're so fucking beautiful, AJ."

My hand tightened on his as Corvus planted his palms against my lower back and pushed himself the rest of the way in, making me scream.

"Give her a minute," he hissed behind me and all movement stopped as I adjusted to the feel of them all, so wet and so turned on that the pain only registered as an afterthought.

"No," I gasped, letting up on Grey's hand. "I need you to move."

They all started up again, slow at first, but gaining speed as they pumped into me. Corvus shifted his grip, grabbing me around my elbows to pull me up, making my back bow as he railed me from behind.

Grey took the opportunity to pull my left breast into his mouth, suckling greedily on my hard nipple, making my pants come faster. My moans louder.

"This is so fucking hot," Rook said on a heavy breath, and I risked a look back to see him bent backwards, his fists pressed into the blanket as he thrusted his hips up and into me, his tatted thighs flexing with each pump. His head tipped back.

"Choke me," I spluttered out, feeling my orgasm start.

Grey wrapped a fist around my throat, never ceasing the teasing pace of his tongue on my breast. I let the sensations overwhelm me, my muffled cries rising to the rafters, joining the grunts, groans, and soft cries of my guys.

I shut my eyes tight as my climax ripped through me, consuming my whole body like hot fire. They held me in place, fucking me through it as they all fell victim to their own releases. One by one like dominos. Grey jerked me close, crying out his release into my mouth as he kissed me. Corvus came next and Rook followed right behind him, shouting a violent curse, making one orgasm roll right into another as their euphoria turned me on to the point of insanity. I rocked my hips against Grey as Corvus popped free of my ass, riding the last wave of my bliss.

Rook exited next and without the weight of us all holding him down, Grey flipped me onto my back, fucking me stupid to prolong my orgasm until I was sure I wouldn't be able to walk right for a fucking month.

I clenched around him, still hard despite his release as my orgasm wore down and he slowed, stopping entirely only once the last of my jerking spasms stopped completely. He laid his cheek on my chest, and I wrapped both arms around him, feeling the ghost of them all still inside me, even as Grey slipped out, flopping onto his back beside me with a laugh.

"That was..." He started but didn't finish.

"Perfect," I finished for him, peeling back my eyelids to find Corvus and Rook watching me.

Rook's lips tipped up at one side in a crooked grin. "I think I just found my new religion."

I glanced from him to Corvus. If this was a church, he was our priest. Leading the sermon. Sweat beaded over his brow and something wicked flashed in his eyes. I knew, somehow, that he was thinking the same thing.

He removed his shirt, bending to press it against my pussy. I winced, realizing just how sore I was, but I opened wider for him, letting him help clean me. "You did so good, Sparrow. Next time it won't hurt so much."

Next time?

An exquisite ache formed in my lower belly at the promise, and I reached down to grab his wrist, hauling him closer to plant a kiss on his lips. He pulled back, his light eyes flashing as he glanced between my eyes and my lips before leaning down to kiss me again. Softly.

When he pulled back, he was smiling, ditching the soiled t-shirt to hold out a hand to help me up. "Want to finish this for good?"

The reminder clawed through me like fingers of ice, waking the darkness that'd retreated into its cave to give me my moment in the sun. I nodded, taking his hand, getting shakily to my feet.

I took Rook's offer of his shirt, lifting my arms to help him pull it over me. It hung past my mid thigh, his scent clinging to it.

Carson attempted to speak again from where he still sat strapped to the chair. I didn't know if he was still making useless threats or begging now. It sounded like a mixture of both. But I was beyond caring. Ready to be done with him for good.

I went to the couch, reaching for my thigh strap to remove my new baby from his holster, feeling the weight of him in my palm. Time for his christening.

The guys split for me to pass before crowding behind me, forming a semi-circle as I closed the gap between myself and Carson, his eyes trained on the Wilson Combat hanging from my grip.

"*Thhdiry whore,*" he spat, but the darkness was gone from his eyes, leaving only a brittle shield that I knew couldn't stand a chance against me anymore.

"Better than a dead one," I replied in a lethal whisper.

He finally shut up, his lips sealed tight as I crouched to his eye level.

"Everything we've done to you was for *them,*" I told him, feeling my skin bristle with heat, goose flesh rolling down my back as I tipped my head to the side, indicating my Crows.

"But this?"

I lifted the gun, turning it this way and that in the harsh overhead lights.

"This is for Becca."

I cocked my weapon, pressing the gun to his chest. I fired and the shot rang through the underground space.

His eyes went wide.

"And this one's for me."

I fired again, letting the second bullet chase the first until blood spurted from the back of the chair, blowing through skin, bone, and wood.

I lowered my smoking weapon, my hands shaking as we all watched the light leave his eyes. Unlike him, my shots were true. I didn't fucking miss.

My shoulders fell as his life's blood pooled in his lap and his last breath pushed past his lips.

I sighed, hanging my head, feeling something almost tranquil settle in my bones, feeling more calm now than I ever had before.

"It's finally over."

42

AVA JADE

I pulled the blanket tighter around my shoulders, cozying up against Rook on the roof of Sanctum. He tugged the blanket corner, and I opened it for him to slide in next to me, shivering against the chill in the midnight air.

Corvus sat in front of the couch I'd asked them to drag up all three flights of stairs, pulling my calf over his shoulder to run his fingers over the skin there in lazy strokes.

The door behind us opened and I felt Corv jerk forward, his hand reaching behind him for his gun, but it was only Grey returning from the kitchens downstairs. Two black trays piled high with golden-fried goodness, sticky wings, and Corvus' cobb salad balanced precariously in his hands.

My stomach rumbled loudly as he came to sit next to me on the other end of the couch, setting one of the trays down in my lap. My mouth watered at the feast, and I shivered as the warmth of the bottom of the tray soaked into my legs.

"This is all for me, right?" I joked, popping a fry in my mouth with a little moan.

"You fucking earned it, Ghost," Rook said with a laugh, fingering his bottle of whiskey from the floor to take a swig before setting it back down, scooping up two fries between his fingers to feed me them one by one.

"Fuck, it's cold up here. How long till the fireworks?" Corvus said in a low growl, and I dragged the other blanket from the arm of the couch beside Rook and dropped it on his head.

He pulled it off, turning to give me an unimpressed scowl that couldn't touch the diamonds still shining in his eyes. "I said I'd watch the fireworks so we're all watching the damn fireworks."

Grey chuckled. "If Thorn Valley does one thing right, it's the new years fireworks. I watch them every year."

"Yeah, and you drag our asses out with you every damn time, too," Corvus said, throwing the blanket over his lap.

I passed him his salad. "Here, eat something before your hangry ass gets you sent to the doghouse."

He raised a brow like he'd love to see me try to put him there, and I let out a laugh, something crumpling in my gut. I didn't know if I'd ever get used to this. Especially now that there was no immediate danger. Nothing to have to do. At least not for a while.

We could just *be*.

I didn't know if I knew how to do that, but I was looking forward to giving it a try.

Two taps on the inside of the roof access door had Grey pausing before stuffing an entire cheeseburger into his face.

Diesel poked his head onto the roof. "Everyone decent?"

Decent? He was joking, right? Rook and I shared a conspiratorial look, and I grinned. We were about as far from decent as it got, clothed or not.

He cleared his throat as he came out onto the roof, checking a watch I rarely saw him wear. "Almost time."

"You joining us?" Rook asked, but Diesel shook his head, and I noticed he was carrying a familiar box in his hands. A thick envelope lay atop it.

"Nah. Just came up to give these to Ava Jade."

I cocked my head at him, and Rook moved the tray of food as Diesel came around to place the box and envelope in my lap.

"What is this?"

"A gift."

"Christmas was a week ago."

I peered at the guys. He hadn't given them anything, but they did mention he usually just did a big family meal and handed them each a wad of cash. I wondered if he'd slipped them a little something on Christmas when we came down to Sanctum to start our work.

He'd been away since then. Combing Lennox for any rogue Kings. Spreading the word that the Saints wouldn't take kindly to anyone breaching their territory, which now stretched to encompass not just Thorn Valley, but Edgewood, and Lennox, too. It was all Saint land now, and Diesel had to work double time to keep it all in check, hunting for new blood worthy of joining his ranks.

"Just open it," he chided. "The box first. The envelope is... something else."

I passed the thick envelope to Grey, trying to get a look at the seal on the front, but he tucked it away under the blanket, giving me a sly wink that told me he might know what was inside of it.

My stomach fluttered as I remembered where I recognized the box from. It was the one I'd put Diesel's leather jacket in when I'd gifted it to him. But, he was wearing that now, so he wasn't returning it in some *fuck you* move. Stupid to even think it.

The guys watched, just as curious as me as I pulled off the lid, which meant they had no idea what their father was giving me, either. I remembered the last gift I'd gotten from my dad. My blades. I only had one left now, another lost in the battle at the factory. The last one stayed at the Nest where it was safe. The last piece of him I had. At least there was a comfort in knowing now that no matter which King killed him, that person was long dead. Who knew? Maybe I was the one that ended him.

A ball formed in my throat as I squinted down what looked like a pile of well worn, supple black leather. "What is this?"

I pulled it from the box and watched Diesel's jaw clench and his eyes harden, betraying some emotion I didn't understand. It was an old leather jacket. A woman's. With a shining silver zipper and the Saint emblem over the right breast. "It's been collecting dust for too long."

Realization hit me like a sucker punch to the gut and my eyes stung. "Was this..."

"It was Jacqueline's."

My throat burned.

"It's yours now," he told me, and I made myself look him in the eyes even though mine were welling. He reached out and put a hand on my shoulder like he often did his sons, squeezing gently. "Welcome to the family, Ava Jade. I'm so glad my sons found you."

I coughed to cover a sob, swallowing hard as Diesel retracted his hand.

"Help me up?" I croaked and stuck out my hand. Diesel took it, lifting me from the warmth of the couch onto my feet. I sniffed, no longer feeling the cold in the air as I pushed my arms through the sleeves of the jacket.

"Fits you like a glove," Diesel said, his voice tight. "I thought it might."

"I can't accept this," I said, even though I was already hugging it, feeling a warmth bloom in my belly where not so long ago there had only been ice.

"You can and you will," Diesel said with a note of finality, holding a hand out to Grey. "Hand me that envelope, Son."

Grey passed it over, and Diesel lifted the top, tugging out three identical form-like sheets. He passed one to each of the boys.

I looked over Rook's shoulder, and my lips parted on a silent intake of my breath as the paper crumpled in his hard grasp. They were name change forms.

"If you boys still want the St. Crow name, it's yours. I've already signed the forms."

Grey dropped his head, pinching the bridge of his nose. I settled back on the couch next to him, feeling him shudder as I wrapped my arms around his shoulders, tears pricking my eyes anew.

He pushed to his feet, slipping out of my grasp to give Diesel a rough embrace. "Thanks, Dad."

"Of course, Son. Of course."

"What happened to waiting until graduation?" Corvus asked, unable to conceal the traces of emotion leaking through in his voice.

Grey pulled away, falling back into his seat next to me, staring down at the piece of paper between his hands.

"Well, I still expect you to," Diesel replied.

I barked a laugh. "I seriously doubt that'll be happening this year."

A smug smile spread on Diesel's mouth. "I've taken care of it. You'll all pass your classes from last term with whatever grade you had when shit hit the fan. So I'd get some *sleep* over the next couple days," he said pointedly. "Classes start again Tuesday. Bright and fucking early."

Diesel turned to leave, but Corvus stopped him, grabbing his good leg from where he sat on the floor, an elbow propped up on his knee as he looked over the form. "Thank you."

Diesel nodded at his son, pausing to fix me with a cheeky smirk. "Ava Jade, there's a little something else in that envelope that might interest you."

He left without another word, and Grey set the still heavy envelope in my lap. Corvus turned around and Rook and Grey folded away their forms, tucking them into their jacket pockets.

"Should I be worried?" I asked, trying to figure out why they were looking at me like they were.

Corvus shook his head. "Just open it, Sparrow."

I did, finding a hefty stack of pages with a legal seal glinting gold in the low lighting on the roof.

"What is this?"

I flipped through a few pages, finding my aunt's name typed in several places along with mine... and some very large numbers.

"No," I said to myself, shaking my head. "She wouldn't have left me anything."

"She didn't have to," Rook crooned, flipping the page for me, pointing to a line that said something about her estate passing to her last remaining blood relative. Her niece. A Miss Ava Jade Mason. "Under state law, you get everything."

A tingle ran down my legs, and I inhaled a rickety breath.

"So I'm..." I trailed off, my mouth going dry.

"Rich as fuck," Grey finished for me, smiling wide.

No. Fucking. Way.

My gut reaction was to refuse it. I didn't want her fucking money. But we could use it. The gang could use it. To rebuild. To become even stronger than they ever were before. So nothing could ever hurt them— hurt *us*—again.

I found myself smiling.

"Happy New Year," Corvus said, leaning in to press a kiss to my stunned lips. Rook roped me in with an arm, crushing me to him as he planted a kiss in my hair and Grey took my hand under the covers.

"Happy New Year," they echoed.

"Oh shit!" I cursed, stuffing the papers back into the envelope to dig around the cushions for my phone. "I was supposed to call Becks when it was done."

"Here," Grey said, passing me my phone.

I pecked him on the cheek and got up off the couch, wandering to the edge of the roof as I tapped the new phone number she'd texted me sometime in the last week while we were busy in the basement.

I stared out over Thorn Valley as it rang, hugging the leather jacket tiger around me as the wind whipped my short hair away from my face.

"Aves?" she answered, her tone apprehensive. "Fuck, girl, it's been a week. I thought—"

"It's done," I told her. "He's gone."

I heard her reedy exhale blow down the line.

"Did you make it hurt?" she asked after a second, surprising me.

I nodded as though she could see me. "I don't think anyone's suffered more."

She hesitated a second before saying, "Good."

Vaguely, I heard music playing in the background of the call and remembered where she was. "How was dinner? Did he take it okay?"

Even though I'd been more than a little preoccupied this week, I did read the message she sent me this morning. About how she'd decided to go against her father's wishes and take the space at CalArts. I was so fucking proud of her. Life was too damned short. I just wished she didn't have to learn that the hard way.

"Let's just say I won't be wearing Louboutin anytime in the imme-diate future." She tried to laugh it off, but I could hear the stress in her voice, and I immediately wanted to go climb into the Rover, drive my ass down there, knock some sense into her father.

"What do you mean?"

"He freaked out," she said. "We had a huge fight. He told me if I go to CalArts instead of MIT I'm cut off."

"So, you aren't going?"

"Fuck yes, I'm going. I told him to shove it. I'm actually packing my shit right now. Going back to Briar Hall. I figure I have until spring to figure my shit out. *Get a job.*"

I could practically hear the distaste in her tone.

"I can help you with money—"

"Nope. I'm going to do this myself, Aves. I just... I feel like I have to, you know? And I can do it. I know I can."

I smiled.

"Damn right, babe. I'm so happy for you."

"You're coming back to the academy tomorrow, right? Say you'll be my roomie until I have to leave? And that we'll stay in touch even while I'm all the way down in SoCal? You'll visit, right?"

I could hear the note of panic in her voice and laughed. "I'll be there, I'll be there," I assured her. "Whenever you need me."

A pop and fizzle sounded behind me, and I whirled to watch a firework splatter the night sky in shades of pink and green.

"They're starting!" Grey hollered.

"I'll see you tomorrow?"

"Tomorrow," Becca echoed. "Love you, girl."

"Love you, too."

I hung up and raced back to the couch, knocking into Rook and Grey, making them snort and whine as I made a space between them, Corvus reaching his arm up to rest it on my thigh as the show started in earnest.

The sky burned bright above, painting colored light over their faces. I watched them watch the fireworks, letting their warmth sink into me. Letting it chase all the ice away until there was none left, and I knew this was it.

Rook was right. Family really was who you chose, not who you were born to. And this? This was mine.

*Skip ahead for a preview from **Kings of Kilborn University**! The complete companion duet to the Boys of Briar Hall series. Don't miss it!*

ACKNOWLEDGMENTS

The crazy idea for this story wrapped its callused fingers around my throat and demanded to be written, and I'll be honest, I wasn't sure I had it in me at first. It was so unlike anything I'd ever written before. So, I have to thank my readers for pushing me to go for it. From the moment I posted that first chapter in The Lair, you were there for it, cheering me on. I am eternally grateful for that support. I don't think I've ever felt more connected to a story or its characters as I have with Ava Jade and the Crows.

This book may not have been possible without the support of my husband. Thank you for taking time off work and doing more than your fair share around the house while I made strange faces at my computer screen all day. Thank you for listening to me rant and complain and gush about these characters while listening to my Crooked Crows playlist on repeat. You are the real MVP.

I doubt this book would be half as awesome without the help of my incredible alpha readers. Casey, Sam, Claire, Frankie, Courtney, Kim, and Amanda, you were all vital to the process of bringing Ava Jade's story into the world. Thank you for all your input, feedback, and support. Most of all, thank you for falling in love with these characters and this story. Without you cheering me on, the finish line would've been much harder to reach.

Jennifer, you total fucking champ. Thank you for always making my words sparkle, and for dealing with last minute changes in my batshit crazy schedule. I couldn't ask for a better editor.

Papa, for believing in me without question and always reading my books. If you read this one (even though I specifically asked you not to), maybe do us both a favor and pretend you didn't?

I also need to thank my author friends for being there, you know who you are. Without you I would have procrastinated the shit out of writing this book. Thank you for being there at all hours of the day and night, ready to write along with me and keep me honest.

Last, but certainly not least, I want to thank the advance reviewers, PR companies, and everyone who has helped or will help to share these Boys of Briar Hall. Without you, I would be nothing but a blimp on the radar of publishing. I see you, and I love the shit out of each and every one of you.